NEVER LET GO

Also by Pamela Nowak

Chances
Choices
Changes

Escaping Yesterday

NEVER LET GO

Based on Historical Events

Pamela Nowak

In the Moment Historical Novels
Albuquerque, New Mexico, U.S.A.

Never Let Go Copyright © 2021 by Pamela Nowak

Published by Pamela Nowak, In the Moment Historical Novels

ALL RIGHTS RESERVED. In accordance with the U.S. Copyright Act of 1976, no part of this publication may be reproduced, distributed, or transmitted in any form or by any means, or stored in a database or retrieval system, without prior written permission of the author.

This novel is a work of fiction. Names, characters, places, and incidents are either the product of the author's imagination, or, if real, used fictitiously.

Paperback ISBN-13: 978-0-9897578-8-1
Ebook ISBN-13: 978-0-9897578-9-8

First Edition. First Printing: January 2021.
Hardcover LCCN: 2019045248

Interior Maps: Lake Shetek Settlers' Cabins, 1862 (courtesy of Jon Isch); Presumed Route of Lake Shetek Captives with White Lodge and the Fool Soldiers (from Minnesota's Heritage, Vol. 4, page 8, courtesy of the Dakota County Historical Society); Southwest Minnesota and the Santee Reservation (courtesy of Pond Dakota Heritage Society, owner).

Cover design by Kathy Heming
Cover photographs © South Dakota State Historical Society, South Dakota Digital Archives: Lake Shetek captives, ambrotype (vault).

For Bill Bolin,
my teacher and friend.
You ignited my passion for history,
taught me the value of its lessons,
and introduced me to the
settlers of Lake Shetek.
Thank you . . . more than you will ever know.

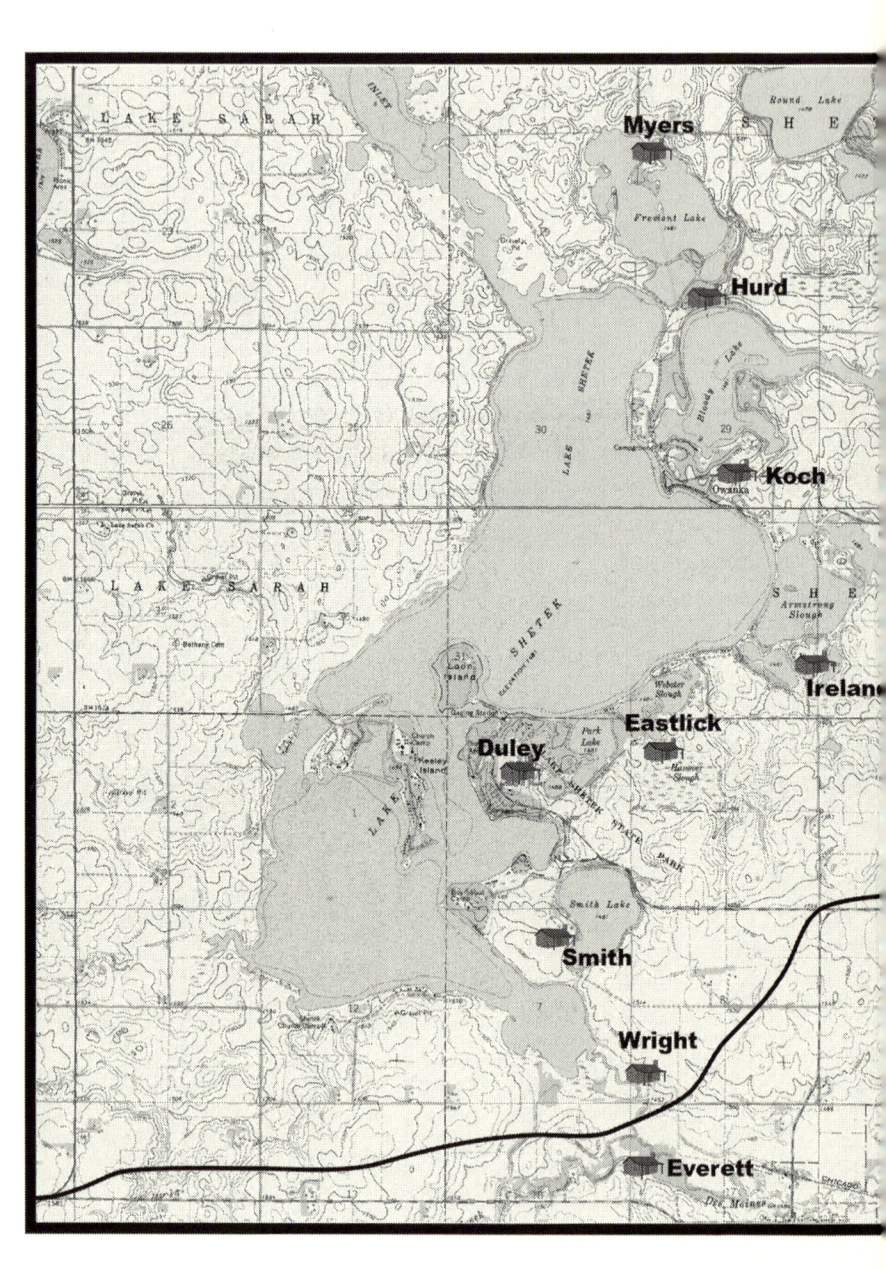

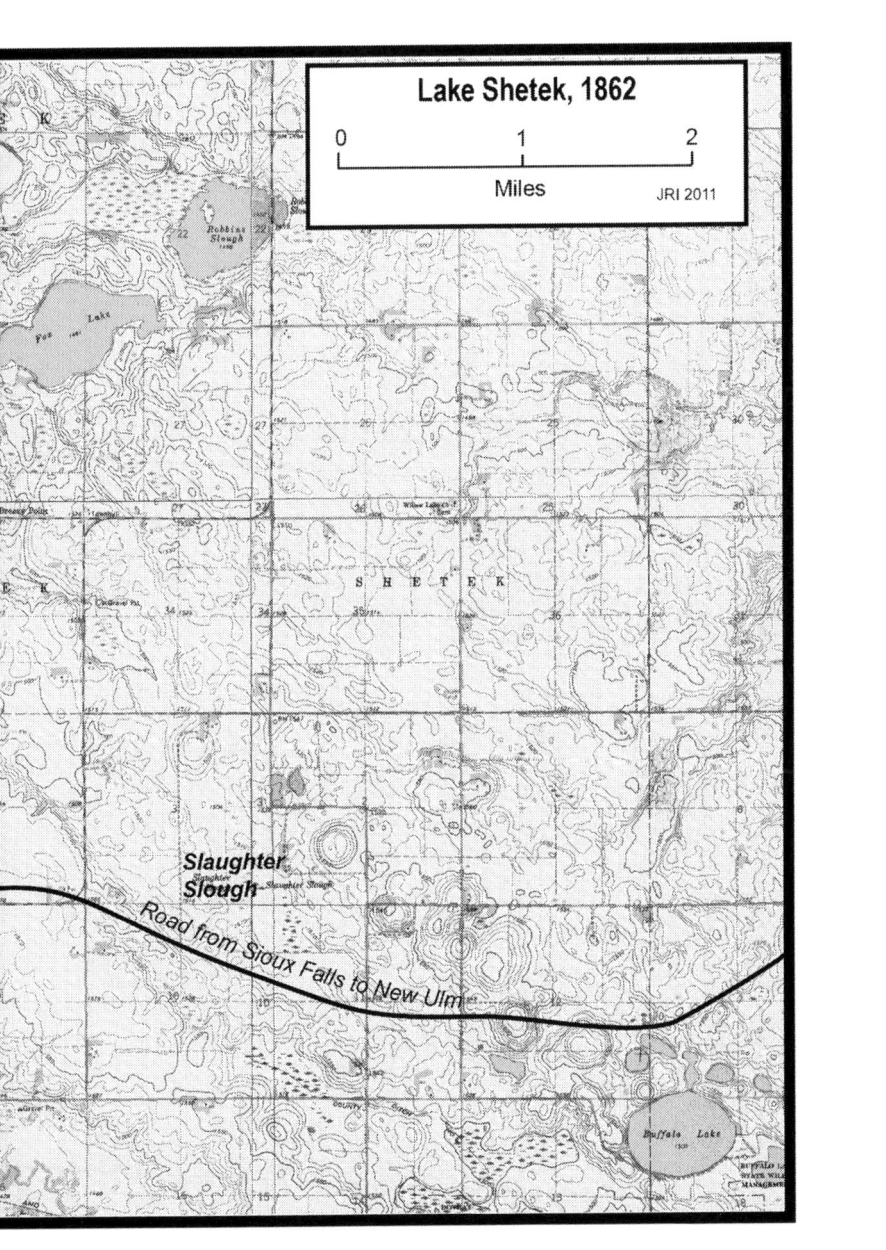

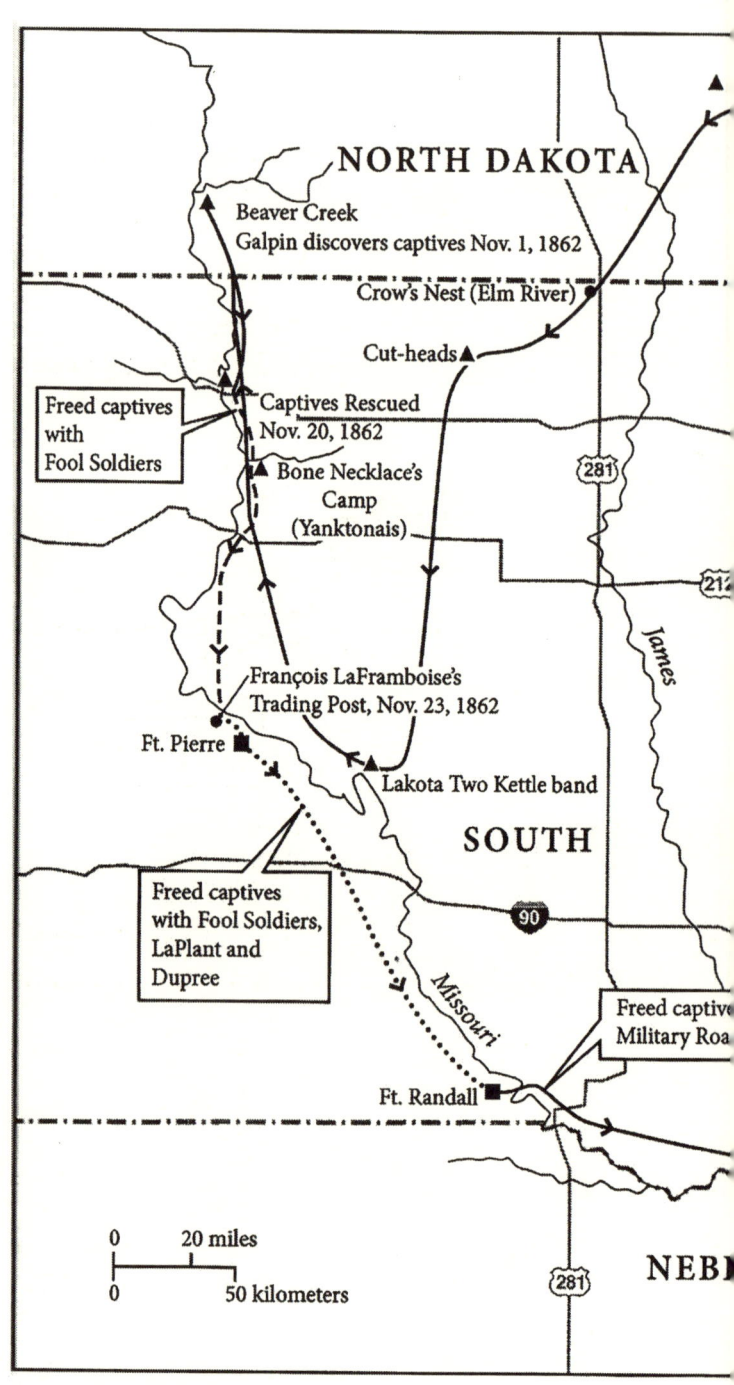

Map by Patti Isaacs, 2011

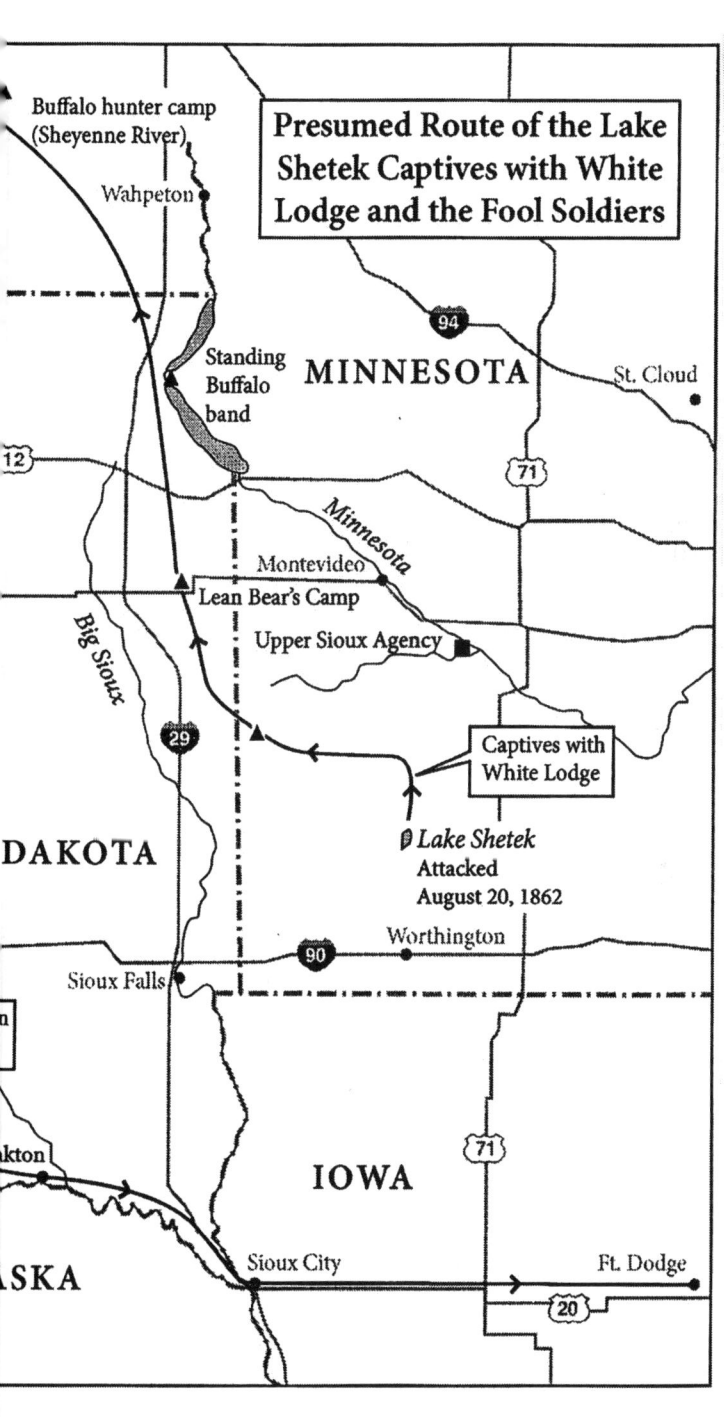

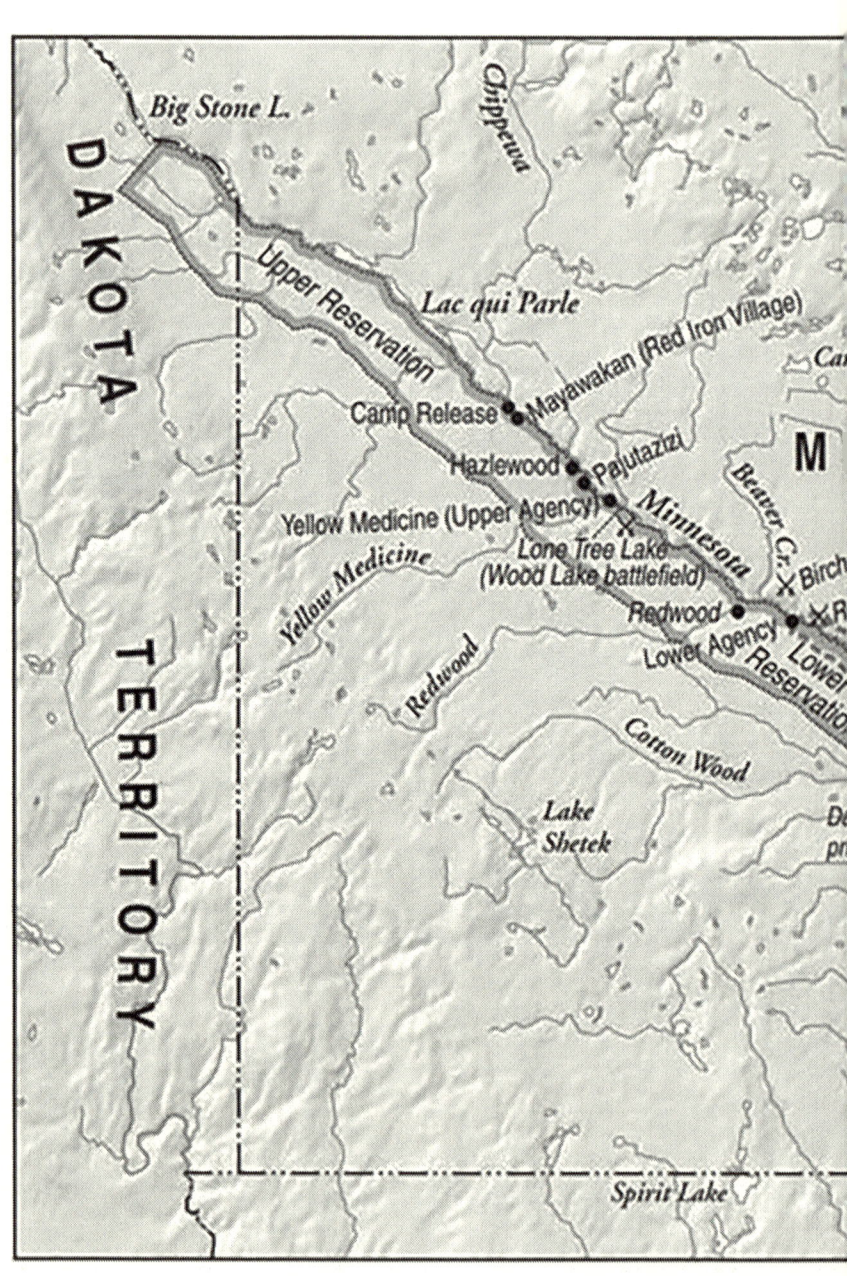

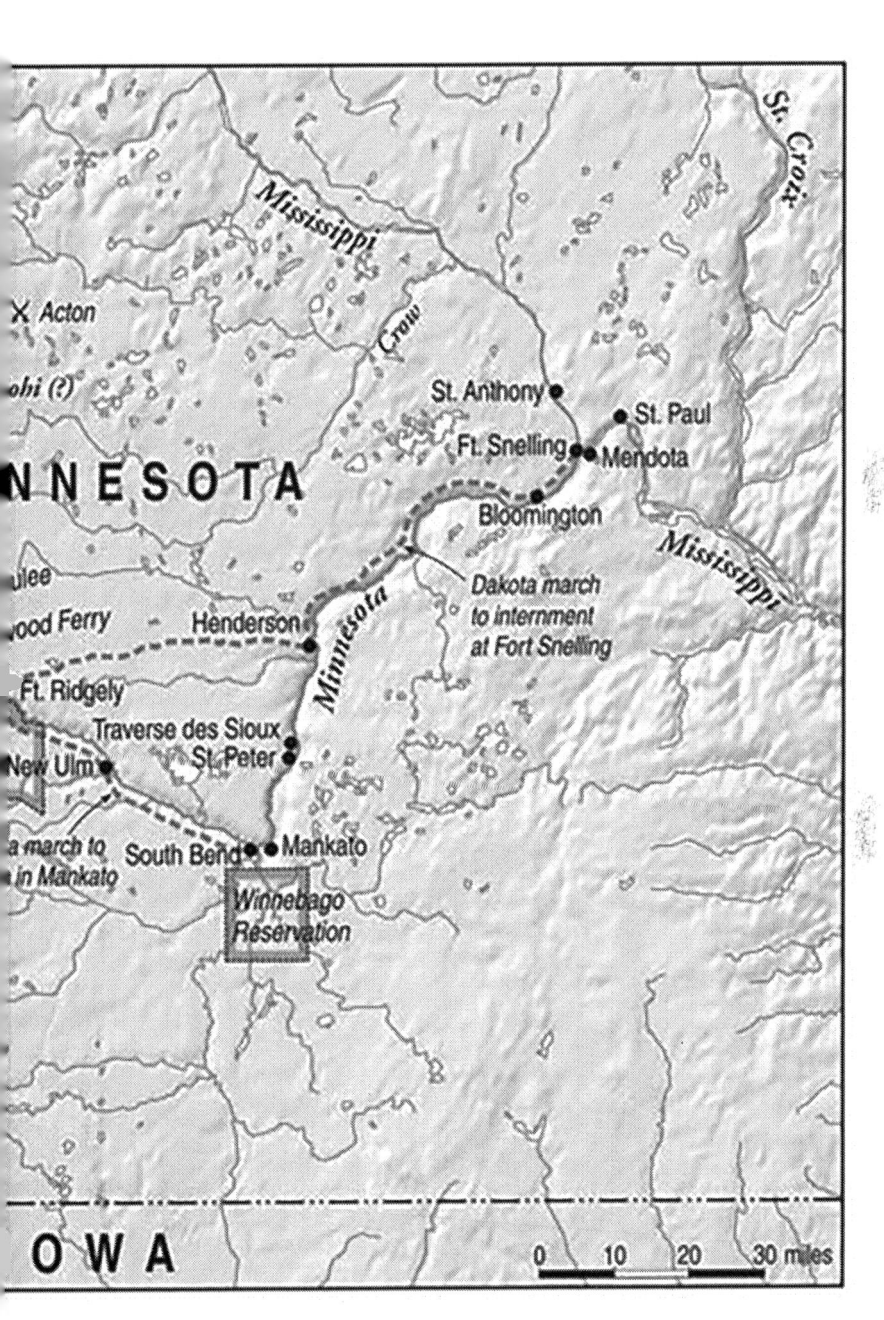

Families at Lake Shetek

On August 20, 1862
(by cabin location, north to south)

MYERS

Aaron (36)
Mary (36)
Louisa (12)
Arthur (11)
Olive (8), away at school
Fred (5)
Abby (1)
Edgar Bentley (30)

HURD

Phineas B. (29), missing
Almena (26), full name Alomina
William Henry (3)
Frank Elmer (18 mos)
John Voigt (??)

KOCH

Andreas (45)
Christina (??), aka Mariah
E.G. Koch (??), not related, absent

IRELAND

EASTLICK

DULEY

[First family — name cut off at left edge]

Thomas (50)
Sophia (??)
Roseanna (8)
Ellen (6), aka Nellie
Sarah (5)
Julianne (3)

[Second family — name cut off at left edge]

John (39)
Lavina (29)
Merton (11)
Franklin (10)
Giles (8)
Freddy (5)
Johnnie (2)
A.A. Rhodes (??)

[Third family — name cut off at left edge]

William (43)
Laura (34)
William, Jr. (10)
Emma (8)
Jefferson (6)
Bell (4)
Frances (2)

SMITH

Henry Watson (42), aka Wat
Sophia (37)

WRIGHT

John (27), absent
Julia (25)
Dora (5), full name Eldora
George (3)

EVERETT

William (31), called Will in novel
Almira (21), called Mira in novel
Lillie (6), full name Ablillian
Willie (5)
Charlie (2)
Charlie Hatch (25)

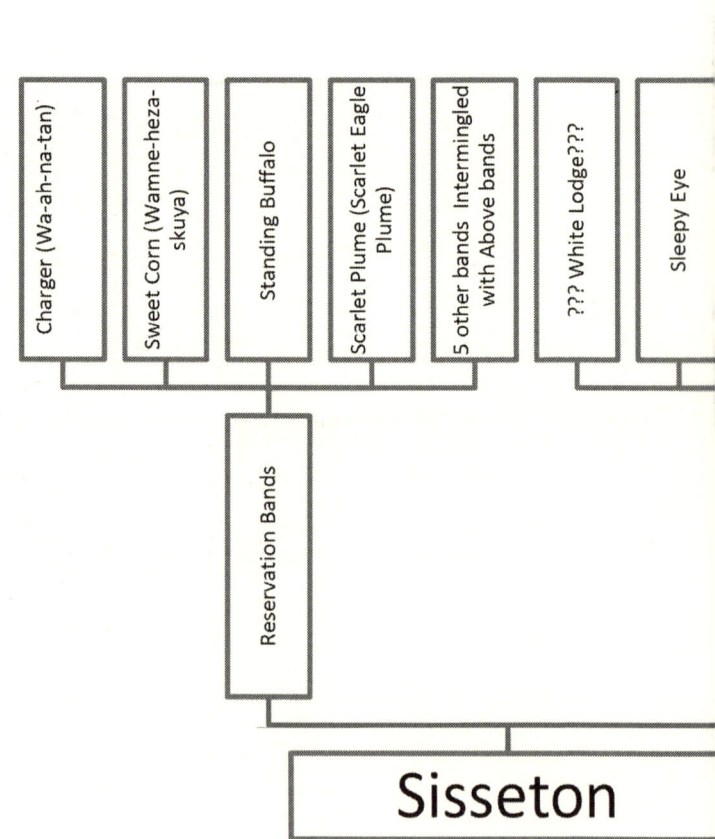

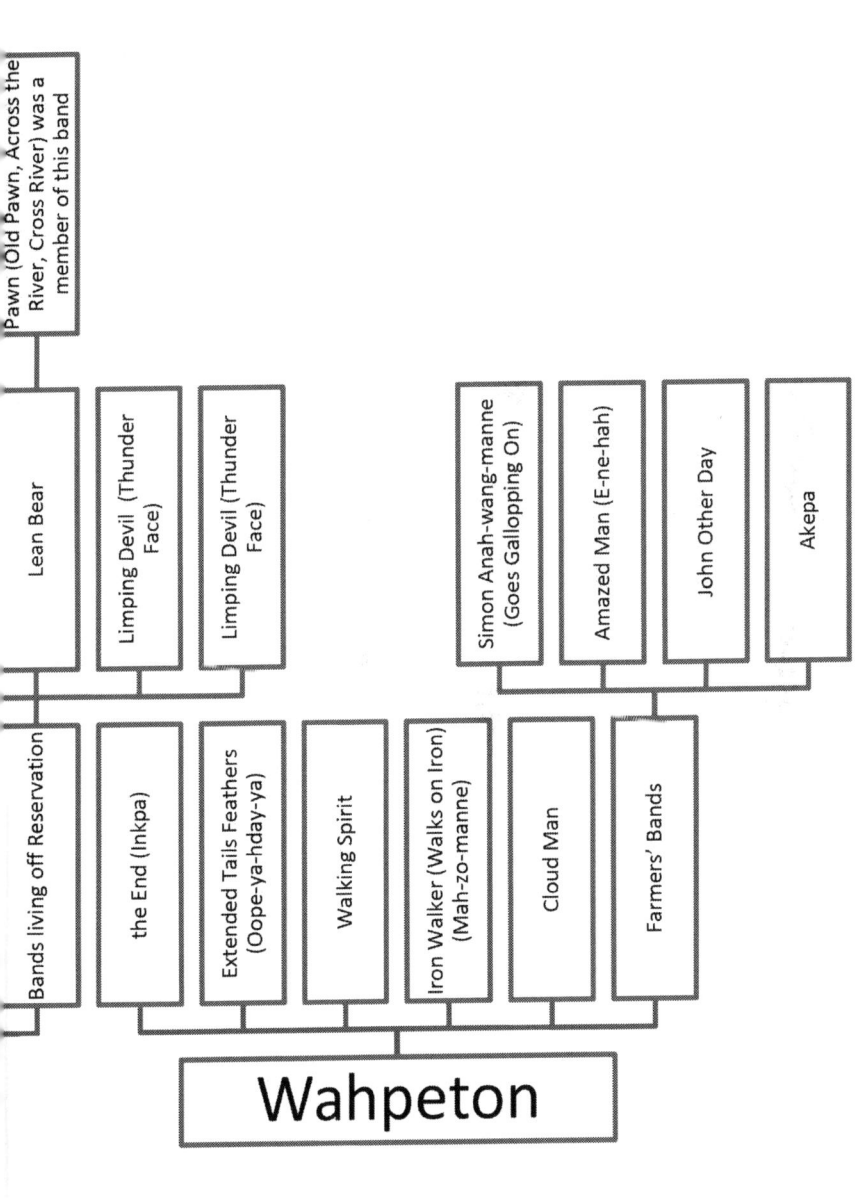

SISSETON BANDS LIVING OFF RESERVATION

White Lodge (*Wakeska*)
This village was located 25 miles west of Big Stone Lake in present South Dakota. White Lodge's sons were Black Hawk and Chased by the Ree.

Sleepy Eye (Young Sleepy Eye)
This village was located 20 miles west of the Yellow Medicine (Upper) Agency. This was the nephew of Old Sleepy Eye and was part of Old Sleepy Eye's band.

Lean Bear (Lean Grizzly Bear, Grizzly Bear)
The village was located at Lake Shaokaton or Bullhead Lake near present day Lake Benton, MN. White Owl and Old Pawn (Cross River, Pawn, Across the River) were members of this band. This was part of Old Sleepy Eye's band, and Pawn's wife was a relative of Old Sleepy Eye. This village was to the northwest of Lake Shetek, about 30 miles.

Limping Devil (Thunder Face)
These were two bands under the same chief. The village was located at the Two Woods, not far from Lake Shetek. Blue Face was his son.

CAST OF CHARACTERS

<u>MAJOR PROTAGONISTS</u> are capitalized, underlined, and in bold.

<u>**Secondary characters**</u> are underlined in bold.

Tertiary characters are in bold.

Minor characters are not bolded.

Characters are grouped by association.

<u>LAURA DULEY</u> (nee Terry): Marries William Duley in Ripley County, Indiana, and expects a fairy-tale life. Instead, they move ever farther West, and she suffers loss and depression. Reflects common biases of her time.

William Duley: Laura's husband, a man always looking for a big break. Aspires to politics and is known as someone who always thinks he's right; has few friends and dislikes Native Americans.

William and Rachel Terry: Laura's parents.

Ellen and Hannah Terry: Laura's closest sisters.

William and (Mother) Emily Duley: Laura's in-laws.

Monroe (Washington Monroe) Duley: Laura's brother-in-law. He lived with William in Iowa before William married Laura.

Hattie Mae Tucker: Laura's neighbor in Iowa, a feisty woman who helps Laura through difficult times. (a created character)

Ellen, Emiley, William Jr., Emma, Bell (Isabella), Rachael, and Frances Duley: Laura's children, in order of birth.

Jo: a half-breed captive who befriends Laura. (a created character)

Old Hag: the name Laura calls one of her captors. (a created character)

<u>LAVINA EASTLICK</u> (nee Day): Goes to live with her brother in Seneca County, Ohio, where she wants to be on her own and become a teacher. Instead, she meets John Eastlick, and they anchor their hopes in acquiring their own farmland. She's practical and takes life as it comes.

Leicester Day: Lavina's older brother who, with his wife, Christine, and young daughters, take Lavina in.

Mr. Beal: an opinionated teacher in Ohio. (a created character)

<u>John Eastlick</u>: Lavina's husband. His goal is to own his own land and support his family.

Mr. Covey, Maggie Knowles (a created character), the

Cast of Characters

Malindy brothers, Dr. Brooks: townspeople in Beaver, Minnesota.

Merton, Frank (Franklin), Giles, Fred, Willie (William), and Johnnie (John) Eastlick: Lavina's children in order of their birth.

A. A. Rhodes: a bachelor settler who meets John in Olmstead County and comes to the lake with John; lives with the Eastlick family.

Sophia and Thomas Ireland: Friends of the Eastlicks from Illinois. They share the Eastlick dream of owning a farm and move West with them. Sophia is a confidant, and "Uncle Tommy" is a hardy man with common sense.

Roseanna, Ellen (Nellie), Sarah, and Julianne Ireland: the Ireland children in order of birth.

ALMENA (ALOMINA) HURD (nee Hamm): left home at age 14 with her younger brother in Caton, New York. She is determined to be self-sufficient and becomes an expert butter-maker; has a strong belief in the importance of family.

Seneca Hamm: Almena's younger brother, put up for adoption.

Chauncy Hamm: Almena's father. He remarries after her mother dies and adopts children out to make room for growing family.

Marilla and Christian Minier: adopt Seneca and take in Almena. Marilla teaches Almena butter-making while

Christian teaches her to read. They later have daughters of their own.

Phineas B. Hurd (Phin): Almena's husband. He works in a mercantile but dreams of owning land. He respects Almena's independent spirit.

William Henry and Frank Hurd: Almena's children in order of their birth.

Bill Jones: a friend of Phin's who travels West with the Hurd family.

Agnes Jones: Bill's ex-wife. (a created character)

John Voigt: a German trader who settles at Lake Shetek, partners with E. G. Koch. He dislikes Indians and is disliked by the Santee locals. He resides with the Hurd family while Phineas is away.

Iltimony and Bad Ox: Dakota men who often trade for cheese with Almena.

Spot: the mail carrier who travels the route between New Ulm and Sioux Falls.

Mr. Berry: an attorney who assists Mrs. Hurd with her depredation claim.

CHRISTINA (Mariah) KOCH: A hearty German immigrant who wants to have her own home within the German community of New Ulm. She's tidy and industrious.

Cast of Characters

Andreas Koch: Christina's husband. He speaks with a heavy accent and dislikes Indians.

Mr. Renicker: A German immigrant from the Lake Shetek community who travels to New Ulm for supplies. Suspected of selling whiskey to the Sioux.

Dutch Zierke (Dutch Charley): A German immigrant who, with his family, lives between Lake Shetek and New Ulm. Travelers often spend the night there.

The Browns: a family living between Lake Shetek and New Ulm. Travelers often spend the night there.

Parmlee and Hammer: bachelor fur trappers who have shacks at Lake Shetek.

E. G. (Ernst) Koch: A German trader who settles at Lake Shetek, partners with John Voigt. No relation to Andreas and Christina. Desires to settle at north end of lake.

Inkpaduta: a Dakota man who visits the Kochs.

Running Bear: a member of White Lodge's band who is responsible for Christina.

Falling Star: a Dakota woman who treats Christina well. (a created character)

JULIA WRIGHT (nee Silsby): An ethical woman who finds herself married to an unscrupulous man. Gifted with language and an understanding of other cultures, she regrets her hasty marriage but is committed to her vows. She is friends with the Dakota who camp near the lake.

Jack (John) Wright: Julia's husband. A heavy drinker, he becomes an Indian trader. He is always looking for ways to get rich without working and is easily talked into breaking the law.

Dora (Eldora) and George Wright: Julia's children in order of birth.

Lorenza (Laura) and George Lamb: Julia's sister and her husband (a trapper), who settle with the Wrights at Lake Shetek for a time. They have several children.

Bill Clark and Charley Wambau: disreputable characters who meet Jack Wright and later come to Lake Shetek.

The Jacques Brothers: horse thieves said to keep stolen horses on land across the lake.

LaBousche: a half-breed fur trapper who camps near the Wright cabin.

Mr. Annadon: an attorney from Sioux Falls.

Aaron and Mary Myers: A couple living at the north end of Lake Shetek. Aaron is known for his medical abilities, though he is not a doctor. He is well-liked by the Santee.

Louisa, Arthur, Olive, Fred, and Abby Myers: the Myers's children in order of birth.

Cast of Characters

Edgar Bentley: a bachelor who lives with the Myers family.

Henry Watson (Wat) and Sophia Smith: a couple living toward the south end of Lake Shetek.

Will (William) and Mira (Almira) Everett: a couple living at the far south end of Lake Shetek.

Lillie (Ablillian), Willie, and Charlie Everett: the Everett children in order of birth.

Charlie Hatch: Mira Everett's bachelor brother. The man who discovers the attack and warns the other settlers.

Old Scalpie: a scarred Dakota woman who cares for Lillie Everett. She was once doctored by Aaron Myers and often camped near Lake Shetek.

Across the River (Pawn/Old Pawn): A Sisseton (Santee Dakota) man who camps frequently at the lake and befriends Julia Wright. He is a member of Lean Bear's band.

Speaks with Strong Tongue: First wife of Across the River. She is prideful and resents Julia. (a created character)
Dances in Water: second wife of Across the River. (a created character)
Tizzie Tonka: a Dakota man who is often with Across the River.

Lean Bear (Lean Grizzly Bear, Grizzly Bear): Leader of a Sisseton (Santee Dakota) band located about thirty miles from the lake.

White Lodge (*Wakeska*): Leader of a Sisseton (Santee Dakota) band who is known for his cruelty. His band joins with Lean Bear's band after the conflict begins.

Black Hawk: White Lodge's son.

Redwood: a member of White Lodge's band; he and his wife adopt Roseanna.

Sleepy Eye (Young Sleepy Eye): Leader of another Sisseton (Santee Dakota) band, nephew of Old Sleepy Eye.

The Fool Soldiers Band: Eight young Yankton Sioux (Lakota) men who disagree with the actions of the Dakota bands to the east and pursue rescue of the white captives. They include **Martin Charger** (*Waneta*), Joseph Four Bear (*Mah to top ah*), Swift Bird (Alex Chapelle), Kills and Comes (Kills Game and Comes Home or *Waktegli*), Mad Bear (*Mato Watogla*), Red Dog, Bears Rib (Kills Enemy), Sitting Bear, Pretty Bear (*Mato Waste*), Charging Dog, Jonah One Rib, Strikes Fire, Big Head, Foolish Bear, and Black Tomahawk.

Major Galpin, Eagle Woman, et al: a trader, his wife, and their party who are traveling on the Missouri River and see the captives.

Little Crow: A Dakota leader who is recognized as the chief and leader of the conflict.

General Sibley: The military leader in charge of the response to the attacks.

Prologue

Murray County, Minnesota
August 20, 1862

Charlie Hatch slogged northward, up the marshy stretch of land between Lake Shetek and Bloody Lake. The mud sucked at his feet in the areas where solid land gave way to water, slowing him. Still, he was grateful for the shortcut that saved him the four-mile detour around the inlet. Already, the summer sun was creeping over the horizon. After he secured Voigt's yoke of oxen, he still had to return the six miles to his brother-in-law's place on the Des Moines River before they even began the heavy work of raising the sawmill. No doubt about it, it would be a long day.

The air filled with the sound of early morning waterfowl, a variety of greetings to the new day, and the glow of sunrise gave way to full light.

A distant shot broke the tranquility, and Charlie chuckled. *Almena Hurd, shooting at blackbirds again.*

On Shetek, the fresh sun glinted off the water, rousing the pelicans from their leisurely nap by the shoreline. Charlie watched one dive for its breakfast, then turned toward the Hurd place where Voigt was serving as hired hand during Phineas Hurd's absence. His very long absence.

Mrs. Hurd is going to have to make some hard decisions unless some sort of miracle happens.

Charlie emerged from the trees and stopped in his tracks.

Holy Mother of God!

Household goods lay strewn across the cleared land in front of the Hurd cabin, feather ticks slashed open, trunks upended.

Eerie silence greeted him. Not even a blackbird chattered. Charlie sprinted toward the cabin, past an overturned milk pail, its souring contents staining the ground. Near the door, Voigt lay on the ground, blood pooling beneath him. Not yet gelled, its coppery stench still hung in the air. Charlie turned away, swallowing against the bile rising in his throat.

Indians. It had to be Indians.

He glanced into the cabin, empty save for larger pieces of furniture flung about the room. He dashed toward the two stables and found the livestock gone. All of it, gone. Almena and the boys were nowhere in sight. Charlie's skin crawled at the implications.

There's nothing more to be done here.

Some forty others lived along the shores of Lake Shetek, most of them to the south, all of them needing to be warned. Chest pounding, Charlie turned back the way he had come and sprang toward the trees.

If the Sioux were attacking the entire settlement, he prayed like hell that he could make it back down the shortcut ahead of them.

★ ★ ★ ★ ★

Part One: Beginnings

★ ★ ★ ★ ★

Chapter One

Laura
Ripley County, Indiana
April 27, 1848

For better or for worse, my new life was about to start.

I drew a shaky breath and peered forward. William waited at the front of the church. Ellen, my closest sister, patted my forehead with a lace-trimmed handkerchief, tucked it into my hand, and bade me to follow her. I clutched the now damp handkerchief in my palm, knowing it would never fit in the tiny watch pocket of my gown, and smoothed the fine cream wool with its delicate floral pattern and pink silk striping. I took Papa's arm, my eyes on William's bright face, and started down the aisle.

The man I loved was making me his. When he'd asked for my hand, he'd pledged to provide me a secure and comfortable life. A smile tugged at my mouth as I recalled his clumsy, albeit romantic promise to make me his fairy princess. I might be leaving the sanctuary of childhood, but my prince awaited me.

The Pipe Creek Baptist Society congregation appeared ready to burst, so eager were they to make my happiness their own. Pride stretched across Mama's face, and she lifted her hands to her mouth as it formed into an "oh." William's warm gaze was firm upon me, his unruly chestnut hair freshly trimmed and tamed for the service. He reached for me, taking my arm as Papa handed me off.

We made our vows, he to love and honor, me to love and obey. From this moment forward, my life would be in his hands. Apprehension over leaving my childhood behind still prickled at me, but my giddiness chased it away. There was nothing but promise in our future. Children of the leading families of Sunman Township, it seemed as if we were destined for one another. We had grown up together, though I a few years behind him. Three years ago, our love had blossomed as if it really were a fairy tale. We turned, William taking my hand in his and squeezing it. Facing the assembly, we felt their admiration and led them out into the spring sunshine to celebrate our arrival as a couple.

Our family of relatives and friends offered congratulations as they spread out upon the church lawn. With the ladies, as a new matron of the community, I set out hams and fried chicken, cakes and cookies on plank tables that were laid across sawhorses. William and I took our place of honor at the front of the line and settled on a quilt to eat. I hardly touched my food. My thoughts were a jumbled mess . . . bliss, desire, nervous anticipation over what would come later. My pulse raced a bit with the realization that tonight I would be in his bed rather than the one I had shared with my sister for so many years.

I was a wife. Laura Duley. Mrs. William Duley.

Reluctantly, I gathered our plates as William folded the quilt. We had obligations. I took the dishes to be washed as he returned the quilt to his mother.

"So, how does it feel?" Hannah, my fifteen-year-old sister intercepted me, always curious about all things adult.

"Oh, ever so grand. I can hardly catch my breath." I exaggerated for her, waiting to see her eyes widen. When they did, I took smug satisfaction in my successful teasing. Gullible as Hannah was, Ellen and I were too often merciless with her. I would miss that.

Never Let Go

In truth, I was no different now than I'd been in my previous score of years. I felt much the same as I had this morning, both nervous and expectant. Though perhaps a bit more of both.

I herded Hannah toward the women gathered at a wash tub. This was my place now, not giggling like a school girl with my sister. Hannah could stay or drift off with the youngsters her own age.

"Well, Mrs. Duley," Mama said as she took the dishes from me, "the Lord has gifted you with a gorgeous day."

"Almost like He is smiling on your union," piped in one of my aunts, her expression as proud as Mama's.

I responded with what I hoped was a sage and knowledgeable expression. "I'm certain He is."

"William is a fine man, of such good stock. The two of you will be pillars of the community," my aunt added, her confirmation of our roles warming me.

"Not to mention that he's already built his fortune," Mama said. "Not many young men are responsible enough to do so before marriage these days. The two of you will want for nothing. William and Monroe did a good thing."

He would be providing well for me, though I hadn't been entirely in agreement during the two years he'd been away. While William had increased his financial footing, the wait and worry had been interminable. After his proposal, he'd left Indiana in the company of his younger brother, Washington Monroe, bound for Iowa. William had preempted land there, Monroe having not yet achieved his majority; they'd cleared the claim and farmed the rich black soil together. Their first harvest had been fruitful, giving both of them a nest egg, one that would be even larger for William once Monroe bought out the claim. This, and the legacy our parents had built, would assure the perfect life he'd pledged to provide.

I looked forward to being well-established, respected, with a solid home and our own land. Few brides were as lucky as I.

Mama tucked a stray strand of my dark hair back into one of the intricate braids that framed my chignon and secured it with a pin.

"There, all beautiful again. A wife should always primp for her husband. Shoo, now. He's likely waiting for you."

I spotted him across the yard, huddled with Monroe and their parents. William and I would live with them for the first year, perhaps starting construction of our own house on the family farm by Christmas. Eventually, the land would become William's inheritance while Monroe grew a new branch of the family out West.

My husband. The strange new proprietorship filled me with warm pride.

I sensed the moment he spied me approaching in my spring-striped gown. His gray eyes softened and their conversation halted.

Halted entirely.

Glancing from one of them to another, I slid my arm through William's. "Am I interrupting?"

"No, not at all." His words came out hurried, and I knew I had stumbled into the midst of a conversation not intended to include me.

A wedding surprise?

I glanced at William and noted his now shuttered eyes. Avoidance? Not a surprise, then, but something else. I knew him well enough; he wasn't likely to say anything more, not unless I pried it from him. I turned to his mother, a woman incapable of keeping a secret. "Mother Emily?"

"I . . . uh . . ."

"Come, Mother, let's leave the newlyweds on their own." Father William raised his brow and steered his wife away.

Monroe cleared his throat, shuffling from one foot to another.

"Guess I'd better tag along."

"That would be best," William prompted. "Leave Laura and me a bit of privacy. We'll talk later."

Their unified evasiveness mystified me. I waited until Monroe was out of earshot, but still William did not speak.

"Well, what is it?"

"Now, Laura, don't get all sharp with me." Chastisement was clear, despite his light tone. A wife should not be prickly on her wedding day.

I drew a breath. Mama had warned me a thorny tongue would not be tolerated in a marriage. I searched for a more suitable way to ask. "I'm sorry. I didn't mean to snap, Husband. I sense there is something you mean to tell me, something you suspect I don't want to hear."

"Let's walk a bit."

He guided me away from the gathering, down the path leading to the river. My chest tightened. This was not good, not good at all. I waited, as should a proper wife, and twisted the handkerchief in my apron pocket.

When we were a distance into the woods, he stopped and settled on a fallen tree. He patted his leg, an invitation to sit.

My skin flushed.

"We're married. There's no shame in a wife sitting on her husband's lap, especially on their wedding day." He winked.

I perched, birdlike, thankful for the care he was taking of my gown, nervous at the intimacy.

He drew me close, kissing my eyelids, my cheeks, the corners of my mouth until I melted into his arms and surrendered to his full kiss, desire running roughshod over my good sense. It was only when his hand, greedy upon my breast, moved to the buttons of my gown that I pulled reluctantly away. We had a yard full of wedding guests waiting for us, and it would not do to return with hints of dishabille.

Besides, I knew my husband in this behavior as well. It wasn't the first time he'd distracted me with his warm mouth.

"William?"

"Please, you won't deny me today?"

"I'm not denying, merely delaying." I kissed his cheek, a promise that we would return to pleasures of the flesh later. "We've company to return to, and you've yet to tell me what needs discussing."

"Laura—"

"What is it?" I winced at my impatience.

He sighed and took my hand as if he were a schoolboy seeking a dance. The sudden formality launched my palpitations anew. "I know we discussed taking over my father's farm, making our life here in Ripley County . . ."

"Yes. We did." The words came out curt. This was the dream we shared, taking our rightful place in the community, building our home and continuing our parents' legacy. His silence frightened me. "What is it?" I said for the third time. "What's happened?"

"Monroe and I have decided he will stay here, and we will go to Iowa."

"We'll do what?" I sprang off his knee and glared at him, hardly proper behavior for a new wife, but I didn't care one whit.

He gained his feet and reached for my shoulders. "Now, Laura." His words were laced with syrup, and I was none too pleased with the condescension.

"Don't you 'now Laura' me." My hands plastered themselves on my hips. "You've no right to make such a decision without consulting me."

William drew back, as if shocked to discover a fishwife had usurped his quiet new spouse. "I have every right."

I ignored his clipped assertion. "But we agreed. We had

everything planned out."

"Plans can change."

"What earthly reason would you have to change something we discussed and agreed upon?" I fought to stay calm. It tore my heart that he would alter our dream, that he would confer with this family but fail to consult me. Hot tears stung my eyes. He'd promised me a life here. Surely I had not bound myself to a man who would make empty pledges?

"Monroe's young." William shrugged. "I don't see him doing well out there alone."

"Why not sell off the land in Iowa? You can both stay here. It was only about building up a nest egg anyway. You can both farm with Father William. There's nothing tying either of you to Iowa."

"Oh, but there is. The soil there is unbelievably rich. It puts my father's land to shame. The yields, Laura, the yields!" His eyes grew animated as the words tumbled from his mouth. "When the Mississippi floods, it leaves such fertile ground behind. Even freshly broken, the land is generous."

"And here, the land is already broken."

"Our farms there are cleared now, too. All that remains is to harvest the bounty."

"Let Monroe harvest it."

I uttered the words in a flat tone, unwilling to surrender the argument.

"Monroe is still a boy. He'll never survive out there alone. I want this, Wife. I want the land, I want the dream."

My chest tightened. This wasn't about Monroe. William had latched on to a fantasy I knew nothing about, and he was dragging me along on the chase. And what's worse, he was so enamored of it that he'd not told me, not even considered me.

"And the struggle? You're willing to give up the ease our parents have created for us?" I knew I sounded petty but he'd promised me comfort and security. I couldn't let it slip away. "We belong here, William. This is our destiny. We're the first of the second generation. The *heads* of the generation."

"And in Iowa, we will be the heads of the first generation, leaders of the entire community, not just the second wave."

"I'll be all alone." Panic seized me as I realized what the words meant. I knew *no one* in Iowa.

"We'll be together, among the founding families of Jackson County. We may not have a township named for us, but we'll form a life there, establish towns and governments, not simply carry on what our parents did. We'll create our own destiny."

"You promised me a perfect life." I laid my head on his shoulder, angry still, but it would be pointless to argue. I wasn't going to win. Not with William so excited. His mind was set, and it was a husband's decision to make, no matter what his wife might feel.

"Ah, Laura, it will still be perfect," he told me, cupping my head in his hand. "The only difference is that it will be perfect in Iowa instead of Indiana."

Two weeks later

Our departure was accomplished with more speed than I imagined possible in order to arrive in time to sow a garden. As it was, the vegetables would be late, but the truck would be too important for our winter food store to ignore it all together. Monroe had agreed to go ahead, on horseback, to sow the early crops as his wedding gift to us, and would return to Indiana once we arrived in Iowa.

We traveled lightly, with only my possessions and the household items I'd deemed necessary: rugs and curtains, quilts, and other items to which William and Monroe had likely paid scant attention. Most of what we would need was already there,

William said; the house built and comfortably furnished. Mama and I had doubts about the items that would truly make the house a home and concentrated on packing the items men tended to forget.

I mourned the loss of the life to which I was accustomed, however temporary it might be. Until we built our community, no one would come calling; I would have no need for my tea service. I would be lucky, even, to be able to purchase tea. For a while, there might be few women to gather with and compare dress patterns. Until we established society, I'd wear serviceable clothes, dark colors that would need laundering less often, and I would have little use for my silk-striped gown.

Though William professed bright hope for our future, I knew much of our early survival would depend on my abilities to grow vegetables, bake bread, and maintain our household. I'd been raised in such tasks, but my family had not relied on me. Perhaps such fright was shared by all newly-wedded wives, but the responsibility weighed heavy upon me. For a few years, there would be no other supply, no one to share the burden. I would not see Mama or Ellen or Hannah for a long time, if ever again. They would not be with me as I birthed my children, and I was terrified that I would be entirely alone with no one to advise or assist me. And I knew not at all whether natives still abounded in that country.

Anxiety pressed upon my heart, one already breaking at the loss of everyone and everything I held dear, and I clung for dear life to William's assurances that we would build that community and enjoy both its comforts and our place within it.

The early weeks were not the ideal start for our marriage with one or the other of us sullen for most of the trip. I still resented William's decision to alter the plans we'd agreed upon during our betrothal, one made without consulting me. Though resigned to his authority, I found myself sulking to convey my dissatisfaction during our first wedded days. I was not the only one, however. William complained at any complication, as if it were my fault that the garden would be late. Some days, we literally drove mile after mile in silence.

We'd not displayed such behaviors to one another during our courtship, and I wondered if every couple experienced such adjustments. I missed William's teasing. Moreover, I wasn't certain if our new conduct was part of both our natures, in which case our future would have its trials, but it seemed to me the long jostling days on the wagon seat aggravated our petulance. Each evening, despite our fatigue, we released our petty behavior. Perhaps it was our removal from the wagon, the sharing of tavern fare and glasses of ale. I cannot recall a night that we took our discontent to our bed, and I was glad of it, for Mama had advised never to sleep with anger between us. And, too, I discovered much joy in William's arms, dispelling all the disparaging words I'd ever heard about those particular wifely duties.

As we neared Iowa, William's enthusiasm for our new home finally began to infect me. Though the country became ever more untamed, my fears grew less sharp. I allowed my anger to play out, committing to his theory that we would become the bedrocks of society in Jackson County and build a comfortable life there.

Emerging from the woods onto the marshlands and sandy prairie along the Mississippi, I had my first view of Iowa. Bellview sat on a wide plateau, surrounded by high hills and rugged bluffs. The river itself was dotted with islands that belied its half-mile width. Everywhere, it was green—bright, lush, unbelievable green in every shade. Such an echo of Indiana's own verdant landscape spurred my hopes.

"Oh, William, it's so pretty." I bounced on the wagon seat. "You never told me there would be such beauty."

Never Let Go

"You wouldn't have listened had I done so."

Though the reminder came with a wink, I hung my head, knowing he was right.

"Our land is about two and a half miles that way." He pointed northwest.

I glanced around, trying to envision it, my gaze settling on the town across the river. An entire host of buildings ran along the shoreline and back toward the hills. This was no burgeoning settlement. William had misled me. This was a town already developed, its businesses firmly part and parcel of daily life, churches and schools raised, leaders no doubt in positions they'd long ago carved out for themselves.

"It looks already well-established," I finally said.

"It was platted in 1835."

"So we *won't* be among the founders of the community." Accusation crept into my voice.

"Not of Bellview." William patted my hand. "We'll be among the founding families in Tetes Des Morts Township."

"But not in town." I fought to keep my voice level, my newfound confidence in William's promises slipping away with most of my hope. Though pleased beyond measure that civilization existed here, I felt off balance, insecure in my trust in him, unsure what else might not be as he'd pledged.

"There's the river crossing." He pointed ahead, subtly shifting the topic, a technique in which I'd come to realize he was quite skilled.

I focused my attention on the small, flat boat. It appeared none too secure, a simple log platform bobbing in the water. With each wave, one side heaved then dipped as the other end rose. "That's the ferry?" I choked out.

"That's it."

I peered at it, my stomach already queasy, anxiety clawing at me. One sudden swell could send me into the water, where I'd most assuredly drown. "But I thought it would be a real boat, with paddlewheels, like the advertisement I saw in Rockford."

William sighed. "We'd have to go all the way up through Galena to the Dubuque crossing."

His stubbornness raised my dander. "I would prefer we cross there. That flat boat is little more than a raft. With the current of a river that size, I can't imagine it being safe."

"It rocks pretty good, but it's safe enough." He halted the wagon. "Guess you'll have to spend the entire trip across in my arms."

I ignored his wink, refusing to be teased away from my concerns. "I would prefer we cross at Dubuque." I made the announcement with all the discontent I could manage to remind him of the discomfort of the situation, of the promises he continued to break.

"Dubuque is nearly fifty miles out of our way, and, when I left for Indiana, toll charges there were close to a dollar."

"We can take it from the pin money Mama sent along with me." I patted my reticule.

"I'll be damned if I pay four times the going rate to cross the river. And I am sure as hell not going to take this wagon twenty-five miles north simply to cross the river and drive back again. That's three or four days, given the condition of the roads."

"But—"

"For God's sake, Laura, it would be a waste of time and money."

I bit my lip, knowing he was right and that my insistence rose more from anger than distrust of the bobbing flatboat. I simmered with the realization that William had misled me. We would not be founders, with the honor of leading a fledgling group of pioneers. We would be forcing our way in, interlopers within an already established society. There wouldn't be any guaranteed prestige and no fairy-tale life.

I'd left that behind in Indiana, along with my faith in my husband's promises.

William made the arrangements for the crossing as I stewed on the hard seat of the wagon. I held my tongue, not wanting to embarrass him in front of the ferry operator, a man who would be within our circle of friends and acquaintances. The two shook hands, and William returned to me.

"They'll take us across immediately."

I remained stubbornly silent.

"Time to get down, Laura."

"I'll stay on the wagon."

At least if the overgrown raft pitched us into the water, I would have something to cling to.

"You'll feel the sway more up there. We'll be an hour or more getting across."

"I don't care. I feel safer on the wagon."

"You'll be safer standing on your own two feet." He pointed to a crude wooden rail that stood like a short fence at the center of the boat. "You can hold on to that. Or me."

"I'll stay on the wagon, Husband."

He muttered under his breath, shaking his head. He led the team down a planked incline, keeping the descent slow and steady. Workers stood at the ready as we neared the shore.

The wagon lurched as the horses pulled it onto the huge flatboat, and I choked back a yelp. The weight dipped the raft, and my hands flew to clutch the seat as the platform rose from the water ahead of me. My stomach rolled.

One of the men tugged the horses forward, speeding them across the platform until the weight was centered. The pitching ebbed much more slowly. Laborers nailed blocks in front of the wheels as well as behind. Though their placement was careless, I knew the blocks were meant to keep the wagon from rolling off should the current become troublesome. Large as the ferry was, each step, each movement, still caused it to bob. My stomach protested, and I straightened, closing my eyes as I told myself not to be sick.

"I'd git down, missus," one of the men uttered.

I shook my head and twisted my handkerchief.

The ferryman disappeared, and I thought I heard him say, "Your funeral."

Oh lord.

The men took their places at the sides of the barge where large poles were threaded through rings. One of them gave a yell, and the operator on the shore released the rope. They shoved off, the raft sliding forward into the vast lane of water. The current caught, and the barge flowed downriver. The polemen, their feet widespread, shifted their weight with each swell and dug deeply to hold the boat on course. With the movement of the water, the wagon slipped forward, rolling until it hit the block, jerking to a stop, and rolling back again.

Acid rose into my throat, making the sour stomach I'd had these past three mornings trivial. I bent over the side of the wagon and heaved, again and again.

It was an inauspicious beginning to life in Iowa.

William lifted me from the wagon and wiped my mouth. Though I longed to simply crumple, he enfolded me into his arms and guided me to the rail, telling me to shift my weight as the boatmen did. I managed to control my nausea by the time we hit shore, but my dress was stained, and my mouth tasted bitter. I left the barge on shaky legs, thankful we'd made it safely across. A woman on the other side handed me a ladle full of water and pointed me to a bench where I waited while the wagon was unloaded from the ferry.

We stopped at the mercantile, buying supplies, and I gained

my first glimpse of life in Bellview. Well-stocked with all the necessary basics, including tea, the store would provision us with all we needed. Luxuries could be ordered, for a price. My apprehension dipped a bit. We would not want for supplies, at least.

As to our role in the community, I accepted it would not be as I'd expected. Despite William's insistence that we would be a leading family in our township, I knew how life worked. We were close to town; our community life would be in Bellview. William had placated me all this time, and I had no choice but resign myself to reality. At least, I would have a fine house to make into a home. In that, I would be able to make our dreams come true.

We trekked northward from town, toward the farm. Verdant green was everywhere. There were abundant trees and bright wildflowers blooming in welcome. I imagined looking out of my lace curtains to gaze upon the flora of this beautiful new land, breathing in the fragrance of summer blooms as I worked in my garden. I'd set the table with an embroidered tablecloth—one of the fine ones Mama said was from England, trimmed with Irish lace. I'd use my fragile china tea set, the other wives sipping and sharing delicate baked treats. Or, we might take our tea in the parlor where imported figurines would grace the side tables and a fine rug would warm the gleaming wood floor.

With town so close, I would be able to hire out laundry like Mama did. I hadn't thought to ask William about a laundress, but I was certain Bellview had one. After all, someone must have done wash for him and Monroe these past two years. I was sure I'd be able to hire a town girl to help out, as well. I'd ride one of the horses into town in the next few days to check. Glad I'd insisted on bringing my side-saddle along, I smiled to myself. We were near enough to town that I would be able to ride in often to attend social events. Never a wallflower, I would soon work my way into the fabric of the community, despite being a newcomer.

"Laura? Are you wool-gathering?"

I looked up. "I am, Husband. Daydreaming a bit."

"You're better?" His expression was soft, concerned, and I knew he loved me, despite our head-butting.

"I am, though I'll not want to do that crossing again."

"You won't need to." He grinned and patted my leg. "You seemed pleased with Bellview, once we were there."

"I was."

"And past your anger at me?"

"Yes." I paused, uncertain whether it was proper for me to lay out my feelings. In this, Mama had offered no advice. "You've been less than honest with me," I said, choosing my words and tone carefully lest I provoke another argument. "That does not bode well."

"I didn't mean to mislead you." His words were contrite, and I took solace in the apology.

Emboldened, I pressed on. "Perhaps it is time we talk about that tendency. We will not have a happy marriage if this continues. I am not a child to be mollified."

"I suspect we've much still to learn about one another." He clutched my hand, and we rode in silence for a while before he found his words. "I am discovering daily that you are a wholly different type of wife than my mother is, and that me being the type of husband my father is will not work well with us."

I thought about Father William's authoritative mannerisms, Mother Emily's quiet acquiescence. "No, it will not. I do not wish to be pacified, nor do I wish you to guide me around like a mule without regard to my opinion."

"And I don't wish to be contradicted."

I recognized his right in that desire and did not want to diminish it. Still, I'd not live with a lifetime of being shut out of planning for our future. "Perhaps if you were to ask me for my thoughts prior to making your decisions, I would not be so argumentative."

"You would still be very vocal, I believe. This is a side of you I had not seen until we were wedded."

No, we'd both taken great care to display only the best of ourselves during our courtship. "Nor had I seen you try to deceive me."

"It appears we have some work ahead of us."

"I will try to curb my tongue if you will treat me as your partner rather than as a child along for the ride."

He offered me a wry smile. "I can manage that."

"We are agreed, then."

We rounded a bend in the river and emerged from the trees where William halted the wagon. A small dwelling stood in front of us, unpainted wood planks forming its sides. A step up from a log cabin, it was coarsely built all the same. Our nearest neighbor, I suspected.

"Well? What do you think?"

I was about to open my mouth with a comment about how glad I was that our home was superior when Monroe opened the door, grinning like a fool.

Where was my grand house?

I waited for the anger to erupt. Instead, I felt only oppressing disappointment. This time, I had misled myself. William had told me we had a comfortable, furnished house. I had filled in my own meaning of comfortable. Tears stung my eyes.

I wanted to go home.

Chapter Two

Lavina
Seneca County, Ohio
The same year (1848)

At fifteen, I think myself quite worldly, venturing off into the unknown all on my own.

Well, almost on my own.

My brother, rocking beside me with the steady rhythm of the wagon, is intent on the plodding horses. I ignore him, having long since decided not to countenance him; he's but my conduit to my new life of independence.

"You doing all right, there, little sister?"

I bristle a bit at the reminder of my role as the baby of the family. "Fine."

"Won't be too long now." Leicester stretches his lanky limbs and flicks the reins.

I let go of my imaginings. I'm not worldly in the least, just plain simple Lavina Day. Still, I have high hopes of making my own way, perhaps as a teacher or a milliner or a seamstress. My father is aging, as is my mother. With both of them in their sixties, I am moving to live with Leicester's family and launch my own life. I'll not be too far, but I do feel grown-up to be leaving my childhood behind me.

I adjust the skirt of my new, full-length dress and pat my inexpert bun, hoping I've used enough pins to hold my heavy tresses. Not sophisticated but definitely all grown-up.

Never Let Go

The wagon rolls to a stop, and I recognize I've been musing again. I completely missed entering the town.

"Well, this is Tiffin."

I peer around, noting all the necessities . . . a general store, a cafe, blacksmith and livery, saloons. Board sidewalks line the street for two whole blocks. "Is there a school?"

"And a church. They're across town along with the courthouse."

Good. I file the fact away and glance up and down the dusty street again. No hat shop, but there is a dressmaker, and a bakery with aromas so delicious my stomach growls despite the fact I ate a sandwich on the road. I'm not much of a baker, or a cook for that matter, but I can learn. I don't want to live with Leicester forever, after all.

"Cinnamon rolls," Leicester comments, reading my thoughts.

"Was my nose twitching?"

"A little. Jump on down, and I'll buy you one to celebrate. It's not every day a girl leaves home."

My excitement patters to a stop. "You think Ma and Pa will be all right?"

"They'll be fine. There's enough family close by if needed."

He climbs from the wagon and hitches the horses to the rail while I scrabble down with more clumsiness than I desire. Long dresses take some getting used to. Leicester rescues me part way through, lifting me to the ground. "Surprised you didn't want to go live with our sister."

I scrunch my face. "Her boys would be the death of me. Besides, I wanted to get away from Trumbell County and make my own way."

"You're a few years away from that, little sister."

"I'm fifteen."

"Fifteen is young still," he says from his vantage point of twenty-five. He heads down the boardwalk. "You've a lot yet to learn before you're ready to be on your own."

I hitch up my skirt a bit, struggling to keep up with him under the bulk of my petticoats. "I went all the way through normal school, graduated from eighth grade. That's two whole grades more than you did."

"Pa got sick, needed my help working the forge. Else Ma would have made me stay in school."

"Well, you didn't, so you got no call telling me I'm not learned."

He stops. "There's more to life than book-learning."

"Pshaw."

"You'll see, little sister; you'll see."

He opens the door to the bakery and waits for me.

I step in, pouting. I'm always *little sister* to everyone. I want to be defined by who I am, not by my place in a long line of siblings. I'll show them all, I will.

"You want one or two?"

I eye the assortment of rolls in the case. Scents of cinnamon and maple fill the small shop along with heady vanilla and yeast. My mouth waters, and I fight a greedy urge to ask for two. One is a splurge. Only a child would ask for two. "Just one."

"One for each of us," Leicester tells the baker.

She hands us each a warm, gooey piece of heaven along with cloth napkins. Sticky caramel covers the top and drips onto my fingers. I peel a section away and stuff it into my mouth. Sweet bliss explodes on my tongue, and I shiver. "Mmmm."

Leicester laughs.

"Well, it's good," I protest.

We sit outside on a wooden bench, both of us wrapped up in enjoyment. I finish my roll, and Leicester pushes the last bit of his—the soft center—toward me. "I'm full," he says, but I know he isn't. I take it anyway, unable to resist the temptation.

"We sure have been looking forward to your help with the girls."

I jerk my head up. "I'd thought to find a job in town."

"A job?" Leicester's brow knits.

"Yes, a job. That's what people do when they strike out on their own." I straighten and wipe my fingers on the napkin like a lady instead of licking them.

"Lavina, you're fifteen."

"And?"

"Fifteen is too young for a girl to be out on her own. You'll be living with us, helping out, gathering experience with children. They've been chattering for weeks about their auntie coming. There'll be more than enough for you to do around the house with a trio of little ones."

I have no doubt about that, with all of the girls under the age of three. I'm sure it *is* an active household, but tending my nieces full time isn't what I'd planned on.

"I wouldn't be out on my own. I'd still be living with you, like a boarder."

Leicester shakes his head. "Ma and Pa put you in my care, and that means you're to mind me." His eyes soften. "You are too young to take a job. If you were a boy, I'd consider it, but you aren't. You'll stay at home and learn more about tending house and family. That's what Ma and Pa want."

"I'm not a child anymore." I stomp my foot, instantly regretting it and feel my face flush. Had he noticed, or had my skirts been enough to muffle the sound?

"No, you're not. But you aren't an adult either, and you will do as I say."

"But—"

"No buts, Lavina." His voice grows stern. "No arguments. You are not out on your own. Understood?"

I nod, the sweetness of the cinnamon rolls souring into a clump of resentment.

Seneca County, Ohio
1849

Six months into my life in Seneca County, I finally surrender to the fact that I'm not as grown-up as I'd thought. The girls humble me quickly, and I grasp I'll need a lot more experience with children before I can hope to be a teacher. Leicester and his wife, Christine, include me in their discussions, revealing I also know little about adult responsibilities. And so, I set about learning all I can, still determined to become independent but knowing Leicester has been right. I'm not ready.

By the time I turn sixteen, however, I gain confidence and earn Leicester's seal of approval. He grants me permission to test for a teaching certificate and I make plans to do so as soon as I study up. In the meantime, I decide to offer tutoring services to local students.

I stride toward the small white schoolhouse just after dismissal. The children have already run past, headlong and eager to leave their studies. Early autumn chill is in the air, and I clutch my shawl tighter around me. Though excited about the prospect of assisting students, I have more than a fair share of trepidation over approaching their severe teacher. I've never seen him so much as crack a smile. I straighten my dress and knock on the door.

"Enter." I recognize Mr. Beal's sharp voice and draw a deep breath before stepping in.

"Hello, Mr. Beal." I pause at the back of the main room, unsure if I should approach or wait for him to rise from his desk.

Intent on reading papers, he sighs and lifts his gaze. Annoyance crosses his features. "Yes?"

"I'm Lavina Day—"

"I know who you are. What do you want?"

Swallowing, I keep my head high and walk toward him, forcing a cheery smile. "I want to offer tutoring services to your students."

"*Your* services?"

"Yes, sir."

"Whatever leads you to believe you're qualified to tutor my students?" Disdain fills his haughty voice.

I shift before him, small as a mouse. "Well, you see, I've been studying for my teacher's examination and—"

Mr. Beal snorts.

Dryness fills my throat. "Sir?"

"You're a female."

I'm not sure what to do with his statement. Deny it? Obviously, I'm a girl.

I have no idea what he wants me to say. "I am," I finally state, feeling even more the fool.

He peers over the rim of his spectacles. "I don't believe females have the qualifications to teach, Miss Day."

"What?" I squawk the word before I've time to stop it. There aren't many women teachers, but it's hardly unheard of.

"Nor do I believe certificates should be awarded them."

"Oh."

He rises with another sigh and gestures toward the door. "Good day."

I step away, heat filling my face as it always seems to do. Silence lies thick in the air save for the clumping of my shoes. Halfway to the door, I stop. Had he misunderstood my intent?

I turn back.

"I'm not applying for your position. I'm offering to tutor any of your students who might need extra help."

He still stands next to his desk. "My students do not need assistance."

"They're all doing well? Even those who miss half the term due to field work?"

"They are proceeding at an acceptable rate for their situations."

"I'd work with them, in the evenings."

"They are busy in the evenings. Their families barely allow them to attend school in the first place. Do not make the mistake of thinking they will be permitted to forsake their chores to study."

"Couldn't you explore it?" Even to me, my voice sounds whiny.

"No, I couldn't. More precisely, I won't. I have exhausted my efforts in getting them into the classroom for a few months each winter, and I will not jeopardize that precarious advancement."

"But—"

"Furthermore, I don't desire your assistance." He speaks over my protest. "You have no business seeking to undertake public instruction. Go home, teach your nieces domestic skills, and keep your nose out of my classroom."

"But—"

"Good day." This time, he marches to the door and jerks it open. I step out, and he slams it behind me.

I bite my lip as the anger I'd suppressed floods through me. How dare he! I turn and reach for the doorknob.

"I wouldn't, Miss. Whatever was said between the two of you won't be advanced by you going back in."

I jump at the deep voice and drop my hand.

"Once he has his dander up, there's no negotiating. He does the same thing with the school board. Folks have learned the hard way to leave things be."

School board? I compose myself and face the man behind me.

Tall, he sits on a well-used wagon; his dirty overalls announce he's a farmer. "John Eastlick." He removes his straw hat, and a shock of black hair tumbles from it. "I'm from Eden Township."

I smooth my clothing and stand tall. "Lavina Day."

"Leicester's sister?"

"Yes, sir." I cross the school yard so we don't have to yell.

"What are you doing at the schoolhouse, Lavina Day?" He grins, showing even white teeth.

"Offering to tutor students."

"Little bird like you? You don't look much out of short skirts."

I want to take offense, but there'd been teasing in his tone. Besides, I can't afford to waste the opportunity to reach my goal via another route. "I'm sixteen and studying for my teacher's examination. Are you on the school board, Mr. Eastlick?"

The grin fades into an easy smile. "A bachelor like me? I'm afraid not. But your offer has merit, and I know some folks who would benefit from your skills. No reason why you couldn't talk to them directly, is there?" He jumps from the wagon and stands beside me, his height indeed making me feel like a bird.

Looking up at him, my pulse races. I tell myself not to get too excited.

"Folks in Eden Township?"

"The Swensons, an immigrant family. Parents don't speak much English. I'm sure the kids could use help with their lessons."

"That sounds perfect." The words come out of my mouth, but my thoughts are a world away wondering if his hair is as soft as it looks. The realization startles me.

"If you're agreeable, I can drive you over there after church on Sunday."

I agree mutely, no longer thinking about tutoring at all, only about spending more time with him.

Sunday service is intolerably long. I fidget, and Leicester frowns at me. He is less than pleased about me spending the day with John Eastlick. He made a fuss about his bachelor status and gossip, but Christine told him to hush and took up my case. His stern expression, days later, tells me he still disapproves. To be frank, I don't care. I squirm again, eager to get on with the day. I have students to acquire, after all.

John sits across the aisle, a little in back of us. I fight the urge to turn and look at him again given I've already stared at him once. His hair is combed today, but I like it better mussed, I think.

Finally, we receive the benediction, and the congregation shuffles outdoors. The day is bright and sunny, and I'm glad I don't need to cover my good Sunday dress with my shawl.

In the churchyard, Leicester approaches John, and they talk quietly before shaking hands. Christine winks at me. Then John turns to me.

"You ready, Miss Day?" he asks.

I've been ready all day but I don't say it. "I am."

"I'll have her home by supper," he tells Leicester.

"I'll be expecting it," Leicester says without a smile.

John points toward the trees, and we leave my brother and his family. I'm glad of it, as stifling as Leicester's mood has been. It's as if he doesn't want me to go talk with the Swensons.

"Your brother is protective."

"My brother doesn't want me to grow up. I can't imagine why it bothers him so that I take on tutoring in Eden Township. It didn't irk him when we talked about me tutoring here in Tiffin."

"I don't believe tutoring is the issue." John mumbles the

words as he leads me to a shiny buggy, *property of Tiffin Livery* marked on its side, and hands me up.

As he crosses round, it dawns on me. The rented buggy, his well-groomed hair, Leicester's attitude and comments about gossips. This isn't merely John being helpful. He's courting me. My telltale face heats, and I am glad he's not looking at me.

He settles onto the seat beside me. "Ready?"

We leave the churchyard, both of us silent. I'm at odds for words, of a sudden, as I work through the realization that John is attracted to me. Perhaps as much as I am to him. That insight frightens me. No one has ever courted me before, and I'm unsure of what to say, how to act.

I feel like a ship in a storm, with no heading and no control against the wind and the waves.

"The Swensons are good people," John says. For a moment, I panic, wondering if I'm wrong, if this is but a business trip after all. But I notice his grip on the reins is tight; he is as nervous as I.

"The parents don't speak much English, especially Mrs. Swenson," he continues, and I'm thankful he's found a topic for us. "There are three daughters in school, and their pa says Mr. Beal doesn't take the time to work with them."

Beal's condescension comes back to me. "It's because they're girls."

"I had it figured it was being immigrants."

"Mr. Beal doesn't much hold with educated females. When he refused my services, he said women weren't qualified. It made me mad enough to spit."

John laughs, easier with me now that we're in conversation. "That wouldn't have helped."

"I've little doubt of that."

We travel on, both of us relaxing a bit, and I glance at him. His eyes are a midnight blue, almost black. He catches my gaze and smiles. "Is that what you want to do with your life, Lavina?"

I startle a bit at the use of my given name but quiet as I interpret it as confirmation of my theory. The air seems charged, as if there is an energy quivering between us. I fight the urge to check my hair for falling tresses and focus on his question.

"I've always been of a mind to be on my own. Teaching is a way to accomplish that. And I like children."

"Most girls dream of marrying and settling down."

I ponder his words and wonder what it means that I've never thought much about love and marriage. "Maybe it's because I grew up the youngest of ten. Everyone always did for me instead of letting me do for myself. There hasn't ever been a time that I didn't want to be independent."

"Even if that means being a spinster? Teachers can't marry, you know. That's usually part of the contract."

"Why is that, do you suppose?"

"Duties of caring for a house and family, taboos against wives working outside the home, women being in a family way, favoring one's own children. I've heard all of those cited as reasons."

"That's not fair."

"Likely not, but it's the way of the world."

His agreement strikes me as significant. Unlike most men, he doesn't relegate women to lesser roles.

I'm not merely attracted to this man. *I like him.*

"Truthfully, I'd not given the marriage aspect much thought. Autonomy overshadowed all else, I guess."

We both digest my words, me with no small amount of trepidation. Was that what I wanted in life?

John turns and guides the horses down a long lane. We're almost there, and already I rue the loss of our private time.

"So you view independence only in light of having a job?" he asks.

"I . . . I guess I always have."

"Me? I see having my own land as independence."

"You own your farm?"

"Not yet. I'm saving toward buying my own place. For now, self-sufficiency is about relying on my own skills to choose what to plant, when to plant, to cultivate and bring in a good crop."

"We both have goals."

He slows the horses, pausing halfway down the lane, and looks straight at me. "Might you imagine meeting your goals in another way? As part of a team rather than on your own?"

"I've never thought about it."

At least not until today.

"Perhaps it's time you do." He reaches for my hand and covers it with his. "Because if ever there was anyone I'd like to work with, it'd be you."

Chapter Three

Laura
Jackson County, Iowa
Upon arrival, May 1848

"What do I think?" Outside the small house, I echoed William's question, unable to find the words to convey my dismay. I blinked away tears before he caught sight of them and drew a breath.

"It's twice the size of our neighbors' houses. I thought you'd like a sleeping room." Excitement filled his tone, and I knew he'd done his best to please me by providing two rooms. It was not a crude log cabin, and it was not a shack. For all its simplicity, it appeared solidly built. I vowed to look past the lack of polish and make the best of the situation. William was not a carpenter, and he'd spent time building this house, time away from clearing land.

I tried to muster enthusiasm. "I . . . uh . . . it's not what I expected."

He glanced at me and must have seen the disappointment still etched on my face. His expression softened, and he took my hand. "It's not as grand as your parents' house, but we need to start somewhere." He kissed my palm before jumping down from the wagon. "Come, look inside."

He lifted me from the wagon as Monroe rushed over to welcome us. We chatted about the trip and the sowing he'd completed. Monroe unhitched the horses while William, beaming with a pride I hadn't the heart to shatter, led me to the house. Noting the rough-shaved boards, I wished he had at least brightened the building with whitewash. The unpainted exterior spoke of poverty. I'd lived all my life in a large, painted, two-story house with clapboard siding, a wide front porch, and pretty flower boxes. This would all take adjustment, but I couldn't fault him for the basic exterior when he'd had so much else to do in clearing the land and reaping its bounty. We could make improvements. A little paint and flower beds would help considerably.

I followed him across the ground-level threshold into the house. With but two rooms, the interior would be cozy. Had he chosen cherry wood or maple for the furnishings? I hoped he'd been wise enough to stick with one for the entire house. Men seldom thought of such things, but surely the proprietor of the mercantile would have steered him when he placed the order.

The room was bare, save for a plank table, two rough, handcrafted chairs, a few crates tipped on their sides and stacked to make shelving, and a flat bench near the fireplace. Dimness dominated, with only a single window set into the opposite wall.

My throat closed.

Hard-packed dirt formed the floor, and mustiness hung in the air. Through the open doorway into the sleeping area, I viewed a few more crates and a bed, which appeared to be the only store-bought piece of furniture in the house. There was no cooking stove, just a fireplace with a crane to hold pots and swing them over the flames.

I stared first at the room, then at William, aghast. "This is the comfortable, furnished house you spoke of?"

"It's furnished." His tone was defensive.

"I've never cooked on an open fire. Never."

"You'll learn." His eyes glinted.

Hot anger flooded me at the thought of all we'd left behind in Indiana, at William's placating lies. I'd trusted him!

"My father said he'd send Mama's old Saddlebag stove, the one that's been sitting in the barn for years. You told him we had no need of it."

"We needed to travel light. A cast-iron stove would have weighed us down."

"He offered us any number of finely crafted pieces, and you told him the house was already furnished."

"It is. We have what we need, and we'll replace it when we can afford to do so. I won't take charity from your father."

My jaw dropped. "Charity? It would have been part of my dowry."

"It's my place to provide for you."

So we'd come to the meat of it. I cursed his pride along with his false pledges. "Well, you aren't doing much of a job of it, are you?"

His glare spoke volumes, but he punctuated it with further comment anyway. "Laura Duley, have you already forgotten your promise to me?"

"You deceived me in this, too, Husband."

"You will hold your tongue."

I held it, biting it until it bled. But I would not live in such a state. I would not. This shanty was not what he had promised me, and I *would* have my stove and my furnishings, if nothing else.

Honoring my end of our fragile bargain was not easy.

I covered the makeshift tables with fine crocheted doilies, tacked up cloth to provide privacy for the bedroom and to hide the stacks of dishes in the open crates, hung my lace curtains at the single window in each room, and covered the dirt floor with an abundance of rag rugs. It was a paltry effort, but the house grew homier in the process. I stitched cushions for the rough chairs and for the bench near the fire (to which William had added a back) and placed my wedding quilt on the bed. Underneath the trimmings, my furniture was still nothing but a hodge-podge of boxes and planks, but I'd no other choice but to make do.

I was not, however, able to adjust so easily to the lack of a cookstove. Cooking over an open fire was not a craft easily mastered. I did all right with the basics such as fried meat, boiled vegetables, potatoes, and stews, but biscuits and bread eluded me. Underdone, overdone, or combinations consisting of burnt crusts and mushy insides were the usual offerings.

My nausea grew worse each day and no longer confined itself to mornings. As the eldest of eight, I suspected the cause after the signs continued on a daily basis. I hid them from William, until I could be certain, choking back sour churning amid bouts of sweat. But, by the time Monroe departed a week later, I could fathom no other reason for my symptoms.

Life shifted into an endless pattern of cooking and housekeeping chores. I sowed the remaining garden vegetables, anxious to get them in before the morning sickness became more acute. William departed the house with his scythe each morning, returning for lunch before heading back to the fields. I learned to keep potatoes baking in the fire and to cook enough meat to serve it cold on laundry day when I had little or no time for anything but the clothes. Strenuous farm work meant I had to wash clothing more often than I had expected, and I now knew we hadn't the money to hire the work out to a laundress, nor for a hired girl.

I also knew the baby meant there were certain things I could not delay until harvest. We would need chickens, I decided, and a milk cow. While occasional purchases of eggs and milk at the mercantile might have worked for two bachelors, it would not do for a family. I craved butter and was already tired of tasteless bread, an added insult when it was over- or under-baked. I would need a varied diet to keep strong and healthy. And, truth be told, I did not have any idea how I was going to cope without a stove. I determined to ask William for all three items at once, for I wasn't sure I had the fortitude to argue with him three times.

I baked Johnnycakes on the day I planned to bring up the subject, having found a jug of maple syrup in the root cellar behind the house. After much experimenting, I'd finally got the timing right for them. I set the rough table with my white ironstone plates in lieu of the tin that William and Monroe had stocked. Adding a vase of wildflowers, I smiled to myself and waited for William to come in from the creek where he was washing up.

He paused as he stepped through the door, a smile lighting his face. "Something smells good."

"Johnnycakes. It took a bit of practice, but I think I got them right." I set the platter on the table, and we sat. It was a good start. "There's syrup."

"This is a nice change, a treat. You used to make such delicious cakes, while we were courting. Perhaps you might make one of those?"

I seized the opportunity, launching into the plan I'd strategized. "Husband, I know very little about raising crops, about when to sow and when to reap, what we will need to sustain us and what can be sold for profit."

"True enough."

"I would suggest that you know very little about cooking and baking and maintaining a household. Would I be correct?"

He glanced up from his plate, confused. "Monroe and I kept house."

"You and Monroe survived. From his accounts, you subsisted

on beans, bacon, and potatoes and wore your clothes until you couldn't stand the stench before taking them to a laundress."

"I guess that's a fair summary."

"And now that I am here, you prefer a more varied diet and your clothes clean?"

"You were taught those skills, so yes. I would expect that. I've been surprised that you never bake decent bread. Didn't your mother teach you to master that?"

Of course my mother taught me bread baking.

I itched to tell him exactly that but knew a moderate tone was needed. My next words would be a delicate balance between biddable and firm but must be devoid of any trace of shrewishness. "My mother taught me all of those skills, but you've tied my hands in applying them."

He looked up in earnest.

"My kitchen skills were learned on a cookstove. Baking bread over an open fire is a very different art entirely. I spend hours making dough, letting it rise, punching it down only to have it ruined because I cannot predict the heat level correctly. Green wood burns differently than dry wood, disrupting the predictions I make based on what happened the day before. I don't know whether to swing the pot over the fire or to set it in the embers, nor do I know how long to leave it there."

"Stoves are expensive."

He'd missed the point entirely, even while spooning the Johnnycake into his mouth. It was time to change tack.

"I can't prepare meals properly. I have to disrupt cooking to use the crane to heat water for the laundry, which has become an all-day process in the heating of one pot of water at a time, let alone the time it takes to do the wash itself. I can't cook a varied menu because I have only a small supply of eggs and milk, purchased on the occasions that you have time to go into Bellview. We have no butter, which further limits me."

"We can't afford—"

"It takes three times as much wood to keep the open fire going," I continued, launching into yet another line of reasoning. "A stove would use less fuel, heat the room in the winter, save me both time and effort, and allow me to provide you with foods more to your liking."

"The cost—"

"If you wish me to keep this house in the manner you expect, I require a stove, a milk cow, and chickens."

There, I'd said it. I let the words sink in. Though I had but one round of ammunition left, he had no clue how powerful it would be. "You promised me a comfortable life, William. You have not provided it. You have bound my hands so that I cannot be a good wife to you, nor a good mother."

"We've a while before we need to worry about that." And with that, he brushed my request away.

Oh, William, you still do not understand, do you? Though I'd hidden my nausea, he'd missed the changes in my body as only an unsophisticated man could. I drew a breath and fired the shot.

"No, we do not have a while. I am sick every morning and have not had my courses. There will be a baby early next year."

He paused, his spoon halfway to his mouth, then set it back on his plate. "A baby?"

"I have all the signs."

"I'm going to be a father!" He pushed from his chair, rushing to engulf me in his arms.

"Do you know much about what women go through during this time? What babies need?" I asked the question against his chest, sure he was naïve in this as well.

"I was still a kid when Monroe came along."

"Already, my chores are more difficult. In the coming weeks and months, there will be days I cannot keep food down, and, when I can eat, I will need milk and eggs to help the babe grow. I will tire easily and cry at the drop of a hat. I will be cranky, and I will grow unable to do much of what I do now. And once the baby is born, it will take more time than you can imagine."

He drew back, looked me in the eye. "I didn't know," he said softly.

"I realize we haven't much extra money. But I am not asking for luxuries nor even for all of what you promised me—"

He shook his head. "Laura, I can't satisfy your whims."

Biddable slid from my grasp, and I crossed my arms, anger seething.

He would not deny me this. Though I suspected my eyes flashed, I did not yell. "This is not a whim," I told him in clipped, no-nonsense words. "You *did* promise me comfort, Husband. What you have provided is not what I envisioned when you gave me that vow. You have supplied enough to meet my needs, but that was *not* what you pledged. For now, I will accept that we cannot afford comfort. But in asking for the stove, the cow, and the chickens, I am requesting you to meet our baby's needs, not my comfort."

"Do you understand the cost of what you're asking?"

"I do not. And I care not."

I met his troubled gaze and held it. "Even if you have to write my father and ask him to ship Mama's cast-off stove or beg him to send money to us, you will do this. This is no longer about me and my 'whims.' Your child is depending on you, and, if you fail to provide for us, I will return to Indiana."

By the end of the week, I acquired a brand new Stanley rotary-top cookstove, a dairy cow, a chicken coop and a dozen laying hens, along with Mrs. Tucker. William purchased the former; Mrs. Tucker arrived on her own.

I found her perched on a stump like one of the hens when I

emerged from the smokehouse one morning.

"You Laura Duley?" she asked. "I'm Hattie Mae Tucker. Ran into Mr. Duley over at the mercantile t'other day. I'd heard he took a bride, so I asked on about you. Got an earful, I did. Made sure your man did, too, once I heard you was having a hard time of it. Told him it weren't fair of him to leave you struggling. So here I am."

I grappled for my social graces. "Would you like to have tea?"

Even to my own ears it sounded odd.

Mrs. Tucker cackled, her wrinkled jowls shaking. "Oh, lordy, girl. I ain't here to have no tea party. I'm gonna learn you what you need to know to get through what's coming." Slapping her hand against her ample thigh, she caught my gaze. "You ready?"

Relief bubbled through me. If this woman was here to make my life easier, I was ready and willing to learn anything she had to offer. "I am."

"Well then, let's get things going. You look pasty. Guess we'd best brew up some tea anyways." She stood and glanced around. "You growing any ginger root?"

Monroe had left me a nicely turned garden plot, fenced to keep the deer at bay, but I knew ginger was not growing there. It required shade, and I'd seen no other plantings. "I don't think so."

"Might be they traded for some. Got a cellar?" She stalked around, looking for evidence of a pair of wooden doors set into the ground.

"Behind the house," I told her.

She turned in her tracks. I followed like a lost sheep, drawn to her take-charge, plain-speaking personality. She was rough around the edges but would be of tremendous help to me, if I could keep up with her. My stomach turned, and I covered my mouth with my hand. She clucked, descended into the cellar, and emerged with a handful of ginger root.

"First thing, you gotta move slow-like. No popping out of bed or sprints across the yard." She thrust the ugly root into my hand. "Peel and slice, boil it up for ginger tea. Else grate a bit in a cup of boiling water. It'll calm your stomach. You know how to bake soda bread?"

"If you've a recipe, I can follow it."

She marched into the house and eyed the new stove, a shiny wonder that took up a large portion of the front room. "Turntable, is it?" She hustled over and turned the crank, rotating the top. "Hmph."

"William thought it would be easier on the baby if I didn't have to do so much lifting." I turned the cooking surface so the pot of water I kept at the back of the stove was over the heat and set about grating the root.

In truth, William had selected the model for its replaceable parts, which would eliminate the need to buy an entirely new stove should anything wear out, but I doubted it was prudent to tell Mrs. Tucker so. It was best she believe he'd provided me the benefit of cooking four pots at once, all at varying heat without the need to shuffle them around as a thoughtful gift.

"And, look, there are two fuel reservoirs." I pointed out the doors, at the bottom and side. "I can keep one hot and the other cool."

Mrs. Tucker rolled her eyes. "You can cook and bake?"

"Now that I have a stove, yes." William had received his first cake last night and spent the entire evening doting on me.

"Got the chores down-pat?" she probed. "Laundry? Milking and collecting the eggs?"

"I do." I gathered the ginger shavings into an infuser and reached for a cup, tired just listening to her rapid-fire questions.

"How 'bout butter-making and putting up the vegetables? Butchering?"

"I know how to make butter, and Mama taught me to can,

though I've never done either on my own. I've never butchered."

"Dip that there cup into the water. No need to go lifting the pot. Keep things easy. I'll sell you a butchered hog this year. Pregnancy don't go so well with that whole mess. Meantime, I'll take you under my wing. I reckon I can spend a day a week with you. Learn you on making soda bread this week, get that morning sickness battled. Lift that water for you on laundry day. See to the butter and cheese making, help you with that garden once the waddle gets bothersome. You'll need a hand with the canning when that time comes, and with the birthing."

I turned, the cup still empty in my hand. "You would do all that for me?"

"Don't mind the company, me being a widow and all. I'll take home a share of what we make, and we both get a boon."

My chin dropped. William would not take kindly to sharing our foodstuffs.

Beside me, Mrs. Tucker cackled again. "He don't know how much butter or cheese a churn of milk makes, and he don't know what comes out of that garden. The secret to managing a man is to keep him in the dark, dear. Never, ever, tell a man more than he needs to know. Now finish up brewing that tea and drink it down."

We sealed our deal, not without a share of trepidation on my part, and William was none the wiser. Mrs. Tucker visited often, providing guidance and wisdom. Well past fifty, she had raised a flock of children and advised that my constant backache was not to be feared and that some mothers did indeed remain sick to their stomachs for months, particularly with their first child.

She also kept me amused with her tales of the early days. She and Mr. Tucker had moved to the frontier early, in the 1820s, when the Sac and Fox tribes still lived in the area. Since that time, they'd given up all their lands in Iowa. The Potawatomi had ceded their lands two years ago, and only the Sioux remained, far away to the northwest.

Her stories explained why we'd seen no natives in the area, and I was glad of it. William had told me not to worry about Indians, but I had harbored fears that he had misled me in that area as well. It was good to not have to worry for our safety in addition to all the other adjustments the frontier, and my pregnancy, brought.

By the time Ellen was born in early 1849, this primitive life I had never expected to live became routine. We named her for my dear sister and found her a true blessing. Hale and robust, she was a perfect baby, sleeping through the night in no time. It seemed as if she'd spent out her difficult days in my womb and was now content to sleep and gurgle and smile. She became the center of my world. William doted on his little girl, proving himself a proud and playful father and an unexpected helpmate as we adjusted to family life.

I came to love time outdoors with Ellen, so alert was she to all that occurred around her. I enjoyed her company immensely as I again sowed my garden, the time flying past. William and I also grew in our relationship. I learned, as Ellen sat and gurgled at us, of William's desire to make his own way rather than to simply follow in the footsteps of our parents and grandparents. This new insight provided me understanding into why Iowa was so important to him. We spent our summer evenings on the porch he had added, talking about our dreams and shaping a new vision for our future.

Ellen's quick transition to sleeping full nights without need of feedings left me unexpectedly fertile, and a second child was on the way. As I grew in girth, we joined a congregation in Bellview, traveling to Sunday services each week and forging our place in the community. William handled butchering in deference to my once-again-daily morning sickness, even into the middle of pregnancy. He'd softened since our early days of marriage, no longer seeking to shape our relationship after that of his parents. Winter offered up blizzards and heavy snowfall, and he took over tending the cow and the chickens during the worst of it, as I grew larger and more cumbersome.

Emiley, named for William's mother, was born just after the new year, again with Mrs. Tucker's help, about the time Ellen took her first steps.

The two kept me busy, and I was thankful the season meant fewer outdoor chores for us. As the snows melted, they left both mud and green buds. They also left swollen rivers. William told me about Minnesota Territory, where the snows were even worse, all of the melt draining into the Mississippi. As it flowed south, a half mile distant, it roared with that run-off. Even our small Spruce Creek filled to the brim before receding and leaving us with true spring in all its green glory.

None of us suspected the storms to come.

Spring exploded into summer. Once again, I relished my outdoor chores, though my attention was now divided among my tasks and the children. Ellen was ever busy, toddling as fast as her little legs could go. Oh, how she gurgled and chattered in her baby language. Emiley was eager to sit on her own, as if she needed to keep pace with her sister, and I suspected she would tackle crawling with the same enthusiasm. I had little doubt the two of them would keep me on my toes.

Though not the life I had once envisioned, it was finally one that fulfilled me. Looking at my two little towheads, I envisioned tiny princesses who would live out their own fairy-tale lives. William and I would make sure of it. Already, we were carving a place for the girls in the community. Our church family had taken us into the assembly and William had been named an officer of the congregation. Our daughters would grow up being part of a leading family, just as William and I had.

Most Sundays, the congregation gathered along the river, a short way from the church, for a group picnic. By tradition, we met near a sandbar that blocked the busy current so that the older children could wade in the river without fear of being swept away. As the summer went on, we craved the cool breezes offered up by the water, and we spread our quilts ever nearer the shoreline. By August, the Sunday respite from the heat became the highlight of our week.

The day was glorious, perfect in its sunny splendor, and I looked forward to a few relaxing hours with William. As church ended, he hinted that he had something to discuss, something that would impact our future, and I was intrigued by the wide smile that had not left his face since he'd clustered with several other men earlier that morning.

He spread the quilt away from the shore in deference to the children's safety. Ellen had developed a habit of following the older children, and we felt it best to put distance between her and those wading in the river. Emiley had mastered sitting, though she still tumbled over from time to time, and was already scooting herself along. She would be crawling soon, which would be a further challenge to our diligence.

We spread out tin plates and jars of tea, and I set down the basket. I'd fried a chicken the evening before, and my family was eager to devour it. We ate, each of us tending to one of the children, and finished the meal off with chocolate cake and faces smeared with frosting.

As I cleaned the girls up and repacked our luncheon supplies, William suggested a walk. Minutes later, we ambled toward the river, Ellen scampering ahead while Emiley fussed in William's arms.

"I've been talking with Riling." The reference was to a leading member of the congregation and businessman who owned a flour mill located a few miles distant, where the river ran fast and steady. "He's offered to take me under his wing."

I glanced at William, curious. "In what way?"

"I'd like to learn a bit more about milling, how it all works."

"As in running the business?"

"As in the millwright trade." He shifted Emiley, who by now was squirming like a little pink piglet. He shushed her and waited for my response.

William's proposal revealed a side of him I'd not previously known. In our conversations about the future, he'd always talked of land and farming. "I had no idea you were interested in machinery."

"I'm thinking ahead. The late spring had me worried. Having trade skills would be a good hedge against the uncertainty of farming." He jostled Emiley again.

"Do you want me to take her?" Sadie, one of the girls from the congregation, approached. "I could take both girls to the river. Ellen could wade at the edge, and Emiley could dangle her feet."

William looked relieved and handed Emiley over to her.

I worried, though. I'd never surrendered them to anyone else's care. "You'll take care with them?" I narrowed my eyes, making sure the fourteen-year-old understood my concern. "They can be a handful."

"I'll keep them near." She took Ellen's hand and walked away, chatting with my excited daughter.

"Stay out of the current," I yelled after her. I shouldn't fret so much. It was the hallmark of young mothers, I guessed, and it was time I allowed the girls a bit of freedom. I stood, watching them go, until William offered a soothing rub to my back.

"Mother Hen," he teased. "They'll be fine. Sadie is good with the little ones." He took my hand and led me to a batch of cottonwood trees where the shade would provide us a measure of relief from the summer heat. "What do you think? About the mill?"

"It's a logical thought, learning a trade," I told him as we sat. "It would be a good thing, should the weather bring problems. That said, how would you be able to do such a thing? The fieldwork takes all your time."

"I'd thought to spend my time with him in the winter months. He'd have to understand I'd only go to the mill on good days. It would mean leaving the three of you on your own." He rubbed my hand. "I could milk before I left, but you would have to handle the afternoon chores."

"We'd need to figure out how to keep the girls occupied. The last thing I need is for them to end up in the manure pile or kicked by the cow. Maybe fence off a small area in the barn for them?"

My gaze drifted toward the river. An entire gaggle of children was gathered there, but Sadie sat, as promised, at the edge of the water, Emiley beside her and Ellen within reach. Satisfied, I turned back to William.

"I could come up with something," he said.

I scrambled to reason out the benefits and drawbacks, to catch the possibilities William might have missed in his excitement. By now, I understood he was wont to do that, and it was my responsibility to sharpen his awareness. "Would you be paying for this training?"

William smiled, appreciation for my careful thought. "I would provide my labor in return for the instruction, learning as I work. Riling's millwright will take charge of me."

I was pleased he'd already thought to address that point, and I marked it into my mental ledger, moving to the next item. "You would bring in the harvest and finish the butchering?"

"Of course."

"And repairs needed on the house and outbuildings? Projects

we've agreed upon?"

"Yes, you have my word."

I paused, noting nothing more in the debit column of the ledger. "What am I not seeing, Husband?"

"I guess that we would lose the winter days together. I've enjoyed those."

He was correct in counting that as a loss. I would rue surrendering that time, but the skills he gained would be an asset. Recalling the past two winters, I found the missing factor—pregnancies. "The winters have been times of ungainliness for me."

He sighed. "There has been that."

This, then, might be the sticking point. I could tell from his scrunched shoulders that he'd not thought of this, and I knew he didn't truly understand how difficult those months were for me. I drew a breath and treaded with care. "You've eased my chores much, each of those times. Would you anticipate I do without that aid should we find ourselves expecting again?"

He started. "You're not, are you?"

"No, but you do realize babies are an inevitable outcome of our relations? Emiley's quick conception indicates I am a fertile woman. Should I conceive in the coming months and find myself in the midst of a difficult pregnancy, I would expect not to endure it alone."

"Women go through pregnancy all the time, Laura."

I'd anticipated his hackles would rise, as they did each time he didn't want to hear my concerns. It was his nature, and, though I hated battering horns with him, it was easier to do so now than after the fact. I'd learned by now that these small confrontations were simply the way it was with us.

"Yes, they do, but it is a different experience for each of us. Not all women retch for month after month, and not all women suffer excoriating back pain throughout. Emiley was easier, but you remember how difficult it was with Ellen? I would not take kindly to you being gone every day if I were to find myself in the same situation again. We are a partnership."

His jaw tightened. "My back hurts every day from sowing until harvest. I sweat until I'm drenched. My hands blister, and my stomach growls. Have you heard me complain?"

"No, and I do not minimize your hard work."

I paused, letting him digest that I understood him. "But, I also work hard. I spend days on my knees in the garden to keep it weeded so we have vegetables for the winter and extra garden truck to sell at the mercantile. Those long days give me pain at night. I milk, tend chickens, smoke meat, put up food for the winter, launder our clothes, feed you three times a day and our children far more often. Every two hours when they are infants. And when they are finally abed, I knit and mend and churn butter until I fall into our bed. At sunrise, I do it all again. Do not make the mistake of assuming all of that occurs without effort simply because you are in the field and do not witness it. We both work hard, William."

"I'm sorry, Laura. I do realize all of that."

"I don't want to have an argument later, if we make this decision now."

"Let's confront that obstacle if we encounter it. I don't want to lose the opportunity by delaying. Riling could easily take on someone else. This is a chance for me to learn a craft that could be important."

We'd not completely settled things, but at least I'd raised the points that needed to be aired. It seemed a sound idea and William had asked for my opinion, as I'd requested of him. It was more than many husbands did, and I had no reason to suspect the winter would bring any change to our circumstances anyway.

"I should go find Riling, tell him I'm his man." William stood and offered his hand. "Want to come with me?"

Shrieking sounded from the river. I glanced toward the children, my breath stuttering.

Someone's dog ran through the water, the crowd of children splashing and squealing in delight. Ellen tottered after it, then plopped on her bottom, spraying water everywhere. She wailed, startled. Sadie stood and headed over to put her back on her feet, the dog still spinning in circles amid the group.

My gaze shifted back to Emiley, anticipating her laughing appreciation for the pup's antics and her sister's sudden splat. Instead she lay in the water, face down, the dog whirling around her.

Panic surged through me, and I sprang to my feet, my legs churning amid my skirts. "Emiley!"

William sprinted ahead of me, reaching the river faster than I, and plucked her from the water. He shook her, called her name, terror in his voice. Sadie stood with Ellen in her arms, her eyes wide with alarm. I reached them just as William began pounding Emiley's limp back, and I knew.

Deep inside me, I *knew.*

Dread clawed at me, shredding every fiber of my being.

Chapter Four

Lavina
New Bedford, Illinois
A few years later, 1857

John and I married the year after we met, a month past my seventeenth birthday. My aspirations of becoming a teacher blew away with the first blizzard of the winter—and John's first kiss. I found I wanted nothing so much as to be a supportive wife. Nearly seven years and three children later, my feelings are still as strong, but being supportive has required more patience than I'd anticipated.

Our own land, John's goal for so long, continues to elude us. We struggled to make a living in Eden Township. With the boys, Merton, Frank, and Giles, born one after another, our budget grew lean. We headed west, to Indiana, but land prices there, too, were beyond our means. And so, we have come to Illinois in hope of easier purchase.

I am weary of relocation but trust in John when he says we will have our dream. Spring holds promise, and, already, John has the crops sown. We anticipate a profitable year and cross our fingers there will be no problems. If all goes well, we will purchase our own land next year.

"Lavina?"

At the sound of my friend's voice, I glance up from my mending. Sophia Ireland stands at the open door, her daughters in tow. "Do you have time to talk?"

I struggle to my feet and waddle like a duck to greet her. My thick hair swings behind me in a heavy braid. I simply have no energy to wrestle with it these days.

"You shouldn't have gotten up," she says and envelops me in a hug. Sophia and her husband Tommy are an unexpected blessing to us. Tommy, more than ten years John's senior, is a fountain of knowledge and the source of much valuable advice.

I shoo Sophia's words away with my hand. "I need to move a bit anyway. This one is kicking up a storm."

The children cluster together, chirping with ideas for play. Roseanna and Giles are both three with Ellen not too far behind. Merton and Frank, pretending to be big boys, shepherd them into the yard to meet John's new dog. Sarah, the baby, stays in Sophia's arms as she sits at my table.

We chatter about my pregnancy while I bustle around, putting water on for tea, but my mind is not on our words. It's rare that Sophia shows up in the middle of the day. Busy lives take precedence over visiting and I wonder more than a little about the unusual visit. Once the tea is ready, I set two cups on the table and ease into the chair across from her.

"Now, what is it?" I ask.

Sophia blows out a heavy breath. "Tommy wants to move."

I gawk at her.

Then I push away my panic at the possible loss of my dearest friend and absorb what this might mean for her. She is a local New Bedford girl and is not accustomed to relocations. I know how she is feeling. I cried when we left my family behind in Ohio, despite all my bluster over being on my own.

"Men talk of moving all the time," I say, not wanting to acknowledge where such talk leads.

"We argued."

Her soft admission reveals much. Tommy dotes on Sophia. She stole his widowed heart when they met, and he never has a sharp word with her. Disquiet fills me. "I thought Tommy was happy here."

"I did, too."

We stare at one another for a moment, both of us uneasy. I can't fathom what has gotten into Tommy to want to leave Illinois. Life is good here, for all of us. "Whatever is in his head to prompt talk of moving?" I finally ask.

"Land. What else?"

I don't understand. While we still lease land, the Irelands own forty acres. "But you have land."

"He says we need more, that there's nothing worth having that edges on our property." She sounds resigned, and my panic returns. I don't want to lose my friend.

"What about nearby?" I ask. There has to be a solution that won't tear them away from us. "You could sell your place and get something in the next county."

"That's what I told him." She sighs.

"And?"

"And he says it's too settled in Illinois; the best land is already claimed. He wants to go west."

West. I know that word too well.

"Where?"

"Minnesota Territory."

"The territories? He does want unsettled!"

She puts her hand to her mouth, and I regret my words.

"He says Minnesota will become a state soon, and this is our chance. The territorial government is trying to build the population. You can preempt whole sections of land. That's four times what we have now. And we can pay for it later."

If all this is true, Tommy will have told John; they will have talked about it in depth. My hand covers my womb as it dawns on me that I may be once again packing up and rocking my way west with an infant in arms.

Olmstead County, Minnesota
The following year, 1858
"Tommy says Rochester has been incorporated," John tells me. We've been in Minnesota for a year now, having left Illinois with the Irelands when Freddy was but a few weeks old. The soil is rich, and the county is filling fast. We were lucky to get here when we did.

I set a bowl of fried potatoes on the table and lurch back to the stove for the ham. The pinch in my back twinges, and I wince. "What's that mean?" I ask John as I return to the table.

"It's now bigger than a town." He grins.

"Ha ha." John is in good humor tonight, and I am glad of it.

"Put Freddy in the high chair for me, will you?"

My back pains have been low and steady, but the cramping heralds a change. I hope I can get the boys fed and settled into bed before the labor pains start in earnest. Together, John and I dish up their meals and cut meat for Freddy and Giles. As usual, by the time we get to our own meals, all is cooling. At least Freddy is eating on his own now, picking up the food with his fingers but thankfully all by himself.

I continue to pad around the kitchen rather than taking my chair, and John raises his brow in question. At baby number five, he recognizes the signs.

He keeps the boys entertained, whistling tunes and telling them how the French explorers paddled their canoes into the area nearly two hundred years ago and met the Sioux and Ojibway and Winnebago Indians. Now, this area is devoid of the natives, and the Dubuque Stage carries travelers. In all, it's a pleasant area, the land fertile and plentiful. We've made a good home here, the Irelands nearby.

Finally, our life has settled, and I believe John will be content. Prosperity and our happiness have a good start here. A contraction grasps me, and I exhale.

"Should I get Sophia?" John asks.

"In a bit." There is little sense in sending for her yet. I calculate it will be some time before I need her.

"Mama, do you need me to put the boys to bed?" Merton asks. At seven, he remembers Freddy's birth and is intuitive enough to sense what John and I have left unsaid.

I smile at my oldest, this wonderful child who is always so responsible. "Can you do the dishes for me?" I ask, knowing Giles and Frank will be likely to pout and cause him problems. "Boys, off to bed."

"But, Mama . . ." they grumble, a nightly ritual.

"Boys," John says as he takes Freddy from the high chair.

The single word is enough, and they trudge into their sleeping room. Soon, we'll need to purchase another bed. Once Freddy leaves the crib, they can sleep crosswise on the mattress, but it will be a stopgap measure, good only until they sprout in height. Merton already is tall for his age.

John tends them as I continue to pace in the other room, my hand at the small of my back where the pangs grow increasingly stronger. I get out my nightgown and change into it before spreading an oilcloth over our feather tick and stacking clean sheets and towels on it.

My back seizes, and I gasp, tears springing into my eyes. Lord, but this one is putting up a fuss.

"Lavina?" John is at my side, concern etched on his face.

"Get Sophia."

He flees out the door. Another contraction grips me, sooner than I anticipated. Hard and vise-like. Still, my water hasn't broken, and I tell myself not to worry. There's time. But my skin grows clammy as time stretches.

I am panting by the time John returns with Sophia.

She eyes me, then John. "Make sure the water's on," she says and waits for John to move away. "Are you close?" she asks.

"I don't know. This doesn't—" Pain grips me and my legs weaken. My hand flounders, seeking something to steady myself. They help me into bed as my stomach ripples. It feels like I am being sliced with a knife.

Sophia spreads my legs, checking my progress. She shakes her head. Another spasm hits me, and I finally feel the warm liquid rush of my water breaking. Again, I contract and scream against the pain.

We bury William Merton Eastlick as soon as I recover the strength to stand at his graveside. I remember very little about the night he was born, save that it seemed to last forever. His middle name honors our oldest, who, at only seven, kept his brothers occupied the entire night. I feel guilty that I somehow caused his death. Sophia tells me it wouldn't have mattered. This one, conceived so soon after Freddy was born, was too weak to survive.

The loss of the life I nurtured for these past nine months nearly chokes the life from me as they lower his tiny little casket into the dark grave. This is the first child I've lost, and, though I know it's common for children to die, it shocks me to my core.

Next to me, John is shaking.

I take his hand, and we both squeeze tightly, taking solace in our shared despair. Life leaves little time to mourn, and I'm thankful we can support one another.

Sophia has charge of my other boys and has explained things to those old enough to understand, holding them close in my stead as they grieve.

But I know that tomorrow, they will have need for me. There will be no room for my sorrow. I must cling to them instead.

Chapter Five

Laura
Jackson County, Iowa
1850, following Emiley's death

The time following Emiley's death dragged on without end. My body was leaden, and it was an effort even to rise from my bed each morning. I wanted to curl up and surrender my soul so that she would not be alone in heaven, and I would not be alone here on earth. I wanted to escape the ever-present grief that racked my body. And I wanted to go home, to my mother and to the calm safety of our family farm.

Ellen's happy chatter brought me no solace those first troubled weeks as I struggled to complete my household duties. Mrs. Tucker visited frequently, helping with laundry and meals. It was August, and William was in the fields from dawn until dusk tending to haying and beginning the harvest. Nights, he was curt and withdrawn. We each lived in our own minds, separate and angry and lost.

In September, nearly a month after Emiley was taken from us, Mrs. Tucker sat down at the table across from me. I'd been sitting in my chair, unfocused but for the handkerchief I twisted in my hands.

"Laura?"

I looked at her and sighed, the exhalation long and drawn. What did she want of me? Couldn't she see I just wanted to be left alone? I was tired, so very tired, and she'd already ousted me from my bed, as she'd begun to do each time she visited. I laid my head on the table and closed my eyes.

"Laura Duley!"

"What?" I murmured, keeping my eyes closed against the sun. Was it time for Ellen's nap soon? I'd lost track. Maybe Mrs. Tucker would let me take back to my own bed. My bones ached, and I was so tired.

"Child, you got to snap out of this." Her voice was stern, nothing like the soothing caretaker I desired her to be.

"No. No, I don't. I need to sleep."

"You need to go outside, into the sun. Jerk some carrots out of the ground. Knead some bread dough, punch it fierce-like."

My head was so heavy, how could I possibly perform chores?

"It's too much."

"You don't get up, you ain't gonna get past this. You lost a child, but you got another, and she's growing as dark and melancholy as you. You owe her better'n that. You must not let go here. A mother can never let go."

"I can't."

"You can, and you will. Else you'll lose two daughters instead of one."

Panic surged through me, and I lifted my head.

"You are driving Ellen to distress. For her sake, you need to quit moping. Put your attention on that little one instead of on yourself. I got work to be done at home, and I can't be here taking care of you and her no more. It's time you get back to your life."

"You aren't going to help me?" My voice sounded pitiful, petulant.

"I am helping you," she bellowed. "Get up out of that chair and go pull carrots. Now."

I stood, wooden, haggard, and trudged outside. The sun blinded me, and I squinted against it as I plodded toward the garden. A blanket and basket awaited me. I sighed, sank to the ground, and stared at the frilly carrot tops. I'd forgotten how pretty carrot tops were.

"Go on, girl. Yank 'em out."

I glared at her brusque orders. She was a witch to make me go out into the sun and do chores when I needed so badly to sleep. Angry, I grasped the leafy top and tugged. Nothing. I cursed the dratted vegetable for its resistance. Finally, I jerked hard, nearly falling over as the carrot erupted from the ground. I slammed it into the basket and wrenched up the next one. With each hostile carrot, I cursed and rebelled until the basket was full, and tears streamed down my face.

I sobbed in that garden for nearly an hour.

True to her word, Mrs. Tucker put me back to work, brooking no argument, and I took out my despair on bread dough, butter churning, and laundry until I had no anger or misery left. Each day, living became easier. The following week, she stopped coming and left me on my own. I set about putting my life, our lives, back in order.

Ellen, who had become silent and woeful, finally received the attention she needed, and I spent every spare minute with her, cajoling her back into the happy little girl she had once been.

William, too, softened as fall wore on, and we tackled butchering and winter preparations together. His eyes were still filled with sorrow, but we found solace in one another again, and in Ellen. We didn't talk of the day by the river.

We'd buried Emiley near the house, a quiet family service sending her off. Sadie had sent a note, full of grief, and I responded, telling her we did not hold her responsible. If anything, it was my fault for sending such a small child with her. It had been an accident, nothing more, a baby who had fallen over face-first into shallow water. But I did not return to

Sundays at church, nor did I allow William to take Ellen with him. Though I recovered from my grief, I would not be careless again with my remaining child. Here, at home, I could remain watchful for danger and keep her protected. Elsewhere, there were too many risks.

As winter descended upon us, Ellen uttered her first clear words; William spent his days at the mill, learning of the machinery vital to its operation. Ellen and I played games, sang nursery rhymes, and read fairy tales. I made a vow, during those months, that Ellen would have the life I had not received, and my mind explored how that dream might be attained.

In becoming a millwright, William was opening doors for that future. He'd be able to operate any mill; whether it be flour or lumber, the basic machinery was the same. One day, we could leave the constant toil of farming and have our own mill. We would live in town, and Ellen would enjoy calls from neighbors and teatime. She, and I, would have the life William had promised.

All we needed to do was hang on until he learned the craft, and we could set aside the money we would need to make that transition.

I could do that. I would.

Winona County, Minnesota Territory
Early 1856, six years after Emiley's death
We left Iowa six years later. Six long, interminable years.

Beaver village would be our new start, one we both desperately needed. Five-year-old Willie and two-year-old Emma rode in the wagon behind us, quietly playing. Ellen lay in a grave next to Emiley. We'd lost her when she was three, while en route home from a visit to Illinois. The raft ferry was struck by a log, heaving so suddenly that she fell and was pitched into the river, drowned like her sister before her. I'd spent months desolate, once again unable to function until Mrs. Tucker took charge and reminded me I must not let go. Leaving them had reduced me to sorrow once again, but I knew our new home would be safer for our remaining children as well as the one kicking inside my womb.

We'd made the decision to move in the year following Ellen's death. I refused to cross that river ever again and feared even nearing its rushing waters or what might happen should it flood. William promised me he would find us a less dangerous home and had staked a claim on farmland in Minnesota Territory two years ago. While there, he'd met several other pioneers. With them, and with my full support, he'd made plans to form a town. The children and I had taken advantage of the break in winter weather to move before the baby came, taking the stage from Dubuque to Rochester, where William met us with the wagon. A freighter would bring our household goods—those that William was not purchasing new.

Now, as the wagon lumbered on, negotiating the rugged hills of Whitewater County, I felt optimistic for the first time in years. With the income from the sale of our land in Iowa, William had built a mercantile, and we planned to live above it. He was also negotiating with two brothers to partner in building a sawmill. I was happy we were going to be in business rather than living by the uncertainties of farming. William would rent out our farmland as the area settled. Life, for once, was going to be good, and I anticipated the comforts we would finally have as William fulfilled the promise he'd made (then broken) eight years ago. I looked forward to achieving our place among respected town leaders.

"There it is!" William's excited voice broke my thoughts.

We'd crested a hill, and Beaver lay in the narrow valley below, Beaver Creek running through it. Just outside of the settlement, the creek flowed into the Whitewater River. The Mississippi, with its violent waters, lay to the northeast, close enough for commerce but not so close as to endanger the community.

I stared at the town. Or lack thereof. "Six buildings?"

"Now, Laura, don't raise a fuss."

I ignored his playful wink. "You told me there was a town. A real town."

"It's not much to speak of now, but it'll grow. We only just platted it. Now that we have the lots laid out, we can advertise and bring in others."

"I thought it would be bigger." The baby kicked in my womb, and I winced.

"It will be. We platted out twenty blocks. If it were already a populated town, we'd hardly be among the founders, now would we?"

I shook my head at his teasing. I'd gotten ahead of myself again. Our grandparents had created Ripley County from nothing. Beaver would be *our* legacy. I spied the stakes as we drew into town and, with them, the ambitious plans the men envisioned for the village. We stopped, and William helped us from the wagon.

"Well, it's good you're safely back." An older man with graying hair approached and slapped William on the back. "This must be your family."

"It is. My wife, Laura. The little ones are Willie and Emma. Laura, this is Mr. Covey. He built the first house here two years ago."

I shook Covey's hand as other residents poured out to greet us, clustering like a gaggle of geese.

Maggie Knowles, like me, was heavily pregnant. She caught my arm and steered me toward a building. "Let's leave these men to catch up. I'd wager you're more interested in this."

"Ours?" I asked, making an assumption. It was the only two-story structure in town.

"Yep. Went up last week."

It was small, fourteen by twenty feet, and was built of logs—not the large frame building I had envisioned from William's description. Of course, he'd never said it was anything but a two-story structure. I'd visualized the size and building materials all on my own. That I had even expected anything more was my own fault.

I loved William, admired his hard work and determination, his teasing and his caring ways with the children. It wasn't so much that his dreams were always bigger than reality (though they often were) but that our dreams were different.

I pushed open the front door, devoid of a lock, and entered. The front room was light and airy. I glanced at the windows along three sides. "William built this?"

"The Malindy Brothers. They've built most of the town."

I recognized the name of the duo who were partnering with William in the sawmill business. Until the mill went up, I realized, there would be no frame structures. Those would come later, and William would be part of making it happen.

The interior space was designed to be heated by the open fireplace at the center of the longer wall. I pictured a cozy area near it to beckon customers. Stairs at the rear led to the second floor, where we would live. The room was small, and the store would be cluttered, but at least it would be light. "I'm pleased they thought to put in so many windows. There's nothing worse than a dim store."

"Most men wouldn't appreciate that, but the Malindys have good heads on their shoulders; they're building our house. We've been doubled up with my brother-in-law."

Maggie showed me the back room and the living quarters upstairs. The sleeping rooms would be tight, but at least there were two of them, and the main room should accommodate the new cookstove with no problem. A tingle of anticipation surfaced as I wondered what model William had decided on and when it would be delivered. Below, we heard the men carrying in our temporary supplies and the new feather ticks William had purchased in Rochester.

The two of us shuffled down the stairs, and Maggie departed for home, leaving me to survey the mess in the middle of the room. The children chased one another around the main room of the store while William spread the ticks on the floor.

"We'll need to sleep down here next to the fireplace until the freighter arrives with the furniture and stove."

I turned to him, trepidation rising. "The freighter from Iowa is stopping to pick up the new stove?"

"What new stove?"

Now, the anger surged. "You didn't buy a stove?"

William's face grew puzzled. "Why would I do that? We have a perfectly good stove. Brand new just eight years ago."

I bit back my dander. Had he completely forgotten our discussion? "We *had* a perfectly good stove. You told me it was too heavy to freight and was best left behind."

"Now, Laura, you knew I was only grumbling."

Good lord how I hated it when he "now, Laured" me. Fury bubbled up, and I let it spew. "No, I didn't know! You did nothing but harp about how much it would cost to transport it here. Over and over again, you said we ought to leave it."

I glared at him, infuriated. "I sold that stove!"

Two days later, the store inventory arrived. I watched it being unloaded, crate by crate and barrel by barrel. There would be a decision to be made once the wagon was empty. With inventory now in hand, were we to unpack it and open for business or continue to live in the store space? The single fireplace heated the main floor. To my knowledge, William had done nothing about purchasing a stove for our living quarters.

I, in turn, cooked him nothing but potatoes and stew, beans and ham.

Burning with resentment that I'd felt forced to sell my wonderful turntable stove, I bristled constantly. I'd barely spoken to William since discovering he'd not meant his emphatic statements and blamed myself for assuming he'd truly meant for me to leave the stove behind. To compound the situation, our household goods were past due for delivery. Without a bed, I struggled in getting up and down from the floor with my huge belly and aching back. My ankles were swollen and my feet so large I could no longer put on shoes. My toes were like ice. The women of Beaver, God bless them, brought me knitted slippers and baked goods, which I fed to the children, leaving William to go without. If I could not have my belongings, he would not have bread and cookies—not if I had anything to do with it.

As the wagon left, I surveyed the pile of mercantile inventory now in the middle of the store. William was nowhere in sight, no doubt working on the dam for the mill. In the short time we'd been here I learned he enjoyed playing politics with the other town founders more than he was wont to be a storekeeper. Every minute he wasn't working on the mill, he was meeting with the men. Unless the store was to remain this hopeless pile of inventory, I would have to organize it.

"What are we gonna do with it, Mama?" Willie asked.

I hugged my boy close and smoothed the cowlick in his hair. Though only five, he had a heart of gold and was ever helpful to me.

"I suppose there's nothing to be done but to start prying the crates open." I eyed the crowbar that had been left atop the largest crate.

"You gonna do it?" Willie's eyes widened.

"You do, Mama?" Emma echoed from the corner where she

sat with her doll.

"I don't see anyone else around," I muttered.

Reaching for the tool, I slid the flattened section beneath the lid and pressed the other end down. Nothing. I drew a breath and pushed harder. Pain cramped my abdomen, and I dropped the crowbar.

"Run," I told Willie. "Get your father and the doctor."

Jefferson was born less than two hours later, coming faster than any of my other children. But he arrived healthy, despite his early appearance, thank heavens.

Now alone with William, the doctor gone and the other children with Maggie, my body slumped with weariness. Jefferson wailed in the crate we'd hastily converted for a cradle. Still waiting for the household freight and our trunks of clothing, we'd borrowed diapers and gowns for him.

Frustrated, I scolded my husband from my bed on the floor. "We should have been settled before this baby arrived. Full and completely settled."

He scooped Jefferson up and rocked him gently. "I know."

Though William's voice was full of remorse, my irritation still simmered.

"I should not have had to birth him on the floor."

"I know that, Laura." He laid the baby in my arms. "But what was there to be done about it? Babies come early sometimes."

Babies come early sometimes.

Oh, of all the infuriating platitudes. I opened my nightgown and helped Jefferson latch to my breast. I drew a breath and leveled my voice. It would do little good to provoke an argument. "They especially come early when their mothers are trying to pry open crates."

William started. "You were trying to open crates? My god,

Laura! What possessed you to do that in your condition?"

"It needed doing, and you were nowhere to be found. We own a business, and the sooner we get that business into operation, the sooner we have income."

To me, this was obvious, but I knew after all this time that obvious to one of us did not always equate to clarity for both.

"It could have waited a few days, for heaven's sake." And there was the gist of it. He didn't view it as I did.

"No, it couldn't. Those goods needed to be unpacked, recorded in an inventory log, arranged, and made ready for sale. I figured I had only a few weeks to get that done before the baby came."

He offered a small smile and shook his head. "Well, that didn't work out, did it?"

"No, it didn't." I kissed our little one on the head and caught his father's gaze. "I could have lost this child. Do you understand that?"

He swallowed. "I was so scared when Willie came for me. You took a big risk, Wife."

I knew his words were true. I had no business trying to open that crate in my condition. But William needed to understand his role in events as well, past *and* future. "You put me at risk, Husband. You put both of us at risk. And you have left me once again with only a fireplace for chores and cooking."

"I never told—" he blustered, defensive.

"Yes. You did." I said the words softly, and he stopped his protest.

"I'm sorry, Laura."

"Then fix it. For Jefferson's sake, if not mine."

Once again, focusing on a baby convinced William to put others' needs first. He spent two days unpacking mercantile inventory. On the third, he traveled to Rochester to find out where our household goods were and purchase me a stove. That same night, the new stove was installed upstairs with our other household items, which had been sitting at the freight station in Rochester. I recovered from childbirth to face the arranging of both our living quarters and the store.

As was usual between us, the incident led to discussion and new commitments from William. He was tender and caring with me, clearly sorry for his actions. I found it difficult to remain angry with him. This husband of mine so often simply didn't comprehend that the rest of us didn't march to the same drummer as did he.

William was a fine, affectionate man, but there were times he became so wrapped up in his own ambitions and his own way of doing things that it became his sole focus. He forgot details and often didn't understand how his actions impacted others. My mother had warned me that was the way of men, and I resolved to be more patient with him. It was my job to stay one step ahead of William, to anticipate him and counter his missteps before they occurred.

He'd done an admirable job of prying off lids and removing items but left the contents in the middle of the floor. I knew he had little idea what to do with all of it, and we determined I would be the one to organize the store. After all, he had little skill in such matters, while I excelled in creating order from chaos. And chaos it was, with piles scattered throughout the building, upstairs and down.

What a mess! With hard work and minimal interruptions from Willie and Emma, I suspected it would take me at least a week to put it all in its place.

I focused first on the household upstairs, which took precedence. I'd packed carefully, crating like goods together, and discovered my planning was a boon. Putting things away took far less time than anticipated.

The store was another matter entirely.

It appeared William had purchased nearly every item necessary for building a town. Hammers, axes, saws, and screwdrivers abounded. I discovered tinned foods, winter jackets, and men's boots. There were barrels of flour and sugar, crackers and pickles, all creating a strange mixture of smells that mingled with the leather goods like every mercantile I'd ever entered. But there was not a pot or pan or women's item in the lot.

There also were no shelves.

I rocked on my heels and shook my head. How on earth could he have neglected to order shelving? Or had he assumed the Malindy brothers would tend to it? I pondered out his thought process, determining he'd likely thought it more prudent to order shelves built once there was a clear idea of need. That was my husband through and through.

The items women would need never entered his mind.

I set off to locate William, children in tow, so he could order the necessary goods. I found him in Dr. Brooks's front office with several other men, all of them poring over a plat of the town.

"Laura!" he said as we entered. "I didn't expect you up and out."

I watched Willie and Emma rush into the living quarters to locate their new playmates as I shifted the baby in my arms. "I have a list for you," I told him. "Shelves and more inventory."

He grinned, but I saw his embarrassment under the action. "My busy little wife."

The men chuckled, but I sensed their disapproval that I'd interrupted their business.

"We're discussing where to locate houses," he told me. "Most folks have been doubled up, and they're ready to buy lots. I've been elected to handle the sales, land agent if you will, and I wanted to make sure we were in agreement on business and residential areas."

"I knew it must be something like that." I handed him the list. "I'll need you to attend to these items today."

One of the men punched William on the arm. "She's a bossy one, Duley."

"She keeps me focused." He glanced at the list. "All of this?"

"All of that."

He drew me into the entryway and spoke softly. "I'll get the shelves built, but I don't believe we need those types of items."

I held his gaze. "You are trying to grow a town. That means women and children will be here, and they will have needs. You can stock the things they'll need, or they can buy them in Rochester. Every time a husband needs to do that, he will buy the other items there as well."

William's jaw dropped. "Do you think so?"

"Wouldn't you?"

Comprehension dawned in his eyes. "What would I do without you!" He embraced me. "You are a gem."

I glowed at the praise. "Just trying to catch all the details."

"Well, you have a head for business. More so than I realized." He smiled, thoughtful. "Perhaps I ought to put the entire store into your hands."

Run a store *and* care for my family? "Well, I don't think—"

"It will free me to get the mill up and operating and focus on selling lots. I'll need to get our land rented out, too. The men have even talked of me running for County Commissioner."

"But—"

"The store is yours." He smiled, the decision setting well with him.

I digested what it would mean for me. Even with tending house and the children, it would be far easier than chasing William all over town. But, to do it effectively, I would need full control.

"You'll put me on the account, so I can order inventory?" I ventured.

He shook his head. "There's no need for that. I can place the orders for you."

Beaver, Minnesota
1858, two years later

Over the next two years, I built a thriving business of the mercantile. It took but a month after putting me in charge for William to grow tired of my constant interruptions and lists to fill when he traveled to Winona for commission meetings. I'd had to make a lot of extra trips to bother him that much, but it was well worth it. He placed my name on the account, and I was able to run the store without his interference. Or his resistance.

Willie started off to school, and William and the Malindy brothers converted the sawmill to a gristmill, once area farming began in earnest. William continued in politics, serving on the Republican delegation to the Constitutional Convention the year Minnesota achieved statehood. Our lives were comfortable and secure. Secure enough that we'd borrowed against the mill toward enlarging the store.

The spring had been unusually wet, delaying our plans. Three days of dry weather had prompted William to seize the chance for travel, and he'd left for Winona, promising to return with construction materials. Looking outside at the downpour that had returned today, I hoped he'd had the sense to delay the trip home. He'd take pneumonia or ague if he hadn't.

The bell on the door tinkled, and I looked up, eager to visit. There'd not been a customer all afternoon. Nor morning, for that matter.

Maggie bustled into the store, dripping wet. "Goodness, will this rain never stop?" She shook her umbrella and propped it near the door.

"Where are the children?" I asked her.

"At home. I figured it was the better choice in this downpour." She glanced down at her muddy boots.

"Leave them. Emma can sweep it up. She'll be happy for something to do. The children were so bored at being inside yet again that I didn't have a bit of protest when I suggested a nap."

Nonetheless, Maggie wiped her feet on the rug before tiptoeing to the counter. "Did the mail make it through?"

I grinned at her. "Is that what brought you out in this weather?"

"I'm desperate for news."

She was lucky. The mail carrier had come yesterday, taking full advantage of the pause in rain. I guessed he wasn't likely to return for a week or more, given how hard it was now pouring. The ground was saturated. I turned to the mail slots and took a newspaper from the one marked as theirs. "Just the *Herald*."

She grabbed the paper and spread it out on the counter. "Let's see what's going on in Wabashaw." She perused the front page, chirping out tidbits of gossip as they caught her eye. Her face soured. "There's another ad for the Dakota Land Company."

I groaned. "Everyone in three counties is talking about moving west. From the sound of it, towns are springing up left and right. This part of the state is hardly settled. I can't for the life of me imagine why anyone would want to go even farther west."

"William hasn't gotten Dakota Fever yet, has he?"

"No. And he would do well not to." Surely he wouldn't, not with all we'd built here. We'd finally caught our dream. I couldn't imagine him giving any of it up for the frontier.

"John has brought it up twice."

"Oh, Maggie, no!"

"I've managed to dissuade him, but it's a battle every time he reads one of these ads." She sighed. "I'm tempted to leave the paper here."

"If you like. You can read it when you stop by." I'd find a place for it behind the counter. Maggie was too good a friend to lose.

"I'd best put it away for today and get back."

We chatted on as I walked her to the door and watched her hustle away into the rain. Water stood in puddles, the ground too wet to absorb any more. I shook my head and closed the door.

Seconds later, it swung back open, slamming against the wall. I turned as one of the Malindy brothers burst into the store. "Is William back?"

"Heavens, Mr. Malindy! Whatever is the matter?"

"The mill! The dam broke, and the mill's sliding down the creek bank. We're gonna lose it all."

Chapter Six

Almena
Caton, New York
During the same period, 1850

Almena Hamm picked up the carpetbag and reached down to take her brother Seneca's hand. Seneca clutched it tightly and edged closer to her.

Scared to death, poor little man.

She was too, for that matter. Maybe not scared to death but more than a little frightened and uncertain. And resentful. She kicked at a rock, sending it flying. Too bad it wouldn't hit her stepmother in the head.

If Ma were still alive, she'd never stand for this. But, then, if Ma were still alive, they'd still be living in Pennsylvania, and Pa wouldn't be married to that horrid woman.

Tears swelled behind Almena's eyes. She fought them back, refusing to cry over spilt milk. What's done was done. But no matter what, for as long as she lived, she would always put *her* children first—if she ever had any. For now, Seneca came first. In that, too, tears would be of little use.

It was a gloomy day, clouds casting pallor over the usual vibrancy of the small farms that dotted Steuben County's green hills.

Appropriate, given our inauspicious mission.

"Slow down, Almena," Seneca whined. He'd never been able to pronounce her given name, Alomina. He knew her by nothing else, and she'd left Alomina behind with the rest of her childhood.

She forced herself to slow her steps so Seneca could keep up. The boy was just five years old, for heaven's sake. Five years old and farmed out to strangers.

"You doing all right?" she asked him.

He nodded, not truly understanding. "Where're we going?"

"We're going to live with the Miniers, down the road."

"With Miss Marilla?" His voice brightened a little.

"Mm hmm." Childless, Christian and Marilla had offered to adopt Seneca. They seemed like good folk, and Almena knew he'd have an easier life with them. At nearly fourteen, Almena was too old to be adopted, but they'd agreed to have her join the household as a hired girl. She was glad of it. Having her there would ease things for Seneca. For them both, really; they'd cope with the change together.

"Why d'we gotta go there?"

Oh, Seneca. How in heaven's name did you explain something like this to a child? "Twelve is too many for a little house like ours."

It was the truth. And a little tyke like Seneca was better off not knowing the whole of it . . . that Pa was willing to split up his family and farm out his kids to make more room for his new wife's brood. Almena understood there'd been a need to remarry. But she'd never expected her new step-siblings to come before Pa's own children. Already, Pa was seeking homes for some of the others. Since his remarriage, the family had doubled in size, and they barely scraped by.

He should have picked a single lady, instead of a widow with a passel of little ones.

He *should* have put his own children first.

Almena huffed and guided Seneca onto the stoop of the Minier house.

Marilla met them at the door, opening it in welcome. The scents of cinnamon and vanilla wafted out.

Almena's stomach growled as she tried to identify the source. She couldn't remember the last time she'd had baked sweets. Not since before Ma passed, and that was more than four years now.

"Well, will you look who's here!" Marilla knelt and drew Seneca into her arms. He stiffened, unaccustomed to such affection. Marilla laughed and drew back. "I have cookies," she announced, gesturing toward the kitchen at the back of the house.

Seneca's face brightened, and he sniffed the air. "Cookies? I don't never get cookies."

"Well, you do now. Come on in and have a couple before I show you your room. We've purchased you a hobby horse."

Seneca's eyes grew wide, and he rushed down the hallway, leaving Almena on the stoop.

Marilla eyed her, her chilly glance moving from head to toe.

Almena stood straighter and wished she'd taken the time to re-braid her ash-blonde hair.

"You going to stand there all day?" Marilla finally said.

Almena swallowed. "No, ma'am." She stepped into the house, and Marilla released the door. It swung shut with a bang.

Halfway down the hall, Marilla stopped and grasped a loop of rope hanging from the ceiling. A trap door dropped open, revealing a set of folded stairs. She drew them down and faced Almena. "Your bed's in the attic." She turned and whisked away into the kitchen.

Almena stood abandoned, shaking and bewildered and completely alone.

Caton, New York
1852

By their second year together, Almena and Marilla had settled into a more comfortable relationship. Still, Almena had been relegated the manual aspects of housework for too long. She hungered to move past the tedious chores of potato peeling, dishwashing, and laundry scrubbing. She wanted to learn the secrets of "housecraft." Secrets Marilla guarded as if she believed Almena would somehow use the knowledge against her. These skills would make the difference in mastering a household and making life better for the family she envisioned in her future.

Almena wanted to be a full-fledged baker, to discover the methods of sweetening preserves so that each fruit tasted the best it could, and to learn how Marilla made such mouthwatering butter. These were the secrets that made Marilla's bread, jams, and dairy products popular enough to sell to others. If Almena could do something like that, she'd have the means to make sure her children never had to be farmed out to others.

She and Seneca had been lucky. Not all her siblings had been able to stay together as they had. And life was good with the Miniers. Seneca now had parents who loved him, an education, and a bright future. Though she hadn't attended school, Almena had learned mathematics and grammar from the primers Seneca brought home, Seneca taking great pleasure in teaching his older sister. And Christian had allowed her use of his library so she could practice her reading and broaden her knowledge. They'd not wanted for anything.

But today, she was determined to stretch that knowledge further.

She hefted the plunger of the butter churn up and down a few more times, working out her strategy before she paused to check her progress.

"Is it ready for me?" Marilla asked

Almena lifted the lid from the churn instead of waiting for Marilla to do so, eager to prove she'd paid attention when she'd watched Marilla do the task. Small granules had begun to form within the cream. But had she churned enough? Were the granules the right size? Almena shushed her insecurities and examined the mixture more closely.

"It's come," she said.

Marilla approached, one eyebrow raised, and looked for herself.

"Sure enough. Good job." Marilla squeezed Almena's shoulder.

Pride surged within her. She'd never truly known how uneducated she'd been, without a mother to teach her. And her stepmother sure hadn't bothered. Almena took a breath and turned to Marilla.

"I was thinking, maybe today would be a good time for me to learn what you do after I finish the churning." There, she'd said it.

Marilla stared at her. "You were?"

"Yes."

"I guard my butter-making, Almena. You know that."

"I'm not trying to steal your secrets."

She shrugged. "Still, they are my secrets. I bring in good money making the best dairy goods in the county."

"I'm nearly sixteen. One day, I'll have my own family. It would serve me well to know how to do the same."

Sighing, Marilla digested her argument. "And how do I know you won't rush out and compete with me?" she finally said.

"In two years you don't know me well enough to recognize that's not my way?" It hurt that Marilla didn't trust her.

"No, I suppose it's not. But if you move out of this house,

that could all change in a minute. A girl on her own is going to do what she has to do."

That made sense. The world was not easy, but she needed to make Marilla understand. "I'm not seeking a way to support myself on my own. I want to be able to assure I can always keep my family together. I don't want my children to ever face being turned out or neglected."

"Oh, Almena . . ."

"Please? I'll give you my word. I promise not to go into competition with you. I'll even sign my name to it."

"Here." Marilla thrust a jar of cold water into her hands. "Toss this in with the cream."

Almena did as instructed, watching the water seep into the crystalizing cream.

"Now put the lid back on and churn the water in a bit. If you can show me you have a talent for it, I'll teach you."

Almena fitted the top on the churn and plunged the agitator up and down.

After a few minutes, Marilla stilled her hand. "That should be enough. Let's go ahead and drain off the buttermilk."

Together, they lifted the heavy churn and poured the liquid into a pail for later use.

Once the churn was back on the floor, Marilla handed Almena a bucket of clean cold water. "Pour it in."

"Why do you add the water?"

"You have to 'wash' the butter. Fill up the churn and let it settle." The answer was terse.

Almena emptied the water into the churn, wishing Marilla had provided more information. It was clear she was ill-at-ease with the situation. The water rested a moment before she and Marilla lifted the churn a second time and drained it off. The liquid flowed out, leaving a mound of butter sitting in the bottom.

"What's next?"

"Wash it again, in the butter-worker." Marilla handed Almena a small scoop and indicated the odd-looking wooden contraption at the edge of the room. The shallow wooden trough, mounted on legs, reminded her of a sawhorse. On either end, the trough was open, with pails set on the floor below.

Nervous, she placed glob after glob of the butter into the butter worker. "I never even imagined such a thing as washing butter."

"If you don't, it won't keep. The better you wash it, the longer it lasts and the better the flavor. You can always tell a butter that isn't washed well. It tastes off."

Almena brightened, glad Marilla had finally relaxed enough to explain the reasoning behind the task. She knew it was vital knowledge, one of the keys to Marilla's success.

"More water?"

"That's right. Then roll it."

Almena poured more water atop the butter and let it soak in. She took the handled roller from its hook on the side of the butter-maker and moved it across the butter until the mound spread out in the trough like thick piecrust. "Like this?"

"Harder. You want to squeeze out the water with it."

She pressed hard, throwing her weight into the effort. Milky water ran off the edges of the trough, caught by the pails beneath.

Marilla handed her another jar of water. "Again. Keep repeating until the water runs off clear instead of cloudy."

Almena continued to repeat the wash and roll sequence, thankful for Marilla's tutelage, reluctant as it was. She glanced down at the butter, watching for the liquid to clear. When it was no longer filmy, she did one more wash, just to be sure.

Marilla smiled. "Good instinct. Mix in salt, to help preserve it, and put it in the crocks."

Warmth filled Almena as she gathered salt and several earthenware crocks. After salting and mixing the butter, she began to place butter into the first crock.

Marilla lifted an eyebrow and shook her head.

Almena paused, a handful of soft butter in her hand, oozing a bit between her fingers.

"Fling it into the crock."

"Fling it?"

"Throw it. Hard. That helps force out the air and any leftover water."

Almena tossed it as hard as she could into the crock. It smacked against the bottom, and Marilla chuckled. A small amount of water oozed to the top, and she drained it off before flinging in the next handful. Once the crock was full enough, Marilla handed her the butter press.

Almena took the stem of the mushroom shaped tool and pushed the rounded top into the butter.

"Ram it down. This is your last chance to get all the water and air out so it won't go rancid."

Almena pressed until her arms ached, draining out liquid each time it appeared. When it finally seemed dry, she stopped.

Marilla smiled at her. "That's it. Put on the lid, and we'll set it in the springhouse."

Almena sat on a three-legged stool, pride warming her. "That was a lot more work than churning."

"You'll soon get strong enough that it won't be so bad. It'll be one of the most important skills you learn."

"How's that?"

"Families who rely on farming alone are often poor. Skilled wives can make extra money. Being a good laundress is one way, but a laundress will work non-stop, ruin her hands, and break her back doing it. If a woman can make good butter and cheese, she can use her time and effort more wisely and still contribute to the household income—all for the cost of a callus or two. Not everyone has milk cows. Women who do can trade their butter and cheese for necessities or sell it at the mercantile."

"How come my stepmother didn't do that?" Extra money for so large a family might have made it possible for the family to stay together.

"Because she's a ninny."

Almena laughed. She hadn't liked the woman anyway, or her passel of kids. Life was better with the Miniers, for her and for Seneca.

"With such a large family, it could be your stepmother never had enough extra milk to make extra butter and cheese."

"We did only have one cow."

"So you see?"

"I'll make sure I have more than one. Thank you, Marilla." Almena jumped from the stool and hugged Marilla tight.

Marilla tensed, withdrawing for a moment before she hugged Almena back. As she pulled away, she caught Almena's gaze.

"Make sure you own milk cows before you marry. Or purchase them in your own right once you do. That way, should your husband be too poor, a lazy cad, or a gambler, you will always have the means to support yourself. If you have a good man, you'll be able to bring even more money into the household. A woman with cows is never a poor woman, as long as she knows what to do with her cream, and her children will never want."

Marilla's gaze softened. "If you continue to do well with this, we'll keep a heifer calf back and you can raise it as yours. What you produce from it will be profit to you. If you learn your craft well, you'll gain a reputation and outsell those who don't wash their butter or pitch their cheese well."

"Truly? You'd give me a cow of my own? And the profits?"

"Under three conditions. You make it your goal to excel at

what I teach you—what you produce will reflect on me. For the first three years, you apprentice; you will produce for the family only." She paused, staring hard at Almena. "And, once you start selling, you don't sell your products to any business that buys from me."

Almena offered her hand. She wasn't sure that left her any options for selling her goods, but she'd always have the skills to preserve her family.

Caton, New York
Three years later, 1855
Almena squared her shoulders and opened the door to Finch's Mercantile. The bell above her tinkled as she stepped in and closed the door behind her. The Miniers marketed with the store at the other end of town, and she'd never stepped inside Finch's establishment. It was the only store in town that didn't buy from Marilla.

"Morning, miss," the man behind the counter said, his amber eyes brightening noticeably. "What can I help you with?"

She approached, fighting trepidation, and set her large basket atop the counter. She was nearly nineteen years old, for heaven's sake, and she could handle this. It was too important to her future to let a little fear impede her. She needed to learn this one last skill—selling—and she'd know her family would always be secure.

"I'm Almena Hamm," she said, her voice strong and confident despite her nerves. "Are you Mr. Finch?"

The clerk appeared to be in his mid-twenties, his rich chestnut hair groomed and a neat apron covering his vest. He looked professional enough to be the owner, but his young age gave her pause.

"Just a clerk. Phineas B. Hurd at your service." He offered his hand.

She shook it and withdrew, enjoying his warm, lingering grasp far too much. She fussed at the callus on her right palm for a moment, wishing she'd put cream on it earlier, then stopped as if it had burst into flame. Lord, she hoped he hadn't noticed!

"Do you have the authority to purchase goods for Mr. Finch?"

He grinned at her. "It depends on what it is."

"I've bread, preserves, cheeses, and butter for sale." She removed the cloth and revealed her assortment of products.

Hurd peeked at them. "They look real good, Miss, but we've got a healthy stock of those type of items already."

She offered him a broad smile. "Not like these, you don't."

He hesitated. "This is a case of me having my hands tied. Mr. Finch has been buying from the same ladies for years and—"

"And I'm sure they keep him well-supplied. You'll find my goods are superior." As Marilla had advised, she gave him no time to turn her down.

"What he offers is good," Hurd protested. But a slim thread of hesitation was wound into the words.

Seizing the opportunity, she plunged ahead, her confidence building. "Not as good as what I have in this basket, Mr. Hurd."

"You're a tenacious woman, Miss Hamm," he said. "I like that." He winked at her.

Almena swallowed. Good heavens but those amber eyes were arresting! "Have you had your lunch yet today?"

"Not yet." He leaned his elbows on the counter, chin in his hands, and stared at her.

Oh, my! She tore her gaze away, wondering if there was a Mrs. Hurd. "Well, get a plate, knife, and napkin." She extracted items from the basket, arranging an assortment on the counter, trying to keep her mind on the sale.

Hurd disappeared into the back, whistling, and reappeared a few moments later, utensils in hand. He eyed the display, then Almena. "Gracious," he said, pausing in his tracks. "That's enough to make a man's mouth water."

Her face heated, and she bustled with the items. She'd brought only one type of bread, basic sourdough, but her preserves included a sampling of different berries. Her butter was stamped with a distinctive floral pattern she'd designed herself and had carved onto a roller. A fine, sharp aged cheddar (her specialty) sat next to several soft and semi-soft varieties.

"Help yourself," she told him.

He sliced off a slab of bread, breaking it, and spread one half with blackberry jam. The other, he slathered with butter. He cut into the cheddar and took a bite. His eyes lit, and he smiled. Setting the cheese down, he took the bread and bit into the buttered slice.

"Good, huh?" she asked, knowing it was.

"Are you joking? This is the best butter I've ever had."

Hah! "I told you so."

"That you did."

"Let's negotiate an order. I can supply daily or weekly per your choice. My preference is cash on delivery, but I am willing to work with you on consignment, if that is an issue."

Hurd's mouth dropped open. "I wish I dared, Miss Hamm, more than you can possibly know. But the ladies Finch buys from now are Mrs. Finch's sisters, and I don't see any way to keep my job if I buy from you instead."

Almena paused for only a second. If she knew anything, she knew Phineas B. Hurd had little chance of holding out for long. She leaned her elbows on the counter, mimicking his earlier pose. "Do you own a cow, Mr. Hurd?"

Corning, New York
Two years later, 1857

Almena and Phin stood on the New York & Erie Rail Road platform along with Seneca and the Miniers. The large broad-gauge locomotive spewed occasional hot cinders from its tall smokestack, and Almena was glad of the numerous cars of cut wood separating it from the passenger cars that lined the platform. Though there was a screen to trap large cinders, small ones still managed to escape, most burning out before they hit the ground. At least they wouldn't have to breathe in coal fumes the entire way.

The cow Phin had gifted her on their wedding day had already been loaded in a stock car, along with the now-grown heifer Marilla had given her two years ago. Only the good-byes remained.

And, the new life ahead of them. They had high hopes, both of them. Phin had secured a position at a mercantile owned by Finch's brother way out west in Wisconsin, where they hoped to buy all the land they could. The storekeeper had agreed to take on Seneca as well, as soon as he was old enough. Almena, well, she planned to make butter—the best butter La Crosse had to offer.

She chased the thoughts away and turned to Christian. "Thank you. For everything."

Christian's face reddened, and he squeezed her shoulders. "You take care of yourself, Mrs. Hurd."

"I will. We will." A week into marriage, she still forgot.

Beside her, Phin laughed. "We'll be fine."

"I know, son." Christian turned and shook Phin's hand.

Almena faced Marilla. *Ah, Marilla* . . . what could she possibly say to Marilla?

"You have a good man," Marilla said, "and cows of your own. There's nothing more you need." Her smile faltered.

Almena slipped into Marilla's arms, hugging her tight.

"You remember everything I taught you, honey, and you will never want."

"I love you, Marilla."

"Oh, girl, I love you, too."

Almena slipped from the embrace and quickly hugged each of Marilla's small daughters. She turned to smile at Seneca. "You ready?"

At twelve, he was in the midst of a growth spurt, arms and legs long and gangly. His face was no longer that of a boy but not yet that of a man. He swallowed.

Phin checked his new gold pocket watch, Almena's wedding gift, and caught her gaze.

"Seneca?" Almena said. "We'll need to board in a few minutes."

His head dipped, and he kicked at a stone. "I'm staying."

Staying? The word tumbled through her, landing in a hard clump. "St—staying?"

Seneca's face was full of anguish. "I can't leave. This is home, Almena."

He was right, and she knew his decision had not been made lightly. Christian and Marilla were his parents. Her lips trembled. "You'll write? And come visit?" she said. The words felt hollow.

"I will."

"You know I love you? That I'm not just leaving you?"

"Aw, I know that. You ain't getting rid of me that easy."

"Ain't?"

"Aren't."

"That's better. I love you."

"I love you, too." He hugged her, crushing her until the whistle sounded. "Better get on there."

She chucked him under the chin and turned away as Phin

bid him farewell. They mounted the steps and made their way into the passenger car. Tears streaked down her cheeks.

Phin wiped them with his finger as they took their seat. "You're sure? You didn't plan on leaving him."

"It's time to start our life together."

"We can do that here . . . wait a few years to leave."

"No. This is what we planned. A couple years working for Finch, and we'll have enough saved to buy that farm and a good idea of where to do it. Besides, I . . ." her voice broke, "I suspected that might happen. He wasn't enthusiastic, just pretending for my sake. This is for the best."

Phin hugged her tight and kissed her on the forehead. "I wish it weren't so far. I hate taking you from him."

"He'll visit. He has a family that loves him, and that's what's important." She peered out the window, found them, and waved. They waved back, adults with long faces, the little girls with excitement, Seneca with choked resignation. Choosing had been difficult for him, but he'd know love in the choice he made. She waved again as the train lurched and left the station.

She'd said good-byes, too, to her other siblings . . . those who still lived in Caton. The Hamm household had given up some children only to be crowded again with five new babies. She'd bitten back her resentment and done her duty, bidding her father farewell. But she'd shed no tears. They'd been shed years ago.

The train rolled through the green hills of central New York, making its way west. Almena slept, lulled by the rocking of the train, her head on Phin's shoulder. At a jerk, she woke, startled. Ahead of them, the gray waters of Lake Erie stretched as far as the eye could see.

"We'll get off, spend the night here," Phin told her. "I telegraphed ahead to reserve a room at the Loder House. I figured you'd want to sleep in a bed instead of sleeping on the train all night." He grinned. "But maybe that wouldn't have been an issue for you."

She smiled back. "Oh, you!"

They gathered their things and disembarked. The city was busy, travelers rushing to and fro. Between the railroads and the boat traffic, the bustle was hectic, and Almena was glad Phin had made hotel arrangements in advance. A few yards past the depot, someone called their names. They stopped and turned.

"Oh, I'm so glad I caught you." A small rotund man approached. "I'm the station master. I'm afraid I have a bit of bad news."

"What is it?" Almena asked.

"It's the cows. We've lost your cows."

Chapter Seven

Christina
New Ulm, Minnesota
The year before, 1856

It is a stupid idea my husband has, and I don't like it one bit. Why should we leave New Ulm? It is a good German town where the old ways are still kept. We are at home here. There are German bakers and beer makers. Everywhere, it looks like Germany, and I can think of no reasons for us to leave.

"You are crazy to even think it," I tell him.

"It is a chance for us, Christina," he says. Like me, he is trying to practice the strange English words but his accent is still so thick. *Ach,* no one will even understand him if we leave here.

"It is stupid." I stomp my foot to make sure he knows I am serious.

"That man Brink, he will pay us to hold the land for him."

Brink again. He has been in the beer hall, drinking with the men, talking about the lands to the west. He is *ein Scheisser,* that one, trying to claim two pieces of land. I want no part of it.

I hold my tongue and do not say the foul word aloud. "He is breaking the law."

Andreas sighs. He is fed up with me, I think. He did not know his wife was so stubborn. But that is how it is. He will have to get used to it.

"What is wrong with trying to get more land? There is more than enough."

His voice is softer, and I know he is trying now to sweet-talk me. He will use those blue eyes of his like he is a puppy, and I will not be able to resist.

"*Nein.* That cabin is in the middle of nowhere, and I will not go." I turn away and start to put dishes in the cupboard so he will know it is my final word.

"It is not so far from New Ulm."

I think again that he is stupid, but he is not. He is trying to trick me.

I slam the tankard on the counter and swing to face him. My blond braid whips with the movement, it is so fast. "I am not such a *Dummkopf,* Andreas Koch. I know what's what. That cabin is a two-day ride from New Ulm. Alma Schmidt told me so."

"And what does Alma Schmidt know of it?"

"A good plenty. She heard from her cousin that a man named Myers lives out there in a village called Saratoga, and he says Brink is miles from it, all alone on that prairie."

All the women in New Ulm know this. We have been spreading the word since we learned Brink was in town.

"He is in the Walnut Grove," Andreas insists, like it is a town. But the women know better and have spread the word about that, too.

"*Ja.* And the Walnut Grove is *nein* but trees in the middle of the prairie." I turn back to the dishes and slam them onto the shelves.

"All in the territory are trees in the prairies. And the lakes. This Walnut Grove will be no different. It is not so important where it is. What matters is that there is already a cabin there that we will not have to build. Brink will pay us to live there, so it is a way to make money for doing nothing. And we can farm the land and sell what we don't need. Think of what that could mean for us. Money to start our lives."

He still does not understand.

"I did not come to *Amerika* to live all alone. We should stay in New Ulm, like the other Germans, where we can buy *bier* and *schnitzel* and pumpernickel. Here we can celebrate a *Richtfest* when we build our own home."

"I am a farmer. You know this. I do not want to spend my life in a town. You knew this before we married."

His reminder hits me in the gut. I did know this. When we came to New Ulm and rented this little house, I knew it would only be for a time, that we would one day move onto land. But I didn't think it would be so far from a town.

Andreas wraps me in his strong arms. "I can make the *bier*, and you can make the *schnitzel* and the pumpernickel. I will build our own *Haus*, and you will make a wreath to hang on it. I will even say a poem to bless it. It will still be a *Richtfest* even if it is only us two. You will honor me as a good *Hausfrau* there as much as you would in New Ulm."

"There will be no one for miles and miles," I say, my head on his chest.

"I will keep you safe. And is it such a bad thing to be all alone? Are you so tired of your husband already that you do not want to be with him?"

"*Ach!* You make fun of me." I step back and slap him playfully.

He smiles. "*Nein, mein Frau. Du bist mein Ein und Alles.*"

You are everything to me, my one and only. I sigh and let those blue puppy eyes draw me in.

Cottonwood County, Minnesota
May 1858
Ja, the Walnut Grove is *nein* but a grove of trees on the prairie. We live here now for almost two years. Andreas does not mind

so much the loneliness, but I am tired of it and wish so much to visit New Ulm. It is not good to live so far from people. Our closest neighbors even are too far to visit by walking, and the trappers who occasionally live at Lake Shetek are at least twelve miles from us.

I have not talked to another woman for two years. Today, I will ask Andreas if I can travel with Mr. Renicker on his trip to New Ulm for supplies.

Renicker is a single man. He lives in Saratoga, a town with a name and not much else. This is about thirty miles from us, along the Nobles Trail. There, Aaron Myers also lives with a wife and children, and a widower with four little girls. But I have never met them. Only Aaron Myers, who takes turns with Renicker to go for supplies at New Ulm. They trade for us, too, and sell our crops, so that Andreas does not have to leave me alone on the prairie.

It is not good, to live like this. The prairie has much to love, with grasses waving and bright flowers, but the winters have a cold that bites and snow so deep that sometimes we cannot walk. When the winds come, we must be careful not to get lost. Those are the times I miss having other women to visit. When we are done at Brink's cabin and ready to have our own land, I will insist we settle near others.

Andreas is lonely, too, even if he refuses to say so. He is always glad when Renicker comes through, for they sit and speak *Deutsch* together. Today, Renicker is much on my mind. It is time for him to go to New Ulm for supplies and make the stop here. I have cleaned until the *Haus* is spotless and do not allow Andreas to wear his shoes inside. Even though the floor is dirt, I have laid down rugs, freshly beaten, and they must be spotless when guests arrive.

I look forward to each visit with excitement. It is good to see someone besides my Andreas. Much as I love him, we get tired and cranky of each other. That is the German in us, I think. It is no good without friends to share the *bier und kaffee*.

All is ready. I have even coiled my braid atop my head for his visit. It is time to talk to Andreas before Renicker is here. I know I should have done this days ago but I do not know what Andreas will say. Now, it is the last minute, and I am even more nervous.

"Andreas?" I call from the *Haus* yard. I know he is near and did not go to the fields today.

"*Ja*, what is it?" In his mouth, he shifts the small sliver of wood he chews on. "Does he come?"

"*Nein*, but I need to talk with you."

"I am busy, trying to clean the stable before he arrives. The stalls for his horses have a need to be mucked."

"I would like to go to New Ulm with Mr. Renicker."

"We cannot go to New Ulm," he says. "We must finish the planting. There is much left in the grain fields. It cannot wait until we go to New Ulm and come back. That is four days it would wait."

"I have sowed my garden and am free to go."

He spits out the toothpick. "You mean to go alone with Renicker to New Ulm?"

"*Ja*, if you will not come."

"*Nein*. It would not be proper."

"*Ach*, it is only riding on the seat of a wagon."

"But you will stop for the night."

"That is at Brown's Cabin. There is a whole family there. It is not like I would be alone with Renicker."

"It is not seemly." He turns and goes back to the stable, leaving me alone in the yard with no answer. I will have to ask again, but it is better not to nag him now. It is always better not to provoke a German temper. I sigh and return to the *Haus* but am not long there before Andreas shouts from the yard.

"Christina! He comes."

I rush to shoo out the cat, who has wandered in through the open door, and straighten the quilt on the bed. As I step outside, Renicker is nearing with his wagon.

"Hello, the house!" he calls, though I know he can see us fine standing in front of it.

Andreas goes to shake his hand and release the horses.

Renicker greets me. "Mrs. Koch, it's good to see you. Mrs. Myers sends her regards," he says in German, thrusting a jar of preserves into my hands from the wife of Aaron Myers. I have not met her, but her husband speaks of her when he travels through.

"*Danke*," I say, then remember to practice my English. "Thank you."

The men care for the animals while I finish with the meal. As usual, Renicker will go on to Brown's Cabin in the morning. Today is for visiting. I am eager for the news of the other settlers and rush to get supper on the table.

Once we are seated, I wait for news to start, my knee almost bouncing with pent up anticipation.

"Well," Renicker begins, "the widower left."

I think about him, all the way in the middle of nowhere with those four little girls and am glad to hear it. "Where did he go?" I ask.

"He said they were going to head up toward Leavenworth. That's the second family that's left now."

"So Saratoga is *kaput*." Andreas punctuates the words with finality.

"Just me and the Myers family now. All those houses built by the government are sitting there empty. You sure you two don't want to move up there and join us?"

I look to Andreas, my pulse skipping.

"*Nein*. We are doing *gut* here."

But I am not doing so *gut*. I am afraid if I do not talk to another woman soon, I will dry up from the loneliness. I will have to ask again, but I have waited too long and now must do so in front of Renicker. Andreas will not be pleased.

"He wasn't happy there, anyway," Renicker continues in German. The whole of our conversation has become a mix of languages. "Came up from the lake when his wife died while back East. He didn't understand how hard it would be to raise those girls. That first winter was pretty hard."

"In Minnesota, all the winters are hard." Andreas shrugs, as if this is not important.

"Some harder. Myers almost went back that year. They ran out of flour and had to live on milk until the weather broke. That was right before you arrived."

"*Ja*, in New Ulm, the snow was deep that year," I say. "It would be good to visit with my old friends there to hear of life since."

I hope that my mention of New Ulm will remind Andreas of my desire to go, but the observation leads to nowhere but a stony glare and awkward silence.

After a while, Renicker finds a new topic. "Parmlee, from Lake Shetek, came through and said there is a new family there. Wat Smith and his wife built a cabin at the end of last year. Took over where Bennet had his shack and added on to that." He turned to me. "I bet Mrs. Smith would be glad to see another woman, if you're inclined to go visiting."

I have not been to the lake, but I know it is large. I wonder how far away this Mrs. Smith is. "Where at on the lake?"

Renicker dips a finger into the leftover gravy on his plate and traces a crude outline of the lake. On the southeast side, he makes an *X*. "Right about here, between Lake Shetek and Beauty Lake."

"How far?"

"That part of the lake, maybe fourteen miles. Oh, and a German named Charley Zierke has settled between here and Brown's Cabin. They call him Dutch Zierke. It will be another place to stop on the way to New Ulm."

Andreas looks to me. I shrug and give him a tiny up-turn of my mouth. He will want to go and visit there, to speak German with someone besides me. We will have a negotiation, I think.

"Maybe Andreas can take a day off tomorrow, and we can travel with you to meet this Dutch Zierke."

"I have field work," Andreas says.

"It could wait one day," I say, "so I could travel on to New Ulm with Mr. Renicker and have a visit with Alma Schmidt?"

Andreas's face hardens. "No, Christina, you will not go to New Ulm with Renicker. This will not be, and you will not ask me again."

Cottonwood County, Minnesota
June 1858

We wait, but Renicker does not return with the supplies. It is one week, and he is not back. "He should have been here two days ago," Andreas says for the third time.

"Maybe he had too much *bier* in New Ulm," I joke.

But Andreas does not laugh. "He is a good man, not a drunk, a man who does his business and returns."

"Maybe he stayed more time at Dutch Zierke's or Brown's Cabin."

"It is possible. But if he does not come by Friday, we will go to look. He would not visit longer than that. If a wheel has broken and he is walking back, we must find him."

I think about him out on the prairie and know Andreas is right. "We will go tomorrow," I say, "if he does not come in today."

Never Let Go

It is less than an hour later that two men ride into our yard. I rush out, and they are already talking with Andreas. They quiet as I approach.

"Renicker?" I ask, my stomach in a knot.

"*Ja*," Andreas says. Just *ja*.

I see in his eyes that the news is not good.

"This is Parmlee and Hammer, from Shetek. They found Renicker between Plum Creek and here."

"What happened?" I ask. Only a few more miles and he would have been safe to the Walnut Grove.

Parmlee turns to me. "Real sorry, ma'am. I know you knew him." He does not answer my question.

The worry builds. Why do they not tell me? "Andreas?"

"He was killed by the Indians," my husband says, his voice soft as be breaks the news.

And now the worry becomes fear. My heart thumps. "Indians? But there has never been trouble with the Indians." I think how close Plum Creek is to us. "We never even see the Indians here."

"They plundered the wagon," Parmlee continues. "Took most of what was in it, from the looks of it. And the team."

"Why would they do that?" I ask.

Then I remember how I had wanted to go with him. I shiver. I would be dead beside him, I think. Or maybe worse. I have heard the stories of Indian attacks in other places.

"They get hungry. Especially if the annuity goods from the government don't get to the reservation on time." This time it is Hammer who answers.

I wonder why they didn't simply take what they wanted rather than kill him.

Parmlee shifts his feet. "Or it was the whiskey."

"The whiskey?" Andreas asks.

"Renicker has been trading whiskey with the Indians. The

keg was still in the wagon but it was empty. Could be they were drunk and fought."

I glance at Andreas, who looks surprised. We did not know that he was selling whiskey.

"Or they wanted more and there was no more. Or they had nothing to trade and Renicker wouldn't give up the goods." Hammer shrugs. "Could have been any of a number of things that led to it. We'll never know."

I clutch Andreas's arm, shaking. "Did they . . . scalp him?" My other hand goes to my coil of blond hair and I think again how I would have been with him if Andreas had not refused to let me go.

Parmlee looks uncomfortable. "No, ma'am. They left him on the side of the road, partly covered in a gopher hole. We buried him proper."

"Do you want to come in? I have *kaffee*."

"We'd best get on, back to the lake and let the others know," says Hammer.

"I'll ride up to Saratoga and tell Myers," Parmlee adds.

Andreas watches them get on their horses, his face a mix of emotions, and I realize he is afraid.

I have never seen him fear anything, and my skin prickles.

"You tell them we must have a meeting," he says. "We must talk about this attack and what we should do."

When they have gone, Andreas turns to me. "Maybe now is the time to leave this place."

We meet at the home of Wat Smith. It is so crowded that we spill into the yard. The cabin is a few hundred feet from the west shore of Beauty Lake, which sparkles in the summer sun and gives the name. The Myers children play along the top of the bank.

Lake Shetek is further west, perhaps a half mile. Smith takes the group to look at it while we wait for the last bachelor trappers to arrive. I am surprised. I have not seen such a big lake in all the time I have been in *Amerika*. It stretches for miles with pelicans everywhere. Smith says Shetek is an Indian word for pelican. His words bring us back to why we have come here, and we look at each other, all of us quiet. My stomach has churned these last few days, and I want nothing more than to return to New Ulm and leave this isolated place. *Ach,* we should have done so as soon as we heard the news.

I walk with Mrs. Smith and Mrs. Myers, excited to finally visit with other women. Mrs. Myers's oldest keeps watch on the children. The men are ahead, and we hang back, since it is not so proper for women to offer opinions. But we itch to do so.

"We shouldn't have even come here," Mrs. Smith says. "It isn't natural to be so alone and unprotected."

Mrs. Myers chimes in. "We are alone in Saratoga now. I told Aaron we are too far away from others, and I won't stay there all alone. We have four children to protect."

"I told Andreas this, too."

In fact, I have told him this non-stop since Renicker was found. I tell him we must return to New Ulm. He has grown tired of my nagging, I think.

"How much danger do you think there is?" Mrs. Smith asks. She is a quiet woman, plain in her patched dress.

"I do not know," I say. "We have not had any Indian trouble. We do not even see Indians. But the killing was not far from our house, and that is not good." I am careful of my words and hide my worry.

Mrs. Myers stops near the house and looks to make sure her brood is safe. We cluster together. The men sit in a group on logs, deep in their talking.

"They've been very friendly with us. Aaron does herb remedies and is good with injuries. He treats them if they come for help and we trade food with them. But, now that Renicker has been killed, we would be out there all alone."

"Parmlee says he was selling whiskey to them," I say.

"Never a good thing. Aaron says trading whiskey to Indians creates problems. So many of them get crazy from it. If we had known Renicker was doing that, we would have had words with him."

"What brought you to Saratoga?" I ask her.

She snorts. "Dakota Fever."

I do not know what this is, and I look at her with my brow raised.

She laughs at my confusion. "We were living in Wisconsin, and the Dakota Land Company plastered handbills all over town telling about new settlements. Aaron went to a meeting, and we ended up coming west with eleven other families, bound for Yankton, in Dakota Territory. When we got to the Cottonwood River, near here, we met a group on their way back East. They said the Indians farther west in Dakota were too wild. Some of our party turned back East with them, others went south to Sioux City, and we claimed land near Saratoga. There were houses already there. It was supposed to be a town."

"My husband heard there was a town here, Cornwell City. We were surprised to find nothing but empty land. But we like the lakes, and he is determined this is the place for us."

We turn to watch the men and send nervous glances to one another. I am a good German woman and know my place, but I do not like that we are not included. I want to know what they are saying.

Mrs. Smith sighs and says, "That's enough, ladies. I'm going over, whether they like it or not." She strides away toward the men. She is stronger than she looks, I think.

Mrs. Myers and I follow.

Andreas frowns at me but does not say anything as we sit on

the logs with them. The men look at each other, their talk at a stall.

Aaron Myers speaks. "Here's where we're at, ladies. None of us have had any problems with the Indians, and we all agree Renicker wouldn't have had any either, if he hadn't been trading whiskey."

"We are farmers," Andreas adds. "We came to plow the lands. We do not want to live in towns where we cannot do this."

I want to scream at him. "We must return to New Ulm," I say. "I do not want to live alone on the prairie."

"Me, either," says Aaron's wife.

"Nor I," Mrs. Smith adds.

"We've talked about that," Smith says. "We agree that we shouldn't be so isolated, miles away from others."

This is good. It means we will go back to places east. We can make our farms near Mankato and New Ulm.

Aaron Myers continues. "We've talked about the lake. The soil is good here, and land is available for the taking. If we spread out our farms along one side of the lake, we can all have what we need for farming but be close enough that we can get to one another easily."

"Since we have already settled here, it makes sense for everyone else to settle on up the lakeshore," says Smith.

"Most of the trappers have small shacks where they stay when we are at the lake. They're in a group, about a mile to the north," Parmlee adds. "My place is a mile or so north of them."

"When we came down from Saratoga, we traveled the length of the lake," Myers says. "There are good spots all along it. I'm thinking we could settle at the north end, the Kochs in between. At most, we would be two to three miles apart, able to walk to our nearest neighbors within an hour's time."

"What?" I stand, gaping at Andreas. "We will not return to New Ulm?"

"I can farm, Christina, and you would not be so alone."

"It's not such a bad idea," Mrs. Myers says. "We would be a community if not a town. We could visit with no problem, and we can get together easily."

Ach, she is right. I know this. New Ulm is not for us anymore. It is time for me to let go of that place and take hold of this new community we will form. "But, will it be safe?" I ask. If it will be safe, I will try this.

Smith smiles at me. "None but Renicker have had problems with the Indians. Myers doctors them, and they regard him as a friend. We'll need to keep on guard if others settle here so whiskey doesn't become an issue."

"Other than that one instance, the Sioux here are friendly and eager to trade with us peacefully," Myers adds. "What other problems could we have?"

Chapter Eight

Julia
La Crosse, Wisconsin
During the same period, July 1856

Reality kicked Julia Wright in the head within days of her ill-considered marriage.

And it ached. It ached something fierce.

She slunk down in the chair and laid her head on the table, trying to block out the ruckus across the room, where Jack and two other men passed a jug of home-brewed corn liquor from hand to hand, all three bragging about their grand plans to sell watered-down whiskey to unsuspecting customers.

Hot anger sent spikes through her throbbing head. She'd thought him an ethical man!

Well . . . she'd be damned if she'd let him drag her good name through the mud. Julia Silsby had character, by God, and she would not be undone by the likes of Jack Wright.

Served her right, leaping without looking, like her sister had warned her she was doing. Jack had wooed her, told her he adored her too-plump curves, treated her like she was the most special woman in the world. He and his dimples and that glorious blond hair combed just so, looking so distinguished and worldly. Well, he wasn't distinguished now, not by any means.

Lord, why hadn't she listened? It had taken less than one week to discover Jack Wright the husband was not at all the same man as the charmer who had pressed his suit.

Stupid, stupid, stupid. With no one else to blame but herself.

How on earth was she going to manage being married to a man without an ounce of integrity? But she was stuck now, completely and thoroughly stuck. Wedded and bedded and bound for life to a dishonorable drunk who had no qualms about hoodwinking others. She'd have to figure out a way to keep him under control, for both their sakes.

She lifted her head and observed the trio in the far corner. Clearly, the whiskey in that jug was not watered. Jack was bleary eyed. His companions, neither of whom she'd seen before this evening, were pretty near in their cups. They'd stretched out, their dirty stockings and smelly feet mucking up the brand-new woven rug her parents had sent as a wedding gift. Their muddy boots were piled in the corner where they'd reluctantly shed them after she'd protested them wearing the detestable things into her clean cabin.

"So, how many d'ya think we hid away today?" Jack asked. It was the third time he'd asked the question, but she still wasn't sure what he was talking about because their drunken rambling had jumped from one topic to another.

"Ten, fifteen, m'be," the stinkiest one answered. He shifted his legs and the nauseous stench of his feet wafted through the close quarters.

I should have kept my mouth shut about their boots.

It would have been easy to shake the dried mud out later but oh, no, she'd insisted, nagged at them until they'd shed their footwear. Now, with so few windows, the stench of their dirty feet hung in the close quarters and would haunt the room until the heat of the day dissipated.

Egad, when was the last time they'd bathed?

Jack hadn't washed more than *his* hands and face since the morning they wed, a week before, despite unloading wagon-loads of furs into his uncle's mercantile these past few days.

Last night, his sweat-soaked skin had turned her stomach as he climbed into bed and started pawing at her. She'd washed the sheets this morning, along with his clothing. He'd been mad as a bear when he'd noticed that she'd grabbed them from the hook on the wall, insisting it was wasteful to wash them before the job was finished.

But the deed had already been done, praise heaven. Jack Wright would learn he hadn't married a weak-kneed woman, no matter how much wool he thought he'd pulled over her eyes.

"Ya hear me?" Stinky shouted. "Ten or fifteen of 'em."

"That ain't much," Jack mumbled.

"S'bout fifty, all t'gether," Stinky countered.

Fifty what? She thought they'd been working all day. Julia put her hand to her nose and focused on their conversation.

"Ought to bring good money." The groggy man in the corner mumbled the question then keeled over.

"They beaver?" Jack asked.

Beaver? Good heavens, they'd been stealing furs. From his uncle! Stealing and selling watered-down whiskey. Oh, she'd married a winner, all right.

"Uh huh."

"Where're they?"

"The shed. Gimme that jug."

But Jack had passed out. Stinky reached for the whiskey and collapsed atop Jack, his mouth gaping open.

Julia shook her head and rose from the table. She pushed up the single window as far as it would go and strode to the door. She threw it open and inhaled the clean air. Evening had settled, and it was cooling. She propped the door open and prayed for a cross breeze. Not that she intended to stay. She'd spend tonight at her sister's house.

But first, she needed to get those beaver pelts back to Uncle's store.

She laid down ground rules the following day, while nursing Jack's scrapes and bruises. Lorenza had advised her it was better done sooner than later, and this time she'd listen to her sister's wisdom.

When they'd discovered the missing pelts, there'd been a whopper of a fistfight among the three men, each one sure the other two had stolen the furs away. None had been able to remember a thing about the night before, which Julia counted a blessing.

"Ow!" Jack flinched as she dabbed at the bloody knot on his head.

"Sit still and be quiet." She eased the pressure of her touch. "I know it hurts, but it's your own fault."

"My fault?"

Julia exhaled, shaking her head. "You brought them here." She wiped the last trace of blood from his hair and dropped the cloth into a bucket of cold water to soak.

"Thought I could trust them," Jack mumbled.

Trust a crook? *Oh, Jack.*

She returned to the table and sat down across from him. "Do you have any idea how badly you stink? I don't know how you lived when you were single, but you're married now, and I share this cabin with you. Don't you ever come in here smelling like that again."

"Aw, Julia." He smiled at her, flashing his dimples—that same beguiling expression that had caught her in the first place.

Her heart stuttered.

She silenced it and concentrated on the task at hand. "You bathed when you were courting me, and you'll bathe now or I'll leave you. I won't live with a man who smells." She said the words firmly, praying he wouldn't call her bluff. She'd vowed to live in sickness and in health, and the Lord likely lumped smelliness into the same bucket.

"You won't." He cast his deep-brown eyes on her.

"Why would you think that I wouldn't? You stink."

"I guess I am a little ripe."

Julia snorted. "You smell like you're rotting."

"Okay, okay."

She leaned forward, vowing to get him a bath as soon as possible. But first, there were things that needed saying. She caught his gaze and chose her words with care. "You are not the same man who courted me. I've been swindled, and I don't like it. Not one bit."

"It was a bad week."

"It's a side of you I don't like. Where did the gentleman go? The one who swept me off my feet?"

"He's still here."

"I haven't seen him since the wedding. All the tenderness, the gentle loving stopped. You started drinking and turned mean and surly without an ounce of consideration for me."

"Whiskey does that to me."

"Then I expect you to stop drinking whiskey."

"Stop drinking? Good lord, Julia. That ain't right."

She drew back, considering. He had a point . . . sainthood wasn't necessary. "At the very least, I expect you to control it." Still, she wanted no more of what happened this week. "I didn't agree to marry a drunk. I agreed to marry an attentive, kind, responsible man. This week, that man disappeared."

"I'm sorry. I'll do better."

"I don't want those men here again." She punctuated the words so he would understand it was not negotiable.

"I'm done with them. Never want to see the thieves again."

"What you did with them, stealing those furs, can't happen

again. Or watering down whiskey to make a profit."

His eyes widened. "You heard all that?"

"Couldn't much help it the way you were all blathering. You're lucky half the town didn't hear."

He grinned, looking abashed. "I got caught up in their plans."

"Plans like that aren't right, Jack. I won't abide dishonesty."

"I—"

She continued, knowing she had to say the words. "I married you with the belief that you were a man of integrity. If you're not that man, you have bound me under false pretenses."

"Well, we're married now." He said the words, swallowed, a bit of shock on his face. But he offered no modifier, and the statement stood like a barricade.

Oh lord. She'd hoped not to have to spell it out completely.

She gathered her courage. "I'll divorce you if you force me."

"You can't do that."

She stared at him, knowing she couldn't back down from the bluff now. She had to make him believe she could and would.

"Then you had best return to being the man you were. The one I've seen this past week is not the one I agreed to marry. That makes our marriage a false contract and contestable. You will not push me, Jack, or we are done."

La Crosse, Wisconsin
Two years later, 1858

Julia stood with her hands deep in dishwater. Her oldest sister, Lorenza, sat in a rocking chair nursing her baby girl while Lorenza's other children played on the floor with Julia's little Dora. The men had escaped to the peace and quiet of Lorenza's front porch.

She'd not visited with her sister enough these past two years and was glad Lorenza had seen fit to set things right between them. It was well past time they repaired their relationship.

Life since marrying Jack had been an up and down journey. Lorenza and Jack butted heads often, with Lorenza seeing right through all Jack's blustering and Jack resenting her interference. Eventually, Julia had found it easier to keep distant and focus on keeping Jack out of trouble.

"I'm not used to others doing my work for me," Lorenza said.

"Hush. You tend to the baby and let me worry about the chores. It was enough that you cooked supper for us." She'd do dishes all day if it meant a visit with Lorenza.

"It's good to have you here, finally."

"With us both having children, it's hard." Julia knew she was prevaricating, but it was easier to hedge than talk about the obvious.

Lorenza shook her head and raised the baby to burp her. "It's not so hard, and you know it. You hide."

Julia looked away. "I do no such thing."

"You do, too."

Lorenza was right—always was, it seemed.

Julia blew out a breath. They'd best talk about it and get it done with. "It's easier," she said.

"I don't like that man of yours, but I love you to death. You are my little sister, and I hate that we don't talk like we used to."

Nostalgia wrung Julia's heart. Lorenza had been so helpful with advice when she'd first wed Jack. Now, they'd lost so much of that closeness. Growing up wasn't easy. At her feet, Dora whimpered, and she scooped her daughter up, jostling her. "Keeping Jack in line takes all my energy."

"I don't doubt that."

Julia crossed the room and hugged her sister, provoking squawks from both little ones. "I'm glad you asked us over. I've missed you, too, Lorenza."

"Is he treating you all right?" Lorenza whispered the words, as if saying them aloud might make the concern valid.

"We have our ups and downs. But he doesn't hit me, if that's what you mean."

"Does he treat you right?" This time, the question was more forceful.

Julia put Dora back on the floor with her cousins and sat down with them, absently stacking blocks to keep them entertained. "I don't know what you want me to say. He's the same man he's always been. At times, he dotes on me. But there's always another wild plan he gets caught up in. He goes off on a tangent, and we fight. He's never yelled at me or talked bad to me. It's such a constant battle trying to keep him out of trouble. He always wants to take the easy way to profit rather than the most ethical."

"Do you love him?"

She caught Lorenza's gaze and sighed. "There are times he makes my pulse pound with excitement, when I look at him and melt. He gets out that jaw harp of his and acts the clown with it until I laugh my head off at him. He knows so many things but has no common sense at all." She paused.

"It was a mistake to marry him, but, as long as he treats me with kindness and respect, provides for us, and keeps out of trouble, it doesn't matter much whether there's love between us. We're happy enough. What's more, I'm bound to him."

"He didn't want to come here, did he?"

"You slapped him on the face the last time we visited."

They laughed uneasily. It had been more than a year ago, and they'd done well enough together today, at least.

"He and George seem to get on," Lorenza said.

"He likes George."

They watched the children, both silent.

"Do you think he can come to tolerate me?"

Julia grinned. "As long as you don't hit him again." *And you don't tell him what to do.*

"How is he with Dora?"

"He's good with her. I don't have any complaints there. And he provides well." What was Lorenza up to?

"He's staying out of trouble?"

"For the most part. His uncle watches him like a hawk at the store. From time to time, he comes up with an idea that's a little on the shady side, and we have words."

"And that works?"

"I told him I would divorce him if he didn't live by my rules. I remind him, and he falls back in line."

Lorenza sucked in a breath. "Would you? Divorce him?"

"I don't think there would be true legal grounds, not for a woman. Besides, I made vows. Before God, for better or worse. I won't break them."

"But he doesn't know that?"

"I think he believes I'd make true on the threat. It always works. He forgets about his schemes, and life becomes normal for a while. Until the next time."

It wasn't the easiest way to make a marriage, but it worked. Jack stayed out of trouble, the family stayed whole, and she was able to keep her own reputation intact.

"Do you think there would be less temptation if he started fresh, in a less populated area where there's not so much to lead him astray?"

"Lorenza Lamb, what are you getting at? Just spit it out."

"George brought home a handbill about the Dakota Land Company. They've had posters up all over advertising they've started a couple towns in the western part of Minnesota near Lake Shetek. We've been talking about going."

Julia stood, already at a loss. "Oh, Lorenza, so far?"

"George loves trapping, and there's land there for the grabbing."

"There's trapping in Wisconsin. Why in the world would he want to traipse into the far reaches? Especially with a family in tow!"

"It's a solid idea, Julia. The fur is playing out here; farmland has been grabbed up. Moving west makes sense, to both of us. I've never shied away from adventure."

So, they'd knit their relationship only to say good-bye. "You've already decided."

"We have."

Julia swallowed. How would she survive without her big sister there to talk her through things? Heavens, Lorenza was her confidant, her strength, the only one she could talk to about Jack.

"What will I do without you?"

"George and I have talked . . ." Lorenza drew a breath. "We'd like you and Jack to come with us."

★ ★ ★ ★ ★

Part Two: Gathering

★ ★ ★ ★ ★

Chapter Nine

Laura
Beaver, Minnesota
The same year, spring 1858

Our future washed down Beaver Creek along with the quagmire that had once been a hillside. The mill broke apart, walls and flooring rushing away with the muddy floodwaters. Helpless in the pouring torrent, I watched the turbulent crest erode and destroy one more part of my life. We would have to wait until the water subsided to determine whether the heavy mill works had survived at the bottom of the creek.

Would we chase our dreams forever without being quite able to grasp them?

I prayed the loan against the mill had been denied, and we wouldn't have to pay for the useless devastation, but I doubted we'd be so lucky. We would have a loan to pay back as well as a new mill to construct. My head ached as I calculated the profits we would need to achieve at the store in order to accomplish so much. Once again, a river had wreaked havoc with our lives.

How I hated that roiling flux. Memories of the Mississippi and the horrid deaths of my little girls flowed within those cursed waters. I shut my eyes against the images and tried to take solace in that my three other children were all safe at home and that our only loss was the mill.

William returned a few days later. Along with the building

materials to expand the store.

We settled the children into bed early. Though we hated facing our options, we needed to determine our course. He sat on the small horsehair-stuffed settee he'd purchased last year—an attempt to win me over when he announced he'd been elected to the statehood convention.

I wished his diverted attention were still my only worry.

"I think we should rebuild the mill instead of expanding the store," he said.

I'd expected him to take that tack but wasn't sure it was the best choice. I perched next to him, determined to express my opinion in a quiet, non-confrontational manner, as I'd done each time I'd needed him to hear my words. I'd learned with that first stove discussion that I had to take care lest he become defensive and stop listening to what I had to say.

"We make more money from the store. It makes more sense to expand the mercantile." I'd carefully summed the returns from each and was prepared to show him the account books, if needed.

"The Malindys are going west. We'd own the entire mill ourselves." Despite the announcement, he looked less pleased about being the sole owner than I would have expected. Worry lines etched his face.

"That means the entire rebuilding cost would be ours."

"So would the profits."

"And who's going to operate it?" I asked. "In the past year, you've been so involved with politics, you've barely been at the mill. You said you intended to run for statehouse."

"I'll have to find a new partner." His voice held little enthusiasm, and I ached for him. Much as I hated it when he had unrealistic dreams, I did not want him to give up entirely.

I chose my words with care, so that I didn't defeat him. "Taking on a partner would eliminate the potential profit. Maybe the mill should wait a few years, until we are back on solid financial footing."

He slumped in the chair. "I guess I should take the building materials back to Winona, return the money to the bank, and get the mortgage released. We wouldn't be able to expand the store, but at least we'd have no debt."

Poor William. I knew what it was like to let loose of one's desire.

"That would be an option." The best, I thought, but I was uncomfortable with his dismay. This was not my usually assertive husband, and it gave me pause. "Or we add on as we planned and double the size of the store."

We would be stretched tightly, but Beaver's residents would bring us steady profit if they were able to purchase more goods locally. With a careful watch on our expenditures, we might be able to rebuild the mill sooner this way.

"Or we could go west." He dropped the suggestion so softly that it failed to register at first. "We can sell the farm property and the store, and take the recovered mill works with us."

My dander rose. "Move? Again?"

What new fantasy had he seized upon that he would disrupt our lives once more? That he would take away *my* dreams? We were part and parcel of this town, leading citizens, with a host of friends and the respect of those who arrived each month to expand the community. He had finally given me what he had promised me more than a decade past and now he wanted to take it away? I bit my tongue, aghast.

"I could go back to farming, partner in milling."

"We have land here. We have lives here. The lives we always dreamed about. How can you possibly think of taking us away from this?"

"Minnesota is being settled faster than ever. There were a lot of new precincts out west that registered during the statehood vote. And that was nearly a year ago. Those towns have been growing ever since."

How could he even ask this of me? I shook my head. "I can't."

We sat there, silent. I was baffled, unable to understand why he wanted to leave here. We'd need to recover financially, yes, but we had everything else we'd envisioned.

"I promise we'll take the stove this time, and everything else you deem necessary."

His offer, so sincere, almost broke my heart. That he would very nearly beg this of me confused me. My thoughts churned trying to fathom his reasons.

"Why, William? We have the means to make a go of things. We may have a few tight years, but we can flourish here."

"Look at this, Laura." He rose and strode to the kitchen area. When he returned, he held Maggie's copy of the *Wabashaw Herald* in his hand.

Lord, why had I not hidden that thing away?

He opened it and pointed to the Dakota Land Company ad. "See . . ."

"What I see is a land company greedy for profit."

"Now, Laura—"

I rose and poked at his chest with my finger. "Don't you dare 'Now, Laura' me. You can't spend your entire life chasing pipe dreams."

"I'm not chasing a dream this time."

I barely heard his words, so intent was I on arguing. "You can't just follow whims, taking us hither and whither. Not when it involves me and our children. It's reckless."

My hand drifted to my again-growing abdomen.

"I won't uproot us and take us there sight unseen. I can scout, find the perfect town, good land."

"I've experienced your scouting results already. Each time, you have settled us where there is fine farmland. But you also like places with fast running rivers that have stolen our children and our livelihood. I cannot abide that happening again. I will die myself if we lose another child."

He caught my hand, stilled it in his, and embraced me.

"I'm scared, Laura." His voice broke as he uttered the words.

"Oh, Husband." This was not a man who expressed trepidation. I wrapped my arms around him, held him.

"I thought this would be the place for us, but the way those hillsides slid away frightens me. Folks in Winona said the town should never have been built here, that the river rages often and consumes the entire valley. I don't want to expand the store only to lose that, too, if the creek floods the town. I never imagined that happening. I avoided the Mississippi, but I didn't think about possible flooding here. I made a mistake in settling us in this place."

He grew quiet. "I don't want to lose another child, either."

My throat tightened. "I don't know that I would be able to do that. Not again."

"It's the ravines. They're too narrow. People in Winona said both the Whitewater and the Beaver flood often. They're such small waterways that I assumed there was no threat. In truth, there's nowhere for the water to go but up."

We held each other as it dawned on me that he was right. Those hillsides had crumbled like they were made of cake batter. A little more rain, and the water would have crested the banks and poured into town. And it hadn't been unusually wet for spring, just a violent, prolonged rain. I shivered.

There truly was danger here, and that it had William worried was significant.

"Where would we go?" I finally asked.

"I don't know yet." He withdrew, his gaze catching mine. "I'll pay back the loan immediately, salvage the mill works, and try to find out what's available out West. I can look at the Dakota

Land Company offerings, visit the towns. I'll find us a place where we won't need to worry about the fickleness of a strong river. I'll spend whatever time we need to find it and avoid hills and ravines that collect water in heavy rains. I can find us a place where it's flat and there are no threats."

I agreed, even as I wondered if there really was such a place.

Lavina
Olmstead County, Minnesota
Summer 1858

I return to household duties and my living children the day after we bury William Merton. Though grief still chokes me, I have to concentrate on the four who remain. It's the way of life.

As summer advances and life returns to normal, Tommy and Sophia Ireland invite us to picnic with them, and we gather, the children running amok, our dog loping with them. It's good to return to normal life, and I'm content in Olmstead County. It feels like home, and I'm glad our family is taking root here.

"Who's up for a stroll?" Tommy asks. It's his usual activity after a meal, and we've come to anticipate the brisk walks. Tommy Ireland has never "strolled" in his entire life.

Sophia laughs at him. "Shall we walk through the woods? It would be cool there."

I look toward the copse of trees lining the small creek where the children are playing hide and seek. My head perspires beneath my hair, piled as it is atop my head like a fur hat. Walking in the shade would be a welcome respite.

"I've a mind to check on the corn," Tommy says.

I eye the trees again and let the desire go.

Tommy marches off, a ball of energy. Sophia, John, and I follow as best we can. Though in his mid-forties, Tommy remains more spry than men half his age. He leads us with a fast pace.

Thank heavens I'm not wearing a corset, or I would faint in my effort to keep up.

Ahead, the corn is already past knee high, a good sign. If we get no hail, if we have no drought, if we do not receive too much rain, the yield will be good. The green stalks stretch for acres. Beyond lie grain fields.

"We managed to get all the land into production." Sophia beams at her husband.

John looks at me. Like us, the Irelands claimed the largest parcels available by the time we got there. Tommy, able to work twice as hard as anyone else, cleared his quickly. We still labor to break ours.

"All forty acres?" John asks. There is a flash of envy in his eyes, but it is soon gone. Even John cannot keep up with Tommy, and there is no sense begrudging his vigor.

"All except the home site and the little batch of trees." Tommy grins at her. He steps among the stalks, peeling away a bit of one husk to check the progress of the ear, and smiles.

"It's good soil," John says. He pokes at the dirt with his boot. "Produces well, like ours."

Tommy glances at him. "Trouble is, it's like Illinois all over again."

Sophia looks at me and rolls her eyes. This, too, is typical Tommy.

"I sense it, too," John says.

Familiar dread fills me at this. *Not again.* I wonder if my husband will ever be content where he is.

"But the land is good," I insist. "It will be years before it's tired and worn. That's why we left Illinois."

Tommy returns to us, his expression unreadable. "That's true. The land here is more fertile. The problem is that we were only able to preempt forty acres. When we came, we anticipated whole sections being available to us. We got here too late."

I looked from him to John, confused.

"What Tommy's saying is that forty acres is not going to be enough," John says.

"But we're doing well." Sophia's voice holds a note of panic, and I know we now both understand this is more than our men grumbling. They are serious. Lunch leaps in my stomach.

Tommy shrugs. "We are surviving. Olmstead County has filled in. With so much land in production, there will be a surplus of crops. Prices will go down, our profits along with them."

"Can't we buy more land?" I take up the cause in earnest and hear the plea in my voice.

"Who will sell it to us? It's like Tommy said. We're boxed in, like Illinois."

"But if we sold our land, others would pay well for it," Tommy says. "We can head farther west, claim more land. But we need to do it before others do or we'll face the same situation all over again."

"Where are you thinking?" Sophia's mouth gapes.

"We saw an ad in the paper. The Dakota Land Company is settling in the western part of the state and beyond, in Dakota Territory."

Now it's my turn to gawk. We? They have already discussed this. The two of them have hashed it out already, and, once again, Sophia and I are the last to know. Though I understand the reasoning, anger stirs.

"They've platted towns in Murray County," Tommy says. "And the company is offering one hundred sixty acres to those who help settle the surrounding area."

"Where's that, now?" she says angrily.

"Western Minnesota, out near Dakota Territory. According to last year's census, there's a community taken hold there." John chimes in like they are a team of tinkers trying to sell their wares.

"So, you're thinking to just pack us up and go?" Sophia's voice already holds resignation.

I look to John. We are partners, and I know he awaits my opinion. Olmstead County has become home, but the points the men raise are valid. Forty acres is enough to support a family but provides little profit to set aside for lean years. That lack of cushion could bring ruin during drought or overly wet years. Even one good hailstorm could wipe a family out.

Still, I'm uncomfortable with the notion of moving to such unsettled areas. An undercurrent of fear has taken the place of my anger. I don't know how wild that part of the state remains.

"I think we need to learn more before we make this decision," I say.

"I think we have time yet," Tommy says, "but we do need to start thinking about it, looking into what's out there."

"While we don't need to be in a hurry, we do need to make plans, before we lose our chance," John adds.

Tommy nods. "We could travel out there once harvest is in, take a look, find the right place."

"After that, we can plan the timing." John holds my gaze, waiting for me to accede.

I look to him, know the men are right. Leasing land, farming small plots, is not part of what we envisioned in our dreams. Independence, true security, still eludes us. I dig into my worry, seeking the cause of my unsettled alarm and remember news accounts of Indian attacks from last year. If we can find our dream, grasp it without putting the family in danger, I will go.

"There were Indian attacks on the frontier. I do not want to settle anywhere near Spirit Lake."

"That was in Iowa. This area is miles from there. We'll find a safe settlement. I can't promise there will be no Indians, but we will make sure any in the area have a reputation of being peaceful."

Almena
La Crosse, Wisconsin
Summer 1858

In the springhouse, Almena covered the milk she'd left to cool and stood. Her back twinged, and she winced. Not even five months into the process, and, already, she couldn't wait for this baby to be born. Hand at her back, she padded to the house and into the small kitchen.

Phin sat at the table, the advertisement Almena had given him in hand. He picked up his spectacles and adjusted the oil lamp until the glow brightened. He peered at the ad.

"It's a good opportunity," she told him. "The land company is offering quarter sections. Do you think we're ready?" She sat across from him and rubbed a dab of homemade hand cream into her callous.

"We've got a good nest egg, between my four years of clerking and your three of selling to my employers."

She grinned. He'd risked his job, back in Ohio, introducing her goods little by little, until customers demanded more and more of them. Once they replaced the lost cows, she'd done well here, too. They'd built their wealth, saving everything they could. He hated clerking, but it was a means to his land-ownership dream.

"The Dakota Land Company is on the frontier, Almena. Are you sure you want to live in the middle of nowhere?"

"The article says they have several settlements. This one is in Murray County, Minnesota. Farther west, yes, but not in the territories. There's a community there already, Cornwell City. The '57 census recorded ninety-two residents. There's a blacksmith, millwrights, a grocer, even a physician. It must be way past a hundred by now."

"But it's still miles away from settled cities."

"But the land! We can pre-empt on one hundred sixty acres of the company land, sign a sales contract, and pay on installments. That'd leave our money for improvements and stock."

"I agree. But is it a safe place to raise a family?"

A prickle of fear needled her. It *would* be isolated.

"I think we need to take care," he said. "Minnesota's only recently become a state. I expect the unsettled areas are still pretty wild."

But the opportunity . . . they had to look at the opportunity. *Surely people wouldn't settle there if it wasn't safe.* She opened her mouth to tell Phin that but paused. He was right—they didn't know about the potential dangers.

"You're right."

"So are you. It's a chance to grab what we want from life." He removed his pocket watch. Opening it, he read the inscription aloud, "Time to follow our dreams."

"It's a big step. We don't have to rush, Phin. There will be other prospects."

"I want us to be safe, but I also want us to provide a good life for our family." He eyed her growing midsection. "Does it say if there's a school? I want our children to be educated."

"I don't know. I guess if there were twenty-three children listed on the census, there should be one, or will be soon."

"Indians?"

Almena drew a sharp breath. *I didn't think about Indians!*

"The Chippewa around here are peaceful, but I don't know a thing about the tribes out West. Sioux? Aren't they more warlike?"

Almena's shoulders slumped. "I think so. If I recall, there have been reservations for a number of years."

"Well, that would make a difference. If they're on reservations, there shouldn't be problems for folks in settled towns. You said there was a doctor in Cornwell City? A hundred people? It sounds no different than La Crosse but for the size. If you're not worried—"

"I'm a pregnant woman. I worry about everything." She covered Phin's hand with hers. "You're tired of working for other people—you come home frustrated. You're not a shopkeeper, Phin; you never wanted to be one. It's time to start on our dream. I looked at a map . . . there's a large lake northeast of the town. We could settle up that direction. The soil ought to be good and the water table high enough to supply a well."

"It sounds perfect. Too perfect."

"Let's do this: let's wait until summer to decide, after the baby is born. We can gather our facts. Find out if anyone has been out that direction and ask them about it."

"A good idea." He grasped her fingers. "I think Bill Jones, at the store, lived near Mankato for a while. Maybe he can offer up more details." Phin's chair scraped across the floorboards. He stepped behind her and circled her with his arms, leaning his head atop hers. "That should give us what we need to make a solid decision."

She pondered the dangers he'd mentioned, the isolation, the unknowns. They'd twisted into a heavy knot that now lay in her stomach, souring her original enthusiasm.

Christina
Lake Shetek, Minnesota
Summer 1858

Andreas and I, we move to the lake as soon as possible, in the same week the Myers also come. We do not want to be alone on the prairie so close to where Renicker was killed. The lake is farther from that place, and there will be others nearby. This will be safer, especially since the Indians are friends with Aaron Myers.

We choose a fine spot for our cabin. It is a small parcel of land that sits between the big lake, Shetek, and a smaller lake that is called Bloody. Parmlee tells us the willow roots surface every few years and turn bright red, which makes the water look like blood. It is not such a good name, I think, but it was not mine to choose. Our cabin is south of it, in a grove among many trees. I will ask Andreas to buy lilac seedlings in New Ulm. These I will plant by the door.

I have never watched a cabin being built before. It is not so easy. Andreas sweats in the summer heat. Even with his chest bare, the sweat runs from his dark hair. I regret he must work so hard, but I do not mind so much seeing his muscles ripple.

"Christina?" he calls.

"*Ja?* What is it?"

"Will you go to Myers now?"

Andreas has all the logs ready. We have chopped off the branches and made chinks where the logs will fit together, working hard for many days. Now, it is time to lift the logs. Myers will come to help, and Andreas will do the same for him.

I do not take my bonnet. It is too hot, and I have been working hard with my husband to prepare. Our house will be seventeen by thirteen feet, big enough for our bed, a table and chairs, and a cabinet or two. That is all we need. We will add another room later. With hard work, Andreas and Myers should raise the walls today.

I tidy my braid and set off to the north. Myers has a spot at the end of a small lake called Fremont that connects into Shetek. It is about two miles from us. I take the shortcut between Lake Shetek and Bloody Lake that Andreas told me about.

As I leave our cabin site, the land becomes mushy, and I am glad I am wearing my old boots. The ground squishes beneath me, and I lift my skirts so they will not get wet. Around me, birds chatter, some trilling complicated songs, others scolding in sharp tones. Pelicans lift from the water and leave ripples that cast sunlit rings. The smell of fish fills the air as I pass the remains of some animal's meal. There is life here, more than on the bare prairie around the Walnut Grove, and I am glad.

I leave the swampy stretch of land and continue around Fremont Lake, waving as I near the Myerses' home site. There, Myers and his wife are preparing their logs. Their older children help while the youngsters play in the grass.

"Mrs. Koch!" Mrs. Myers rushes to me and stops, unsure. We are strangers still.

I take her hands in mine. "You must call me Christina. We are neighbors now." The Smiths are at the south end of Lake Shetek, four miles from us with the bachelor Parmlee half-way between, and so I am the Myerses' closest neighbor. We should not be formal.

"And you can call us Mary and Aaron," she says.

"Are you ready?" Aaron asks. Andreas has already warned him that today will be the day.

"*Ja*," I tell him and see that his walls will soon be ready to raise, too.

Aaron has a yoke of oxen, and he makes them ready as I chat with Mary. The oxen will ease the work, so that the men do not have to lift all the weight of the logs.

"I'm so glad we've moved from Saratoga. The prospect of living there all alone was dreadful," Mary says.

"*Ja*. I have been lonely at the Walnut Grove. I think the men do not understand." I think about how Mary and I will become friends and visit. I will put up my braid, and we will call on each other like the women did in New Ulm.

"Men understand very little about women, sometimes." Mary leans close and lowers her voice. "I birthed Fred with only Aaron there. He's a good doctor, but I missed having a woman with me."

For a moment, I do not know what to say. I cannot imagine such a thing as having a baby without another woman there. I think about the rest of her words. "Aaron is a doctor?"

This will be a good thing, to have a doctor.

Mary raises her hands and makes a motion as if to shoo the words away. "Not a real one. But he has a gift with herbs and healing."

"That is good to know, if we have need."

"Do you have family, Christina?"

A pang of sadness swarms me. "I came to *Amerika* from Germany with them, but only my brother came West. He did not like it and went back to the others."

"You stayed alone?" She sounded surprised, and I know I must explain.

"I met Andreas and was married."

"Christina?" Aaron calls out.

I turn and see he has the team ready. I say my good-byes to Mary, and we depart in his wagon, filled with rope and tools he says will ease the work. At Bloody Lake, he veers east, to take the oxen around the inlet. It will be longer, but he says the oxen will drive easier that way. We cover the four miles quickly.

Andreas is waiting for us.

But, with him are three other men. They are dressed in wool trousers tucked into leather leggings. Long dark hair, tamed by leather bands, flows down their backs.

Indians.

Julia
St. Peter, Minnesota
Fall 1858

"So, what do you think?"

Julia stared at Jack. Had she heard him right? What did *she* think? It was more than a little late to ask, given the way he'd just announced his new hare-brained idea. Good lord, he was about to destroy the strategy she and Lorenza had so carefully crafted to keep him out of trouble.

He was supposed to fur trap with George, clear land in the middle of nowhere, and keep his nose clean!

"You've decided already, that's what I think." She'd folded up the newspaper she'd laid in her lap when he started talking.

Jack paced the shabby hotel room, his pent-up energy ready to burst. "Aw, Julia, you know it's a good plan."

A good plan? Was he crazy? And where ever had he come up with such an idea? She forced herself to stay calm and concentrate on the why of it and not the how.

"What in heaven's name makes you think you would be a good Indian trader? I thought we were going to farm."

Jack took the rickety chair on the opposite side of the tiny side table. It creaked as it absorbed his weight. He had insisted on the "best" room in the establishment, and, if this was it, Julia shuddered to think what the other rooms were like. They should have picked a better place.

"I'll farm, too," he said.

She suspected he meant what he said. Still, if she knew anything, it was that Jack was easily led astray. She let out a heavy breath. "We planned this all out, before we left Wisconsin."

"Plans can change."

The way his eyes lit told her she hadn't much chance of changing his mind, but she'd do her best. Letting Jack run amok was best avoided when at all possible.

She crossed her arms and settled against the back of the chair. This might take a while. "Where did you come up with this idea, anyway?"

"The other day, when George and I were in the saloon."

Well, that made things a lot clearer. The saloon, Jack, and whiskey—that explained most of it.

"George thinks it's a good idea."

"Oh, he does, does he?" Wouldn't Lorenza be delighted to hear that? "When did you and George end up on the same side of things?"

"We had a few drinks." Jack had the good grace to look sheepish, at least. "George doesn't want to farm, either, you know."

She leaned forward, elbows on the arms of the chair. "Really?"

Jack shrugged, his enthusiasm dampening the way it usually did once he caught on that she wasn't buying what he was selling. "He's a trapper at heart. Always has been."

Julia suspected that much was true. But she also knew George Lamb was a responsible man who recognized what was what. "And now he has a family," she said. "George knows trapping won't support them. He said as much to Lorenza. Even Minnesota will get trapped out before long."

"But if we work the land together, it'll be less farming for both of us. Trapping and trading will supplement our income and decrease the risk if we have a bad crop year."

Heaven help her, he had a point. Still, this was Jack, and she didn't see the scheme working. "You've worked in a mercantile. That's not the same thing as being a trader."

"Uncle traded for furs all the time."

"Your uncle did, not you."

"Yeah, but I know their worth." He stood and walked to her, crouching in front of her. "And you know Indians."

Her mother had descended from a long line of trappers, many of whom had intermarried with Iroquois and the Chippewa.

Probably with others she didn't even know about. "Just because my uncle has an Ojibwa wife doesn't mean I know anything about the Dakota. It's a different tribe that lives out here."

"You pick up languages easy enough. You can do the same with the Sioux."

Julia sighed. "They prefer to be called Dakota. Sioux is a white man's word." In fact, the Dakota defined themselves by their bands, but she didn't want to try to explain all that to Jack. He'd never understand, and she wasn't sure she even had a firm grasp on the differences.

"See! You already have insight." He jumped up and paced again. "Think about it: with George spreading the word that we'll buy their furs, why wouldn't they sell to us? We'd be right there, with trade goods on hand to pay them. With you to help me communicate, it will be simple to do this in addition to the farming. Hell, they won't be there much of the time."

"Are you sure it's wise to create reasons to attract the Dakota to the settlement?" She'd heard stories. The Dakota had not adjusted well to the recent infusion of whites. Farmers were not trappers. They treated the Indians differently.

"They'll be attracted anyway. That's human nature. Curiosity, food, and things they need. We might as well take advantage of it and have goods for them. Otherwise, they'll just steal what they want."

"Jack!" She rose. "That's hardly fair. In their world, people share with those in need, no questions asked. Hospitality is a given. They don't regard it as stealing."

"So, are the customs the same across tribes?"

She shifted, unsure how to answer. "Some."

"We'll do fine."

She sighed. "I'll think about it. For now, let's stick with the original plan, pick out land, and get settled. We can decide later on the trading idea."

"All right." Jack headed for the door.

"There is one other thing," Julia said.

He turned. "Now what?"

She'd not wanted to tell him this way, but it might have bearing on the issue. Besides, it was time, and he certainly hadn't been observant enough to figure it out on his own. "I'm expecting."

"We're having another baby?" His voice grew quiet with the slightest trace of awe.

"I think it will be March or so."

"That's wonderful!" He drew her into his arms and kissed her on the mouth. "Damn!"

"Jack . . . I don't want to go until the baby is born. I want to stay where there's a doctor."

He drew back, piecing it together. "But—"

"I am not having this child out in the middle of nowhere. I agreed to settle out there, despite learning the advertised towns don't exist but I am *not* having this baby there."

"We can't stay here all this time. Good heavens, it would cost a fortune."

Even in this dump. "George has relatives in Mankato. We can stay with them."

"That will be one whole trapping season we miss."

"Then we will just need to miss it."

"But Charley Wambau and Bill Clark said—"

"Who?" Inexplicable unease rippled up and down her spine. Nothing good ever came from Jack quoting people he'd recently met. Generally, it boded ill.

"Wambau and Clark. I met them the other night, after George left the saloon. They had this great idea. Did you know there's hardly anywhere out there that sells whiskey?"

Oh, Jack, no!

Of all the things she didn't need right now! Easy money

always caught Jack's attention, usually leading him in the wrong direction. And whiskey and Indian trading was definitely the wrong direction. If this Wambau and Clark were introducing temptations like that, she needed to get Jack away from them as soon as possible.

"How about you and Lorenza and George head out to Shetek ahead of me?" she said, grasping at the first solution that came to mind.

His eyes brightened with enthusiasm. "That might work. You'll think about the trading idea?"

"I'll think about it. You and George go ahead and make plans to travel. I'll talk to Lorenza about me staying in Mankato until spring."

"I love you, Julia."

"And, Jack?"

"Yeah?"

"No whiskey, no Wambau, and no Clark. No matter what I decide on the trading."

Chapter Ten

Lavina
Olmstead County, Minnesota
March 1859

The harvest is a good one, giving pause to the idea that this land will not support us. But I know all years will not be so bountiful and accept we don't have enough land. The birth of any more children will strain our resources. The men are right; the future lies to the west.

We've wintered well, but it will soon be time to plant, and a decision must be made. I don't relish it, for the thought of living in such a wild place is unnerving, no matter how necessary it might be. I hold on to the knowledge that this town, Cornwell City, holds over a hundred souls and that we will be safe among such a number.

I clear the supper dishes and wash them as Merton and Frank dry, both of them whistling as John so often does. Merton's pitch is off key; Frank's, as true as his father. The cat folds back its ears at the lack of harmony and slinks outdoors as the boys get louder and seek to outdo one another in volume.

The time has come to make firm plans and set a date for our departure. We've eaten early, and the Irelands will be here soon. Poor tabby will not be pleased about relocating, and I wonder if we would be better to leave her here with whomever buys the property.

I'm tucking stray pieces of hair back into my bun when the Irelands arrive with their brood. John welcomes them as Merton and Frank change into their nightclothes. Sophia ushers her girls inside and settles them with my boys in the bedroom. Merton will once again take charge of them. I have been blessed in this child and his remarkable sense of responsibility. He is my bedrock.

The adults arrange our chairs near the fire, for the early spring evenings remain chilly. John stirs the logs, and they pop, the sound sharp in the quiet of the room. He tosses an evergreen sprig on the flames, and its scent fills the air.

"We made a good profit last year," my husband says.

"Us, too, but not all years will be that way."

"I don't want us to jump the gun."

"But, if we wait too long, the best land will be taken there, too. I'm tired of arriving too late. I think we need to get there soon," Tommy replies to him.

Sophia and I remain quiet, listening to their back-and-forth.

"Have you heard any more about Cornwell City? How many are there now? If we can gauge how fast it's growing, we can better judge whether we need to get there this year."

"I haven't. But it must be growing. The latest Dakota Land Company ads say the company-owned land around the town is going fast, and that worries me. We'll need to buy from the company if we want to take advantage of the time payments."

"Lavina, get that paper, will you?" John says. "The one we got yesterday. Let's check to see if there's any news on it."

I rise and retrieve the newspaper I had tucked away until we had time to read it in detail. "The front page is a story about election fraud. You'll likely need to page through it." I hand it to John, check on the children, and return to my chair next to Sophia.

John pages through, refolds the paper. "Nothing."

He hands the paper to Sophia. She takes it to the kitchen table, pausing as something catches her eye.

"I think we need to head out there in April or May," Tommy says. "If we arrive early, we'll have time to get gardens in and cut a couple crops of wild hay to support livestock through the winter. The first year will be tight, but that would get us through until we can break more land."

"We'd need to put in a big garden if we're going to rely on its produce all winter." John's lips move as he calculates in his head. "April might be best, given we'll have to break ground."

"April?" I say. I'd not thought we would leave that soon. I fight to hold my argument, knowing it must be. "That gives us only a few weeks to pack."

John puts his hand on mine. "If we're not putting in crops here, Tommy and I can help you."

"We'll sell the livestock before we go, buy new once we get near, maybe Mankato or New Ulm. That'll make travel faster."

"Tommy . . . look at this." Sophia rushes over and hands him the paper. "The article on the election."

"I'll read it later."

"You'd best read it now." Her voice is stern.

Tommy blows out an exasperated breath and takes the paper. "What? Fake precincts in an election two years ago?"

"You didn't read it all." She points to a section in the middle of the page. "Oasis Precinct is among them. It doesn't exist. Never did."

"What's that got to do with anything?"

"It's in Murray County, where we're going. For Pete's sake, read the article, will you?"

Tommy reddens, and I recall John saying he doesn't read well. Whatever is in the article, it has Sophia rattled to the point that she's forgotten it entirely. I take the paper from him and read the section Sophia pointed at. My breath catches. Cornwell

City does not exist?

I read it again to make sure.

"I'm confused. It says Oasis Precinct was never legally formed and that it was mistakenly listed in Murray County instead of Cottonwood County. The next bit is unclear, where it talks about Cornwell City. It claims no one has lived there since the middle of '57. I can't tell if they mean no one has lived in the real Oasis Precinct or in Cornwell City."

"*No one* lives there?" Sophia's skin has gone white. "You said there were two hundred people!"

I sense I'm also pale. "I don't know," I say, "But we'd darn well better find out before we pack up and go there, now hadn't we?"

Julia
Lake Shetek, Minnesota
April 1859

Julia settled baby George on her lap and buttoned her bodice. She cast a glance into the wagon bed, where Dora lay asleep, lulled by the constant rocking. Ahead of them, endless spring prairie stretched.

"It's pretty empty."

Compared to the lush woods of Wisconsin and the Minnesota River valley near St. Peter and Mankato, the land looked barren. Oh, there were hills, endless rises and falls of nothing but prairie grass, already green and growing. She suspected there'd be flowers but saw precious few of them yet.

"You'll love the lake," Jack said. "The sun glints off the surface, all sparkles and colors, and you should hear all the birds."

Whatever it was like, she'd make do. She always did. You couldn't change what life brought, only what you did with it. At least, she and Lorenza would be together. That was the blessing in all of this, one she anticipated beyond measure.

But, still, please let it be as nice as Jack described.

The road was rough, barely worthy of being called a road at all, but at least it was a clear trail. "You said this is a mail route?" she asked Jack.

"Runs from New Ulm to Sioux Falls, in Dakota Territory. Spot, the mail carrier, goes through once a week or so."

"Then we aren't entirely cut off from the world."

Jack laughed. "Not quite."

They topped a rise, and she spied the lake with a scattering of trees to the west. The waters stretched forever. They'd never want for fish, that was for sure.

"That big house, just off the trail—that's ours."

She followed his gesture. A large cabin sat on an open patch of land.

"Two stories?" Julia gaped. "Whatever do we need such a big house for?"

"Second floor's only a half story. Your sister and family are living there for now. Once they get a place of their own, we'll move up and use the first floor mostly for business—it's one big room with a small one we can use for storage. Maybe we can turn it into a full-fledged store."

"Are there enough people out here to support that?" Somehow, she doubted it. She hadn't noted another cabin anywhere.

"I'm hoping for a steady trade with the Dakota, and we'll need space for the trade goods and the furs. Or, maybe we'll fill it up with kids." He smiled at little George. "I sure wouldn't mind a few more boys."

Then maybe you ought to pay a bit more attention to me.

Or not. All the fine loving she'd expected during their courtship had never come to fruition, and she'd long since tired of his all-too-routine ministrations. The babies were blessings, but Jack's baby making she could live without. That, too, was what life had brought.

Even so, she'd not trade the children for anything. She nestled George on her shoulder, burped him, and wiped his curds of spittle with a rag.

"The trail runs right by the place. I thought we might get travelers, once the area starts attracting more folks. Easier for bringing in supplies, too."

She looked up, a bit surprised Jack had thought ahead so much. Maybe there was hope for him as a trader after all.

"Tell me about the settlement," she asked. "There are *some* families here, aren't there?"

"There are a handful of trappers who stay here part time. The Smiths, no children, live about a mile north. The trappers have temporary shacks a mile farther on; one of them, Rhodes, puts up a tepee when he's at the lake. There's the bachelor Parmlee, the Kochs—another couple—and the Myers family. It's about a seven-mile stretch all together."

"Five families." That was pretty sparse. When folks said there was no Cornwell City, they didn't say it was this unsettled. Julia bit her lip. More making do. At least it would keep Jack out of trouble. Nobody to get into trouble *with*.

"Julia!" Lorenza ran from the house, a smile stretching across her pretty face.

Julia fought to keep from leaping from the wagon. "Lorenza!" She leaned forward, waving. "We're here!"

As they neared, Julia noticed her sister's plump belly. She was glad she'd stayed in Mankato to have George. Lorenza better be planning to do the same.

Jack set the brake, and Lorenza rushed forward. "Let me hold that darling little boy."

Julia handed George down to her sister's eager arms and

climbed off the wagon. Jack was already halfway to the house.

Dora roused. "Are we here?" Her tiny voice was still sleepy.

"Yes, pet." Julia bussed her head and lifted her from the wagon.

Once on the ground, Dora wobbled a bit, searching for her land legs. She spied Jack on his way to the house and ran off after him. "Papa, wait for me."

Jack stopped and held out his arms for her, smothering her with kisses when she tumbled into them.

At least, he's good with the children.

Julia scolded herself. Jack was never unkind to them, always tender. He just . . . well, he just hadn't lived up to her expectations.

"The birth went well? Is he a good baby?"

"Yes and most of the time." Julia laughed. It was good to be with Lorenza again. "How's your brood? Growing, it would appear."

Lorenza patted her belly. "That happens."

"You aren't having it here, are you?"

Lorenza shook her head. "When I get close, we'll go to Mankato. If you'll tend the other children."

"I will." They walked, Lorenza veering toward the lake rather than the house. They skirted through the trees toward the bank, where she stopped. Sun glinted off the surface of the water, golden ripples forming as waves undulated. A trio of geese honked and splashed at one another, their noise punctuating the gurgle of the waves.

"It's bigger than I thought it'd be."

Lorenza sat on a log, looking out on the water. "Big enough so every settler here can claim a quarter-section of land, if they're inclined to want that much."

"A hundred sixty acres?" Julia asked, finding her own spot on the log.

"Jack claimed three hundred twenty."

"He what?" Had she heard right? Julia looked at her sister, but Lorenza kept her eyes on the water. "I thought there was a limit."

"There is."

"Then how . . . ?"

Lorenza pointed to a piece of land across the lake. "That peninsula is the abandoned Brown claim. Jack jumped it and filed as his father. The land we're on is filed in Jack's name."

"Oh, good lord." Julia shook her head in disbelief.

"My George isn't too happy with him."

"I imagine not. Jack plays far too loosely with the law." She sighed. "Why in the world would he want that much land, anyway?"

"It's not the land so much as it is *that* land."

Julia looked across the lake again. "What's so special about that peninsula? All the way across the lake, how can he even think it would be practical?"

"It's not. It's isolated and tough to get to."

"What's the point of filing on it?"

Even as she asked the question, worry knotted her stomach. There were few reasons a man would want to own an isolated peninsula of land full of trees. It'd be no good for farming, completely inconvenient, hard to get to . . .

Oh, no! What on earth are you planning, Jack?

"Rumor has it that two brothers use the woods over there to hide stolen horses."

No, no, no. "Is that true?"

"One of the settlers helped them put up hay one year. For their cows, they said. They never did bring any cows, but folks say there've been some nice looking horses there from time to time."

"So, a rumor."

"Yes, but one I thought you'd want to know about, Jack being Jack and all."

Julia watched the waves lap against the shore. They made soft slapping sounds, and the smells of algae and fish drifted through the air. Peaceful . . . except for Jack. She was only fooling herself, dismissing the rumor as simple gossip. Where there was smoke, there was usually fire.

"It didn't take him long, did it?"

"There's nothing to suggest he's involved with them," Lorenza said, "other than claiming the land."

No, but it implied Jack knew about the place. And that meant he was anticipating a way to make money from it, legal or not. Putting the welfare of the family and her own reputation at risk and leaving it up to her to find a way to prevent both before it was too late.

"Do he and George argue?"

"Frequently."

"I worried about that." George was too ethical not to get upset.

"Julia . . ." Lorenza paused. "Has Jack said anything to you about a man named Clark? Or Wambau?"

The knot in her stomach clenched tight. "They're one of the reasons I suggested you all go on ahead. They met in the saloon, and Jack had a suspicious gleam in his eyes when he mentioned them. I thought it best to get him away before they started scheming in earnest. Why?"

"Clark is a thief. They're the sort that would be in league with the Jacques brothers. George is worried they could show up here, hiding loot on the island."

No, there would be no peace here, despite the tranquility of the lake.

"I'll keep an eye on Jack."

"I think you'll need to." Sadness filled her sister's eyes.

"I'm sorry, Lorenza."

"Me, too, sweetie. I'd hoped this would be a new beginning." She offered a wavering smile, drowned away by glistening tears. "You need to know that if Jack brings trouble to us, George and I will not be staying."

Laura
Beaver, Minnesota
May 1859

It's been a year since baby Isabelle (Bell, as William called her) made her appearance, not long after our mill floated away in the turbulent waters of Beaver Creek. The turmoil of those waters remained with me, churning my fears. Within days of Bell's arrival, I became paralyzed with fear.

I was convinced life was conspiring against us. I couldn't stop thinking that those same waters would find a way to claim Bell as the Mississippi had her two sisters. I feared we would be unable to meet our financial obligations and that William would lose everything. But I was also frightened about moving yet again, especially farther west, where I'd heard the Sioux were still wild and untamed. I wanted a life free from all such dangers.

Each day, I became more and more despondent. It was an effort to rise from the bed and nurse Bell, let alone make my way down the stairs to tend the store. I drew my curtains closed against the bright sun and slept long endless hours. My body grew heavier and heavier with the need to sleep. Emma, just four, pleaded with me to rise and care for Bell as well as for toddler Jefferson. Seven-year-old Willie finally laid Bell with me in the bed, opening my nightgown so she could suckle. When I no longer rose to change diapers, it was Willie who went to his father.

My poor William. He didn't know what to do, as plain-spoken

Mrs. Tucker had back in Iowa. We struggled for months. He tended the store, the children, and me, with occasional relief from Maggie, who said I had the "baby blues." But Maggie's own little ones needed her, and she could offer little respite.

At long last, William wrote to Mrs. Tucker and received her response. The next day, he turned me from my bed and sent me out into the blinding sun to pull weeds. The warmth nurtured me, though I found no relief in the physical work. There was no grief, no anger, only an all-encompassing worry. But the children . . . running and laughing and playing without a care in the world . . . that's what finally turned me around. I knew I must hold on for them.

My recovery took nearly an entire year before life returned to normal. William had taken over the store during my illness and claimed to enjoy it. I began to hope we would remain in Beaver after all, without the worry of the mill, and convinced myself the town would never flood.

"Laura?"

"I'm here. In the side yard."

"We have visitors. Can you mind the store for a bit while we handle some business?"

I rose from the garden and brushed the dirt from my work-dress. Visitors, not customers. I set aside my tools and entered the store, giving my eyes time to adjust at the doorway. Two men stood at the counter, men I didn't know.

"Laura, this is Thomas Ireland and John Eastlick. They've come from Olmstead County."

"Good afternoon," I told them and stepped behind the counter. With no one shopping, I picked up a feather duster and busied myself with straightening and dusting goods. William and the two men took seats on the benches I'd asked William to install near the fireplace, a place for the children when I needed to bring them with me. I eyed the men. The one called

Ireland was tall and hale with a full beard and a shock of graying hair. Eastlick was dark, trim. I wondered what they wanted of William.

"Gentlemen, what brings you to Beaver?"

Eastlick drew out a newspaper and handed it to William. "We read this article, about the election fraud."

"It isn't very clear," Ireland said. "Since you're the nearest member of the Constitutional Congress, we're hoping you might be able to shed some light on the matter."

I narrowed my eyes, confused. The congress had dissolved over a year ago, after approval of the state constitution. Curious, I moved to a closer shelf where I could better eavesdrop.

"I was indeed a member of the congress. Honored to have been elected, proud to serve."

I dusted around a display of whitestone dinnerware. I knew how much pride he took in that service, and, though I couldn't see his chest from where I stood, it was likely puffed out like a rooster.

William continued on. "This fraud you're referring to is a matter related to the election itself. The congress certainly wasn't involved in that. I'm sorry, gentlemen, but I had no part in either the election or the fraud. I don't think I can help here."

Ireland raised a finger to stop him. "We're not concerned about who committed the fraud. We have a question about the fake precincts and thought a person like you might know about the places mentioned."

"Well, now, let me take a moment. My wife has been ill, and I haven't kept up with the news."

I stepped to the right and watched William peruse the paper, his face growing paler by the minute.

"My God," he said, his eyes seeking the two men. "I had heard there were issues with voter registration fraud, but I had no idea entire precincts had been created out of thin air."

Eastlick rose and pointed to the article. "It's this paragraph here we're concerned about. We need to know if this means no one resided in Oasis Precinct, which was registered in the wrong county, or if no one resided in Cornwell City."

"We figured you might have the answer, or at least know who to ask," Ireland added.

"Well, as you can see, I didn't even know about the details." William looked uncomfortable. He was not a man who favored being the last to know anything. I knew he was stalling them while he thought about how to respond. He reviewed the news again. "Hmm. The article makes several errors with names of towns. It's going to take research."

"Can you get to the bottom of it?" Eastlick asked, reclaiming his seat.

"I'm not sure. Do you men have a particular interest in this Cornwell City?"

Ireland sighed. "We were going to settle there."

"But if it doesn't exist . . ."

William lowered the paper. "Maybe the best thing would be to go and look."

"We heard the town's not too far from Lake Shetek," Ireland said. "If there is one."

I picked up a cup and rubbed at a smudge of dirt. It would be foolhardy to take families out to the middle of nowhere if no towns existed, but I resented them coming here. They should have simply gone and looked for themselves. William had no responsibility for solving their problems.

The men rose and shook hands, the matter settled.

"I'll make it an official expedition," William announced. "I'll set off as soon as I make arrangements here. If the land's good, I've a mind to relocate there myself. If three families went, we wouldn't need a town."

Relocate? Just three families on their own in the middle of nowhere?
I dropped the cup I'd been dusting, and it shattered on the floor.

Almena
South Bend Township, Minnesota
June 1859

Almena relaxed her shawl, enjoying the unexpected heat of the June afternoon. They'd left La Crosse behind, with Phin's storekeeping. His friend, Bill, had been enthusiastic about Minnesota. After weeks of discussion, they'd agreed to pursue the opportunity, claim their land, and make their home in Cornwell City. Bill had jumped at the chance to come with them. Together, they'd signed a contract with the Dakota Land Company agent and preempted 160 acres of land on Lake Shetek.

She liked the prairie and its colorful palette of wildflowers. Already, she looked forward to their new life and all the openness. The cloudless blue sky stretched forever, and the air smelled fresher.

Of course, Phin and Bill might not think so, shepherding livestock as they were, back behind the double-box wagon. Her two best milk cows were tied securely to the wagon—there'd be no losing them this time. Along with them, the two friends tended three new cows and ten pigs. Phin's new dog nipped at the livestock's heels when they strayed; Bill's aging canine trailed behind. Crates of chickens hung on the wagon box, their clucking erupting with each lurch. Even with a baby to tend to, she had the easiest of the responsibilities. Minding William Henry and driving the team had to be better than walking behind a passel of animals.

She wrinkled her nose and grinned. Nope, she wouldn't want

to be trailing pigs and cows.

Phin had rigged up a hammock for William Henry, and he'd taken to it right off. The bumps and jars of the ill-made roads hardly bothered him. This last short trek from Mankato to South Bend had taken awhile, though, and he'd soon be awake and demanding her breast. She was glad they'd waited to purchase most of what they needed in Mankato rather than bringing everything from Wisconsin. As it was, they'd be trailing pigs and cows for the next hundred miles or so. Between the animals and the now heavily-loaded wagon, progress would be slow. They had one more stop to make, at Bill's old farmstead, to pick up the few belongings he'd left there when he'd gone back east to La Crosse. From there on, they'd be sleeping under the wagon, which was now full to the brim with farming implements and household goods.

She looked forward to spending a peaceful, comfortable night in the farmhouse. Tomorrow, they'd launch the final leg of their journey. With luck, they'd be in Cornwell City this time next week.

"Swing right," Bill shouted.

Almena spotted an overgrown lane ahead, a small dwelling at its end. Finally.

She guided the horses down the path, and they neared the house. Smoke rose from the chimney, and a riot of flowers bloomed in a tended garden along the foundation.

What in the world?

Bill had said the place was abandoned. Apprehension filled her at the unexpected sign of occupation. Who was here?

She stopped the wagon and waited for Bill and Phin to catch up.

A tall, severe woman emerged from inside. Almena thought she'd once been pretty. Her eyes were a beautiful blue but were now overshadowed by tired lines, and her mouth was set in a resentful scowl. She lifted the shotgun in her hand and pointed it at Bill. "You!" she shouted. "You no good, dirty piece of scum."

As Almena shifted in the seat, placing herself between William Henry and the woman, she told herself not to panic. It was obvious the woman knew Bill. Things would be straightened out in a minute. Phin circled the wagon and laid his hand on Almena's leg. An unspoken question filled his eyes.

She lowered her gaze to the floorboard.

He grasped the rifle and slid it off, holding it in his hand, out of the woman's line of sight.

"Agnes." Bill stood along the other side of the wagon, his stance firm and protective. Whoever the woman was, he didn't care much for her. "I didn't expect to find you here."

"Obviously not." She barked the words out, angry and hostile, jerked the barrel of the gun toward the wagon. "Who's this with you? Your paramour?"

Almena stiffened in her seat.

Next to her, Phin raised the rifle and trained it on the woman. "If you're speaking of my wife, I'd advise you to keep a civil tongue in your mouth."

The woman's eyes narrowed. "Being your wife don't make her any less what she is." She shifted her attention back to Bill, and Almena released the breath she'd been holding. "I heard all about your little threesome. Gossip travels fast from Mankato."

Almena sucked in a breath. "How dare you! That's a ludicrous implication. You don't know a thing about me."

"Put the gun down, Agnes," Bill said. "This is Mr. and Mrs. Hurd, my traveling partners. Phin and Almena, this is my wife, who seems to have returned after all these years."

His wife? He'd told them nothing about a wife. A wife? Oh, dear lord, he didn't expect to bring her along, did he? She wasn't about to expand their group to include this lying shrew.

Agnes lowered the gun but continued to glare at all of them. "You're not welcome here, none of you. Get out."

"I came for my things. I'll get them, and we'll be on our way."

Thank goodness.

"What things?" Agnes demanded.

"My trunk, my tools . . . household things." Bill approached the door and grabbed the gun from her hands, leaning it against the house a few feet away from her.

"You mean my things?"

"I assumed you took what you wanted when you hightailed it back east to your mother."

Almena shifted in her seat and looked at Phin. It didn't feel right, sitting there listening to their personal conversation. Should she get down? Stay where she was?

Phin shrugged, looking as uncomfortable as she felt. They hadn't much choice.

Almena turned and looked in on William Henry. At least, she wouldn't sit there staring, even if she couldn't block their words.

"Well, you didn't appear to want them much. You left them behind. Guess that makes them mine."

"What are you doing here?" Bill's voice dropped.

"Mother died. I had nowhere else to go."

"You can't stay here."

"I can, and I will."

Their conversation shifted into a calmer vein, no longer loud enough to hear. William Henry stirred, and Almena reached for him, eager to keep him quiet and avoid Agnes's attention. Phin took him from her and moved behind the wagon as Almena climbed down, taking care to keep silent. She joined Phin, and they sat, sheltered. She opened her bodice and took the baby, guiding him to suckle.

"The bank owns it!" Bill shouted, his voice full of frustration.

Almena winced. So much for letting them discuss things in private. She sighed, and Phin shook his head.

"You sold it out from under me?" Agnes nearly screeched the words.

"Sold it? They foreclosed on it. It's been sitting here empty for nigh onto three years."

"What am I going to do?"

"I don't know, and I don't much care. You left me."

"You can't just turn me out."

"We were divorced six months after you left."

"Don't matter none."

Almena turned to Phin, rising. "Let's get him out of here."

Phin stood with her. "Stay here." He stepped toward the horses.

"I just want my things, and I'll be on my way. I don't have any responsibility for you." Bill turned and headed toward the stable.

Agnes jerked his arm. "Can't have 'em."

He stopped. "What do you mean?"

"Burned what was in the trunk. Sold the tools. Things in the house are mine." The bitterness in her tone was like a slap.

Phin circled the horses and coughed. Neither Bill nor Agnes paid any attention.

"You burned my things?"

"I sure didn't want them."

"Damn, Agnes."

"Bill," Phin called, "let's be on our way."

Bill sighed. He turned and walked toward the wagon.

Phin threw a smile in Almena's direction. She waited for him to return to help her into the wagon. With William Henry, she couldn't do it alone. She loosened him from her nipple, hoping he wouldn't bellow. The sooner they were out of here, the better.

"Heard you're headed to Cornwell City," Agnes called out, baiting.

"What business is that of yours?" Bill muttered.

"That where you're going?" she continued to taunt. "Good luck to you."

Almost at the wagon, Bill turned. "We don't need your luck."

"Do, too. There ain't no Cornwell City." She spat out the words, then cackled, *cackled,* at them.

Like a witch.

Almena had no other word to describe her. William Henry squawked, and Phin hastened to get them into the wagon. She set the baby in the hammock without burping him and reached for the reins.

Bill took off at a run, storming past Agnes into the house. Moments later, he returned with a small trunk in his hands. Phin took it from him and found a place for it in the wagon as Bill rushed into the small stable. Phin ran after him.

Agnes eyed Almena. "I ain't lying, you know. That town was all made up."

Almena froze, William Henry hollering like the dickens. She should turn the wagon around. The woman was only making trouble; that was all. She'd proven herself a liar, and there was no reason to put stock in any of her words.

"You sleeping with both of them?"

Almena's mouth dropped open. "You *are* a witch." She spat the words out and flicked the reins.

Phin and Bill emerged from the stable, each carrying a box of tools. Without words, they loaded them in. "Let's go."

They herded the animals together, and Almena led them back down the lane.

"Serve you all right to go all the way out there and find nothing," Agnes called from behind them.

At the intersection, Almena paused.

"Head back to Mankato," Phin advised. "She's more than likely messing with us, but we need to find out if there's anything to what she said and what to do about it before we go all the way out there."

Almena turned the team to the left, the woman's words about Cornwell City ricocheting in her head. They'd already signed the contract! Had their dream just turned into a nightmare?

Christina
Lake Shetek, Minnesota
August 1859

One of the Indians who came when we built our cabin is called Inkpadutah. For a moment, when I heard the name, I panicked, but Aaron Myers, who knows the Indians here, said he was Inkpadutah the son and not Inkpadutah the father, who killed so many in Iowa a few years ago. For this, I am glad. Aaron says the Indians do not understand Andreas's English and have named my husband "Yappee Seicha" which means "Bad Talker."

A year later, I know them better, and I no longer fear so much when Indians come to the door. We are careful whenever any of them visit so we do not disturb the peace between our groups. In the winter, they grow hungry, and the women offer us goose down for vegetables. It is a good bargain for us because we trade weight for weight, and they are happy with it. Imagine, having a feather bed out on the prairie for the cost of a few vegetables.

Our settlement is growing. Last year, the Browns built a house on the peninsula across the lake from the trappers but did not stay long. In the fall, Mr. Lamb and his family along with Jack Wright, who is a brother in some way, took a claim southeast of the Smiths. I have also heard that Wright jumped Brown's claim. In April, Julia Wright and her children joined them; their house has a second story, and Andreas says Jack Wright is trading with the Indians, grains and supplies for furs. This is a good thing, I think, for the Indians don't like Andreas so much; perhaps they will stay at that end of the lake and not visit us.

A family named Everett has built a cabin near the traders' shacks, and a man named William Duley was here in July. He set stakes to land south of Wright where the lake flows into a creek. Duley will build a mill there when he returns with his wife, Laura, and their children. The houses will be in a string along the east side of the lake, about a mile apart.

"Christina?" Andreas calls from the yard. "A wagon is coming."

I rush out of the *Haus,* anxious to see who has come.

There *is* a wagon, cows and pigs trailing behind it. I smooth my apron so I do not look so messy and think I should have put up my braid. Andreas waves, his wooden toothpick still in his mouth. I wish he would spit it out.

When the wagon nears, it is a woman driving it, and my heart sings. Two men walk behind, with the animals.

"Hello," I say. "I am Mrs. Koch. Christina. This is my husband, Andreas."

The woman smiles, looking as glad to see me as I am to see her. She is plain of face, but her smile draws me in. She is a good woman, I think.

"I'm Almena Hurd," she says. "My husband, Phineas, and his partner, Bill Jones." She climbs down as the men all begin talking about land and farming.

She shakes her head, and I want to laugh.

"Have you come far?" I ask her.

"From La Crosse, with a stop in South Bend. We were coming to Cornwell City but learned there was no such place."

I have heard of this Cornwell City, but it was never built.

One of the trappers told us it was to be a few miles south of the lake. "*Nein.* There is no town here, only settlers along the lake."

"So we learned. But we already signed the contract to buy the land, so, when we heard there was a settlement starting after all in such a beautiful place, we decided to come anyway. We traveled along the New Ulm Road and stopped at the Wrights."

"*Ja*, they are not long here, either." I have not had much chance to visit with Julia Wright all the way down there at the end of the lake. Perhaps once the harvest is in, we will have time to take the wagon there.

"Wright showed us a map he'd drawn of the lake. We're headed a little farther north, about halfway between you and the Myers family. The men have their eyes on the land east of Fremont Lake."

"That will be a good spot, a mile or two from here. But you will have to travel around the inlet. Andreas will show you. There is a shortcut, but the land there is too mushy for the wagon. We will be able to walk to visit if you build near the big lake."

She leans close, whispering to me. "There are Indian tepees near the Wright place. We weren't expecting that."

I think maybe she does not wish her husband to know she is afraid, but I hear it in her voice.

"*Ja*, Wright is a trader. He will get you feathers for a bed if you have vegetables to offer them." I know I should say more, let her know they are not violent. "There was trouble a little ways east last year, with drunken Indians." I do not tell her Renicker was murdered. "But these at the lake have been peaceful. In the old days, they had ceremonies in this place, and now they come to hunt. The one called Old Pawn has been friendly with the whites, and the others listen to him."

"That's good to hear. I worried." She brightens again.

Just in case, though, I must tell her they come to this part of the lake, too. "Aaron Myers, who is at the north end, is an herb doctor. There are sometimes Indians camped near him, but he has no trouble with them."

"Good."

We pause in our talking, still too new with one another for our words to come easily. I point to her animals. "You have cows and pigs and chickens already. This is good."

"I make excellent butter and cheese." She blushes, and I see she is not a braggart but a modest woman. That, too, is good.

"Then we will trade, too," I tell her. "I'm not so skilled at that."

She glances toward the cabin. "Do you have children?"

"*Nein.* Not yet. You?"

"William Henry, sleeping in the hammock. He's only a few months old."

I look at the little one in the clever swing they have made. He is chubby and perfect, sleeping soundly. His milky baby smell drifts to me, and I wonder if Andreas and I will ever have one like him. We are married now for several years, and still there is no baby.

"Almena?" her husband calls. "It's time we head on. Parmlee said he'd come up in the morning and help us start on a cabin, so we'd best figure out where we want to put it."

She climbs back onto the wagon and makes sure the baby is secure. "I look forward to seeing you again soon."

"*Ja.* It will be good to have someone near."

I watch the wagon turn and head east, as Andreas told them. In the distance, there is a man on a horse, watching.

I hope I have told Almena the truth about our Indians being friendly.

Chapter Eleven

Laura
Beaver, Minnesota
February 1860

I'd not been happy with William since he returned from that blasted trip west to tell me he filed on one hundred sixty acres of land in the midst of nowhere. A fifth child was on the way, and I was once again shuffling with my dress stretched tight and my feet unseen. Cranky, I resented it that he'd left me alone so much these past few miserable months.

Like my first pregnancies, this one was nearly unbearable. Sick from the first month, I cursed William more than one can imagine and looked forward to being delivered. I persuaded myself that the months of morning sickness and backaches were good omens. If William was determined to take us to the ends of the earth, I wanted this infant as healthy as possible. Still, my handkerchief was in shreds from all the wringing I'd put it through.

The bell on the door of the mercantile chimed, and a woman entered. She wore no bonnet, and her lush, thick hair shimmered in the sunlight that streamed through the windows. Oh, to have such hair!

"Laura Duley?" she asked. Confidence filled her voice.

"Yes?" I answered. I was sure I sounded far less self-assured, and unwelcome envy tinged at me.

"I'm Lavina Eastlick. I came over from Rochester with my husband, John. It sounds as if we and our good friends Tommy and Sophia Ireland are going to be traveling west together with you. I wanted to stop and introduce myself."

She looked about my age, thirty-two, or perhaps a few years younger, and moved with determination. I suspected she was a woman who could deal with anything that came her way. As she neared the counter, I wondered what she thought of all this. Was she as worried as I was? With so much conviction in her carriage, I doubted it.

Perhaps I'd once again overreacted to William's moving plans.

Lavina paused, and a smile warmed her face. "John said you had little ones but he didn't mention the one on the way."

"Men tend not to think about such things." I bit my tongue, hoping I hadn't sounded waspish.

"Travel will be more difficult for you." Genuine concern filled her tone, but her words reminded me of how, once again, my husband had made decisions without regard for my comfort.

"William has decided we'll go this summer, so we'll go. He's paying off the last of our land and has located buyers. That makes things about as firm as they can get." My face heated.

Heavens, had I just talked about finances to a complete stranger? I'd completely forgotten my social skills. What she must think of me!

She laughed, though surely she must have been uncomfortable, plunging through the awkwardness without pause. "John and I have boys: Merton, Frank, Giles, and Freddy. The Irelands have four girls."

"We have a mix," I said, glad for the shift in topic. "Willie, as well as Emma, Jefferson, and Bell."

"It will be a lively trip."

With so many children, there was little doubt it would be difficult as well. We would have need to band together. "Did your husband stake a claim?" I asked.

"No. John hasn't been to Shetek yet. Tommy Ireland went with your husband on his second trip. We'll select land near the Irelands, I suppose. We've known Tommy and his wife for years—since back in Illinois—and they're like family."

I'd be the outsider, traveling without the support they would provide one another. Jealousy nipped at me, and I shooed it away, hating that I'd become so negative. "They put up thirty tons of wild hay, William said."

"Tommy said the grass had never been mowed there. It'll be good, these first years, to rely on the prairie grasses instead of having to sow our own hay."

"William went back a third time." The words sprang from my mouth, and our conversation paused.

Lavina blinked, regrouped. "He did?"

"He took cows and oxen, wintering them with the Wrights, one of the families already there." There, I'd established a new thread.

"Goodness, he's eager to get settled, isn't he?" She laughed, the sound tinkling and carefree.

"Chasing his dream," I muttered. *Oh, dear lord!*

"What?"

"William. He's chasing his dream."

"I suppose that's what we're all doing. Looking for a better life."

"I have a good life here, Mrs. Eastlick. This settlement on the lake, it's not my dream. My dream vanished a long time ago."

She peered at me, quite uncertain, I was sure, what to make of me.

I knew my words must have sounded bitter. But they were true; I no longer had a dream. There was no safe future here, and I'd agreed to go west, but it was not to chase my dream. A few years ago, I might have grieved the loss of the excited young woman I had once been, looking for my happily-ever-after in each new place. Now, I simply accepted that my castle in the sky had vanished like a cloud in the wind.

"Mrs. Duley? Laura?"

I stared back at her.

"I think I'd best run for the doctor." She pointed to the floor.

Numb, I glanced down at the liquid pool beneath my feet and swayed.

Julia
Lake Shetek
June 1860

Dusk was falling as Julia lit the lamps. In the kitchen, Lorenza finished up the dishes, the children reading stories at the table. It was a peaceful night, crickets chirping and a breeze drifting off the lake. With chores nearly done, they could all walk down to the shore and catch the wonderful orange and purple sky and its glistening reflection as the sun sank behind the lake.

The front door of the house flew open, and Julia jumped. What now?

Panting, Charley Wambau rushed in and slammed the door.

Julia groaned.

Two months ago, Wambau and Clark had shown up, ready to re-instigate whatever scheme they'd hatched out with Jack at the saloon in St. Peter. She'd stomached them for as long as she could and finally managed to get them out of her house by suggesting they hire on to complete odd jobs around the settlement. She'd thought Wambau was nicely settled at the north end of the lake, digging a cellar.

"I thought you were at Aaron Myers's place."

"I was. But Clark showed up drunk. Says he's gonna kill me."

"Oh, good heavens." Julia hustled toward the back door.

Lorenza stood in the doorway to the kitchen, concern etched on her face.

"There's trouble," Julia said. "Take the kids down to the lake."

She opened the back door and stuck her head out. "George? Jack?"

The men turned at her yell.

"Finish with the fence later. Wambau's here, and Clark's threatening him again. This time, he's drunk."

She shut the door and strode back to Wambau. It was always something with these two, and she was sick to death of dealing with them. "What is it this time?"

"He wants the stuff." Wambau's hands flew in the air in a strange gesture she didn't understand. In fact, she understood very little about him except that he was an irksome little man who'd showed up as if he had an engraved invitation, and she wanted him gone.

"What stuff?"

"The stuff we took in St. Peter." As if that explained anything.

"What's going on?" Jack asked, coming into the house. George and Mr. Annadon, the attorney from Sioux Falls who'd come to check on the condition of the mail route, trailed him.

"Clark's gonna leave. He wants his share," Wambau said.

"Share of what?" George said.

Stuff they took.

The words finally dawned on her. Hot anger roiled, and she marched toward the little weasel. "You didn't bring stolen goods onto this property, did you?"

"Julia!"

She turned at Jack's shout. Good lord, he sounded stricken. She leveled a glare on him. "I told you no good would come of those two being here."

George looked at Wambau, disbelief etched on his face. "You stole things and came here?"

"Get your clothes and get out," Julia said.

She turned back to Jack. "I want them out, right now, and away from here, or I swear I will walk out with the kids and never come back."

"It's only a few trinkets, a bit of ammunition." Wambau nearly squeaked the words.

Julia shook her head and charged past lawyer Annadon to fetch Wambau's things from behind the stairs. She shoved his knapsack into his hands and pointed to the door. "Get out!"

George pointed to the rifle in his hand. "That your gun, Wambau?"

"Belongs to Myers. I told his wife I was going hunting."

"Myers didn't take it with him?" Jack asked. "Why would he and Jones head off to New Ulm without a gun?"

"Spare."

Julia shook her head. *Good god, Jack, who cares about Jones and Myers right now?*

"Just leave it here." She took the gun from Wambau, handed it to Annadon, and yanked the door open.

Bill Clark stood in the yard, raising his own gun. A blast sounded, the shot hitting the doorframe.

Inside, everyone ducked.

Julia's chest pounded. She lifted her head and looked outside.

Clark waved the gun around, wobbling on his feet.

"Damn it," George muttered. He strode into the yard and grabbed the gun Clark was now leaning on. "Give me the damn thing."

The two tussled with it, and George wrenched it from Clark's hands. Clark stumbled away.

"Best listen to my missus, Wambau," Jack said. "I'll go grab your horse from the stable."

Jack tramped out the back door, Julia alongside him. "Gone. Away. Both of them. And don't you dare bring people like that here again."

"I didn't exactly bring them this time."

"You told them where you were headed. Did you actually think they'd fail to show up? Don't you think, Jack?"

"I—"

"Jack!" George yelled. "We've got more problems! Clark's on his way back."

Jack dropped the halter and ran for the front yard, Julia on his heels.

As they neared the corner of the house, a shot rang out. They skidded to a stop and peered around the side. Wambau lay in the dirt, hands around his head. Clark and George struggled over Clark's second gun. At the edge of the tree line around Beauty Lake, the neighbors Smith and Parmlee stood clutching their sides and breathing heavily. Annadon stood in the doorway, his eyes wide.

George shoved Clark to the ground and jerked the gun away. "Get out."

Clark scuttled to his feet and wiped drool from his mouth with his hand. "You'll be sorry. All a'you are gonna be sorry. I'm a' go up t'the Redwood Agency an' bring a bunch of 'em renegade Sioux down here. They'll kill Wambau, and they'll kill all a'you. Ever' single one."

He stumbled up the trail.

George strode back to Jack and Julia. "Good God, Jack. You got no sense letting men like this come here."

"You reckon we ought to follow him?" Jack asked. "Make sure he doesn't go up to the reservation?"

"Yeah, we got no choice. Get our guns. He's so drunk it won't be hard to trail him, but it'll be dark soon."

Julia hastened into the house to get the guns. *So much for a peaceful, quiet evening.*

She just hoped George and her idiot husband could find a way to control this senseless mess.

Christina
Lake Shetek
June 1860

I have had a good visit with Almena and am on my way down the shortcut. It has grown dark, and I think I should have come home sooner, but we were having such a fun time. It is a good thing, having people so close, and I think it will be even better when the new families come with William Duley. I think maybe tomorrow we should plan something with our neighbors to the south. We do not know them well enough.

There are voices as I near the edge of the trees, from around our cabin, and I stop. A chill embraces me. Who would be at our house at night? Indians have never come after dark, but perhaps this is an attack. I do not know their ways. I strain my eyes to make out who is here and wish I had a shotgun with me. Lord, where is Andreas?

There is a group of men . . . the men from the south end of the lake. My heart settles a bit.

Wright, Lamb, Parmlee, Smith, Wambau, and a man I do not know are clustered together, whispering in that loud way of men, thinking they are being quiet. I stay in the shadows, waiting until I know what is happening. It is strange for them to be here like this, and I do not know these men as well as I should.

"What should we do?" Smith asks. "Clark's shooting his mouth off pretty good in there."

"Koch'll get fed up with him soon and kick him out," Lamb tells them.

I hear Andreas speak, calm, in control but can't make out his words. But Lamb is right, Andreas will tire of the ranting and tell the man to leave.

Smith looks at my house, then back at the men. "Clark still drunk?"

Hah, I think. *Of course he is drunk. If he were sober, he would hear you out here talking about him!*

Clark is nearly shouting, his words slurred enough that I cannot follow what he is saying from where I am hiding.

Parmlee laughs. "He's angry."

There was something off about his laughter. A chill creeps up my spine. This is not good, and I should check on Andreas, tell them all to go home. But fear freezes me where I am.

The man inside stops yelling. Wright strides to the window and cocks his head, then returns to the group.

"What's he saying?" Smith asks.

"He's still ranting on about inciting the Indians but sounds more serious. He's threatening to bring them here."

Inciting Indians? The chill in my spine becomes a shudder. Who would do such a thing?

Lamb looks at the group. "He's drunk off his rocker. For whatever reason, he's fixated on causing the settlement problems, and, if he remembers Koch has a horse, he'll be halfway to Redwood before we can mount a chase."

I think about how many Indians live at the Redwood Agency and what would happen if they were to come here. My pulse sounds in my ears like a drum. Why are they just standing there?

"Do we take that chance?" Smith says.

"We can't." Wright gestures, frustrated. "Even if we stop him tonight, how do we know he won't go later?"

The man I do not know points at the house. "I say we storm the cabin."

Wright shakes his head. "Not all of us. He's sitting by the stove and likely to grab Koch's gun before we get through the door. Let's split up, provide cover from the windows."

"Do we shoot him?" Smith asks.

"Wing him," says Lamb.

I pray Andreas has the sense to drop to the floor. I do not want them to shoot a man inside my house, but I know he must be stopped.

The men move to the cabin and separate, Wright and Wambau to the west window, the others circling the cabin toward the door and the other window. I follow, ready to run to Andreas and make sure he is safe.

At the window, Wambau raises his gun.

"Go on, give it to him," Wright urges.

Wambau fires. Acrid smoke fills the air. Inside, the cabin there is a commotion, and I hear Andreas shout that Clark has been murdered.

I exhale a heavy breath as I grasp my Andreas is safe.

But I remember Wright's words. *Go on, give it to him.*

Ja, I think, Andreas is right. It *is* murder, and Jack Wright is as much to blame as Wambau.

Almena
Lake Shetek
July, 1860

Cresting the hill on the trail, Almena spied the Wright place ahead. Five tepees nestled in the meadow beyond, and the camp bustled with activity. The remains of several deer hung in a nearby tree, women trimming strips from the meat. Scattered campfires fed smoke beneath racks of drying meat. Everywhere, women were busy with butchering, cooking, or tanning hides. Julia Wright moved among the visitors, chatting with several of them.

Almena's lips lifted. It sure didn't look like there was anything to be feared from these people, despite all Clark's bluster. But, if there was nothing to fear, then the shooting had been groundless, just like Andreas maintained. Her smile faltered. Neither scenario set well.

She clicked the reins and urged the horses on. Up at the north end of the lake, Aaron Myers and Andreas Koch had been sharply critical of the killing, refusing to interact with the men who had been involved. She and Phin were caught in the middle, and it was high time someone bridged the chasm that yawned in their close settlement.

That meant it would be up to the women. She needed Julia's perspective.

Julia spotted her and strode toward the house, waving as she approached. "I sure hope you brought butter."

"And cheese." Almena set the brake and looped the leather around it, then climbed down. "How much are you needing?"

"We're pretty much out." She peered into the wagon. "I can take everything you brought. Between those who live here and our visitors, we always manage to trade well."

They hoisted boxes from the wagon bed and carried them to the cabin, chatting along the way. Once inside, they set their loads on the counter.

Julia gestured toward the trade goods. "Have a look around; stack what you need here while I tackle your list."

Almena left her notes on the counter and began exploring the shelves. She always enjoyed Julia's direct, open personality. What a shame such a pleasant woman was saddled with the likes of Jack Wright.

"There was a census taker through at the beginning of the month," Julia said. "A prissy little man. He made it clear he'd anticipated a town and didn't want to 'cavort around the lake,' looking for everyone's cabins."

"Since we didn't see him, I assume he flat-out refused to do so."

"Exactly. Jack gave him everyone's names and the ages from that list he keeps. We weren't sure if Phin's mother was still visiting or not so he included her. I hope that was all right."

"Either way. She's gone home, thankfully."

Julia laughed. "I take it she didn't realize you're expecting."

Almena's cheeks heated. How on earth did Julia know? She was barely showing.

"You've put your hands on your womb twice already. I do that when I'm carrying."

Perceptive, as usual. "I didn't even realize it." She took supplies and carried them to the counter. "Phin's mother is a good woman, but far too fussy to stand for too long at a time. And you're right, she didn't know. Otherwise, she'd have nested with us for the entire time."

"In-laws can be a trial." Julia measured coffee beans from a large wooden barrel and tied off the bag. "Things are strained between Jack and my sister and her husband."

"The Clark business?" Almena asked. Knowing Jack, there would be more to it, but it was an opening to discuss what had happened. And to determine if there was a cause for alarm.

"Among other things."

"What happened with Clark has divided the entire community."

"It was a disaster, from start to finish."

Julia set a bag of flour on the counter and began to factor the total but said no more, and Almena wondered how much Jack had told her. Likely the barest of details. Jack talked a lot, but only when it suited his interests.

"I helped Christina scour the blood from the floorboards of her cabin. The wood sucked every drop of it in. The stain wouldn't yield until we poured lye on it."

"I saw the lye on your supply list and wondered if that wasn't the case. I'm sorry it came to that."

"You know Christina was there?"

Julia's eyes widened. "In the cabin?"

"No, outside. She'd been at our place and was just returning. She was in the trees."

"Dear lord."

"She told me the details. I'm glad Phin wasn't with them."

"Jack didn't say much. Just that Clark was so drunk, and they'd feared he would ride up to the agency and incite the Dakota."

That was the story all the men had told, as well, and what they'd put on the witness affidavit they'd signed. All but Andreas.

"He was drunk, but Christina swears it was mostly ranting, that he'd have passed out soon."

Julia put down her pencil and sighed. "Do you think they shot him without reason?"

"I don't know. I imagine it was a difficult decision, and it would be best if we all move past it. Andreas and Christina will always see it differently than the men who were outside."

"Different experiences. They didn't fight with Clark earlier, didn't chase him up the lakeshore, didn't know him as well. He was a despicable man, a thief, and worse, I suspect. I'm not sorry to see him gone, but I wish our men hadn't killed him." Her voice held regret. "But I've no doubt he would have brought ruin to us. If not that night, another."

"Wambau's gone?"

"He hightailed it as soon as the judge in New Ulm cleared him. Thank God. Jack should never have gotten involved with either of them. But, then, Jack's not too good at doing what he should."

They shared gazes, understanding what went unsaid.

"Would the Indians have turned on us?" Almena asked.

"I don't know. I don't know those who live up at the agency, the ones Clark threatened to involve." Julia placed the supplies in the empty box as she spoke. "I think there are many there who hate whites. They survive almost entirely on annuities, and, most years, the supplies are either late to arrive or the supply is short. The Indian agents cheat them. It's not a good situation."

"I never have any problems with those who come to our place to trade."

"Nor do we. And Aaron Myers has a long history with some of them. When he lived up at Saratoga, the year the winter was so bitter, he often let them sleep inside his place. And he treated their medical needs . . . still does."

"He told us an old woman named Teeny broke another woman's arm, and he set it for her. Her brother gave him a buffalo robe in appreciation."

"I think that's true. There's a special bond in Dakota culture between brothers and sisters, a unique relationship. The tribe values kinship in all its forms."

"What about those who camp here?"

"It's a steady group. Old Pawn seems to be the leader among them."

"I've heard Myers mention him."

"Over six feet tall. You'd know him if you saw him. Fierce looking, but he's never been anything but friendly with us. I think his real name is Across the Water. His first wife is related to old Sleepy Eye."

Almena recognized the reference. Though now dead, the chief had befriended whites, and a town near New Ulm had taken his name. His nephew of the same name, rumor had it, was not so friendly.

"Are they here much? Are you ever afraid?" she asked Julia.

"They bring their tepees a few at a time, mostly to hunt,

sometimes to trade. They stay a few days, move on. It's fascinating, really. There are bands of them that live together, some on the reservation and some in villages. But there are larger divisions, I guess you'd call them sub-tribes, and the larger tribes. Sort of like how Norwegians and Swedes and Danes are all Scandinavian, and Scandinavians are all European."

"Goodness. However did you learn all that?" Almena had never suspected Indian society was that complicated.

"I talk with them, listen. Everything I learn makes understanding them easier."

"I suppose that's good for all of us."

Julia set the last bag of beans in the box. "Their ways are very different from ours, and as complex. There are even different language groups and identifications based on geographical areas. I can hardly keep track."

"Goodness, if we fail to understand that much about Indian society, no wonder there are problems between us."

"We're done here—works out as an even trade for me if that works for you?"

At Almena's nod, Julia continued. "Come with me, then, and I'll give you a little glimpse." She grabbed Almena's hand and led her outside, veering toward the small encampment.

"We're visiting them?"

"Of course, we are. How else are you going to learn?"

She steered Almena to a woman who sat on the ground, her legs tucked primly to one side. In front of her lay a stretched hide. As they approached, she looked up from scraping it and said something to Julia.

Julia greeted her with a few words, then turned to Almena.

"This is Dances in Water. She is second wife to Pawn and is glad to meet you. She has heard of the woman who makes butter."

Almena nodded, flattered but uncertain. "Tell her I am

pleased to meet her."

Julia translated then waited for the woman's response. "Will you sit?" she relayed. "There is stew in the pot, and she offers to share it with you."

"I'm not hungry."

"It's a custom—hospitality. To be polite, you should have some."

They sat while Dances in Water rose and fetched wooden bowls. The woman dipped them into the pot hanging over the fire and extended a bowl to each of them before returning to her place on the ground.

Almena accepted the bowl, watching Julia, and sipped from it as her friend did. It was good, an artful blend of venison and wild vegetables.

"This is a hunting trip; only a few couples have come. The men bring in the meat, and the women prepare it to take back to the village. That's why you see all the meat drying. They work on the hides, too, scraping them for later use."

Almena glanced around. The industry was clear, as was a pride in doing it well. Christina would appreciate their diligence. The savory soup would reap her praise as well. "Tell Dances in Water the stew is very good."

"She is pleased to honor you with it."

Almena smiled at the woman, thinking about the men who stopped by her cabin on occasion.

"The men who visit us, who ask for food . . . I thought it was because they were hungry or because they wanted to trade. But maybe they're visiting and expect us to know the hospitality custom?"

"Sometimes, they come to trade and will make an offer to you for food. In those cases, it may be hunger that drives them or maybe a desire for your butter and cheese. But they may also come to visit; I don't know. Hospitality is always offered to guests."

Almena thought of Bad Ox's visits. The tall Indian often came, asking in English to trade for cheese. But he sometimes came into the cabin and sat at her table, as if waiting for food. She'd never viewed one as any different from the other.

"When I provide a meal, they always give something to me. I thought it was a trade."

"They are returning the honor you gave them with your hospitality. I think trading is different. They offer the trade goods first."

I need to return the honor to Dances in Water.

Almena searched her apron, wishing she had brought a cheese with her. Deep in her pocket, her fingers latched onto a tin of her homemade hand cream. She drew it out and extended it to the woman.

"Tell her this is for her, to soften her hands."

Julia spoke, and Dances in Water smiled. She opened the tin and smelled the cream, then dabbed a bit on her palm. She worked it into her skin and spoke.

"She thanks you and says it smells much better than grease."

Almena laughed. "Tell her to mix rosehip into the grease." It wouldn't be quite the same as mixing dried flowers into her unsalted butter, but it would be better than smelling like an animal. "Tell her I will always have more for her."

She and Julia stayed a few minutes longer, then returned to the house.

"See?" Julia prompted. "More complicated than you thought."

"Much more. I had no idea."

"We would do well to understand the differences in our cultures and not to slap our own interpretations on actions."

"So, do you think there is any basis for fear?"

"I trust the Dakota who camp here, Pawn and the others we've come to know."

"But if Clark had gone to the agency, would there have been violence?"

Julia shrugged. "Just because certain Dakota have become our friends does not dictate what other Dakota do. Those who don't know us misinterpret us as much as we do them. We are all too much in our own worlds. Problems are created by some; assumptions are made; entire groups are blamed. Both our cultures do that."

They quieted, digesting the complexities. Then Julia turned to her again.

"We're friends with the few small groups who visit the lake. But many others are angry that whites have settled in the area. It wouldn't take much to stir them. I think the men were right to fear what might have happened if Clark had gone to them.

"We're isolated here, but what happens in one place impacts what happens everywhere else, isolated or not."

Lavina
Olmstead County, Minnesota
Fall 1860

John enters the house without his usual whistling, sheds his overcoat, and kicks off his boots. He doesn't say a thing, and I cast an inquiring glance his direction. He shrugs.

My stomach tumbles a bit. We are to start toward western Minnesota next week, and John has been in Rochester, attending to final details. Our land has been sold, the house along with it. Most of our goods are packed. We are already months behind our original schedule. Now is not the time for things to go amiss.

I tuck up a tress of fallen hair and finish frosting the cake while I wait. He will tell me in his own time. I wipe up a dollop of frosting that has dripped onto the table and lick it off my finger. John sits in the chair near the fire and slumps his head into his hands.

With that, I can hold back no longer. "John?"

"They aren't going." The words drop like lead.

"What?" For a moment, I wonder if I have heard him correctly. But his hunched shoulders say otherwise. "Who?" I ask.

He lifts his head and faces me. "William and Laura Duley are not going. Not this year, anyway."

He says nothing of the Irelands, forcing me to ask. "Tommy and Sophia?"

"They've decided to wait as well."

Resentment churns in large, rumbling waves. "What do you mean, they're not going? How can they simply say they're not going?" At the last minute? I'm unable to believe everyone has simply decided not to go. My mouth hangs open, and I blink several times.

John swallows. "Rachael, one of the new Duley babies, died."

"Oh, John, no." Memories of my dead baby flood back, and my hand hugs my womb. "Just now?"

"Early June. She was three months old."

In June, four months ago. It surprises me that no one sent word. But why would they? We're not family, after all, or even close friends. Babies die. Life goes on. It is a harsh way to think, but that is the way of it. The living remain. We must hold on for their sake.

John rises and takes me in his arms. We embrace one another, remembering our pain.

Eventually my thoughts shift to the tiny little twin girls born the day I stopped to visit Laura in the store. "They were so small, so weak."

"William didn't say what took the baby, only that Laura took to her bed with melancholy when it happened. She's still not healthy and refuses to risk the surviving baby."

I've known other women to suffer long periods of despondence but have never experienced it myself. I try to imagine what she must be feeling, but my brain doesn't allow it. Though I know she is grieving and that each woman does so in her own way, I am unable to glimpse such surrender in my mind's eye, not when other children would have need of me. But I do understand her refusal to travel when the other babe is not yet strong.

John releases me and paces the room, worry clouding his eyes. "Duley thought she'd be all right by now, that the other baby, Frances, would be stronger. That's why he didn't send word earlier."

I pity Laura, struggling so with both grief and worry. "Oh . . ."

I'm unable to say anything more.

"So, Tommy and I talked about it. Given the time of year, Tommy wants to wait until spring."

My thoughts come back to the move, unease accompanying them. Tommy has not yet sold his land; of course he has no problem waiting until spring. But we've already sold. I glance at John. Will we even be able to stay?

The answer is etched on his face without me even needing to voice the question.

Anxiety surges. "When do we have to be out?"

"The buyer will give us until November first."

Two weeks. Two weeks in which to head off to an unknown place on our own or find a place to rent, spending what we'd intended to use to start out at Lake Shetek. Neither choice is appealing, and I grow afraid.

I do not mention the baby I suspect I am carrying. Not today, when death and despair hang in the air, piercing me with memories. I will need to push it away, chase away the fear before it takes root.

We will have too much to do in this next handful of days, and others will have need of me.

CHAPTER TWELVE

Julia
Spring 1861

The rich aroma of buffalo roast filled the house. Julia figured she'd need to head out to LaBousche's tepee and let him know the meal would be ready soon. She'd kept the last roast back, to share with the half-breed trapper when he returned to the area, inviting him over from the peninsula across the lake especially for that reason. LaBousche had shot it before Christmas, claiming it might well be the last buffalo in the area. Even the elk and moose had moved on to less settled areas. Oh, the deer and waterfowl were still plentiful, but the big game—that was a thing of the past.

She glanced into the other room, where Dora was singing to baby George. Happy as larks, those two. The community was once again at peace, and Jack had taken on Will Everett as a partner. For a return on profits, he was allowing Jack to store goods in one of the abandoned trapper shacks on his property, two miles north. Everett was a solid man, a positive influence on Jack. It was about time her husband settled into being an honest man. Finally, they could operate this business the way it should be run.

Julia smiled to herself, prideful of her good fortune. Until guilt surfaced. The Lambs had not been so lucky, after all. She'd best remember that pride goeth before a fall.

Her sister's baby had not survived, born too early at the lake, despite Lorenza's intentions of going to Mankato, and George's fur trapping had not gone well this year. Those animals, too, were moving on. Truth be told, she worried George and Lorenza would be leaving the lake. Neither was too pleased with Jack, and they talked of settling a ways east, near the town of Iberia.

Julia held back a sigh. She didn't have to like it.

"Lorenza?" she called up the stairs. "I'm headed out to let LaBousche know what time to expect supper. I'm leaving Dora and George here."

"I'll keep an eye on them, if you're willing to risk Frank teaching her to pass gas on command."

Julia laughed. Leave it to Lorenza's little ruffian! At eleven, he thought farts were hilarious.

"I'll hold my nose when I get back."

Hearing Lorenza descend, Julia grabbed her shawl and swung it across her too plump shoulders. She opened the door and strode across the yard to LaBousche's tepee. She'd grown used to having them in the yard, a few at a time, when the Dakota came. This time, it was just the trapper, but the lodge was the same. The structures fascinated her—easily transported, well-insulated, and surprisingly roomy. There were times she found them more comfortable than the log house she lived in, where air grew sultry in the summer and icy in the winter.

"Hello," she called, alerting LaBousche to her arrival before she lifted the flap and stuck her head in. Warm heat poured out, filled with the scent of sage. "Supper will be ready in about an hour."

Once the smokiness cleared, she realized Will Everett sat next to the trapper.

"Well, hello, Will. I didn't notice your horse."

Everett offered a wan smile. "Tied it up next to your barn. Jack isn't around?"

Julia's skin prickled. Something was off. "He went up to Smiths'."

"Ah."

Everett's response fueled her unease. She'd learned to trust her instincts, and his reserve was unusual. Normally, he'd be chatting a mile a minute.

"*Madame* Wright, *entrez-vous, s'il vous plaît.* There is something we must speak about."

"With me?"

"*Oui.*"

"It's a thing you need to know."

She stepped into the tepee and adjusted the flap to keep the heat in. She circled left as Dakota women did and sat. "Something that involves me?"

"Unfortunately, yes." Everett shifted.

"That doesn't sound good." She looked from one man to the other. Nervous, both of them.

"*Madame,* there are rumors."

"It's not good, Julia."

Men. "Oh for heaven's sake, just tell me what it is."

LaBousche leaned forward. "When I was at Yellow Medicine, Tizzie Tonka, who has camped here before, he was there. He said the Sioux, they are buying whiskey *ici.* From your husband."

"Here? But Jack doesn't stock whiskey. I won't allow it."

"He claimed they bought it at my place," Everett said.

She looked at him, trepidation knocking like an impatient child. "Your place?"

"Made me mad as hell when LaBousche told me, pardon my language." Everett's face grew beet red.

Julia waved the language issue away with a gesture. She was used to worse than that. It was the whiskey rumor that was important. "Is it true?"

"I found four barrels in the cellar of one of the shacks. They were hidden under the stairs, behind a stack of crates."

"Oh, Will, no."

Not again, Jack, not again.

"It was rot-gut swill. Homemade, I think. There were a bunch of bottles there with fancy labels. I suspect he's been filling them and selling by the bottle, passing it off as good stuff."

"*C'est dangereux* to trade whiskey with the Sioux. And to cheat them. You *comprendez* this, *oui?*"

"I do." She understood all right. Selling whiskey in any form to the Dakota was a bad idea. Many of them handled alcohol—especially moonshine—less well than whites. Not that drunks of any sort were easy to deal with. Bad enough on its own, but to add deception . . .

She shuddered to think what they must consider Jack. No wonder the Dakota had taken to calling him *Tonka Tensena*. Big Liar. It fit, all right.

"You, they trust, but not your husband." LaBousche's words warmed her. She'd worked hard to establish a good relationship with the bands that visited the lake, allowing them to camp in the yard, interacting with them. That Jack was sabotaging all her goodwill was infuriating.

It was dangerous, it made them distrust whites, and it made the Dakota suspect *her* word.

Didn't Jack know this?

"Two of the barrels were empty, so I think he's had this side business for a while." Everett's gaze met hers. "Mira and I won't be involved in it. It's dishonest, and it's dangerous. He's apt to get himself or the rest of us killed."

The incessant foreboding hammered harder. "What is he thinking?"

"If he got the idea anywhere, it was likely from Clark and Wambau. It's the sort of scheme they'd promote. I drained the barrels, Julia, every drop. I'm dissolving the partnership, and he'll need to move the legitimate goods from the other shack."

Of course he'd dissolve the partnership.

One step forward, two steps back—the story of her life ever since she'd had the misfortune of meeting Jack Wright. She drew a breath, already exploring solutions. For the trade goods, at least.

"We'll move things to our barn again. Can you give us a few days?"

"I can do that."

"*Je suis désolé* to bring such news to you."

She smiled at the trapper's concern. "It's not your fault, LaBousche. It needed to be done."

Everett began to stand. "Julia, I was going to come up to the house, tell Jack what I told you—"

"Sit, Will. I'll tell him when he returns." She rose and straightened her skirt. "I have a few other things to say to him, and it's best you not have to hear them."

"Perhaps I should bring my plate here?" Again, LaBousche and his concern for others.

"That might be best." She circled to the door flap and pushed it away.

"*Merci, Madame.*"

Turning, she caught both their gazes. "*Non, merci* to you, both of you."

Julia left the tepee and trod back to the house, worry chasing her with every step.

Almena

Summer 1861

Almena tucked the hair that had escaped from her limp braid behind her ears. The summer afternoon heat bore down with burning intensity, and humidity hung heavy in the air. She glanced at the group of Sioux men—Dakota, Julia said they called themselves—that were mounting their horses. *Titonhah Seachah,* Bad Ox, and two others she didn't know, had traded her six geese for two rounds of cheddar.

She smiled and waved to the group. She still wasn't too sure she cared for Bad Ox, but he liked cheddar cheese and showed up every three or four weeks to restock his supply, and occasionally to visit and enjoy her hospitality. They'd established a routine relationship, and she no longer felt threatened when Bad Ox and his friends rode up to the cabin. It was funny, how she'd thought the Indians would be the worst part of living here.

She'd never in a thousand years anticipated the biggest problem would be blackbirds.

She and Phin had selected a beautiful place for the cabin, with Bloody Lake to the south and the waters that connected Lake Shetek and Lake Fremont to the north. The cabin sat in a grove of oak trees, and their farmland lay in the open prairie to the east. In all, it was a protected spot, isolated, with glistening waters nearly everywhere they looked. This year, Bloody Lake had borne true to its name, the willow roots at its edge turning deep red in the shallow water, casting a blood-red glow all along the shoreline.

But the blackbirds.

Lord help them, she and Phin hadn't reckoned on the blackbirds. She had no idea what attracted them like flies, but she aimed to get rid of them once and for all. Shooting them didn't work. Every day, she killed a few; every day there were more of them. Though they occasionally sang in harsh-sounding melody, it was the screeching call of the males that drove her most crazy. Two short notes then that long screech.

Propping the new scarecrow up against the makeshift pole, Almena fished a hank of rope from her pocket and tied the straw-stuffed thing to the post. It flopped a bit, bending at the waist, and she sighed. He'd need rope around his neck, too.

"Almena?"

She turned to Phin's voice and lifted her braid to cool her neck. "Over here."

He wiped his dirty hands on his pants as he approached—the mark of a farmer, for sure.

"Phineas B. Hurd," she chastised.

"Sorry." He had the good grace to look abashed, at least, and she couldn't find it within her to be mad at him. "The boys in the house?"

"Napping, both of them. Though I expect Frank will be waking soon for a feeding."

Phin grinned at her. "He's a hungry one. More so than William Henry."

"William Henry's going to be our easy one, I suspect."

Together, they walked toward the house and settled on a shaded log they used as a bench. Phin mopped sweat from his face. "The birds have been at the grain again."

"Oh, Phin, no." The birds had become the bane of their existence this summer. Though they'd mostly flocked in the trees around the house last summer, they'd now discovered the fields were an easy food source.

"They're at the fields, they're in the trees, they're on the ground. I hate the things."

"I'm hoping the scarecrow helps."

"The one in the field hasn't done a lick of good," he pointed out. "I don't understand why we're the only ones plagued like this."

"I hear the blasted things in bed at night and can't tell whether it's real or if I'm having a nightmare."

Conk-a-lee! Conk-a-lee! Except the *lee* was more like a

leeeeeeee. And it wasn't just a solo, it was a whole choir of them.

"I'm thinking I might have to move the fields farther out," Phin said. "It might be the water or maybe the acorns from the oak trees. We might have to move the cabin, too."

Almena scrunched her face at him. "I like this spot. Except for the noise and the feathers and the bird droppings."

"Maybe this isn't the right place for us."

She shivered. The way he said that didn't sound good. "Phin?"

"Maybe it's a sign. Maybe we should have moved into Dakota Territory."

She stood and faced him, hands on her hips. He hadn't just said what she thought he had? "Phineas."

"Bill and I have been talking. Maybe we ought to explore farther west. Maybe near Yankton—a real town, not an imaginary one."

"Oh, no, you don't! I don't want to move farther west." They'd been misled about the size of this settlement, and they'd take no more chances.

"I know. But at least we wouldn't lose anything more if we left before I pay up on the rest of the claim."

She shook her head. "We'd lose what we put into this place."

"Mostly logs and hard work."

"No." *No, no, no, no, no.* "Look at the livestock we have. We have crops in. We have too much invested here."

"We take the animals along, or sell them."

"I don't like the idea." Almena's mouth tightened into a thin, hard line. She hated the idea.

"All I want is for you to think about it. It's an idea, that's all. Not anything we'd do right now."

"I'll give it consideration, but don't raise your hopes." Her voice was brittle, but she didn't care.

"I'm not hoping anything, except to be rid of these darn

blackbirds." Phin stood and wrapped his arms around her. "I like it here, Almena. The neighbors are friendly, the land is fertile, the weather is tolerable—except for scorchers like today and the three-day blizzards." He dropped a kiss on her forehead.

"All I'm saying is that if the blackbirds keep at our crops, we might not have any choice."

Christina
October 1861

In the fall, we have another German at the lake, another Koch.

Though I wish it were a child, instead it is an immigrant, fresh from the Old Country. Ernst Koch shares our name—one that is common in Germany—but is not a relation, at least not that we know. Of course, when he arrives, he comes to us.

Andreas is glad of it. They spend hours speaking German to each other, and I think I am again in Dresden. Ernst brings *beir* from New Ulm and the two sit together like old friends. The only other German in the area is Charles Zierke, whom everyone calls Dutch Zierke, but he lives twenty miles away, on the road to New Ulm.

It is an interesting thing, about Ernst. Even though he is newly to this country, he speaks English better than my Andreas. We have a good laugh about that.

Ernst has a partner named Voigt, who will come to us soon. They are making plans to open a trading house; it sounds like they will have many goods for the settlers. Wright, who trades at the south end of the lake, has mostly things to trade to the trappers and the Indians. The settlers, we must still make trips to New Ulm for all but the basics. We will be glad if we do not have to do this so much. We also hear Wright does not give the trappers a fair price, so Ernst may have their business, too.

I invite Phin and Almena Hurd to dinner, to help welcome

Ernst and hear the news he brings of the southern rebellion. He will also need to find a place for his cabin, and I think it will be a good thing if Andreas and Phin can offer advice. We are much like a family at this end of the lake, and I look forward to many years of the same.

Bright leaves have all fallen from the trees and have become a crunchy rust and ochre carpet. There is a chill in the air that stings when the wind blows, as it does nearly every day now. Snow will come to us soon.

Crackling leaves and chattering children catch my attention. I jump and dash from the house. If my braid were not coiled up, it would fly behind me like a rope.

"Almena!" I rush to my friend and hug her. Little Frank wriggles in her arms. He is growing and not so little any more.

William Henry jumps up and down and tugs at my skirt. "Aunt Christina," he says. His young voice mangles my name, but I do not care. I scoop him up, and we walk together to the house, Phin and his partner, Bill Jones, trailing behind us.

Andreas and Ernst welcome us at the door, and we make introductions.

"Come into the house," Andreas says. "It is too nippy out here. We have a good fire and *beir*. And Christina made us strudel."

"Beer," Phin says. "I haven't had a beer since we left La Crosse. Show me the way."

We all laugh and enter the small cabin, tossing wraps on the bed. The men move chairs and sit by the window while Almena and I settle the boys on the bed. Almena gives them small stuffed animals to keep them occupied. The two of us go to my small stove behind the table. We are crowded, but we make do.

"Ernst will bring bolts of cloth for his trading house," I tell her.

"I can supply him all the cheese and butter he wants, bread

and preserves, too." Almena has five milk cows and makes the best butter and cheeses.

"I have told him already."

She mouths a silent thank you to me and blows kisses to her boys. William Henry has made a parade with the animals, all but the one Frank chews on. Almena laughs before going to my cupboard to gather dishes and silverware for the table. I am glad she is my neighbor—she has a joyful spirit and is such a good mother.

"Where will you locate?" Phin asks.

"I have not decided." Ernst gestures with his hands. "I will look when Voigt gets here so we can decide together."

"Voigt is his partner," Andreas says. "Another German." He raises his *beir* in a toast. *Ach.*

"Are you planning to trade with the Indians?" Jones asks.

"More with the settlers, I think. Voigt does not like Indians much, and Wright already has that trade."

I think this is a good decision. Germans and Indians are not a good mix. The Germans, we are stubborn and set in our ways. And the Sioux, they cannot understand the German accent.

"Did you hear they killed one of Wright's oxen?" Phin asks.

We, the Kochs, stare at him. We did not know.

Almena sets the plates on the table. "Old Pawn told Julia it was because Wright cheated them, and they were owed."

"*Ja,* I don't doubt that." Andreas has a bitter tone in his voice; his dislike for Wright is still strong.

But I think about other things than Wright. I think about the Sioux killing an animal that belongs to a settler. "Should we be worried?" I ask.

Phin scowls. "No, I'm sure Wright had it coming. He's not an honest man."

"We haven't had a lick of trouble with them," Almena says. "I trade cheeses to Bad Ox all the time."

"The squaws trade us feathers for our mattresses," I tell Ernst. Too late, I remember that Julia says we should not use that term, that it is demeaning. But I have said it already. She is the only person I know who worries about it anyway. Julia is like that. I think I will not worry so much. Even the Sioux men call them that, after all.

"If you locate at the north end of the lake, you wouldn't be in direct competition with Wright or need to worry about so many Indians around," Jones says and drains the last of the *beir* from his stoneware bottle.

"But Andreas says most of the north end land has been claimed."

"True enough. But you might be able to buy from someone," says Phin.

Beside me, Almena drops the silverware, and it clatters on the table.

Laura
November 1861
The wind grew bitter on the road to Lake Shetek, biting into our skin, and we were forced to stop for days to wait out snowstorms. It was cold, constantly cold, and I didn't think I would ever forgive William for waiting so long into the fall to make the journey. But the Irelands had needed to bring in their harvest and complete the sale of their property, and John said they changed their plans for us last year, when we lost Rachael. So we had waited. It had been a difficult trip for me, filled with constant worry, and I wanted so much to finally be at our new home and settle into a warm, comfortable cabin.

Traveling with two other families grated upon me. I was easily provoked and grew snappy without warning. Always, children demanded attention, taxing my patience. Oh, to be in our home with a bit of privacy.

"Laura?"

I turned to William, trying to muster a bit of enthusiasm. "Yes, Husband?"

"Are you all right?"

I winced. He kept asking this. For months, now, he'd asked it.

I was as good as I was going to get.

I was not abed, and I was caring for the children. I cooked his meals and did what needed doing. He always wanted more, tried to cajole smiles and laughter where there were none to be had.

"Yes," I answered. "I'm fine."

"I just wond—"

"I said I'm fine. Leave it be."

We sat in silence again, the wagon rocking.

William had made several trips to Lake Shetek. He'd cleared land, mowed hay, and taken the remains of the mill works on ahead. Business had dwindled at the store, but we'd managed to locate a buyer for it as well as for our land, turning a decent profit. I was glad to have the responsibility out from under us and looked forward to a quiet life as a farmer's wife.

I no longer yearned for leading roles in the community, where William would be tempted to become involved with politics and spend hours serving others. I wanted nothing but a peaceful existence. A private existence where no one bothered me.

"We're almost there."

Good. I was tired of this bump-filled mail road. Up and down hills it went, the frozen ground refusing to yield, stuck as it was in a churned up mess from the last rain of the season. We cleared yet another hill, and I spied a building in the distance.

"Wright's place," William said.

We rolled in, the Irelands and Eastlicks behind us, and

stopped near the house. It was a story-and-a-half high or perhaps even two stories, and larger than any cabin we'd seen on the cold, brown prairie.

A woman rushed out of the house. Bright eyed and a little plump, she possessed a degree of excitement I simply could not dredge from myself. A blond man and two young children followed.

"Welcome to Lake Shetek."

I sat on the wagon seat as the others clustered together, chattering like magpies. My own children clambered out the back of the wagon—all except Frances, who was asleep under mounds of blankets. Finally, William came to lift me down. I went, albeit grudgingly. I was tired and had little tolerance for an extended welcome.

We made introductions, and I shook hands with the woman, Julia.

"We're so glad to have you here. Three more families!"

"Is it always this cold here?" I winced at the rudeness of my words.

Julia laughed. "Not always. But the air off the lake holds a lot of moisture, so it can be pretty biting. You'll learn to live with it."

I doubted so, but I nodded anyway.

Julia offered a brilliant smile before moving to welcome the other women. "The Everetts are expecting the lot of you up at their place, so we'd best let you head on up."

"We'll see you soon," I heard Lavina say in that confident way of hers.

Shivering, we loaded back up and drove the two miles north, gusts blowing off the lake. Gray waves rushed across its surface each time I spied it through the trees, turbulent and inhospitable. William turned and headed straight into the gale, up a small strip of land. Ahead was a small, two-room cabin, twelve by sixteen at the best. In the distance stood two less solid buildings I could only call shacks.

My heart plummeted.

The wagons ground to a halt, and the whole bunch climbed out. This time, I went with them. It seemed we had reached our destination.

A family emerged from the log cabin, and I met the Everetts: Will and Mira and their children Lillie, Willie, and the baby, Little Charlie. Mira's brother Charlie, the baby's namesake, was to arrive after the first of the year.

Again, the entire group babbled on, until Mira Everett announced, "Let's get everyone settled. Make yourselves at home, folks." Taking armfuls of belongings, the Eastlicks made for one of the shacks, the Irelands for the other, as if it had been prearranged.

Of course it had.

And William had not informed me once again. Where in heaven's name were we going to live?

William smiled at me. "I figured you wouldn't want to make do in one of the trappers' shacks," he said.

The words warmed me, and a tiny spark of eagerness ignited. He must have already built our cabin. A small, timorous smile rose. "Shall I get the children back on the wagon?"

"What for?" He looked puzzled.

"To go to our cabin."

"Oh, we don't have a cabin yet. I'll build that in the spring." He guided me forward. "I figured, since Will and I plan to partner in the mill, we'll live with the Everetts this winter."

Lavina
November 1861

Without words, the men lead us down a travois trail through

the mature trees, created by the trappers who used to live here, and we neared the shacks. Dear lord, when John told me there would be a place for us to live, I never imagined such a dilapidated place. No wonder he's not whistling.

Though my journey to Lake Shetek has been made with far less enthusiasm than my first journey out into the world all those years ago with my brother Leicester, I'm determined to make this an adventure as well. Even though it is early winter, and our first months will be filled with cold and snow, I've observed the beauty of this place as well as its possibilities. The lake is huge, full of geese and loons most of the year, we're told. Though the water is choppy now, it reflects the sun with a glittering brilliance. The place is raw and wild and will certainly test our independence, but I resolve to maintain a positive outlook and forge a happy home here.

The shack gives my resolution pause.

I enter, Johnnie in my arms. Inside, it's dim. Though there is a window, it is oiled paper rather than glass, and the muted light is less pure, less brilliant. It's also chilly. I'm glad to note the stone fireplace at one end, but wind blows through the spaces between the logs. And through the roof.

The children scamper in and hop onto a pile of bedding stacked in one corner. Straw ticks, I imagine.

John enters behind me and stops.

"Did you see the roof?" I ask.

"I see it."

"And the walls?"

"Mm hmm."

"We can't live here, John. Not during this season. Johnnie's six months old, for heaven's sake. We'll freeze in here."

"It was supposed to be habitable. William Duley said he'd make sure of it while he was out here cutting hay."

"Well, he evidently didn't. I suspect he was too busy boasting about his accomplishments to think about it."

I bite my tongue at my uncharitable comment. Duley isn't all bad, but he does tend to puff up like a rooster more often than not. He'd served on the state constitution committee, he'd founded a town, he'd owned two businesses, he'd—

"I'll go talk to Everett about it. Will you be all right? Do you want me to start a fire first?"

"No, we can do that. At least there's been wood stacked."

I lay Johnnie on the mattresses. Goodness, they're stuffed with feathers. Feather ticks way out here! I remove my bonnet from atop my thick bun and start assigning chores.

"Merton, fetch in wood and lay a fire. Frank and Giles, start bringing in what you can carry from the wagon. Start with quilts and foodstuffs. Fred, you mind Johnnie."

I spy a broom in the corner and sweep the hardened dirt floor to clear the scattered bits of mud and leaves that have blown in. Already, I understand we will have to live here; there is nowhere else for us. My mind whirls, exploring ways to make the shack more habitable. I wonder if the Irelands are encountering the same conditions. I think about the Duleys crowded into that one-room cabin with the Everetts. None of us are too satisfied right now, I suspect.

John reenters the shack with Uncle Tommy, another man behind them.

"Lavina, this is Parmlee, another of the settlers here."

"Mr. Parmlee." I shake his hand and hope the men can come up with an idea. We can't all move in with the Everetts, after all.

"Good to meet you, Mrs. Eastlick," he says. He looks around the cabin, his gaze lingering on the ceiling.

"See what I mean?" John says.

"Yep. Didn't know it had gotten this bad."

"What do we do about it?" I ask, eager to press the issue.

Parmlee's brow knits. "My place is about a mile and a half

from here. I cut blocks of sod over the summer, was going to build a stable with them. Looks like a new roof here is more important right now. Those last few windstorms we had must have shredded the roofs. They weren't much to start with, but they were better than this. I can haul them up tomorrow, but you'll have to cut them."

"I don't have anything to trade you for it." I know John's pride prickles with the admission.

"Not to worry. I've pretty much decided I'm headed back east in the spring anyway. Whoever takes over my place will have to worry about his own stable."

"We can use the canvas from the wagon for tonight, and I can work on the roof tomorrow." John looks to me for agreement.

"I can tack up quilts on the walls for now, but the logs will need to be chinked."

"We'll pitch in and give a hand to get that done," Tommy says.

John catches my gaze. "The other shack is even worse. I've told Tommy to let it be for now. We'll get this one weatherproofed first, and they can stay with us until we can do theirs."

"I know it will be crowded, Lavina," says Tommy, "and I hate imposing but—"

"Nonsense. What's another six people?" If nothing else, the body heat will keep us warm.

Chapter Thirteen

Laura

January 1862

I snapped the quilt atop the sole bed in the cramped room the Everetts had provided for our use. The colorful patchwork lent cheer to the dull gray of the morning. Emma and Jefferson shoved the spare feather tick—the one the children slept upon—under the bed, giggling as they struggled with the ungainly mattress. The experience of so many living under one roof was an adventure to them, and I was glad of it. Even so, I envisioned a time when we would move into our own cabin and planned to raise the issue with William.

"Everyone dressed and ready for breakfast?"

A chorus of yesses sounded, and we headed in a group for the main room of the cabin, knocking to alert the others before we opened the door.

Mira Everett stood at the small stove, cracking eggs into a frying pan. "Good morning, all you little sleepyheads." She turned and beamed at the children.

They chimed replies and scrambled to chat with their playmates. Emma had become fast friends with Lillie Everett; Jefferson and Bell played nicely with their Charlie. Our William typically sought out Frank Eastlick, the two being of an age.

I neared the kitchen area and grabbed plates and silverware from the shelf. With so little room and too small a table, we had become accustomed to eating picnic style.

"Thought we'd have the last of the bacon." Mira indicated a pan on the back of the stove.

The winter had come hard and fast, and supplies had thinned. Yesterday, William and Mr. Parmlee had left for New Ulm to purchase a wagonload of foodstuffs for the settlement. Mira said it was common practice during the winter, but she thought there might be two trips this year, given how many of us there were.

"I think William volunteered for the trip just to have a break from the monotony," I said.

Mira laughed. "Too bad we don't get that luxury."

She dished up plates of bacon and eggs, and we handed them off to the children. They assembled in a group upon a quilt the girls had spread on the wooden floor. Mira and I sat at the table.

"Where's Will?" I asked.

With "William" being such a popular name in the settlement, I was glad Mira's husband preferred the shortened nickname. It was hard enough dealing with three boys called "Willie" without confusion in referring to our men.

"He ate early, went out to do chores. I think he likes the barn better than the house, once everyone is up and at it."

I laughed. "That's not a surprise. We're packed pretty tightly. I suspect the Eastlicks are much relieved the Irelands have moved out of the shack and into their own cabin."

"I have no doubt. Despite their long friendship, fourteen in one room would be far too many to abide. The Irelands must have jumped at Parmlee's offer."

A few days after our arrival, Tommy Ireland had negotiated a purchase of Parmlee's land and cabin. The entire family had moved two miles northeast immediately, with Parmlee to remain there as well until his move back East in the spring.

"When is your brother arriving?"

Mira's face lit with a smile. "I think Charlie plans to be here in the next month or two."

We finished eating and gathered plates for washing, my thoughts drifting forward. By March, we would have one more soul in a cabin that was already packed to the gills. "Where are we going to put everyone?" I asked.

"If we're fortunate, spring will come early and allow the men to get a cabin built on your land. If not, we'll figure it out."

"I imagine we will, though it'll be left to the two of us, I'm sure." The men would simply escape to the barn or clear land or other tasks to take them from the house.

We finished stacking the dishes, and Mira set the coffee on. We pulled out our mending, taking chairs near the stove, while the children scattered throughout the two rooms in play.

"I keep thinking about Charlie and where he'll claim land. John Eastlick said they plan to take their claim between here and the Irelands. That means the only available land near us is to the east, away from the lake, out on the prairie. I worry that he'll be more vulnerable out there all alone."

"He's a grown man."

"But he's my little brother, and I worry about him."

"I know. I worry about my sisters, too."

Mira rose and fetched two cups of steaming black coffee for us, setting a small container of precious sugar on the table for me, along with a spoon, before sitting back down. "Has William taken you to your claim?"

"Our first week here."

I stirred a tiny bit of the sweetener into my cup, careful not to take too much. Steam rose from the surface, and I set it back on the table to cool a bit so I wouldn't scald my tongue.

"Did you decide where to put the house, Laura?"

"In truth, no. William wants to locate near the Des Moines

River." I paused, wondering if I should share my concern. "We argued about it. Rivers have not been good to my family."

I left it at that, not telling her about my two drowned girls or the ruin of the mill.

"I didn't think you were too enthused about it."

"And it's so far away from most of the settlement. The Wrights and Lambs would be our only neighbors." And if the Lambs leave like they're planning, there would be only one family. "Neither William nor I am keen on the Indians who camp on the Wright place."

Mira waved a hand in dismissal. "Oh, the Indians have never been a problem. There's usually not more than two or three tepees there at a time and not too often at that. It's the hard winter that's had them here more these last months. We've gotten to know a few of them pretty well."

"They've come begging for food?"

"They're hungry; game's scarce. Julia said they're supposed to get annuity supplies on the reservation, but Mr. Lincoln's war has delayed delivery."

I shook my head. "I'd just as soon not have them here."

"Just be glad they're a friendly bunch."

I glanced out the window, musing. "This must be a beautiful spot in the summer months."

"It is. We set the cabin here, smack in the middle of the peninsula, for that very reason. The lake is close enough to get to, but far enough that the kids aren't tempted all the time. Lots of trees, calm water, gorgeous sunsets. But it is off the main trail. I think Will would prefer it weren't so quiet."

As for me, I thought the Everett place was one of the most picturesque cabin sites, set far back from the water, among a grove of fully matured trees. A few of the others favored the Ireland place, but this cabin's distance from the lake held special appeal for me.

I lifted the coffee and breathed in the aroma before taking a sip. It warmed my mouth and slid down my throat, a treat I'd not had for days. Coffee, too, was in short supply. I savored each sip and watched Mira do the same. We might not agree on what made a perfect location for a house, but we did both agree that coffee was a pleasure to be enjoyed.

An idea popped into my head so suddenly that I nearly spilled the treasure. "Mira? What if we traded claims?"

"Traded?"

"There's lots of land around the southern side of the lake, and it's near the New Ulm Trail. Charlie could take a claim right next to you, and Will wouldn't feel so isolated."

"Oh, my! And you would be nearer people you know, farther from the Indian encampment."

"I do like it here."

"And if we lived on the river, Will and Charlie could take on running the mill more easily. Your William could be a silent partner, the way he's been saying he wants. It's a perfect idea."

I thought so, too. Now, I just had to convince William.

Julia
April 1862

Dora rushed into the house, breathless. "Mama! Old Pawn is back again."

"Is he now?" Julia ruffled her daughter's head. Five-year-old Dora was fascinated with the huge Dakota man, despite his fierce appearance. In fact, other settlers called him the ugliest Indian they'd ever seen. To her way of thinking, Julia found him a big—very big, given his height—pussycat, but she wasn't about to tell anyone else that. The last thing she wanted to do was insult the man. "And what did he have to say?"

"He and the others have come to hunt again."

Lake Shetek remained a valued hunting ground and ceremonial area, even now, after many of the Dakota had moved onto the reservation. But, hunting here was more than their tradition now. Folks all said food was scarce at the agency. Their farming didn't support them, and the annuities ran out far too soon. And the situation had worsened since the fighting between the states.

She supposed life on the reservation could be pretty miserable.

The Sioux were a complicated people, with three different dialects (Dakota being one of them), two major geographic divisions, and seven tribes or bands. It still confused her, trying to sort it all out, but she'd at least learned the Dakota dialect and made efforts to understand and respect them. Jack sure as goodness didn't.

The first thing she'd learned was that they disliked being called Sioux, which was an Ojibwa word meaning "little snakes." Dakota was preferred, because it meant "ally." Others called themselves Santee, which referred to any of the eastern tribes.

"One of the men wanted to know if Papa had any more whiskey for sale," Dora said.

"Oh, for heaven's sake." Julia sighed and grabbed her shawl. "You stay here and watch George."

She strode out the front door, crunching across the new spring grass and ruing the day she'd met Jack Wright. What in the world was that man doing this time? She neared Pawn's tepee and paused to alert him of her presence. "Pawn? It's Julia Wright."

Pawn lifted the flap. "*Hau.* It is *waste* to see you. Do you wish to enter?"

Julia spoke to him in his own language. "It is good to see you, too. I don't need to come in. I wanted to tell you that Jack isn't selling whiskey any longer. One of the men asked Dora."

Pawn shrugged his shoulders. "There are rumors there *is* whiskey again, sold from the barn."

She closed her eyes and drew a slow breath. A year of compliance from Jack and peace of mind for her seemed to be Jack's limit. She needed to take care of the issue before it went too far.

"Tell your men I am sorry," she said. "If there is whiskey, it is no longer for sale."

"I will tell them." The way in which his mouth thinned told Julia he understood the situation completely. "You are well?"

"I am. And you?"

"Yes, my friend. I will come later to talk, to tell you of the news among my people."

Julia returned to the house, slammed the door, and marched toward the area that had been curtained off as a bedroom. Jack lay abed, snoring heavily. She yanked the blanket from him and kicked the bed.

"Get up, you louse!"

Jack jumped, glared at her with bleary eyes. "Damn it, Julia, I was sleeping."

Sleeping it off, maybe. Now, she knew why he'd gone to check on the livestock last night. "It's time to get up. It was time two hours ago."

He crumpled back to a prone position and drew the blanket back up over his head. "What d'ya want, anyway?"

"Do you have whiskey hidden in the barn?"

"What?" he mumbled.

She jerked the quilt off and let it fall to the floor. "Do. You. Have. Whiskey. In. The. Barn?"

"Don't know what you're talking about." He attempted naiveté but failed miserably. He'd never been a good liar, ought to not even try.

Still, it was a saving grace that she could always see through him. Lord help her if he ever learned to lie well.

"I will go out there myself and tear that barn apart."

This time he sat up, sighing. "Aw, Julia, why does it matter so much?"

"Why? Because you promised me you wouldn't. Because it drags my reputation through the mud along with yours. Because it's dangerous."

He reached for his pants and tugged them on. "A little whiskey never hurt anybody."

"A little whiskey gets the Dakota drunk, especially if it's that rotgut stuff you were selling before. It got Renicker killed a few years ago."

"Nobody's gonna kill us."

Julia stared at him. Did he truly believe there was no danger in what he was doing?

Of course he did. Arguing that point would get her nowhere. She crossed her arms and glared. "I will not have it here."

"Ain't that much anyway."

"Where is it, Jack?" Her foot tapped the wooden floor, tapping out a rhythm of growing impatience.

"It's my business."

"You already drove away George and Lorenza with your foolish whiskey business. Don't you realize they were afraid? That the other families are concerned? Selling whiskey impacts all of us. It's everyone's business."

"Stay out of it, will you?"

"No, Jack, I won't. Finish getting your lazy butt dressed, go out to the barn, and show me where those bottles are hidden. And any barrels, too, inside the barn or out of it."

He glanced up. "And if I don't?"

"I will pack up the kids and take them to Iberia, and we'll live with George and Lorenza. You're putting lives in danger, and I will not be a part of that. Not now, not ever."

Christina
May 1862

I am glad the spring has finally come. My lilac bushes have buds, and I look forward to the scent of the purple flowers filling the air. I think, maybe, the turn of season will brighten our moods. The winter was long, and we had to make two supply runs to New Ulm. The second trip, Andreas and William Duley went. It was not a good trip, and it lingers on like a bad taste in Andreas's mouth.

"He is a loud-mouth know-it-all," Andreas says.

All the way, Duley kept trying to tell Andreas how to drive the team. I think my husband knows how to drive a team! But Duley thought he knew better. If there is one thing I know, it is that telling Andreas how he should do something is not a good thing. Telling any German such a thing is not good.

Ach, I can see them in my mind: Duley all puffed up like he is a peacock and Andreas stubborn as a kicking mule. A stubborn German, though, can cut off his nose to spite his face, and my husband did exactly that. He drove straight into a patch of quicksand at the Cottonwood River. Oh, and didn't Duley have a great time preaching how he should have more sense? Andreas says they almost came to blows, and he will never go anywhere with the man again.

Ja, I am glad we are past the winter, and my husband can work out his anger in the field instead of telling me over and over about it.

"Hello?"

Almena! I stop kneading my bread and rush to the door to hug my friend, and little Frank who is on her hip.

"I brought butter." She hands me a basket, and I peek into it, my mouth already watering. Almena's butter is a treat, and our mouths will have pleasure tonight at suppertime.

She removes her shoes at the door and reminds William

Henry to do the same. Only then do they enter my tidy cabin. How well she knows me. She is the only one I do not have to remind of this. As usual, I have swept every spot of dirt outside. A good *Hausfrau* keeps everything clean.

Almena sets Frank down on the rug to play with his brother. The two boys are charmers, that is sure, and I am proud the rug is freshly beaten and a good spot for them. Their blond heads bob as they play with carved animals together—William Henry takes them everywhere with him. These boys are darlings, and they bring me such happiness.

I motion for Almena to sit as I return to the bread dough. "How are you?" I ask.

"Fine, fine," she says, but I am not sure she tells the truth.

Silence stretches with only the boys babbling and me punching dough. "Were there many Indians at your place this winter?"

"More than usual. I fed them as often as I could." I know we are both thinking about how cold and hungry they were this winter. "Julia Wright said there were problems getting food on the reservation. Were there many here?"

"*Nein*, not so much. Andreas and Voigt saw to that." Andreas has never wanted to trade with them, and, in the fall, Voigt became angry when they came to trade for food and shot at their feet to make them leave. It was not good, because they were only women and children. Now, the Sioux regard Voigt as an enemy. Me, I do not mind helping them when they are hungry. "Old Scalpie came a few times, when the men were not here." I shape the dough into loaves, which I put on the back of the stove to rise.

"I wish we knew her true name," Almena says. My friend has a softness that wants to avoid this awful nickname, but I have no answer for her. The woman has been called this name ever since being attacked and nearly scalped by hostile Indians.

"Even the Indians call her that," I finally say. "Is there any other gossip?"

Almena laughs at my question. She knows I will only ask this of her. "You heard about Hatch and Bentley arriving?"

"Charlie Hatch is Mira Everett's brother, I know. Who is Bentley?"

"He came with Charlie. He's staying with the Myerses for now but plans to take a claim south of the Everetts. He's a millwright. Looks like the mill operation is growing."

"Isn't Duley a millwright?" I think of the man and his bragging about his skills. He will not like it that Charlie has brought another.

Almena laughs again, understanding. "He's likely a bit put out, but Bentley's already here; what can he do? I guess they plan to start on the mill this summer. Oh, and the Eastlicks have a cabin up. It's not quite finished, but they've moved into it. They built at the edge of the timber near that small slough southeast of the Irelands. Everett moved the trapper shack the Eastlicks were in down to the Des Moines River as temporary quarters until he can build a bigger place."

She pauses, and I glance at her. I know her. She is making small talk with me instead of talking like sisters as we usually do.

"You have heard much news," I say.

She shrugs. "Phin has been up and down the lake."

I raise my brow. This is not usual for him, and I wonder if it is linked to what bothers her. I probe a little. "Just to gather news?"

"No. He went out with Ernst when he was looking at land." Almena's mouth trembles, and I rush to crouch next to her.

"What is it?"

"Phin and Bill Jones have made a provisional sale of our place to Ernst and Voigt. They are back there at our cabin now, working out the details. I couldn't stay there another minute."

"No!" I put my hand to my mouth. It cannot be. "You are not leaving us?"

"Phin and Bill want to go west, to Dakota Territory. They've been talking about it for months." Her tone is wooden, resigned.

"But why? I thought you were happy here."

"It's the blackbirds. We can't get rid of them, and they've taken over the crops."

Ach, I know about their blackbirds but to let the pesky birds push them away from here? This I do not understand. "But there's plenty of land. Can't you take another claim?"

Almena's face tightened. "I tried to tell Phin that, but he and Bill have heard about a settlement called Yankton, in Dakota Territory. And with the new Homestead Act, the land will be free."

Ja, this I do understand. It is difficult to sway a man when he has heard about something that seems to answer all his hopes.

"So far?" I am not sure even where this Yankton is, but I think it is on the Missouri River far to the west. Days and days of travel.

"I'm afraid so. The two of them will go out to look things over before we move. We don't want any surprises this time. If Yankton isn't the right place, they'll scout other areas."

"What will you do while they go?"

"The sale includes an agreement that I can stay in the cabin until they return and we pack up the place. Voigt will come up and stay in the second room to keep the place in order while they are gone. And watch over the boys and me."

I sigh. "Voigt and Ernst don't care about the blackbirds?"

"Not so much, no. They plan to make the place into a trading house."

I think Ernst will be a good trader but Voigt, not so much, not as an enemy to the Sioux. "How will Voigt handle it when Bad Ox comes to trade for cheese?"

Almena's eyes close for a moment, and I know she feels bad. "There won't be any cheese for him, I suppose. I'll warn Bad Ox about the change, if I have the chance. In the meantime, Voigt will need to keep his opinions under control."

Almena
July 1862

Almena placed the boys down for their naps and sank into the kitchen chair. She dropped her head into her hands.

Where were they?

Phin and Bill had been gone for six weeks, two weeks longer than they'd said they would be. Phin had *promised* her they'd be back by Independence Day. Instead, she'd picnicked with the other families in the wooded area between the Duleys and Smiths, pretending to be as happy and joyous as the rest of the settlers. She'd watched Frank totter after William Henry, laughing at their antics while worry battered her head. She'd eaten green peas and spring chicken, licking her fingers and chatting with the other women. But, all the time, she'd been anxious and fretting.

And every day since, the trepidation had grown, growling and churning so that she could barely eat. She'd fought to hide it from the boys, feigning that life was normal. But Phin was never late, had never broken his word. She'd been fighting the thought that wouldn't stop roiling in her stomach.

What if he doesn't come back?

Lord help her, for the boys' sake, she needed to make plans.

"Almena?" Julia Wright's voice sounded from outside.

Gracious, what was Julia doing all the way up here?

Almena patted her cheeks, stepped over Bill's near-deaf dog, and rushed to the door. She pasted on a bright smile she didn't feel. "You're about the last person I expected to ride into my yard."

"I suppose I am." Jumping from the wagon, Julia looped the reins around one of the oak trees. She swatted an errant blackbird away. "You do have a lot of them here, don't you?"

"We're infested with the damn things." Almena put a hand to her mouth as soon as the curse came out, but it was too late. She flushed. What must Julia think of her?

But Julia only laughed.

Relieved, Almena relaxed a bit. "At times, they're so thick we fire off the shotgun to scatter them. I don't know why . . . they just come back." She glanced at the wagon. "Do you want me to get Voigt to tend the horses?"

"No, no, don't drag him in from the fields. He looked busy when I passed him. I won't be too long. They can stay in their braces."

"Come on in." Almena tipped her head toward the house.

"Are the boys inside?"

A strange question. Unease crept up Almena's spine, and she kneaded her callus. "Asleep," she said, "but we can chat."

Julia shook her head. "Let's sit out here. How about on the log?" She pointed to a spot about halfway between the cabin and Bloody Lake. "The shade looks refreshing." She strode away and lowered herself onto the fallen oak.

Almena followed, apprehension growing. This was odd, Julia not wanting to come in, being worried about the boys. "What is it? Something about Phin?" She whispered the words and sank down next to Julia. Tension coiled through her.

Julia drew a breath. "The New Ulm postmaster sent word that there was a letter from Fort Pierre."

"Fort Pierre?"

"It's in Dakota Territory, about two hundred miles north of Yankton, on the Missouri River. There's a trading post there."

Dakota Territory. Almena's pulse stuttered. "Phin?"

"The letter was from a trader, who had received goods in trade from a group of Dakota." She paused and reached for Almena's hand.

No, no, no, no, no.

"—horses, a wagon, and a gold watch with an inscription."

Air whooshed from Almena, and she swayed. "Phin's watch." The words were so softly uttered, she wasn't sure she'd said them aloud until Julia answered.

"It appears so, yes. It was his name, and an inscription."

Almena's head fell back, and she scrambled to suck air into her mouth. She gulped once, twice, and squeezed her eyes shut. But the implication wouldn't be blocked out so easily. She clutched at Julia's hand.

"I gave him that watch," she croaked out before her voice broke and she could say no more.

Julia gripped her hand, grasping it until she breathed more evenly.

Almena composed herself. Emotional breakdown would do her no good, not now. She sensed Julia knew her anguish, but they were not familiars. With Christina, she would share her tears. Right now, she needed to hold herself together.

"From what the trader gathered from the Dakota, he reasoned they'd had the items since early June, maybe as early as June third."

One day after he'd left.

Almena tamped the anguish. "Maybe they found it. Or stole it."

"Maybe."

But neither of them believed it. She certainly didn't, and she spied the doubt in Julia's eyes, heard it in her voice. There was only one scenario that made sense.

"Or maybe not," Almena conceded. She removed her hand

and smoothed her skirt. Realizing what she was doing, she stilled the errant motion and stood. She needed to move, to get away from this spot.

"What do you want to do?" Julia asked, rising to join her.

"Could we . . . do you think the men would . . . ?"

"I think we could get a search party together."

Almena strode toward the lake. "Phin said they'd go to Sioux Falls first—they wouldn't have even gotten that far."

From behind, Julia caught her arm, stalling her escape.

"Almena, if they search, are you ready for what they might find?"

If they found his body, she would be ready. But until that time, he was still alive in her heart.

Lavina
August 17, 1862

The summer is hot and humid. Thunderhead clouds roll through the sky in the late afternoons, bringing streaks of lightning and threatening hail. We watch carefully for any telltale swirling that might form tornados. Something ominous weighs on me, and I'm not sure what it is. I tell myself it's only the weather and return to the field with Merton and the dog to check the crops.

Perhaps it's only that John has been away so much this summer. I'm pleased he is due home today from his trip east to work the harvest there.

Despite our house still needing a bit of work, he went with the search party in July with Everett, Wright, Duley, and Smith. Estimating where Phin Hurd and Bill Jones might have been on their second day out, the group rode to Split Rock, on the Rock River, and spent time scouting the area. Though they found traces of the men's trail, it led them no further. The search party itself became separated and returned in two groups. John told me his group thought there were Indians in the area and thought it best to come home immediately.

We laughed about it when the lost members of the search party straggled in late that same day, having found the note John had left for them after they got lost. John said nothing to the others about his Indian fears, and we dismissed it as errant worry. After all, small groups of Sioux camped along the lake all winter, begging for food. They played with our children, teaching them their language. We'd all gotten on well together. In late spring, they'd left, and we've glimpsed little of them since. It is hard to imagine violence coming from any of them.

"Mother?" Merton asks, rousing me from my thoughts.

"Yes, my boy?" I'm proud of him. Now eleven, he has a keen sense of what's needed around the farm. He and Frank complete their chores without fuss, whistling all the while. Even Giles steps up to help, Merton supervising them.

"Will you look at this corn? I'm thinking we may need to bring it in soon."

He's pulled back a portion of the husk on one ear, and I examine it with him. It looks ripe, ready to be picked. "The corn first," I say. "Then the potatoes. We can start tomorrow."

Merton looks pleased. His father taught him well.

The dog leaps off, barking, and we follow him to the house, Merton chattering about who will do what in the morning. As we near, I notice John's horse in the yard, along with one I don't recognize, and rush to locate him. I find him in the barn, hefting the saddle onto a rail.

"John!"

He turns and opens his arms. I run into them, and we share a kiss in the dimness. At someone's throat clearing, we draw apart. When I turn to see a strange man, my face heats and I'm glad for the darkness. I tuck in stray locks of hair and wait for

John to introduce him.

"Lavina, this is Mr. Rhodes. We met in Olmstead County, and he's decided to settle here at the lake. I told him he could stay with us until he settles on a claim."

I welcome Rhodes, shaking hands and ask, "How was Olmstead County?"

"Full of work. I was glad Wright suggested hiring out back there. The money will help, with the limited crops I got in this first year."

"Merton and the boys will bring the corn in tomorrow."

As the men finish with the tack and the horses, we chat about their work, the progress of our crops, the thunderstorms, and the news from back East. They met sixteen Indians on the way back, in traditional loincloths and red face paint, but found them friendly and talked with them. As well, Lincoln's war continues, and Minnesota men are leaving their farms to enlist. Rhodes hands me a pile of newspapers so that I may read about the details. We walk together to the house.

"Have the Indians been around?" John asks, a hint of disquiet in his voice.

"Not at all," I answer, waiting for him to say more.

"That's good. Good," is all he says, and I wonder what has prompted him to ask, what has made him uneasy.

"Should I be worried?"

"No, no. I just wondered." He looks at Rhodes, and something passes between them. "Wright stayed in New Ulm for a couple days. He thought he spotted Phin Hurd's dog with an Indian yesterday. He was going to dig into it a little, try to find out more."

"That's not a good sign."

"No, it's not." He pauses but says no more about it. "You go ahead in, get washed up, my little field hand. We'll be in soon."

I roll my eyes at the strange endearment and enter the house.

I wonder if the stew will feed an extra mouth and begin setting the table. Outside, John and Rhodes speak in low tones, and I catch only a few words here and there.

". . . good idea to build a fort, don't you think?"

I stop, my heart racing. A fort? I rush to the doorway.

"Why do we need a fort? What have you heard? Are we in danger?"

John glances toward me, and I swear his eyes hold distress. Rhodes shifts his feet.

"John?"

"Nothing to worry about. Phin disappearing, seeing his dog, it got us talking about how the settlement was growing. With more of us, it wouldn't hurt to explore the idea of a fort."

I don't believe him, but he will say no more.

Part Three: Ordeal

Chapter Fourteen
August 20, 1862
It Begins

Almena

5:00–6:00 a.m.

Almena crept from the house, taking care to keep as silent as possible. William Henry and Frank were still asleep in the bed they'd shared since Voigt had taken over the second room of the cabin. If she was to get her five cows milked, it was to her advantage that the children stay asleep. Hungry toddlers usually made for uncomfortable delays for the cows. Besides, this was the day Charlie Hatch planned to borrow Voigt's oxen, and he'd likely be here around sunrise.

Outside, the pre-dawn air held a chill she hadn't anticipated. She debated returning for her shawl but shrugged the idea off. It would only get in the way, and she'd warm up once she started milking. She fetched her milking stool from the barn and headed to the paddock.

"Good morning, ladies," she called, patting each of the cows with affection as they gathered around her. Hungry girls, she thought. She dumped feed into the trough and eyed the cows. Their udders were heavy; there would be a lot of milk today. Maybe she'd make an extra sharp cheddar this time, have it waiting for Phin when he returned.

When he returned.

She'd denied reality for so long now that such thoughts were almost a given. *When he returned.* But he was now months late, and she had to accept that hope was useless.

A soft neigh reached her ears. Charlie already. She sighed at the poor timing, with feed already in the trough. The cows would be less cooperative later, and they wouldn't be happy at the lack of relief for their full udders.

"Be right there," she said. Maybe Charlie would round up the oxen by himself and be on his way so she could finish milking. She turned to suggest just that, but it wasn't Charlie after all.

Ten Dakota men were in the yard, one of her trading partners, Iltimony, among them. He scratched the dog's ears as another group reined in a distance away. *"Hau,"* he said, raising a hand.

Almena sucked in a breath. Goodness, they'd come in quietly. She'd not even heard them arrive, and Bill's old dog had long since gone deaf. Her patience prickled at the inconvenient arrival—she'd need to offer breakfast. She acknowledged him and several others she recognized. Most had been at the cabin before but had never caused any problems.

"Have you come for cheeses?" she asked, hoping to send them on their way with just a trade this time.

Iltimony slid from his mount in that fluid way of their people. "We come to hunt buffalo, but we will visit with you."

Sighing, she patted the cows in apology and strode toward the house. She shouldn't be so resentful with her hospitality.

The group in the yard dismounted and followed her into the cabin.

Inside, Voigt stood near the stove. The heavy aroma of coffee filled the room. It was their usual habit, Almena laying the fire before the milking, Voigt starting the coffee. He glanced at them, a scowl forming as the Indians filed in.

Almena mouthed a silent "shh" to him, hoping he'd keep his

mouth shut. There was enough bad blood between Voigt and the Dakota, and the last thing she needed was an altercation. Thankfully, he moved to the corner of the room and remained silent.

She went to the stove, gathered a frypan, and carved ham from the hock she'd brought in from the smokehouse late last night. There were only a few potatoes. It wouldn't go far, not with the four of them and the Dakota men, but it would have to do.

The men took out pipes and lit them. Fragrant tobacco smoke wafted through the air. Voigt exaggerated a cough.

"So do you think you'll find buffalo?" she asked, hoping to distract them from Voigt's antagonism.

They conversed in the Dakota language. Over the past few months, she'd become more skilled at understanding it. What she didn't grasp, or was unable to say, was translated by Iltimony and the half-breed among the group. They chatted, mostly about the wildlife and late annuities until little Frank woke, fussing. Almena supposed it was the sight of so many Indians all at once.

She glanced toward the bed. William Henry was stirring, wide eyed. Frank was frantic.

"I will tend him," Voigt said and scooped Frank up. He headed toward the door.

Almena breathed easier. She knew Dakota children were brought up not to cry, and the men were likely judging her. Taking Frank outside would calm him and avoid the men's displeasure. One of the men she didn't know rose and followed them outside.

Seconds later, a shot rang out, and the dog began frenzied barking.

Almena dropped the fork, her pulse thundering. Frank! She raced for the door.

Voigt lay on the ground, blood pooling beneath him, Frank still in his arms.

Almena sank to the ground and met Frank's wide, startled eyes. The moment he saw her, he wailed. She grabbed him, pulling him from Voigt's limp arms. The German's lifeless eyes stared up at her, and she gagged.

Nearby, the dog squealed. Then silenced.

She heard only the sounds of horses and people running, shouting in Dakota. She turned. The dog lay still on its leash. The other group of Indians had ridden into the yard, and a host of women emerged from behind trees. They rushed into the house.

Almena followed, desperate to rescue William Henry. He was still on the bed, his mouth gaping as women rummaged through their belongings, shattering china and ripping window curtains from their anchors. One of the women yanked on the handle of the largest trunk, edging it toward the door in staccato movements. Another rustled through a second trunk, flinging belongings far and wide.

Almena shoved her way past them, and William Henry scampered into her arms. She turned and fled the cabin, a child on each hip. She turned away from Voigt, so that the boys would not catch sight of his dead and bloody body, lying there on the ground with a hole in his chest.

Outside, one of the women piled up cheeses and cakes of butter. Months of hard work sat before her—twenty-three cheeses and nearly three hundred pounds of butter. Someone had hauled a feather tick from the house and another woman sliced it open. The crash of furniture being tipped over rang out.

Horses pranced among the havoc, and Almena scrambled to avoid being trampled. She glanced back.

Oh dear lord, that's Phin's horse!

A few feet from it pranced one of the dogs Phin and Jones had taken with them.

Almena gulped, panic racing through her veins. At that moment, she *knew*.

Someone grabbed her arm and swung her around.

She cried out and clutched the boys close.

"If you go, we will not kill you," the man said.

The words were rough, and she barely heard them.

"We have no quarrel with you. Go to your mother." The Indian pointed eastward.

To her mother?

William Henry struggled in her arms, whimpering in his nightclothes. He had wet himself and shivered in the cool air.

"All . . . all right," she said. "Let me get my boys dressed."

The man shook his head. "No. You go."

"But they need clothing, and their shoes."

"If you wish to live, you will take them now and go. Otherwise, you will all die."

Still dazed, Almena stood silent.

The Indian grabbed her again. He shoved her and she began walking.

"Be quiet, William Henry, be quiet," she told the wriggling boy.

Usually argumentative, he must have heard the urgency in her voice. He gulped back sobs and clung to her as she headed east, accompanied by seven Dakota men.

Christina
5:30–6:20 a.m.

The sun is peeking into the day when I hear the hoofbeats of a horse.

"*Ja*, that will be Charlie Hatch," says Andreas. He is pulling on his boots and does not yet have his shirt buttoned. "He is going up to borrow Voigt's ox to raise the mill today. I told him he should leave the horse here so he will not have to worry about it when he is leading the oxen down the shortcut."

We hear a distant shot and glance at one another, grinning. Almena and the blackbirds.

I think she has it in her mind to shoot them all before Phin returns. I sober, and my heart is in pieces for her because I know he will never return, no matter how much she hopes. Before I choke up, I turn to Andreas and make conversation.

"Are you going to the lower end?" I ask. The mill will be built south of the lake, where the Des Moines River flows out, about four miles from us.

"*Nein*, there is much to get done here."

I am glad of it, for both corn and wheat are ready for harvest and should be brought in before we are hit with a hailstorm. When we finish our chores, we will work in the fields. This is the way of things, hard work and good weather. That is how we survive.

Andreas comes to the table, and I set his plate of bacon and eggs before him before I sit with my own.

"The Indians are back," he says. "Old Pawn is camping by the Wrights."

"*Ja*, Julia says he is a good man."

"He is ugly."

I laugh. Andreas does not like the Indians any more than they like him. They do not bother me so much. We finish breakfast, and Andreas heads outside to tend the livestock before we go to the fields. There is time, I think, to sweep out the *Haus*, and I make use of it. I do not like the dirt that has gathered on the floor. No matter how many times I sweep each day, the dirt comes back, blowing in with the breeze and clinging to our clothes.

Never Let Go

I hear more horses and step out of the cabin, wondering if visitors have come.

Andreas is talking to a group of Indians. One of the men asks him for water. He grabs a pail, and they dismount to follow him around the *Haus* to the well at the bottom of the hill near the lake. It is not long before I hear shots. We will not get to the fields so early now, if they are having a shooting competition. I think perhaps Andreas should not have set up the targets for that, but it is a harmless thing.

The shooting stops after only a few shots, as if the contest has halted too soon.

Worry snakes through me, and I drop the broom. I rush around the house, my heart thumping. Charlie Hatch's horse is spooked, loose in the yard, and the Indians are chasing it. I do not see Andreas.

My gaze darts to the barn, and I notice him on the ground in the stockyard. He does not move.

Mein Gott! They've shot Andreas!

I dart forward, Indians scurrying all around. Not my Andreas, not like this! The horse thrashes in front of me, its hooves flying. I screech to a halt, quivering.

In that moment, I realize Andreas is dead and that I will very likely be next.

Almena
6:15–7:15 a.m.

The seven men took Almena to a little used trail, escorting her on horseback as she walked. The sun had emerged, its brightness and warmth in stark contrast with the brutality that had just ripped her world apart.

William Henry's weight grew heavy, and Almena stumbled, landing on her knees. She bit back a sob, wondered how she could keep carrying both boys. Despair crowded her soul. Phin was dead, despite how she'd tried to avoid accepting it, and she yearned to curl into a ball and cry until the loss was numbed. And, if the Dakota didn't like it, it would matter little if they killed her, too.

And, while she gave in to the grief, the Dakota would take the boys away from the only family they had left. Or worse.

She gulped a breath and dredged up a smile for William Henry.

"How about you walk a little bit?" she asked him, filling the suggestion with as much enthusiasm as she could muster.

The toddler shook his head, defiant.

The half-breed tugged on her arm. "Go. Now." He spoke Dakota now, not English as he had in the cabin, and glared at her.

Get up, Almena, get up and go. It's all up to you, now.

She made her way to her feet, adjusted Frank, and took William Henry's hand. He tugged it away, and his mouth scrunched into an angry pout.

"We need to go, my little man. We must." She pulled, and he trudged along, plodding his way across the still-dewy grass in his bare feet.

"It's wet, Mama."

She squeezed his hand. "I know, Sweet. It's all right."

"I don't want to go nowhere. I want to go home." He looked back, tugging away.

"We have to go this way. Let's have a game of it, like we're on an adventure."

"I don't want to." His lip trembled.

One of the men pushed at her.

"We must go." She grasped William Henry's arm, dragging him behind her. Her eyes burned. *Walk, William Henry, walk.*

In the distance, two shots rang out, and Almena jumped.

Christina!

She faltered, stumbling in panic. Christina would need her.

The clawing fear gave way to reality as she stood, her son clinging to her legs. "I'm scared, Mama. I want to go home."

There was no home. Christina was likely already dead.

The men grunted, and Almena took William Henry's hand again. If they did not go, they would be killed. All of them. Being allowed to leave with their lives was a gift. Though she had no clue of the reasons behind it, they needed to take what was offered and *go*.

She caught her son's gaze and forced a stern tone. "You will do as I say. You will take my hand, and you will come with me. Now. You will not let go."

He cried, wailing, then hiccupped as his sobs became whimpers. But he no longer resisted her confusing orders.

They'd gone about two or three miles when the men reined in their horses. "Go straight to the east to your mother, to your people. Do not stray. Do not come back. If you come back, if you go to the others, we will kill you."

Almena nodded. Her husband was surely dead, her home destroyed, and her friends being killed. Ahead of her were seventy-five miles of open prairie. Her children had no clothing, and there was no food. But she would go, and she would not turn back.

She clutched William Henry's hand and strode away.

Lavina
7:00–8:00 a.m.

The house is crowded, now that Rhodes is boarding with us. We don't have an extra feather tick for him, and he's forced to sleep on a pallet in the side room where the five boys have their bed. There are no extra chairs, either, and it takes two rounds at the table to feed everyone. The oldest boys have eaten and are doing their chores. Only Johnnie sits at the table with us, boosted upon a wooden box so he can reach his breakfast.

The extra furniture will need to wait until winter. Getting settled is taking more time than we anticipated, but, eventually, we will carve out a comfortable home. For now, we make do. I long ago learned to be practical about life. Events do not go as expected; when they don't, we do what we must.

I serve Rhodes and my husband and set a small bowl in front of Johnnie, giving him a spoon so he can eat his porridge. The children awoke so early that I haven't even had time to put on my shoes yet and have no idea if the boys have donned theirs.

It will be good to sit and have a few moments of peace before we start our busy day.

"Ma!" Merton calls from outside, the dog barking along with him. "Ma!"

I sigh and hustle to the doorway, my few moments of quiet and my breakfast both delayed. "What is it?" I ask.

"Charlie Hatch is coming, as fast as he can run!"

I glance across the yard and spy Charlie emerging from the waist-high grass. He is panting and can barely catch his breath by the time he reaches me. I wonder if there has been an accident in raising the mill. But he has come from the wrong direction.

I shiver. "What is it?"

"The . . . Indians are . . . upon us."

Our Indians? I'm unable to believe our friendly group has turned on us. My mind doesn't want to accept his words. "That can't be," I say.

"They've shot Voigt, and Hurd's household is strewn across the yard. Mrs. Hurd and the children are missing. When I got back to Koch's, I saw them shoot Andreas. I'm pretty sure he's dead, too."

Now, my heart thunders in earnest, but I stand paralyzed. "What about Christina?" I ask as Merton rushes into the house.

"I don't know. I didn't see her. My horse—the wild colt—was tied up there, and he spooked when they shot Andreas. They were busy chasing him. I figured I'd better run while I had the chance. I came down Stump Pass to the Irelands."

Stump Pass—the marshy shortcut between the lake proper and a water-filled slough. The shortcut saved miles and precious time. Thank God it existed!

Oh, dear Lord, an Indian attack. Of all the things I have imagined might go wrong here, this was not one of them. I turn around, looking for John. In my panic, I don't know what to do.

"Tommy said we should all meet at the Smith cabin," Charlie says, as if he recognizes my dilemma. "I came here while the Irelands went there."

"Have you warned the others?" John asks. He has Johnnie in one arm and guns in the other. I don't know when he came from the house or how long he has been standing there.

"Not yet. Can I take a horse?"

"I'll grab a saddle," Rhodes calls out and veers to the barn.

"No time. Just a bridle," Charlie says.

I stare at him, still numb with shock. "How far away are they?"

"The bridle?" he asks again, and the request finally breaks through my haze. I remember Rhodes was working on the leather last night and rush into the house. Where is it? I check the table, run to the side room.

John calls out, "Merton, get the boys together."

I grab the bridle from next to the bedroll, hasten outside, and hand it to Rhodes.

John catches my gaze. "We've got to go."

The children are barely dressed. "I'll gather our clothes."

"There isn't time." Now, John's tone is urgent, and my skin

crawls. I tell myself to focus. Do what needs to be done.

I am barefoot, the boys as well. "Our shoes?" We cannot leave without shoes.

"There's no time. Let's go." He tugs at me and sets off. I forget the shoes.

Charlie rides out of the yard, toward the Duley cabin. I turn, count the boys, and start to follow John.

"For God's sake, at least take ammunition with you!" Rhodes yells.

Rhodes is right. The shoes can be left, but we will need the ammunition. "Go," I tell the boys, "to the Smiths' as fast as you can."

I turn back and lift the front of my skirt. Rhodes dumps powder, shot, and lead into it, and I dash after John and the boys, weighed down by the heavy lead. Rhodes follows, carrying more guns. He flashes past us to the front of our scattered group. The dog trails us, ever faithful.

I run as fast as I am able with the extra weight, my feet striking the hard ground without cushion, the grass cutting my feet. Lead jounces out of my skirt, and I stop again and again to scoop it up. Panting, I call out to John, and he trots back to me, urging the boys to continue on.

"The lead—"

"We don't have time. Leave what spilled, and hike your skirt up further. Maybe that will keep the remainder secure."

I run after him, the load still heavy. I lurch on the uneven ground and flounder. "I can't keep up, John."

He rushes back to me, his face knotted with anxiety. "Grab my coat."

I imagine us both being caught. "No, go ahead."

"I won't go without you," he says. "I don't care how hard it is. You can't give up. The boys need you. I need you."

I swallow. He's right. I can't give in to the pain or the fatigue.

We rush on. My side pinches, and the rocks cut my tender feet. We run the two miles to the Smith place only to find it closed up tight.

"Smith? You here?" John calls out.

"Wright's." I gasp for breath. "They must have gone to Wright's." We race past the end of Beauty Lake. The boys, Rhodes, and the Smiths are ahead of us.

Winded and panting, we crest a hill. The Wright house is below, several Indians gathered around it.

Julia
7:30–8:30 a.m.

Julia had just finished dressing Dora and George when she heard the horse. Before she could open the door, Charlie Hatch burst into the house.

He appeared a wild man, his hair windblown, his shirt drenched with sweat. "The Sioux are attacking. We have to arm."

"What do you mean, attacking? There are three tepees in the meadow, and the whole bunch of eight was up here for coffee not more than a half hour ago."

"Voigt's dead, shot through the chest, and Mrs. Hurd and the kids are missing; household contents scattered. I saw them shoot Koch and headed out to warn everyone. They seem to be headed from the north, and we don't have much time."

His panic was real. Old Pawn and his group might be having coffee with her, but that didn't mean squat about any others.

"I'll get our guns," she told Charlie.

His eyes filled worry. "I still need to warn my sister."

"Go. Send them here." Theirs was the biggest house, nearest the Sioux Falls Trail. It made sense that they gather here.

He ran out the door, and she turned to the children. "Go

upstairs," she told them. "I want you to stay there until I tell you to come back down."

"But, Ma . . ."

"Go."

They trudged up the staircase as Julia assembled guns and ammunition from the trade stock. There wasn't as much as she'd hoped. Jack had planned to purchase more in New Ulm, on his way back from working the harvest.

New Ulm . . . he was likely there now. She offered a small prayer for his safety as she piled the arms on the kitchen table. What else needed doing?

She thought of Pawn and the lodges outside. She'd need to determine if they would stand with the settlers. She drew a breath and rushed outside.

"Pawn?" she called.

He stepped from the group he'd been talking with and approached. "The rider had urgent news?" he asked. His was even, without panic.

Julia weighed his tone. "He said an attack has been made on the settlement. Do you know about this?" She watched his face, searching for any sign that he already knew of the events.

"I do not."

A note of surprise. Easy enough to fake, but it sounded sincere. Still Julia pressed further, needing to be sure. "He said it was Dakota warriors."

"Sisseton?" he asked, referring to his band, one of seven among the Sioux people.

"I don't know."

Pawn's brow knit, worry evident.

Julia weighed his response, unwilling to distrust her friend.

"We will fight with you, if they come here. You have been friends to us, and we wish to keep you safe."

His words held the ring of truth, and her gut told her to trust him. The additional defense would be valuable, and a go-between might prove of benefit.

"Make plans. We will need you."

She ran toward the house, her mind flying to the other tasks necessary for a possible siege. In the distance, a group of people approached, and she recognized the Smiths. She waved them on, told them about the weapons, and rushed back to the yard. Rhodes was sprinting down the hill, followed by the Eastlick children.

"Merton, take the boys into the house and upstairs," she directed. "I will need you to keep them there until we call you down."

The boy straightened to his full height. "I can help shoot, ma'am."

Poor kid. He'd be a solid defender and wanted to prove himself a man.

"I know," Julia answered, putting her hand on his arm, "but we'll need assurance the children are all safe, and that will be your responsibility. If necessary, we will arm you, but I think it best if we keep the little ones away from that so they don't panic. I need you and Frank and Willie Duley to take charge of it. You three are the oldest. Can you do that?"

"We'll do it. Come on, boys. We need to get set, find ways to keep 'em all busy. There's gonna be a hoard of kids up there." The five boys disappeared into the house.

Julia glanced around, realizing three Eastlicks were missing. "Where are John and Lavina and the baby?" she asked Rhodes.

"On their way."

She mentally tallied the group. "Charlie didn't mention the Myerses. Are they coming?"

"No one knows. Charlie had to make a choice. He came south."

She thought of the Myerses, alone at the north end of the

lake, and lifted a silent prayer for them. It made sense for Charlie to have come this way instead—more families to be warned in doing so—but she hoped the remaining family had found a way to escape.

Rhodes shifted, uneasy. "You haven't been attacked?" He waved toward the tepees.

Julia eyed him. Rhodes was new to the settlement, and she'd yet to take his measure. "Old Pawn and a few others, set to head south to hunt buffalo. They've given us their allegiance."

Rhodes's eyes held skepticism. He pointed to the north. "Here come the Eastlicks. And Tommy Ireland. Looks like William Duley is with him."

Good heavens, Lavina was on her last legs. Julia rushed forward as they came down the hill, and Lavina collapsed in her arms.

"She barely made it," John said.

And no wonder. She smothered a gasp as she caught sight of Lavina's bloodied feet. "Someone take that lead from her, get her up to the house, and see if any of my shoes fit her." She turned her friend over to John and watched him usher her toward the house.

Rhodes still stood beside her, as if waiting to be told what to do. *Idiot.*

He had to be in shock, much like the others, even if he didn't appear as stupefied. "You. Gather up buckets of water from the well out back and get them inside the house. Use the pails on the shelves. The Smiths can help you."

In her mind, she knew she should be just as traumatized, but if her years cleaning up after Jack had taught her anything, it was that there was little time for panic when things needed doing, and, right now, she might well be the only person thinking clearly at all. She could fall apart later.

"Where are the rest?" she called out to Duley and Ireland.

Tommy raced to her. "They attacked before we got out of the yard. We were trying to load up supplies. They chased me while Sophia led the kids into the woods. We don't have much time."

"Laura's in the woods, too, hiding with the kids," William Duley confessed. "She couldn't keep up."

"We will go." Pawn stepped forward. Dances in Water and another Dakota woman stood behind him. "We will find them and bring them here. You make things ready."

Laura
8:00–8:30 a.m.
I huddled in the bushes, shaking, my children clustered around me. Their eyes were nearly bursting with fear. My heart pulsated with more trepidation than I'd ever known. We were going to die here, in this isolated place, and no one would ever know.

We should never have come to Shetek.

Already we have suffered so much loss and now this. We should have stayed in Ripley County or even in Iowa. Or kept the store in Beaver. A thousand regrets filled my head, and still I stood quaking, knowing none of it mattered. It would not change where we were nor what we would likely encounter.

Emma held four-year-old Bell in her arms, comforting her. Willie and Jefferson were likewise embraced. I carried Frances. The minutes stretched on, and I wondered if William were still alive, or if savages had already murdered him. Would that be our fate? Had he abandoned us here in the scrub, leaving us to perish?

I couldn't move, didn't know if I should take us onward or remain hidden. Tears streamed down my cheeks, and I remained frozen in place.

The sound of rustling leaves broke through the heavy silence of our hiding. I clutched Frances closer and stifled a scream.

The brush parted, and a haggard Christina Koch stood there. "Laura, is that you?"

"You're alive!" The words fell from my mouth, so astounded was I that she had survived.

"*Ja*, I got away, but my Andreas has been killed." Grief filled her voice, but she didn't waver as she stepped closer to us. Her dress was torn from the brush, its hem wet and muddy. Her blond hair had escaped her usually tidy braid and hung about her face, full of sticks.

"William?" she asked, seeking my husband.

"He went ahead. To Wright's."

"He should not have left you. We must go on. I saw the Indians at the Irelands. They barely escaped. We cannot stay here, or they will come upon us."

I shrank at the accusation in her words and did not respond to them. William *had* left us, and I could not refute it. Still, I did not want to leave our refuge. I didn't want to emerge from the forest to cross the open ground.

"William said to stay in hiding," I protested.

"If we stay here, we will be murdered for sure." Christina was firm, resolute.

I envied her courage and shrank smaller into my green nest. I glanced at each one of my children. "No."

"*Ach*, you do as you want, but I am going on. I will not be killed hiding in the woods."

She stood and stepped out of the bushes just as three Indians appeared on the trail.

Julia
8:30–9:00 a.m.

Julia thanked the two Dakota women who ushered the Irelands, Duleys, and Christina Koch into the yard and urged the settlers into the house.

Lavina rushed forward to greet them and drew Christina into her arms.

"My Andreas is killed." The words were wooden. "They shot him for nothing."

"We may likely all be widows before the day ends," Lavina noted and wiped Christina's face with her thumb.

Laura Duley's chin quivered, and Julia drew a breath. The last thing anyone needed right now was a gaggle of weeping women. "Lavina, take Christina into my room and find her dry clothes. Did you find shoes?"

"None that fit these big feet." She lifted her skirt and raised one foot, then gave a short laugh that hung in the air.

"Laura, take your young ones upstairs. You, too, Sophia."

Understanding fills Sophia Ireland's eyes. "Come on along, Laura." She wrapped an arm around Laura's waist and guided her up the narrow stairs.

With the women all busy, Julia turned back to the men. Edgar Bentley had arrived. She tallied the numbers. Thirty-four of them. Only the Hurds and the Myerses were missing, along with her husband and Ernst Koch, who were both in New Ulm. She suspected the missing neighbors had been killed hours ago. This would be all of them.

Of their total number, most were children. There were eight women—all could shoot, she supposed, except maybe Laura Duley—and eight men.

She glanced at the table. Three squirrel rifles, some shotguns, a few sacks of shot, and a keg of powder. "That's all?" she asked. It was as sparse a collection as she'd ever seen.

"Some of us didn't even have a chance to grab guns," Tommy Ireland said.

"It's going to make for a difficult defense," John Eastlick noted. He held his rifle in his hand; it was the best in the community and he, the best shot.

"*Ja,* you will need these, too." A freshly dressed Christina Koch dumped a collection of butcher knives and hatchets onto the table. "I took from the shelves."

"Gather up the axes, too," Julia said.

Eastlick moved to the center of the group. "There aren't enough guns for all of us. I think it best for the men to take the guns and defend from the holes we've been notching out of the chinking. The women can take the other weapons and go upstairs. Let us know when you spot them coming."

"What about the Indians outside?" Smith asked. "I'm surprised they haven't attacked."

Julia sighed at her nearest neighbor, a man of less than keen intelligence by her reckoning. "You know as well as I do they've been camped here for the past three days without a single problem."

"That's true. They're planning to head down the Des Moines River to hunt buffalo."

"You believe them?" Duley scoffed. "I don't trust the whole bunch of 'em."

"Pawn's been a friend." *For heaven's sake, I shouldn't even have to remind them of that.* "I didn't note anything in his reaction that led me to believe his intentions are evil. He offered their help. I think we need to trust them."

"You mean give them some of our arms?" Smith shook his head.

Ireland caught Julia's gaze and rolled his eyes. "Oh for Pete's sake. If they wanted us dead, we'd be dead already."

"I'm not inclined to let them in here with us, that's for sure," Duley said.

"I think Julia is right. Let's trust them. Tizzie Tonka stopped me outside, said he'd fight for us. I gave him a small horn of powder already." Ireland shrugged his shoulders. "We don't have much to lose."

"Enough already. We're wasting time." Eastlick eyed the group. "If they prove friends, we'll have need of them. Give them powder and lead and have them take up defense from the barn. That's more tactical anyway."

"And if they do turn on us?" Lavina asked from the edge of the room. "John, you asked one of them earlier if he would fight for us, and he said he didn't know."

"Uncle Tommy is right. If they had killing in mind, we'd already be dead." Julia scooped a few bags of shot from the table and strode toward the door. Ireland followed with two of the guns.

Pawn and Tizzie Tonka stood in the yard, scanning the distance. "Will you still defend us?" she asked Pawn.

"We will."

She tossed the shot to him. "Thank you, my friend."

Ireland handed him the guns. "You can take a stand in the barn."

Tizzie Tonka motioned to the others and the Dakota moved away with guns, bows, and knives.

Pawn pointed to the northwest. Ponies circled the prairie near Beauty Lake, and war whoops began to sound.

Ireland caught Julia's gaze and drew a breath.

She swallowed. It wouldn't be long.

Lavina
9:00–9:30 a.m.

In a burst of speed, Julia and Uncle Tommy flee into the house and bar the door.

Tizzie Tonka and Old Pawn have come in with them. These are old friends. I cannot believe they would be any part of savagery, but apprehension fills me, and I can't dismiss the cloying fear. Ever since the Indian in the yard responded he was unsure he would fight for us, my pulse has raced nonstop. Everything I know about these people is now topsy-turvy.

I huddle behind the counter with Christina; the other women have gone above. She shakes, her eyes narrow, upon glimpsing the two Sioux. I can only imagine the thoughts in her mind after seeing her husband lying dead at the hands of their tribesmen. I wrap my arm around her and offer her as much strength and comfort as I can muster.

Julia stands with Pawn and Tizzie Tonka as the men in the room take notice. Suspicion hangs in the air like heavy morning fog on the lake.

"It looks like they're making camp," my Merton reports from the stairs. "The women are putting up tepees near Smith's place."

"They're coming!" Laura shouts, terror in her voice.

"Two riders only," Mira Everett clarifies.

I drag Christina with me to the nearest window, unable to stay back simply waiting for the attack. Better to know what is coming, to confront it. She draws a breath and comes with me, and I realize we are of one mind in this. There's nothing to be gained in hiding in fear.

Pawn and Tizzie Tonka are at windows, too, their guns in their hands. Seeing them, I breathe easier. I believe they remain the friends I knew them to be.

Outside, two Sioux ride to the edge of the field, fire off their guns, and return to their camp, whooping. In a moment, another surges forth, aiming at a stray cow and downing it.

"What are they doing?" Duley asks. His shoulders are tense, his face filled with panic.

"They're baiting us," Uncle Tommy says.

Pawn straightens. "They are showing their bravery by riding in front of you. They are also making you fear them."

"I've heard of this," John says.

One after another, the Indians emerge. Some moments apart, others at longer intervals. I tense at the waiting, and it stretches on and on.

Christina stands at the window, her face drawn. I clutch her hand, and she says, "It will be all right. Whatever happens, it will be all right."

I am not so sure if she believes that, or if she is trying to chase her fear away.

"What do we do?" Everett asks.

Tizzie Tonka turns from his post. "Show they do not make you afraid. If you all fire your guns, they will know this and will be frightened away."

The men whisper among themselves, gather their guns. In a group, they move to the door and lift the bar.

They're going out.

My skin grows hot with sweat even as a cold shiver creeps up my spine. When they exit, Julia Wright goes with them, her husband's gun in her hand, a shot pouch and powder horn slung over her shoulder like a warrior. The woman must know no fear. I envy her.

They line up in front of the cabin as I watch from the door. As one, they raise their guns and fire toward the attackers.

All but Pawn and Tizzie Tonka.

My knees nearly buckle, and I fear they will turn on us after all. I rush out to John. "Do not discharge further," I plead, "lest they turn on you when your guns are all empty."

"Go inside," my husband orders.

The Indians continue to taunt us. We have failed to convince them we are unafraid.

Julia
9:30–10:00 a.m.

Julia stood firm as they fired. The sound echoed in her head, her ears ringing. She blinked her eyes, coughing as the combined smoke of their multiple rifles stung her lungs. From the corner of her eye, she saw that Pawn and Tizzie Tonka had held their fire.

Strategy against the settlers? Had she made an error . . . a tremendous, horrid error?

"That did no good," Smith muttered.

"What now?" As usual, Ireland got to the meat of the matter.

Pawn grunted, low in his throat. A single note of resignation. "I will go parlay." He strode away.

Julia watched him go as Lavina and most of the men stomped back inside. She debated with herself. It was possible Pawn had seen this result coming, that he'd held his fire in order to maintain an illusion of neutrality so he could better negotiate. It made sense. But she was no longer as sure of him as she'd been before. There was too much she didn't understand.

Several Dakota rode from the field at breakneck speed, directly toward Pawn. He stopped, facing them. Julia held her breath as the riders continued on, hell-bent for him. He did not flinch, and they reined the horses to a stop. They shouted back and forth before Pawn approached the riders.

Julia glanced at Ireland, who waited outside with her. His face was etched with worry.

She shivered and realized she was afraid.

We are at their mercy, and there is no way this is going to end well.

When her pulse started racing, she tamped the thought down. Fear was her enemy, as much as that group of Dakota, and she couldn't let herself fall prey to it.

"Julia," Ireland whispered, "Pawn's coming back."

She lifted her head and watched the tall Dakota man jog toward them. "I have news," he told them.

They clustered inside, so that all could hear.

"Grizzly Bear leads two hundred warriors and many squaws."

Julia recognized the name as the man who had become chief after Old Sleepy Eye died a while back. Some called him Lean Bear, but she knew both were the same man. "Sisseton?" she asked, trying to sort out whether or not the group belonged to the same band as Pawn.

"Yes. White Lodge and Strike the Pawnees are with him," Pawn said. "They wish to kill the whites."

"I say we go out there and kill them!" someone shouted from the back of the room.

"I speak for you, tell them you have been friends. I ask them to let you leave. They say you may go, if you do not fight them. But you must hurry and take nothing, or they will burn this house with you in it."

Julia turned and faced the men. Their faces were taut with fear. Their comments blurred together as they talked over one another.

"It doesn't sound like much of a choice."

"The house has green shingles, but it wouldn't last long."

"There's women and children to be considered."

"We can't be thinking of trusting that savage, can we?"

"It's seventy-five miles!"

She emerged from the fog, stuck her fingers in her mouth, and whistled until all was quiet. "We can't delay this, or it will be understood as a rejection of the offer."

"Then we go," Eastlick said. When a majority agreed, he spoke to Pawn and Tizzie Tonka. "Tell them."

They turned and left the house.

"Should we get supplies?" Lavina asked.

Christina stepped forward. "*Ja*, I can do that, get the blankets and food."

Julia shook her head. "They said to take nothing. We would be wise to take note of it."

"We cannot take twenty children across this prairie on foot," Everett said. "Charlie, you and Rhodes go out the back, take two horses, and ride for our place to get a wagon, blankets, and food. If we're lucky, you can get through the woods along the river without them noticing. They'll be focused on the rest of us. Meet us down the Sioux Falls Trail a bit."

"I'll get the others," Lavina said.

Julia watched her ascend the stairs.

Leave now, leave peaceably, take nothing.

She shivered again.

Chapter Fifteen
August 20, 1862
Flight Interrupted
10:00 a.m.–2:00 p.m.

Almena

10:00 a.m.

Almena trudged across the prairie, Frank limp on her hip. William Henry plodded alongside her. She blew at the strand of hair that had strayed across her face, sticking fast to her sweaty skin. Damn merciless humidity. It had to be near ninety already. She sighed and glanced at the sky, trying to factor the time. She couldn't reconcile location and the sun.

She stopped and glanced around. How had she been so careless? There was no longer any visible trail, and she had no idea how long they'd simply walked on, oblivious. Were they still going east?

Think, Almena!

Their path seemed correct, felt on course. It couldn't have been more than a few minutes since she'd last glimpsed the faint path across the prairie. It had become less distinct with each step so it wasn't difficult to imagine it had faded completely. It was but an Indian trail, after all. They had to be going east. She glanced upward and found the sun.

Was it only early morning still? No, the sun was too high. Wasn't it? She thought they'd been walking for hours, but that could be an illusion. Carrying twenty-two pounds for any length of time seemed an eternity. It was hot, more like late morning, but it was also August, and the Minnesota heat rose early.

Stupid, stupid, stupid.

Hot wetness exploded under Frank, and the smell of urine filled the air.

"Frank peed, Mama."

Almena sighed. "He sure did." She guessed she should be thankful he hadn't soiled himself yet. Wet as his diaper was, it would fail to hold that, either.

"He stinks."

They all stank, she imagined.

"My feet hurt."

"Sit a little. I need to put Frank down for a while anyway."

They both sank to the ground. She shifted Frank to the grass and pain surged down her arm and into her hand. She grimaced and shook it until the sting eased and only numbness remained. Years of butter-making had made her arms strong, but, lord above, it hadn't prepared her for this!

"I didn't get no breakfast."

"I know, sweet one. I didn't either." She reached for one of his feet and took it in her hands, wincing at the sight of the bloodied cuts from the grass. "This hurt?"

"Yes'm."

She rubbed first one, then the other, hoping to ease his pain and her own numb fingers. He lay back, sighed, and fell asleep, his thin nightclothes up around his knees.

Almena shook her head. The light cotton would be a blessing through the day, but the boys would both be cold tonight. She'd need to find a sheltered spot before nightfall.

She lay on the grass next to them. The last time she'd left her home on foot with a little one had been twelve years ago with her brother Seneca. She'd thought herself frightened and uncertain, but it had been nothing. Nothing like now. After all, there'd been another home waiting at the end of that road.

Now there was naught. There was no home. There was no money, and there were no cows to help them survive. Her eyes stung with unshed tears.

Most of all, there was no Phin, with his laughing eyes and silly teasing.

There was only her, and she had no idea how she was going to hang on.

Christina
10:00 a.m.

It is like thunder, with twenty children coming downstairs at once.

"Go, go," Mrs. Everett urges from above.

They flood down with their faces dazed. Parents rush behind them, and the cabin is thick with people.

"Bell? Where's Bell?" Laura Duley is frantic, almost wild. She spins around like a *dreidel* to find her daughter.

Gott im Himmel, I think. It is all upside down. Parents run about hysterical and the children stand in stupors.

"Go to your mothers," I tell the older ones, those who are not so shocked and are looking around with terror on their faces. They have need of something to do.

Merton Eastlick herds his brothers close and shoos them to Lavina. Lillie Everett clutches her brother's hand. Emma Duley's mouth quivers even though she tries to hold it in a frozen line, but she has Bell with her. Laura sees them, puts her hand to her chest, and exhales a long, wavering sigh. Her hands are shaking. The Ireland girls dance around their mother, and I know they are nervous, because it is not how they usually behave. Julia Wright leads Dora and George outside to the sun.

Others follow in a desperate tide.

Laura and her children seem unable to move, and I go to her.

"Will they kill us? We can't leave here; we can't. There's a cellar. Can't we hide in the cellar?" Her voice has too much alarm, and I think her terror has taken over her mind.

"Listen to me, Laura Duley. You must hold on to yourself. You must be a leader for your children." I point to Emma. "Already Emma is so afraid she might break. Your husband is too busy telling the men what to do, so it is up to you. If you let go, what will happen to them?"

"But—"

"There is no choice. You will all die in the cellar if they burn the house. I think you must hold on now and go to pieces later, when this is over."

Laura draws in a breath and steers her children to the door. It is a good thing, that she finds a way to do this.

We must all find a way to do this. I think about what Lavina said to me, that the day could end with many women alone, their husbands dead. Widows.

I am a widow.

My shoulders quiver. My good, strong Andreas lies on the ground, shot dead. He will never hold me in his arms again or call me his *Leibchen* or tell me I am his *Ein und Alles*. I will never look into his soft, blue eyes.

I choke down my grief and my own worries. It does no good to do this now. The children will need the women to be strong. Already, they have noticed Laura's alarm and heard guns and whooping. It is not good if they are so panicked that they cannot be handled. This we do not need.

It will be a long day, and we must keep everyone moving.

"Are you coming," Mrs. Smith asks. "Christina?"

"*Ja.*"

I see I am the last one. I go out the door with one last look toward the supplies. I do not know how we will cross all the miles to New Ulm without food and blankets, but Julia is right. We cannot take the risk.

It would not be a wise thing to defy the Dakota at a time like this.

Laura
10:15 a.m.
We scrambled out onto the prairie, clutching our children close. I struggled to keep my fear at bay, glad that Christina forced me to surrender my selfishness and focus on my little ones. I'd lost too many children already. I would not, could not, lose my remaining family to those demons.

Ahead, Mira Everett began to run. Like falling dominoes, the rest of us followed suit. All but Julia Wright.

"Stop," she shouted. "We need to pace ourselves."

Everyone halted, a few running into those ahead of them.

"She's right," my William said. "Stay together. Hurry along, but don't run."

"Men, fan out around the women and children," Uncle Tommy advised.

Smith shouted, "Carry the littlest ones, and keep your kids together."

The men were full of instructions, but the women had already followed their instincts. They'd already clustered the children together and herded them as faithful sheepdogs caring for lambs.

"Mama!" someone called.

"Shhh, come along now."

A few followed along the Sioux Falls Trail, but most of us were stretched out on the prairie so we were not so bunched up. Older children parted the tall prairie grasses for their siblings, and we rushed forward. A few dogs ran among us, loyally following their masters.

I cast a look back. The eight Indians who had given their word to protect us remained at the cabin. The other group had now moved in and were plundering the house. A few had climbed onto the roof to watch our progress.

Tommy Ireland was pointing in that direction. "They're keeping watch."

"Move on! Don't look back," my William directed. "Don't give them cause."

We moved as quickly as we were able, more than thirty of us streaming forth. The uneven ground beside the trail dipped, and our party undulated down, then up as we encountered a rise. Though the hills were not high, the route was difficult, and we soon tired, not even a half mile from the cabin.

"The wagon!" Merton shouted.

We surged forward, over the crest.

Hatch and Rhodes were approaching, driving two horses and a wagon as fast as possible. They halted. The horses were lathered, their sides heaving.

"Up. Get them up."

We loaded the children in, bidding them to crowd together. Charlie Hatch began handing women up, and Rhodes followed suit.

As he lifted me into the wagon bed, I glanced west one final time. More Indians had clustered on the roof, gesturing at us with sharp, hostile movements. I could almost feel the intensity of their anger.

A chill flashed up my spine.

Julia
10:30 a.m.
Julia set George into the wagon and bent to pick up Dora.

"Sit and hang on tightly, little ones. I love you."

"Aren't you coming up?"

Julia eyed the wagon and the two horses. The poor animals were already tired, and it would be a heavy load. "I'll walk for a while."

Next to her, Lavina was handing up her own children. "I'll do the same," she said. "Merton, Frank . . . you two can stay with me."

Julia extended a smile and choked back resentment that the other women had settled in the bed of the wagon. A nip of guilt struck her, and she chided herself for being judgmental. Later, after they recovered a bit, they would walk.

"Let's go!" the men shouted.

Mrs. Smith, at the reins, gave them a slap, and the horses started off. The wagon lurched and moved forward.

Julia glanced back from the top of the rise. The Dakota had merged into one group.

What? Had she expected Pawn and Tizzie Tonka to come along?

She guessed there were thirty or forty in total, not the two hundred or more as they'd been told. A scare tactic, likely. She wasn't sure if Grizzly Bear had made the exaggeration or if Pawn had done so. In any case, it had worked.

They'd left as commanded.

But she had no doubt the Dakota lookouts on the roof had noticed that they'd taken horses, a wagon, and blankets with them.

Lavina
10:45 a.m.

The war call sounds out of nowhere when the wagon has gone a scant mile or so down the road. Laura screams. At once there is a panic in the wagon.

Julia is wide eyed with realization.

"Merton, Frank! On the wagon." I scale the front of the wagon box while the boys clamber into the back. Julia tosses her gun up, and the other women heave her into the box. The men rush aboard, crawling over children until every space is filled. Those who do not fit begin to run.

Mrs. Smith starts the horses, and we jerk forward at a crawl. Too slow! I grab the whip from its holder and fling it overhead, lashing the poor animals with all my strength. They flinch and strain but still manage no more than a walk.

"They are coming!" Christina yells.

"Move those horses faster!" William Duley shouts, as if I can do anything more. "Get a man up there."

I risk a look back. Dust plumes in the air. The Indians are chasing us, gaining on us.

"Ya!" I yell and lash the horses yet again. The shouts of the war party drown my words.

"We shouldn't have taken the wagon," Julia mutters.

"Stop!" Duley shouts. "Stop and leave the damn horses and wagon."

The men's voices converge as they all shout orders.

"Everybody out. Out now."

"Run for your lives."

"Men at the rear!"

"Do we shoot?"

"We need those horses, and I'll shoot any of them that touches them."

Women and children pour from the wagon. Merton jumps down, and I force little Johnnie into his arms. "Run, Merton, but do not let go of Johnnie. Don't let go. You are responsible for him."

He nods and rushes away.

I tumble from the wagon, stepping on the hem of my dress. The skirt rips from the waistband. I clutch it so I won't trip and rush the other children forward. Confusion and panic reign around us, and I struggle to keep them in my sight. The little ones whimper at being hurried, but the older children understand and push them forward. Women and children swarm across the prairie as the men stand firm. Julia grabs her husband's gun and takes her place with the men.

Shots fill the air but come from too far away. It won't be long until their fire will reach us. The Indians have spread out in a line, their horses rearing as they yell and whoop. They fire again.

We rush on, frantic. Children flinch as shots sound. Mothers urge them on, into the tall grass. So far, they have shot above our heads, but that could change at any moment, and we must get the children away.

Several of the Indians reach the wagon and dismount near our horses. They struggle with the harness, and one of them begins to cut through the leather with his knife.

"Grizzly Bear," Christina whispers beside me, "the chief."

Four shots ring out, and the Indian with the knife drops to the ground. The others jerk, wounded.

The shooters—Duley, Ireland, Everett, and my John—are lowering their guns to reload.

"Everyone into the slough!" Duley shouts.

We run downhill, into the tall reeds to hide. Shots rain upon us. Near me, the smallest Ireland girl stumbles and screams, her three-year-old voice shrill amid the gunfire. Two of the Duley children fall; Laura tows them into the marsh.

"Laura?" I whisper. "How bad?"

"Willie's hit in the shoulder, Emma in the arm."

On the road above, Smith and Rhodes run to the east, and the other men shout at them. One of them turns, and the Indians fire on them. They both rush down from the road into the far end of the slough.

"Julianne got it in the leg," Sophia Ireland says.

One by one, mothers report in low whispers. We keep our children still so the movement of the reeds does not give away our locations. Above, the Indians continue to fire, shots falling randomly into the quagmire.

We quiet, squatting in the wetness. My bare toes squish into the mud. The water isn't deep but creeps past my ankles, and my dress soaks it upwards. Despite the heat of the day, I shiver. Freddy's teeth chatter, and I hug him close to warm him. My little Johnnie's eyes are wide with fear, but he plops his bottom into the water and digs his hand through the mud. I make no move to chastise him, for the distraction fades his distress.

Dear lord in heaven, how can this be happening?

"Eastlick? Take a shot!" someone calls. My John has the best rifle among us and is a good marksman, so it's no wonder the other men call on him. The Indians show themselves only one or two at a time on the ridge above us, shooting before moving quickly out of range. Others pop up as the first group reloads. Each time our men fire, they reveal our places, draw more fire. Dull thuds sound as targets are found, quick gasps of pain, muted groans.

The balls fall fast, and my children flinch. I crawl through the stifling reeds, hot and sticky with sweat. Mud sucks at my hands and knees, but the children do not follow, so I halt and draw them close.

"Aaaah!" someone screams. Mira Everett, I think. "My neck."

Sharp pain explodes in my side. I bite my tongue but cannot stop the moan from escaping my lips.

"Lavina?" John calls.

"I'm hit."

"Are you much hurt?" His voice is tight.

"It feels like I'm dying."

The grasses move, and I gasp. "Stay still! There's nothing you can do, and you'll draw their fire. Just keep shooting."

White hot fire bursts in my head. I clutch my scalp with my hand. My mind clouds, throbbing. The thick, sticky blood seeps through my fingers, and at least I know I am still alive.

"They've noticed me. I'm moving," John whispers. He crawls away through the tall grass. My senses haze.

He reloads, the sounds crisp and distinct, then nothing. In the quiet, more thuds and gasps.

"John?"

He groans, so faintly I can barely hear him, and I inch toward him.

"Do not, for God's sake." Christina's plea halts me. "Stay with your children. If you stir, they will all be killed."

She whispers more, but I can no longer make out the words. In shock, I grasp for my boys.

The time stretches, and I no longer have any idea how long we have been here.

Nor how long we have yet to remain.

Christina
Late morning or early afternoon

"He is dead already, and you can do him no good. Stay put." I whisper the words to Lavina and hope she hears. I think that she does, because she no longer tries to crawl to John. She hugs her children, and I wonder if she will die, too. I think she has been shot in the head.

It is muggy in the slough. Flies and mosquitoes bite, but we dare not swat them. The mud here is stagnant and cloying. I think this will be a miserable place to die.

The sun is high in the sky, and I try to figure the time but cannot see enough. I know only that we have been here for some time. We whisper among ourselves, passing news.

"Rhodes and Smith ran," someone says. "I think they made it out the east end."

"Cowards." Tommy Ireland's voice is bitter, even in a whisper.

I am not sure I agree. A chance was there, and they took it. But I cannot imagine how Mrs. Smith must despair being left alone.

I wonder now if I should also have fled at dawn, when I had a chance. I could be safe, fleeing east on the prairie. Regret claws at me but lasts only a second. I would not have made more than a few steps before turning back. Leaving all the others to die when I had the chance to warn them, to spare them, would have plagued my soul forever. I could not have left them.

"Charlie's shot," Mira Everett says. "He's got two shotguns but can't raise them."

I hear the panic in her voice and know what she is planning. If she crawls to him, she will show where she is.

"Do not go," I tell her.

"I know. He told me already. He has the guns ready, if they come into the slough, and will fire with his other hand."

"I think Duley's shot in the wrist," someone says, passing news along the line.

"I think there are many of us shot," Mira says.

Too many.

I do not know what to say to her. "Does it hurt bad?" I finally ask.

"I can't feel much anymore." She pauses. "There's so much blood."

"Can I do anything?" Empty words, even to me.

"If I die, promise you will tell Will and the children I love them."

I shudder. "*Ja*, I will promise this, but you will not die."

I say the words to her, but I do not believe it. I think that we will all die here in this miserable swamp.

Chapter Sixteen
August 20, 1862
Difficult Choices
2:00 p.m.–4:00 p.m.

Julia

The endless day wore on as Julia sat in the mud, George and Dora on either side.

"I gotta potty," George whispered, his voice urgent.

"Me, too." Dora wriggled, and Julia halted her with a sharp glance.

"Just go." Why not add the reek of urine to the sluggish mud and stench of blood and black powder?

"Right here?" George asked.

"In our clothes?" Dora's voice held shock at the suggestion.

"Shhh . . ." Julia whispered, "we're all wet anyway."

George giggled, and Julia felt his warm urine heat against her hip. He squirmed, and a muddy cloud rose. She stilled him with the same look she'd given Dora.

Dora worried her lip, distress pulling her mouth down as she continued to hold her bladder.

Aw, hell. The poor little thing had learned her manners well.

"Go ahead," Julia encouraged. "We might as well all go." She heaved a sigh and released her own bladder into the slop so that Dora would know it was all right. Moments later, Dora made a face and peed.

Julia's attention focused on the sounds around her . . . or lack thereof. The gunfire from the slough had all but stopped. She rejoiced that shots no longer drew return rallies from the

Dakota, but only for a second.

My God, they're dead.

She shuddered. She still had Jack's gun but had long since set it aside. Thank heavens she'd had the sense to do so. There had been little hope of killing any of the Dakota, and she hadn't wanted to risk the children's lives in a useless attempt to do so. Tremors consumed her as she thought it through. She'd be as dead as the men had she not done so.

Who the hell fired anyway? And at Grizzly Bear!

If they'd gone on foot, without resisting, they might have had a chance.

It would have been much easier to kill the settlers back at the cabin, if that had been the Dakotas' intent. Instead, the group had won a concession, only to waste it away by killing the Dakota leader.

She shook as bitter anger plowed its way through her core. It wouldn't have been this way. She *knew* it. The rage ran into her grief and fear, and the emotions scattered in a thousand directions. She sucked breaths in, one after the other, and wondered if there would be any way out of this.

Pawn had risked his stature by bargaining for their lives. She knew this, even if the others didn't. And they'd brought shame upon him when they broke their word. They'd behaved with dishonor and disrespect, and she doubted there was much that would help them now.

"Are you tired of fighting?" one of the Dakota called.

"Women, come out so you will not die," said another. Pawn?

"Go to hell, you heathens!" Everett shouted back.

"Everett? You have called me friend, but now I am your enemy?" Pawn said.

"You said you would defend us."

Pawn continued, "Come out with the women, Everett, and we will talk."

"I'm wounded. I can't walk. You come to me."

"You lie. I think you can walk if you wish."

Two shots rang in the air.

"Will!" Mira shouted.

Everett whispered, "My elbow's shattered. Tell him I'm dead."

The grass moved, and Mira Everett rose from the slough, wavering on her feet. Blood soaked the side and front of her gown.

"You've killed him," she called out. "He's dead." Her voice quivered with despair.

"Come out and talk peace, and we will stop shooting," Pawn told her. "We will talk how to let the women and children live, and I will take you and Julia Wright into my tepee."

Mira glanced down at her husband.

"It might be best," he whispered. "Obey for now, escape when you can. Otherwise, I think they'll kill you."

"Lavina, will you come with me?" Mira said.

"I don't think I know enough of the language to negotiate with them. Besides, my head . . ." Lavina's words were soft, pained.

Mira turned. "Julia?"

Julia sighed. She and Mira knew the language best. She kissed her children's foreheads, hoping like hell she was making the right choice.

"I'll go, if Christina will keep George and Dora."

"I will do this."

Julia stood, her pulse loud in her head. "Do not shoot my children," she called. "They are moving to Mrs. Koch."

She waited while they crawled to her friend. Christina would have the strength to keep them safe, if things went wrong. She turned to Mira. "Are you ready?"

Julia slogged toward her, mud sucking at her feet. Her dress was heavy with water, and she shivered as the air hit her.

"You're weaving. Can you walk?" Julia asked.

Mira nodded, wincing as her neck muscles strained at the wound. "I'm faint, but the pain has mostly numbed."

"Blood loss. Try to avoid moving your head." Julia wrapped an arm around her neighbor's side, and Mira leaned into her. "Let's go."

Now that she was standing, she saw the clouds building to the west, and she prayed the storm would skirt them. That was the last thing they needed right now.

She ushered Mira forward. "Be strong and choose your words with care," she whispered. "What happens next depends upon us."

"Do you still trust Pawn?"

"We didn't keep our promises. He spoke for us, and we've brought dishonor on him. I don't know how much influence he has anymore or how he feels."

They emerged from the slough and struggled up the hill, crested the ridge.

Pawn stood just beyond, amid a pair of Dakota Julia didn't recognize. She nodded to him, an acknowledgment of his superiority.

"It is good you come to speak, Julia Wright," he said.

"We are honored you asked us to do so."

He motioned for them to sit, and the trio joined them on the ground. Pawn gestured to the others. "We will speak in Dakota so all may understand."

Mira looked at Julia. "My Dakota is not good. You will need to speak for us."

Julia knew Mira had to be part of this. It was a duty she did not want to shoulder alone. "If Mrs. Everett does not understand, I must tell her in English. If I do not understand, I must ask you to use English. We have much responsibility."

Pawn grunted an agreement. "There is much disagreement among the Santee, and the Sisseton are only a small voice. Our brothers, the Mdewakanton and Wakpekute, are much displeased with your people and have attacked many settlements in the past days."

He paused, and Julia relayed the information to Mira, explaining that these were three tribes of the eastern Sioux known collectively as Santee, whom she called Dakota because of their dialect. Pawn was a Sisseton, several villages of which populated this part of the state.

"Many whites have been killed, but some have been spared on the promise they will leave. Even among the Sisseton, there are those who wish to kill the whites rather than let them leave these lands. Even among those here today, there is disagreement. I asked my brother Grizzly Bear to let you go, but, when his terms were broken, I had no power." He stopped again, waiting to make sure the women understood.

At their assent, he continued. "Now, Grizzly Bear is dead at the hands of your men. There is a thirst for vengeance and much confusion among his followers. For now, I have been delegated to speak on behalf of all here, but my power is not strong. Because I spoke for the whites and they did not keep their word, I have been cast between your world and ours. Do you understand this?"

Shots rang out from the area of the slough, and the women jumped.

Oh God, oh God.

Mira glanced at Julia, her eyes wide with fear, and she looked ready to jump up. Julia reached for her and placed her hand on her leg, shaking her head with steady intent. Mira quieted.

Julia drew a breath and searched for the right words. "I understand what you have said and wish you to know, in the white world, women have very little voice. Our men act without consulting us and often do not have clear understanding of the impact their actions have. I am honored you are speaking with two women, but we, too, have limited power."

She halted, hoping she had worded things correctly. If she had, the Dakota would know she had integrity and had made promises in good faith. If others broke the promises she made, the Dakota would know she did not intend that to happen. This would save Pawn face among the Dakota and might help gain her family's safety, should things go wrong.

"I see that we understand one another. I have asked my brothers to spare the women and children, and this they have agreed. There must be no resistance, and all must do as they are told. If that does not happen, my brothers will view any promises to be dishonored. We will take with us those who are able, but we will take no men, and we will not take those who are unable to keep up with us."

"I understand." The survivors, women and children only, would be taken with the Dakota; the severely wounded would be left behind with the men. It was harsh, but it was more than she'd hoped for.

She didn't ask if those left behind would be killed. She didn't want to know. Either outcome was too bitter to think about.

"You must also know that there is much anger among Grizzly Bear's people. His wife and mother mourn him and wish revenge, as do the families of the others killed. I have been given power to negotiate with you, but there is much dissent among the bands here. I will do my best to honor what has been said, but it is a risk."

"I will do my best to honor the agreement we make, but there is much anger among the settlers as well, and many do not view things as I do."

"I see we understand one another."

"Let me now make sure Mrs. Everett has understood and see if she agrees."

"This you may do."

Julia faced Mira. "Did you understand what he said?"

"That the Santee tribes are attacking many settlements. Those here disagree about what to do with us. We broke the promise we made this morning when we tried to take the wagon and shot Grizzly Bear and the others. Some wish to kill us all but allowed Pawn to negotiate. We must agree to surrender without resistance. They will spare those who are able to walk. If we agree, we do so knowing there is a risk that some may still be violent."

"That's what I heard, too."

"What about those who are injured? Will they save them?"

"I don't think so. He said they will leave those who are unable to come with them."

Mira shuddered. "Will they be killed or just left here?"

Oh, Mira. Her husband would be among that group.

"I don't know. I fear to ask."

"And if we don't agree to this?" Mira blinked, hard.

Julia clutched her hand. "I think they will kill us all."

"We haven't much choice, do we?"

"I'll ask that we be allowed to confer with the others."

"That's the best we can do."

Julia asked for permission to return to the slough and consult with those there.

Pawn looked to the other men, and they spoke before he turned back to Julia. "You may do this, but you must decide soon, or my brothers will withdraw the offer. When you come back, you will bring the guns with you."

Laura

When Julia and Mira started from the slough to speak with Pawn, I crouched low, with the children still close around me. I clutched my handkerchief in my pocket, worrying it through my fist. I couldn't fathom how they could trust that vile creature yet again. Had he not already betrayed us?

"I'll shoot that son of a bitch," William muttered from beside me. "Now, while he's up there waiting for them. It's too good a chance to throw away. They're going to kill us all sooner or later, and he'll be one less to deal with." He began to rise from the slough.

"No, Husband, no!" I called, the other women chorusing the same.

Ice cold fear sliced through me. If William stood and shot, he would surely draw fire to us, and we would all perish. "If you do so, you will be shot. I beg you, stay alive! Stay alive and escape from here. Go to New Ulm and relay what has happened."

He eased back to the ground, and I sighed with relief that he had, for once, listened to me. My children would be safe. I couldn't lose any more children, not like this.

Tommy Ireland rose, shouting that the women and children must be saved. Before the words were out of his mouth, buckshot exploded. Two of the Indians had moved to the edge of the slough, shooting him at close range. Blood erupted from his chest and several other wounds.

Ireland fell. "Oh God, I am killed." The choked words were enough to quiet any others who had thoughts of rising.

Muffled screams echoed through the reeds, Mrs. Ireland's among them.

Stuttering sounds poured from my mouth, and my entire

body shook. Emma and Will, Jr. quieted me with gentle words, and I went limp.

Christina

Buckshot explodes, and I throw myself over Julia's children. Tommy Ireland calls out, and I know he was the one. I think that the men have almost all been wounded now. Why they keep making challenges I do not know.

We wait. The silence is long. In it, I hear insects buzz and children whimper. It is a strange mix, the peace of nature and the fearful cries of children. Mothers comfort, but their voices hold panic.

I hold George and Dora close. Dora is five, and she draws stuttered breaths. I know she understands more than her brother. George seems only to be bothered by having to sit still.

"*Ach*, do not worry so," I tell Dora and ruffle her blond hair. "Your mama is talking with them, and she will make sure we are safe."

"Will they kill her?"

"*Nein*. They respect her." I think of my friend, who is married to such a man as Jack Wright, who has no respect from anyone. She worries so about how we regard her. She does not know how much we think of her. I am glad of her. She will be our way out of this slough, I think, if only the men will stop their fighting.

We are quiet again, waiting. Julia and Mira return. Julia wades back into the slough to where most of us cluster. The reeds shake as she nears.

"If the women and children come out and do not resist, we will be spared to the best of Pawn's ability."

She does not say anything more but lets us discuss the offer. I hear in her words what she does not say more about: to the best of his ability. I wonder if the others have heard this, but I do not raise questions. I think that it will only lead to argument and make the men rise up again.

"Do you think they will honor their word?" someone asks.

"I think it will depend on us, how well we obey," Julia answers. "If we resist at all, I don't know what will happen."

"If we don't go, what will happen?" Laura asks.

"I think we'll all be killed," Mira says.

"This is our only chance," I say.

Julia stands tall among us. "You all need to know there is much anger among them. They've attacked many settlements, and Grizzly Bear's death makes them unstable. Pawn will do his best."

Lavina groans. "You can't still trust him?"

"I don't believe he is lying, but he's one man among many." Julia glances around. "What do you say? We don't have much time before the offer expires."

I rise. "I will go."

One by one, women agree and move out of this wet, sucking place. Each step bogs us down, and I pick up George. Dora holds my hand. Julia moves about, gathering rifles and shotguns. Three Indians wait for us at the edge of the marsh.

Lavina comes with four of her boys. Merton carries the baby, Johnnie. Frank and Giles help Lavina, who has been shot and has trouble walking. She puts her hands on their shoulders and limps along. She stops and whispers, "John."

She crumples.

As I walk past her, she is clutching her dead husband. He lies with his rifle in one hand and the other over his face. His hat is still on his head. His dog, who rushed after us, lies beside him. Lavina weeps over him and takes his hand in hers. "Oh, John." She whispers words of love and kisses him on his brow. Then she rises and continues with the boys. All of them carry sorrow on their faces but remain strong for her, I think. I do not know if she even comprehends Freddy is missing.

I pass Tommy Ireland. He is still alive, but blood and froth ooze from the hole where he is shot. I think it is his lung. His wife and children bend over him, saying good-bye. I do not think he will remain long, he gurgles so. They rise and leave him, trudging as they go.

Julia stops and picks up his gun.

"Please, Julia, end this for me. Shoot me before you go."

"Oh, Uncle Tommy . . . I wish so much I could help, but I can't kill a friend, even to ease his suffering." She bends and takes his hand. "I am so sorry."

Ireland closes his eyes, and Julia moves away to join me where we wait for her.

"Charlie Hatch lives," she whispers. "I left a gun with him. Mrs. Smith is wounded in the hip, and she can't move. Ireland's little Sarah got buckshot in the bowels."

"Dead?"

"Not quite. But her face is splotched, and she's spitting blood and foam. I think it won't be long."

I shake my head, numb. We reach solid ground and join the others. There are no men.

Six Dakota surround us and command us to sit.

The sky darkens with clouds. They build and churn, signs of a coming storm.

Almena

Almena's feet ached. Beside her, William Henry cried to be carried. Frank whimpered on her hip. She sank to the ground and sighed. She should have come to a road by now.

The air grew heavy, darkness creeping upon them. She glanced up. Heavy, gray clouds roiled overhead. The wind rose with them, its violent force building.

"I'm hungry," William Henry pleaded. "Please, Mama."

"There isn't any food. Mama has nothing to give you."

"My tummy hurts."

"Mine, too. Come on, let's go a little further."

They gained their feet and moved on, plodding at a three-year-old's pace. The wind built. Thunder cracked and lightning flashed above them, and the rain began. Sharp torrents poured down on them, stinging in their force.

William shivered against her wet skirt, his thin nightclothes drenched and dripping.

Almena gathered him up, settling his thirty-plus pounds on her left hip. Frank clung to her right hip. She shifted, trying to balance their combined weight, and trudged on, forcing one foot in front of the other.

Hold on. Hold on to them. They can't do this without you.

The boys wrapped their legs about her the best they could, struggling for purchase. Finally, they clutched each other's arms tight around her middle and fell asleep, heavy with fatigue.

She trudged on, the dead weight of their limp, sleeping bodies growing more arduous with each step. Her arms throbbed. The sodden tendrils of her hair plastered themselves against her face.

One step. Two.

She saw nothing but the rain streaming down on them amid the growing darkness.

Surely, they'd come to the road soon. Surely.

Lavina

I edge away from John, refusing to cry further. My boys have need of me, and I must be strong for them. I will grieve him later, when I am able to do so. For now, I must be strong. This is the only way to get my children through this.

The sky above is turbulent, thunder and lightning moving

fast upon us. The Indians hurry to catch their ponies. We will soon be moving away. The clouds unleash a torrent of rain, and we shiver with cold, drenched to our cores.

I emerge from the slough, dazed. One of the Indian men takes Christina Koch with him; another herds one of the Ireland girls. A third approaches me. He already has Laura Duley by one hand, and he grabs me with the other. Laura's shoulders are slumped in defeat, and I resolve to go with as much grace as possible. I will not surrender my strength.

"Laura," I whisper, "be strong."

She lifts her head. Despair fills her face.

The Indian hauls us along. I go without resistance but not in defeat. Within steps, it dawns on me that my boys are not here.

I stop, turning back to the slough. Where are my boys?

Freddy, my five year old, rises from the grass. "Mama!" he calls out and begins to run to me.

A squaw, hideous and old, runs into the slough and chases Freddy, yelling something about Lean Bear.

"Freddy!" I call, wrenching to go to him. My captor holds me tight, and I struggle to break away.

The woman reaches Freddy and knocks him on the back of the head with something, a rock, perhaps. His face fills with terror, and he slumps.

I thrash against my captor. Still, the hag beats Freddy, again and again with her weapon . . . until she doesn't.

For the first time, tears flood my eyes. *Oh, my boy!*

Somehow, Freddy rises, unsteady but alive. Blood streams from his nose, his mouth, his ears. He looks at me, glazed, and starts forward.

The woman rushes back to him and hammers at him again and again. Finally, she stops, lifts him up and dashes him upon the ground.

Never Let Go

"Let me go," I beg and tug repeatedly but am too weak to get away.

When Freddy is still upon the ground, the squaw takes out a knife.

My captor jerks my arm and drags me along with him. He hauls us across the prairie, Laura in one hand, me in the other. At the slough, the woman leaves my Freddy and grabs Laura's four year old, Bell, who is running to catch up with us. Laura screams and wrestles with our captor. He strives to keep his hold on the two of us.

"Mother! Mother!" It is Frank's voice, and I look to him. My ten year old stands with blood streaming from his toothless mouth. His thigh and abdomen drip blood. I startle, realizing I hadn't even known when he was shot.

I wrench from my captor's grasp. He lets me fall and drags Laura away.

Pawn passes by with Julia and her children. He orders them upon a horse, sends them toward the others who are running west to the shelter of the cabins. Pawn returns to me and orders me to rise and go after Julia.

"Go," he says. "You can do them no good. That is Grizzly Bear's mother, and she takes their lives because their father killed her son."

I struggle to my feet and turn toward the slough.

"It will be worse for them if you go back."

My heart breaks into pieces and stabs into me in a thousand places. I take a step, stop. It is like Solomon telling me I must cut them in half! To leave them goes against all my instincts and rips me apart. Yet, if I go, and they are cruelly murdered . . . I collapse, unable to move.

Mira Everett runs back into the slough to her husband. An Indian pursues as another fires at her. She falls, wounded in the back.

Another shot rings out, and Laura screams. Her oldest son, wounded earlier, has fallen a few steps from her. She screams again and pleads with Pawn to spare her other children. She stands with Frances in one arm, Emma clutching her other hand. Jefferson runs toward her, desperately fleeing the slough. Bell is not with them, and I fear Lean Bear's mother has killed her as she did my Freddy. She cannot know which man fired the fatal shot, and perhaps her revenge will be upon us all.

Laura's face is pale, haunted, and filled with anguish, but her eyes are full of fierce protectiveness. I know how much this costs her, to be so strong. When Pawn tells her the others will be spared, she turns and rushes the remaining children away. Willie lies where he fell.

In that moment, I know I must leave Frank and Freddy. I can do nothing to help them. Three other boys depend on me to assure their safety.

Pawn returns and stands over me, leaning on his gun.

"What do you intend to do with me? Will you kill me, too?" I ask him.

"You must go with the others. You must hurry."

I crawl to my feet and limp after the others, refusing to look back at the boys I am leaving. Each step is full of agony. I struggle to hurry, but the distance between me and the others widens. My head has stopped throbbing where the ball settled. The wound in my side bleeds with each step; I no longer feel it. I risk a glance back and see Pawn reloading his gun. I try to hurry more. I enter a small slough and wade through it, following the others. Weakness swallows me, and I fall behind.

White-hot pain explodes in the small of my back. The ball rips through me and passes through my lower right arm. I fall to the ground, face down, and lie there, waiting. I'm on the trail and know the Indians will find me, so I crawl away from it, inching my way with my good arm, unable to use my legs at all.

Footsteps approach. I hold my breath, pretending to be dead.

From the corner of my eye, I spy a man's moccasins, the butt of a rifle. He stands, watching me. Surely he will think me dead. He must. But he doesn't. He swings his rifle up.

Blows land upon the back of my head, so hard that my head bounces on the hard ground. Again and again until I lose count and can only focus on the throbbing pain shooting through me. He strikes my right shoulder in the same way. I tell myself to hold my breath, but I can't do so. I nearly smother, my face pushed deeply into the ground. I gasp and gasp.

Finally, the blows stop, and I realize he believes me to be dying.

I'm numb with fear and don't think I will even feel it if he reaches down and cuts into my head to scalp me.

Chapter Seventeen
August 20, 1862
The Long Night
4:00 p.m. through morning

Julia

Julia rode back toward Lake Shetek, George and Dora in front of her on Pawn's horse. They shivered, rain pouring down upon them. Their lives were now in Pawn's hands, and she hoped she'd laid the groundwork for his continued respect and that she could negotiate their captivity in a way that didn't destroy it.

She tried not to think about what was happening behind her, the men and women still lying in the slough, clinging to life. Whether they would be left to suffer and die slow, agonizing deaths or whether they would be savagely killed by Dakota with anger in their hearts, she didn't want to contemplate. Neither was a vision she wanted in her head, and the definition of "mercy" was no longer clear to her.

Back in the slough, Mira Everett had said a brief silent good-bye with her solemn eyes. Then, she'd run back to her husband and certain death. Julia tried not to mourn her closest neighbor, told herself it was a choice Mira had made and that she had understood the consequences. Julia wished her a quick and peaceful end.

The killings she had witnessed lingered more strongly.

She'd looked back, seen Lavina fall, and watched the Dakota man lift his rifle and bring it down on her head.

We will not take those who are unable to keep up with us.

Never Let Go

She hadn't watched any more than that, had kept her eyes focused ahead. But she'd been unable to keep herself from flinching as she heard the shots and screams from those who had been deemed too injured to keep up.

Julia accomplished the three miles to the Ireland cabin, where Pawn had told her the Dakota would be encamped, in a surreal haze and reined the horse to a stop. Lodges and bustling people filled the usually calm home site. The cabin had been built on a point of land surrounded by a slough on one side, the lake on another. It was one of the most idyllic areas of the settlement.

Until tonight.

Rough hands jerked the children from her, and she gasped. *No, not my children.*

In the next instant, someone grabbed her off the horse and threw her to the ground.

"White squaw too proud," said one of the women. "You now a dog."

Another woman spat at her, the glob landing square on her chest.

Julia fought the urge to stand tall and lowered her eyes instead. These people were angry, still driven by the emotion of warfare, and challenge would do her no good. Instead, she needed to draw on everything she'd learned about the Dakota these past few years.

"Pawn sent us to the camp and will follow." She used the Dakota language and kept her tone submissive, hoping the strategy of conveying she was under Pawn's protection was enough to forestall a beating.

The women glared at her, but Julia knew her words had worked. They were uncertain if she was to be a prisoner or Pawn's personal property. One of them *tsk*ed and pointed to a familiar-looking tepee. "Wait there."

She started toward his lodge, the children on either side of her. "Keep your eyes lowered," she told them.

"Julia!"

She turned and saw Christina being led into camp by one of the men.

He jerked on Christina's arm, muttered a few words, and slapped her. She recoiled, defiance in her eyes. That would not bode well for her. He dragged her to a teepee near Pawn's and dumped her on the ground.

Julia resisted the urge to help her up. Instead she told the children to wait and crossed the open area. She looked around and bent to speak to her friend before those in the camp noticed them.

"They'll come soon; there isn't much time. Stay meek, eyes down, don't talk unless spoken to, and use their language. This is war for them, and they may not treat us well."

"Will they kill us?"

"No, but they may beat us. The Dakota don't often take captives, usually only to adopt them into the tribe. This is different, fueled by anger and revenge. I sense they may not agree on what to do with us. Pawn said some of the leaders wanted to kill all the whites. Everything is in chaos, and I can't predict what will happen. Don't be defiant. Watch what they do and do things the same way. If one of the men takes you as a wife, you'll be the lowest in the tepee. Work hard and do as you are told, and you have a chance."

"*Ja*, I understand. Will . . . will the men . . . will they . . . ?"

Julia understood her unspoken words. *Will they rape us?*

She tempered her fear, knowing there was nothing she could do about the situation. "In their culture, women who are taken are welcomed as part of the family and become respected new wives, but this is war. It could change things."

"I cannot do that, I cannot."

"If that does happen and you don't submit, you risk being killed. And, if you're made a wife, it will be expected of you." Julia paused and touched her friend's cheek. "I can't make that decision for you; it's up to you. Just understand what may happen before you do so."

"*Ja*, I will think."

"I need to go back to Pawn's lodge, before the women return. Stay strong, and we'll get through this." She hugged Christina, then rushed across the small stretch of open ground to George and Dora.

Everything she did, from this point forward, would be for them.

She tapped against the side of the tepee, guessing that they were meant to wait inside, hoping they wouldn't be beaten for doing so. She'd never seen the Dakota display such anger. When there was no answer, she lifted the flap. "Come," she said, holding open the flap until the children entered, Dora grim, George curious. She slipped into the darkened tepee, lit by a low fire in the center.

Lord, how good that fire feels.

Blessedly, there was no one else inside. That would change soon. Pawn's wives were no doubt being informed about the prisoners and would come soon. She knew her moments alone with the children would be short.

Dances in Water had been a friend, but she didn't know his first wife. She hoped Dances in Water would remember their visits and speak for her.

Around the fire, sleeping robes lined the circular perimeter of the lodge. Cooking pots and other household goods were still bundled, yet to be unpacked. Julia's gaze rested on the sleeping robes, knowing that she would be taken to one of them and made Pawn's wife. She wouldn't resist, not with George and

Dora needing her. She would do what was necessary to assure they were treated well.

She settled them on a buffalo robe near the fire. "Dry near the fire, my little ones, then you can sleep."

Once the two were seated, Julia paced back and forth, letting the warmth of the fire reach her own damp clothing. Her mind was too busy to sit. She hoped she could vanquish the demons so she could deal with what was at hand.

A short time later, the flap opened, and she steeled herself. But it was Pawn who entered the lodge, not his women.

"Julia Wright, I am glad you are at my fire. Please sit."

She exhaled, relieved that they would talk rather than moving directly to the robes. Near the fire, George and Dora slept. She moved each of them to a robe and sat near the fire where Pawn had already taken his seat.

"I am honored you have asked us here," she said, keeping her voice humble and her eyes downcast.

"It has been a day with much regret."

Wasn't that the truth!

"It has," she agreed.

Pawn lifted her chin so that their gazes met. "You understand there are many bands here, many chiefs?"

She'd thought as much.

"Did you know the others were attacking?" The words she'd wanted to ask all day leaped out, and she drew a breath, hoping she'd not been too forward.

Pawn shrugged. "Attacks on settlements started several days ago. I did not think Shetek would be spared."

She ached to ask him if he had come to camp there for that reason, if he had meant to intervene, but she wasn't sure if it was her place to do so. "How many bands came here?" she asked instead, hoping to gain a sense of the bigger picture and how she was to fit into it.

"Those of White Lodge and Grizzly Bear are here. Part of Sleepy Eye's band, some from Limping Devil's two villages."

She'd heard the names, had recognized Grizzly Bear from his prior visits to Lake Shetek. They were small bands of Sisseton that chose to live away from the reservation. If she had her facts right, there were five such villages and five on the reservation. She wasn't sure how many bands comprised them.

"And these are the bands that are attacking?"

"All of the Sisseton, most of the Wahpeton and Mdewakanton and Wahpekute."

My God, nearly all of the Santee. The entire state was under attack. Had her husband been killed on the prairie between New Ulm and Lake Shetek? Was she, too, a widow? Though she hadn't loved Jack for a long time, she sent a prayer he had managed to survive.

"I belong to Grizzly Bear's band. He was the one I spoke to at your cabin."

She pushed her mind to process what he was saying, what he had not articulated. She thought he was trying to give her a renewed sense of his limitations. "So you are only one voice here, and not a chief?" she asked, to clarify.

"I am a small voice, Julia Wright. I did what I could. I will try to keep you safe. Some of the leaders wished to kill the whites. Grizzly Bear and White Lodge were at the war council when the fighting started. They were among those who wished to kill all the whites. Others said they would not kill if the whites left. Today, I reminded them you have been a friend and have treated us with respect. I did not want to see your people killed."

And there it was, her answer. He had sought to intervene, had not tricked the settlers. That knowledge would make things easier, when he claimed her.

"Am I to be your wife?" she asked. Better to know for sure.

"It will go better for you if you are a wife. There is much

anger, and I do not know if our traditions will be honored. Making you a wife will keep you under my protection."

"And the other women?"

He shrugged. "In normal times, my people would treat them well, but these are not normal times, and many say kinship should not be offered to the whites this time. White Lodge says he will keep the captives for ransom, to protect our bands from white attacks, and they will not become part of our people. There is much discontent, much disagreement. Some say they will be made slaves."

She shut her eyes, thinking it through. They would fare better as wives than property. "The children?"

"Some may be adopted in the usual Dakota way, or they may also become slaves. No one knows what should be done."

"You have two other wives?"

"Yes. You already know Dances in Water. My first wife is Speaks with Strong Tongue. They are honorable women. You will not be mistreated."

"I understand."

"I must go, now, to take part in the celebration. My wives will come and tell you what you are to do."

He rose and strode toward the door, then turned.

"Know, Julia Wright, that you must not disrespect me or my wives. If that happens, you *will* be punished. Tell your children this when they waken."

He lifted the flap and exited, leaving her to ponder what, exactly, he had meant by "disrespect."

Laura

The Indian man yanked me along with him. My feet moved of their own volition. My soul was in shreds, left behind with Willie and Bell, their lives so violently wrenched from them. Oh, to see

Bell beaten so and not be able to intervene! I could not fathom the reasons for such cruelty and was glad my William was among those who shot the men who were taking the horses. I hoped his was a kill shot, and I hoped those men's families were suffering as I was.

I would never again consider the Dakota to be friends but would instead forever view them as savages.

Frances was still in my arms, heavy and limp with sleep, her poor little body drenched. Somehow, I'd managed to hold on to her through all of this torturous day. Emma and Jefferson trotted next to me, clutching my wet skirts. They were all I had left. Grief and despair threatened, and I choked it all back. I could not let it take hold, could *not* let it paralyze me. Not now. I had to hang on for these three who were left.

The Indian jerked my arm, and I stumbled to my knees. He let go, and I realized we had entered the camp and were in front of a tepee. I'd been so involved in my thoughts that I'd not noticed. The man opened a flap and pointed inside. I crawled in, the children following. Christina Koch was huddled near the fire. Her blond hair hung about her face, her tidy braid long gone.

I rose, intent on seeking warmth and speaking to Christina. Emma and Jefferson were shivering. Once at the fire, they smiled for the first time since morning, but they said nothing, the horrors of the day likely rendering them mute.

I laid Frances on a robe and shook out my deadened arm.

"I am so sorry, my friend," Christina said. She embraced me, held me close for a few moments.

"We lost so many," I said.

It sounded inane. I thought of my husband, of Willie and Bell left at the slough. It was painfully obvious there had been severe losses and hardly needed stating. Still, I was unable to say much else and fought to keep my sobbing under control.

"Julia survives," Christina said in the vacuum of silence. "She says we must obey, that the Dakota are very angry. We may be taken as wives or become slaves."

Slaves. I shuddered at the thought. Oh, to be brought so low that women of standing should be slaves. Did these people not know we were respected leaders of our community?

A rustle sounded, and I looked toward the entrance. Two women stepped in and glared at us. I trembled at their hostility. Thank heavens their tunics were not bloodstained. I would have fainted had they been the hags who killed my precious children.

The two, both around my age, muttered together. I knew very little of their language and couldn't make out their words. One of them came to us, shoved Jefferson down, and seized Emma's hand.

No.

I stepped to them, and she slapped my face, saying something in a bitter tone. I hadn't even the chance to bring my hand to comfort my stinging cheek before she grabbed it and dragged both Emma and me toward the door. I glanced back at Jefferson. His eyes were filled with fear.

"She says to come," Christina told me. "We are to work."

I tried to scuttle away, to return to my little ones, but I was yanked out of the tepee. Outside, the woman released Emma, pointed to pots, and motioned for Emma to pick one up. She turned her bony finger on me and glared.

Pick up the pot. Just pick it up.

I nodded, and she released my hand. I glanced back to the tepee flap, fear flooding me at what might happen to Jefferson and Frances in my absence. The squaw raised her hand. I stopped, remembering the sharp sting on my cheek, and picked up the pot.

Christina already held hers.

The squaw marched away. We followed. We were near the

Never Let Go

lake, at the Ireland cabin. The contents of the cabin were strewn about, feather ticks ripped to shreds as if their value meant nothing to these coarse beings. That they preferred to sleep on the ground rather than in comfort told me volumes. We went to the lake, gathered water, and trudged back to the tepee.

"What happens next?" I whispered to Christina.

The woman turned and spoke to us, her guttural gibberish harsh on my ears. It was hard to imagine that I had treated them with such charity, only to be repaid with murder.

Again, I hoped my William's shot had been one of those that downed her clansman.

Christina replied to her, then spoke to me. "We are not to talk, except for me to relay her words."

I looked around the camp to take my mind from the injustice of it all. There were many tepees, twenty or thirty at least. People bustled, all of them busy. The women never stopped moving, and the children played as if the events of the day were nothing out of the ordinary. The Ireland girls were ordered about, but I kept my head down and did not interact with them. Heaven only knew what might happen if I did.

The afternoon edged into evening; all the time we were kept busy with chores. Thankfully, the rain eased, though the air grew chilly, and I craved the fire once again.

A large meal had been prepared, each tepee contributing. The scent of roasting beef filled the camp. Our cows, I supposed. Our vegetables likely filled their pots, too. The heady aromas lingered, and my stomach rumbled.

Emma glanced at me once and opened her mouth to talk, but I shook my head, and she held her words. We sat where we were directed and listened to our impatient stomachs until the Sioux had all eaten before we were allowed to have our meals. We gobbled them with no regard to manners, and I wiped my greasy fingers with my handkerchief, the only napkin at hand. I glanced around, looking for the tepee where we'd left Jefferson and Frances.

"They eat. You stay." The words were barked in clipped English by a nearby woman.

I stayed, holding Emma close as we finished our meals. The camp swelled as more Indians arrived. The circle around the main campfire grew as they joined those already there.

"Pawn new chief," the woman said. "We dance."

Several Indians stood and formed a circle. Drums and chanting sounded. They jumped and twisted, their feet hammering in a strange, barbaric rhythm. The children trampled in the shadows, mimicking the adults.

Christina edged closer and whispered to me. "Did you hear her? That Pawn is to be the new chief."

"I thought he was a chief," I muttered.

"Grizzly Bear was. He was one of those shot at the wagon."

I sucked in my breath. "Our men shot the chief?"

"*Ja*, they were very angry with us."

Yes, and we were very angry that they killed our husbands and children!

One of the Indian women returned. "No white talk," she ordered. As the woman stood guard, Emma fell asleep, her head on my lap, and the evening grew ever darker and the dancing more frenzied, furious.

Later, the woman prodded us. "I take girl to tepee. You go there." She pointed to another tepee near the center of the camp. "We will see if anyone wants you as a wife."

I watched them usher a dazed Emma away while two others shoved Christina and me toward the tepee where a crowd clustered. They pushed us through the door, and we shuffled toward the center. Pawn and several other men entered behind us.

My heart began to pound.

Christina

I shudder, knowing the time has come that Julia spoke of. The time when I must decide what I will do.

The men speak, arguing about what to do with us. Their voices are hostile, their eyes angry as they look at us. I do not think Laura and I will be claimed as wives. I think we will be slaves, and it will not go well for us. I think these men intend to violate us. I understand too little of the language to figure out exactly what the disagreement is about. But I recognize the tone of vengeance.

Laura's breath is fast in her chest, and her eyes are not focused. I think she understands what will happen. She is a frail woman, not stout like me. I think she will not last long before she passes out.

Me, I am strong. For the first time, I wish I was not.

There are dogs in the tepee, and they sniff at us, wander away. A woman says something about us being unfit even for dogs.

The men still argue, but their words flow too fast for me to understand.

Women come from the shadows and lead us to the robes. Then they leave with the men, still arguing together.

Only Pawn remains. He comes to me, and I know it is the time Julia told me about.

I shudder. I do not want this.

Pawn sits on the robe. "There is much anger tonight among these men. They wish to punish the women captives for what happened today, for the killing of Grizzly Bear and the others.

Revenge is strong in their hearts, and they do not wish to respect our usual ways. I have told these men you will be my wife. It is better to do this now, before they change their minds."

He waits, but I do not say anything. I cannot agree to this.

But when I do not refuse, he lifts my skirts.

I fight to push them back down, my legs churning.

Nein, I will not do this. I will not lie with a man other than my Andreas. I will not. Even if I am killed, I will not do this.

The skirts fly back up.

"Be still, German Woman. It is better this way, so you are in my protection." He is between my legs.

I thrash and bring my knee up.

He cries out and stops. When he moves away, he is clutching himself, and I know my aim was true. He crawls to the side and glares at me.

I have shamed him, and I know I will pay the price.

Other men rush in, alerted by his cry. When they see him cradling his privates, they yell and swarm to us.

I hear Julia's words in my head. *This is war. It could change things.* I have sacrificed my chance to be respected. My defiance will make these already angry men forget their traditions. My heart seizes—I have done this to myself.

One of them slaps me and forces my knees apart.

I push at him, resisting. I turn my head and glimpse Laura nearby.

She struggles, too. Fighting and kicking like I do. The man holds her down, and she weakens. *Ja,* she is not so strong as I am. He takes her, pounding into her as she screams. She faces me, terror in her eyes, tears streaking her cheeks.

But I have my own battle.

The man slaps my face again, and someone holds my legs so I cannot fight back. I wince when he enters me, hear his hoarse grunting as he pumps and his cry when he releases.

I am shamed and I will never tell anyone of this. Never.

Almena

The afternoon slid into evening and the rain thinned, stopped. Almena glanced up, weary beyond all measure. She'd managed to keep walking, despite the deluge, but only in intervals. She knew they would need to stop soon.

"I'm cold, Mama."

"I know, William Henry. Me, too." She bent down and drew her three year old close. "But we have nowhere to go, sweet boy. Nowhere to get warm."

They'd had the same conversation every few minutes. Either that or one about hunger. She cursed the prairie, the rain, and the Dakota. Seconds later, she recanted the curse.

They could have killed us.

Thank God she'd always welcomed them, fed them, traded with them. Had she not, they might not have been spared.

"I'm tired. Carry me?"

Lord, I can't. I can't do this.

She'd transferred Frank from one hip to the other and back again as her arms had grown too numb to support him. William Henry had been forced to trudge beside them. She had to find a place for them to spend the night, now, before it became any darker.

She glanced around, searching for a dry location. Water pooled in every low spot, and the grasses dripped. Everywhere, the ground undulated. Up and down and up again. She knew that only too well, having walked its terrain for the entire day.

Finally, a small rise with no grass. *A sand hill.*

She'd be able to dig out sleeping spots for the boys.

"There." She pointed so that William Henry would see.

"That's where we're going. Can you get there before me?"

He sighed and started away from her, his tired little body managing the uneven ground in spurts. His wet nightclothes clung to him. From behind, she noted his limping gait.

Oh, William, your poor little feet.

Tears bit her eyes. Reaching him, she scooped him up, gritting her teeth at the additional weight. She struggled up the hill. Each step was a gain, each sank into the sandy ground. But she felt the difference in the movement of it. She crested it and sank down, laying Frank on the ground. Despite the aches that stung her arms, she hollowed out a small hole, avoiding too much depth so water would not fill it, and laid Frank into the nest. She did the same for William Henry, who watched her efforts with curiosity.

"Lie down, Sweetie. Sleep."

He crawled into the space and curled up.

Almena reached for one of his feet, felt the cuts on his sole. She began to rub.

William Henry jerked from her grasp. "Hurts, Mama," he said and nodded off.

Almena sat, sighed. In his spot, Frank was tossing and turning, whimpering in his sleep. He'd likely waken soon . . . he'd slept so much of the day away. She glanced at the sky again, hoping to find the stars, but the clouds hung heavy, and darkness grew thick around them. She lay down next to the boys, fatigue overwhelming her.

But when the raindrops fell again, dripping onto her face, she crawled to the boys and lay atop them, sheltering them as best as she could.

The night would be as long as the day had been.

Lavina

I hold as still as possible, but no hand reaches for me; and no cold knife slices my scalp. I remain as if dead, praying I will be spared. In my haze, I hear others moaning and crying.

"Mama? Mama, are you there?"

My heart! It's Merton. The urge to crawl to him overwhelms me. I still it and stifle my voice. If Merton is to remain alive, I cannot reveal myself. I know with dreadful certainty that he would come to me, and I can't risk the Dakota noticing him. I pray he will keep quiet. I force myself to stay strong, hating that I must deny him comfort.

Lord, how much longer will this day last?

Sounds of people moving away seep through my consciousness. Then, nothing.

I shiver, wet and cold. I open one eye, then the other. The day is still dark, the rain drenching, but the Indians have gone.

I shudder a breath and shake in earnest—I am alive.

I am alive, but I don't know when they will return.

With my good arm, I push off the ground. Pain shoots through my body, and my head feels as if it will explode. I slow my movement, inching upward little by little. Vomit rises with the agony, but I fight and finally sit.

Congealed blood cakes the hand that was under my head. That the rain did not wash the blood away from the wound, that it clotted so much among my fingers, tells me just how much it has bled. I wonder if my skull is still there, or if I have left it on the ground.

My gaze darts to where I'd lain. There's blood, a good deal of blood, but no chips of bone. I raise my arm and touch my head. Within my thick hair, there is the hole, where I was shot, but only numbness. I can't feel the damage from the beating. I turn my head from side to side.

Bone fragments grate against one another, reminding me of

the sound of teeth grinding together. The sound echoes through the back of my head. Bile rises in my throat. I'm unable to choke it back. It flows down my chin, lodges bitter and stinging in my nose.

I wait for the rain to wash it away and marvel that my brain is not lying on the ground. I can't fathom how that is possible. I touch my head again.

My hair—my long, thick hair that I have so loathed piling atop my head. Though it now hangs in a tangled mess, it must have cushioned the blows enough to keep my skin intact.

Slowly, awareness sharpens. I hear sounds around me. Children still cry at odd intervals.

Johnnie . . . is that my Johnnie?

The cries come from the slough, and I wonder if Merton still has charge of him, if he has taken him back to the men who are lying among the reeds.

Oh, my boys . . .

I push to my feet, fighting the pain of my many wounds. I take a step, stagger, holding up my torn skirt with my left hand so I do not stumble on it. Each movement stirs more pain. I remember my feet are bare, cut and blistered. The wound in my side pinches as I move, my back screams, my hip twinges. My wounded arm hangs limp, and the throbbing is unbearable, so I hold it with my good arm—the one already holding my tattered dress. I take one step, two and grit my teeth. If I can continue on, the pain will eventually numb, I think.

I hope.

The route back to the slough stirs the horrendous memories of my Freddy being so savagely murdered. Determined, I fight the visions. He is gone. I must focus on Merton and Johnnie, who are still in that bog . . . on Giles and Frank, who are missing.

The air cracks, and I duck. I squelch my panicked cry so I

Never Let Go

don't draw more fire. Only then do I realize no one shoots. It's just thunder.

An insane urge to laugh surges, ebbs away. I'm thankful, for there is no room for hysteria now. I must find my boys.

A child calls out for his mother. Willie Duley is somehow still alive. He calls out again.

The urge to comfort him rises, but I know I can't save him; he's injured too severely to survive. I can do nothing for him, and my own boys need me. I swallow and continue past.

Again, I think I hear Johnnie and lurch toward the sound.

It is not my Johnnie.

Little Charlie Everett, two years old, lies among the reeds. He breathes sluggishly, death imminent. His six-year-old sister, Lillie, sits next to him, sheltering him from the storm.

"Lillie?"

"Mrs. Eastlick?" She looks up at me, her face bereft. "They haven't killed us all?"

"Not quite. There are a few left."

"Will you take care of Charlie?"

Sorrow stabs at me. He will last but a few minutes longer, and I don't know how to tell her. I long to sit and wait with her, to comfort her when he slips away, but those few moments could mean death for my own boys.

"Oh, Lillie, I wish I could. But I must find my own Johnnie. He is here, crying for me. He'll surely die if I don't find him."

"I know." She is calm, resigned.

"I'm sorry, Lillie. Will you come with me?"

"I need to stay."

"I'll come back, after I find Johnnie. Maybe then you can come with me." It is all I can offer her.

"I'm thirsty. Do you have water?"

"I don't, dear." I take a moment to show her how to squeeze water from her clothing.

She swallows and scrunches her face at the muddy taste. "Is there better water in heaven, do you think?" Her clear, sweet voice sounds older than her years.

"I think there is. I think when you get to heaven, you will never suffer again and never be thirsty."

"That's good." A wavering smile crosses her face, and she lies across her little brother and closes her eyes.

Sobbing, I move on, searching. I'll return for Lillie when I can and take her with me.

I find the bodies of Mrs. Smith and my dear friend Sophia Ireland. Both are dead, their clothing disturbed. Oh, Sophia. I do my best to cover them so they have more dignity. Little Sarah Ireland lies on Sophia's chest, unmoving. I spy Mrs. Smith's heavy canvas apron. It would make a good cloak in the increasing chill. I struggle to remove it. Inching my good arm under her to unfasten it, I choke back my discomfort at touching death so closely. I discover pins in their pockets and take them to pin my skirt back to my waistband so I don't have to hold it up.

In the growing darkness, I find yet more remains, a boy. *Giles.* I lower my aching body, unable to do anything else. He's been shot through the chest and is dead. He looks peaceful. I sit with him but a moment before leaving him. He no longer needs me.

The sound of breathing draws me to another child.

Oh, God, it's Freddy, still alive after his savage beating. How many hours has he lain here? He's face down, his clothes torn to shreds. I shudder at the agony he must be suffering. But I hear the rasp in his throat and know his death will also come soon. An urge to lie down next to him and hold him, to die beside him, overwhelms me.

Then, I remember Merton and Johnnie are still out there and have need of me.

I make my choice and rise.

Mrs. Everett is close by, shot through the lungs. She breathes still, the effort creating a gurgling rattle. My skin crawls at the sound, and terror fills me. I call her name, but she doesn't respond, and I hurry away, unable to listen to that haunting sound any longer.

I call out for Merton, but there is no answer. Several times, I think I hear my husband, but the sound comes from all about me, and I know I must be imagining it. I wander in circles, fatigue overtaking me. A strange light floats atop the grass, pale red, circling round and round me.

I stumble to the ground, unable to go on, waiting for the light to consume me.

CHAPTER EIGHTEEN
August 21, 1862
Christina, Julia, and Laura
Becoming Captives

Julia

"Get up, you lazy dogs." The bitter voice broke into Julia's sleep, and she forced herself to find wakefulness. Today would be the day that defined her role in Pawn's family. She opened her eyes. A Dakota woman stood over her, her dark eyes hard in the dim, pre-dawn light.

Good lord, what time was it?

Julia nudged Dora and George and rose from her buffalo robe pallet. She stood before the woman but did not lower her gaze. Pawn had made it clear she was a wife, not a servant. She'd be damned if she'd let this one lose track of the distinction.

Dances in Water stood some distance away, deferring to the other woman, the first wife. Speaks with Strong Tongue, if she recalled correctly. Wasn't that fitting?

"Tell me, sister, what I am to do." She used the Dakota language.

"Sister, bah!" Strong Tongue said. She spat at Julia's feet.

"We need water and firewood," Dances in Water said.

"And the pots need scrubbing." The older wife still glared at her.

Julia refused to flinch and met her gaze. "My name is Julia Wright. My children are called George and Dora." She gestured to the children, still abed, but sitting upright, thank goodness. "We are honored to be part of Pawn's family. I will do as you ask. Are they to help me?"

"Go yourself, Julia Wright. These two will help us pack. We have much to do before we leave this place."

She'd won this round, but she dared not push things any further. She glanced down at George and Dora. "Get up— quick now, so you do not anger these women. You must do as they tell you and help them pack."

"Are we slaves?" Dora asked.

"They are wives of Pawn, and you must obey as if they are your mothers, too. But know if you do not do as you are told, they may discipline you. Get up and go to work. *Now.*"

She gave them a stern look and exited the lodge. Lord, she hoped Dora understood all she hadn't said, that Dances in Water would protect her from Strong Tongue's bitterness.

Outside, she stirred the embers in the dying fire and added the last remaining logs. She grabbed the pots and strode toward the lake. It made most sense to wash the pots, bring water, then locate more wood. She hoped she'd chosen wisely, that she was being efficient.

The sun was barely rising. It was early but not as early as she'd thought. She'd found sleep, her fatigue saturating her. She crossed the far edge of the Irelands' yard and stepped down to the water's edge. Other captives were already there, performing similar chores. A Dakota youth stood on the bank above them. A guard, she supposed.

She waded into the water and bent to rinse out the pot. Dried stew caked the inside of it and would bear scrubbing. She tugged out a few grasses from the shoreline and lifted the hem of her skirt for use as a dishrag. Her dress was far past the ruined state, so there was little sense taking care with it at this point.

"*Ja*, a good idea," Christina whispered from beside her.

"Who claimed you?"

"Wakeska, White Lodge, gave me to Running Bear as a slave. He took me to his tepee early this morning."

Julia's gaze drifted over her friend. Christina moved stiffly, stepping with care. She'd been ill-used; rage had led some of the men to dishonor the Dakota ways.

"The others?" she asked, fighting the urge to comfort her friend with a hug.

"Laura passed out, but I heard she was taken by Sleepy Eye. The Ireland girls are with Tizzie Tonka. This is all I know."

"Enough talk. Work," the teen advised. From his tone, Julia knew they'd best obey. She moved away from Christina and scoured the pot. Eight-year-old Roseanna Ireland stepped into the lake, gathered water, and returned to shore with her eyes downcast. Julia wasn't even sure she'd noticed anyone else. No doubt Ellen, being younger, had been put to work in the tepee.

Finished scrubbing the pot, she scooped water into it and returned to Pawn's lodge without speaking to anyone else. Laura staggered from a tepee, barely able to walk, but Julia didn't pause. A Dakota woman stood nearby, and it wouldn't go well for Laura if they spoke now. Besides, it was starting to drizzle again, and she knew the fire would need nursing if the rain continued. For that, she'd need more wood.

Julia quickly gathered wood from the stack Tommy Ireland kept near the cabin. There was little left, but it would be enough to keep the fire going until they broke camp. Already, the women were tearing down tepees. Her arms loaded, she turned back to the encampment.

"Julia Wright."

Julia jumped at the familiar bitter voice of Pawn's first wife.

She hadn't even heard the woman approach. She turned and faced her.

"You have much to learn," the woman said in Dakota. "I am called Speaks with Strong Tongue and am the first wife of Across the River, whom you call Pawn. I am a daughter of old Sleepy Eye, cousin to young Sleepy Eye, who is a strong leader. I am also a favorite of White Lodge, who knew my father and treats me like a daughter. As the elder of the leaders, White Lodge is much respected by all the Sisseton and has great power. It is because of my stature that Across the River has been named to follow Grizzly Bear as chief of our village."

Julia lowered her eyes. *It may have been a mistake, challenging this one.*

"I am honored to know you, Speaks with Strong Tongue."

"You think you are important because you join Across the River's tepee, but you are much risk to him. He lost importance because of you, because he negotiated for your people. My cousin Sleepy Eye and White Lodge, who have far more influence among our people, did not like his interference. His support was not strong, and there was much dissent about him becoming leader. Last night, he took pity on another of the captives, and she brought him shame when he let her knee his manhood. Now, the people laugh at how he walks this morning, and his authority is weakened further."

"I'm sorry." She'd known yesterday that he'd taken a risk, but she'd had no idea how much it had cost him. She swallowed. Maybe she wasn't as protected as she'd thought.

Strong Tongue's gaze bore into her. "Know this. It is your fault that these things have happened. Your fault that my husband does not have the status he should, that I have lost standing. I will not extend kinship to you because of that. He has made a mistake taking you as a wife, and he will soon be forced to trade you or lose his rank. You will not work your power on him to bring him more disgrace. In my tepee, you will be a dog."

No, that wasn't right. Pawn had told her she'd be treated as a wife. His other wives were supposed to make her part of the family. "Pawn . . . Across the River . . . will decide these things," she said, but doubt stabbed at her.

Strong Tongue's hand landed against her cheek, the sound sharp, the pain instant.

Julia flinched and fought to keep from soothing her face with her hand. She would not cower before this woman.

"You are impudent, Julia Wright. The band will decide. Without their support, Across the River will lose his new position. He leads with their consent. Within his lodge, I will determine how things are to be. Without my support—my position as cousin of Sleepy Eye and favorite of White Lodge, who knew my father—Across the River is nothing."

Julia's sense of control slipped further. No, this was not a woman to be toyed with. "I will not cause trouble."

"You are nothing but trouble, and I will see you dead rather than enjoying a wife's comfort."

Christina

I have been raised to be a good German *Hausfrau* and try to hold on to that this morning. Used to rising early, I did not mind so much when I was roused to do chores before dawn. I do not mind the cooking and cleaning. I am used to such things. But I do not know the ways of these people and struggle to do as they expect. Running Bear's wife has cuffed me three times for mistakes in packing.

I will learn. I have no choice. I will learn, and I will do what I can to help the children among us.

My stomach growls, and Falling Star, the wife, glares at me.

Several gunshots sound, and I jump.

This time, Falling Star does not glare. Her dark eyes soften. "Go, sit, eat," she says, pointing to where Laura is already sitting, her surviving children with her. The Ireland girls are across the camp, helping to fold a tepee. I do not see Julia.

I scoop a portion of the remaining corn mush into my hand, as the others have done. There is not much left, after all the camp has eaten, but I remind myself to be grateful I am allowed to eat at all. I shuffle toward Laura, stiff and aching. The night was long, and I hope I will not endure such as that again. I think, now that I have been claimed, that it will be easier.

"*Gutenmorgen*," I say as I sit next to her.

She looks puzzled, and I remember this is my greeting to Andreas and that he is no longer here. I exhale. Is it only twenty-four hours?

"Good morning," I translate.

"Is it?" she mumbles.

"We are alive. It is good."

"You can say such a thing when your husband lies dead? When I have lost three of my family?"

"They are gone. We remain and must stay strong."

"For what? More of what they did to us last night?"

"I will not talk of that. Their wrath is spent. I think now it will be better. You must be strong for your children."

She sighs. For a moment, she smiles as she looks at the three clustered near her. Her face saddens again. This will be a difficult thing for her, I think. She will need to find strength.

A horse gallops into camp—the one that belonged to Charlie Hatch, I think. The rider eases a body to the ground. He speaks to those who greet him, but I cannot make out the words. When he rides away, I see that six-year-old Lillie Everett has been brought to us, still alive. They shove a bowl of food into her hands and push her toward us. She is wounded in her side, blood drying on her dress. Laura and I make a place for her between us, and she stumbles forward. Her eyes look empty.

"Lillie, come sit," I say.

Emma and Jefferson Duley greet her and urge her to join us. She sits.

"You are hurt?" I ask.

"It hurts, but the blood stopped, and I didn't go to heaven."

Laura hugs her close. "Oh, you darling girl. You spent the whole night out there alone?"

"I wasn't alone. I sat with Mama and baby Charlie."

I look at her. "Do they live?"

"Mama went to heaven, but Charlie was still alive. They found us when they were searching pockets and made me leave him. I think he will be with Mama soon."

"Was there anyone else left?" Laura asks.

"Mrs. Eastlick was there last night, and I heard others moving. This morning, I saw only us and one of Roseanna and Ellen's little sisters. They left her there with baby Charlie."

She eats the porridge with her fingers and looks to us for instruction.

Concern for this poor little orphan fills me, and I take her hand in mine as we stand. "You will come with me, and I will keep you safe. *Ja?*"

"I would like that," she says.

There is a shot. The bullet rips through the bottom of my dress, and we all move apart, too startled to think.

"No more talk," one of the Indians says as he lowers his gun. "This one is not yours."

"She has no mother. I will keep her," I say.

Running Bear's wife slaps my face. "Quiet, German Woman. She will go to Grizzly Bear's wife. Or, if you still want to argue, they can give her to his mother, the one who took out her rage on the children whose fathers shot her son."

Freddy Eastlick and Bell Duley, the two who were beaten to death.

I look at Lillie and weep, unwilling to risk further protest. Will Everett also fired at the chief. "I'm sorry," I say and hope she does not suffer too much.

Laura

We let them take poor little Lillie away from us. We had no alternative; we couldn't let her be turned over to that wicked woman to be beaten to death. Images of Bell flashed through my mind at the suggestion, and I am ashamed that we left Lillie with no one to care for her, but there was no choice to it— anything would be better than turning her over to such a fate. Besides, I could not risk my remaining children by disobeying.

I returned to the tepee, now lying on the ground, and gathered up the poles as instructed. They were heavy, and I struggled to lug them to the travois. My body ached beyond all measure. I could hardly walk, but I knew I had to continue on, to satisfy the shrews who commanded me.

"Do you need help?" Julia Wright asked from her campsite. "We've finished, and I haven't been given any other chores."

"Oh, that would be a boon indeed. I am so sore, my muscles enraged from sitting so many hours in the slough and then . . . last night." My face heated, and I could say no more.

Julia grabbed one end of the pole, and we carried it to the travois. "Did they hurt you?" she whispered.

I squeezed my eyes shut for a moment. I didn't want to talk about it—the night was long and torturous. I fought to keep the white-hot fury at bay but could not. "Of course they hurt me," I snapped. "How could they not, doing what they did? I tried to fight them, as Christina did, but I was too weak."

I couldn't block out the visions of what was done to me, the despicable horror of the night. The dogs sniffing at me, women cackling in snide laughter that I was so worthless not even a dog would have me, the shame of being held down, my body exposed and violated.

"I'm so sorry, Laura. This is war for them, and those who did that to you abandoned their ways."

She would defend them? I paused to let my anger dissipate, telling myself she meant only to show her concern. I finished the story, forcing myself to say it out loud this once, so that I would never have to do so again. "I just lay there and let it happen and forced my thoughts to visions of the children running about with laughter, squealing in delight. I don't know how many used me. I passed out, finally."

"Do you know where we're going?" Julia said after a while.

"No, only that we are moving. They tell me nothing, and I understand very little of what they do say."

"You'll learn." She stopped and glanced around. "Is that the last pole?"

"How are we going to survive among these heathens? Did you notice how savage they were in their celebration?" I couldn't forget how they forced me to watch their gleeful dance. One by one, they declared they had killed and danced about in reenactment of how it had happened. They jumped as if hit by bullets, staggered to the ground, groaning as the others whooped and danced around him like demons. I think they did it to torture those of us who survived.

"I think it was a ritual."

"It was horrible. It's all horrible. I would give anything to escape this."

Julia looked around, leaned close. "Would you run, if you had the chance? If you could escape, before we leave the area we know, would you do so?"

If I could flee a future of nightly violations, daily beatings, savage mockery? If I could leave behind a life of toil and despondency?

I turned and met Julia's gaze. "I would take my children and run like the wind."

Julia

"You, white women! Hitch the oxen."

Julia stepped forward, her arms tired. The early morning rains had stopped, and sun peeked through the clouds to signal it was time to start on their way. Many of the tepees had been loaded onto the settlers' wagons. Already, they'd put the available horses into harnesses, and one wagon remained.

"I will get the yoke," Christina said. She strode to the Ireland barn, where a wooden ox yoke lay.

Julia joined her. There was little reason Christina should drag it alone. Her arms were likely sore, too.

They grasped the yoke, one per side, and carried it back to the wagon.

"You know how to manage oxen?"

"*Ja.* This I know." She talked Julia through yoking the animals and looping the reins through the rings.

Julia pondered the exchange she'd had with Laura. If *she* had the chance to run, would she? In truth, she wasn't sure. Last night, she would have placed her lot entirely with Pawn, trusting that she would be kept safe. Now, she no longer had faith that was the best option. Pawn . . . Across the River . . . did not have the backing of his people, and her fortunes could turn in a minute.

Would it be better to attempt an escape?

"You, German Woman, you drive this wagon. You know the ox."

Julia trudged back to Strong Tongue and shouldered the pack

she'd been assigned earlier. Pawn lay on a travois, his face tight. Christina had done damage, that was for sure. Strong Tongue had grown tired of his lurching walk—or perhaps of the thinly suppressed laughter that followed him—and had prepared the travois. Now, Julia carried much of the bulk that would normally be transported there.

Strong Tongue glanced in her direction. "You think you are above carrying our goods, Julia Wright?"

"No, but it is a labor I haven't done before."

"Hah! You will get used to it. It is your burden now. Across the River would not need to ride like an old woman if you had not begged for lives to be spared."

"I will do it." She shifted the pack, trying to balance the weight, but was unable to stand erect. She was certain Strong Tongue had distributed it so it would rest high on her back instead of low, as fur trappers carried their loads.

Strong Tongue laughed. "Move. Can't you see we are leaving?"

Julia looked up from her hunched position and stepped forward.

As they headed north, she lagged behind. George and Dora stayed close, each shouldering their own burdens. Each step became more and more difficult, and the weight pressed down on her. The group circled around the Koch place and turned northwest toward the Hurds, crossing a narrow strip of land between two bodies of water. Under her feet, the ground grew soft, mushy, and walking became more difficult.

She glanced at the children, saw them struggling as well. Tears streamed down Dora's cheeks. George barely walked. In the next moment, he dropped to the ground.

Julia and Dora halted. As one, they shrugged from their packs and freed George. Julia glanced at the party, now quite far ahead of them. She eyed the land around them, the water, the trees.

I would take my children and run like the wind.

CHAPTER NINETEEN
August 21–24, 1862
Almena and Lavina
Seeking Dutch Zierke's

Lavina

August 21

Dawn breaks as I lurch across the prairie. Once the strange light disappeared, I'd again crawled to my feet, trying to move as far as possible from the slough under the cover of darkness. I couldn't find Merton and Johnnie, and I tell myself they're still alive, escaped from this dreadful place. I must save myself for their sake. I will find them, no matter what.

As muted light spreads across the prairie, I stumble to a patch of tall weeds and fall to my knees, hoping the grasses will hide me from any Indians still roaming the area. I find little comfort. The drizzling rain lessens as I lie there and finally stops. The sun emerges, warming me.

Oh, what a mess I am. My thick hair droops about me. At nearly three feet long, it will warm me, once it finally dries out. My dress is in tatters, gaping open where it tore from the waistband. The pins I took from Sophia Ireland hold it here and there. Blood has stained the cloth brown.

But what does it matter? There is no one to see me. I am alone.

I staunchly refuse to let melancholy overtake me. John's dead, and I can do nothing about it. Freddy and Giles lay where they fell, all now with John. I'm glad they're free of the pain and suffering that filled their last minutes, and I pray that Frank didn't linger long. I must focus on Merton and Johnnie and hang on for them.

Time crawls. I hear children calling out and know I'm still near the slough. The cries continue throughout the day, in spurts. Sometimes, they shriek in pain. Other times, there is low whimpering. I long to crawl back and help, but I'm so weak. It's hellish to lie and do nothing, and my soul weeps.

Mid-afternoon, I hear three shots, and the wailing stops. Finally, they've been given peace.

I hold fast to the hope that Merton and Johnnie escaped.

But my mind doesn't rest. It conjures visions of Merton and Johnnie among those who suffered all day, among those now dead. I think I'll lie here and let myself die. There are enough wounds to my body, to my head, that it shouldn't take more than a few days.

Yet, what if Merton and Johnnie do live? I told Merton to never let his brother go. Merton, the man that he is despite his youth, wouldn't give up, and I must not either.

With all quiet and twilight upon me, I push myself to a sitting position and look around. I need to make my way to Dutch Zierke's. The old German is the closest settler, sixteen miles east of Lake Shetek. I spy timber on the horizon. I must be close to Buffalo Lake, which lies along the mail route a few miles from the slough, one third of the distance to Zierke's place.

I gain my feet and begin to walk to the timber as evening descends. I trudge for hours at a snail's pace, barely able to move. I dig in, drawing on every ounce of strength, until I can go no further. I lie on the damp ground, the dew seeping into my dress. I try to scoop up the moisture with my hand to quench my thirst but to no avail. My failure makes me even more aware that I've had nothing to eat or drink for two days now. Finally, I sop at the dew with the hem of my skirt and suck on the cloth.

I ease Mrs. Smith's apron over me and close my eyes. I blow onto my cold hands and shiver, my teeth chattering. Finally, as I warm, I hear footsteps approach. I keep my eyes closed and still myself, but my heart thrashes.

An animal sniffs at my head. It moves, nudging me, licking the old blood in my hair. When the wolf nears my face, I can feel its hot breath, and the stench of death bathes me as it stands over me.

I thrash at the animal, and it jumps back.

Hah, you thought me dead, did you?

Surprised the wolf didn't snap at me, I gape at it. It's too dark to see the animal's eyes; they are but a glint in the darkness. It sits a few feet away, watching me. I push to my feet, shocked it has not lunged at me, has not torn me apart. With my good arm, I snap the apron, and the wolf rises and saunters away.

There is no need for it to bother taking down a live being, even one as weak as I. As long as it knows I am alive, it will leave me alone and seek an easier meal.

The macabre reality is that the wolf will not go hungry tonight, and I will be safe because of it.

As long as I do not sleep like the dead.

Almena
August 21
That same morning, Almena woke early, still as tired as she'd been the night before. Frank had fussed most of the night, and she'd caught only snatches of troubled sleep. She stretched her aching muscles. Oh, how she wished Frank could walk. But he

Never Let Go

couldn't, and she'd best put the thought out of her head. It would do her no good. As the sun rose, around 5:30, by her reckoning, she stood and woke the boys. It was time to move on. Today, she hoped to reach Dutch Zierke's place.

Frank's diaper was both soaked and soiled. She shook it out, rubbing it in the grass to clean it as well as she could while William Henry looked on.

"It's still dirty, Mama."

"I know, little man. I can't get it any cleaner."

"Why don't you leave it?"

The idea was tempting. The cloth did little good, but it was an extra layer that might keep Frank's thin little nightgown from the soil of his waste. "We might have to, later. We'll use it as long as we can."

"Are we having breakfast today?"

Almena kissed his little head. "We have nothing, my sweet." Frank had suckled a few times, but her milk had dried. "You and I will have to be strong and go without again today. We'll eat when we get to Dutch Zierke's."

William Henry's lower lip trembled, but he didn't cry. He simply started walking.

Almena gathered Frank, settled him on her hip, and strode after her little one. His thin nightclothes flapped with each step, and he limped worse than ever. The rain had ceased during the night, but the clouds hovered, low and gray, and she knew they held more water.

Progress was slow, between William Henry's short steps and his poor little feet, and Almena had little clue how much distance they were covering. Time dragged on, and she heard shots.

"Oh, lord." She stopped and sat on the ground, her shoulders slumping as she released Frank.

"What's a matter, Mama? You got tears."

She wiped her eyes and gazed at William Henry.

"I think we're still near Lake Shetek, honey. We've been walking in circles." The shots had to have come from Shetek. There were no other settlements west of Dutch Zierke's. She sank her face into her hands and sobbed. An entire day, and they were still at the lake.

"It's okay, Mama, don't cry." William Henry wrapped his little arms around her and hugged her tight. "Maybe we can go back and get bread and milk."

"I wish we could, but we can't go near the lake. I think the Indians are still there, and we'll only be safe if we go away."

"I'm hungry, Mama."

"Me, too. Come on, let's head on." She pointed, showing him a new route, one which veered away from the direction she'd heard the shots. "This way." She stood, and they travelled on.

The day proved as wet as she'd anticipated, with the clouds dipping lower, misting at intervals.

The boys shivered, William Henry begging often for food, all of them resting frequently. Toward dark, he dropped to the ground, retching.

Almena lowered Frank and kneeled next to the three year old, rubbing his back as he vomited onto the wet prairie grass. She wiped his spittle with the edge of her skirt, and they sat while he whimpered, his head on her lap. At last, she roused them, hefting both boys as she stood, one on each hip, and trudged on again. They had another half hour before complete dark, and they needed to find a better spot for the night.

They crested a hill, and she stopped. *A road. The mail road.* She lowered the boys and glanced around, trying to get her bearings. And when she realized where they were, she plopped down with them and sobbed.

Another entire day of walking, and they were but four miles from her own cabin.

Lavina
August 22

I wake before dawn and find the wolf gone and my body still fully intact. Rising, I set my sights again on the tree line and set off. Today, I will reach Dutch Zierke's and send out word I've survived. I'll find Merton and Johnnie, and we'll strive on.

My steps this day are more painful. The numbness of yesterday is wearing off. My feet are bloody, cut by the prairie grass, and they throb with each step. I don't know what the soles look like, but the tops of my feet are lashed nearly to the bone. I enter a slough and wade in it, craving the cool caress of the mud. In seconds, I grasp it is water, not mud. I stoop and scoop it up, drinking again and again.

I slog on, parting the shoulder-high reeds and wading through two-foot-deep water. At the bottom, my feet squish, and mud sucks at me. Finally, when I think I can go no further, I emerge and find dry ground on which to rest.

As the sun edges up and light blooms, I realize I'm but a short distance from the timber. I stand, swaying with weakness. I'm light-headed and must wait before I move. I drag myself onward.

The squawk of geese startles me, and I look up. Despair crashes over me. This isn't Buffalo Lake! I'm back at Lake Shetek.

I sway on my feet. How can I have wandered for days and gotten nowhere? Dejected, I crawl into the nearest patch of weeds. Mosquitos swarm, and I cover my face with the apron and retch, my stomach protesting the lack of food. Misery claws at me as I think about lying here, where I started, dying of starvation while I hide from the Indians.

But I'll die either way. I can't lie in the weeds until dark, sacrificing another day. The risk of being discovered is less than the certainty of perishing if I fail to find food. And so I stand and push on toward the house—Tommy Ireland's, I think.

I wade through another small slough and clutch my way up the bank. The weeds are so tangled I simply stop and lie among them, too exhausted to move.

Maybe I should have gone around the slough. No, better to take the short route, isn't it? It's not so bad here, now that I'm not crawling through the weeds. I could lie here and sleep. Just a little while. The sun will be so warm. I'm shivering, after all. It would feel so nice.

A while later—an hour? a lifetime?—I drag myself up the bank, grabbing onto the underbrush with my hands until I reach the top. Uncle Tommy's cornfield is in front of me, and I stagger to it, wobbling with each step, and pluck the first ear of corn I spy. I remove the husks, wondering why it's so difficult, and strip off the corn silk. I attack the ear like a wild animal. The kernels are milky, not yet ripe, but I don't care. I eat two rows before my stomach rebels, and I retch my puny meal back up and collapse.

When I finally rise, I totter to the house. The slaughtered remains of a bull and several pigs clutter the yard. Clothing and dishes are scattered all about, feathers strewn far and wide, the mattresses emptied.

Shoes! I should search for shoes.

But I haven't the energy. I stumble to the cabin. A dog lies dead in the corner. I spy a crock on the table and rush to it, releasing the sour smell of spoilt buttermilk, mold crusting it. I vomit again, but there is nothing but spittle.

I lurch back out and take a cup of water from the spring before crawling into a plum thicket.

When I wake, it's evening, and darkness is thickening. I stand, still weak but no longer staggering. I return to the cabin, manage to catch a chicken, and kill it. I skin it. Desperate, I sink my teeth into its flesh and tear it apart. I don't remember until later that there was surely a knife at the cabin. I rip the raw meat from the bone, dip it all into the salt brine at the bottom of the pork barrel to preserve it, wrap it, and put it in a tin pail with three ears of corn.

Afterwards, I head east, to locate the mail route and the road to Uncle Charley's. It takes me all night to cover the two miles to the road. My heel, where it was shot, is swollen, and I can barely walk on it. Why didn't I look for shoes? Around eleven o'clock, I reach Buffalo Lake. The road crosses an inlet via a makeshift bridge.

Halfway across, I hear the sound of splintering wood, and the bridge breaks apart.

I fall into the inlet, water filling my nose and mouth. I sputter. My food pail bobbles, and I flounder in the water, unable to use my limbs to make my way to shore.

Almena
August 22

Almena roused herself to discover another foggy day. During the night, she'd gone back and forth between despair over having wandered about for two days and a sense of joy over having found the road at last. She'd again slept very little, and fatigue had lodged itself in the body, working its way deep into her muscles and her bones. She stretched, but it did little good.

She stood and surveyed her surroundings in the light of day. The road was marked but overgrown with grass. Still, she was no longer lost. Today, at last, they would reach civilization.

She wakened the boys and began the long trek. William Henry

lagged, and she stopped frequently to wait for him. When he collapsed, she gathered him up, as she had done much of yesterday, and staggered forward with both boys. But, today, the fifty-plus pounds wore on her, and she swayed under the weight, able to take only a few steps.

Weak, I'm so weak.

Setting the boys down, she sat next to them to catch her breath. She spied a puddle of water at the edge of the road, scooped it up, and drank, then showed the boys how to do the same. They both sipped but showed little interest in other activity.

If we don't cover these twelve miles today, we might not make it at all.

The thought hit her with enough force to make her faint. It was up to her, all up to her. She would need to dig deep if William Henry and Frank were to survive. No matter how much she wanted to sit here next to this pool of water and sleep, she couldn't.

Sighing, she tilted William Henry's face so he was looking at her. "You must listen to me. I need to leave you here, next to the water, for a little while."

"No, Mama, no! Don't leave me!"

"I'll come back."

"No, Mama."

"Mama can't carry both of you today. I can't. But I can carry one of you. I'll take Frank a little ways and set him down and come back for you."

"Promise?" His lips trembled.

"I promise. I won't leave you for long. But you must wait right where I leave you so I can find you. Can you do that?"

He lay down at the side of the road. "I'll be right here, Mama."

"Drink a little more while I'm gone."

"I will."

Almena drew a breath and picked up Frank, and headed east. Though she knew it was the only way, her heart broke leaving her boy behind. But she walked on, covering about a quarter mile. Once she found a good spot, she stopped, set Frank down, and gave him the same instructions.

Then she returned for William Henry.

The day passed, endless hours of back and forth treks that tripled her steps and the time it would have taken under normal circumstances. Almena was glad for the puddles of water that quenched their thirst and gave each of them the strength to go a little farther.

Late in the afternoon, a shout sounded from behind her. Fear catapulted through her, stalling as she realized it was a child, not an Indian. Clutching Frank close, she turned.

Merton Eastlick trudged up the road, his little brother in his arms.

"Mrs. Hurd? Is that you?"

"Oh, dear boy, it is." She waited, questions swirling in her mind, as he struggled forward.

"We didn't know where you were," Merton said as they continued together.

"The Indians killed Voigt but let me go as long as I went right away and didn't warn anyone." She paused, unsure if she wanted to ask her next question. "What happened, at the lake?"

Merton stopped. The boy wouldn't look at her. His breath came faster and faster.

At last, he settled. "They killed Andreas Koch, but Charlie Hatch escaped and gave the alarm. We all went to the Wright place. Old Pawn was there, and he said he'd help us. The other ones, the ones who killed Koch, they said we could go."

"So everyone is safe?" Almena held her breath, hoping Merton and Johnnie had simply become separated from the group.

But his eyes grew dark, haunted. "No." He paused. "Everything went wrong. They tried to take the horses, and a bunch of the men shot them. We all ran into a slough, and they started killing us. Mother told me to take Johnnie and not to ever let him go. I ran when I could."

Oh, Merton.

She set Frank down and knelt in front of him, her hand on his arm. "The others?"

"I don't know." He gulped air, swallowed. "Father's dead. Mother got shot. A lot of people got shot. I think a lot of them died. Uncle Tommy got away, but he told me to go without him. He was shot a bunch of times." The words came in a rush.

Almena hugged both boys, holding them as Merton sobbed against her shoulder. "And you made it all this way on your own?"

He freed himself of her arms. "I found the road, and we stopped at Buffalo Lake for the night. That's when Johnnie got all bit up by mosquitoes." He shifted, and Almena saw the little one's face, full of scabs where he'd scratched at the bites. "It rained all night. I tried to keep Johnnie dry. And the wolves came and howled for hours. I yelled at them, though, and they went away."

She gave him a wavering smile and picked up Frank. They walked on as he told her more about the journey. She didn't ask him any further questions about the events at the slough. He'd said enough for her to put it all together.

She pointed down the path. "There's my William Henry, waiting."

They stopped, Merton setting Johnnie down.

"Why don't you rest while I take William Henry on ahead. I'll be back for Frank."

"That'd be real good." He dropped to the ground.

After two hours more of going back and forth, as twilight

settled, they spied the cabin ahead. She pushed through her pain and fatigue in a burst, rushing to the door.

"Are we here, Mama? Is this it?" William Henry asked.

"We're here." She pounded on the door and called out. "Hello the house!"

No one answered.

Lavina
August 23

By the time I finally make it out of the inlet, I'm exhausted. I wring out my dripping hair and remove my wet clothes. After squeezing the water from them, I hang them on bushes to dry. As well, I hang strips of the salted chicken out to dry in the sun—it's too slimy for me to choke down as is. I can do no more. My body craves rest, and I again must lie in the grass and recover my strength. I'm weary of having to do this so often, but I can't go on.

When I wake, the sun is high in the sky. I dress, wrap my feet in bits of cloth I tear from my skirt, and eat a bit of corn and meat—which is improved but still slippery. I force it down anyway. I'm finishing when a crane and several ducks rise from the lake in a sudden flurry.

I dive behind a tree so the Indians won't glimpse me when they come over the hill. I lie there, waiting, hoping they will not hear my ragged breath.

But it's not Indians!

The horse draws a small cart, and I recognize the driver as Spot, our mail carrier.

I hope it's not a mirage and crawl from the grass.

"Help," I call. It comes out in a hoarse croak.

Spot reins the horse to a stop and speaks in Dakota with the strong guttural accent of the Germans.

I don't understand him but try to tell him the Indians have killed all the whites at the lake.

He speaks again, this time in English. "You look too white to be a squaw."

I finally comprehend he'd asked if I was Indian. It's no wonder, given the filth of my clothing and my undone hair flowing in the wind. "I'm Mrs. Eastlick. You've met me at the Everetts'. I'm badly wounded." I limp out of the brush.

He jumps from the wagon. "Here, now. Let's get you in the sulky."

He guides me to the small vehicle. The dam holding my despair breaks, and I sob while he holds me.

"There, there," he says. When I'm through telling him of the attack, he looks at my wounds and deems me solid enough to travel. He edges me up onto the seat and climbs aboard. It's crowded, with two of us, but I don't care. I'm safe.

We near Dutch Zierke's in the late afternoon, and Spot stops the cart. "I think you should stay here," he says, "while I check the house."

I creep down, hiding in the grasses while he goes to the cabin. Moments later, he returns.

"It is safe. There are no Indians here. Only a man who says he is from Shetek."

"Who is it?"

"I don't know him. Come, let's get you to the house."

A few minutes later, we arrive, and the door flies open.

"Uncle Tommy!" I scream.

My dear friend stands in the doorway, pale and gaunt, his eyes sunken. But he has a smile for me as I make my way from the cart. Spot helps me to him. Tommy opens his arms, and I fall into them.

"Dear Lavina, I never expected to see you again." His voice is a tired rasp, barely audible.

Never Let Go

"Nor I you," I say. We both weave a bit on our feet, and I know we must sit. "Let's go in."

We stumble into the house and find chairs, collapsing into them.

"Merton and Johnnie escaped," Tommy says, a smile brightening his ghostly face.

Fresh tears drip down my face, and my lips tremble.

"They made it out the day of the attack. I'm thinking they may have made it here before the Zierkes left, that they're safe, maybe in New Ulm."

"Then we'll find them there."

"Will Everett made it out, and Charlie Hatch, and Bentley. They left ahead of us. I thought I was going to die there."

"But you didn't." I pat his trembling hand.

"When Merton said he was going to take Johnnie across the prairie, I'm ashamed to say I told him not to go, to stay and die with me." His voice cracks. The admission has cost him much.

"Oh, Tommy . . ." I can do nothing but hold his fingers.

"The boy would have none of it. He said he promised you he'd keep Johnnie safe, that he'd never let him go."

Pride swells. "That's my Merton."

"I decided to go with him to the road, to make sure he found it, but I only made it a half mile. I couldn't go further. I lay in the grass and prepared to die."

"Yet, here you are." I smile, realizing I shouldn't have been surprised. If I had the strength to make it out, then a hardy man like him most certainly did.

"I think I laid there for a day and a half. Far enough away the Indians didn't find me when they came back. When I didn't die, I forced myself to get up and walk. I got here last night."

"I'm so glad, Tommy. Now we've only to go on, to find my boys."

"Lavina . . . Frank . . . Frank was still alive. He tried to go with Merton, but he was hurt so bad. His thigh, his stomach, his mouth. He couldn't even make it out of the slough."

I gasp, my hand flying to my mouth.

"Merton sobbed. He couldn't take them both. I couldn't take him."

"I know. I couldn't either." *Oh, my boy.*

"He's gone now. I don't see how he could have lived."

"I know."

The door creaks, and Spot steps in. He searches the house, finds cheese for our hungry stomachs, and we rest a bit. Before we leave, I wrap up the rest of the cheese and a few turnips from the garden, and we're on our way.

The sulky is too small for all of us, and Tommy walks, his gait shaky at first. But he gains his feet and soon manages to keep up. We camp for the night, feasting on cheese and turnips, sheltered by a quilt and Spot's oilcloth blanket, which he gives to us when it begins to rain. At morning light, we continue on.

"There's someone ahead," Spot says. His voice is tense. "A group."

"Indians?" Tommy asks.

"I don't know. I think I will take us in the ravine for a while." He turns the sulky off the road. We keep quiet, looking at one another, fear evident in all our faces. Spot stops and climbs the bank. When he fails to see anyone, he returns.

"Well, what shall we do?" he asks. "We can go back the way we came, all the way to Sioux Falls."

"If you think it's safer for you," I say, "but I won't go back west. You can leave me, and I'll make my way to New Ulm."

"Same here," Tommy adds.

"I'll not leave you. If it's New Ulm you want to go to, I will go with you."

"I don't want you to risk your life for me," Tommy says.

"We'll be fine."

Never Let Go

"*Nein*, we all go." We continue on, Spot going ahead to check for the Indians, Tommy and me following as he signals it's safe. Together, we all regain the road and travel on. But as we crest a hill, we spy them again, and Spot halts the horse.

"It's a woman," he says, "and children."

We close the distance. I think for a moment it's Laura Duley and call out for her to stop. She turns.

It's Almena Hurd.

"Almena!" We rush the horse forward and stop beside her and her two boys. "You're safe!"

She stands in shock for a few moments, shakes it off, and greets us all. Her glance settles on me, and she smiles. "Merton and Johnnie are ahead, just over the hill."

"My boys," I choke out.

Spot urges the horse forward, and suddenly we're upon them.

Merton turns and stares at us. Spot stops the cart, jumps down, and takes Johnnie from his wearied arms. He hands the little one up to me, and I kiss his poor little head and scabby face. I open my other arm, and Merton tumbles forward, his face against me. I brush his head and embrace him.

"I didn't let go, Mother. Not once."

"My brave hero," I say before my voice breaks.

"Are we safe?" he asks me.

"We're alive, and I'll keep you safe," I say as Uncle Tommy and the Hurds catch up to us. But I have no confidence this will be an easy thing. There are eight of us now, and it won't be so easy to hide nor to find enough food to sustain a group of this size. With the Zierkes having fled, I sense the Indians have been on the attack here, too, and I don't know what we'll find in the miles ahead.

Almena catches my gaze, and I know we agree. For now, we hang on and make it to where the next whites live, the Browns, halfway between Dutch Zierke's and New Ulm. The house is there, in the distance, and my heart sings.

It's but a few minutes later when we hear the bark of dogs in the distance.

Chapter Twenty
Late August 1862
Christina, Julia, and Laura
Among the Dakota

Julia

August 21

"You, Julia Wright." Speaks with Strong Tongue stood at the top of the rise. Several men on horseback joined her.

Panic seized Julia, and she jerked the children to a halt. She hadn't been fast enough, hadn't even made it into the trees.

Think, think.

"Dora," she whispered, "pretend you need to potty."

Dora's chin dipped, and Julia knew she understood the situation.

The men approached, cantering across the prairie. "Where do you go, Julia Wright?"

"To the trees. My daughter needs to relieve herself."

"She made water before we left. Do you try to escape us?"

"But I do have to go," Dora said. She gazed up at the Dakota with an innocent expression worthy of the stage, grimaced, and farted loudly.

George giggled, but Julia grasped the slim hint of hope. She sure as heaven would never chastise the children again for their uncouth abilities to expel gas on command.

"Please," Dora whimpered.

"Take her," the man told Strong Tongue. "You," he told one of the other men, "report back to Across the River."

The woman grasped Dora's arm and hauled her into the woods.

Julia prayed Dora could produce something.

"I think you lie to us," the man said. "You will not do this again."

They waited, Julia's concern rising. Would they be beaten? Killed? Her pulse thundered, but she did not show her fear to her captors.

Finally, Dora and Strong Tongue returned.

"She makes gas like a demon," Strong Tongue said, "but she does not go."

"I thought I needed to."

"Maybe. Maybe not." Strong Tongue pushed her toward Julia. "Go back to the others. Across the River will decide what must be done with you."

Christina
August 21
We stop at the Myerses' house. There is no one here, but the wagon is gone. I do not know if the family escaped or if the Dakota have taken it. But there are no bodies, and I think they may have gotten away.

"Come here," Running Bear's wife tells me. She has tied together three of the heaviest of the tepee poles, and they are raised high above. "Take one."

I grasp it, the weight catching me by surprise, but I hold firm. I must learn what is expected of me.

The wife takes another, and a third woman takes the last. "Now, go." She points, and I move away from the group until we form a triangle, the poles crossed above.

She looks at me and points again. "Go more."

I step further from them until my pole extends more than the others. It looks strange to me, but I do not argue. I push the point at the bottom into the ground as they do. We gather smaller poles, four each, and Falling Star shows me where to put the points, how to cross them on the others, all four at once. When we are done, there is a circle, but the top is not centered. I look around. Other tepees are being formed the same way. I had not noticed this before and wonder about it.

We push the poles into the ground. Falling Star takes the rope hanging from the three main poles and steps outside the ring. She walks around the ring four times, keeping the rope tight, then goes back inside. At the center, she tightens the rope and ties it to a stake.

"Come," the other woman says. She is standing at the long end of the circle with a folded bundle of hides. When I am there, she places one end of the heavy bundle in my arms. "Stretch out." She points beyond the ring. I unfold the bundle as she brings another long pole. She lays the pole next to it and attaches it to ties sewn to the largest fold. "Watch."

Falling Star and the other woman work together to raise the pole and the attached hides and prop it against the others. Falling Star turns it, and the fold falls open. Several hides are stitched together. They are scraped thin—not like the hides inside the tepee that are used for beds. "Pull out."

We move away from the fold at the pole, each hauling a section of hide that continues to unfold as we move around the tepee. I struggle under the weight but continue until we meet at the front. When we are done, Falling Star points to the back of the tepee, the long side. "Smoke hole," she says. "Above the fire. Smoke less this way."

The other woman has attached another flap of hide there. Falling Star sets a pole against a flap of hide and shows me how to open and close the smoke hole. So that is why the top is off center. The skins around the top are draped closed, and the poles will not catch fire. It is a good design, I think.

"Go in. Tie skins."

I enter the tepee and see there are ties that hang down. She follows and knots them around the poles. I do the same, and, with that, I have helped to raise my first lodge. It has taken only a few minutes. She is pleased with me, and I am glad.

Like good Germans, the Dakota seem to value industrious work. This I know how to do.

When I leave the tepee, I notice the others also working. Lillie works with Grizzly Bear's wife, and her captor does not seem so pleased. She cuffs Lillie again and again.

Guilt swarms me, and I want to go to her, to hit the woman as she hits Lillie. But I do not move. If I go to her, she will be beaten worse. I turn away, unable to watch.

Roseanna Ireland works with Redwood's wife. This woman talks to Roseanna and smiles often. I think I will not have to worry so much about her.

Then, I see Pawn with Julia. He is yelling at her. Something bad has happened, and I have a sick feeling Julia will not have so much favor as she did our first night.

Laura
August 21

Wearied and hungry, I stumbled into the tepee and dropped my load of wood onto the pile near the door. Sleepy Eye's wife glared and stalked toward me. I flinched.

"You are a useless fool," she yelled and slapped my face.

I cowered, my cheek stinging. It was the third time she had hit me since making camp, and I feared my skin would be bruised purple before long. I didn't know what I'd done wrong. Tears threatened. How could I do better if I didn't know what

I'd done wrong?

"Stack it neatly," Emma said. "Do it right and they won't be displeased with you."

I knelt next to the wood and restacked it. Who would have thought these people cared about neatness? As far as I was concerned, they were dirty as pigs, with their greasy stains on their clothing and dirty hair.

Then I remembered how I looked and sighed. I was reared a lady and never thought to be brought so low as this. I stood and walked toward the fire.

"Other side, Mama," Emma advised. "One side for women, one for men."

However did my little girl know such things? I switched directions and approached, then sat next to her. She was kneeling, some sort of tool in her hand. She was sewing hides, shoving a bone needle through them. Lord, had it taken but one day for her to become an Indian?

Frances sat on a buffalo robe, intently watching her sister. I hugged my frailest girl close. I knew I had only a short time before the old hag would force a new chore upon me. It was only the solace of having my little ones near that kept me struggling to do as I was told. I had never worked so much or so hard in my entire life, not even when on our first farm, back in Iowa.

Oh, to be back in that shoddy little cabin. I wouldn't even care about lack of a cook stove.

Jefferson bounded headlong into the tepee.

The wife yelled and cuffed him.

"Always go the other way, Jefferson," Emma said. "This is the women's side."

He hung onto me and muttered an acknowledgement. I comforted him, stroking his back. How I loved these three that were left to me. I would do whatever I had to do to protect them.

Someone rapped on the tepee skins, and the wife responded. "Enter," she said in Dakota; I was proud I'd understood her this time.

Another squaw poked her head in and said a few words before leaving. I remembered that Julia had said the word was disrespectful, but I didn't care. I did not hold much regard for these people.

"All go out," the wife said.

We stood and went outside, each of us this time minding our routes. The sun was setting, its rays casting orange and purple across quiet ripples of Fremont Lake. We were camped near the Myers farmstead, north of Lake Shetek. Tomorrow, we'd strike off across the prairie, into places unknown. I hated to leave the lakes. It was one more home I was being forced to leave behind.

Christina had whispered their plans to me earlier. She said they would move us faster in the coming days. My loins still pained with each step; I'd not even been allowed to wash the small tears I'd suffered last night, much less to treat them with any salve. My muscles ached from walking the seven miles from the Ireland cabin. I wasn't sure I'd survive more than that, but I couldn't surrender to my distress; my children needed me.

We moved to the center of the camp, where Pawn sat before a fire. Julia and her children were standing before him, as were the Ireland girls. Christina approached with Lillie Everett, and we joined them.

Lined up as we were, I could almost *feel* hostility emanating from Pawn. I twisted my handkerchief in my fingers. Emma was stiff, Jefferson clutching my dress. I looked to Christina. She was biting her lip. Julia stood firm but kept her head downcast instead of up, as she normally held it.

"I am much concerned," Pawn said in English. "This day, my

wife Speaks with Strong Tongue tells me there was an escape plan."

I gasped and glanced at Christina again. She shook her head. Julia? I couldn't believe it. Christina was the rebel, I thought. Julia had been nothing but dutiful. Then I remembered our discussion. Had someone overheard? Had someone heard me say I would run? I staggered a bit.

"I have trusted too much." His gaze bore into Julia's, and she lowered her head more.

What had she done?

"Though I wished to give my white captives comfort, my hand has been forced. As leader, I must prevent such things." He paused and looked at each one of us, his expression deadly serious.

His wife, Strong Tongue, grinned.

"Dora and George Wright. Emma Duley and the little girl, come here."

"No!" Julia and I cried out together.

"Silence!" Pawn's face reddened as he saw how we clung to our children. "Take them."

Women came forward, grabbing our little ones, holding us back as they were dragged forward. I struggled against the hands securing me as my children were taken to stand with the man who had betrayed us all so grievously yesterday.

Oh, how I hated him.

"Stop, women! I can easily kill these children."

I stopped. Julia did the same.

"Laura Duley, your boy I will leave with you. Sleepy Eye's wife has need for him. These others, I now give to other lodges."

Emma and Dora, old enough to understand, turned to look at us, their eyes full of questions, lips trembling.

"Please," Julia said, "please don't do this. I only meant to stop for a moment. It won't happen again."

"I cannot take that chance. I am the leader, and you have pushed me to take this step. From now on, these children will not live with or walk with their white mothers."

Women approached and herded the children away. The older girls struggled but were hauled apart anyway. A young squaw grabbed Frances from Emma's arms, and her cries rent the air.

"Please, do not punish all of us," I pleaded. "Please!" I fell to me knees.

"I have spoken," Pawn said. "It is this, or their death."

Julia
August 24

Evening was falling by the time the party set up camp a few miles outside the Redwood Agency. The group was smaller now—White Lodge and his followers had split off to attack Sioux Falls—and they moved faster. Julia's feet ached from the day's long march. Her legs ached, her arms ached, her back and bruised skin ached. And . . . her heart ached. The last three days had provided her new perspective, and she chided herself for having considered taking her former position for granted. And for being prideful.

From here on out, she would think before she acted.

She brushed sweat-drenched hair from her face and shrugged off the heavy pack in the spot Strong Tongue had indicated. By her reckoning, they'd covered twenty miles today. It had been the longest day thus far. She had precious little time to dump the pack and fetch the lodge poles.

Julia's muscles sighed with relief, but the respite was short lived. The minute she straightened from her hunched position, they seized up on her. With stiff steps, she returned to the wagons. A crowd of women clustered around it.

As a leader, Pawn's lodge poles were at the top of the stack, and Julia knew others were waiting. If she didn't get her poles off the wagon, the other captives might be punished for taking too long. She'd found that out the second night, at their camp on Long Lake. She'd lingered too long, and Laura had been beaten for not returning promptly with her poles.

They were all interconnected now.

Julia reached for the roll of twelve poles, grasping the rope that tied them together. She wrapped the rope around both hands, turned with the rope over her shoulder, and began to walk. The rope bit into the scabs on her hands, opening the wounds. She strained forward, wincing as the rope sliced her shoulder.

Laura stood at the edge of the group, watching her. Julia tugged harder. She didn't want to see the scowling in Laura's eyes, the blame.

In the next moment, Christina was there, grabbing the rope with her, moving the dreadful weight with her.

"How's George?" Julia asked. Thankfully, Running Bear's wife had taken George, easing Julia's worry by half.

"He cries, but he eats and does as he is told."

Julia's throat closed. Her poor little boy, too young to understand why he'd been jerked away from his mama and taken to live with a stranger. Thank heaven for Christina, that he had her there with him.

Dances in Water had told her removing the children was not a punishment but instead was a way to prevent the women from running away. Neither she nor Laura would leave children behind.

"Have you seen Dora today?" she asked.

"*Ja*. She was gathering wood and works hard."

That was Dora. At five, she knew what was expected. Old enough to obey, but hardly old enough to comprehend all this. Julia damned herself for giving in to temptation, for failing to think about consequences.

"If you get a chance, tell them I love them and that I'm sorry." Her voice broke.

"*Ja*. This they know, but I will tell them." Christina's words were soft, comforting. She was a good friend.

The logs dropped from the wagon behind them, the sudden movement ricocheting up the rope. It slapped against Julia, and she jumped. "Ouch!"

Christina shook her head. "The wife of Pawn does not help with this?"

"No." Strong Tongue helped with very little anymore. Except to berate her and hit her. And it was only when Strong Tongue wasn't watching that Dances in Water assisted. Julia envied Christina, who was aided in heavy tasks by Running Bear's wife. Then she squelched the green-eyed monster. She had no one to blame but herself. "I think she is very bitter to defy Dakota customs so much."

"I would help more, but I dare not."

"I know. It's all right. Thank you."

"*Ja*." Christina squeezed her arm before returning to the wagon, where Running Bear's wife waited.

Julia turned and jerked the poles along behind her. When she arrived at the lodge site, she untied the logs and grouped them together, the three main poles, the three sets of four, and the extra pole. She tied the main poles together and left them for Strong Tongue and Dances in Water, who would erect the lodge. She hurried to unpack the skins so they would be ready when it was time.

"What took you so long?" Strong Tongue asked.

"I am not yet strong."

"You are lazy." Strong Tongue's eyes glinted, and she slapped Julia's face.

Julia's head dipped forward, her skin and eyes both stinging.

"I will work harder," she choked out.

Strong Tongue spat at her and walked away.

Dances in Water, Pawn's second wife, bit her lip, her gaze full of pity. But she said nothing.

It was enough, though. Julia gave her a quavering smile, letting her know she understood the hierarchy of the lodge prevented any interference. Julia turned away and started meal preparations, hoping she would do well enough to avoid another slap.

Routine filled the rest of the evening, and Julia was bone weary by the time she finished cleaning up the meal.

Full darkness had descended when Pawn approached. "Julia Wright, I would have you walk with me."

This was the first he had spoken to her since the night of the attack. "You are well?"

"Much better. German Woman is strong." He gave a wry grin, out of place on his hardened face and guided her to the bank above the Minnesota River. He motioned for her to sit and lowered himself to the ground beside her.

"I have seen you are sad. For this, I am sorry. You have been a good friend. I walk a thin line and could not let your actions go unpunished."

It was both an apology and the explanation, she realized. "I was not trying to escape," she told him—a stab in the dark. She doubted it would ease things, but she damn sure wasn't ever going to admit her guilt.

"That may be. Or may not be." He shrugged. "This I don't know, but it does not matter. It appeared you were trying to escape, and that was enough. I cannot be weak and continue to be leader of my village."

"I understand."

"Do not put me in that position again."

"I won't."

He watched her for a while, and she tried to keep her ease under the scrutiny.

"Speaks with Strong Tongue voices her displeasure with your work," he finally told her.

She looked up. She'd never please that woman, and they both knew it. "I'm trying."

He laughed, a short grunt-like sound. "I know this, but you must know she is honored as daughter of old Sleepy Eye. Her word carries weight.

"I would have you welcomed into my family in the way of the Dakota, yet my wife chooses to put herself first in this. She ignores our kinship traditions but it is her lodge and her decision." He stood and looked down at her. "Take care, Julia Wright, for I will not be able to spare you punishment if you fail to obey her."

If it came down to her words against those of Strong Tongue, it wouldn't matter whether she'd obeyed or not. Her life was now dependent upon the whim of a bitter woman who hated and resented her.

She suspected it would only be a matter of time before Pawn's warning became reality.

Chapter Twenty-One
September 1862
Almena and Lavina
Recovery

Almena
Brown's Cabin
September 2

Almena tucked the boys into bed, warmth filling her. It was good to watch them asleep so soundly, their tummies full and William Henry's little feet healing. She kissed them on their heads and prayed the night would be quiet.

"Hear anything?" she asked Lavina.

Her friend sat in a chair, bolstered by pillows, her leg propped on an empty crate so her swollen heel hung over the edge. Beside her lay one of the dogs that had so frightened them the day they'd arrived, some nine days ago now.

"Not tonight," Lavina answered.

It had become their standard exchange in the days since they'd reached this place. After the mail carrier had assured the house was safe, he'd returned with food he'd found inside and left them, headed east for help. They'd remained in hiding until dark, in case the Dakota were still around, before moving to the cabin. Those words—*hear anything?*— had been their constant refrain. Days later, they remained diligent.

"I still worry," Almena admitted.

The dog moved to lay its head in Lavina's lap, and she scratched the animal's ears. "I'm glad we figured out these fellows belonged to the Browns, or we'd still be shaking out there in the plum thicket thinking they were Indian dogs."

Now, one dog slept inside with them, the other two just outside the door.

"Do you think Spot made it to Sioux Falls yet?" The mail carrier had reached New Ulm only to discover no horses or people about, just burned buildings and Indians creeping among the ruins. After stopping to report the news, he'd left them again, this time heading west.

Lavina shrugged. Neither voiced their fear that he'd met trouble. Instead, they sat in silence, both of them weary, until Lavina dozed in the chair.

Almena shook her awake. "Go on to bed. You're going to fall off the chair. I'll wait up a while." Though dead tired herself, she knew Lavina needed the rest more than she did. When they both retired, neither of them slept. At least this way, they could trade off.

"Do you think Uncle Tommy made it?" Lavina asked, only half awake.

He, too, had left them, determined to obtain more food, even if he had to sneak past the Dakota to do so.

"Stubborn as he is, of course." She had her doubts, but she wouldn't discuss them. Though he appeared to have regained his strength, his injuries were severe, and it was hard to believe he was as well as he pretended. She hoped he wasn't lying on the prairie somewhere.

Lavina inched across the room, still nursing her inflamed heel. She crawled into the bed, and the room quieted.

Almena watched her sleep. Like Tommy, Lavina was a survivor. Her stories of the horrors at the slough, the deaths of her husband and children, proved it. And her injuries, like Tommy's, should have killed her days ago.

Thank God they let us go.

She blew out the lamp and sat in the dark, listening.

Lavina
Brown's cabin
September 3

I wake with a start. Outside, the dogs are barking fiercely. "What is it? Do you hear anything?"

"No," Almena says. She is at the window, peering into the darkness. "Maybe it's just cattle moving through." Her words are casual, but concern fills her voice.

Chills rush up my spine, and I reach for Mrs. Brown's wrapper. We'll need to gather the children.

"The dogs are frightened," she says, confirming my own thoughts. "They're running back and forth."

"I'll rouse the boys." I leave the wrapper and grab my clothing instead, throwing it on. I hurry across the room.

"My God," Almena says. "It's Koch!" She runs to the door and throws it open.

For a moment, I think she speaks of Christina, who was taken away from the slough by Indians.

"Ernst Koch, is that you?" Almena says.

"*Ja!* And Jack Wright."

I dash to the door, forgetting about my heel. The German trader who had left the lake before the attack stands there with Julia Wright's husband.

"Tommy Ireland sent us for you," Wright says. Beyond them, a group of soldiers ride in with a wagon.

The boys, stirring from their beds, appear behind us, curious.

Wright fetches a lantern, and light engulfs us.

Chapter Twenty-Two
September–November 1862
Christina, Julia, and Laura
Different Routes

Laura

Encamped near Redwood Agency

Early September 1862

During the two weeks we had been encamped near the Redwood Agency, the Sioux were much unsettled, and we captives suffered dearly for it. Each day, riders brought updates of attacks and battles along the frontier. Not understanding the language, I had little grasp of the details beyond that Sioux victories brought celebrations, and defeats often led to beatings for us. Julia and Christina tried to communicate with me surreptitiously, but we were allowed little time together, and I lived isolated, enduring the travails of this new, horrifying life with no one but Jefferson to talk to.

Julia insisted she'd not tried to run, and I struggled not to blame her for causing my children to be taken from me. I couldn't, really, when all I wanted was to slip away to one of the many towns within the settled Minnesota River valley. But I dared not with two of my children in other lodges. Nor did I have any idea about what was happening in the area.

And so I hung on, for that was the only thing I could do with any certainty.

I had to find a way to be strong in this and shun any surrender to despair. There was no one here to force me from it. It would be up to me.

Never Let Go

"Mama?"

"Hmm?" I stayed put where I was. I needed to complete the chore I'd been assigned before the Old Hag returned. She'd never told me her name, and I'd never asked. She called me Dog.

"Can we go home today?" My boy asked this each day, and each day I'd been forced to tell him no.

"Not today. If you've finished stacking the firewood, go out and tell the Old Hag you're done. Otherwise, she will hit you again."

He left the tepee, pausing to hold the flap so a woman could enter. I didn't recognize her and drew a breath, resigning myself to yet more abuse.

"Is this Sleepy Eye's lodge?" she whispered.

Her English took me by surprise, and I looked at her more closely. She was dressed as most of the women in the camp, a combination of worn white woman's clothing and Indian dress, her hair in braids.

"It is," I said, still trying to sort out who she was. "Are you Sioux?" I finally asked.

"Half. I'm a captive."

"A half-breed captive?"

"My husband and I had a farm in Renville County. He was killed three weeks ago, on August eighteen, when the attacks first started. I've been kept in Little Crow's camp."

So Pawn had told Julia the truth . . . the attacks were not isolated to our settlement. But it hadn't occurred to me Indians might turn upon one another. I considered it for a moment.

"What are you doing here?" I asked, unsure how direct I should be.

"Sleepy Eye traded a locket for me."

"A locket?" She must have been valued very little.

"We're not worth much once they tire of us." She approached me and sat. "I'm Josepha; they call me Jo."

"Laura; they call me Dog."

I grappled with the fact that she was part Sioux, wondering if she'd been sent by the Old Hag to entrap me. "Why are *you* a captive?" I finally asked, weary of trying to process it.

"We didn't live as Dakota, and we refused to join the attacks."

"Oh." I appraised her anew. A farmer Indian, I think they called those who abandoned Sioux ways. This woman might have more knowledge, and I needed to seize the opportunity.

"Do you understand Sioux? Why are they doing this?" Of all the questions I had, this remained foremost in my mind. I couldn't fathom why they'd turned on us. We had been friendly, many of us trading with them.

Jo bit her lip. "It's complicated. The Sioux on the reservation were starving. Annuities were months late. The day before the attacks, there was an argument when a group of settlers refused to give food to four young Dakota men. The Dakota killed them and fled to their village for protection. A soldiers' lodge met—leaders from all the bands—but they didn't agree. Some decided to attack; others did not. Some wanted to chase away the whites; others wanted to kill them."

"How widespread?"

"New Ulm, Fort Ridgely, all along the Minnesota River north to Fort Abercrombie. East to Acton and Hutchinson, west to Sioux Falls. All the small settlements in between."

"Oh, my stars!" I felt faint, glad I had not tried to escape. "Are there no soldiers defending?"

"General Sibley leads a force but has few men. Everyone has been sent to fight the Rebels."

I'd forgotten . . . it had been so long since I'd heard news about Lincoln's war. "There was a big celebration a few days ago, and the men brought fifty horses and a herd of cattle into camp. What was that?"

"Sibley's burial detail was attacked at Birch Coulee. It was a huge victory for the Sioux. Sibley started peace negotiations, but Little Crow refuses to surrender."

"How many are dead?"

"Hundreds or more, and hundreds are captives." She paused. "How is it here?"

I shrugged. What could I tell her?

"It's harsh. My daughters were given to others. I see little of Emma and pray she is not beaten too severely. Frances is two, but very frail. Every night, I hear her crying, wailing for hours, and I don't know why. I worry she's being tortured. They left my boy here, with me."

"They did?" She looked surprised.

I thought about it for a moment. "I think it is to keep me in line." I looked down, unsure if I should reveal more, but she was a captive, too, and she'd likely experienced similar treatment. And, if not, she should know what was ahead for her. Still, I could not look her in the eyes. "Every night," I whispered, "when Sleepy Eye has his way, the Old Hag sits beyond the fire with Jefferson. I am afraid she would burn him if I resisted."

Jo's eyes grew wide. "This does not sound like the way of a Dakota woman. Perhaps it is an illusion?"

"I wouldn't put it past the—"

Jefferson burst into the tepee. "The Old Hag says to pack up. The soldiers are coming, and we need to leave."

Jo's hand flew to her mouth, but I scrambled. There was much to gather if we were to be away. The last thing I wanted was to be in the middle of a battle.

I'd survived too much to die that way.

Christina
Ten miles north of Yellow Medicine
Early September 1862

Our camp is near the place where Sleepy Eye has his village. We fled Redwood and unpacked little at the camps along the way. I think the leaders are very afraid the soldiers will catch them. They do not look so pleased now, and their faces are angry. Sleepy Eye's wife says we will move again. That means the soldiers are close. We always move when such news comes, breaking camp very quickly.

I take the stewpot and hurry to the river to rinse it.

Around me, Dakota children play, unaware of the tenseness. The boys pretend to be hunters, the girls care for dolls. I have watched them and seen the respect they have for their elders, how the older children teach the younger ones this. When a toddler misbehaves—a rarity—the oldest sibling is disciplined with quiet reserve.

In all, they are a happy people and enjoy one another. The women laugh while they work, like good German *Hausfraus,* and the children are much loved. I do not see the Dakota even slap their children. I have learned, in normal times, captives would not be hit either. Instead, they would be taken only to be adopted into a family.

Ach, these are different times, though.

This is a large war instead of a single raid on the enemy, and there are many unexpected captives. No one knows what to do with us. There is so much hatred that it changes how the Dakota respond. I think this is a bad thing for all of us.

Julia is at the river, and I go to her, eager for a few words. This is our first chance to talk in days, since she was shot for doing chores the wrong way. I think it was because Pawn's first wife resents her. I am thankful Running Bear's wife is not so bitter. Now that I have learned my chores, she treats me well.

"How is your heel?" I ask her. I step into the river and scrub at the pot.

"Scabbed, sore, but getting better. Just a flesh wound."

So, Pawn's shot glanced off. I think he had to do something because Strong Tongue made such a ruckus, but that he did not want to hurt Julia too much. He respects her, I think.

"How is George?"

"He does as he is asked, a good boy, and is not beaten. He sleeps on my robe and cries for you but says he is glad he is with someone he knows."

"Give him hugs and kisses from me. Tell him I love him and wish we could be together."

"I will."

"Do you see Dora?" she asks.

"She works hard as well. I think she is not mistreated."

We finish and climb the bank. Julia limps and does not put much weight on the heel. I think it hurts her badly. "You are limping."

"Limping but I still have my foot, still have my life."

I know she is right. She is still the same Julia and will not let this defeat her. But when we leave the river, she moves away from me, and I know she takes care not to anger Strong Tongue. Again, I am glad I am not mistreated.

We tear down the tepee and move minutes later. I drive the wagon, as usual, and George is allowed to sit with me. It is a good thing I was given such a job and do not have to walk with heavy packs like Laura and Julia. Today, the Ireland girls herd the cattle that will be butchered for food. The herd is growing smaller all the time. Lillie Everett is still with the wife of Grizzly Bear and suffers greatly.

After about ten miles, we stop to make camp again, and the tepee goes up as fast as it went down. White Lodge and part of his group are here already. We have not been with them since before the Redwood camp. Tonight, news will be exchanged. The women in his group have already cooked the meal, and we hurry to join them in the circle.

"Sioux Falls is destroyed," White Lodge reports. He is an old man but has much power among his people. I think he has been a chief for a long time.

They speak in Dakota, and I am glad I am able to understand.

"Are there soldiers to the west?" someone asks.

"No settlements are left. The soldiers come from the forts along the Missouri River. But I've heard they're thick here, along the Minnesota River."

"They move upriver. Many of our people are weary of running from them and talk of surrender."

"I will need to ponder this, decide what will be best," White Lodge says.

The men continue to talk of recent events while the captives and Indian women clean up the camp and finish unpacking. I am putting out the sleeping robes, George at my side, when Running Bear comes to the door.

"Come," he says. "Both of you. White Lodge wishes to see the captives."

I usher George out, and we follow Running Bear across the camp. White Lodge, who is also called *Wakeska*, is the man who first took me, who gave me to Running Bear. My stomach is in knots as I wonder what this is about. Ahead, the prisoners line up in front of the leader. Their captors stand in a group. I take George by the hand, and we join the line.

White Lodge paces in front of us. He looks at us as if we are prizes. When he stops in front of me, my feet want to sidestep, but I force myself to stand firm.

"This one," he says.

I look up at his words. This one what?

Running Bear steps forward. In the distance I spy Falling

Star, who has treated me so well. She strides to him and whispers in his ear.

"Well?" says White Lodge.

I swallow.

"She is a good worker. My wife doesn't wish to trade her."

The knots in my stomach tighten. When fighting first began, White Lodge wanted to kill all the whites.

"That's the reason I want her. German Woman is sturdy, and she raises your lodge well."

"My wife—"

"She also understands Dakota, and that is important. I will offer a horse for her."

I hear Julia gasp, and I hold George close.

Running Bear exchanges glances with his wife, and her lips draw tight. She whispers to him again, and he says, "What will you give for the boy?"

"I do not need the boy."

"My wife does not want the boy without the woman. Too much work for her."

"Why should I pay for something I don't want?"

"Perhaps the woman won't be such a good worker without the boy."

White Lodge sighs. "The horse has a good bridle. You can have that. This is all I will offer."

Running Bear pushes us forward, and I choke back my fear of what will happen next. Falling Star has given a gift, sending George with me, and I must be grateful and do all I can to make sure he remains safe.

White Lodge grins at me, and I cringe.

Julia
Ten miles north of Yellow Medicine
Mid-September 1862

Camp was in an uproar, despite the misty weather. Julia held fast to her chores, trying to avoid the hullabaloo. In the past ten days, more captives had been brought into camp. Some were sold away immediately but a few half-breeds were still being traded within camp. Though originally distributed among lodges in case they were needed as bargaining chips, the captives were now being sold and traded for other reasons. Bands were constantly on the move, and food was growing scarce.

Traditional rules no longer seemed to apply, and, despite Pawn making her a wife, Julia feared Strong Tongue would offer her up in a minute.

News of soldiers came daily, and tempers were short as the men bickered about what to do. White Lodge wanted to move to his own village and rejoin those who had stayed there. Others preferred to maintain the camp where it was.

A few days earlier, young Frances Duley had wailed the entire night, dying before morning. The child had been but two years old; Laura was bereft and had taken to her buffalo robes, unable to bear the grief of losing another daughter, and Sleepy Eye's wife had beaten her severely for refusing to work. Now, she finally emerged from her lodge, her face mottled with bruises.

Julia gasped. *She must be in such pain.*

But her attention was drawn away by a woman who entered camp with Lillie Everett in her arms.

Oh, no.

Julia started forward but was stopped by Dancing in Water's grip on her arm.

"It doesn't concern you," she said. "You must not go."

"What happened to her?"

"Grizzly Bear's wife continues to beat her for being the daughter of Will Everett."

"Because Will was one of those who shot him?"

"She cannot get past the hatred. It is an eye for an eye to her."

"This hatred is very strong."

"It destroys us. We are not a hateful people, Julia Wright. We should be offering hospitality and kinship to our guests. Too many are forgetting our ways, and this will leave a bad mark on our people."

Dances in Water offered a wan smile. "I must go. Speaks with a Strong Tongue will soon return and will expect you to be at work."

Julia turned away and dropped to the ground, marveling at how different the two wives were. With a simple reminder, Dances in Water had pointed out the need to remain productive. Strong Tongue would have hit her out of spite, even though it was not the Dakota way.

She focused on scraping the hide in front of her, but her attention was on Lillie. As they passed, Julia saw it was not Grizzly Bear's wife but an old woman, familiar somehow, who carried the girl. Lillie's body was limp and drenched with blood.

Lord, will it never stop?

"She takes Lillie to her lodge," Christina said.

Julia looked up and brushed away a damp lock of hair. It was the first time she'd seen her friend since Christina had been sold to White Lodge.

"Are you safe? George?"

"We are both fine, thank *Gott*. White Lodge is old. His eyesight is not so good, and he sits a lot. Sometimes he talks to me, asking questions, but otherwise he does not bother with us. We work hard, and his wives like us."

"Grizzly Bear's wife beat Lillie."

"With a stake, I heard. Two women found her lying on the ground, the cow bellowing next to her."

Poor Lillie; thank goodness she'd been rescued. Then, she realized why the woman looked familiar. "Was that Scalpie? The Scalpie who visited Shetek?" The elderly woman was a regular, scarred from being nearly scalped by a hostile band many years ago.

"*Ja*. This is good, is it not?"

"Very good. Scalpie was a patient of Myers, and I think she worked for Lillie's mother. If she recognized her, she'll take care of her."

"Laura is up."

"Did you see her face?"

"*Ja*. But she is up, and this is good."

"German Woman!"

Julia and Christina both looked toward the voice.

One of White Lodge's wives approached. "White Lodge has need of you," she said. "He has decided to go to his village and will take you with him."

Christina
Ten miles north of Yellow Medicine
Mid-September 1862

White Lodge's sons complain about his decision. "He should not take her. It would be better to leave her here," they say again and again.

"You should not go," one of the wives says. "Here there is more food. The village has nothing to eat."

"Hah, they will eat you," says another.

I do not want to go to this place, to leave my friends and be alone, but now I am afraid, because of their words. I think the village will be a harsh place if everyone has such bad words to say.

"German Woman, I am ready. Come." White Lodge beckons.

George rushes to me, and I hug him tight. "Be good, and these women will take care of you," I say, hoping it is the truth. He is sobbing, and everything in me breaks as I join White Lodge. One of the wives picks him up and holds him as we walk away.

When we get to his horse, he hands me his gun and mounts. I start to hand the gun back to him, but he grunts and says, "You carry it."

I walk alongside the horse. The mist becomes drizzle, and the air cools. I am cold and wet, and each step takes me farther from everything and everyone I know. My insides squirm.

The gun grows heavier, and I shift it from one shoulder to the other. Though I am strong from hard work, I think if I go on, I will never be found. The powder horn hangs from the gun and bumps against my chest, and the rain becomes miserable.

On the horse, White Lodge drones on about how the whites should have all been killed.

I re-shoulder the gun, and rain runs into my eyes. Oh, how Andreas hated rain like this when he hunted with his percussion gun; he had to take such care to keep moisture out of the powder charge when reloading.

My foot catches in an animal burrow. I struggle to keep my balance and nearly drop the gun.

"Take care, German Woman," White Lodge says, "or you will shoot yourself."

I pause, regain my footing, and see he has not stopped. Now, I will need to catch up. But I do not go right away because his words sink in.

I cannot shoot myself unless the gun has already been primed to shoot.

If it has been primed with powder already, I can shoot him. Then I pause, thinking it through—this would be a risk, if I miss. But if the powder got wet . . . he would not be able to shoot me, and perhaps I can run. A plan forms in my mind.

Glancing forward, I see the horse still moves, and I start to walk in case he looks back. But I move slowly so the distance grows. When he is enough in front of me that I think he will not be able to see clearly through his old and cloudy eyes, I ease back the hammer until I can reach the percussion cap. I remove it and hold it in one hand while I shift the gun so rain runs into the hole to the barrel, where the powder is.

"You are slow, German Woman. Keep up."

"I am coming, but my ankle hurts."

"Come faster. A good woman does not let pain stop her."

"Yes, White Lodge."

He continues, slowing a bit. I do not have much time before he will stop entirely. I know he will not let me get too far behind, especially since I carry the gun. I am thankful he does not realize I know how to fire it.

I squeeze water from my hair, and it fills the tube. I put the cap back on, ease the hammer down, and catch up to him. I am careful to limp when I get near. We continue on, and I keep up the limp—not much, but enough so he will believe I slowed because of it.

"Your wives say the Sissetons in the village have little to eat," I challenge.

"This is true, but we will hunt."

"*Ja*, but game is scarce."

"Then we will move camp."

I can see he does not like me arguing, but, still I push, unable to hold back my quarrelsome German tongue. "Your sons say it is a bad idea to take me with you."

"My sons are impudent."

My heart pounds. "I don't wish to go with you."

"It does not matter what you wish. You are mine, and you will go where I say." He is angry now.

Ach! No more!

I stop and raise my voice. "I will not. I will go no further with you."

He turns, faster than I think possible, and jerks the gun away from me. "You will obey me, German Woman." He raises the gun and points it at me, and I pray the powder is wet through. Either way, I have had enough.

"*Nein*, I will not." I step back and thrust out my chest, inviting him to shoot.

Laura
Big Stone Lake
Late September 1862

White Lodge returned to the camp with Christina, deferring to her as if she had special power and causing much speculation. It was five days until the focus of gossip shifted, when the riders came with news of a large battle at Wood Lake. General Sibley's forces attacked Little Crow's men, roundly defeating them. Worried they would soon be upon us, we disassembled the tepees in haste and fled northwest.

Jo had taught me more of the Sioux language, enough to understand the Old Hag's instructions and pick up the news around camp, and I chastised myself for not learning sooner. I thought of all the beatings I might have been spared and my new security in knowing what was happening in the world. I resolved anew to remain strong for my two remaining children.

Our new camp was at a place called Big Stone Lake, a widening of the Minnesota River. The gray waves reminded us fall had descended, and the prairies stretched brown and dry beyond the lake. We'd crossed into Dakota Territory, and the remaining Indians spoke of moving farther west if the soldiers gave chase. But some had broken away, refusing to leave Yellow Medicine. They said they were tired of fighting and would surrender or join the camps of the friendly Indians who had refused to take up arms in the first place.

"Did you hear?" Jo asked.

"Hear what?"

"White Lodge didn't bring Christina when we moved."

I jerked up my head. "What?"

"He sent her and George with a group of younger men who went to the west when we left Yellow Medicine."

"He sold her away?" I was surprised. I couldn't imagine he'd sold her. She was such a good worker.

"Maybe he got tired of all her fretting about going back to the whites."

And no wonder. She'd talked of it constantly. And, with indulgence other captors did not exhibit, he'd allowed it. "Maybe so," I agreed.

It was unfortunate, for her new captors would likely not be so accommodating. In fact, if she'd gone west, her life would likely be much harsher.

Oh, Christina, what did you do?

CHAPTER TWENTY-THREE
September–November 1862
Wandering

Christina

Yellow Medicine

Late September 1862

After my trick with the gun, White Lodge is very different. My plan to run was not well thought out—I'd forgotten to consider his horse. But now, I think he believes I worked magic. He tells me I am the bravest woman he has ever seen and gives me more freedom. I am glad of the honor he gives me, and I tell him I want to go back to my people, hoping he will consent.

But this morning, he gives me to the young men, and now I do not know what to think. The men march me away, before it is even daylight.

Ach, this is not a good thing. I fear we are going back where White Lodge was headed when I did the gun trick. Perhaps I was talking too much of wanting to leave, and White Lodge decided to punish me. Now, I am all alone, except for George Wright, who was sold to these men, too.

I pick him up and carry him for a while.

The five-year-old is confused. His face is pale, and he calls for his mama. Though he did not see her often, he knew she was in the camp. Now, the camp is gone, and we are the only whites with this smaller group. George shivers and drops his head on my shoulder.

"German Woman, keep up."

I move faster. I do not know if I am stronger or if George is losing weight, but he feels lighter. I think maybe he is wasting away and hope I can keep him safe. I promised Julia I would do this and know it will be harder if we go onto the prairies in Dakota Territory. Winter is coming, and our life will be harsh. I have heard stories of how the wind blows there.

We walk into the night and stop many hours after dark comes. I have no idea where we are, and no one tells me. I am ordered to help one of the women with a lodge. Her child has a cough, and she doctors it with teas and tells me she is also a captive and was married to a white man. She says now is a good time to escape because there are fewer men in the group. She vows to do so as soon as her child is well enough. I think at least this night I will have nothing to fear.

I put George on a buffalo robe and lie next to him hoping this will be true.

When the woman wakes me, I have hardly rested.

"German Woman, get up."

The fire has died down, and I am sure she will tell me to go and fetch wood.

"It is time to go."

I stand and start to the door.

"No," she whispers. "Take the boy along but do not let him make a sound."

Only now do I realize she is whispering.

"Quick, quick," she says. "The men rode out early, and we must go, before the rest of the camp wakes."

Her words do not make sense, not unless no one is to know we are going. Hope floods me, but I dam it. I must get George and follow her. I pick him up. He stirs but settles as I put him against my shoulder.

"Hurry."

I slip out into the night, and she follows with her child, who no longer coughs. With sharp hand signals, she directs me, and we jog away into the darkness. The camp dogs stand to follow us but return to their places, not caring much that we are going. An owl hoots, and I trip, but she catches my arm and steadies me.

After about thirty minutes, I dare to speak. "Where are we going?"

"I am taking you to your people."

Hope surges within me, but I must be sure. "To White Lodge's camp?" I ask.

"Away from the Dakota."

I quicken my step, new energy flowing in my veins. We wade through water, and she tells me this will hide our tracks, and the dogs will not have our scent if the men search for us. The children sense the need for quiet and do not fuss. Through the day, we rush on, going back and forth across the Minnesota River. We say little, even when the water is deep, and we struggle for our footing. Our clothes are wet, cold in the autumn wind, but I try not to think about it. We take no roads, and my guide says this is because she cannot be seen. I trust she is right.

Near nightfall, we approach a camp. I stop, fearful she has led me into a trap.

She turns. "It is all right, German Woman. This is Red Iron's village, and they wait for the white army. They have no will to fight and will surrender. There are many whites there, waiting."

"Why do you do this?" I ask her.

"Because you have been favored."

I do not understand her meaning, and she explains no further.

We enter the camp, and she speaks to someone there, then takes me to a tent. "This a half-breed family of a Frenchman. I know them, and they will keep you safe." She pushes me forward. "I go to find my friends."

"Thank you," I say. I want to hug her but smile instead, unsure.

She smiles back. "Go. It is time." She disappears into the darkness.

A few days later, three days after the Battle of Wood Lake, General Sibley's troops arrive. He names the place "Camp Release" and accepts the surrender of friendly Indians camped there. That day, ninety-one whites and one hundred fifty mixed-blood captives are freed.

I clutch George's hand, and we walk forward to give our names. Today is a good day, and we have survived.

Julia
Big Stone Lake
Late September 1862

Julia swayed on her feet, unable to digest Laura's words. George was gone? She grabbed the tree branch to steady herself. "When?" she asked.

"Yesterday. White Lodge sent them with another group."

"Where to?" She looked from side to side, stopped herself. *Stupid thing to do—he's not here.*

"No one knows. They left camp very early."

Tears stung behind her eyelids. "Oh my God."

"I tried to get to you last night but couldn't."

"Oh my God." A sob escaped, and she wavered on her feet.

Laura held open her arms, and Julia fell into the embrace. She'd never thought she'd be brought this low. "I thought I'd escape losing them."

"I hoped you would. Just hang on to the fact that he lives, that they didn't kill him."

"Yet."

"Christina will protect him."

Julia drew a breath. It would do no good to give in to despair. None. "How did you get through the pain?"

"I haven't. But if I surrender to it, I won't be here for Emma and Jefferson. They are all I have left."

Guilt nipped at Julia. Laura had needed comfort, too, and she'd not given it. "I'm so sorry if I didn't seem to care when—"

"I know you cared. But you had your children about you, and they needed you."

"What he must be feeling, ripped away like that!" How would a boy of three even begin to understand?

"Christina will make it better for him. She'll tell him it's only for a little while. He'll be all right. Focus on Dora. She's smart as a whip, and she'll figure out what's happened. She'll need to see you being strong, even if from across camp."

"I'm usually the one offering advice."

"I know. Strange how events turn. You've taught me much about being strong. I guess it's a fair turn-about for me to help you."

Julia gave her a wavering smile. Laura was right. But it was strange, her being the strong one now. Laura Duley had been frightened of her shadow for the entire time Julia had known her, that or weeping about her fate.

"Ellen Ireland was sold, too. To Talking Spirit." Talking Spirit was young, recently married. His new bride would be much honored with the gift, but Julia doubted the teen would know what to do with the six year old. But, who knew? There could well be a baby on the way for her to tend.

"I hope they treat her well. Pawn talks of more of the main group splitting off. It'll be hard to travel in large numbers once the snow flies."

Laura shivered. "Not what I want to think about."

Julia turned, knowing she had no more time to spare before Strong Tongue came for her. She trudged back to camp, water vessels in each hand. Near the lodge, Pawn stood talking with White Lodge. She neared and set the water down.

"What is that one called?" White Lodge asked.

"Julia Wright."

"She is strong, like German Woman."

Julia sharpened her ears. White Lodge spoke of Christina.

"She is a good woman, despite what Speaks with Strong Tongue thinks."

"I have need for her to replace German Woman."

Julia held her breath. This was not good.

"I took her as a wife."

"She is not a wife, not in our old ways. She is a captive like the others. Your wishes do not matter to me, Across the River. Your stature is not secure. I will buy this Julia Wright. You may have three buffalo robes for her."

"I do not need any more buffalo robes."

"I will give you a cow."

"I will keep her, thank you."

"Robes, cows, take your pick." White Lodge shrugged his shoulders. "Either way, she comes to my lodge now. I like speaking with the white women, and I have need of her."

And, with that, White Lodge reached out, grabbed Julia's arm, and yanked her away.

Laura
Sheyenne River, Dakota Territory
October 1862

There was a rush of trading before we left Big Stone Lake, and I was sold for a blanket. At the time, it was like a slap, to be valued so little. With the first snowfall, I realized the value of blankets and rethought my assumption.

"I'm so cold," Lillie Everett mumbled. Trudging next to me,

Never Let Go

she tightened her scrap of wool around her shoulders.

"You were lucky Old Scalpie gave that to you," I said.

My teeth chattered, and I despaired of ever being warm again. I prayed Jefferson, sold into a different lodge, was faring better than I. The wind blew bitter ice fragments into my face, stinging it red. I had no need to look into a mirror to know how chapped it had become—I could feel it burning.

"Maybe she'll give me one for you."

"It's better not to ask. It will only cause trouble." I longed for my flannel shawl, for my knitted scarf, but I'd survive. I had to. Emma and Jefferson needed me to be strong so they could be strong. I envied Lillie, but I rejoiced for her good fortune as well.

"I'm glad she rescued me."

"Me, too. You're a lucky girl." It was hard to imagine these people having the kindness and warmth the old woman had shown Lillie after rescuing her from Grizzly Bear's wife. She'd hauled the six year old on a travois, enduring chastisement from the other women. When they'd taken the travois away, Old Scalpie had carried her on her back.

"That's because my mama was good to her. She remembered."

Too bad more of them hadn't remembered the kindnesses given them by our little group of settlers. I'd never been able to understand what Julia saw, to trust Pawn as she did. In my view, he'd betrayed us, led us straight into death.

"You can use my blanket for a while, if you want."

I smiled at Lillie and shook my head. She needed it more than I. "I have my calico." I drew the piece of cotton around my shoulders. It was a remnant, full of holes, but offered extra protection to the tattered dress I'd worn for nearly two months.

"Look! The camp!"

I glanced up and followed Lillie's pointing finger. Across the wide expanse of tall, brown prairie grass ahead of us, I spotted tepees. The buffalo hunters' camp. My stomach growled.

"Tonight, we'll have meat," I told Lillie.

"Truly?"

"That's what the Indian women say." The cows had all been butchered long ago, and our only foodstuffs came from dried meats, berries, and wild game—which was too scarce to support us. Hunger became a constant companion this past week.

We neared the encampment, and a group was dispatched to secure our welcome. The buffalo hunters were not Sisseton but, rather, members of a local band. One of the men returned with word we would camp near them for a day or two.

With renewed energy, we hurried to make camp. There were forty or fifty lodges in our group, and we swamped the other group. Lillie returned to Old Scalpie, I to my new owner. This woman barked orders but had not yet hit me as did the Old Hag. She'd yet to tell me her name, so I called her Loud Talker. It seemed appropriate.

"Hurry," she said. "There will be a feast, and we do not want to be late."

"They'll feed us all?"

"We are guests, and guests are always fed."

I wondered if that applied to captives as well but didn't ask the question. I helped her pitch the lodge and put our sleeping robes inside. My feet ached, and I wished I could sink down and remove my shoes. They were worn thin, the soles full of holes, the tops torn where the grasses had cut through the leather. Some days we'd covered nearly thirty miles.

I could find no rhyme or reason to our path, save we were perhaps avoiding soldiers or trying to confuse pursuers with our zigzag route. Up until a few days ago, we'd often traveled by night, sleeping during the day. Many times, we'd camped without fires.

"Hurry, woman," Loud Talker said.

I followed her from the tepee.

"Go there. Tonight, you may all sit together." She pointed.

Across the camp, the captives were clustering together, the whites in one group, the half-breed women in another. My lodge-mate, Jo, was no longer among them, having been sold away en route west.

I rushed to my friends, and we exchanged hugs, mindful of those who watched us.

"Why do we get to sit together tonight?" I asked Julia.

"I think because they don't want to bother with us during the feast. We have no idea where we are, so there's little chance we'll escape."

"We're near the Sheyenne River," I told her, repeating what I'd heard Loud Talker say.

"As if any of us knows where that is."

We traded news about new owners, most of us now traded at least once. Only Roseanna Ireland remained with her original captors. The couple favored her and named her *Ondee*, which meant Rain. She was treated well and often released to play with the children of the camp. Julia said there might be an adoption ceremony for her, if we ever stopped fleeing.

"Mama!"

I turned at Emma's voice and took her into my arms. "My sweet girl, look at you." Her beautiful hair was in tangles and her dress a dirty mess. But she looked healthy, save for her haunted eyes. I clutched her.

Jefferson bounded into us, and I showered him with kisses. "Oh, darling! Do you stay warm? Do they treat you well? Do you eat?" The words tumbled from my mouth.

We chattered on, I with my children, Julia with her Dora, the Ireland girls and Lillie. All of us were cold, tired, and hungry, but we'd learned the way of things and how to avoid beatings.

Hard work was prized among these people, and it had become our way now, too.

"How's White Lodge?" I asked Julia.

"His wives are tolerant of me, not like Strong Tongue. He spends much time asking me about the whites."

"Have you heard where we go from here?"

"He's mentioned Elm River, wherever that is."

Like her, I was no longer familiar with the landmarks we encountered. We were hopelessly lost. "How far do you think we are from Shetek?"

"I don't have a clue. All I know is that we haven't reached the Missouri River yet."

"Do you think we'll be captives forever?" I asked, already suspecting we would.

Julia shrugged. "It gets more likely every day."

Julia
Near the Big Bend of the Missouri River
October 1862

Julia set down her pack and watched the people in the other camp. They called this place the Big Bend. It was a distinctive curve in the Missouri River, and, if she remembered correctly, Jack had said the Big Bend was due west of Lake Shetek, halfway across Dakota Territory. White Lodge had led the group north, then back south.

This other camp spoke Lakota, still Sioux but speakers of a different dialect. They were western Sioux—Tetons—the village led by Two Kettles. He was not happy about them being here; that much was obvious to everyone.

She straightened, aching from the rough use these past three nights. Her newest owner's preoccupation with her had also angered his wife, and she'd been beaten daily. Today, her ribs were sore, and she hated to think about how bruised her face must be. From across the camp, Pawn looked at her, and she thought his eyes held apology.

But they were no longer friends.

The loss should have caused her sorrow, but she was numb to it. She was on her own, and all she needed to do was hang on. She could endure anything. She had to.

White Lodge neared and stopped in front of her.

"Julia Wright, I have missed you."

Odd as it was, she had missed him—*if that's what one called it.* Though she hated him with every fiber of her being for having been among those who led the attack on Shetek, he was a tolerant captor.

"Yet you sold me," she said.

"I needed the blankets for my wives. They were cold."

Practical, matter of fact—she could relate to that as well. Didn't mean she had to like it, though. "And are they still cold?"

"They are warmer than you. But now I am much lonely, and my wives miss you. You are a good worker and a good cook."

Julia had learned straight off that work was valued in this culture. Jack had valued that, too. It'd be nice to be valued for herself sometime.

"My wives think they would like to have you back in the lodge."

"That does not involve me," she said.

"They will share blankets, so I may offer one to buy you back. You will go to my lodge again."

"Hmmpf."

"It has already been done. Come now."

Julia followed White Lodge, accepting the change with little emotion. She was beyond any mourning or celebration regarding who owned her. But she couldn't help hoping the man she was leaving preyed on his wife tonight and left *her* bruised and battered. Maybe, the wife would hit him. That would be just as good.

They neared White Lodge's tepee, and he paused. "I wish you to come with me. I go to smoke the pipe with Two Kettles. I would have him see my fine white captive so he will know I have good medicine and agree to be my ally."

Being valued simply because she was a white captive wasn't exactly what she had in mind, either.

When they entered the other camp, White Lodge led her through the circles of lodges to the center. There, he told her to sit while he met with Two Kettles. She settled outside the lodge, and a few of the women neared.

"You are White Lodge's captive?"

"One of them." She heard the hollow tone in her voice and wondered when she'd stopped caring.

"How many does he have?" another asked.

"Two white women, six white children, six half-breed women."

"So many."

The women chattered among themselves in Lakota. The words were hard to distinguish, but she understood the gist of the conversation. They spoke about the captives and disagreed about the strategy of taking white captives as well as about their treatment. They'd noticed the bruising on her face, her slow gait.

One of the women gave her a bowl of stew, and her stomach growled. She forced herself to eat it slowly so her empty stomach wouldn't rebel. She had one handful remaining when White Lodge exited the tepee. She quickly ate the last of it and handed the bowl back to the women, offering her thanks. She followed White Lodge back to his tepee.

As he'd told her, the wives were glad of her return, and White Lodge welcomed her into his own robe that night. Though he whispered he would wait until she healed instead of taking her that night, he'd not asked her to be a wife. The old traditions had become a casualty of war, and she was nothing now but a possession to be passed from one man to another.

She felt his hardness against her back as he spooned her, and she wept.

Laura
Along the Missouri River, near Beaver Creek
November 1, 1862

Winter came on with full force, dumping snow often as we traveled north. White Lodge's big plans to unite with Two Kettles failed miserably when the leader sent word his people had no quarrel with the whites and did not wish to join in the fighting. The band supplied them with food and told them to move on.

Bitter winds accosted us as we trudged north. A few days ago, we'd camped near a band of Yantonais, another band of the Teton Sioux, and White Lodge was attempting to recruit them to his cause.

I shivered as I neared the shoreline, my fabric scrap shawl no longer of much use. My shoes had gone by the wayside miles ago—I'd cut off the soles and tied them to my feet. But now, those, too, were worn beyond use. I sat on a rock to attend to my feet. My chores could wait. I'd stolen two strips of leather from the tepee. I didn't care if I was beaten. My feet were nearly frostbitten, and I could go no further in this condition.

Julia walked the bank collecting dried buffalo dung, water vessels hanging from her shoulder. I waved to her and began working on my new footwear. I untied the rag strip holding the useless sole and peeled it from the bottom of my foot, wincing as my tortured skin went with it. The cloth was in shreds. Sighing, I ripped the cotton I'd used as a shawl and used half to wrap my foot. My arms would have to go bare—there was nothing else for it. I bound the stolen leather around it, round and round, and tied it off around my ankle. From my pocket, I took strips of sinew and lashed them around my foot to help hold everything secure. Not fashionable in any sense, but much better than before.

No fairy-tale glass slippers, certainly.

With unexpected suddenness, I laughed at how my priorities in life had changed. It was the first time in months that I'd found humor in anything.

I crossed my other foot onto my lap and repeated the procedure.

Julia had disappeared to the south, but I heard a commotion from upriver. Afraid they'd come to search for me, I grabbed my own bag of buffalo dung and hastened back the way I'd come.

Treading up a low rise, I spied sails and dropped the bag in my rush up the hill. It was a Mackinaw boat! The wooden sailboat was common among fur traders.

Whites?

A group of Santee, mostly from our camp of Sisseton, were at the edge of the water, beckoning the group in the boat to shore. Three men jumped from the boat, and I recognized them as Yanktonais from the group camped north of us. They yelled for the rest of the group to move on, no matter what. Then the Santee raised their guns toward the boat.

Oh, please go on. Do not let these people take you.

I wanted to shout, but I held my tongue. I couldn't risk a warning if I was to keep Emma and Jefferson safe. But another man had already waded ashore. He *was* white, as were a number of his party in the boat.

I approached, keen to hear what was happening, but took care to stay out of sight. The Santee were arguing with the three

Yanktonais men, their voices loud.

"We must kill all of them," one of the Santee said.

"No, the woman is Yanktonais and must be spared."

I glanced at the boat, where an Indian woman sat atop a high pile of goods. She watched the man on shore closely.

"What is she hiding, there on the boat?" the Santee asked.

"Eagle Woman doesn't hide anything," the white man said. "She is with the body of our son, and we're taking him home for burial."

"Galpin tells the truth," said one of the Yanktonais. "We were on the boat, and we saw this."

"And the other men?"

"They are miners, riding with us. We mean no harm," Galpin said.

"We will spare you if you give us all you have aboard, the food and the trade goods."

Galpin agreed and beckoned to the boat. One of those still aboard tossed a rope, and the Santee hauled the boat close, wading into the water to take possession. The two groups continued to argue about what Eagle Woman might be hiding. Finally, one of the Yanktonais men became angry.

"You will let these people go or the Yanktonais will turn on the Santee."

Eagle Woman stood in the boat and screamed at her husband to come. She pointed to the shoreline. More Santee had crept through the grass. Eagle Woman cut the rope, and Galpin jumped aboard as the boat floated away. Aboard, everyone crouched low. The Santee raised their guns and fired.

I jumped at the sound, tears biting my eyes. Heaven only knew when I would again see whites. I moved back, afraid to let the Santee witness me spying, unwilling to let them glimpse my tears. My dung bag had slid down the hill. I sighed and turned back to fetch it.

In the distance, Julia ran along the shore shouting at the boat.

I held my breath.

But the boat passed her by and continued downriver.

Chapter Twenty-Four
November–December 1862
The Fool Soldiers

Julia

Along the Missouri River

November 1, 1862

Julia watched the boat pass by, disappointment squeezing every fiber of her being.

Damn, damn, and damn!

The vulgar words, foreign to her a few months before, no longer shamed her. She'd hardened. She was no longer the lady she'd been raised to be, the wife who fought to maintain her reputation, or the woman who rescued her scoundrel of a husband.

She'd fought too hard, survived too much, *allowed* too much. It was enough to make her want to curl up and die. How could they have sailed past, as if they hadn't cared one whit about there being white captives? She'd made a split-second decision, had staked her life—and Dora's—on calling out to them. And they'd gone on past.

The boat floated away, well out of earshot now, and she watched it until it disappeared. When it was gone, she picked up the water vessels and the bag of dung she'd dropped on the ground and trudged back to camp.

She supposed it was too much to ask that no one had noticed.

"Julia Wright."

She looked up at the sound of White Lodge's voice. His face was stern, his voice hard. She stopped in front of him and waited to be disciplined.

"I do not know why you keep doing these things."

"It did little good."

"And I am glad of that. Still, it cannot go unpunished. Pack up your things. I am trading you back to Across the River. Speaks with Strong Tongue will deal with you. My wives are not strict enough."

So, back to Pawn and his embittered wife. She took the buffalo dung and water vessels back to White Lodge's wives before trudging to Pawn's lodge.

"What a disgrace you are that you have to be traded to me so you stay in line." Strong Tongue kicked her, spat at her. "You are worthless."

Julia lowered her head. She knew that wasn't true. She was a good worker as well as a good cook. But she was also known for disobedience. She'd tried to be like Christina, but she guessed it wasn't in her nature.

"Well, take down the lodge. The Yanktonais withdrew their hospitality. We've been asked to leave."

Less than an hour later, the camp was packed and ready to go, back south this time, to the Grand River. Julia hefted her pack and marched forward with the rest of the band. She spotted Dora and waved.

A smile lit her daughter's face, and Julia smiled in return.

Heavens, how did I let myself forget?

She needed to count her blessings. White Lodge could easily have traded her to the Yantonais before they departed. And, though she didn't have control over what others did to her, she *did* control how she responded. She was strong, damn it, and she was done with simply enduring.

Though she had no quarrel with Pawn, he refused to interfere with Strong Tongue. Life was easier with White Lodge. She'd find a way to persuade him into buying her back. His wives liked her, he liked her, and he would have need of a white captive again when he made yet another plea to another band to join his cause and attack settlements in the spring. Then, she'd focus on finding a way to get Dora into his lodge.

Ahead, Laura slowed, and Julia caught up. The band had grown more lax, now that they were so far from civilization, and didn't bother to keep the captives separated so much. In the evenings, Julia sat with the children, making sure they were all right and offering them encouragement. There were fewer beatings now that all knew what was expected of them. Lillie was treated well by Old Scalpie, and Roseanna was a favorite of Redwood's wife.

"They didn't stop," Laura said.

"You saw?"

"I was too frightened to call to them and so proud of you. You're always the one taking risks for the rest of us, bolstering us when we need it the most."

The words warmed her. "We're pretty close to out of food, again. There will be hungry nights ahead. Maybe we should start stashing roots and berries. I've had enough of watching them eat while we starve." The only good thing about wasting away was that neither had conceived a child.

Laura lifted her tattered skirt hem. "Did you see my new shoes?"

"Very fine. White Lodge's second wife gave me her old moccasins, holes and all."

"Will we wander from camp to camp all winter, do you think?"

Julia thought for a moment. "Game is so scarce that I doubt they'll make a permanent winter camp. Besides, White Lodge is so determined to recruit among the Teton so he can renew fighting the whites in the spring."

"I hear mumblings. Not all his people agree anymore."

"Mumblings, yes, but I doubt enough to change his course. We're in for a hard winter, friend of mine."

Laura
On the Missouri River, near the mouth of the Grand River
mid-November 1862

I limped to a log and sat down, my buckshot heel paining. For reasons that bewildered me, my owner's wife had grown angry and shot at my feet, one of the balls landing in my heel. A week later, I still had no idea what had prompted her outrage. I was fortunate it had been a light wound and that they'd sold me to someone with compassion enough to dress it.

The camp was busy with chatter. A small group of men, perhaps from the Two Kettle Band where we'd camped several weeks ago, was setting up lodges a mile or so distant. The gossips were having a fine time speculating about them. Though they'd come from the direction of Bone Necklace's camp—where we'd seen the boat—everyone agreed they were from further south. Perhaps they'd broken from Two Kettle to join with White Lodge. If so, they would be the first Tetons to do so.

White Lodge paraded back and forth, preparing to welcome the young men to his cause. What that meant for us, I did not know, and I was eager to talk to Julia. She was back in White Lodge's tent again; he constantly sold her and bought her back. She joined me at the log, both of us watching him.

"Look." I pointed to two young men entering camp on horseback. They both dismounted and walked through camp.

"I recognize them," Julia said. "They *were* at Two Kettle's village. I saw them when White Lodge took me to the council there."

"What do you suppose they want? Will they join the Santee, do you think?"

"I don't know. Come on." She grabbed my hand, and I limped along with her, weaving through the tepees. I glanced around, fearing we would be observed and punished for leaving our work. I halted, out of sight, as we neared White Lodge. This was close enough.

Julia huffed but stayed beside me.

The men looked to be in their late teens or perhaps early twenties. They passed us, speaking quietly. "There are too many warriors here to fight, but they are starving. We will use that."

Fight? Who were these men? I glanced at Julia, and she shrugged.

The two approached White Lodge with the deference due an elder and leader and stopped.

"I am known as *Wa Anatan,* or Charger," said the taller.

"I am called *Wa Yaya,* or Kills Game," said the other.

White Lodge grunted. "You are from Two Kettle's band."

"Yes, there are ten of us," Charger confirmed.

"And ten more who left you and turned back." White Lodge flung out the insult, but neither young man flinched.

"They were from Bone Necklace's camp," Kills Game stated.

Though the explanation meant little to me, White Lodge nodded as if the distinction was important. "What is it you want, Charger and Kills Game? You have come a long way."

"We wish to hold council with the Santee," Charger said.

"We have little food to offer you." The admission seemed to pain White Lodge.

"We have food and will bring it to share with your people," Charger answered. "We want to speak about your captives."

I gasped and reached for Julia's hand. Her eyes were wide. She motioned for me to keep still with her finger to her lips. We stepped backward, quietly, until we were a distance from the trio.

"What do you think is going on?" My head spun with possibilities.

"I'm afraid, Laura. Very afraid. Before this night is done, some of us may well be sold away."

Julia
On the Missouri River, near the mouth of the Grand River
mid-November 1862

Julia sat at the back of the council lodge, against the outer wall, well behind the elder members of the tribe. She knew she was present only because White Lodge might need to display her. If not, she would remain unseen behind the men.

But she would be able to hear and might have at least a chance of warning the other captives about which of them were to be traded.

The two Teton men, Charger and Kills Game, boys really, sat with White Lodge. Together, they shared the pipe, until White Lodge lowered it and gestured for them to speak.

"You see us here. Our people call us crazy, but we want to do something good." Charger paused, and Julia held her breath, waiting.

At Kills Game's agreement with his words, Charger continued. "If a man owns a thing, he will not part with it for nothing. We have come here to buy the white captives."

Julia fought to draw a breath.

White Lodge grunted, stiffening at the words.

"We will give horses for them, all the horses we have. That proves we want the captives very much."

All their horses. The cost for captives had dropped from guns and horses to blankets, a pair of pants, and measly trinkets. This was a generous offer, and White Lodge might very well accept it. Julia leaned forward.

"You speak of doing a good thing. I wish to know what you mean by this."

"We wish to return the captives to their friends."

They want to ransom us? Set us free?

"Hah!" White Lodge said. "In the east, the sky is red from the fires that burn the homes of the whites. I have taken these captives after killing many of their people and can never again be considered a friend of the whites." He paused. "I have chosen my path and now must follow it, fighting until I die. I may have need of the captives so the whites will not attack and risk their lives. Or I may ransom them to the whites. I will not sell them to you."

Oh, White Lodge, no! Take the horses; please take the horses.

Charger signaled with his hand, and others in his party brought goods forward.

Julia strained for a glimpse. Bread, sugar, coffee, she thought, perhaps more.

Charger waited until the other men dropped back again. "Here is food. Eat what you want and go home, and we will take the captives and go home."

White Lodge grunted again and gestured for his tribal elders to eat. They did so, taking what was offered them. No one said a word. The tension was thick, the air heavy with lingering traces of smoke and unspoken words. Julia's pulse beat loud and fast, ringing in her ears. She prayed no one could hear it in the silence.

White Lodge stared at the two guests and finished the last of the food.

"Your people are right to call you crazy. You think you are like soldiers, coming to rescue the captives, but you are fools. The whites care nothing for you and would cut your throats in an instant. You are boys who should go home in shame rather than attempt to be men. You bring shame to the Teton and to the Santee. I spit on you."

He rose and left the council, a final insult to the two petitioners.

No, the captives would not be separated, but neither would they be rescued.

Laura
On the Missouri River, near the mouth of the Grand River
November 19, 1862

The Fool Soldiers, as everyone was calling them, returned, and the gossips had another holiday discussing whether captives would be sold. This time, White Lodge did not invite them into his lodge. He insulted them by meeting outdoors.

I snuck from my tepee and crouched behind another, as closely as I dared get. I prayed I wouldn't be discovered, but I had to learn as much as possible. Julia had not been able to get word to me about the first meeting, and I knew only what I'd gathered via the rumors—that White Lodge had refused to discuss a sale.

The young man, Charger, spoke, but I couldn't distinguish all of his words. He spoke in Lakota, which was foreign to me, enough different from Dakota that I had difficulty comprehending when he spoke rapidly.

"Go home," White Lodge said. "You are boys, and I will not sell these captives to you."

So it was true! I grasped the last shreds of my handkerchief in my fist. Who did they wish to purchase? Which of us would be sent away? Lord, please not my children.

"Again, I say to you we will offer all we have." It was the young Charger again.

"And, again, I say to you I will not sell."

Silence stretched, and I could imagine them looking at one another, White Lodge with his face stony and resolute.

"You talk big, White Lodge. You speak of killing white men who had no guns. You steal women and children and run away with them. Where is the bravery in that? If you are truly brave, why did you not fight the white soldiers instead?"

I held my breath, waiting for White Lodge to spring up and attack Charger for the insult. He'd spoken slowly, each word deliberate, and the leader must be seething with anger.

"Three times . . . we will take the captives . . . Teton will come against you . . ." This time, the words came too fast. I understood only that the captives might be stolen away, and fighting might be imminent.

My breath stalled.

We'd battled in the slough near Shetek and experienced only death and despair. For the first time since being taken, I prayed we would be sold.

White Lodge said nothing, but other men whispered of warriors riding back and forth in the distance. I remembered when they'd done that at the Wright house, before the attack at the slough, and I shivered.

A new voice joined in, a young man from White Lodge's camp. "Black Hawk, son of White Lodge, why do you not speak? Why sit so still?"

Black Hawk had been the one who had advised Christina not to go with White Lodge back at Big Stone Lake. After a few moments, he spoke. "You boys have courage in your hearts and strong intent. You bring us good food, and you are respected among your people. This I know. But my father does not know you."

Several voices mumbled.

I sat, tense, waiting.

Black Hawk continued. "It is winter, and we are starving. I have one white child that I will give up. Let the others do the same and give up their captives. It is time for them to go."

One of the Ireland girls. How in heaven's name would the girl survive alone? I struggled to hear the mumbling among the men. Many of the voices affirmed the Santee might survive better, be welcomed more easily by those who lived in the area, if the captives were not with them.

Panic crushed in on me as I realized there might be more sold, that my children might be separated from me.

White Lodge made a low grunt. "My own son believes the captives should leave us. Go, Charger, and return with all you have to trade. I will let each family who has claimed a captive decide for itself."

I limped away as fast as I could. I had to keep Emma and Jefferson with me, no matter the cost. Even if it meant offering myself as wife to one of these heathens.

Julia
On the Missouri River, near the mouth of the Grand River
November 19, 1862

"What are they doing?" Julia asked White Lodge's wife. Across the camp, a large lodge was being raised, much bigger than the lodges they lived in. She wasn't sure what it was for, though she suspected it had to do with the Fool Soldiers. She'd heard enough about what had happened that she knew they would be returning.

"Putting up the council lodge. The meeting will be large, many more than just the elders."

Julia tried to stay calm. If they needed space, the rumor about White Lodge consenting to the sale of the captives was true. She glanced at the woman who had always treated her well.

"We're being sold?"

The woman looked at Julia as if weighing her response. Julia held her breath.

"Each family with a captive will hear what is being offered. Each may negotiate or not."

"My daughter . . ."

"There is nothing you can do, Julia Wright." She motioned to the tepee. "We have work inside—go."

Julia took a last glance at the council lodge, wondering when they would go. An hour later, when people began to move outside, Julia dropped her needlework and rushed to the door. "They're going to the lodge," she told the wife.

The woman stood behind her, both of them watching. The Ireland girls, Lillie Everett, the Duleys, and Dora were ushered in. Laura looked anxious.

Julia's pulse quickened. She glanced at the woman behind her. "Shouldn't we be going?"

"We are not going."

Julia's mouth dropped open, words clogging in her throat. Was she not to be sold? *They're selling Dora without me?* That couldn't be. She'd been sold again and again. Maybe White Lodge planned to make a production of it. That had to be it. She'd misunderstood, that was all. He was saving her for last.

"Go back inside. White Lodge does not wish to sell you."

"No!"

"It is not for you to decide."

"I won't lose Dora."

She slipped through the opening and rushed forward, toward the council lodge. Behind her, the wife yelled. Hands grasped her and lifted her from the ground. Her feet churned as she fought to get away, but it was no use.

Laura
On the Missouri River, near the mouth of the Grand River
November 20, 1862

I sat inside the big lodge, my eyes glazing with fatigue. I'd tried to stay awake through the night, to keep up with the negotiations, but had fallen asleep several times, my head jerking as I awoke. We'd been lined up in a row, whites and half-breeds. Everyone but Julia. I didn't know where she was or why she wasn't with us, and I was afraid for her.

They'd offered her daughter first, negotiations going back and forth for over an hour before agreement was reached, and Dora had been sent to sit with the Fool Soldiers. She'd sat there, looking back at us with terror in her eyes, and I'd tried to signal to her that it would be all right. But I didn't know if it would be. I didn't know what would happen.

Then they'd sold my Jefferson.

I'd screamed and raged, offered myself to his owner, been slapped into silence with a warning that Emma and Jefferson could still be killed at any time. I resigned myself and prayed I would not be left behind.

By the time late morning came, all of the children had crossed to the Fool Soldiers. Now, there was me.

There wasn't much left to offer, by my accounting. I tried to force myself to listen to the offers going back and forth, but I was so weary I could barely keep track. My gaze settled on my children, and I held on to hope. They'd offered for me, and that was a good thing.

I was jerked to my feet and shoved across the room. I rushed to my children, and they fell into my arms, all of us in tears. At least we would remain together. With that, we could survive.

"We have been told there is one more," Charger said.

Julia! In my panic, I'd forgotten about Julia.

"The last one is mine. I will not sell her," White Lodge said.

"She is a fine cook, and I will make her a wife."

Dora looked to me, her eyes filled with fear. All I could do was open my arms to her, hug her tight with my own family.

"We need to be done with these captives," one of White Lodge's sons said.

White Lodge glared at him. "I have spoken."

A heated argument broke out among White Lodge and his sons, Charger standing with them.

The other Fool Soldiers gathered us together and told us to make ourselves ready to leave. They spoke rapidly, and I had trouble understanding them. Lillie Everett explained what I failed to grasp. We stood, ready. Only Roseanna had belongings to take, a necklace of blue beads given to her by the woman who had treated her as a daughter and cried as she'd been sold away. But the necklace was hidden, under Roseanna's tunic, and there was nothing to gather.

Suddenly, one of White Lodge's sons strode from the lodge, returning with Julia as we exited. Confusion filled her eyes but vanished as she saw her daughter. The man released her and told her to go with us. He told the Fool Soldiers to go quickly while he and Charger completed the last sale.

The men ushered us away onto the snow-filled prairie, and Charger joined us soon after.

"We must hurry," he said in English. "White Lodge is not happy, and we have one hundred miles to the nearest white outpost."

We walked faster, in our threadbare clothing. I glanced around, limping and dazed by the events. There was one horse remaining, a tepee and a few blankets, two rifles. Snow began to fall.

Julia
Along the Missouri River,
Late November 1862

Julia trudged beside Charger, each step an effort in the deep snow. During the three days since leaving White Lodge's camp, they'd moved in spurts. Each time her eyes grew heavy or her legs protested, she told herself to move on. *Move on or you will die.*

The first day had been the hardest. She'd heard the Fool Soldiers' comments on the rags they wore, their emaciation. They'd hoisted Laura onto the single horse and given up their blankets. Charger had walked barefoot, giving his moccasins away. They'd carried the children most of the time and pushed a rapid pace, resting when necessary but walking into the dark of the night before the men had finally stopped and erected tepees.

Julia knew the hectic pace had been because of her. White Lodge had been angry at his sons for bringing her to the council lodge. Though her ransom had been completed, he'd threatened to follow. Indeed, he'd appeared in the distance with five Santee the next morning. They'd trailed the group, on foot, through the increasing snow until his companions had turned back. Later in the day, White Lodge had finally done the same.

"How much farther, do you think?" Julia asked Charger.

"I think today, we will reach Fort LaFramboise."

They'd stopped at the village of Bone Necklace, near the place where she and Laura had seen the boat. The Yanktonais had supplied a cart, food, and more moccasins to the group, and they'd pushed on. The snow had been heavy, but the bulk of the blizzard had been ahead of them. They'd come across the bodies of the ten men who had split off from the Fool Soldiers before arriving at White Lodge's camp, frozen in the snow a few miles from the Yanktonais village. They'd died unaware of how close they were to safety.

"Why are you doing this?"

Charger gave her a small smile and shrugged. It had been his answer each time she asked. She'd not pushed. Instead, they'd talked of Teton life and white life. But if they reached the trading post today, she might not have another chance to ask.

"Charger, I wish to know."

"Because it is the right thing."

"I saw you, at Two Kettle's village, when White Lodge asked for an alliance."

"You have keen eyes and a good memory."

"The village was divided."

"It was," he agreed. "Some of the young men had gone east, in the summer. Some were at the war council of the Santee, before the attacks."

"In Minnesota?"

"In the east, yes. There was much discussion at that council. Some wished to chase the whites away, some wished to kill them."

"Were you there?"

"I was. I did not agree to killing or taking white captives. We left that place and returned home. It is one thing to fight soldiers; it is another to kill those who cannot fight."

"And you just decided to rescue us?"

"There is no honor in harming women and children. When White Lodge bragged of his captives, we were much dismayed. We made a pact, though our people thought us fools."

"That's why you are called Fool Soldiers?"

"That is why. But we have displayed honor. We have also set the Teton apart from the Santee and hope the white soldiers will remember this."

"I will remember it."

"The woman you call Laura, does she respond today?"

"I think she's in shock. Her mind is flooded with all she couldn't think about before, when she worried about her children, about surviving."

"How long have you been captives?"

"I think about three moons."

"Look. There is Fort LaFramboise." He pointed ahead.

Not much of a fort, but solid buildings nonetheless. The small post sat across the river. Three men were at the shore, waving and calling to the group. Women stood near the buildings.

"There are the traders, LaFramboise and Dupree and LaPlant. Now you will have better clothing and more food."

Julia smiled after him as he jogged ahead. On the opposite shore, the men readied a small boat. Ice was forming on the river, and she knew the boat would have to be navigated carefully. They weren't safe yet, but a little ice was nothing.

Nothing at all.

★ ★ ★ ★ ★

Part Four: Aftermath

★ ★ ★ ★ ★

Chapter Twenty-Five
1862-1864
Decisions

Christina

Camp Release, Minnesota

Late-September, 1862

The camp is crowded though not so much as it was last week when General Sibley rode in celebrating victory. Sibley may think it was his actions, but the captives know it was the poor conditions among the Dakota that brought them here so they can surrender and have food and shelter again.

Ach, we know how it was.

The refugees, we are trickling away to make our lives again. I do not again meet the woman who helped me escape and I never make sense of her words to me. I do not know if it was good luck that put us in the same place that night or if White Lodge was swayed by my words and provided a way for me to leave.

I am thankful and that is enough. I think how it was only one month that I was a captive and I cannot believe it. It seemed a lifetime.

"Mrs. Koch?"

I poke my head out of the tent where many women are crowded together. "*Ja,* I am here."

"There are two men looking for you and the boy. They're over at the headquarters tent."

"We will come." I duck back into my tent and smile at George. "Get your things. Your father has come for you."

"Papa?"

"*Ja*, come now." We leave our blankets for the others and walk through the camp. Little George trots beside me and there is a spring in our steps. Jack Wright sent word he was alive and would come. I do not know who else is with him.

"Will Mama be there? And Dora?"

"*Nein*, I think only your papa."

George clutches my hand tight and we go on. A man waves us into the big white tent and we stop.

"George!" Jack Wright kneels and opens his arms.

"Papa!"

My face almost cracks with my smile. To see that tough little boy run to his papa so happy fills my soul.

Ernst Koch, who boarded with us at Shetek, is also here and I step into his embrace. It is not so proper but I cannot do otherwise. I thought him dead.

"*Ach*, Christina, it is good to see you."

"*Ja*, I feel the same."

He leads me to chairs and we sit to visit while George and his papa are still hugging and talking together.

"I heard about what happened at the lake," Ernst says.

"Who survived to tell?"

"Several." He hands me a newspaper with a headline *The Boy Hero of Lake Shetek*. "Merton Eastlick carried his brother out." He lists the others: Lavina, Tommy Ireland, Will Everett, Bentley, Charlie Hatch, Wat Smith, William Duley, Rhodes, and Almena Hurd and her boys. Even the Myers family, all but Mary who died of pneumonia during their escape.

"More than I thought," I say.

"*Ja*, I am surprised."

I tell him a little of my story and what I heard this week of

Frank Eastlick, who was shot in the mouth and left for dead. "There is gossip here that he somehow crawled away from the slough, to one of the houses and the half-breed trapper, La-Bousche, found him there and took him west. Someone thought they went to a fort. Another said he left the boy with a friendly band of Indians. No one knows for certain."

"This is news his mother will want to hear. She is in Mankato or St. Charles, I am not sure. She's been moving around."

He tells me about the attacks on New Ulm when he and Wright were there and I tell him what I know of Julia and Laura and the children still captive. Jack hears us and comes closer with George to hear.

"She's still with them?" he says. "She didn't escape with you?"

"She did not have the chance," I say. "She was taken with the larger group." There is a tone in Wright's voice. It sounds like accusation, and I want to defend my friend. "I was lucky when George and I were sold away and there were not so many watching us."

"Thank you for bringing my boy back to me."

"*Ja*, you are welcome."

"We'll be on our way, Ernst. I want to get us back as soon as possible."

I turn to George and think I am losing a bit of myself. I squeeze him tight in my arms. "Be a good boy for your papa." I kiss his head as my eyes start to sting.

"Bye, German Woman," he says, using the name given by the Dakota.

"Good-bye, Little Man," I say, doing the same.

Wright takes his hand and leads him out of the tent. He looks back once, at the doorway, and waves. Finally, they are gone and I let the tears flow.

Ernst gives me a handkerchief.

"You'll see him again. Wright's been staying in Mankato."

I sniffle. "That is where you are?"

"*Ja*, I will stay there. Or go to New Ulm when they rebuild. It won't take Germans long to put things in order."

I think he is right. We are an orderly people. I will need to put my life in order, too. Perhaps I will go to Mankato. There is little use in wandering about—it is time for me to make plans. Mankato is civilized, a good place, safe, where a person can have a *Haus* instead of a cabin and keep it as it should be.

I think I will do this.

Julia
Fort Randall, Dakota Territory
January, 1863

Julia paced the small room. Jack and George would arrive soon and her stomach was in knots. She'd wept, hearing they both lived, her first tears since the Fool Soldiers had moved them across the river to Fort LaFramboise over a month ago. She'd rejoiced. But with reunion close at hand, she was all nerves about Jack and his sharp views.

She forced herself to stop pacing and glanced at Dora. Her clothing was still neat and tidy. As good as it's going to get, she supposed. They still looked a wreck, but there was nothing more to be done.

A knock sounded, and she jumped.

Oh, God, they're here.

She smoothed her dress and opened the door, her stomach in knots.

Jack stood there, George at his side.

Her eyes stinging, she stilled her heart. *Oh, George!*

"Mama!"

Julia knelt and scooped him into her arms, smothering him

with kisses. "I am so glad you are safe, my little man."

"German Woman took care of me."

"I'm glad she was with you." So Christina was safe, too. Julia's anxiety loosened, edged out by warmth and thanksgiving. How on earth was she ever going to thank her friend for keeping George safe?

She drew a breath and stood, George in her arms. He was heavy again, no longer the thin little boy who'd been sold away at Big Stone Lake. A good thing, along with the likelihood he'd remember little of the horror as he grew. There were blessings in being young.

Glancing at Jack, she smiled. He held Dora. Her little arms were stretched around his neck. If she was lucky, Dora, too, would forget much.

"Hello, Julia," Jack said. His tone was soft, but discomfort hid behind the words. "Your hair?"

She fingered her shorn locks, cut short at Fort Randall when they couldn't get the tangles out. "It was knotted, full of grease."

"Oh." He released Dora, and she scrambled away to play with the doll she'd been given by one of the women at the fort.

Julia set George down, and he ran to his sister. Then she drew a breath and faced Jack. "I'm glad you're safe."

He closed the door and sat in a straight-back chair as silence stretched tight between them.

Stilted, as she'd feared.

"I thanked Mrs. Koch . . . heard the story from her, at least through her escape."

"When you wired that you found George safe, I wondered what had happened." Typical of Jack, he'd supplied no details. She'd wondered for days.

"They got away, near Big Stone Lake." So, not long after they'd parted. Good.

"That's where she and George were sold away."

"I heard in October you were a captive there, with Pawn. But you were long gone when I got the news."

"In Dakota, by that time. Sold to White Lodge."

Jack's expression remained stoic.

"Where did you end up?" Julia asked. "When it started, I mean?"

"I helped with the defense of New Ulm, led a burial detail to the lake. Since, I've mostly been in the Mankato area."

It was hard to imagine him helping with the defense of New Ulm. He was more the type to run. But, perhaps he'd found his backbone. "I'm glad you weren't at Shetek," she said.

"Me, too. Dead in a slough is not the end I'd want. Imagine them attacking after all we did for them." His voice was bitter, and Julia ached to tell him about how traders like him, bent on cheating the Dakota at every turn, had laid the foundation for the hatred.

But she didn't. He wouldn't grasp it.

"It was awful, watching our friends die."

His eyes darkened. "Dirty savages."

She'd heard so many use those words. She comprehended part of it, knew women like Laura who had watched family die in brutal ways who would never get past hating. She hated, too, but she refused to label an entire people for the acts of a few.

"Not all of them. A few tried to save us."

Jack's eyes grew dark, accusatory. "They tricked you, and you fell for it."

The comment stung, though she'd expected the sentiment would come at some point. "You weren't there, Jack. You don't know."

"I know they're back-stabbing sons of bitches, and anyone who thinks otherwise has been duped. It'll do you no good to voice such opinions once we return. An Indian lover is not what you want to be."

And there it was, the core of the matter. Or at least the beginning of it. Julia's hand pressed against her abdomen, again in knots.

"If it weren't for ten Sioux men, I'd still be a captive." It seemed a better place to start. She had no idea if he'd accept the concept that there were good people and bad people within any culture, but Charger and his Fool Soldiers deserved a defense.

"The military was on its way. Another week and they would have been there."

"And there would have been a battle during which we might have been killed."

Jack shook his head. "You should have escaped when Christina Koch did. Or before you left Shetek."

"I had two children to protect."

"And did you protect them? No. You let those heathens take them on an eight-hundred-mile trek through the cold and subject them to Lord knows what."

Oh, the man! Did he actually think she just willingly went along?

"I tried to escape, Jack. The second day. They shot me and took the children away."

"You shouldn't have even let it go to the second day. From what I heard, you were the one who told the women and children to give up. You should have crawled away with them instead."

Julia glanced at the children and lowered her voice. Jack had no idea of what it had been like, none. "Crawled away? We were in a slough, at the bottom of a rise. How the hell could we have crawled anywhere?"

He leaned forward, glaring. "You didn't even try. At least Mira Everett had the sense to run back and be shot instead of surrendering to them."

"You'd rather we died?"

"You let them *have* you."

She let his words hang. This was it—the very heart of what bothered him the most. That she'd been used by Dakota men. She'd known this would stab at him, suspected he'd never get past it. That it might even end their marriage entirely.

"I didn't *let* them do anything," she said. "I endured it to keep the others alive. To keep my children alive."

"You weren't anyone's keeper, Julia."

She opened her mouth to tell him she was but shut it. She'd spent their entire marriage keeping Jack from trouble, assuring respectability for her family, fixing things in the community because she felt responsible. And, yes, she had fought to keep the other captives safe. She'd endured because her children depended on her. She'd borne it all.

Until it nearly defeated her and the only choice left was to fight for herself.

In the end, the only vow that mattered had been the one she'd made to survive, and, if Jack wanted to divorce her, she'd welcome it. He didn't define her anymore, and her vows to *him* didn't matter anymore.

"I'm my own keeper, Jack. I chose to survive, and I'll be damned it I let you take that away from me."

"I don't know if I can be with you anymore, Julia."

"Then we're agreed."

She waited for grief to rise, for the mourning of her marriage to overtake her, but it didn't. There was only serenity in the decision.

She'd found herself, and she was never letting go.

Laura
Fort Dodge, Iowa
January 1863

I glimpsed William from the window of the stagecoach as it came to a stop. He looked worn, haggard, as if he, too, had been through hell. I knew not what he'd think when he saw us.

I patted my short hair and brushed the wrinkles from my calico dress. Julia had sewn the simple garments for each of us while we rested at Fort LaFramboise. Jefferson's matched mine. He was not pleased at being in a dress rather than pants, but we'd had little time, and I'd pacified him by fastening a neckerchief for him so he wouldn't appear girlish. Emma's frock was of differing fabric but just as simple. We were glad to have them, after the rags we'd given up, and had worn them for the pictures taken at Fort Randall.

My nervous mind was wandering. I refocused and turned to the children. "Stand up, now. Your father waits." I glanced at Lillie Everett, who had traveled with us, and she readied herself, as well.

My joy in hearing William lived had brought me strength these last weeks. I'd traveled much of the way through the snow thinking we'd again been sold, moving ever farther away from civilization. We'd arrived at the trading post, and I finally accepted we *were* free, that it wasn't something Julia had latched onto as a dream.

I must confess, I took to my bed for nearly two weeks, secure in the knowledge my children were finally safe. I'd let the good women of the fort tend them and surrendered to fatigue and grief. But when word came from William, I'd risen, put myself in order, and prepared to return to life.

And here he was, at last.

He opened the door, and Emma tumbled into his embrace.

"Me, too, Papa!" Jefferson squawked.

William set Emma down and withdrew our son from the coach, kissing him soundly. He stood him next to his sister and held out his arms for me.

I stepped out with care. Though my heel was better, I remained weak, and I waited until he held my weight. He pulled me close, smothering me with kisses.

"I thought I'd lost you, Wife."

"And I, you."

We must have been a spectacle, kissing so in public, but I hardly cared. Until a week ago, I'd thought myself a widow. I rejoiced in his welcome, touching his face, my finger tracing the worry lines that hadn't been there before.

"Oh, William," I choked out.

"I can't believe I have you back. All of you." He smiled at Emma and Jefferson. He said nothing about our three missing children, and I was thankful. My eyes misted as the loss jabbed at me. I had two left, and I reminded myself to delight in them.

William let me go and helped Lillie from the stage. She'd patiently stood there, waiting while we'd said our hellos, still the fine, sweet girl she'd always been. Once she was on the ground, she walked past us.

I turned. There was Will Everett standing near a bench, leaning on a cane. We'd thought him dead, and I remembered how his wife had turned back to die with him. Shocked, I brought my hand to my mouth. I'd not expected him to be present, and warmth filled me when he drew Lillie to his breast. She clung to him, neither saying a word as tears poured down both their faces.

"Oh, William," I said, "no one knew!"

"I thought her uncle, Charlie Hatch, would come for her. I didn't know Will was coming until he showed up. Charlie's here, too, but wanted to give them a moment."

We left them with privacy, and William unloaded our meager

Never Let Go

belongings—a basket of food sent by the women of Yankton and a valise with donated clothing. We made our way to the hotel, where we'd stay until we traveled to Mankato.

Once the children were settled down for naps, William and I retired to the sitting area. We'd been five months apart and had much to catch up on.

William told me of his return to Shetek in late October, with soldiers. He, Tommy Ireland, and Charlie Hatch had identified twelve bodies and buried them in a common grave. The two Everett boys and one Eastlick boy had not been located. I told him of Frances being taken from me and how she had cried without ceasing until she had died or been killed—I never knew which.

"And you, Laura? Did you suffer much?"

"It was not easy. That first night, I couldn't fight them off. I'm sorry."

William held me while I cried. "There is no shame, Wife. You did the best you could."

"I was much damaged. I fear there will be no more children."

"Then we will smother Emma and Jefferson with our love."

"I heard . . . you were there . . . when they hanged the Sioux." In truth, I'd been told he served as hangman.

"I was. They hanged thirty-eight. Lincoln commuted the sentences of the rest. I was asked to cut the rope." He paused. "There was so much hate in me that I said yes. I didn't know it would be so difficult. The first time, I missed the rope and had to swing the ax again."

"One rope, for thirty-eight?"

"A pretty complex scaffold. There were angry crowds there. A man offered me money to take my place. I refused. I was bitter, thought you'd all been murdered, and I wanted to get even, any way I could."

"I know. I've felt the same. Julia tries to understand, says whites treat the Indians as badly. I can't grasp it. Not anymore."

We sat in quiet, knowing our lives would never be the same, until William caught my gaze. "I'd like to join up as a scout, help track down White Lodge's band."

"Is that to be your new dream?" I thought of him being gone from me, and resentment burned.

"Not a dream, just something I have to do."

That, I did understand. But there were things that still needed to be discussed. "And after that?"

William shrugged. "I don't know."

"We've spent our entire lives chasing dreams."

"Mostly mine." The humble admission told me volumes.

"Always yours," I said in soft agreement. "I left my dreams in Indiana."

"I'm sorry, Laura. I'm not good at perceiving things from others' points of view." This, too, I knew. But I sensed his realization of it might be a turning point for us.

"We have a second chance, Husband. I think this time, we need to pursue common dreams."

He smiled, offering no argument. "I think we can do that."

"The frontier has not been good to us. We've lost all of our children but two. We've lost our property and our land. I'd like to start somewhere different. Away from farming, away from rivers, away from Indians. No more new settlements, no more being a 'first family,' no more politicking. Let's focus on us."

"That sounds like an idea I can live with. This experience, what happened at Shetek and after, has changed me."

"We're agreed?"

"We are." William smiled at me and kissed my hand. "Just as soon as I help Sibley track down and purge the Dakota who escaped justice."

Almena
St. Peter, Minnesota
April 28, 1863

"You realize many were in tears, don't you?" Almena's attorney said as they exited the room where the U.S. Indian commissioners were meeting.

She carried Frank in her arms; William Henry held Mr. Berry's hand.

"They were?" She exhaled a heavy breath. Telling her story had been the most difficult thing she'd done since living through the events, and she was glad to have it over. Besides, the crying was more likely due to the boys being there in the room than her words. Those boys could melt hearts; she doubted she could.

"Indeed." Mr. Berry patted her arm. "It was exactly what the commissioners needed to hear. I think it will help when they process the claims."

"I didn't relish telling it." She'd been shaking the whole time, more so once she'd spotted reporters taking notes.

"The damages claim has been officially filed—depredation claims, they're calling them—and is now in their hands. Once I hear on the findings, I'll notify you. I don't expect that to happen for a while. Government moves slowly."

"How does the government expect all of us to live? We lost everything we had."

Mr. Berry opened the door of the courthouse, and they exited into the crisp spring air. Almena breathed in the warmth, a blessing after the bitter winter. To her, it heralded new life.

"I don't expect you'll get the entire amount you claimed. There aren't many women who claim their own property in addition to household property."

She'd thought as much when she listed the items lost and their worth. She'd cited the highest values she could justify. It was like negotiating a sale. Start high in expectation of settling lower. That was the way of things. But her pride hadn't allowed her to dismiss that she'd owned her own property, and she'd listed it separately.

"I owned livestock in my own right. Why should I not claim that as a loss?"

"I understand that, Mrs. Hurd." He escorted her down the quiet boardwalk. "It might have been wiser to lump it all into household property, to which you are entitled as a widow. Government officials won't know what to do with this."

"Property is property, whether I claimed it as Phin's or as mine. They'll merge it, and they'll award only a portion of it, either way. That's how government operates. By the time you get your percentage, there will be little left."

"But at least there will be something," he placated as they stopped at his office door. "Will you be staying on in St. Peter?"

Almena shook her head. She'd thought about it, but this wasn't where she wanted to rebuild their lives. There was nothing left here—no land, no home, no livestock. She'd lived the last few months on the charity of others, and she refused to continue in that vein.

"It's time to leave. Minnesota has little to offer me anymore, save for the ties to my fellow survivors, and those will not support us."

"You are a strong woman, Mrs. Hurd. I suspect you could make your way." His words held encouragement, but Almena had made up her mind.

"You'll be able to reach me in La Crosse for the next few months. I have friends there."

"And after that?"

"Caton, New York." Home . . . as much home as anywhere. Her boys needed family more than ever. In truth, so did she.

"That's a long way."

"I've always sworn my children would have family. I can't

bring back their father, but I can give them an uncle." Seneca, his wife and children, the Miniers—all waited for them. And there were her other siblings, maybe even her father and stepfamily. "It's time those ties are renewed."

Mr. Berry smiled and offered his hand. "I think you'll do just fine."

"I'm sure we will. My brother has already bought a cow for me."

Lavina
Ellenboro, Wisconsin
1864

After dinner, I ask Leicester to stay at the table so we can have a discussion. Christine herds the children—teenagers now—out of the kitchen along with Merton and Johnnie. I face my brother, anxious to have his input.

"I've been thinking," I start.

"Not unusual." He grins at me, gray hair and wrinkles reminding me we've both aged.

"Do you remember, all those years ago, when I first came to live with you?"

"Hah! You were fifteen and thought you owned the world."

I smile at him, recalling my naiveté. "I wanted adventure, independence, and didn't think I needed anyone."

We laugh, then sober. "And now?" Leicester asks.

"Well, I've certainly had more adventure than I ever imagined and not the type I'd envisioned."

"That's true." He pats my hand. Neither of us needs to say anything more about what happened.

"And, now I'm forced to be independent and discovering it not quite what I'd imagined."

I think back to the weeks after reaching safety, scrambling for hand-outs, petitioning to the government, fighting tooth and nail to be treated fairly when so many were attempting to take advantage of my widowhood. I'd been forced to stand up for myself and the boys, even becoming a bit of a shrew at times.

"It can be a troublesome responsibility," he says.

"I've thought much about it, how I can take care of the boys. I don't want to live here with you and Christine forever."

"You know you're welcome here." His voice is warm, brotherly. My parents in Ohio said the same, but it's time I stop making the rounds of my relatives and stand on my own feet.

"I know. But it's not what I want."

"And you have an idea, I take it?"

"Remember me telling you about that man in Minnesota, the artist?"

"Mr. Stevens? The one who was painting the panorama about the uprising?"

"I had a letter from him. As planned, he's taken the paintings on tour and has had a good response. I suppose it's human nature, being drawn to tales of horrific events without having to experience them in reality."

"And?"

"I've written about the events at Lake Shetek." I lift a notebook from my lap and lay it on the table. "I'd like to get it published and sell copies."

Leicester picks up the tattered notebook and reads bits, here and there. Finally, he looks at me. "You're sure you want to do this, share this with the public? You'd have to travel around, promote it, speak about it."

"I'm sure," I say. "It will provide me a way to support the boys." I meet his gaze and draw a breath. "Besides, what happened to us there is too important to be forgotten."

Epilogue
Reunion

Lake Shetek,
July 1895

Charlie Hatch walked across the dry summer prairie, retracing the route he'd taken thirty-three years before. He moved slowly, images flashing through his mind . . . sun glinting off the water, mud sucking at his feet, the first distant shot that hadn't seemed at all ominous. Then, Voigt dead in front of Almena's doorway, the realization and his frantic flight down the lake to warn the others. And, finally, the taste of fear and panicked faces as they rushed for the slough and the carnage that came after. Though he'd told the story often, his skin crawled at being here again.

Five of the survivors had returned—plus the Burns Brothers who had once lived at Walnut Grove—responding to an invitation by Dr. Workman, a local man who was compiling a collection of accounts to assure future generations would know of the event. They'd told him the stories again, showed him where things had happened.

And they'd sat and talked.

"There's so much I'd pushed out of my memories," Lavina said, suddenly beside him.

Cold sweat chilled Charlie's spine. He hadn't even heard her approach. "Mine, too. Even in telling reporters over the years, it was never this sharp."

"It's odd. Johnnie and I couldn't even locate exactly where the cabin used to be. But I remember everything that happened.

As soon as I stepped out of the wagon with Uncle Tommy, it flooded back. I don't think I'll ever come here again."

She turned away, back toward where the others had gathered.

Charlie let her go. She had her own memories and was best left to deal with them on her own.

He stood alone, his gaze on the slough while the images took life in his mind, then died. In the silence, he honored them: those who had died and those who had found the strength to survive.

At length, he, too, left.

There's nothing more to be done here.

AFTERWORD ON LAKE SHETEK SURVIVORS

Laura and William Duley resided in the Mankato, Minnesota, area until some time in the 1870s. Secondary sources claim she "lost her mind" for two years after being released and spent time institutionalized. There is no record of her being a patient within the Minnesota State (psychiatric) Hospital during that time, a time during which William would also have been away from home serving as an army scout, and Lavina Eastlick reports in her 1864 booklet that Laura's children lived with Laura during William's absence. According to obituary accounts, William was discharged from military service on February 10, 1865, and, by the summer of that year, was farming eighty acres in Blue Earth County. Anecdotal accounts say William provided wood from his sawmill in Mankato to build a fence around the graves at Lake Shetek. Sometime in the 1870s, the Duleys relocated to Colbert, Alabama, where William worked as a millwright and, in 1880, was appointed as justice of the peace and notary public. Emma Duley married and moved to Texas. Around 1890, Laura and William moved to Gig Harbor, Washington, near Tacoma, where Jefferson served as chief of police. William worked as a machinist and carpenter and died there in 1898; Laura died on March 2, 1900. She was seventy-one.

Lavina Eastlick returned to Minnesota and published "A

Personal Narrative of the Indian Massacres 1862" (first printing 1864). Merton stayed briefly with John Stevens and his wife in Minnesota, touring with the panorama show, while Lavina went to visit family, and he returned to her while she was with her sister in Wisconsin. On April 1, 1865, she married widower Henry W. (Wat) Smith, who had also resided at Lake Shetek. In June of the same year, she left him. According to divorce documents, they were never compatible, Lavina complaining he did not love her or her children and Wat complaining she was away peddling books and disregarding her wifely duties. Divorce was filed for in July 1866 and granted on January 24, 1867. In the 1870 census, she is recorded under "Eastlick" as a widow with a farm of 145 acres near Mankato that she bought with the proceeds of her depredation claim award. On November 30, 1870, she married Solomon Pettibone (marriage documents list her as "Smith"). Three months later, he left her, went to Ohio to visit his sister, and disappeared. Lavina was pregnant at the time and gave birth to a daughter, Laura, in August 1871. Merton worked while Johnnie, age ten, cared for the baby and Lavina worked the fields. Merton married in 1873 and moved to Rochester, Minnesota. He died in 1875. Johnnie married in 1885 and settled one mile from Lavina. Records indicate he did not own land but operated a threshing business. Laura married Angus McDonnell in 1895. The couple farmed near Lavina, then moved to Alberta, Canada, in 1906. Lavina joined them in 1915. She died there on October 9, 1923.

Almena Hurd relocated to her former home of Canton, New York, where she married Elbridge George Woodward on August 11, 1864. Elbridge is listed as a carpenter with his own land in the 1874 census. The two had several children: John, Carrie, Albert (Bertie), Fredrick, Charles, and Seneca. They moved to

Afterword on Lake Shetek Survivors

Roulette, Pennsylvania, in 1883, where they farmed and ran a boarding house. A daughter, Alice, is listed as being adopted. Almena was widowed in 1905 and died in 1922 at age eighty-six.

Christina Koch resided in Mankato, Minnesota, for the remainder of her life. By 1870, she had married Charles H. Heinze (sometimes recorded as Heinz, sometimes as Charles A. Heinze), who made his living as a baker. Property value listed in the 1870 census is sufficient to indicate he likely owned the bakery. They were listed in the 1880 census as well. Charles died in December 1883, and Christina married Carl F. W. Hohmuth (Hohmith, Holmeth) on October 15, 1884 (Oct. 16 also cited). He is identified as a laborer in the 1885 census. In 1894, Christina provided an interview to Dr. Harper Workman, who recorded her story of the events of 1862. In 1900 and 1905 censuses, Carl is listed as a small farmer. Christina died March 1, 1907 (also reported as March 5) of cancer of the liver. She never had any children. In all official records, she is listed as Christina, although Dr. Harper Workman always referred to her as Mariah in his historical accounts, as do those local to the Lake Shetek area today.

Julia Wright disappeared from history. Though Lillie Everett later thought Julia had given birth to a mixed-race baby soon after her release and that John Wright had divorced her because of it, there are no records of such a birth or of a divorce in either Minnesota or Wisconsin. On July 8, 1863, she provided sworn testimony on John's depredation claim, identifying herself as his wife. In February of 1865, daughter Eldora died in Minnesota. No record of Julia is found after that date. There are unsubstantiated reports that John married a woman from Austin, Minnesota, then left her. A marriage record for a John Wright is recorded in Winona in 1872, but there is no way to know if this is the correct John Wright—Wright was a common name. A John G. Wright shows up in the 1875 census for La Crosse, Wisconsin, but La Crosse was full of Wrights, and the state census lacks enough vital statistics to verify identity. There were also reports that Julia remarried and moved to Nebraska, but there are no census or marriage records to prove or disprove this. She shows up in an online family tree as marrying a James Cart in Alamosa, Colorado, in 1877, but the reference offers no citation of source, and Colorado records indicate Cart married Annie Julia Coal, aka Aimee Julina Kohl (died September 1880), and there is no evidence this was Julia Wright. A search of census records for Minnesota and surrounding states reveals many possible Julia Wrights and Julia Silsbys but none matching in all vital details. When Dr. Workman and Neil Currie were collecting information on the 1862 events, they attempted to contact George and John Wright (identified as living in Utah and California at that time), but there was no response.

Thomas Ireland: Thomas married Sally Haddock, and the couple lived on the Myers property at Lake Shetek. Widowed after sixteen years, Thomas then married Sarah Ridgeway and resided in Mankato. Roseanna moved to Butte, Montana, after the death of her father in 1897. She worked as a domestic before marrying Joseph R. Miller. After Miller's death, she married Samuel VanAlstine. Roseanna died in 1936. Ellen (Nellie) married Albert Hotaling and resided in Mankato until her death in 1946.

Edgar Bentley, who came to Lake Shetek with Charlie Hatch,

Afterword on Lake Shetek Survivors

enlisted in the army, serving until the end of the war. There is no record of him thereafter.

Frank Eastlick was never seen again, though rumors continued to surface that he survived and was taken to Dakota Territory by Joe LaFramboise. Aaron Myers claimed to have spoken to LaFramboise in 1873, at the Minnesota state fair, and that LaFramboise confirmed the story.

William Everett recovered, though he suffered pain from a ball in his leg for the rest of his life. He married Amelia Addison in 1865 and moved to Waseca, Minnesota, where he founded Eaco Mills. He died in 1892. Daughter **Lillie** (Ablillian, Lily) Everett Keeney died in 1923 in Oakland, California.

Charlie Hatch: Charlie enlisted in the Union Army in 1864. After the war, he married Hattie Bangs, and they farmed near Huntly, Minnesota. In later years, he moved to Tappen, North Dakota, and died there in 1907.

Aaron Myers and his family escaped the attack on Lake Shetek. Around 6:00 a.m., Myers spotted a Dakota tearing down his fence, yelled at him to stop, and reminded him of past friendship and medical attention. The Dakota left. Son Arthur discovered Voigt's body around 10:00 that morning, and Aaron found Andreas Koch soon thereafter. He loaded his ill wife and children (daughter Olive was boarding with the Lambs in Iberia) into a wagon, and they headed to Dutch Charley's, warning the Zierke family. The journey to New Ulm was fraught with narrow escapes, but the family did arrive safely. Mary Myers died of pneumonia a day after they reached safety. Aaron eventually settled in Garretson, South Dakota. He and son Aaron provided their stories to Workman's history.

The Fool Soldiers dispersed not long after successfully ransoming the Shetek captives and six half-breed women. Their names were Martin Charger (*Waneta*), Joseph Four Bear (*Mah to top ah*), Swift Bird (Alex Chapelle), Kills and Comes (Kills Game and Comes Home or *Waktegli*), Mad Bear (*Mato Watogla*), Red Dog, Bears Rib (Kills Enemy), Sitting Bear, Pretty Bear (*Mato Waste*), Charging Dog, Jonah One Rib, Strikes Fire, Big Head, Foolish Bear, and Black Tomahawk. Exact membership varies among sources with most sources indicating there were initially eleven members. Martin Charger is usually named as the leader. The story of the role these young Lakota men played in freeing the captives was largely lost. Nearly all official military reports fail to mention them and magnify the role of the military instead. One is reported to have been killed by the military for stealing rations. It is suspected others were part of the group rounded up in 1863 when they admitted they had been present "in the east" at the war council meeting that occurred prior to the initial Minnesota attacks (even though they voted not to participate and left the area). For many years, the only records of the Fool Soldiers were the oral stories passed down to their descendants. These oral histories are now part of the South Dakota Oral History Center collections at the University of South Dakota. The stories differ, a natural result of oral histories repeated through multiple generations and translation issues. Their history was lost until the 1970s, when interest was renewed.

AUTHOR'S NOTE ON HISTORICAL ACCURACY

As a historian as well as a novelist, I took great pains to remain true to the historical record wherever possible. However, my purpose was to make the stories of Laura, Lavina, Christina, Almena, and Julia come alive rather than to offer a scholarly reporting of events. While I was able to locate clues to their major life events, I could only surmise their personalities, their family interactions, their dreams and motivations, conversations, or what they thought and did in their daily lives. I have not changed any of the facts I was able to uncover. However, to create my story, I filled in the gaps and developed the women as characters, from my imagination, around factual events. This is a novel, not a history.

To shape each of the women's personalities, I relied on clues within census records, local histories, personal accounts, and descriptions related by others. The Workman and Currie Papers contained recollections from many of the early Shetek settlers, though there were discrepancies in dates and details.

In a few cases, I altered names to eliminate confusion due to duplication of the same name. John Wright became Jack (a common nickname), Laura Lamb became Lorenza (her middle name), Almira Everett became Mira, and variations were used to differentiate all the many Williams and Johns.

Laura Duley: Through census records, I noted that Laura's

Author's Note On Historical Accuracy

family owned more valuable property than other families in the township and that the family was one of the first in the area, which was confirmed by county histories. It made sense that she might have been used to a comfortable life and may (or may not) have expected to continue in that lifestyle upon her marriage to William, who was also from an established family. I could not verify William and Washington Monroe were brothers, since early census records do not list children's names, but their ages and parental references matched, so I made them brothers as a mechanism to launch the story. William did claim land in Iowa prior to marriage, and he and Laura moved there shortly after marrying. Online obituaries indicate two daughters drowned in the Mississippi while they lived there. Census and land records trace movement to Beaver. Local histories reveal Willian operated a mill and a mercantile. Birth and death records trace their children. Workman's collected histories provide information on the arrival at Shetek and the events there. There is no direct evidence that Laura suffered from depression other than references that she "lost her mind." Given the number of children she lost, I chose to create this as part of her personality. Other settlers reported William as pompous; I adapted from that. Laura's short account of her captivity reports being raped repeatedly on her first night of captivity. Physically, it would be unlikely she could endure the treatment as she reported. The Duleys' personal accounts were bitter and indicated they had little positive interaction with the Dakota and were likely very biased in their opinions. Still, stigma of the time would have made most women reluctant to admit being raped. Thus, I treated her account of the night as exaggerated but holding some truth, despite rape being an unacceptable behavior within Dakota culture. I chose to adapt her story,

Author's Note On Historical Accuracy

motivating the incident with anger and revenge for her husband being one of the men who fired on Grizzly (Lean) Bear.

Almena Hurd: Census records indicate Almena and her brother lived with another family—he listed as adopted, she as a laborer. Previous records list them with the Hamm family, with the change coming after her father remarried. I used this as a defining influence for Almena's character. Census records and birth records trace the Hurds' journey to Wisconsin and Lake Shetek. Accounts given to Workman and Currie indicate there was a rumor at some point about her relationship with Phin's partner, Bill Jones, but that no one who knew her believed it. Accounts also mention her great butter that was sold to others; and her own depredation claim cites the amounts of butter and cheese destroyed in the attacks. The current owner of the Hurd cabin site reports the blackbirds are still a problem. Almena did not contribute to the Workman collection but did leave a detailed account of the attack in her depredation claim. A newspaper account, printed after her testimony to the commission, relates the events with a more sensationalistic tone. Her own words reveal she was educated and practical. Because she was released and told to go east "to her mother" (in Dakota, it would mean to her people), it is likely she had a respectful relationship with them.

Lavina Eastlick: Lavina's early life events were taken from census records as well as her own personal narrative. I have no idea why she went to live with her brother at age fifteen, but I sensed, from her personal narrative, that she was not afraid of adventure despite being apprehensive about the move to Shetek. She was also practical. She had to have been to leave dying children and crawl east for the two she thought had survived. Much of the detail on the fight in the slough and her escape was taken from her account as well as the accounts in the Workman Papers.

Christina Koch: No one knows her maiden name or when she married Andreas or when she emigrated to the U.S. from Germany. Online family trees are fraught with errors and a lack of supporting citations. She provided little information about her captivity to Workman beyond a short statement that "the way Mrs. Duley and I were treated cannot be told and from what Mrs. Wright told me afterwards, she fared no better. Many of the horrible reports are not true. I was not outraged" (despite Laura Duley's statement saying otherwise). The report of her resistance to Pawn was reported by a newspaper just after her release. Those living in the Lake Shetek area always refer to her as Mariah, but I could find no documents with that name. As a German, she may have used her middle name rather than her first name. (Germans had a custom of naming children after a close relative, which made for confusion, and thus they were usually called by their middle names instead.) All vital records list her as Christina. She provided a short account to Workman about dates they settled at the Walnut Grove (and, yes, that's the same Walnut Grove that later became the town of Laura Ingalls Wilder fame) and life at Lake Shetek.

Julia Wright: Her birth and marriage as well as the births of George and Dora can be traced through vital and census records. Her ancestors may have included fur trappers who intermarried with native women. There is little clue to her personality except via the comments of other settlers that she

Author's Note On Historical Accuracy

was caring and supportive and upstanding. Remembrances provided to Workman left little doubt about her husband's reputation. The accounts of the attack all say she took on a leadership role and that she was of good character. I chose to make her a woman in conflict with her husband. As well, she became my filter through which I provided a glimpse of Dakota culture and history. An account provided by one of the men who accompanied the ransomed captives to Fort Randall referenced her discussing the displeasure she expected from her husband for having been a "wife" during captivity.

The Fool Soldiers: It was difficult to reconcile the history of these young men. White historians dismissed them, for the most part. Officers' reports from Fort Randall gave them no credit (although a lesser report clearly stated their role). The stories passed to their children and grandchildren were later recorded as oral histories. Most of them indicate the Fool Soldiers were taken prisoner and some of them were killed. No military reports claim this. However, a deeper study of military records indicates a force was dispatched in the months after the release and that some Teton were taken prisoner; one is recorded as dying in the guardhouse. There is note that several answered they had been in the "east" when the fighting started. This may have been a translation issue for members of the Fool Soldiers who had been in attendance at the War Council on August 17 and left the area without becoming involved in the fighting because they disagreed about the path of action chosen by the council. The discrepancies with the oral histories are likely due to natural corruption of details over the years and issues with the meanings of words used (example: "when the snows stopped" was translated as "spring," when it likely meant a blizzard stopped).

Author's Note On Historical Accuracy

Dakota Culture: Within Dakota culture, there is a huge emphasis on kinship—whether family or social in nature. The Dakota were not known for taking captives and usually only did so in situations where a person reminded the raiding party of someone who had died. In those cases, they would be taken captive and soon adopted into the tribe in an official ceremony. My Dakota advisors tell me they would have been treated as social kin, a member of the tribe, and not abused. The Dakota did not hit their children nor did they beat others. Women who were taken captive were adopted or taken as wives if they consented. However, consent might be an ambiguous statement or a statement about wives that white women might not have understood. A ceremony may or may not occur. Hospitality and industry were both highly important. Adults and teens would have been expected to know this, and white women may have seemed woefully ignorant or lazy when they failed in that understanding.

In the days following the outbreak of hostilities in Minnesota, the Dakota found themselves in a position of having captives that would be used as shields or kept for ransom, and it is likely many were unsure how to treat them. Clearly, they were not being made part of the tribe, and captives as property would have been an alien idea. While the Dakota did practice "an eye for an eye" in warfare (allowing family members to be killed in revenge for a death), rape was not practiced in their culture. That some Dakota men did give testimony to having done so indicates this war was different. This was *not* part of their traditional culture. Other native testimony of the time indicates some Dakota made an effort to hide captives from groups of angry young men who would have mistreated them. This was a time of intense hostility toward the whites that blurred traditional lines of behavior, fueled by months of suffering and insult. Further, these were not captives in the usual sense, and there was an ongoing state of

Author's Note On Historical Accuracy

war that was much different from the quick raids usually practiced by the Dakota. I believe this was a time when some broke with tradition. I chose to strike a middle ground with some Dakota characters behaving outside the bounds of traditional behavior. I hope I have not been too disrespectful in doing so.

ACKNOWLEDGMENTS

As with every book I write, there is an endless list of people who contributed. Whether through inspiring me, supporting me as a writer, easing research tasks, or participating in the edit process, their roles were essential to making this project a reality.

This novel began in my head while I was still in elementary school, shaped by the knowledge and love of history shared by Bill Bolin, my ninth-grade history teacher at Tracy High School. Bill was a friend and neighbor, father of my friend Kelli. In that role and as seasonal naturalist at Lake Shetek State Park, he introduced me to the history of Lake Shetek. Later, in his class on Minnesota state history, he provided more detail, and my imagination took off. When I pursued my B.A. in history a few years later, I had no clue I would return to the story again all these years later. In 2017, when I traveled to Minnesota to re-walk in the footsteps of my characters, Bill was there to share his boxes of research materials and take me on tour of the cabin sites and Slaughter Slough, despite his struggle with cancer. His wife, Sandy, welcomed me into their home and put up with five solid days of listening to us. I wish he had lived to read the finished book.

A huge debt is owed to Dr. Harper Workman and his determination to record the Shetek history. His extensive interviews during the 1880s assured memories of the original settlers would survive. His foresight in providing a copy to the

Acknowledgments

Minnesota Historical Society all those years ago guaranteed his collection would endure. Neil Currie's dedication to pursuit of additional remembrances was an additional invaluable contribution. Without their efforts, we would not know what happened at Shetek.

In college, years before I thought of this book, I wrote my senior research paper on the duality of historical event and fiction. All those years ago, I conducted research at the Minnesota Historical Society with Dr. Alan R. Woolworth as my personal guide. Alan was a friend of my late husband, and he took care to provide me access to the Workman Papers and other information I would need for that paper—and later, for this project. I also had the opportunity to visit with author Frederick Manfred at his home near Luverne, Minnesota. His novel, *Scarlet Plume,* was inspired by the Dakota Conflict and at the heart of my study then. His insights stayed with me. Both of these men passed away years ago; their generosity remains.

During my 2017 visit to Minnesota, many old and new friends and professionals assisted me. Jeff (Jesse) James, my former English teacher, also stepped up to the plate. Knowing of Bill's ailing health, Jesse invited me to ride along on a Road Scholar tour of the Shetek area to assure I would be able to visit sites as well as obtaining more detail on them. The program, *Minnesota's Dakota Conflict,* was a great addition to my research arsenal. Jesse's passion was infectious (he lives on the Hurd site!), and I was pleased to connect with Roseann Schauer, current seasonal park naturalist at Lake Shetek State Park, and with Janet Timmerman, who coordinated the Road Scholar module. Jon Wendorff and Billie Jo Lau graciously pulled files and allowed me to access the entire collection of Lake Shetek materials at the Wheels Across the Prairie Museum in Tracy, including a copy of Christina Koch's depredation claim, which couldn't be located in the National Archives. And, to Dan Dries,

Acknowledgments

my Airbnb host and his wonderful Lake Shetek cabin—within walking distance of many of the sites—thank you so much for your hospitality and allowing me to spend time in the footsteps of the settlers.

Many thanks to Dakota Conflict historians Curtis Dahlin, John Isch, and Elroy Ubl. Elroy welcomed me to his home where he and Curt shared their files and information and were available via email to answer questions as they arose. John was always ready with guidance and provided the map for the book.

Research professionals were critical to this project, and a long list of them assisted. A huge debt of gratitude is owed the Minnesota Historical Society for having digitized the entire Dakota Conflict collection and making it available online. Josh Jordan, Site Coordinator, and the End-O-Line Railroad Park & Museum in Currie, Minnesota, provided assistance in acquisition of research materials as did Rebecca J. Snyder, Director of Research & Publishing at the Dakota County Historical Society in St. Paul, Minnesota. Darla Gebhard and Dan, the volunteer whose last name I missed, provided assistance prior to and during my visit to the Brown County Historical Society in New Ulm, Minnesota. Matthew Reitzel, Manuscript Archivist at the South Dakota State Historical Society Archives/Cultural Heritage Center in Pierre, South Dakota, assisted me with review of records from Fort Randall.

There were a host of professionals who responded to my online inquiries as I tried to chase down vital records: Karen S. Myers, Deputy Director Taxpayer Services of Blue Earth County (Mankato, Minnesota); Krista Lewis, Archivist, History Center of Olmsted County (Rochester, Minnesota); Walt Bennick, Archivist, Winona History (Winona, Minnesota): thanks for all your help.

Several professionals at the National Archives and Records Administration in Washington, D.C., assisted with tracking

Acknowledgments

down specific depredation claims and military documents. My thanks goes to DeAnne Blanton, Archives I Reference Section; Rose Buchanan, Archives Technician, Archives I Research Rooms Section; and Danielle Marie Eyre, Archive Technician, Archives I Reference Section.

When staff of the National Archives was unable to track down information, I was fortunate to have Ranel Capron, friend and BLM archeologist, who was in the D.C. area and willing to spend time researching my project. Ranel—your dedicated line by line reading of Fort Randall military records provided me with previously unknown/unconfirmed details about the Fool Soldiers and their ransom of the Shetek captives. I owe you!

Sam Herley, Ph.D., Curator at the South Dakota Oral History Center, University of South Dakota, also provided me access to the oral histories left by family members of the Fool Soldiers. The perspectives offered in these recordings were invaluable.

As I completed my manuscript, I found input from Dakota tribal members and experts on Dakota history and culture invaluable. To my Facebook friends—Mike Lord, Bud Johnston, Terri Bischoff, and Adrienne Zimiga . . . thanks for extending connections. Barbara Britain . . . thank you for the review of the manuscript and comments. And Breon Lake . . . your input on tribal culture, history, names, and sensitivity issues was critical. Thank you for your willingness to share it with me. I hope I have represented the culture fairly.

Of course, my critique groups and beta readers, who helped immeasurably in shaping my craft, hold my everlasting appreciation. To my home team, my RMFW Critique Group (Alice, Carla, Cate, Denee, Janet, Jessica, Kay, Peggy, Robin, Steven, and Thea): thanks for always being there and getting me through the worst of those awful early chapters! Many thanks to my WFWA Critique Group (Amanda, Debby, and Karen) for their

Acknowledgments

genre insight, their input made such a difference. And, my beta readers: thank you Elke, Janet, Liz, Peggy, Sharon, and Susan for the time you took to provide me such valuable feedback on the manuscript as a whole—though I hated the edits, I appreciate you making me do them.

The support of my family means more than I can say. My parents, Dick and Vauna, fostered my imagination daily and encouraged me to pursue my dreams. My siblings and their loved ones—Judy and Dave, Mike and Brenda—couldn't be more supportive of my writing. My daughter Katrina and her family (Don, Asher, and Xander) are always there and always cheering me on as are Ilka (and Edger, Luca, Enzo, and Giulio) and Danika (and Sergio, Kathia, and Erik). Thank you all!

And then there's Ken, my love. Daily, he allowed me time closed up in my office, listened to me rant and rave about history and the story and challenges and worries, and took me in his arms when I needed to be held. He shares his life with my writing and loves me all the same. His support means the world to me, as does his love.

SOURCES

Documents, Manuscripts, and Transcripts (Including Primary Sources On-line)

1790 United States Federal Census [database on-line]. Provo, Utah, U.S.A.: Ancestry.com Operations, Inc., 2010. Images reproduced by FamilySearch.

1820 United States Federal Census [database on-line]. Provo, Utah, U.S.A.: Ancestry.com Operations, Inc., 2010. Images reproduced by FamilySearch.

1830 United States Federal Census [database on-line]. Provo, Utah, U.S.A.: Ancestry.com Operations, Inc., 2010. Images reproduced by FamilySearch.

1840 United States Federal Census [database on-line]. Provo, Utah, U.S.A.: Ancestry.com Operations, Inc., 2010. Images reproduced by FamilySearch.

1850 United States Federal Census [database on-line]. Provo, Utah, U.S.A.: Ancestry.com Operations, Inc., 2009. Images reproduced by FamilySearch.

1860 United States Federal Census [database on-line]. Provo, Utah, U.S.A.: Ancestry.com Operations, Inc., 2009. Images reproduced by FamilySearch.

1870 United States Federal Census [database on-line]. Provo, Utah, U.S.A.: Ancestry.com Operations, Inc., 2009. Images reproduced by FamilySearch.

1880 United States Federal Census [database on-line]. Provo, Utah, U.S.A.: Ancestry.com Operations, Inc., 2016. Images reproduced by FamilySearch.

1900 United States Federal Census [database on-line]. Provo, Utah, U.S.A.: Ancestry.com Operations, Inc., 2006.

1910 United States Federal Census [database on-line]. Provo, Utah, U.S.A.: Ancestry.com Operations, Inc., 2006. Images reproduced by FamilySearch.

Canada, Find A Grave Index, 1600s-Current [database on-line]. Provo, UT, U.S.A: Ancestry.com Operations, Inc., 2012.

Claim #1 (Almena Hurd), filed 4/28/1863; Box 1709; Indian Accounts (Entry 3503A); Records of the Accounting Officers of the Department of the Treasury, Record Group 217; National Archives Building, Washington, DC—copy in files of Brown County Historical Society.

Claim #2 (Henry W. Smith), filed 1863; Box 1709; Indian Accounts (Entry 3503A); Records of the Accounting Officers of the Department of the Treasury, Record Group 217; National Archives Building, Washington, DC—copy in files of Brown County Historical Society.

Claim #4 (John G. Wright/Weight), filed 8/15/1864; Box 1709; Indian Accounts (Entry 3503A); Records of the Accounting Officers of the Department of the Treasury, Record Group 217; National Archives Building, Washington, DC.

Claim #9 (William J. Duley), filed 11/12/1862; 13E2A, 35/22/2, Box 1709 (tabbed); Indian Accounts (Entry 3503A); Records of the Accounting Officers of the Department of the Treasury, Record Group 217; National Archives Building, Washington, DC.

Claim #26 (Thomas Ireland), filed 8/17/1863; 13E2A, 35/22/2, Box 1709 (tabbed); Indian Accounts (Entry 3503A); Records of the Accounting Officers of the Department of the Treasury, Record Group 217; National Archives Building, Washington, DC.

Claim #53 (Estate of John Eastlick—deceased), filed April 29, 1863; Box #1710; Indian Accounts (Entry 3503B); Records of the Accounting Officers of the Department of the Treasury, Record Group 217; National Archives Building, Washington, DC.

Claim #63 (E. G. Koch), filed July 15, 1863; 13E2A, 35/22/2,

Sources

Box 1710 (tabbed); Indian Accounts (Entry 3503B); Records of the Accounting Officers of the Department of the Treasury, Record Group 217; National Archives Building, Washington, DC.

Claim #1161 (Ernest Koch, on behalf of Christina Koch); Box 3; Record Group 75; National Archives Building, Washington, DC—partial copy in files of Wheels Across the Prairie Museum.

Currie, Neil, 1842–1921, compiler. "Information of Victims of the Lake Shetek Massacre Obtained by Correspondence and Personal Testimony," 1894, 1946. Dakota Conflict of 1862 Manuscripts Collections. Minnesota Historical Society, #1925.

Duley, William J., 1819–1898. "Notes on the Sioux Massacre of 1862," 1885. Dakota Conflict of 1862 Manuscripts Collections. Minnesota Historical Society, #4546.

Eastlick, L. (Lavina), 1833–1923. "The Lake Shetek Indian Massacre in 1862," 1890. Dakota Conflict of 1862 Manuscripts Collections. Minnesota Historical Society, #6868.

Guetzlaff, R. E., *Letter to George V. Staeburg.* June 26, 1912.

Hamm, Mary A. (Pew). *Letter to Sylvia Ham Lightzer.* Undated copy.

Hatch, C. D. "Massacre of 1862." *1897 transcript of article.* Prepared for the *Fulda Republican* and reprinted in the *Martin County Independent* (April 22, 1897). From files of Brown County Historical Society.

Hatch, Charles D., 1837–1907. "Narrative of Charles D. Hatch's Experiences in the Indian War in Minnesota in 1862," undated. Dakota Conflict of 1862 Manuscripts Collections. Minnesota Historical Society, #7817.

Illinois, State Census Collection, 1825–1865 [database on-line]. Provo, UT, USA: Ancestry.com Operations, Inc., 2008.

Indiana Marriage Index, 1800–1941 [database on-line]. Provo, UT, USA. Ancestry.com Operations, Inc., 2005.

Iowa, State Census Collection, 1836–1925 [database on-line]. Provo, UT, USA. Ancestry.com Operations, Inc., 2007.

Kansas State Census Collection, 1855–1925 [database on-line].

Provo, UT, USA: Ancestry.com Operations, Inc., 2009.

Michigan, Compiled Marriages for Select Counties, 1851–1875 [database on-line]. Provo, UT, USA: Ancestry.com Operations, Inc., 2000.

Minnesota, Births and Christenings Index, 1840–1980 [database on-line]. Provo, UT, USA. Ancestry.com Operations, Inc., 2011.

Minnesota, County Marriages, 1860–1949, database with images. FamilySearch.com. Intellectual Reserve, Inc., 2016.

Minnesota, Death Index, 1908–2002 [database on-line]. Provo, UT, USA. Ancestry.com Operations, Inc., 2001.

Minnesota, Marriages Index, 1849–1950 [database on-line]. Provo, UT, USA. Ancestry.com Operations, Inc., 2011.

Minnesota, Territorial and State Censuses, 1849–1905 [database on-line]. Provo, UT, USA. Ancestry.com Operations, Inc., 2007.

Minnesota Territorial Census, 1857, database with images. FamilySearch.com. Intellectual Reserve, Inc., 2014.

Myers, Aaron, 1825–1906. "Aaron Myers reminiscence and biographical data," 1900, 1906. Dakota Conflict of 1862 Manuscripts Collections. Minnesota Historical Society, #2048.

Myers, Aaron. Untitled transcript. Received from Rick Myers, grandson, Nov. 14, 1961. Files of Brown County Historical Society.

New York, State Census, 1855 [database on-line]. Provo, UT, USA. Ancestry.com Operations, Inc., 2013.

New York, State Census, 1875 [database on-line]. Provo, UT, USA. Ancestry.com Operations, Inc., 2014.

Ohio, County Marriages, 1774–1993 [database on-line]. Lehi, UT, USA. Ancestry.com Operations, Inc., 2016.

Pattee, Major John, 41st Iowa Infantry, Commanding, to Charles Poimeau, Esq., Fort Randall, DT, Nov. 15, 1862; 9W2; 34/8/9; Letters and Telegrams Sent (Entry 370-2, Vol. 3 of 17 Ft. Randall, SD, Post Letter Book); Record Group 393,

Sources

National Archives Building, Washington, DC.

Pattee, Major John, 41st Iowa Infantry, Commanding, to Capt. F. H. Cooper., Fort Randall, DT, Nov. 16, 1862; 9W2; 34/8/9; Letters and Telegrams Sent (Entry 370-2, Vol. 3 of 17 Ft. Randall, SD, Post Letter Book); Record Group 393, National Archives Building, Washington, DC.

Pattee, Major John, 41st Iowa Infantry, Commanding, to Major Gen. John Pope, Fort Randall, DT, Nov. 26, 1862; 9W2; 34/8/9; Letters and Telegrams Sent (Entry 370-2, Vol. 3 of 17 Ft. Randall, SD, Post Letter Book); Record Group 393, National Archives Building, Washington, DC.

Pattee, Major John, 41st Iowa Infantry, Commanding, to Brig. Gen. G. Cook, on the March from Fort Randall to Fort Pierre, Dec. 1, 1862; Part V, Entry 2, Vol. 3 of 17; Ft. Randall, SD, Post Letter Book; Record Group 393, National Archives Building, Washington, DC.

Pattee, Major John, 41st Iowa Infantry, Commanding, to Major Gen. John Pope, Fort Randall, DT, Dec. 1, 1862; 9W2; 34/8/9; Letters and Telegrams Sent (Entry 370-2, Vol. 3 of 17 Ft. Randall, SD, Post Letter Book); Record Group 393, National Archives Building, Washington, DC.

Pennsylvania, County Marriages, 1885–1950, database with images. FamilySearch.com. Intellectual Reserve, Inc., 2016.

Racou, J. C., 1st lt., Co. H, 41st Iowa Infantry, Fort Randall, DT, Jan. 13, 1863, Report of Expedition; Part V, Entry 2, Vol. 3 of 17; Post Letter Book—Ft. Randall, SD, Record Group 393, National Archives Building, Washington, DC.

Somsen, Henry N., Jr. *Letters to Mrs. Clark Kellett, New Ulm Public Museum*. Feb. 26, 1963, and May 23, 1963. Copy in files of Brown County Historical Society.

United States Bureau of Land Management. *Minnesota Land Records* [database on-line]. Provo, UT, USA: Ancestry.com Operations, Inc. 1997.

United States Bureau of Land Management. *Minnesota, Homestead and Cash Entry Patents, Pre-1908*, [database on-line]. Provo, UT, USA: Ancestry.com Operations, Inc. 1997.

United State Census of Union Veterans and Widows of the Civil War,

1890, database with images. FamilySearch.com. Intellectual Reserve, Inc., 2016.

U.S. City Directories, 1822–1995 [database on-line]. Provo, UT, USA: Ancestry.com Operations, Inc., 2011.

U.S., Find a Grave Index, 1600–Current [database on-line]. Provo, UT, USA: Ancestry.com Operations, Inc., 2012.

U.S. General Land Office Records, 1796–1907 [database on-line]. Provo, UT, USA: Ancestry.com Operations, Inc., 2008.

U.S. Returns from Regular Army Infantry Regiments, 1821–1916 [database on-line]. Provo, UT, USA: Ancestry.com Operations, Inc., 2011.

Web: International, Find a Grave Index [database on-line]. Provo, UT, USA: Ancestry.com Operations, Inc., 2013.

Wisconsin State Census, 1875, database with images. Family Search.com. Intellectual Reserve, Inc., 2016.

Workman, Harper M., 1855–?. "Early history of Lake Shetek Country," undated and 1924–30. Dakota Conflict of 1862 Manuscripts Collections. Minnesota Historical Society, #3470.

Books, Documentaries, Letters, Interviews

Anderson, Gary Clayton, and Alan R. Woolworth. *Through Dakota Eyes: Narrative Accounts of the Minnesota Indian War of 1862.* St. Paul, Minnesota: Minnesota Historical Society Press, 1988.

Barbier, Charles P. "Recollections of Ft. La Framboise in 1862 and the Rescue of Lake Chetek [sic] Captives." *South Dakota Historical Collections* (Doane Robinson, ed.), vol. XI, 1922: pp. 232–42. Digital version.

Britain, Barbara, producer. *Return to Lake Shetek: The Courage of the Fool Soldiers.* White Bear Lake, Minnesota: Barbara Britain, undated.

Bryant, Charles S., and Abel B. Murch. A History of the Great Sioux Massacre by the Sioux Indians in Minnesota. Cincinnati: Rickey & Carroll, 1864.

Sources

Carley, Kenneth. *The Sioux Uprising of 1862.* St. Paul, Minnesota: The Minnesota Historical Society, 1976.

Charger, Sam. "Biography of Martin Charger," *South Dakota Historical Collections* (Doane Robinson, ed.), vol. XXII, 1946: 1–25.

Child, James E. *Child's History of Waseca County, Minnesota.* Owatonna, Minnesota: Whiting & Luers, 1905.

Dahlin, Curtis A. *Calamity at Lake Shetek.* Roseville, Minnesota: Curtis A. Dahlin, 2015.

Deloria, Ella Cara. *Speaking of Indians.* Pickle Partner Publishing. www.pp-publishing.com, 2015; originally published 1944. Digital version.

Deloria, Ella Cara. *Waterlily.* Lincoln, Nebraska: University of Nebraska Press, 1988. Digital version.

Eastlick, Mrs. (Lavina). *A Personal Narrative of Indian Massacres 1862.* No publication data listed, 1864, 1959, 1967.

Eastman, Charles Alexander. *From the Deep Woods to Civilization: Chapters in the Autobiography of an Indian.* No location: Little Brown and Company, 1916. Digital version 2017.

Eastman, Charles Alexander. *The Collected Complete Works of Charles Alexander Eastman.* No publication data. Digital version.

Greene, Jerome A. *Fort Randall on the Missouri, 1856–1892.* Pierre, South Dakota: South Dakota State Historical Society Press, 2005.

Haymond, John A. The Dakota War Trials of 1862: Revenge, Military Law and the Judgment of History. Jefferson, North Carolina: McFarland & Company, Inc., 2016. Digital version.

Heard, Isaac V. D. *History of the Sioux War and Massacres of 1862 and 1863.* Ann Arbor, Michigan: University of Michigan Library, 2005. Digital version.

Hibschman, Harry Jacob. *The Shetek Pioneers and the Indians.* New York: Garland Pub., 1976.

Sources

History of Winona County, 1883. H. H. Hill and Company, 1883. Digital version.

Isch, John. *A Battle for Living: The Life and Experiences of Lavina Eastlick.* New Ulm, Minnesota: Brown County Historical Society, 2012.

Isch, John. *The Dakota Trials: Including the Complete Transcripts and Explanatory Notes on the Military Commission Trials in Minnesota 1862–1864.* New Ulm, Minnesota: Brown County Historical Society, 2012, 2013.

Johansson, Eric J. *Letters to Bill Bolin.* 1985–1987, from files of Bill Bolin.

Kelly, Fanny; Clark Spence and Mary Lee Spence, eds. *Narrative of my Captivity among the Sioux Indians.* New York: Barnes & Noble Books, no date.

Manfred, Frederick. Interviews with Pamela Gieser. Brookings, SD, and Luverne, MN. Jan. 9 and Mar. 9, 1983.

Manfred, Frederick. *Scarlet Plume.* New York: Frederick Feikema Manfred, 1964.

Michano, Gregory, and Susan A. Michano. *A Fate Worse than Death: Indian Captivities in the West, 1830–1885.* Caldwell, Idaho: Caxton Press, 2009. Digital version.

Morris, Lucy Leavenworth Wilder. *Old Rail Fence Corners: Frontier Tales Told by Minnesota Pioneers.* St. Paul: Minnesota Historical Society Press, 1914. Digital version.

Native South Dakota: A Guide to Tribal Lands. Pierre, South Dakota: South Dakota Department of Tourism, 2014.

Pattee, Colonel John. "Report of Colonel Pattee," *South Dakota Historical Collections* (Doane Robinson, ed.), Vol. V, 1910: 273–96.

Schwandt, Mary. *The Captivity of Mary Schwandt.* Fairfield, Washington: Ye Galleon Press, 1975.

Seymour, John. *The Forgotten Arts and Crafts.* New York: Dorling Kindersley Publishing, Inc., 2001.

Sharp, Abbie Gardner. *The Spirit Lake Massacre and Captivity of*

Sources

Miss Abbie Gardner. Big Byte Books, 2015 (original publication 1912). Digital version.

Silvernale, John A. *In Commemoration of the Sioux Uprising Aug. 20, 1862.* Tracy, Minnesota: Tracy Publishing Company and the Murray County Historical Society, 1962, 2006.

Sneve, Virginia Driving Hawk. *Betrayed.* New York: Holiday House, 1974.

Wakefield, Sarah F. *Six Weeks in the Sioux Tepees.* Guilford, Connecticut: Globe Pequot Press, 2004.

Newspapers

"125th Anniversary Set at Shetek," *Tracy Headlight Herald.* Aug. 19, 1987, p. 1.

"Arrival of Mrs. Duly [sic] and Children," *The Stillwater Messenger.* February 19, 1863, p. 1.

"Arrival of Mrs. Duly [sic] and Children," *The Wabashaw County Herald*, vol. 3, no. 24: Feb. 26, 1863, p. 1.

"Arrival of Mrs. Duly [sic] and Children," *Mankato Free Record.* Jan. 31, 1863, p. 2.

"Author Has Special Feeling for Pioneers," *Tracy Headlight Herald.* August 19, 1987, pp. 1–2.

Bolin, Bill. "Hatch Kin Still Linked to Shetek," *Southwest Sailor,* July 199?.

Bolin, Bill. "Pioneer Mothers Escaped Indian Slaughter at Shetek," *Southwest Sailor.* July 199?, pp. 12, 14.

Bolin, Bill. "Shetek's 'Paul Revere' Rides On," *Southwest Sailor,* July 199?.

Brown, Curt. "Forgotten Survivor of a Frontier War," *Minneapolis Star Tribune.* October 16, 2016, p. B4.

Brown, Curt. "Minnesota History: Image Surfaces from a Grim Chapter," *Minneapolis Star-Tribune.* November 1, 2015, p. B4.

"Dakota Conflict at Shetek: 1862–1987 Year of Reconcilation

Sources

Edition," various articles, *Tracy Headlight Herald.* August 19, 1987.

Dakota Land Company ad, *St. Paul Pioneer & Democrat.* Dec. 15, 1861, p. 1.

"Early Events Recalled: An Interesting Story Connected with the Outbreak of the Sioux," *The Mankato Review.* July 6, 1892, un-paginated copy.

"Elmira [sic] Descendants of Hurd Family Recall," *The Sunday Telegram.* Dec. 1931, un-paginated copy.

"First Settler in Lyon County Believed Found," unidentified, undated newspaper clipping. Files of Brown County Historical Society.

Golden, T. C. "The Indian War-Expedition to Lake Shetek—Letter from the Chaplain of the 25th Wisconsin," *St. Paul Pioneer.* Nov. 11, 1862.

Hatch, Charles. "A Part of the History of Murray County: Scenes of the Lake Shetek Massacre," *Southwest Minnesotian* (reprinted from the *Waseca Herald*). Weekly series April 7, 1887–June 7, 1887.

Hatch, Chas. D. "Story of Indian Massacre Told by a Survivor," *Minneapolis Tribune.* Aug. 18, 1912, clipping.

"Held by Indians for Many Weeks," *Blue Earth County Enterprise.* Jan 24, 1927, clipping.

"Heroine of War with Sioux Dies: Captive of White Lodge Passes Away at Mankato," *Mankato Review.* Mar. 6, 1907.

"Heroism of Elmira [sic]: Pioneer Saves Lives of Her Babies," *The Sunday Telegram.* Dec. 14, 1931, un-paginated copy.

"Historic Claims Paper Reveals Contents of Koch Cabin at Time of Massacre," *Tracy Headlight Herald.* July 4, 1963, p. 1.

"The Indian War—Lake Shetek Massacre—More Bodies Found," *St. Paul Pioneer-Democrat.* Sept. 10, 1862.

"The Indian War—The Massacre at Lake Shetek: Statement of Mr. Everett," *The St. Paul Pioneer.* Sept. 3, 1862.

Johnson, F. W., Mrs. "Hurd's Heart-Rending Story of Sioux Massacre," *Journal.* August 11, 1937, un-paginated copy.

Sources

"Lake Shetek Massacre Edition," *Tracy Headlight Herald.* Various articles, Aug. 16, 1962.

Lee, Zion. "The Fool Soldiers," *Pierre Capital Journal.* July 21, 2016. Digital version.

"Left for Dead: The Story of Thomas Ireland," *Mankato Free Press.* April 6, 1893, clipping.

"Mankato Woman, 80, Recalls Horror of Indian Massacre," *Mankato Free Press.* June 8, 1936, clipping.

Mathis, Tedd. "At the End, 38 Men Hanged," *Worthington Daily Globe.* Aug. 27, 1987, pp. 1, 10.

"Mrs. Hotaling Survivor of Indian Massacre," *Mankato Free Press.* Feb 2, 1946, clipping.

"Notice of Departure of Wm J. Duly and Family," *Ft. Doge Republican.* Jan 21, 1863, p. 1.

Olson, Corrinne. "Descendant Offers 'Thank You' for 1862 Rescue," *Sioux Falls Argus Leader.* Undated, un-paginated copy in Brown County Historical Society files.

"Personal," *The New York Times,* from the *St. Paul (Minn) Press.* September 28, 1862.

"Pioneer Recalls Massacre at Shetek 69 Years Ago," *Mankato Free Press.* Aug 21, 1931, clipping.

"Released Captives," *Mankato Weekly Record.* Jan. 24, 1863, clipping.

"Remembering the Battlegrounds," *Worthington Daily Globe.* August 14, 1987, p. B3.

"She Asks for a Pension," *Mankato Review.* March 2, 1898.

"Shetek Hero," *Tracy Headlight Herald.* Aug. 16, 1962; Section 1, p. 12.

"Shetek Massacre Edition," *Tracy Headlight Herald.* Various articles, Aug. 19, 1932.

"The Sioux Barbaritie [sic]-Narrative of Mrs. Phineas B. Hurd before the United States Commissioners," *Goodhue Volunteer.* Vol. 7, no. 45, June 3, 1863, p.1.

"The Sioux War—From Sibley's Camp," *Mankato Semi-Weekly*

Record. October 18, 1862, pp. 1–2.

"The Sioux War—Statement of a Released Prisoner," *Mankato Semi-Weekly Record.* October 18, 1862, pp. 1–2.

"Sudden Death of Mrs. Hohmuth," *The Mankato Review.* March 5, 1907, un-paginated copy.

"Where Are They Buried? Heroic Fool Soldiers Killed and Left in Gregory Co.," *Gregory Times-Advocate.* Vol. 110, no. 14, April 2, 2014, pp. 1, 10.

Periodicals

Britain, Barbara. "Gifts from the Fool Soldiers." *Minnesota's Heritage,* vol. 4, July 2011: 36–43.

Carpenter, Paul. "Charles Hatch, Survivor of Slaughter's Slough-Lake Shetek, Minnesota 1862," unpublished article in files of Bill Bolin.

Gray, John S. "The Santee Sioux and the Settlers at Lake Shetek," *Montana: The Magazine of Western History,* vol. XXV, no. 1; winter 1975: pp. 42–54.

Ketcham, Jim. "The Fool Soldiers." *Minnesota's Heritage,* vol. 4, July 2011: 6–19.

Laut, Agnes C. "Pioneer Women of the West II: The Heroines of Lake Shetek," *The Outing Magazine,* vol. 52, 1908: 271–86.

Nelson, Jim. "The Fool Soldiers' Story Told Many Ways." *Minnesota's Heritage,* vol. 4, July 2011: 20–35.

Oral Histories

Plummer, Stephen. "American Indian Research Project Field Notes," *Institute of American Indian Studies, South Dakota Oral History Center, University of South Dakota.* 1972. Mss. #0850, 0851, 0852, 0854, 0855, 0856, 0858, 0875.

"South Dakota Oral History Project," *Institute of American Indian Studies, South Dakota Oral History Center, University of South Dakota.* Mss. #1616, 1967, 1968.

Sources

Online Websites

"Beaver, Minnesota," *Wikipedia*. https://en.wikipedia.org/wiki/Beaver,_Minnesota: last accessed May 20, 2019.

Curtiss-Wedge, Franklyn, Editor. "History of Whitewater Township, Winona County, Minnesota," *The History of Winona County, Minnesota*. Chicago: H. C. Cooper, Jr. & Co., Publisher, 1913. http://history.rays-place.com/mn/wi-whitewater.htm: copyright 2003–2013: accessed Feb. 18, 2017.

"Dakota People," *Wikipedia*. https://en.wikipedia.org/wiki/Dakota_people: May 14, 2019. Last accessed May 21, 2019.

"During the War," *Minnesota Historical Society: The US-Dakota War of 1862*. http://www.usdakotawar.org/history/war/during-war: Last accessed May 21, 2019.

"Early West Murray County Minnesota History," *USGW Archives*. http://www.usgwarchives.net/mn/murray/history/116-117.htm. Last accessed May 21, 2019.

Eckles, Polly, transcriber. "1854 State Census of Iowa, Jackson County, All Townships," *IAGenWeb State Census Project*. http://iagenweb.org/census/: 2008: accessed Feb. 18, 2017.

"Ferryboats," *Encyclopedia Dubuque*. From Oldt, Franklin T. *History of Dubuque County, Iowa*. Chicago: Western Historical Company, 1880. http://www.encyclopediadubuque.org/index.php?title=FERRYBOATS: Creative Commons BY NC-SA, 15 Nov 2015: last accessed May 20, 2019.

Find a Grave www.findagrave.com

Capt Wiliam J. Duley, Sr. Memorial #59962077; Oct. 11, 2010. Cindy K. Coffin, sponsor.

Jefferson M. Duley. Memorial #56823287; Aug. 8, 2010. Nolte, Gwen, creator; maintained by Cindy K. Coffin.

Laura Terry Duley. Memorial #59962127; Oct. 11, 2010. Cindy K. Coffin, sponsor.

Lavina Day Eastlick. Memorial #61103083; Nov. 4, 2010. Bill Cox, creator.

Sources

Fool Soldiers Band Monument. Memorial #2385551; Jan. 22, 2011.

Andreas Koch. Memorial #37509095; May 25, 2009. Cindy K. Coffin, creator.

Rachel Sunman Terry. Memorial #60686252; 12/16/2016.

Almena Hamm "Alomina" Hurd Woodword. Memorial #63748588; Jan. 5, 2011. Created by Bill Cox.

Eldora Wright. Memorial #174942797; Jan. 6, 2017. Created by Candy.

"Flood of 1851," *Wikipedia*. https://en.wikipedia.org/wiki/Flood_of_1851: Feb 15, 2017.

Flora, Stephanie. "The Covered Wagon," *The Oregon Trail and Its Pioneers*. http://centralthirdgrade.weebly.com/uploads/7/3/9/0/7390012/ covered_wagon.pdf: 2007. Last accessed May 21, 2019.

Gerischer, Debbie Clough, transcriber. "Crossing the Mississippi," *IAGenWeb Project*. From Parish, John C., editor. "The Palimpsest," *Iowa History, vol. 1. no. 5*. State Historical Society of Iowa: December 1920. http://iagenweb.org/history/palimpsest/1920-Dec.htm: last accessed May 20, 2019.

Greene, William A. "The Erie Railroad," *Allegany County Historical Society Local History and Genealogy*. 2003–2012. http://www.alleganyhistory.org/culture/transportation/railroads/ erie-railroad/1060-the-erie-railroad: last accessed May 20, 2019.

Grey, Jim. "About the Road" and "Traveling the Road," *The Historic Michigan Road*. https://historicmichiganroad.org/: 1/16/2016. Last accessed May 20, 2019.

Harris, Howell. "Henry Stanley and the Rotary Stove," *A Stove Less Ordinary*. Aug. 20, 2016. https://stovehistory.blogspot.com/2016/08/ henry-stanley-and-the-rotary-stove.html: accessed Feb. 18, 2017.

Harris, Howell. "The Pioneer Cooking Stove, Indiana, Late 1830s," *A Stove Less Ordinary*. https://stovehistory.blogspot.com/2013/04/ the-pioneer-cooking-stove-indiana.html: April

Sources

2, 2013: accessed Feb. 18, 2017.

Hintz, Susan. "Roseanna Ireland Miller VanAlstine (1853–1936)," *Susan's Space*. https://sooze471.wordpress.com/2011/09/25/ rose-anna-ireland-miller-vanalstine-1853-1936/: Sept. 25-2011. Last accessed May 21, 2019.

"History of South Dakota," *Wikipedia*. https://en.wikipedia.org/wiki/History_of_South_Dakota: Feb. 20, 2019. Last accessed May 21, 2019.

"History of Weather Observations-Fort Ridgely, Minnesota 1853–1867," *MRCC*. http://mrcc.sws.uius.edu/FORTS/histories/MN_Fort_Ridgely_Boulay.pdf. Last accessed May 21, 2019.

Hubbard, Lucius F. "Wahpeton Chiefs," *Minnesota in Three Centuries*. 1908. www.archive.org/stream/minnsotainthree03 bubbuoft/minnesotainthreeo3hubbuoft_djvu.txt: Dec. 28, 2009. Accessed May 21, 2019.

Iowa Land Records. https://iowalandrecords.org. Last accessed May 23, 2019.

"Ishtakhaba," *Wikipedia*. https://en.wikipedia.org/wiki/Ishtakhaba: May 2, 2019. Last accessed May 21, 2019.

"Jackson County Cemetery Directory," *IAGenWeb Project*. http://www.usgwarchives.net/al/jackson/cemetery.htm: 2008-2017: accessed Feb. 17, 2017.

Knox, Douglas, and Michael Conzen. *The Electronic Encyclopeida of Chicago*. c. 2005, from *Encyclopedia of Chicago*. Chicago: Chicago Historical Society, 1848. http://www.encyclopedia.chicagohistory.org/pages/500003.html: last accessed May 20, 2019.

Krogman, Mary Kay, transcriber. "Jackson County, Iowa," *Genealogy Trails*, from "About Bellevue, Iowa," *The History of Jackson County Iowa*. No publisher listed, November 1879. http://genealogytrails.com/iowa/jackson/towns_current.html, copyright 2017. Last accessed May 20, 2019.

Krogman, Mary Kay, transcriber (from various sources). "Murray County, Minnesota: Dakota War-Victims and Survivor Stories," *Genealogy Trails History Group*. http://genealogy

trails.com/minn/murray/history_massacre.html. Last accessed May 21, 2019.

"Lakota and Dakota Sioux Fact Sheet," Native American Facts for Kids. http://www.bigorrin.org/sioux_kids.htm: Native Languages of the Americas website, 1998—2015. Last accessed May 21, 2019.

"Lakota Phrase Archive," Akta Lakota Museum & Cultural Center. http://aktalakota.stjo.org/site/News2?page=NewsArticle&id=8577. Last accessed May 21, 2019.

"Legislators Past & Present: Duley, William J. 'W.J'," *Minnesota Legislative Reference Library*. https://www.leg.state.mn.us/legdb/fulldetail?ID=12622: last accessed May 20, 2019.

Leigh, Ray, and Kathy Leigh, "The Tragedy of Minnesota," *US-Roots*. http://www.us-roots.org/colonialamerica/ pioneer/chap26_1.html: Oct. 26, 2001. Last accessed May 21, 2019.

"Michigan Road," *Wikipedia*. https://en.wikipedia.org/w/index.php?title=Michigan_Road&p;dod=745612427: 22 Oct. 2016: last accessed May 20, 2019.

"Minnesota Weather for the Year 1862," *Climate Stations*. https://www.climatestations.com/minnesota-weather-for-1862/. Last accessed 5/21/2019.

"Mrs. Alomina Hurd: A Story of Border Suffering," *Civil War*. http://www.civilwar.com/people/21-union-women/ 148422-mrs-alomina-hurd.html: last accessed May 20, 2019.

Pridmore, Jay. " '1848: Chicago's Turning Point' Exhibition Lives Up To Its Billing," *Chicago Tribune*. Nov 6, 1998. https://www.chicagotribune.com/news/ ct-xpm-1998-11-06-9811060472-story.html: last accessed May 20, 2019.

Sherman, Bill. "Tracing the Treaties: How They Affected American Indians and Iowa," *Iowa History Journal*. http://iowahistoryjournal.com/ tracing-treaties-affected-american-indians-iowa/: last accessed May 20, 2019.

"The Start of Ripley County, Indiana," *Ripley County Historical Society Library*. http://www.rchslib.org/ripleyformed.html: accessed Feb. 17, 2017.

"Sunman, Indiana," Wikipedia. https://en.wikipedia.org/wiki/

Sources

Sunman,_Indiana: last accessed May 20, 2019.
"Sycamore Row (road)," *Wikipedia:* 12 Jan. 2016. https://en.wikipedia.org/wiki/Sycamore_Row_(road): Feb. 15, 2017.
Sykora, Jason, and Matt Robertson. "Koch Cabin Lake Shetek," *RRCNET.* http://www.rrcnet.org/~historic/kcabin.html: last accessed May 21, 2019.
"Tete Des Morts. Jackson County 1893. Iowa. 1893," *Historical Map Works Residential Genealogy.* From *Jackson County 1893, Iowa.* Northwest Publishing Company: 1893. http://www.historicmapworks.com/Map/US/54824/Tete+Des+Morts/Jackson+County+1893/Iowa/: last accessed May 20, 2019.
Weeks, John A., III. "Dubuque-Wisconsin Bridge," *Highways, Byways, and Bridge Photography.* http://www.johnweeks.com/river_mississippi/pagesA/ umissA09.html: accessed Feb. 13, 2017.
Whitaker, Beverly. "The Chicago Road and the State Road," *Road Trails: Early American Roads and Trails.* http://freepages.rootsweb.com/~gentutor/genealogy/trails.html: 2006: last accessed May 20, 2019.

BOOK CLUB DISCUSSION QUESTIONS

1. Westward expansion is a major thread in *Never Let Go*. What factors motivated the Shetek settlers to move west? Do you feel those reasons were valid? How much of a role did restlessness play? In what ways did land companies lure and manipulate settlers? Would such techniques work today?

2. Cultural misunderstandings and biases were rampant in nineteenth-century Minnesota. In what ways did white settlers fail to understand the Dakota? What parts of white culture were not understood by the Dakota? How were such biases perpetuated? Which of the Shetek women do you think displayed the most prejudice? The least? How did this impact them as events unfolded?

3. The novel takes places during a time when gender roles were defined much differently than they are today. Which of the women was most bound by these expectations? Do you think her adherence to these "rules" made her weak? Why or why not? What methods did the five women use to "work around" such expectations?

4. All of the women in the novel discovered their adult lives to be different than the expectations of their youth. Which of the women did you identify with most? Why? How did you feel

Book Club Discussion Questions

about the ways in which she adjusted? At what point in the story did she discover her strength?

5. Laura may have suffered from depression. Do you feel she was predisposed to mental illness, or did external factors shape her response? How so? If she were alive today, how might her "treatment plan" have differed from that created by Mrs. Tucker? Do you believe she was weak? In what ways did she exhibit strength?

6. Julia coped with a husband who was irresponsible, willing to break the law, and who drank heavily. Why do you feel she was willing to remain with such a man? Do you feel those reasons were valid, given the era in which she lived? Would she have behaved differently if she were alive today?

7. Christina and her husband had very strong opinions about the shooting of Clark. Based on what happened, do you think the settlers handled the threat in the best way? What other solutions might they have explored?

8. Lavina was forced to make life and death decisions concerning her children. How did you feel about what she decided? If you had been in her position, what would you have done?

9. Almena's adult life was much shaped by her early years. What traits did she exhibit that might be traced back to those events? What other paths might she have taken in her life?

10. Which woman do you feel had the largest spirit of

Book Club Discussion Questions

adventure? The most courage? Was most ill-suited for frontier life? Why?

11. What actions of the settlers, over time, contributed to the events of August 20, 1862? On the day of the attack, what decisions were made that impacted the outcome of the day? Do you think the day might have turned out differently if those decisions had not been made? Why or why not?

12. Do you believe the decision to attack white settlements was one with which all Dakota agreed? What unexpected issues did the Dakota have to deal with as a result of the decision to attack? How did the taking of captives differ in this instance? How did it complicate Dakota life?

13. Published accounts of the time (book and newspaper) told stories of atrocities. Do you believe these accounts fairly represented what occurred? Why or why not? What impact do you think these accounts had on Dakota/white relationships thereafter?

14. The Fool Soldiers did not receive credit for their role in ransoming the Shetek captives until recently. Why did the army fail to recognize these young men? Why has it been so difficult to trace the real story of events surrounding the Fool Soldiers?

15. Scars of the Dakota Conflict still remain in both white and Dakota societies today. Why do you think this the case? What role have bias and misunderstanding played? What impact have the atrocity stories played in this? What retaliatory actions occurred? Do you believe either or both cultures have avoided negative history? In what ways? How might these scars be healed?

ABOUT THE AUTHOR

Pamela (Gieser) Nowak was born and raised in southwest Minnesota. She has a B.A. in history and was a teacher, preservationist, project manager for the Fort Yuma National Historic Site, and administrator of a homeless shelter prior to her writing career. Her four historical romance novels have won numerous national awards and garnered critical acclaim for her ability to weave actual people, events, and places into her plotting. Now writing women's historical fiction with a heavy basis in fact, she's returned to her roots. The voices of these five Shetek survivors have called to her since she first learned about the Dakota Conflict and walked in their footsteps along the shores of Lake Shetek.

Made in the USA
Middletown, DE
24 January 2023

A General Discussion

on

*Time-Resolved Chemistry:
From Structure to Function*

A General Discussion on Time-Resolved Chemistry was held at the University of Manchester, UK on 24th, 25th and 26th June, 2002.

Contents

1 Introductory Lecture: Time-resolved chemistry at atomic resolution
  Philip Coppens and **Irina V. Novozhilova**

13 The realization of sub-nanosecond pump and probe experiments at the ESRF
  Michael Wulff, Anton Plech, Laurent Eybert, Rudolf Randler, Friedrich Schotte and **Philip Anfinrud**

27 Femtosecond mid-infrared spectroscopy of condensed phase hydrogen-bonded systems as a probe of structural dynamics
  Matteo Rini, Andreas Kummrow, Jens Dreyer, Erik T. J. Nibbering and **Thomas Elsaesser**

41 What we can learn about fast chemical processes from slow diffraction experiments
  Hans-Beat Bürgi

65 The frontiers of time-resolved macromolecular crystallography: movies and chirped X-ray pulses
  Keith Moffat

79 General Discussion

89 Achieving photo-control of protein conformation and activity: producing a photo-controlled leucine zipper
  Janet R. Kumita, Daniel G. Flint, G. Andrew Woolley and **Oliver S. Smart**

105 First investigations of the kinetics of the topochemical reaction of *p*-formyl-*trans*-cinnamic acid by time-resolved X-ray diffraction
  G. Busse, T. Tschentscher, A. Plech, M. Wulff, B. Frederichs and **S. Techert**

119 Nanosecond time-resolved crystallography of photo-induced species: case study and instrument development for high-resolution excited-state single-crystal structure determination
  Jacqueline M. Cole, Paul R. Raithby, Michael Wulff, Friedrich Schotte, Anton Plech, Simon J. Teat and **Graham Bushnell-Wye**

131 Time-resolved and static-ensemble structural chemistry of hydroxymethylbilane synthase
  John R. Helliwell, Yeu Perng Nieh, Jarjis Habash, Paul F. Faulder, James Raftery, Michele Cianci, Michael Wulff and **Alfons Hädener**

145 Structural dynamics of the receptor-binding domain of colicin E9
  Ruth Boetzel, Emily S. Collins, Nigel J. Clayden, Colin Kleanthous, Richard James and **Geoffrey R. Moore**

163 The dynamic transition in proteins may have a simple explanation
  Roy M. Daniel, John L. Finney and **Jeremy C. Smith**

This journal is © The Royal Society of Chemistry 2002

171	General Discussion
191	Mechanism of formation of DNA–cationic vesicle complexes **Paula C. A. Barreleiro, Roland P. May** and **Björn Lindman**
203	Following the formation of nanometer-sized clusters by time-resolved SAXS and EXAFS techniques **Florian Meneau, Gopinathan Sankar, Norberto Morgante, Rudolf Winter, C. Richard A. Catlow, G. Neville Greaves** and **John Meurig Thomas**
211	Application of stopped flow techniques and energy dispersive EXAFS for investigation of the reactions of transition metal complexes in solution: Activation of nickel β-diketonates to form homogeneous catalysts, electron transfer reactions involving iron(III) and oxidative addition to iridium(I) **M. Basyaruddin B. Abdul Rahman, Peter R. Bolton, John Evans, Andrew J. Dent, Ian Harvey** and **Sofia Diaz-Moreno**
223	Direct dynamics calculations of reaction rate and kinetic isotope effects in enzyme catalysed reactions **Gary Tresadern, Sara Nunez, Paul F. Faulder, Hong Wang, Ian H. Hillier** and **Neil A. Burton**
243	Time-resolved computational protein biochemistry: Solvent effects on interactions, conformational transitions and equilibrium fluctuations **Alexander L. Tournier, Danzhi Huang, Sonja M. Schwarzl, Stefan Fischer** and **Jeremy C. Smith**
253	Theoretical studies of time-resolved spectroscopy of protein folding **Jonathan D. Hirst, Samita Bhattacharjee** and **Alexey V. Onufriev**
269	General Discussion
283	Chemistry, physics and time: the computer modelling of glassmaking **David Martlew**
299	A SAXS/WAXS XAFS study of crystallisation in cordierite glass **G. N. Greaves, W. Bras, M. Oversluizen** and **S. M. Clark**
315	Excited state molecular structure determination in disordered media using laser pump/X-ray probe time-domain X-ray absorption spectroscopy **Lin X. Chen**
331	Recent results from the *in situ* study of hydrothermal crystallisations using time-resolved X-ray and neutron diffraction methods **Richard I. Walton, Alexander Norquist, Ronald I. Smith** and **Dermot O'Hare**
343	Are metastable, precrystallisation, density-fluctuations a universal phenomena? **Ellen L. Heeley, C. Kit Poh, Wu Li, Anna Maidens, Wim Bras, Igor P. Dolbnya, Anthony J. Gleeson, Nicolas J. Terrill, J. Patrick A. Fairclough, Peter D. Olmsted, Rile I. Ristic, Micheal J. Hounslow** and **Anthony J. Ryan**
363	*In situ* neutron diffraction studies of single crystals and powders during microwave irradiation **Andrew Harrison, Richard Ibberson, Graeme Robb, Gavin Whittaker, Chick Wilson** and **Douglas Youngson**
381	General Discussion
395	Concluding Remarks: Time-resolved chemistry: from structure to function. A summary **John Meurig Thomas**
401	List of Posters
403	List of Participants
405	Index of Contributors

Introductory Lecture

Time-resolved chemistry at atomic resolution

Philip Coppens* and Irina V. Novozhilova

Department of Chemistry, State University of New York at Buffalo, Buffalo, NY 14260-3000, USA

Received 19th July 2002, Accepted 19th July 2002
First published as an Advance Article on the web 8th October 2002

Though time-resolved studies are still at an early stage, the field is rapidly being developed and applied to an increasingly broad spectrum of problems with timescales varying from seconds or more down to femtoseconds. In this overview a number of different techniques are discussed, with emphasis on chemical applications in which information is obtained at the atomic level. The need to correlate with theory, both for calibration of theoretical methods and to obtain related information not accessible experimentally, is stressed.

Background

The importance of time resolution in the study of a wide variety of chemical processes can hardly be overestimated. While molecular structure is a basic concept and must be known before a fundamental understanding can be reached, chemical processes are dynamic, and reaction pathways and their transition states play a crucial role in determining the products of chemical reactions.

Time-dependence in chemistry is implied in the century-old Arrhenius equation, which expresses the rate of a chemical reaction in terms of an activation energy in the exponent and a pre-exponential factor. More detailed understanding of the physics underlying the kinetics followed from the work of Polanyi and Wigner, Eyring, Karplus, Polanyi and Zewail and others. It soon became apparent that to follow rapid atom dynamics the existing experimental methods needed vast improvement, as motions of several ångstroms are achieved in picoseconds or less, so that to reach a reasonable precision, time resolutions of femtoseconds are needed. The stopped flow kinetics widely applied in the forties have now been complemented by flash photolysis, and especially laser-triggering of photochemical reactions. The increasing time-resolution achieved in the past decades has been described by Zewail in his Nobel lecture as an experimental 'arrow of time', proceeding to ever shorter timescales.[1]

Though studies of kinetic processes, and in particular vibrational energy transfer within molecules, are essential, the elucidation of time-dependent geometry changes remains one of the crucial requirements for the understanding of chemical dynamics. Examination of time-dependent geometry implies the study of transient species, intermediate in chemical processes. They are in general highly reactive and can be precursors in important chemical and biological processes. How far have we progressed in time-resolved structure determination and what are the prospects?

Time resolution

The concept of time-resolution implies that that time is sliced and that a direct image, scattering or diffraction pattern is recorded instantaneously, before significant changes occur. We will concentrate here on timescales of a millisecond or less, but note that this volume gives abundant evidence of the important information that can be provided by studying slower processes such as nucleation[2,3] and crystallization,[4] while slower-moving solid-state reactions[5] must also be mentioned.

A distinction can be made between reversible processes, which can be repeated a very large number of times, and irreversible processes such as fast moving chemical reactions which can be measured only once along their path, because of read-out limitations of current detectors. However, such processes can be repeated with a different pump–probe delay time t, to give an image of the changes along the reaction path. Such methods have been applied with great success in time-resolved biochemical crystallography,[6–8] and in a first study of a solid-state dimerization reaction reported in this volume.[9] Alternatively, it may be possible to 'stop the clock' and stabilize an otherwise short-lived state by cooling. The trapped metastable state may correspond to a transient state under ambient conditions. Such freezing allows much longer periods of data collection, and thereby affords higher spatial resolution, thus providing important information not otherwise accessible. Examples of such studies are our diffraction and IR spectroscopy measurements on low-temperature metastable states of transition metal complexes with small ligands such as NO, N_2[10] and SO_2,[11] and the trapping of short-lived intermediate species along the reaction pathway of the enzyme cytochrome P450cam.[12]

The stroboscopic technique, applicable to reversible processes, is intermediate between repeated measurement of different samples with different delay times and the study of trapped species. The stroboscopic technique is very well suited for the study of molecular triplet states, generated through intersystem crossing from the initially formed excited singlet states. They often have lifetimes of microseconds or more, especially at reduced temperatures. If the pump and probe pulses are sufficiently narrow, the stroboscopic technique can also be applied to faster reversible processes and the evolution with time followed by varying the delay time between the pump and the probe pulses in a series of runs. The observations are made in rapid succession, sometimes thousands of times per second on a single specimen. Measurements with pump-on conditions can be followed immediately (but within the limitations imposed by the detector read-out time) by measurement without the periodic pump pulses. Precise measurement of the intensity *change* has important advantages, as it eliminates variations in intensity from, for example, long-range beam instability and allows toleration of moderate sample decay, and thus increases the sensitivity of the method. In monochromatic single crystal diffraction studies, in which a large number of reflection intensities are to be measured, the light-on phase may consist of the recording of a single area-detector frame, followed immediately by the measurement of the same oscillation range under light-off conditions.

Geometry information from spectroscopic studies

a Geometric information derived from vibrational fine structure of the UV absorption and emission spectra

Franck–Condon analysis of the intensity and spacing of the vibrational fine structure of the UV and visible absorption and emission spectra (when resolved) allows determination of the distortion upon excitation, provided the vibrational spectrum is dominated by a single mode.[13,14] The technique often gives information on one prominent distortion that occurs, as in a recent study of nitridorhenium complexes,[15] and for binuclear Pt and Rh complexes as discussed in more detail below.

b Time-resolved Raman and IR studies

Pump–probe time-resolved IR and infrared spectroscopy are extremely useful in providing information on the rate and mechanism of photochemical reactions. New equipment development[16] and commercial availability of the equipment is facilitating more widespread application. The results are in many ways complementary to those obtained by diffraction techniques, but can, through analysis of group frequency changes, be used to infer information on the strengths of bonds associated with identified frequencies, and thus indirectly on geometry changes.

c Time-resolved XAFS

Time-resolved X-Ray absorption fine-structure analysis (XAFS) has the great advantage that it can be performed in the condensed phase and at relatively low concentration, and is thus highly relevant for processes occurring under ambient conditions. The inner coordination sphere of the resonating atom is probed by analysis of the extended fine structure, while near edge features can give information on changes in oxidation state or coordination number that are taking place. The studies by Chen and coworkers on the transient intermediate produced by photoexcitation of nickeltetraphenyl porphyrin-piperidine$_2$,[17] and on photooxidation and exciplex formation of Cu(I) (dmp)$_2$, reported at this conference,[18] are the first examples of nanosecond timescale EXAFS experiments.

Amorphous phase *vs.* crystal diffraction experiments

Diffraction experiments in the gas phase pose major challenges because of the low number density of the molecules and the lack of the constructive interference typical of the scattering by periodic arrays. Nevertheless, a number of very high temporal resolution studies of chemical reactions have now been accomplished by ultrafast electron diffraction (UED). First among these is the iodine elimination reaction of 1,2-diiodotetrafluoroethane to give tetrafluoroethylene,[19] and more recently the ring opening reaction of 1,3-cyclohexadiene.[20] In the latter case the pump laser beam was derived from the same laser that generates the electron beam.

The random orientation of the molecules in the gas phase necessarily limits the results to a radial distribution curve, which means that the method is suitable for not too complicated reactants, a condition also imposed by the need to achieve a reasonable vapor pressure. In the case of diiodotetrafluoroethane,[19] the radial distribution difference function clearly shows non-concerted disappearance of the two C–I vectors in 17(2) ps, indicating a two-step iodine elimination, with an intermediate non-bridged radical state. The radial distribution function changes and their interpretation are shown in Fig. 1. Typically the *differences* between the light-on and light-off patterns are analyzed, a recurring theme in many of the time-resolved studies.

The ring opening of 1,3-cyclohexadiene to give 1,3,5-hexatriene is in some respects a more challenging experiment, as strongly-scattering heavy atoms are absent, analysis of light-on/light-off difference patterns becomes imperative. Changes in the interatomic vectors are clearly evident from the difference electron diffraction patterns, but the analysis of the time-resolved pattern is complicated by the fact that at least four different product structures, related by rotations around the C–C bonds must be considered.

Time-resolved studies of processes in crystals have the great advantage that three-dimensional structural changes are accessible. In contrast with macromolecules, in which the active site is usually within the molecular envelope, in smaller unit cell crystals the molecular environment can play an active role. The advent of supramolecular crystallography allows incorporation of one type of guest molecule in a variety of host structures,[21] and opens the possibility of using dilute, yet crystalline media.

While few chemically- rather than biologically-motivated solid-state diffraction studies have been reported so far, the number of studies may be expected to grow rapidly in the coming years. In both studies discussed in the following section information from other time-resolved techniques is available to complement the diffraction results.

Comparing information from parallel time-resolved techniques: two examples

a 4-(Dimethylamino) benzonitrile DMABN

In the molecule of DMABN a donor and acceptor group are linked by an aromatic ring.

4-(dimethylamino)benzonitrile

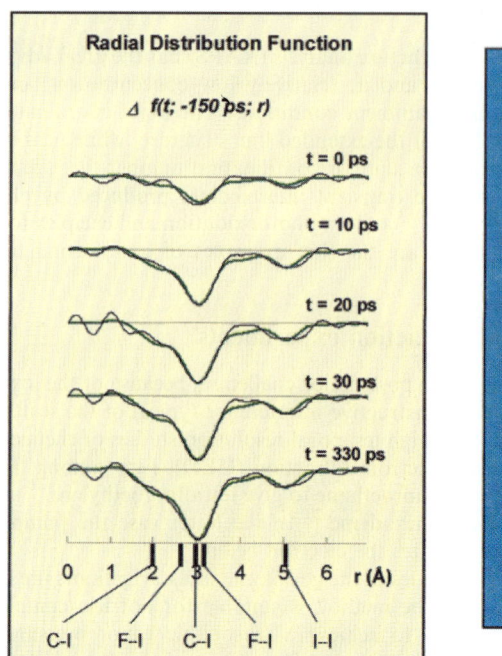 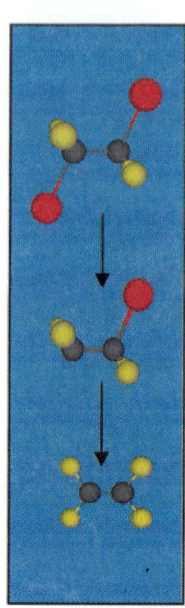

Fig. 1 Difference radial distribution function of diiodotetrafluoroethylene after excitation from time-resolved electron diffraction and interpretation. (Reprinted with permission from ref. 1. Copyright 2000 The American Chemical Society.)

The molecule is regarded as a typical example of a species in which intramolecular charge transfer (ICT) occurs on photoexcitation. In non-polar solvents DMABN shows a single fluorescence component in the UV, while in polar solvents an additional spectral component is observed in the visible region, corresponding to a highly polar ($\mu = 17$ D, compared with 6.7 D for the ground state[22]) charge-separated singlet state. It is generally accepted that the latter is due to a 'twisted intramolecular charge transfer (TICT) state, though other models have been proposed. A shorter (S_0) and a longer lifetime (S_1) fluorescent state are observed. Picosecond transient IR measurements ruled out structures for the S_1 state in which the negative charge was confined to the phenyl ring, or the C–N(CH$_3$)$_2$ bond order increased.[23] Subsequent time-resolved resonance Raman measurements including D and ^{15}N substitution,[24] indicated a 96 cm^{-1} frequency downshift of the phenyl–N stretching vibration, which supports electronic decoupling of the amino and benzonitrile groups, and thus the twisted TICT model, but is not in agreement with the planar intramolecular charge transfer (PICT) model. The spectra further indicate sp^3 pyramidal character of the dimethylamino substituent in the excited state. This is of interest as theoretical predictions of this distortion are frequently dependent on the level of theory used. A full optimization of the excited state structure was not available at the time the experimental work was reported.[24]

The crystal experiment by Techert et al. used a powder sample with a room-temperature fluorescence lifetime of 1.9 ns.[25] The diffraction pattern shortly after excitation ($\sim 10^{-10}$ s) was refined to give an initial excited state population of 28–32%, and an increase in torsional angle around the exocyclic C–N bond from 0 to 10(1) °, thus confirming the TICT model. While the ground state molecule is slightly pyramidal at the amino nitrogen atom (the angle between NCC and benzene planes $\theta_{inv} = 13°$ before excitation), the experiment indicates that the nitrogen atom becomes less inverted upon light induced charge transfer ($\theta_{inv} = 3°$ at 80 ps). Interestingly, the relaxation time of the diffraction pattern of 520 ps is shorter than the electronic lifetime of the excited state as indicated by the fluorescence lifetime. This discrepancy suggests a complex mechanism before return to the ground state and requires further analysis.

In addition to the radiative decay of DMABN directly back to the ground state, intersystem crossing (ISC) occurs to a phosphorescing triplet state ($^3T_1$), the structure of which has been investigated by nanosecond resolution resonance Raman spectroscopy.[26] The results indicate the $^3T_1$ state to be a $\pi\pi^*$ charge-separated state of planar or near-planar structure, in agreement with the increased dipole moment of 12 D,[22] and as predicted by several theoretical studies.

b The $[Pt_2(pyrophosphate)_4]^{4-}$ ion (pyrophosphate, $(H_2P_2O_5)^{2-}$)

The Pt–Pt distance in the $[Pt_2(pyrophosphate)_4]^{4-}$ (Ptpop) ion is bridged by four ligands in a paddlewheel type arrangement (Fig. 2). At room temperature, the $^3A_{2u}$ excited state has a lifetime of 9–10 µs in water and acetonitrile solutions, and a high quantum yield ($\phi_r = 0.5$–0.6) for phosphorescence.[27] As a result of spin–orbit coupling, the triplet level is split into two sub-levels: a lower-lying A_{1u} level, and a second E_u level $\sim$42 cm^{-1} higher in energy.[28] As the lower A_{1u} level has a much longer lifetime than the E_u level, at ambient temperature, at which the spacing is much smaller than kT, the phosphorescence is mostly from this state, while at very low temperatures (below $\approx$30 K) the A_{1u} level with a lifetime of 6.06 ms dominates the emission process.[28] As a result, the lifetime is strongly temperature dependent in the region in which the 42 cm^{-1} splitting is comparable with kT, a feature that can be used for temperature calibration purposes.[29]

Franck–Condon analysis of the vibrational fine structure of the absorption and emission spectra indicated a shortening of the Pt–Pt bond by 0.21 Å (with an error estimated at 10–15%), based on the assumption that the spectrum is dominated by the metal–metal stretch.[30] In combination with the X-ray value of the ground state distance, this result corresponds to a Pt–Pt excited state bond length of 2.71 Å. A second spectroscopic study based on Raman data and application of the empirical Badger's rule, which relates a change in stretching frequency with a change in bond length, gives a value of 2.81 Å for the excited state bond length.[31] A time-resolved EXAFS study has also been reported. It gives a shortening of the Pt–phosphorus bond by 0.047(11) Å, but the EXAFS curve is not sensitive to the longer Pt–Pt distance. To infer the gross molecular changes, the authors therefore used a spectroscopic excited state Pt–Pt distance of 2.75 Å to derive a movement of 0.52(13) Å of the planes through four P atoms attached to one platinum along the Pt–Pt axis.[32]

The stroboscopic X-ray diffraction study was done at 17 K with a repeat frequency of 5000 Hz and a 33 µs X-ray pulse length, which may be compared with the 50 µs lifetime of the triplet state at 17 K. In the experiment sensitivity was enhanced by immediately following collection of a light-on frame with that of a light-off frame (Fig. 3).

Since the three-dimensional structure is refined in the single-crystal diffraction analysis, the light-induced structural change can be illustrated by a *photodifference* map,[33] obtained by Fourier summation with coefficients equal to the difference between the 'on' and 'off' structure factors. The photodifference map shows the *change* in electron density upon light exposure. The map (Fig. 4)

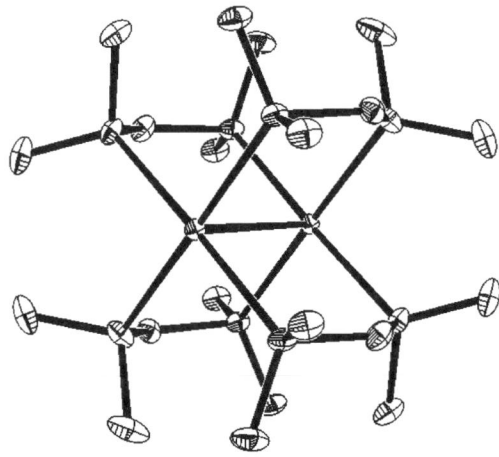

Fig. 2 ORTEP drawing of the $[Pt_2(pyrophosphate)4]^{4-}$ ion.

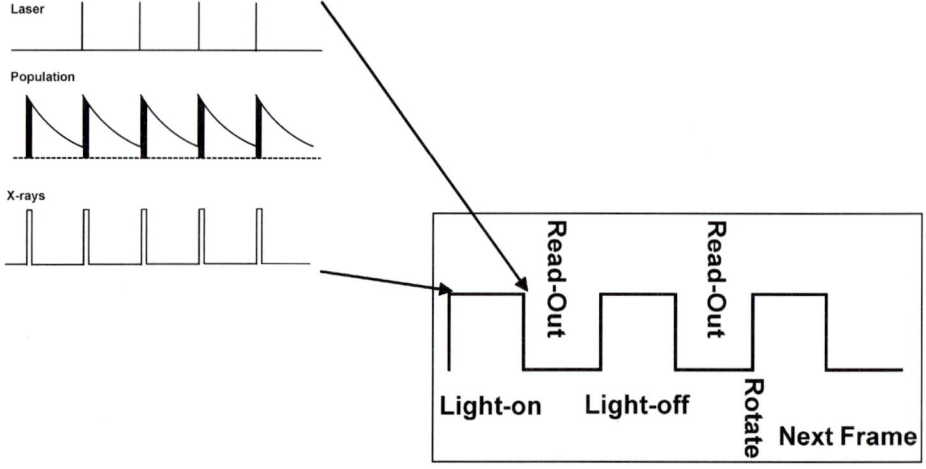

Fig. 3 Time structure and data collection strategy of the stroboscopic diffraction experiment.

gives clear evidence for a displacement of the Pt atoms in a direction towards the other Pt atom in the molecular ion and shows that the direction of the displacement does not coincide exactly with the intramolecular Pt–Pt vector, indicating that a small molecular rotation ($\approx 3°$) accompanies the shortening of the Pt–Pt bond on excitation. Least-squares analysis of the response ratios, defined as $\eta = (I_{on} - I_{off})/I_{off}$,[34] gives a shortening of the Pt–Pt bond by 0.28(9) Å, in satisfactory agreement with the spectroscopic results. It must be emphasized that this time-resolved X-ray study is but a first result, that can be improved by the use of a more intense beam and smaller samples, the former

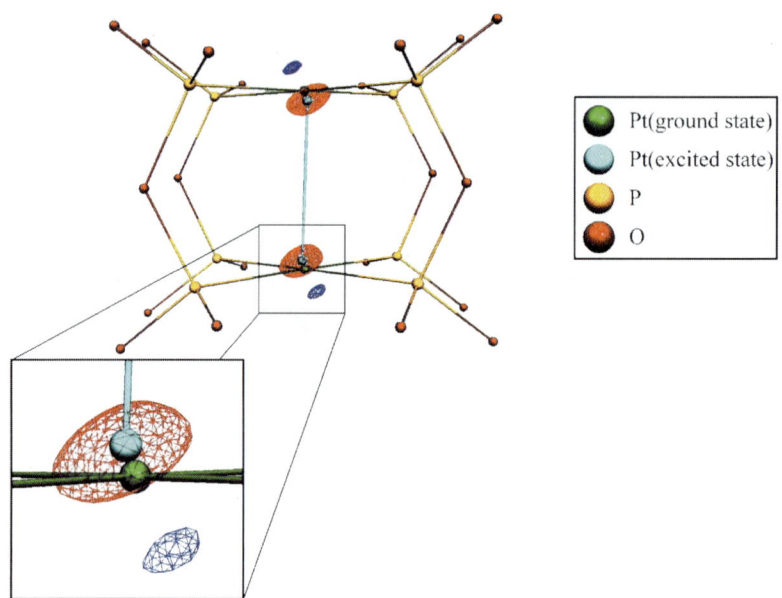

Fig. 4 Three-dimensional photodifference map along the Pt-Pt bond in the $[Pt_2(pyrophosphate)4]^{4-}$ ion.

to speed up data collection so that larger data sets can be collected before crystal damage becomes prohibitive, the latter to improve the photon/active-molecule ratio to obtain larger conversion percentages in the crystal than achieved in the first experiment ($2.0 \pm 0.1\%$).

All studies agree on the contraction of the molecule, which theoretical calculations discussed in the following section attribute to a transition of an electron from a $5d\sigma^*$ Pt–Pt antibonding orbital to a $6p\sigma$ orbital, which is bonding with regard to the Pt–Pt interaction.

The interplay between theory and experiment

Given the dramatic increase in power of computational methods over the last decade, it is now possible to routinely perform parallel theoretical calculations, and to examine which, if any, of the theoretical results are ambiguous and method-dependent, so that experimental information becomes crucial.

Upon initiating a theoretical calculation of a complex molecule one is confronted with a large number of choices of Hamiltonians and basis sets, which produce quantitatively different results, though the qualitative trends predicted are often robust and independent of method. In our calculations on the metastable states of the ruthenium–sulfur dioxide linkage isomers, for example, both smaller and larger basis set DFT calculations reveal, in addition to the observed (S,O) bound isomer, a third, non-yet observed, O-bound metastable state.[11] But this state is more stable than the ground state according to the smaller basis set calculation, an obviously unrealistic result that is corrected by the larger basis set.

From DFT calculations of the ground state of the $[Pt_2(pyrophosphate)_4]^{4-}$ ion with the Amsterdam density functional (ADF) program package,[35] the spread between the various values for the Pt–Pt bond distance is ≈ 0.1 Å depending on the functional selected (B88LYP, B88P86, PW86LYP)† and the relativistic treatment adopted (Pauli or ZORA),[36] compared with an experimental standard deviation in each of the available analyses of less than 0.001 Å and a variation among the different solids of not more than 0.01 Å. Other bonds behave very much in the same manner. The local density approximation (LDA) with the functional of Vosko–Wilk–Nusair (VWN) was rejected,[37] as it produced too short Pt–Pt and Pt–P bonds and thus did not reproduce the ground state geometry satisfactorily. In addition to the geometry information from spectroscopy, EXAFS and diffraction, summarized above, spectroscopic energy differences are available for comparison with the theoretical results. The relative merits of the different calculations in reproducing the combined experimental information are depicted in Fig. 5, which shows the variation in Pt–Pt and Pt–P bond lengths and the excitation energy as predicted by different calculations and measured experimentally. The wide spread among the theoretical values for both the Pt–Pt shortening ($\Delta d \approx -0.2$ to -0.5 Å) and the excitation energy ($\Delta E \approx 1.9$–3.2 eV) is evident. The Pt–P bond length is invariably calculated to be larger in the excited state. This is intuitively acceptable, as a strengthening of the Pt–Pt interaction may be accompanied by a weakening of the other bonds to Pt, but is contrary to the EXAFS results, which have to be re-examined. As the ZORA FC PW86LYP gives reasonable results for both the Pt–Pt shortening and the ΔSCF excitation energy, it has been selected for the calculation of excited-state properties which are not accessible experimentally, such as the frontier molecular orbitals (Fig. 6), the charge density in the molecule, topological properties in the Pt–Pt bonding region, and the spin density in the excited state. The spin density is related to the high chemical reactivity of the excited state, which includes abstraction of hydrogen and chlorine atoms from a range of organic substrates, including DNA.[38]

---

† The valence atomic orbitals of platinum, oxygen, phosphorus and hydrogen atoms were described by triple-ζ Slater-type basis sets with one polarization function added on the O, P and H atoms (ADF database IV). Relativistic effects were taken into account using either of two methods implemented in ADF: a quasi-relativistic method which employs the Pauli Hamiltonian and the zero order regular approximation (ZORA). The $(1s2s2p)^{10}$ and $(1s)^2$ shells of P and O, respectively, were treated by the frozen core (FC) approximation in all calculations. The $(1s2s2p3s3p4s3d4p4d)^{46}$ core shells of Pt were either kept frozen or all electrons of Pt (with the ZORA formalism) were used in the computation in which case the core was described by double-ζ quality basis set (the Pt all-electron calculations are labeled AE_{Pt} in the text).

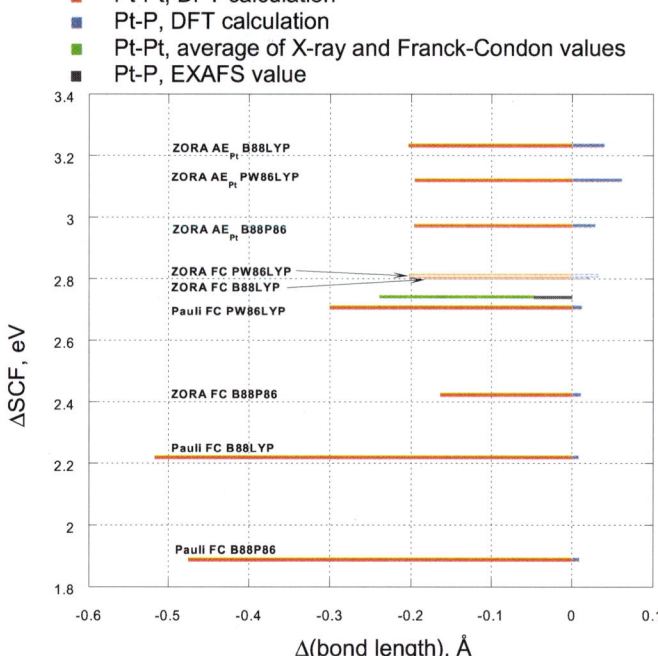

Fig. 5 Summary of theoretical and experimental Pt–Pt and Pt–P bond length changes and excitation energies for the [Pt$_2$(pyrophosphate)4]$^{4-}$ ion. Red bar: theoretical Pt–Pt bond shortening, blue bar: theoretical Pt–P bond length change, vertical axis: energy of excitation, green bar: average of X-ray and Franck–Condon values for Pt–Pt bond shortening and grey bar: EXAFS results for Pt–P bond change.

The calculation shows the spin density to be mostly located on the Pt atoms, which are the likely reactive sites.[36]

A theoretical prediction of an excited state distortion

The tetrahedrally coordinated Cu(I) complexes distort towards a more planar geometry upon metal-to-ligand-charge-transfer (MLCT). A prototype example is Cu(I)bis(1,10-phenanthroline),[39–41] the excited state distortion of which, and thereby its lifetime and other photophysical properties, can be manipulated by variation of the 2,9-substituents. The Cu bisphenanthrolines absorb light in the visible spectral region, and may show intense long-lifetime luminescence. In solution the luminescence tends to be quenched by exciplex formation, even with weak Lewis bases, but this cannot occur in the solid state, unless solvent molecules can be included with the guest in one cavity of a supramolecular solid, a possible avenue for investigation. Changes in coordination of the Cu atom upon excitation in solution have now been measured by EXAFS.[18] Full information on the geometry changes is not yet available, but the geometry can be calculated for the isolated molecule. Calculations of Cu(I) bis(2,9-dimethyl-1,10-phenanthroline) cation with the ADF2002.01 program‡,[35] indicate a flattening of the complex (Fig. 7), with the dihedral angle

---

‡ DFT calculations were performed using the VWN local density functional and the gradient-corrected B88LYP functional. The copper atom was described by a triple-ξ basis set (ADF database "TZP"), the C, N and H atoms were described by double-ξ basis set augmented by one polarization function (ADF database "DZP"). The (1s2s2p) core shell of Cu and (1s) core shell of C and N were treated by the frozen core approximation. Relativistic effects were taken into account using the ZORA formalism. The calculations were symmetry-restricted to the D_2 point group.

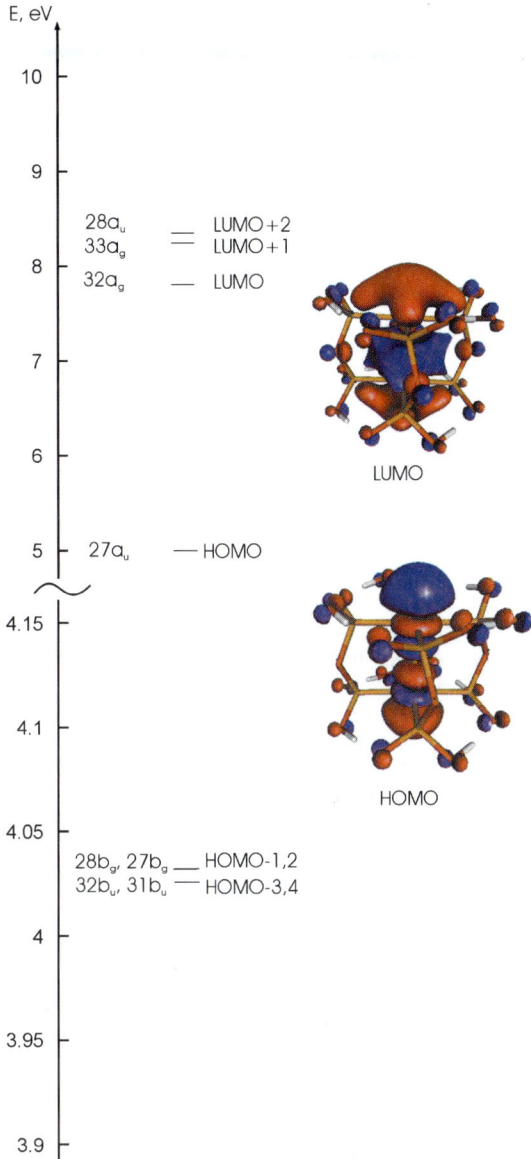

Fig. 6 Ordering of the frontier molecular orbitals in the ground state of [Pt$_2$(pyrophosphate)4]$^{4-}$ ion (ref. 36) Plotted isosurface value 0.025 a.u. Orbital designations refer to the C_{2h} point group.

between the phenanthroline planes decreasing from ≈80 to ≈65° and a shortening of the Cu–N distances by ∼0.04 Å on MLCT.

This is in agreement with the predicted distortion from the essentially tetrahedral§ geometry of the ground state. Calculations of an exciplex with five-coordination of the Cu atom are now being pursued and will be reported separately.[42]

---

§ The distortion of the ground state from the perfect tetrahedral geometry is due to the limiting N···N chelate bite size, which restricts the N–Cu–N angles.

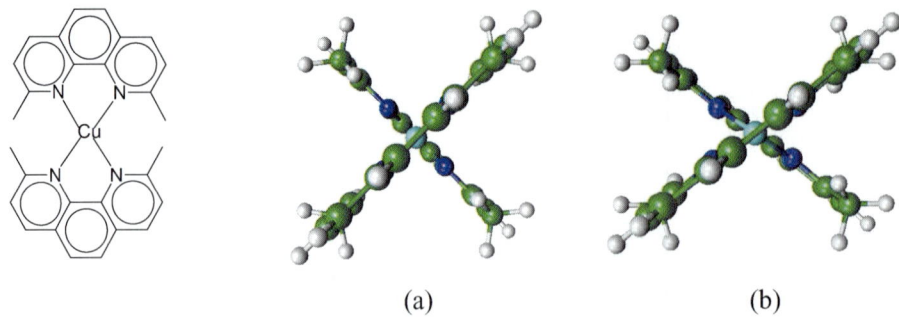

Fig. 7 Ground (a) and excited (b) state structure of Cu(I)bis(2,9-dimethyl 1,10-phenanthroline).

Concluding remarks

The interplay between theory and experiment is an essential component of time-resolved studies at atomic resolution. The combined approach opens a way for resolving theoretical as well as experimental ambiguities and for selecting the most reliable theoretical treatments for calculation of other quantities, such as molecular orbitals and excited state spin and charge densities, which are not experimentally accessible but are important for understanding excited-state properties. In future work non-reversible chemical reaction should attract increased attention as experimental methods are becoming more sophisticated and photon sources more powerful. The increasing application of theory to the study of mechanisms of chemical reactions,[43] should be a further impetus for collaboration between experimentalists and theoreticians.

Finally, notwithstanding the significant progress evident from what is presented in this issue, time-resolved chemistry at atomic resolution is still in its infancy, but will undoubtedly become a major research topic in the coming years.

Acknowledgements

Financial support of our work by the National Science Foundation (CHE9981864) and the Petroleum Research Fund of the American Chemical Society (PRF32638-AC3 and PRF37614-AC3) is gratefully acknowledged. The computations reported were performed on the 64-processor SGI Origin3800, 32-processor Sun Blade 1000 (UltraSparc III) and 48-processor Sun Ultra-5 (UltraSparc IIi) supercomputers at the Center for Computational Research of the State University of New York at Buffalo, which is supported by grant (DBI9871132) from the National Science Foundation.

References

1 A. H. Zewail, *J. Phys. Chem. A*, 2000, **104**, 5660.
2 F. Meneau, G. Sankar, N. Morgante, R. Winter, C. R. Catlow, G. N. Greaves and J. M. Thomas, *Faraday Discuss.*, 2002, **122**, 203.
3 E. L. Heeley, C. K. Poh, L. Wu, A. Maidens, W. Bras, I. P. Dolbnya, A. J. Gleeson, N. J. Terrill, J. Patrick, A. Fairclough, P. D. Olmstead, R. I. Ristic, M. J. Hounslow and A. J. Ryan, *Faraday Discuss.*, 2002, **122**, 343.
4 R. I. Walton, A. Norquist, R. I. Smith and D. O'Hare, *Faraday Discuss.*, 2002, **122**, 331.
5 See for example P. Norby, *J. Appl. Crystallogr.*, 1997, **30**, 21.
6 Z. Ren, B. Perman, V. Srajer, T.-Y. Teng, C. Pradervand, D. Bourgeois, F. Schotte, T. Ursby, O. R. Kort, M. Wulff and K. Moffat, *Biochemistry*, 2001, **40**, 13788.
7 V. Srajer, Z. Ren, T.-Y. Teng, M. Schmidt, T. Ursby, D. Bourgeois, C. Pradervand, W. Schildkamp, M. Wulff and K. Moffat, *Biochemistry*, 2001, **40**, 13802.
8 R. Helliwell, Y. P. Hieh, J. Habash, P. F. Faulder, J. Raftery, M. Cianci, M. Wulff and A. Hädener, *Faraday Discuss.*, 2002, **122**, 131.
9 G. Busse, T. Tschentscher, A. Plech, M. Wulff, B. Frederichs and S. Techert, *Faraday Discuss.*, 2002, **122**, 13.

10 P. Coppens, I. V. Novozhilova and A. Y. Kovalevsky, *Chem. Rev.*, 2002, **102**, 861.
11 A. Y. Kovalevsky, K. A. Bagley and P. Coppens, *J. Am. Chem. Soc.*, 2002, **124**, 9241.
12 I. Schlichting, J. Berendzen, K. Chu, A. M. Stock, S. A. Maves, D. E. Benson, R. M. Sweet, D. Ringe, G. A. Petsko and S. G. Sligar, *Science*, 2000, **287**, 1615.
13 T. C. Brunold and H. U. Gudel, in *Inorganic Electronic Structure and Spectroscopy, Volume I: Methodology*, ed. E. I. Solomon and A. B. P. Lever, Wiley, New York, 1999, p. 259.
14 J. I. Zink, *Coord. Chem. Rev.*, 2001, **21**, 69.
15 S. E. Bailey, R. E. Eikey, M. M. Abu-Omar and J. I. Zink, *Inorg Chem.*, 2002, **41**, 1755.
16 X. Z. Sun, M. W. George, S. G. Kazarian, S. M. Nikiforov and M. Poliakoff, *J. Am. Chem. Soc.*, 1996, **118**, 10525.
17 L. X. Chen, W. J. H. Jager, G. Jennings, D. J. Gosztola, A. Munkholm and J. P. Hessler, *Science*, 2001, **292**, 262.
18 L. X. Chen, *Faraday Discuss.*, 2002, **122**, 315.
19 J. Cao, H. Ihee and A. H. Zewail, *Proc. Natl. Acad. Sci. USA*, 1999, **96**, 338.
20 R. C. Dudek and P. M. Weber, *J. Phys. Chem. A*, 2001, **105**, 4167.
21 P. Coppens, B. Ma, O. Gerlits, Y. Zhang and P. Kulshrestha, *CrystEngComm*, 2002, **4**, 302.
22 W. Schuddeboom, S. A. Jonker, J. M. Warman, U. Leinhos, W. Kuhnle and K. A. Zachariasse, *J. Phys. Chem.*, 1992, **96**, 10809.
23 H. Okamoto, *J. Phys. Chem. A*, 2000, **104**, 4182.
24 W. M. Kwok, C. Ma, P. Matousek, A. W. Parker, D. Phillips, W. T. Toner, M. Towrie and S. Umapathy, *J. Phys. Chem. A*, 2001, **105**, 984.
25 S. Techert, F. Schotte and M. Wulff, *Phys. Rev. Lett.*, 2001, **86**, 2030–2033.
26 C. Ma, W. M. Kwok, P. Matousek, A. W. Parker, D. Phillips, W. T. Toner and M. Towrie, *J. Phys. Chem. A*, 2001, **105**, 4684.
27 (*a*) A. E. Stiegman, S. F. Rice, H. B. Gray and V. M. Miskowski, *Inorg. Chem.*, 1987, **26**, 1112; (*b*) S F. Rice and H. B. Gray, *J. Am. Chem. Soc.*, 1983, **105**, 4571.
28 J. T. Markert, D. P. Clements and M. R. Corson, *Chem. Phys. Lett.*, 1983, **97**, 175.
29 L. Ribaud, G. Wu, Y. Zhang and P. Coppens, *J. Appl. Crystallogr.*, 2001, **34**, 76.
30 S. F. Rice and H. B. Gray, *J. Am. Chem. Soc.*, 1983, **105**, 4571.
31 P. Stein, M. K. Dickson and D. M. Roundhill, *J. Am. Chem. Soc.*, 1983, **105**, 3489.
32 D. J. Thiel, P. Līviņš, E. A. Stern and A. Lewis, *Nature*, 1993, **362**, 40.
33 M. D. Carducci, M. R. Pressprich and P. Coppens, *J. Am. Chem. Soc.*, 1997, **119**, 2669.
34 Y. Ozawa, M. R. Pressprich and P. Coppens, *J. Appl. Crystallogr.*, 1998, **31**, 128.
35 (*a*) E. J. Baerends, D. E. Ellis and P. Ros, *Chem. Phys.*, 1973, **2**, 41; (*b*) L. Versluis and T. Ziegler, *J. Chem. Phys.*, 1988, **88**, 322; (*c*) G. te Velde and E. J. Baerends, *J. Comput. Phys.*, 1992, **99**, 84; (*d*) C. Fonseca Guerra, J. G. Snijders, G. te Velde and E. J. Baerends, *Theor. Chem. Acc.*, 1998, **99**, 391.
36 I. V. Novozhilova, A. Volkov and P. Coppens, manuscript in preparation.
37 S. H. Vosko, L. Wilk and M. Nusair, *Can. J. Phys.*, 1980, **58**, 1200.
38 D. M. Roundhill, H. B. Gray and C. M. Che, *Acc. Chem. Res.*, 1989, **22**, 55.
39 P. A. Breddels, P. A. M. Berdowski, G. Blasse and D. R. McMillin, *J. Chem. Soc., Faraday Trans.*, 1972, **78**, 595.
40 D. V. Scaltrito, D. W. Thompson, J. A. O'Callaghan and G. J. Meyer, *Coord. Chem. Rev.*, 2000, **208**, 243.
41 N. Armaroli, *Chem. Soc. Rev.*, 2001, **30**, 113.
42 I. V. Novozhilova and P. Coppens, manuscript in preparation.
43 (*a*) A. Michalak and T. Ziegler, *J. Am. Chem. Soc.*, 2001, **123**, 12266; (*b*) E. Zurek and T. Ziegler, *Organometallics*, 2002, **21**, 83.

The realization of sub-nanosecond pump and probe experiments at the ESRF

Michael Wulff,[a] Anton Plech,[a] Laurent Eybert,[a] Rudolf Randler,[a] Friedrich Schotte[b] and Philip Anfinrud[b]

[a] *European Synchrotron Radiation Facility, 6 rue Jules Horowitz, BP 220, Grenoble Cedex 38043, France*
[b] *Laboratory of Chemical Physics, NIDDK, National Institutes of Health, Building 5, Bethesda, MD 20892-0520, USA*

Received 18th March 2002, Accepted 29th April 2002
First published as an Advance Article on the web 7th October 2002

We present beamline ID09B that is designed for pump and probe experiments to 50 ps time-resolution. The beamline has been refurbished with a narrow-bandwidth undulator for Laue diffraction and diffraction from liquids. The new undulator has 235 poles, a 17 mm magnetic period and is operated at 6.5 mm gap. It produces a spectral flux of 2.0×10^8 photon/0.1% bw/pulse (10 mA) at the fundamental at 15.5 keV and an integral flux of 1.1×10^{10} photon pulse^{-1} in a 2.5% bandwidth. The optics has been renewed with a high-precision toroidal mirror and a cryogenic monochromator. The X-ray chopper used for single pulse selection is also described together with the femtosecond laser. Finally the diffraction from excited iodine molecules in CCl_4 is investigated on the nanosecond time-scale. It turns out that the high-angle scattering is insensitive to the thermal chock from the laser; these oscillations are therefore readily used for structure determination. Conversely, the low-angle scattering probes the hydrodynamics of the liquid over longer length scales and the oscillations are believed to originate from thermal stress and expansion of the solvent.

1. Introduction

The intensity of the pulsed radiation from undulators from the European Synchrotron Radiation Facility (ESRF, 6 GeV), the Advanced Photon Source (APS, 7 GeV) and Spring8 (8 GeV), has made it possible to conduct pump and probe experiments on chemical and biochemical systems down to a time-resolution of 50–200 ps. In these machines, the undulators produce polychromatic beams with a spectrum of harmonics caused by the interference of single electrons.[1] The spectrum of the new U17 undulator from beamline ID09 at the ESRF is shown in Fig. 1. The figure shows the spectral flux, *i.e.* the photon count in a 0.1% bandwidth, as produced by one bunch of electrons traversing the insertion device (10 mA single-bunch mode). The bunch contains 1.8×10^{11} electrons and produces 1.1×10^{10} photons in 145 ps (fwhm)! Although the pulse length is a thousand times longer than the time it takes to form and break chemical bonds, the intensity is orders of magnitude greater than from second generation synchrotrons and rotating anodes. Plasma sources can provide sub-picosecond pulses and deliver up to 5×10^4 photon pulse^{-1} on the sample[2] and that is sufficient for surface studies but insufficient for biological molecules. So until the arrival of the

DOI: 10.1039/b202740m

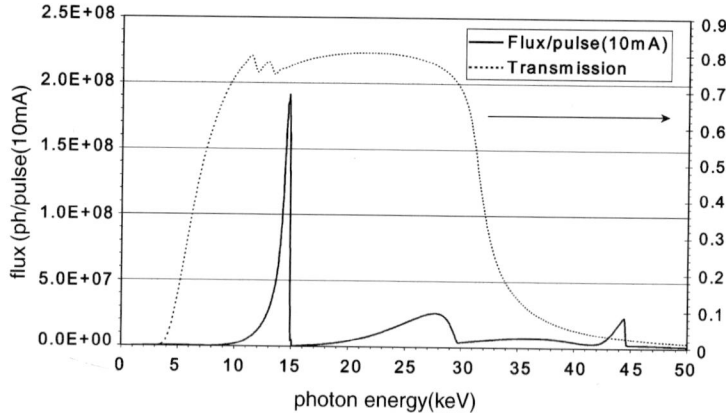

Fig. 1 Spectral intensity of the in-vacuum undulator U17 from a single bunch (10 mA, 28.2 nC/bunch). The apertures in the calculation have been set to accept 99% of the central cone. The transmission of the front-end, the beamline beryllium window and the toroidal mirror at 2.68 mrad are shown to the right.

X-ray free electron laser towards 2010, third generation synchrotrons are the only source for time-resolved experiments in chemical and biochemical systems.

We have used the short X-ray pulses to probe the moving structure of molecules that have been initiated by a short laser pulse. The experiments use pump and probe: a short optical pulse initiates the molecules and a delayed X-ray pulse takes a snapshot of the moving structure at a given delay. The scattering pattern is normally recorded on a CCD detector and the experiment repeated for improved statistics. The experimental methods that have been developed include Laue diffraction from macromolecules,[3–5] diffraction from smaller molecules[6] and diffraction from liquids.[7,8] The Laue program has benefited enormously from having abandoned the wiggler approach with a narrow-bandwidth undulator, the latter of which gives much superior data quality.[9] In addition it is also very fortuitous that many reactions are active in the crystal. That makes it possible to construct the three-dimensional electron density in sharp contrast to the one-dimensional information from a liquid.

A high integral-flux per pulse is of crucial importance for these studies since it reduces the exposure time and makes the data less sensitive to drifts and radiation damage. For these reasons we have upgraded the ID09 beamline with an in-vacuum undulator, a new toroidal mirror and a cryogenic monochromator. We will briefly describe these developments.

2. The high-flux undulator U17

The straight sections at the ESRF can accommodate three 1.6 m long in-air undulators or two 2.0 m long in-vacuum undulators. The in-air undulators are normally operated at 11.0 mm gap whereas the in-vacuum undulators operate at 6.0 mm. The U17 undulator has been designed for very high flux between 14 and 18 keV at the expense of tunability. The emission at closed gap is dominated by the fundamental at 14.8 keV, but the second and third harmonics are also usable. The strong emission from the first harmonic comes from the fact that the critical energy in the sinusoidal orbit is close to the fundamental energy of the device. The undulator parameters are listed in Table 1. Its spectral flux is 1.9×10^8 photon pulse^{-1} for a 28.2 nC bunch charge (10 mA

Table 1 Undulator parameters on ID09. The (low-beta) source size is 0.117 mm horizontally and 0.024 mm vertically (fwhm). The U17 produces 546 W in the central cone at 200 mA

Period/mm	Poles	Minimum gap/mm	B_{max}/T	E_f/keV	E_c/keV	K	P (W/200 mA)
17	235	6.0	0.544	14.84	13.2	0.86	2740
46	71	16.0	0.643	0.64	15.6	2.76	3116

Table 2 The parameters of the new toroidal mirror

Shape	Cylindrical (in gravity → toroidal)
Dimensions: $L \times W \times H$ (mm^3)	$1000 \times 114 \times 52$
Material	Silicon crystal
Sagittal radius (mm)	71.6
Coating	Pt
Surface roughness (Å; rms)	1.3
Incidence angles (mrad)	2.684
Energy range (keV)	4–34
P = source–mirror distance (m)	33.05
Q = mirror–focus distance (m)	22.37
Demagnification M	0.677
Slope-error (µrad; rms)	0.7 µrad (intensity weighted)
Residual meridional radius (km)	25.0
Gravity curvature (km)	9.9

operation), see Fig. 1. We believe that this is close to the theoretical limit for an undulator on a third generation machine.

3. The X-ray optics

The layout of the new optics is shown in Fig. 2. The incoming beam is first reduced by the primary slits that remove the diffuse halo around the central cone. The radiation is then passed through the heatload shutter, which relieves downstream components from the heatload of the focused beam. The shutter consists of a rotating copper-block with a tunnel. The shutter is water-cooled and the water runs through the rotation axis. The shutter can open down to 20 ms at a frequency of 3 Hz. The next element is a cryogenic monochromator based on channel-cut silicon 111 crystal. The energy can be varied between 4.0 and 50.0 keV. The orthogonal distance between the crystal surfaces, *i.e.* the crystal gap, is 4.0 mm. The monochromatic beam, which is parallel to the white beam, is shifted upwards by up to 8.0 mm. The next element is a bend cylindrical mirror. The platinum-coated mirror receives the beam at 2.68 mrad, and reflects between 0 and 34 keV. The mirror is placed 33.0 m from the source and the focus is 22.4 m downstream ($M = 0.679$). The sagittal and meridional radius are 71.6 mm and 9.95 km respectively. The mirror is 1000 mm long, 114 mm wide and 52 mm thick. These dimensions have been chosen so that the gravity-bend mirror is close to an ideal toroid. A stepper motor pushes from below the mirror and fine-tunes the curvature. The intensity distribution and figure errors along the mirror are shown in Fig. 3. The

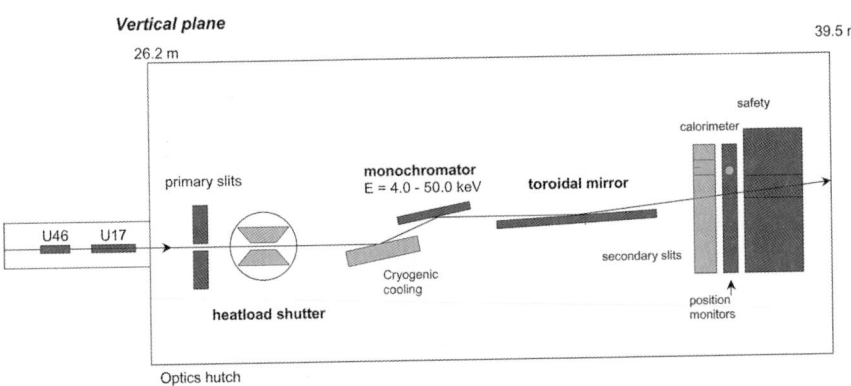

Fig. 2 Layout of the optics hutch on beamline ID09B.

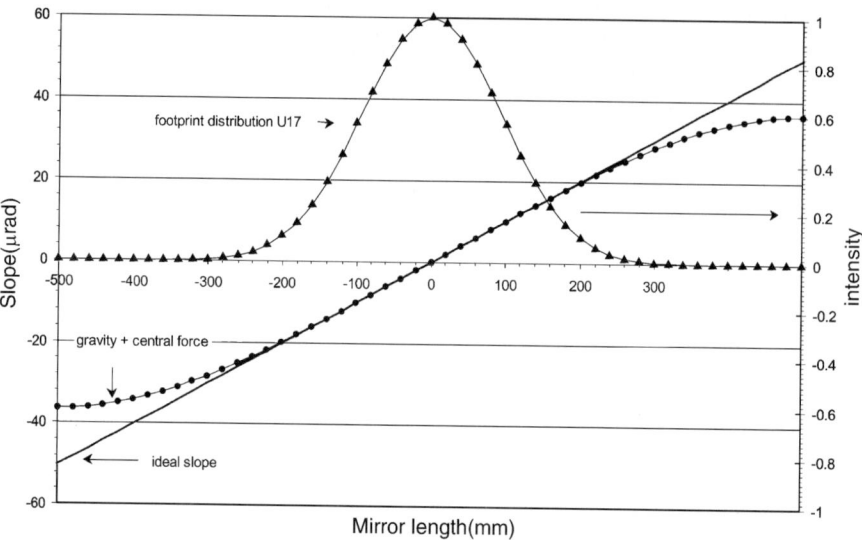

Fig. 3 The intensity distribution on the toroidal mirror from the U17 undulator (–▲–). The mirror receives the beam at an angle of 2.68 mrad. The slope produced by gravity and the (compensating) central force is shown (–●–). The theoretical slope, parabolic in shape, is shown (—). The figure error in the zone from −200 to +200 mm is less than 0.1 mrad.

ideal slope profile, corresponding to a parabolic shape, is a straight line. Note that the deviation from the straight line is below 0.1 μrad between $-200 < x < 200$ mm. The slope error of the optical surface of the cylindrical mirror is specified to be less than 0.7 μrad (rms) in the 400 mm central zone. In the absence of vibrations, the vertical focal size should thus be as small as 75 μm (fwhm). Note the vertical size is determined solely by the slope error! We are aiming at a tight vertical focus to optimize the transmission in the chopper in 16-bunch mode, where the tunnel height has to be as small as 145 μm to produce an opening window around 0.3 μs. The mirror is loaded with 546 W of beam of which 134 W is absorbed. The heat is extracted laterally by cooling plates that are dipped into indium gallium filled channels running parallel to the optical surface, see Fig. 4. Stress and vibrations from the cooling system are thus eliminated. The measured focal spot

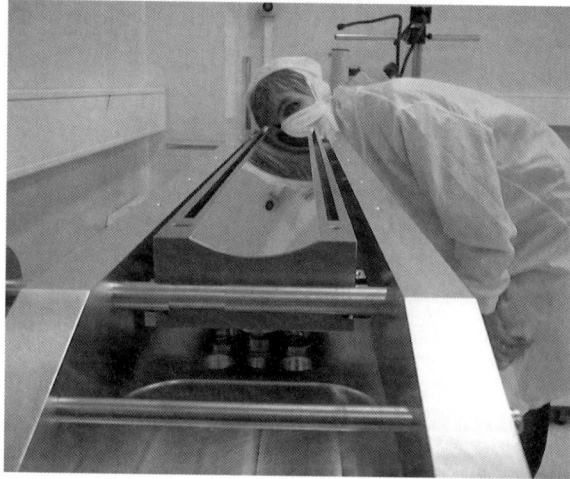

Fig. 4 The new toroidal mirror is cooled by copper plates that are dipped into the two indium–gallium filled channels. Vibrations and stress from the cooling system are hereby eliminated.

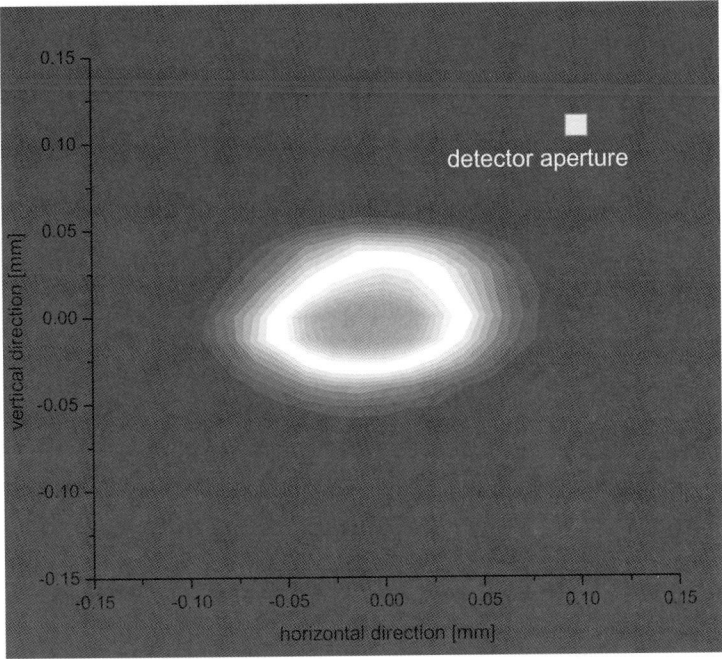

Fig. 5 Polychromatic focus of the U17 undulator produced by the toroidal mirror in Fig. 4. The focus is 0.100 mm horizontally and 0.070 mm vertically.

Table 3 Flux numbers for pump and probe experiments

Beamline configuration	Single-shot flux/ photon (10 mA pulse)$^{-1}$	Flux at 896.6 Hz/ photon s^{-1} (10 mA)$^{-1}$
Si(111) + toroidal mirror	2.4×10^7	2.2×10^{10}
Multilayers + toroidal mirror	1.7×10^9	1.5×10^{12}
Toroidal mirror	1.1×10^{10}	9.6×10^{12}

is shown in Fig. 5. The flux values of the new beamline are summarized in Table 3. The important number for Laue diffraction is the photon integral per pulse. By contrast, for diffraction experiments on a circulating liquid, it is the stroboscopic flux per second. The flux level from an ESRF bending magnet, monochromatised by silicon 111, is 5×10^9 photon s^{-1}.

4. The single-bunch chopper

The chopper consists of a triangular rotor made of titanium, which rotates about its centre of gravity. The rotation axis is horizontal and perpendicular to the beam. The rotor has a groove in one of its sides. The groove is covered (or roofed) by small plates at its extremities. The groove is thus made into a semi-open tunnel. The rotor, which is suspended in magnetic bearings, rotates at 896.6 Hz, which produces a supersonic speed of 545.3 m s^{-1} at the tips of the rotor. It is thus mandatory to keep the rotor in vacuum. The 896.6 Hz frequency is the 396th sub-harmonic of the orbit frequency of the storage ring. The chopper is shown schematically in Fig. 6 and its parameters are summarised in Table 4. The rotor speed is controlled by a feed back which stabilises the rotor to an accuracy $\delta\omega/\omega$ of 1×10^{-5}. The frequency has been limited to 896.6 Hz since the rotor shaft has a resonance at 998 Hz and breaks down from the centrifugal force at 1300 Hz. The opening window, *i.e.* the transmission *versus* time, is generally trapezoidal in shape.

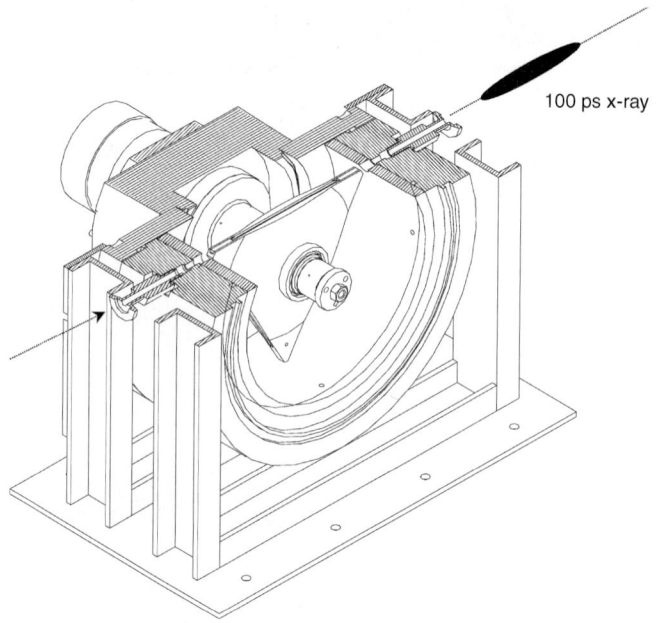

Fig. 6 The chopper for single-pulse selection. The rotor is synchronized to the bunch clock.

Table 4 The chopper parameters

Tunnel length (mm)	165.0
Maximum radius (mm)	96.8
Tunnel off-set (mm)	47.35
Minimum frequency (Hz)	10.0
Maximum frequency (Hz)	896.6
Tunnel width (mm)	4.0
Tunnel height (mm)	0.05 to 0.90
Minimum opening: δt_{min} (s)	0.10×10^{-6}
Maximum opening: δt_{max} (s)	0.17×10^{-3}
RMS phase jitter (s)	10.5×10^{-9}

The base line of the trapezoid is:

$$\tau = \frac{a}{2\pi R f \sqrt{1 - (h/R)^2}}$$

where a is the height of the tunnel, R is the maximum radius of the triangle, h is the (orthogonal) distance of the tunnel to the centre of rotation and f is the rotation frequency. $a = 0.70$ mm, $R = 96.8$ mm, $h = 47.4$ mm and $f = 896.6$ Hz gives $\tau = 1.472$ µs. The opening time, at the highest speed, can be varied by having a variable tunnel height. That is done by the use of a trapezoidal tunnel cross-section: the tunnel is 4.0 mm wide and the height increases linearly from 0.05 to 0.90 mm. The opening time can thus be varied from 0.10 µs to 1.89 µs by translating the chopper horizontally. The time between two pulses in single bunch mode is 2.82 µs and it is 0.176 µs in the 16-bunch mode. As the opening window has to synchronise to the centre of three pulses, the opening time has to be slightly shorter than twice the inter-pulse distance. A PC controls the frequency of the chopper and displays the deviation from the desired frequency. This jitter is

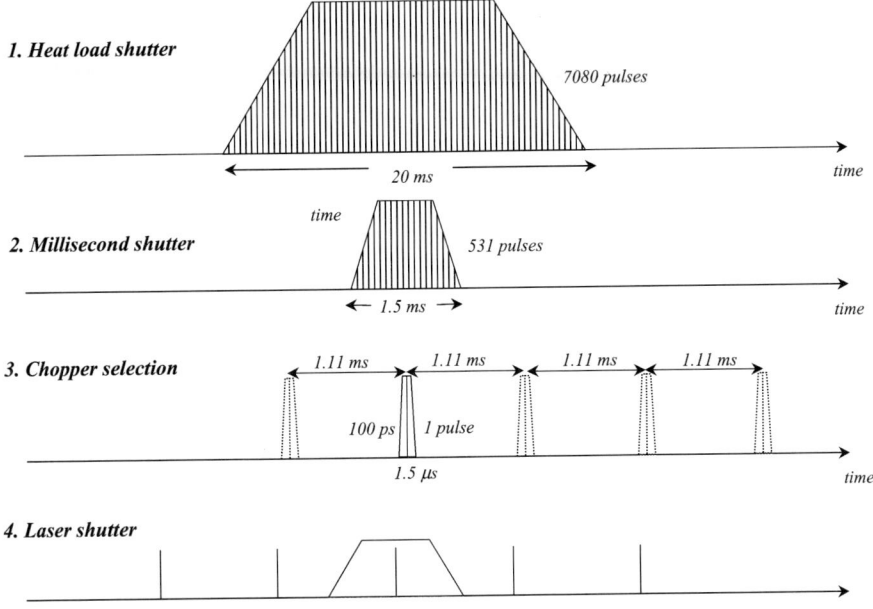

Fig. 7 The synchronization of the four shutters used in single-bunch Laue diffraction. The first shutter, the heatload shutter, allows one to load the focused white beam on the (uncooled) chopper.

recorded every two minutes; it is typically 10.5 ns (rms) at full speed. The synchronisation of the open position is based on a phase shifted reference clock at 896.6 Hz, which also controls the cavity dump in the femtosecond laser. The sampling of the pick-up signal from the chopper is done at 44.02 MHz(RF/8).

The chopper selects pulses continuously at 896.6 Hz giving a pulse on the sample every 1.11 ms. The femtosecond laser also runs at 896.6 Hz and by moving it relative to the fixed X-rays, one can probe photosensitive systems in a pump/probe fashion to about 100 ps resolution. However, there are not many bio-crystals that can tolerate a laser running at 896.6 Hz. In the case of Laue diffraction on myoglobin, hemoglobin and PYP, the laser repeat frequency is normally slower than 1 Hz. For these *slow repeat* experiments, the chopper and femtosecond laser are gated by two millisecond shutters. The X-ray ms-shutter is installed in vacuum upstream of the chopper. It consists of a 60 mm long bar with a tunnel along its length. The tunnel cross section is also trapezoidal: it is 5 mm wide and the height increases from 0.3 to 2.0 mm. The tunnel is positioned on the axis of rotation. The tunnel-bar is rotated by a stepper motor that is mounted in air. The shortest opening time is 0.2 ms, which is obtained by accelerating the tunnel from $-90°$ to $+90°$. It takes 48 ms to move from $-90°$ to the open position at $0°$. The laser shutter is a commercial UniBlitz shutter, which can open down to 1 ms. The timing of the four shutters is shown in Fig. 7.

5. The femtosecond laser for reaction initiation

The femtosecond laser is used to initiate photoreactions and to trigger a jitter free streak camera. The laser comprises four stages. The first stage is a continuous wave (CW) diode-pumped laser from Coherent (VERDI). It produces 5 W of frequency-doubled light at 532 nm. The VERDI pumps a Ti: sapphire crystal in the MIRA femtosecond laser from Coherent. The optical cavity in this laser runs in phase with the RF clock at RF/4(88.05 MHz). This oscillator produces, via the Kerr-effect in the Ti: sapphire crystal, weak 100 fs pulses at 800 nm. The frequency is adjusted to RF/4 by adjusting the length of the cavity. The third stage, the Hurricane Laser from Spectra Physics, is a chirped pulse amplifier (CPA) which stretches, amplifies and compresses a sub-train of pulses at 896.6 Hz. The pulses are amplified to 1.1 mJ pulse^{-1} at 800 nm and the pulse duration is

130 fs. The laser system is phased to the X-rays in the following way. First the X-ray chopper is centred on a single bunch which produces a train of 100 ps X-ray pulses at 896.6 Hz. The MIRA oscillator will now have a pulse that is less than half a period away (5.7 ns). By shifting the phase of the 88.05 MHz reference clock, the two pulses can be put into coincidence. This pulse needs to be amplified at 896.6 Hz. The starting point is to use the phase from the chopper and then fine-tune the delays for the seed, the pump and the cavity dump. There are two reference signals: a bunch clock at 352.201 MHz and a single-bunch clock at 355.042 kHz. The single-bunch clock marks the position of the bunch in single-bunch mode. From that we divide by 396 to get to the chopper frequency of 896.6 Hz. Now the precise phasing of the chopper requires a phase-shift, which has to be determined experimentally. A Stanford delay generator (DG535 no 1) generates the delay, which is a machine constant. Once determined, the chopper will automatically phase with the single bunch.

The fourth stage in the laser is the optical parametric generation (OPG)/optical parametric amplification (OPA), which uses frequency mixing to obtain wavelengths between 460 and 760 nm. It can produce 20–30 μJ per pulse.

From Table 4 it is seen that the laser can produce more than 3×10^{13} photon pulse^{-1}. That is comparable to the number of unit cells in a (100 μm)^3 myoglobin crystal. It is thus possible, at least in principle, to excite such a crystal to a very high degree. In practice one would like to have 5–10 times more photons to compensate for losses between the laser and the sample. The laser is focused by a lens that is mounted on an (x, y, z) alignment stage. The focal spot can thus be scanned into a pinhole on the sample goniostat.

The timing between the laser and the X-rays is measured using a GaAs photoconductor with a fwhm resolution of 50 ps.[10] The signal is recorded on a 3 GHz oscilloscope from a Tektronix TDS 694C. The setting of time zero is defined to an accuracy of ± 10 ps which is sufficient for the 60 ps resolution of the set-up.

Finally we note that very short laser pulses have a finite bandwidth. For a Gaussian pulse shape, the relation between pulse width and bandwidth is:

$$\Delta \nu \Delta t > 0.441$$

Let us consider a 100 fs pulse at 800 nm as an example. The frequency is derived from $\Delta \nu = c$, which gives $\nu = 3.75 \times 10^{14}$ Hz. Consequently $\Delta \nu / \nu = \Delta \lambda / \lambda = 1.2\%$. This distribution tends to smear out the excited state for very short pulses.

6. The recombination of molecular iodine in CCl$_4$

As an example of a pump and X-ray probe experiment in a dilute disordered sample, we will measure the X-ray scattering from excited I$_2$ and describe results following the model developed by Harris.[11] More recently Savo Bratos et al. have worked out a theory for ultrafast X-ray scattering in the presence of a laser excitation and applied this theory to molecular iodine.[12] The potential energy of two iodine atoms is shown in Fig. 8. The ground state X-curve is shown with the first two vibrational levels. For a Morse potential, the vibrational levels are[13]

$$E_{\text{vib}} = (\nu + 1/2)\omega_e - (\nu + 1/2)^2 \omega_e \chi_e.$$

where ω_e is the eigenfrequency and x_e is a constant derived from the Morse potential. For he first level $(n = 1)$, the zero point motion, is 26.52 meV and for the second $(n = 2)$ 79.56 meV. The thermal occupancy is determined by the Boltzmann factor $g = \exp(-\Delta E_{\text{vib}}/kT)$. At 300 K the ground and first excited state are 64.9% and 23.4% populated respectively. This leads to dispersion in the excited state. The optical absorption band is shown in Fig. 9.

In our experiment, the molecule is excited vertically to the B-state by a 150 fs pulse at 2.340 eV (530 nm). Note however that the second vibrational level is sent to the $^1\pi_u$ state. A calculation of the Franck–Condon factors, shows that the B and the $^1\pi_u$ state are excited in the ratio 5.18:1 respectively.[14] Both curves are repulsive and the molecule moves apart at increasing speed. At the curve crossing between B and $^1\pi_u$, the B molecules may cross to $^1\pi_u$ from where it continues to expand until they reach the liquid boundary at 4.5 Å. Some molecules remain in the B-state after the first passage of the curve crossing. After one full oscillation they return to the crossing and

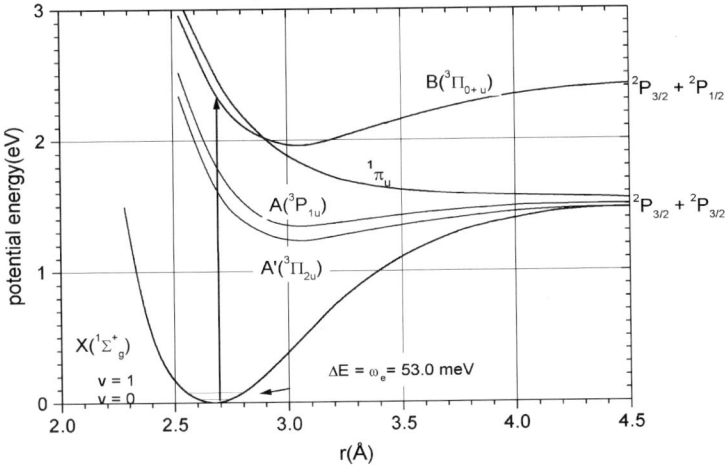

Fig. 8 The potential energy of the iodine molecule for different wavefunctions X, A/A' etc. The molecule is dissociated by a 150 fs pulse at 530 nm that excites the molecule to the B state (vertical arrow).

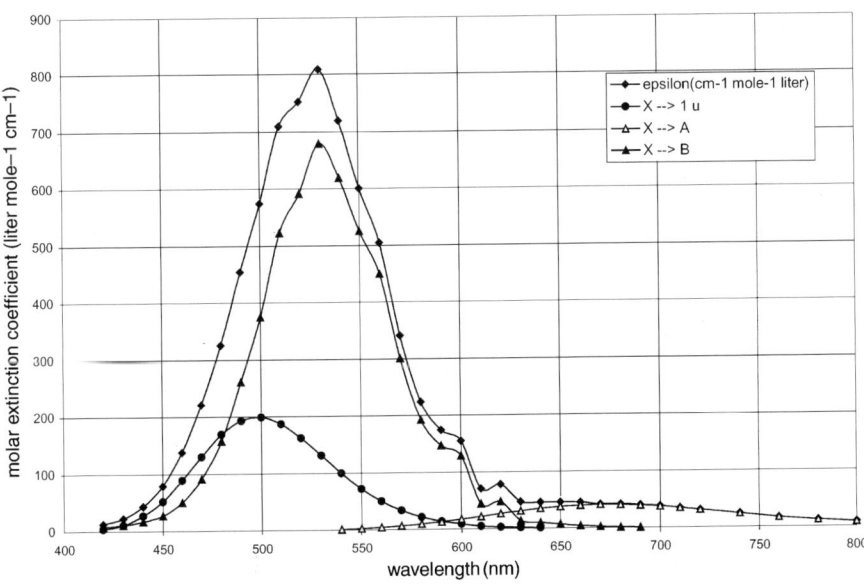

Fig. 9 The molar extinction coefficient of iodine (after Tellinghuisen). The partial absorption to the 1u, A and B branches is also shown.

dissociate at a certain probability. After a few oscillations lasting 1–2 ps, the B-state is depleted. The solvent molecules surrounding the hot atoms form a cage that more or less traps the atoms and then catalyze the recombination process. However, a solvent molecule may slide in between and force them to separate. The probability of cage escape depends on the viscosity of the solvent and varies between 30 and 90%. The separated atoms recombine diffusively in microseconds. The information about the solvent cage from optical spectroscopy is limited and X-ray scattering may eventually be used to measure the size of the cage at the different stages in the recombination. The in-cage atoms recombine diffusively in 1–10 ps and form I_2^* on the A/A' or X curve. Collisions with the cage cool the molecules and the molecule relaxes towards the potential minima on the X, A or A' curves. Molecules on the X potential thermalise in 50–200 ps by transferring energy to the solvent. The A/A' molecules thermalise in about 10 ps to a new stable position at 3.1 Å. This process is faster than the X cooling due to the lower energy transfer. The lifetime of the A/A' state depends on the polarity of the solvent; it varies from 60 ps in alkane solvents to 2.7 ns in CCl_4. The Franck–Condon factors for a vertical transition A/A' → X are low and it is believed that the A/A' molecules decay to the ground state through collisions with the solvent that stretches the molecule to the cage boundary where the energy-gap to the ground state is small. That enables the molecule to curve cross to the ground state.[15,16] To summarize the picture developed by Harris, the molecules recombine in four processes:

1. Vibrational cooling along A/A' in 10 ps.
2. Vibrational cooling along X in 50–200 ps
3. Intersystem crossing from A/A' to X in 60–2700 ps.
4. Non-geminate recombination in µs.

With the exception of process 2, synchrotron experiments can resolve these processes.

7. Experimental configuration

The diffuse scattering was recorded on a MARCCD detector, which was centered on the incident beam. The iodine was dissolved at 20 mM in CCl_4 i.e. the ratio of I_2 to CCl_4 was 0.0019. The liquid was injected into the joint focus between the X-rays and the laser in a 0.3 mm diameter capillary, see Fig. 10. The capillary was used to make the flow stable and to avoid fluctuations in the vapor pressure. The iodine was excited with yellow light (580 nm) from a nanosecond laser. The pulse width was 2.2 ns, which became the time-resolution of the experiment. At this wavelength and concentration, the optical absorption μ^{-1} is 1.0 mm.[14] The laser beam was focused to 0.7×1.0 mm^2 and the incident energy was 9.0 mJ pulse^{-1}. The X-rays were delivered by the single-line undulator U20 and the synchrotron was operated in single-bunch. The spectrum of the U20 has one harmonic at 16.45 keV and its bandwidth is 2.37%. The increase in flux, as compared to a conventional monochromatic beam from a Si(111) monochromator was 460! The beamsize on the sample was 0.20 mmh × 0.32 mmv and the flux 3.2×10^8 photon pulse^{-1} for a 10 mA bunch. The experiment was repeated at 10 Hz and the liquid exposed for 100 s per time delay. The data were collected in pairs of *laser on* and *laser off* for every time point. The Ø132.5 mm detector was positioned 40 mm

Fig. 10 Sample chamber for liquid experiments. The liquid enters from above and is collected in a funnel below the interaction point. The pumping speed is set such that the sample is replaced between two pulses (1.1 ms apart). The scattering pattern is collected on a CCD detector centered on the incident beam. Cell designed by Armin Geis (ESRF).

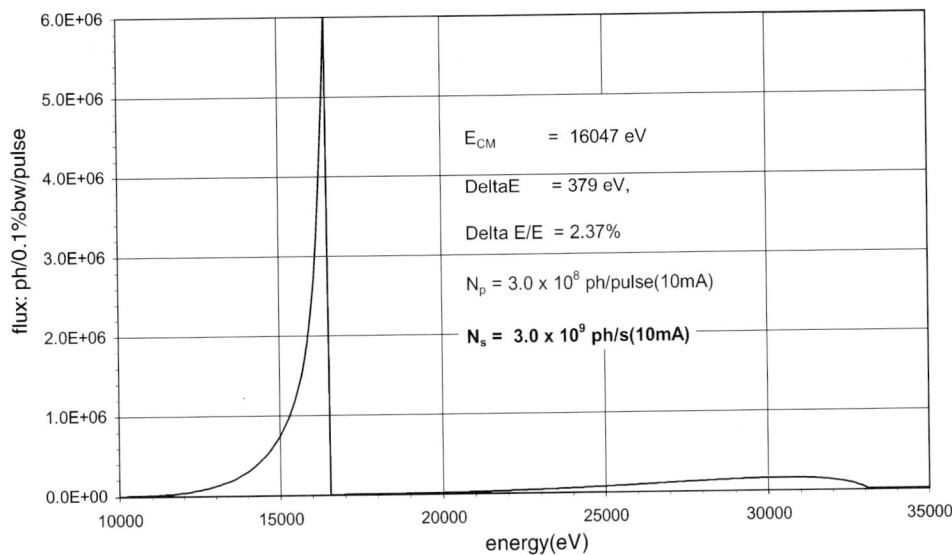

Fig. 11 The spectral flux in one pulse from the single-line undulator U20. The second harmonic is neglected in the analysis.

from the jet and the 2θ-angle was recorded between $2.05°$ and $58.55°$. The corresponding Q-range was 0.29–7.94 Å, which is calculated for a center of mass wavelength of 0.774 Å. The spectrum of the U20 undulator is shown in Fig. 11.

8. Experimental observations

The radial distribution from a 100 s exposure of 20 mM of I_2 in CCl_4 is shown in Fig. 12. The data have been integrated radially using the program fit2d, cleaned for cosmic rays and radioactive impurities in the fiber optics and space-angle corrected. The pixel size is 64.689×64.689 µm^2 and

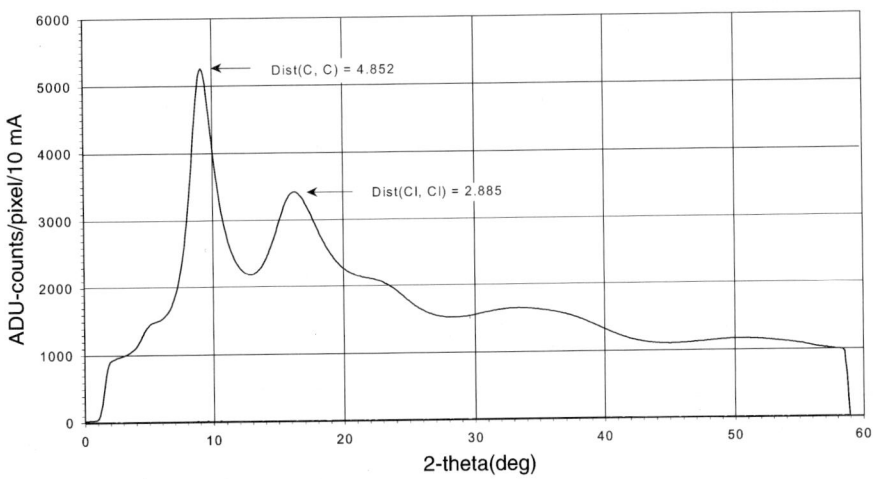

Fig. 12 Radial distribution function for 20 mM I_2 in CCl_4 without laser excitation.

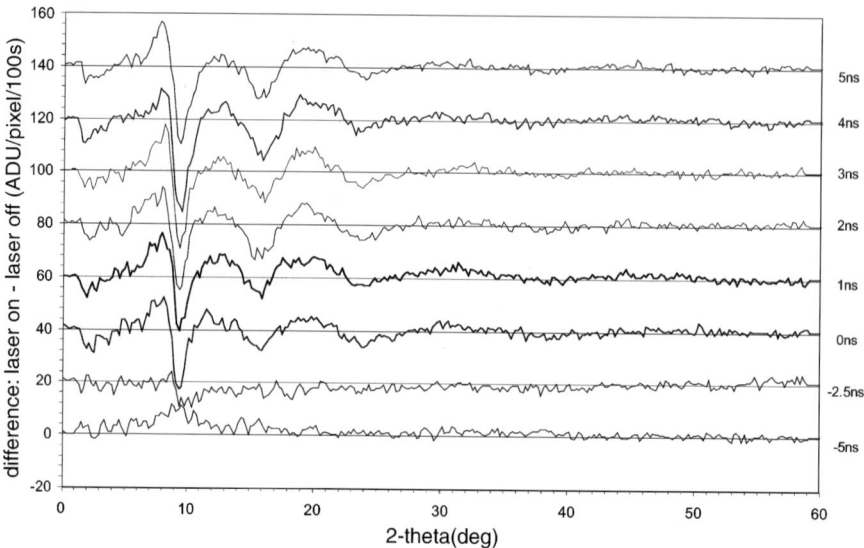

Fig. 13 Difference maps for time delays between −5 ns and 5 ns. The exposure time was 100 s and the integral flux: 3×10^{11} photons.

the software corrects the counts making the pixel perpendicular to the 2θ scattering angle at a distance of 40 mm. Note the oscillatory nature of the (dominating) solvent scattering. The main peak is found at 9.25°, which represents the distance between two CCl_4 molecules, *i.e.* it corresponds to a C–C distance of 4.852 Å. A second peak is seen at 16.45°, which is assigned, to the internal Cl–Cl distance of 2.885 Å in CCl_4.

The difference between frames *laser on* and *laser off* for time points between −5 ns and 5 ns are shown in Fig. 13. The data have been scaled such that the high-angle region oscillates around zero. The first two negative time-points at −5 ns and −2.5 ns are control points used to determine the confidence level of the experiment. In this case the X-ray pulse arrives before the laser and the difference pattern should be zero. The slight peak seen near the solvent peak is possibly due to the trailing edge of the laser pulse that initiates the solvent very slightly. In the high-angle range, the difference curve oscillated below +/−1 ADU per pixel which has to be compared with the liquid background of about 1000 ADU. The difference oscillations are due to the change in I_2 structure and its environment. The high-angle range 25–58°, taken at a delay of 1.0 ns, is shown in Fig. 14. The difference oscillation curve is a mixture of (formfactor) transitions from the ground state to the stretched A/A′-state and from the ground state to atomic iodine. The analysis shows that 78% of the excited molecules are in the A/A-state at 1.0 ns and 22% have broken through the cage. The bondlength of the A/A′-state is found to be 3.14 Å in good agreement with the total-energy calculations in Fig. 9.

The relative number of excited molecules can be determined by scaling the difference oscillations to the high-Q part of the CCl_4 scattering (neglecting the I_2 contribution) which above a Q of 2.5–3.0 Å equals the scattering from free molecules at the solvent density. One finds that 69% of the I_2 molecules are excited. At low angles, the interpretation is more complicated: the photolysis produces an overall temperature rise in the solvent, which, even on the nanosecond time-scale, leads to a small but significant expansion in the CCl_4 to CCl_4 distance. This point is being scrutinized at the moment and we will limit our discussion to a calculation of the temperature rise:

$$\Delta T = \frac{E}{A} \frac{\varepsilon c}{c_p \rho}$$

where E is the energy of the laser flash, A is the illuminated area, ε the molar extinction coefficient, c_p the heat capacity and ρ the CCl_4 density. The values are given in Table 6; they give a ΔT of 4.3 K.

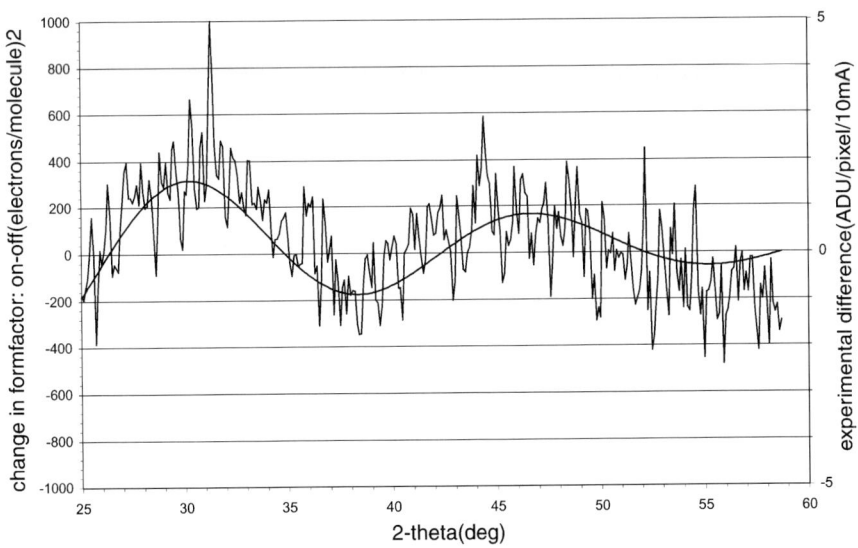

Fig. 14 Difference oscillation from the recombination of iodine. (—) Fit assuming that 78% of the molecules have recombined into A/A' with a bondlength of 3.14 Å and 22% of the molecules have escaped the cage.

Table 5 The performance of the Ti: Sapphire laser. The pulse length is 150 fs

	Wavelength/nm	Energy/eV	Energy/µJ pulse^{-1}	photon pulse^{-1}	photon s^{-1}
1 harm.	800	1.55	750	3.0E + 15	2.7E + 18
2 harm.	400	3.10	150	3.0E + 14	2.7E + 17
3 harm.	267	4.64	25	3.4E + 13	3.0E + 16
OPG/OPA	460	2.95	35	7.4E + 13	6.6E + 16
OPG/OPA	760	1.63	35	1.3E + 14	1.2E + 17

Table 6 Parameters for the temperature jump in CCl_4

Absorption of iodine at 580 nm	ε	224	cm^{-1} M^{-1}
Thermal capacity of CCl_4	c_p	842	J kg^{-1} K^{-1}
Density of CCl_4	ρ	1590	kg m^{-3}
Concentration of I_2	c	20	mM
Energy of laser flash	E	9	mJ
Laser focus (0.7 × 1 mm^2 FWHM)	A	0.7	mm^2

Acknowledgements

The authors wish to thank Savo Bratos, Rodolphe Vuilleumier, Fabien Mirloup, Richard Neutze, Armin Geis, Wolfgang Reichenbach, Dominique Block and Peter Trommsdorff and for discussions and assistance on the beamline.

References

1. F. Schotte, S. Techert, P. A. Anfinrud, V. Srajer, K. Moffat and M. Wulff, in *Third-Generation Hard X-ray Synchrotron Radiation Sources*, ed. Dennis Mills, Wiley, New York, 2002, pp. 345–401.
2. A. Rousse, C. Rischel, S. Fourmaux, I. Uschmann, S. Sebban, G. Grillon, Ph. Balcou, E. Forster, J. P. Geindre, P. Audebert, J. C. Gauthier and D. Hulin, *Nature*, 2001, **410**, 65–68.
3. V. Srajer, T. Teng, T. Ursby, C. Pradervand, Z. Ren, S. Adachi, W. Schildkamp, D. Bourgeois, M. Wulff and K. Moffat, *Science*, 1996, **274**, 1726–9.
4. V. Šrajer, S. Crosson, M. Schmidt, J. Key, F. Schotte, S. Anderson, B. Perman, Z. Ren, T. Y. Teng, D. Bourgeois, M. Wulff and K. Moffat, *J. Synch. Radiat.*, 2000, **7**, 236–244.
5. V. Srajer, Z. Ren, T.-Y. Teng, M. Schmidt, T. Ursby, D. Bourgeois, C. Pradervand, W. Schildkamp, M. Wulff and K. Moffat, *Biochemistry*, 2001, **40**, 13 802–13 815.
6. S. Techert, F. Schotte and M. Wulff, *Phys. Rev. Lett.*, 2001, **86**(10), 2030–2033.
7. R. Neutze, R. Wouts, S. Techert, J. Davidson, M. Kocsis, A. Kirrander, F. Schotte and M. Wulff, *Phys. Rev. Lett.*, 2001, **87**(19), 195 508.
8. A. Geis, D. Block, M. Bouriau, F. Schotte, S. Techert, A. Plech, M. Wulff and H. P. Trommsdorff, *J. Lumin.*, 2001, **94–95**, 493–498.
9. D. Bourgeois, U. Wagner and M. Wulff, *Acta Crystallogr., Sect. D*, 2000, **56**, 973–985.
10. R. Wrobel, B. Brullot, F. Dainciant, J. Doublier, J.-F. Eloy, R. Marmoret, B. Villette, O. Mathon, R. Tocoulou and A. K. Freund, *SPIE*, 1998, **3451**, 156–163.
11. A. L. Harris, J. K. Brown and C. B. Harris, *Annu. Rev. Phys. Chem.*, 1988, **39**, 341–366.
12. S. Bratos, F. Mirloup, R. Vuillemier and M. Wulff, *J. Chem. Phys.*, 2002, **116**(24), 10615–10625.
13. G. Herzberg, *Molecular Spectra and Molecular Structure I. Spectra of Diatomic Molecules*. Robert E. Krieger, Malabar, FL, 1991.
14. J. Tellinghuisen, *J. Chem. Phys.*, 1973, **58**(7), 2821–2834.
15. D. F. Kelley, A. N. Abul-Haj and D.-J. Jang, *J. Chem. Phys.*, 1984, **80**(9), 4105–4111.
16. J. T. Hynes, R. Kapral and G. M. Torrie, *J. Chem. Phys.*, 1980, **72**(1), 177–188.

Femtosecond mid-infrared spectroscopy of condensed phase hydrogen-bonded systems as a probe of structural dynamics

Matteo Rini, Andreas Kummrow, Jens Dreyer, Erik T. J. Nibbering* and Thomas Elsaesser

Max Born Institut für Nichtlineare Optik und Kurzzeitspektroskopie, Max Born Strasse 2A, D-12489, Berlin, Germany. E-mail: nibberin@mbi-berlin.de

Received 29th January 2002, Accepted 12th April 2002
First published as an Advance Article on the web 18th July 2002

We report the first time-resolved site-specific mid-infrared study of the photo-induced excited state hydrogen transfer reaction in 2-(2′-hydroxyphenyl)benzothiazole (HBT) with 130 fs time resolution. The transient absorption of the C=O stretching band marking the keto*-S_1-state appears delayed on a time scale of 30–50 fs after electronic excitation to the enol*-S_1-state. Its line center subsequently shifts up by about 3–5 cm^{-1} after excitation, depending on the excitation wavelength tuned between 315 and 349 nm. This effect is attributed to intramolecular vibrational energy redistribution (IVR) and vibrational energy relaxation (VER) processes. We observe for the first time the coherent effects of anharmonic coupling of low frequency modes ($\approx$60 cm^{-1}, $\approx$120 cm^{-1}), on the C=O mode marking the product state. We ascribe the 120 cm^{-1} mode to a Raman-active in-plane deformation mode that is coherently excited by the UV-pump pulse. We tentatively explain the coherent excitation of the infrared active 60 cm^{-1} out-of-plane deformation mode by nonradiative processes within the excited enol state after electronic excitation.

I. Introduction: Ultrafast structural dynamics in the condensed phase

When dealing with ultrafast chemical reaction dynamics in the condensed phase, the object of research is not only to decipher the underlying molecular parameters determining femtosecond chemical events of bond breaking and formation (known as femtochemistry [1,2]), but also to gain a clear picture of the roles that nearby solvent molecules have in the chemical reaction dynamics. Solvent motions occur with a broad range of time scales, with ultrafast components at femtosecond and picosecond time scales having a major impact on the outcome of these reactions due to processes such as molecular conformation (de-)stabilization, electronic and vibrational energy exchange, electronic and vibrational coherence decay and the cage effect in molecular dissociation.[3]

The ideal method for time-resolved studies of chemical reaction dynamics would be a technique where the spatial parameters of the structural dynamics are resolved for the molecular probe under study as well as for the nearby solvent molecules. We focus on femtosecond mid-infrared pump–probe and four-wave mixing techniques (photon echoes) as an alternative method to probe ultrafast structural dynamics, since methods such as ultrafast X-ray diffraction,[4–7] ultrafast X-ray spectroscopy [8,9] or ultrafast electron diffraction[10,11] are still in their infancy. It is well known that with time-resolved vibrational spectroscopy one can grasp the dynamics of specific chemical bonds in the case where the probed vibrations can be regarded as local modes. In contrast, by probing

DOI: 10.1039/b201056a

electronic states with optical frequencies additional arguments are necessary to determine whether certain chemical bonds are involved in the reaction pathways.

Following a description of several major advantages, well-known from stationary vibrational spectroscopy, that enable one to gain detailed structural information on molecular geometries and interactions in section I, we review ultrafast spectroscopic work on hydrogen bonding dynamics and hydrogen transfer reactions in section II. We then give a short overview in section III of earlier ultrafast mid-infrared spectroscopic studies on the hydrogen bond dynamics of Coumarin 102. We present our new results on ultrafast site-specific mid-infrared spectroscopy on excited-state intramolecular hydrogen transfer in 2-(2′-hydroxyphenyl)benzothiazole in section IV, and conclude with some prospects for our method in section V.

A. Site-specific information from inspection of vibrational bands

In the case where a molecular vibration is coupled to the reaction coordinate, leading to marked frequency shifts and intensity changes, this mode can be used as a spectator for the state of the chemically reactive bond. For instance, we have demonstrated the potential of probing site-specific hydrogen bond cleavage and rearrangements in the case of hydrogen-bonded complexes of Coumarin 102, a standard probe in solvation dynamics studies.[12–17]

B. Geometric information from vibrational band patterns

Vibrational marker modes can appear, shift or disappear, indicating the occurrence of a rearrangement of nuclear coordinates when crossing occurs from the reactant state towards the product state. Moreover, comparison of experimental vibrational patterns with results of quantum chemical calculations leads to determination of geometric structures of transient states, as demonstrated in the case of the locally excited and charge-transfer states of 4-(dimethylamino)-benzonitrile.[17–24]

C. Structural information from anharmonic coupling between vibrational modes

Direct geometric information can be obtained from mid-IR pump–mid-IR probe experiments on vibrational bands that exhibit features of anharmonic coupling between vibrational modes. By inspection of one specific mode not only the dynamics of this mode can be followed, but also the dynamics of a second mode is monitored due to anharmonic coupling between these modes. In principle, due to the implicit geometrical dependences of the anharmonic couplings between vibrational normal modes the potential of the method lies in resolving information on the molecular structure. In addition, due to the inherent time-resolution, structural dynamics of evolving molecular species can be grasped.

As an illustration of the potential of IR spectroscopy of probing anharmonic coupling we note here recent results obtained on intramolecular hydrogen bonds of organic molecules in the electronic ground state. A modulation of the IR pump–probe signal in phthalic acid monomethylester (PMME) with a period of 330 fs has been observed, indicating a coherent motion of the hydrogen bond.[25] The coherent motions have been ascribed to anharmonic coupling between the O–D stretching mode and a low-frequency out-of-plane motion of the two sub-groups that are connected to each other through the hydrogen bond. Similar features have been obtained for 2-(2′-hydroxyphenyl)benzothiazole (HBT), where the hydrogen bond distance is modulated by a 120 cm^{-1} in-plane deformation mode.[26]

Determination of molecular structure is also pursued by investigation of excitonic coupling between vibrational modes with comparable transition frequencies by use of two-dimensional IR spectroscopy.[27] Examples on which structural information has been obtained include small peptides,[28–33] N-methylacetamide[34,35] and Rh(CO)$_2$(C$_5$H$_7$O$_2$).[36,37] Two-dimensional IR spectroscopy can be extended towards resolution of transient structures by means of an additional optical trigger pulse.

II. Hydrogen bonding dynamics and hydrogen transfer reactions

The structural dynamics of protic solvents such as water and of biomolecular polymers such as proteins and DNA are largely determined by the special properties of hydrogen bonds. The dynamics of the structural properties of hydrogen bonding are crucial to understanding such systems on a microscopic level. In addition proton exchange along hydrogen bonds occurs frequently in hydrogen-bonded networks such as water (proton hops, Grotthuss mechanism).[38–40] Proton pumps through membranes also operate by proton transfer along "water wires" to maintain a certain pH gradient along membranes, *e.g.* in the case of photosynthetic reaction centres.[41] The dynamics of hydrogen bonds occur on ultrafast time scales, mainly set by motions of the hydrogen donor and acceptor groups, both in thermal equilibrium and for non-equilibrium excitations. In thermal equilibrium, *i.e.* in the electronic ground state, vibrational and translational motions of the nuclei comprising the hydrogen-bonded system cause fluctuations in the geometrical parameters of the hydrogen bond, leading to *e.g.* proton transfer. In addition, fluctuating solvent configurations may alter the relative energies of the donor and acceptor moieties of the hydrogen-bonded complex, thereby stabilising or de-stabilising the newly formed configuration after proton transfer.[42,43]

Static and dynamical properties of hydrogen bonds are intensively studied using a multitude of spectroscopic techniques, varying from X-ray diffraction, electronic and vibrational spectroscopy, and nuclear magnetic resonance. In particular, it has been shown that steady-state infrared spectroscopy of the O–H/O–D stretching mode has the potential to reveal the strength of the hydrogen bond due to a direct relationship to the red-shift of the vibrational frequency of the O–H stretching band.[44] The same applies for N–H/N–D or F–H/F–D stretching vibrations. In addition similar correlations have been found for C=O, C=N, C–O and C–N vibrations when these groups are part of a hydrogen-bonded system.

The ultrafast dynamical properties of intermolecular hydrogen bonds, in the electronic ground state, in water, alcohols and acids have been studied intensively during the last 5 years after triggering a non-equilibrium vibrational excitation of an O–H vibration with an ultrafast mid-IR pump, after which the non-equilibrium dynamics are determined by transmission changes of a mid-IR pulse or by anti-Stokes Raman emission. Important information has been obtained on vibrational lifetimes with typical values in the subpicosecond time range,[45–48] vibrational dephasing and spectral diffusion,[49,50] energy redistribution,[51–54] energy transfer to neighbouring molecules,[55] band substructures[56,57] and band shifts due to the dynamical Stokes shift[53,58–61] or due to local heating,[62] and orientational dynamics.[63,64]

III. Hydrogen bond dynamics in solvation studies

Solute–solvent interaction in liquids has so far mainly been studied by monitoring transient redshifts of electronic emission bands or the electronic coherence decay of the chromophore in order to characterize the time scales of solvent response. Such solvation experiments provide ensemble averaged time-correlation functions for liquid motion, but give very limited information on changes of microscopic solvent structure. An important issue to be inspected is how a hydrogen-bonded complex in the condensed phase responds to electronic excitation. In this solvation scenario, changing local hydrogen bonds lowers the energy of the transition dipole. A prototypical case is hydrogen-bonded complexes embedded in a nonpolar aprotic solvent, as the relative concentrations of the species forming the complex and, thus, the site geometry and molecular interactions can be varied over a wide range. With this the problem is simplified as compared to the case of a solute hydrogen-bonded to protic solvents like water, where the staggering magnitude of the hydrogen-bonded networks makes the interpretation a formidable task. New and highly specific insight has been obtained into the ultrafast structural dynamics of hydrogen-bonded complexes between an organic chromophore, Coumarin 102 (C102), serving as hydrogen acceptor, and hydrogen-donating phenol molecules dissolved in the nonpolar solvent tetrachloroethene, C_2Cl_4. The advantage of these complexes as compared to the case of a hydrogen-donating solvent like chloroform ($CHCl_3$) is that one can study the dynamics on both the acceptor and donor sides.

From femtosecond vibrational spectroscopic experiments, where C102 is excited electronically and the spectator carbonyl-stretching mode of C102 and the spectator O–H-stretching mode of phenol are probed, one has learnt that:[13,14,16,17]

(1) The hydrogen bond between C102 and (phenol)$_{1,2}$ breaks within 200 fs (time resolution of the experiments), similar to C102–CHCl$_3$ complexes.[12,15]

(2) The time-dependent features in the O–H region show in addition that: (a) the solute dipole change induces strong changes of vibrational transition moments; (b) the released (phenol)$_2$-moiety reorganizes itself to its equilibrium configuration with an 800 fs time constant.

(3) In the reported studies, dynamics is described involving the phenol-unit not directly bonded to C102. With this result a demonstration is given of the ability of femtosecond vibrational spectroscopy for probing dynamics in that part of the hydrogen-bonding network that is not directly linked to the initially excited acceptor. This is a result that by no means can be directly determined with techniques where only electronic transitions are probed, such as photon echoes or time-resolved Stokes-shift measurements.

Since hydrogen bonding occurs in a wide range of solvents, the above-mentioned results have far-reaching consequences for interpretation of solvation studies.

IV. Ultrafast mid-infrared study of the excited state intramolecular hydrogen transfer

The transfer of hydrogen atoms or protons represents one of the most elementary structural changes occurring in chemical and biological processes.[65–71] In general, hydrogen transfer between excited singlet states displays ultrafast dynamics and, thus, spectroscopy with ultrashort light pulses represents a powerful technique to monitor and analyze such reactions. So far, most work has concentrated on dynamics in the condensed phase, where both intramolecular hydrogen transfer and the release of protons from so-called photoacids into the surrounding solvent have been studied. In pump–probe experiments, the reaction has been initiated by pico- or femtosecond excitation to a higher electronic state and the subsequent time evolution of the system has been monitored through changes of electronic absorption or emission spectra. Time-resolved studies of photoacids have shown proton transfer dynamics on time scales of tens to hundreds of picoseconds.[72–76] In contrast, early picosecond studies of intramolecular hydrogen transfer gave an upper limit for the transfer time of the order of a few picoseconds, even at low temperatures of the samples.[77–81] The first femtosecond study of intramolecular hydrogen transfer was performed on the enol*–keto* transformation of 2-(2'-hydroxyphenyl)benzothiazole (HBT) and gave a rise time of the red part of the keto*-emission of 170 fs.[82] After this work, a number of similar studies with a time resolution of about 100 fs have been reported for other intramolecular hydrogen transfer reactions, giving rise times of the product species between 50 and 200 fs.[83–87] Recent experiments with a time resolution of about 20 fs allow the observation of vibrational coherences occurring during and after excited state hydrogen transfer. This has been demonstrated for the first time for 2-(2'-hydroxy-5'-methylphenyl)benzotriazole where two low-frequency modes at 299 and 470 cm^{-1} are elongated upon electronic excitation and give rise to oscillatory features in the rise of product emission.[88] An analysis of the microscopic motions connected with such modes, based on resonance Raman studies and theoretical calculations,[89] led to a qualitative microscopic picture of hydrogen transfer in which motions along low-frequency modes determine the pathway of the reaction on the excited state potential energy surface. Though such experiments have provided substantial insight into ultrafast hydrogen transfer, the study of electronic spectra does not allow for a direct characterization of transient molecular structures during and after the reaction. Here, ultrafast vibrational spectroscopy monitoring local changes of molecular geometries provides much more information.

The object of our studies is the hydrogen transfer reaction of 2-(2'-hydroxyphenyl)benzothiazole (HBT) dissolved in tetrachloroethene (see Fig. 1). After excitation to the enol*-S$_1$-state, the keto* product structure is formed in its first excited state Already 15 years ago it was shown with picosecond infrared spectroscopy that a clear signature of the keto*-S$_1$-state population density of HBT is the mid-infrared (MIR) absorption band around 1535 cm^{-1} corresponding to the C=O double bond stretching mode.[90] In such measurements, the transfer reaction was not temporally

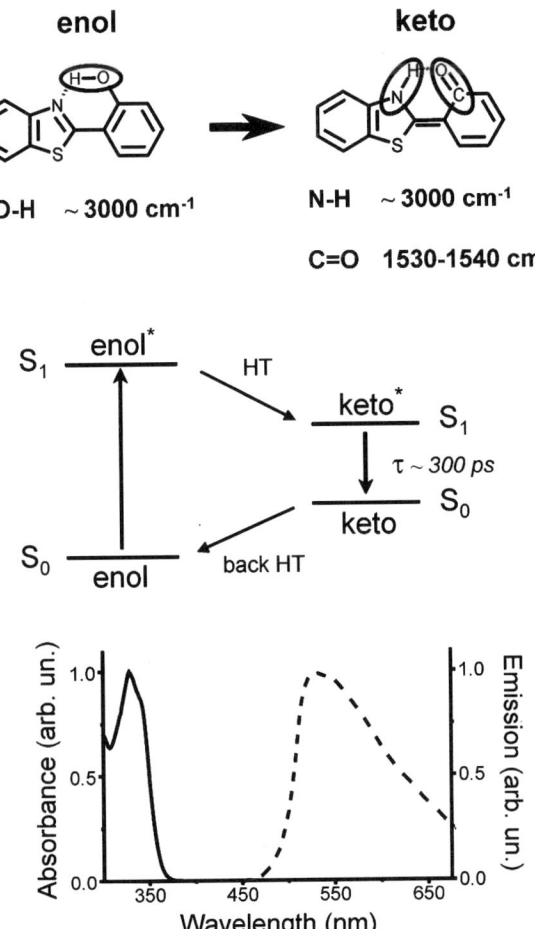

Fig. 1 Molecular structures of HBT in the enol and keto-tautomer configurations. Hydrogen transfer (HT) occurs after electronic excitation of the enol*-S1-state. The keto*-S$_1$-state decays on subnanosecond time scales to the keto-S$_0$ state by photo-emission. HBT relaxes then to the enol-S$_0$ state by back hydrogen transfer (back HT). The optical spectra show the large Stokes-shift between absorption and emission bands that typifies the excited state hydrogen transfer reaction.

resolved. Femtosecond pump–probe studies of stimulated emission in the red part of the keto S$_1$–S$_0$ emission spectrum gave a rise time 170 fs for the emission which was attributed to hydrogen transfer.[82,83] Very recently, this process has been studied with a substantially improved time resolution of 30 fs and over a spectral range covering the full keto*-emission band.[91,92] At short wavelengths, emission rise times of about 60 fs were found, whereas a substantially slower rise was detected at long wavelengths, in quantitative agreement with the data of Laermer et al.[82] The delayed onset of stimulated emission was explained by a ballistic reaction on the excited state potential surface leading to delayed population of the keto*-S$_1$-state of HBT. The 60 fs rise time of emission at short wavelengths was attributed to the hydrogen transfer. The occurrence of pronounced oscillatory features on these UV/pump–probe measurements has been ascribed to coherent motion of four low-frequency modes induced by the nuclear rearrangement that occurs during the hydrogen transfer process. It should be noted, however, that such modes are strongly elongated upon excitation of the enol*-S$_1$-state, as they couple strongly to the electronic transition.

In the following we show that with ultrafast vibrational spectroscopy one can monitor changes in the vibrational spectra of relevant functional groups, in this way providing direct site-specific access to molecular structure and nuclear motions. In particular, we monitor the dynamics of the C=O carbonyl stretching mode formed by hydrogen transfer, and, thus, representing a direct probe of the formation of the keto species. In this way, the ambiguity resulting from the wavelength dependent rise time of keto*-emission is avoided. In addition, the shape of the band is potentially sensitive to vibrational energy redistribution after hydrogen transfer, either when the C=O stretching mode is vibrationally excited, or by anharmonic coupling to other intramolecular modes that are on their own transiently excited.

A. Experimental procedure

The pump–probe set-up was similar to the one used earlier for femtosecond mid-IR spectroscopy on hydrogen bond dynamics of Coumarin 102 complexes[13] and intramolecular charge transfer of 4-(dimethylamino)benzonitrile[20] with three modifications used to improve time resolution, tunability and signal to noise ratio. First, electronic excitation was performed using near-UV pulses generated by sum frequency mixing of the fundamental of a 1 kHz amplified Ti : sapphire laser and visible pulses generated by a noncollinear optical parametric amplifier as described elsewhere.[93] In the experiments the excitation wavelength was tuned from 315 nm to 350 nm. The excitation pulse energy was 2–4 µJ and the pulse duration around 40 fs. The pump pulses could be variably delayed and were focused on the sample with a concave mirror with a beam diameter of approximately 150 µm.

Second, the mid-infrared pulses were generated using double-pass collinear optical parametric amplification followed by difference frequency mixing of signal and idler.[94] The center frequency was tuned to 1550 cm^{-1} and the output energy was around 400 nJ. Probe and reference pulses were derived using reflections from a BaF$_2$ wedge, and focused in the sample with off-axis parabolic mirrors (focal diameter 100 µm). The whole pump–probe set-up was purged with nitrogen gas to avoid spectral and temporal reshaping of the MIR pulse by the absorption of water vapor and CO$_2$ in air.

Third, probe and reference pulses were dispersed in a polychromator and complete spectra were recorded simultaneously for each shot using a liquid nitrogen cooled 2 × 31 HgCdTe detector array. Normalizing probe and reference signal on a single shot basis provides highly reliable spectra. The polychromator was not tuned during measurements to avoid the repositioning error (± 2 cm^{-1}). Synchronous chopping of the UV-pump pulses was used to eliminate long term drift effects. Experimental curves shown here represent an average of 100–200 delay time traces each taking 100 shots average per delay step.

HBT was dissolved in C$_2$Cl$_4$ and pumped through a free streaming jet (nominal thickness 100 µm). The group velocity mismatch between UV-pump pulse and the MIR-pulses was measured to be 880 fs mm^{-1} in the neat solvent, the UV-pulse traveling more slowly. In order to minimize the effect of temporal walk-off between the pulses a relatively high concentration of 4 g l^{-1} was chosen, leading to an effective jet thickness of less than 30 µm. Nevertheless the high extinction of the UV pulse does not lead to substantial temporal reshaping, since excitation was performed around the peak of the broad absorption band, which leads to spectrally uniform attenuation.

For reference purposes the jet was replaced by a polished ZnSe window to determine the zero delay point (including the chirp of the infrared pulse) and to control the time resolution of the cross correlation (FWHM 120–140 fs).

B. Transient spectra obtained on the ESIPT reaction of HBT

We investigated the mid-IR spectral region between 1400 and 1600 cm^{-1}, where the C=O stretching absorption of the keto*-state can be found. We have also inspected the spectral region of the O–H stretching band of the enol-form and the N–H spectral region of the keto*-form. However, since the broad O–H and N–H stretching bands overlap significantly with implicit complications in the interpretation of the experimental data, we focus here on our results obtained on the C=O stretching band.

Typical experimental transient UV-pump–mid-IR-probe data of HBT in C_2Cl_4 are shown in Fig. 2 and 3. In this case the UV excitation pulse was tuned at 335 nm. In Fig. 2 we present transient infrared spectra, *i.e.* the change of vibrational absorption recorded between 1410 and 1590 cm^{-1} together with the infrared spectrum of the enol ground state. Negative contributions to the absorbance change ΔOD (bleach) can be observed already at negative delay times at those frequencies where ground state bands are located. These signals result from perturbed free induction decay contributions in the pump–probe signal due to bleaching of ground state modes upon UV-excitation.[95,96] In addition, around zero delay, a contribution of the solvent occurs, of which the response is identical at all detected frequencies of the probe pulse.

A prominent new band is formed at 1530 cm^{-1}, representing the C=O stretching band of the keto*-species. The strength and spectral position of this band agree with earlier picosecond measurements.[90] The new C=O band builds up with a delay of 30–50 fs (Fig. 3A), representing the formation time of keto*–HBT.

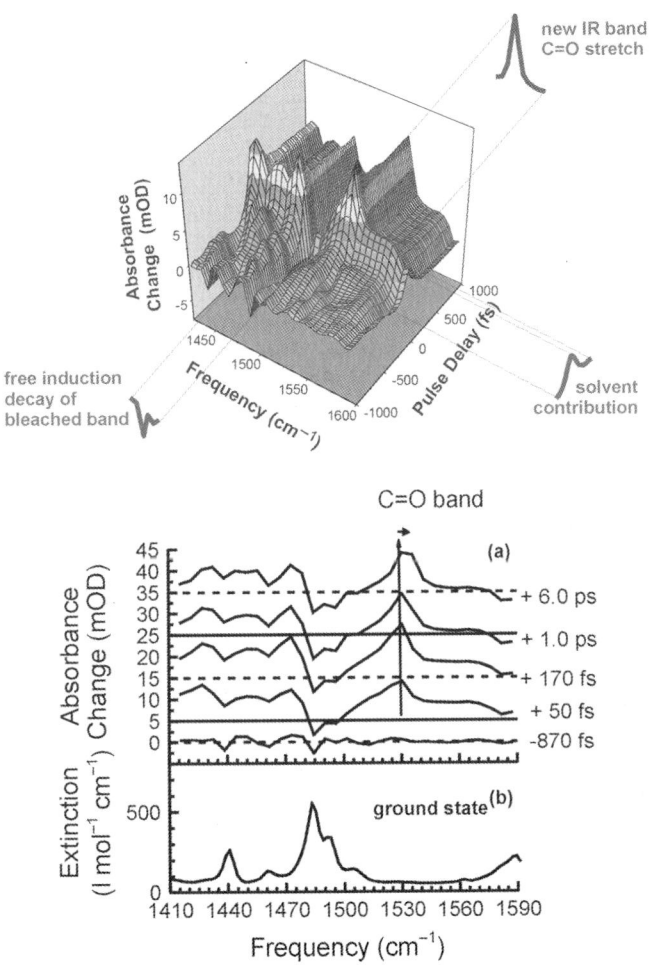

Fig. 2 Three-dimensional plot of the spectrally and time-resolved pump–probe signals of HBT with electronic excitation at 335 nm (upper graph). The data show typically perturbed free induction decay contributions at negative delays, solvent-signals around zero delay, and bleaches and induced absorptions of transient vibrationl bands at positive delays. Transient spectra at several pulse delays are shown in the lower graph (a), indicating the rapid rise of the C=O stretching band and subsequent up-shifting at picosecond time scales. The ground state infrared spectrum of HBT is shown in (b).

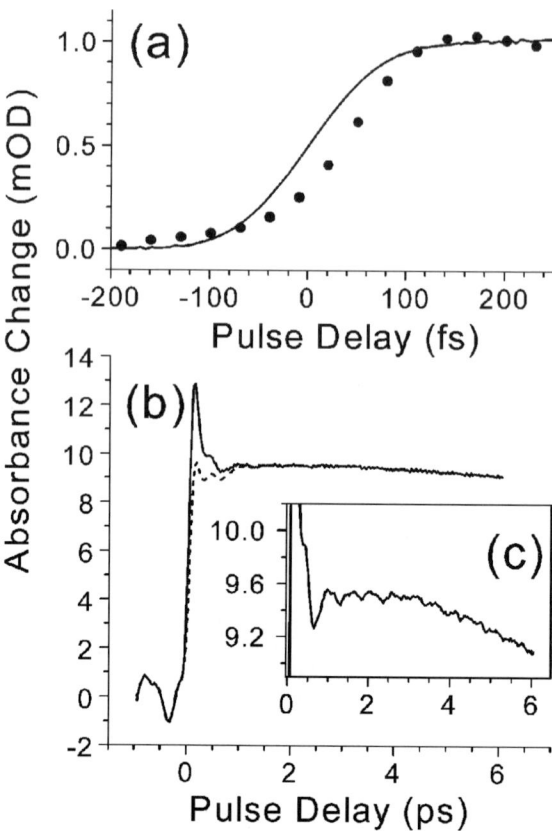

Fig. 3 Transient signals measured at 1530 cm^{-1} with excitation at 335 nm. In (a) the initial delayed dynamics of HBT (dots, after solvent signal subtraction) are compared with a cross-correlation signal measured in ZnSe (solid line). In (b) the dynamics are shown over a larger time range, with the measured signal (solid line) compared to that of HBT only after substraction of the solvent contribution (dashed line). In (c) a blow-up is presented of the signal due to HBT and solvent indicating the oscillatory contribution due to the anharmonically coupled low-frequency modes.

We performed Gaussian fitting of the C=O band to derive the temporal development of the strength, width and line centre, of which results for excitation at 335 nm are shown in Fig. 4. We observe that the strength and width of the C=O band does not change at longer delay times. From this we deduce that the C=O mode is populated in its $v = 0$ state, since a feeding of the $v = 1$ state would lead to both transient stimulated emission and absorption contributions to the pump–probe signal for the following reasons. For a harmonic oscillator one would not expect to observe any changes in absorbance of the probe signals, since the excited-state $v = 1 \rightarrow v = 2$ absorption has a cross section which represents twice that of stimulated emission from the $v = 1 \rightarrow v = 0$ transition. Any changes in absorbance do not occur when the $v = 1$ state decays to the $v = 0$ state by population relaxation. For an anharmonic oscillator similar ratios in transition moments occur for moderate anharmonicities.[97] However, for an anharmonic oscillator the anharmonic shift between the $v = 0 \rightarrow v = 1$ and the $v = 1 \rightarrow v = 2$ leads to spectrally displaced excited-state absorption and stimulated emission bands. For the C=O stretching mode with an estimated anharmonic shift of 15–20 cm^{-1}[127] an initial feeding of the $v = 1$ state and subsequent decay should thus be clearly observable.

Moreover, a second even stronger argument that the C=O stretching mode is created in the $v = 0$ state can be derived from the observed spectral width of 12.5 ± 0.5 cm^{-1} of the C=O stretching

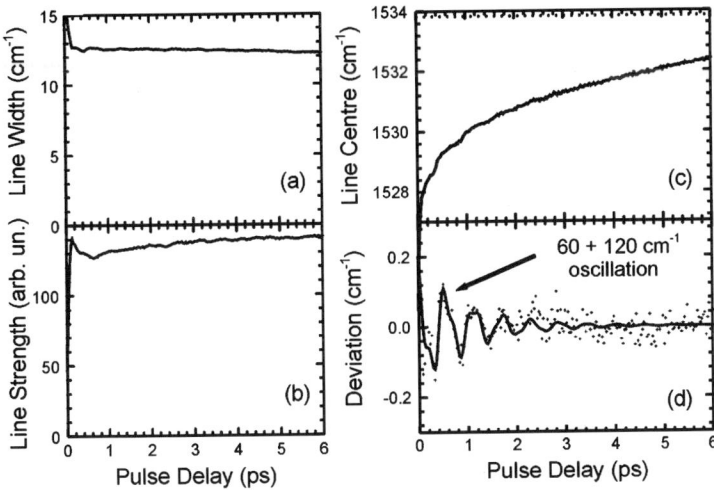

Fig. 4 Results of the fitting procedure of the measured C=O band (excitation at 335 nm) with a Gaussian line shape. The width (a) and strength (b) of the C=O band do not change at longer delays. At early times the fitting routine is affected by the additional solvent contribution. In (c) the line centre of the C=O band (dots) shows a frequency up-shift with components of 0.5 ps and 5 ps. The coherent modulation of the line centre is clearly visible in (d), where the residue (dots) is shown after substraction of the biexponential fit on the data in (c). The solid line in (d) shows a function consisting of two oscillating contributions with frequencies of 60 and 120 cm^{-1} and a decaying constant of 1 ps.

band directly after generation of the keto*-state. Such a value for the width of a vibrational band indicates that even for the extreme case of a line shape completely determined by population relaxation, the $v = 1$ state of the C=O transition has a lower limit of the population lifetime T_1 of 424 fs. More likely the T_1-value will be larger, since pure dephasing processes will also contribute to the line width.

C. Energy redistribution and dissipation

The centre frequency of the C=O band blue-shifts by about 2.5–5.5 cm^{-1} after the hydrogen transfer reaction is finished (Fig. 2 and 4). Biexponential fitting shows a temporal behaviour with a 0.5 ps component (relative weight 30%) and picosecond component (70%) with a time constant depending on excitation wavelength. Blue-shifts of vibrational bands after a photo-induced chemical reaction have been observed before in the picosecond time regime in the case of for instance *trans*-stilbene[98] and azobenzene.[99] In these studies it was assumed that at picosecond time scales the excess energies are thermally distributed amongst the vibrational modes. Specific spectator modes appear shifted due to anharmonic coupling with low-frequency modes that are highly populated. Usually a red-shift results upon excitation since most anharmonic coupling terms have negative values. However, the same red-shift behaviour would occur when only a limited set of highly populated normal modes takes place. This may be the case for HBT, since a full equilibration of excess energy is unlikely on the time scale of 50 fs. We expect that only a limited number of accepting normal modes strongly coupled to the hydrogen bond coordinate will initially redistribute the excess energy between the enol* and keto* excited states.[100,101]

The subsequent up-shift of the C=O transition frequency of HBT is understood to be a consequence of ongoing IVR among intramolecular modes and vibrational relaxation of the highly populated intramolecular modes towards thermal equilibrium through dissipation of the excess energy towards the surrounding solvent (vibrational energy relaxation, VER). We tend to ascribe the initial subpicosecond component to IVR, and the longer picosecond dynamics of the blue-shift as an indicator of cooling of the excited molecule towards ambient temperatures. For medium-sized molecules typical values for time scales of cooling are found to lie in the picosecond range.[102–105]

The hydrogen transfer reaction of HBT occurs on such a fast time scale that we expect that energy equilibration over all intramolecular modes is highly unlikely to occur on the same time span of 50 fs. It would be very interesting to identify the vibrational modes that accept the excess energy generated when HBT converts from the enol* to the keto* state. These accepting modes are extremely effective in redistributing the energy in such a way that the reverse ESIPT reaction from keto* to enol* state is prevented. We note that transient anti-Stokes Raman spectroscopy is selective for vibrationally excited modes, and with that technique non-equilibrium populations of vibrational (Raman-active) modes can be grasped.[98,106,107] This method is thus, in principle, ideal for identifying the energy flow in reactive systems. In the case of HBT, however, one would have to rely on coherent techniques such as femtosecond CARS[108] with sufficient time resolution.[109] Subpicosecond time-resolved detection of transient incoherent resonance Raman signals implies loss of frequency resolution. In addition, due to small Raman cross-sections, the latter form of transient Raman spectroscopy often fails for fluorescing molecules.

D. Coherence phenomena in photoinduced chemical reactions

Inspection of the transient recorded at 1530 cm^{-1} after excitation at 335 nm shows that oscillatory components are present in the response of the C=O mode (Fig. 3). The Gaussian fitting procedure of the transient C=O stretching mode band shape reveals that the temporal behaviour of the line centre exhibits these oscillatory features superimposed on the dynamical blue-shift in a more pronounced way (Fig. 4). Fourier analysis of the transient line centre recorded with UV excitation at 335 nm reveals two components with frequencies of about 60 and 120 cm^{-1}. In contrast, with UV excitation at 349 nm only the 120 cm^{-1} component is observed.

Oscillatory features on vibrational bands have been observed before in IR-pump–IR-probe studies on O–H and O–D stretching modes in intramolecular hydrogen bonds in the electronic ground state.[25,26] In these works the oscillatory parts of the pump–probe signals are caused by coherent modulations of the O–H/O–D stretching band positions due to anharmonic coupling with coherently excited low-frequency modes. In the present study we ascribe our observation that the frequency position of the C=O stretching mode is modulated by anharmonic coupling to one or two low-frequency modes, respectively. We thus detect, for the first time, such a spectral modulation by coherently excited low-frequency modes of a *vibrational* band marking the product state after a chemical reaction.

The assignment of these low-frequency modes in the keto*-product state can be made by comparison to the well-known vibrational mode spectrum in the enol-ground state[89,110] (see also Fig. 5). Although there is no guarantee that the vibrational mode spectrum is similar, ultrafast electronic pump–probe spectroscopic data have not shown substantial differences for the low-frequency Raman-active modes.[91,92] One could anticipate that this also applies for other (infrared-active) modes. With this in mind one can correlate the 120 cm^{-1} vibrational mode to an in-plane bending motion of the two ring systems modulating the hydrogen bond length.[89,110] This mode has been observed in electronic resonance Raman spectra indicating a strong displacement between the two enol potential energy surfaces. An out-of-plane twisting motion of the ring systems can be ascribed to the 60 cm^{-1} mode, also modulating the hydrogen bond length. This mode has an extremely low electronic resonance Raman cross section, in contrast it is known to be infrared active.[89] A third mode is present at the low-end of the vibrational spectrum. This mode however involves an out-of-plane tilting motion of the two ring systems without strong motions of the atoms that constitute the hydrogen bond. We tentatively discard the involvement of this mode in the dynamics of photo-excited HBT in the following discussion.

At this point we want to make a clear distinction between ultrafast UV-pump–VIS-probe and UV-pump–IR-probe spectroscopy in relation to what one can expect in terms of coherently excited wave packet motions in the system under study. The ultrashort UV-pump coherently excites vibrational coherences on the enol-excited and enol-ground states of those modes that are strongly Raman active, and whose frequency lies within the bandwidth of the UV excitation pulse.[1,111–118] These light-field driven coherences then evolve on the respective potential energy surfaces, and may even survive level crossings if the modes are not strongly coupled to the reaction coordinate. Another option is that vibrational wave packets are generated by rapid nonradiative processes from the initially excited reactant state to a product state.[119–123] In the latter case the surface

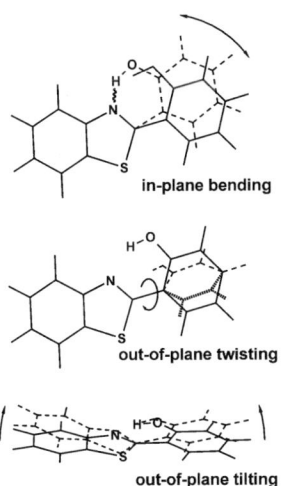

Fig. 5 Schematic representation of the low-frequency in-plane bending, out-of-plane twisting and out-of-plane tilting modes. These modes are similar in the enol- and keto-tautomers.

crossing along the reaction coordinate is accompanied by the creation of vibrational coherences along the coordinate of the vibrational mode that, in contrast to the previously mentioned case, is strongly coupled to the reaction coordinate. In the case of probing the product state the transient absorption or emission of a UV/VIS probe pulse is modulated by coherences in Raman-active vibrational modes. If no other knowledge than the Franck–Condon factors of the electronic transition induced by the UV-pump pulse exists on the particular molecular systems, one cannot decide whether the coherences are induced by the applied light pulse or by the subsequent chemical reaction. With regard to HBT for instance the Franck–Condon factors of the enol-S_0 to enol*-S_1 state transition are well known,[89,110] however this is not the case for the keto*-S_1- to keto-S_0 state. Only when a coherence in the keto*-S_1-state is observed that cannot be correlated to one of the modes that are Raman-active in the enol → enol* transition, can one safely conclude that the coherence is driven by nonradiative processes.

In the case of our ultrafast UV-pump–IR-probe experiment we probe the keto*-S_1-state by inspection of a C–O stretching vibrational marker mode. Vibrational coherences in low-frequency modes are observed if the anharmonic coupling constants to the C=O stretching mode are sufficiently large. The factors determining the magnitude of coherent modulation of the infrared-signals by anharmonic coupling are different from those for coupling of vibrational modes to electronic transitions, and it should be no surprise that coherences in both infrared- and Raman-active modes are visible.

With regard to our observation of the frequency and damping time of the 120 cm^{-1} mode we confirm within experimental error earlier UV-pump–VIS-probe observations.[91,92] Higher frequency oscillations, most notably the 254 cm^{-1} mode, are not detectable in our experiment due to limited time resolution in comparison to the UV-pump–VIS-probe experiment. The observation of the 60 cm^{-1} mode, however, is a surprising result. The fact that this mode is not observed in the UV-pump–VIS-probe experiment suggests that the mode is infrared active (not Raman active) in the keto* → keto transition. Moreover it is known that the mode cannot be coherently excited by the UV-pump pulse as it has a low Franck–Condon factor in the enol → enol* transition. Excitation of this mode is thus driven by nonradiative processes *after* preparation of the excited enol*-state. One could regard this fact as an indication that the mode is impulsively excited by the hydrogen transfer reaction, where the reaction time is only one tenth of the oscillation period of the mode. From the observations that (a) the 60 cm^{-1} mode is not observable at 350 nm where the electronic origin (0–0) transition is located, whereas (b) the reaction time appears to be independent of the excitation energy, we are led to the tentative explanation that the coherent excitation of the infrared-active 60 cm^{-1} out-of-plane deformation mode is driven by an IVR mechanism in the enol excited state.

V. Conclusions and prospects

We have studied the excited state intramolecular hydrogen transfer reaction of 2-(2′-hydroxyphenyl)benzothiazole (HBT) with femtosecond site-specific UV-pump–IR-probe spectroscopy. For the first time we observe a delayed onset of the C=O stretching mode band, indicating that the time scale of the actual hydrogen transfer process lies in the range of 30–50 fs. After hydrogen transfer we observe that the spectral width and intensity of the C=O band does not change within experimental error, indicating that the C=O vibrational mode is generated in the $v = 0$ state. The line centre of the C=O stretching band blue-shifts after excitation, from which we deduce a subpicosecond component assigned to intramolecular vibrational redistribution (thermalization) within the HBT-molecule, and a picosecond component that is correlated to cooling by vibrational energy relaxation to the solvent. We also observe oscillatory contributions to the position of the C=O stretching band that are due to anharmonic coupling with two coherently excited modes: a 120 cm^{-1} Raman active mode and a 60 cm^{-1} infrared active mode. The coherence of the latter mode, that is only observed when the electronic transition of HBT to the excited enol*-state occurs with significant excess energies, cannot directly be coherently driven by the UV-pump light field, and should thus be impulsively generated by nonradiative processes during the hydrogen transfer reaction. We tentatively assign a mechanism of coherent feeding by IVR within the excited enol*-state as the origin of this phenomenon.

The experimental results on excited-state intramolecular hydrogen transfer obtained with femtosecond mid-infrared spectroscopy demonstrate the potential of this method. We aim to extend this method to investigate excited state intermolecular proton transfer of photoacids.

Acknowledgements

Our progress has benefited from the financial support of the Deutsche Forschungsgemeinschaft through the *Schwerpunktprogramm "Femtosekunden-Spektroskopie elementarer Anregungen in Atomen, Molekülen und Clustern"*. The expertise of Dr. P. Hamm on mid-IR generation and detection has been extremely helpful in the pursuit of success in this project.

References

1. A. H. Zewail, *Science*, 1988, **242**, 1645.
2. A. H. Zewail, *J. Phys. Chem. A*, 2000, **104**, 5660.
3. G. R. Fleming, *Chemical Applications of Ultrafast Spectroscopy*, Oxford University Press, Oxford, 1986.
4. C. Rischel, A. Rousse, I. Uschmann, P.-A. Albouy, J.-P. Geindre, P. Audebert, J.-C. Gauthier, E. Fröster, J.-L. Martin and A. Antonetti, *Nature*, 1997, **390**, 490.
5. C. Rose-Petruck, R. Jimenez, T. Guo, A. Cavalleri, C. W. Siders, F. Raksi, J. A. Squier, B. C. Walker, K. R. Wilson and C. P. J. Barty, *Nature*, 1999, **398**, 310.
6. C. W. Siders, A. Cavalleri, K. Sokolowski-Tinten, C. Tóth, T. Guo, M. Kammler, M. Horn von Hoegen, K. R. Wilson, D. von der Linde and C. P. J. Barty, *Science*, 1999, **286**, 1340.
7. A. Rousse, C. Rischel, S. Fourmaux, I. Uschmann, S. Sebban, G. Grillon, P. Balcou, E. Förster, J. P. Geindre, P. Audebert, J. C. Gauthier and D. Hulin, *Nature*, 2001, **410**, 65.
8. F. Raksi, K. R. Wilson, J. Zhimig, A. Ikhlef, C. Y. Cote and J. C. Kieffer, *J. Chem. Phys.*, 1996, **104**, 6066.
9. M. Bauer, C. Lei, K. Read, T. R. Tobey, J. Gland, M. M. Murnane and H. C. Kapteyn, *Phys. Rev. Lett.*, 2001, **87**, 25 501.
10. J. C. Williamson, C. Jianming, I. Hyotcherl, H. Frey and A. H. Zewail, *Nature*, 1997, **386**, 159.
11. H. Ihee, V. A. Lobastov, U. M. Gomez, B. M. Goodson, R. Srinivasan, C.-Y. Ruan and A. H. Zewail, *Science*, 2001, **291**, 458.
12. C. Chudoba, E. T. J. Nibbering and T. Elsaesser, *Phys. Rev. Lett.*, 1998, **81**, 3010.
13. E. T. J. Nibbering, C. Chudoba and T. Elsaesser, *Isr. J. Chem.*, 1999, **39**, 333.
14. C. Chudoba, E. T. J. Nibbering and T. Elsaesser, *J. Phys. Chem. A*, 1999, **103**, 5625.
15. E. T. J. Nibbering and T. Elsaesser, *Appl. Phys. B*, 2000, **71**, 439.
16. E. T. J. Nibbering, F. Tschirschwitz, C. Chudoba and T. Elsaesser, *J. Phys. Chem. A*, 2000, **104**, 4236.
17. E. T. J. Nibbering and J. Dreyer, in *Femtochemistry*, ed. F. C. de Schryver, S. de Feyter and G. Schweitzer, Wiley-VCH, Weinheim, Germany, 2001, p. 345.
18. C. Chudoba, A. Kummrow, J. Dreyer, J. Stenger, E. T. J. Nibbering, T. Elsaesser and K. A. Zachariasse, *Chem. Phys. Lett.*, 1999, **309**, 357.
19. J. Dreyer and A. Kummrow, *J. Am. Chem. Soc.*, 2000, **122**, 2577.

20 A. Kummrow, J. Dreyer, C. Chudoba, J. Stenger, E. T. J. Nibbering and T. Elsaesser, *J. Chin. Chem. Soc.*, 2000, **47**, 721.
21 H. Okamoto, *J. Phys. Chem. A*, 2000, **104**, 4182.
22 W. M. Kwok, C. Ma, P. Matousek, A. W. Parker, D. Phillips, W. T. Toner and M. Towrie, *Chem. Phys. Lett.*, 2000, **322**, 395.
23 W. M. Kwok, C. Ma, D. Phillips, P. Matousek, A. W. Parker and M. Towrie, *J. Phys. Chem. A*, 2000, **104**, 4188.
24 W. M. Kwok, C. Ma, P. Matousek, A. W. Parker, D. Phillips, W. T. Toner, M. Towrie and S. Umapathy, *J. Phys. Chem. A*, 2001, **105**, 984.
25 J. Stenger, D. Madsen, J. Dreyer, E. T. J. Nibbering, P. Hamm and T. Elsaesser, *J. Phys. Chem. A*, 2001, **105**, 2929.
26 D. Madsen, J. Stenger, J. Dreyer, E. T. J. Nibbering, P. Hamm and T. Elsaesser, *Chem. Phys. Lett.*, 2001, **341**, 56.
27 P. Hamm and R. M. Hochstrasser, in *Ultrafast Infrared and Raman spectroscopy*, ed. M. D. Fayer, Marcel Dekker, New York, 2001, p. 273.
28 P. Hamm, M. Lim, W. F. DeGrado and R. M. Hochstrasser, *J. Chem. Phys.*, 2000, **112**, 1907.
29 S. Woutersen and P. Hamm, *J. Chem. Phys.*, 2001, **114**, 2727.
30 S. Woutersen and P. Hamm, *J. Chem. Phys.*, 2001, **115**, 7737.
31 M. T. Zanni, S. Gnanakaran, J. Stenger and R. M. Hochstrasser, *J. Phys. Chem. B*, 2001, **105**, 6520.
32 S. Woutersen, Y. Mu, G. Stock and P. Hamm, *Proc. Natl. Acad. Sci. USA*, 2001, **98**, 11 254.
33 M. T. Zanni, N.-H. Ge, Y. S. Kim and R. M. Hochstrasser, *Proc. Natl. Acad. Sci. USA*, 2001, **98**, 11 265.
34 M. T. Zanni, M. C. Asplund and R. M. Hochstrasser, *J. Chem. Phys.*, 2001, **114**, 4579.
35 S. Woutersen, Y. Mu, G. Stock and P. Hamm, *Chem. Phys.*, 2001, **266**, 137.
36 O. Golonzka, M. Khalil, N. Demirdoven and A. Tokmakoff, *J. Chem. Phys.*, 2001, **115**, 10 814.
37 N. Demirdöven, M. Khalil, O. Golonzka and A. Tokmakoff, *J. Phys. Chem. A*, 2001, **105**, 8025.
38 R. Pomès and B. Roux, *J. Phys. Chem.*, 1996, **100**, 2519.
39 M. E. Tuckerman, D. Marx, M. L. Klein and M. Parrinello, *Science*, 1997, **275**, 179.
40 P. L. Geissler, C. Dellago, D. Chandler, J. Hutter and M. Parrinello, *Science*, 2001, **291**, 2121.
41 R. A. Mathies, S. W. Lin, J. B. Ames and W. T. Pollard, *Annu. Rev. Biophys. Biophys. Chem.*, 1991, **20**, 491.
42 D. Borgis and J. T. Hynes, *J. Chem. Phys.*, 1991, **94**, 3619.
43 D. Borgis and J. T. Hynes, *Chem. Phys.*, 1993, **170**, 315.
44 D. Hadži and S. Bratos, in *The Hydrogen Bond: Recent Developments in Theory and Experiments*, ed. P. Schuster, G. Zundel, and C. Sandorfy, North Holland, Amsterdam, 1976, vol. II, p. 565.
45 S. Woutersen, U. Emmerichs and H. J. Bakker, *Science*, 1997, **278**, 658.
46 S. Woutersen, U. Emmerichs, H.-K. Nienhuys and H. J. Bakker, *Phys. Rev. Lett.*, 1998, **81**, 1106.
47 H. K. Nienhuys, S. Woutersen, R. A. van Santen and H. J. Bakker, *J. Chem. Phys.*, 1999, **111**, 1494.
48 G. M. Gale, G. Gallot and N. Lascoux, *Chem. Phys. Lett.*, 1999, **311**, 123.
49 J. Stenger, D. Madsen, P. Hamm, E. T. J. Nibbering and T. Elsaesser, *Phys. Rev. Lett.*, 2001, **87**, 27 401.
50 J. Stenger, D. Madsen, P. Hamm, E. T. J. Nibbering and T. Elsaesser, *J. Phys. Chem. A*, 2002, **106**, 2341.
51 R. Laenen, C. Rauscher and A. Laubereau, *Chem. Phys. Lett.*, 1998, **283**, 7.
52 L. K. Iwaki and D. D. Dlott, *J. Phys. Chem. A*, 2000, **104**, 9101.
53 J. C. Deak, S. T. Rhea, L. K. Iwaki and D. D. Dlott, *J. Phys. Chem. A*, 2000, **104**, 4866.
54 L. K. Iwaki and D. D. Dlott, *Chem. Phys. Lett.*, 2000, **321**, 419.
55 S. Woutersen and H. J. Bakker, *Nature*, 1999, **402**, 507.
56 R. Laenen, C. Rauscher and A. Laubereau, *Phys. Rev. Lett.*, 1998, **80**, 2622.
57 R. Laenen, C. Rauscher and A. Laubereau, *J. Phys. Chem. B*, 1998, **102**, 9304.
58 G. M. Gale, G. Gallot, F. Hache, N. Lascoux, S. Bratos and J. C. Leicknam, *Phys. Rev. Lett.*, 1999, **82**, 1068.
59 S. Woutersen and H. J. Bakker, *Phys. Rev. Lett.*, 1999, **83**, 2077.
60 S. Bratos, G. M. Gale, G. Gallot, F. Hache, N. Lascoux and J. C. Leicknam, *Phys. Rev. E*, 2000, **61**, 5211.
61 G. Gallot, N. Lascoux, G. M. Gale, J. Leicknam, S. Bratos and S. Pommeret, *Chem. Phys. Lett.*, 2001, **341**, 535.
62 A. J. Lock, S. Woutersen and H. J. Bakker, *J. Phys. Chem. A*, 2001, **105**, 1238.
63 H. K. Nienhuys, R. A. van Santen and H. J. Bakker, *J. Chem. Phys.*, 2000, **112**, 8487.
64 H. J. Bakker, S. Woutersen and H. K. Nienhuys, *Chem. Phys.*, 2000, **258**, 233.
65 *Proton-transfer Reactions*, ed. E. Caldin and V. Gold, Chapman and Hall, London, 1975.
66 A. Weller, *Die Naturwissenschaften*, 1955, **42**, 175.
67 A. Weller, *Progr. React. Kinet.*, 1961, **1**, 187.
68 M. Eigen, *Angew. Chem. Int. Ed. Engl.*, 1964, **3**, 1.
69 E. Vander Donckt, *Progr. React. Kinet.*, 1970, **5**, 273.
70 W. Klöpffer, *Adv. Photochem.*, 1977, **10**, 311.
71 M. Kasha, *J. Chem. Soc., Faraday Trans. 2*, 1986, **82**, 2379.
72 E. M. Kosower and D. Huppert, *Annu. Rev. Phys. Chem.*, 1986, **37**, 127.
73 E. Pines, B. Z. Magnes, M. J. Lang and G. R. Fleming, *Chem. Phys. Lett.*, 1997, **281**, 413.

74　D. Huppert, L. M. Tolbert and S. Linares-Samaniego, *J. Phys. Chem. A*, 1997, **101**, 4602.
75　L. Genosar, B. Cohen and D. Huppert, *J. Phys. Chem. A*, 2000, **104**, 6689.
76　T. H. Tran-Thi, T. Gustavsson, C. Prayer, S. Pommeret and J. T. Hynes, *Chem. Phys. Lett.*, 2000, **329**, 421.
77　P. F. Barbara, L. E. Brus and P. M. Rentzepis, *J. Am. Chem. Soc.*, 1980, **102**, 5631.
78　K. Ding, S. J. Courtney, A. J. Strandjord, S. Flom, D. Friedrich and P. F. Barbara, *J. Phys. Chem.*, 1983, **87**, 1184.
79　S. R. Flom and P. F. Barbara, *Chem. Phys. Lett.*, 1983, **94**, 488.
80　D. B. O'Connor, G. W. Scott, D. R. Coulter, A. Gupta, S. P. Webb, S. W. Yeh and J. H. Clark, *Chem. Phys. Lett.*, 1985, **121**, 417.
81　M. Lee, J. T. Yardley and R. M. Hochstrasser, *J. Phys. Chem.*, 1987, **91**, 4621.
82　F. Laermer, T. Elsaesser and W. Kaiser, *Chem. Phys. Lett.*, 1988, **148**, 119.
83　W. Frey, F. Laermer and T. Elsaesser, *J. Phys. Chem.*, 1991, **95**, 10 391.
84　B. J. Schwartz, L. A. Peteanu and C. B. Harris, *J. Phys. Chem.*, 1992, **96**, 3591.
85　T. Elsaesser, in *Femtosecond Chemistry*, ed. J. Manz and L. Wöste, Wiley-VCH, Weinheim, Germany, 1995, vol. 2, p. 563.
86　T. Fiebig, M. Chachisvilis, M. Manger, A. H. Zewail, A. Douhal, I. Garcia-Ochoa and A. de La Hoz Ayuso, *J. Phys. Chem. A*, 1999, **103**, 7419.
87　S. Ameer-Beg, S. M. Ormson, R. G. Brown, P. Matousek, M. Towrie, E. T. J. Nibbering, P. Foggi and F. V. R. Neuwahl, *J. Phys. Chem. A*, 2001, **105**, 3709.
88　C. Chudoba, E. Riedle, M. Pfeiffer and T. Elsaesser, *Chem. Phys. Lett.*, 1996, **263**, 622.
89　M. Pfeiffer, K. Lenz, A. Lau, T. Elsaesser and T. Steinke, *J. Raman Spectrosc.*, 1997, **28**, 61.
90　T. Elsaesser and W. Kaiser, *Chem. Phys. Lett.*, 1986, **128**, 231.
91　S. Lochbrunner, A. J. Wurzer and E. Riedle, *J. Chem. Phys.*, 2000, **112**, 10 699.
92　A. J. Wurzer, S. Lochbrunner and E. Riedle, *Appl. Phys. B*, 2000, **71**, 405.
93　A. Kummrow, M. Wittmann, F. Tschirschwitz, G. Korn and E. T. J. Nibbering, *Appl. Phys. B*, 2000, **71**, 885.
94　P. Hamm, R. A. Kaindl and J. Stenger, *Opt. Lett.*, 2000, **25**, 1798.
95　K. Wynne and R. M. Hochstrasser, *Chem. Phys.*, 1995, **193**, 211.
96　P. Hamm, *Chem. Phys.*, 1995, **200**, 415.
97　E. E. Nikitin, C. Noda and R. N. Zare, *J. Chem. Phys.*, 1993, **98**, 46.
98　K. Iwata and H. Hamaguchi, *J. Phys. Chem. A*, 1997, **101**, 632.
99　P. Hamm, S. M. Ohline and W. Zinth, *J. Chem. Phys.*, 1997, **106**, 519.
100　P.-T. Chou, S. L. Studer and M. L. Martinez, *Chem. Phys. Lett.*, 1991, **178**, 393.
101　M. A. Ríos and M. C. Ríos, *J. Phys. Chem. A*, 1998, **102**, 1560.
102　A. Laubereau and W. Kaiser, *Rev. Mod. Phys.*, 1976, **50**, 607.
103　A. Seilmeier and W. Kaiser, in *Ultrashort Laser Pulses. Generation and Applications*, ed. W. Kaiser, Springer, Berlin, 2nd edn., 1993, p. 279.
104　T. Elsaesser and W. Kaiser, *Annu. Rev. Phys. Chem.*, 1991, **42**, 83.
105　J. C. Owrutsky, D. Raftery and R. M. Hochstrasser, *Annu. Rev. Phys. Chem.*, 1994, **45**, 519.
106　S. Hogiu, W. Werncke, M. Pfeiffer and T. Elsaesser, *Chem. Phys. Lett.*, 1999, **312**, 407.
107　S. Hogiu, W. Werncke, M. Pfeiffer, J. Dreyer and T. Elsaesser, *J. Chem. Phys.*, 2000, **113**, 1587.
108　A. P. Shkurinov, N. I. Koroteev, G. Jonusauskas and C. Rulliere, *Chem. Phys. Lett.*, 1994, **223**, 573.
109　A. Vierheilig, T. Chen, P. Waltner, W. Kiefer, A. Materny and A. H. Zewail, *Chem. Phys. Lett.*, 1999, **312**, 349.
110　M. Pfeiffer, K. Lenz, A. Lau and T. Elsaesser, *J. Raman Spectrosc.*, 1995, **26**, 607.
111　M. J. Rosker, F. W. Wise and C. L. Tang, *Phys. Rev. Lett.*, 1986, **57**, 321.
112　S. Ruhman, A. G. Joly and K. A. Nelson, *J. Chem. Phys.*, 1987, **86**, 6563.
113　Y.-X. Yan and K. A. Nelson, *J. Chem. Phys.*, 1987, **87**, 6240.
114　Y.-X. Yan and K. A. Nelson, *J. Chem. Phys.*, 1987, **87**, 6257.
115　H. L. Fragnito, J. Y. Bigot, P. C. Becker and C. V. Shank, *Chem. Phys. Lett.*, 1989, **160**, 101.
116　W. T. Pollard and R. A. Mathies, *Annu. Rev. Phys. Chem.*, 1992, **43**, 497.
117　M. H. Vos, F. Rappaport, J.-C. Lambry, J. Breton and J.-L. Martin, *Nature*, 1993, **363**, 320.
118　T. S. Yang, M. S. Chang, R. Chang, M. Hayashi, S. H. Lin, P. Vohringer, W. Dietz and N. F. Scherer, *J. Chem. Phys.*, 1999, **110**, 12 070.
119　R. M. Bowman, M. Dantus and A. H. Zewail, *Chem. Phys. Lett.*, 1989, **156**, 131.
120　U. Banin, A. Waldman and S. Ruhman, *J. Chem. Phys.*, 1992, **96**, 2416.
121　N. Pugliano, D. K. Palit, A. Z. Szarka and R. M. Hochstrasser, *J. Chem. Phys.*, 1993, **99**, 7273.
122　Q. Wang, R. W. Schoenlein, L. A. Peteanu, R. A. Mathies and C. V. Shank, *Science*, 1994, **266**, 422.
123　T. Kuhne and P. Vöhringer, *J. Phys. Chem. A*, 1998, **102**, 4177.

What we can learn about fast chemical processes from slow diffraction experiments

Hans-Beat Bürgi

Laboratory of Crystallography, University of Berne, Freiestr. 3, CH-3012, Berne, Switzerland. E-mail: hans-beat.buergi@krist.unibe.ch

Received 13th February 2002, Accepted 13th March 2002
First published as an Advance Article on the web 24th July 2002

The potential energy surface is an important determinant of a chemical reaction. Three ways of deducing non-trivial properties of such surfaces from the results of crystal structure analyses are discussed and illustrated with examples. (1) The mapping approach brings together structures of the same molecular fragment from different environments to outline reaction coordinates and vibrations. (2) Correlations between molecular structures and activation energies for a given reaction type reveal general and quantitative relations between seemingly independent entities such as ground state structure, force constants, reaction path length, activation energy and catalysis. (3) The evolution of atomic mean square amplitudes (displacement parameters) with temperature uncovers frequencies and atomic displacement patterns of large-amplitude vibrations in molecular crystals. Examples include the vibrations of molecular zeolite building blocks, the crankshaft motion of stilbenes, the dynamic coupling between pyramidal deformation of the amide NH_2 group and hydrogen bonding, the bowl inversion of corannulenes and nucleophilic addition/elimination reactions.

1. Introduction

At first sight the title of this article implies a contradiction: what does a diffraction-experiment lasting kiloseconds reveal about the transformation of a molecule happening within femtoseconds? Physicists and chemists are proficient in resolving such apparent contradictions, because they are capable of drawing far-reaching conclusions from relatively simple experiments. A pertinent example is transition state theory. In the mid 1930s Eyring and, independently, Evans and Polanyi expressed Arrhenius' empirical relation between reaction rate constant and temperature, $k(T) = A\exp(-E_a/RT)$, in terms of a potential energy surface and statistical mechanics, $k(T) = (k_B T/h)(Q^\ddagger/Q_A Q_B) \exp(-E_0/k_B T)$. The theory made it possible to relate the rate constants measurable in those days (milliseconds) to the much higher frequency for the passage of a molecule through the transition structure (~200 fs at room temperature, corresponding to $k_B T/h \sim 10^{12}$ s^{-1}).[1] In this contribution the structural aspects of chemical reaction path and molecular vibrations are studied with a combination of two tools: the traditional, slow variety of crystal structure analysis and the well-known theoretical concepts underlying fast molecular processes. A spectroscopist has succinctly summarized the goal of such efforts: 'short-time dynamics from long-time experiments'.[2]

Of course, not even the most far-reaching conclusions can anticipate all the results to be gained from more and more sophisticated experiments. Given order-of-magnitude improvements in experimental technology, *e.g.* ever shorter laser pulses and more intense synchrotron radiation, exciting discoveries and marvellous surprises follow. In comparison, conventional experiments convey much less of the sense of adventure and excitement and fewer surprises than an expedition into the uncharted land of time-resolved chemistry; they are, nevertheless, the firm point of departure for such journeys. As we hope to demonstrate, the old fashioned approaches have contributed significantly to the understanding of chemical reactivity and thus to one of the topics of this discussion: 'from structure to function'.

2. A few basics

2.1 Structure–energy diagrams

Many aspects of chemical reactivity and molecular motion are conveniently summarized with the help of potential energy surfaces (PES). Fig. 1 shows a highly simplified version of a PES, the prototypical diagram familiar to chemists. To be useful in practice the schematic picture needs embellishment: the nature and sequence of intermediates and transition states must be characterized, the corresponding energies given explicitly and the generalized reaction coordinate elaborated. We will consider two kinds of fast processes on such surfaces: (1) molecules move between minima by transiting one or more saddle points of the PES, $i.e.$ they undergo a chemical reactions and (2) molecules move within a single minimum, $i.e.$ they vibrate.

Here the focus is on structure, $i.e.$ on the nature of reaction coordinates. They are usually much more complex than suggested by the single dimension in Fig. 1. The chemical process determines their characteristic major components, $e.g.$ one or two bond distances in a bond-breaking bond-making reaction, or torsion angles in a conformational interconversion. The main components tend to be the same along the entire path, but are accompanied by adjustments of other distances and angles whose nature and importance may well differ at different points along the path. The 'reaction coordinate' of a vibration usually involves changes in several distances or angles, which together form the atomic displacement pattern corresponding to a 'normal coordinate'. The nature of reaction coordinates may be determined indirectly through detailed interpretations of extensive spectroscopic experiments,[1] or directly from quantum chemical modelling. In the subsequent discussion we show how crystal structure analysis complements these techniques.

Reaction energies are most easily obtained from other than diffraction experiments, $e.g.$ from equilibrium constants or from thermodynamic quantities. Activation energies follow from the temperature dependence of kinetic constants. Energies of vibrations and force constants are best

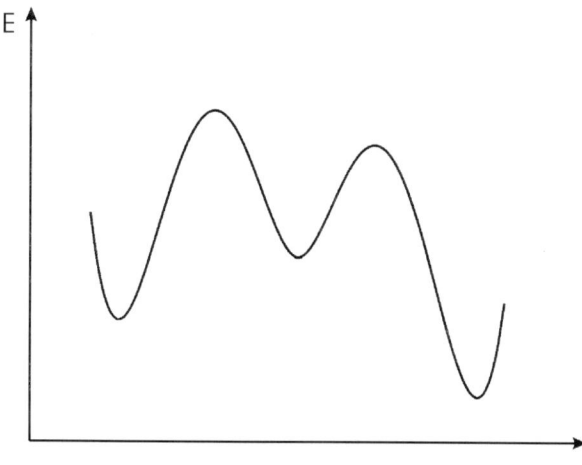

Fig. 1 Structure–energy diagram showing stable starting, intermediate and product states, as well as two transition states of a chemical reaction. The energy coordinate is generic and stands for potential energy, enthalpy or free energy. The reaction coordinate is a one-dimensional rendering of a curve on a multi-dimensional potential energy surface.

obtained from infrared and Raman spectroscopy or from inelastic neutron scattering. However, as will be shown below, diffraction experiments at different temperatures are an alternative source of information on equilibria between different molecular states and on low frequency, large amplitude vibrations.

2.2 Time and space averaging in crystal structure analysis, physical significance of results

The structure of a unit cell determined from a Bragg diffraction experiment represents the average over space and time of all unit cells in the crystal. Both types of averaging have consequences, either on the way an experiment is performed or on its interpretation. In order to get a representative space averaged structure, diffraction experiments must be conducted on the same volume element of a crystal or, preferably, on its entire volume, unless there is evidence or good reason to assume that the crystal is homogeneous throughout.[3] Time averaging encompasses all structures connected by processes faster than typical exposure times. Note that first order reactions with activation energies as high as ~ 14 kcal mol^{-1} are still fast on this time scale because their rate constants at room temperature are ~ 10 s^{-1}, about an order of magnitude faster than conventional exposure times.

Refined atomic coordinates represent mean atomic positions. In well-ordered structures they are usually a good approximation to the equilibrium positions of atoms. At higher temperatures they need to be corrected for effects of thermal motion.[4] Likewise mean positions, especially of light atoms, are affected by anharmonic vibrations.[5] Atomic displacement parameters (ADPs) represent mean-square displacements and are an expression of harmonic thermal motion. Coordinates and ADPs from disordered structures are more difficult to interpret. If an atom is distributed over several positions less than the atomic diameter apart, these positions must be determined indirectly from an interpretation of a mean position and the associated ADPs, which include contributions from thermal motion and positional disorder.[6] If the distance between the positions of a disordered atom exceeds its size, the separate atomic positions are associated with an additional parameter, a site occupation factor.

3. What can we learn about fast chemical processes from single crystal diffraction experiments? An overview

To the extent to which chemistry can be pictured as taking place on PESs, the title question may be answered at three different levels: (1) conventional crystal structure investigations provide many qualitative and quantitative features of PESs. The structures themselves define the start and end points of reaction coordinates. Structure comparisons and experiments at different temperatures reveal less trivial aspects of PESs such as reaction coordinates and vibrational coordinates. (2) The new time-resolved experiments allow one to study the kinetics of fast solid-state processes. More importantly, they give access to crystal structures of short-lived intermediates. Such evidence complements mechanistic studies, which become less dependent on indirect reasoning based on solution experiments. This topic is not developed further, as it is the main theme of most other contributions to this discussion. (3) Molecular dynamics in crystals cannot be followed yet with crystallographic diffraction experiments. There are two main reasons: first, even the fastest, state-of-the-art diffraction experiments on crystals are still too slow (hundreds of ps) to photograph moving molecules at arbitrary points of a reaction coordinate, and, second, the problem of producing a large enough, sufficiently long lived ensemble of molecules moving coherently is not yet solved.

The next two sections give a general introduction into two approaches for deriving properties of PES from crystal structure data. They are summarized in Table 1. Applications to specific problems, chemical reactions and molecular vibrations, will be discussed in sections 4–6.

3.1 The mapping approach

This approach is based on the profoundly chemical notion according to which molecules and even molecular fragments can be distinguished and separated, at least conceptually, from their environment consisting of nearest neighbours or substituents or both. The hypothesis underlying the

Table 1 Inferring features of potential energy surfaces from crystal structure data. (The letters and numbers in brackets indicate the type of crystallographic data used and the sections in which pertinent examples are given)

Single-minimum potential (Vibrations)	Single structures (S) or series of structures (SS) (the same molecular fragment in different environments, from structural data bases)	Temperature evolution of ADPs and occupation factors (T). Structures combined with activation energies (E)
	Mapping deformation patterns of molecular vibrations (SS, 4.1)	Frequencies, force constants and atomic displacement patterns of large-amplitude vibrations (T, 6.1–6.4)
Multiple-minimum potential (Chemical reactions)	Ground state structures (S)	Estimates of transition state structures (E, 5)
Bond breaking–bond making reactions, conformational interconversions, *etc.*	Mapping reaction coordinates (SS, 4.2)	Structure–reactivity correlations (E, 5)
Multiple molecular states present in the same crystal (disordered structures)	Resolution of structures of different molecular states (S), (*e.g.* ground and excited state)	Estimating energy differences between different molecular states from occupancy (T, 6.5)

mapping approach presumes that the general appearance of a PES is characteristic of the fragment and largely independent of environment. Changes in environment may slightly perturb the positions of the stationary points and the details of the pathways connecting them, but leave their topology unaffected.

In practice the approach requires one to search structural databases for a fragment structure in as many different environments as possible.[7] The structures are analysed for gradual distortions, *i.e.* for correlations between the distances and angles of interest. If a correlation can be found, the various molecular or fragment structures are considered to constitute a series of 'frozen-in' points, or snapshots, taken along a reaction pathway, which, when viewed in correct order, yield a cinematic film of the reaction (principle of structure–structure correlation, section 4.2).[8,9] The same approach applies to molecular vibrations (section 4.1). Intermolecular perturbations, as found in different polymorphs or solvate structures, tend to be weak and move the fragment structure within the low lying parts of its PES. Intramolecular perturbations, as induced by different substituents, are generally stronger and give access to higher lying portions of a PES.

Although the energetic suppositions of the mapping approach are usually not assessed in detail, they can be tested in specific cases by combining structural data with activation energies, normally taken from kinetic experiments in solution. Correlations between structures and energies of related molecules undergoing the same reaction have shown that the respective energy profiles are indeed related by simple, continuous energy perturbations (principle of structure–energy correlation).[9] As a bonus, such correlations allow estimates of transition state structures (section 5). Various applications of the mapping approach excluding and including energy have been summarized in several reviews and a two volume book.[9–11]

3.2 Temperature evolution of ADPs, occupation factors and atomic coordinates

Thermal motion implies departure of an atom from its mean position. Displacements increase with increasing temperature. It follows that ADPs measure molecular deformation energies thus probing the PES. However, interpretations of ADPs from a single diffraction experiment in dynamic terms are subjected to severe limitations: ADPs say nothing about the correlation of motion between atoms, and dynamic contributions to ADPs cannot be distinguished from static ones. If it can be assumed that a molecule in a crystal is moving in an ordered averaged environment, energies and deformation patterns of low energy vibration modes may be derived from the temperature evolution of ADPs (sections 6.1–6.4).[6,12] Such studies are complementary to vibrational spectroscopy because the atomic displacements are investigated directly rather than deduced indirectly from vibrational energies and isotope effects on these energies.[13]

Occupation factors measure the mole fractions associated with different atomic positions, molecular orientations, molecular states, *etc.*, in disordered structures (called A and B below). In many cases occupancy (or concentration) depends on temperature and may even obey the equilibrium condition $\Delta G = -RT\ln\{[A]/[B]\}$, thus providing a measure of the energy difference between different minima of a PES. If the dependence is more complicated, intermolecular cooperative effects are indicated and the simple picture, according to which a molecule acts in an averaged environment, must be modified (section 6.5).

4. Inferences from static structures

In this section the mapping approach is illustrated. Deformed molecular structures are related to vibrational motion (section 4.1), and unusual interatomic distances to chemical reactions in which bonds are made and broken (section 4.2).

4.1 Vibrations of molecular zeolite fragments

Spherosilasesquioxanes are a family of oligomers built from tetrahedral $RSiO_{3/2}$ fragments with variable organic substituent (H, CH_3, C_6H_5, *etc.*). The Si-atoms form a closed polyhedron: a cube with symmetry O_h in the case of the octamer, a pentagonal prism with symmetry D_{5h} in the case of the decamer (Fig. 2) and a closed arrangement of four five-membered and four four-membered rings with approximate D_{2d} symmetry in the case of the dodecamer. Oxygen atoms bridge the edges

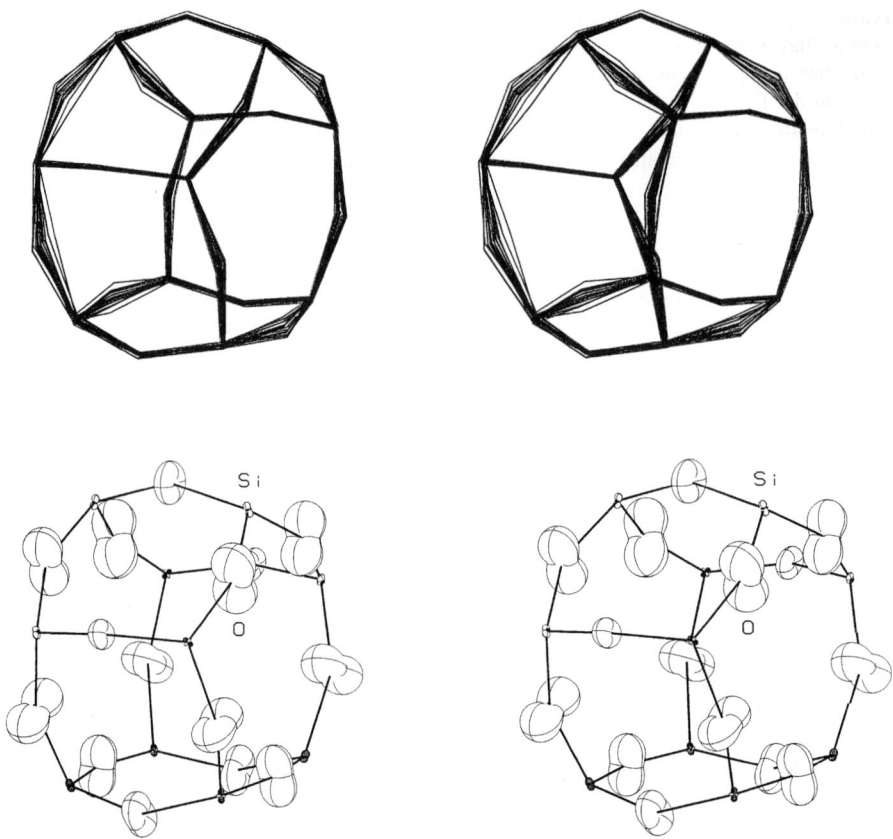

Fig. 2 Top: a least-squares superposition of the Si atoms of 10, 10 and 20 isometric images of $H_{10}Si_{10}O_{15}$ (180 and 295 K) and of $(CH_3)_{10}Si_{10}O_{15}$, respectively. Bottom: difference root-mean-square displacement surfaces for $H_{10}Si_{10}O_{15}$ (180 K, {ADP(obs)−ADP(rigid body, Si-atoms only)}$^{1/2}$, scale factor 3.08, solid outlines: positive differences, dotted outlines: negative differences[17]).

of the polyhedra. The $RSiO_3$ tetrahedra are quite rigid. In contrast, the Si–O–Si fragments connecting them behave like freely moving ball joints and convey a high degree of flexibility to these molecules, which are easily deformed in the crystal lattice by intermolecular, non-bonded interactions. The actual symmetry of $H_{10}Si_{10}O_{15}$ in its crystal structures at 180 and 295 K is C_2, that of $(CH_3)_{10}Si_{10}O_{15}$ is only C_1. Because the groups D_{5h}, C_2 and C_1 comprise 20,2 and 1 symmetry operations, respectively, it follows that there are 10 energetically equivalent (or isometric) ways to deform the former, and 20 ways to deform the latter. Fig. 2 (top) shows a least-squares superposition of the Si-atoms of the sets of 10, 10 and 20 isometric structures, 40 in all. Whereas the Si-atoms superimpose well, the O-atoms on the prism edges show some scatter and the O-atoms on the pentagon edges are spread even more. The distributions of the oxygen atoms indicate the degree of distortion. In order to compare these distributions to the atomic displacements associated with the actual vibrations, we have analysed the ADPs. Molecular translation and libration amplitudes have been determined from the ADPs of the Si-atoms [4] and subtracted from the observed ADPs of all atoms. The differences are shown at the bottom of Fig. 2. Residual atomic displacements are very small on the Si-atoms and much larger on the O-atoms, in agreement with the picture gained from static deformations. Note the semi-quantitative agreement between the two pictures. The scatter of the O-atoms corresponds to their residual mean square amplitudes: both quantities are smaller for the five O-atoms on the prism edges than for the remaining ten O-atoms. A more detailed picture of the deformations is obtained from a principal component analysis, which reveals individual deformation modes and their contributions to the total deformation.[14] Analogous observations apply to the octamer and the dodecamer.[15] The flexibility of spherosilasesquioxanes is germane to that of zeolites. Deformations of these infinite framework structures that are important for their chemical properties are well described in terms of a 'rigid unit mode' model.[16] Quite generally, molecules and fragments with low frequency vibrations tend to show noticeable structural differences when in different environments.

4.2 Bond breaking and bond making

Bond lengths are separated from van der Waals contacts by a window of distances considered 'forbidden' in the context of ground-state structures. From a structural point of view bond making implies the continuous shortening of a van der Waals distance into a covalent contact, bond breaking implies the reverse process and both instances require transit through the energetically unfavourable window which for first and second row non-metal atoms is ~1.6 Å wide.[18] Crystal structures with distances in the 'forbidden' window may be the result of inadequate experimentation or, more interestingly, they may show rare and very unusual structural motifs of chemical significance. For example, contacts between atoms with complementary electron donating and accepting properties are sometimes substantially shorter than the van der Waals limit and their lengths reflect the strength of donor–acceptor interactions, as has been recognized more than thirty years ago.[19] The plasticity of van der Waals interactions invites application of the mapping approach illustrated above for deformations of bond angles and torsion angles to describe bond making and breaking. To our knowledge the earliest application of the mapping approach was to the formation of I_3^- from I_2 and I^-, to the reverse breakdown[19] and to the interchange of ligands in four-coordinate Cd^{+2}-complexes.[20] In both cases the changes in the structures are reminiscent of those occurring during an S_N2 reaction at carbon with inversion of configuration.

The best-known example of a mapping is probably the nucleophilic addition of an amine nitrogen to a carbonyl carbon atom of a ketone. This path was first mapped in 1973 on the basis of 6 crystal structures.[21] By now there are 97 entries in the Cambridge structural database pertaining to N···C=O interactions (CSD, version 5.22, October 2001).[7] Their N···C distances cover the range 3 to 1.7 Å, almost the entire window between van der Waals and covalent distances (3 to 1.45 Å). With decreasing N···C distance the carbon atom becomes increasingly pyramidal and the angle N···C=O covers a decreasing range, converging to a value between 100 and 110° (Fig. 3, top). The fragment structures provide an almost complete picture of the main changes of distances and angles along the pathway. This picture has not changed since 1973. What has changed in the meantime is the total number of entries in the CSD; it has increased from 15 000 to 250 000! This heap of information has stimulated a broad search for N···C=O and O···C=O interactions in ketones, carboxylic acid and amide fragments.

Apart from two outliers, the N···C contacts to carboxylic acid fragments cover a less broad range than those to ketones (Fig. 3, middle). The shortest distances are 2.6 Å, distinctly longer than for ketones, but still significantly below the van der Waals limit. The carbon atoms show a slight pyramidalization, mostly towards the nitrogen atom, and the N···C=O angles converge from a 30–40° range at 3 Å towards 100° at 2.6 Å. The N···C contacts to amides are yet somewhat longer and the pyramidal deformation of C is less pronounced and not always towards the N atom (Fig. 3, bottom). The smaller and especially the negative values of pyramidal deformation found in all classes of contacts, are not necessarily related to the donor–acceptor interactions, but may be intramolecular in origin.[22] The O···C=O contacts in ketones, carboxylic acid and amide fragments show a similar picture (Fig. 4). They tend to be shorter for ketones and carboxylic acid fragments than for amide fragments. Pyramidal distortions are most pronounced for ketones, intermediate for carboxylic acid fragments and smallest for amide fragments, but always predominantly towards the nucleophilic O atom. O···C=O angles cover a range of ~70° for the largest contacts and converge to ~100° at the shortest distances. Whereas individual points in these distributions may be considered as incipient or even advanced stages of nucleophilic addition reactions, the scatter plots as a whole reflect the electrophilicity and thus the relative reactivity of the respective carbonyl compounds: carboxylic acids, esters and anhydrides with their O–C=O-fragments are known to be more reactive than amides with their N–C=O-fragments.

It is interesting to note that O···C=O interactions are much more numerous than N···C=O interactions (~1100, 4000 and 1200 vs. ~80, 100 and 110 for ketones, O–C=O– and N–C=O–

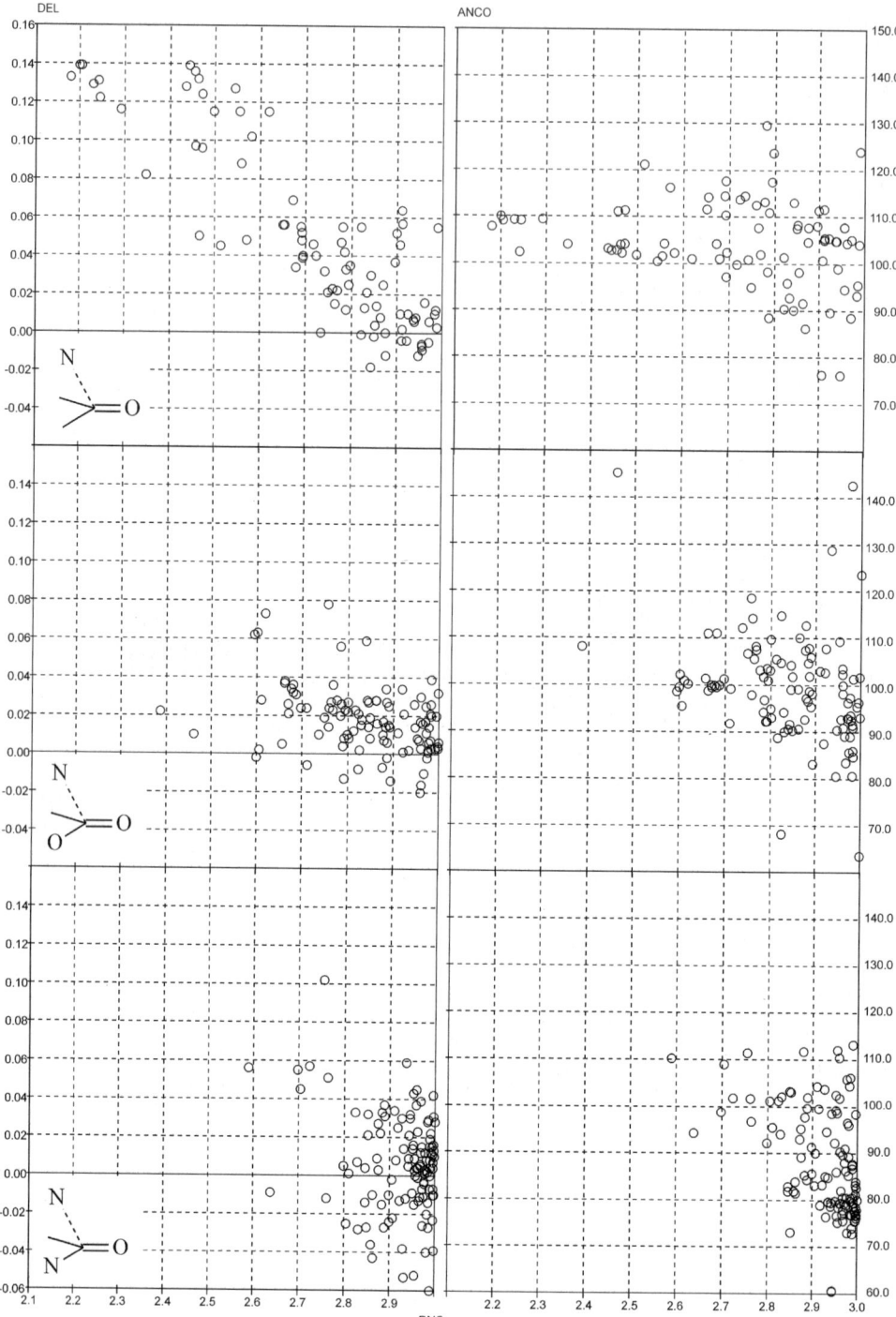

Fig. 3 Scatter-plots of N···C=O distances DNC vs. N···C=O angles ANCO and pyramidal deformations DEL of carbonyl carbon in ketones (top), carboxylic acids, esters and anhydrides (middle) and amides (bottom). Two points well beyond the range of the top two figures have been excluded: CLIVOR10 with 1.993 Å, 0.213 Å, 110.2°, and GICPAJ with 1.713 Å, 0.289 Å, 110.4° (CSD, version 5.22, October 2001, search criteria: DNC < 3 Å, R < 10%, no disorder, error free).

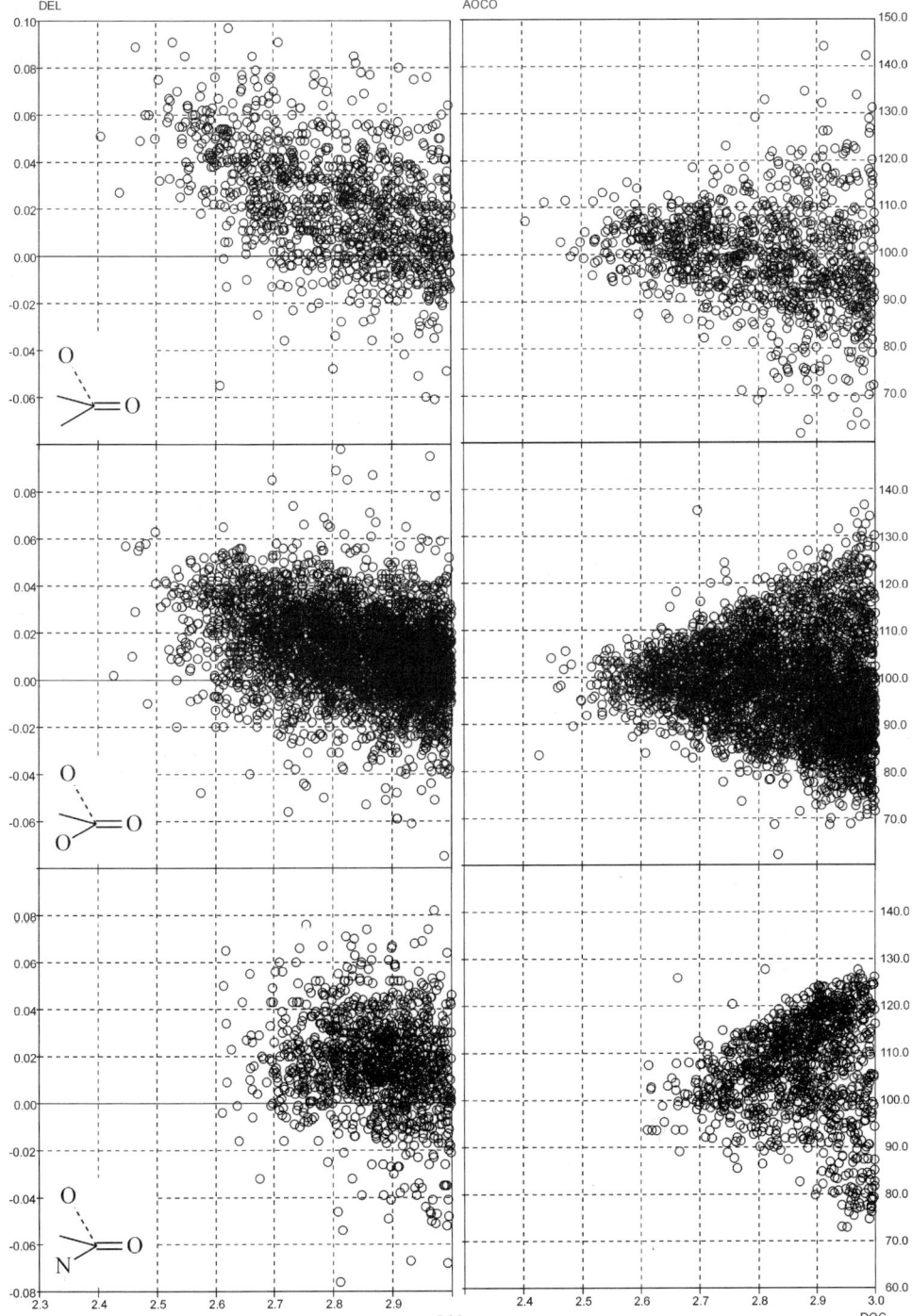

Fig. 4 Scatter-plots of O···C=O distances DOC *vs.* O···C=O angles AOCO and pyramidal deformations DEL of carbonyl carbon in ketones (top), carboxylic acids, esters and anhydrides (middle) and amides (bottom). (CSD, version 5.22, October 2001, search criteria: DOC < 3 Å, R < 10%, no disorder, error free).

fragments, respectively; CSD, version 5.22, October 2001). Given the large numbers of O···C=O contacts, these data sets will have to be broken down into chemical classes of nucleophiles and electrophiles to produce a more refined picture of group reactivities. In a study along these lines the donor–acceptor interactions in 16 *peri*-substituted naphthalenes (**1, 2**) with OCH_3 or $N(CH_3)_2$ as nucleophiles and aldehydes, ketones, carboxylic acids, esters and amides as electrophiles have been compared.[23] The trends found are similar to those presented above, but other factors, *e.g.* the conjugation between the nucleophile and the naphthalene π-system, become apparent.

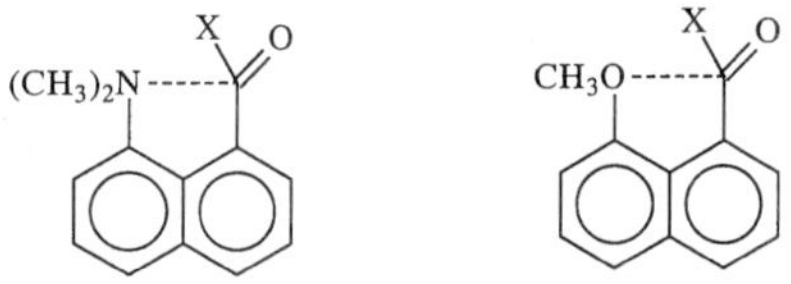

(X = H, CH_3, OCH_3, OH, $N(CH_3)_2$)

1   2

The structural basis of peptidase and esterase activity has been investigated extensively by X-ray crystallography and NMR spectroscopy. Early work on trypsin and trypsinogen complexed to several inhibitors indicated that the nucleophilic group of the enzyme, O_γ of serine-195, is at distances between 1.7 and 2.8 Å from the carbonyl carbon of the inhibitor. A pyramidal distortion of the latter has also been reported; it decreases from ~0.35 to ~0.1 Å.[24] Irrespective of these details, the relative arrangement of the nucleophiles and electrophiles are in essential agreement with the reaction paths sketched in the preceding paragraphs. In more recent work the high acyl-transferase activity between two substrate molecules in the presence of a catalytically active antibody has been studied on the basis of an NMR structure determination. Binding interactions with the antibody place the nucleophilic hydroxy group of one substrate in contact with the carbonyl group of the other. The angle of attack is between 80 and 117°, in agreement with the data given in Fig. 4.[25] Conversely, it has been argued that displacement of serine O_γ from its normal position in the active site of a proteinase B prevents nucleophilic attack on the carbonyl carbon of a complexed inhibitor.[26] As more and more very high-resolution protein structures become available, finer details of active site geometries can be measured with high precision and local deformations identified reliably. The significance of such deformations for enzymatic activity remains to be shown. In the meantime the highly accurate results from small molecule structure analyses are a rich source of information for the chemical validation of protein structures and a source of inspiration for the understanding of chemical reactions. As discussed above, both aspects need not be confined to questions of hydrogen bonding.

A real chemical reaction provides an interesting illustration of these ideas. The peptide bond linking an acylated *N*-methyl-α-aminoisobutyryl residue to the *N*-terminus of an amino acid is unusually labile towards hydrolysis (*e.g.* AcNMeAib, Scheme 1). Crystal structure analyses show a molecular conformation with intramolecular distances of ~2.6–2.7 Å between the oxygen atom of

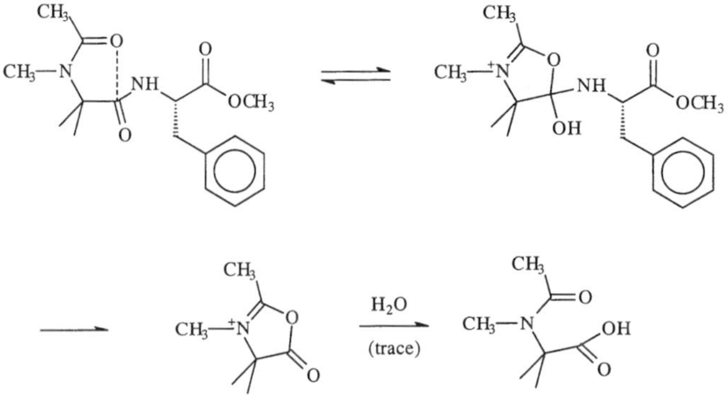

Scheme 1

the acyl group and the carbonyl carbon atom of the NMeAib residue. These distances are among the shortest observed for this type of interaction (Fig. 4, bottom). The relatively fast reaction rates confirm the idea that the structures of these compounds represent advanced stages along the reaction pathway to the tetrahedral intermediate of amide hydrolysis. Based on these observations a new, tuneable protecting group has been developed: the terminal acetate is replaced with a benzoate group whose rate of cleavage can be controlled to some extent by varying the substituents on the phenyl ring.[27]

5. Inferences from static structures combined with kinetic data, catalysis

The hypothesis underlying the mapping approach states that a chemical fragment is associated with its characteristic PES and that changes of substitution or of other aspects of the fragment environment modulate its PES without changing it fundamentally. This idea is now tested by comparing structural data of starting materials with corresponding activation energies for dissociatively activated reactions on one hand, and for conformational interconversions on the other (sections 5.1 and 5.2). Energies correlate strongly with small differences of the starting structures. The nature of the dependence allows identifying factors contributing to catalysis (section 5.3).

5.1 Acetal hydrolysis

This is the reverse of the nucleophilic addition reaction of an alkoxide anion to an $R_2C=O^+R$ cation. Activation energies for the spontaneous, unimolecular hydrolysis of tetrahydropyranylacetals **3** decrease as the scissile $C-O_1$ bond increases in length. The decrease is very pronounced, $\sim$30 kcal mol^{-1} for a bond length increase of 0.1 Å, corresponding to a change in rate constant of $\sim 10^{20}$ at room temperature.[28] A correlation between a relatively small structural change and a rate acceleration that dwarfs a good many enzymes raises the question whether or not the two observations can be traced to a common origin. They can.

R = alkyl, phenyl, acyl

3

A simple, one-dimensional structure–energy diagram together with a consideration of the stereoelectronic properties of acetals do the job, qualitatively and quantitatively. The energy profile E is expressed as a polynomial in the simplest reaction coordinate possible, the deviation $(d-d_0)$ of the $C-O_1$ bond length from its equilibrium value d_0:

$$E = k_2(d-d_0)^2/2 + k_3(d-d_0)^3$$

(Fig. 5, top). The harmonic force constant k_2 is >0, the anharmonicity k_3 is <0. Apart from the minimum at d_0 this profile has a transition state at $d_0^{\neq} = -k_2/(30k_3)$ with activation energy $E_0^{\neq} = k_2^3/(54k_3^2)$. The $C-O_1$ equilibrium distance in a given molecule depends on the nature of the substituent. Exchanging R for a better electron acceptor R′ withdraws electrons from O_1, lowers the antibonding σ^* orbital on the $C-O_1$ bond and facilitates the delocalisation of an antiplanar lone pair on O_2 into this σ^* orbital. The $C-O_2$ bond becomes shorter and the $C-O_1$ bond longer. Proceeding along the reaction path, the distance d increases and the energy of the σ^* orbital is lowered even more. The concomitant stabilization energy is again expressed in the simplest possible form, as a linear perturbation of E in $d-d_0$ with proportionality constant k_1 characterising R′ relative to R:

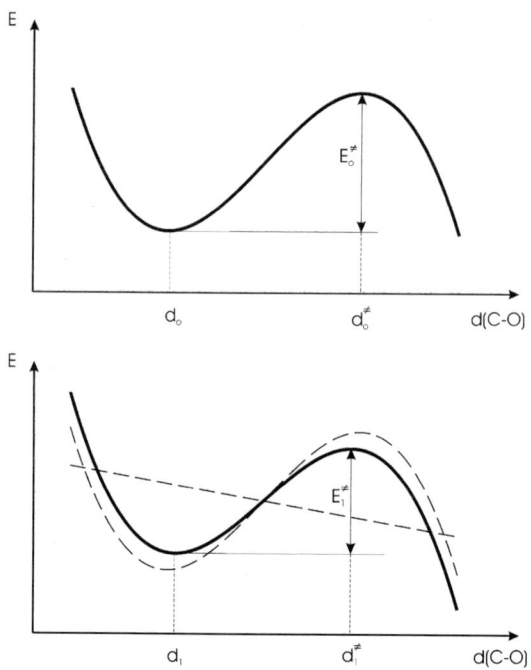

Fig. 5 Top: energy profile for breaking the C–O$_1$ bond in the spontaneous hydrolysis of acetal **3** with equilibrium structure d_0, transition state structure $d_0^{\neq}$ and activation energy $E_0^{\neq}$. Bottom: replacement of the leaving group R in **3** by a better electron acceptor R' is represented by a perturbation (dashed straight line) on the original energy profile (dashed curve). The perturbation brings the ground and transition state structures closer together, to d_1 and $d_1^{\neq}$, respectively, and reduces the activation energy to $E_1^{\neq}$ (solid curve).

$$E = k_1(d - d_0) + k_2(d - d_0)^2/2 + k_3(d - d_0)^3$$

The perturbation is shown in Fig. 5 (bottom); it moves ground and transition state structures closer together and reduces activation energy as expected from Hammond's postulate.[29] The equilibrium distance d_0 changes by $\Delta d = -2k_1/3k_2$ (to first order) and the activation energy by $\Delta E^{\neq} = 2k_1k_2/(9k_3)$. The resulting rate of change is

$$\Delta E^{\neq}/\Delta d = -(6E_0^{\neq}k_2)^{1/2}$$

Note that $\Delta E^{\neq}/\Delta d$ depends only on the activation energy and the force constant of the unperturbed molecule! Introducing typical values of $E_0^{\neq}$ (~25 kcal mol^{-1}) and k_2 (~700 kcal mol^{-1} Å^{-2}) the rate of change is ~32 kcal mol^{-1} Å^{-1}, in good agreement with the value of ~30 kcal mol^{-1} Å^{-1} derived from experimental activation energies and X-ray structural data.[30]

The agreement between the rate of change observed experimentally and that predicted from the model not only confirms the concept of a linear perturbation and its interpretation as representing the varying nature of R, it also validates the hypothesis underlying the mapping approach. And it arouses curiosity about other predictions this model might make, especially about the length of the scissile bond in the transition state. It is

$$d_0^{\neq} = d_0 - k_2/(3k_3) = d_0 + (6E_0^{\neq}/k_2)^{1/2}$$

With the same typical values as used above $d_0^{\neq} - d_0$ is ~0.45 Å implying a C–O$_1$ distance in the transition state of ~1.9 Å, approximately midway between the covalent distance of ~1.45 Å and the shorter nonbonded distances of ~2.5 Å shown in Fig. 4 (top). The estimate agrees with the limited amount of independent evidence available.[31] The same treatment explains the structure–

reactivity patterns observed for other dissociatively activated processes, *e.g.* ligand substitution of nickel(II)aquo, nickel(II)amine and some cobalt(III) and chromium(III) complexes, as well as $S_N 2$ substitution at boron.[9,10d]

5.2 Bowl inversion in corannulene derivatives

The molecular structures of corannulene and its derivatives **6** and **7** are bowl shaped.

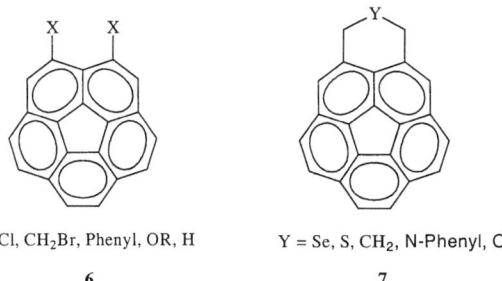

X = Cl, CH$_2$Br, Phenyl, OR, H   Y = Se, S, CH$_2$, N-Phenyl, O

6   **7**

The bowl depth of the parent molecule, *i.e.* the distance between the plane of the central five-membered ring and the plane of the ten peripheral carbon atoms, is 0.85 Å. The bowl inverts with an activation energy of 11.5 kcal mol^{-1}. Two substituents in *peri* positions as in **6** tend to repel each other, thereby reducing the depth of the bowl and the inversion barrier. A ring connecting two *peri*-positions as in **7** tends to pull them closer together, thereby increasing both quantities. As in the case of acetal hydrolysis the effects of a small structural change on activation energy are stunning. The decamethyl derivative has a bowl depth of ~0.58 Å, about 2/3 that of corannulene itself, but a barrier that is only 1.3 kcal mol^{-1}, about 1/10 that of the parent compound. Increasing the bowl depth by only 1/4, as in acecorannulene ($X_2 = CH_2–CH_2$), more than doubles the barrier to ~28 kcal mol^{-1}.[33]

Inversion of corannulenes is a symmetric double minimum problem that can be described with a quartic-quadratic potential E in the bowl depth d

$$E = -k_2 d^2/2 + k_4 d^4$$

The stationary points are the transition state at $d^{\neq} = 0$ corresponding to a planar molecule and the ground state at $d_0 = (k_2/k_4)^{1/2}/2$. The activation energy is $\Delta E^{\neq} = k_4 d_0^4$ (Fig. 6). A change in

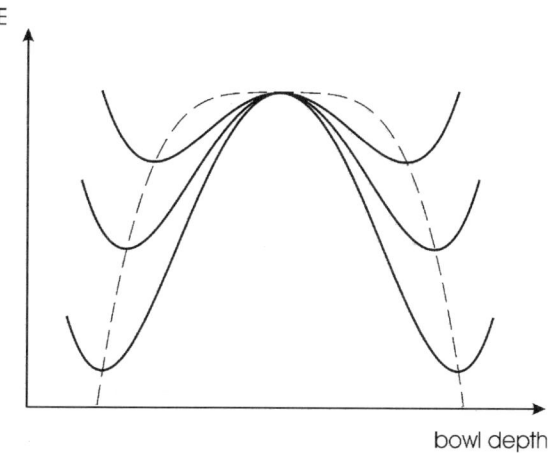

Fig. 6 Double minimum potential for bowl inversion of corannulenes with different depths (solid curves) and dependence of activation energy on bowl depth (dashed curve).

substituents translates into a change in k_2. With increasingly negative k_2 the bowl and the well get deeper; as k_2 approaches zero they get shallower, until for $k_2 = 0$ the two minima coalesce into a single, planar ground state. Activation energies for bowl inversion are proportional to the fourth power of the bowl depth

$$\Delta E^{\neq} = k_4 d_0^4 = (k_2/4)^2/k_4$$

This relationship, with $k_4 \sim 24$ kcal mol^{-1} Å^{-4}, fits the available structural and energetic data extremely well. An analogous treatment relates the ring inversion barriers of differently substituted metallacyclopentenes to the flap angles between the C–M–C and the C–CR=CR–C planes of the five-membered metallacycle.[34]

5.3 Energy diagrams, catalysis and catastrophe theory

Acetal hydrolysis, corannulene inversion and all the other processes mentioned in the two preceding sections are chemically quite diverse and yet they all show the same type of quantitative relationship between structures, force constants and energy. The empirical findings summarized in these equations must be quite general. A recent investigation based on catastrophe theory has reproduced these relationships.[35] The general energy profile mentioned in section 5.1 is now expressed relative to the point of inflection at $d = (d_0 + d_0^{\neq})/2$. This leads to the antisymmetric function

$$E = k_3 x^3 - (k_2^2/(12k_3) - k_1)x = ax^3 - bx$$

where x is the distance from the inflection point. If b equals zero, the linear term disappears and the point at $x = 0$ is a so-called non-Morse critical point.[36] At such a point the potential cannot be decomposed by a smooth coordinate transformation into a sum of simple, one-dimensional quadratic terms in the individual coordinates. For positive b two Morse stationary points emerge and move apart both in structure and energy with increasing b. A similar analysis applies to the symmetric function introduced in section 5.2

$$E' = a'x^4 - b'x^2$$

If b' equals zero, the potential has a single minimum at $x = 0$ corresponding to another non-Morse critical point. For positive perturbations b' two Morse stationary points develop moving further apart and to lower energies as b' increases. Catastrophe theory requires that at points in parameter space where basins and passes disappear (b or $b' \to 0$), the local geometry is described by catastrophe functions. E and E' with $b = b' = 0$ are such functions for one-dimensional energy profiles.

Several aspects of the mathematical discussion and the empirical findings are relevant. First, the even and odd functions E and E' are universally applicable to the description of corresponding reaction profiles provided the ground and transition states are not too far apart,[35] i.e. provided no higher order terms are necessary for a decent description of the energy profile. Within this limitation the relationships between reaction paths, barrier heights and vibration frequencies are general. This is illustrated by the finding that the relationships hold for vastly different chemical systems and processes, including organic and organometallic compounds, molecules and clusters, ligand dissociation and conformational interconversion processes.[9,10d,30,33,34] The second important result of our analysis is pre-eminently chemical: structural fragments belonging to the same family share one of the two potential constant (a or a') independently of substitution; differences in substitution are associated with differences of the second constant (b or b'). The constancy of a and a' in a given family of compounds is an empirical finding; it does not follow from catastrophe theory. It is surprising and not yet understood. In any case, the above findings justify interpolating and extrapolating trends in structure, dynamics and barrier height in families of related compounds and provide general insight into the structure–reactivity problem, a central issue in physical (organic) chemistry.

How do these results relate to current views of catalysis? In both examples discussed above reactivity is tuned by tuning electronic or steric properties of substituents, which are not involved in the process directly and may therefore be considered as a kind of 'intramolecular catalyst'. For example, the negative charge at O_1 of acetal **3**, which the leaving group is acquiring on its way to the transition state, is better stabilised by a phenyl or an acyl group than by an alkyl group. This is an example of transition state stabilization. In the corannulene family the transition state is always planar for symmetry reasons. The substituents affect the ground state structure thus providing an example of ground state (de)stabilization. Of course the (de)stabilizing factor need not be associated directly with the reacting molecular fragments. Both the methoxy- and the alkoxy-group in ketal **4** are poor leaving groups. However, the reactivity of the latter is enhanced due to the presence of a hydrogen bond originating in a carboxylic acid group located in a part of the molecule that is separated from the ketal. As might be expected from the discussion above the enhanced reactivity is visible in the ground state structure. The O–CH$_3$ distance is 1.383(4) Å, the O–CR$_3$ distance is 1.424(3) Å, to be compared with average values of 1.398(16) and 1.408(7) Å, respectively (derived from six acetals with a tertiary alkoxy group, CH$_3$O–CH$_2$–OCR$_3$, for which accurate structures are found in the CSD).[37] Kinetic measurements on the closely related compound **5** indicate a rate acceleration of 10^{10} fold corresponding to a transition state stabilization of $\sim$14 kcal mol^{-1} relative to the compound without the carboxylic acid group. The effect is attributed to an intramolecular hydrogen bond said to be particularly strong in the transition state.[37] In molecules **4** and **5** the reactive and catalysing groups are juxtaposed with the help of a molecular scaffold. Similar juxtaposition and consequent catalysis is achieved in an enzyme by docking the substrate into the active site. It seems reasonable to expect that the perturbation models accounting for intramolecular substituent effects are equally applicable to modifications in the active sites of enzymes and other catalytically active molecules.

The models developed here have one virtue and many shortcomings. Shortcomings first: the models are one-dimensional, expressed in terms of potential energy rather than enthalpy and neglect entropy altogether. These shortcomings are not fundamental, however. The example of acetal hydrolysis has also been treated on a two-dimensional energy surface taking into account changes of both the C–O$_1$ and the C–O$_2$ bond lengths. The results are essentially the same as those of the one-dimensional treatment.[30] In addition, the structure–energy correlations have been established mostly from $\Delta G^{\neq}$ and $\Delta H^{\neq}$, not from potential energies. The virtue of the treatment is to provide a language for discussing substituent effects, structure–reactivity relationship and catalysis for different molecules and different chemical processes from the same vantage point.

6. Inferences from the temperature dependence of crystal structures

In section 4 inferences were drawn from structural data alone, from so-called structure–structure correlations. In section 5 structural data were combined with independent kinetic measurements into structure–energy correlations. In this section energy is brought into the discussion more directly by considering the temperature evolution of crystal structures. ADPs show the most obvious temperature dependence and, in disordered structures, occupancy may be temperature dependent as well. The former are primarily an expression of vibrational dynamics, the latter measure the concentration of species belonging to different minima of an energy profile.

Single crystal structure analysis is usually not the method of choice for studying crystal and molecular dynamics, because interpretations of ADPs pertaining to a single temperature suffer from two severe shortcomings alluded to in section 3.2. First, it is impossible to distinguish mean square amplitudes of motion from those due to unresolved crystallographic disorder. Second, the dynamic information cannot be unravelled unambiguously, even in the absence of disorder, because *ADPs say nothing about the correlations of atomic motions*, at least not directly.

In section 6.1 we outline a general method that remedies both shortcomings. We explain how to extract low frequency-large amplitude dynamics from the temperature evolution of ADPs, not only for rigid,[4] but also for flexible molecules.[12] In section 6.2 we show how to distinguish dynamic mean square amplitudes from static ones and answer a long-standing question concerning the determination of the molecular structure of benzene by single crystal diffraction experiments. In section 6.3 we describe low frequency dynamics of a crystalline stilbene derivative and show differences to the gas phase. The case of crystalline urea, discussed in section 6.4, illustrates that deforming a molecule may be energetically less costly than distorting the hydrogen bonds to its nearest neighbours.

6.1 Vibrational motion from ADPs

Our interpretation of ADPs is based on an explicit expression of their temperature dependence and on the simplifying assumption that molecules move in a mean crystal field. Within the confines of this model the temperature dependence of ADPs is given by

$$\Sigma^x(T) = AgV\delta(T)V^{\mathrm{T}}g^{\mathrm{T}}A^{\mathrm{T}} + \varepsilon$$

Although the equation looks complicated, its essence is not so difficult to grasp. The 3×3 diagonal blocks of Σ^x are better known as ADPs and are available from Bragg diffraction experiments. The 3×3 off-diagonal blocks of Σ^x represent interatomic vibrational correlations and are not accessible from Bragg diffraction. The matrices $\delta(T)$ and V are the quantities of central importance. The former is a diagonal matrix with the mean square displacements of the normal modes. Its elements are

$$\delta_i = \hbar/(2\omega_i)\coth(\hbar\omega_i/2k_{\mathrm{B}}T)$$

They establish the connection between vibration frequencies ω_i, temperature T and the ADPs. V describes the coordination of atomic motions. The transformation $V\delta(T)V^{\mathrm{T}}$ produces the mean square displacements of the mass-weighted internal and external coordinates, such as angle bending, torsion, molecular libration and translation. The transformation by g removes the mass weighting and the multiplication by A transforms mean square displacements of internal coordinates into mean square positional displacements, the elements of Σ^x. The correction term ε accounts for contributions to the ADPs showing little or no temperature dependence, especially contributions from high-frequency molecular vibrations ($\hbar\omega_i \gg 2k_{\mathrm{B}}T$), but also from disorder.

The problem is to determine the frequencies ω_i, the coordination of atomic motions expressed by the eigenvector matrix V and the correction terms ε from an incompletely known mean square amplitude matrix Σ^x, namely from its observable diagonal 3×3 blocks. We have solved this problem by measuring ADPs at multiple temperatures in the zero-point motion and classical regimes, and by determining V, δ and ε from these multiple measurements by a least-squares procedure. The matrices g and A present no problem. They are purely geometric transformations depending only on the choice of molecular coordinates. The whole treatment is closely related to normal mode analysis from vibrational spectra of isotopomers.[12,38]

6.2 The structure of benzene

The solution of an old problem concerning the molecular structure of benzene illustrates the power of the model sketched in the preceding section. The question is whether a single crystal structure determination can prove the delocalised structure of benzene with six equal bond distances and angles. The answer is 'no' which may seem counterintuitive.[39] The reasoning is as follows: superposition across a centre of inversion of two localized cyclohexatriene molecules with bond lengths differences of ~0.1 Å, would add a disorder contribution of about 0.0008 Å^2 to the tangential in-plane component of the carbon ADPs (Fig. 7). At 15 K this component is observed to be 0080 Å^2, ten times larger than the putative disorder contribution. It is therefore impossible to conclusively exclude disorder, even at a temperature as low as 15 K.

ADPs of C$_6$D$_6$ from neutron diffraction experiments at two temperatures (15 and 123 K)[40] are sufficient to resolve the ambiguity. Three translation and three libration frequencies (ω_i), the orientations of the respective axes of motion (V) and correction terms ε_{C} and ε_{D} have been determined from them (18 parameters, 72 independent observations, wR2 = 0.019). The tangential component of ε_{C} is found to be 0.0007(1) Å^2. It has the same magnitude as the putative disorder contribution; it is also the same as the zero-point mean square amplitude due to the high-frequency intramolecular vibrations (0.0008 Å^2).[41] Given the laws of quantum mechanics, the small temperature independent component of ε must correspond to the zero-point amplitudes and cannot be

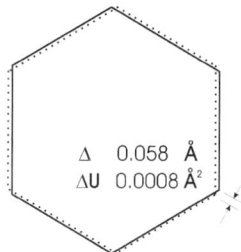

Fig. 7 Best centrosymmetric superposition of two cyclohexatriene molecules (difference in bond lengths 0.1 Å, Δ is the distance between two disordered carbon atoms, ΔU is the corresponding disorder contribution to the tangential ADP-component).

due to disorder. This finding corroborates the sixfold symmetric structure of benzene and eliminates the cyclohexatriene model of Fig. 7. Of course, this result is well known from other lines of evidence, *e.g.* high level *ab initio* calculations. However, the analysis demonstrates that static structures become much better defined, if ADPs measured at different temperatures are interpreted in terms of an appropriate model of their temperature dependence. At the same time a detailed picture emerges of the dynamics of molecules in crystals.

6.3 Crankshaft motion in 2,2′-dimethylstilbene

In the temperature range 118–298 K this molecule shows an unusually short C=C bond.[42] Its length is between 1.321(2) and 1.283(3) Å to be compared with 1.349 Å as calculated from density functional theory (DFT).[43] It has been argued that the shortening is due to a 'dynamical disorder in a direction approximately perpendicular to the molecular plane which mainly originates from the torsional vibrations of the C–Ph bond'.[42] This conclusion is based on crystallographic refinements of structural models in which two rigid molecules with different C–Ph torsion angles and different occupation factors are superimposed. Empirical force field calculations indicate a C–Ph torsion potential with essentially a single minimum, albeit a very asymmetric one.[44] Both models explain not only the large ADPs perpendicular to the mean molecular plane, but also the unusual observation that the ADPs of the carbon atoms in the centre of the molecule are as large as or larger than those of the carbon atoms at the molecular periphery. In-plane bending about the *ipso*-carbon atoms has also been suggested.

To test the conclusions from the static refinements in dynamic terms the thermal evolution of the ADPs has been analysed for the postulated vibrations. To gain a first impression of the flexibility of this centrosymmetric molecule, its vibration frequencies and corresponding displacement patterns in the gas phase were calculated by DFT. Four modes of motion with low frequencies are of particular interest because they might contribute substantially to the ADPs. Modes destroying the centre of symmetry are labelled u ('ungerade'), those preserving the centre are labelled g ('gerade'). The lowest mode (15 cm^{-1}, u) has the two phenyl rings rotating in opposite directions (when looking down the respective Ph–C bonds). The corresponding g-vibration has a much higher frequency (88 cm^{-1}). The two other low frequency modes bend the molecule into an arc, either in its mean plane (67 cm^{-1}, u) or perpendicular to it (55 cm^{-1}, u). The model chosen to explain the ADPs observed at five temperatures between 15 and 235 K includes 7 modes with frequencies less than 100 cm^{-1}. Three of them are g; they are composed of a total of ~205% libration about the three inertial axes of the molecule, and of ~95% torsion. The torsion dominates one of the three modes (~85%, at 45(5) cm^{-1}, Fig. 8, top) and mixes somewhat into the other two (~15%, ~35–55 cm^{-1}). The four u modes are composed of the three translations and the in-plane bend deformation. The bending mode largely maintains its identity in the solid state (~95%, at 60(5) cm^{-1}, Fig. 8, bottom) and mixes somewhat with the three translation modes (~5%, ~30–40 cm^{-1}). The arc deformation out of the mean plane is of minor importance, it merely mixes into the three translational modes to a limited extent (~5%). The 'ungerade' torsional mode contributes insignificantly to the ADPs and was not included in the model. Comparison of the results from the gaseous and solid state shows, not unexpectedly, that crystal packing strongly affects the low-frequency

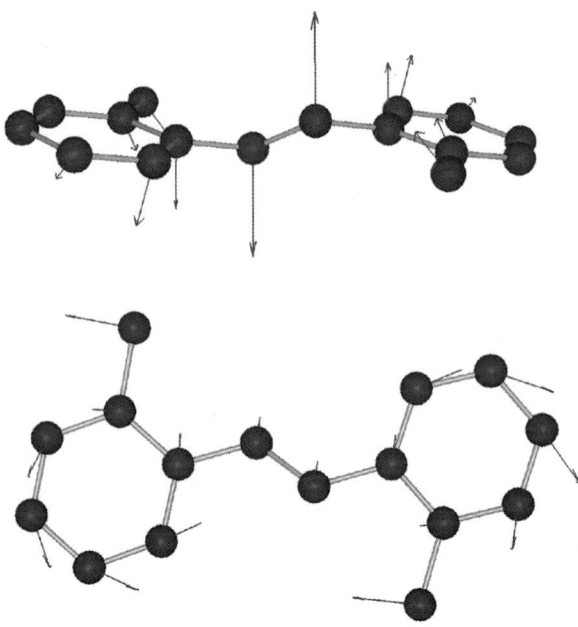

Fig. 8 Motions in crystalline 2,2′-dimethylstilbene from the thermal evolution of ADPs. Top: crankshaft motion (~45 cm^{-1}); bottom: in-plane bending (~60 cm^{-1}).

motions. Modes with significant out of plane displacements of the phenyl rings are among the lowest in the gas phase, but need not be considered in the solid state as they affect the thermal evolution of the ADPs very little. The 'gerade' torsional motion is the only low frequency, out-of-plane mode that is seen in both phases, apparently because only the central ethylenic carbon atoms show really large displacements (Fig. 8, top). It is the mode responsible for the unusual shortening of the central C=C bond. The bending motion with predominantly in-plane displacements is also very similar in both phases (Fig. 8, bottom). In summary, this example shows that the energy of large amplitude modes can be measured and the corresponding pattern of atomic displacements visualised from the thermal evolution of ADPs.

The torsional mode, if enhanced into a continuous motion, resembles a rotating crankshaft or pedal motion and accounts for the conformational disorder in stilbene itself, several stilbene derivatives and azobenzenes.[45] In these compounds the atoms connecting the two phenyl rings are disordered over two positions that are 180° apart along the crankshaft coordinate. Crankshaft motion is also discussed widely in the context of polymer dynamics and multiple polypeptide conformations.

6.4 Dynamic distortion of the peptide fragments in crystalline urea

This molecule is not only small enough to have been investigated extensively in the solid and in the gas phase by neutron diffraction, different spectroscopic methods and *ab initio* calculations, it also has two peptide bonds which may be considered as (over)simplified models of corresponding bonds in polypeptides. The equilibrium structure of urea in the gas phase is not planar; the two NH$_2$ groups are pyramidal, the molecular symmetry being C_2.[46] Urea molecules are described as being planar in the solid state,[47] but appear to be soft with respect to pyramidal deformation of the NH$_2$ groups. Evidence for this comes again from the temperature evolution of the ADPs obtained from elastic neutron diffraction experiments.[41] In the simplest of several models compatible with the experimental data, the lowest frequency out-of-plane mode (64 cm^{-1}) is mainly a libration about the C=O bond (~94%) coupled with some pyramidal deformation of the NH2 group (~6%). Although this admixture is small, it affects atomic displacements in a significant way: libration would move the NH$_2$ groups out of the plane thereby distorting hydrogen bonds to neighbouring

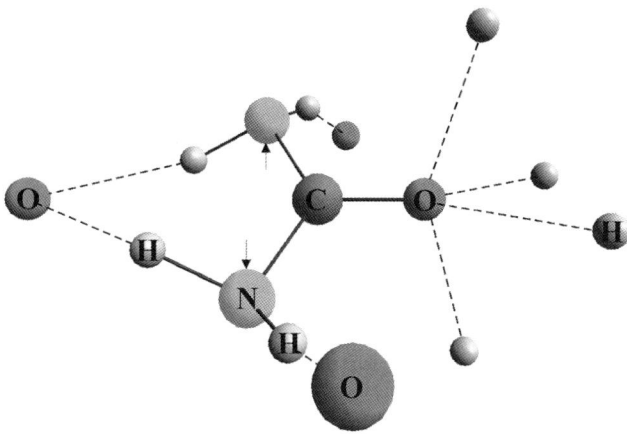

Fig. 9 Motion in crystalline urea. Note the way molecular libration couples with out-of-plane deformation of the NH$_2$ groups.

molecules; the combination of libration with NH$_2$ deformation ensures that the hydrogen atoms move very little thus keeping the strain on the hydrogen bonds minimal (Fig. 9).

So far no analogous study has been done on amides. However, several structural and quantum chemical investigations have addressed the question of nitrogen flexibility in amides. The structure of N,N-dimethylacetamide has been determined by electron diffraction in the gas phase. The equilibrium structure at nitrogen is either planar with a large-amplitude, out-of-plane vibration or pseudo-planar with an inversion barrier below the vibrational ground state.[48] Deviations from planarity of up to 15° in the CC–NC torsion angle appear to cost less than 0.1 kcal mol^{-1} in strain energy. In a study mapping the *cis–trans* isomerization pathway of amides from crystal structures, out-of-plane deformations of 90 R(X=)C–NR$_2$ fragments have been compiled. Deviations of nitrogen from planarity by as much as 10° are not uncommon in amides (X=O).[49] A study of the deviations from planarity of the amide bond in peptides and proteins arrives at similar conclusions.[50] Recent quantum chemical calculations on formamide[51] and N-methylacetamide[52] indicate planar or non-planar structures depending on the basis set used, the method of accounting for electron correlation, the presence or absence of solvent molecules and external electric fields. A substantial amplitude of pyramidalization is reported from a molecular dynamics simulation on formamide in water using density functional theory and classical potentials.[53] The persistent finding in these investigations is the flexibility of the nitrogen atom with respect to pyramidal deformation, irrespective of the details of its equilibrium configuration. It is difficult to judge the significance of this flexibility for protein structure. On the basis of the dynamic and static structural findings we speculate that these soft hinges are another degree of freedom helping proteins to find the fold that is best suited for performing their function.

6.5 Measuring concentration from occupancy in disordered crystal structures

With improved instrumentation and experimentation many more crystal structures turn out to be disordered, sometimes in subtle ways. In molecular crystals occupational disorder is most common: different forms of the same molecular entity occupy the same position in different unit cells. Here we mention a few specific examples for which the temperature dependence of occupancy has been studied in some detail. Proton migration associated with a keto–enol equilibrium has been observed in citrinin **8**[54] and in salicylideneanilines **9**,[55] double proton migration in the cyclic hydrogen bonded dimer of benzoic acid **10**.[56] Metal ion transfer between different double bonds of the same ligand has been studied by solid-state NMR and by crystallography (**11**).[57] There are several processes in which electrons are shuffled between orbitals or between atoms with consequent changes in structure. In high spin–low spin equilibria electrons move from strongly σ-antibonding to weakly π-antibonding orbitals or *vice versa*. The change compresses or expands the molecules (**12**).[58] Electron transfer in the mixed-valence, polynuclear complexes **13**[59] and **14**[60] and dynamic Jahn–Teller distortion in transition metal complexes with high spin d^4 and d^9 electronic configurations (**15**)[61] redistribute short and long bonds among the ligands. There are conformational changes in organic molecules, *e.g.* inversion of pyramidal nitrogen in **16**,[62] chair–boat conversion in **17**[63] and the pedal motion in the stilbenes and azobenzenes with a double minimum in the crankshaft coordinate.[45] Finally, there is the spherical molecule C_{60} rotating between two well defined, but crystallographically distinct orientations.[64]

In disordered structures, like the ones mentioned above, atoms belonging to the different forms of a molecule usually overlap and measuring occupation factors becomes difficult. Their change with temperature cannot be determined directly but must be deduced from changes in the mean atomic positions and from the (disorder contribution to the) ADPs. Disorder models need to be refined with great care and making prudent use of restraints and constraints. Once these problems are solved, the concentrations of the two (or more) species change continuously with temperature and show van't Hoff behaviour: $\ln K = [A]/[B] = -\Delta H/RT + \Delta S/R$. This gives direct access to the relative energies of A and B in the crystalline environment. If A and B are the same chemically, as in **10**, **11**, **13** and **14**, the equilibrium is a sensitive probe of intermolecular interactions, one that so far has been exploited very little. In some cases the transition between different species takes place in a relatively narrow range of temperature. Such behaviour usually indicates a cooperative effect whereby the changes in some molecules influence the changes in others. The conditions for the presence or absence of cooperative effects remain poorly understood in most molecular crystals. However, cooperative effects belong into the realm of phase transitions, a topic that is way beyond the scope of this work.

7. Problems with and opportunities for slow diffraction experiments

One limitation of slow experiments is obvious: they are unsuitable for measuring transient phenomena. However, their weakness is also their strength. With sufficient time available for the experiment diffraction data can be measured accurately and detailed, high quality structural information is relatively easy to obtain. The various ways of interpreting structural data in terms of PESs have very different requirements with respect to quality of data. Dynamic studies have the highest demands. In order to obtain accurate ADPs, high-resolution neutron data or, often more conveniently, high-resolution X-ray data are needed. In the latter case it is important that deformation electron densities are properly accounted for. The accuracy needed for structure–energy correlations depends on the rate of change of activation energy with structure $\Delta E^{\neq}/\Delta d$. A large rate of change is often associated with small structural changes, of the order of a few hundredths of an Å, and thus experimental accuracy needs to be high. The mapping approach is usually least demanding. For structure correlations covering distance changes of the order of an Å, atomic positions accurate to several hundredths of an Å are sufficient.

There are aspects other than accuracy. For example, the syntheses of molecules mapping a particular reaction path may be difficult and are often beyond the competence of a structural chemist. His or her mappings will depend largely on whatever structures are available in the CSD. In return for this limitation, the method often benefits from an element of serendipity. Many an outlier in a scatter plot, after careful scrutiny, turns out to represent an interesting structure, one that may well become the beginning of a new study. Structure–energy correlations have problems of their own. All too often kinetic data do not match corresponding structures and *vice versa*. Calculations sometimes help. In the case of the corannulenes several molecules where synthesized and their barrier measured by NMR. Most structures and the extreme points to the correlation come from DFT calculations:[33] the one with the largest and, more important, the one with the smallest barrier, which would be very difficult to measure.

Single crystal diffraction studies of large-amplitude motions of flexible molecules have hardly begun. Until recently neither the theoretical background nor the experimental possibilities for such studies were sufficiently well developed. Nowadays synchrotron radiation, CCD detectors, easy-to-use flow cryostats operating to 10 K and powerful computers allow the measurement and interpretation of high-resolution diffraction data at many temperatures in a few days. In spite of these advances, diffraction experiments still measure averages over ensembles undergoing a plethora of motions. In comparison, modern methods of laser spectroscopy are much more selective with respect to energy and thus with respect to the processes they probe and the molecules they see. However, diffraction experiments have a specific advantage over spectroscopic ones. Displacements patterns of atoms, closely related to vibrational eigenvectors, are observed directly rather than being derived indirectly, *e.g.* from spectroscopic isotope effects. They reveal details of atomic motion that are of chemical interest, but are very difficult to pinpoint from spectroscopy. The coupling of libration with molecular deformation in urea has been discussed above,[33] the coupling of molecular translation with bond length deformation in $Ru(H_2O)_6^{2+}$ is another example.[6,65] In both cases the ADPs are a direct probe of the influence the hydrogen bond environment has on these molecules.

Studies of temperature dependent disorder would also seem to hold some promise, because chemical processes may be followed in an environment that is still highly ordered compared to that in solution. A more detailed understanding of these processes requires knowledge about the short-range correlations between the different molecular states in the crystal. Information on such correlations comes from diffuse scattering,[66] a phenomenon whose interpretation is very much less developed than standard structure determination.

We hope that this article has conveyed some of the fun we have with the good old and relatively slow diffraction techniques. We also hope to have shown that they still have something to offer with regard to the understanding of fast chemical processes and expect that for some time they will remain complementary to the new and exciting time resolved experiments. The main gain from mapping approaches will always be the culling of different structures from databases and putting them together into a collage, into a whole that is more than the sum of its parts. It is difficult to say what will come from the dynamical studies, except that the door to a little known aspect of crystal structure analysis has been pushed open.

Acknowledgements

We thank Dr Jürg Hauser for his help with illustrations and with retrieving data from the CSD.

References

1 (a) A. H. Zewail, *Angew. Chem. Int. Ed. Engl.*, 2000, **39**, 2587–2631; (b) A. H. Zewail, *J. Phys. Chem. A*, 2000, **104**, 5660–5694.
2 B. R. Johnson and J. L. Kinsey, in *Femtosecond Chemistry*, ed. J. Manz and L. Wöste, VCH, Weinheim, 1994.
3 This is not always the case. For a recent example see T. Weber, M. A. Estermann and H. B. Bürgi, *Acta Crystallogr., Sect. B*, 2001, **57**, 579–590.
4 V. Schomaker and K. N. Trueblood, *Acta Crystallogr., Sect. B*, 1968, **24**, 63–76.
5 C. K. Johnson, in *Crystallographic Computing*, ed. F. R. Ahmed, Munksgaard, Kopenhagen, 1970, p. 220–226.
6 For a review see H. B. Bürgi, *Annu. Rev. Phys. Chem.*, 2000, **51**, 275–296.
7 F. H. Allen, *Acta Crystallogr., Sect. A*, 1998, **A54**, 758–771.
8 T. P. E. Auf der Heyde and H. B. Bürgi, *Inorg. Chem.*, 1989, **28**, 3960–3969.
9 H. B. Bürgi and J. D. Dunitz, in *Structure Correlation*, ed. H. B. Bürgi and J. D. Dunitz, Verlag Chemie, Weinheim, 1994, p. 163–204.
10 (a) H. B. Bürgi, *Acta Crystallogr., Sect. A*, 1998, **54**, 873–885; (b) V. Feretti, P. Gilli, V. Bertolasi and G. Gilli, *Crystallogr. Rev.*, 1996, **5**, 3–98; (c) A. G. Orpen, *Chem. Soc. Rev.*, 1993, 191–197; (d) H. B. Bürgi, in *Perspectives in Coordination Chemistry*, ed. A. F. Williams, C. Floriani and A. E. Merbach, Verlag Helvetica Chimica Acta, Basel, 1992, p. 1–29; (e) H. B. Bürgi and J. D. Dunitz, *Acc. Chem. Res.*, 1983, **16**, 153–161; (f) H. B. Bürgi, *Angew. Chem. Int. Ed. Engl.*, 1975, **14**, 460–473.
11 *Structure Correlation*, ed. H. B. Bürgi and J. D. Dunitz, Verlag Chemie, Weinheim, 1994, vol. 1 and 2.
12 H. B. Bürgi and S. C. Capelli, *Acta Crystallogr., Sect. A*, 2000, **56**, 403–412.
13 E. B. Wilson, J. C. Decius and P. C. Cross, *Molecular Vibrations*, McGraw-Hill, New York, 1955.
14 H. B. Bürgi, K. W. Törnroos, G. Calzaferri and H. Bürgy, *Inorg. Chem.*, 1993, **32**, 4914–4919.
15 (a) K. W. Törnroos, H. B. Bürgi, G. Calzaferri and H. Bürgy, *Acta Crystallogr., Sect. B*, 1995, **51**, 155–161; (b) A. M. Bieniok and H. B. Bürgi, *J. Phys. Chem.*, 1994, **98**, 10 735–10 741; (c) H. B. Bürgi, *Acta Crystallogr., Sect. B*, 1995, **51**, 571–579.
16 K. D. Hammonds, V. Heine and M. T. Dove, *Phase Transitions*, 1997, **61**, 155–172.
17 W. Hummel, J. Hauser and H. B. Bürgi, *J. Mol. Graphics*, 1990, **8**, 214–220.
18 L. Pauling, *The Nature of the Chemical Bond*, Cornell University Press, 3rd edn.,1960.
19 H. A. Bent, *Chem. Rev.*, 1968, **68**, 587–648.
20 H. B. Bürgi, *Inorg. Chem.*, 1973, **12**, 2321–2325.
21 H. B. Bürgi, J. D. Dunitz and E. Shefter, *J. Am. Chem. Soc.*, 1973, **95**, 5065–5067.

22 (a) A. S. Cieplak, *J. Am. Chem. Soc.*, 1985, **107**, 271–273; (b) A. S. Cieplak, in *Structure Correlation*, ed. H. B. Bürgi and J. D. Dunitz, Verlag Chemie, Weinheim, 1994, p. 205–302.
23 J. O'Leary, P. C. Bell, J. D. Wallis and W. B. Schweizer, *J. Chem. Soc., Perkin Trans. 2*, 2001, 133–139.
24 (a) M. Marquart, J. Walter, J. Deisenhofer, W. Bode and R. Huber, *Acta Crystallogr. Sect. B*, 1983, **39**, 480–490; (b) R. Huber and W. Bode, *Acc. Chem. Res.*, 1978, **11**, 114–122.
25 E. M. Driggers, C. W. Liu, D. E. Wemmer and P. G. Schulz, *J. Am. Chem. Soc.*, 1998, **120**, 7395–7396.
26 K. S. Bateman, K. Huang, S. Anderson, W. Lu, M. A. Qasim, M. Laskowski, Jr. and M. N. G. James, *J. Mol. Biol.*, 2001, **305**, 839–849.
27 C. J. Creighton, T. T. Romoff, J. H. Bu and M. Goodman, *J. Am. Chem. Soc.*, 1999, **121**, 6786–6791.
28 P. G. Jones and A. J. Kirby, *J. Am. Chem. Soc.*, 1984, **106**, 6207–6212.
29 G. S. Hammond, *J. Am. Chem. Soc.*, 1955, **77**, 334–338.
30 H. B. Bürgi and K. C. Dubler-Steudle, *J. Am. Chem. Soc.*, 1988, **110**, 7291–7299.
31 We were unable to find a recent high-level quantum chemical calculation on this or a closely related system. Transition state structures for the hydration of formaldehyde catalysed by one or two water molecules show C–O distances of ~1.65 Å.[32] It has been argued that this is a lower limit for the C–O distance in the transition state of spontaneous acetal hydrolysis (ref. 30).
32 S. Wolfe, C. K. Kim, K. Yang, N. Weinberg and Z. Shi, *J. Am. Chem. Soc.*, 1995, **117**, 4240–4260.
33 (a) T. J. Seiders, K. K. Baldridge, G. H. Grube and J. S. Siegel, *J. Am. Chem. Soc.*, 2001, **123**, 517–525; (b) U. D. Priyakumar and G. N. Sastry, *J. Org. Chem.*, 2001, **66**, 6523–6530.
34 H. B. Bürgi and K. C. Dubler-Steudle, *J. Am. Chem. Soc.*, 1988, **110**, 4953–4957.
35 D. J. Wales, *Science*, 2001, **293**, 2067–2070.
36 (a) J. Morse, *Trans. Am. Math Soc.*, 1931, **33**, 72; (b) R. Thom, *Stabilité Structurelle et Morphogénèse*, Benjamin, New York, 1972.
37 (a) A. D. Bond, A. J. Kirby and E. Rodriguez, *Chem. Commun.*, 2001, 2266–2267; (b) E. Hartwell, D. R. W. Hodgson and A. J. Kirby, *J. Am. Chem. Soc.*, 2000, **122**, 9326–9327.
38 S. J. Cyvin, *Molecular Vibrations and Mean Square Amplitudes*, University of Forlaget, Oslo, 1968.
39 O. Ermer, *Angew. Chem. Int. Ed. Engl.*, 1987, **26**, 782–784.
40 G. A. Jeffrey, J. R. Ruble, R. K. McMullan and J. A. Pople, *Proc. R. Soc. London Ser. A*, 1987, **414**, 47–57.
41 S. C. Capelli, M. Förtsch and H. B. Bürgi, *Acta Crystallogr., Sect. A*, 2000, **56**, 413–424.
42 K. Ogawa, T. Sano, S. Yoshimura, Y. Takeuchi and K. Toriumi, *J. Am. Chem. Soc.*, 1992, **114**, 1041–1051.
43 T. Lüthi, K. Ogawa and H. B. Bürgi, unpublished (B3LYP functional, 6-31G** basis set).
44 S. Galli, P. Mercandelli and A. Sironi, *J. Am. Chem. Soc.*, 1999, **121**, 3767–3772.
45 J. Harada and K. Ogawa, *J. Am. Chem. Soc.*, 2001, **123**, 10 884–10 888.
46 S. G. Raptis, J. Anastassopoulou and T. Theophanides, *Theor. Chem. Acc.*, 2000, **105**, 156–164.
47 (a) S. Swaminathan, B. M. Craven and R. K. McMullen, *Acta Crystallogr., Sect. B*, 1984, **40**, 300–306; (b) B. Rousseau, C. Van Alsenoy, R. Keuleers and H. O. Desseyn, *J. Phys. Chem.*, 1998, **102**, 6540–6548; (c) R. Keuleers, H. O. Desseyn, B. Rousseau and J. Van Alsenoy, *J. Phys. Chem.*, 1999, **103**, 4621–4630.
48 H. G. Mack and H. Oberhammer, *J. Am. Chem. Soc.*, 1997, **119**, 3567–3570.
49 V. Ferretti, V. Bertolasi, P. Gilli and G. Gilli, *J. Phys. Chem.*, 1993, **97**, 13 568–13 574.
50 M. W. MacArthur and J. M. Thornton, *J. Mol. Biol.*, 1996, **264**, 1180–1195.
51 G. Fogarasi and P. G. Szalay, *J. Phys. Chem.*, 1997, **101**, 1400–1408.
52 I. N. Demetropoulos, I. P. Gerothanassis, C. Vakka and C. Kakvas, *J. Chem. Soc., Faraday Trans.*, 1996, **92**, 921–931.
53 S. Chalmet and M. F. Ruiz-Lopez, *J. Chem. Phys.*, 1999, **111**, 1117–1125.
54 R. Destro, *Chem. Phys. Lett.*, 1991, **181**, 232–236.
55 K. Ogawa, Y. Kasahara, Y. Ohtani and J. Harada, *J. Am. Chem. Soc.*, 1998, **120**, 7107–7108.
56 C. C. Wilson, N. Shankland and A. J. Florence, *J. Chem. Soc., Faraday Trans.*, 1996, **92**, 5051–5057.
57 R. Kumar, F. R. Fronczek, A. W. Maverick, A. J. Kim and L. G. Butler, *Chem. Mater.*, 1994, **6**, 587–595.
58 For an introduction into this wide field see a recent review by P. Gütlich, Y. Garcia and H. A. Goodwin, *Chem. Soc. Rev.*, 2000, **29**, 419–427.
59 A. Darovsky, V. Kezerashvili and P. Coppens, *Inorg. Chem.*, 1996, **35**, 6916–6917.
60 C. Wilson, B. B. Iversen, J. Overgaard, F. K. Larsen, G. Wu, S. P. Palii, G. A. Timco and N. V. Gerbeleu, *J. Am. Chem. Soc.*, 2000, **122**, 11 370–11 379.
61 (a) C. Simmons, *New J. Chem.*, 1993, **17**, 77–95; (b) J. Bebendorf, H. B. Bürgi, E. Gamp, M. A. Hitchman, A. Murphy, D. Reinen, M. J. Riley and H. Stratemeier, *Inorg. Chem.*, 1996, **35**, 7419–7429.
62 G. A. Sim, *J. Chem. Soc., Chem. Commun.*, 1987, 1118–1120.
63 G. A. Sim, *Acta Crystallogr., Sect. B*, 1990, **46**, 676–682.
64 (a) W. I. F. David, R. M. Ibberson, T. J. S. Dennis, J. P. Hare and K. Prassides, *Europhys. Lett.*, 1992, **18**, 219–225; (b) H. B. Bürgi, E. Blanc, D. Schwarzenbach, S. Liu, Y. Lu, M. M. Kappes and J. A. Ibers, *Angew. Chem. Int. Ed. Engl.*, 1992, **31**, 640–643.
65 H. B. Bürgi and A. Raselli, *Struct. Chem.*, 1993, **4**, 23–31.
66 (a) T. R. Welberry and B. D. Butler, *Chem. Rev.*, 1995, **95**, 2369–2403; (b) F. Frey, *Z. Kristallogr.*, 1997, **212**, 257–282.

The frontiers of time-resolved macromolecular crystallography: movies and chirped X-ray pulses

Keith Moffat

Department of Biochemistry and Molecular Biology, Institute for Biophysical Dynamics, and Consortium for Advanced Radiation Sources, The University of Chicago, 920 East 58th Street, Chicago, Illinois 60637, USA

Received 12th February 2002, Accepted 19th March 2002
First published as an Advance Article on the web 7th October 2002

Three important frontiers of ultrafast time-resolved macromolecular crystallography are presented: extension of this technique to other biological systems; further developments in the elucidation of mechanism through the analysis of time-dependent movies to extract the underlying, time-independent, intermediate structures; and enhanced time resolution. The last is intimately linked with the nature of the pump–probe experiment itself, with the sources of random and, particularly, systematic experimental error, and with the factors that contribute to overall time resolution. All experiments to date have utilized the unchirped X-ray pulses that are emitted by synchrotron sources. Chirped pulses offer certain advantages for ultrafast X-ray experiments such as those based on Laue diffraction. An energy-chirped pulse maps photon energy into time; a Laue diffraction experiment maps photon energy into detector space. Hence, a Laue experiment with an energy-chirped pulse maps time into space. The proposed sub-picosecond photon source could provide an excellent source of intense, chirped hard X-rays for such experiments.

Introduction

In time-resolved macromolecular crystallography, a structural reaction is initiated at a defined time in the molecules in a single crystal at near-room temperature, where full structural transitions are possible. The reaction progress is monitored through the subsequent time dependence of the X-ray structure amplitudes, $|F(hkl,t)|$. The ultimate goal of such an experiment is to identify the structural mechanism: that is, to determine the structures of reactants, of all intermediates and of products; and the pathways and rates by which these structures interconvert.[1] This is challenging. The differences between these structures are expected in general to be small; accurate measurements and high crystallographic resolution are necessary to reveal them. Certain intermediate structures may have very short lifetimes and interconvert rapidly; excellent experimental time resolution is required. Yet others may be long-lived; data must be collected over many decades in time. Unless the reaction mechanism is simple and the magnitude of the rate coefficients for the structural interconversions particularly favorable, the crystal contains, at all times, a time-dependent mixture of structural states; this mixture must be resolved. That is, the time-independent structures of each intermediate must be extracted at the data analysis stage, "analytical trapping". This overall, time-resolved approach may be contrasted with other crystallographic approaches that seek to isolate and study homogeneous, intermediate structures by manipulation of the chemistry of the system, "chemical trapping", or by lowering the temperature, "physical trapping".[2,3]

DOI: 10.1039/b201620f

It is clear that successful ultrafast, pump–probe, time-resolved experiments can be conducted, in which a light-driven reaction is initiated or pumped by a brief laser pulse and the X-ray diffraction pattern is acquired or probed after a suitable time delay by a brief X-ray pulse.[4,5] This paper explores briefly three of the frontiers of such experiments, then describes how a novel type of chirped X-ray pulse might reduce systematic experimental errors and aid in attacking the third of these frontiers, time resolution.

Frontiers

(a) Biological systems

To date, ultrafast time-resolved experiments have been published on only two systems, myoglobin[4] and photoactive yellow protein.[5] A first and obvious frontier is therefore to apply the technique to light-sensitive systems of wider biological interest. Light directly influences many organisms, for example through light-harvesting complexes harnessed to efficient photosynthesis, and through light-driven signal transduction. In the latter, photons of a particular wavelength range and intensity are absorbed by a detector molecule or domain, a signal is generated and transmitted in both an intramolecular and intermolecular fashion to at least one output molecule or domain, and a measurable output is produced. Examples of such outputs include altered swimming behavior of bacteria, or phototropism in plants. The molecular and structural bases for the light-driven generation and transmission of signals are not well understood. The recent availability of, for example, the complete genome sequence of the experimental plant Arabidopsis[6] enables many such light-sensitive systems in the plant to be cataloged. The Arabidopsis genome encodes at least 58 proteins that respond to light, including 9 that are homologous to known signal transduction proteins.[6] Each of these 9 proteins represents an upstream component; each must interact with other, downstream components, many of which are kinases, to form an entire signal transduction pathway. Light-dependent structural studies of the members of a pathway will reveal how the initial structural signal is generated, and how it is transmitted.

As one specific example, the blue-light photoreceptor known as phototropin controls phototropism, chloroplast relocation and other processes in plants.[7,8] Absorption of a blue photon by the FMN chromophore in a small domain of phototropin known as the LOV domain leads to the rapid but transient and fully reversible formation of a covalent bond between a cysteine side chain in the FMN pocket and C(4a) of the FMN.[9,10] Phototropin also contains an integral serine–threonine kinase, which confers autophosphorylation activity on phototropin that is modulated by the structure of the LOV domain. Thus, phototropin contains a light-driven molecular switch, the LOV domain, which confers light sensitivity on an enzymatic domain, the kinase. The structural basis for this is completely unknown.

(b) Determination of the mechanism: from movies to time-independent intermediates

How shall "analytical trapping" best be conducted, to establish whether a chemical kinetic mechanism with well-defined intermediate states exists? If it does exist, how shall the time-independent structure associated with each state be cleanly extracted and refined? Answering these questions constitutes a second frontier.[1]

Variations in the magnitude of the features in time-dependent (difference) Fourier maps arise from variation in the concentrations of the intermediates. These variations may be modelled and realistically presented as "movies" (see for example ref. 4 and 5) in which the electron density varies smoothly with time. However, interest lies not so much in the smooth variation of concentrations, but in the nature of the individual, distinct, intermediate structures. Progress along the reaction coordinate is not smooth, but may be visualized as a "hopping" of molecules from basin to basin in a complex energy landscape, in which each basin is associated with an intermediate state of the system.[11] Molecules do not spend significant time between basins. In particular, their residence time in the transition states that are represented by the mountain passes in this energy landscape lies in the femtosecond range. The best representation of reaction progress is therefore not a smoothly varying movie; it is a set of time-independent intermediate states or structures, and the accompanying rate coefficients for their interconversion. However, the number of such intermediates, how they interconvert and the time courses with which their concentrations vary are not known *a priori*. These quantities must be extracted from the time-resolved crystallographic data, and constitute determination of the mechanism.

If the mechanism is simple, then direct inspection of the "movie" may reveal it,[4] but a more general approach is needed. A promising strategy is to examine simultaneously the variation of the (difference) electron density at all grid points for all time points, using the mathematical tool of singular value decomposition, SVD.[12] SVD has been widely and successfully used for many years, for example to separate the time and wavelength variables in time-resolved absorption spectroscopy (for an example, see ref. 13) and, more recently, to analyze on a genome-wide basis the patterns of temporal expression of genes.[14] SVD can be readily adapted to the analysis of time-dependent (difference) electron density maps. SVD analysis yields a set of singular values, the species-associated (difference) electron density distributions or maps, each identified with a particular singular value, and the time course with which each distribution varies.

SVD is playing three main roles.[12] First, it separates the time and structure variables. Second, it acts as a noise filter which is "best" in a least-squares sense; and this property can be employed in an iterative mode to improve phase information (M. Schmidt *et al.*, unpublished results). Third, the time courses can be fitted by suitable functions such as a sum of exponentials, the exponents of which reveal macroscopic rates; and the species-associated distributions may be separated into a sum of underlying distributions, each of which arises from a desired, time-independent intermediate. The relationship between the species-associated distributions and the intermediates, and between the macroscopic rates and the microscopic rate coefficients, constitutes the mechanism. Preliminary results on both mock and real data (M. Schmidt *et al.*, unpublished results) suggest that this is a promising approach to the elucidation of mechanism.

(c) Enhanced time resolution

A substantial challenge is offered by experiments that seek to examine very fast processes in the fs to 100 ps time range. Typically, the processes are light-sensitive and their initiation is readily obtained by illumination of the sample with a short, high power, laser pulse. Experiments in the fs time range are particularly attractive since ultrafast structural dynamics in condensed matter occur on the time scale of the period of an interatomic vibration, below or around 100 fs. For example, certain important biological processes such as photosynthesis have their origin in events that occur on the fs time scale.[15] As discussed in more detail below, these processes are experimentally inaccessible with much longer, synchrotron X-ray pulses of around 100 ps duration. Enhancing the time resolution into the fs range to elucidate the nature of these processes thus constitutes a third frontier.

In considering how to attack this frontier, the limitations of pump–probe experiments should also be taken into account.[1,4] The time-resolved X-ray structure amplitudes $|F(hkl,t)|$ have to be acquired in a four-dimensional space spanned by the three variables in reciprocal space and by time. Changes in these structure amplitudes with time are small and error-prone. Reference values of these amplitudes $|F(hkl,0)|$ must be obtained prior to the initiation of any structural reaction if accurate measurements are to be made of the differences in structure amplitudes in time, $|F(hkl,t)| - |F(hkl,0)|$. Radiation damage limits the amount of data that can be acquired on any one crystal, which introduces systematic errors through crystal-to-crystal variation. If, as has been the case in experiments to date, the (hkl) variables are scanned rapidly and time is scanned slowly, then the evolution of the structural process must be pieced together from separate measurements made at different values of t, often on different crystals. Since each time point requires a separate reaction initiation, comparison of these measurements to extract the time-dependent signal is inaccurate and error prone. Further errors will be introduced if the probe X-ray pulse is destructive, since each time point now requires a separate crystal, not merely a separate measurement. Finally, it is a rule of thumb that the faster the structural reaction, the more limited are the underlying structural changes. Thus if the time resolution is improved, the precision of the structural measurements must also be improved.

An experimental strategy that both offers enhanced time resolution and minimizes systematic sources of error has appeal. Chirped X-ray pulses offer one such strategy.

Chirped X-ray pulses

In an unchirped pulse of electromagnetic radiation, the spectrum and direction of propagation are constant across the pulse and do not vary with time (Fig. 1a). In contrast, in a chirped pulse, a property of the radiation such as its energy or direction of propagation varies across the pulse and hence depends on time. For example, in a simple form of energy-chirped pulse the spectrum is monochromatic at all time instants but varies between a minimum energy E_{min} at the earliest, leading edge of the pulse and a maximum energy E_{max} at the latest, trailing edge (Fig. 1b). In a spatially-chirped pulse, the spectrum is again monochromatic but is constant in time. However, the direction of propagation of each ray varies with time and thus the rays incident on a sample sweep out a fan of radiation: the angle of incidence of the earliest ray differs from that of the latest ray (Fig. 1c). A pulse may combine features of an energy chirp and a spatial chirp, in which both the spectrum and the direction of propagation vary with time (Fig. 1d). The key feature of a chirped pulse is that it provides intrinsic time-tagging of photons : there is a one-to-one correspondence between a given energy or direction of propagation of photons and their temporal location in the pulse.

Chirped pulses are widely used in the microwave and visible regions of the spectrum. For example, the amplification of chirped pulses and their compression in time forms the basis for all high power, short pulse lasers.[16] However, chirped pulses have not been utilized in the hard X-ray region of the spectrum. Such pulses are not readily available, since synchrotron beamlines normally deliver almost entirely unchirped pulses.[17]

In the following sections, I point out that chirped hard X-ray pulses are particularly well-suited to ultrafast X-ray experiments with high time resolution, and discuss their applicability to single crystal Laue diffraction experiments in some detail. The proposed sub-picosecond photon source,

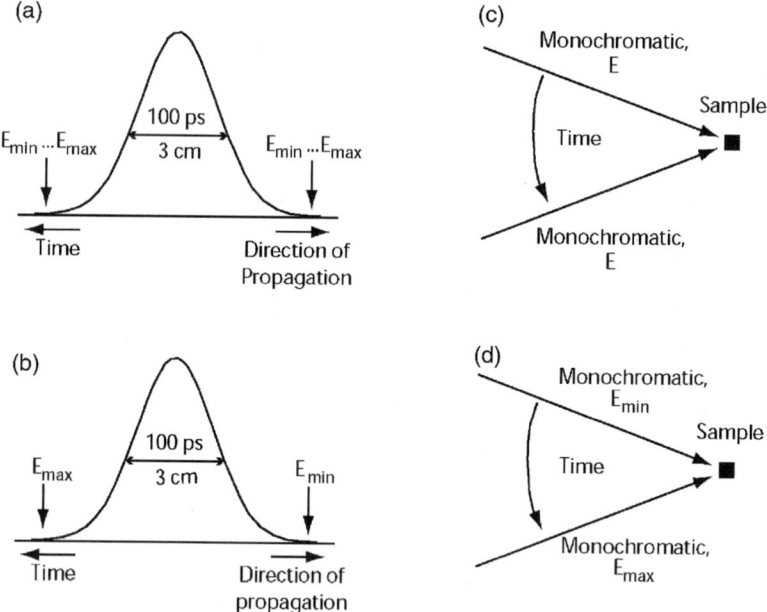

Fig. 1 Unchirped, energy- and spatially-chirped pulses. (a) Schematic of an unchirped pulse. All instants in the pulse contain the same range of X-ray energies E_{min}.........E_{max}. (b) Schematic of a simple energy-chirped pulse. The X-rays are monochromatic at all instants in the pulse, but this energy varies from E_{min} at the earliest, leading edge of the pulse to E_{max} at the latest, trailing edge of the pulse. (c) Schematic of a simple spatially-chirped pulse. The X-rays are monochromatic with energy E at all instants but their direction of propagation i.e. their angle of incidence on the sample varies across the pulse. (d) Schematic of a combined energy- and spatially-chirped pulse. Both the energy and the angle of incidence of the pulse on the sample vary with time.

SPPS, a precursor to the LCLS at Stanford, could be an excellent source of chirped hard X-ray pulses.

Ultrafast time-resolved X-ray experiments

(a) Time resolution

High time resolution is usually achieved by one of two routes: using a time-slicing X-ray detector such as a streak camera that directly provides a time resolution around 1 ps;[18] or by conducting the experiment in pump–probe mode, in which the evolution of the processes after a laser, pump pulse is monitored at a suitable and variable time delay t by an X-ray, probe pulse.[4,5] However, there are limitations on both routes. The active area of streak cameras is small and this restricts the classes of experiments to which they can be applied. They are either zero-dimensional, recording the time dependence of the flux of X-rays falling on one pixel, or one-dimensional, recording the flux on a short linear array of pixels. No ultrafast, time-slicing, two-dimensional detector exists. If it did, measurements could be made on the same sample, continuously in time.

The time resolution $\Delta\tau$ of conventional pump–probe experiments is set by three contributions: the duration of the pump laser pulse Δt_L that initiates the structural process, the duration of the probe X-ray pulse Δt_Z, and the jitter in the time delay between the two pulses Δt_J, eqn. (1):

$$\Delta\tau = (\Delta t_L^2 + \Delta t_Z^2 + \Delta t_J^2)^{1/2}. \tag{1}$$

It therefore appears that achieving a value of $\Delta\tau$ around 100 fs requires that each of Δt_L, Δt_Z and Δt_J be significantly lower than that value. It is non-trivial to achieve values of Δt_J much below 1 ps. Although ultrafast laser pulses with values of Δt_L in the tens of fs time range are readily obtained, this is not the case for X-ray pulses. The X-ray pulse length Δt_Z emitted by near-circular synchrotron sources is determined by the electron bunch pulse length, which in turn is limited to 50 to 100 ps by essential, long-term stability requirements on the electron beam. Considerable effort has therefore been put into the development of novel fs hard X-ray sources. Examples include laser-driven plasmas[19] and diode sources,[20] and sources based on high order harmonic generation[21] or interaction between a laser pulse and a relativistic electron beam.[22] However, at present the X-ray flux per pulse that these sources can deliver to the sample is too low to be experimentally useful for much more than proof-of-principle experiments.

A very promising, proposed source is the hard X-ray free electron laser, XFEL. In this device, extremely bright, fully spatially and temporally coherent, 100 fs pulses of X-rays are to be generated by the self-amplified spontaneous emission or SASE process[23] as a brief electron pulse derived from a linear accelerator traverses a very long undulator of roughly 100 m in length. However, the X-ray pulses from an XFEL are associated with electric fields believed to be sufficiently high to cause full ionization of all atoms and the complete destruction of the sample,[24] and the SASE process has not yet been demonstrated at hard X-ray wavelengths. No decision has yet been made on the proposal to construct the first such device at Stanford Synchrotron Radiation Laboratory, to be known as the Linear Coherent Light Source, LCLS.

Chirped X-ray pulses provide a third route to obtaining high time resolution. What is required is not necessarily a 100 fs X-ray pulse but rather, a much longer, non-destructive X-ray pulse at the sample whose characteristics still permit excellent time resolution. Although X-ray experiments and detectors cannot readily distinguish photons in time, they can easily distinguish photons in energy or in direction of propagation. The time tagging of photons inherent in a chirped pulse maps time into energy in an energy-chirped pulse, or into direction of propagation in a spatially-chirped pulse. The time variable is established by the nature of the chirp. In essence, chirped pulses map a variable that cannot be readily measured, time, into a variable that can be more easily measured, energy or direction of propagation.

(b) Time-resolved single crystal Laue diffraction

A straightforward example of how a chirped X-ray pulse would be utilized is provided by an ultrafast time-resolved X-ray diffraction experiment.

When a polychromatic, quasi-parallel pulse of X-rays falls on a stationary single crystal, a Laue diffraction pattern is generated that consists of an array of diffracted X-ray beams. Each beam is characterized by the set of crystal planes (*hkl*) that give rise to it, by its direction with respect to the incoming beam, by its intensity and by its X-ray energy. When the beams fall on an area detector such as a CCD or image plate, they generate an array of spatially-separated spots, the Laue spots, that comprise a single Laue image. It is straightforward to derive the unit cell dimensions and crystal orientation from the locations of the spots, and hence to index each spot (*hkl*) and identify the energy that stimulates it.[25] That is, Laue diffraction automatically maps the energy of each spot into its spatial location (Fig. 2). The X-ray structure amplitudes $|F(hkl)|$ can also be obtained by measurement of the integrated intensity of each spot, and the derivation and application of energy-dependent correction factors.[25]

As described above, time-resolved Laue experiments in macromolecular crystallography have been conducted in pump - probe mode.[4,5] The experiments yield the time dependence of the structure amplitudes $|F(hkl,t)|$ that arises in response to a structural perturbation which alters the spatial distribution of electrons in the unit cell but leaves the crystal lattice unchanged. When the X-ray phases associated with each value of $|F(hkl,0)|$ are known, the time-dependent, space average electron density distributions $\rho(xyz,t)$ and the time-dependent difference electron density distributions $\Delta\rho(xyz,t) = \rho(xyz,t) - \rho(xyz,0)$ are obtained. From these distributions, structural and mechanistic information may be deduced.[4,5]

Depending on the unit cell dimensions of the crystal, its limiting crystallographic resolution and the complexity of the structural mechanism being examined, a complete set of four-dimensional, time-resolved data may contain of order 10 000 unique values of (*hkl*) and 100 values of *t*. Laser pulses in the ns to 100 fs range have been used as the pump,[4,5,26] and unchirped synchrotron X-ray pulses of around 100 ps duration as the probe.[4,5] The time resolution $\Delta\tau$ achieved (eqn. (1)) ranges from a few ns, determined largely by the duration of the pump laser pulse Δt_L, to a few hundred ps,

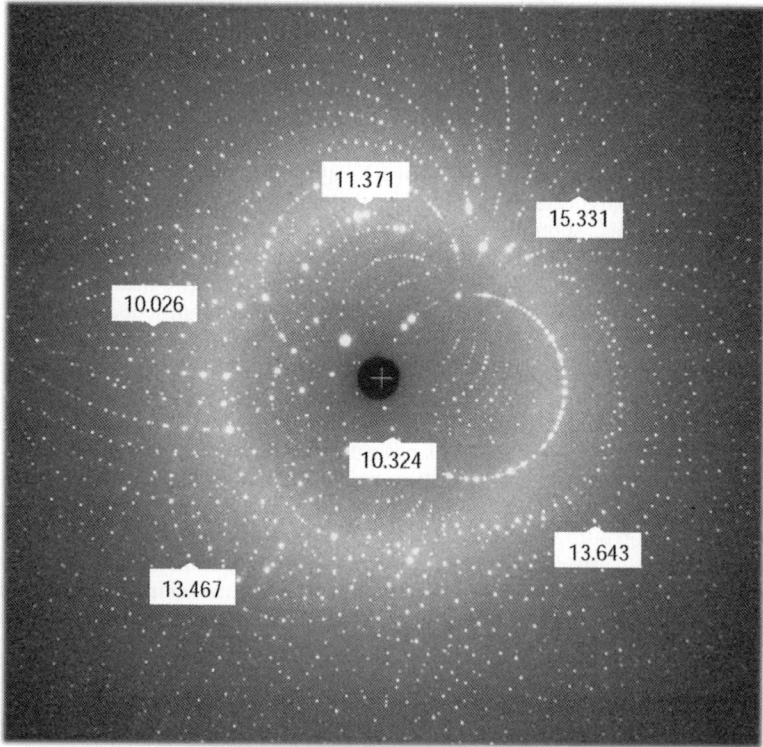

Fig. 2 A representative Laue pattern from a protein crystal. The X-ray energy that gives rise to certain spots is identified.

determined by the duration of the probe X-ray pulse Δt_Z and the jitter in the delay time Δt_J. Sources such as the ID9 beamline at ESRF or 14 ID-B at BioCARS/APS deliver around 10^8 photons per 0.1% bandpass per X-ray pulse through a 200 μm aperture to the crystal, with a duration of around 100 ps.

The limitations on pump–probe experiments can be addressed if an energy-chirped X-ray probe pulse replaces the unchirped pulse. Suppose that a simple, perfectly energy-chirped X-ray pulse of 100 ps total duration (Fig. 1a) falls on a crystal and generates a Laue diffraction pattern. Laue spots stimulated by the lowest energies near E_{min} correspond to the earliest times of arrival of the X-ray pulse at the crystal, and those stimulated by the highest energies near E_{max} to the latest times of arrival. Suppose further that the pump laser pulse occurs during the probe X-ray pulse, at a time when the incident X-ray energy is E. The structure amplitudes derived from all Laue spots stimulated by energy E_{spot} where $E_{min} < E_{spot} < E$ arise from the unperturbed structure and yield $|F(hkl,0)|$. Each spot where $E < E_{spot} < E_{max}$ arises from a perturbed structure and yields $|F(hkl,t_{spot})|$ where t_{spot} is the time after the laser pulse that corresponds to E_{spot} (Fig. 3). Thus, each Laue image automatically contains the internal control $|F(hkl,0)|$ for certain values of (hkl) and a set of time-resolved data $|F(hkl,t)|$ for a range of values of t, for other values of (hkl). This time range is set by the total duration of the chirped pulse and by the time of arrival of the laser pulse. No time-resolved X-ray detector is required. The experimental diffraction pattern itself contains information on the delay time between the laser and X-ray pulses; jitter in the delay time is irrelevant. Finally, suppose that the energy-chirped X-ray pulse contains the same number of photons per 0.1% bandpass as the original, unchirped pulse; the photons are simply redistributed in time within the pulse in a more experimentally-convenient manner. Hence, we see that the intensity of each Laue spot, the background underlying the spots and the exposure time per diffraction image are unaltered in replacing the unchirped by the chirped pulse.

The Laue diffraction pattern obtained from one crystal orientation contains only a subset of values of (hkl). If the experiment is repeated at a set of slightly different orientations of the crystal, then complete coverage of the unique volume in reciprocal space can be achieved. As the crystal is re-oriented, each spot samples a different energy E_{spot} corresponding to a different value of t_{spot} and yields $|F(hkl,t_{spot})|$. If the total duration of the chirped pulse does not cover the complete time range needed, then the time of arrival of the laser pulse can be adjusted to precede all of the chirped X-ray pulse. In this case, no automatic measurement of $|F(hkl,0)|$ occurs.

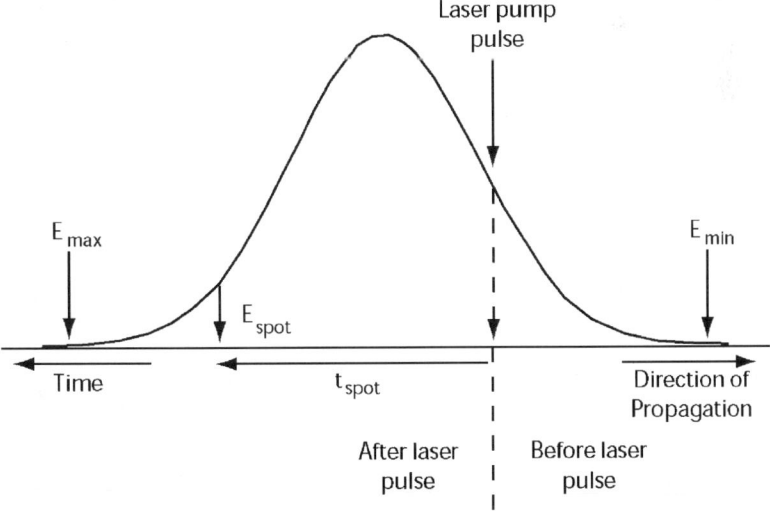

Fig. 3 Schematic of a simple energy-chirped pulse, in which a laser pump pulse occurs during the X-ray pulse when the X-ray energy is E. All spots that arise from energies between E_{min} and E diffract before the laser pulse; all spots that arise from energies between E and E_{max} diffract after the laser pulse. In particular, a spot with energy E_{spot} diffracts at a time t_{spot} after the laser pulse.

A similar experiment is possible if a spatially-chirped X-ray pulse replaces the unchirped pulse. When a nearly parallel, monochromatic X-ray beam is incident on a stationary crystal, a "Laue still" diffraction pattern is generated that contains only those spots (hkl) lying on the corresponding Ewald sphere. As the direction of propagation of the incident beam changes, the Ewald sphere also changes and gives rise to a new set of spots. In a spatially-chirped pulse, each direction of propagation (that is, each incident ray) corresponds to a different time of arrival of the probe pulse and all rays together constitute a fan (Fig. 1c). If the pump laser pulse arrives at a time corresponding to one particular ray in the fan, all earlier rays generate spots from which values of $|F(hkl,0)|$ may be obtained. Each later ray corresponds to a known value of the time delay t and generates spots that yield $|F(hkl,t)|$.

There are disadvantages to the use of a spatially-chirped pulse. The spots on the Laue still generated by each ray are displaced relative to their neighbors; the spots derived from the fan are elongated. Although each spot retains the same number of photons, the peak height of each and the signal to noise will be diminished. The possibility of overlap between adjacent spots with different values of (hkl) is increased. The properties of each ray (if they are discrete) or of the fan of rays as a whole (if they are continuously distributed in angle of incidence) must be such as to generate the integrated intensities necessary to yield accurate structure amplitudes.

In effect, a chirped pulse allows the four-dimensional space spanned by (hkl) and t to be scanned in an unusual way: an individual Laue diffraction pattern contains spots that arise from both a subset of the values of (hkl) and a range of values of t, notably including 0. This should be contrasted with the two normal ways of spanning this space. In the first (as for example in ref. 4 and 5), t is kept fixed and data are collected at a series of orientations of the crystal to cover all of (hkl); then t is altered and the process repeated (if necessary with new crystals), until all desired values of t are covered. Data at $t = 0$ are obtained in a separate experiment. In the second (S. Anderson et al., unpublished results), the crystal is kept in a fixed orientation and data are collected over all desired values of t including 0; then the crystal orientation is altered and the process repeated (if necessary with new crystals) until all unique (hkl) values are covered. The systematic errors that affect data acquisition and reduction in both these ways should be greatly minimized by the use of chirped pulses, in which the (hkl) and t variables are intermingled.

(c) Application of chirped pulses to other energy-dispersive experiments

An effective strategy for an X-ray absorption experiment is to conduct it in energy-dispersive mode. The beamline optics deliver a polychromatic X-ray beam to the sample that is highly collimated in one angle dimension but strongly convergent in the other. In the fan of X-rays falling on the sample, each ray corresponds to a different X-ray energy.[27] The X-rays transmitted by the sample are collected on a one-dimensional detector (Fig. 4). Though the experimental geometry is quite different from the Laue diffraction case, there is again a one-to-one correspondence between spatial location on the detector and photon energy. If an energy-chirped X-ray pulse is used, each spatial location on the detector corresponds to a different time of arrival at the sample. A time-resolved X-ray absorption experiment can then be carried out in the same manner as the Laue experiment:

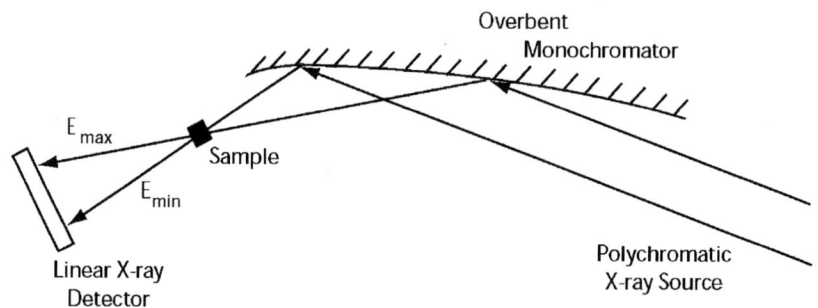

Fig. 4 Dispersive X-ray absorption experiment.

lower X-ray energies correspond to earlier times of arrival of the probe, X-ray pulse relative to the pump, laser pulse, and higher energies to later times. To obtain complete coverage of the energy- and time-dependent absorption spectrum $\chi(E,t)$, one strategy is to vary the time of arrival of the laser pulse relative to the X-ray pulse. Alternatively, the X-ray optics may be adjusted to alter the relation between energy and angle of incidence on the sample.

In energy-dispersive powder diffraction, a point detector with excellent energy resolution is positioned at a fixed scattering angle with respect to the polychromatic, highly collimated, incident X-ray beam. If an energy-chirped X-ray pulse is used, the energy resolution automatically maps into time resolution. To obtain the complete set of $I(E,t)$ values, variation of the time of arrival of the laser pulse relative to the X-ray pulse will be necessary.

Generation of chirped X-ray pulses

(a) Introduction

The potential applications of chirped X-ray pulses have not been widely considered because until very recently, there was no suitable source of such pulses. In a conventional synchrotron source, the radiation from each electron as it traverses a bending magnet, wiggler or undulator is independent of that from all other electrons in the bunch and in particular does not depend on longitudinal position in the bunch. The pulse of radiation from the bunch is therefore unchirped.[17]

Two novel methods have been proposed of manipulating an individual particle bunch in a synchrotron with the goal of obtaining a pulse of X-rays short with respect to the normal bunch length of 50–100 ps. Both methods also produce a chirped X-ray pulse, though that was not their explicit object. The first[28] employs an unusual RF cavity that in effect turns the bunch on its side; it has not been tested experimentally. The second[29,30] modulates the electron energy of a small slice of the electrons in a bunch as they pass through an undulator, by interaction with a fs laser pulse that co-propagates with the electron beam. Electrons of different energies pass through an immediately downstream dispersive element, which separates them in space according to their energies. Since electrons of different energy traverse different path lengths, they are also separated in time. That is, the source exhibits both an energy and a spatial chirp. Initial experiments confirm that this method works.[30] A limiting feature is that only a small fraction of the electrons in a synchrotron bunch are affected, and hence only a small fraction of the total number of X-rays that would be emitted by the electron bunch are chirped.

Chirped pulses in the UV–visible region of the spectrum are obtained by passing an unchirped, polychromatic pulse over a grating pair in which photons of different energies traverse different path lengths.[31] Equivalent schemes in the hard X ray region of the spectrum would utilize, for example, multilayer pairs or asymmetric-cut crystals.[28,32] Indeed, all X-ray dispersive elements automatically introduce an X-ray chirp, but its magnitude is in general extremely small. Hard X-ray delay lines can therefore be envisaged. However, all such schemes are subject to Liouville's Theorem on the conservation of phase space volume. If a chirped pulse is derived from an initially unchirped pulse, it is expanded in time; and conversely, a lengthy, chirped pulse can be compressed into a brief, unchirped pulse. Thus, application of a hard X-ray delay line to an unchirped, 100 ps synchrotron X-ray pulse would result in a chirped pulse of much longer duration, say 1 ns. Further, the time resolution can never be less than the original pulse length, here 100 ps. It cannot approach the desired fs time range.

(b) The sub-picosecond photon source (SPPS)

The experimental situation has been transformed by initial conceptual and experimental steps towards the LCLS. A precursor known as the SPPS has very recently been proposed[33] that does not depend on the SASE principle but is designed to generate very brief X-ray pulses of under 100 fs. The SPPS is based on modifications to the existing SLAC linac. Briefly, the SPPS exploits the fact that if the low emittance requirements essential to the SASE principle are relaxed, then it is possible to substantially compress the electron beam in longitudinal phase space (that is, in time) without excessive blow-up in the transverse phase space (that is, in position and momentum). These

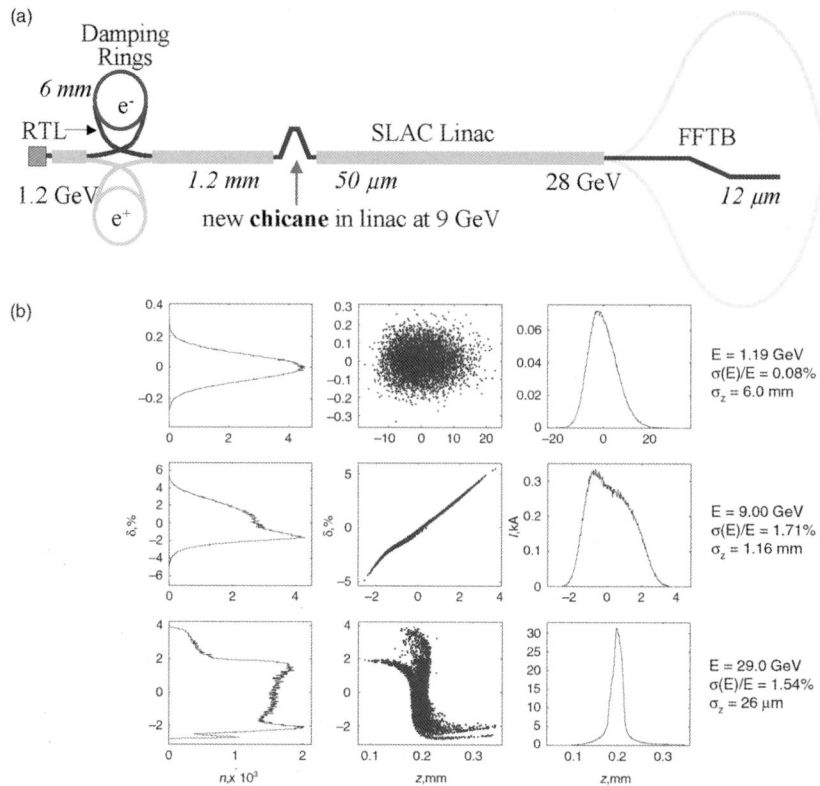

Fig. 5 Above: The overall layout of the SPPS. Adapted from Fig. 1 of ref. 33. Below: The electron bunch compression process at various locations. Left column, the energy distribution; center column, the phase space distribution; right column, the longitudinal distribution. Upper row, at extraction from the damping ring; center row, prior to new chicane; lower row, after FFTB bends. Adapted from Fig. 5 of ref. 33.

compressed, high energy electron bunches then generate very short X-ray pulses as they pass through a suitable undulator.

The full SPPS scheme[33] proposes three stages of compression of the electron bunches as they traverse the SLAC linac (Fig. 5): a damping ring to linac compressor and bends (electron energy at the exit 1.19 GeV, bunch length σ_z around 1.16 mm i.e. 3.86 ps), a new chicane compressor (9 to 10 GeV, around 50 µm, 165 fs) and a second new chicane compressor at the entrance to the Final Focus Test Beam (FFTB) facility (28 GeV, around 26 µm, 86 fs). The final result would be an almost entirely unchirped electron bunch of 80 fs FWHM duration, with an energy spread σ_E/E_{el} of 1.5% around its mean of 28 GeV and a peak current of 30 kA.[33] If this electron bunch then passes through a 10 m undulator, unchirped hard X-ray pulses of less than 100 fs duration and an X-ray flux of around 3×10^7 photons per 0.1% bandwidth per pulse would be produced. This value is nearly comparable with that delivered by ID9 at ESRF and 14 ID-B at BioCARS/APS of around 10^8, used successfully for our time-resolved experiments. That is, this form of the SPPS would deliver polychromatic X-ray pulses comparable to those available today from the ESRF and APS undulators, but in a pulse that is three orders of magnitude shorter in time.

These 100 fs SPPS pulses could, in principle, be used directly for pump–probe single crystal X-ray diffraction experiments, exactly as with the present 100 ps APS pulses. However, jitter in the relative timing of the fs pump laser pulses and the 100 fs X-ray pulses becomes critical to the time resolution of the entire experiment, as discussed above; any structural changes on this very short time scale are likely to be very small and prone to being masked by systematic and random error in the time-dependent X-ray structure amplitudes; and if non-linear effects turn out to be significant, the 100 fs X-ray pulses may be more damaging to the crystals than otherwise comparable 100 ps pulses.

These limitations can be addressed by a modification to the full SPPS scheme that utilizes the less-compressed, chirped electron bunches at lower energy. Note that the electron bunch immediately prior to the new 9 GeV chicane is highly chirped, with an energy spread of 1.7% or 154 MeV. The chirp is nearly linear, and the bunch length σ_z is 1.16 mm or 3.86 ps. The full electron energy range of $-3\sigma_E$ to $+3\sigma_E$ then spans 8.54 GeV to 9.46 GeV, and a full duration of 23.2 ps (Fig. 6A). Suppose that this electron bunch is delivered to an undulator whose specifications are those of an APS undulator A with 100 poles and a period of 3.3 cm, operated at $K = 0.5$. (These specifications are used simply for definiteness; the optimum insertion device for this source is likely to have rather different parameters). The X-ray photon energy E_{photon} of the n-th harmonic is given by:

$$E_{photon} = \frac{0.95 n E_{el}^2}{(1 + K^2/2)\lambda_u}$$

and

$$dE_{photon} = \frac{1.9 n E_{el} dE_{el}}{(1 + K^2/2)\lambda_u}$$

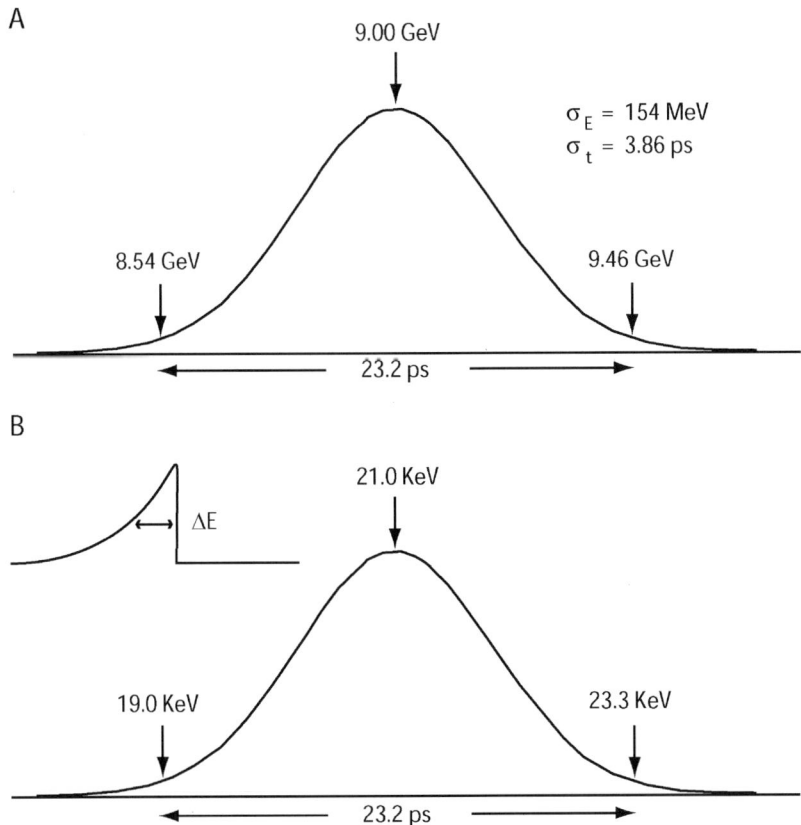

Fig. 6 A. Schematic of the profile of an energy-chirped electron pulse at 9.00 GeV with $\sigma_E = 154$ MeV. The $\pm 3\sigma_E$ energies are noted. B. Schematic of the profile of the energy-chirped X-ray pulse obtained by passing the electron pulse in A through an undulator (see text). At each point, the X-ray energy spans a small spectral range of width ΔE, shown schematically in the inset.

E_{photon} thus ranges for the first harmonic from 19.0 KeV at the leading edge of the pulse (lowest electron energy) to 23.3 KeV at the trailing edge (highest electron energy), in an X-ray pulse of around 23.2 ps full duration (Fig.6B).

Four main factors contribute to the time resolution available with such an X-ray pulse. First, the chirp in the electron bunch is not perfect; electrons of a given energy occupy a small range of longitudinal positions in the bunch, which corresponds to a small time range Δt_{chirp}. Second, the chirp and hence the mapping of energy into time may not be stable from pulse to pulse, and gives rise to Δt_{pulse}. This factor will not be significant if the zero time can be successfully extracted from each diffraction pattern, as suggested above. Third, electrons of a given energy generate an X-ray spectrum in the nth harmonic of width ΔE_{photon} where

$$\Delta E_{photon}/E_{photon} \sim 1/nN$$

where N is the undulator period (Fig. 6B, inset). X-rays of a given energy thus originate from electrons of a small range of energy, and hence from a small range of time, $\Delta t_{spectrum}$. Fourth, indexing of the Laue diffraction pattern generated when such a chirped X-ray pulse falls on a single crystal assigns an energy E_{spot} to each spot with an uncertainty ΔE_{spot}, corresponding to Δt_{spot}. The overall time resolution is therefore given by

$$\Delta \tau_{experiment} = (\Delta t_{chirp}^2 + \Delta t_{pulse}^2 + \Delta t_{spectrum}^2 + \Delta t_{spot}^2)^{1/2}.$$

Of these four factors, the third appears to be the most significant. In particular,

$$dE_{photon}/\Delta E_{photon} \sim 2nNdE_{el}/E_{el}.$$

The larger this quantity, the better the time resolution. This suggests that the largest electron energy chirp consistent with pulse stability, and a high harmonic n derived from an undulator with many periods N, should be employed.

The above discussion has concentrated on the use of the chirped 9 GeV electron bunch. There is another possibility: pass the final, compressed, nearly unchirped, 28 GeV electron bunch through an expander, to generate a longer bunch with a suitable chirp prior to entering the undulator.

Conclusions

Achieving an experimental time resolution in the 100 fs range will be challenging. The conventional pump–probe experiment using an unchirped X-ray pulse will be limited by jitter in the relative timing of the two pulses; and the unconventional experiment proposed here using a chirped X-ray pulse will be limited by the characteristics of the X-ray chirp. Nevertheless, the effort will be worth while if important biological problems can be addressed.[15]

Acknowledgements

These ideas were developed during a short leave at the University of California at Berkeley/Lawrence Berkeley Laboratory, and at the European Synchrotron Radiation Facility in Grenoble, France. It is a pleasure to acknowledge the hospitality of Professor Graham Fleming (UC Berkeley) and Drs Michael Wulff and Peter Lindley (ESRF); and discussions with them and with Roger Falcone, Howard Padmore, Robert Schoenlein, Charles Shank, Sasha Zholents and Max Zolotorev (UC Berkeley and LBL); Dominique Bourgeois and Andreas Freund (ESRF); and Vukica Šrajer and Zhong Ren (BioCARS). Supported by NIH grants RR07707 and GM36452.

References

1. K. Moffat, *Chem. Rev.*, 2001, **101**, 1569.
2. K. Moffat and R. Henderson, *Curr. Opin. Struct. Biol.*, 1995, **5**, 656.
3. B. Stoddard, *Nature Struct. Biol.*, 1996, **3**, 907.
4. V. Šrajer, Z. Ren, T.-Y. Teng, M. Schmidt, T. Ursby, D. Bourgeois, C. Pradervand, W. Schildkamp, M. Wulff and K. Moffat, *Biochemistry*, 2001, **40**, 13 802.
5. Z. Ren, B. Perman, V. Šrajer, T.-Y. Teng, C. Pradervand, D. Bourgeois, F. Schotte, T. Ursby, R. Kort, M. Wulff and K. Moffat, *Biochemistry*, 2001, **40**, 13 788.

6 Arabidopsis Genome Initiative, *Nature*, 2000, **408**, 796.
7 J. M. Christie, M. Salomon, K. Nozue, M. Wada and W. R. Briggs, *Science*, 1998, **282**, 1698.
8 T. Kinoshita, M. Doi, N. Suetsugu, T. Kagawa, M. Wada and K. Shimizaki, *Nature*, 2001, **414**, 656.
9 S. Crosson and K. Moffat, *Proc. Natl. Acad. Sci. USA*, 2001, **98**, 2995.
10 S. Crosson and K. Moffat, *Plant Cell*, 2002, **14**, 1067.
11 *Simplicity and Complexity in Proteins and Nucleic Acids*, ed. H. Frauenfelder, J. Deisenhofer and P. Wolynes, Dahlem University Press, Berlin, 1999.
12 E. R. Henry and J. Hofrichter, *Methods Enzymol.*, 1992, **210**, 129.
13 A. Ansari, C. Jones, E. R. Henry, J. Hofrichter and W. A. Eaton, *Biochemistry*, 1994, **33**, 5128.
14 O. Alter, P. O. Brown and D. Botstein, *Proc. Natl. Acad. Sci. USA*, 2000, **97**, 10101.
15 J.-L. Martin and M. H. Vos, *Annu. Rev. Biophys. Biomol. Struct.*, 1992, **21**, 199.
16 D. Strickland and G. Mourou, *Opt. Commun.*, 1985, **56**, 219.
17 J.-F. Eloy, B. Brullot, J. Doublier, A. K. Freund, R. Marmoret, O. Mathon, R. Tucoulou, B. Villette and R. Wrobel, *SPIE*, 1998, **3451**, paper 12.
18 Z. Chang, A. Rundquist, J. Zhou, M. M. Murnane, H. C. Kapteyn, X. Liu, B. Shan, J. Liu, L. Niu, M. Gong and X. Zhang, *Appl. Phys. Lett.*, 1996, **69**, 133.
19 C. Rose-Petruck, R. Jimenez, T. Gou, A. Cavalleri, C. Siders, F. Raksi, J. A. Squier, B. C. Walker, K. R. Wilson and C. P. J. Barty, *Nature*, 1999, **398**, 310.
20 T. Anderson, I. V. Tomov and P. Rentzepis, *J. Appl. Phys.*, 1992, **71**, 5161.
21 Z. Chang, A. Rundquist, H. Wang, M. M. Murnane and H. C. Kapteyn, *Phys. Rev. Lett.*, 1997, **79**, 2967.
22 R. W. Schoenlein, W. P. Leemans, A. H. Chin, P. Volfbeyn, T. E. Glover, P. Balling, M. Zolotorev, K.-J. Kim, S. Chattopadhyay and C. V. Shank, *Science*, 1996, **274**, 236.
23 *Linac Coherent Light Source (LCLS) Design Study Report*, ed. The LCLS Design Study Group, Stanford Linear Accelerator Center, 1998.
24 R. Neutze, R. Wouts, D. van der Spoel, E. Weckert and J. Hajdu, *Nature*, 2000, **406**, 752.
25 K. Moffat, *Methods Enzymol. B*, 1997, **277**, 433.
26 M. Wulff, F. Schotte, G. Naylor, D. Bourgeois, K. Moffat and G. Mourou, *Nucl. Instrum. Methods Phys. Res., Sect. A*, 1997, **A398**, 69.
27 T. Matsushita and U. Kaminaga, *Jpn. J. Appl. Crystallogr.*, 1980, **13**, 465.
28 A. Zholents, P. Heimann, M. Zolotorev and J. Byrd, *Nucl. Instrum. Methods Phys. Res., Sect. A*, 1999, **425**, 385.
29 A. A. Zholents and M. S. Zolotorev, *Phys. Rev. Lett.*, 1996, **76**, 912.
30 R. W. Schoenlein, S. Chattopadhyay, H. H. W. Chong, T. E. Glover, P. A. Heimann, C. V. Shank, A. Zholents and M. Zolotorev, *Science*, 2000, **287**, 2237.
31 E. B. Treacy, *Phys. Lett*, 1968, **28A**, 34.
32 J.-F. Eloy and A. Freund, *SPIE*, 1997, **3154**, 152.
33 M. Cornacchia, J. Arthur, L. Bentson, R. Carr, P. Emma, J. Galayda, P. Krejcik, I. Lindau, J. Safranek, J. Schmerge, J. Stohr, R. Tatchyn and A. Wootton, SLAC-PUB-8950, LCLS-TN-01-7, 2001.

General Discussion

Prof. Helliwell opened the discussion of the Introductory Lecture: Your conversion efficiency in the Pt–Pt complex experiment was only 2%; have you explored, *e.g.* by simulation or calculation, the limits of applicability to lighter, *i.e.* weaker scattering, elements than Pt due to this?

Prof. Coppens responded: We believe that we can reach higher conversion percentages by working with smaller crystals at more intense sources, or by using more complex solids in which the active species are diluted. The 'limiting percentage' depends on the distortion, for example, for the large change in dihedral angle predicted to occur (for the isolated molecule) on excitation of benzophenone, the limiting percentage will be lower than for small changes. We have done some simulations; you are right that in general the conversion percentage must be higher when the scattering is not dominated by one or a few strongly scattering atoms.

Prof. Bürgi asked: An illuminated crystal of $TEA_3HPt_2(H_2P_2O_4)_4$ is composed of two species, 98% ground state molecules, 2% excited state molecules. Does the difference in Pt–Pt distances give rise to a diffuse scattering signal?

Prof. Coppens answered: We have assumed here and in our work on transition metal linkage isomers that the distribution of the excited molecules in the crystal is random. This assumption is supported by the lack of additional diffraction spots and the results of the structural analyses. So there should be a diffuse scattering contribution, but we have not looked for it.

Dr Schmidt asked: (i) Did you see changes in the crystal parameters, since your observed atomic displacements are significant relative to the unit cell parameters? (ii) If yes, how did you correct for these?

Prof. Coppens replied: Yes. In the case of the binuclear Pt complex the excited state population was too small to observe an effect on the cell dimensions. However in our work on photoinduced metastable transition-metal nitrosyl and sulfur dioxide complexes, the conversion percentages were much higher (sometimes close to 50%), and significant cell dimension changes were observed. The sign of such changes correlates with the change in the molecular shape. For example, we observed the largest effect in (pentamethylcyclopentadienyl)nitrosyl-nickel, $[Ni(NO)(\eta^5\text{-}Cp^*)]$, in which the NO groups are closely aligned with the *b*-axis. This axis shortens by 0.28 Å on photoinduced conversion of 47% of the molecules to the metastable state, while the *c*-axis shows a smaller decrease. In the combined analysis of the light-on and dark data it is necessary to take such changes into account. For the photodifference maps in which the ground state density is subtracted, the fractional coordinates must be converted to the new cell in order to prevent a bond length change on transfer to the new cell. In least squares refinement of the response ratios we use two sets of cell dimensions, in the metastable state work we use a slightly different procedure in which the ground state molecule is allowed to undergo rigid body motions after it has been included with corrected fractional coordinates to preserve the intramolecular distances.

Dr Chen said: I am not sure about the Pt–Pt distance in the compound, but we have encountered difficulties in determining the Rh–Rh distance in another similar compound. This distance was too long for EXAFS in solution at room temperature. (i) What were your excited state structure calculation results on the nearest neighbour to Cu distance? (ii) Would you please comment on any problem in making comparisons between your calculations that were carried out on a single molecule and your experimental results that were obtained in single crystals where the effect of crystal packing was significant?

Prof. Coppens replied: (i) We find that the Cu–N distance decreases by about 0.04 Å upon metal-to-ligand charge transfer. The shortening is as expected from the change in oxidation state of copper. We are working on the calculation of the five-coordinate exciplex, and hope to have results shortly. (ii) There are crystal structures for three different salts of the binuclear Pt complex. They are very different in terms of intermolecular interactions, two are acid salts with infinite hydrogen bonded networks, while the third, the potassium salt, is held together by cation–anion contacts. The variation in ground state distances between the three structures is about 0.01 Å at most, which makes it seem unlikely that the excited state distances would be very much affected by the crystal packing, in this case at least. The variation between distances from the various theoretical calculations for either the ground or excited state is about ten times larger.

Prof. Helliwell opened the discussion of Prof. Wulff's paper: Your beamline at ESRF encompasses the spectrum of chemistry fields from biochemistry through to "pure" chemistry what features are common to all the chemical experiments in terms of structure to function rather than 'simple' characterization?

Prof. Wulff responded: The main focus of our work has been to follow structural changes following breakage or formation of a chemical bond in condensed systems. For systems such as myoglobin and iodine, the cage around the photo-activated molecule determines the reaction pathways and to some extent their time course.

Dr Nibbering said: Most of the I_2 recombines very fast because of the cage effect, and what you observe is only the minor fraction that can escape the cage, diffuse away and finally recombine again. Would it not be beneficial if one were to persue an experiment where I_2 is inside a nano-cavity, so that all I_2 molecules can dissociate to larger internuclear distances, and the expected signals in X-ray diffraction will be more pronounced.

Prof. Wulff replied: The photo-induced signal indicates that 15–50% of the photolysed iodine molecules dissociate (solvent dependent), *i.e.* break through the solvent cage. The signal from atomic iodine is therefore already quite strong.

Dr Techert said: One advantage of time-resolved X-ray scattering is the extended q range, which can be scanned in one measurement. Therefore, it is possible to determine intra- as well as intermolecular distances of a system within one experiment, in contrast to spectroscopic methods. This is summarised in Figs. 12 and 13 of your paper. In the reported experiment a ns laser was used as excitation source. In Fig. 13, the experimental difference maps at low q range are interpreted as thermal heating effects. How can the found thermal effects be affected by energy flow? Can, in general, energy flow be studied by time-resolved scattering techniques? How does the thermally induced change in the Boltzmann distribution function (see the paper) influence the difference map at high q?

Prof. Wulff answered: When two iodine atoms recombine to form a molecule, the binding energy is transferred to the solvent, *i.e.* the solvent cools the nascent molecule. The flow of energy is slaved to the recombination. It proceeds though at three stages: direct recombination *via* vibrational cooling on the X-state potential (100 ps), intersystem crossing from the A-state (500–2700 ns) and atomic recombination *via* diffuse motion (µs). The result is that the solvent starts to expand. If the expansion was instantaneous, the distance between nearest neighbours, as measured by the angular position of the liquid peak, would be a direct measure of the energy flow. In a real liquid, the expansive motion and its time scale have to be included. The expansion is seen starting from 25–50 ns onwards. After about 1 µs, the expansion stops, *i.e.* the system reaches thermal equilibrium. We are currently working with Savo Bratos, University of Paris, to separate the thermal expansion from the energy flow. Concerning your second question, if an iodine molecule is (thermally) excited to a vibrational level near the ground state, its average bond length will increase. A distribution of bond lengths will shift and broaden the difference oscillations and the effect is largest at high q. However this broadening does not prevent us from seeing oscillations up to a $Q = 9.0$ Å^{-1} in iodine and we have the impression that the effect is small in iodine. The effect should be treated as a Debye–Waller factor as in crystallography.

Dr May asked: Is there any chance of activating the C–Cl bond and what would be the consequences?

Prof. Wulff replied: From recent studies of CH_2I_2 in the solvent CH_2Cl_2, we know that this solvent can be activated *via* two-photon absorption. It is our impression that the solvent CCl_4 is completely transparent to the (softer) 515 nm laser pulse used here. We are planning an experiment to check this point.

Prof. Greaves said: You use the molecular potential for iodine to interpret your laser excited X-ray scattering data. Do these new experiments enable you to refine the potential in any way or do they simply demonstrate its correctness?

Prof. Wulff replied: Our initial fit functions, based on simple molecular form factors with the solvent cage, are not very sensitive to the bond length of the A/A-state. We will soon include cage effects and hope that that will enhance our sensitivity. In addition, new multi-layer optics will reduce the polychromatic bandwidth from 3–4% to about 1%. Combined, we hope to enhance our model selectivity.

Prof. Coppens asked: Is your spatial resolution affected by the use of a 3% band width. As the lineshape of your undulator harmonic is asymmetric does it introduce a bias?

Prof. Wulff answered: The polychromatic X-ray spectrum from a single-harmonic undulator leads to a slight increase in the background of the radial intensity on a CCD detector and that dampens the oscillation amplitude in the difference pattern. Simulations show that the damping is small and greatly compensated by the 250–500 fold gain in flux over conventional monochromatic methods.

Dr Techert opened the discussion of Dr Nibbering's paper: In the reported work the out-of-plane-twisting mode was found to be 60 cm^{-1}, which is surprisingly high if it is compared with the twist motion of stilbene (*ca.* 11 cm^{-1}). Is this high value due to the rigidity of the system, which enhances the harmonic contribution (in contrast to the rotational contribution in stilbene) to this vibrational mode?

Dr Nibbering responded: The high value is indeed due to the strong intramolecular hydrogen bond, making the molecular structure more rigid. We compared the out-of-plane mode of 2-(2'-hydroxyphenyl)benzothiazole (HBT) with that of its anion (where the proton is removed by a strong base) in quantum chemical calculations. In the case of the anion, where no hydrogen bond exists, the frequency of the out-of-plane mode is very close to that of stilbene.

Prof. Moffat asked: Have similar ultra-fast spectroscopic measurements been made either in single crystals or in HBT bound to a small protein? In other words, how does the "solvent" environment affect the mechanism and rates of reaction?

Dr Nibbering answered: The observed H-transfer reaction in HBT in tetrachloroethene represents a clear case of intramolecular H-transfer with minor solvent contributions. When dissolving HBT in polar solvents, like DMSO, alcohols or water, the efficiency of intramolecular hydrogen bond formation will be affected and compete with intermolecular hydrogen bonds with solvent molecules. Since these changes in the hydrogen bond have pronounced effects on the optical spectra, HBT in polar solvents has been studied in optical pump–probe experiments, where different proton transfer times have been deduced from the observed transients. We have not performed femtosecond IR experiments on HBT in polar solvents yet. We expect to see different dynamics dependent on the hydrogen bond configurations.

Dr Techert asked: How is *excitonic coupling* defined in the liquid phase (or does this only refer to IR studies on peptides)?

Dr Nibbering replied: Excitonic coupling refers to coupling of vibrational modes within a larger molecular system, that may itself be in the condensed phase (liquids, proteins, solids) or even in the gas phase. These vibrational modes have a mutual coupling when their vibrational bands spectrally overlap or are at very small detuning. Coupling might take place by a through space transition dipole–dipole coupling mechanism with angle and distance dependences. Another mechanism might involve a through bond coupling scheme. Examples include the amide I band in amino acid subunits in peptides, or hydrogen bonded OH-groups in dimeric systems, such as the acetic acid dimer or the DNA base pairs in the double helix.

Dr Chen asked: How do you distinguish anharmonic coupling in the proton transfer processes that you are probing from heterogeneity of H-bonding distribution that was disturbed by the laser excitation, which may also result in the spectral shift of the O–H shielding band?

Dr Nibbering answered: The theory of O–H stretching vibration line shapes shows that anharmonic coupling of the high-frequency O–H stretching mode to other vibrational modes leads to (i) a red-shifting, a consequence of the weakening of the O–H stretching vibration; (ii) a Franck–Condon progression due to coupling with underdamped low-frequency modes; (iii) a broadening, due to coupling to overdamped low-frequency modes; (iv) level splitting due to Fermi resonances with vibrational overtone or combination modes. We probe here the carbonyl stretching mode marking the formation of the keto*-product state. We observe in a clear way the effects of anharmonic coupling of coherently excited underdamped intramolecular low-frequency modes. We observe these coherently excited low-frequency modes also in the O–H/N–H stretching region. Interpretation is more problematic though due to the above mentioned other contributions to the overall line shape of O–H and N–H stretching bands. Since the O–H and N–H stretching bands spectrally overlap to a significant extent, it is difficult to distinguish the coherent motions in the keto*-product and enol-ground states.

Prof. Coppens said: Is the time scale of H-transfer distance dependent? Would it be slower for intermolecular transfers?

Dr Nibbering replied: The time scale of H-transfer is first and foremost determined by the shape of the potential energy surfaces. If barriers exist, reaction times may be longer, and even the surrounding solvent may play a decisive role. For the photoacid molecules we currently study the dynamics appear to take place on picosecond time scales. However, even in these cases recent findings suggest that the H-transfer distance is not the most important parameter, but a more complex relaxation scenario through different electronic states may be the rate-limiting step.

Prof. Wilson said: You are correct that determination of hydrogen atoms is difficult with X-ray diffraction but the accurate "end-point" structures can be examined by a "slow technique"— neutron diffraction. Such precise/accurate structural techniques provide the ideal basis for setting up *e.g.* theoretical chemical modelling as identified by Prof. Coppens in his Introductory Lecture. In addition, such static methods can show "precursor" effects which set up conditions for processes such as proton transfer. For example, variable temperature or variable pressure studies can begin to probe the average shapes of potentials, for example in low barrier potentials.

Dr Nibbering responded: I agree that for a full understanding of the dynamics one needs to determine the structural information in real time. While awaiting the development of time-resolved structure resolving techniques with femtosecond time resolution, such as ultrafast X-ray spectroscopy, X-ray diffraction, electron diffraction or even neutron diffraction, we pursue femtosecond vibrational spectroscopy. However, for a full interpretation of our studies the understanding of the potential energy surfaces is a necessary requirement. Here the mentioned "slow techniques", or I would rather say "steady-state techniques with averaging over a broad range of time scales" may be helpful in giving part of that information on the steady-state configurations, with high accuracy as well as the option to study temperature or pressure dependences. Nevertheless, for the study of transient states time resolved techniques are the only experimental approaches that potentially reveal the structural dynamical information.

Dr Cole asked: If you were to isotopically enrich the subject sample and perform an otherwise identical experiment to that described, could you use the comparison of the data, *via* exploitation of the isotope effect, to draw out more quantitative information from the results, *e.g.* with regard to force constants, and the alike? If experimental complications could be overcome, I wondered if it would prove very useful, not only for this quantification of the results, but also to help highlight the harmonic frequencies which could be used to give further consistency to the results in hand.

Dr Nibbering answered: It is known that in numerous H-transfer studies a kinetic isotope effect exists. Isotopic labelling will then give information on the potentials (*i.e* the force constants). For the case of HBT the currently adopted model ascribes the finite H-transfer time to the motion of a low-frequency mode modulating the hydrogen bond distance. Since in this case the dynamics involve relative motions of the O and N atoms constituting the hydrogen bond, no significant H/D-exchange effect on the reaction time scale can be expected. This is reflected by the fact that the low-frequency modes do not alter signifcantly their frequencies upon H/D exchange.

Prof. Helliwell said: You are advocating in your conclusions the femtosecond IR spectroscopy method but what systems do you have in prospect to apply it to? (Finding systems that are appropriate can be difficult and of course it is the proposition of this meeting that such research can be scientifically rewarding at the "Smoking Gun" level.)

Dr Nibbering replied: We are currently studying the dynamics of intermolecular proton transfer of photoacids in liquid solution, and we aim to extend these studies to photoacids in protein surroundings. In a different line of experiments we now also use femtosecond IR spectroscopy in the study of the photoinduced dynamics of photochromic switches. In principle the method can be extended to any chemical process induced by an ultrafast trigger, that may be an optical light pulse (for dynamics in electronic excited states), but could also be an IR pump pulse, initializing reactions in the electronic ground state.

Prof. Helliwell opened the discussion of Prof. Bürgi's paper: Central to your approach is that the structure database scatter plot reveals sampling of metastable intermediate structures but, if I may use the analogy of jumping off a cliff, at the cliff and on the beach you have a larger population of structures than you do falling to the beach. How do you really reveal snapshots between the top and the bottom? (After all to isolate structural intermediates *via* time-resolved experiments requires considerable ingenuity to trap them in time.)

Prof. Bürgi responded: Structural databases sample stable structures only. For a set of structures with a particular fragment in common, the structures of the common fragment—the only part comparable among the members of the set—may vary considerably. The variation in bond lengths and angles reflects the influence of those parts of the structures, which are not common to the set, *i.e.* the influence of the environments. Our approach does not presume one cliff and one beach, but rather a series of closely related energy surfaces whose minima delineate a (more or less well defined) region of parameter space such as a reaction path (see Fig. 6 of our paper, for example).

Dr Sagi asked: How can a dynamic process be elucidated from a collection of data points that were taken in different crystallization conditions. For example, ionic strength, pH, solvent *etc*.

Prof. Bürgi replied: Techniques in time resolved chemistry localize chemical processes along the arrow of time. In our approach we attempt localization in the structural domain. The approach is based on the hypothesis that a given class of ground state dynamic processes is associated with a common reaction path on a generic energy surface. The details of the path and the surface for a specific process, *i.e.* its minima and transition states, depend somewhat on the specific molecule undergoing this process. Our hypothesis implies that the stationary points characterizing the various molecules tend to congregate in the low-lying parts of the generic surface, which—by definition—includes the reaction path of the process. They can be said to 'map the reaction path' along the structural coordinate (principles of structure–structure and structure–energy correlation, see section 3.1). Empirically the hypothesis has been found to hold for many different chemical systems (see ref. 11 of the paper). (My answer to Prof. Helliwell's question is also relevant.)

Dr Techert asked: How would the presented simulation change if the assumptions of the Eyring theory/transition state theory (equilibrium reactant ↔ TS) were to break down?

Prof. Bürgi answered: I assume that you refer to the empirical correlations between ground state structures obtained from crystal structure analyses and activation energies derived from reaction rate constants measured in solution (see section 5 of the paper). These correlations apply to thermally activated processes and illustrate the Hammond principle from a structural point of view. They are similar in a way to correlations that can be understood in terms of a Marcus relationship, which emphasises the energy point of view. The reactions you are interested in are initiated by a photo-excitation and followed by vibrational relaxation. These processes lead to a more or less long lived intermediate associated with a structure on an excited-state surface that usually differs significantly from the original ground state structure. Therefore the simple correlations described in section 5 will not apply.

Dr Hirst said: One section of your paper mentions the non-planarity of amides, referring to deviations of up to 10° in proteins. Do you believe that protein crystallography can resolve such deviations reliably? And if so would you like to expand on your speculation that this extra degree of freedom is important in protein folding?

Prof. Bürgi replied: To measure the non-planarity of amides accurate positions of the atoms C_{i-1}', N_i, αC_i and HN_i are needed. For a number of high-resolution X-ray structures several torsion angles $\omega(\alpha C_{i-1} - C_{i-1}' - N_i - \alpha C_i)$ have been reported to deviate from 180° by more than 10° (for a recent example see ref. 1). The position of HN_i cannot be determined accurately from even the highest-resolution X-ray diffraction experiments, but could be determined by high-resolution neutron diffraction (< 1 Å). The hinge-like flexibility associated with this degree of freedom could help to minimize strain energy of protein folds, especially with respect to N–H···X hydrogen bonds. It could also facilitate domain motions associated with protein function. Even though the energy increment associated with the flexibility of a single N–H···X hydrogen bond may be small, a substantial contribution to the total energy may result, because of the large number of such hydrogen bonds. However, these are speculations and require experimental verification.

1   J. Symersky, Y. Devedjiev, K. Moore, C. Brouillette and L. DeLucas, *Acta Crystallogr., Sect. D*, 2002, **58**, 1138–1146.

Prof. Sir John Meurig Thomas commented: Prof. Burgi's persuasive arguments about how much we can learn about fast chemical processes from slow diffraction experiments prompts me to draw to the Discussion's attention to how much it becomes possible to gain quite useful insights into the process of catalytic turnover at a well defined active site from steady-state measurements of X-ray absorption fine structure coupled with density functional theory computations. In papers that my colleagues and I have published elsewhere[1–3] we showed that the commercial Ti–SiO$_2$ catalyst for the epoxidation of olefins has an active site which is a Ti^{IV} ion tripodally attached , *via* oxygens, to the underlying silica support. This ion has also attached to it an OH group. In the presence of hydroperoxide oxidant and the alkene, the XANES fingerprint of the Ti^{IV} unmistakably shows it to be 6-coordinated,[3] and EXAFS analysis yields precise bond distances and quite good bond angles in which the Ti^{IV} is involved (see the figures in the paper). These tally well with the corresponding values deduced from DFT. Taking all experimental factors into consideration we may plausibly portray the key catalytic act as the "plucking away" of one of the oxygens of the bound peroxide, which leaves the active site in its original 4-coordinated state, ready for further catalytic turnover. Fuller details are described in a recent paper.[4] (A fictional animation of the conversion of cyclohexene to its epoxide was shown during this contribution.)

1   T. Maschmeyer, G. Sankar, F. Ray and J. M. Thomas, *Nature*, 1995, **378**, 159.
2   J. M. Thomas, G. Sankar and C. R. A. Catlow, *Top. Catal.*, 2000, **10**, 225.
3   J. M. Thomas and G. Sankar, *Acc. Chem. Res.*, 2001, **34**, 571.
4   G. Sankar, J. M. Thomas C. R. A. Catlow, C. M. Baker, D. Gleeson and N. Kaltsoyannis.

Prof. Greaves said: In your intriguing video which models the structural changes taking place during the catalytic event around Ti^{IV}, the start and end configurations come directly from static experiments.

Prof. Wilson commented: To emphasise the point of *in situ versus* quenching experiments, often *in situ* experiments with extrapolation can give more accurate (and less misleading) information than more traditional methods which often involved quenching and the implicit assumption that the state frozen-in by the quenching process is actually of relevance to the reaction under study.

Prof. Helliwell opened the discussion of Prof. Moffat's paper: (i) Re your target proteins, how many are membrane bound (*i.e.* which would then be very difficult to crystallise)? (ii) Re Fig. 1 of your paper. A monochromatic chirping approach will involve a profile method. What accuracy of intensity measurements are to be expected?

Prof. Moffat responded: (i) The target proteins are identified only by sequence homology. Some such as the photosynthetic reaction center and light-harvesting complexes are indeed integral membrane proteins; others such as phototropin are loosely membrane-associated and can readily be solubilized, yet others are probably cytoplasmic and soluble in aqueous media. The experimental distribution into these three subsets, to my knowledge, has not been established. My point is that experimental organisms such as *Arabidopsis* offer several light-sensitive target proteins (and even more targets if domains of the full-length proteins are considered, or of the light-insensitive components that lie further downstream in the overall, light-driven signal transduction pathways). (ii) This has not yet been explored. The accuracy will depend on, among other factors, the nature of the spatial chirp, the mosaicity of the crystal and the resolution of the spot being considered. One way to approach this problem is to introduce time-dependent Ewald spheres into the static treatment for oscillation spot size and shape developed 20 years ago by, for example, Greenhough *et al.*[1-3]

1   T. J. Greenhough, J. R. Helliwell and S. A. Rule, *J. Appl. Crystallogr.*, 1983, **16**, 242 250.
2   T. J. Greenhough and J. R. Helliwell, *J. Appl. Crystallogr.*, 1982, **15**, 493–508.
3   T. J. Greenhough and J. R. Helliwell, *Prog. Biophys. Mol. Biol.*, 1983, **41**, 67–123.

Dr May asked: (i) You mentioned that there are 58 photosensitive proteins in *Arabidopsis*. How many proteins are not photosensitive? Only direct photoreactions are very rapid. (ii) You may not be able to observe all reactions (and their consequences) that are going on in the protein within a crystal, because the movement may not be possible in the crystal.

Prof. Moffat answered: (i) The exact number of proteins in *Arabidopsis* that are not photosensitive is now known; but it is certainly orders of magnitude larger than 58. That is, only a small fraction of proteins in an organism are naturally photosensitive. Yes, only direct photoreactions are very rapid, but this is characteristic of all naturally light-sensitive proteins. Attempts to confer light sensitivity on otherwise light-inert reactions by preparing so-called "caged" compounds, such as caged ATP, suffer at present from the fact that the initial, direct photoreactions are followed by much slower, dark reactions that ultimately liberate the desired product, such as ATP. It may be possible to develop other forms of caged compounds that do not suffer from this limitation.
(ii) Yes, but the intermolecular forces that stabilize the crystal lattice in biological macromolecules are weak, roughly 1 kcal mol^{-1} per interface. I find it worrying that activity in the crystalline state is seldom directly examined, let alone quantitated; we blithely assume that crystal structures always provide an accurate foundation for assessing mechanism. In any case, it is highly

desirable to check by optical means that the reaction in the crystal firstly can proceed at all, secondly that it does so by the same reaction mechanism as in dilute solution, and thirdly that the rate coefficients associated with each step in this mechanism are not significantly different from those in dilute solution. ("Significant" here must be thought of in energetic terms; by how much is the free energy of activation for the particular step affected?)

Prof. Sir John Meurig Thomas said: Do you feel that, in using Laue time-resolved and other X-ray crystallographic techniques on enzyme crystals, one is addressing the active sites and other regions of the enzyme under realistic (pseudo-physiological) conditions?

Prof. Moffat replied: Yes—provided always that one can demonstrate that chemical or biochemical activity is quantitatively retained in the crystalline state. If this is NOT the case then time-resolved experiments are of no relevance and indeed, the static enzyme structure itself comes into question.

A historical note on this point—I was first stimulated to consider time-resolved crystallography in 1969 by a key paper by Parkhurst and Gibson[1] who examined quantitatively the reactivity of haemoglobin towards carbon monoxide in the physiological environment of the erythrocyte, in the biochemist's environment of dilute solution, and in the crystallographer's environment of the intact crystal. They concluded that, at least for the reaction studied, the kinetic behaviour of haemoglobin was very closely similar in these three, very different environments. This provided strong supporting evidence for the physiological relevance of the crystal structures of haemoglobin then being determined by Perutz and colleagues. It took a further 25 years before it became clear that the kinetic properties of haemoglobin are in fact significantly different, both qualitatively and quantitatively, in the crystal compared with dilute solution.[2]

1 L. J. Parkhurst and Q. H. Gibson, *J. Biol. Chem.*, 1967, **242**(24), 5762.
2 C. Rivetti, A. Mozzarelli, G. L. Rossi, E. R. Henry and W. A. Eaton, *Biochemistry*, 1993, **32**(11), 2888–2906.

Prof. Greaves commented: If you can bring the time scale of diffraction experiments into the regime of ps or shorter, will this possibly open the door to penetrating the co-operative elements of photostructural phenomena in macromolecules.

Prof. Moffat added: It might bring coherent structural transitions into view—an exciting challenge.

Dr Chen said: I am always very impressed by the movies of protein movement from your studies. However, I would like to understand what happens in the later time after the initial coherent atomic movement triggered by the laser pulse are lost in the protein molecules. One can envision by the potential energy landscape in the protein that multiple conformations exist after the initial protein quake?

Prof. Moffat replied: Coherence is presumably maintained only for a very short period of time after the laser pulse, perhaps a few hundred fs but in any case, a time much shorter than the present time resolution of our experiments. Thereafter, we believe that structural processes evolve purely stochastically; coherence is lost. That is, the subsequent time evolution arises from the build-up and decay of the populations of intermediate structures, exactly as in dilute solution. A consequence is that at all time points, there is indeed a mixture of multiple conformations present. Our challenge is to unscramble this mixture (for example, by singular value decomposition and associated techniques) and to recover the time-independent structures of all intermediates. This is in progress, as illustrated by the poster by Schmidt, Rajagopal, Ren and Moffat presented at this meeting.

Prof. Bürgi asked: How does the information from a chirped pulse in a time slice of 1 ps, say, compare with that of a typical Laue experiment?

Prof. Moffat answered: In a time slice of 1 ps, say at a time t after the laser pulse, only a subset of the Laue spots on a "normal" Laue image would be stimulated. This subset corresponds to those spots stimulated between an X-ray energy E and $E + dE$, where the values of E and dE depend on t, d*t* (here, 1 ps) and the nature of the chirp. Thus the information content would be a subset of that present in a "normal" Laue image. However, I emphasize that each "chirped" Laue image contains all the spots that would be present in the corresponding "normal" Laue image.

Prof. Greaves said: You say that the time resolution for Laue diffraction from a chirped source in principle is greater than that from an unchirped source even though the former is far longer than the latter. Is this because you have created a more manageable instrument function?

Prof. Moffat replied: The time resolution from an unchirped pulse is today set by the total duration of the X-ray pulse, say 100 ps. If such a pulse is manipulated to produce a (much longer) chirped pulse, the time resolution can never be better than 100 ps since phase space volume must be conserved. Equally, if a 100 fs unchirped pulse from the proposed SPPS or LCLS (Linac Coherent Light Source) is stretched to provide a 1000 times longer, chirped pulse of 100 ps total duration, it may be possible to retain near-100 fs time resolution by the strategies outlined in the main paper. This is not really due to an "instrument function"; rather, it results from the experimental design that maps time into X-ray energy and X-ray energy into space, on the detector.

Prof. Finney asked: Do you have any good physical evidence to justify a statement that, as you improve the resolution towards ~100 fs, you will have a coherent target system? Light takes 1 ps to cross a 0.3 mm crystal. Does this not raise a basic problem with approaching 100 fs time resolution?

Prof. Moffat answered: Yes it does; the physical dimensions of the crystal (likely to be somewhat smaller than 0.3 mm, say 0.075 mm in typical dimension) does enter into the time resolution. Rather than a disadvantage this fact may be exploited as proposed by Neutze and Hajdu;[1] but this will be very challenging experimentally.

1 R. Neutze and J. Hajdu, *Proc. Natl. Acad. Sci. USA*, 1997, **94**, 5651–5655.

Dr Nibbering asked: Did you consider the effects of group velocity mismatch between the optical pump pulse and the X-ray probe pulse? How thin do your crystals have to be to maintain the anticipated time resolution of about 100 fs (100 μm or less)?
What do you expect will happen when probing a molecular wave packet motion that will spread out in the course of time? Will the diffraction signal initially be strong and wash out with the dephasing time (typically 0.5–2 ps)?

Prof. Moffat replied: As in my reply to Prof. Finney, crystal dimensions do inescapably enter into the time resolution.
The initial diffraction signal will presumably arise from coherent motion of the excited species; and then evolve (but not "wash out") as coherence is lost over the few ps time frame when stochastically independent structural processes begin to come into play. (My replies to Prof. Greaves and to Dr Chen are also relevant here.)

Prof. Greaves said: If the pump pulse occurs during the chirped pulse and the X-ray detector has no time resolution, how are the ensuing changes in diffraction differentiated from those that are unperturbed if neither are known beforehand—or is this simply a question of normalising against a pulse-free pattern?

Prof. Moffat responded: Laser-pulse-free patterns will normally be acquired, interleaved in time with the laser-pulse-present patterns. Comparison of the structure amplitudes derived from the latter (which correspond to time zero) with those of the former (which correspond to different times after the laser pulse depending on their X-ray energy) will yield the desired, time-dependent differences in structure amplitudes.

Prof. Wilson said: As I understand it, there is no time (energy) or space resolution on the detector. Also, the method does not improve the overall data collection time resolution, but instead is improving the intrinsic time resolution of the Laue sections taken in each shot.

Prof. Moffat replied: There is indeed no time resolution in the detector but it certainly has excellent spatial resolution; and energy resolution is afforded by indexing the Laue pattern and hence assigning an energy (or more accurately stated, a small energy range) to each spot. In conventional Laue experiments, the time resolution is at present limited by the total duration of the X-ray pulse from the synchrotron, typically 100 ps. The time resolution of a Laue experiment conducted with a chirped X-ray pulse is not limited by the total duration of this pulse but can be much shorter. Exactly how much shorter depends on many factors, among them the nature of the chirp itself.

Achieving photo-control of protein conformation and activity: producing a photo-controlled leucine zipper

Janet R. Kumita,[a] Daniel G. Flint,[b] G. Andrew Woolley[a] and Oliver S. Smart[b]

[a] *Department of Chemistry, The University of Toronto, 80 St. George Street, Toronto M5S 3H6, Canada*
[b] *School of Biosciences, The University of Birmingham, Edgbaston, Birmingham, UK B15 2TT. E-mail: o.s.smart@bham.ac.uk*

Received 24th January 2002, Accepted 1st March 2002
First published as an Advance Article on the web 17th July 2002

We have recently developed a technique that has great potential in producing proteins with photo-control of conformation and consequently activity (J. R. Kumita, O. S. Smart and G. A. Woolley, *Proc. Natl. Acad. Sci. U. S. A.*, 2000, **97**, 3803–3808). The method is based on incorporating two cysteine residues into the sequence of a polypeptide. An azobenzene derivative is subsequently used to produce an intramolecular cross-link between the cysteine sulfhydryl groups. In previous work photo-isomerisation of the azobenzene moiety has been used to control the helicity of a monomeric peptide. In the experiments described here this method has been applied to the coiled coil leucine zipper peptide GCN4-p1. The aim was to produce a variant of GCN4-p1 whose helicity and consequently dimerisation is under direct photo-control. We have produced a modified GCN4-p1 incorporating two cysteine residues. The mutations introduced are shown to interfere with the ability of the uncross-linked peptide to form a coiled coil. After the peptide was cross-linked with the azobenzene derivative more normal coiled-coil behaviour was restored. Irradiation of the peptide producing a conformational change in the azobenzene cross-linker was accompanied by an increase in the helicity of the peptide. The work presented here highlights the potential of the use of photo-isomerisable cross-linkers to control protein activity through induced conformational change. In addition, the methodology has the potential to provide a fast trigger for the initiation of protein conformational changes.

Introduction

The selective control of the activity of a protein through the application of an external source of light has many potential applications.[1] Photo-isomerisable chromophores are most suitable in this area as they introduce the possibility of rapid yet reversible control. Work to date has concentrated on the selective introduction of photo-isomerisable compounds, in particular azobenzene, into peptides. The azobenzene chromophore has been introduced into the backbone of cyclic β-turn peptides by Moroder, Chmielewski and co-workers.[2–5] Others have investigated the effect of amino acids with azobenzene side chains on biological systems.[6,7] In general these studies, although encouraging, have not led to a general and easily applied method of achieving photo-control of the conformation and activity of a protein.

DOI: 10.1039/b200897a

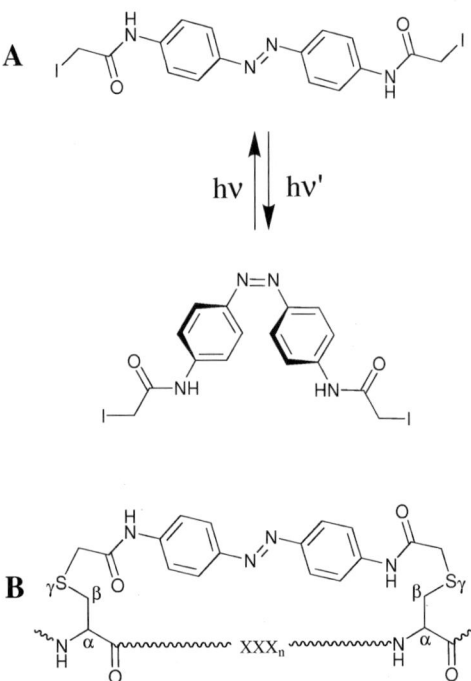

Fig. 1 The structure of the azobenzene-based cross-linker. (A) Chemical structure[8] of the azobenzene cross-linker **1** showing how it can be photo-isomerised. (B) How the compound **1** can cross-link a pair of cysteine residues within a peptide or protein.

In recent work we have developed an alternative approach[8] which has great promise. The method employs compound **1** where the photo-isomerisable azobenzene chromophore is flanked by two iodoacetamide functional groups (Fig. 1A). Compound **1** can be used to cross-link a pair of cysteine side chains within a polypeptide chain as the iodoacetamide group reacts selectively with the sulfhydryl group of the cysteine side-chain (Fig. 1B). This allows the compound to be used to cross-link either peptides that have been produced by conventional solid-phase synthesis methods or recombinant proteins.

The initial application of the cross-linker was in the photo-control of the conformation of a monomeric 16-residue peptide.[8] Molecular modelling was used to design a peptide that would be α-helical when the azobenzene cross-linker was in the *cis* (photo-isomerised) conformation but unfolded when the cross-linker adopted the *trans* (dark adapted) form. It was predicted that a relative spacing of i to $i+7$ between the cysteine residues would result in this behaviour. In practice, circular dichroism spectropolarimetry (CD) was used to show that photo-isomerisation of the cross-linker dramatically increased the helicity of the peptide. Using the CD signal at 222 nm as a gauge of α-helix content, results indicate that the dark-adapted cross-linked peptide was 12% helical (at 11 °C). Upon illumination with 370 nm light (the optimum wavelength for inducing cross-linker photo-isomerisation) apparent helix content increased to 48%.[8] It should be noted that a limitation of the azobenzene chromophore is that it is not possible to switch the entire population of the cross-linker to a *cis* conformation and that for this peptide only 77% photo-isomerisation was achieved (unpublished results; using the method set out below). When this is taken into account the percentage helicity of the peptide with the cross-linker in a *cis* conformation can be estimated to be around 60%.

In a series of studies we have extended these initial results. In the original peptide with a cysteine spacing of $(i, i+7)$ α-aminoisobutyric acid (Aib), an unnatural amino acid, was incorporated under the cross-linker at the $(i+4)$ site.[8] This limited the use of the cross-linker to peptides that could be synthesised by solid-phase methodology to facilitate the incorporation of Aib. However, further work has demonstrated that the presence of coded amino acids at this position results in conformational changes similar to those seen in the original system.[9a] This shows that the cross-linker is functionally applicable for peptides and proteins containing only coded amino acids.

Furthermore, we have shown that the cross-linker can be used with different spacings between the cysteine residues.[9b] Improved molecular modelling procedures indicated that a relative cysteine spacing of $(i, i+4)$ could be used to produce a peptide that would form an α-helix when the cross-linker was in the *cis* isomeric form. A cross-linked peptide with this spacing would be unable to adopt a helical conformation with the *trans* isomer (similar to the original peptide). In contrast, a spacing of $(i, i+11)$ is suitable for producing a peptide that is helical when the cross-linker is in the dark-adapted *trans* conformation and is forced to unfold upon photo-isomerisation of the cross-linker to the *cis* form. Peptides incorporating these features were synthesised and shown to behave as expected.[9] This knowledge will be most useful when applied to proteins, we can now choose the direction of photo-control as well as the size of the region affected.

The cross-linker has great potential in aiding time-resolved studies of protein conformational changes. The photo-isomerisation process of azobenzene compounds is fast, typically occurring[10] in less than 10 ps. This means that if, for instance, the folding of a protein was coupled to the photo-controlled formation of an individual helix this methodology could provide a sensitive and selective trigger for the change. An alternative approach utilising the photolysis of an aryl disulfide cross-linker demonstrates that photo-control can be fruitfully applied as a trigger for peptide conformational change.[11]

In this work, we seek to apply the method to control the conformation and behaviour of a coiled coil peptide. The coiled coil is one of the most ubiquitous assembly motifs found in proteins.[12] As exemplified by GCN4-p1, it normally consists of two parallel amphipathic α-helices that wrap around each other to form a homodimeric left-handed supercoil[13] (Fig. 3(A), below). This results in favourable interactions between hydrophobic residues spaced every 4 then 3 residues apart in the sequence, a pattern defined as a heptad repeat[13] (abcdefg)$_n$ (Fig. 2). Hydrophobic residues occur at positions a and d (Fig. 2B). For a family of coiled coils these hydrophobic residues are predominately leucine leading to the name leucine zipper.[14] Flanking the hydrophobic core heptad repeat positions e and g are often occupied by charged residues that form inter-helical salt bridges[13]

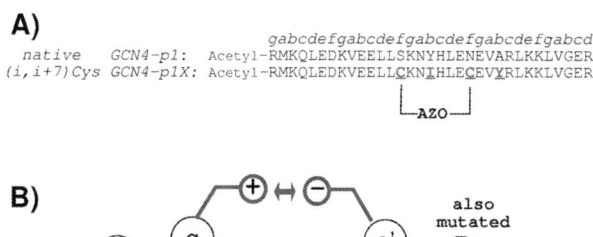

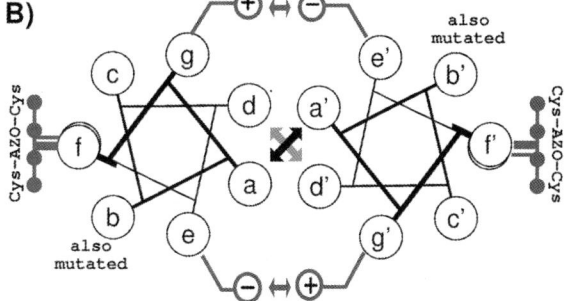

Fig. 2 The proposed cross-linked GCN4-p1. (A) The primary structure in one letter code of the modified GCN4-p1 compared to the native sequence, with the heptad repeat shown at the top. (B) How the modification fits on a helical wheel diagram for GCN4-p1. The arrows at the centre of the interface represent the hydrophobic interaction between residues in the *a* and *d* positions of the heptad repeat. The modifications to the native sequence are limited to the *f* and *b* positions of the heptad repeat and should not disrupt the dimer interface.

(Fig. 2B). Amino acids in positions b, c and f lie on the external faces of the coil and are tolerant of amino acid variability.[15]

We have chosen to work with the leucine zipper[13] from the yeast transcriptional activator protein GCN4. GCN4-p1 is a 33 residue peptide found at the C-terminus of the protein that forms a coiled coil.[13] This peptide is attractive because it has been very widely studied and has a two-state folding mechanism from random coil monomers to folded helical dimers.[14] This means that CD can be used as a powerful tool in the analysis of the behaviour of GCN4-p1 since the signal at 222 nm can generally be directly related to association.[14,16]

The leucine zipper GCN4-p1 is also an attractive system for photo-control as it should be possible to extend these studies to the longer (56 residue) GCN4-bZIP protein that comprises a basic DNA binding helix followed by the leucine zipper. An X-ray crystal structure of GCN4-bZIP bound to its cognate DNA shows it to be a Y-shaped dimer of two extended α-helices.[17] The zipper forms the body of the Y and joins the two arm-like basic regions, each of which binds into the major groove of DNA.[17] By controlling the helix propensity and, as a consequence dimerisation, of the leucine zipper part of the protein we can expect a major influence on the DNA binding ability of the longer protein. This is because even small changes in the helix propensity of the zipper region can have dramatic effects on the DNA binding ability of a bZIP protein. This is elegantly demonstrated in a study conducted by Vinson and co-workers[18] where the phosphorylation of a residue in the zipper region had a small effect on the percentage helicity of an isolated zipper peptide but produced a dramatic 100-fold effect on DNA binding. Our approach differs markedly from that of Mascareñas and co-workers[19] who have used an azobenzene-based compound to produce an intermolecular cross-link between a pair of basic DNA binding helices taken from GCN4-bZIP. An encouraging degree of photo-control of DNA binding was found, albeit with a problem of irreversibility.[19]

By incorporating the cross-linker into GCN4-p1, we aim to produce a coiled coil peptide whose helicity and, consequently, dimerisation is under direct photo-control. Such a peptide would be the first example of a widely applicable methodology that could potentially allow the external control of the dimerisation of a macromolecule.

Materials and methods

Synthesis of azobenzene cross-linking reagent

The azobenzene cross-linking reagent containing two cysteine-reactive iodoacetamide groups (structure **1**) was synthesised as reported previously.[8]

Peptide design

Peptide design was based on the high-resolution X-ray crystal structure for GCN4-p1.[13] Molecular Graphics and modelling were performed using the SYBYL package (Tripos Inc) and the AMBER4.1[20] potential energy function as described below. VMD[21] and Raster3D[22] were used to produce pictures of the molecular structures. A Silicon Graphics Octane2 workstation was used for all computational work.

Peptide synthesis

Standard fluorenylmethoxycarbonyl-based solid-phase peptide synthesis methods were used to prepare the modified ($i, i+7$)Cys GCN4-p1: acetyl-RMKQLEDKVEELLCKNIHLECEVYRLK-KLVGER and native GCN4-p1: Acetyl-RMKQLEDKVEELLSKNYHLENEVARLKKLVGER (Fig. 2A). The peptides were constructed on Fmoc-Arg(Pbf)-Wang resin (capacity 0.35 mmol g^{-1}) (Novabiochem, San Diego CA). Coupling used 3 equiv. HATU {O-(7-azobenzotriazol-1-yl)-1,1,3,3-tetramethyluronium hexafluorophosphate} (Sigma-Aldrich, Canada), 6 equiv. DIPEA (*N*, *N*,-diisopropylethylamine), 3 equiv. amino acid (Novabiochem, San Diego CA). Peptides were purified by HPLC (Zorbax SB-C18 column) using a linear gradient from 0 to 75% acetonitrile/H$_2$O (+0.1% trifluoroacetic acid) over 50 min for ($i, i+7$)Cys GCN4-p1 (eluted at 49.8% acetonitrile) and native GCN4-p1 (eluted at 46.2% acetonitrile). The peptide primary structure was confirmed by MALDI-MS for ($i, i+7$)Cys GCN4-p1 (observed: 4083.0 Da; calculated (C$_{178}$H$_{302}$N$_{51}$O$_{52}$S$_3$):

4083.4 Da) and for native GCN4-p1 (observed: 4037.7 Da; calculated ($C_{176}H_{297}N_{52}O_{54}S$): 4037.7 Da). The purity by HPLC was >95%. Peptide concentration was determined in triplicate under denaturing conditions in 6 M GdnHCl (pH 6.5) by monitoring the tyrosine absorbance at 275 nm, using an extinction coefficient[23] of 1470 M^{-1} cm^{-1}.

Cross-linking (i, i+7)Cys GCN4-p1

Intramolecular cross-linking of Cys residues by **1** was performed. It was found necessary to perform the cross-linking reaction in the presence of guanidinium hydrochloride to disrupt the dimeric coiled coil interaction of (i, i+7)Cys GCN4-p1. In a total volume of 500 µL, 47 mM Tris-HCl buffer (pH 8.0), uncross-linked (i, i+7)Cys GCN4-p1 (0.75 mM), TCEP (0.83 mM) and GdnHCl (2.3 M) were combined and incubated for 18 h at room temperature, under nitrogen to ensure the cysteine residues were in their reduced state. To the aqueous solution, 500 µL DMSO containing 0.6 µmol of **1** was added, giving a reagent concentration of 0.6 mM. This solution was stirred for 20 min protected from light in a 40 °C waterbath, followed by the addition of 60 µL of a 10 mM solution of **1**. The reaction mixture was stirred in a 40 °C waterbath for a further 20 min protected from light followed by 20 min exposed to light. The solvent was removed by high vacuum pump and the peptide was purified by HPLC (Zorbax SB-C18 column) using a linear gradient from 0–75% acetonitrile/H_2O (+0.1% trifluoroacetic acid) over the course of 50 min for (i, i+7)Cys GCN4-p1-X (eluted at 47.4% acetonitrile). The peptide primary structure was confirmed by MALDI-MS: (i, i+7)Cys GCN4-p1-X (observed 4377.05 Da; calculated ($C_{194}H_{314}N_{55}O_{54}S_{3}$): 4377.09 Da). Concentration of the dark-adapted cross-linked peptide was determined by monitoring the azobenzene crosslinker absorbance at 367 nm, using a molecular extinction coefficient[8] of 28 000 M^{-1} cm^{-1}.

Circular dichroism measurements

Circular dichroism measurements were performed using a Jasco Model J-710 spectropolarimeter. All measurements were carried out in thermostatted quartz cuvettes (0.1 cm or 1.0 cm pathlength). Temperatures were measured using a microprobe placed directly into the sample cell. All samples were dissolved in 5 mM acetate buffer (pH 5) or 5 mM phosphate buffer (pH 7). DTT (3 mM) was present in the uncross-linked peptide samples to ensure that cysteine residues were in the reduced form. Spectra reported are averages of three individual experiments of five scans each, with the appropriate background spectrum subtracted. A scan speed of 10 nm min^{-1}, with a 0.5 nm bandwidth and a 4 s response time was used. All CD signals are reported using mean residue ellipticity. The mean residue weight used for native GCN4-p1 was 122.4 and for (i, i+7)Cys GCN4-p1 in the uncross-linked and cross-linked form was 123.7.

Guanidinium hydrochloride (GdnHCl) denaturation curves were measured by monitoring the mean residue ellipticity at 222 nm ($\theta_{222\,nm}$) as a function of GdnHCl concentration. Thermal denaturation studies were performed by monitoring $\theta_{222\,nm}$ at various temperatures ranging from 10 °C to 70 °C in 5 °C increments. The samples were allowed to equilibrate at each temperature for 5 min prior to data acquisition.

UV/VIS spectroscopy and photo-isomerisation

UV/VIS absorbance spectra were measured with a Perkin-Elmer Lambda 2 spectrophotometer using the same thermostatted quartz cuvettes (0.1 cm or 1.0 cm pathlength) in which the CD data were collected. To obtain rates of thermal isomerisation, the dependence of the absorbance at 367 nm was recorded with respect to time. The resulting curve was fitted to an exponential decay expression using the program IGOR (Wavemetrics).

Photo-isomerisation was accomplished by irradiating thermostatted peptide solutions with a 70 W metal halide Tri-Lite Lamp (World Precision Instruments Inc, FL) coupled to a 370 nm ± 10 nm band pass filter (Harvard Apparatus Canada, PQ). Photo-isomerisation was complete (as judged by the lack of any further changes in UV spectra) in ⩽10 min. A limitation of the azobenzene chromophore is that it is not possible to achieve a complete isomerisation of a sample to the *cis* form.[8,9] The proportion of the sample converted to *cis* upon irradiation of cross-linked peptide was determined by fitting its UV/VIS spectra with those of pure *trans* and *cis* samples obtained by

HPLC separation[9] of a monomeric peptide containing the same azobenzene moiety. Given a measurement of p_{cis} (the proportion of a sample converted to cis) it is possible to estimate the CD spectrum of a sample with 100% conversion to cis:

$$\theta_\lambda^{100\%cis} = \{\theta_\lambda^{irradiated} - (1 - p_{cis})\theta_\lambda^{dark}\}/p_{cis}$$

where $\theta_\lambda^{irradiated}$ is the CD signal at a wavelength of λ nm after irradiation and θ_λ^{dark} is the corresponding signal for the dark-adapted peptide. This extrapolation makes the assumption that the observed CD spectrum is a linear combination of the CD spectra of pure cis and pure trans peptides. The possibility that a coiled coil formed from one cis and one trans peptide gives a CD spectrum different from the spectrum of an equimolar mixture of cis–cis and trans–trans peptides is neglected. Nevertheless, the expression provides a useful estimate of the helicity for a sample with complete conversion of the cross-linker to the cis conformation.

Results

Peptide design

The starting point for the design of a GCN4-p1 derivative incorporating the azobenzene-based cross-linker **1** was the high-resolution X-ray crystal structure of O'Shea et al.[13] It was decided to incorporate the cysteine residues to be cross-linked at a relative spacing of i to $i+7$ as the utility of this approach had already been demonstrated for a 16-residue monomeric peptide.[8] In addition it was decided that the position $i+3$, occupying a position under the cross-linker, should be set to a β-branched amino acid such as isoleucine. This idea had its origin in preliminary modelling studies that indicated that such a bulky residue would increase the degree of photo-control by participating in steric interactions with the trans form of the linker.[8] Subsequent experimental work and improved modelling has shown this idea to be in error. In fact, the residue types below the cross-linker have little effect on the degree of photo-control.[9a]

Once the decision had been made to mutate three residues to cysteine, isoleucine and cysteine with a relative spacing of (i, $i+3$, $i+7$) the next step was to determine where in the sequence to introduce these changes. Consideration of the sequence variability of coiled coils[15] complemented by a sequence alignment of GCN4-p1 with homologous protein sequences from the SWISS-PROT databank,[24] indicated that the b, c and f positions from the heptad repeat are most tolerant to alteration. It was decided that the mutation to cysteine of two consecutive f heptad-repeat positions was advantageous and produced the required relative inter-cysteine spacing of i to $i+7$. This would ensure that the cysteine/cross-linker/cysteine moiety would lie on the solvent exposed side of the coiled coil (Fig. 2B). Thus the ($i+3$) residue, which is to be mutated to isoleucine, would lie in the b heptad position and as such would also be amenable to change (Fig. 2B). Given this decision the next question was where in the sequence of GCN4-p1 (Fig. 2A) to introduce the changes. The only places where the desired changes could be made without altering the charge of the peptide were S14C, Y17I, N21C (Fig. 2A). Substitution of residue Tyr17 removes a useful means of assessing the concentration of the peptide spectroscopically.[14] As a consequence of this a further modification A24Y was included, thereby reintroducing a tyrosine residue (in the b position of the next heptad repeat).

The final stage of the design involved checking whether the modifications outlined above would result in obvious structural problems. The amino acid modifications were incorporated into the high-resolution X-ray crystal structure[13] of GCN4-p1 (Fig. 3A) using the SYBYL package. Examination with molecular graphics showed that no obvious conflict was produced by the changes. To assess the compatibility of the cross-linked structure with coiled coil formation, two models were produced: one with the azobenzene group in a cis conformation and the other with the azobenzene in the trans form. The conformation of each form of the azobenzene cross-linker was the result of ab initio geometry optimisation using the 6-31G* basis function with Gaussian 98. The GCN4-p1 dimer structure was then separated into two monomers. For each of the monomers the cross-linker was joined to the cysteine side chains. Each cross-linked monomer was then subjected to energy minimisation with the AMBER4.1 force field,[20] while the cross-linker was constrained to its ab initio low-energy conformation. After energy minimisation the two monomers modelled with the cross-linker in a cis conformation, remained fully helical and could be rejoined to form a dimer

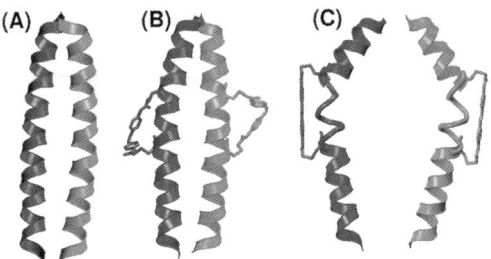

Fig. 3 Molecular models of the proposed cross-linked GCN4-p1. A comparison between the structures of (A) the X-ray crystal structure[13] for GCN4-p1, (B) a model for ($i, i+7$)Cys GCN4-p1X with both cross-linkers in a *cis* conformation and (C) a model for ($i, i+7$)Cys GCN4-p1X with both cross-linkers in a *trans* conformation. In all cases α-helical sections of the structure are marked with ribbons and areas where helicity is disrupted are marked by a tube, an atomic representation is used for both cysteine residues and the cross-linker. Picture produced using VMD[21] and Raster3D.[22]

(Fig. 3B). In contrast, the *trans* conformation of the cross-linker forced a considerable bend in the helix (Fig. 3C) that was expected to substantially destabilise coiled coil dimer formation.

Characterisation of uncross-linked ($i, i+7$)Cys GCN4-p1 in comparison to native GCN4-p1

After synthesis and purification of the peptide the conformation of uncross-linked ($i, i+7$)Cys GCN4-p1 was analysed by CD spectropolarimetry (Fig. 4). All experiments were conducted in the presence of DTT to ensure that the cysteine side chains were in a reduced form. The concentration of the peptide was varied in the range 6 μM to 50 μM (Table 1). Due to problems with solubility in the cross-linked form of ($i, i+7$)Cys GCN4-p1 (see below), the majority of CD analysis was performed at pH 5. For comparison with previously published studies, the un-crosslinked ($i, i+7$)Cys GCN4-p1 was also analysed at pH 7. As a control, native GCN4-p1 was synthesised by solid-phase peptide synthesis and analysed at pH 5 and pH 7 to allow comparison with previously published results (Table 2).

CD analysis of native GCN4-p1 at 10.5 °C gave $\theta_{222\,nm}$ of $-28\,970$ degrees cm^2 dmol^{-1} (50 μM, pH 7) which compares to $-33\,200$ degrees cm^2 dmol^{-1} (35 μM, 0 °C, pH 7) reported by Lumb and co-workers.[25] The native GCN4-p1 was also analysed at pH 5 (5 μM, 10.5 °C) and gave $\theta_{222\,nm}$ of $-21\,670$ degrees cm^2 dmol^{-1} which compares well with a reported $\theta_{222\,nm}$ value of $-22\,500$ degrees cm^2 dmol^{-1} (12–15 μM, 10 °C, pH 5.5) for a GCN4-p1 Ser14Ala mutant in which no change in stability was observed from the native peptide at pH 5.[26,27] These control experiments demonstrated that the conditions and techniques used here are not inconsistent with work reported by other groups.

Comparison between the values in Tables 1 and 2 shows that the amino acid mutations introduced into ($i, i+7$)Cys GCN4-p1 have resulted in a substantial destabilisation of coil-coiled formation compared to native GCN4-p1. This is true at both pH 7 and pH 5. It should be noted, however, that the marked concentration dependence of $\theta_{222\,nm}$ indicates that some peptide association is occurring. A similar concentration dependence is also observed in thermal denaturation curves (Fig. 4 inset). It should be noted that melting occurs at temperatures around 40 °C lower than native GCN4-p1.[14]

To test whether this unexpected destabilisation was a result of an alteration of the intrinsic helicity of the peptide or the disruption of the coiled coil interface, the effect of the solvent trifluorethanol (TFE) was assessed. This solvent promotes the formation of α-helices in monomeric peptides[28] producing a marked increase in the size of the 209 and 222 nm minima in CD spectra. Its effect on coiled coil peptides is more complex.[29,30] The presence of 50% TFE causes the breakdown of dimeric coiled coils into monomers.[30] This effect is accompanied by changes to the CD spectrum: a slight decrease in the magnitude of the 222 nm minimum and an increase by a similar amount in the size of the minimum at 209 nm.[29]

For uncross-linked ($i, i+7$)Cys GCN4-p1 the addition of 50% TFE produced a marked increase in the size of the 209 and 222 nm minima in the CD spectra (Fig. 4B). The $\theta_{222\,nm}$ signal showed

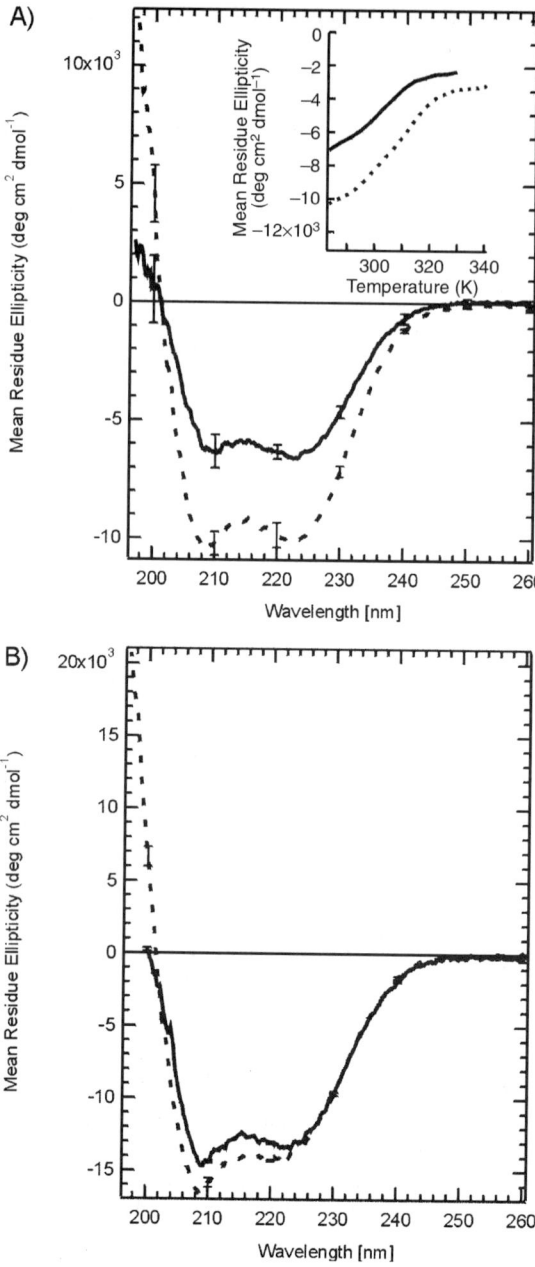

Fig. 4 Secondary structure of un-crosslinked $(i, i+7)$Cys GCN4-p1. (A) CD spectra of 6 µM (solid line) and 50 µM (dashed line) un-crosslinked $(i, i+7)$Cys GCN4-p1 (5 mM sodium acetate buffer pH 5.0, 3 mM DTT, 10 °C). (Inset) thermal denaturation of 6 µM (solid line) and 50 µM (dashed line) un-crosslinked $(i, i+7)$Cys GCN4-p1. (B) CD spectra of 6 µM (solid line) and 50 µM (dashed line) un-crosslinked $(i, i+7)$Cys GCN4-p1 in the presence of 50% TFE /50% 5 mM sodium acetate buffer pH 5.0, 3 mM DTT, 10 °C.

only a slight dependence on the concentration of the peptide (Table 1), consistent with the formation of a monomer. Furthermore, the minimum at 209 nm falls to a greater extent than that at 222 nm. Taken together these observations suggest that 50% TFE breaks down a partially formed coiled coil present in a purely aqueous environment. Even in 50% TFE the peptide is of only limited

Table 1 Analysis of un-crosslinked $(i, i+7)$Cys GCN4-p1 by circular dichroism spectropolarimetry[a]

$(i, i+7)$Cys GCN4-p1 concentration /μM	$\theta_{222\ nm}$	
	pH 5	pH 7
6	-6520 ± 500	-7030 ± 700
12	-8600 ± 100	-9770 ± 80
25	-10010 ± 200	
50	-10020 ± 500	-10690 ± 900
6 with 50% TFE	-13330 ± 200	
50 with 50% TFE	-13940 ± 200	-14290 ± 600

[a] All CD measurements were performed at $10 \pm 1\ °C$ in 5 mM NaOAc (pH 5.0) or 5 mM NaPO$_4$ (pH 7.0) with 3 mM DTT. Mean residue ellipticity ($\theta_{222\ nm}$) is reported in degrees cm^2 dmol^{-1}. The average of three individual experiments is quoted, followed by the standard deviation.

Table 2 Analysis of native GCN4-p1 by circular dichroism spectropolarimetry[a]

GCN4-p1 concentration /μM	$\theta_{222\ nm}$
5 (pH 5)	-21670 ± 100
50 (pH 7)	-28970 ± 200
50 (with 50% TFE pH 7)	-30860 ± 200

[a] All CD measurements were performed at $10 \pm 1\ °C$ in 5 mM NaOAc (pH 5.0) or 5 mM NaPO$_4$ (pH 7.0) with 3 mM DTT. Mean residue ellipticity ($\theta_{222\ nm}$) is reported in degrees cm^2 dmol^{-1}. The average of three individual experiments is quoted, followed by the standard deviation.

helicity (comparing values in Tables 1 and 2). This shows that the amino acid changes made affected the helix propensity of the peptide both in the monomeric and associated (presumably coiled coil) forms.

Characterisation of cross-linked $(i, i+7)$Cys GCN4-p1

The $(i, i+7)$Cys GCN4-p1 peptide was cross-linked as described above and is denoted here as $(i, i+7)$Cys GCN4-p1X. The conformation of $(i, i+7)$Cys GCN4-p1X was assessed using CD analysis both for the dark-adapted state and following irradiation. Initial results from experiments conducted at pH 7.0 presented a complication. The peptide was soluble in the dark and immediately after irradiation. However, if the sample was left following irradiation a precipitate formed over a number of hours. This precipitate formed at peptide concentrations as low as 3 μM. This complication was alleviated by altering the experimental conditions. At pH 5.0 the precipitation was not observed for irradiated samples with concentrations up to 12 μM. At this lower pH the *trans* form of the cross-linked peptide showed no formation of precipitate at concentrations up to 50 μM (Table 3). Analysis of a GCN4-p1 system at pH 5 has been reported previously by Sosnick and co-workers.[27] Although we are currently unable to explain this phenomenon, there is a histidine residue (residue number 18) under the cross-linker (in the $i+4$ position relative to cysteine 14) that might lead to the pH dependent tendency of the peptide to precipitate.

The CD analysis for the cross-linked peptide is illustrated in Fig. 5 and the corresponding $\theta_{222\ nm}$ values are reported in Table 3. A fit of the UV/VIS absorption spectrum (Fig. 5A) with "pure" cis

Table 3 Analysis of $(i, i+7)$Cys GCN4-p1X by circular dichroism spectropolarimetry[a]

$(i, i+7)$Cys GCN4-p1X concentration /µM		$\theta_{222\text{ nm}}$	
		pH 5	pH 7[b]
5	Dark adapted	−13 020 ± 370	−10 550 ± 500
	Irradiated[c]	−16 330 ± 640	−13 340 ± 200
	Estimated 100% cis[d]	−18 350	
12	Dark adapted	−16 590	
	Irradiated[c]	−18 800	
	Estimated 100% cis[d]	−20 200	
50	Dark adapted	−16 310 ± 330	
	Irradiated[c]	−18 990 ± 160	
	Estimated 100% cis[d]	−20 600	

[a] All CD measurements were performed at 10 ±1 °C in 5 mM NaOAc (pH 5.0) or 5 mM NaPO$_4$ (pH 7.0). Mean residue ellipticity ($\theta_{222\text{ nm}}$) is reported in degrees cm^2 dmol^{-1}. The average of three individual experiments is quoted, followed by standard deviation. [b] Upon thermal relaxation of $(i, i+7)$Cys GCN4-p1X at pH 7, precipitate was formed, therefore was not fully reversible. [c] After exposure to 370 ± 10 nm light for 10 min (70 W source). [d] Estimated value for a peptide sample where all the cross-linker is in the cis conformation. Estimate derived from dark and irradiated values and a measurement that the irradiated sample represents a mixture of 62% cis and 38% trans (see text).

and trans spectra showed that the irradiated sample was composed of a mixture of 62% cis and 38% trans azobenzene chromophore (see Methods). Taking this into account it is possible to estimate both the CD spectrum (Fig. 5B) and $\theta_{222\text{ nm}}$ for a sample composed of only the cis cross-linker conformation. All spectra are characteristic of a partially formed α-helix. Furthermore, the increase in the magnitude of the $\theta_{222\text{ nm}}$ minimum with concentration shows that the degree of helicity is concentration dependent (Table 3). The irradiated and corrected "pure" cis spectra clearly show the features consistent with coiled coil formation:[14,29] namely that the 222 nm minimum is lower than that at 209 nm (Fig. 5B).

There is a clear difference in the signal size with more helicity in the illuminated and "pure" cis spectra than that for the dark-adapted peptide (Table 3). Furthermore the 222 nm minimum is lower than 209 nm minimum and this tendency increases as the signal magnitude is increased. A similar effect has been observed for native GCN4-p1.[14] Comparison of the magnitude of the $\theta_{222\text{ nm}}$ signal for $(i, i+7)$Cys GCN4-p1X at a concentration of 5 µM (Table 3) with that for the native GCN4-p1 (Table 2) is instructive. Expressed as a proportion of the value for the native peptide the $\theta_{222\text{ nm}}$ signal for the dark-adapted state is 60% and upon illumination this increases to 75%. Taking into account the correction to estimate a "pure" cis the signal increases to 85%. This demonstrates that the cis conformation of the cross-linker is helix stabilising and therefore able to restore a large proportion of the coiled coil formation disrupted by the amino acid modifications incorporated in $(i, i+7)$Cys GCN4-p1. In contrast the helicity, and consequently coiled coil formation, of the dark-adapted state is considerably lower than that for the "pure" cis showing that a degree of photo-control has been achieved. The greater concentration dependence found for the $\theta_{222\text{ nm}}$ signal for the dark-adapted case compared to illuminated or pure cis (Table 3) is consistent with decreased coiled coil stability.

An unexpected observation was that the trans (dark-adapted) conformation effects helix stabilisation (Table 3) in comparison to the uncross-linked peptide (Table 1). When expressed as a proportion of the value for the native peptide the $\theta_{222\text{ nm}}$ signal for the dark-adapted state, at 5 µM, is 60%. In comparison the uncross-linked peptide at 6 µM exhibited only 30% of the native $\theta_{222\text{ nm}}$ signal. In previous studies of monomeric peptides using the cross-linker with an $(i, i+7)$ or an $(i, i+4)$ inter-cysteine spacing,[8,9] we have observed that the trans form of the linker destabilises the structure compared to the uncross-linked form of the peptide. Increased stability in the trans form

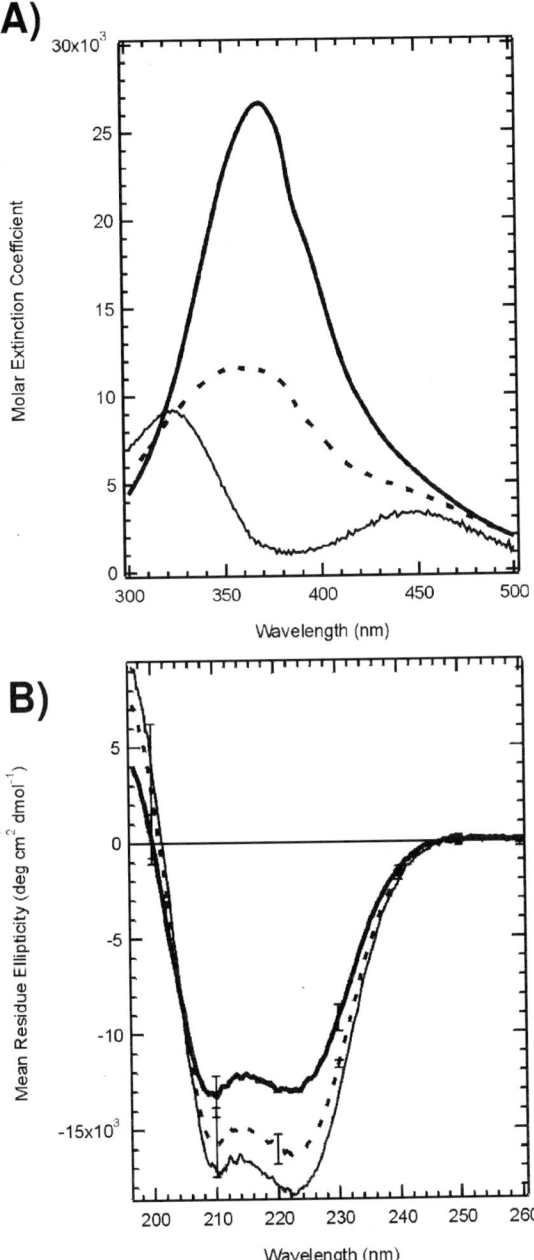

Fig. 5 Effects of photo-irradiation on $(i, i+7)$Cys GCN4-p1X. (A) UV Spectra of $(i, i+7)$Cys GCN4-p1X, dark-adapted (solid line), irradiated (dashed line) and 100% cis (thin solid line). (B) CD spectra of 6 μM dark-adapted $(i, i+7)$Cys GCN4-p1X (thick solid line) and irradiated $(i, i+7)$Cys GCN4-p1X (dashed line). Conditions 5 mM sodium acetate buffer, pH 5.0, 10 °C; irradiation used 370 nm light for 10 min, 70 W source. Calculated 100% cis CD spectrum represented by thin solid line.

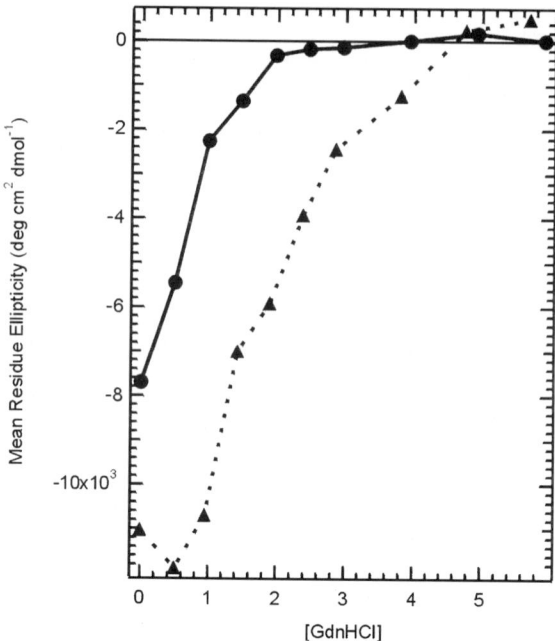

Fig. 6 Chemical denaturation of uncross-linked and cross-linked $(i, i+7)$Cys GCN4-p1. Effect of increasing GdnHCl concentration on CD signal of 6 µM uncross-linked $(i, i+7)$Cys GCN4-p1 (solid line, circles) and 6 µM dark-adapted (*trans*) cross-linked $(i, i+7)$Cys GCN4-p1 (dotted line, triangles) (5 mM sodium phosphate buffer, pH 7, 3 mM DTT, 10 °C).

was further confirmed by performing GdnHCl denaturation experiments on both the uncross-linked $(i, i+7)$Cys GCN4-p1 and the (*trans*) cross-linked $(i, i+7)$Cys GCN4-p1X at the same concentration (Fig. 6). From this analysis it was apparent that the cross-linked form behaves differently from the uncross-linked system in that it is more stable to chemical denaturation by GdnHCl.

A point of interest is the influence that the environment has on the photo-isomerisation properties of the azobenzene-based cross-linker. As discussed above, it was found that in this case the photo-stationary state on illumination with 370 nm light was 62% *cis*/38% *trans*. This can be compared to results obtained for monomeric peptides where the limiting percentage of molecules in the *cis* conformation was 77% to 90%.[9] It was also noted that a longer irradiation time was necessary to reach a photo-stationary state (unpublished results). Table 4 shows the thermal relaxation half-lives for the *cis* conformation to revert to a *trans* conformation at two different temperatures. The half-times obtained at these temperatures were similar to those previously reported for the original monomeric peptide.[8] Therefore the behaviour of the cross-linker upon relaxation found here is similar to other applications, despite distinct differences in the properties of the photo-isomerisation process.

Table 4 Temperature dependence of thermal relaxation of the *cis* cross-linked peptides in the dark

Temperature /°C[a]	JRK{ValAib}-X[b] $\tau_{1/2}$/min	$(i, i+7)$Cys GCN4-p1X $\tau_{1/2}$/min
25	22	20
31	7.8	10

[a] Temperatures are accurate to ±1 °C. [b] Values from ref. 8.

Discussion

The results obtained are encouraging. We set out to produce a coiled coil peptide whose helicity, and as a consequence dimerisation, is under photo-control. Fig. 5 shows clear evidence that this has been achieved. This success is tempered by the fact that the mutations introduced to allow cross-linking caused a radical disruption of the coiled coil prior to the cross-linking step. The addition of the cross-linker restored a more native conformation with the exception of the need to avoid neutral pH to avoid precipitation.

Could such a disruption have been expected? It is instructive to make a comparison with results obtained by Zitzewitz and co-authors.[31] These authors produced a series of modified GCN4-p1 peptides in which all four of the external heptad repeat f positions: Asp7, Ser14, Asn21 and Lys28 (see Fig. 2A) were mutated.[31] The peptides produced were designated by the mutations made at the f positions: f-DSNK is the native wild type sequence whereas f-AAAA refers to a mutant where all four f position residues are mutated to alanine.[31] It was found[31] that the experimental differences in the free energy of coiled coil formation could be reasonably reproduced using a simple consideration of the helix propensity free energy scale developed by O'Neil and DeGrado.[32] This scale was itself derived by determining the effect on the stability of modifications at the heptad repeat f position of another coiled coil peptide,[32] and so is particularly applicable to this situation.

Applying a similar consideration to that applied by Zitzewitz and co-authors[31] we can estimate the effect of the mutations introduced into $(i, i+7)$Cys GCN4-p1 (Fig. 2). The effect expected from the individual mutations on the free energy of coiled coil are as follows S14C: $+0.24$ kcal mol^{-1}, Y17I: -0.12 kcal mol^{-1}, N21C: -0.32 kcal mol^{-1}, A24Y $+1.20$ kcal mol^{-1}. Overall, we could expect that the four mutations would result in the destabilisation of the coiled coil by 1.0 kcal mol^{-1} (compared to a free energy of folding for the native coiled coil of -10.6 kcal mol^{-1}[31]). This can be compared to the estimates produced by this method for reductions in the folding free energy produced by mutations f-NNNN and f-GGGG of 1.88 and 2.44 kcal mol^{-1} respectively. These estimates are in reasonable agreement with the experimental values for differences found.[31] Comparing the values shows that we could expect that the mutations introduced into $(i, i+7)$Cys GCN4-p1 would have a smaller destabilising effect than f-NNNN and considerably lower than that found for f-GGGG. Experimentally the f-NNNN peptide is 90% folded at a peptide concentration of 10 μM while f-GGGG is ~70% folded at a 100 μM concentration.[31] From these considerations it is not unreasonable to expect that $(i, i+7)$Cys GCN4-p1 would be at least 90% folded at concentrations above 10 μM. However, comparison between values for pH 7 from Tables 1 and 2 shows that less than 35% of the peptide is folded at a concentration of 12 μM. The deviation between expected and observed effects is dramatic.

It is clear that the destabilisation of $(i, i+7)$Cys GCN4-p1 before cross-linking cannot be accounted for by a simple consideration of the effects on the helix propensity. What other factor could account for the phenomenon? Coiled coil peptides have been reported to accommodate cysteine residues without large disruption of their structure.[32-34] The mutations introduced (S14C, Y17I, N21C and A24Y) involve the substitution of reasonably hydrophilic amino acids with larger hydrophobic residues. It should be noted that cysteine is a hydrophobic amino acid, occurring next to alanine in a scale of hydrophobicity.[35] Consideration of the helical wheel diagram for a coiled coil (Fig. 2B), shows that the mutations are introduced in the b and f positions of consecutive heptad repeats. In addition the residue Leu13 lies in a solvent exposed position[13] (heptad repeat e) next to the mutations. This, in effect, creates a stripe of hydrophobic amino acids on what should be the external face of the coiled coil (Fig. 7). The major force in the assembly of a coiled coil is the association of the hydrophobic surfaces at the centre of the coil opposite this external face. It can be imagined that interactions between the hydrophobic residues introduced by the mutations and partly formed coiled coils could interfere with normal assembly and may be involved in the precipitation. Analysis of a model for the uncross-linked mutant (Fig. 7) shows that the solvent exposed surface area for hydrophobic residue types (C, V, I, M, L, F, W and Y) is increased by around 570 Å^2 compared to that of the crystal structure for the native peptide.[13] The free energy cost of exposing such a hydrophobic surface area to solvent can be roughly estimated[36] using a coefficient of 20 cal mol^{-1} Å^{-2}). This gives a free energy cost for exposure of 11.4 kcal mol^{-1}. Given that the residues would not be completely shielded from

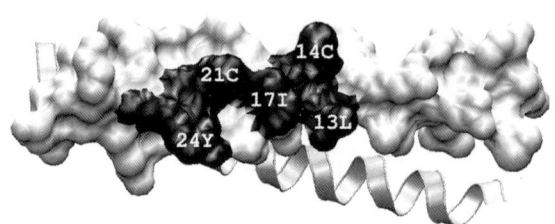

Fig. 7 The hydrophobic stripe created by the mutations introduced into $(i, i+7)$Cys GCN4-p1. The model for the uncross-linked peptide incorporating the mutations was modelled with SYBYL from the crystal structure of GCN4-p1.[13] For clarity the molecular surface of one of the monomers is shown in isolation with the other helix shown as a ribbon. The hydrophobic patch on the molecular surface created by the mutations is shown in black. Picture produced using VMD.[21]

solvent in an unfolded state, this provides an upper limit to the effect. This upper limit is comparable to the free energy of folding of GCN4-p1[31] of -10.6 kcal mol^{-1}. So if an unfolded state provides a degree of protection from solvent of the mutated residues a large effect on coiled coil formation could be expected.

An additional consideration is that the mutations have been introduced into the region of three helix-breaking residues (Asn16, Tyr17, and His18) that have been suggested to be important in the folding of the coiled coil.[31] It is particularly unfortunate that two (Y17I and A24Y) of the four mutations were introduced as a consequence of the suggestion that the presence of a β-branched amino acid would enhance photo-control.[8] This has now been shown not to be the case.[9a]

The conjecture that the mutations created a stripe of hydrophobic amino acids could also account for the ability of the cross-linker to restore more native characteristics, as observed experimentally (Tables 1 and 3). The cross-linker modifies the two cysteine residues and is reasonably hydrophilic (containing two peptide moieties, Fig. 1). What is more, it can be expected to partly bury the Ile17 residue introduced below it (even in a partially folded peptide conformation). It can therefore be expected that cross-linking will have a large effect on any hydrophobic association event that involves the residues introduced by the mutations. We hypothesise that this effect may explain the promotion of helicity and coiled coil formation by the cross-linker (as seen by comparing values from Tables 1 and 3). In the case of the dark-adapted *trans* conformation, that was expected to be helix disrupting, it can be proposed that the prevention of unnatural hydrophobic interactions is the overriding factor.

In conclusion, we have produced a coiled coil peptide with a degree of photo-control of its helicity. However, by the injudicious choice of mutations to the cross-linker we have seriously altered the behaviour of the peptide. The current sequence is unsuitable for the ultimate aim of producing a photo-controlled GCN4-bZIP DNA binding protein. An advantage of the cross-linking method is that it can be applied in various ways. Future work aims at improvement, in particular by utilising the demonstrated ability of the cross-linker to control the helicity of peptides with an i to $i+4$ inter-cysteine residue spacing.[9] This offers a number of advantages, most notably that mutations can be made in a smaller area reducing the possibility of complicating effects. In addition the shorter spacing promises greater helix destabilisation in the dark-adapted *trans* cross-linker conformation as well as the potential to switch a larger proportion of the cross-linker into a *cis* conformation.[9] We are confident that the development of photo-controlled variants of proteins will have many scientific applications.

Acknowledgements

We would like to acknowledge NSERC (Canada) (GAW), the Volkswagen Stiftung (Germany) (GAW) and the U.K. MRC and BBSRC Research Councils (grants G.4600017 and B/16000) (OSS). DGF was supported by a U.K. MRC Bioinformatics studentship. JRK was supported by a NSERC studentship.

References

1. I. Willner and I. Rubin, *Angew. Chem. Int. Ed. Engl.*, 1996, **35**, 367.
2. L. Ulysse, J. Cubillos and J. Chmielewski, *J. Am. Chem. Soc.*, 1995, **117**, 8466.
3. R. Behrendt, C. Renner, M. Schenk, F. Wang, J. Wachtveitl, D. Oesterhelt and L. Moroder, *Angew. Chem. Int. Ed. Engl.*, 1999, **38**, 2771.
4. C. Renner, J. Cramer, R. Behrendt and L. Moroder, *Biopolymers*, 2000, **54**, 501.
5. C. Renner, R. Behrendt, S. Sporlein, J. Wachtveitl and L. Moroder, *Biopolymers*, 2000, **54**, 489.
6. R. Cerpa, F. E. Cohen and I. D. Kuntz, *Fold. Des.*, 1996, **1**, 91.
7. D. Liu, J. Karanicolas, C. Yu, Z. Zhang and G. A. Woolley, *Bioorg. Med. Chem. Lett.*, 1997, **7**, 2677.
8. J. R. Kumita, O. S. Smart and G. A. Woolley, *Proc. Natl. Acad. Sci. U. S. A.*, 2000, **97**, 3803.
9. (a) J. R. Kumita, D. G. Flint, O. S. Smart and G. A. Woolley, *Protein Eng.*, 2002, in press; (b) D. G. Flint, J. R. Kumita, O. S. Smart and G. A. Woolley, *Chem. Biol.*, 2002, **9**, 391.
10. J. Wachtveitl, T. Nagele, B. Puell, W. Zinth, M. Kruger, S. Rudolph-Böhner, D. Oesterhelt and L. Moroder, *J. Photochem. Photobiol. A*, 1997, **105**, 283.
11. M. Volk, *Eur. J. Org. Chem.*, 2001, 2605.
12. W. D. Kohn, C. T. Mant and R. S. Hodges, *J. Biol. Chem.*, 1997, **272**, 2583.
13. E. O'Shea, J. D. Klemm, P. S. Kim and T. Alber, *Science*, 1991, **254**, 539.
14. E. K. O'Shea, P. Rutkowski and P. S. Kim, *Science*, 1989, **243**, 538.
15. R. S. Hodges, A. K. Saund, P. C. Chong, S. A. St-Pierre and R. E. Reid, *J. Biol. Chem.*, 1981, **256**, 1214.
16. S. Betz, R. Fairman, K. O' Neil, J. Lear and W. DeGrado, *Philos. Trans. R. Soc. London, Ser. B*, 1995, **348**, 81.
17. T. E. Ellenberger, C. J. Brandl, K. Struhl and S. C. Harrison, *Cell*, 1992, **71**, 1223.
18. L. Szilák, J. Moitra, D. Krylov and C. Vinson, *Nature Struct. Biol.*, 1997, **4**, 112.
19. A. M. Caamaño, M. E. Vázquez, J. Martínez-Costas, L. Castedo and J. L. Mascareñas, *Angew. Chem. Int. Ed. Engl.*, 2000, **39**, 3104.
20. S. J. Weiner, P. A. Kollman, D. A. Case, U. C. Singh, C. Ghio, G. Alagona, S. Profeta, Jr. and P. Weiner, *J. Am. Chem. Soc.*, 1984, **106**, 765.
21. W. F. Humphery, A. Dalke and K. Schulten, *J. Mol. Graphics*, 1996, **14**, 33.
22. E. A. Merritt and D. J. Bacon, *Methods Enzymol.*, 1997, **277**, 505.
23. H. Edelhoch, *Biochemistry*, 1967, **6**, 1948.
24. A. Bairoch and R. Apweiler, *Nucleic Acids Res.*, 2000, **28**, 45.
25. K. J. Lumb, C. M. Carr and P. S. Kim, *Biochemistry*, 1994, **33**, 7361.
26. A. Kentsis and T. R. Sosnick, *Biochemistry*, 1998, **37**, 14613.
27. T. R. Sosnick, S. Jackson, R. R. Wilk, S. W. Englander and W. F. DeGrado, *Proteins: Struct., Funct., Genet.*, 1996, **24**, 427.
28. A. Cammers Goodwin, T. J. Allen, S. L. Oslick, K. F. McClure, J. H. Lee and D. S. Kemp, *J. Am. Chem. Soc.*, 1996, **118**, 3082.
29. S. Y. M. Lau, A. K. Taneja and R. S. Hodges, *J. Biol. Chem.*, 1984, **259**, 3253.
30. S. Y. M. Lau, A. K. Taneja and R. S. Hodges, *J. Chromatogr.*, 1984, **317**, 129.
31. J. A. Zitzewitz, B. Ibarra-Molero, D. R. Fishel, K. L. Terry and C. R. Matthews, *J. Mol. Biol.*, 2000, **296**, 1105.
32. K. T. O'Neil and W. F. DeGrado, *Science*, 1990, **250**, 646.
33. N. E. Zhou, C. M. Kay and R. S. Hodges, *Biochemistry*, 1993, **32**, 3178.
34. N. E. Zhou, C. M. Kay and R. S. Hodges, *J. Mol. Biol.*, 1994, **237**, 500.
35. S. D. Black and D. R. Mould, *Anal. Biochem.*, 1991, **193**, 72.
36. P. A. Karplus, *Protein Sci.*, 1997, **6**, 1302.

First investigations of the kinetics of the topochemical reaction of *p*-formyl-*trans*-cinnamic acid by time-resolved X-ray diffraction

G. Busse,[a] T. Tschentscher,[b] A. Plech,[c] M. Wulff,[c] B. Frederichs[a] and S. Techert*[a]

[a] *Max-Planck-Institute for Biophysical Chemistry, Dept. 010, D-37070, Göttingen, Germany. E-mail: stecher@gwdg.de*
[b] *Hamburger Synchrotronstrahlungslabor HASYLAB at Deutsches Elektronensynchrotron DESY, Notkestraße 85, D-22607, Hamburg, Germany*
[c] *European Synchrotron Radiation Facility, B. P. 220, F-38043, Grenoble Cedex, France*

Received 20th March 2002, Accepted 12th April 2002
First published as an Advance Article on the web 1st August 2002

Under UV irradiation *p*-formyl-*trans*-cinnamic acid (p-FCA) crystals in the β-phase dimerise irreversibly to solid 4,4′-diformyl-β-truxinic acid. The experimental conditions were chosen in such a way (non-aqueous environment and room temperature) that the product formed is amorphous. The kinetics of this bimolecular reaction, which has not yet been characterised, was investigated by picosecond time-resolved X-ray diffraction. From the experimental results a mechanism for this topochemical reaction is proposed including two observed time constants, one less than 100 ps and another of several seconds. The feasibility of investigating this class of substances by time-resolved X-ray diffraction from third generation synchrotron sources and future free-electron lasers is discussed.

1. Introduction

One of the fundamental bimolecular reactions in the solid state is the light-triggered reaction according to the so-called topochemical principle. Topochemical reactions were first introduced in 1931[1] and since this time this reaction class in the crystalline state has been a permanent topic of experimental studies in different solid-state schools.[1–20] Crystal systems, which follow the topochemical principle, undergo a [2 + 2] photodimerisation, if the reactants pack in a molecular mode with intermolecular double bond distances of $r < 4.2$ Å (Fig. 1).[3–5] Crystal modifications of the same chemical species with intermolecular double bond distances $r > 4.2$ Å are photo-inactive. Therefore, depending on the chromophore packing, photoactivity is selectively produced or not. The photoactive morphologies are further distinguished between so-called α-type crystals, where the chromophores stack in opposite directions, *i.e.* head–tail ↔ tail–head, leading to centrosymmetric products, and β-type crystals, where the chromophores order in a parallel way, *i.e.* head–tail ↔ head–tail, forming mirror-symmetric products.

In another formulation of the topochemical postulate, chromophores in crystals can be visualised as existing in rigid, three-dimensional cavities formed by their nearest neighbours (concept of reaction cavity)[8,10] (Fig. 2). As the central molecule reacts, its geometry changes within the cavity. Reactions that involve minor changes in reactant geometry are topochemically allowed, since they

DOI: 10.1039/b202831j

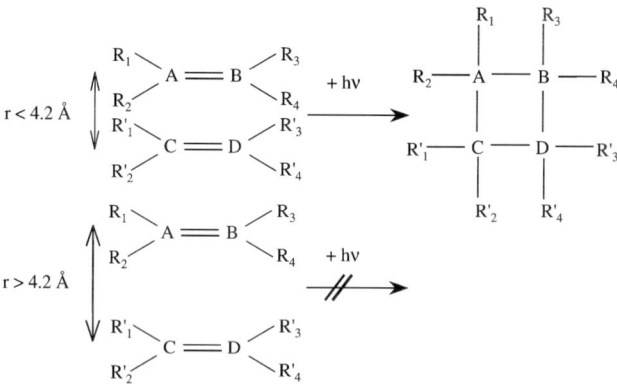

Fig. 1 Scheme of the topochemical principle.

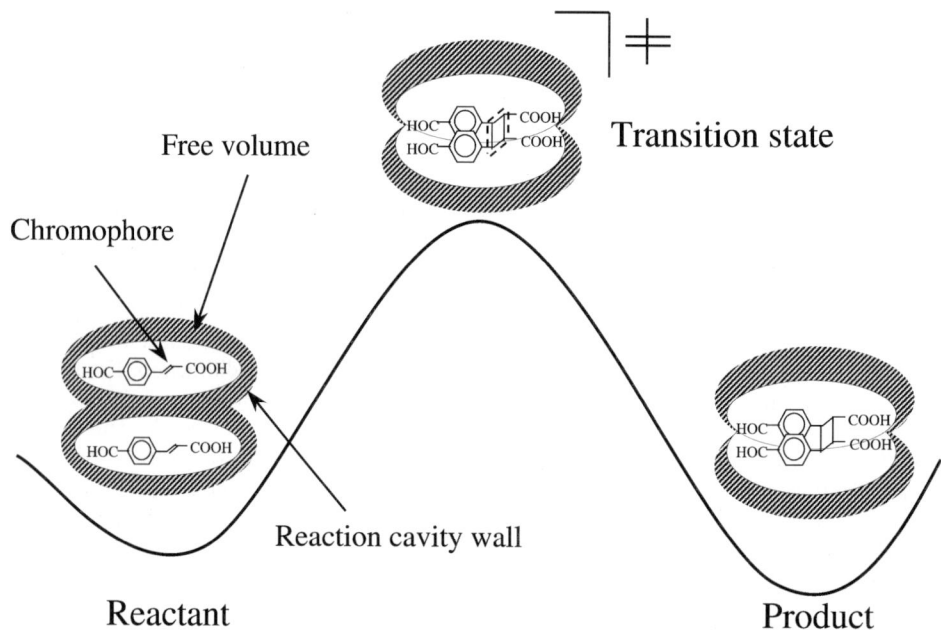

Fig. 2 The definition of the reaction cavity and transition state of the [2 + 2] photodimerisation.

proceed without restriction from the cavity walls. Reactions with transition state geometries that do not fit within the cavity will be strongly disfavoured.

The crystal-packing properties of the reactant, which result from the thermodynamic crystallisation conditions of the material, have far-reaching consequences, *e.g.* for optical applications of such materials. Systems, which follow the topochemical principle might be used as, *e.g.*, photo-driven nanometre-scale actuators or holographic and three-dimensional memories, as the reversible morphological changes of blue–white photochromic diarylene crystals show.[14]

In the present work, we will concentrate on the time-resolved investigations of the "classical" topochemical reaction of *trans*-cinnamic acid derivatives (see Fig. 3). Also here, three kinds of crystal structures are distinguished: centrosymmetric α-type crystals, mirrorsymmetric β-type crystals (both with $r < 4.2$ Å) and photo-inactive γ-phases ($r \approx 4.7$ Å). The observed reaction is the [2 + 2] photodimerisation of the non-aqueous, crystalline β-phase of *p*-formyl-*trans*-cinnamic acid

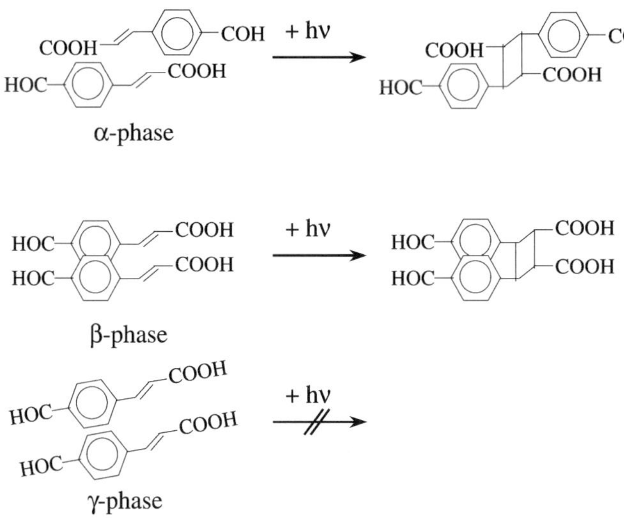

Fig. 3 Structure of the photoactive and photo-inactive phases of *trans*-cinnamic acid.[3,7,13]

(p-FCA) to the solid, amorphous 4,4′-diformyl-β-truxinic acid (product). Picosecond time-resolved X-ray diffraction using synchrotron radiation at the European Synchrotron Radiation Facility (ESRF) was chosen as the experimental method.

Though a lot of experimental work has been undertaken to understand the thermodynamical properties of the solids which result from the spatial arrangements of the molecules in the lattice,[4–8] so far no detailed time-resolved studies have been carried out in order to understand the *kinetics* and the *mechanism* of this solid state reaction. Until now work has been focused on the optimisation of the *thermodynamic* conditions of such reactions like the choice of the environment (protic or aprotic solvent in which the crystals were dispersed), or studies on the temperature-dependence of the reaction. Assuming an Arrhenius behaviour of the light-induced dimerisation it was found spectroscopically that the overall reaction rate of the reactant varied between less than 1 minute and a few minutes (with a mercury flashlamp as excitation source).

This work was focused on the question *how*, according to Fig. 2, the reactant forms some kind of "transient phase" by the absorption of a photon and if it would be possible to characterise, by X-ray diffraction on the picosecond time-scale, the fast intermediates of the reaction cavity which drive the reaction to the product state. A further aim was to explain why, under the chosen reaction conditions, the product state is amorphous and whether information about the early states might explain this.

As stated, time-resolved X-ray powder diffraction was used as the experimental method. With respect to the chosen system, this method has several advantages: the investigated reaction is irreversible. Therefore the most complete information about the reciprocal space is obtained within the smallest amount of exposure time of the sample. Since topochemical systems crystallise in lower crystallographic symmetry, monochromatic studies, which need a high sampling of the reciprocal space, are not applicable to such systems. A disadvantage of powder diffraction is surely the lack of structural resolution. However, because of the short sampling time of one pattern, a whole series of time-scans can be recorded on the same sample using powder diffraction. p-FCA was chosen as the substance for study since some optical characterisation of the powder phase has already been reported.[15–19]

The time-resolved set-up at ID09b at the ESRF, which was used in this work, follows a classical pump–probe scheme, with a Ti : Sapphire laser as the pump source and the synchrotron-generated X-ray pulses as the probe. Pioneering work in the field of time-resolved X-ray crystallography came first from biology by following the light-induced structural changes of myoglobin–CO complexes or photoactive yellow protein (PYP) from the millisecond up to the nanosecond time-scale.[21–25] In chemical research, picosecond time-resolved X-ray diffraction (TR-XRD) was applied in order to study light-induced relaxation phenomena on the electron spin-singlet excited state potential energy surface of crystals,[26] to study ultra-fast dissociation processes like the unimolecular dissociation of iodine in methanol[27] or the dissociation of HgI_2 in methanol.[28]

In this context it should also be mentioned, that microsecond long-living intermediates of reversible light-driven processes in the crystalline state can be characterised for a fixed time window by a stroboscopic approach first realised in ref. 29 for an X-ray home source and, e.g., in ref. 30 using synchrotron radiation. The presented method is very strong for measuring accurate structures of intermediates on the microsecond time-scale, the time-scale, at which mostly electron spin-triplet states are populated via intersystem crossing processes. Characterising the structure of triplet states requires highly accurate crystallographic data, since triplet states commonly differ only slightly from the structures of the non-excited ground state.[31]

Finally, in the present work, the applicability of time-resolved X-ray diffraction to the study of irreversible structural transformations using X-ray radiation from future X-ray free-electron lasers (X-FEL), like the TESLA X-FEL project at the DESY in Hamburg (Germany)[32,33] is discussed. Future X-FEL sources seem very interesting for the study of irreversible processes since they propose X-ray pulse durations of the order of 100 fs at photon fluxes, even higher than present-day synchrotron radiation sources. The faster time-scale should make it possible to study femtosecond intermediates of chemical (and biological) reactions and the higher flux should make it possible to study irreversible reactions in a much more convenient and intensive way, since just one X-ray laser shot should be sufficient to collect a complete highly intense X-ray diffraction pattern on the detector.

2. Experimental

Sample preparation

The β- and γ-modifications of p-FCA were grown according to the crystallization procedure described in ref. 15–19. p-FCA was supplied by Sigma Aldrich, acetone (spectroscopic grade) and ethanol (Uvasol) by Merck. For the spectroscopic measurements the dry, grained powder was dispersed on a 1 mm thick quartz plate (thickness of the powder: max. 15 µm). For the X-ray diffraction experiment p-FCA powder was dispersed with different layer thickness (10–40 µm) on 5–12 µm thick mica plates.

Spectroscopic characterization of the dimerisation

The dimerisation reactions were initiated with two different light sources, i.e. with a 40 W high-pressure mercury lamp (equipped with a water cut-off filter) and with the third harmonic (267 nm) of a 300 fs Ti:Sa laser system (power: 5–9 µJ). The lamp was used in order to verify the photo-activity of the β-phase and the laser system to reproduce and check the dimerisation with a weaker monochromatic, pulsed light-source. The dimerisation was followed by steady-state absorption spectroscopy using a commercial Cary-5E spectrometer. In the wavelength range 200 nm to 500 nm the band-pass of the absorption spectrometer was 0.5 nm, resulting in a resolution of 55 cm^{-1} at 350 nm.

X-ray diffraction (XRD) experiments

The data were collected at the ID09b beamline of the ESRF. The time-resolved set-up at ID09b (Fig. 4) follows a classical pump–probe scheme, with a Ti:Sapphire laser as the pump source and the synchrotron-generated X-ray pulses as the probe source.[34]

The pump wavelength of the mode-locked laser, which runs synchronously with single pulses of the X-rays, was generated by frequency tripling to λ_{exc} = 267 nm. The laser power varied between 5 and 9 µJ with a pulse width of 300 fs and the laser beam was focused down to 400 µm diameter. The sample did not tolerate either higher laser power or tighter focus without visible degradation. Both higher laser power and tighter focus led to a visible degradation of the sample (the degradation product was dark-yellow, the dimerisation product white/white-yellow).

The X-ray probe pulses were selected from the 16-bunch filling of the storage ring using a synchronized chopper. For a pulse width (X-ray) of 70 ps a flux on the sample = $0.5-2 \times 10^8$

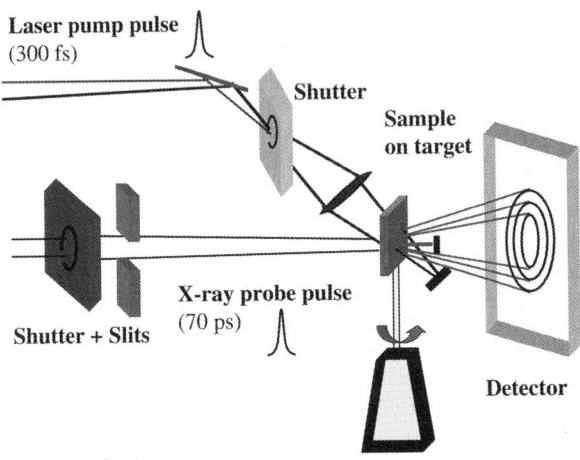

Fig. 4 The time-resolved set-up at ID09b following a pump–probe scheme.

photon (s 100 mA)$^{-1}$ was obtained in a 200 × 200 µm² focal spot. The monochromatic X-ray probe beam at 16.5 keV ($\lambda_{\text{X-ray}}$ = 0.753 Å) was selected by a Si$_{111}$ monochromator. Diffraction data were collected with a MAR133 CCD camera (diameter = 133 mm, pxl-size = 64.7 × 64.7 µm²) at a sample-to-detector distance of 160 mm. During the measurement, the decay of the storage ring current was monitored online and later included in the intensity correction of the diffraction pattern.

The XRD experiments were carried out at room temperature. The repetition frequency of the experiment was 897 Hz. The laser and X-ray beams hit the sample in a quasi-parallel configuration resulting in the greatest overlap between pump and probe volume. The overall heating of the sample could be determined from the 2Θ shift of the Bragg peak maxima to ΔT = 3–4 K by comparing the diffraction pattern under light illumination with the dark diffraction pattern. One-dimensional diffraction patterns were obtained by integrating the two dimensional images with Fit2d.[35] The patterns were normalized against the background signal. Further details of the experimental set-up are described elsewhere.[26,27,34]

Since in this work an irreversible dimerisation reaction was studied, a sophisticated time sequence and data treatment had to be applied to extract information about the ultrafast and slow time domains of this reaction simultaneously. Fig. 5 illustrates the principle of the time slices used. Under the chosen experimental conditions of sample thickness and laser power the light-induced transformation from the crystalline β-phase to the amorphous dimer product took between 20 and 50 min. In order to determine the time constant of this slow sample kinetics the intensity decay of X-ray diffraction spots was followed at detector integration times of Δt_{det} = 4–10 min. The ultrafast timescale could be measured in the common approach by tuning the laser pulses with respect to the X-ray pulses on the picosecond time-scale. At the beginning of one measurement cycle, time zero (t = 0) was set by monitoring the pulse sequence of the direct laser and the X-ray beam using a fast GaAs detector. Negative time points (t_i < 0) were defined as time points where the X-ray pulse arrived before the laser pulse, and positive time points were defined as time points where the X-ray pulse arrived after the laser pulse. The time intervals of this fast time-scale varied between Δt_{fast} = 30 and 120 ps.

In order to determine transient signal changes at the fast, picosecond, and slow, minute, time-scales, the change in the diffraction signal is plotted as a function of both time-scales. If the signal changes were an effect of the slow time progress, they should coincide at the same slow time point. If the signal changes were an effect of the fast time-scale, the transient signals should all appear at the same fast time point. Provided that a small enough time raster is used, this method should be independent of the interval size and lead to coincident signal changes at the slow and/or fast time-scales.

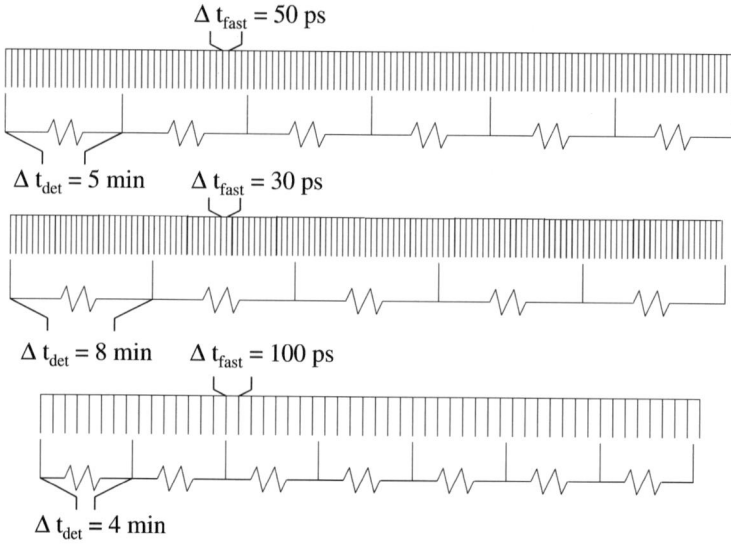

Fig. 5 Probing irreversible reactions: Timing scheme suitable for X-ray probe pulses suitable to measure very slow and very fast components of structural changes during chemical reactions.

3. Results and discussion

Both, the steady-state X-ray diffraction pattern and the UV spectra of the β-phase, the γ-phase and the product state support that the previously discussed solid-state reaction occurred. The clearly distinguishable powder diffraction pattern of the photoactive p-FCA β-phase and the photo-inactive p-FCA γ-phase are shown in Fig. 6 top (β-phase) and bottom (γ-phase, see also ref. 18–20). In Fig. 7 the normalized UV spectra of the sample before and after the time-resolved X-ray diffraction experiment are presented. These spectra are in agreement with those published in ref. 15, indicating that the correct reaction was observed.

Fig. 8 shows the time propagation of a typical Bragg diffraction peak of the β-phase of p-FCA for several time points. As can clearly be seen, the peak splits into two components before it

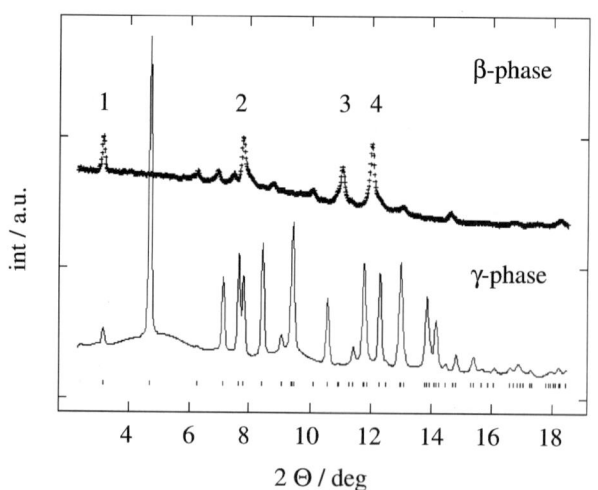

Fig. 6 Powder diffraction pattern of the β-phase (top) and γ-phase (bottom) of p-FCA reactant.

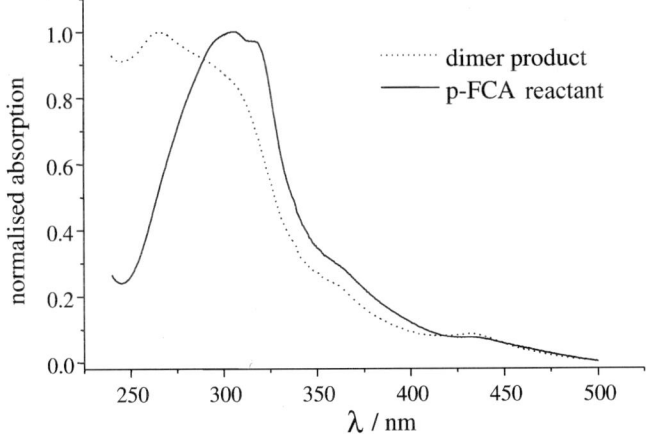

Fig. 7 Normalized UV spectra of the sample before and after the time-resolved X-ray diffraction experiment.

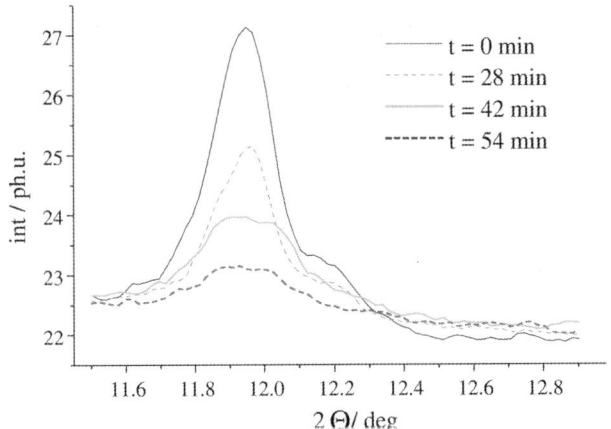

Fig. 8 Time propagation of the most prominent Bragg diffraction peak (No. 4) of β-p-FCA to the product state.

completely degrades at times longer than 45 min. The corresponding diffraction pattern of the product state shows a broad scattered signal without structure, thus indicating an amorphous product state.

Fig. 9 shows the time dependence of the overall correlation function $C_{tot}(t)$. Similar to the kinetic treatment of time-resolved spectroscopic data like e.g. the time evolution of a dynamic Stoke shift in fluorescence spectroscopy[36] $C_{tot}(t)$ is defined as

$$C_{tot}(t) = \sum_n C_n(t)/n.$$

$C_{tot}(t)$ is an averaged correlation function of the normalised correlation functions $C_n(t)$ of the nth Bragg peak of the pattern. The Bragg peaks could best be refined by a Lorentz profile (not a pseudo-Voigt profile). From the intensity of the Bragg peak C_n is calculated as:

$$C_n(t) = \frac{A_{2\Theta}(t) - A_{2\Theta}(t = \infty)}{A_{2\Theta}(t = 0) - A_{2\Theta}(t = \infty)}.$$

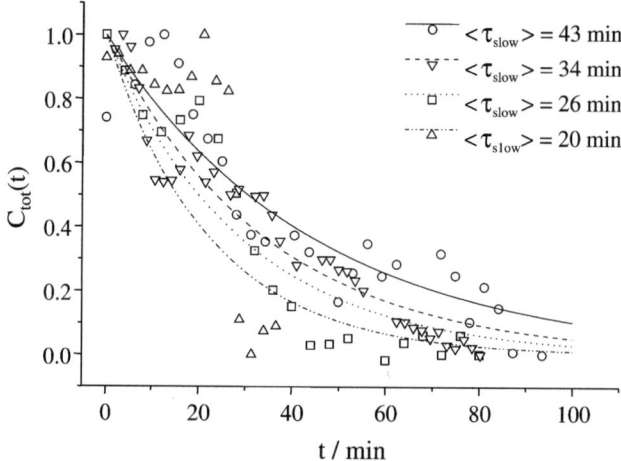

Fig. 9 Time dependence of the overall correlation function $C_{tot}(t)$.

where $A_{2\Theta}(t=0)$, $A_{2\Theta}(t)$ and $A_{2\Theta}(t=\infty)$ are the integrated intensities of a Bragg diffraction peak at the start of the experiment $t=0$, the time point t and the end of the experiment or $t=\infty$ respectively. The peak profile is refined according to

$$I_p(2\Theta) = \frac{2\int I(2\Theta)\mathrm{d}(2\Theta)\Delta_{\mathrm{FWHM}}2\Theta}{\pi(4(2\Theta-2\Theta_c)^2 + \Delta_{\mathrm{FWHM}}2\Theta^2)}$$

giving the integrated peak intensity $A_{2\Theta} = \int I(2\Theta)\mathrm{d}(2\Theta)$. $\Delta_{\mathrm{FWHM}}2\Theta$ is the full width at half maximum of the peak and $2\Theta_c$ is the peak centre in 2Θ.

Since the integrated intensity of a peak depends on the height and the FWHM, a change in the correlation function might be introduced by height changes or by FWHM changes (or both). Since the observed intensity of a diffraction peak is related to the squared structure factor $|F_{hkl}|^2$ also the following correlation function can be defined:

$$C_n(t) = \frac{|F_{hkl}(t)|^2 - |F_{hkl}(t=\infty)|^2}{|F_{hkl}(t=0)|^2 - |F_{hkl}(t=\infty)|^2}.$$

However, in this work we will concentrate on the expression $A_{2\Theta}$. Though different attempts were made (in this work and ref. 7 and 14), till now the crystallographic refinement of the pure β-phase has failed. Since the effects found were very strong, we nevertheless think that one can get important information about the mechanism of the structural transformation of the β-phase to the amorphous dimer state.

The time dependence of the overall correlation function $C_{tot}(t)$ is shown in Fig. 9. From the *slow* time behaviour of $C_{tot}(t)$ the overall degrading of the p-FCA to the dimer product can be derived. The time decay of $C_{tot}(t)$ has been fitted by monoexponential curves using a Marquard fit routine with a least square convergence method. Decay times between 20 and 43 min were found for the slow component. After normalisation against the sample thickness and the laser power, an averaged transformation time of $<\tau_{slow}> = 28$ min (10 μm)$^{-1}$ (7 μJ)$^{-1}$ was found. This result is reasonable comparing the photon flux per second of the laser and flashlamp experiments. Note, that the values for the correlation function $C_{tot}(t)$ scatter very much for $t < 30$ min. In the following we will show that these perturbations are not arbitrary but follow some reproducible modulations on the *fast* time-scale since, as shown in Fig. 5, both time-scales are measured *in parallel*. However, on the slow time-scale no coincident perturbed signals are found.

As in Fig. 8, for all Bragg diffraction peaks it was observed that the peaks split before the sample becomes amorphous. In Fig. 10 this splitting is presented for the Bragg diffraction peak No. 3 of Fig. 6 at $2\Theta_c = 11.02°$. On the left-hand side (open circles), the peak centre $2\Theta_c$ is plotted as a

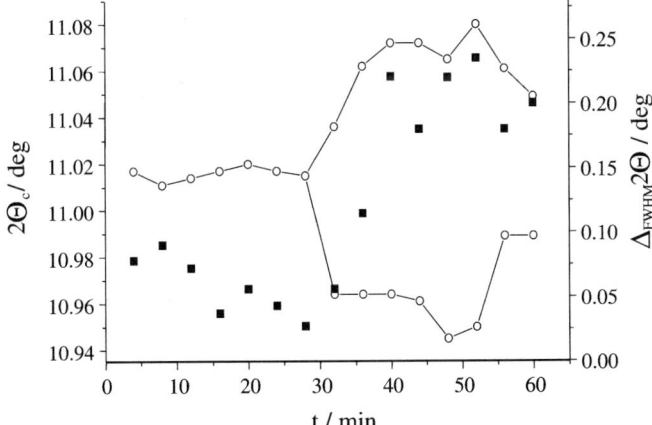

Fig. 10 Splitting of the Bragg diffraction peak No. 3 at $2\Theta_c = 11.02°$. Open circles on the left-hand axis: Time evolution of the peak centres $2\Theta_c$. Filled squares on the right-hand axis: Time-dependence of the full width at half maximum $\Delta_{FWHM}2\Theta$ of the 11.02° peak.

function of time and compared with the full width at half maximum of the peak $\Delta_{FWHM}2\Theta$ on the right-hand side (filled squares). After 32 min the width broadens so much within 12 min that a refinement of two peaks is possible.

If one plots the correlation function $\tilde{C}_1(t)$ of the most prominent Bragg diffraction peak (peak No. 4 in Fig. 6) as a function of the *fast* picosecond time-scale at early times a coincident perturbation of $\tilde{C}_1(t)$ is found (see Fig. 11 for three representative samples). Note that the scaled correlation function $\tilde{C}_1(t) = aC_1(t)$, with a(sample1) = 0.875, a(sample2) = 1.285 and a(sample3) = 1.402, is shown for clarity. In all three cases, a local perturbation of the decay curves around $t = 0$ ps is observed, where an extremely fast intensity decrease is followed by a fast $\tilde{C}_1(t)$ increase. The whole perturbation takes place within 140 ps (or 70 ps for the decrease and 70 ps for the increase) and therefore directly reflects the time resolution of the apparatus, suggesting that the modulation is even faster than the value found. Note that *in parallel* the sample degrades on the slow time-scale. The local intensity drop around $t = 0$ ps might be explained as some kind of structural distortion *similar* to temporal "heating" of the sample. The modulation of the

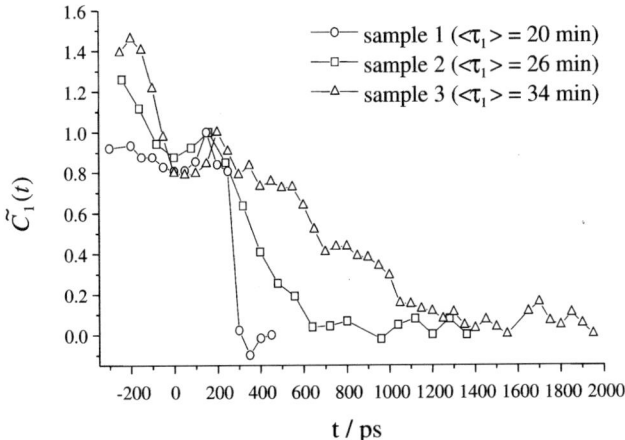

Fig. 11 Fast time behaviour of the correlation function $\tilde{C}_1(t)$ of the most prominent Bragg diffraction peak (peak No. 4) for three representative samples. Note that the scaled correlation function $\tilde{C}_1(t) = aC_1(t)$ with a(sample 1) = 0.875, a(sample 2) = 1.285 and a(sample 3) = 1.402 is shown for clarity.

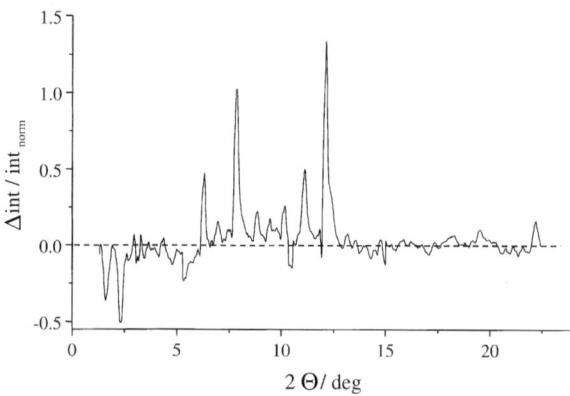

Fig. 12 Difference map of the powder diffraction pattern for $t = 200$ ps–0 ps. The difference map is averaged over three experiments.

correlation function was also observed for the other Bragg diffraction peaks, however, it was less pronounced and not always observable as an intensity decrease. Fig. 12 shows the difference map for $t = 200$ ps–0 ps which was averaged over 3 experiments. Both, intensity increases and intensity decreases (at low 2Θ values, $2\Theta = 10°$ and $2\Theta = 15°$) are reproducibly found. The relative signal change Δ int/int $_{norm}$ is normalised against 100%, leading to a maximal intensity change of 1.5%. The difference map shows that simple laser heating effects, which would uniformly lower the Bragg intensities via an increase in the Debye–Waller factor, can be excluded.

However, it cannot be clarified without doubt whether the temporary structural distortion results from the excess energy of the 267 nm excitation light leading to a phonon-assisted intermolecular vibrational energy redistribution, which then forms the product state. It is also not clear if this excess energy is necessary to initiate the reaction or if an excitation in the vibronic $S_1^0 \leftarrow S_0^0$ ground state would be sufficient. However, in liquid phase reactions, it is well known that excess energy plays an important role for photochemical processes and is absolutely required in order to initiate e.g. isomerisation reactions.[17] Definitely, excitation with 800 nm excitation light did not initiate the reaction and did not lead to the temporal modulation of the diffraction pattern found here. The experimental results of ref. 15 also indicate that in this solid-state dimerisation the excitation of a particular phonon branch is necessary for initiation of the reaction. Therefore, for an efficient photo-dimerisation process the reaction cavity has to be activated,[10] which allows changes or distortions in the crystal lattice in such a way that the dimerisation reaction can proceed.

From the time-resolved X-ray diffraction measurement we propose the following mechanism (Fig. 13): we interpret the picosecond modulation of the correlation function as a light-induced phonon motion, which, similar to Peierls distortion, forms a pair-like metastable crystal state. In coincidence with this, small, distortion of the lattice, a reaction cavity with a transient pair-like state is formed, guiding the reaction to the product dimer. Since the lattice deformations are very strong during product formation, the periodic lattice is split into smaller domains (and crystal pieces) with progressing transformation. Thus amorphisation is completed within 30 min. However, recrystallisation to a crystalline dimer product would be possible if the chosen environment of the reaction was a suspension of the crystals in water.[14–16]

One general problem of all reported time-resolved experiments is to clearly distinguish between the wanted light-induced phenomena and their observation and the unwanted observations of perturbing heating effects. As pointed out in ref. 26 and in the present work, one approach to exclude heating-induced structural changes might be to excite the sample optically with an infrared wavelength far from the electronic absorption band. Provided the heat capacity is known, the temperature rise of the sample can be calculated from the 2Θ-shift of the Bragg diffraction peaks (in the sample used the temperature increase was about $\Delta T = 3$ K). However, since most heat travels through the crystal as low-frequency phonon motions this temperature rise might be sufficient to induce phonon-distortions. Line broadening of the Bragg diffraction peak can also be

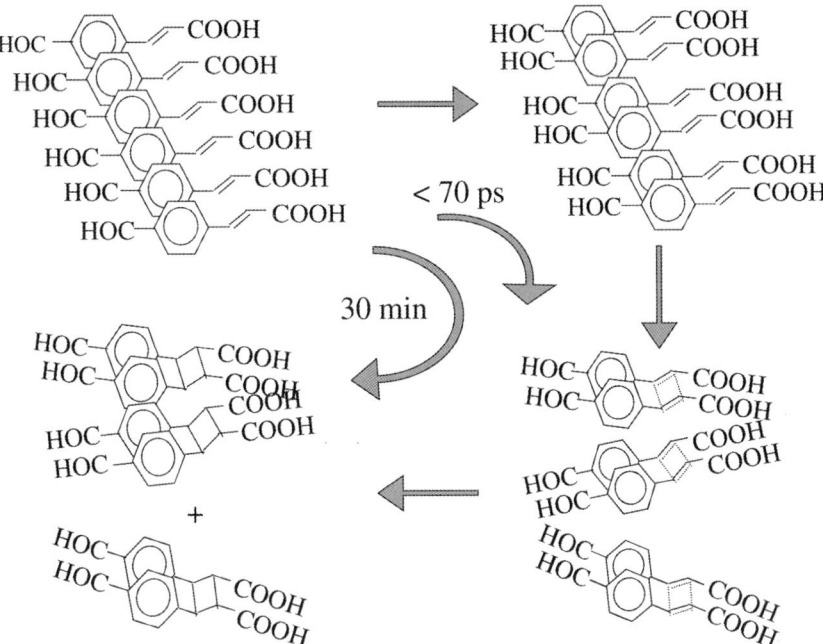

Fig. 13 The picosecond increase of the FWHM can be interpreted as a light-induced phonon motion, which, similar to Peierls distortion, forms a pair-like metastable crystal state. Coinciding with this, small, distortion of the lattice a transient pair-like state is formed guiding the reaction to the product dimer. Since the lattice deformations are so strong during the product formation, with progressing crystal transformation it splits into smaller domains (and pieces) leading to a complete amorphisation after 30 min.

used as an experimental hint. A separation of time-scales can be performed if the size of the crystals or crystallites is known, since phonons travel with the speed of light.

4. Conclusions and outlook

In the present work the dynamics of the irreversible, topochemical reaction of *p*-formyl-*trans*-cinnamic acid crystals to 4,4′-diformyl-β-truxinic acid was investigated. Time-resolved X-ray powder diffraction was chosen as the experimental method. The observed changes in the Bragg diffraction pattern at early times were interpreted as an initial distortion assisted by a phonon motion on a time-scale faster than 70 ps leading to the dimer. The formation of the product state results in the generation of at least two phases after about 30 min. The reaction is finished after 40–60 min ending in a complete amorphisation of the sample.

We have shown that time-resolved X-ray diffraction using undulator radiation of the third generation synchrotron sources, *e.g.*, the European Synchrotron Facility (ESRF) in Grenoble (France), the Advanced Photon Source (APS) in Chicago (USA) and SPring-8 in Harima (Japan), provide powerful new tools, which allow for tracking of structural changes during the course of chemical reactions down to the picosecond time-scale. As pointed out in this work, the major part of these fast experiments employs the pump and probe scheme. With sophisticated timing schemes it is also possible to investigate irreversible reactions. In this context, X-ray powder diffraction is a good choice to follow such reactions, since the exposure time of the sample is quite limited, allowing a complete time scan. However, with the chosen set-up the powder diffraction pattern lacks resolution so that the structural statements which can be given are quite limited. Therefore, future experiments will concentrate on the quality of the crystals and whether structural distortions, which initiate the reaction, can be "slowed down" *via* chemical modification.

Table 1 Basic features of a monochromatic X-ray beam produced in a third generation synchrotron compared to a monochromatic X-ray beam of an X-FEL

$E_{\text{X-ray}}$/keV	$\lambda_{\text{X-ray}}$/Å	Photons pulse^{-1}/ photons (0.1%bw)$^{-1}$	ν_{rep}/Hz	Pulses per measurement	$\Delta t_{\text{X-ray}}$/fs
ESRF (ID09-TR U20)					
11	1.13	10^6	896.6	10^5–10^6	50 000
X-FEL					
12.4	1.00	10^{12}	10	1–2	100

The time-resolution of time-resolved experiments using synchrotron radiation is limited by the pulse duration of about 50–70 ps. In order to achieve faster time domains the duration of the X-ray pulse has to be reduced. In contrast to pulse slicing techniques, which have severe limitations in the obtainable flux of the sample, future X-ray free electron laser sources seem most interesting as they propose X-ray pulse durations of the order of 100 fs at photon flux even higher than present-day synchrotron radiation sources. According to refs. 32–34, Table 1 summarises some key parameters concerning flux and time resolution of a synchrotron of the third generation and an X-FEL.

In present day experiments 10^6 X-ray pulses with 10^5–10^6 photons pulse^{-1} have to be accumulated on the detector in order to obtain an X-ray signal of sufficient intensity, using a two-dimensional CCD camera as detector. Using the X-FEL as source, few X-ray pulses yield the same or even better intensity at the detector. Due to the higher photon flux and the faster exposure times, the investigations of irreversible reactions will also benefit from this source. Sub-ps resolution can be obtained at synchrotron sources if an IR-laser pulse triggered X-ray Streak camera is used as detection system.[37] However, the low sensitivity of this device is not favourable for diffraction or diffuse scattering experiments with weak signal modulation. Since X-ray pulses generated by X-FELs have a natural pulse-width of 100 fs these sources will also offer better experimental conditions for the investigation of processes in the time domain from 100 fs to a few picoseconds, *e.g.* ultrafast structural relaxation experiments.[38]

Acknowledgements

The authors wish to thank Prof. J. Troe for his permanent support and interest in this work. I. Dreger is acknowledged for technical assistance with the manuscript. S. T. is grateful to the DFG for the research grant TE 347/1–1.

References

1 F. Hertel, *Z. Elektrochem.*, 1931, **37**, 536.
2 A. Mustafa, *Chem Rev.*, 1951, **51**, 1.
3 M. D. Cohen and G. M. J. Schmidt, *J. Chem. Soc.*, 1964, 1996.
4 M. D. Cohen, G. M. J. Schmidt and F. I. Sonntag, *J. Chem. Soc.*, 1964, 2000.
5 G. M. J. Schmidt, *J. Chem. Soc.*, 1964, 2014.
6 G. M. J. Schmidt, *Pure Appl. Chem.*, 1971, **27**, 647.
7 J. M. Thomas, *Philos. Trans., R. Soc. London*, 1974, **277**, 251.
8 M. D. Cohen, *Angew. Chem. Int. Ed. Engl.*, 1975, **14**(6), 386.
9 G. Kaupp, *Angew. Chem. Int. Ed. Engl.*, 1992, **31**(5), 592.
10 R. G. Weiss, V. Ramamurthy and G. S. Hammond, *Acc. Chem. Res.*, 1993, **26**, 530.
11 G. Kaupp and M. Plagemann, *J. Photochem. Photobiol A*, 1994, **80**, 399.
12 H. Ihmels, D. Leusser, M. Pfeiffer and D. Stalke, *Tetrahedron*, 2000, **56**(36), 6867.
13 M. Chorev and M. Goodman, *Trends Biotechnol.*, 1995, **13**(10), 438.
14 M. Irie, S. Kobatake and M. Horichi, *Science*, 2001, **291**, 176.
15 F. Nakanishi, H. Nakanishi, T. Tasai, Y. Suzuki and M. Hasegawa, *Chem. Lett.*, 1974, **1974**, 525.
16 F. Nakanishi, H. Nakanishi, M. Tsuchiya and M. Hasegawa, *Bull. Chem. Soc. Jpn.*, 1976, **49**(11), 3096.
17 M. Hasegawa, H. Katsuki and Y. Iida, *Chem. Lett.*, 1981, 1799.
18 K. D. M. Harris and I. L. Patterson, *J. Chem. Soc., Perkin Trans.*, 1994, **2**, 1201.
19 K. D. M. Harris and J. M. Thomas, *J. Solid State Chem.*, 1991, **93**, 197.
20 H. Nakanishi, *Act. Crystallogr. Sect. C*, 1985, **41**, 70.

21 D. Bourgeois, T. Ursby, M. Wulff, C. Pradevand, V. Srajer, A. LeGrand, W. Schildkamp, S. Laboure, C. Rubin, T.-Y. Teng, M. Roth and K. Moffat, *J. Synchrotron Radiat.*, 1996, **3**, 65.
22 V. Srajer, T.-Y. Teng, T. Ursby, C. Pradevard, Z. Ren, S. Adachi, W. Schildkamp, D. Bourgeois, M. Wulff and K. Moffat, *Science*, 1996, **274**, 1726.
23 V. Srajer, Z. Ren, T.-Y. Teng, M. Schmidt, T. Ursby, D. Bourgeois, C. Pradervand, W. Schildkamp, M. Wulff and K. Moffat, *Biochemistry*, 2001, **40**(46), 13 802.
24 B. Perman, V. Srajer, Z. Ren, T.-Y. Teng, C. Pradervand, T. Ursby, D. Bourgeois, F. Schotte, M. Wulff, R. Kort, K. Hellingwerf and K. Moffat, *Science*, 1998, **279**, 1946.
25 Z. Ren, B. Perman, V. Srajer, T.-Y. Teng, C. Pradervand, D. Bourgeois, F. Schotte, T. Ursby, R. Kort, M. Wulff and K. Moffat, *Biochemistry*, 2001, **40**(46), 13 788.
26 S. Techert, F. Schotte and M. Wulff, *Phys. Rev. Lett.*, 2001, **86**(10), 2030.
27 R. Neutze, R. Wouts, S. Techert, A. Kirrander, J. Davidson, M. Kocsis, F. Schotte and M. Wulff, *Phys. Rev. Lett.*, 2001, **87**(19), 195 508.
28 A. Geis, D. Block, M. Burieau, F. Schotte, S. Techert, A. Plech, M. Wulff and H. P. Trommsdorff, *J. Lumin.*, 2001, **94**, 493.
29 M. R. Pressprich, M. A. White, Y. Vekhter and P. Coppens, *J. Am. Chem. Soc.*, 1994, **116**, 5233.
30 C. D. Kim, S. Pillet, G. Wu, W. K. Fullagar and P. Coppens, *Acta Crystallogr. Sect. A*, 2002, **58**, 133.
31 M. Klessinger and J. Michl, *Lichtabsorption und Photochemie organischer Molekuele*, VCH, Weinheim, 1989.
32 *TESLA Technical Design Report, Part V, The X-ray Free Electron Laser*, eds. G. Materlik and Th. Tschentscher, TESLA-FEL **2001–05**, DESY, Hamburg, March 2001.
33 Th. Tschentscher, *Proc. SPIE*, 2001, **4500**, 1.
34 F. Schotte, S. Techert, P. Anfinrud, V. Srajer, K. Moffat and M. Wulff, in *Third Generation Hard X-ray Synchrotron Radiation Sources: Source Properties, Optics, and Experimental Techniques*, ed. D. Mills, Wiley, New York, 2002.
35 (a) A. P. Hammersley, M. Svensson, M. Hanfland, A. N. Fitch and D. Haeussermann, *High Press. Res.*, 1996, **14**, 235; (b) A. P. Hammersley, S. O. Svensson and A. Thomson, *Nucl. Instrum. Methods Phys. Res. Sect. A*, 1994, **346**, 321.
36 S. Techert, A. Wiessner, S. Schmatz and H. Staerk, *J. Phys. Chem. B*, 2001, **105**, 7579.
37 G. A. Naylor, K. Scheidt, J. Larsson, M. Wulff and J. M. Filhol, *Meas. Sci. Technol.*, 2001, **12**(11), 1858.
38 S. Techert and R. Neutze, in *TESLA Technical Design Report, Part V, The X-ray Free Electron Laser—Ultrafast Chemistry*, eds. G. Materlik and Th. Tschentscher, TESLA-FEL **2001–05**, DESY, Hamburg (March 2001), p. 133.

Nanosecond time-resolved crystallography of photo-induced species: case study and instrument development for high-resolution excited-state single-crystal structure determination

Jacqueline M. Cole,*[a] Paul R. Raithby,[b] Michael Wulff,[c] Friedrich Schotte,[c] Anton Plech,[c] Simon J. Teat[d] and Graham Bushnell-Wye[d]

[a] *Department of Chemistry, University of Cambridge, Lensfield Road, Cambridge, UK CB2 1EW. E-mail: jmc61@cam.ac.uk*
[b] *Department of Chemistry, University of Bath, Claverton Down, Bath, UK BA2 7AY*
[c] *ESRF, B.P. 220, F-38043, Grenoble Cedex, France*
[d] *SRS, Daresbury Laboratory, Warrington, UK WA4 4AD*

Received 11th April 2002, Accepted 29th April 2002
First published as an Advance Article on the web 30th July 2002

This work describes one of the first stages in the development of time-resolved photo-induced small-molecule single-crystal diffraction, whereby transient electron density perturbations, with lifetimes down to the *nanosecond* level, can be resolved at the *atomic* level. Knowledge of such ephemeral electronic effects is likely to yield key information regarding the origins of certain important physical properties, *e.g.* luminescent and non-linear optical effects, since it will allow the dynamics of electron density to be identified and quantified, and it is this that underpins such phenomena in a given molecule. The experimental methodology employs phase-locking pump–probe techniques such that the inherent time-structure of a synchrotron X ray beam (nanoseconds) is harnessed and time-gated in-phase with a femtosecond laser. The resultant beams, made coincident on the crystal in a periodic manner, and a diffraction pattern are recorded as a function of the Bragg angle, θ. Such technology is based upon the pioneering work carried out in sub-nanosecond time-resolved crystallography of macromolecular biological moieties (non-atomic resolution) at the ESRF, although one crucial difference here is the use of monochromatic irradiation and oscillatory motion rather than Laue 'snapshot' methodology, so that atomic resolution is possible. The experimental details of a case study conducted on ID9 at the ESRF, France, are described, whereby the feasibility of the excited-state structure determination of a luminescent rhenium carbene complex, $[HNCH_2CH_2NHCRe(2,2'-bipyridine)(CO)_3]Br$, is realised. Key experimental parameters that are required for the success of such an experiment are discussed in the light of this study, together with other feasibility work conducted at the SRS, UK, and in the laboratory. Plans, designs and tests for the implementation of this technique in the UK, first at the SRS, and then at DIAMOND, the forthcoming UK synchrotron, are described, in particular with reference to the world-leading potential that DIAMOND could lend toward the development of this technique.

DOI: 10.1039/b203552a

1. Introduction

The photophysics of organic[1] and organometallic[2] complexes has attracted a wide level of interest over recent years on account of the very applied nature of their light emissive properties: *e.g.* for semiconductor devices, non-linear optical components and light-emitting diodes.[3,4] The origin of these properties lies in the nature of the excited states of these materials, whose lifetimes typically range from μs to ps.[2,5] The photolysis process excites electrons into otherwise inaccessible states, thus inducing a redistribution of electrons that can also lead to atomic displacement within the material or, more severely, isomerism or solid-state chemical reactions. The effects are prevalent in organometallic species due to their low-valent metal centres and the high degree of covalency between the metal and its ligands which results in the presence of various types of low energy excited states.[6] The accessibility of these various states, and thus the energy, intensity and lifetime of the associated light emission, depends inherently on the metal type and the nature of the ligands. In principle, one could therefore tune materials to exhibit specific emissive properties by judiciously varying the metal and ligand type. However, this requires a thorough knowledge of the exact nature of the excited state that is responsible for the emission. This is no trivial matter, since this emissive state is usually a mixture of various types of low-lying excited states. One can infer a certain level of information *indirectly* through UV/vis spectroscopic measurements, by comparing the different emission wavelengths, lifetimes and quantum yields for a given series of complexes, and such inferences can be supported by theoretical molecular orbital-based calculations. More direct information can be obtained by recent developments in time-resolved infrared vibrational spectroscopy.[7] Such work undoubtedly provides invaluable information. However, in order to be able to ascertain both *direct* and *quantitative* information regarding the excited-state structure of such materials, stroboscopic pump–probe techniques are being developed for time-resolved small-molecule single-crystal X-ray diffraction, such that photo-induced crystal structures which exist on a timescale of μs to ns become accessible.[8,9] The resultant ability to build up excited-state structure/photophysical property relationships leads to the ultimate goal of being able to engineer materials with desired physical properties for a given photonic application. Whilst this paper concentrates on organometallic complexes, on account of the case study, the majority of arguments and results expressed herein also pertain equally well to organic materials where, for example, photo-induced charge-transfer processes give rise to non-linear optical effects. One of the great assets of organic non-linear optical materials over their inorganic counterparts is their fast optical response times (typically ns to ps). Therefore, analogous studies of the excited-state structure of such organic materials using the technique described herein are also underway.

Given that the changes in electronic and/or atomic configuration of the excited state of a molecule, relative to its ground state, can be subtle and/or localised, for example, primarily between one metal-to-ligand interaction, obtaining excited-state crystal structures at the highest possible atomic resolution is paramount in observing these changes. In terms of nanosecond time-resolved X-ray diffraction studies to date, the pioneering work has been reported on macro-molecular biological moieties (non-atomic resolution) using the instrument, ID9, at the ESRF.[10–12] These studies use the Laue 'snapshot' methodology, owing to the delicate nature of the samples with respect to an intense X-ray and laser beam, and because atomic resolution is not usually possible and/or required to observe the biologically important conformational changes ensuing. Such bio-structural studies have proven to be very successful and the coming of age of the Laue method in this respect is described by Ren *et al.*,[13] including a survey of ten successful Laue time-resolved bio-structural studies. Corresponding software for recording and processing Laue data has also been well developed.[14] However, whilst the Laue method exploits the use of the entire 'white' X-ray beam, its coverage of the Ewald sphere can be patchy and there is significant wavelength overlap of reflections. The resolution of the resulting structure is significantly compromised as a result, relative to an analogous experiment where monochromatic irradiation and oscillatory scans as a function of the Bragg angle, θ, are used. Given the more stringent resolution requirements for small-molecule excited-state crystallography, the feasibility of conducting a nanosecond time-resolved pump–probe experiment on ID9 using the oscillatory scanning method in tandem with time-gating to a femtosecond laser was investigated. A perspective of this technical route has been described previously by Coppens.[8] The subject study is a luminescent rhenium carbene complex, [HNCH$_2$CH$_2$NHCRe(2,2'-bipyridine)(CO)$_3$]Br.[15] Experimental details are described herein and key experimental parameters relating to the sample are discussed. Related preliminary feasibility tests both on Station 9.8 at the Synchrotron Radiation Source (SRS), Daresbury, and in the laboratory are also described. Station 9.8 is the world-leading small-molecule single-crystal synchrotron facility and these tests form the first stages of a pilot project to develop time-resolved pump–probe X-ray diffraction in the UK. The more major developments will take place on Station 9.8. Whilst the SRS is scheduled to see its demise by the end of the decade, the methodology herein proposed is being designed, taking into account the construction specifications of the new synchrotron source, DIAMOND, as they unfold. In this way, the technology developed will be readily transferable, together with the instrumentation, when DIAMOND comes on-line in ~5 years time.

2. Experimental

Structure simulations

A set of single-crystal X-ray diffraction data was obtained on a suitable crystal of [HNCH$_2$CH$_2$NHCRe(2,2'-bipyridine)(CO)$_3$]Br, using a Bruker–Nonius Kappa CCD diffractometer, molybdenum-K$_\alpha$ radiation ($\lambda = 0.71069$ Å), with the crystal cooled to 150 K, using an Oxford Cryostream crystal cooling device. The co-ordinates reported by Xue et al.[15] were used as a starting model for the structure which was refined successfully using SHELXL-97.[16] The structure of the rhenium carbene cation is shown in Fig. 1 along with an indication of the direction that the Re → C(carbene) vector, x, is expected to shift upon photo-excitation as a result of metal–ligand charge transfer (MLCT).

Following crystal structure refinement, a set of F_c^2 values for all the unique data was computed and used as the ground-state values in simulations to determine which reflections are most likely to be affected by the expected lengthening of the Re=C(carbene) double bond upon excitation to the excited state. The magnitude and direction of the Re–C vector for the ground state were computed (Re=C 2.153(4) Å), and then the co-ordinates of the carbene ligand recomputed when this ligand was moved away from the Re atom, along the Re–C vector, in successive steps of 0.01 Å between 0.01 and 0.1 Å, and in steps of 0.02 Å for increases between 0.1 and 0.4 Å [using the MOVE instruction in SHELXL-97]. For each of these 25 sets of co-ordinates (all non-metal atoms not in the carbene group were assumed to retain their ground-state co-ordinates) a set of F_c^2 values for all the unique data was calculated using SHELXL-97. The F_c^2 dataset relating to an increase in the Re–C vector of 0.1 Å was compared with the F_c^2 dataset for the ground state structure. 0.1 Å is the expected level of change in bond-length upon excitation since the 'formal' double bond character

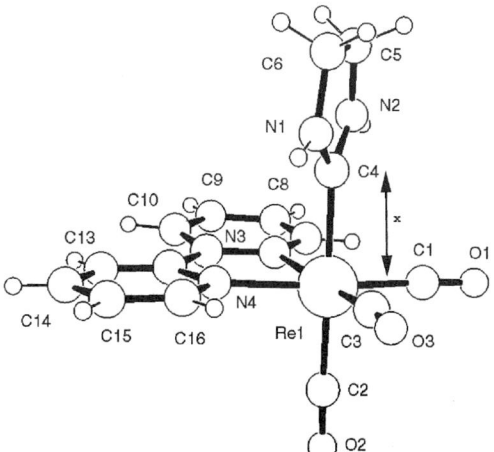

Fig. 1 The structure of the [HNCH$_2$CH$_2$NHCRe(2,2'-bipyridine)(CO)$_3$]$^+$ cation showing the direction of the displacement of the diimine carbene ligand used to compute the simulated F_c^2 values.

of the Re=C bond is reduced, Re–C single bonds being of the order of 0.1–0.2 Å longer than Re=C double bonds. A wide variety of changes in reflection intensity were observed for all Miller indices. It should be remembered that all these calculations are based on a 100% conversion of the structure to the excited state.

The X-ray diffraction experiment

The pump–probe time-resolved single-crystal X-ray diffraction experiment was performed on beamline ID9, at the ESRF, Grenoble, France. The X-rays emanate from the synchrotron *via* a low-K undulator with a 20 mm period. This produces a polychromatic spectrum with only one harmonic at 16.45 keV ($\lambda = 0.7537$ Å). The polychromatic beam was monochromated using a Si(111) double crystal monochromator and the beam was focused onto the sample in a 0.25 mm diameter spot. The average flux was 3×10^7 photons s^{-1}. The inherent X-ray pulse length was 110 ps after injection at 90 mA and reduced to 90 ps at the end of a fill (full width half maximum). Sub-nanosecond X-ray time-resolution was achieved by using the 16-bunch mode of the synchrotron, which has a bunch spacing of 176 ns; a chopper on the beamline running at 896.6 Hz with a vertical tunnel aperture of 0.145 mm, defines an opening time of 280 ns. One bunch is selected exclusively by centring it in this window relative to its neighbouring bunches.

A mode-locked Ti: sapphire femtosecond laser was synchronised to the radio frequency of the synchrotron in order to achieve pump–probe X-ray diffraction. The 800 nm fundamental wavelength of the laser beam, operating at a repetition rate of 896.6 Hz, was frequency doubled, giving a $\lambda = 400$ nm laser beam of 50 µJ which was focused onto the sample in a 0.25 mm diameter spot, and made coincident to match the cross-section of the X-ray beam.

A crystal sample with dimensions $60 \times 50 \times 40$ µm^3 was mounted onto the ϕ-axis of the diffractometer and cooled to 77 K, using an Oxford Cryosystems Cryostream cooling device. Data were collected using a MAR-CCD detector. Three data sets were collected with the crystal maintained at 77 K, corresponding to (i) a 'reference' ground-state structure determination, no laser irradiation (dataset **1**); (ii) a ground-state structure determination, incorporating laser heating effects by imposing a -10 ns time-delay of the X-ray pulse with respect to the laser pulse (dataset **2**); (iii) the excited-state structure determination, where the laser and X-ray beams are synchronised, using a time-delay of $+0.5$ ns (dataset **3**). These time delays between the X-ray and laser were achieved by delaying the 88.05 MHz reference pulse train that controls the synchronisation of the femtosecond optical cavity. The delay can be shifted between -1.11 ms and 1.11 ms. For the 'reference' ground state structure determination, data were collected in frames as the crystal was rotated about the ϕ-axis, through 251°, in 2° steps, but with 1° of overlap, in each case the exposure time per frame being 13 s. These details were replicated for the other two data collections, except that in these cases, data were recorded through the full ϕ-rotation of 360°.

3. Results and discussion

I. Case study at the ESRF

The focus of the work presented here is a feasibility study for the structure determination of the rhenium carbene organometallic complex [HNCH$_2$CH$_2$NHCRe(2,2'-bipyridine)(CO)$_3$]Br while under synchronised laser irradiation, so that a percentage of the molecules within the crystal are promoted into an excited state and maintained there by irradiation from a femtosecond laser. This complex was chosen for the study because it is luminescent, with the origin of the emission being assigned to a ^{3}MLCT state. A combination of detailed UV/vis spectroscopic studies and theoretical calculations indicates that the emission is ^{3}[d(Re) → π*(diimine)], with the latter exhibiting partial σ* parentage. This indicates that in the excited state the double bond character of the rhenium–carbene bond should be reduced, and that the expected increase in Re–C should be of the order of 0.05–0.20 Å. Although the lifetime of this excited state is only 230 ns, in dichloromethane, at room temperature, this difference should be observable in the solid state using nanosecond time-resolved pump–probe photocrystallographic methods combined with oscillatory-based data collection. Under the experimental conditions, it should be borne in mind that up to a maximum of ~20% of the molecules can be typically excited at any one time without crystal fracture resulting.

Thus the experiment affords the combined excited and ground-state structure of the given compound. By first measuring the ground state with a −10 ns time-delay between the laser and the X-ray pulse such that all photo-excitation has decayed before each subsequent X-ray measurement, and then collecting analogous data but with the X-ray and laser pulses synchronised to a time-delay of +0.5 ns, to ensure laser-excitation before X-ray exposure, the electronic perturbations of the excited-state can be obtained exclusively by taking the difference between the two experimental sets of electron density distributions. This type of time-resolved pump–probe experiment that uses the time structure of synchrotron radiation is only required for compounds with sub-microsecond lifetimes. For materials with longer lifetimes, a mechanical chopper can be used to create a suitable X-ray pulse time-resolution with the chopper being synchronised to the laser,[17] and for samples with *metastable* excited states, *steady state* methods can be used.[8,18–21]

When considering the optimum conditions for data collection for time-resolved photo-crystallographic experiments, a large number of factors have to be taken into consideration. The complex [HNCH$_2$CH$_2$NHCRe(2,2'-bipyridine)(CO)$_3$]Br was selected for a number of reasons in addition to the expected significant change in one bond length and the lifetime of the excited state being in the sub-microsecond range. The complex readily affords good quality single crystals, and the crystal system is orthorhombic which is relatively high for common organometallic complexes. This level of crystal symmetry is, in fact, crucial for experiments run on beamline ID9, at the ESRF, because the instrument is optimised for 'cutting-edge' time-resolved macromolecular crystallography and so the sample axis allows only one degree of rotational freedom, thus restricting data collection to the equatorial plane. With the capability of rotation about only one axis it is not possible to obtain complete coverage of the unique part of reciprocal space in samples that crystallize in lower crystal systems, and thus the high resolution required for this type of detailed analysis is compromised. With the beamline in its present configuration, this crystal symmetry restriction can only be overcome by either removing the crystal mid-data-collection and mounting it at a different orientation or by using a goniometer head fitted with tilting stages or with a suitable external attachment and changing the crystal orientation mid-data-collection. Both of these alternative methods compromise significantly the resolution, since the merging of the data from different tilted orientations contains systematic errors owing to manual crystal recentring and/or angular definition of any imposed tilt; the sphere of confusion about the crystal is simply not small enough. The use of compounds that crystallize in high symmetry crystal systems is also generally very helpful, and sometimes critical, to the success of this type of experiment since the intense lasing conditions imposed upon the sample commonly cause crystal decay; the higher the inherent crystal symmetry, the fewer unique data that have to be collected for a given size of problem, and so the faster the collection of a full unique data set. In favourable cases, where the crystal survives long enough to collect all unique data, multiple equivalent reflections that can be used for data averaging and scaling can also be readily obtained.

The wavelength of laser radiation chosen is also crucial to the success of the experiment. While the laser must provide enough energy to produce enough excited-state molecules to be detected, the radiation must not be absorbed so strongly that a high enough proportion of the energy is converted to heat and the crystal destroyed. Laser wavelengths at or close to absorption maxima should generally be avoided as this will lead to all the photons within the laser pulse being absorbed within the first few microns depth of the crystal. In this experiment with [HNCH$_2$CH$_2$NHCRe(2,2'-bipyridine)(CO)$_3$]Br, the laser wavelength used was 400 nm whereas the absorption maxima occur at 365, 318 and 273 nm, in dichloromethane at room temperature, and an emission maximum lies at 565 nm. Related to the wavelength of the laser is the size of the crystal and with it the associated optical penetration depth. For the molecule studied here, the crystal contains *ca.* 1.9×10^{21} molecules per cm^3. Given a lasing energy of 50 μJ at $\lambda = 400$ nm, there are approximately 1×10^{14} photons per laser pulse. Calculations using the Beer–Lambert law, assuming an absorption cross section of 5×10^{-17} per molecule, show that >99% of the photons should be absorbed in less then 1 micron of the crystal. This equates to only a fraction of a percent of the total number of molecules within the crystal being excited. However, experiments on several different sized crystals, all using the laser in the same configuration as that used for the primary experiment reported herein, indicate that this value is largely underestimated; the laser was fired at eight crystals ranging from 40 to100 μm diameter in the direction of the laser beam path. Laser ablation was observed in all crystals where the laser path through the crystal exceeded 50 μm. An example of the laser

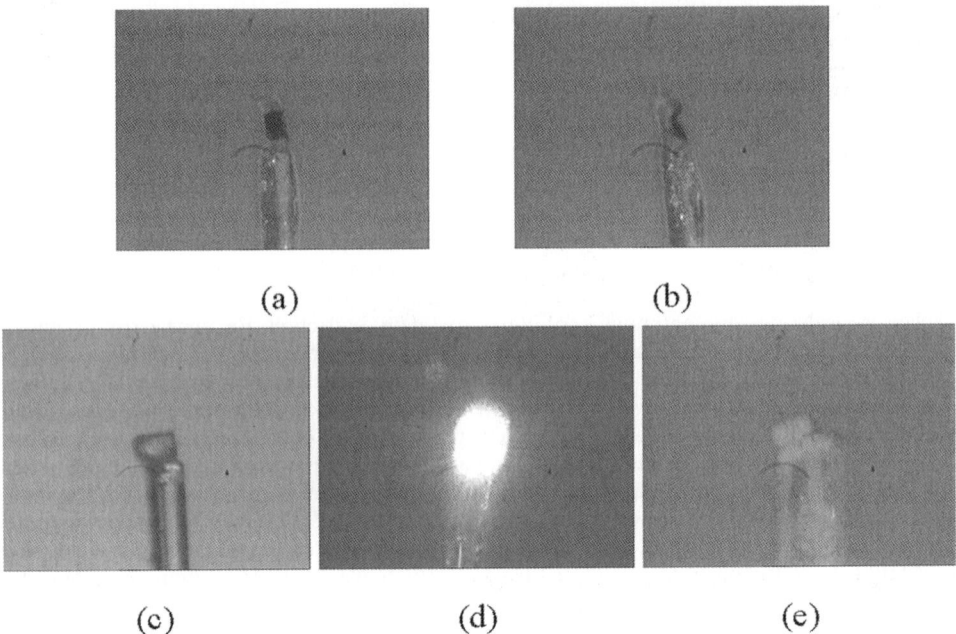

Fig. 2 Crystals of [HNCH$_2$CH$_2$NHCRe(2,2′-bipyridine)(CO)$_3$]Br mounted on a glass fibre and centred on the ϕ-axis of ID9 at the ESRF and subjected to a laser beam of $\lambda = 400$ nm at 50 μJ. Photos (a) and (b) are different views of a crystal of 90 μm diameter in the laser beam direction post-irradiation; photos (c), (d) and (e) relate to a $40 \times 50 \times 60$ μm^3 crystal ultimately used in the case study before, during, and after laser irradiation, respectively. Note that the view of the crystal in (e) is slightly obscured by ice that formed around the crystal during the experiment. Only amorphous contributions due to the icing were observed in the diffraction patterns.

damage on one such crystal (90 μm diameter in the laser beam path) is shown in Fig. 2(a) and (b): as the laser cannot pass entirely through the crystal, local heating effects at the maximum point of optical penetration become extreme and the crystal is gradually 'eaten away' by the laser over a period of several minutes. Both crystals tried with either 40 or 50 μm diameters in the laser beam path direction did not suffer any observable crystal damage, and were stable in the laser beam over several hours of irradiation. Fig. 2(c), (d) and (e) show the crystal ultimately used for this experiment before, during, and after laser irradiation, respectively. Moreover, sustained laser irradiation of a 50 μm diameter crystal rendered a noticeable photochemical colour change (to orange) of the formerly yellow sample throughout the bulk of the crystal, thus indicating optical penetration greater than 50 μm. The calculations based on the Beer–Lambert law rely intrinsically on the value of the extinction coefficient. This parameter is normally measured using solution-state UV/vis spectroscopy, at room temperature, as in this case study and in general, solid-state spectroscopic data is rarely available for compounds of interest. A sharpening of the absorption bands is observed typically when comparing solution-state spectroscopic measurements with analogous solid-state spectra and lowering the temperature stands to alter considerably not only the width of this band but also its general profile, since the accessibility of excited states toward absorption from the ground state will vary according to energy. However, even when bearing in mind these assumptions and calculating the optical penetration depth with large tolerances for the extinction coefficient, only values much lower than 50 μm were obtained. This suggests that whilst these calculations are very useful as a guide, they may not represent fully the optical effects on the crystal bulk, perhaps due to the influence of competing multi-photon processes and/or temporal optical changes in the environment local to a ground-state molecule that neighbours one or several in its excited state, for example.

As the determination of the excited-state structure relies on the accurate measurement of small differences in intensities between the ground and excited-state data collections, it is necessary to

Table 1 Data reduction and integration statistics for datasets 1, 2 and 3

Data set	No. full reflns.	No. partial reflns.	Total no. obs. reflns.	Total no. unique reflns.	No. outliers rejected	No. reflns. measured only once	No. observed reflns.	R_{merge} all reflns.
1	51 512	13 909	81 560	3241	288	176	3714	0.064
2	79 993	19 314	120 096	3729	581	8	3729	0.100
3	79 411	19 295	119 719	3730	791	10	3729	0.090

maximise atomic scattering power and definition of the atomic coordinates for each part of the experiment. For this reason the crystal was cooled to 77 K as this enhances the definition and intensity of the diffraction data by reducing the level of thermal motion within it. In addition, lowering the temperature generally enhances the lifetime of the excited state, as shown in this case by UV/vis spectroscopy taken at room temperature and 77 K (as a glass).[15] Thus excited-state data can be captured with a greater population inversion than would otherwise be possible, when the operating limits of the time-resolution of the pump–probe instrumentation are comparable with the excited-state lifetime of the crystal, thus enhancing the contrast between ground and excited-state structures. Indeed, for materials with particularly short lifetimes, lowering the temperature will make possible photocrystallography of some compounds that is otherwise impossible at room temperature.

All data reduction and initial processing were carried out using the MOSFLM suite of programs,[22] which are usually used for processing macromolecular data. Details of the three data collections including the number of reflections measured, the level of reflection redundancy, and the merging R factor for equivalent reflections are presented in Table 1. A notable feature of the data is the 32-fold redundancy of total reflections measured to unique reflections in data sets **2** and **3**. The corresponding R_{merge} values are also relatively low. Since the software parameters for integration in MOSFLM are optimised for macromolecular crystallographic structure determination, non-standard settings need to be used for small-molecule crystallographic data. The full optimisation of the parameters for small-molecule data processing is currently in progress[23] and it is anticipated that the statistics given, whilst already favourable, will improve in the final processing. In addition, accurate absorption correction procedures are being tested out. A good absorption correction is particularly important for this compound, as it will be in most organometallics of interest for pump–probe photocrystallography, since not only are heavy atoms present in the structure, but also the photoinduced structural changes expected pertain principally to the local metal environment, owing to the dominant triplet MLCT character of the excited state. Therefore, care must be taken to ensure that structural changes observed in this area can be distinguished from possible artifacts relating to X-ray absorption effects. Full details of the data analysis and structure refinement for the compound used in the case study will be presented in a future publication.

In the experiments described above, over 100 000 reflection data may be recorded. Since the expected differences in reflection intensities between ground and excited state may be small and there are many reflections to compare, it has been found helpful to augment the diffraction experiments with additional information. Simulation studies that indicate which reflections in a data set may be subjected to the greatest change in magnitude if the predicted structural changes occur upon excitation can prove very useful in this respect. Since, in the case of [HNCH$_2$CH$_2$NHCRe(2,2'-bipyridine)(CO)$_3$]Br, spectroscopic data and theoretical calculations indicate that the rhenium–carbene bond will lengthen upon excitation, and, as a consequence, the diimine ligand will move further away from the rhenium along the Re → C(carbene) vector, a series of simulations, as described in the previous section, were performed. In addition to identifying the reflections affected most by this structural change, consistent with the reduction in 'formal' bond order, the simulations were also used to establish the minimum bond length change that might show significant differences in the intensity data. Five strong reflections whose F_c^2 values changed between 15 and 80% upon excitation were selected from the unique data. The variation in the F_c^2 value of these reflections, (0, 0, 10), (3, 3, 8), (10, 2, 7), (4, 12, 9) and (4, 0, 2), as a function of increasing Re–C distance was determined (see Fig. 3). The reflections all follow a non-linear

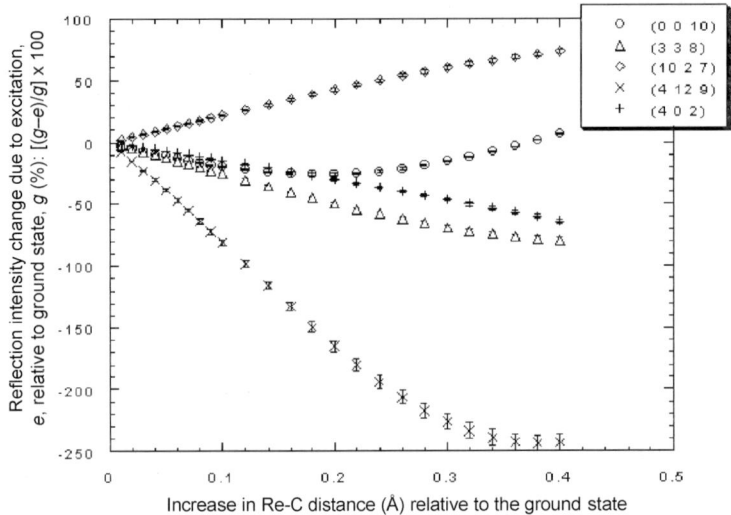

Fig. 3 A plot of the percentage change in intensity of five selected reflections as the Re–C(carbene) bond length is increased in the simulated structures. [(ground − excited)/ground] × 100.

variation in the range 0.01–0.4 Å, the (10, 2, 7) and the (4, 12, 9) reflections being the most sensitive to distance. Given that the error in experimentally determined intensities for all reflections in the dataset varies by a considerable amount, the estimated standard deviation associated with each photoinduced intensity perturbation must be calculated for individual reflections. Such uncertainties were computed for the five selected reflections by assuming the same percentage error of a structure factor whether derived from theory or experiment. An inspection of the level of these uncertainties, shown in Fig. 3 (the estimated standard uncertainties are all less than 4%), indicates that intensity changes corresponding to greater than 0.02 Å increases in the Re–C bond length will be observable if the excited-state conversion is 100%. Clearly, as has been stated previously, only a maximum of 20% conversion is likely to occur without crystal degradation and so the calculated differences must be scaled down to account for this incomplete conversion. It may be possible to determine the exact percentage conversion for a particular sample from spectroscopic studies and then a scale factor could be included in the calculation.

II. Plans, designs and feasibility studies for the development of photocrystallography in the UK

ID9 at the ESRF is truly world-leading in terms of pump–probe time-resolved X-ray diffraction and has far-reaching applications, including photocrystallography as shown above. However, it is formally a beamline for macromolecular crystallography and thus is understandably optimized for Laue experiments. Moreover, its unique ability to realize time-resolved data on sub-nanosecond photo-induced processes puts it in very high demand for experiments requiring 100 ps to ns time-structure. Therefore, whilst experiments focusing on longer-lived processes (μs or greater) can be carried out on the beamline, the availability of alternative instrumentation that could use a mechanical chopper to obtain the required time-structure from a multi-bunch synchrotron beam for such work would optimize resources in this rapidly growing area of research. The requirements for X-ray flux are also much less demanding for microsecond time-resolved studies and so a medium energy synchrotron would be well suited for such developments. Such developments using chopper design are already underway in the USA but European access to these resources will inevitably be restricted. The current developments for the new UK synchrotron, DIAMOND, due to come on-line in 2006, would make the building of such a beamline here an optimal choice for Europe since, in addition to the possibility of designing the instrument from scratch and optimising it for time-resolved studies, it will provide a unique opportunity to tailor the type of insertion device to such studies, and characteristics that are more fundamental to the synchrotron ring could also be considered, pending similar demand from other proposed beamlines, since many of the exact specifications of the synchrotron are still fluid at this stage.

Station 9.8, at the SRS, the current UK synchrotron, is world-leading in its capacity as a single-crystal diffraction synchrotron facility, and so the exploitation of the leading instrumentation and expertise in this remit, that is readily transferable to DIAMOND, provides strong additional scientific reason for the UK being the proposed site for these developments in Europe. Developing time-resolved diffraction on a dedicated single-crystal diffraction beamline will also make it highly desirable for the study of more transient species, that possess crystal symmetry lower than orthorhombic (approximately 75% of all reported crystal structures are either triclinic or monoclinic, as deduced from a statistical search in the Cambridge Structural Database, Version 5.23, April 2002[24]) since this is problematic on ID9 in its present configuration, if high atomic resolution is to be realised, as stated earlier. Given the availability of a high enough brilliance off an insertion device on DIAMOND, and a suitable bunch mode of the synchrotron, the realization of ps to ns time-resolved photocrystallography on DIAMOND is eminently possible and would offer excellent complementarity to studies at the ESRF. Developing time-resolved photocrystallography at a medium energy synchrotron, where the inherent temporal structure of the synchrotron is used, also means that even shorter-lived photo-induced structures than those that are presently possible could be captured. The lower energy characteristics of such a synchrotron compared to those of a high energy synchrotron, such as the ESRF, result in less electron–electron repulsion such that shorter bunches are possible. The ESRF, for example, has a 100 ps bunch width, whilst if the tentative specifications of DIAMOND are met, a bunch width of 10–30 ps will be realized.[25] Given the enormous range of important photonic processes that occur on the picosecond time-scale, let alone other photo-induced phenomena, the ability to study photocrystallography in the time regime, 10–100 ps, would allow a myriad of new structural science to be studied. The direct and quantitative acquisition of three-dimensional structural information at this time-scale would also be highly complementary to recent advances in time-resolved spectroscopy at the picosecond level.

Technical designs for the development of a single-crystal diffraction beamline on DIAMOND that will encompass photocrystallography are currently underway. A 2 T multipole wiggler is proposed as the insertion device. This will suit well the proposed photon energy range of 5–65 keV which will be directed to the instrument *via* a plane bent collimating mirror and a fixed exit sagittal focusing monochromator, and optimized for 5–40 keV by a following plane bent focusing mirror. This energy range would allow the contrast sought between ground and excited-state data in photocrystallography measurements to be maximised by the exploitation of wavelength tuneability: depending on the chemical nature of the target compound, atomic scattering factors may be enhanced by conducting experiments at longer wavelengths than the 16 keV at which most conventional single-crystal experiments are carried out, whilst shorter wavelengths would be optimal in cases where absorption is high. The possibility of collecting data at shorter wavelengths is particularly pertinent for the study of the type of organometallic materials highlighted in this paper, since the dominant structural differences expected lie close to a heavy metal and care must therefore be taken to discern between real structural differences and artifacts due to residual X-ray absorption effects. Moreover, the energy range proposed for this instrument would inherently allow the contrast local to the metal environment in the excited-state to be increased by using anomalous X-ray scattering techniques: 5–65 keV will allow access to the absorption K-edges for vanadium to ytterbium and absorption L-edges from Caesium to the end of the periodic table. A multipole wiggler is the best option to cope with the requirements of wavelength precision and selectivity over the dynamic range proposed. In order to realize an X-ray time-structure, a double-wheel rotating chopper system and associated time-gating equipment has been designed to produce X-ray pulses of lengths tunable down to 1–10 μs.[26] The proposed instrument has been designed to be able to accommodate ancilliary equipment for achieving the more technically demanding ps–ns time-structure. A full feasibility study will be conducted, as soon as the relevant design specifications of DIAMOND unfold, to assess the viability of using this time structure. One of the crucial specifications in this regard is the type of bunch modes that will be available. The option that may suit all parties is a hybrid structure where a multibunch component lies at the opposite side of the μs orbit to a single bunch. In this case, the rotating chopper mentioned above could be readily adapted to time-gate out the single bunch from the rest of the beam whilst other beamlines, not needing the temporal resolution of the synchrotron, could continue to receive high flux during this time. The diffractometer itself will comprise a three-circle goniometer and possess a helium open-flow cryostream for operating at temperatures down to about 30 K. Several detectors are envisaged so as to cover the maximum solid-angle possible per unit time. However, since CCD detector technology is advancing so rapidly at the moment, these specifications will be designed at a later stage. A reliable incident beam monitor will also be important to ensure optimal data normalization, given the small differences sought in these experiments and a fluorescence detector will be added to quantify that arising from the crystal. The type of laser remains unspecified, since this technology is also rapidly advancing at the moment, but a laser encompassing a widely tunable wavelength is envisaged.

Feasibility testing for photocrystallography has recently begun using Station 9.8 at the SRS, where it is planned to run a pilot-project to start developing this technology, keeping in mind the technical specifications of DIAMOND as they unfold, such that the technology developed at the SRS will be readily transferable to the new UK synchrotron. In a commissioning period, the viability of the instrumental set-up for this technique on Station 9.8 was assessed. A suitable instrument set up together with a laser and an Oxford Cryostream Helix apparatus, capable of cooling crystals to 26 K, was realised and tests showed that it could readily be used to study crystalline materials with excited state lifetimes in the micro to millisecond range. In parallel to these tests, the feasibility of steady state excited state structure determinations has been also been investigated in the laboratory, at the University of Bath, using a Bruker–Nonius Kappa CCD diffractometer, which is equipped with a sealed-tube X-ray source, together with a 10 Hz Continuum 8010 seeded Nd:YAG pump laser (6–7 ns pulse width) with ND6000 dye laser component, borrowed from the Central Laser Facility Laser Loan Pool, UK. Complementary laboratory studies are crucial to the optimisation of key experimental parameters for the synchrotron-based work. Similar steady-state laboratory studies in the UK have also been shown to yield long-lived excited-state crystal structures of technological importance.[21]

4. Conclusions

A feasibility study on nanosecond time-resolved single-crystal X-ray diffraction *via* the oscillation method, carried out on ID9 at the ESRF, has been shown to be successful. Key experimental parameters relating to the sample have been identified. In particular, considerations of the optical penetration depth through a crystal at a given wavelength, temperature and X-ray absorption effects, and the effects of crystal symmetry on data collection methodology are paramount to the success of an experiment. In addition, simulations have shown that the level of atomic resolution that can be obtained is sample specific and in the case study is sensitive enough to the subtle changes expected. Data collection methodologies and means by which intensity differences upon excitation can be accessed and optimised have been identified. An outlook for developing photocrystallography in the UK is described and associated technical design specifications and initial feasibility tests are outlined. If the potential proposed herein can be harnessed, time-resolved photocrystallgraphy stands to become an important new area of structural research, not only for photonics, as the discussion is restricted to here, but also it is equally applicable to scientific endeavours in areas such as photoisomerisation studies, solid-state reactions, spin cross-over transitions in magnetic materials, and understanding electroluminescent and triboluminescent phenomena.

Acknowledgements

The authors wish to thank the Central Laser Facility (CLF) for laser loan pool (Mike Towrie and Sue Tavender) for preliminary experiments; Tony Parker and Pavel Matousek at the CLF for valuable discussions; Harry Powell at the Laboratory of Molecular Biology, MRC, Cambridge, for assistance with MOSFLM analysis; SRS for use of commissioning time on Station 9.8 for feasibility testing; ESRF for access to synchrotron beamtime and facilities; St. Catharine's College, Cambridge, for a Bibby Research Fellowship (JMC) and the Royal Society for a University Research Fellowship (JMC).

References

1. (a) J. H. Burroughes, D. D. C. Bradley, A. R. Brown, R. N. Marks, K. Mackay, R. H. Friend, P. L. Burn and A. B. Holmes, *Nature*, 1990, **347**, 539; (b) J. M. Halls, C. A. Walsh, N. C. Greenham, E. A. Marseglia, R. H. Friend, S. C. Moratti and A. B. Holmes, *Nature*, 1995, **376**, 498.
2. (a) N. Chawdhury, A. Köhler, R. H. Friend, W.-Y. Wong, M. Younus, P. R. Raithby, J. Lewis, T. C. Corcoran, M. R. A. Al-Mandhary and M. S. Khan, *J. Chem. Phys.*, 1999, **110**, 4963; (b) J. S. Wilson, N. Chawdhury, M. R. A. Al-Mandhary, M. Younus, M. S. Khan, P. R. Raithby, A. Köhler and R. H. Friend, *J. Am. Chem. Soc.*, 2001, **123**, 9412; (c) M. S. Khan, M. R. A. Al-Mandhary, M. K. Al-Suti, A. K. Hisahm, P. R. Raithby, B. Ahrens, M. F. Mahon, L. Male, E. A. Marseglia, E. Tedesco, R. H. Friend, A. Köhler, N. Feeder and S. J. Teat, *J. Chem. Soc., Dalton Trans.*, 2002, 1358.
3. I. R. Whittall, A. M. McDonagh, M. G. Humphrey and M. Samoc, *Adv. Organomet. Chem.*, 1999, **34**, 349.
4. J. B. Torrance, in *Low Dimensional Conductors and Superconductors, NATO ASI Series 155*, ed. D. Jerome and L. G. Caron, Plenum Press, New York, 1987, p. 155.
5. H. F. Wittmann, R. H. Friend, M. S. Khan and J. Lewis, *J. Chem. Phys.*, 1994, **101**, 2693.
6. A. J. Lees, *Chem. Rev.*, 1987, **87**, 711.
7. M. W. George and J. J. Turner, *Coordination Chem. Rev.*, 1998, **177**, 201.
8. P. Coppens, D. V. Formitchev, M. D. Carducci and K. Culp, *J. Chem. Soc., Dalton Trans.*, 1998, 865.
9. W. K. Fullager, G. Wu, C. Kim, L. Ribaud, G. Sagerman and P. Coppens, *J. Synchrotron Radiat.*, 2000, **7**, 229.
10. V. Srajer, T.-Y. Teng, T. Ursby, C. Pradervand, Z. Ren, S. I. Adachi, W. Schildkamp, D. Bourgeois, M. Wulff and K. Moffat, *Science*, 1996, **274**, 1726.
11. M. Wulff, F. Schotte, G. Naylor, D. Bourgeois, K. Moffat and G. Mourou, *Nucl. Instrum. Methods Phys. Res., Sect. A*, 1997, **398**, 69.
12. B. Perman, V. Srajer, Z. Ren, T.-Y. Teng, C. Pradervand, T. Ursby, D. Bourgeois, F. Schotte, M. Wulff, R. Kort, K. Hellingswert and K. Moffat, *Science*, 1998, **279**, 1946.
13. Z. Ren, D. Bourgeois, J. R. Helliwell, K. Moffat, V. Srajer and B. L. Stoddard, *J. Synchrotron Radiat.*, 1999, **6**, 891.
14. J. R. Helliwell, J. Habash, D. W. J. Cruickshank, M. M. Harding, T. J. Greenough, J. W. Campbell, I. J. Clifton, M. Elder, P. A. Machin, M. Z. Papiz and S. Zurek, *J. Appl. Crystallogr.*, 1989, **22**, 483.
15. W.-M. Xue, M. C.-W. Chan, Z.-M. Su, K.-K. Cheung, S.-T. Liu and C.-M. Che, *Organometallics*, 1998, **17**, 1622.
16. G. M. Sheldrick, SHELXL-97. Program for the Refinement of Crystal Structures using Single Crystal Diffraction Data, University of Göttingen, Germany, 1997.
17. C. D. Kim, S. Pillet, G. Wu, W. K. Fullagar and P. Coppens, *Acta Crystallogr. Sect. A*, 2002, **58**, 133.
18. M. Rudlinger, J. Schefer, G. Chevrier, N. Furer, H. U. Gudel, S. Haussuhl, G. Heger, P. Schweiss, T. Vogt, T. Woike and H. Zollner, *Z. Phys. B*, 1991, **83**, 125.
19. M. Kawano, A. Ishikawa, Y. Morioka, H. Tomizawa, E.-I. Miki and Y. Ohashi, *J. Chem. Soc., Dalton Trans.*, 2000, 2425.
20. D. V. Formitchev, K. A. Bagley and P. Coppens, *J. Am. Chem. Soc.*, 2000, **122**, 532.
21. M. Marchivie, P. Guionneau, J. A. K. Howard, G. Chastenet, J.-F. Létard, A. E. Goeta and D. Chasseau, *J. Am. Chem. Soc.*, 2002, **124**, 194.
22. A. G. W. Leslie, *Crystallographic Computing*, Oxford University Press, Oxford, 1990.
23. J. M. Cole, H. R. Powell and P. R. Raithby, unpublished results.
24. F. H. Allen, J. E. Davies, J. J. Galloy, O. Johnson, O. Kennard, C. F. Macrae, E. M. Mitchell, G. F. Mitchell, J. M. Smith and D. G. Watson, *J. Chem. Inf. Comput. Sci.*, 1991, **31**, 187.
25. See *Report of the SR User forum's Time Structure Workshop*, May 1999, and http://www.diamond.ac.uk
26. J. M. Cole, A. Beeby, J. A. K. Howard and P. R. Raithby, unpublished results.

Time-resolved and static-ensemble structural chemistry of hydroxymethylbilane synthase

John R. Helliwell,*[†][a] Yeu Perng Nieh,[a] Jarjis Habash,[a] Paul F. Faulder,[a] James Raftery,[a] Michele Cianci,[a] Michael Wulff[b] and Alfons Hädener[c]

[a] *Laboratory of Structural Chemistry, Department of Chemistry, University of Manchester, Manchester, UK M13 9PL*
[b] *ESRF, BP 220, Grenoble CEDEX, France*
[c] *Department of Chemistry, Universität Basel, CH-4051, Basel, Switzerland*

Received 6th February 2002, Accepted 9th April 2002
First published as an Advance Article on the web 5th August 2002

The enzyme hydroxymethylbilane synthase (HMBS, EC 4.3.1.8), 313 amino acid residues and MW 34 kDa, also known as porphobilinogen deaminase (PBGD), catalyses the stepwise polymerization of four molecules of porphobilinogen (PBG) to the linear tetrapyrrole 1-hydroxymethylbilane. Several crystallographic structures of HMBS have been previously determined, most recently including by time-resolved Laue protein crystallography of the Lys59Gln mutant form with reaction initiation undertaken by use of a flow cell carrying the substrate PBG. In this paper we review these structures and add new molecular graphics representations and analyses. Moreover we present a new structure refined at 1.66 Å resolution using diffraction data recorded at cryo-temperature (100 K) in an attempt at trapping the polypeptide loop (residues 47 to 58) in the vicinity of the enzyme active site, missing in all previous structure determinations. This loop still has not appeared in the electron density maps, in spite of the advantage of cryo-temperature, but nevertheless the 1.66 Å cryo-structure extends the ensemble of known HMBS structures. The cryo-model of protein, cofactor and 320 bound water molecules has been refined to a final *R*-factor and *R*-free of 0.198 and 0.247 respectively; the PDB deposition codes, coordinates and structure factors are 1GTK and R1GTKSF respectively. Finally a protein comparison study is presented of the *Mycobacterium tuberculosis* (MTb) HMBS, with the *E. coli* HMBS. This has been done as preparation for future structural studies on the MTb HMBS from this important disease bearing organism. The overall amino acid sequence identity is 41%. Most interestingly there is a two-residue reduction in length of the loop referred to above (Asp 50 and Gly 58 being missing in the MTb form). This gives the hope that this loop will be less flexible and thus might become visible to crystallographic analysis.

1 Introduction

The enzyme HMBS is found in all organisms, except viruses. Hydroxymethylbilane (HMB) formed by the enzyme (Fig. 1) is subsequently transformed into uroporphyrinogen III by

[†] Present address: CCLRC, Director of SR Science, Daresbury Labratory, Warrington WA4 4AD, Cheshire, UK. Email: j.r.helliwell@dl.ac.uk.

DOI: 10.1039/b201331b

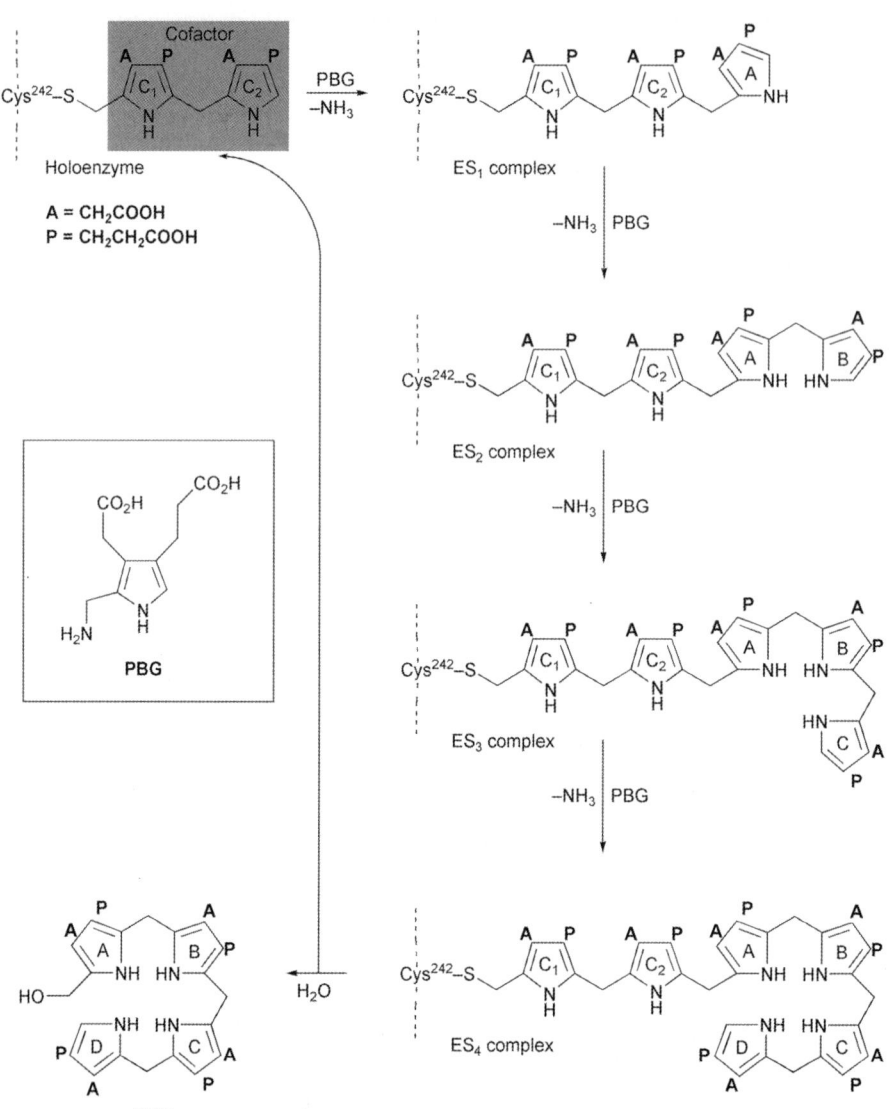

Fig. 1 Overall course of the reaction catalysed by HMBS.

uroporphyrinogen III synthase in a reaction involving rearrangement of ring D and cyclisation. Uroporphyrinogen III is the common precusor of natural tetrapyrroles such as haem, chlorophyll and vitamin B_{12}. *In vitro*, and in the absence of uroporphyrinogen III synthase, however, HMBS cyclises spontaneously (with a half life of *ca.* 4 min at 37 °C and pH 8.25) without rearrangement to give uroporphyrinogen I.[1] In the presence of air, the latter is readily oxidised to uroporphyrin I, which is red in colour. To accomplish the assembly of the bilane, HMBS uses a dipyrromethane cofactor to which the growing chain remains attached during oligomerisation. The cofactor is covalently bound to the enzyme from *Escherichia coli via* the sulfur atom of Cys 242.[2] The catalytic cycle of the HMBS reaction involves the stepwise, head-to-tail polymerisation of four molecules of PBG with expulsion of ammonia at each of these steps and a reaction with water when HMB is finally cleaved from the enzyme.[3,4] Reduction in the activity of this enzyme in humans, due to natural induced mutations, causes the hereditary disease 'acute intermittent porphyria'[5] (the 'madness of King George III').

There are two forms for the enzyme; the reduced 'active' form and the oxidised 'inactive' form.[6] Both crystal structures, at room temperature, of both the catalytically inactive enzyme, carrying the cofactor in an oxidised state, and the catalytically active enzyme, carrying the cofactor in the reduced state, have been determined, respectively, by MIR (1.9 Å room temperature, PDB code 1PDA[7]—in a later study the structure is expanded to 1.76 Å[8]) and selenomethionine MAD X-ray crystallography (2.4 Å room temperature, PDB code 1AH5[9]). The latter study also determined the positions of the C-terminal residues 308–313 not determined by the former. The two dipyrromethane cofactor rings, C1 and C2, are 11° from coplanarity in the oxidised form but 61° apart in the reduced form.

In addition the wild-type active protein structure has been refined at 2.3 Å resolution against Laue protein crystal data (2.3 Å room temperature, PDB code 2YPN[10]). These experimentally determined structures established the structure of the enzyme. Moreover the MIR structure report[7] proposed that the oxidised cofactor ring 2 position was a likely binding site for the first substrate. This is in keeping with earlier evidence that the C2 ring atom C4B is the atom to which the first PBG unit is attached during the catalytic cycle.[11,12] Louie *et al.*[7] also proposed that there would be relative movement of the three domains of the protein to accomplish subsequent, successive, ring coupling steps. The enzyme active site cavity was estimated as being sufficient in any case as being capable of accommodating three and a half PBG molecules.[6]

2 The 3-dimensional structure

The secondary structure is a combination of α-helices, β-strands and loops and the tertiary structure forms three domains[7] (Fig. 2). The first includes residues 4–99 and 200–217, the second 105–193 and the third 222–313.

There is a mobile loop in the polypeptide chain involving residues 42–63 which connects α-helix and β-strand and is important due to its proximity to the active-site cleft. Likewise the cofactor

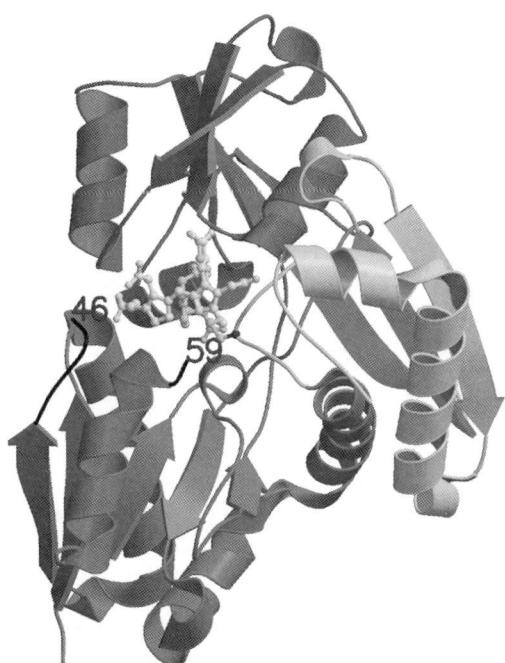

Fig. 2 Ribbon diagram of wild-type HMBS with the cofactor in the reduced catalytically active state (PDB code 1AH5) and the cofactor in the oxidised state (PDB code 1PDA). The lighter shade cofactor (ring C2 is at left and face on) is the oxidised inactive state.

dipyrromethane lies proximal to the cleft between domain 1 and domain 2. Its C1 ring is covalently linked directly to the side chain of Cys 242 which is in a loop on domain 3. The C2 ring atom C4B is the reactive atom towards PBG as substrate. The acetate and propionate side chain groups (marked A and P in Fig. 1) of the cofactor are involved in an extensive network of interactions (salt-bridges and hydrogen bonds) with the polypeptide chain, and which thus cross-links the three domains.[7] Residues Arg 131, Arg 132 and Arg 155, Lys 83, Ser 129 and Thr 127 (largely from domain 2) form the cofactor site C (*i.e.* C1 and C2). Arg 11, Arg 149, Arg 155 and Ser 13 (largely domain 1) form the substrate-binding site S.[6] The carboxyl side chain of catalytic Asp 84 (an invariant residue across species) forms hydrogen bonds with both pyrrole NH groups and is within hydrogen bonding with substrate thus implicated in stabilising intermediate states throughout the reaction cycle.

3 Resume of the time-resolved Laue structural studies

HMBS exhibits several features that made this enzyme suitable for time-resolved crystallography.[13] It is a slow enzyme with $k_{cat} = 0.1$ s^{-1} at 310 K and pH 7.5 for the saturated enzyme from *E. coli*,[14] compared to $k_{cat} = 1\text{--}10^7$ s^{-1} for most enzymes. An even slower reaction rate can be achieved by using a mutant, lower pH or lower temperature.

Thus an ensemble of refined time-resolved Laue protein crystal structures of HMBS K59Q mutant as substrate flowed over the crystal was determined.[15] These were at time points of 1 min, 2 min and 8 min, using data merged from several crystals, but each at essentially identical time-slices, and then, using one crystal each, also at 25 (+/−10) min and 2 h (+/−10 min). In addition a 'static' crystal structure was refined using monochromatic data recorded at 12 h (+/−30 min) *i.e.* 10 h after flow of substrate over a crystal in the flow cell had ceased. These various structures are described in detail.[15,16] A gradual build up of extended electron density running from the position of the oxidised C2 cofactor ring position was observed in the enzyme active site cavity. The elongated electron density was most pronounced at 2 h and this crystal structure was refined and examined in detail and coordinates deposited in the Protein Data Bank (2.3 Å room temperature, PDB code 1YPN[15]). The elongated density fits within the large cavity that forms the active site (Fig. 3). The elongated density at one end sat in the C2 ring oxidised position (Figs. 4 and 5) thus experimentally supporting the proposal of Louie *et al.*[7] that this place was most likely the substrate first PBG molecule binding site. The density commences adjacent to and above residue Asp 84. It then extends past residue Arg 149, then past residue Arg 155 (residues whose mutation causes build up of ES$_1$ and ES$_4$ intermediate enzyme–substrate complexes, respectively[17,18]), and out towards the open solvent channel of the crystal. There is also density enhancement around both ends of the 42–63 polypeptide loop *i.e.* residues 42–47 and 58–63 show increased ordering *versus* the wild-type

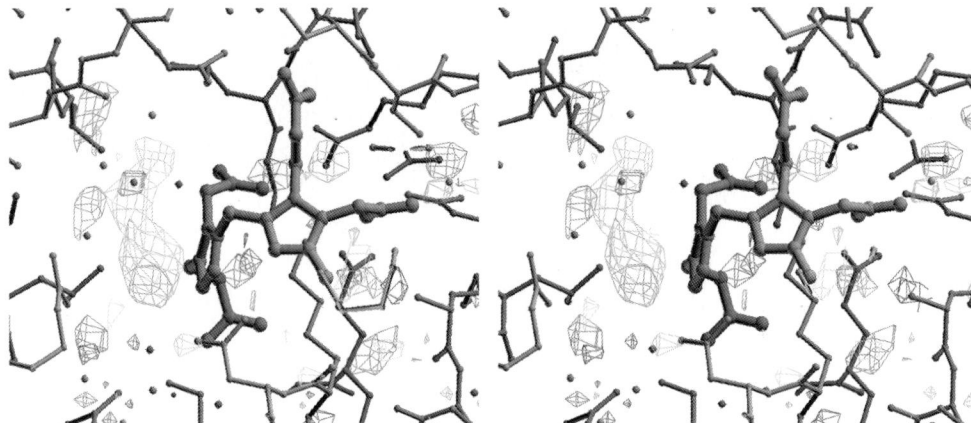

Fig. 3 Close in view in stereo of the enzyme active site with the cofactor in its reduced *i.e.* active form (PDB code 1AH5) and the 2 h experimentally observed electron density difference map from the time-resolved Laue diffraction studies included.

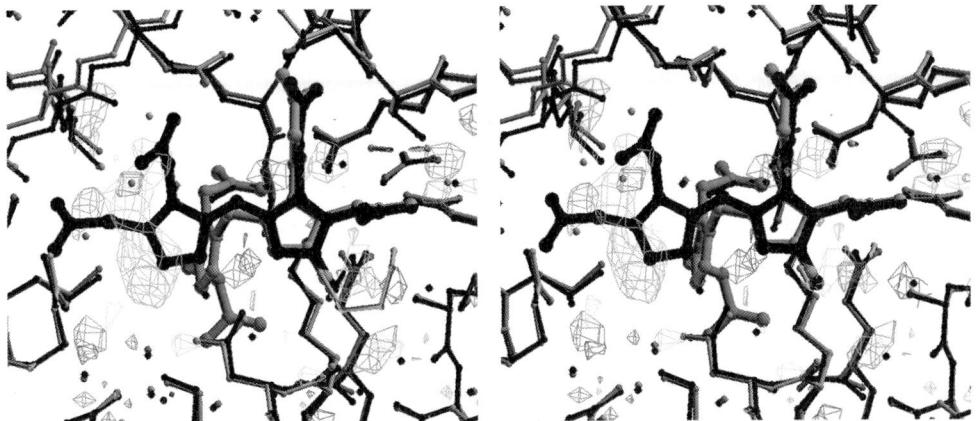

Fig. 4 As Fig. 3 but with the model of oxidised cofactor (in black) added. The start of the elongated density overlaps nicely with the C2 oxidised ring position (PDB code 1PDA).

Fig. 5 As Figs 3 and 4 but with the protein (PDB code 1AH5), and active cofactor, in space filling mode. Carbons in light grey, oxygens in darker grey and nitrogens as darkest. The elongated density and oxidised C2 ring (shown in 'stick representation'; PDB code 1PDA) sit nicely in the cavity void that is the enzyme active site.

reduced form structure (2YPN). However residues 48–57 do not obviously become visible. There are also electron density peaks sitting on some key residues near the active site (*e.g.* Cys 242, Arg 149, Arg 11 and Arg 132) and on the cofactor showing that the active site becomes more rigid 'at 2 h'. After flow of substrate had ceased, a situation represented by the data set at 12 h, the elongated electron density feature had disappeared, as had the density enhancement of the loop region. By this time, and for the later Laue data sets, the crystal had gone a pronounced red colour characteristic of HMB fully released and cyclised to uroporphyrin.

4 Structure of wild-type active form HMBS at cryo-temperature in order to try to trap the 'missing polypeptide loop (48–57)'

4.1 Crystallization

Crystallization[9,10,14] was carried out at pH 5.3 by the use of sitting drops of 50 µl volume. Each drop contained 6–7 mg ml^{-1} of protein, 0.3 mM EDTA, 15 mM dithiothreitol, 10% (w/v) polyethylene glycol 6000 and 0.01% NaN$_3$ in 0.1 M sodium acetate. This was equilibrated by vapour diffusion at 293 K against a reservoir containing 10–20 mg of solid dithiothreitol. Crystallization was undertaken afresh at the ESRF/EMBL laboratories in France immediately in the weeks prior to data collection. Crystals obtained in this way contained active, reduced, HMBS and were colourless as expected,[14] whereas crystals of inactive HMBS containing the oxidised cofactor are yellow in colour.[8]

4.2 Data collection and analysis

Data were collected at the ESRF, beamline 3 (ID09). A single crystal at cryo-temperature was exposed to X-rays of wavelength 0.8611 Å and data recorded with a high read out image intensifier/CCD detector system. Two subsets of data were collected. The first included 135° of low resolution data images recorded in 3° oscillations per image, at a long distance of the detector from the crystal so as to capture the reflection spots bordering the ice rings that unfortunately were present due to lack of an ideal cryo-protectant. [This latter also led to diffraction resolution (and B factors) not superior to the previous best room temperature cases.] The second data set comprised 135° of high resolution data images in 1° oscillations per image. The data were processed in DENZO and merged in SCALEPACK.[19] The space group was $P2_12_12$ and the refined unit cell parameters were $a = 87.5$, $b = 75.9$ and $c = 50.1$ Å. The statistics for data reduction for the two subsets are shown in Table 1. Comparison of Table 1a and 1b confirms that the low resolution ice ring around 3.5 Å does not affect completeness in the 'low resolution' data set. A final composite data set for use in the refinement of the structure was made by combining the two subsets. Table 2 shows details for this final data set; the completeness breakdown is reasonable although some reflections have still been lost at low resolution presumably due to spots saturating the detector.

4.3 Structure refinement

The starting model was that of the wild-type native structure determined at room temperature at 2.3 Å resolution (2YPN). This was subjected to rigid body refinement along with overall temperature factor refinement (5 cycles) using CCP4 'Refmac5'.[20] Assessment of phase accuracy was made by cross validation and was applied throughout the refinement.[21] The overall R-factor, R-free and figure of merit (FoM) reached 0.262, 0.290 and 0.727 respectively. The input and output models in this rigid body refinement exhibited high temperature factors for the atoms of the residues 3, 42, 60, 61, 62 and 305–313. The model then was subjected to restrained isotropic temperature factor refinement (5 cycles). The overall R-factor and R-free dropped to 0.212 and 0.252 respectively and overall FoM rose to 0.761. By generating Fo–Fc and 2Fo–Fc maps *via* the FFT programme[20] and inspecting the 2Fo–Fc map using the O molecular graphics system[22] it became evident that at 1 r.m.s. these same residues represented poorly defined density of the model structure. Careful inspection of further Fo–Fc and 2Fo–Fc maps was made to check for any linking electron density between residues 42 and 60 that would define the missing loop *i.e.* residues 43 to 59, but no meaningful density was found. For the third iteration of the model refinement, TLS B-factor refinement (10 cycles) was made, and the overall R-factor, R-free and overall FoM converged at 0.208, 0.248 and 0.771 respectively. At this stage Lys 26, Met 41, Ser 128 and Arg 184 were partially modelled according to Fo–Fc and 2Fo–Fc densities.

The refinement was carried out for a further 10 iterations essentially to define the bound water structure using the ARP/wARP programme.[20] The details of each iteration of the refinement are shown in Table 3 and the final parameters in Table 4. The final model contained 320 bound water molecules and the overall R-factor, R-free and overall FoM were 0.198, 0.247 and 0.767 respectively. Fig. 6 shows the variation of the reliability index R as a function of each iteration in the cryo-refinement.

4.4 Results and discussion of the cryo-structure

No meaningful density (either in Fo–Fc or 2Fo–Fc) was observed for the final model linking the missing loop between residues 42 and 60. The cofactor dipyrromethane generally shows continuous 2Fo–Fc density but the pyrromethane C1 ring is more resolved than the C2 ring, as is reflected in the temperature factor values. The average temperature factor for the C1 pyrromethane atoms is 27.0 Å^2, but 30.4 Å^2 for the C2 ring. Cys 242 is within a mobile region but is well resolved despite

Table 1 Cryo-data reduction statistics

(a) Low resolution subset

Resolution shells/Å	R-merge	Number of reflections	Completeness (%)
100.00–6.79	0.041	609	89.4
6.79–5.39	0.039	571	91.9
5.39–4.71	0.035	573	92.7
4.71–4.27	0.033	559	93.6
4.27–3.97	0.056	554	93.1
3.97–3.73	0.041	564	94.0
3.73–3.55	0.058	538	91.5
3.55–3.39	0.052	548	93.8
3.39–3.26	0.061	566	94.8
3.26–3.15	0.064	560	96.1
3.15–3.05	0.067	552	93.9
3.05–2.96	0.082	568	96.4
2.96–2.89	0.206	541	92.6
2.89–2.82	0.183	507	88.8
2.82–2.75	0.114	418	71.1
2.75–2.69	0.050	30	5.1
All shells	0.052	8258	86.4

(b) High resolution subset

Resolution shells/Å	R-merge	Number of reflections	Completeness %
100.00–4.48	0.062	2012	89.9
4.48–3.55	0.058	766	36.2
3.55–3.11	0.052	1835	88.3
3.11–2.82	0.052	1952	95.1
2.82–2.62	0.052	1974	96.1
2.62–2.46	0.057	1958	95.9
2.46–2.34	0.063	1986	96.5
2.34–2.24	0.082	685	33.7
2.24–2.15	0.113	1286	63.0
2.15–2.08	0.138	1968	97.8
2.08–2.01	0.167	1983	97.7
2.01–1.96	0.211	1953	96.3
1.96–1.90	0.239	1278	63.7
1.90–1.86	0.332	1899	94.1
1.86–1.82	0.320	1974	97.4
1.82–1.78	0.324	1950	97.2
1.78–1.74	0.359	1884	92.6
1.74–1.71	0.360	1710	85.3
1.71–1.68	0.344	1593	80.7
1.68–1.65	0.364	492	24.3
All shells	0.077	33 138	81.1

exhibiting a rather high temperature factor and is covalently bonded to the CH atom of the C1 ring of the cofactor (CH–SG bond length 1.87 Å). The COO$^-$ group of the catalytically important residue Asp 84 is within hydrogen bonding distances of the two NH groups of the dipyrromethane cofactors, and is sitting in a nice well-formed electron density (Fig. 7). The hydrogen bond distances OD1–N1 (C1 ring) and OD2–N1 (C2 ring) are 2.88 and 3.20 Å respectively. The Asp 84 side chain is also within hydrogen bonding distance to the putative substrate binding site.

The bound water structure comprises 320 water molecules mostly with well defined densities. The average temperature factor for the waters is 35.6 Å^2 with a minimum and maximum B of 18.5 and 61.8 Å^2 respectively. The bulk of the waters lie within a B value range of 20–50 Å^2.

An Fo–Fc omit density map was generated with the cofactor, Asp 84 and Cys 242 removed from the model. These residues play key roles in the catalytic process for the enzyme and are shown in the omit map (Fig. 7).

Table 2 Statistics for the combined dataset

Resolution shells/Å	Number of reflections	Completeness (%)
57.74–5.23	1300	90.7
5.23–3.70	2258	93.3
3.70–3.03	2884	94.1
3.03–2.62	3393	94.5
2.62–2.35	3911	96.3
2.35–2.14	2337	52.4
2.14–1.98	4708	97.5
1.98–1.85	4262	82.9
1.85–1.75	5273	95.9
1.75–1.66	4091	70.7
All shells	34 417	87

4.5 Alignment of E. coli HMBS and Mycobacterium tuberculosis HMBS amino acid sequences

The homology modelling for *Mycobacterium tuberculosis* HMBS was done with Swiss-Model and PDBViewer[23,24] and BLAST2.0.[25] The amino acid sequence alignment for *M. tuberculosis* HMBS with *E. coli* HMBS was optimized with BLAST2.0. The overall sequence identity is 41%. (Table 5 illustrates the results.) This information was used, together with coordinates of the related crystal structure (PDB code 1AH5,[9]), to derive with Swiss-Model and PDBViewer a theoretical model for *Mycobacterium tuberculosis* HMBS. The core parts of the structure appear to be highly conserved. The catalytic residues Arg 11, Asp 84, Arg 132, Arg 149, Cys 242 (using 1AH5 sequence numbering) have conserved positions. There are two residue deletions (His 31 and Pro 32) for the loop region 29–36 and nine residue insertions in the loop region 255–256. The most interesting feature, however is in the loop region 46–59 that is shorter by two residues (Asp 50 and Gly 58). This aspect could result in the loop region 46–59 being more rigid and then reducing the turn-over rate in changing its conformation.

Mycobacterium tuberculosis HMBS could then be a better target for time-resolved crystallographic studies and crystallographic studies in order to understand the role of the loop region 46–59 in the reaction mechanism.

5 Discussion and concluding remarks

The time-resolved Laue crystallographic studies of Lys59Gln HMBS have opened up a completely new window on the structural chemistry of the HMBS enzyme system. Since the monitoring of the enzyme substrate intermediate complexes (ES_1, ES_2, ES_3 and ES_4, which are not coloured) individually by microspectrophotometry is not possible, the time evolution of this enzyme system functioning in the crystalline state has been established by Laue diffraction. Some success has been achieved by this approach. By 2 h *i.e.* much later than anticipated (2 min for the build up of ES_2 and 10 min for ES_3 had been expected[3] based on kinetic studies of immobilised Lys59Gln HMBS) elongated electron density of substantial volume appeared in the active site.[15] The slow build-up could be due to the pH of the crystal mother liquor being non-optimal, or the crystalline state itself. The density is located adjacent to and above the critical Asp 84 side chain and at the oxidised C2 ring position of the cofactor previously proposed to indeed be the PBG binding site position. It then extended towards Arg 149 and past Arg 155, amino acid residues whose mutation causes build up of ES_1 and ES_4 respectively, and then out towards the crystal open solvent channel. As was discussed in ref. 15 previously, whilst the first pyrrole ring and its side chains overlapped the start of the elongated density in some detail, the subsequent pyrrole rings do not have density for their side chains. It was noted then that the elongated density could possibly be a mixture of bound PBG and ordering of the missing loop *i.e.* residues 48–57. Nevertheless the construction of a Beevers molecular model (not shown here but available at the FD122 meeting itself) allowed the exploration of the various positions of the mobile loop whilst tethered at its known end points (residues 46 and 58), which was generally distant from the position of the elongated electron density. This, and the juxtaposition of the residues Arg 149 and Arg 155, favoured the

Table 3 Iterations of the cryo-model refinement

Iteration	Refinement	R-factor	R-free	FoM	Molecular graphics
1	Rigid body, B = overall	0.262	0.290	0.727	—
2	Restrained, B = isotropic	0.212	0.252	0.761	—
3	Restrained, B = TLS, B = isotropic	0.208	0.248	0.771	—
4	Restrained, B = TLS, B = isotropic	0.207	0.245	0.770	Fitting Lys 26, Met 41, Ser 128, Arg 184. Deletion 66 waters.
5	Restrained, B = TLS, B = isotropic	0.222	0.255	0.764	Deletion all waters. Input 129 waters calculated by DDQ.[26]
6	Restrained, B = TLS, B = isotropic	0.221	0.257	0.763	Fitting Glu 305. Total waters 132 from DDQ.
7	Restrained, B = TLS, B = isotropic	0.208	0.250	0.769	ARP/wARP determines 55 waters, removes 1. Total waters 186.
8	Restrained, B = TLS, B = isotropic	0.203	0.246	0.768	ARP/wARP determines 55 waters, removes 4. Total waters 237.
9	Restrained, B = TLS, B = isotropic	0.199	0.245	0.769	Fitting Glu 305. ARP/wARP determines 50 waters, removes 3. Total waters 284.
10	Restrained, B = TLS, B = isotropic	0.196	0.243	0.768	ARP/wARP determines 40 waters, removes 3. Total waters 321.
11	Restrained, B = TLS, B = isotropic	0.196	0.245	0.766	ARP/wARP determines 25 waters, removes 5. Total waters 341.
12	Restrained, B = TLS, B = isotropic	0.196	0.246	0.767	ARP/wARP determines 5 waters, removes 2. Deletion 17 waters. Total waters 327.
13	Restrained, B = TLS, B = isotropic	0.198	0.247	0.767	ARP/wARP determines 1 waters, removes 2. Deletion 6 waters. Total waters 320.

Table 4 Final iteration cryo-model refinement parameters

Resolution range high	1.66 Å
Resolution range low	43.85 Å
Data cutoff	None
Completeness for range	87%
Number of reflections in refined set	32 708
Free R value test set size	5%
Free R value test set count	1709
Number of non-hydrogen atoms used in refinement	2578
Mean B value	22.2 Å^2
Estimated overall coordinate error	
Coordinate error based on R value	0.118 Å
Coordinate error based on free R value	0.122 Å
Coordinate error based on maximum likelihood	0.066 Å
Error for B values based on maximum likelihood	1.946 Å^2
Correlation coefficient Fo–Fc	0.961
Correlation coefficient Fo–Fc free	0.937
Bond lengths refined atoms (r.m.s.)	0.021 Å
Bond angles refined atoms (r.m.s.)	2.0°
Torsion angles (r.m.s.)	5.0°
Non-bonded contacts refined atoms (r.m.s.)	0.281 Å
Isotropic thermal factor restraints (r.m.s.)	
Main-chain bond refined atoms	1.17 Å^2
Main-chain angle refined atoms	1.98 Å^2
Side-chain bond refined atoms	3.14 Å^2
Side-chain angle refined atoms	4.70 Å^2
Ramachandran plot statistics[a]	
Residues in most favoured regions	91.6%
Residues in additional allowed regions	7.2%
Residues in generously allowed regions	0.8%
Residues in disallowed regions	0.4%

[a] Calculated *via* Procheck. The rest of the values were determined by Refmac5 (both of the CCP4 programme suite[20]).

interpretation of the elongated density as not only bound PBG but also bound HMB. The lack of bridging density to the C4B position of ring C2 and steric arguments (bond angles) preclude interpretations in terms of any of the four covalent enzyme–substrate complexes ES$_1$, ES$_2$, ES$_3$ or ES$_4$, but allow interpretations in terms of ES and EP.[3] In particular, the red colour of the crystals at 2 h, due to uroporphyrin I, presumes the presence of HMB within the crystals. The structure at 2 h (PDB code 1YPN) may therefore allow a glimpse of a Michaelis-type enzyme–substrate and/or enzyme–product complex of HMBS.

A 'static' cryo-temperature HMBS native form crystal structure has been presented here. Again, unfortunately, the 'missing loop' is still not determined. The ensemble of HMBS structures has been extended however in the process (Fig. 8 shows the ensemble of positions of the side chain of Arg 149 which shows quite some variation, and is in the vicinity of the elongated 2 h Laue electron density at the end remote from the C2 position), and the coordinates deposited in the Protein Data Bank (1.66 Å cryo-temperature, PDB code 1GTK). In addition to this new experiment we also have presented a new space filling rendering of the HMBS structure with the "2 h" elongated electron density and the C2 ring oxidised position included (Fig. 5). This then both confirms the Beevers molecular model work referred to above and extends it *via* space filling rendering of the structure on the graphics. The elongated density sits nicely in the void that is the active site region. As discussed at the CIBA Foundation Symposium[6] the void is big enough in volume without interdomain movement to accommodate up to three and a half pyrroles. Presumably the final step of the full HMB being synthesised must stimulate interdomain movement to release the HMB after the final EP complex (enzyme product complex) is formed. However, as emphasised by Louie *et al.*,[7] interdomain movement has also been suggested in the formation of ES$_2$ onwards due to the presence of only one conserved Asp (Asp 84) in the active site region. Such studies of interdomain movement, as remarked by Helliwell *et al.*,[15] would have to involve a quite different experimental

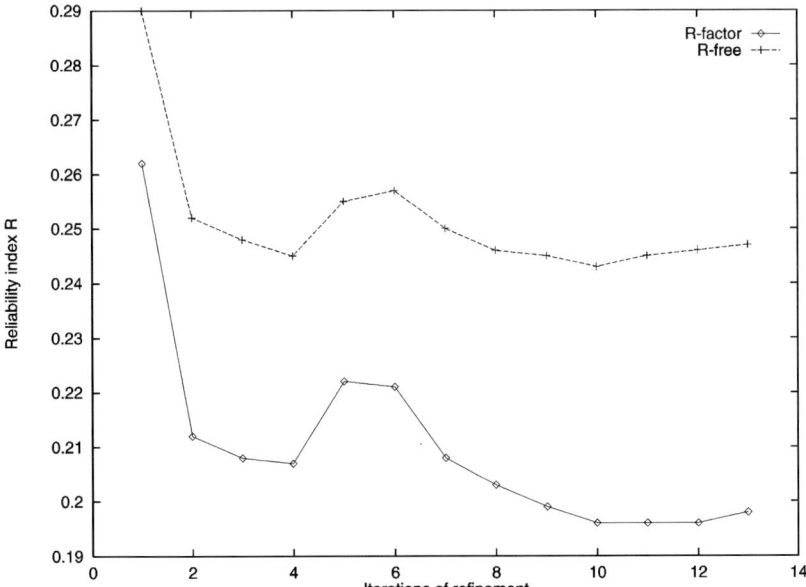

Fig. 6 Reliability index R versus iterations of the cryo-refinement.

approach such as time-resolved solution X-ray scattering *i.e.* so as to avoid the constraints of the crystal lattice.

Finally we suggest two further approaches to seek understanding of the structural chemistry of this fascinating, important, molecular system whose complexity verges on that of a molecular machine. Firstly, as NMR continues to expand its scope in molecular weight capability, perhaps NMR solution studies could be harnessed to study this 34 kDa protein, although the time needed to record a 3D NMR pulse sequence would prevent perhaps the necessary fast glimpse of the EP complex that would be required. Secondly, genomic sequencing data are accumulating. Thus the knowledge of which amino acid residues are conserved across species continues to expand. A putative HMBS has been identified for example in the *Mycobacterium tuberculosis* genome and its

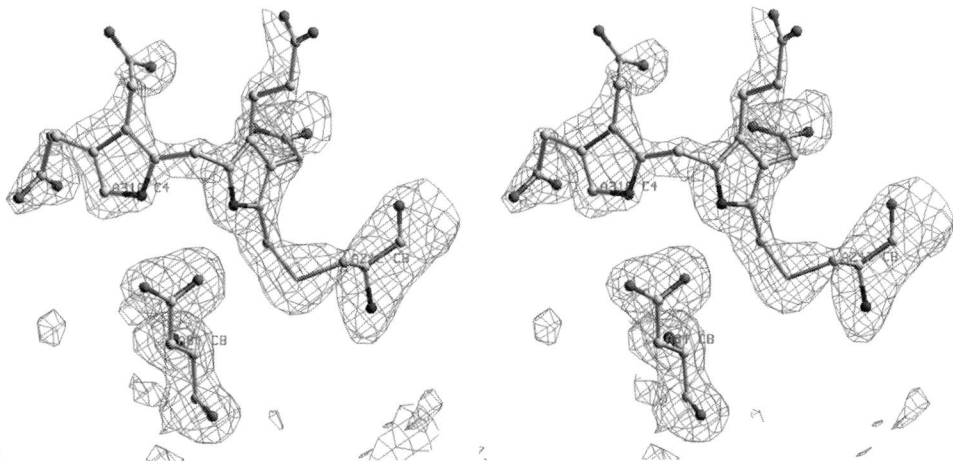

Fig. 7 Stereo omit electron density map (Fo–Fc at 2.2 r.m.s.) of the cofactor, Asp 84 and Cys 242 at 1.66 Å resolution *i.e.* for the 'cryo-structure'.

Table 5 Alignment of HMBS amino acid sequences from *E. coli* and *Mycobacterium tuberculosis* (SWISS-PROT entries P06983 and Q11173, respectively). Vertical bars denote identical amino acids

```
E. coli           1     MLDNVLRIAT RQSPLALWQA HYVKDKLMAS HPGLVVELVP MVTRGDVILD TPLAKVGGKG
                                      ||||  |       |                  |      |   ||||
M. tuberculosis   1     ---MIRIGT RGSLLATTQA ATVRDALIAG --GHSAELVT ISTEGDRSM- APIASLG-VG

E. coli          61     LFVKELEVAL LENRADIAVH SMKDVPVEFP QGLGLVTICE REDPRDAFVS NNYDSLDALP
                         |  |  |    |  |  |  |    |     |   |||| ||   | ||  |       | |
M. tuberculosis  53     VFTTALREAM EAGLVDAAVH SYKDLPTAAD PRFTVAAIPP RNDPRDAVVA RDGLTLGELP

E. coli         121     AGSIVGTSSL RRQCQLAERR PDLIIRSLRG NVGTRLSKLD NGEYDAIILA VAGLKRLGLE
                         ||||||||   |  |||    ||  |  ||| |  |||   |   |  ||||    ||  |||
M. tuberculosis 113     VGSLVGTSSP RRAAQLRALG LGLEIRPLRG NLDTRLNKVS SGDLDAIVVA RAGLARLGRL

E. coli         181     SRIRAALPPE ISLPAVGQGA VGIECRLDDS RTRELLAALN HHETALRVTA ERAMTRLEG
                         |  | | ||    ||| | |    |   |||  ||   ||  |   | | ||| ||   | |
M. tuberculosis 173     DDVTETLEPV QMLPAPAQGA LAVECRAGDS RLVAVLAELD DADTRAAVTA ERALLADLEA

E. coli         241     GCQVPIGSYA ELIDG----- ----EIWLRA LVGAPDGSQI IRGERRGAPQ DAEQMGISLA
                        || |  | |      |           |     |||  ||   |        |         |
M. tuberculosis 233     GCSAPVGAIA EVVESIDEDG RVFEELSLRG CVAALDGSDV IRASGIGSCG RARELGLSVA

E. coli         292     EELLNNGARE ILAEVYNGDA PA
                            |  |||       |  |
M. tuberculosis 293     AELFELGARE LMWGVRH-- --
```

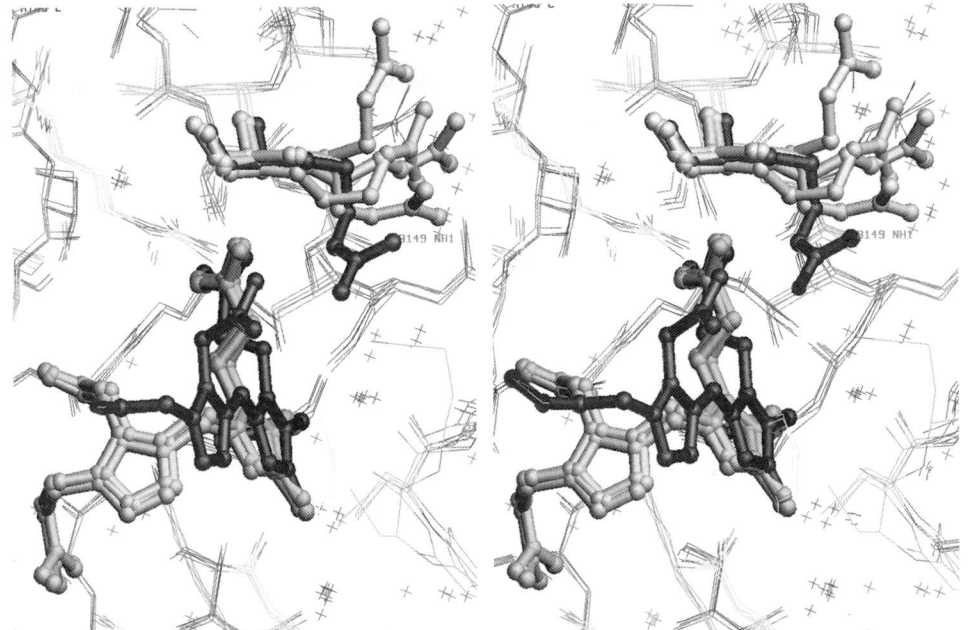

Fig. 8 The ensemble of known HMBS enzyme crystal structures. Again the cofactor conformers sit essentially in the centre of the graphics picture with those atoms highlighted (in black = the oxidised inactive form PDB code 1PDA). Also highlighted in solid stick (with atoms as spheres) is the side chain of residue 149 (as labelled) which displays a range of positions (PDB codes 1AH5, 2YPN, 1YPN, 1GTK and 1PDA, the latter is in black).

3D structure targeted for study (see http://www.nwsgc.ac.uk/), with a comparison study presented here for the first time between MTb and *E. coli* HMBS cases.

Acknowledgements

JRH thanks The Leverhulme Trust for a grant award (partial salary support of JH) and EPSRC for a studentship award to PFF. The BBSRC and The Wellcome Trust are thanked for a research grant to JRH for the Manchester Structural Chemistry computing suite and partial salary support of JR (BBSRC). AH gratefully acknowledges financial support from the Swiss National Science Foundation and the Ciba-Geigy-Jubiläums-Stiftung. Thanks are also extended to ESRF in Grenoble for the provision of synchrotron radiation at beamline ID09 'monochromatic mode' for the cryo-temperature data set collection, and the time-resolved Laue work was undertaken also at ESRF ID09 'Laue mode', both under beamtime awards to AH and JRH. The time-resolved data analyses, which have been reviewed here, were undertaken mainly by Dr Y. P. Nieh in Manchester whilst a PhD student with JRH, and funded by the ORS and the Nieh family. YPN is now based at the Fred Hutchinson Research Center in Seattle.

References

1 A. R. Battersby, C. J. R. Fookes, K. E. Gustafson-Potter, E. McDonald and G. W. J. Matcham, *J. Chem. Soc., Perkin Trans. 1*, 1982, 2427.
2 G. J. Hart, A. D. Miller and A. R. Battersby, *Biochem. J.*, 1988, **252**, 909.
3 A. C. Niemann, P. K. Matzinger and A. Hädener, *Helv. Chim. Acta*, 1994, **77**, 1791.
4 P. M. Anderson and R. J. Desnick, *J. Biol. Chem.*, 1980, **255**, 1993.
5 A. Kappas, S. Sassa, R. A. Galbraith and Y. Nordmann, in *The porphyrias, in the metabolic and molecular bases of inherited disease*, ed. C. R. Scriver, A. L. Beaudet, W. S. Sly and D. Valle, vol. II, McGraw-Hill Inc, New York, 1995, p. 2103.

6 *The Biosynthesis of the Tetrapyrrole Pigments*, Ciba Foundation Symposium 180, John Wiley & Sons, 1994, p. 70 and p. 97.
7 G. V. Louie, P. D. Brownlie, R. Lambert, J. B. Cooper, T. L. Blundell, S. P. Wood, M. J. Warren, S. C. Woodcock and P. M. Jordan, *Nature (London)*, 1992, **359**, 33.
8 G. V. Louie, P. D. Brownlie, R. Lambert, J. B. Cooper, T. L. Blundell, S. P. Wood, V. N. Malashkevich, A. Hädener, M. J. Warren and P. M. Shoolingin-Jordan, *Proteins: Struct., Genet.*, 1996, **25**, 48.
9 A. Hädener, P. K. Matzinger, A. R. Battersby, S. McSweeney, A. W. Thompson, A. P. Hammersley, S. J. Harrop, A. Cassetta, A. Deacon, W. N. Hunter, Y. P. Nieh, J. Raftery, N. Hunter and J. R. Helliwell, *Acta Crystallogr.*, 1999, **D55**, 631.
10 Y. P. Nieh, J. Raftery, S. Weisgerber, J. Habash, F. Schotte, T. Ursby, M. Wulff, A. Hädener, J. W. Campbell, Q. Hao and J. R. Helliwell, *J. Synchrotron Rad.*, 1999, **6**, 995.
11 G. J. Hart, A. D. Miller, F. J. Leeper and A. R. Battersby, *J. Chem. Soc., Chem. Commun.*, 1987, 1762.
12 P. M. Jordan and M. J. Warren, *FEBS Lett.*, 1987, **225**, 87.
13 J. R. Helliwell, Y. P. Nieh, A. Cassetta, J. Raftery, A. Hädener, A. C. Niemann, A. R. Battersby, P. D. Carr, M. Wulff, T. Ursby, J. P. Moy and A. W. Thompson, in *Time-Resolved Diffraction*, ed.. J. R. Helliwell and P. M. Rentzepis, Oxford University Press, 1997, p. 187.
14 A. Hädener, P. K. Matzinger, V. N. Malashkevich, G. V. Louie, S. P. Wood, P. Oliver, P. R. Alefounder, A. R. Pitt, C. Abell and A. R. Battersby, *Eur. J. Biochem.*, 1993, **211**, 615.
15 J. R. Helliwell, Y.-P. Nieh, J. Raftery, A. Cassetta, J. Habash, P. D. Carr, T. Ursby, M. Wulff, A. W. Thompson, A. C. Niemann and A. Hädener, *J. Chem. Soc., Faraday Trans.*, 1998, **94**, 2615.
16 Y. P. Nieh, PhD Thesis, University of Manchester, UK, 1997.
17 M. Lander, A. R. Pitt, P. R. Alefounder, D. Bardy, C. Abell and A. R. Battersby, *Biochem. J.*, 1991, **275**, 447.
18 P. M. Jordan and S. C. Woodcock, *Biochem. J.*, 1991, **280**, 445.
19 Z. Otwinowski and W. Minor, *Methods Enzymol.*, 1997, **276**, 307.
20 CCP4 Collaborative Computational Project, Number 4, *Acta Crystallogr.*, 1994, **D50**, 760.
21 A. T. Brünger, *Acta Crystallogr.*, 1993, **D49**, 24.
22 T. A. Jones, J. Y. Zou, S. W. Cowan and M. Kjeldgaard, *Acta Crystallogr.*, 1991, **A47**, 110.
23 N. Guex and M. C. Peitsch, *Electrophoresis*, 1997, **18**, 2714.
24 M. C. Peitsch, *Biochem. Soc. Trans.*, 1996, **24**, 274.
25 S. F. Altschul, T. L. Madden, A. A. Schaffer, J. Zhang, Z. Zhang, W. Miller and D. J. Lipman, *Nucleic Acids Res.*, 1997, **25**, 3389.
26 F. van den Akker and W. G. J. Hol, *Acta Crystallogr.*, 1999, **D55**, 206.

Structural dynamics of the receptor-binding domain of colicin E9

Ruth Boetzel,[a] Emily S. Collins,[a] Nigel J. Clayden,[a] Colin Kleanthous,[b] Richard James[c] and Geoffrey R. Moore*[a]

[a] *School of Chemical Sciences, University of East Anglia, Norwich NR4 7TJ, UK. E-mail: g.moore@uea.ac.uk*
[b] *School of Biological Sciences, University of East Anglia, Norwich NR4 7TJ, UK*
[c] *Division of Microbiology and Infectious Diseases, School of Laboratory Sciences, Queen's Medical Centre, University of Nottingham, Nottingham NG7 2UH, UK*

Received 30th January 2002, Accepted 4th April 2002
First published as an Advance Article on the web 7th October 2002

Colicin E9 is a 61 kDa antibacterial protein secreted by *E. coli*. In order for it to enter the cytoplasm of susceptible bacteria and kill them by hydrolysing their DNA, the colicin must first interact with an outer membrane receptor on the target cell, BtuB, and a translocation pathway involving Tol proteins. The receptor binding, translocation and DNase functions of colicin E9 are housed in discrete structural domains, which have been independently expressed and characterized. The minimal receptor-binding domain is a 76 amino acid protein (min-R). X-ray structure determination of a related colicin shows its receptor-binding domain to have a helical hairpin structure (S. Soelaiman, K. Jakes, N. Wu, C. Li and M. Shoham, *Molecular Cell*, 2001, **8**, 1053). Our solution NMR studies of min-R have confirmed it has a helical hairpin structure, and shown it has multiple slowly interchanging conformers and a flexible inter-helix loop. A plausible interpretation of these data is that in solution the helical hairpin can adopt a variety of structures differing in the spatial relationship of the two helices. A possible biological role for this involves the hairpin opening during translocation into bacteria.

Introduction

Atoms in proteins are constantly moving, ensuring that all proteins have dynamic features to their structures. The full characterisation of structural dynamics for any protein involves determining the variation in its atomic coordinates as a function of time, which is a major technical challenge. In favourable cases, NMR spectroscopy allows the amplitudes and rates of motions to be measured, providing some insight into the dynamic characteristics of a protein. However, establishing that a particular movement of atoms has biological relevance is difficult. In this paper we present NMR data on a sub-domain of colicin E9, a bacterial protein antibiotic,[1] which reveals it has both slow and fast dynamic features to its structure that may be relevant for the biological action of the intact protein.

Colicins are plasmid-encoded proteins induced *via* the SOS response to selectively destroy competing microorganisms,[1,2] and kill susceptible cells by utilising their nutrient uptake pathways to deliver either a depolarising ionophore to the inner membrane, or a cytotoxic enzyme to the periplasm or cytoplasm. The producing cell is protected against the action of its own colicin by a specific immunity protein that binds to the colicin and inactivates its toxic action.[1,3] Colicins are classified into groups on the basis of the cell surface receptor on the target cells to which they bind. The E colicins all bind to BtuB, the product of the chromosomal *btuB* gene, which is an essential component of the high-affinity transport system for vitamin B_{12} in *E. coli*.[4] Based on immunity tests the E group colicins have been subdivided into nine types that fall into one of three cytotoxic classes: a membrane-depolarising agent[2,5] (colicin E1), DNases[1,6] (colicins E2, E7, E8 and E9), and RNases[7,8] (colicins E3, E4, E5 and E6). In common with most colicins,[1,2,5,9] the enzymatic E-type colicins consist of three functional domains: a central receptor-recognition domain that binds the outer membrane receptor, an N-terminal translocation domain that interacts with proteins in the periplasm, and a C-terminal cytotoxic domain. The recently reported[8] 3 Å resolution X-ray

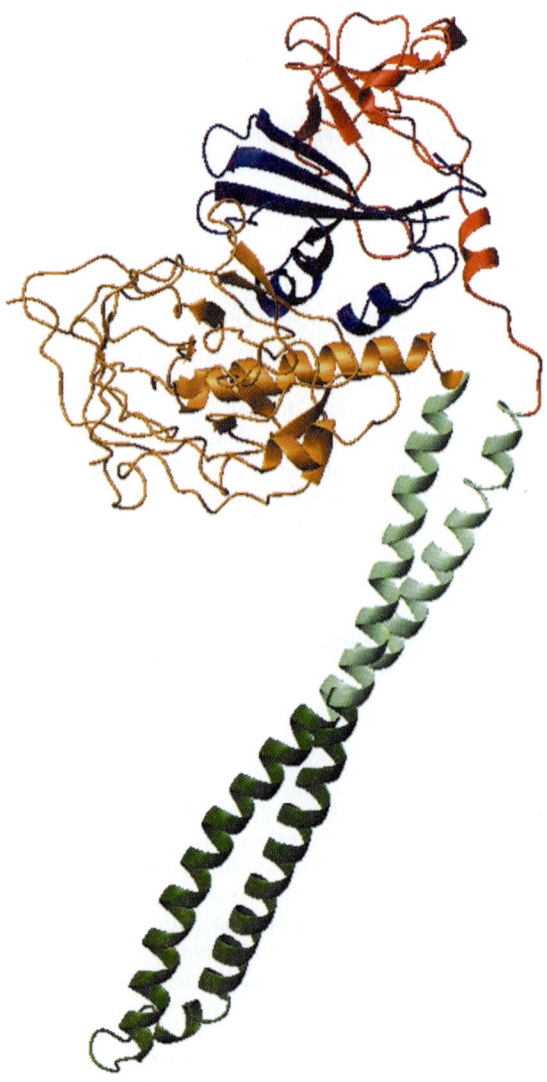

Fig. 1 Structure of the colicin E3–Im3 complex[8] and the probable structure of min-R (this paper). The complete receptor-binding domain of colicin E3 is shown in light green and min-R in dark green. The N-terminal region of colicin E3, apart from residues 1–83, is shown in orange, its RNase domain in red, and the immunity protein Im3 in blue.

structure of colicin E3 shows that it has a hairpin-like structure, with each of its three domains located at the ends and middle of the hairpin (Fig. 1). The pore-forming toxin colicin Ia has a similar structure,[10] though unlike colicin E3 the helices of the coiled-coil of colicin Ia are long enough to span the periplasm. Colicins appear to at least partially unfold on binding to cells,[2,11] allowing them to simultaneously contact their outer membrane receptor and proteins in the periplasm that assist in their translocation into the cell. Structural details of this stage of colicin-induced cell death have not been reported for nuclease colicins, but for pore-forming colicins, a variety of biophysical approaches in combination with X-ray structures have led to proposed models in which molten globule forms are intermediates.[5,12]

Colicin E9 exhibits a wide variety of dynamic characteristics on timescales varying from 10^{-9} s to 1 s. The isolated DNase domain interchanges between different conformations with forward and backward rate constants[13] of 1.0–1.6 s^{-1}. Binding of the immunity protein Im9 perturbs this interchange but does not abolish it.[14] However, introduction of a single disulfide bond by mutation of Asp 20 and Glu 66 to cysteine residues does abolish it and, moreover, a similar disulfide bond in the intact colicin renders it non-toxic to *E. coli*.[15] Hence, we know the rates of this motion and have an indication that it may be biologically relevant. However, we do not know the actual difference between the two conformers, though they are likely to be small and to involve a buried tryptophan residue.[14] At the other end of the molecule, and the other end of the timescale range, the backbone of the region containing the sequence directing the colicin to interact with the periplasmic TolB[16] of the target cell is flexible, with motions on the ns timescale.[17] NMR studies of the intact colicin show that this region is largely unstructured, though the TolB recognition sequence is more constrained than other parts of the N-terminal sequence. Some of the flexibility is lost when the colicin binds to TolB but even in the 114 kDa complex of TolB-colicin E9-Im9, parts of the N-terminal region of the colicin retain considerable flexibility.[17] Such flexibility is likely to be important for binding to other proteins of the translocation machinery or for passage across the membranes of the target cell.

The receptor binding activity of colicin E9 has been mapped to a central region of the protein, through mutagenesis and BtuB binding assays.[18] The smallest fragment that has receptor binding activity encompasses residues 343–418; hereafter called min-R. Investigation of min-R with multinuclear NMR methods is the subject of this paper. The amino acid sequence of min-R is identical to the corresponding region of colicin E3,[8,19] whose X-ray structure[8] reveals it to form the helix–loop–helix part of the central coiled-coil (Fig. 1). Our goals with NMR were to determine if min-R retained the helix–loop–helix structure of the intact colicin, and to investigate its dynamic properties.

Results and discussion

Assignment of resonances and secondary structure of min-R in solution

Investigating the structure of min-R with NMR is dependent upon resonance assignments being obtained for isotopically labelled samples. The NMR characteristics of a ^{15}N labelled sample then enable the issue of structural dynamics to be addressed. His-tagged min-R showed characteristics of a folded protein in ^{1}H NMR spectra; namely, resonances below 0.0 ppm and a spread of amide resonances indicative of helical regions.[17] The appearance of the ^{1}H–^{15}N HSQC spectrum confirmed the presence of structure in having a dispersion of resonances quite different from that expected for an unfolded protein (Fig. 2). However, extensive sequential assignments from HNCA, HNCACB and CBCACONH[20] spectra (Table 1) were not possible due to severe resonance overlap. In part, this arose because the sequence contains 17 alanines[19] (Fig. 3). HCCONH, CCONH and ^{1}H–^{1}H–^{15}N-TOCSY[20] experiments (Table 1) provided additional information to clarify ambiguous amino acid types, and an 800 MHz ^{1}H–^{1}H–^{15}N-NOESY spectrum[21] helped establish sequential connectivities, allowing us to assign >60% of all resonances as well as most of the resonances of the His-tag.

CSI[22] analysis indicates helical stretches (Fig. 4), all of which are also helical in the X-ray structure of colicin E3 (Fig. 1), and shows that the sequence from Ala 38 to Gly 44 lacks regular secondary structure.

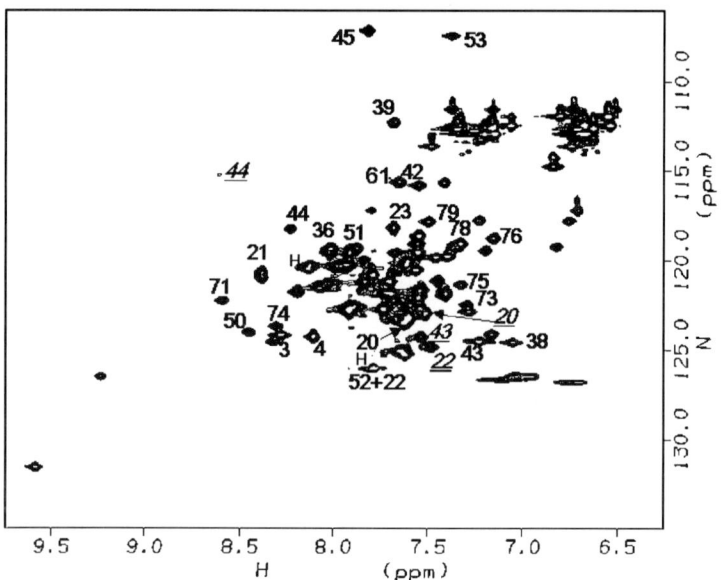

Fig. 2 The 600 MHz ^{1}H–^{15}N HSQC spectrum of 1.0 mM ^{15}N labelled min-R in 90% H_2O/10% D_2O and 50 mM potassium phosphate buffer, pH 6.2, and at 298 K. Resonance assignments are indicated with the residue numbers using the sequence numbering given in Fig. 3. Note that there is conformational heterogeneity giving rise to multiple signals for some residues (see text). Resonances from the minor conformation are indicated by the italicised labels.

Min-R exists in two slowly inter-converting conformations in solution

A major complication during the assignment process was the discovery of the existence of two conformers in solution. Resonances of ten residues were identified unambiguously to be present in two forms (Ala 20, Thr 23, Met 42, Ala 43, Gly 44, Gly 45, Asn 64, Ala 69, Phe 70 and Asp 71), with relative populations of about 60:40. The complexity of spectra indicated other amino acids also had multiple resonances, and, importantly for the diffusion measurements, methyl resonances shifted to below 0 ppm were split into two with a 60:40 intensity ratio. The amide protons of Ala 20, Thr 23, Gly 45, Asn 64 and Phe 70 showed chemical exchange cross-peaks between the two forms of min-R in NOESY spectra (Fig. 5), indicating that a dynamic equilibrium between them exists. However, the chemical shift difference between the corresponding signals of the two conformers was too small for the rate constant for the exchange process to be determined, though an upper estimate for the rate based on the chemical shift difference at 800 MHz is 300 s^{-1}.

Does min-R exist as a mixture of monomer and dimer in solution?

There are several possible reasons for the occurrence of two forms of min-R, one being the presence of an equilibrium between monomer and dimer forms. The X-ray structure of the colicin E3–Im3 complex shows two molecules per unit cell closely packed together; and furthermore, Levinson et al.[24] showed that free colicin E3 dimerizes in solution. Analysis of diffusion coefficients (Fig. 6) and hydrodynamic or Stokes radii, R_h^{prot}, is a well-established approach for addressing molecular size and shape,[25] and gradient NMR methods allow these parameters to be measured. The translational diffusion coefficient, D_t, is particularly sensitive to molecular size, decreasing as the size increases.

Values of D_t and R_h^{prot} measured for min-R are listed in Table 2, along with values of D_t calculated with the program HYDROPRO[26] assuming that min-R has the same structure as in the intact colicin (Fig. 1). Table 2 also presents values for Im9 and hen lysozyme, the former of which

Table 1 Summary of experimental NMR parameters for assignment experiments[20,21]

Experiment	^1H B_0/MHz	^1H SW^a/Hz	^1H NP^a	F1 Nucleus	F1 SW^a/Hz	F1 NP^a	F2 Nucleus	F2 SW^a/Hz	F2 NP^a
HNCA	500	6000.2	1024	^{15}N	2500.0	32	^{13}C	3770.9	48
HNCO	500	6000.6	1024	^{15}N	1800.2	32	^{13}C	2000.0	64
CBCACONH	500	6000.2	1024	^{15}N	1800.2	32	^{13}C	7050.0	41
HNCACB	500	8000.0	1024	^{15}N	1800.2	32	^1H	7050.0	160
HCCONH	500	8000.0	1024	^{15}N	2500.0	48	^1H	8000.0	140
CCONH	500	8000.0	1024z	^{15}N	2500.0	48	^{13}C	10055.7	160
^1H–^{15}N-NOESY–HSQC	800	16025.6	1536	^1H	10863.0	128	^{15}N	3333.3	36

^{a} SW is the spectral width and NP the number of data points.

```
               10                    20
       mrQAKAVQVYnsrkSelDaA
               30                    40
       NKTlADAiaeIkqfnRFAHd
               50                    60
       PMAGGHRMWQMAGlKaqraQ
               70                    80
       TDVNnkqaAFDaAAAKEkSHh

                HHHH
```

Fig. 3 The amino acid sequence of min-R.[18,19] Residues whose ^{1}H–^{15}N NH resonances have been assigned in this work are indicated by upper case lettering; underlining indicates those residues with multiple NH resonances.

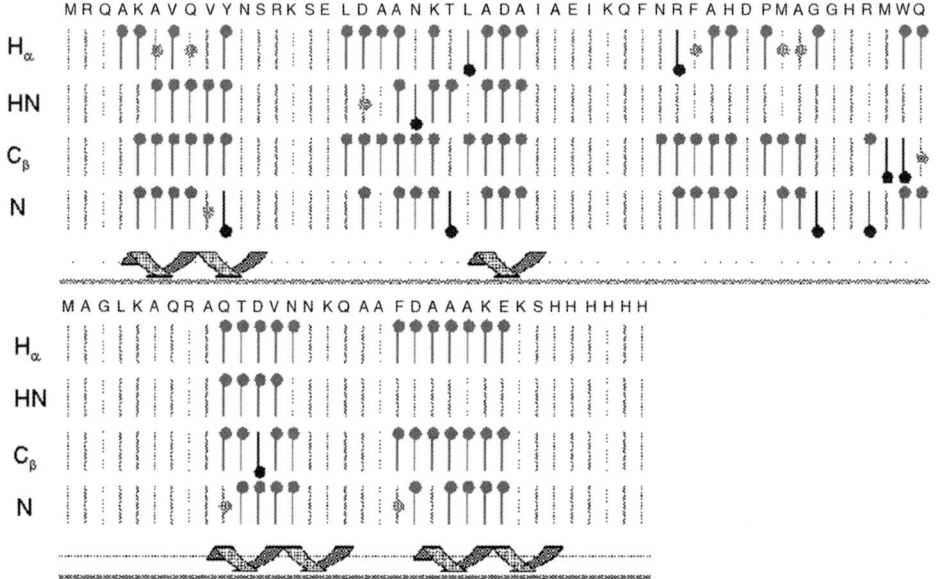

Fig. 4 Plot of CSI[22] for H_α, HN, C_β and N vs. sequence for min-R from NMRView.[23] Filled black circles indicate a CSI of -1, filled grey circles refer to a CSI of $+1$ and patterned grey circles indicate a CSI of 0.

has a similar molecular weight to monomeric min-R, and the size of the latter corresponding to that of a min-R dimer. The min-R D_t shows only a small concentration dependence, with the absolute values of D_t being larger than that of lysozyme.[27] The Im9 D_t is significantly smaller than the value observed for min-R at either concentration, suggesting that min-R is either a smaller molecule or has a more compact shape, both of which rule out the presence of a dimeric form of min-R in solution. Comparison of the experimental hydrodynamic radii for min-R, Im9 and lysozyme (Table 2), and the lack of concentration dependence to the min-R R_h^{prot}, further strengthens our view that min-R exists as a monomer in solution. Finally, from the empirical formulae relating chain length to the hydrodynamic radii of proteins reported by Wilkins et al.,[29] monomeric min-R would have an R_h^{prot} of 17.2 Å, while the dimer should exhibit a higher value of ~21 Å. Calculations in **HYDROPRO** are in broad agreement, yielding radii of 19.4 and 25.2 Å for monomer and dimer, respectively. These calculated values are higher than our experimental value. Thus we conclude that the exchange process does not result from monomer–dimer equilibrium.

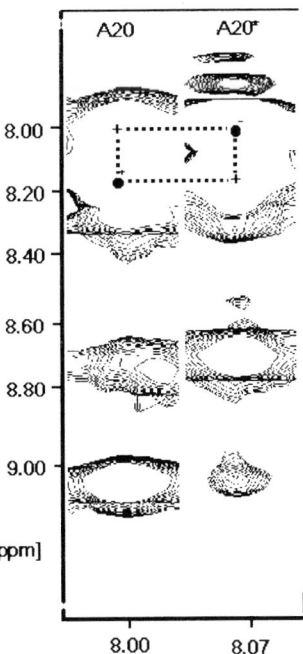

Fig. 5 ^{1}H–^{1}H strips from the 800 MHz ^{1}H–^{1}H–^{15}N-NOESY spectrum showing chemical exchange cross-peaks, indicated by +, for the two forms of Ala 20. The respective diagonal peaks are marked by ●.

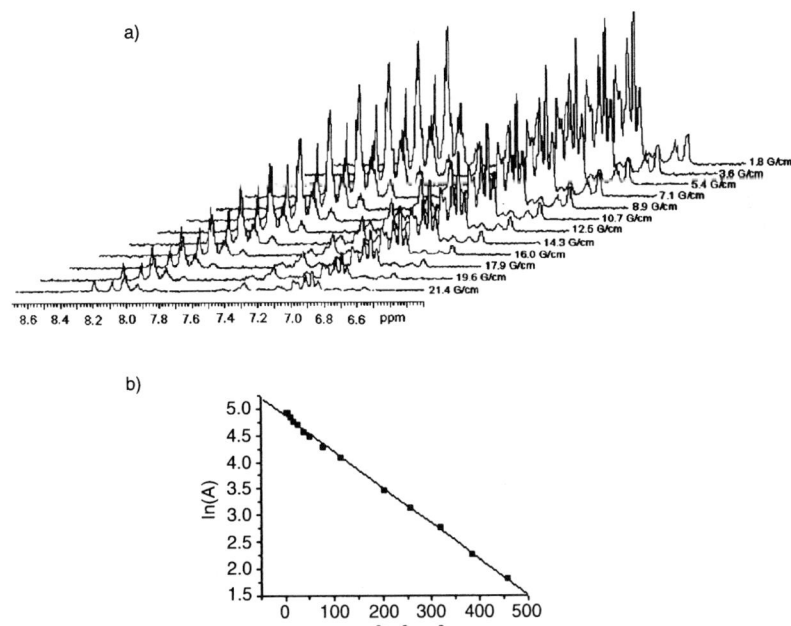

Fig. 6 (a) Stacked plot of ^{1}H NMR spectra for diffusion coefficient measurement of 0.5 mM min-R in D$_2$O; and (b) representative plot for intensity decay with increasing gradient strength according to eqn. (1). The data points encompass the error bars, and are for the peak at 8.21 ppm.

Table 2 Experimental and calculated hydrodynamic properties of min-R

	Number of amino acids	D_t(experimental)/cm^2 s^{-1}	D_t(calculated)/cm^2 s^{-1}	R_h^{prot}(experimental)/Å	R_h^{prot} (calculated) [Å]
Min-R (1.0 mM)	84	$1.29 \times 10^{-6} \pm 1.12 \times 10^{-8}$	1.11×10^{-6}	15.9	19.4
Min-R (0.5 mM)	84	$1.38 \times 10^{-6} \pm 5.15 \times 10^{-8}$	1.11×10^{-6}	15.9	19.4
Im9 (1.5 mM)[a]	86	$1.18 \times 10^{-6} \pm 1.13 \times 10^{-8}$	1.18×10^{-6}	18.6	18.3
Lysozyme (1.0 mM)[a]	129	$1.17 \times 10^{-6} \pm 2.46 \times 10^{-8}$	1.07×10^{-6}	15.9	19.9

[a] Im9 and lysozyme are monomeric at the concentrations used.[27,28]

Is one form of min-R in solution unfolded?

Another possibility for the presence of two species is equilibrium between folded and unfolded species. However, the CSI analysis[22] of the HN, N, C_β and H_α chemical shifts of the two forms suggests that both contain significant amounts of helical structure. Importantly, residues from the N-terminus of the first helix and the C-terminus of the second helix exhibit multiple signals whose chemical shifts indicate the presence of helical structure. This observation suggests that neither min-R helix unravels from its terminus. In addition to this, the hydrodynamic radius for an unfolded form would be significantly bigger, about 25 Å, than the ones observed for min-R. Therefore the presence of unfolded min-R in solution can be ruled out.

Relaxation properties of the backbone NH groups of the major conformer of min-R

A third possibility for the multiple forms of min-R is motion in the loop connecting the two helices of min-R (Fig. 1) leading to several structures that vary in the angles between their helices or in their alignment. The differences in chemical shifts for resonances of the loop between Ala 38 and Gly 44 (Fig. 7) are consistent with this model in suggesting a large difference in environment for the nuclei in the loop between the different forms of min-R. Since the other residues exhibiting multiple conformers show no consistent stretches of chemical shift differences between the forms, but rather isolated residues, indicating that there is not a large difference in the environments of their nuclei between the conformers, the loop may be acting as a hinge. Support for this comes from studying the backbone relaxation characteristics of min-R. However, before we can analyse relaxation times on a residue-by-residue basis it is necessary to determine the influence of the general tumbling motion of min-R upon them.

Backbone NH groups of ^{15}N labelled proteins are good probes of protein dynamics because they are relatively far from other magnetic nuclei to be significantly affected by them, and because NH bond distances are similar throughout the backbone. This means that they can be considered to be isolated IS spin systems whose relaxation is dominated by dipole–dipole interactions of their ^{15}N nuclei with their attached protons and the chemical shift anisotropy, these being modulated by changes in orientation of the NH bond vector with time.[30,31] The overall rotational diffusion of a protein, defined by the rotational correlation time τ_R, is a key influence on the relaxation properties of the backbone, generally determining the magnitude of the NH relaxation parameters. Fig. 8 illustrates this for Im9.[32]

For Im9, there is only a small variation in ^{1}H–^{15}N NOE values and ^{15}N T_1 and T_2 relaxation times along the sequence, except at the two termini. The residues at each terminus have high T_1 and T_2 times and low NOE values, with Gly 86 being particularly notable with a negative NOE. The increase in T_1 and T_2 times, and decrease in NOE values, indicates that these residues are subject to

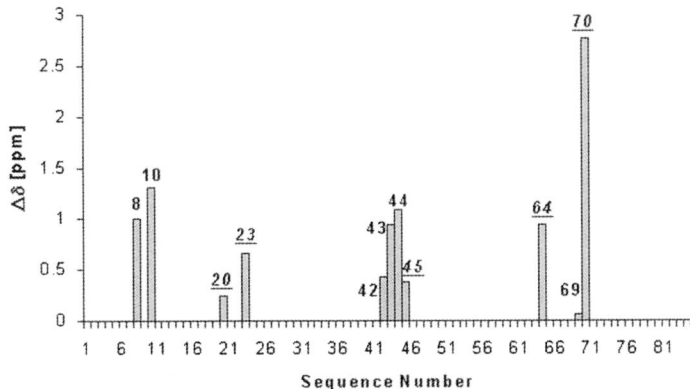

Fig. 7 Differences in weighted average chemical shifts $\Sigma(\Delta_i/\Delta_{max})$ (HN, N, C_β, H_α) for corresponding resonances of the different min-R conformers as a function of sequence number. Underlined and italicised labels indicate residues showing exchange cross-peaks.

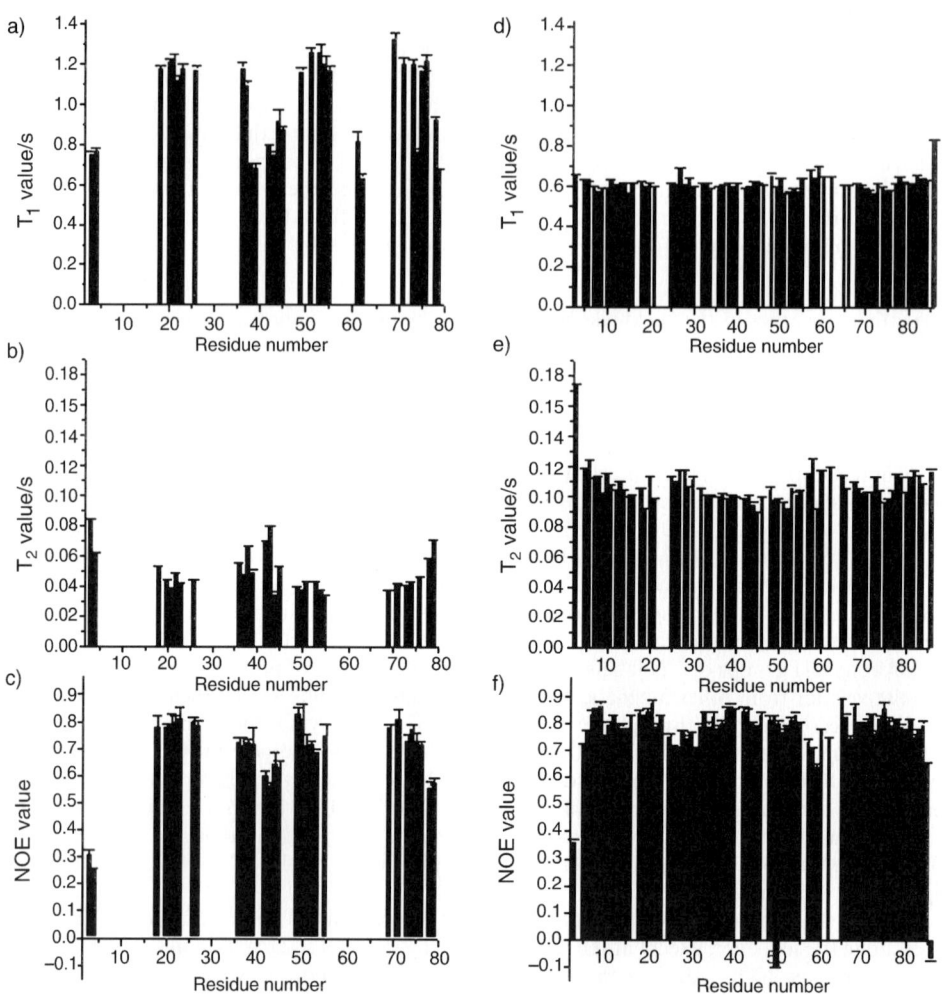

Fig. 8 Histograms of (a and d) T_1, (b and e) T_2 and (c and f) ^{1}H–^{15}N NOE values for the backbone amides of Im9 (right) and min-R (left). Average error values (as determined from the error bars shown) are <1% for Im9 and between 1.5–3.7% for the min-R measurements.

fast motions on the ps–ns timescale and of a larger amplitude than is seen for the protein as a whole. The similar NH relaxation properties of residues 5–84 are consistent with them being determined by tumbling of Im9 with a τ_R of ~7 ns.[32]

The NH relaxation properties of min-R are different from those of Im9 (Fig. 8 and Table 3) with its T_2 values generally being much lower, and T_1 values longer, than those of Im9, and ^{1}H–^{15}N NOE values being variable throughout the sequence. The T_1/T_2 ratios of 24.75 ± 7.70 for min-R and 5.84 ± 0.51 for Im9 emphasise the difference. For both Im9[32] and min-R, the quality of the time-decay curves for the T_1 and T_2 measurements were good, as the typical plots of Fig. 9 illustrate, and thus the different relaxation characteristics indicate very different dynamic behaviour for the two proteins. Lower than expected T_2 values can be indicative of chemical exchange on the ms timescale,[31] and since slow chemical exchange between different conformers of min-R is seen (Fig. 5) this might seem to be an explanation for the low T_2 times. However, this would not account for the relatively high T_1 values and therefore we favour an alternative explanation for why the relaxation times of min-R differ so substantially from those of Im9. Though Im9 and min-R are similar in size, Im9 is roughly spherical[33] and min-R approximately cylindrical (Fig. 1). This means

Table 3 Backbone relaxation parameters of min-R and Im9

NMR parameter	Average for min-R	Major form of min-R	Minor form of min-R	Im9
Average T_1 for resolved resonances	1.03 ± 0.21 (70)			0.62 ± 0.04 (68)
Average T_1 for resolved and assigned non-terminal resonances		1.05 ± 0.21 (27)	1.03 ± 0.17 (2)	0.61 ± 0.03 (66)
Average T_2 for resolved resonances	0.053 ± 0.03 (69)			0.106 ± 0.012 (68)
Average T_2 for resolved and assigned non-terminal resonances		0.046 ± 0.011 (25)	0.046 ± 0.011 (2)	0.105 ± 0.008 (66)
Average NOE for resolved resonances	0.69 ± 0.11 (71)			0.78 ± 0.12 (75)
Average NOE for resolved and assigned non-terminal resonances		0.74 ± 0.07 (27)	0.81 ± 0.09 (2)	0.80 ± 0.05 (73)

[a] ± indicates standard deviation. Number in brackets indicates number of resonances used to obtain average value.

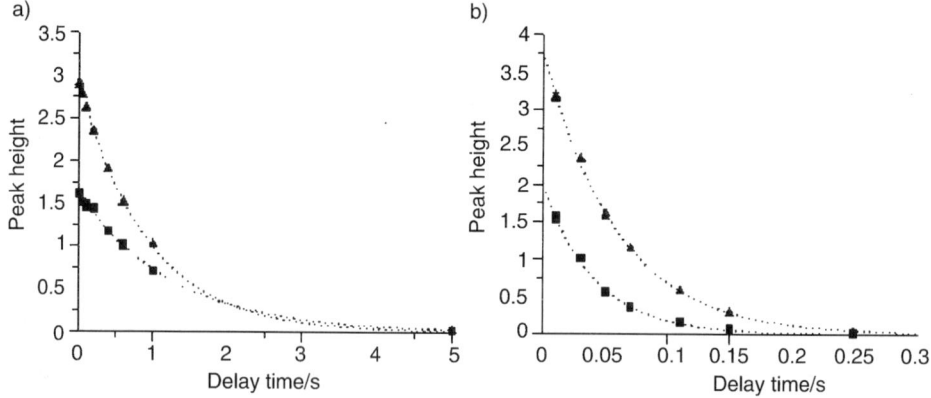

Fig. 9 Example decay curves and 2-parameter exponential fitting for (a) T_1 and (b) T_2 min-R measurements. The resonances of Ser 53 and Glu 78 are represented by squares and triangles, respectively. Peak height uncertainties are smaller than the size of the data points. T_1 and T_2 values are 1.26 s and 0.042 s (Ser 53) and 0.93 s and 0.058 s (Glu 78).

they will tumble differently in solution, Im9 isotropically and min-R anisotropically, with major consequences for their relaxation characteristics. For isotropically tumbling molecules, the orientation of the NH bond vector with respect to the principal axes of the molecular diffusion tensor is not important, but anisotropically tumbling molecules rotate at different rates around the orthogonal axes and so the orientation of the NH vector relative to these influences the relaxation rate. Cylindrical molecules rotate faster around their long axis than the two axes perpendicular to it, and motions about an axis parallel to the NH bond vector do not reorient the vector and so do not contribute to its ^{15}N relaxation. The NH bond vectors in a helix are roughly parallel to the axis along the helix, and if the helix is contained within a cylindrical protein such as min-R (Fig. 1) their relaxation rates will be determined by the slower rotation about the axes perpendicular to the helices. The linear behaviour (Fig. 10(a)) of the min-R T_1/T_2 ratio with the function $(3\cos^2\theta - 1)$, where θ is the angle between the NH vector and the principal axis of the diffusion tensor derived from the output of HYDROPRO,[26] confirms that min-R tumbles anisotropically, with further support provided by the calculated moment of inertia, whose principal components are in the ratio 1.000:0.982:0.108. The smallest component of the moment of inertia lies along the crystallographic y-axis, coincident with the long axes of the helices, and the other axes are close to the crystallographic x and z axes. Calculations using HYDRONMR[34] also show that the principal axis

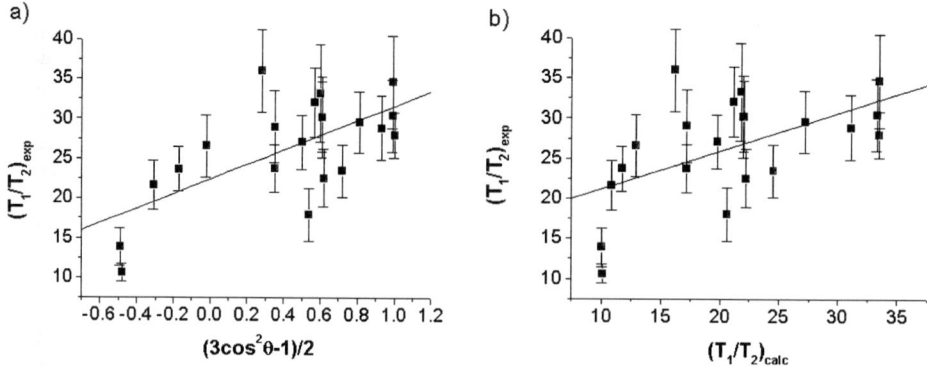

Fig. 10 (a) Variation of experimental T_1/T_2 ratios of min-R as a function of $(3\cos^2\theta - 1)$ (see text); and (b) correlation of experimental and calculated T_1/T_2 ratios, based on rotational diffusion tensor components calculated from hydrodynamic values as determined by linear regression.

system of the rotational diffusion tensor is coincident with the crystallographic axes, with the principal components being: $D_{xx} = 1.057 \times 10^7 \text{ s}^{-1}$, $D_{yy} = 3.347 \times 10^7 \text{ s}^{-1}$ and $D_{zz} = 1.046 \times 10^7 \text{ s}^{-1}$. These calculations confirm that min-R in solution has faster rotation around its long helical axis than along it, and they also show that the rotational diffusion tensor has near axial symmetry.

Despite the clear evidence for anisotropic rotational diffusion, direct fitting of the experimental T_1/T_2 ratio to an anisotropic rotation model[35,36] did not lead to reasonable values for the anisotropic rotational diffusion tensor components (not shown). This is a consequence of the difficulty in identifying backbone residues lacking independent motion relative to the overall tumbling of the protein for use in determining the global rotational diffusion co-efficient. Standard criteria[36] based on the range of errors of the T_1/T_2 ratio are not applicable when the ratio is expected to vary by a factor of 5 or more as a consequence of anisotropic tumbling, and because of this the experimental T_1/T_2 values were compared with calculated ratios (Fig. 10(b)), which gave a correlation coefficient of 0.556. Despite the relatively low correlation co-efficient, which is typical for this kind of analysis,[37] the overall trends in the range of T_1/T_2 ratios are reproduced, from the large values seen for the majority of residues in the α-helices to the smaller values observed for the loop residues.

What is the structure of the minor conformer of min-R?

The CSI analysis for the minor conformation of min-R suggests it has a helix–loop–helix structure similar to that of the major form (not shown). Since it was only possible to measure T_1 and T_2 times for two residues of the minor conformer, namely Ala 20 and Ala 43, it is not possible to say whether there is any major difference in the dynamical properties of the two forms; though the disparity in T_1, T_2 and NOE values between the conformers for the Ala 20 and Ala 43 resonances of 0.31 s, 0.01 s and 0.031 for Ala 20 and 0.4 s, 0.04 s, 0.31 for Ala 43, is suggestive of a difference for Ala 43. The T_1/T_2 ratio of 18 for Ala 20 is consistent with an anisotropically tumbling monomer form as described above for the major form of min-R. The relaxation parameters for the minor Ala 43 suggest it is more constrained than that of the major Ala 43. Other assigned resonances of the minor conformer were too weak or overlapping with other resonances for accurate relaxation values to be determined.

The D_t values determined for signals shifted to below 0 ppm for both the major and the minor conformer were similar, which indicates the same shape for each conformer. The differences in chemical shifts for the two forms (Fig. 7) occur mainly for hydrophobic residues in the loop and near the end of the helices, consistent with only minor structural differences, such as a slight twisting of the helices around each other linked to movement at the loop.

The inter-helix loop has motion independent of the tumbling of min-R

To determine if there is any variation in dynamical properties along the sequence of min-R it is necessary to look at the consensus between the T_1, T_2 and NOE values (Fig. 8). There is reasonable agreement between these in that there is a subset of residues that have high T_2 and low T_1 values and relatively low NOE values. These include the two ends of the protein and residues 38–45, which are likely to be experiencing extra motions in addition to the overall tumbling of the protein. Confirmation that residues 38–45, which form the loop between the two α-helices in min-R (Fig. 1), are more mobile than other parts of the structure comes from comparison of the min-R relaxation times and colicin E3 crystallographic temperature factors, which correlate well (Fig. 11). Crystallographic B-factors are a measure of the spread of the electron density of an atom as a function of its position in the crystal, and both static disorder and dynamic disorder can contribute to B-factor magnitudes. Perhaps for this reason, NMR backbone relaxation data do not always correlate well with B-factors,[38] and where they do, as in the present case, it is likely to be because fast motions contribute to dynamic disorder.[38,39]

Having established that the loop region shows increased mobility compared to the rest of the molecule the question is now what sort of hinge motion is possible. The most obvious choice is an opening and closing of the two helices, up to the extreme of the helix angle being 180°. From the colicin E3 X-ray structure we generated six structures with inter-helix angles between 30° and 180°, by rotation about the peptide bond between residues 40 and 41, and calculated their corresponding diffusion coefficients and hydrodynamic radii (Fig. 12). The experimental values for D_t are higher

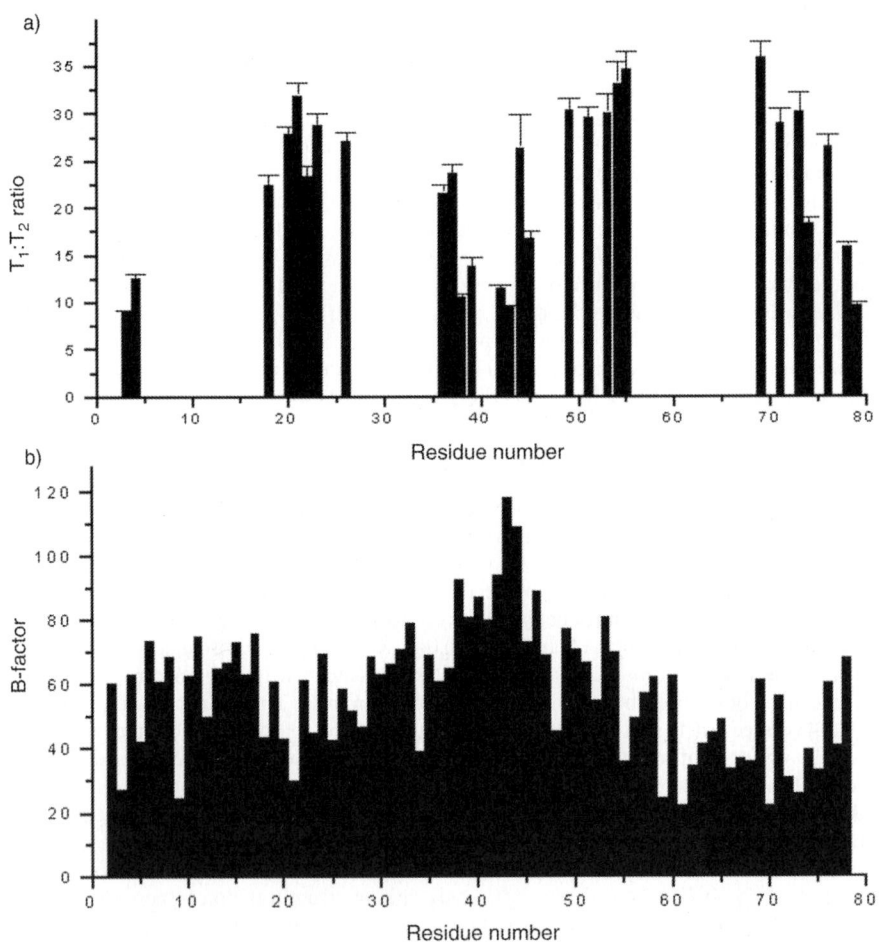

Fig. 11 (a) Histogram of T_1/T_2 ratios for min-R; and (b) X-ray B-factors for the min-R region of the colicin E3–Im3 complex obtained from the X-ray structure of Soelaiman et al.[8] Note that the N- and C-terminal residues of the min-R region of colicin E3 (b) are anchored by extending into the remainder of the coiled-coil region (Fig. 1) while the corresponding residues of min-R itself (a) are not anchored.

than any of the calculated values, while for R_h^{prot} they are smaller, indicating min-R has a more compact structure with a small inter-helix angle, tying in well with the X-ray structure and ruling out an open conformation. Furthermore, an analysis of the distribution of hydrophobic residues in min-R reveals the presence of large patches of internal apolar residues (Fig. 13), which would make an extended conformation energetically unfavourable in water. Therefore we conclude that an extended helix–loop–helix conformation is unlikely to occur in solution. This leaves small range motions with just the loop adopting different orientations, which leads to a small displacement of the helices relative to each other while preserving the interhelix angle at approximately 0°.

The inter-helix loop may be the BtuB binding site

Soelaiman et al.[8] have suggested that the hairpin loop of the coiled-coil region of the colicin structure (Fig. 1) constitutes the interaction site on colicin E3 for the receptor BtuB, consistent with the earlier identification of min-R as a BtuB binding partner.[18] The relative flexibility of this loop compared to the helices of min-R, may be related to the recognition events between the colicins and BtuB, in which flexibility of one of the binding partners assists with recognition of the partner

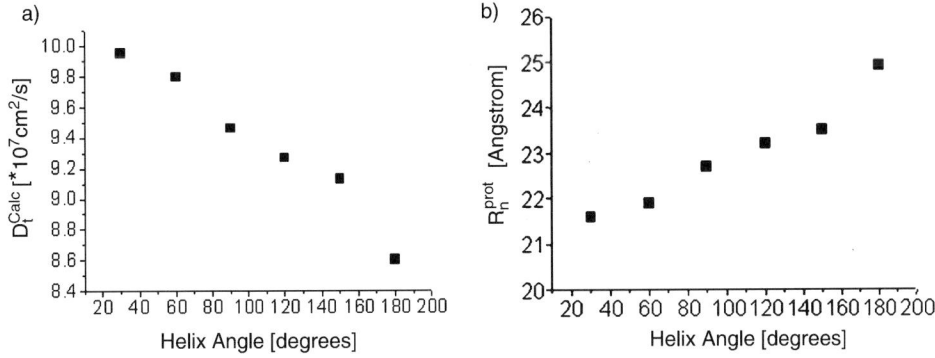

Fig. 12 The translational diffusion coefficient (a) and hydrodynamic radius (b) of min-R, calculated as a function of the angle between the two helices (see Materials and methods for details).

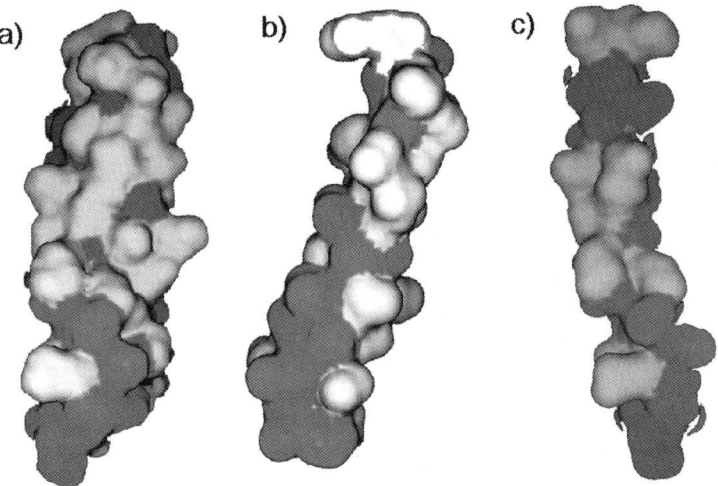

Fig. 13 Hydrophobic residues (in dark grey) of min-R on (a) the outer surface, (b) the inner surface of helix 1, and (c) the inner surface of helix 2.

proteins and formation of a well-packed interface between them leading to a tight inter-protein complex.[40] In connection with this, the indication from the limited characterisation of the minor form of min-R reported here that movement of loop residues is related to movement of residues approximately 20 Å away at the ends of the min-R helices (but midway in the coiled-coil structure of the full receptor-binding domain) may be significant. Opening the helix angle of the coiled-coil structure would make it possible for the hydrophobic residues on the inside of the helical hairpin to make contact with residues of the binding partner, thereby enhancing the interaction energy. Such hinge opening may also be involved with transport of the colicin into the cell since opening the helix angle creates a more elongated, and less compact, structure than that of the free inhibitor-bound colicin (Fig. 1). This would then have parallels with the pore-forming colicin Ia, which has a long helix that spears the outer membrane to deliver the toxic domain to the inner membrane.[10]

Experimental

Isotopically-labelled min-R was obtained as previously described.[17,18] Protein concentrations for NMR were 0.5–1.0 mM, in 90% H_2O/10% D_2O, and 50 mM phosphate buffer (pH 6.2) containing

0.01% sodium azide. Except for a ^{1}H–^{1}H–^{15}N-NOESY–HSQC spectrum[21] (τ_M = 100 ms) measured on a Bruker 800 MHz spectrometer (BBSRC National Facility, Cambridge), all NMR spectra were acquired with Varian Unity Inova 500 or 600 spectrometers. One-dimensional ^{1}H spectra were measured using a 90°–acquisition sequence, over 8000 Hz with 16k data points and 512 scans, and processed using VNMR (Varian, California) and FELIX 95.0 (Biosym/MSI, California). Multidimensional spectra were acquired with pulse sequences incorporated in the Varian 'Protein Pack' suite of experiments, and processed using NMRPipe.[41] Prior to Fourier transformation, a sine-squared bell-shaped window function with a 60°–70° shift was applied to each dimension for apodization. The indirect dimensions were linear predicted once and the spectra zero-filled in all dimensions to double the number of data points. Proton chemical shifts were referenced to external TSP and the carbon and nitrogen chemical shifts were referenced indirectly to TSP.[42] Spectra were analysed with XEASY[43] and FELIX 95.0.

Values of D_t were obtained with the longitudinal encode–decode gradient–echo sequence[44,45] through acquisition of spectra with varying gradient strengths, and plots of variations in signal intensity as a function of gradient strength, according to eqn. (1).

$$A(2\tau) = A_0 \exp[-(\gamma \delta G)^2 (\Delta - \delta/3) D_t] \quad (1)$$

where A refers to the peak intensity for a given gradient strength G; A_0 to the peak intensity in the absence of gradients; Δ denotes the separation between leading edges of the gradients; δ is the duration of the gradient pulse of strength G, and γ the magnetogyric ratio of ^{1}H.

Values of R_h^{prot} were measured with the same gradient–echo experiment and with a non-invasive compound, in our case dioxane (with R_h^{ref} = 2.12 Å), added to the protein solutions.[46] R_h^{prot} was obtained from the slopes, s_{prot} and s_{ref}, of the semi-logarithmic fits of eqn. (1) for resonances of the protein and reference compounds, respectively, according to eqn. (2):

$$R_h^{prot} = \frac{s_{ref}}{s_{prot}} (R_h^{ref}) \quad (2)$$

The experiments[45] were performed on min-R and Im9 in 100% D$_2$O containing 20 μl of 1% dioxane in D$_2$O,[46] with gradient strengths between 1.7 and 21.5 G cm^{-1} at 298 K. The gradient strength was calibrated using the diffusion coefficient of water at 298 K (2.3 × 10^{-5} cm^2 s^{-1}). The delays Δ and δ were held constant for all experiments, at 113 ms and 7.8 ms, respectively. Peak intensities for several peaks across the spectrum in the aromatic and aliphatic regions were measured, including those for the His-tag of min-R and two signals for the minor conformer, using VNMR. The slope of plots of ln(A) against the square of the gradient strength yielded the translational diffusion coefficients for the respective peaks, which were then averaged to give the final D_t value. All data fitting was performed in Origin 4.1 (Microcal Software Inc., Massachusetts, USA).

Backbone NH ^{15}N relaxation times for min-R at 600 MHz were measured with standard procedures[30,31] using spectral widths of 8000 Hz (^{1}H) and 2500 Hz (^{15}N), and with 1024 × 64 and 1024 × 68 complex points respectively with either 32 (T_1) or 36 (T_2) scans per transient point. The delay time between scans was 7 s for the T_1 measurements and 3 s for the T_2 measurements; the τ delay times are in Table 4. Steady-state heteronuclear NOE spectra were measured from spectra recorded in the presence and absence of proton saturation.[30] The spectra were recorded as 1024 × 128 complex data points with 64 transients per point. Proton saturation was achieved with a pulse train of 120° pulses every 5 ms for 3 s. For the spectra recorded with proton saturation a 2 s relaxation delay was followed by a 3 s period of saturation whilst those recorded without proton saturation used a relaxation delay of 5 s. For the determination of peak height uncertainties, three sets of spectra with and without proton saturation were acquired. Relaxation times and

Table 4 Delay times used for T_1 and T_2 relaxation time measurements of min-R

Experiment	τ Delay times/ms								Repeated values/ms		
T_1-600 MHz	10	50	100	200	400	600	1000	5000	10	100	600
T_2-600 MHz	10	30	50	70	110	150	250		10	50	150

heteronuclear NOEs were obtained from peak heights as previously described.[17] The determination of the Im9 Backbone NH ^{15}N relaxation times and NOEs has been described elsewhere.[32]

Calculations of hydrodynamic parameters were performed with the programmes HYDROPRO 3.C[26] and HYDRONMR,[34] using PDB files (6lyz.pdb, 1imq.pdb and 1jch.pdb) as input. Atomic coordinates for min-R were generated by removal of all residues from 1jch.pdb apart from residues 342–417. The unit cell of colicin E3 (1jch.pdb) contains two protein molecules in close contact along the extended helices of the receptor-binding domain. The coordinates for residues 342–417 of this 'head-to-tail' arrangement were used as a model for the dimer min-R calculations. To obtain conformations with varying angles between the two helices, rotations of 30°, 60°, 90°, 120°, 150° and 180° around the peptide bond between the loop residues 382 and 383 (42 and 43 starting with the N-terminus of min-R as residue 1) were performed in SPOCK.[47] Moment of inertia calculations and fitting of the relaxation time ratio T_1/T_2 to an anisotropic rotational diffusion model[35,36] were carried out using in-house programs, MOMENT and R2R1MC respectively (N.Clayden, unpublished work). The HYDRONMR calculations were at the temperature of the T_1 and T_2 measurements, and with a solution viscosity of 0.0118 poise.[48]

Abbreviations

ColE9, colcin E9; E9 Dnase, the nuclease domain of ColE9; Im9, the colicin E9 immunity protein; min-R, residues 343–418 of ColE9; HSQC, heteronuclear single quantum coherence; PDB, protein data bank; ppm, parts per million; TSP, sodium 3-trimethylsilypropionate.

Acknowledgements

We gratefully acknowledge the Wellcome Trust for a 600 MHz NMR spectrometer and its support of the UEA Colicin Research Group; HEFCE for a 500 MHz NMR spectrometer; and BBSRC for its award of a studentship to ESC. We are grateful to Dr D. Nietlispach (Cambridge) for the 800 MHz NOESY–HSQC spectrum of min-R, and Prof. M. Shoham (Cleveland, Ohio) for providing the coordinates of the colicin E3–Im3 complex. We also thank Colin MacDonald and Ann Reilly for expert technical assistance.

References

1 R. James, C. Kleanthous and G. R. Moore, *Microbiology*, 1996, **142**, 1569.
2 (a) W. A. Cramer and C. V. Stauffacher, *Ann. Rev. Biophys. Biomol. Struct.*, 1995, **24**, 611; (b) C. J. Lazdunski, E. Bouveret, A. Rigal, L. Journet, R. Lloubès and H. Bénédetti, *J. Bacteriol.*, 1998, **180**, 4993.
3 (a) K. S. Jakes and N. D. Zinder, *Proc. Natl. Acad. Sci. USA.*, 1974, **71**, 3380; (b) J. Sidikaro and M. Nomura, *J. Biol. Chem.*, 1974, **249**, 445; (c) C. Kleanthous and D. Walker, *Trends Biochem. Sci.*, 2001, **26**, 624.
4 R. Taylor, J. W. Burgner, J. Clifton and W. A. Cramer, *J. Biol. Chem.*, 1998, **273**, 31 113.
5 Y. V. Griko, S. D. Zakharov and W. A. Cramer, *J. Mol. Biol.*, 2000, **302**, 941.
6 P. C. K. Lau, M. Parsons and T. Uchimura, in *Bacteriocins, Microcins and Lantibiotics*, ed. R. James, C. Lazdunski and F. Pattus, NATO ASI Series H65, Springer-Verlag, Berlin, 1992, p. 353–378.
7 (a) H. Masaki, S. Yajima, A. Akutsu-Koide, T. Ohta and T. Uozumi, in *Bacteriocins*, ed. R. James, C. Lazdunski and F. Pattus, NATO ASI Series H65, Springer-Verlag, Berlin, 1992, p. 379–395; (b) T. Ogawa, K. Tomita, T. Ueda, K. Watanabe, T. Uozumi and H. Masaki, *Science*, 1999, **283**, 2097.
8 S. Soelaiman, K. Jakes, N. Wu, C. Li and M. Shoham, *Molecular Cell*, 2001, **8**, 1053.
9 (a) R. Wallis, A. Reilly, K. Barnes, C. Abell, D. G. Campbell, G. R. Moore, R. James and C. Kleanthous, *Eur. J. Biochem.*, 1994, **220**, 447; (b) L. J. A. Evans, S. Labeit, A. Cooper, L. H. Bond and J. H. Lakey, *Biochemistry*, 1996, **35**, 15 143; (c) E. Bouveret, A. Rigal, C. Lazdunski and H. Bénédetti, *Mol. Microbiol.*, 1997, **23**, 909.
10 M. Wiener, D. Freymann, P. Ghosh and R. M. Stroud, *Nature*, 1997, **385**, 461.
11 (a) H. Bénédetti, R. Lloubès, C. Lazdunski and L. Letellier, *EMBO J.*, 1992, **11**, 441; (b) K.-F. Chak, S.-Y. Hsieh, C.-C. Liao and L.-S. Kan, *Proteins: Structure, Function and Genetics*, 1998, **32**, 17.
12 (a) F. G. van der Groot, J. M. González-Mañas, J. H. Lakey and F. Pattus, *Nature*, 1991, **354**, 408; (b) P. Elkins, A. Bunker, W. A. Cramer and C. V. Stauffacher, *Structure*, 1997, **5**, 443; (c) M. Lindeberg, S. D. Zakharov and W. A. Cramer, *J. Mol. Biol.*, 2000, **295**, 679; (d) I. R. Vetter, M. W. Parker, A. D. Tucker, J. H. Lakey, F. Pattus and D. Tsernoglou, *Structure*, 1998, **6**, 863.

13 S. B.-M. Whittaker, R. Boetzel, C. MacDonald, L.-Y. Lian, A. J. Pommer, A. Reilly, R. James, C. Kleanthous and G. R. Moore, *J. Biomol. NMR*, 1998, **12**, 145.
14 (*a*) S. B.-M. Whittaker, M. Czisch, R. Wechselberger, R. Kaptein, A. M. Hemmings, R. James, C. Kleanthous and G. R. Moore, *Protein Science*, 2000, **9**, 713; (*b*) R. Boetzel, M. Czisch, R. Kaptein, A. M. Hemmings, R. James, C. Kleanthous and G. R. Moore, *Protein Science*, 2000, **9**, 1709.
15 K. Mosbahi, C. Lemaître, A. H. Keeble, H. Mobasheri, B. Morel, R. James, G. R. Moore, E. J. A. Lea and C. Kleanthous, 2002, submitted.
16 (*a*) H. Pilsl and V. Braun, *V. Mol Microbiol.*, 1995, **16**, 57; (*b*) E. Bouveret, A. Rigal, C. Lazdunski and H. Bénédetti, *Mol. Microbiol.*, 1998, **27**, 143; (*c*) C. Garinot-Schneider, C. N. Penfold, G. R. Moore, C. Kleanthous and R. James, *Microbiology*, 1997, **143**, 2931.
17 E. S. Collins, S. B.-M. Whittaker, K. Tozawa, C. MacDonald, R. Boetzel, C. N. Penfold, A. Reilly, N. Clayden, M. J. Osborne, C. Kleanthous, R. James and G. R. Moore, *J. Mol. Biol.*, 2002, in press.
18 C. N. Penfold, C. Garinot-Schneider, A. M. Hemmings, G. R. Moore, C. Kleanthous and R. James, *Mol. Microbiol.*, 2000, **38**, 639.
19 T. Eaton and R. James, *Nucleic Acid Res.*, 1989, **17**, 1761.
20 (*a*) M. Ikura, L. E. Kay, R. Tschudin and A. Bax, *Biochemistry*, 1990, **46**, 59; (*b*) S. Grzesiek and A. Bax, *J. Am. Chem. Soc.*, 1992, **114**, 6291; (*c*) D. R. Muhandiram and L. E. Kay, *J. Magn. Reson. B*, 1994, **B103**, 203; (*d*) L. E. Kay, G. Y. Xu and T. Yamazaki, *J. Magn. Reson. A*, 1994, **A109**, 129; (*e*) M. Wittekind and L. Mueller, *J. Magn. Reson. B*, 1993, **B101**, 201; (*f*) T. Yamazaki, J. D. Forman-Kay and L. E. Kay, *J. Am. Chem. Soc.*, 1993, **115**, 11054.
21 (*a*) L. E. Kay, P. Keifer and T. Saarinen, *J. Am. Chem. Soc.*, 1992, **114**, 10663; (*b*) O. W. Zhang, L. E. Kay, J. P. Olivier and J. D. Forman-Kay, *J. Biomol. NMR*, 1994, **4**, 845.
22 (*a*) D. S. Wishart and B. D. Sykes, *J. Biomol. NMR*, 1994, **4**, 171; (*b*) S. Schwarzinger, G. J. A. Kroon, T. R. Foss, J. Chung, P. E. Wright and H. J. Dyson, *J. Am. Chem. Soc.*, 2001, **123**, 2970.
23 B. A. Johnson and R. A. Blevin, *J. Biomol. NMR*, 1994, **4**, 603.
24 B. L. Levinson, C. A. Pickover and F. M. Richards, *J. Biol. Chem.*, 1983, **258**, 10967.
25 R. L. Haner and T. Schleich, *Meth. Enzymol.*, 1989, **176**, 418.
26 J. G. de la Torre, M. L. Huertas and B. Carrasco, *Biophys. J.*, 2000, **78**, 719.
27 A. S. Altieri, D. P. Hinton and R. A. Byrd, *J. Am. Chem. Soc.*, 1995, **117**, 7566.
28 R. Wallis, A. Reilly, A. Rowe, G. R. Moore, R. James and C. Kleanthous, *Eur. J. Biochem.*, 1992, **207**, 687.
29 D. K. Wilkins, S. B. Grimshaw, V. Receveur, C. M. Dobson, J. A. Jones and L. J. Smith, *Biochemistry*, 1999, **38**, 16424.
30 (*a*) L. E. Kay, L. K. Nicholson, F. Delaglio, A. Bax and D. A. Torchia, *J. Magn. Reson.*, 1992, **97**, 359; (*b*) N. A. Farrow, R. Muhandiram, A. U. Singer, S. M. Pascal, C. M. Kay, G. Gish, S. E. Shoelson, T. Pawson, J. D. Forman-Kay and L. E. Kay, *Biochemistry*, 1994, **33**, 5985.
31 (*a*) J. Engelke and H. Rüterjans, in *Biological Magnetic Resonance: Structure Computation and Dynamics in Protein NMR*, Kluwer Academic/Kluwer Publishers, New York, 1999, vol. 17, p. 357–417; (*b*) A. G. Palmer III, *Annu. Rev. Biophys. Biomol. Struct.*, 2001, **30**, 129.
32 E. S. Collins, PhD Thesis, UEA Norwich, 2001.
33 M. J. Osborne, A. L. Breeze, L.-Y. Lian, A. Reilly, R. James, C. Kleanthous and G. R. Moore, *Biochemistry*, 1996, **35**, 9505.
34 J. G. de la Torre, M. L. Huertas and B. Carrasco, *J. Magn. Reson.*, 2000, **147**, 138.
35 (*a*) G. Lipari and A. Szabo, *J. Am. Chem. Soc.*, 1982, **104**, 4546; (*b*) G. Lipari and A. Szabo, *J. Am. Chem. Soc.*, 1982, **104**, 4559.
36 N. Tjandra, S. E. Feller, R. W. Pastor and A. Bax, *J. Am. Chem. Soc.*, 1995, **117**, 12562.
37 J. J. A. Huntley, S. D. B. Scrofani, M. J. Osborne, P. E. Wright and H. J. Dyson, *Biochemistry*, 2000, **39**, 13356.
38 J. H. Davis and D. A. Agard, *Biochemistry*, 1998, **37**, 7696.
39 J. Kördel, J. J. Skelton, M. Akke, A. G. Palmer III and W. J. Chazin, *Biochemistry*, 1992, **31**, 4856.
40 (*a*) R. J. P. Williams, *Eur, J. Biochem.*, 1989, **183**, 479; (*b*) R. S. Spolar and M. T. Record, *Science*, 1994, **263**, 777; (*c*) P. E. Wright and H. J. Dyson, *J. Mol. Biol.*, 1999, **293**, 321.
41 F. Delaglio, S. Grzesiek, G. Vuister, G. Zhu, J. Pfeifer and A. Bax, *J. Biomol. NMR*, 1995, **6**, 277.
42 D. S. Wishart and D. A. Case, *Methods Enzymol.*, 2001, **338**, 3.
43 C. Bartels, T. H. Xia, M. Billeter, P. Güntert and K. Wüthrich, *J. Biomol. NMR*, 1995, **6**, 1.
44 E. O. Stejskal and J. E. Tanner, *J. Chem. Phys.*, 1965, **42**, 288.
45 S. J. Gibbs and C. S. Johnson, *J. Magn. Reson.*, 1991, **93**, 395.
46 J. A. Jones, D. K. Wilkins, L. J. Smith and C. M. Dobson, *J. Biomol. NMR*, 1997, **10**, 199.
47 J. A. Christopher and T. O. Baldwin, *J. Mol. Graph. Model*, 1998, **16**, 285.
48 *CRC Handbook of Chemistry and Physics*, 1984–5, 65th edn., p. F-37, CRC Press Inc., Florida.

The dynamic transition in proteins may have a simple explanation

Roy M. Daniel,[a] John L. Finney[b] and Jeremy C. Smith[c]

[a] *Department of Biological Sciences, University of Waikato, Hamilton, New Zealand*
[b] *Department of Physics and Astronomy, University College London, Gower Street, London, UK WC1E 6BT*
[c] *Lehrstuhl für Biocomputing, IWR, Universität Heidelberg, Im Neuenheimer Feld 368, D-69120 , Heidelberg, Germany*

Received 25th January 2002, Accepted 19th March 2002
First published as an Advance Article on the web 3rd July 2002

The transition that has been observed in the dynamics of hydrated proteins at low temperatures (180–230 K) is normally interpreted as a change from vibrational, harmonic motion at low temperatures to anharmonic motions as the temperature is raised. It is taken to be an intrinsic property of proteins and has been associated with the onset of protein functions. Examination of the dynamic behaviour of proteins in solution within a defined timescale window suggests that certain observations can be explained without the need to invoke a discontinuity in the dynamics of proteins with temperature, *i.e.* the existence of a dynamical transition is not required. This is discussed in the context of recent evidence that enzyme activity is independent of the activation of anharmonic picosecond dynamics and declines steadily with temperature through the apparent dynamic transition, in accordance with the Arrhenius relationship. That similar timescale dependent dynamical behaviour has been observed experimentally in chain polymers, and seen also in computer simulations of silica glasses, suggests that the phenomenon may be of wide general relevance in both simple glassy and more complex polymeric systems.

Introduction

Protein function involves structural changes, sometimes small and barely detectable, and sometimes involving significant, correlated motions over relatively large length scales. Determining which motions exist in proteins and which of these are required for function is thus a fundamental challenge.

Several techniques have shown a transition in the dynamics of hydrated proteins at low temperatures.[1–16] Much of this work has been done on myoglobin using Mössbauer spectroscopy[3,6,8] neutron scattering[10,11] or X-ray crystallography[2] of hydrated crystals, powders, or frozen solutions, but similar results have been found in X-ray crystallographic studies of ribonuclease A[12] and in Mössbauer[14] and neutron scattering[15] studies of membrane proteins. Some protein functions have been observed to cease with the loss of equilibrium anharmonic dynamics as the protein is cooled through the dynamic transition. Among these are electron tunnelling in *Rhodospirullum rubrum* chromatophores,[14] some elements of the photocycle of bacteriorhodopsin in hydrated membranes of *Halobacterium salinarum*,[15] and ligand binding/release in ribonuclease A crystals.[16]

This discontinuity is interpreted as a transition from vibrational, harmonic motion at low temperatures to anharmonic motions as the temperature is raised. Most experimental results arise from studies of hydrated protein powders, or crystals, using a range of techniques. These include Mössbauer spectroscopy of the Fe ion in myoglobin, X-ray scattering measurements of the temperature factor in protein crystals, Rayleigh scattering of Mössbauer radiation, and neutron scattering to probe the global dynamics of a relatively limited number of proteins.[1–16] Depending on the technique and possibly the protein or the nature of the preparation, the sharpness and temperature of this transition may vary somewhat, but has been generally observed between about 180 and 230 K. It is taken to be an intrinsic property of proteins and, as indicated above, has been associated with the onset of protein function.[14–20]

Recent neutron scattering measurements on a thermophilic glutamate dehydrogenase enzyme in solution, *under conditions in which enzyme activity is both possible and measurable*, failed to show any relationship between an observed dynamical transition at around 220 K and the onset of activity[13] (Fig. 1). The activity was observed to maintain an Arrhenius temperature dependence to well below this temperature, indicating that the transition observed in this system has no effect on the catalytic activity of this soluble, multisubunit enzyme. Results from a similar study carried out on a xylanase enzyme suggest that the behaviour of single subunit enzymes are also unaffected by the observed transition, although activity measurements were made here down to only 200 K.[21] We have now measured activity in a number of enzymes between 200 K and 170 K,[22] and there is so far no evidence for any intrinsic lower temperature limit for enzyme activity, although the lowest temperature at which enzyme activity has been measured to date is 170 K.[22] The association of the dynamical transition with the onset of enzyme activity is thus brought into question.

We need however to be aware of a number of points in considering the possible relationship between enzyme activity and dynamics. For example, there is the possible dependence of the results on the experimental or computational probe used. Diffraction methods such as X-ray crystallography on protein crystals produce time-averaged information *via* temperature factors. Due to their time-averaged nature, these results also contain static disorder effects. Other techniques such as Mössbauer spectroscopy of fluorescence depolarisation measure *localised* signals on specific timescales. Neutron scattering is a probe of faster motions (ps to ns depending on the instrument used) of mainly the hydrogen atoms in the system, and is hence a probe of *global* dynamics of the molecule. Finally molecular dynamics simulation can provide detailed modelling results on either global or localised dynamics over timescales stretching from ps to ns. Furthermore, we need to be sensitive to the environment of the proteins examined. For good experimental reasons, dynamical transition measurements have been made in the main on proteins under conditions of low hydration or in lipoprotein membranes rather than in the solution conditions in which the protein

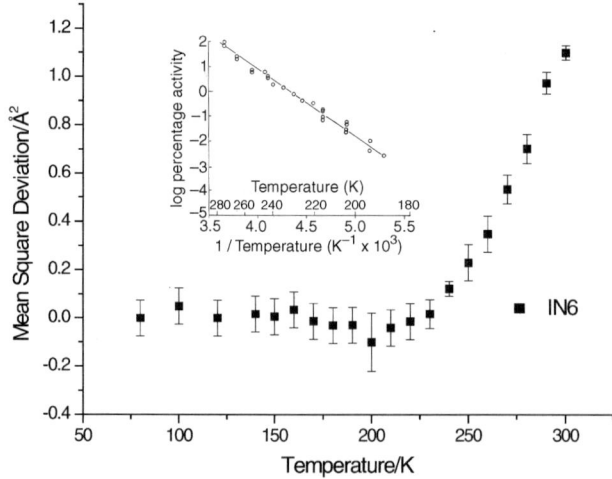

Fig. 1 Mean square displacement, measured on IN6, of GDH in 70% methanol in water, as a function of temperature *T*. The inset shows the activity of this enzyme under the same conditions, which is seen to be Arrhenius over the whole temperature range covered.

is normally active. Hence our insistence, in the parallel activity/dynamics measurements mentioned above, on performing the dynamics measurements under the same solvent conditions as those under which the activity measurements are made. The variation of dynamics with solvent conditions is therefore in itself a relevant area of study.[23]

We focus here on the possible dependence of the dynamical transition on the timescale of the motions probed. For such measurements, neutron scattering is a particularly useful technique, as the timescale of the motions measured depends on the resolution of the instrument used. As the sample requirements are similar for different resolution instruments, the dynamics of the same system under the same environmental conditions can be probed using different timescale windows. In the results given below, we use the two instruments IN6 and IN16 at the Institut Laue-Langevin, Grenoble, France. IN6 probes motions in the timescale faster than about 100 ps, while the motions reported by IN16 are faster than about 5000 ps.

Methods

The glutamate dehydrogenase enzyme used is from *Thermococcus* strain AN1 (now known as *T. zilligii* strain AN1) (DSM 2770), and was purified, assayed and prepared for neutron scattering as described elsewhere.[13,24,25] The xylanase enzyme was obtained from an *E. coli* clone containing the gene from the extremely thermophilic bacterium *Thermotoga maritima* strain FjSS3-B.1.[21,26] Its purification, assay and preparation for neutron scattering are described elsewhere.[22]

The neutron scattering measurements were performed on the IN6 time-of-flight spectrometer and on the IN16 backscattering spectrometer at the Institut Laue-Langevin, Grenoble. The incident neutron wavelengths were 5.12 Å on IN6 and 6.28 Å on IN16. All data were collected with the sample holder oriented at 135° relative to the incident beam. The samples were contained in aluminium flat-plate cells, of 0.3 mm and 0.5 mm path length on IN6 and IN16 respectively.

Samples were of between 50 and 100 mg ml^{-1} of enzyme in 70% v/v CD_3OD/D_2O solvent. The samples were cooled to 80 K then heated progressively to 320 K over 16–24 h. Raw data on the two instruments were corrected in identical fashion. The elastic intensity was determined by integrating the detector counts over the energy range of the instrumental resolution. The detectors were calibrated by normalising with respect to a standard vanadium sample. The cell scattering was subtracted, taking into account attenuation of the singly scattered beam. Finally, the scattering was normalised with respect to the scattering at the lowest measured temperature, 80 K, and to the lowest wave vector q.

The elastic incoherent scattering intensity $S_{inc}(q,\omega = 0)$ (where q is the magnitude of the scattering wave vector and ω is the energy transfer) was used to obtain the average mean square displacement $\langle u^2 \rangle$ using the relationship $\ln S_{inc}(q,\omega = 0) = -\langle u^2 \rangle q^2 / 3$ which is valid in the regime $q^2 \langle u^2 \rangle / 3 < 1$. $\langle u^2 \rangle$ was thus obtained by fitting a straight line to a semi-log plot of $S(q,\omega = 0)$ versus q^2 in the linear regime which was found at 0.12 Å^{-2} < q^2 < 1.07 Å^{-2} and 0.10 Å^{-2} < q^2 < 1.13 Å^{-2} in the IN6 and IN16 experiments, respectively. The linear regime was found to be well-separated from the Bragg scattering of the solution which was found at 1.4 Å^{-1} < q < 2.0 Å^{-1}, and no evidence was found for a low-q protein–protein interaction peak. As the scattering was normalised with respect to the 80 K intensities, the $\langle u^2 \rangle$ determined is equal to $(\langle u^2 \rangle_T - \langle u^2 \rangle_{80})$ where $\langle u^2 \rangle_T$ is the absolute mean-square displacement at temperature T. In practice, the measured $\langle u^2 \rangle$ corresponds to the H atoms, whose scattering cross section is strongly dominant. Depending on the concentration of the sample, between 70% and 80% of the incoherent signal is due to the enzyme, respectively. The $\langle u^2 \rangle$ obtained for these samples are therefore dominated by the enzyme motions. The energy resolution of IN16 is 1 µeV whereas that of IN6 is 50 µeV. The inverses of these energy resolutions correspond to times of 5 ns and 100 ps, respectively.

Results

Glutamate dehydrogenase

The temperature dependence of the rms displacement of this multisubunit (hexameric) enzyme in 70% methanol (the cryosolvent in which activity measurements have been made at low temperature[24]) is given in Fig. 2 for the two different instruments. There is a clear indication from Fig. 2 of

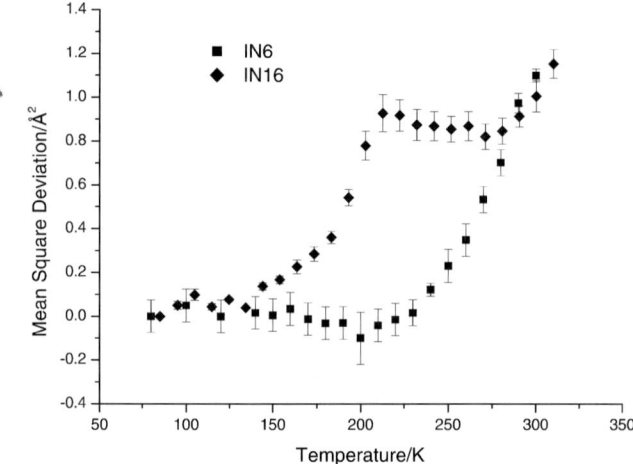

Fig. 2 Mean square displacement of GDH in 70% methanol in water, as a function of temperature T, measured on both IN6 and IN16.

a timescale-dependence of this dynamical transition. The onset of anharmonic motion occurs at $\sim$140 K on IN16 (motions $<\sim$5 ns), and $\sim$220 K on IN6 ($<\sim$100 ps). Further measurements on a spectrometer of intermediate resolution (IRIS at the ISIS pulsed spallation neutron source, Rutherford Appleton Laboratory, UK) shows a dynamic transition at an intermediate temperature.[28] Referring to the IN16 data in Fig. 2, in addition to the dynamical transition at $\sim$140 K, there are inflections in the IN16 $\langle u^2 \rangle$ at $\sim$185 K, $\sim$210 K and $\sim$280 K. If one defines a 'dynamical transition' as an inflection in $\langle u^2 \rangle$, then the IN16 profile demonstrates the presence of *four* dynamical transitions in the sample. The three highest-temperature transitions do not correspond to transitions from anharmonic to harmonic behaviour, rather to modification of the anharmonic behaviour itself. Focussing on the lowest transition at each timescale, this result implies that, for this protein solution, the temperature of the observed onset of anharmonic motion does indeed depend on the timescale of the motions explored ($\sim$100 ps and $\sim$5 ns in Fig. 2). Parallel differential scanning calorimetry and synchrotron X-ray powder diffraction measurements on both the enzyme preparations and the pure cryosolvent confirm[27] that the lowest transitions measured on each instrument are not related to phase changes in the solvent.

Xylanase

Because of the possibility that this initially surprising result might hold only for a multisubunit enzyme, where we might perhaps expect longer timescale motions to relate to subunit motions, we have recently made a series of similar measurements on the smaller, single subunit enzyme xylanase, in the same solvent.[21,29] The mean square displacement as a function of temperature measured on the two different instruments is shown in Fig. 3. The trend of the results is similar to that found for glutamate dehydrogenase (Fig. 2), confirming that the temperature of the observed onset of anharmonic motion depends on the timescale of the motions explored, and that this conclusion is valid for both the hexameric and single subunit enzymes examined.

Discussion

We recall that IN6 probes motions faster than about 100 ps, while IN16 covers a wider range up to 5 ns. If we therefore subtract these two data sets for the same sample, we will obtain information on motions of that sample within a timescale window delimited by 100 ps at the faster end and 5000 ps at the slower end. The difference will therefore show the temperature dependent behaviour of enzyme motions within a defined timescale window of between 100 and 5000 ps. The subtraction also has the advantage of largely removing the residual 20–30% contribution of the solvent motions from the data. The results of this subtraction for the two enzymes are shown in Fig. 4.

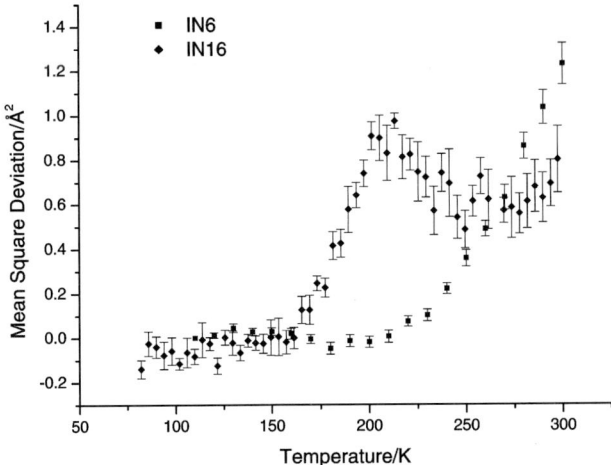

Fig. 3 Mean square displacement of xylanase in 70% methanol in water, as a function of temperature T, measured on both IN6 and IN16.

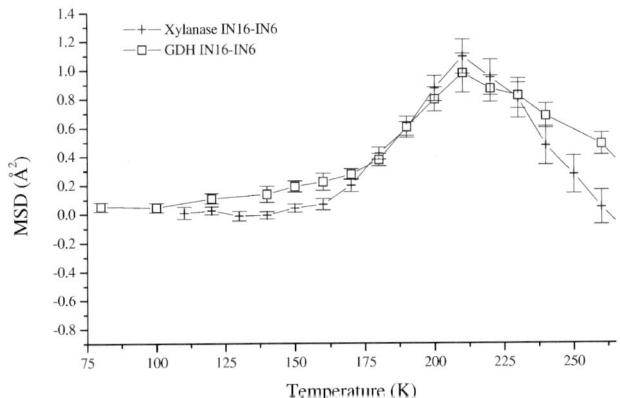

Fig. 4 Protein global dynamics in a 100 to 5000 ps timescale window. This figure shows the subtraction of the average mean square displacements of the protons observed up to 100 ps (instrument IN6) from those observed up to 5000 ps (instrument IN16), for xylanase and glutamate dehydrogenase in 70% methanol; *i.e.* the difference plot shows the motions for each protein within a timescale window of 100 to 5000 ps. The data used is that presented in Figs. 2 and 3.

Within the experimental uncertainties, Fig. 4 shows that the difference results for the two (very different) enzymes are remarkably similar, giving a roughly symmetrical peak at around 240 K. At the lowest temperatures, no motions faster than the slowest motions that will be visible in this window (characteristic times of around 5000 ps) are observed. As the temperature is raised above about 160 K, the slowest motions towards the observational limit of 5000 ps are detected. As temperature is increased further, faster (higher energy) motions are excited, and begin to contribute to the increase in observed mean square displacements. With a further temperature increase the mean square displacements decline, as the frequencies increase further and pass out of the 100 to 5000 ps timescale window.

This behaviour is consistent with that of simple activated dynamics, observed through a defined timescale window. A key distinguishing feature of a discontinuity arising from such behaviour would be its dependence on the instrument timescale. The implication of timescale dependence is that if the dynamics gradually and continuously slow as the temperature decreases, then any technique which observed only a part of the dynamic timescale would record a transition in the dynamics at the point where it could no longer record the motions because they were too slow. Thus, in this simplest interpretation of the observed timescale dependence, the existence of a dynamical transition is not necessary to explain the experimental results to date.

We now conduct thought experiments on what might be seen using two spectrometers of different energy resolution. Three scenarios may be considered. In the first there is a change in the long-time (equilibrium) dynamics of the enzyme system, and both spectrometers are considered to be of high enough resolution to resolve the motions concerned at all temperatures. In this case there will be a transition in the data that is independent of instrumental resolution. In the second scenario there is no change in the long-time dynamics of the enzyme system with temperature but the characteristic relaxation times pass into the resolved energy window of each instrument as the temperature increases. In this case a transition will also be observed in the data, and this will be dependent on instrumental resolution. The third scenario is similar to the first in that there is a change in the long time dynamics of the enzyme system, but differs from the first in that the instrumental resolutions are such that *not* all motions are resolved at all temperatures. Depending on the resolutions of the instruments with respect to the enzyme system dynamics, this could also lead to a temperature-dependent transition behaviour.

The first scenario is somewhat theoretical in that the spectrometers used are unlikely to be of high enough resolution to fulfil the stated conditions. Moreover, it is not consistent with the observed behaviour of our two enzyme solutions. Given the wide range of timescales in which motions in proteins exist, and X-ray diffraction evidence of a time-averaged (long-time) change in dynamics with temperature (but admittedly made more complex by the difficulty of separating out the effects of static disorder) it is possible that the third scenario could apply. If it does, then we have the problem of explaining why this dynamic transition has no effect on enzyme activity in solution, which is expected to be dependent on dynamics. However, the second scenario, which explains the observed temperature dependence of an apparent dynamical transition in terms of the resolution windows of the spectrometers used, is all that is necessary to explain the observed behaviour. It is the simplest explanation, and therefore passes the Occam's razor test. Moreover it does not require the existence of a dynamic transition, the observed behaviour being consistent with a simpler dynamical picture in which the motions of the enzyme in solution slow continuously with temperature, as the activity is observed to do.

The interpretation based on this second scenario clearly raises questions concerning the direct association observed in some experiments of a dynamic transition with the onset of protein function.[14–20] The processes for which these associations have generally been made, such as electron transport or ligand binding,[14–16] are those involving relatively fast reactions (and under conditions of relatively low hydration, rather than in solution). This is presumably because of a dependence upon the faster motions, which become too slow to allow normal function. Enzyme function however, usually occurring over millisecond timescales, is probably dependent upon slower motions, and thus likely to be independent of the activation of the picosecond-timescale dynamical transition observed in solution. This is consistent with our results that demonstrate conclusively that enzyme activity in solution is completely independent of any possible transition in picosecond motions: no departure from Arrhenius behaviour is observed down to the lowest temperature at which activity has been measured, 173 K.[13,21,22,24,27] Thus, if any observed dynamical transition is to be related to the onset of protein function, account must be taken of the timescales of the relevant processes. If there is indeed no dynamic transition, then our activity and dynamics results can be explained very simply on the basis of slower motions resulting in lower activity.

Conclusions

The absence of a relationship between the picosecond-timescale dynamic transition observed in solution and the onset of activity demonstrates clearly that at 220 K activated picosecond dynamics are not necessarily coupled to the motions that are important for the rate-limiting step of enzymes in solution. The lower temperature at which the nanosecond-timescale transition occurs in Figs. 2 and 3 may or may not be associated with the onset of enzyme activity; activity measurements at such low temperatures have not yet been possible. But it is clear that the simple association of a dynamical transition with enzyme activity cannot be made independent of a consideration of the timescale of the measured transition. The evidence to date is consistent with a model in which the motions of proteins in solution slow continuously with temperature. Thus the observed dynamical transition may be no more than the appearance of motions within the observational timescale window of the instrument used.

In conclusion, we note two further relevant points. First, similar timescale dependences of the dynamics of large molecules have also been made in neutron scattering measurements of chain polymers.[30,31] They have also been seen in computer simulations of silica glasses.[32] Thus, the behaviour discussed here may well be much more general than just its presence in enzymes in solution. Secondly, a recent theoretical model of Becker et al.[33] shows that the kind of timescale dependence observed for the dynamics of these two enzymes can be reproduced if the characteristic relaxation frequencies of the protein are assumed to be temperature dependent. This model, which does not require a change in the time-averaged dynamics, gives good agreement with the experimental neutron scattering data discussed here.

Acknowledgements

We thank the Marsden Fund (NZ) and the Royal Society (UK) for financial support, and the Institut Laue-Langevin, Grenoble, and ISIS, Rutherford Appleton Laboratory, for the use of neutron beam facilities.

References

1 F. Parak and H. Formanek, *Acta Crystallogr., Sect. A*, 1971, **27**, 573.
2 H. Frauenfelder, G. A. Petsko and D. Tsernoglou, *Nature*, 1979, **280**, 558.
3 H. Keller and P. G. Debrunner, *Phys. Rev. Lett.*, 1980, **45**, 68.
4 F. Parak, E. N. Frolov, R. L. Mössbauer and V. I. Goldanskii, *J. Mol. Biol.*, 1981, **145**, 825.
5 S. G. Cohen, E. R. Bauminger, I. Nowik, S. Ofer and J. Yariv, *Phys. Rev. Lett.*, 1980, **46**, 1244.
6 E. W. Knapp, S. F. Fischer and F. Parak, *J. Phys. Chem.*, 1982, **86**, 5042.
7 H. Hartmann, F. Parak, W. Steigman, G. A. Petsko, D. R. Ponzi and H. Frauenfelder, *Proc. Natl Acad. Sci. USA*, 1982, **79**, 4967.
8 F. Parak, E. W. Knapp and D. Kucheida, *J. Mol. Biol.*, 1982, **161**, 177.
9 E. R. Bauminger, S. G. Cohen, I. Nowik, S. Ofer and J. Yariv, *Proc. Natl Acad. Sci. USA*, 1983, **80**, 736.
10 W. Doster, S. Cusack and W. Petry, *Nature*, 1989, **337**, 754.
11 S. Cusack and W. Doster, *Biophys. J.*, 1990, **58**, 243.
12 R. F. Tilton, J. C. Dewan and G. A. Petsko, *Biochemistry*, 1992, **31**, 2469.
13 R. M. Daniel, J. C. Smith, M. Ferrand, S. Hery, R. Dunn and J. L. Finney, *Biophys. J.*, 1998, **75**, 2504.
14 F. Parak, E. N. Frolov, A. A. Kononenko, R. L. Mössbauer, V. I. Goldanskii and A. G. Rubin, *FEBS Lett.*, 1980, **117**, 368.
15 M. Ferrand, A. J. Dianoux, W. Petry and G. Zaccai, *Proc. Natl Acad. Sci. USA*, 1993, **90**, 9668.
16 B. F. Rassmussen, A. M. Stock, D. Ringe and G. A. Petsko, *Nature*, 1992, **357**, 523.
17 J. Fitter, R. E. Lechner and N. Dencher, *Biophys. J.*, 1997, **73**, 2126.
18 U. Lehnert, V. Réat, M. Weil, G. Zaccai and C. Pfister, *Biophys. J.*, 1998, **75**, 1945.
19 X. Ding, B. F. Rassmussen, G. A. Petsko and D. Ringe, *Biochemistry*, 1994, **33**, 9285.
20 A. Ostermann, R. Waschipky, F. G. Parak and G. U. Nienhaus, *Nature*, 2000, **404**, 205.
21 R. V. Dunn, V. Réat, J. L. Finney, M. Ferrand, J. C. Smith and R. M. Daniel, *Biochem. J.*, 2000, **346**, 355.
22 J. M. Bragger, R. V. Dunn and R. M. Daniel, *Biochim. Biophys. Acta*, 2000, **1480**, 278.
23 V. Réat, R. Dunn, M. Ferrand, J. L. Finney, R. M. Daniel and J. C. Smith, *Proc. Natl Acad. Sci. USA*, 2000, **97**, 9961.
24 N. More, R. M. Daniel and H. H. Petach, *Biochem. J.*, 1995, **305**, 17.
25 R. C. Hudson, L. D. Ruttersmith and R. M. Daniel, *Biochim. Biophys. Acta*, 1993, **1202**, 244.
26 D. J. Saul, L. C. Williams, R. A. Reeves, M. D. Gibbs and P. L. Bergquist, *Appl. Environ. Microbiol.*, 1995, **61**, 4110.
27 R. M. Daniel, J. L. Finney, V. Réat, R. Dunn, M. Ferrand and J. C. Smith, *Biophys. J.*, 1999, **77**, 2184.
28 J. L. Finney and R. M. Daniel, *ISIS Experimental Report 1998*, Rutherford Appleton Laboratory, Chilton, Didcot, Oxon, UK, 1998, RB8790.
29 J. L. Finney, R. M. Daniel, J. C. Smith and V. Réat, ILL report on Expt 8–05–341, http://www.ill.fr/.
30 B. Frick and D. Richter, *Science*, 1995, **267**, 1939.
31 C. A. Angell, *Science*, 1995, **267**, 1924.
32 C. A. Angell, *Comput. Mater. Sci.*, 1995, **4**, 285.
33 T. Becker, J. L. Finney, R. M. Daniel and J. C. Smith, in preparation.

General Discussion

Prof. Finney opened the discussion of Dr Smart's paper: How can you ensure that you are not cross-linking between molecules? Could not such cross-linking explain the peptide association you mention on the seventh page of your paper?

Dr Smart responded: The association you refer to occurs before the $(i,i+7)$GCN4-p1 is cross-linked. We find that the circular dichroism signal at 222 nm is anomalously small in comparison with previously published values (ref. 22 and 27 of the paper) yet it shows a marked concentration dependence (Table 1 of the paper). The presence of 3 mM DTT would ensure that the sulfhydryl groups of the cysteine residues are reduced, thus precluding the formation of disulfide bonds. As set out in the Discussion and presented in Fig. 7 we believe that the effect is probably due to the mutation of a number of residues that would create a hydrophobic stripe on the surface of the intact coiled-coil.

Dr Sagi said: The cross-linked peptide has an additional spacer which links the two cysteines. Such an artificial spacer may affect the DNA binding properties of the cross linked peptide to the DNA in terms of affinity and/or the "correct" binding.

Dr Smart replied: The peptide we have described here is a variant of GCN4-p1 which lacks the DNA basic binding helix found on the longer GCN4-bZIP. A clear aim of this work is to produce a variant of GCN-bZIP whose DNA binding is under reversible photo-control. The strategy presented here is to control the dimerisation properties of the zipper part of the protein that is distant from the DNA. A clear alternative would be to try to alter the conformation of the DNA binding helix. As explained in the Introduction of the paper based on the results of Vinson and co-workers (ref. 18 of the paper) we expect control of the leucine zipper part to produce a high degree of photo-control. An advantage of controlling an area distant from the DNA is that the binding specificity of the protein is unlikely to be affected.

Dr Techert said: 23% of the peptides do not isomerise. What are the alternative reaction channels?

Dr Smart answered: We find for the cross-linked $(i,i+7)$GCN4-p1X coiled-coil peptide that illumination with 370 nm for long periods of time resulted in only 62% of the azobenzene chromophores switching to the *cis* state, the other 38% remaining in a *trans* conformation. This is a feature of using the azobenzene chromophore—the dark-adapted state is generally >99% of the *trans* isomer whereas the maximum percentage of the *cis* isomer that can be achieved by irradiation varies but is typically from 70 to 90%.[1] It is interesting to note that the maximum percentage conversion achievable with the cross-linker used here varies with the application it is used for. In recent work (ref. 9b in the paper) we have shown, in a peptide where the cross-linker is used to link two cysteine residues with a relative spacing of $(i,i+4)$, that a proportion of 90% can be switched to the *cis* state by irradiation. The half-life for thermal relaxation back to the *trans* state is also found to be longer than in the application presented here.

1 H. Rau, in *Photochemistry and Photophysics*, ed. J. F. Rabek, CRC Press, Boca Raton, 1995, p. 119.

Prof. J. C. Smith asked: Can one follow the time course for helix folding in these compounds using molecular dynamics and/or fast spectroscopy? Certainly for molecular dynamics (MD) one now has sufficient computer power to sample peptide conformational equilibria and maybe combining MD with your and other experiments one might learn something about helix initiation and propagation.

Dr Smart answered: We have supplied the original cross-linked monomeric peptide (ref. 8 in the paper) to a number of groups for fast time resolved spectroscopic studies (ORD, absorption/photoacoustic spectroscopy and FTIR methods). Initial preliminary results show that it is possible to trigger photoisomerisation of the chromophore using a laser pulse and that the conformational change in the peptide that follows this is fast (< 30 ns), although these results need to be confirmed. Your suggestion for molecular dynamics studies is certainly a good one. In this context Watchtveitl and co-authors have just published a study where molecular dynamics simulation is linked to femtosecond time resolved spectroscopy results for a seven residue peptide that is backbone-cyclized with an azobenzene derivative. Upon photoisomerization of the chromophore the peptide switches between two distinct coil conformations (in DMSO) and an encouraging correspondence of results between simulation and experiment is observed.[1]

1 S. Spörlen, H. Carsten, H. Satzger, C. Renner, R. Behrendt, L. Moroder, P. Tavan, W. Zinth and J. Wachtveil, *Proc. Natl. Acad. Sci. USA*, 2002, **99**, 7998.

Mr Teriete asked: Can the observed difference in relaxation of the azobenzene switch be correlated to internal kinetic processes involved in the formation and folding of the helix? Has the system been investigated using NMR spectroscopic methods?

Dr Smart replied: As detailed in the response to the question of Dr Techert both the maximum percentage conversion of the azobenzene chromophore to the *cis* form and its thermal relaxation lifetime do depend on the ground state structure of the peptide to which it is attached. To what extent the isomerization of the linker and the refolding of the peptide are temporally coupled is presently unknown.

We have been studying the original cross-linked monomeric peptide (ref. 8 in the paper) by NMR methods and will report the results soon.

Dr Hädener said: Is it clear that the wavelengths of the light used to induce isomerisation of the azo groups will be the same for the free crosslinker as compared to the crosslinker attached to the cysteines? In the latter case the isomerisation will be sterically hindered and this may affect the energy of the photon needed to isomerise the azo groups.

Dr Smart responded: We have not observed such an effect. The absorption spectrum of the azobenzene cross-linker before reaction, once attached to a number of peptides or reacted with glutathione, is essentially identical.[1] As noted in the paper and in previous replies, both the maximum percentage conversion of the azobenzene chromophore to the *cis* form and its thermal relaxation lifetime do vary with the context. It should be noted that the absorption spectrum of azobenzene derivatives does depend on the nature of the substituent on the ring. Unmodified azobenzene in the *trans* form has an absorption maximum around 340 nm.[2]

1 G. A. Woolley, personal communication.
2 H. Rau, in *Photochemistry and Photophysics*, ed. J. F. Rabek, CRC Press, Boca Raton, 1995

Prof. Wilson said: I am interested in the possibility of gaining more information on the "recoiling" of the helix in the slow 10–30 min relaxation process. Has this been examined and is there potential there to use this system (admittedly in the presence of the zipper) as a model for protein folding.

Dr Smart replied: The relaxation process that has a half-life of 10 to 30 min is the thermal revision of the azobenzene chromophore from its *cis* to the dark-adapted *trans* form. It is quite possible to use circular dichroism to monitor the secondary structure of the peptide during this revision. However, because conformational changes of peptides occur on time scales that are very many orders of magnitude faster the results would simply reflect the particular proportions of *cis* and *trans* forms at each particular time. It can be noted that for the three different monomeric peptides that we have studied in detail (ref. 8 and 9b in the paper) CD results show isodichroic points. This is consistent with a simple two-state equilibrium between the disordered and helical states of the proteins.

Prof. Wilson said: By how much can the relaxation process (from *cis*-azobezene/uncoiled helix to *trans*-azobenzene/coiled helix) be altered *e.g.* by the use of laser/light flash. Further, by how much is the process speeded up if the azobenzene is removed/excised from the uncoiled protein by chemical means.

Dr Smart answered: In the coiled-coil peptide we have described we have produced a system where the *trans* form of the cross-linker produces a coiled-coil with a lower helicity than that produced by irradiation with 370 nm light. In monomeric peptides it is possible to initiate photoisomerisation using a pulse of laser light (as described in a previous reply). It would be difficult to specifically remove the cross-linking compound from the peptide by chemical means without destroying the peptide. In the paper we have described in detail the properties of the GCN4-p1 derivative prior to cross-linking.

Dr Hirst asked: In your paper, you report that the helicity of native GCN4 drops by about 25% when the pH changes from pH 7 to pH 5. Why might that be?

Dr Smart answered: We have indeed found this effect, in agreement with the previous results of Sosnick and co-workers (ref. 26 and 27 in the paper), but can offer no explanation. That such a subtle change in pH produces a large effect on the circular dichroism signal of a well-understood coiled-coil is of interest.

Dr Grant asked: Have you ever considered using the technique of Raman optical activity (ROA) as it gives more detailed structural information than just CD, although ROA is not a time-resolved technique, if revision back to *trans* is slow enough, it may be possible to employ this technique.

Dr Smart replied: That is a very good suggestion. We are also interested in the possibility of using synchrotron radiation circular dichroism as this offers the potential to acquire more detailed information with good time-resolution.

Prof. J. C. Smith asked: A speculative question—various groups are working on using synthetic metal chelates to design sequence-specific DNA cleavage systems *i.e.*, artificial restriction enzymes. Is there any chance (or interest) in photoactivating such processes?

Dr Smart answered: The chemical nucleases produced by Bailly and co-workers[1] do not have a peptide component and so our approach is not immediately applicable. However, in this context Komiyama and co-workers have produced impressive results in oligonucleotides incorporating azobenzene in place of a DNA base.[2,3] Most notably they have produced an oligonucleotide whose binding to DNA can be utilized to photo-regulate the action of DNA polymerase enzyme on the complimentary strand.[4]

1 S. Routier, H. Vezin, E. Lamour, J. L. Bernier, J. P. Catteau and C. Bailly, *Nucl. Acid Res.*, 1999, **27**, 4160.
2 X. G. Liang, H. Asanuma and M. Komiyama, *J. Am. Chem. Soc.*, 2002, **124**, 1877.
3 H. Asanuma, X. G. Liang, T. Yoshida and M. Komiyama, *ChemBioChem*, 2001, **2**, 39.
4 A. Yamazawa, X. G. Liang, H. Asanuma and M. Komiyama, *Ang. Chem. Int. Ed.*, 2000, **39**, 2356.

Prof. Moffat said: What would be the ideal set of properties for a light-dependent, artificial transcription factor (or DNA binding protein)?

Dr Smart replied: An ideal light-dependent transcription factor would have:
(i) A complete photo-control of the DNA binding process, that is absolutely no DNA binding in the light but completely normal binding upon irradiation.
(ii) Use a chromophore that is altered by a long wavelength of light in comparison to azobenzene. This is important to avoid both scattering and radiation damage effects to living cells.

Furthermore the chromophore should have a high quantum yield so that only short irradiation would be required.

(iii) Have rapid reversible photo switching between the on and off states such that it is possible to turn on the protein for a given time and by using an alternative wavelength. This would allow the equivalent of single turnover experiments on enzymes by watching the effect in a cell of a small "dose" of the active protein.

(iv) Be easily produced—most ideally *in vivo* by standard molecular biology procedures with no chemical intervention so that it can be assayed in the cell in which it is expressed.

Prof. Helliwell asked: What are the applications in biotechnology?

Dr Smart answered: The technology is still in a development phase. We have demonstrated how a photo-isomerisable crosslinker can be used to control the conformation of peptides and coiled-coil molecules. The next stage is to apply the method to recombinant proteins and show how activity can be controlled. The initial application will be to DNA binding proteins and work is in progress.

Prof. Moffat said: Biological systems have evolved various forms of chemistry for absorbing light and harnessing its energy to drive certain biological processes. Can you learn from nature, to direct your chemical approaches?

Dr Smart replied: Compared to the natural biological systems you refer to our approach must be seen to be crude. The subtlety involved in the mechanisms of the rhodopsins and other photochromic proteins is impressive. Compared to a chemical approach where it is necessary to purify and modify proteins *in vitro* a biologically based method of photo-control would have great advantages. For instance if it might be possible to achieve photo-control by using a fusion method where a given target was produced together with a natural photosensitive protein. This would have the advantage of being easily applied to *in vivo* systems.

Prof. Sir John Meurig Thomas opened the discussion of Dr Techert's paper: Your interesting work on the topochemical photodimerization of *p*-formyl-*trans*-cinnamic acid, where the crystalline monomer is converted to a polycrystalline (amorphous?) dimer, prompts me to draw to your attention a very nice example of photodimerization where a single-crystal → single-crystal transformation occurs. This (diffusionless) 2+2 photodimerization takes place[1] in the archetypal molecule, 2-benzyl-5-benzylidenecyclopentanone (BBCP) and in its *p*-bromo derivative (B*p*BrBCP). My colleagues and I were able to record in a time-resolved fashion (on a 4-circle diffractometer) detailed crystallographic measurements on these materials at various stages of solid-state conversion at room temperatures. In particular, for the case of BBCP, the gradual formation of the cyclobutane ring between the two monomers in an incipient dimer could be directly identified[2] (see Fig. 1 presented here).

I am also prompted to raise some more general issues concerning topochemical photo-induced transformations in organic molecular crystals. My own interest in such phenomena began when it emerged that the topochemical postulates of Schmidt and Cahen were, in some cases, vitiated. For example, anthracene may be photo-converted in the solid state to yield the diplanar-dimer, yet the structure of the stable, monoclinic form of anthracene should not permit such a transformation to occur. Even more puzzling was the observation that 9-cyanoanthracene (9CNA) yields the "wrong" dimer, *i.e.* the *trans* rather than the *cis* form, although the packing in the solid state of 9CNA suggests ready formation of the *cis* dimer, just as your cinnamic acid monomers yield the truxinic acid dimer. Why is this so? It is because crystalline defects hold sway. Excitation energy migrates through the crystal and is trapped at defects, where the local structure is what matters.

At stacking faults (bounded by two partial dislocations) in 9CNA juxtaposed incipient dimers are in the *trans*, not the *cis* configuration. And in anthracene, certain types of strucutal faults—like those favoured by the application of gentle pressure that facilitates the production of a metastable form of anthracene in which incipient dimers are brought within the distance (*ca.* 4 Å) required for photodimerization—are also implicated in the photoreactivity.

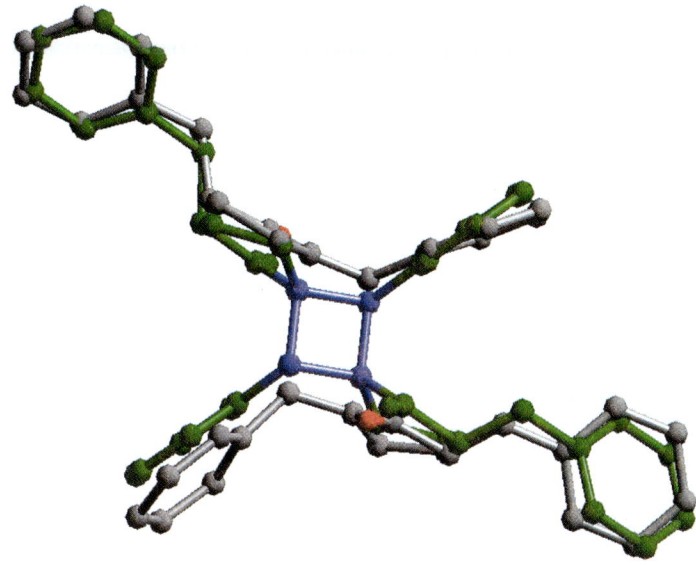

Fig. 1 The gradual formation of the cyclobutane ring between the two monomers of BBCP in an incipient dimer.

There are many other examples (*e.g.* 1,8-dichloro-9-methylanthracene and 1,8-dichloro-10-methylanthracene), where my colleagues and I found that photodimerization yields the "wrong" dimer; and the explanation in each case is to be found in the role of structural faults.[5]

With the refined techniques that Techert, Wulff and coworkers report in their paper, it would be profitable to re-investigate some of these seemingly anomalous instances of topochemical reaction.

1 H. Nakanishi, W. Jones, J. M. Thomas, M. B. Hursthouse and M. Motevalli, *J. Phys. Chem.*, 1981, **85**, 3636.
2 J. M. Thomas, *Nature*, 1981, **289**, 633.
3 M. D. Cohen, J. M. Thomas, J. O. Williams and Z. Ludmer, *Proc. R. Soc. London, Ser. A*, 1971, **324**, 459.
4 J. M. Thomas, G. M. Parkinson, S. Ramdas, M. J. Gorringe, C. M. Gramaccioli, G. Filippini and M. Simonetta, *Nature*, 1980, **284**, 153; see also S. Ramdas, J. M. Thomas, J. O. Williams and G. M. Parkinson, *Eighth Molecular Crystals Symp.*, Santa Barbara, 1977.
5 J. M. Thomas, *Philos. Trans. R. Soc. London, Ser. A*, 1974, **277**, 251.

Dr Techert responded: Indeed, the suggested 2 + 2 photodimerisation you refer to in ref. 1 came to our attention recently and we decided to work on it in more detail since it is a full single-crystal–single-crystal transformation. In this context it will be particularly interesting to measure and to understand the differences in the kinetics if, as in the presented work, the product state is amorphous (or less ordered) or if the product state is fully periodically lattice ordered.

9CNA and other derivatives are also classical and interesting candidates for investigations of topochemical reactions.

Prof. Coppens asked: What drives the condensation of the phonon mode into the metastable state you propose. Can you reproduce the intensity changes reproduced in Fig. 12 (of the paper) with the model? What is the percent conversion by each X-ray flash that gives rise to your signal?

Dr Techert answered: In Fig. 1 (of the paper) only the *effective* reaction mechanism with the effective reaction coordinate of the dimerisation process is shown. However, if one looks more carefully into photo-induced dimerisation processes (*e.g.* taking the Woodward–Hoffmann rules into consideration), then one has to study in more detail the shape of the potential energy hypersurface (PES) of the ground state as well as of the electronically excited state or states in which the sample is excited by 267 nm excitation wavelength. Depending on the interactions of the different PESs of the excited states, level-crossings and adiabatic transitions between the different excited states drive the reaction to particular product states. Here, we think that the proposed metastable state is connected with a local minimum on the excited state PES decaying from there to the product state. This local minimum is populated *via* an optically allowed vibronic transition where the electronic state and one (or more) phonon modes are excited.

At the moment we are performing simulations employing density functional theory of this system in order to obtain a more detailed understanding of the found transient signal changes. In this context it is necessary not only to study the geometrical aspects but also to simulate the energy levels of the (different distorted) lattices in the ground state as well as the electronically excited state PESs.

Taking the preliminary state of the simulation into consideration, the intensity changes in Fig. 12 are reasonably well reproduced. However, the quality of the measurements as well as the quality of the theoretical simulations have to be improved further in order to obtain a complete and quantitative picture of the dimerisation mechanism.

Due to laser damage problems, p-FCA cannot be excited with too high a laser power. From spectroscopic measurements we approximated that a maximum of 5–8% of the chromophores are excited in one laser flash. This corresponds to a relative change in X-ray signal of about 2–4% (maximum) in the reported system.

Dr Nibbering asked: Are the phonons that are supposed to play a role in the reaction dynamics of the acoustic or optical type? If they are optical phonons, one could drive these with optical light pulses through the mechanism of impulsive stimulated Raman scattering. As a consequence, the reaction dynamics will be influenced when the phonons are light-driven, and one may hope to perform some form of optical control of the reaction dynamics.

Dr Techert answered: According to the selection rules, the proposed mechanism is based on optically active phonons, which drive the process. Concerning the energies of these phonon modes, frequencies in the THz regime are assumed—as, *e.g.*, in solid beryllium or InSb.[1] Controlling the reaction dynamics by the impulsive stimulated Raman scattering technique is a very interesting approach, in particular since only a little work has been carried out concerning the vibrational spectroscopy/analysis of this type of reaction.

1 D. A. Reis, M. F. DeCamp, P. H. Bucksbaum, R. Clarke, E. Dufresne, M. Hertlein, R. Merlin, R. Falcone, H. Kepteyn, M. M. Murnane, J. Larsson, Th. Misalla and J. S. Wark, *Phys. Rev. Lett.*, 2001, **86**, 3072.

Prof. Bürgi asked: How does the wavelength of the light used for dimerization affect the lack of crystallinity of the product?

Dr Techert replied: This is indeed a very interesting question. At the moment we do not know the answer. Using 267 nm as the excitation wavelength is surely far above the resonant state of the vibronic transition which is necessary to initiate the reaction. Part of the excess energy will be transformed in heating of the sample, which can lead to structural disorder and loosing the crystallinity of the product state. To answer this question, a systematic study of the amorphism of the product state as a function of excess excitation energy is necessary.

Prof. Helliwell said: Please comment on the X-ray laser potentional *versus* radiation damage issues for your particular compounds.

Dr Techert[†] commented: The proposed X-ray FELs will deliver pulses of approximately 10^{12} photons with a duration of about 100 fs that will create an ideal source for the investigation of ultra-fast processes, like structural (re)organisation. The high flux also will enable one to investigate irreversible processes much more easily as well as *e.g.* nonlinear properties of material. Furthermore the coherence of the XFEL radiation certainly will pave the way to new types of X-ray diffraction experiments.

---

† Also Dr Th. Tschentscher, Hamburger Synchrotronstrahlungslabor HASYLAB at the Deutsches Elektronen-Synchrotron DESY, Hamburg.

It is clear, however, that sample damage due to the high number of photons must be considered carefully when defining experiments. Here one must take into account the reduced photon flux at the sample due to the throughput of mirrors and monochromator and due to collimation. This flux has to be compared to the photon flux required to measure the effect under investigation. Beam attenuation techniques (as already practised at synchrotrons of the third generation) may be applied to match both values.

To estimate the sample damage one has to take into account the particular time structure of the XFEL radiation. The short duration of the pulse, and therefore the short sampling time in diffraction experiments, allows one to extract information before diffusion controlled processes can play a role.

Processes occuring at the sub-picosecond timescale therefore are important to consider. If sample damage effects are found to alter the experiments single sample exchange methods can be applied, like liquid jets or sweeping beam techniques. It is also important to consider sample damage due to laser excitation. Here already sample exchange techniques are practised.

Dr Techert opened the discussion of Dr Cole's paper: What is the concrete application of the rhenium carbene complex and why is it important to know the triplet structure?

Dr Cole responded: The rhenium carbene complex is one in a series of compounds that has potential as a candidate for a building block as a 'molecular wire', and it also has attractive prospects in catalysis (its photolysis might alter the reactivity of the carbene ligand through population of the ^{3}MLCT state).

Prof. Coppens said: You mentioned a life time of 0.5 μs but did not mention the temperature. The life times of excited states of metalloorganic complexes are often quite temperature dependent. Did you obtain the spectra at the same temperature?

Dr Cole replied: The emission spectra of the sample were measured at both room temperature and 77 K in dichloromethane solvent and a 4:1 ethanol–methanol glass matrix, respectively. Their profiles are very similar in both cases thus indicating that the nature of the dominant ^{3}MLCT band remains the same at both temperatures, *i.e.* the lifetime, measured at room temperature, is not significantly altered at 77 K.[1]

1 W.-M. Xue, M. C.-W. Chan, Z.-M. Su, K. K. Cheung, S. T. Liu and C.-M. Che, *Organometallics*, 1998, **17**, 1622.

Prof. Wilson said: We heard that changing temperature dramatically affects the timescales of the process under study. Does it also affect the degree of transformation in the process?

A related point—why not "quasi-continuously" pump to achieve higher degrees of transformation and allow higher resolution diffraction experiments (*e.g.* charge density). Is the problem that molecules are knocked out of the excited state by further irradiation?

Dr Cole responded: It could affect the degree of transformation, but more drastically, it could affect the entire nature of the emissive-state of the sample, *e.g.* a compound with a dominant ^{3}MLCT type emission at room temperature could be overridden by an intraligand (IL) state which dominates at low temperature. (See for example, compound 7 in ref. 1.)

By quasi-continuously pump–probing a sample, one is likely to destroy the sample *cf.* a typical continuous laser provides $\sim 10^{18}$ photons per pulse, compared with a pulsed laser of 10^{14}–10^{16} depending on its repetition rate.

1 W.-M. Xue, M. C.-W. Chan, Z.-M. Su, K. K. Cheung, S. T. Liu and C.-M. Che, *Organometallics*, 1998, **17**, 1622.

Dr Chen asked: In your paper, the excited state lifetime was measured in dichloromethane glass at 77 K. However, the diffraction experiments were carried out in the single crystal. The triplet lifetime of the molecule therefore is likely to be shortened. Have you measured the lifetime in the single crystal? With ~20% excitation states in your paper, how do you deal with triplet–triplet annihilation?

Dr Cole answered: No. Lifetime measurements of samples on a single crystal are practically very difficult although we are presently investigating this as an option. The triplet lifetime may indeed be different in the glass compared with the single-crystal since the solvent viscosity will prevent thermal equilibrium in the rigid 77 K glass in a time comparable with the emission lifetime. Moreover, the nature of the surrounding frozen and disordered solvent environment is likely to affect the lifetime.

20% is stated in the paper simply as a likely maximum level of excitation (based on observations from the literature on other samples). The level of excitation for this compound is not reported in this paper, since data refinement is still underway. Therefore, triplet-triplet annihilation is not necessarily a significant effect here.

Dr Techert asked: In Fig. 2 of the paper, a laser power of about 50 µJ is used. Does one need these high energies in order to reach a sufficient excitation level in the crystal?

Dr Cole replied: Tests were carried out to assess the maximum level of laser power that could be used without destroying the crystal during the experiment. As a result, we arrived at a chosen laser power of 50 µJ. The greater the laser power, the greater the level of excitation and the larger the crystal that one can use for the experiment (*c.f.* optical penetration depth calculations). Therefore, by using the maximum feasible laser power, we were able to maximise the intensity of X-ray diffraction, as well as the level of excitation, thereby ensuring the best possible contrast between excited and ground state.

Prof. Coppens addressed Dr Techert: You asked why Cole *et al.* need a power as high as 50 µJ per pulse. We have used 200 µJ per pulse on a 50 µm crystal and found this to give a marginal photon/molecule ratio, so in fact more than 50 µJ per pulse is needed. This leads to the next question. How did you get away with a lower power pulse in the DMABN experiment?

Dr Techert responded: In the experiments reported till now[1,2] the samples were prepared in such a way that the size of the crystalline powder sample never reached the upper limit of 1 µm guaranteeing an optical density of less than 1. Having such small samples (and calculating the number of chromophores per unit volume), higher laser power than the reported one was not necessary for an efficient excitation.

1 S. Techert, F. Schotte and M. Wulff, *Phys. Rev. Lett.*, 2001, **86**(10), 2030.
2 G. Busse, T. Tschentscher, A. Plech, M. Wulff, B. Frederichs and S. Techert, paper presented at this meeting..

Prof. Moffat addressed Dr Cole: (i) Are your crystals optically isotropic or anisotropic? (ii) What is the polarization of the incident laser beam? How do (i) and (ii) affect the ability to uniformly stimulate the molecules in the crystal, in all orientations?

Dr Cole responded: (i) They are probably anisotropic. (ii) A vertically polarised beam was used, arriving at the sample from above at an angle of 45 degrees.

The level of excitation is therefore likely to vary with changing orientation of the sample, since excitation is based on the transition molecular dipole moment of the molecule. This varying level of excitation may be averaged out, but it is possible to correct for the geometrical effect if one knows the faces of the crystal at two given oscillation angles.

Prof. Helliwell commented: On your data collection strategy, atomic resolution with Laue is possible.[1]

1 See D. Gomez de Anderez, M. Helliwell, J. Habash, E. J. Dodson, J. R. Helliwell, P. D. Bailey and R. E. Gammon, *Acta Crystallogr., Sect. B*, 1989, **45**, 482–488; M. Helliwell, D. Gomez de Anderez, J. Habash, J. R. Helliwell and J. Vernon, *Acta Crystallogr., Sect. B*, 1989, **45**, 591–596.

Dr Cole responded: Yes, atomic resolution is of course possible for small molecule compounds. However, better resolution is generally achieved using the monochromatic oscillatory method, since this is void of any problems of wavelength overlap and the more restricted coverage of the Ewald sphere, common in Laue experiments.

Prof. Helliwell said: The monochromatic rotating single crystal method will be very sensitive to unit cell changes, unlike Laue geometry, and thus could provoke intensity change errors. (I agree of course that the stroboscopic approach creates a stable transient species for which the conventional monochromatic approach is definitely suited.)

Dr Techert said: Three years ago we tried to investigate at ID09b of the ESRF time-resolved Laue diffraction on small molecules (in collaboration with Dr S. Arzt). However, at that time with the old set-up, the collected Laue pattern (unit cell size of the system of investigation: about $20 \times 30 \times 20$ Å^3) contained 10–20 diffraction spots and we were not able to index the Laue pattern with the available software. Today, the beamline as well as the software have been improved and further attempts would be useful.

Prof. Coppens said: I would like to clear up a possible misconception about the effect of a cell dimension change on the accuracy of the monochromatic stroboscopic method. In fact two diffraction patterns are measured by alternate light-on light-off measurements; each can be integrated separately with the appropriate cell dimension, if the change is indeed sufficiently large to warrant such a treatment. So there is no reduction in accuracy of the results associated with the change in cell dimensions. It is of course necessary to take a change in cell dimensions into account when transferring ground state molecular geometry from a dark experiment to the light-on structure.

Prof. Cernik asked: Are third generation SR sources the best way to achieve short bunch structure as the pulse length is limited by the RF structure? What are the possibilities of using FELs or the lower stimulated femtosecond X-ray[1] at ALS?

1   For example, R. W. Schoenlein, S. Chattopadhyay, H. H. W. Chong, T. E. Glover, P. A. Heimann, W. P. Leemans, C. V. Shank, A. Zholents and M. Zolotorev, *Appl. Phys. B*, 2000, **71**, 1–10.

Dr Cole replied: The use of FELs are likely to provide X-rays that are too damaging for the crystal, and the ALS developments for achieving femtosecond X-rays are said to give too low flux. I refer to the paper of Moffat presented in this Discussion Meeting where the viability of these options are specifically discussed [see the section 'Ultra-fast time-resolved X-ray experiments', part (a)].

Prof. Moffat said: Femtosecond laser based "slicing" of 100 fs synchrotron X-ray pulses[1] is indeed feasible; but the number of X-rays emitted by the perturbed "slice" is small; too small for all but experiments that have very strong scatterers or absorbers. The fs free electron laser looks like a more promising route to short X-ray pulses (which are also extremely intense, with full temporal and spatial coherence).

1   R. W. Schoenlein, W. P. Leemans, A. H. Chin, P. Volfbeyn, T. E. Glover, P. Balling, M. Zolotorev, K.-J. Kim, S. Chattopadhyay and C. V. Shank, *Science*, 1996, **274**, 236–238.

Prof. Moffat opened the discussion of Prof. Helliwell's paper: With the benefit of hindsight, this is a remarkably complicated reaction with numerous chemically-distinct microstates. Nevertheless, the crystals are active. Please comment on the overall suitability and/or desirability of this system for time-resolved studies.

Prof. Helliwell responded: I agree that this is a complicated reaction but hydroxymethylbilane synthase (HMBS, EC 4.3.1.8) is a very important enzyme[1,2] because of its fundamental position in the metabolism of all organisms, except viruses, in the production of haem, vitamin B$_{12}$, chlorophyll *etc*. The complexity of the reaction constitutes a challenge, to all available techniques, to examine the enzyme's structure and function if we are to understand it.

Time-resolved crystallographic studies are a valuable option for the following reasons: (i) HMBS is a rather slow enzyme ($k_{cat} = 0.1$ s^{-1} for HMBS from *E. coli* under optimal conditions) and can therefore readily be examined under pre-steady-state conditions; (ii) the substrate can gain access to the crystalline enzyme's active site which is open to the solvent channels of the crystal; (iii) the crystal habit has a favourable shape (thin plates) for quick diffusion of small molecules into the crystal so that the flow-cell method of reaction initiation would work; (iv) the time-dependent changes of electron density are expected to be substantial, as movements of a number of aromatic rings are involved during a single, polymerisation-like, catalytic cycle (see Fig. 1 of our paper); (v) the crystals are relatively resistant to white radiation and the crystal mosaicity remains small also even after substrate diffusion and colour transformation from colourless to red have occurred; (vi) several mutant variants of HMBS have been constructed that exhibit altered reaction kinetics; among these is the Lys59Glu mutant known to accumulate ES$_2$ as a predominant intermediate (after 2 min for Lys59Gln HMBS immobilised on an anion-exchange column).[3] These are technical feasibility reasons of choice. In addition it is worth emphasising that there are no good competitive inhibitors of HMBS known that could allow traditional inhibitor soak experiments followed by crystallographic analysis to determine the location of the inhibitor in the active site in three-dimensional space; a new approach was needed.

The fruits of the time-resolved Laue protein crystallography approach thus far are: (i) the three-dimensional binding site for substrate and/or product within the enzyme active site has been experimentally located; (ii) protein engineering results, namely that mutations of Asp 84, Arg 149, Arg 155, *i.e.* residues proximal to the elongated electron density, which are known to affect the various stages of the enzyme reaction, are supported; (iii) the present results now guide future experiments, involving *e.g.* when to freeze-trap the reaction in the crystal, and provide the basis for further efforts to determine the function of the mobile loop of residues 43 to 59. Overall the HMBS enzyme structure–function relationship, including the correlation of electron density changes with the colour transformation from colourless to red in the crystal, has been successfully probed by direct experiment.

1 A. R. Battersby, C. J. R. Fookes, G. W. J. Matcham and E. McDonald, *Nature*, 1980, **285**, 17–21.
2 A. R. Battersby and F. J. Leeper, *Chem. Rev.*, 1990, **90**, 1261–1274.
3 A. C. Niemann, P. K. Matzinger and A. Hädener, *Helv. Chim. Acta*, 1994, **77**, 1791–1809.

Prof. Wilson asked: What is the rationale for the difference in timescales for the build-up of enzyme–substrate complexes (2 h in the diffraction *cf.* 2–10 min expected)? Is this a solid state effect (*e.g.* compared with solution)?

Prof. Helliwell answered: There may be several reasons as to why the elongated electron density builds up slowly in the enzyme active site: (i) the crystal lattice may restrict conformational change(s) for optimal enzyme reaction; (ii) the pH at which the crystals are grown is non-optimal for the enzyme reaction; (iii) the delivery of the substrate to the enzyme active site through the solvent channels of the crystal may cause delay (however, as Helliwell *et al.*[1] analyse, the HMBS crystal habit of thin parallelepipeds, 50 μm thick, and the substrate size are estimated to facilitate diffusion of PBG into the crystal in seconds. The flow delivers approximately one substrate molecule per enzyme molecule per second which is far in excess of what Lys59Gln HMBS, even if it were to be saturated with substrate, can turn over at room temperature and pH 5.3). Reason (ii) above is probably the most likely but since the crystals are not stable at the enzyme's optimum pH this is not testable.

1 J. R. Helliwell, Y.-P. Nieh, J. Raftery, A. Cassetta, J. Habash, P. D. Carr, T. Ursby, M. Wulff, A. W. Thompson, A. C. Niemann and A. Hädener, *J. Chem. Soc., Faraday Trans.*, 1998, **94**, 2615–2622.

Prof. J. C. Smith asked: Is the reason that the 'missing loop' remained undetected that there is static disorder in the crystal at low temperatures *i.e.*, the loop is trapped in different energy minima, and, if so, might there be a diffuse scattering signature for this disorder?

Prof. Helliwell replied: This is possible but the specific-to-this-loop diffuse scattering signature is likely to be difficult to extricate from other contributors to the X-ray background notably from solvent and the rest of the protein diffuse scattering. Nevertheless it is an interesting suggestion especially if it were possible to make some of the residues on the loop selenomethionine variants (*i.e.* those that are hydrophobic could be substituted by selenomethionine). Then the diffraction recorded at two wavelengths, at the f' dip of the selenium K edge and a 'remote' wavelength, would allow a difference, $\Delta f'$, diffuse scattering pattern to be measured. The precise localization of the loop from such measurements would be difficult but could involve matching to computational models to ascertain where the loop might be. This is an interesting suggestion. Thank you.

Mr Teriete said: On the flexible loop, are there any glycines or prolines on dominant start and end positions, where the glycines could work as hinges or the proline cause an alteration between two conformations, through *cis–trans* isomerisation?

Prof. Helliwell replied: The *E. coli* loop amino acid sequence is, starting from residue 43, Thr-Arg-Gly-Asp-Val-Ile-Leu-Asp-Thr-Pro-Leu-Ala-Lys-Val-Gly-Gly-Lys, *i.e.* finishing with residue 59. So, 'yes' there are glycines located at putative hinge positions to facilitate conformational change. Regarding prolines, it is established that these (staying in *trans*-configuration) tend to restrict conformational change of a polypeptide.[1] The proline near the centre of the mobile loop may therefore restrict conformational freedom near this part of the loop. *Cis–trans* isomerisation, however, as you suggested, seems unlikely to me, since *cis*-prolines are quite rarely found in proteins (within a database of 571 representative proteins, only 5,2% of the Xaa-Pro peptide bonds are in *cis*-, the rest are in the *trans*-configuration.[2] It is notable also that the conserved residues between HMBS from *E. coli* and *M. tuberculosis* here are Thr 43, Gly 45, Asp 46, Pro 52, Ala 54, and Gly 57 (*E. coli* numbering).

1 C. Branden and J. Tooze, *Introduction to Protein Structure*, Garland Publishing, New York, 1991, p. 259.
2 M. S. Weiss, A. Jabs and R. Hilgenfeld, *Nature Struct. Biol.*, 1998, **5**, 676.

Prof. J. C. Smith asked: Is time-resolved solution X-ray scattering sensitive enough to resolve the inter-domain changes you are looking for?

Prof. Helliwell answered: Time-resolved solution small angle X-ray scattering (SAXS), involving synchrotron radiation, could resolve changes in radius of gyration of around 1 Å. This might not be enough but perhaps more helpful is the current practice in SAXS of recording as high angle diffraction as possible. Thus the shape of the protein is estimated.[1] Inter-domain movements could lead to significant changes of the HMBS protein shape. It is nevertheless a challenging experiment.

1 D. I. Svergun, *J. Appl. Cryst.*, 2000, **33**, 530–534.

Prof. Moore said: I am interested in the influence of pH in this system because the cofactor has four carboxylic acid groups and the substrate and product also have carboxylic acid groups. (i) Is the enzyme activity pH dependent? (ii) What are the pK_a values of the cofactor, substrate and product substituents? I imagine they will be 5–5.6 in the absence of carboxylate–carboxylate electrostatic interactions (which could be substantial). (iii) Was the pH of the crystallisation solution 5.3? (iv) Do you have a mixture of forms in the crystal, and could this contribute to disorder thus making the 'loop' invisible in the electron density map?

Dr Hädener replied: (i) At 37 °C, the optimal pH for wild-type HMBS from *E. coli* is 7.4, with values for k_{cat} and K_m being 0.1 s^{-1} and 7 μM, respectively, but the enzyme still exhibits *ca.* 20% of its maximal activity at pH 6.2 and at pH 8.7.[1,2] At pH 7.4, the Lys59Gln mutation does not affect k_{cat} but it increases K_m approximately 30-fold.[2] At room temperature and pH 5.3, the kinetic parameters of crystalline Lys59Gln HMBS can be estimated to be $K_m \geqslant 1.9$ mM and $k_{cat} \leqslant 1.9 \times 10^{-3}$ s^{-1}.[3]

(ii) The pK_a values of the substrate (PBG) are known. They are 10.1 (aminomethyl substituent), 4.95 (propionic acid substituent), and 3.70 (acetic acid substituent).[4] The formation of a favourable ion pair between the negatively charged acetate substituent and the protonated aminomethyl side chain[5] is probably the reason for the latter low value. The pK_a values of the substituents of the cofactor and of the product (HMB) have not been determined as far as I know. The formation of intramolecular ion pairs is not possible in the HMB case, so you would expect the pK_a values to be around 5 including those of the acetic acid substituents, in the absence of the enzyme and in the absence, as you said, of carboxylate–carboxylate electrostatic interactions. In the case of the cofactor and enzyme-bound PBG and HMB, however, ion-pair formation between the carboxylate groups and positively charged side chains of amino acids may have a substantial influence on individual pK_a values.

(iii) This is correct.

(iv) This may well be the case. There are a number of charged residue side chains in the mobile loop (aspartates and lysines, two each, and one arginine). They are disordered in the structure of the holoenzyme but during catalysis they may find a suitable charged group for ion pairing among those of the growing oligopyrrole or of the side chains of amino acids.

1   G. J. Hart, C. Abell and A. R. Battersby, *Biochem. J.*, 1986, **240**, 273–276.
2   A. Hädener, P. R. Alefounder, G. J. Hart, C. Abell and A. R. Battersby, *Biochem. J.*, 1990, **271**, 487–491.
3   J. R. Helliwell, Y.-P. Nieh, J. Raftery, A. Cassetta, J. Habash, P. D. Carr, T. Ursby, M. Wulff, A. W. Thompson, A. C. Niemann and A. Hädener, *J. Chem. Soc., Faraday Trans.*, 1998, **94**, 2615–2622.
4   S. Granick and L. Bogorad, *J. Am. Chem. Soc.*, 1953, **75**, 3610.
5   P. M. Jordan, in *The Biosynthesis of the Tetrapyrrole Pigments*, ed. D. J. Chadwick and K. Ackrill, 1994, Ciba Foundation Symposium, vol. 180, pp. 70–89, Wiley, Chichester.

Dr Techert asked: What is the biological reason for the unusually low k_{cat} value of 0.1 s^{-1}?

Dr Hädener answered: The product of the reaction, hydroxymethylbilane (HMB), is not stable at physiological conditions. With release of H_2O, it cyclises to uroporphyrinogen I with a half-life of less than 5 min.[1] Uroporphyrinogen I, however, is not an intermediate of the biosynthetic pathway leading to the tetrapyrrolic pigments. An isomer of it in which ring D (see Fig. 1 of our paper) is rearranged, uroporphyrinogen III, is the true intermediate.[2] A companion enzyme, formerly called 'cosynthetase', now uroporphyrinogen III synthase, has evolved to take charge of HMB by ring-closing it at high rate to the correct isomer uroporphyrinogen III with release of H_2O. Uroporphyrinogen III synthases exhibit relatively high k_{cat} values such as 500 s^{-1} for the enzyme from *E. coli*.[3] The evolutionary aspects of the biosynthetic pathway of which this enzyme system is part have been thoroughly discussed by Eschenmoser.[4]

1   A. R. Battersby, C. J. R. Fookes, K. E. Gustafson-Potter, E. McDonald and G. W. J. Matcham, *J. Chem. Soc., Perkin Trans. I*, 1982, 2427–2444.
2   A. R. Battersby, C. J. R. Fookes, G. W. J. Matcham and E. McDonald, *Nature*, 1980, **285**, 17–21.
3   A. F. Alwan, B. I. A. Mgbeje and P. M. Jordan, *Biochem. J.*, 1989, **264**, 397.
4   A. Eschenmoser, *Angew. Chem. Int. Ed. Engl.*, 1988, **27**, 5–39.

Prof. Watts asked: So the HMBS constitutes the rate limiting and regulating step for the much faster subsequent reactions?

Dr Hädener replied: This is certainly true regarding the conversion of PBG to uroporphyrinogen III. There are, however, preceding reactions that are precisely regulated to control the entire pathway leading to the tetrapyrroles by preventing even the formation of PBG if it is not needed. This regulation affects *e.g.* porphobilinogen synthase, 5-aminolevulinate synthase, and, in plants and many anaerobic bacteria, glutamyl-tRNA^{Glu} reductase and glutamate-tRNA ligase, which are all inhibited by haem.[1] A reason for the prevention of PBG being accumulated *in vivo* might be its intrinsic lability with respect to oligomerisation.[2,3]

1   G. Michal, *Biochemical Pathways*, Spektrum Akademischer Verlag, Heidelberg, 1999.
2   G. H. Cookson and C. Rimington, *Biochem. J.*, 1954, **57**, 476–484.
3   D. Mauzerall, *J. Am. Chem. Soc.*, 1960, **82**, 2605–2609.

Prof. Watts opened the discussion of Prof. Moore's paper: In Fig. 4 of your paper, you indicate far less α-helix structure from the NMR data, than shown in the modes or crystal structures of related colicins. Why?

Prof. Moore responded: The only relevant X-ray structure for Fig. 4 is the structure in Fig. 1 of the paper. This shows a high content of helix in the min-R region of the protein. Fig. 4 is the output of the chemical shift index, which is a conservative empirical procedure for obtaining information on secondary structures from NMR chemical shifts. This procedure requires a run of NMR data for four or more sequential residues to all indicate a helix before one is indicated. Because of the incomplete resonance assignment for min-R we cannot provide a complete secondary structure map for it. However, what information the CSI does provide is fully consistent with the X-ray structure of Fig. 1; and with the shape analyses and relaxation time study later in the paper that provides strong confirmation that min-R has a helix–loop–helix structure.

Prof. Finney asked: What relationship do you expect between the two conformers and the structure determined crystallographically? Are the structural differences between the two conformers such that you might expect both of them to be accommodated within the crystal, or force the selection of one of them?

Prof. Moore replied: In connection with the DNase domain of colicin E9 referred to in the Introduction to the paper, one possibility is that there is only a small difference between the two conformers in solution,[1] with both co-existing in the crystal though the quality of the crystallographic electron-density map is not sufficient to resolve the different conformers. A second possibility is that the crystallisation process selects only one of the two conformers. At present we don't know which happens but we do know from NMR data that the difference between the conformers is very small and so I favour the first possibility. Another possibility is that the X-ray structure was determined at 100 K (ref. 2) while the NMR data were measured at room temperature. Perhaps at 100 K the protein preferentially populates the lowest energy conformer?

The story with the conformers on the min-R protein that is the subject of the paper is different. The X-ray structure is only at 3 Å resolution, and it is for a full-length protein while the NMR study was carried out on a fragment of the structure. So the conformational exchange we detect by NMR may be a consequence of min-R being a sub-domain of the coiled-coil or it may be a feature of the coiled-coil itself with the X-ray structure not revealing it because it has a relatively low resolution. We plan to carry out NMR studies of the full-length coiled-coil domain and these should show whether the two conformers are an intrinsic property of it.

1 S. B.-M. Whittaker, M. Czisch, R. Wechselberger, R. Kaptein, A. M. Hemmings, R. James, C. Kleanthous and G. R. Moore, *Protein Sci.*, 2000, **9**, 713.
2 C. Kleanthous, U. C. Kühlmann, A. J. Pommer, N. Ferguson, S. E. Radford, G. R. Moore, R. James and A. M. Hemmings, *Nature Struct. Biol.*, 1999, **6**, 243.

Prof. J. C. Smith asked: Could you comment on ways of analysing the contribution of internal motion to NMR spin relaxation in terms of collective dynamical variables, such as that being developed by Brueschweiler *et al.*—this may be a way of linking the relaxation results to the interdomain dynamics you appear to have identified here.

Prof. Moore answered: I can't give a full answer to your question, partly because the approach advocated by Prompers and Brüschweiler has only recently appeared in the literature.[1] Nuclear spin relaxation results from the modulation of inter-nuclear interactions by motions of the nuclei, and relevant motional modes are the overall tumbling of the protein and independent nuclear motion, usually described as internal motions. In order to define the internal motions of amino acid residues, which are really the dynamic information we seek, we have to be able to separate the contributions these two factors make to the experimentally determined relaxation parameters. There are a number of approaches for analysing the contribution of internal motions to NMR spin relaxation, with the Lipari–Szabo 'model-free' formalism[2,3] most widely used. The usual starting point for model-free analysis is to decide which residues have relaxation characteristics determined by the overall protein tumbling rate and using these to determine the rotational correlation time.[4] Those residues with significant internal motion can then be characterised. This benchmarking process is a key stage of the analysis and if it looks as if all the residues have internal motion then alternative procedures, such as reduced spectral density mapping,[1,5] is employed. This is less powerful than the model-free approach in the details it provides, but for disordered proteins in particular it is the most widely used approach. A key feature of the method described by Prompers and Brüschweiler[1] is that it does not require separation of the residues into those whose relaxation parameters are affected only by the overall tumbling of the molecule and those with significant additional internal motions. This seems to offer a substantial advance over other methods. However, it does involve molecular dynamics simulations in the analysis so it is not as straight-forward to apply as the model-free or reduced spectral density mapping approaches.

1. J. J. Pompers and R. Brüschweiler, *J. Am. Chem. Soc.*, 2002, **124**, 4522.
2. G. Lipari and A. Szabo, *J. Am. Chem. Soc.*, 1982, **104**, 4546.
3. For example, A. G. Palmer III, *Curr. Opin. Struct. Biol.*, 1997, **7**, 732; V. A. Feher and J. Cavanagh, *Nature*, 1999, **400**, 289.
4. N. Tjandra, S. E. Feller, R. W. Pastor and A. Bax, *J. Am. Chem. Soc.*, 1995, **117**, 12562.
5. J. F. Lefevre, K. T. Daye, J. W. Peng and G. Wagner, *Biochemistry*, 1996, **35**, 2674.

Dr Sagi said: One of the main goals in biocatalysis or bio-molecular recognition processes is to correlate dynamics with the actual biological process (*e.g.* catalysis, molecular recognition). However, NMR probes only equilibrium states therefore one cannot really probe a real molecular recognition process or catalysis and correlate then with dynamics. How much can we stretch NMR to give direct information about correlating catalysis with dynamics?

Prof. Moore replied: You are right to say that NMR is looking at equilibrium states—to use Prof. Helliwell's analogy, the cliff edge and the beach. NMR is too slow to measure what happens to a body after it has jumped off the cliff until it lands on the beach, but what it can do is to characterise—sometimes in considerable kinetic and structural detail—dynamic processes taking place before the jump. With some proteins such dynamic processes are extremely significant for determining molecular recognition events, and in some enzymes a relationship between such dynamics and catalysis has been suggested. The clearest examples of dynamics affecting molecular recognition involve proteins that only fold into a globular form when they bind to their partner[1]— so-called intrinsically disordered[2] or natively unfolded proteins.[3] Coupling of protein folding to intermolecular complex formation has only been discovered to be a widespread phenomenon with the development of NMR spectroscopy for studying proteins and with estimates that as many as 50% of the proteins in humans contain at least one domain that is intrinsically disordered[2] this is clearly an important field. The way in which a newly synthesized protein folds from its unfolded state to its folded form is related to intermolecular interactions involving at least one disordered protein—in this case the interacting surface is intramolecular—and again NMR is one of the major experimental methods for determining what is happening to the polypeptide chain at key stages of the folding process. Of course, protein folding is generally very rapid so NMR is limited in the states it can inform on, but it is already clear from NMR studies of unfolded protein chains that some are not random coils, even at low pH[4] or in high urea of guanidine·HCl concentrations.[5] Colicin E9 is a member of a related class of natively unfolded protein that interacts with other proteins in that its unfolded domain contains some ordered non-random structure that is highly dynamic and forms the binding epitope for its partner protein.[6] Our NMR studies have shown that even when a ternary protein complex of 114 kDa is formed that anchors the previously dynamic binding epitope, the residues upstream and downstream of it retain considerable flexibility.[6] We have speculated that this is because this region is like a fishing line, with many hooks on it to bind to specific proteins in constructing a complex of many proteins; however, the biophysical characterization has moved ahead of the biological studies and additional interaction partners have not yet been identified. Even when the binding of a protein to a partner molecule does not involve folding of the protein, NMR relaxation studies are providing new insights into the molecular recognition events,[7] which include not only identification of residues that interact with the partner molecule but also information on changes in conformational entropy of the protein on binding obtained in a residue-specific fashion. Investigating catalytic events themselves is as difficult with NMR as it is with any structural technique, and perhaps even more so. However, as indicated above, NMR is giving unique information on the dynamics of enzyme interactions with inhibitors and substrate analogues,[7] and coupled with other data, including that obtained with site-directed mutagenesis, I believe that NMR will turn out to be valuable for characterising catalytic events. Crucially, as my answer to Prof. Smith indicated, this application of NMR will benefit considerably from being combined with theoretical studies of protein dynamics, which themselves may be tested by spectroscopic examination of mutants.

1. H. J. Dyson and P. E. Wright, *Curr. Opin. Struct. Biol.*, 2002 **12**, 54.
2. A. K. Dunker, C. J. Brown, J. D. Lawson, L. M. Iakoucheva and Z. Obradović, *Biochemistry*, 2002, **41**, 6573.
3. V. N. Uversky, *Eur. J. Biochem.*, 2002, **269**, 2.
4. J. Yao, J. Chung, D. Eliezer, P. E. Wright and H. J. Dyson, *Biochemistry*, 2001, **40**, 3561.
5. J. Klein-Seetharaman, M. Oikawa, S. B. Grimshaw, J. Wirmer, E. Duchardt, T. Ueda, T. Imoto, L. J. Smith, C. M. Dobson and H. Schwalbe, *Science*, 2002, **295**, 1719.
6. E. S. Collins, S. B.-M. Whittaker, K. Tozawa, C. MacDonald, R. Boetzel, C. N. Penfold, A. Reilly, N. J. Clayden, M. J. Osborne, A. M. Hemmings, C. Kleanthous, R. James and G. R. Moore, *J. Mol. Biol.*, 2002, **318**, 787.
7. V. A. Feher and J. Cavanagh, *Nature*, 1999, **400**, 289; J. J. A. Huntley, S. D. B. Scrofani, M. J. Osborne, P. E. Wright and H. J. Dyson, *Biochemistry*, 2000, **39**, 13 356; R. Ishima and D. A. Torchia, *Nature Struct. Biol.*, 2000, **7**, 74; A. J. Wand, *Nature Struct. Biol.*, 2001, **8**, 926; F. A. A. Mulder, A. Mittermaier, B. Hon, F. W. Dahlquist and L. E. Kay, *Nature Struct. Biol.*, 2001, **8**, 932.

Prof. Wilson said: You mentioned that the function in this system involves allowing a 100 Å coiled coil to traverse a 150 Å cell membrane. How are the dynamics you have elucidated related to this function?

Prof. Moore replied: How the dynamics of the helix–loop–helix region of the receptor binding domain we have observed relate to the activity of the colicin is not clear at present. The relatively high degree of flexibility of the inter-helix loop compared to the remainder of the coiled-coil might be connected to the loop being part of the binding site for the BtuB receptor on the outer membrane of the target cell, as indicated by site-directed mutagenesis studies.[1,2] As we have discussed already (in the discussion with Dr Sagi), flexibility in an intermolecular interaction site may help in the recognition events leading to the complex formation.

Perhaps it is more interesting to consider whether the coiled-coil unfurls. This is our current hypothesis[3], which assumes that the helices remain largely intact, partly because they are interacting with other proteins in the system (including the outer membrane receptor BtuB and periplasmic Tol proteins). If the helices of the now unfurled coiled-coil remain attached helices, and one of them extends into the periplasm from the loop of the min-R region attached to BtuB it will not be long enough to cross to the inner membrane unless the periplasm is reduced from its normal size. This occurs at contact points. Alternatively, the helix may partly or completely unwind, which would give it sufficient length to cross the periplasm. This is something we are studying with a combined luminescence spectroscopy and protein engineering approach. In the NMR studies reported in this paper we have detected that the two helices of the min-R helix–loop–helix sub-domain move relative to each other in a way that retains the helix–loop–helix structure; and possibly the two helices slide across the surfaces of each other. Such motion may be related to events that lead to unfurling of the coiled-coil in the colicin, though in our model binding to a receptor is the key event that triggers this unfurling and it is not an intrinsic feature of the unbound colicin.

1. S. Soelaiman, K. Jakes, N. Wu, C. Li and M. Shoham, *Mol. Cell*, 2001, **8**, 1053.
2. C. N. Penfold, C. Garinot-Schneider, A. M. Hemmings, G. R. Moore, C. Kleanthous and R. James *Mol. Microbiol.*, 2000, **38**, 639.
3. R. James, C. N. Penfold, G. R. Moore and C. Kleanthous, *Biochimie*, 2002, in press.

Mr Teriete asked: Has dynamic data been gathered on the loop, which is believed to be involved in the activity, by using RDCs?

Prof. Moore answered: Not yet.

Prof. Watts opened the discussion of Prof. Finney's paper: All co-operative transitions have an on-set and completion point. Yours are defined by the dynamic range of the method in some cases, in others, only a single transition is observed. But there must be a tool where the whole dynamic range is concerned and onset and completion are encompassed for this 220 K transition, or perhaps not.

Prof. Finney responded: We are not aware of any experimental technique that can give such information across the whole dynamic range. Encompassing the whole dynamic range implies, in neutron scattering parlance, elucidation of the elastic incoherent scattering function which is determined by the infinite time limit of the van Hove single particle space–time distribution function. Accurate determination of this is possible in some systems where the relaxation times are well within reach of the instruments concerned. For protein solutions the range of motions is such that it has not yet been possible to reach this limit with neutron techniques alone. A range of experiments will be required.

Dr Schmidt said: Data shown trace Doster and Settles:[1] On IN13 and IN6 at the ILL, all data show the same transition temperature despite different time scales. The Mossbauer data from Parak and Knapp[2] show the same transition point at 180–190 K. What type of motions do you expect, which account for your transitions? Are these transitions motions of the entire molecule, or are these motions of domains of the molecule?

1 W. Doster and M. Settles, The dynamical transition in proteins: the role of hydrogen bonds, 1998; Les Houches Lectures: workshop on hydration processes in biology: theoretical and experimental approaches, ed. M. C. Bellisent-Funel and J. Teixera, IOS Press.
2 F. Parak and E. W. Knapp, *Proc. Natl. Acad. Sci. USA*, 1984, **81**, 7088–7092.

Prof. Finney and **Prof. J. C. Smith** responded: IN6 and IN13 measure motions on very similar time scales, so you would not expect to get a large change in the apparent temperature of the dynamical transition. The measurements you mention are taken on samples at low hydration, while the ones discussed in our paper are in solution, where the behaviour is likely to be different (as we find it is experimentally). Moreover, the method used to determine the mean-square displacements in the paper cited is unclear. IN13 in principle works only at relatively high Q, where the Gaussian approximation for individual atoms fails—this is required for a model-free determination of mean-square displacements. Concerning the kinds of motions involved, determining these is one of the objects of the work. The experimental technique measures motions of all the non-exchanged hydrogen atoms of the enzymes, and hence averages over the whole molecule.

Prof. Sir John Meurig Thomas said: Your arguments, which seem to me to be convincing, would become irrefutable if you (or others) were to try and do measurements of the onset of anharmonicity and of the change of enzymatic activity under *in situ* conditions. This is obviously not an easy thing to do; but one of the reasons for discussion such as this is to identify crucial (time-resolved) experiments. Could you comment on that?

Prof. Finney‡ replied: We have tried this. The 'fastest' enzyme known is catalase. We have measured its activity down to 173 K, and see no deviation from that expected from Arrhenius behaviour. 173 K does appear to be well below the onset of anharmonicity for all proteins looked at so far. However, the assay at 173 K requires ~10 h to obtain measurable product. Nanosecond assays appear to be quite out of reach with current technology.

In these circumstances, where it is not possible to measure both dynamics and activity at the same time, it is crucial that the neutron measurements are made under the same conditions as those under which the activity is measured. This was an important aspect of our experimental protocol: the solvents in which the neutron measurements were made were those in which activity was measured at these temperatures. To ensure that the enzymes were still active after the neutron experiments, the samples were recovered and assayed subsequently, confirming that they retained their activity.

Dr Cole said: The error bar at 200 K on Fig. 1 is notably larger than any other in the graph. Since this temperature pertains to the vicinity of the transition, is the size of the error bar a physical consequence of the transition is some way, or does it show the model breaking down here, or does it just emanate from an experimental effect?

---

‡ Also Prof. R. M. Daniel, University of Waikato, New Zealand.

Prof. Finney answered: The error bars on the points relate to those estimated by the extrapolation procedure described in the paper, and for the point you mention, the errors were larger for experimental reasons. This larger error may relate to the phase behaviour of the solvent, though this is not definite. However, the determination of the temperature of the so-called transition does not really depend on this one point. As is seen from a number of papers in which a transition temperature is assigned, it is obtained rather by drawing straight lines to the data above and below the transition, estimating the transition temperature as that at which these lines cross. The points in the vicinity of the transition have little effect on this geometrical construction.

Prof. Watts addressed Dr Cole: In any transition phenomenon, there are highly disordered intermediates formed which are neither initial nor final state related. These are often very small in population compared with the majority and can account for significant errors in determination of experimental parameters.

Prof. Helliwell addressed Prof. Finney: (i) Re Fig. 1 of the paper: Isn't the functional assay resting on the last data point (that the enzyme behaviour is Arrhenius over the full temperature range)?
(ii) Is the xylanase also from a thermophile (*i.e.* Zaccai is saying (personal communication) that the stiffness of proteins in extremophiles is higher and therefore you could look at non-extremophiles too)?

Prof. Finney and **Prof. J. C. Smith**§ responded: (i) I don't think so. Close examination of the figure shows that there are several data points at temperatures lower than the 220 K transition. These show no deviation from linearity. If there were a deviation from Arrhenius behaviour in this region, these results would have shown it.

(ii) The xylanase was from a thermophile. I would point out however that we started out using thermophiles for these measurements as it was thought that their expected greater 'stiffness' might shift the transition temperature upwards, which would ease the enzymology. However, where we have taken measurements on equivalent thermophilic and mesophilic enzymes, we find no measurable difference in their dynamic behaviours as measured by these techniques. Thus we find no evidence for greater 'stiffness' as measured by transition temperature of the thermophiles. Furthermore, other comparative activity measurements on non-thermophile enzymes give similar results.[1,2]

1   J. M. Bragger, R. V. Dunn and R. M. Daniel, *Biochim. Biophys. Acta*, 2000, **1480**, 278–282.
2   N. More, R. M. Daniel and H. Petach, *Biochem. J.* 1995, **305**, 17–20.

Prof. Moore said: (i) Dehydrating proteins can perturb properties even though they may appear to be active. I recall that Kaminsky *et al.*[1] reported freeze-dried cytochrome *c* on dissolving in water undergoes a structural change detected spectroscopically, even though the dehydrated protein retains electron-transfer capability. (ii) In your 70% CH_3OH/30% H_2O solutions how is the protein solvated? Does it have a water shell surrounded by H_2O/CH_3OH?

1   S. Kaminsky, K. M. Ivanetich and T. E. King, *Biochemistry*, 1974, **13**, 4866.

Prof. Finney replied: (i) There is a significant amount of data looking at changes in protein structure on dehydration. In summary, it seems that these are generally quite small (see *e.g.* ref. 1 and 2), though they may have functional significance.

(ii) This is an interesting observation, and is discussed in an earlier paper on the solvent dependence of the enzyme dynamics.[3] Interestingly, we found that the dynamics did not vary significantly with methanol concentration except when going to pure D_2O. One possible interpretation of this observation is that the solvent in the near neighbourhood of the protein is relatively unperturbed by the change in concentration of the bulk, but there may well be other interpretations of the observation.

1   P. L. Poole and J. L. Finney, *Biopolymers*, 1983, **22**, 255.

---

§ Also Prof. R. M. Daniel, University of Waikato, New Zealand.

2   N.-T. Yu and B. H. Jo, *Arch. Biochem. Biophys.*, 1973, **156**, 469.
3   V. Réat, R. Dunn, M. Ferrand, J. L. Finney, R. M. Daniel and J. C. Smith. *Proc. Natl Acad. Sci. USA*, 2000, **97**, 9961.

Prof. Moffat said: The techniques for determining MSDs are as you state—sensitive to time scale. The activities presented by you are essentially on a single time scale for various enzyme systems. Some proteins exhibit "activity" over a very wide range of time scales, fs,µs → s, *e.g.* the individual steps in the photocycles of lR or photoactive yellow protein. Could you envisage parallel activity and dynamic measurements on such systems?

Prof. Finney replied: Enzyme activity measurements are confined to the rate limiting step (as defined by the turnover number), and these certainly vary over at least seven orders of magnitude depending upon the enzyme, and vary by another several orders of magnitude with conditions such as temperature. All other events, including all the other reaction steps, must take place over the same or shorter time scales. Ideally we need to correlate activity with a full dynamic 'spectrum' of motions, but all techniques have either time scale windows (often defined at only one end) or are time averaged. But the good news is that activity varies predictably and smoothly (in an Arrhenius sense) with temperature, suggesting that the real need may be to identify the groups/motions involved in activity rather than their time scales.

Prof. Watts said: Lets try and find out what each approach and method of the papers by Prof. Helliwell, Prof. Moore and Prof. Finney can bring to the systems we have heard about. Loops are ill defined in Prof. Helliwell's crystal structure whereas Prof. Moore defines loops, both of which are functionally important. Prof. Helliwell, what can you do for Prof. Moore's system and *vice versa*, and Prof. Finney finally, where do you see global dynamics fitting into each of these systems?

Prof. Moore responded: I have been asked how NMR could help clarify what is happening with the 'missing' loop in the X-ray data of HMBS. The first experiment would be to look at ^{15}N labelled HMBS. I would expect sharp NH ^{1}H–^{15}N HSQC peaks from the loop and broader peaks from the remainder of the protein. The cofactor NH signals may also be sharp. Peaks of the loop could be assigned from triple-resonance spectra of the ^{13}C/^{15}N labelled material (^{2}H labelling may also be needed given the 34 kDa size of HMBS—the loop residues should not need this); and backbone relaxation parameters measured for the loop with the ^{15}N labelled samples. Monitoring the loop signals during the reaction cycle, and as functions of pH and temperature, should establish whether they are playing a role in the reaction. The pK_a values of the carboxylic acid groups of the cofactor and its adducts might be determined with specifically labelled samples.

Prof. Finney commented: In general terms, the 'elastic scan' neutron scattering measurements we used in the work reported here give information on the global dynamics of the protein through the average mean square displacements. As the signal is dominated by the scattering from the hydrogen atoms, it is the motions of the non-exchangeable hydrogens on the protein that will be largely reported. As the contributions of deuterium atoms to the measured signal are much less than those of hydrogens, if the protein were selectively deuterated, then we could focus on the motions of those regions that remained hydrogenated. The time scales of the motions that can be accessed depend on the instrument used, and can broadly range from picoseconds to tens of nanoseconds. Furthermore, by making quasielastic and inelastic scattering measurements, we can also begin to obtain more detailed information on the natures of the motions involved and the density of states.

Prof. Watts said: New genetically engineered labelling methods permit protein domains to be labelled. The case of PBDG seems an ideal one where NMR visible isotopes placed specifically in the 'invisible' loop, could be studied by NMR (solution or solid state in an amorphous or semi-crystalline state) to resolve structures, or an ensemble of structures. Ligand labelling too, could help here.

Prof. Moore replied: Probably yes, a set of atomic coordinates can be determined. However, I wonder if this is what is really needed. Given the probable dynamic nature of the loop there are likely to be large uncertainties in an ensemble of structures for this. I would put the effort into the relaxation characteristics of the loop under various conditions. Perhaps the NMR and X-ray data combined might be data used in MD calculations rather than as an attempt to define the "structure" of the complete enzyme as a static entity.

Prof. Helliwell commented: A simulation approach perhaps could be the best benefit of NMR information on the loop, *i.e.* to resolve where the HMBS loop is, and its excursions. Also, the hypothesis of the role of inter-domain movements of the 3-subunit protein in the enzyme reaction could be assessed. At present, it seems, simulation cannot readily approach longer time scales than ~10 ns simulations and such a loop might be expected to have slowly moving aspects.

Prof. Helliwell addressed Prof. Moore: Re: Fig. 11 and the 3 Å X-ray structure: crystal annealing could improve the resolution of the protein crystallographic study and B factor estimates would be much better (to compare with your T_1/T_2 ratios).

Prof. Moore replied: We clearly need a better X-ray structure and more complete NMR data to fully characterise the structural dynamics of these colicins, but the comparison of X-ray B factors and T_1/T_2 ratios is suggestive. Remember that the X-ray data is for a full-length protein whilst the NMR data is for a fragment. The reduction in the T_1/T_2 ratio for residues 4 and 5, and beyond residue 70, of min-R (Fig. 11(a)) are because they are its N and C termini while the corresponding residues of colicin E3 (Fig. 11(b)) are in the middle of the coiled-coil helices!

Prof. Finney said: Neutron scattering measurements are essentially limited to probing global dynamical processes on time scales of ~1 ns or faster. Yet processes relating to the enzyme activity are likely to be occurring on slower time scales. Mössbauer offers timescales of ~10^{-7} s, but requires the presence of Fe and cannot be effectively used under solution conditions. NMR would seem to offer a way forward to both (a) probing longer time scales under realistic solution conditions and (b) (through selectively focussing on particular nuclei) probing motions locally through the enzyme. How realistic are such measurements, and how long a programme of work would be needed to characterise fully the dynamics of an enzyme of, say 50 kDa?

Prof. Moore responded: Let me rephrase your question into 3 parts and then answer them in turn. (i) Can NMR fully characterise the motions in small proteins (say up to 20 kDa)? (ii) How long would it take to do so? (iii) How feasible is it for an enzyme of 50 kDa mass?

I assume you will want to do this over the temperature range used in your neutron scattering studies to look at the dynamic transition. The first point to note is that the NMR approach I described is for solutions; solid-state NMR of proteins is a rapidly developing field but cannot yet provide a global description of protein structure and dynamics in the way that you want. The reason size of the protein is important is that the overall tumbling time of the molecule in solution is a key determinant of the nuclear relaxation properties, with slow tumbling producing efficient relaxation and broad lines. Along with the size of the protein, the viscosity of the solvent is important. If the water–alcohol mixtures you use have a viscosity at 200 K and above that allows relatively sharp NMR lines to be observed, you will be set to get the data you need with a small enzyme. This will have to be produced by an expression system that allows isotopic labelling with ^{13}C and ^{15}N; most NMR groups employ bacterial systems growing on minimal media for this. Starting from scratch with ^{13}C/^{15}N labelled samples, it will take 6–8 weeks to collect and analyse spectra that allow the NH resonances observed in the ^{1}H–^{15}N HSQC spectrum to be assigned. A further 2 weeks data collection with ^{15}N labelled samples allows the backbone ^{15}N T_1 and T_2 and ^{1}H–^{15}N nuclear Overhauser enhancements[1] to be collected at one field strength. It is likely that the level of detail you want will require the relaxation parameters to be determined with at least one other spectrometer operating at a different field strength to the first. This should also take 2 weeks. The dynamics of the side chains can be determined by ^{13}C relaxation times,[1,2] and also with selective ^{2}H labelling,[1] and both of these require samples with different isotope labelling patterns to those needed for the assignments and for ^{15}N relaxation measurements. However, provided the samples are sufficiently stable once you have them you can readily carry out a temperature dependence study. Provided the protein does not undergo substantial temperature-induced conformation changes it is unlikely that you will have to repeat much of the assignment work with $^{13}C/^{15}N$ labelled samples at each temperature. So, assuming a stable protein of less than 20 kDa at a concentration of about 1 mM it may take a year to measure the temperature dependence of the ^{15}N relaxation properties. ^2H and ^{13}C relaxation analyses will take longer. Probably you should concentrate on the backbone characteristics first to determine if the dynamic transition is reflected in these. If you pick a protein that is already well-studied by NMR then you will save time; for example, the 14 kDa hen egg white lysozyme may be suitable.

An enzyme of 50 kDa presents major problems because of slow tumbling in solution[3]. Proteins of this size have been studied by NMR but in general, in order to obtain full assignment of the NH $^1H-^{15}N$ HSQC spectrum the non-exchangeable protons of the protein have to be replaced by ^2H. NMR experiments to measure the relaxation properties of the backbone will be somewhat different to those for similar proteins in which deuteration has not been done but unlike the latter proteins, which are routinely studied in many laboratories by these approaches, deuterated proteins are still in the hands of relatively few groups. Moving onto side chain dynamics, deuterated proteins will require specific labelling protocols; for example, introducing protonated methyl groups of particular amino acids into an otherwise deuterated protein. So, the methodology may all be in place for you to characterise the global dynamics of a 50 kDa enzyme over a wide range of temperatures but note that although various groups have described methods that may lead to the fold of a large protein being determined by NMR,[4] a high-resolution NMR structure of a monomeric protein greater than 30 kDa has not been reported.

1 A. G. Palmer III, *Curr. Opin. Struct. Biol.*, 1997, **7**, 732.
2 J. Engelke and H. Rüterjans, in *Biological Magnetic Resonance: Structure Computation and Dynamics in Protein NMR*, Kluwer Academic/Kluwer Publishers, New York, 1999, vol. 17, p. 357–417.
3 K. Pervushin, *Quart. Rev. Biophys.*, 2000, **33**, 161.
4 B. T. Farmer III and R. A. Venters, *J. Biol. NMR*, 1996, **7**, 59; B. O. Smith, Y. Ito, A. Raine, S. Teichmann, L. Ben-Tovim, D. Nietlispach, R. W. Broadhurst, T. Terada, M. Kelly, H. Oschkinat, T. Shibata, S. Yokoyama and E. D. Laue, *J. Biol. NMR*, 1996, **8**, 360; W.-Y. Choy, M. Tollinger, G. A. Mueller and L. E. Kay, *J. Biol. NMR*, 2001, **21**, 31.

Mechanism of formation of DNA–cationic vesicle complexes

Paula C. A. Barreleiro,*[a] Roland P. May[b] and Björn Lindman[a]

[a] *Centre for Chemistry and Chemical Engineering, Physical Chemistry 1, University of Lund, P.O. Box 124, S-221 00, Lund, Sweden. E-mail: Paula.Barreleiro@fkem1.lu.se*
[b] *Institut Laue–Langevin, BP 156, F-38042, Grenoble Cedex, France*

Received 24th January 2002, Accepted 8th March 2002
First published as an Advance Article on the web 5th August 2002

Cationic vesicles and DNA form complexes that are promising gene delivery systems. Despite the increasing number of publications on their morphology and structure, the mechanism leading to their formation is not yet understood due to a lack of kinetic data. In the present study the kinetics of the interaction between DNA and cationic vesicles were followed using stopped-flow turbidity and small-angle neutron scattering techniques. The neutron real-time experiments were performed on a high-flux diffractometer, the D22 at the ILL, using a stopped-flow set-up. Extruded mixed vesicles of dimethyldioctadecylammonium bromide (DODAB) with various amounts of dioleoylphosphatidylethanolamine (DOPE) were investigated at 25 °C. The results show that the transition from unilamellar vesicles to a multilamellar structure upon DNA addition occurs in three steps. The first step, on the millisecond time scale, is currently not accessible to neutron scattering but was observed by stopped-flow turbidity and fluorescence experiments. The second step, on a time scale of seconds, corresponds to the formation of an intermediate with a locally cylindrical structure. As time progresses this unstable intermediate evolves to a multilamellar structure, on a time scale of minutes. An understanding of the mechanisms behind the DNA–cationic vesicle complex formation event will allow the production of more homogeneous, efficient delivery systems in pharmaceutically acceptable forms.

Introduction

DNA and cationic vesicles form complexes that are prospective candidates for gene therapy.[1] These non-viral carriers appear promising because of their simplicity, apparent lack of immunogenicity and inflammatory response, larger carrier capacity and higher fusogenic potential as compared with viral carriers. A major drawback is their low transfection efficiency. There is a lack of knowledge regarding DNA–cationic vesicle interactions, the properties of the resulting complex and the relationship between system characteristics and transfection efficiency. A significant number of studies dealing with the structure and morphology of DNA–cationic vesicle complexes have been reported. Synchrotron X-ray scattering,[2,3] cryo-transmission microscopy (TEM),[4,5] freeze–fracture electron microscopy,[6] optical and fluorescence microscopy and atomic force microscopy have given a fairly good picture of the structure of the DNA–cationic vesicle complexes as a function of the two most important parameters: vesicle composition, *e.g.*, type and quantity of the helper lipid, presence of cosurfactants and charge ratio between cationic lipid and DNA. The

DOI: 10.1039/b200796g

structures observed are not specific for a certain DNA/lipid system but have been observed for different types of DNA and different cationic and neutral lipids.

Despite the increasing number of publications describing the structure and morphology, little is known about the thermodynamics and kinetics of the formation of DNA–cationic lipid vesicle complexes. A clear definition of the pathway and associated critical parameters is lacking. This lack is partly due to the complexity of the self-assembly process and the numerous parameters that contribute to the complex formation and structure. Our goal is to study the kinetics and pathway of DNA–cationic vesicle complex formation. Here, we investigated unilamellar vesicles of DODAB containing varying amounts of DOPE prepared by extrusion. Extrusion was the method chosen to prepare the vesicles since it allows the preparation of monodisperse unilamellar vesicles of controlled size. The key role of the cationic lipid is to provide an electrostatic attraction between the vesicle and the DNA molecule. The introduction of neutral or zwitterionic lipids in the cationic vesicle has been shown to increase the transfection efficiency of the complexes *in vitro* as well as *in vivo*. However their role is not well understood. DNA–cationic vesicle complexes in aqueous solution are usually prepared by pipetting DNA solution (or cationic vesicles dispersion) into a tube containing a dispersion of cationic vesicles (or DNA solution). It was observed that the sequence of mixing as well as the speed influenced the characteristics of the lipoplex. If the mixing was fast there was a good dispersal and growth of many small complexes. Slow mixing led to a growth of larger complexes.

Recent stopped-flow fluorescence experiments have been reported by our group[7] and three time scales were obtained from the fluorescence data. However, fluorescence measurements only give information about the conformational changes of DNA, thus scattering measurements are necessary to probe the structure of the different intermediates that occur during the formation of DNA–cationic vesicle complexes.

We used small-angle neutron scattering (SANS) since it has the unique feature of providing information on each member of a multi-component mixture by adjusting the contrast.[8] Also it allows one to study native biomolecules in aqueous solution thereby eliminating structural artifacts that can be introduced for example by adding a probe. Thus, using different mixtures of normal and deuterated water we can observe separately the lipids and the DNA. Recent developments in SANS instrumentation have allowed the improvement of time and space resolution. We combined the SANS diffractometer with a stopped-flow apparatus to allow measurements at times shorter than seconds.

The knowledge of the time-dependent structural changes will contribute to future developments and biological applications of DNA–cationic vesicle complexes.

Experimental

Materials

The cationic lipid DODAB and the zwitterionic lipid DOPE with purity better than 99%, as determined by HPLC by the manufacturer, were purchased from Avanti Polar Lipids (Alabaster, AL, USA) and used without further purification. Salmon sperm DNA (2000 ± 500 bp as determined by 1% TAE agarose gel analysis and free from DNase and RNase as stated by the manufacturer) prepared from highly pure, phenol extracted DNA was purchased from Gibco, BRL. The DNA concentration was measured by its absorbance at 260 nm, $\varepsilon_{260} = 6600$ M^{-1} cm^{-1}. The ratio of the absorbance at 260 nm to that at 280 nm was about 1.8–1.9 and the absorbance at 320 nm was negligible, so no contamination by protein was observed. The conformation of DNA in aqueous solution was confirmed by circular dichroism (CD) measurements. A transition temperature of 49 °C was measured by differential scanning calorimetry.

Vesicle preparation

The vesicles were prepared by mixing the cationic and zwitterionic lipids in chloroform in the desired mole ratio. A film of the lipid mixture was made by evaporation of the chloroform under a stream of N$_2$. It was dried under vacuum overnight to remove residual organic solvent. The film was then hydrated in water and sonicated for 10 min in an ultrasound bath above the gel to liquid-crystalline phase transition temperature (T_m) to suspend the lipids. An extrusion system from Avanti Polar Lipids (Alabaster, AL, USA) was used to prepare unilamellar vesicles of the desired size. Extrusions were performed manually through two stacked 13 mm polycarbonate filters with nominal pore diameter of 200 nm, above the T_m of the lipids; the extrusion was repeated 25–29 times. An odd number of passages were used, in order to collect the solution in the syringe opposite to the one used to fill the extrusion system, to avoid the presence of multilamellar vesicles that might not have crossed the filter. After extrusion the vesicle dispersions were cooled to room temperature at which they were stored for 2 h before use. Sizes were determined by dynamic light scattering, which revealed a narrow size distribution with a variation of 10%. No multilamellar vesicles were observed by cryo-electron microscopy (cryo-TEM).

Turbidity

Kinetic recordings were obtained in a stopped-flow spectrometer (Applied Photophysics SX.18MV SK.1E). The wavelength was set to 410 nm and the temperature was 25 °C. Two important measurements to be made before using a stopped-flow instrument for the first time are those of the mixing efficiency and deadtime. The deadtime of a stopped-flow instrument is the time that elapses between mixing and observation. The dead time of the instrument was determined from a test reaction described elsewhere[9] and it was estimated to be 10 ms for a 1:1 mixing. The purpose of the mixing chamber is to induce turbulent as opposed to laminar flow. To determine experimentally that this occurs the protonation of pH indicators is used. Another common problem is the presence of air bubbles in the observation cell. These effects can be reduced by using degassed solutions. Suitable control experiments can usually indicate whether the reaction observed is a true process or an artifact. The control experiments performed were the mixing of a lipid vesicle dispersion with water and a DNA solution with water and measuring the change in intensity as a function of time. In the control experiments, no change in intensity was observed, thus, the lipid vesicles were stable upon dilution.

Small-angle neutron scattering

SANS studies were carried out on the instrument D22[10] at the Institute Laue–Langevin, Grenoble, France. D22 has a large dynamic range of momentum transfers, a high neutron flux and large storage memory that allows time-resolved (stopped-flow) measurements. The samples were transferred into quartz cells (Hellma, Müllheim, Germany) with 1 mm optical path length. A 128×128 pixels ^{3}He multidetector was used. The pixel size is 0.75×0.75 cm. A momentum transfer q, $q = (4\pi \sin \theta)/\lambda$, between 0.01 and 0.18 Å^{-1} was covered with a sample-to-detector distance of 4 m. The full scattering angle is 2θ. The incident wavelength (λ) was 8 Å with $\Delta\lambda/\lambda = 10\%$. Neutron transmission measurements were carried out to verify that each sample had the correct ^{2}H$_2$O/H$_2$O content. The data was radially integrated and the samples corrected for the transmission as described elsewhere. The neutron scattering curves were corrected for nonuniform detector response and put on an absolute scale by dividing by the scattering of pure water. All the SANS measurements reported here were made at 25 °C. The kinetic experiments were performed by rapidly mixing equal volumes of solutions containing cationic vesicles (200 nm diameter) and DNA (length 2000 base pairs) and measuring the time evolution of the scattered intensity as a function of the scattering vector. Suitable control experiments were performed by mixing vesicles with water and DNA with water and following the intensity as a function of q and time. The process was observed for a total of about 600s using exponential exposure times, *i.e.*, the initial 2D spectrum was recorded for 1 s, and subsequent spectra were recorded for a duration of 1.053 times the preceding one. For improved statistics, each reaction was repeated at least 10 times, and the respective runs of each sample were summed and analysed.

From the scattering curves the pair distance distribution function $p(r)$ was calculated using a methodology described elsewhere.[11,12] $p(r)$ represents the probability of finding a distance r

between any pair of volume elements of the particle, weighted with the product of the scattering-length densities of the two volume elements. The calculation of $p(r)$ using the equation:

$$p(r) = \frac{1}{2\pi^2} \int_0^\infty I(q)(qr)\sin(qr)dq, \quad (1)$$

requires scattering data in the range $0 \leq q \leq \infty$, and a preliminary desmearing of the wavelength effect. The limited q range available from the experiment would lead to strong oscillations (termination effects) in such a direct Fourier transformation. The method we used, indirect Fourier transformation (IFT) solves the problem with an iterative algorithm.[11] It can simultaneously perform the four steps of least-squares fitting, smoothing, desmearing, and Fourier transformation assuming a limitation in the pair distance distribution function, i.e., $p(r) = 0$ for $r > D_{max}$, where D_{max} is the maximum distance found in the particle.

Results and discussion

We investigated the reaction between double-stranded DNA and cationic lipid vesicles in solution using stopped-flow turbidity and small angle neutron scattering measurements as a function of charge ratio between lipid and DNA, $\rho_{+/-}$. The charge ratio, $\rho_{+/-}$, is defined as the ratio of positive charge equivalents of the cationic component to negative charge equivalents of the nucleic acid. Although equilibrium studies appear frequently in the literature, the kinetics and pathways of the transition under nonequilibrium conditions have not been addressed. An understanding of the pathways that lead to the final equilibrium and the plausible steps involved in the nonequilibrium states are important for the production of dispersions of DNA complex of optimal size and composition.

Turbidity

We followed the formation of DNA–cationic vesicle complexes first by stopped-flow turbidity measurements because we observed, by ocular inspection, an increase in the vesicle lipid dispersion turbidity upon addition of DNA. Our vesicle system comprised a cationic lipid, DODAB, and a neutral lipid, DOPE mixed in equal molar amounts and extruded. We used a wavelength of 410 nm since the absorption at this wavelength is exclusively due to the lipid vesicles. Fig. 1a shows the turbidity as a function of time for the mixing of DNA with DODAB : DOPE (1 : 1) vesicles at 25 °C. These vesicles are in the fluid state, i.e., the temperature of the measurement was above the main transition temperature (or gel to liquid-crystalline phase transition temperature) of the lipid vesicles.[13] The final charge ratios, $\rho_{+/-}$, are given in Fig. 1a. Addition of DNA caused an increase in the turbidity as a function of time. The increase in the turbidity was higher for charge ratios close to one as shown in Fig. 1b, where the change in intensity, ΔI, is plotted as a function of charge ratio. The change in fluorescence intensity for different charge ratios obtained with the stopped-flow fluorescence technique in our group[7] is also given in the plot. The change in intensity for turbidity and fluorescence follows roughly the same behavior. A maximum of ΔI as a function of the charge ratio is observed close to the point of charge neutrality ($\rho_{+/-} = 1$).

A plot of the intensity *versus* the logarithm of time t yielded two separated steps (graph not shown). Thus, the data was fitted to the two-step-function:[14]

$$I(t) = A_1(1 - e^{-t/\tau_1}) + A_2(1 - e^{-t/\tau_2}) \quad (2)$$

where $I(t)$ is the turbidity at time t, A_1, A_2 the prefactors, and τ_1, τ_2 the time constants. The Nelder–Mead simplex method was used to minimize eqn. (2) and the quality of the fits was assessed from the χ^2 value. From the fit to eqn. (2) two time scales are obtained, one in milliseconds and the other in seconds. The first rate constant ($k_1 = 1/\tau_1$) is fast and invariant with the charge ratio in the two regimes, i.e., complexes with excess DNA ($\rho_{+/-} < 1$) and complexes with excess lipid ($\rho_{+/-} > 1$). The second rate constant ($k_2 = 1/\tau_2$) increases with charge ratio. In previous stopped-flow fluorescence measurements in our group,[7] three steps in the formation of DNA–cationic vesicle complexes were identified. The first time constant is roughly the same in both turbidity and

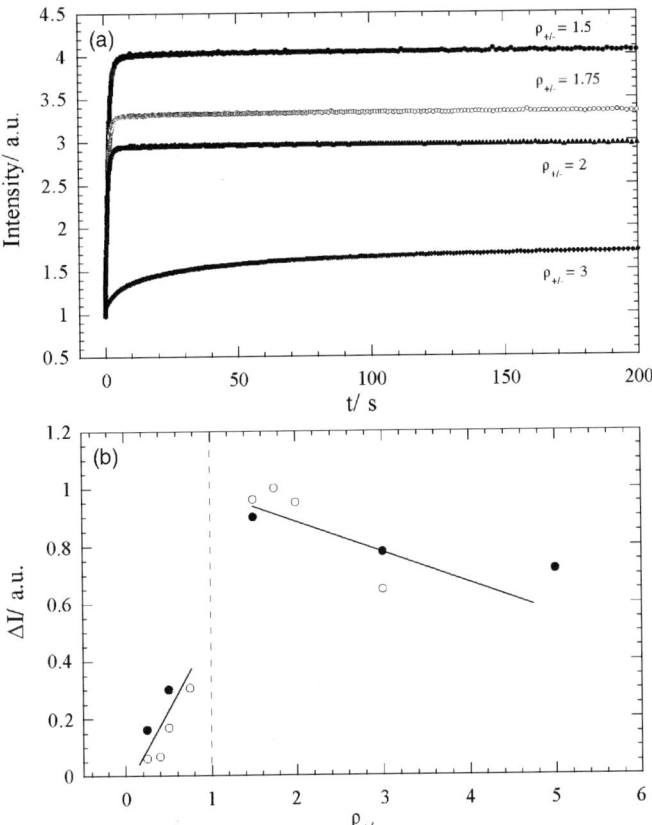

Fig. 1 (a) Stopped-flow recordings corresponding to the turbidity intensity (given as photomultiplier tube output voltage) for the mixing of DODAB : DOPE (1 : 1) vesicles with salmon DNA ($C_i = 0.075$ mg ml^{-1}) at 25 °C. The charge ratios are indicated in the plot. (b) Total intensity change, ΔI, for the mixing of DODAB : DOPE (1 : 1) vesicles with salmon DNA ($C_i = 0.075$ mg ml^{-1}) as a function of charge ratio for (○) turbidity data and (●) fluorescence data.[7]

fluorescence; it was assigned to the binding of cationic vesicles to DNA leading to the formation of a larger particle (from turbidity measurements) and a change in DNA conformation (from fluorescence measurements). The approach of vesicles and DNA will be diffusion controlled. The second step consists most likely of the formation of an intermediate. Since the third step observed in the fluorescence measurements[7] was not observed in the turbidity measurements, structural studies were necessary in order to try to understand the apparent discrepancy, as well as to obtain structural information about the intermediates formed, and thus, the nature of the second step.

Small-angle neutron scattering

Static experiments. Before performing kinetic measurements it was necessary to characterize the vesicles and the structure of the reaction product (the DNA–cationic vesicle complex). The match point of the vesicles, *i.e.*, the contrast where their zero-angle neutron scattering disappears, was determined by plotting the square root of $I(q \to 0)$ as a function of the molar ratio of ^{2}H$_2$O/H$_2$O as described elsewhere.[8] The match point is found to be about 5% ^{2}H$_2$O for the mixed cationic vesicles DODAB : DOPE (1 : 1). The match point for DNA was found to be 70% ^{2}H$_2$O. We chose to work at 70% ^{2}H$_2$O or higher, even though at the DNA concentrations used in this work no scattering from the DNA was observed. Fig. 2 shows the measured scattering intensity of cationic vesicles and

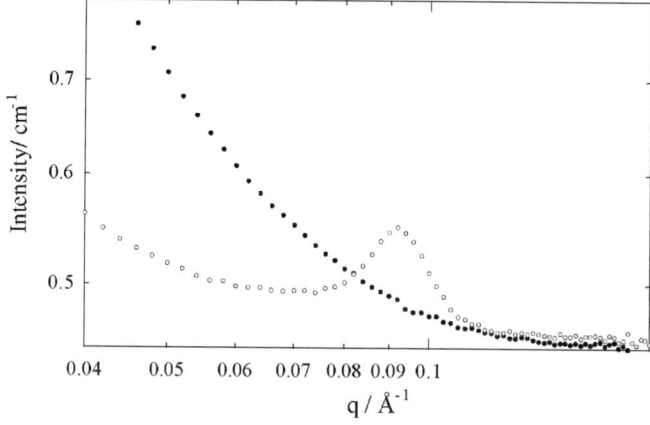

Fig. 2 Radially averaged SANS scattering intensity of the extruded DODAB : DOPE (1 : 1) vesicles in 70% ^2H_2O at 25 °C as a function of the scattering vector (log I –log q plot) in the (●) absence and (○) presence of salmon DNA ($C_i = 0.132$ mg ml^{-1}), charge ratio $\rho_{+/-} = 2$.

DNA–cationic vesicle complexes at a charge ratio $\rho_{+/-}$ of 2 and in 70% ^2H_2O (match point of DNA). Closed unilamellar vesicles (filled circles) exhibit no Bragg peak. In the presence of DNA (open circles) the cationic vesicles dispersions exhibit a single Bragg peak. This confirms that in dilute solution the DNA–cationic vesicle complexes also show a multilamellar structure with DNA intercalated between lipid bilayers as observed by synchrotron X-ray measurements for the precipitate of the systems DNA/DOTAP : DOPC (*i.e.*,1,2-dioleoyl-3-trimethylammonium propane/dioleoylphosphatidylcholine) and DNA/DOTAP : DOPE.[2,15] The scattering peak at position $q = 0.09$ Å^{-1} corresponds to a lamellar spacing of about 70 Å. The lamellar spacing is roughly constant with charge ratio. With $d = d_m + d_w$, where d_m is the thickness of the lipid bilayer and d_w is the thickness of the DNA double strand and one layer of water (25 Å), then the thickness of the lipid bilayer would be 45 Å. Since the second-order reflection was not observed the lamellar stacking presumably does not extend over large distances (over ~ 5 periods).

Kinetic experiments. For this purpose SANS was combined with a stopped-flow apparatus, in which the two solutions are injected rapidly into a measuring cell, to investigate the structural changes occurring upon the interaction of DNA with cationic vesicles. The complexes studied are in solution in the aqueous phase since they are away from charge neutralization ($\rho_{+/-} = 1$). The amount of precipitate is negligible and thus, the scattering comes from soluble aggregates. Representative scattering curves of a time-resolved small-angle scattering experiment are shown in Fig. 3. These curves result from the addition of DNA to fluid lipid bilayers of DODAB : DOPE (1 : 1) vesicles for a final charge ratio, $\rho_{+/-}$, of 2. Neutron scattering measurements in the presence of a high concentration of H_2O are complicated by an intense background of incoherently scattered (*i.e.*, phase-randomized) neutrons. The experiment was performed in 98% ^2H_2O to reduce the incoherent scattering background and to enhance the contrast of the lipids. At 98% ^2H_2O the scattering is mainly due to the lipid vesicles. The effect is also present in 70% ^2H_2O but is less visible because of the higher noise.

In Fig. 3, we can observe a sudden drop in the intensity within the first 2 s. After 2 s the SANS intensity at low q decreases with time as shown in Fig. 4a for a fixed momentum transfer $q = 0.01$ Å^{-1}. This decrease, which levels out after about 7 s, stems from the mixing of the vesicles with DNA, since no change in the structure was observed when mixing vesicles with water. The decay is nearly single exponential with a time constant of 5 s. We then observe the intensity at low angles to increase until it levels off after about 40 s. At high q, a Bragg peak forms and the intensity, for a fixed momentum transfer $q = 0.09$ Å^{-1} (Fig. 4b), increases with time. We interpret this peak to be due to the multilamellar structure where the DNA is intercalated between lipid bilayers, as discussed above. The intensity increases with time and levels out after about 40 s.

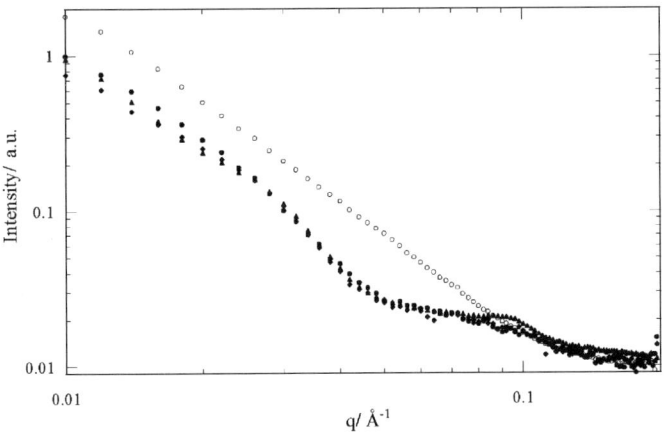

Fig. 3 Small angle neutron scattering intensity as a function of time (log I– log q plot) for the mixing of DODAB : DOPE (1 : 1) vesicles with salmon DNA ($C_i = 0.075$ mg ml^{-1}) at a charge ratio, $\rho_{+/-}$, of 2, 98% ^{2}H$_2$O and 25 °C for a time of (○) 0 s, (●) 2 s, (◆) 6.8 s and (▲) 100 s.

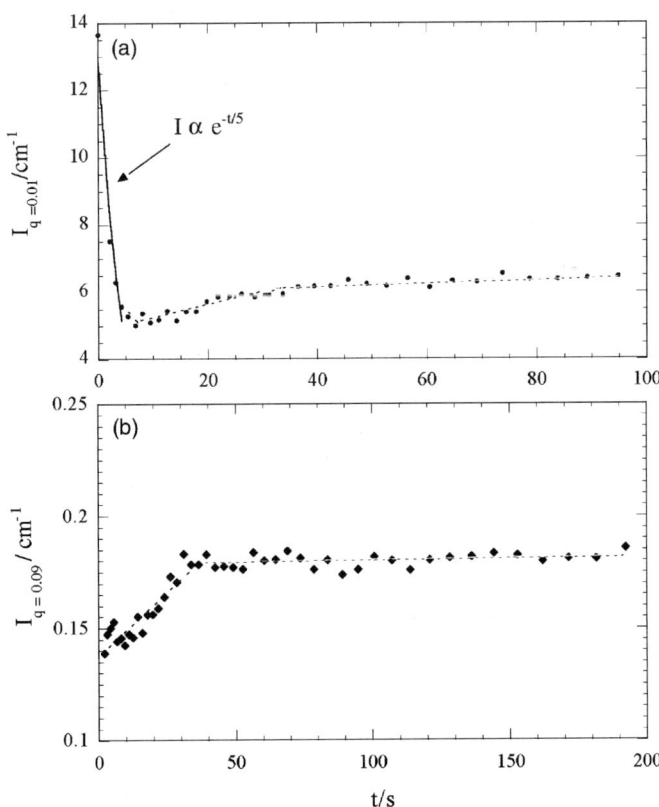

Fig. 4 (a) Scattering intensity at $q = 0.01$ Å^{-1} as a function of time. Solid line represents a single exponential decay with a time constant of 5 s; (b) Scattering intensity at $q = 0.09$ Å^{-1} as a function of time.

The two times suggest that the reaction occurs in at least two steps. The first time constant obtained by SANS is in agreement with the second time constant observed in the stopped-flow turbidity measurements under the same conditions as in Fig. 1a. The second time constant obtained by SANS is made evident both by the Bragg peak appearance and the increase of the low q intensity (Fig. 4a). The second time constant is of the same order of magnitude as that of the third step measured in stopped-flow fluorescence measurements by our group.[7] It is attributed to the reorganization of the complex, resulting in the formation of multilamellar structures. The fact that we do not observe the slower rate constant in the stopped-flow turbidity measurements (Fig. 1a) indicates that it does not include a significant increase in the size of the DNA–cationic vesicle complex but is associated with an internal rearrangement of the complex.

To obtain information about the geometry of the intermediates, information in real space is needed. The indirect Fourier transform that was calculated does not assume a geometry of the particle. Then the geometry can be obtained by comparing the pair distance distribution function, $p(r)$, obtained from the scattering data with those calculated theoretically for a given geometry.[16] The only assumption when comparing with the theoretically calculated curve is the monodispersity, i.e., that all the particles have the same size and shape. Fig. 5a gives the shape of the pair distance distribution function, $p(r)$, for DODAB : DOPE (1 : 1) vesicles calculated from the q range 0.01–0.18 Å^{-1} for time zero (i.e., before the addition of DNA). The shape of the distribution function is qualitatively similar to the pair distance distribution for a locally flat particle. This is expected for large polydisperse vesicles whose outer radius ($R = 1000$ Å) is much larger than the bilayer thickness ($d_m = 45$ Å). The $p(r)$ function for lamellar structures initially increases as r^2 but becomes

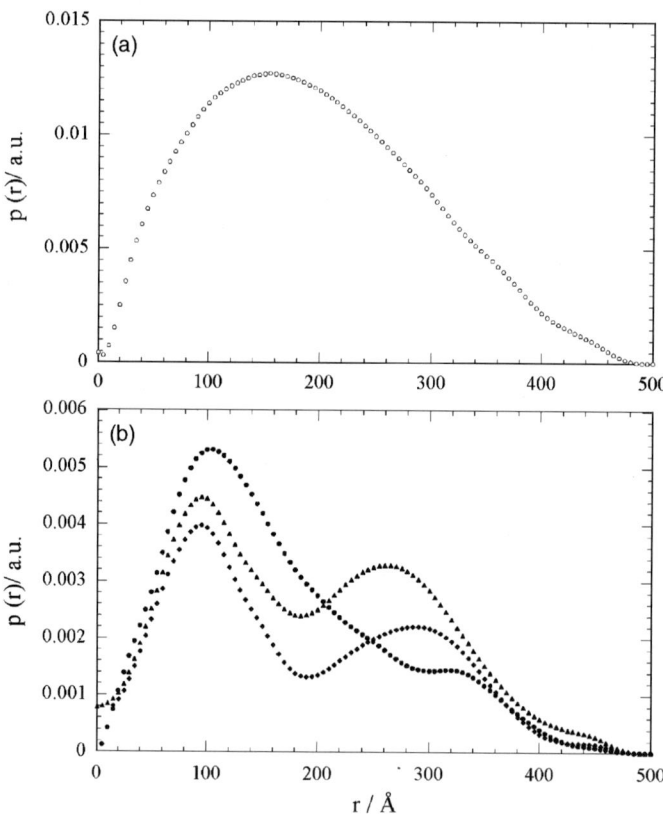

Fig. 5 Pair distance distribution function $p(r)$ for (a) DODAB : DOPE (1 : 1) vesicles and (b) DNA–DODAB : DOPE (1 : 1) complexes at a charge ratio of positive to negative charges of 2 for a time of (●) 2 s, (◆) 6.8 s and (▲) 100 s. The $^2\text{H}_2\text{O}$ content is 98% and the temperature is 25 °C.

linear in r at a distance corresponding to the thickness of the bilayer. The r^2 to r transition is often clearly displaced in graphs of relatively thick lamellae. For the data presented in Fig. 5a, the situation is less clear but a bilayer thickness of about 40 Å can be estimated at the intersection of the r^2 to r transition.

Fig. 5b shows $p(r)$ curves resulting upon addition of DNA for various times. After 2 s the shape of the $p(r)$ curve resembles that of a cylindrical aggregate with an outer diameter, D, of about 125 Å. The resolution in real space due to the sampling theorem is expected to be π/q_{max}, i.e., within the range of ± 17 Å. The cylinder diameter may correspond to $D = 2d_m + d_w$, where d_m is the thickness of the lipid bilayer and d_w is the thickness of the DNA double strand and 1 water molecule (25 Å), as described above. The axial length of the cylinder is responsible for the linear region of $p(r)$ for large r. However, the length of the cylinder was not possible to calculate due to the limited q range used. With increasing time, the $p(r)$ function shows the appearance of a peak at longer distances that increases intensity and moves to smaller distances.

For 100 s, the peak is centered at about 250 Å. The $p(r)$ function in Fig. 5b for a time of 100 s, resembles the pair distribution function for a locally layered structure as reported by Gröhn et al.[17] which seems to be the multilamellar structure discussed above. It was not possible to calculate the total diameter of the aggregates due to the limited q range used.

The SANS results suggest that the second step in the formation of DNA–cationic vesicle complexes corresponds to an intermediate with a local cylindrical geometry. The formation of cylinders as an intermediate is in agreement with the concept of the flexible surface model[18] since the curvature of cylinders lies in between planar bilayers and vesicles. The flexible surface model of surfactant interfaces has been used to understand the phase behavior of amphiphilic systems in terms of the parameters associated with this model, such as bending rigidity and spontaneous curvature of the interfacial surfactant film.[19] The intermediate formed is transformed into multilamellar structures where the DNA helix is sandwiched between lipid bilayers. We believe that the cylindrical geometry arises from the rolling up of the cationic bilayers around the DNA double helix axis. In Fig. 6, we present a possible pathway for the formation of DNA–cationic vesicle complexes. Other groups using cryo-TEM[5] and atomic force microscopy[20] have also suggested a three-step mechanism. Electron micrographs[5] indicate that the cationic vesicles rupture and wrap their whole bilayer around another vesicle (denominated "template" vesicle). Clusters of DNA-coated vesicles where the vesicles are deformed and flattened in the contact region and finally multilamellar complexes consisting of a stack of alternating sheets of DNA and lipid bilayers were observed by Huebner et al.[5] and are in agreement with the proposed mechanism from SANS measurements.

Conclusions

Stopped-flow scattering was used as a tool for the characterization of solution structures of DNA–cationic vesicle complexes. The combination of turbidity, fluorescence and small-angle neutron scattering measurements gave us information about the minimum number of stages and time scales for the formation of DNA–cationic vesicle complexes, as well as information about the structures of intermediates.

The binding followed first-order reactions and occurred step-wise. The electrostatic interaction drives the coverage of one DNA strand with initially one single vesicle (first step). This process is rapid (ms) as observed by turbidity and fluorescence measurements.[7] Since no salt is added to the system, the interaction is strong enough to rupture the vesicle upon its contact with a DNA molecule. The bilayers roll up around the DNA-cylinder axis. This intermediate with locally cylindrical structure appears within seconds (second step). Layer-to-layer association of previously ruptured vesicles leads to continued aggregation and growth of the DNA–cationic vesicle complex into a multilamellar structure (third step).

In this work, we only discuss the pathway under our particular experimental conditions and in our particular system since the results may vary with the initial conditions chosen. Further studies of the detailed structural evolution of the cationic vesicle upon addition of DNA under different conditions are being performed in our group.

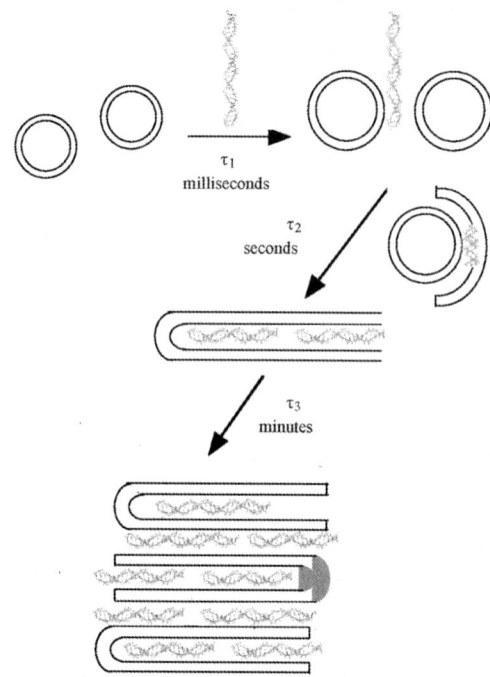

Fig. 6 Schematic representation of the formation of DNA–cationic vesicle complexes derived from stopped-flow turbidity, fluorescence and small-angle neutron scattering experiments, in conditions of excess lipid. The proportions of lipid and DNA have been distorted for clarity. The vesicles are 200 nm in diameter and the DNA has a contour length of 680 nm.

Acknowledgements

We acknowledge the Institute Laue–Langevin in Grenoble, France for providing the neutron scattering facilities, where the measurements were done on the instrument D22. We are also very grateful to Manfred Rössle for the use of and help with the stopped-flow apparatus. Support from the Swedish Natural Sciences Research Council (NFR) is acknowledged. P.C.A.B. also would like to acknowledge the PRAXIS XXI, JNICT for financial support, scholarship BD/13788/97.

References

1. P. L. Felgner, T. R. Gadek, M. Holm, R. Roman, H. W. Chan, M. Wenz, J. P. Northrop, G. M. Ringold and M. Danielsen, *Proc. Natl. Acad. Sci. USA*, 1987, **84**, 7413.
2. J. Rädler, I. Koltover, T. Salditt and C. Safinya, *Science*, 1997, **275**, 810.
3. D. D. Lasic, H. Strey, M. Stuart, R. Podgornik and P. Frederik, *J. Am. Chem. Soc.*, 1997, **119**, 832.
4. J. Gustafsson, G. Arvidson, G. Karlsson and M. Almgren, *Biochim. Biophys. Acta*, 1995, **1235**, 305.
5. S. Huebner, B. J. Battersby, R. Grimm and G. Cevc, *Biophys. J.*, 1999, **76**, 3158.
6. B. Sternberg, *J. Liposom. Res.*, 1996, **6**, 515.
7. P. C. A. Barreleiro and B. Lindman, *Langmuir*, submitted.
8. J. P. Cotton, *Adv. Colloid Interface Sci.*, 1996, **69**, 1.
9. B. Tonomura, H. Nakatani, M. Ohnishi, J. Yamaguchi-Ito and K. Hiromi, *Anal. Biochem.*, 1978, **84**, 370.
10. H. G. Büttner, E. Leliévre-Berna and F. Pinet, *The Yellow Book, Guide to Neutron Research Facilities at the ILL*, Institute Laue–Langevin, Grenoble, 1997.
11. R. P. May and V. Nowotny, *J. Appl. Crystallogr.*, 1989, **22**, 231.
12. O. Glatter, *Acta Phys. Austriaca*, 1977, **47**, 83.
13. P. C. A. Barreleiro, G. Olofsson and P. Alexandridis, *J. Phys. Chem. B*, 2000, **104**, 7795.
14. M. Eigen and L. De Maeyer, in *Techniques of Organic Chemistry*, ed. S. L. Friess and A. Weissberger, Interscience, New York, 1953, vol. VIII, part 2, p. 895.
15. I. Koltover, T. Salditt, J. O. Rädler and C. R. Safinya, *Science*, 1998, **281**, 78.

16 O. Glatter, *J. Appl. Crystallogr.*, 1979, **12**, 166.
17 F. Gröhn, B. J. Bauer, Y. A. Akpalu, C. L. Jackson and E. J. Amis, *Macromolecules*, 2000, **33**, 6042.
18 W. Z. Helfrich, *Naturforsch.C*, 1973, **28**, 693.
19 S. A. Safran, *Statistical Thermodynamics of Surfaces, Interfaces and Membranes*, Addison-Wesley, Reading, MA, 1994.
20 V. Oberle, U. Bakowsky, I. S. Zuhorn and D. Hoekstra, *Biophys. J.*, 2000, **79**, 1447.

Following the formation of nanometer-sized clusters by time-resolved SAXS and EXAFS techniques

Florian Meneau,[a] Gopinathan Sankar,*[a] Norberto Morgante,[a] Rudolf Winter,[b] C. Richard A. Catlow,[a] G. Neville Greaves[b] and John Meurig Thomas[a]

[a] *Davy Faraday Research Laboratory, The Royal Institution of Great Britain, 21 Albemarle Street, London, UK W1S 4BS*
[b] *The Department of Physics, University of Wales, Aberystwyth, Ceredigion, UK SY23 3BZ*

Received 2nd April 2002, Accepted 7th May 2002
First published as an Advance Article on the web

Time-resolved *in situ* SAXS and XAS measurements were carried out to monitor the formation of nanoparticles of the sulfides of cadmium and zinc, from solutions containing the corresponding acetate, and thioacetamide under solvothermal conditions. Analysis of the SAXS data shows that particles of *ca* 5 nm in radius form within the first few minutes of the reaction and then grow uniformly to *ca* 20 nm over a period of two hours resulting in a highly mono-dispersed particle distribution. EXAFS data of the CdS particles also prepared by solvothermal methods and recorded at 20 K, support the formation of nano-meter sized particles.

Introduction

Time-resolved measurements are essential if we are to understand the processes that take place at the initial stages of any chemical reaction. To do so, a variety of spectroscopic and structural tools are either already available or being developed. Here we focus on the use of X-ray based techniques, since both diffraction and absorption spectroscopy are well suited to determine the atomic-architecture of materials that are undergoing reactions.[1] We prefer to combine these two techniques wherever appropriate, since, on the one hand, we are often concerned with systems that transform from an amorphous phase to a crystalline solid and on the other, with highly dispersed and randomly substituted crystalline solids that contain a metal or metals, and possessing no long-range order.[1-3] The power of these combined measurements with time-resolution on the time-scale of milliseconds to minutes have been employed successfully by us and others over the last 10 years in the study of solid-state reactions and in particular, catalyst formation, activation and during reaction.[1-30] Among the various solid state reactions, processes associated with crystallization of solids, nucleation and growth, in particular, have been the most challenging since it is difficult to employ a specific technique and to achieve good time-resolution in order to obtain information on the nature of the particles that promote the crystallisation process. The specific technique that is chosen depends on the type of *in situ* system that is required for the reaction. For example, for the study of solvothermal (which include hydrothermal) synthesis, using "real" autoclave systems, it is necessary to use highly-penetrating X-ray radiation, including "white beam". Indeed energy-dispersive diffraction is most appropriate and, more importantly, although the data are not useful for structure refinement, they are of sufficient high-quality to enable us to obtain time-resolution

DOI: 10.1039/b203142f

(on the scale of seconds) to determine detailed information on the kinetics of reactions.[21,22,31,32] Time-resolved diffraction studies, using monochromatic radiation is also possible, but with the use of miniaturized sealed systems using thin walled glass capillaries or other *in situ* cells that have path-lengths of less than 1 mm are used as opposed to the autoclaves that are normally used in conventional synthesis procedures.[3,33–35] The advantage in utilizing this miniaturized system is that this can be adapted for the particular *in situ* study, employing not only high-resolution diffraction measurements that enables the refinement of X-ray data but also small angle-X-ray scattering and X-ray absorption spectroscopic techniques.[3] Time-resolved studies using SAXS, XRD and XAS have been used extensively for the study of crystallisation of microporous materials, dense oxides and many other systems to determine the processes that take place prior to and during crystallization of inorganic solids.[3,30,36–38] Here we report a time-resolved study of the formation of semiconducting nano particles of the sulfides of cadmium and zinc employing SAXS, XAS and diffraction studies, under solvothermal conditions.

Most of the research has concentrated on the area of synthesis of semiconducting particles belonging to II–VI and III–V groups of the periodic table, since these materials show significant quantum confinement effects.[39,40] Owing to this confinement effect both electrical and optical properties of these materials vary significantly with particle size, and the ability to tune the physical properties by controlling the growth (or particle size) can find potential uses in a variety of applications. Various preparative methods have been explored to produce nano-sized particles which include control of particle growth employing matrices or stabilizers such as thiols, glasses, polymers, reverse micelles, zeolites, xerogels *etc*. We also focus here on the production of small cadmium- and zinc-based sulfide particles, where one of the commonly used methods for their preparation is to react cadmium or a zinc salt with a sulfur-containing organic reagent such as thiourea or thioacetamide, under solvothermal conditions. There are several *ex situ* investigations related to the study of the nature of the reaction conditions on the particle size and its effect on optical properties. Although there are some reports on time-resolved studies using optical spectroscopic measurements, in particular of the change in the absorption edge of a growing cadmium or zinc particle, the particle size determination is carried out only indirectly using the information derived from *ex situ* study.[27,39–44] Here we report the study of the formation of nano-sized CdS particles by reacting thioacetamide with cadmium acetate. As in many other reactions, the rate of crystallisation and the size of the particle increase with temperature. We found that particles below the size of 20 nm can be prepared by conducting the reaction at *ca* 30 °C over a period of two hours.

Experimental

In a typical reaction, 0.02 M of cadmium acetate dissolved in water is reacted with 0.05 M thioacetamide just before introducing the mixture into a specially designed *in situ* cell that consists of 50 μm mica as the window material. *In situ* SAXS and XAS measurements were carried out at station 8.2 and 9.3, respectively, of the SRS, Daresbury laboratory which operates at 2 GeV. Station 8.2 is equipped with Si(111) monochromator to obtain the incident beam wavelength used here of 1.54 Å, an INEL detector for measuring wide angle X-ray scattering (WAXS), a quadrant detector for measuring the SAXS data. Both these measurements were performed simultaneously at two minute time-intervals (to obtain good signal to noise) and over a period of *ca* 2 h, with a camera length of 3.5 m corresponding to a scattering vector range ($q = 4\pi\sin\theta/\lambda = 2\pi/d$) of 0.006–0.2 Å^{-1}. In a typical experiment, the required amount of the reacting liquid was inserted in to the cell and the cell was loaded immediately in a pre-heated system, kept at a specific temperature, and the scans were started immediately afterwards. However the typical time taken to start the measurement after reacting cadmium acetate and thioacetamide is approximately 3 min. The SAXS data were processed using the XOTOKO program available at the Daresbury Laboratory.

Cd and Zn K-edge XAS measurements were performed at station 9.3 of the SRS, Daresbury Laboratory. Experiments were carried out in an identical time-square way to that of the SAXS measurement. We concentrated only on the XANES region for reasons mentioned in the Results and discussion. No attempt was made to record XRD data, Data were collected employing the QuEXAFS mode and the Si(111) monochromator for the Zn K-edge and Si(220) for the Cd K-edge and the measurement time was restricted to 3 min in order to get as close to that used for the SAXS data. The XAS data were processed employing the EXCALIB and EXBROOK suite of programs and whenever necessary EXCURV98 was used to refine the EXAFS data.

Results and discussion

As mentioned in the Introduction, our aim was to follow the formation of cadmium and zinc sulfide particles from a reaction medium. First we discuss the XAS results and subsequently the SAXS data and show how we estimated the particle sizes.

Cadmium sulfide is known to be present in two different structures/types, namely sphalerite and wurtzite. In both of these the first shell around the cations comprises 4 sulfur atoms and the second neighbor consists of 12 cadmiums. However, by careful examination of the EXAFS data and their associated Fourier transforms (FTs) (see Fig. 1) for both bulk and small sulfide particles prepared using the solvothermal procedures (different temperature and time of reaction), employing *ex situ* methods, we find that there are no significant differences between the data for various materials, irrespective of whether they are bulk or small particles. Similar observations are made for zinc sulfide materials prepared under various solvothermal conditions. The main reason being that there appears to be a large thermal disorder associated with the Cd–Cd (or Zn–Zn) shell,[45] which is very well reflected in the data collected at 50 K and below, shown in Fig. 1. To determine the particle size from EXAFS, accurate estimates of the coordination number of this second shell are all important, since the first shell is always surrounded by 4 sulfurs, a typical observation made for many other oxides where the particles are terminated by the anions. This lack of information on the second shell prevented us from analyzing the EXAFS data obtained from these time-resolved measurements. However, although there are changes in the XANES (see Fig. 2) during the reaction when going from an oxygen environment to sulfur neighbors, it is difficult to conclude the nature and shape of the growing particle, since both the unreacted solution and resulting solid contribute to the XANES data. Nevertheless it was possible to monitor the extent of reaction employing the time-resolved XANES measurements. Hence measurements were restricted to the XANES data. It is clear from Fig. 2, both for cadmium and zinc containing systems, that there is a gradual change in the white line intensity (the top of the absorption edge is usually referred to as white line intensity) with time, approaching that of the sulfided form. The decrease in white line intensity is more clear for the cadmium system than for the zinc. Nevertheless, the decrease in white line intensity as a function of time suggests that this reaction results in the formation of sulfided particles.

In Fig. 3 we show the stacked time-resolved SAXS data collected during the solvothermal reaction of cadmium acetate with thioacetamide. It is clear from this figure that a gradual increase in the scattering intensity in the low q region is also accompanied by the appearance of a 'bump' which is caused by the scattering structure factor and indicates a monodisperse system. This 'bump' shifts to lower q values with reaction time, indicating that small particles are gradually replaced by bigger particles. This is typically observed for many systems that represent a nucleating and growing particle processes, which ultimately yield highly monodispersed particles.

The invariant Q measures the electron density contrast $\Delta(\rho)$ independent of particle shape or number. For a simple two-phase system, cadmium sulfide nanoparticles crystallizing out of a water solution, Q is defined by:

$$Q = \int_{q=0}^{q=\infty} I(q) q^2 \mathrm{d}q = \phi(1-\phi)(\Delta\rho)^2 \tag{1}$$

where $\Delta\rho$ is the electron density difference, q the scattering vector ($q = 1/d$) and ϕ is the fraction of one phase and a maximum is predicted when ϕ is equal to 50%. Q obtained from the *in situ* SAXS is plotted against the time of the reaction in Fig. 4. Q increases rapidly to a maximum value at around $t = 50$ min and then begins to fall slowly and linearly as the growth process slows down, reaching its lowest value at $t = 120$ min, when the reaction has been stopped. By extrapolating this linear fall, it is possible to approximate the time required for converting all the cadmium sulfide particles and it is estimated to be *ca* 250 min. The maximum in Q at $t = 50$ min in Fig. 4 can be

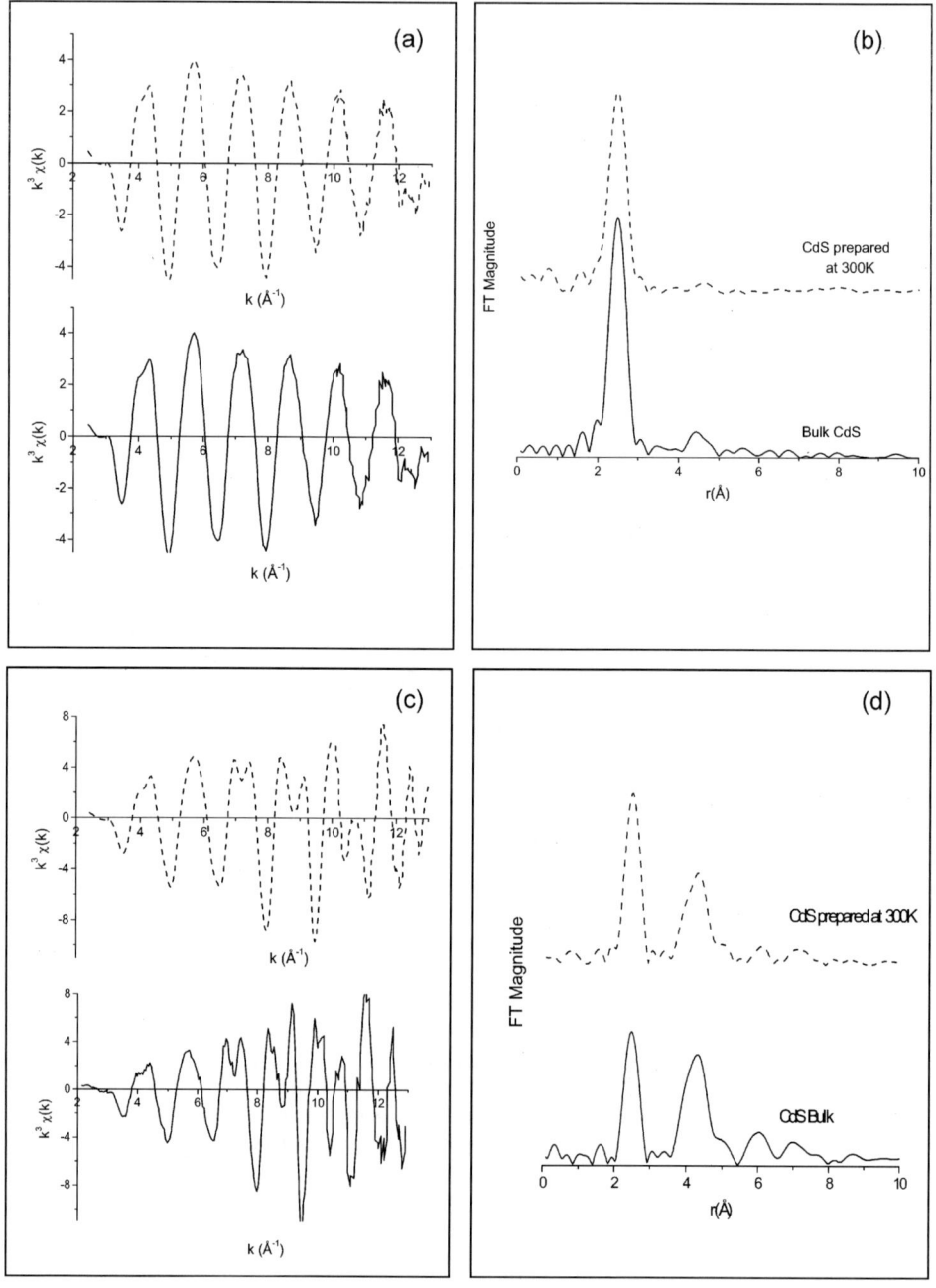

Fig. 1 Comparison of Cd K-edge EXAFS of the bulk CdS sample and the one prepared under solvothermal conditions at 300 K (a) EXAFS recorded at 300 K, (b) associated FTs of the EXAFS data recorded at 300 K, (c) EXAFS recorded at 20 K and (d) associated FTs of the EXAFS data recorded at 20 K. The solid line represents the bulk CdS and the dashed curve for the one prepared under solvothermal conditions at 60 °C for 15 h.

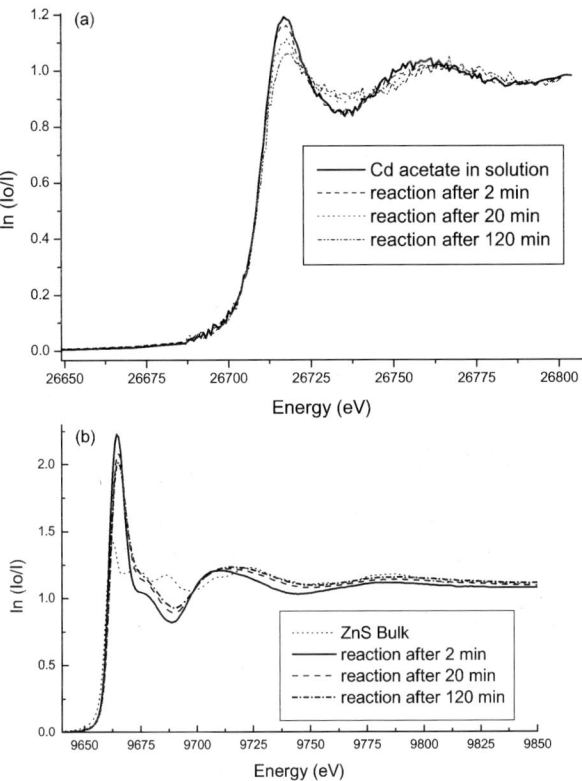

Fig. 2 (a) Cd and (b) Zn K-edge XANES data recorded over a period of two hours during the reaction of thioacetamide with cadmium acetate. XAS data were collected over a period of 5 min for each scan. Only a few scans are shown for clarity, along with the data of the bulk CdS and ZnS systems.

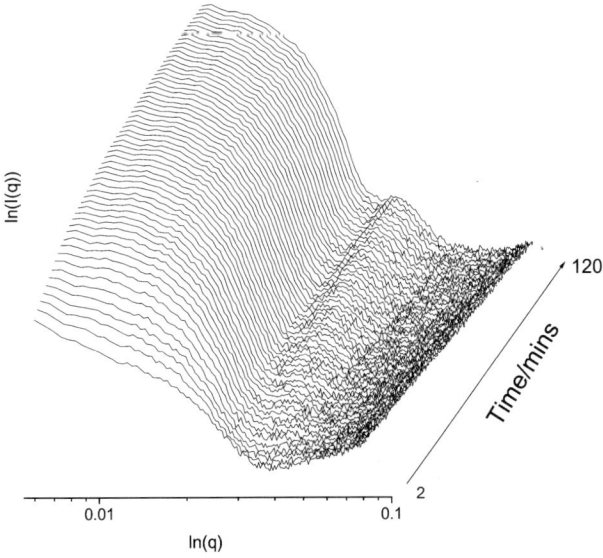

Fig. 3 Stacked SAXS data recorded every two minutes during the reaction of thioacetamide with cadmium acetate at 300 K.

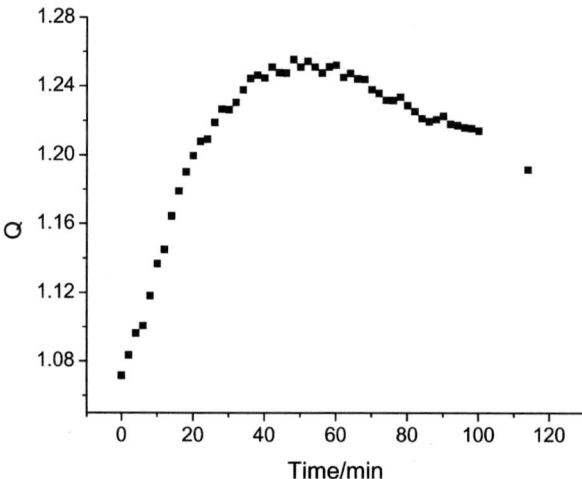

Fig. 4 Q invariant calculated eqn. (1) plotted as a function time.

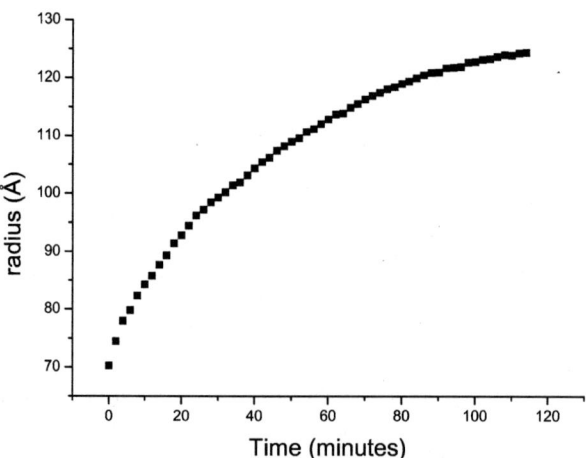

Fig. 5 Particle radius estimated using eqns. (2) and (3), plotted as a function of time.

interpreted as the point at which approximately half the cadmium sulfide nanoparticles have formed. From Fig. 5 we find that Q_{max} corresponds to particles with a radius of 110 Å.

From the small angle region ($q \rightarrow 0$) the Guinier radius can be determined by:

$$I(q) = C\exp\left(-\frac{R_g^2 q^2}{3}\right); \quad q = 2\pi/d \tag{2}$$

where R_g is the Guinier radius or radius of gyration, q is the scattering vector and C a scaling factor. It should be noted that the Guinier approximation is only valid only for monodispersed systems ($Rq < 2\pi$).

We assume that the cadmium sulfide nanoparticles are spherical in shape and for such particles the radius r of the CdS nanoclusters is related to R_g via the following expression:

$$R_g^2 = \frac{3}{5}r^2 \tag{3}$$

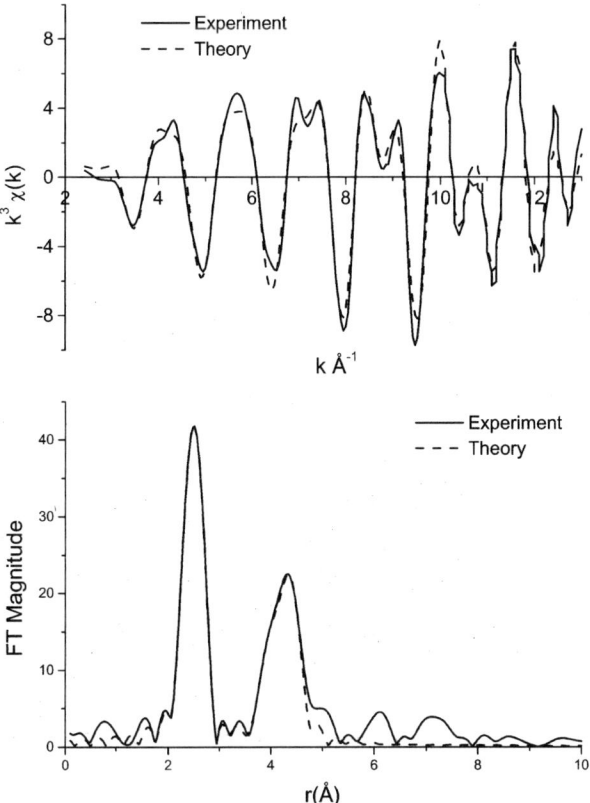

Fig. 6 Best fit to the (top) EXAFS data of the sample prepared at 300 K and the (bottom) associated FTs. Note that the Cd K-edge EXAFS data were collected at 20 K in order obtain the information on the second shell more accurately to determine the particle size. The analysis of the EXAFS data yielded a coordination number of *ca* 10.4 for the Cd–Cd shell; the coordination number for the bulk is 12.

During the reaction, the particle radius of the cadmium sulfide ranges from 7 nm (at time t_0) to a maximum of 12.5 nm after 120 min. (Fig. 5) above which there is no further increase in the size.

We prepared both cadmium- and zinc-sulfided systems taking into account this *in situ* observation and prepared materials to be examined by X-ray absorption spectroscopy. The analysis of the EXAFS data recorded at 20 K (see Fig. 6) revealed that the coordination number for the second Cd–Cd shell is *ca* 10, which is smaller than that of the bulk value of 12. However, we note that a simple Gaussian description for the Debye–Waller factor is used in the present analysis which will result in the under-estimation of the particle size. Further detailed studies are in progress, in particular, the use of a cumulant method to determine accurately the coordination number and Debye–Waller factor to determine the size of the particle.

This *in situ* time-resolved study clearly allows us to track the formation of the sulfided cadmium and zinc nanoparticles.

Acknowledgements

We thank EPSRC for the provision of beam time and CLRC for various facilities. We also thank EU-NUCLEUS program for their financial support. We thank Professor F. Schuth, his colleagues and Dr S. Cristol for useful discussions. We also thank Dr N. Terrill for helping us with the SAXS measurements and Dr I. Harvey with XAS studies. The use of ICSD database is gratefully acknowledged.

References

1. G. Sankar and J. M. Thomas, *Top. Catal.*, 1999, **8**, 1.
2. G. Sankar, P. A. Wright, S. Natarajan, J. M. Thomas, G. N. Greaves, A. J. Dent, B. R. Dobson, C. A. Ramsdale and R. H. Jones, *J. Phys. Chem.*, 1993, **97**, 9550.
3. G. Sankar, J. M. Thomas, F. Rey and G. N. Greaves, *J. Chem. Soc., Chem. Commun.*, 1995, 2549.
4. R. Frahm, J. Wong, J. B. Holt, E. M. Larson, B. Rupp and P. A. Waide, *Jpn J. Appl. Phys. Part 1*, 1993, **32**, 185.
5. G. N. Greaves, C. Aletru, G. Sankar, C. R. A. Catlow, V. Kempson and L. Colyer, *Jpn J. Appl. Phys. Part 1*, 1999, **38**, 202.
6. J. Harford and J. Squire, *Rep. Prog. Phys.*, 1997, **60**, 1723.
7. Y. Inada, *Bunseki Kagaku*, 2000, **49**, 563.
8. J. I. Langford and D. Louer, *Rep. Prog. Phys.*, 1996, **59**, 131.
9. D. Lutzenkirchen-Hecht and R. Frahm, *J. Synchrotron Radiat.*, 1999, **6**, 591.
10. D. Lutzenkirchen-Hecht and R. Frahm, *J. Phys. Chem. B*, 2001, **105**, 9988.
11. S. Pascarelli, T. Neisius and S. De Panfilis, *J. Synchrotron Radiat.*, 1999, **6**, 1044.
12. L. M. Reilly, G. Sankar and C. R. A. Catlow, *J. Solid State Chem.*, 1999, **148**, 178.
13. T. Ressler, J. Wienold, R. E. Jentoft, O. Timpe and T. Neisius, *Solid State Commun.*, 2001, **119**, 169.
14. M. Richwin, R. Zaeper, D. Lutzenkirchen-Hecht and R. Frahm, *J. Synchrotron Radiat.*, 2001, **8**, 354.
15. M. A. Roberts, G. Sankar, C. R. A. Catlow, J. M. Thomas, G. N. Greaves and R. H. Jones, *Eur. Powder Diffraction: Epdic Iv, Pts 1 and 2*, 1996, **228**, 417.
16. G. Sankar, J. M. Thomas, D. Waller, J. W. Couves, C. R. A. Catlow and G. N. Greaves, *J. Phys. Chem.*, 1992, **96**, 7485.
17. G. Sankar, M. A. Roberts, J. M. Thomas, G. U. Kulkarni, N. Rangavittal and C. N. R. Rao, *J. Solid State Chem.*, 1995, **119**, 210.
18. G. Sankar, J. M. Thomas and C. R. A. Catlow, *Top. Catal.*, 2000, **10**, 255.
19. I. J. Shannon, F. Rey, G. Sankar, J. M. Thomas, T. Maschmeyer, A. M. Waller, A. E. Palomares, A. Corma, A. J. Dent and G. N. Greaves, *J. Chem. Soc., Faraday Trans.*, 1996, **92**, 4331.
20. I. V. Tomov, D. A. Oulianov, P. L. Chen and P. M. Rentzepis, *J. Phys. Chem. B*, 1999, **103**, 7081.
21. R. I. Walton and D. O'Hare, *Chem. Commun.*, 2000, 2283.
22. R. I. Walton, F. Millange, D. O'Hare, A. T. Davies, G. Sankar and C. R. A. Catlow, *J. Phys. Chem. B*, 2001, **105**, 83.
23. J. Wark, *Contemp. Physics*, 1996, **37**, 205.
24. J. Wong, M. Froba and R. Frahm, *Physica B*, 1995, **209**, 249.
25. A. Yamaguchi, T. Shido, Y. Inada, T. Kogure, K. Asakura, M. Nomura and Y. Iwasawa, *Bull. Chem. Soc. Jpn*, 2001, **74**, 801.
26. A. Yamaguchi, A. Suzuki, T. Shido, Y. Inada, K. Asakura, M. Nomura and Y. Iwasawa, *Catal. Lett.*, 2001, **71**, 203.
27. N. Yoshida and T. Nagamura, *Rev. Sci. Instrum.*, 1995, **66**, 52.
28. B. S. Clausen, H. Topsoe and R. Frahm, *Adv. Catal.*, 1998, **42**, 315.
29. F. Dacapito, F. Boscherini, F. Buffa, G. Vlaic, G. Paschina and S. Mobilio, *J. Non-Cryst. Solids*, 1993, **156**, 571.
30. W. Bras and A. J. Ryan, *Adv. Colloid Interface Sci.*, 1998, **75**, 1.
31. R. J. Francis and D. O'Hare, *J. Chem. Soc., Dalton Trans.*, 1998, 3133.
32. A. T. Davies, G. Sankar, C. R. A. Catlow and S. M. Clark, *J. Phys. Chem. B*, 1997, **101**, 10 115.
33. P. Norby, A. N. Christensen and J. C. Hanson, *Inorg. Chem.*, 1999, **38**, 1216.
34. D. O'Hare, J. S. O. Evans, R. J. Francis, P. S. Halasyamani, P. Norby and J. Hanson, *Microporous Mesoporous Mater.*, 1998, **21**, 253.
35. A. N. Christensen, P. Norby and J. C. Hanson, *Microporous Mesoporous Mater.*, 1998, **20**, 349.
36. P. de Moor, T. P. M. Beelen, R. A. van Santen, L. W. Beck and M. E. Davis, *J. Phys. Chem. B*, 2000, **104**, 7600.
37. P. de Moor, T. P. M. Beelen, R. A. van Santen, K. Tsuji and M. E. Davis, *Chem. Mater.*, 1999, **11**, 36.
38. P. de Moor, T. P. M. Beelen and R. A. van Santen, *Microporous Mater.*, 1997, **9**, 117.
39. H. Weller, *Adv. Mater.*, 1993, **5**, 88.
40. H. Weller, *Angew. Chem., Int. Ed. Engl*, 1993, **32**, 41.
41. G. Z. Wang, W. Chen, C. H. Liang, Y. W. Wang, G. W. Meng and L. D. Zhang, *Inorg. Chem. Commun.*, 2001, **4**, 208.
42. G. Z. Wang, G. H. Li, C. H. Liang and L. D. Zhang, *Chem. Lett.*, 2001, 344.
43. G. Q. Xu, B. Liu, S. J. Xu, C. H. Chew, S. J. Chua and L. M. Gana, *J. Phys. Chem. Solids*, 2000, **61**, 829.
44. M. Pattabi and J. Uchil, *Sol. Energy Mater. Sol. Cells*, 2000, **63**, 309.
45. J. Rockenberger, L. Troger, A. Kornowski, T. Vossmeyer, A. Eychmuller, J. Feldhaus and H. Weller, *J. Phys. Chem. B*, 1997, **101**, 2691.

Application of stopped flow techniques and energy dispersive EXAFS for investigation of the reactions of transition metal complexes in solution: Activation of nickel β-diketonates to form homogeneous catalysts, electron transfer reactions involving iron(III) and oxidative addition to iridium(I)

M. Basyaruddin B. Abdul Rahman,[a] Peter R. Bolton,[a] John Evans,[a] Andrew J. Dent,[b] Ian Harvey[b] and Sofia Diaz-Moreno[c]

[a] *Department of Chemistry, University of Southampton, Southampton, UK SO17 1BJ*
[b] *CLRC Daresbury Laboratory, Warrington, UK WA4 4AD*
[c] *ESRF, F-38043, Grenoble cedex, France*

Received 20th March 2002, Accepted 18th April 2002
First published as an Advance Article on the web 16th July 2002

Stopped-flow techniques of rapid mixing have been combined with energy dispersive X-ray absorption spectroscopy to monitor the reaction of Ni(dpm)$_2$ {dpm = Bu^{t}C(O)CHC(O)Bu^t} by aluminium alkyls (AlEt$_2$X, X = OEt and Et) to form the active species for the catalytic di- and tri-merisation of hex-1-ene. Acquisition times down to *ca.* 30 ms were achieved on Station 9.3 of the SRS using a photodiode array detector. The EXAFS features of the resulting solution complexes are of the form [Ni(O–O)(R)(alkene)]. In the presence of PPh$_3$, [Ni(O–O)(R)(PPh$_3$)] appears to be the predominant type of species. The reduction of aqueous Fe(III) by hydroquinone was investigated on ID24 at the ESRF by Fe K-edge energy dispersive EXAFS with a CCD camera as detector; spectra were obtained in 1 ms or longer. No intermediate inner sphere complex was detected prior to the formation of aqueous Fe(II). Finally the oxidative addition of CH$_3$SO$_3$CF$_3$ to [IrI$_2$(CO)$_2$]$^-$ was monitored on Station 9.3 with a silicon microstrip detector. A single acquisition of 400 μs was feasible, with spectra recorded in multiples of 1.2 ms. In that time, the first stage of the reaction had been completed, with a slower stage thereafter. The results are consistent with the two-stage ionic oxidative addition mechanism.

Introduction

The capability of simultaneous acquisition over the energy range of an X-ray absorption spectrum has afforded energy dispersive EXAFS (EDE) a significant status as a technique for investigating structure as well as kinetics.[1] In addition to the advantage of multiplexing data acquisition, an important adjunct of the energy dispersive optical geometry is the focusing of the X-ray beam on the sample. Hence the technique is well suited to sampling arrangements in small chambers, such as diamond anvil or stopped flow cells. EDE has been successfully synchronised with a stopped flow experiment in which the oxidation of Fe$^{III}_{aq}$ by hydroquinone was investigated.[2] This experiment utilised a triangular cut monochromator and a photodiode array detector with a Gd$_2$O$_2$S : Tb fluorescent screen. Using a concentration of 100 mM, near edge spectra were acquired with a total illumination time of 2–3 s (Photon Factory BL 4A). Direct illumination of a photodiode array was demonstrated to achieve a high degree of response linearity (Station 9.3 of the SRS),[3] and this was subsequently applied[4] to an investigation of the activation of a [Ni(acac)$_2$]$_3$ by AlEt$_2$(OEt) to form a hexene di- and tri-merisation catalyst.[5] In this case EXAFS analysis (to $k \sim 9$ Å^{-1}) was achieved on a 70 mM solution using similar total acquisition times. These results demonstrated the potential of EDE for achieving structure/activity correlation directly on a reacting solution. In this report we show how refinements of this technique have widened the scope in terms of the lower limits of timescale and concentrations; we illustrate it with three cases (i) from the SRS using a photodiode array as detector, (ii) from the ESRF using a CCD camera as detector and (iii) from the SRS using a silicon microstrip as detector.

The successful acquisition of good quality EXAFS data by the EDE technique places stringent demands upon the light source, optics and detector.[6] The high K device ("wundulator") light source on ID 24 of the ESRF provides both more X-ray flux on the sample, and a smaller beam size than is achievable at the SRS, which uses light from a 3-pole wavelength shifter (Station 9.3). However, until horizontal and vertical feedback systems were installed on the electron beam at ID24, these advantages could not be translated into reliable EXAFS data. Since the background spectrum is not recorded simultaneously to the spectrum of the sample, beam movement between these events has a strongly deleterious effect on the resulting absorption spectrum. The feedback systems did substantially alleviate this problem. The optical arrangement is also highly demanding. The earlier triangular silicon crystal monochromators were shown to produce considerable aberrations, with the effect of having a variation of energy profile within the X-ray focal spot. Hence different parts of the recorded spectrum were from weighted contributions of different physical regions of the sample. A solution stopped flow system should provide a homogeneous sample, thus minimising these effects. Nevertheless, the incorporation of 4-point bending mechanisms (on ID24[7] and Station 9.3[8]) has greatly improved focal size and purity. Finally, detectors must combine sensitivity, good time resolution and very high linearity. This has been achieved using a directly illuminated photodiode array at the SRS,[4,8,9] a CCD camera with a phosphor screen on ID 24[7] and the XSTRIP detector[10] using a silicon microstrip array.

Experimental

Energy dispersive EXAFS were recorded on Station 9.3 at the SRS (2 GeV electron energy, multibunch mode with 150–250 mA) and on ID24 at the ESRF (6 GeV electron energy, 2/3 filling, 150–200 mA). Silicon (111) Bragg geometry monochromators were used on both beamlines. The following detectors were employed:

(i) The Ni K-edge studies were performed on station 9.3 a 1024 element Hamamatsu S4874 photodiode array.[11] A deadtime of up to one acquisition time (15 ms) was required from the firing of the stopped-flow system to the recording of the first spectrum to achieve synchronisation.

(ii) The Fe K-edge studies were carried out on beamline ID24 using a Princeton CCD camera with 1242 elements horizontally and stripes of 64 elements vertically. Eighteen stripes can be acquired prior to the readout of the CCD chip. In this study, 15 of the stripes were collected to provide that number of time resolved spectra.

(iii) The Ir L(III) edge experiments were performed on Station 9.3 of the SRS using the silicon microstrip detector XSTRIP with a single spectrum exposure of $ca.$ 400 μs.[10]

Two different stopped flow systems have been utilised in this study. At the SRS, a specially designed cell system based on a HiTech Scientific SFA20 was used, fitted with a 3 mm pathlength and Kapton windows. At the ESRF a Biologic stepper motor driven stopped flow system was employed, using a PTFE cell with pyrocarbon (200 micron) windows.[12]

Ni(dpm)$_2$ (dpm = Bu^{t}C(O)CHC(O)Bu^t),[13] Ni(dpm)$_2$(PPh$_3$)$_2$[14] and NBu$^n_4$[IrI$_2$(CO)$_2$][15] were synthesised as previously described. Other chemicals were purchased from the Aldrich Chemical Company.

Electronic spectra were recorded on a Perkin Elmer Lambda 19 UV–visible–near IR spectrophotometer.

Background subtraction and EXAFS extraction were carried out using the program PAXAS,[16] and data analysis using EXCURV98.[17] Standard deviations are quoted as derived directly, but normally errors of 1.5% are to be expected in interatomic distance[18] and 10–20% in coordination numbers.

Results

Activation of Ni β-diketonates by aluminium alkyls to form hexene oligomerisation catalysts

The system of [Ni(acac)$_2$] {acac = CH$_3$C(O)CHC(O)CH$_3$} and AlEt$_2$(OEt) has been known to provide an active catalyst for the di- and tri-merisation of hex-1-ene under mild conditions.[5] This provided the basis for our earlier studies on the application of EXAFS to the characterisation of homogeneous catalysts by scanning XAFS[19] and energy dispersive methods.[4] The mixing time within the flow cell that was employed proved to be of the order of 1 min and therefore inappropriate for monitoring rapid reactions.[20,21] In this report, the nickel precursor chosen was a related species, Ni(dpm)$_2$, in which the bulky *tert*-butyl groups of the β-diketonate restrict the trimerisation of the complex, resulting in a mononuclear, square planar precursor. The EXAFS-derived parameters for the complex Ni(dpm)$_2$, in the crystal and in solution, are presented in Table 1. In addition to the 4 atoms in the coordination shell, the other carbons in the planar chelate rings could also be identified. The deviation from the distances for these non-bonded by the X-ray diffraction is rather higher than the expected range for a single determination (*ca.* 0.05 Å), probably due to their relatively small contributions to the total EXAFS. Results from EDE are comparable to those from scanning EXAFS.

The formation of the catalytic solution from Ni(dpm)$_2$/AlEt$_2$(OEt)/hex-1-ene in toluene was monitored by Ni K-edge QEXAFS (Quick EXAFS), with analysis of the data obtained after 20 min at 0 °C presented in Table 2. The presence of a single dpm ligand was evident from the characteristics of the Ni···C and Ni–O shells of the coordinated carbonyl groups. In addition, there is additional intensity due to a first row element that could be fitted to a Ni–C shell. Distinguishing between the Ni–O and Ni–C shells was generally difficult, but it this case a distinct minimum could be observed for the refinement of the two separate shells, as shown in the contour map of the fit index for variations in the interatomic distances of these two components (Fig. 1). These results are consistent with the reaction shown in Fig. 2. The formation of the alkyl/alkene coordination pairing is consistent with the results previously reported using Ni(acac)$_2$[4,19,20] and Ni(1,5-

Table 1 Structural parameters derived from scanning EXAFS (solid state, E_F = 5.5 eV, R = 27%) and EDE (80 mM in toluene, 1000 × 30 ms scans, E_F = 5.2 eV, R = 29%) measurements on Ni(dpm)$_2$

Coordination number (EXAFS)	Coordination number (EDE)	R/Å (EXAFS)	R/Å (EDE)	R/Å (XRD)[21]
4.0(2) O	4.0 (1) O	1.818(1)	1.832 (2)	1.836
4.0 (4) C	4.0 (3) C	2.752 (5)	2.743 (4)	2.829
2.3(3) C	2.0 (2) C	3.104 (5)	3.014 (5)	3.212

Table 2 Structural parameters derived from EDE measurements on the reaction of Ni(dpm)$_2$, AlEt$_2$(OEt) and hex-1-ene ([Ni] 80 mM in toluene, Ni : Al : hex-1-ene = 1 : 2 : 20) at 0 °C after 20 min (scan time 5 min). E_F = 3.5 eV, R = 21%

Shell	Coordination number	R/Å	$2\sigma^2$/Å^2
O	2.3 (5)	1.874(7)	0.004(2)
C	3.3 (3)	2.07 (1)	0.007 (2)
C	2.1 (6)	2.86 (2)	0.008 (4)

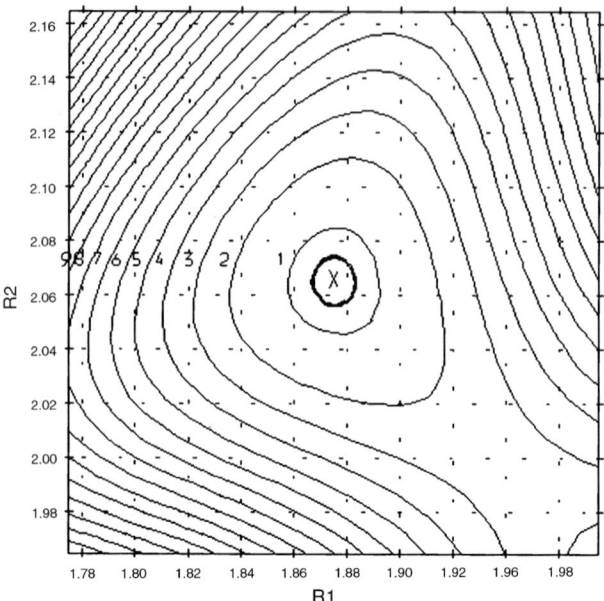

Fig. 1 Fit index contour map for the correlations between the Ni–O and Ni–C bond lengths derived from Ni K-edge QEXAFS measurements on the reaction of Ni(dpm)$_2$, AlEt$_2$(OEt) and hex-1-ene ([Ni] 80 mM in toluene, Ni : Al : hex-1-ene = 1 : 2 : 20) at 0 °C after 20 min (scan time 5 min). $E_F = 3.5$ eV, $R = 21\%$.

cyclooctadiene)$_2$/PPh$_2$CH$_2$C(CF$_3$)$_2$OH.[22] It provides a mechanism for alkene catenation *via* alkene insertion into the Ni–alkyl bond.

To understand this reaction in more detail, stopped flow techniques were applied with differing Ni : Al ratios. An increase in the intensity of a UV band at 460 nm could be used to monitor the kinetics of the process (Fig. 3), and this was carried out in a single wavelength time drive mode. At room temperature, the initial stages of the reaction could be modelled with Michaelis–Menton type kinetics consistent with the formation of a Ni–Al complex (Fig. 4(a)). Although not directly observed with β-diketonate ligands, this type of interaction with a Ni–C–Al bridge has been observed for nickel halide complexes.[19]

This reaction was also monitored by Ni K-edge EDE, with the results for Ni(dpm)$_2$: AlEt$_2$(OEt) : hex-1-ene = 1 : 6 : 20 and [Ni] = 60 mM presented in Fig. 5. These show changes in a pre-edge feature and in the XANES region, indicative of a modification in the nickel coordination sphere. A series of these spectra are extracted and plotted in Fig. 6 and the results of EXAFS analysis depicted in Fig. 7. The standard errors in coordination numbers derived for two closely spaced shells are larger than those in which the shells are significantly different (as for Pt–O and Pt–Pt[23]), and therefore the results are less clear-cut. Nevertheless the data in Figs. 6 and 7 imply a change in the first coordination sphere of nickel by frame 2 (32 s after mixing). Further changes in the XANES and pre-edge region take place over a longer period, and are essentially complete after frame 20 (320 s after mixing). This suggests some additional modification to the coordination geometry, which may accompany the formation of the hex-1-ene dimers (and trimers) as the coordinated alkene; alternatively an equilibrium with an η^3-enyl complex may also come into effect. These results cannot distinguish these alternatives.

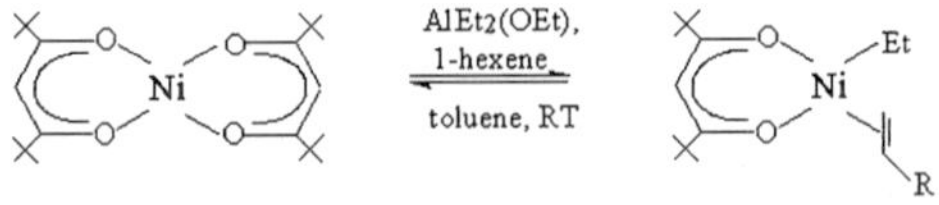

Fig. 2 Scheme for the reaction of Ni(dpm)$_2$ with AlEt$_2$(OEt) and hexene in toluene.

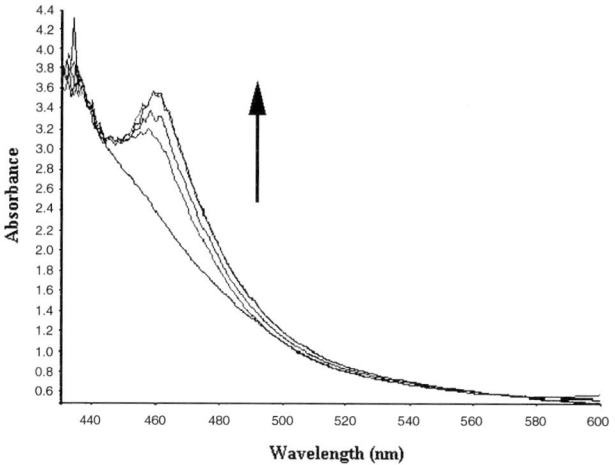

Fig. 3 Monitoring of the reaction of Ni(dpm)$_2$ with AlEt$_2$(OEt) and hex-1-ene (1 : 4 : 20, [Ni] 60 mM) in toluene over 1 min by UV–visible spectroscopy (spectra recorded every 12 s).

The effect of the addition of a potential catalyst modifier, PPh$_3$, was also studied, and the results of EXAFS analyses presented in Table 3. This identifies the *bis* adduct of PPh$_3$, Ni(dpm)$_2$(PPh$_3$)$_2$.[14] Only one of the carbon shells of the chelating rings could be detected on the solid sample, and this could not be refined successfully on the EDE data. The catalytic reaction in the presence of PPh$_3$ effected a change in the nickel coordination sphere, again consistent with the loss of one β-diketonate. From the QEXAFS data, it was not possible to split carbon and oxygen shells in the presence of a third atom type (Ni–P), but the results are consistent with the model in Fig. 8; again these observations are similar to results previously reported from Ni(acac)$_2$.[19]

The initial stages of the reaction were again monitored by UV–visible spectroscopy, and the results of the kinetic study shown in Fig. 4(b). The addition of the PPh$_3$ ligands reduces the K_M value of the binding of the aluminium alkyl but increases the limiting rate of the reaction. The spectra from a Ni K-edge EDE study of this reaction are shown in Fig. 9, with a plot of the coordination number of Ni–P and Ni–O presented in Fig. 10. These indicate that the detectable changes in the coordination sphere were complete within 3 frames (3.6 s) with, again, development of a pre-edge peak being apparent over a longer timescale.

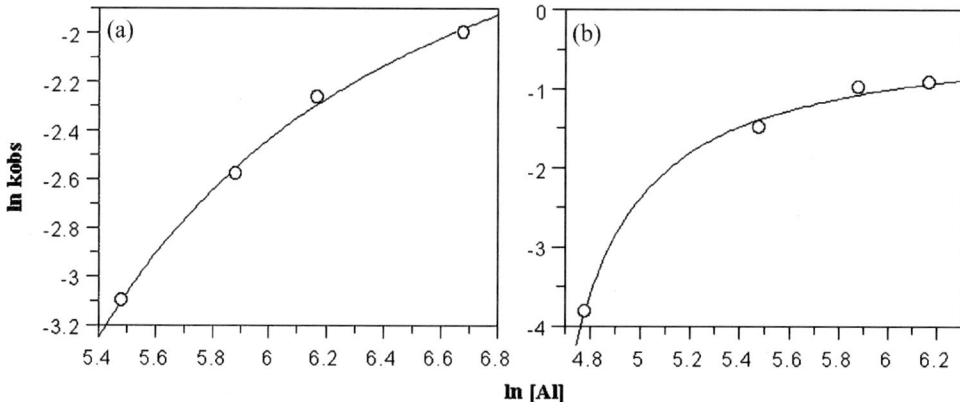

Fig. 4 Plot of ln k_{obs} and ln[Al] at room temperature over the initial 30 s of (a) the reaction of Ni(dpm)$_2$ (60 mM), AlEt$_2$(OEt) and hex-1-ene (1.2 M) in toluene. $k_{max} = 0.47$ s^{-1}, $K_M = 0.016$ M; (b) the reaction of Ni(dpm)$_2$(PPh$_3$)$_2$ (60 mM), AlEt$_2$(OEt) and hex-1-ene (1.2 M) in toluene. $k_{max} = 0.77$ s^{-1}, $K_M = 0.012$ M.

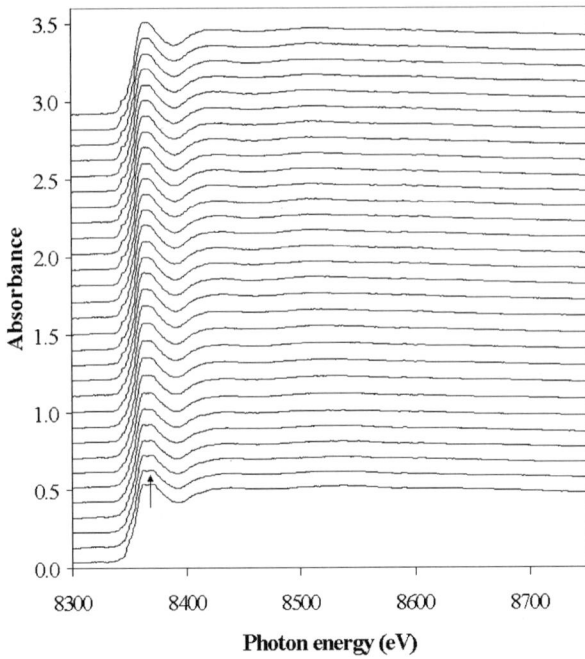

Fig. 5 Ni K-edge EDE spectra for the reaction of Ni(dpm)$_2$ (60 mM), AlEt$_2$(OEt) and hex-1-ene (1 : 6 : 20) in toluene. Thirty spectra were recorded each of 1000 accumulations and 16 ms acquisition time (*i.e.* 16 s per spectrum).

The reaction between Ni(dpm)$_2$ and AlEt$_3$/hex-1-ene was also investigated in toluene, and a plot of 10 successive spectra is presented as Fig. 11. It would be anticipated that this more reactive aluminium alkyl would increase the reaction rate. The spectra are of a single accumulation of 16 ms, and the most evident change is the creation of a pre-edge feature, this being complete by the

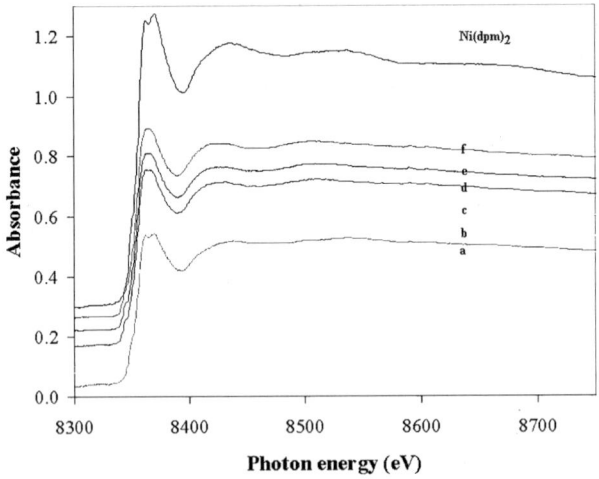

Fig. 6 More detailed comparison of the Ni K-edge EDE spectra following the reaction of Ni(dpm)$_2$ (60 mM), AlEt$_2$(OEt) and hex-1-ene (1 : 6 : 20) in toluene: top Ni(dpm)$_2$ in toluene, and a sequence of spectra after mixing (16 s per spectrum): (a) 1st , (b) 2nd, (c) 9th (d) 20th (e) 30th and (f) after 20 min reaction time.

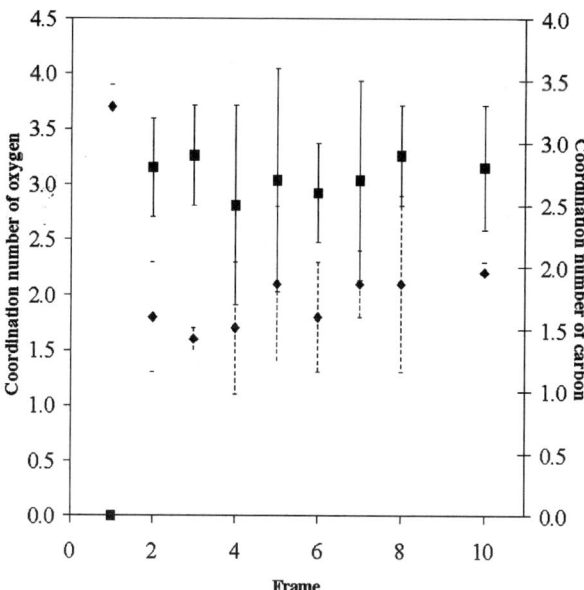

Fig. 7 A plot of the coordination numbers for Ni–O (♦) and Ni–C (■) shells *versus* frame number for the reaction of Ni(dpm)$_2$ (60 mM), AlEt$_2$(OEt) and hex-1-ene (1 : 6 : 20) in toluene Each frame took 16 s to acquire (1000 accumulations and a 16 ms acquisition time.

second or third frame. With a 15 ms deadtime for synchronisation of the detector system with the stopped flow system, and a 16 ms acquisition time, this indicates that the reaction is essentially complete within 60 ms. This example, and the previous system studied, demonstrate the need for improving the time resolution of the instrumentation in order to probe these rapid reactions.

Electron transfer reaction of aqueous Fe(III) and hydroquinone

The additional brilliance of ID24 at the ESRF compared to Station 9.3 of the SRS would be anticipated to provide higher time resolution. This was tested using the same reaction as reported by Yoshida *et al.*[?] The reduction of aqueous Fe(III) by hydroquinone was carried out at a series of pH values. The Fe K-edge XAFS spectra were acquired as individual stripes on the CCD prior to reading out the entire dataset. Improvements in the signal/noise ratio may be achieved by repeating the injections, and averaging the resulting datasets. The XAFS data on concentrations of

Table 3 Structural parameters derived from the EXAFS of solid Ni(dpm)$_2$(PPh$_3$)$_2$ ($E_F = 4.0$ eV, $R = 21\%$), the complex in toluene (80 mM) studied by EDE (1000 × 18 ms, $E_F = 4.1$ eV, $R = 32\%$), and QEXAFS data on the reaction of Ni(dpm)$_2$, PPh$_3$, AlEt$_2$(OEt) and hex-1-ene ([Ni] 80 mM in toluene, Ni : P : Al : hex-1-ene = 1 : 2 : 2 : 20) at 0 °C after 20 min (scan time 5 min, $E_F = 4.0$ eV, $R = 32\%$)

Sample	Coordination number	R/Å	$2\sigma^2/Å^2$
Ni(dpm)$_2$(PPh$_3$)$_2$, solid			
	4.0(5) O	1.968(1)	0.007(0)
	2.0 (1) P	2.305 (8)	0.032 (2)
	4.0 (4) C	2.851 (5)	0.011 (2)
Ni(dpm)$_2$(PPh$_3$)$_2$/toluene			
	4.2 (2) O	1.902 (4)	0.012 (1)
	2.3 (5) P	2.278 (3)	0.019 (0)
Ni(dpm)$_2$, PPh$_3$, AlEt$_2$(OEt), hexene (1 : 2 : 2 : 20)			
3.2(3) O	1.887 (6)	0.006 (1)	
1.2 (5) P	2.18 (1)	0.016 (3)	

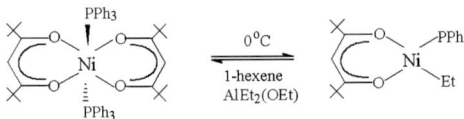

Fig. 8 Proposed reaction scheme for the reaction of Ni(dpm)$_2$, PPh$_3$, AlEt$_2$(OEt) and hex-1-ene (1 : 2 : 2 : 20) in toluene.

100 mM of each reagent and at pH 1.9 are presented in Fig. 12. Of the pH values studied, this afforded the fastest reaction. At such a pH, the predominant Fe(III) species present will be a mixture of [Fe(OH$_2$)$_6$]$^{3+}$ and [Fe$_2$(μ-OH)$_2$(OH$_2$)$_8$]$^{4+}$, with [Fe(OH)(OH$_2$)$_5$]$^{2+}$ as a minor species. The energy range of the spectrum does not allow any structural differentiation between these alternatives, but does provide an estimate of the Fe–O distance of 2.0 Å. In Fig. 12(a), an acquisition time of 100 ms was employed. The first of the 15 spectra indicates that the reaction had already proceeded to some extent, with the final spectrum corresponding closely to that of aqueous Fe(II), with a longer Fe–O distance of 2.1 Å. The intermediate in the electron transfer process is considered to be an adduct: [(Fe^{III}–H$_2$Q)$_{aq}$], observable as a blue species in concentrated solutions.[24] Spectra were therefore acquired with shorter acquisition times (down to 1 ms). The spectra obtained with a 10 ms acquisition time are shown in Fig. 12(b). No evidence of any intermediate was observed, with isosbectic points typical of a single step process.

Changes in near-edge structure and the low k EXAFS region can therefore be monitored on a timescale of the order of ms. In this example, the initial spectra observed may be a mixture of the various forms of aqueous Fe(III) and also the precursor (rather than the successor) complex to the electron transfer from hydroquinone. In all these structures there is an octahedral environment around Fe(III) with 6 oxygen donor ligands. Hence it would have been extremely difficult to differentiate these species. In effect such changes are invisible. The Fe K-edge also provides a relatively narrow energy bandspread for a given focal length of the bent monochromator; longer k ranges are attainable for absorption edges of lower wavelength, such as the Ir L(III) edge.

Oxidative addition of methyltrifluoromethylsulfonate (CH$_3$OSO$_2$CF$_3$) on [IrI$_2$(CO)$_2$]$^-$

The oxidative addition of iodomethane to the square planar Ir(I) complex [IrI$_2$(CO)$_2$]$^-$ is considered to be the initial step in the *Cativa*[25] process for the manufacture of acetic acid by the carbonylation of methanol. A highly reactive methylating agent was employed to model this process under ambient conditions. Using the silicon microstrip detector, XSTRIP,[10] spectra could be acquired in multiples of 400 μs, with an average of 3 accumulations providing a time resolution

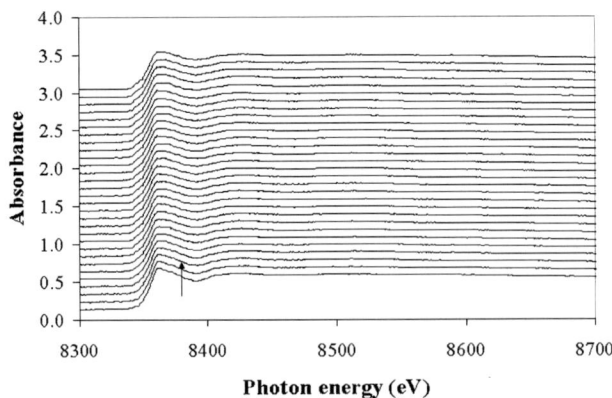

Fig. 9 Ni K-edge EDE spectra for the reaction of Ni(dpm)$_2$ (60 mM), PPh$_3$, AlEt$_2$(OEt) and hex-1-ene (1 : 2 : 4 : 20) in toluene. Thirty spectra were recorded each of 50 accumulations and 24 ms acquisition time (1.2 s per frame).

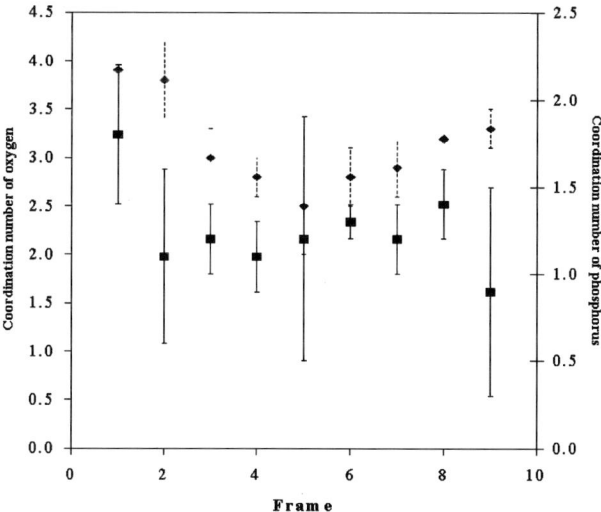

Fig. 10 A plot of the coordination numbers for Ni–P (■) and Ni–O (◆) shells *versus* frame number for the reaction of Ni(dpm)$_2$ (60 mM), PPh$_3$, AlEt$_2$(OEt) and hex-1-ene (1 : 2 : 4 : 20) in toluene Each frame took 1.2 s to acquire.

of 1.2 ms as the minimum used. The readout time is relatively low (*ca.* 12 μs per spectrum), and the number of spectra that may be acquired is 1500. Hence a much wider time frame can be sampled with a single reaction. The reaction was studied with series of 200 spectra, with multiple of 3, 30 300 and 3000 accumulations per spectrum, covering a timescale from 1.2 ms to 240 s. Some results are presented in Fig. 13. These show the Ir L(III) spectra of the starting material NBu$^n_4$[IrI$_2$(CO)$_2$] in acetonitrile (80 mM) and the results of mixing this solution with CF$_3$SO$_3$Me (80 mM) in MeCN (1 : 1) are also presented. Significant changes in the immediate post edge region and in the position of the first EXAFS oscillation are evident, even in the first of the more rapid spectra recorded (1.2 ms after mixing). Further changes in the post edge peak are also apparent over a period of 180 s. The mechanism of the oxidative addition reaction is anticipated to be an ionic one, with initial addition of a carbocation to the iridium centre and then binding of the counter ion to complete an

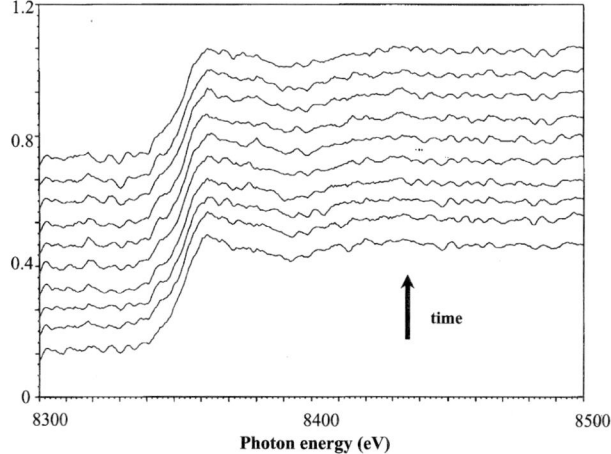

Fig. 11 The 10 consecutive spectra were performed at 16 ms integration time, and 1 accumulation. Single frames took 16 ms for the reaction of Ni(dpm)$_2$: AlEt$_3$: 1-hexene of 1 : 1 : 20, [Ni] (60 mM) at room temperature.

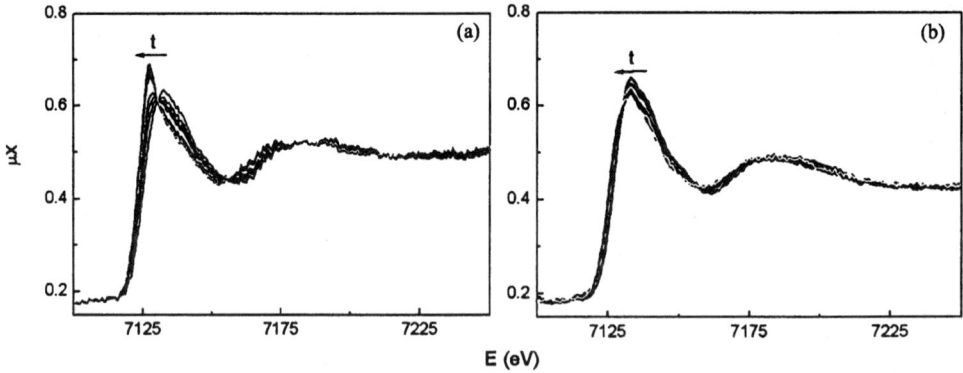

Fig. 12 Fe K-edge EDE spectra observed from 0.1 M Fe(ClO$_4$)$_3$ and 0.1 M hydroquinone in aqueous ethanol (3 : 1), pH = 1.9. 15 successive spectra of (a) 100 ms and (b) of 10 ms acquisition time.

octahedral coordination sphere. This methylating agent provides a weakly bonding anionic ligand, CF$_3$SO$_3^-$, and so it appears that the two steps are discernible. Analysis of scanning EXAFS data on the initial and final solutions are consistent with the presence of initially the Ir(I) complex [IrI$_2$(CO)$_2$]$^-$. Refinement of EXAFS data for this anion afforded, when incorporating multiple scattering and linear Ir–C–O-units, r(Ir–CO) = 1.852(5) Å, r(Ir–I) = 2.673(2) Å and r(Ir···CO) = 2.930 (5) Å. The final complex could be refined to the Ir(III) complex [Ir(CH$_3$)(O–SO$_3$CF$_3$)I$_2$(CO)$_2$]$^-$ {r(Ir–CO) = 1.96(1) Å, r(Ir–CCH$_3$) 2.2(3) Å, r(Ir–OSO$_2$CF$_3$) = 2.05(2) Å, r(Ir–I) = 2.686(2) and r(Ir···CO) 3.034(6) Å; as in the case of the related complex [RhI$_3$(CO)$_2$-{C(O)CH$_3$} (solv)]$^-$, refinement of the 3 metal to light element shells was indicative of, but, by itself, not conclusive proof, of the presence of all three coordination types.[26] There is a significant lengthening of the Ir–CO bonds with this oxidative addition from Ir(I) to Ir(III), indicative of reduced back bonding to the CO groups from the higher oxidation state metal centre. These structural changes cause the change in the position of the first EXAFS oscillation near 11 270 eV. The first, rapid step affords a species with a similar spectrum to that of the final state, but with small changes in the XANES region indicative of a subtle change in coordination geometry. The proposed intermediate would be a square pyramidal complex [Ir^{III}(CH$_3$)I$_2$(CO)$_2$] with the

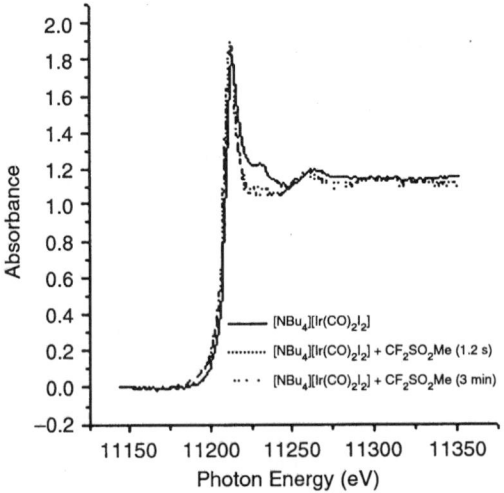

Fig. 13 Ir L(III) edge EDE spectra of the reaction of NBu$_4$[IrI$_2$(CO)$_2$] (40 mM) with CH$_3$SO$_3$CF$_3$ (40 mM) in acetonitrile solution at room temperature.

$CF_3SO_3^-$ group unbound. This group contributes relatively little to the EXAFS and thus this binding will not cause a substantial change in the EXAFS features. The similarity of the position of the first EXAFS maximum to that of the final product suggests that this also is indeed attributable to a Ir(III) centre.

Discussion and future prospects

These results show a progression of capability with detector development and beamline improvements. Acquisition times of under 500 µs have been demonstrated and these closely match the optimum performance of state of the art stopped flow devices. It is thus apparent that, for concentrations in the region of 10^{-1}–10^{-2} mol dm^{-3}, time resolutions of 10^{-3}–10^{-4} s are obtainable at the present time. In other experiments using the XSTRIP detector on ID24, both these guidelines were improved (5–10 × 10^{-3} mol dm^{-3}; 2–10 × 10^{-5} s).[10] In the fastest spectrum attempted (35 µs), only about 12 orbital revolutions had occurred, so the potential for EDE measurement in a single bunch mode becomes tantalising. Time resolution would be governed by activation times and the single bunch pulse width (~10^{-11} s). To accommodate this, much faster reaction initiation procedures would have to be adopted, such as microchannel reactors and photochemical excitation. When the capabilities of all these techniques are combined, it can be envisaged that chemical processes from the steps (ps) through rapid transients (ns–ms) to conventional reaction times (s) may be monitored in solution. Direct observation of structural parameters of transients should also be attainable.

Acknowledgements

We wish to thank the following for financial support: University of Southampton, EPSRC, BP Chemicals and The Royal Society. We also wish to thank the Directors and staff of the Daresbury Laboratory and ESRF for their help and access to their facilities. We are particularly grateful to Jo Salvini and Jon Headspith for their creativity with detector systems.

References

1. (a) T. Matsushita and R. P. Phizackerley, *Jpn. Appl. Phys.*, 1981, **20**, 2223; (b) E. Dartyge, A. Fontaine, A. Jucha and D. Sayers, in *EXAFS and Near Edge Structure III*, ed. K. O. Hodgson, B. Hedman and J. E. Penner-Hahn, Springer, Berlin, 1985, p. 336; (c) R. P. Phizackerley, Z. V. Rek, G. V. Stephenson, S. D. Conradson, K. O. Hodgson, T. Matsushita and T. Oyanagi, *J. Appl. Phys.*, 1983, **16**, 220.
2. N. Yoshida, T. Matsushita, S. Saigo, H. Oyanagi, H. Hashimoto and M. Fujimoto, *J. Chem. Soc., Chem. Commun.*, 1990, 354.
3. D. Bogg, A. J. Dent, G. E. Derbyshire, R. C. Farrow, A. Felton, C. A. Ramsdale and G. Salvini, *Physica B*, 1995, **208/9**, 229.
4. D. Bogg, M. Conyngham, J. M. Corker, A. J. Dent, J. Evans, R. C. Farrow, V. L. Kambhampati, A. F. Masters, D. N. McLeod, C. A. Ramsdale and G. Salvini, *J. Chem. Soc., Chem. Commun.*, 1996, 647.
5. J. R. Jones and T. J. Symes, *J. Chem. Soc., C*, 1971, 1124.
6. M. A. Newton, A. J. Dent and J. Evans, *Chem. Soc. Rev.*, 2002, **31**, 83.
7. M. Hagelstein, A. San Miguel, T. Ressler, A. Fontaine and J. Goulon, *J. Phys. IV*, 1996, **C2**, 303.
8. A. Dent, J. Evans, M. Newton, J. Corker, A. Russell, M. B. Abdul Rahman, S. Fiddy, R. Mathew, R. Farrow, G. Salvini and P. Atkinson, *J. Synchrotron Radiat.*, 1999, **6**, 381.
9. D. Bogg, A. J. Dent, G. E. Derbyshire, R. C. Farrow, C. A. Ramsdale and G. Salvini, *Nucl. Instrum. Methods Phys. Res., Sect. A*, 1997, **392**, 461.
10. (a) C. Anderson, A. J. Dent, G. Derbyshire, R. C. Farrow, J. Headspith, T. Rayment, G. Salvini and S. Thomas, http://detserv1.dl.ac.uk/xstrip/; (b) G. Iles, A. Dent, G. Derbyshire, R. Farrow, G. Hall, G. Noyes, M. Raymond, G. Salvini, P. Seller, M. Smith and S. Thomas, *J. Synchrotron Radiat.*, 2000, **7**, 221.
11. G. Salvini, D. Bogg, A. J. Dent, G. E. Derbyshire, R. C. Farrow, A. Felton and C. Ramsdale, *Physica B*, 1995, **208&209**, 229.
12. S. Diaz-Moreno, in *From Semiconductors to Proteins: Beyond the Average Structure*, ed. S. J. L. Billinge and M. F. Thorpe, Plenum Press, New York, 2002, p. 203.
13. M. J. Collins and H. S. Heinneike, *Inorg. Chem.*, 1973, **12**, 2983.
14. J. P. Fackler, Jr., S. J. Kopperl and P. E. Rakita, *J. Inorg. Nucl. Chem.*, 1968, **30**, 2139.
15. D. Forster, *Inorg. Nucl. Chem. Lett.*, 1969, **5**, 433.

16 N. Binsted, *PAXAS – Programme for the Analysis of X-ray Absorption Spectroscopy*, University of Southampton, 1988.
17 N. Binsted, J. W. Campbell, S. J. Gurman and P. C. Stephenson, EXCURV98, Daresbury Laboratory.
18 J. M. Corker, J. Evans, H. Leach and W. Levason, *J. Chem Soc., Chem Commun.*, 1989, 181.
19 J. M. Corker and J. Evans, *J. Chem. Soc., Chem. Commun.*, 1991, 1104.
20 J. M. Corker, A. J. Dent, J. Evans, M. Hagelstein and V. L. Kambhampati, *J. Phys. IV*, 1997, **7**, C2-879.
21 F. A. Cotton and J. J. Wise, *Inorg. Chem.*, 1966, **5**, 1200.
22 P. Andrews and J. Evans, *J. Chem. Soc., Chem. Commun.*, 1993, 1246.
23 S. G. Fiddy, M. A. Newton, A. J. Dent, J. Evans, G. Salvini, J. M. Corker, S. Turin, T. Campbell and J. Evans, *Chem. Commun.*, 1999, 851.
24 J. H. Blaxendale, H. R. Hardy and L. H. Sutcliffe, *Trans. Faraday Soc.*, 1951, **47**, 963.
25 (*a*) G. J. Sunley and D. J. Watson, *Catal. Today*, 2000, **58**, 293; (*b*) M. J. Howard, G. J. Sunley, R. J. Watt and B. K. Sharma, *Stud. Surf. Sci. Catal.*, 1999, **121**, 61; (*c*) J. H. Jones, *Platinum Metals Rev.*, 2000, **44**, 94.
26 N. A. Cruise and J. Evans, *J. Chem. Soc., Dalton Trans.*, 1995, 3089.

Direct dynamics calculations of reaction rate and kinetic isotope effects in enzyme catalysed reactions

Gary Tresadern, Sara Nunez, Paul F. Faulder, Hong Wang, Ian H. Hillier and Neil A. Burton

Department of Chemistry, University of Manchester, Manchester, UK M13 9PL

Received 31st January 2002, Accepted 1st March 2002
First published as an Advance Article on the web 2nd September 2002

Direct dynamics calculations employing hybrid quantum mechanical and molecular mechanical (QM/MM) potentials and molecular dynamics simulation methods have been used to explore the important dynamic role that enzyme structure has on proton transfer in the C–H bond breakage of a methylamine substrate by methylamine dehydrogenase (MADH). Canonical variational transition state theory with optimised multidimensional tunnelling corrections has been used to predict deuterium kinetic isotope effects corresponding to a range of enzyme conformations and to show the importance of donor–acceptor separation, and transition state and product stabilisation within the active site. Large kinetic isotope effects can be predicted for proton transfer with both semi-empirical and *ab initio* electronic structure methods.

1. Introduction

The chemical basis for enzyme catalysis has been extensively studied[1] and a wide variety of reaction mechanisms can now be predicted from known protein structural motifs. Although there is a general consensus that there are two major factors responsible for rate enhancement, pre-organisation due to protein–substrate binding and transition state stabilisation effects, there are other important features of these complex systems which contribute to their effective function. Computational approaches are now contributing to an understanding of these processes,[2] particularly through the direct study of the energetic and structural behaviour at an atomic level. A number of issues associated with the computational study of enzyme reactivity are addressed in this paper:

The large size of the enzyme means that the whole enzyme cannot be treated at a high level of theory. In view of this, new strategies have been developed to allow the calculation of reaction activation barriers and to study the mechanisms of enzyme reactions. Here we utilise hybrid quantum mechanical and molecular mechanical (QM/MM) methods[3–8] to accurately treat the electronic structure of the active site and include important interactions with the enzyme environment.

The large kinetic isotope effects observed for some alcohol dehydrogenases suggests the importance of quantum mechanical tunnelling[9–15] which requires a description beyond that of conventional transition state theory. Here we shall study the rate limiting proton transfer reaction of methylamine dehydrogenase (MADH) using semi-classical variational transition state theory[16,17] with multidimensional tunnelling corrections[18] to calculate rate constants and hence predict primary deuterium kinetic isotope effects which can be directly correlated with recent experimental data.[9]

DOI: 10.1039/b201183m

Although activation barriers and transition state stabilisation can often explain the kinetic behaviour observed for many enzyme systems, we find that the shape of the entire potential energy surface may be critically important, especially in proton transfer reactions. Such calculations are extremely computationally intensive, even using present day resources. To reduce the computational effort required we have used both semi-empirical and small basis set *ab initio* Hartree–Fock methods.

Enzyme motion will affect the reaction coordinate and thus a single conformer of the enzyme would not be representative of the protein structure. In order to fully understand MADH we must also consider how the dynamical behaviour of the enzyme directly affects the shape of the potential energy surface. We have therefore used molecular dynamics simulations to study multiple enzyme configurations in order to relate enzyme conformation to the reaction kinetic data.

Methylamine dehydrogenase (EC 1.4.99.3) catalyses the oxidative demethylation of methylamine to formaldehyde and ammonia.[9,19] Recent stopped flow kinetic studies of this enzyme from *Methylophilus methyltrophus* have shown an unusually large, temperature independent primary deuterium kinetic isotope effect (KIE) of 16.8 ± 0.5, but strongly temperature dependent reaction rates, that were interpreted as indicating a thermally induced vibrationally driven extreme tunnelling mechanism for the rate limiting hydrogen abstraction step:

Previous experimental studies[20] on MADH from *Paracoccus denitrificans* showed similar kinetic and energetic behaviour recording a large KIE of 17.2 ± 0.6 and a free energy of activation of 14.2 kcal mol^{-1} at 303 K.

Following the success of computational approaches for the study of small gas phase molecular processes, there has been a great deal of activity to develop methods to accurately account for condensed phase interactions in electronic structure calculations.[21] Amongst these are a range of continuum-based solvation methods which account for the electrostatic free energy of interaction between solute and solvent. However, this approach has had little impact upon studies of enzyme reactivity due to the non-uniformity of protein structure. Hybrid quantum mechanical and molecular mechanical (QM/MM) methods[3–8] are well suited to the study of enzyme reactive paths since they include an accurate quantum mechanical description of the active site, where the electronic structure is important and bonds are broken and formed, whilst approximating the explicit effects of the surrounding enzyme framework with a molecular mechanical (MM) potential. To account for the dynamical nature of the enzyme reaction, or entropic contributions, methods are being developed to find the potential of mean force along a reaction coordinate.[22,23] One such approach is based upon free energy perturbation (FEP) methods where the free energy of interaction between the quantum mechanical and the classical enzyme regions is obtained from a canonical ensemble of structures generated by Monte Carlo or molecular dynamics simulations. Such QM-FEP calculations[24,25] have been particularly successful in predicting solvation properties but are limited in that the interactions between solute or enzyme active site and the surroundings have often been approximated using empirical potentials. Recently, potentially more accurate semi-empirical hybrid or empirical valence bond potentials have been used together with umbrella sampling dynamics approaches[26–28] but such calculations are extremely computationally demanding and the use of accurate potentials is prohibitive at present.

The approach taken to analyse the reaction mechanism in this study acknowledges the fact that there may be multiple trajectories which lead from reactant to product and that the definition of reactant and product are in fact ensembles of different enzyme–substrate or enzyme–product structures. For small systems rate constants can be statistically obtained *via* direct simulation,[29,30] but the rarity of the reaction event and re-crossing effects generally preclude widespread use of such an approach and semi-classical approximations of transition state theory are preferred. Although we shall not attempt to calculate an overall rate constant statistically, we shall calculate a number of rate constants (and KIEs), using variational transition state theory, which correspond to a somewhat arbitrary set of reaction paths which approximate the reaction trajectories. We assume in our calculations that only the atoms within the active site, that are described quantum mechanically, will relax during a reaction event since a typical reaction coordinate usually involves the displacement of only several key atoms. This is particularly true for hydrogen transfer events where the mass of the proton is very light relative to the accepting and donating groups. We have summarised our approach in Fig. 1 which shows the time evolution of an equilibrated classical molecular dynamics trajectory. For selected enzyme conformers, reaction paths corresponding to proton transfer are generated using the QM/MM method to give an ensemble of transition states and reaction energetics. Each reaction path differs in the conformation of the enzyme defining the active site so that the position of essential stabilising amino acid residues binding the substrate and tryptophan tryptophylquinone (TTQ) cofactor will differ in each case. This strategy has allowed us to probe the dynamical effects of the enzyme upon the reaction mechanism. We will discuss how the rare reaction event may be driven by a promoting vibration bringing proton acceptor and donor together or by strengthening specific hydrogen bonds to stabilise an enzyme configuration which is suitable for quantum mechanical tunnelling of the proton from the cofactor intermediate to Asp_{428}. We may expect such active configurations, which could be generated by specific vibrational motion or random thermal motion of the enzyme, to promote the large deuterium KIEs which are observed experimentally.

It is perhaps useful at this stage to relate our approach to the influence of near attack conformers (NACs) in enzyme catalysis, a concept recently reviewed by Bruice and Benkovic.[31] In essence this theory argues that rare reaction events are most likely to take place when the reacting groups are suitably pre-aligned into NACs and that the percentage occurrence (~1–50%) of these so called NACs is related to the free energy barrier to reaction, $\Delta G^{\ddagger}$. Such a relationship has been demonstrated for a range of enzyme reactions by studying equilibrium ensembles of enzyme–substrate complexes obtained from long time molecular dynamics simulations. We have however found in our study that ensembles generated using standard molecular mechanical force fields may be inadequate to predict important reactive conformers, due in particular to omission of important polarization effects. In order to account for the increased stabilisation afforded by polarization we have considered two additional strategies. We have generated enzyme structures using product-like potential parameters and secondly we increased the size of the quantum mechanical region. Both methods allow the enzyme to form a structure which preferentially stabilises the transition state rather than the reactant complex in line with Paulings theory of catalysis. Fig. 1 also illustrates how these alternative conformers can be obtained from a simulation using transition state or product-like MM parameters. This approach therefore improves upon some previous hybrid calculations

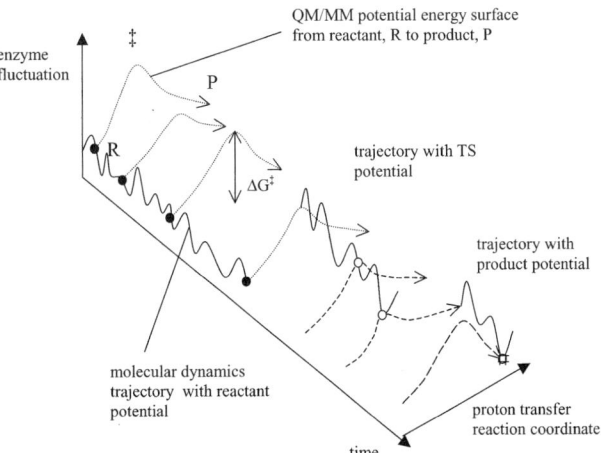

Fig. 1 Schematic showing our computational approach to analyse how the barrier to reaction for proton transfer can depend on enzyme configuration.

which typically use single enzyme structures, optimised to bind the Michaelis complex, and usually remain close to the crystal structure.

2. QM/MM direct dynamics computational approach

Hybrid quantum mechanical and molecular mechanical (QM/MM) methods allow us to accurately study a small region of the system quantum mechanically using semi-empirical, *ab initio* or density functional methods, whilst including the effect of the surrounding enzyme with a molecular mechanical potential. The link atom method was used to describe the covalent junctions between the two regions.[5] Our implementation of the QM/MM method using the GAUSSIAN[32] and the AMBER[33] programs and associated force field[34] has been described previously.[35] In this research we have used both *ab initio* Hartree–Fock and semi-empirical PM3 electronic structure methods including van der Waals, bonding and electrostatic contributions from the MM potential, the latter being explicitly included in the QM Hamiltonian. Although geometry optimisations can be performed on both QM and MM regions simultaneously,[35] we have chosen here to vary only the nuclear positions of the QM region, keeping the MM region and any link atoms fixed along a reaction path. Analytic and numerical harmonic frequency calculations were employed to characterise stationary points with the Hartree–Fock and semi-empirical methods respectively.

For each enzyme configuration, points along an approximate reaction path were first obtained with the QM/MM method by a coordinate driving procedure, often termed a potential energy (PE) scan, by choosing a geometric variable to approximate the reaction coordinate and minimising all other degrees of freedom. In this study we have found that a suitable coordinate is the O(Asp$_{428}$)–H(transferring proton) distance (see reaction scheme above). This reaction profile is then used to obtain the stationary points corresponding to reactant, product and transition state by employing conventional geometry optimisation techniques.

Accurate minimum potential energy paths (MEP) were generated using the Page and McIver intrinsic reaction coordinate (IRC) algorithm.[36] This algorithm starts from a fully characterised QM/MM transition state structure (‡), at reaction coordinate value $s = 0$, and takes quadratic steps of 0.01 u$^{1/2}$ a_0 along the reaction coordinate towards reactant ($s < 0$) and product ($s > 0$). It is necessary to stay close to the minimum energy path and hence gradients were calculated at all points, second derivatives of the energy at every second or third point within the range of at least $s = \pm 0.8$ u$^{1/2}$ a_0, and extrapolation to finally take the path to reactant and products. Since the process is computationally intensive, requiring as many as several hundred hessians to be evaluated, an approach commonly adopted is to use a semi-empirical Hamiltonian to generate the path and then to employ a dual level method,[37–39] using higher level calculations to scale the low level PM3 path. In this work we have also directly used the MEP at the Hartree–Fock level with a small 3-21G basis set.

Direct dynamics calculations utilise these MEPs with canonical variational transition state theory (CVT),[16,17] as implemented within the POLYRATE[40] code and interfaced to our QM/MM program *via* a modified version of GAUSSRATE.[41] Multidimensional tunnelling effects[17,42–45] were subsequently calculated to predict reaction rates and finally deuterium KIEs.

The generalised transition state rate constant[17] is evaluated with respect to s for a given temperature T according to

$$k^{GT}(T,s) = \sigma \frac{k_B T}{h} \frac{Q^{GT}(T,s)}{Q^R(T)} e^{-\Delta V_{MEP}(s)/k_B T}, \qquad (1)$$

where k_B is the Boltzmann constant, h is Planck's constant, $Q^{GT}(T,s)$ and $Q^R(T,s)$ are the generalised transition state and reactant partition functions respectively, σ is a symmetry factor and $V_{MEP}(s)$ is the potential energy. The CVT rate constant is then defined for the position on the MEP that yields the minimum $k^{GT}(T,s)$ (equivalent to maximising the free energy), according to

$$k^{CVT}(T) = \min_s k^{GT}(T,s) = k^{GT}[T, s_*^{CVT}(T)], \qquad (2)$$

where $s_*^{CVT}(T)$ is the location of the CVT transition state for temperature T. For the enzymatic reactions studied here, a major aim was to investigate the role of quantum mechanical tunnelling.

The effects of tunnelling through the barrier and non-classical reflection were included *via* the transmission coefficient, $\kappa^{\text{CVT/OMT}}$, in the final rate constant,

$$k^{\text{CVT/OMT}}(T) = \kappa^{\text{CVT/OMT}}(T) k^{\text{CVT}}(T). \tag{3}$$

The optimised multidimensional tunnelling (OMT) method[17,18,42–45] selects the largest transmission coefficient calculated by three tunnelling approximations: zero curvature tunnelling (ZCT), small curvature tunnelling (SCT) and large curvature tunnelling (LCT). Since LCT calculations are more time consuming, involving extra calculations in regions of the MEP, and as in previous studies on MADH[46] the SCT scheme was found to be most important for tunnelling, we have used here only the SCT method. These calculations feature tunnelling through the adiabatic potential energy, $V_a^G(s)$, given by

$$V_a^G(s) = V_{\text{MEP}}(s) + \frac{1}{2}h\sum_{i=1}^{F-1} \nu_i(s), \tag{4}$$

where ν_i is the generalised normal mode frequency. The transmission coefficient is calculated as the ratio of the thermally averaged quantal transmission probability, to the thermally averaged classical transmission probability,

$$\kappa^{\text{CVT/G}}(T) = \frac{\int_0^\infty P^G(E) e^{-E/k_B T} dE}{\int_{V_a^G[s_*^{\text{CVT}}(T)]}^\infty e^{-E/k_B T} dE}. \tag{5}$$

We have used the centrifugal dominant small curvature semi-classical adiabatic ground state (G = CD-SCSAG) method[42,43] for $P^G(E)$, including a contribution due to reaction path curvature. The total reaction path curvature is defined as

$$\kappa(s) = \left\{ \sum_{i=1}^{F-1} [B_{iF}(s)]^2 \right\}^{1/2}, \tag{6}$$

where the components, $B_{iF}(s)$, are scalar products of the normal mode vector, and its derivative for vibration i with respect to s. If $B_{iF}(s)$ is significant then the motion along the reaction co-ordinate is coupled to the transverse vibration. In regions of increased reaction path curvature the effective reduced mass for the motion along s is reduced, which simulates corner-cutting tunnelling. The transmission coefficient (eqn. (5)) can be factored into quantal, κ^G and classical effects, $\kappa^{\text{CVT/CAG}}$,

$$\kappa^{\text{CVT/G}}(T) = \kappa^{\text{CVT/CAG}}(T) \kappa^G(T). \tag{7}$$

$\kappa^{\text{CVT/CAG}}$ is defined[47,48] as,

$$\kappa^{\text{CVT/CAG}}(T) = \frac{\int_{\max V_a^G(s)}^\infty e^{-E/k_B T} dE}{\int_{V_a^G[s_*^{\text{CVT}}(T)]}^\infty e^{-E/k_B T} dE}, \tag{8}$$

where the numerator is the thermal average of the classical transmission probability for the adiabatic ground state barrier and the denominator is the thermal average of the classical transmission probability calculated by CVT. The factor $\kappa^{\text{CVT/CAG}}$ is employed to ensure consistency between TST and CVT calculations, and is typically $\sim$1. However, for some of our calculations we found that due to the large changes in vibrational frequencies and associated free energy profiles, there were significant amounts of re-crossing, manifesting itself in very small $\kappa^{\text{CVT/CAG}}$ factors and unrealistic KIEs.

The representative tunnelling energy (RTE)[44,49] is the energy at which tunnelling is most likely to occur for a particular temperature. This quantity is defined as the energy at which the integrand of the numerator of the ground state transmission coefficient, $\kappa^{\text{CVT/G}}(T)$, is a maximum. There is competition between the Boltzmann factor that decreases with energy and the tunnelling probability that increases with energy. There are two points on the reaction path where the RTE equals the adiabatic energy and the straight line between these two points is termed the representative tunnelling path, which allows us to more easily compare the relative amounts of tunnelling for different reaction paths.

3. Extreme tunnelling mechanism for proton transfer in MADH

Hydrogen transfer, of both protons and hydride ions, occurs in many enzyme mechanisms and is often the rate limiting step. Kinetic isotope effects are probably one of the most widespread experimental predictors for understanding such reactions, and large deuterium KIEs have been largely attributed as arising from quantum tunnelling effects. However, it has been shown that in addition to a large KIE, the temperature dependence of the KIE is also a very important factor in understanding the role of tunnelling. There is currently great interest in the possibility of enhanced hydrogen tunnelling arising from protein flexibility,[50–52] particularly in the case of the alcohol dehydrogenase family of enzymes.[9–15,53–55] Perhaps the most studied enzyme in this series, both experimentally[56,57] and theoretically,[58–61] is liver alcohol dehydrogenase (LADH) where it has been shown that protein flexibility correlates with hydride tunnelling for thermophilic and mesophilic enzymes although the measured KIEs are quite small (2–3), in contrast to the value for the proton transfer reaction in MADH studied here.

Hybrid QM/MM methods have recently been combined with semi-classical variational transition state theory methods[8,58] to study hydride shift reactions and their associated KIEs. We have recently applied our QM/MM approach to study both the hydride transfer in LADH[61] and the proton transfer in MADH,[46] which allows direct comparison of the two mechanisms. In LADH we found that there is appreciable hydride tunnelling but that this was considerably smaller than the extreme tunnelling found for the transfer of the proton in MADH. Analysis of the reaction profile for MADH (Fig. 2) indicated that a combination of quantum tunnelling (> 90%) and classical protein motion is responsible for the large primary deuterium KIE, which was predicted to be 11.1 at 300 K. The initial part of the classical reaction coordinate was found to be an approach of donor and acceptor groups to within 2.6 Å followed by a further barrier of 2–4 kcal mol^{-1} corresponding to transfer of the proton. In contrast to MADH, the reaction coordinate for hydride transfer in horse LADH involves heavy atom motion to within approximately 0.2–0.4 kcal mol^{-1} of the transition state and thus promotes a more classical over barrier hydrogen transfer mechanism and results in a smaller KIE. This results in predictions that ~40% of the reaction occurs classically in LADH[58,61] compared with only ~4% in MADH.[27,46]

Our preliminary study on MADH,[46] which forms the basis for discussion in this research, used a semi-empirical Hamiltonian (PM3) which had proved relatively reliable in the study of other enzymes[6–8] and enabled the large number of hessians required for the direct dynamics calculation to be evaluated along the reaction path. In our previous work a single enzyme configuration was

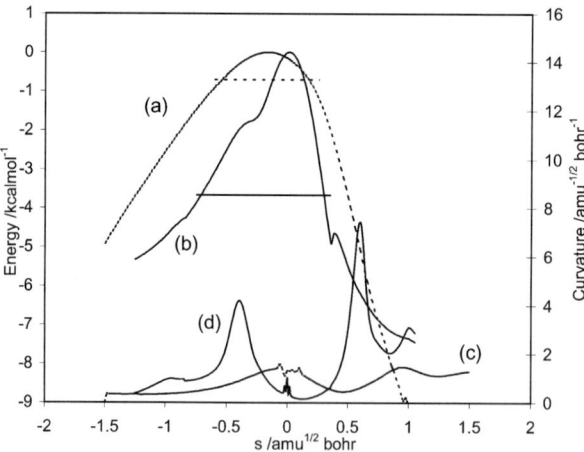

Fig. 2 Comparison of hydride transfer in LADH, HF/3-21G///AM1, and proton transfer in MADH, PM3 level. Relative energetics (left scale) and total reaction path curvature (right scale). (a) V_a^G for hydride transfer in LADH. (b) V_a^G for proton transfer in MADH. (c) LADH hydride transfer total reaction path curvature. (d) MADH proton transfer total reaction path curvature. Horizontal lines are the RTEs through V_a^G.

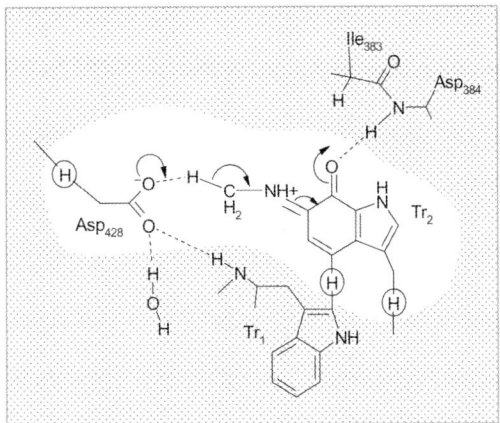

Fig. 3 31 atom active site of MADH. QM region is shown unshaded with link atoms circled.

used to generate the reaction potential energy surface. The initial iminoquinone reactant structure was constructed from the crystal coordinates of MADH taken from *Methylophilus methylotrophus*[62] by replacing the carbonyl oxygen[63] of the TTQ cofactor with methylamine as shown in Fig. 3 (the two tryptophan residues of TTQ are labelled separately as Tr_1 and Tr_2). The entire dimer was protonated, solvated and then minimised using the AMBER molecular mechanics force field. We shall refer to this enzyme structure as R0.

For the hybrid calculations, the QM region was limited to 31 atoms (see Fig. 3) which include the catalytic base, Asp_{428}, and the catalytically active rings of one tryptophan (Tr_2) of the TTQ cofactor after reduction with methylamine. This QM region was subsequently minimised to find an optimised reactant complex, using the QM/MM method employing the PM3 Hamiltonian. Product and transition state structures, corresponding to proton transfer from the methylamine to Asp_{428}, were also found starting with the reactant enzyme structure but optimising only the QM region.

There are several important features of the potential energy surface from this preliminary study which can depend on enzyme configuration, as we shall later discuss later.

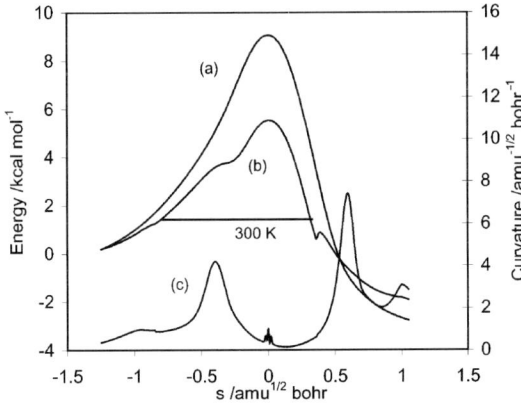

Fig. 4 Energetics and curvature of the adiabatic surface along the reaction coordinate using the QM/MM PM3 potential and enzyme configuration R0. (a) Potential energy relative to reactant. (b) Vibrationally adiabatic potential energy relative to reactant. (c) Curvature of the vibrationally adiabatic potential energy surface. The RTE at 300 K is shown as a horizontal line.

Table 1 Calculated KIE for proton transfer in MADH with the R0 enzyme configuration at the PM3 level

T/K	TST	CVT	TST/W	CVT/OMT
273	7.2	7.2	11.5	13.2
298	6.1	6.1	9.6	11.1
323	5.3	5.4	8.2	9.5

A potential energy barrier to reaction of 9.1 kcal mol^{-1} (Fig. 4(a)) which is lower than the experimentally determined enthalpic barrier of reaction (10.7 kcal mol^{-1}) determined from the temperature dependence of the rates.[9]

The reaction profile (see Fig. 4(a)) shows a narrow potential energy barrier. The transition state occurs at an O–H distance of 1.31 Å compared to the product OH distance of 0.99 Å and has an imaginary frequency of 2000i cm^{-1}.

The reaction is exothermic with a rapid drop in potential on the product side (corresponding to positive mass weighted reaction coordinate, s) as the proton bonds to the aspartate oxygen. The considerable curvature of V_a^G, particularly on the reactant side, is an important factor in promoting tunnelling.

A very low vibrationally adiabatic potential energy ($\Delta V_a^{G\ddagger}$) barrier (Fig. 4(b)) (5.1 kcal mol^{-1}) is due to the large change in the zero point energy (ZPE). The large degree of coupling between the C–H stretch and the reaction coordinate causes the ZPE to change rapidly at the start of the proton transfer, resulting in the well defined shoulders on the PE surface.

In order to bring the proton to a position where it can tunnel significantly, approximately 3.7 kcal mol^{-1} below the classical barrier, there is a region of classical atomic motion within the active site bringing the acceptor O-atom of Asp$_{428}$ and donor C-atom of the methylamine group to close proximity at 2.6 Å.

The predicted primary deuterium KIEs for this hydrogen shift are reproduced in Table 1 for later comparison with other models of this reaction. Transition state theory (TST) and canonical variational TST (CVT) predict relatively large KIEs but we see the importance of inclusion of quantum mechanical tunnelling from the large transmission coefficients, κ: For hydrogen and deuterium, the optimised multidimensional tunnelling (OMT) transmission coefficients are predicted to be 23.1 and 12.6 respectively and are somewhat larger than the simpler Wigner (W) tunnelling corrections[64] (κ = 4.9 and 3.1 respectively). The CVT/OMT method predicts a KIE of 11.1 at 298 K, which is in qualitative agreement with experimental observations. We note that the variation in the total reaction path curvature (Fig. 4(c)) shows a sharp increase in the strong coupling region of closest C–O approach. This region also corresponds to a sharp reduction in the effective reduced mass of the proton resulting in the large KIE.

A particular concern of the preliminary study was the low potential energy and vibrationally adiabatic barriers to reaction. These could result from two factors: the inadequacy of the PM3 Hamiltonian to quantitatively predict reaction energetics to experimental accuracy, and the use of a single MEP to calculate the rates. These factors will be discussed later.

We should emphasise here that an important factor determining the amount of tunnelling is the shape of the potential energy surface. For hydrogen transfer in both MADH and LADH, the potential energy barriers are quite similar at the semi-empirical level ($\approx$8 kcal mol^{-1}). However the curvatures of these potential energy surfaces are very different. From the shape of the vibrationally adiabatic PE reaction path for MADH (Fig. 2(b)) we can see that the sudden drop in energy on the product side is very important for the prediction of the transmission coefficients when the small curvature tunnelling correction is applied (CVT/SCT in Table 1). Indeed, conventional transition state theory with the Wigner tunnelling correction (TST/W in Table 1), which relies only on the curvature of the potential energy curve at the transition state, underestimates the kinetic isotope effect. We will later show that the shape of the entire potential energy curve will be a key factor in determining large KIEs and that it can be substantially affected by the enzyme configuration.

4. Alternative enzyme configurations

In this section we will discuss the effect that alternative enzyme conformations have on the proton transfer potential energy surface for proton transfer since the use of a single enzyme configuration (R0) may not give sufficient insight into possible origins of the temperature independence of the KIE or the importance of interactions and atomic motion within the enzyme and active site.

As an alternative to using a quantum mechanical or a hybrid QM/MM Hamiltonian to generate an ensemble of rare reaction trajectories or just an ensemble of reactant-like structures, we have chosen here to select structures from a standard molecular dynamics trajectory using AMBER[65] and force field.[34] Starting with the enzyme coordinates described earlier as R0, the dimer structure was re-solvated in a box of pre-equilibrated TIP3P water molecules and minimised. Following initial minimisation, the system, keeping the enzyme fixed, was heated gradually to 300 K over a period of 12.5 ps and maintained at this temperature for a further 12.5 ps. The restraints were then relaxed, constraining only the iminoquinone intermediate and 3 active site waters, and the simulation continued for a further 30 ps. Finally all restraints were removed and molecular dynamics was performed for 300 ps at 300 K sampling the enzyme configuration every 0.1 ps. The simulation was carried out under NVT conditions[66] using a time step of 1.0 fs. The particle mesh Ewald algorithm[67]

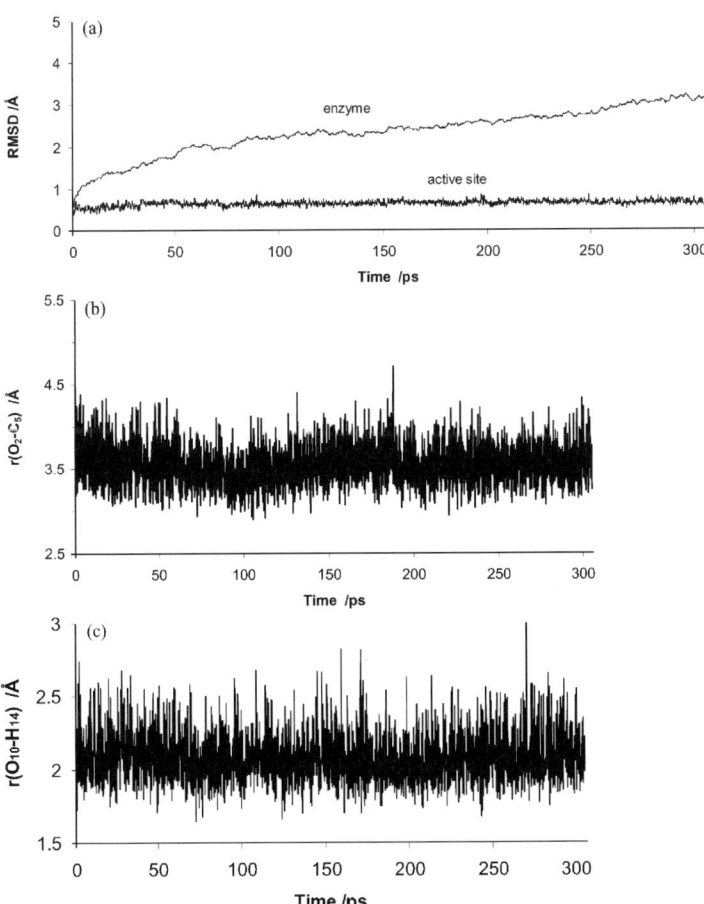

Fig. 5 Simulations using the reactant potential (a) RMS deviation (RMSD) of enzyme and active site coordinates from the minimised structure, (b) variation of the O_2–C_5 distance showing the separation of Asp_{428} from the iminoquinone intermediate and (c) O_{10}–H_{14} distance between Tr_2 and protein backbone.

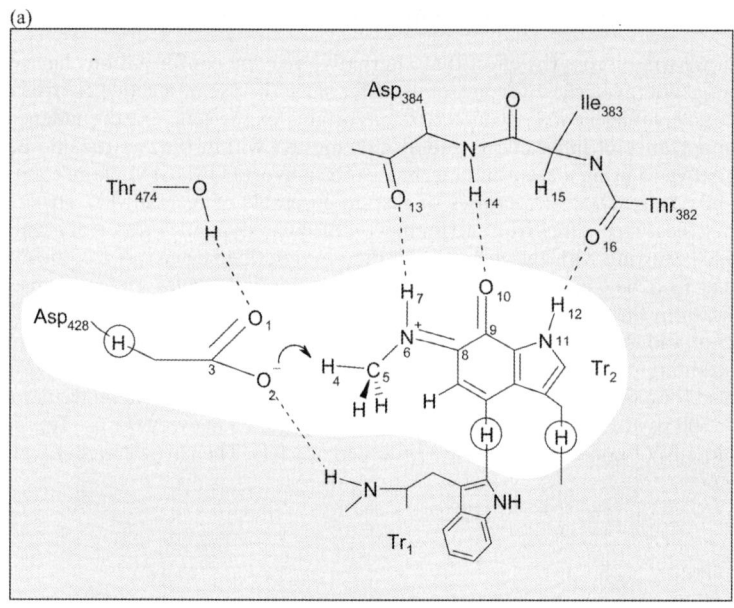

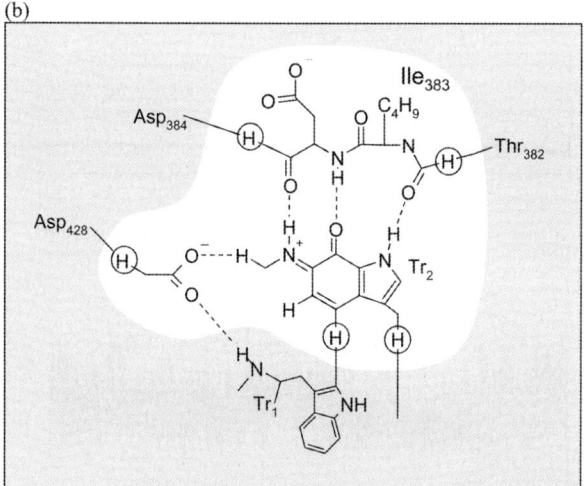

Fig. 6 Equilibrium active site obtained during the molecular dynamics simulation using the reactant potential. QM regions are shown unshaded for (a) 31 atom QM region with atom labelling and (b) 66 atom QM region. Link atoms are circled.

was used to simulate the remaining bulk water, a van der Waal cut-off of 9 Å and the SHAKE algorithm[68] was applied to constrain bonds containing hydrogen to their equilibrium values.

These simulations (Fig. 5(a)) show that although considerable fluctuation in the structure of the enzyme occurs, the active site (residues Tr_2, Asp_{428}, Thr_{382}, Ile_{383}, Asp_{384} and Thr_{474}) is particularly stable after a few picoseconds and there are no significant conformational changes which may affect the reactivity.

From the simulation enzyme structures were selected for further analysis at 2.9, 9.9, 45.9, 134.4 and 188.0 ps and will be referred to as 'reactant' ensemble structures, R1 to R5 respectively. These configurations were each selected as being potentially reactive having short O_2–H_4 distances (for atom labelling see Fig. 6(a)) such that the methyl group proton was already aligned with the Asp_{428}

O_2-atom and this avoids the first period of the reaction path involving rotation of the methyl group.

During the early stages of the MD simulation the three waters in the active site, included as part of the initial solvation process of R0, drifted away from Asp_{428} and a hydrogen bond formed between O_1 and the OH group of Thr_{474} (see Fig. 6(a)). There is some uncertainty in the position of any explicit water molecules at this stage of the reaction since the crystal structures are of an earlier inhibited step of the reaction and the active site is relatively hydrophobic.[19] Since these water molecules were important in the original conformation, reducing the basicity of the proton acceptor (Asp_{428}), we performed a number of other simulations for 150 ps, restraining aspects of the active site and water positions before removing the restraints. In each case the waters drifted away when the restraints were removed, and a new hydrogen bond was formed to Thr_{474}. This new interaction results in a different orientation of Asp_{428} than in R0, with this residue now straddling the C_5–N_6 and N_6–C_8 bonds. By performing PM3 calculations on the QM region alone we find that this new arrangement, which occurs in R1–R5, results in the reactant structures being more stable than in R0 by 4–6 kcal mol^{-1}, thus contributing to the increased calculated barriers.

Molecular dynamics simulations using classical molecular mechanical force fields have been very successful in predicting the equilibrium properties of proteins but the conformations generated will be strongly limited by the parameters and the type of energy function used. For example, the harmonic potential used in the AMBER force field does not allow bonds to stretch much beyond their formal equilibrium values and the parameters must be chosen to reflect the bonds involved. Also, electrostatic parameters cannot reflect polarisation during simulation. As the enzyme structure fluctuates many interactions will dynamically polarise, potentially resulting in increased stabilisation and shorter bonds, a process which will continue until a balance is met with repulsive interactions. Although such configurations may arise as rare high energy structures in a standard MD simulation, their frequency of occurrence may increase if we use appropriate potentials. By choosing molecular mechanics parameters which can describe the transition state structure, a simulation would be biased towards transition state stabilising conformations which may lower activation barriers. For this proton transfer mechanism we will show the importance of product stabilisation in order to obtain a narrow barrier and it will be seen that the same interactions which will stabilise the product structures should also stabilise the transition state. For this reason, we have performed a molecular dynamics simulation of the product of this reaction, after the proton has transferred to Asp_{428}, and have used parameters appropriate for protonated Asp_{428} and the deprotonated iminoquinone group. New partial charges were obtained using the standard Merz–Kollmann electrostatic potential fit[69] with the HF/6-31G** method[70] and the Tr_2 structure taken from a larger R1 QM/MM product with a water molecule placed at 2.0 Å from O_{10}. The small changes do reflect delocalisation of the charge onto the ring resulting in a change in the $N_6H_7^+$ and O_{10} charge densities from 0.06 e and -0.46 e in the reactant MM potential to 0.21 e and -0.65 e in the new product potential. A molecular dynamics simulation was subsequently performed for 130 ps, using the same protocol as for the reactant simulation described earlier, after re-solvation and minimisation of the enzyme. Fig. 7 shows that the separation of the Asp_{428} and Tr_2 groups, $r(O_1-C_5)$, varies considerably more than during the reactant simulation and that the groups are on average further apart, particularly after approximately 60 ps. Thus four potentially reactive configurations labelled P1, P2, P3 and P4, taken earlier at 0.2, 10.0, 11.0 and 50.6 ps respectively, were used for the direct dynamics calculations presented in the next section.

5. Prediction of KIEs and analysis of the PE surfaces

QM/MM reaction paths were calculated using the semi-empirical PM3 method for each of the reactant enzyme configurations, R1–R5 using the 31 atom QM region shown in Fig. 6(a). A selection of bond lengths of the QM/MM stationary points corresponding to the five enzyme configurations is shown in Table 2.

The KIEs for all the configurations were calculated at the CVT/SCT level and are presented in Table 3 with the reaction barriers ($\Delta V_{MEP}^{\ddagger}$) and energy change from reactant to product ($\Delta_r V_{MEP}$).

Comparing the different reaction paths we can see that the reaction barriers are consistently higher than for the reference configuration R0, which has a low barrier of 9 kcal mol^{-1}. However

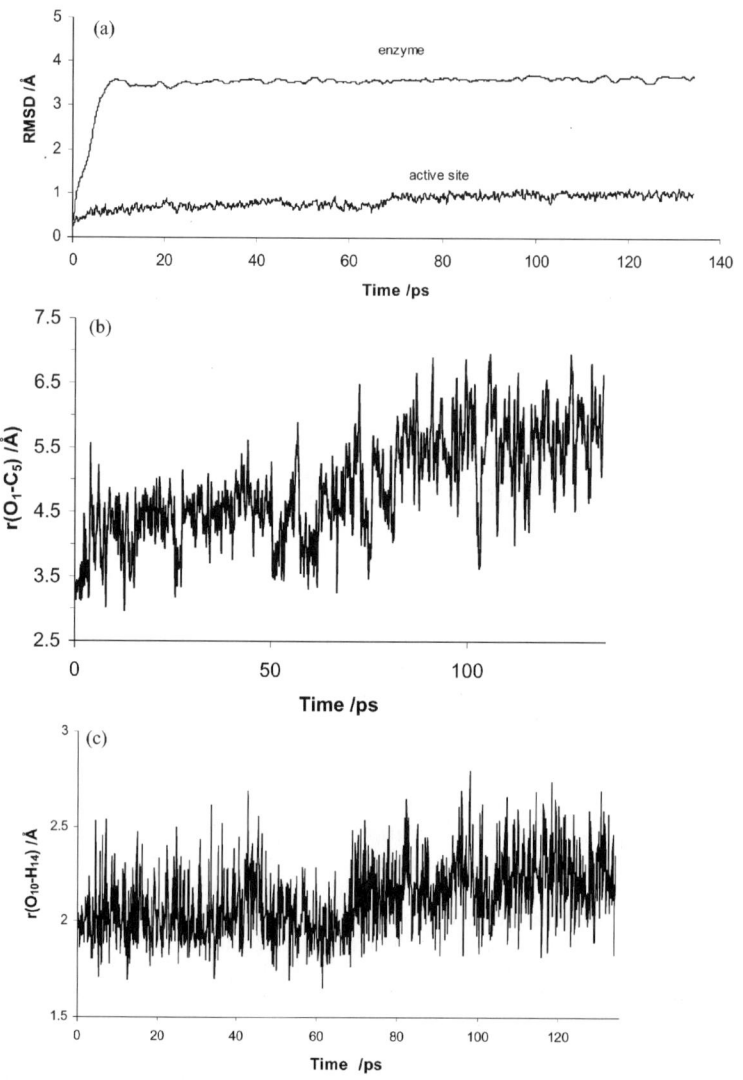

Fig. 7 Simulations using the product potential (a) RMS deviation (RMSD) of enzyme and active site coordinates from the minimised structure, (b) variation of O_1–C_5 distance showing the separation of Asp_{428} from the iminoquinone intermediate and (c) O_{10}–H_{14} distance between Tr_2 and protein backbone.

the reaction using enzyme configuration R0 was slightly exothermic whereas all of the predicted profiles R1–R5 are endothermic. We shall see that low tunnelling coefficients and KIEs are predicted as a result of the lack of rapid decrease in the PE on the product side. This is due in part to the endothermicity of the reaction caused by the subtle differences in active site interactions. More detailed analysis of the stationary points from the reactant ensemble showed few major structural differences from R0.

During the reactant simulation we can see that Asp_{428} has a tendency to approach and then move away from the methyl iminoquinone cofactor as shown by the general oscillation of the O_2–C_5 distance between approximately 3.0 and 3.6 Å (Fig. 5(b)) with a period of approximately 100 ps. The variation of the C_3–C_5 and O_1–C_5 distances have an almost identical trend. In the study discussed in section 3 on R0, a significant part of the reaction coordinate was the decrease in the

Table 2 Structural parameters for selected active site interactions of enzyme configurations R0, R1 to R5. Distances (Å) are specified for the MD configurations[a] and QM/MM stationary points[b] for the reactant, TS, and product using the PM3 method

Enzyme configuration	Structure	$r(O_2–H_4)$	$r(C_5–H_4)$	$r(H_7–O_{13})$	$r(O_{10}–H_{14})$	$r(O_2–C_5)$
R0	Reactant	1.74	1.14	2.81	2.51	2.75
	TS	1.31	1.32	2.81	2.50	2.63
	Product	0.98	1.75	2.81	2.48	2.73
R1	MD[a]	2.11	1.09	1.81	2.51	3.21
	Reactant	1.76	1.14	1.98	2.89	3.14
	TS	1.26	1.39	2.03	2.84	3.16
	Product	0.99	1.79	1.98	2.85	3.18
R2	MD[a]	2.59	1.09	1.71	2.12	3.60
	Reactant	1.74	1.15	1.99	2.20	2.89
	TS	1.27	1.37	2.03	2.19	2.64
	Product	0.99	1.76	1.98	2.18	2.74
R3	MD[a]	2.55	1.09	1.98	2.07	3.38
	Reactant	1.82	1.14	2.00	2.15	2.95
	TS	1.24	1.43	2.12	2.18	2.66
	Product	1.00	1.81	2.03	2.16	2.80
R4	MD[a]	2.66	1.09	1.95	1.93	3.53
	Reactant	1.81	1.15	1.98	2.02	2.96
	TS	1.24	1.43	2.10	2.02	2.67
	Product	1.00	1.79	2.04	2.02	2.79
R5	MD[a]	3.16	1.09	1.75	1.98	4.03
	Reactant	1.78	1.14	1.95	2.03	2.92
	TS	1.25	1.41	2.02	2.02	2.66
	Product	0.99	1.80	1.95	2.03	2.78

[a] The configuration is not a stationary point but is a snapshot taken from the simulation. [b] QM/MM optimised structure within the environment of the fixed MM enzyme configuration.

separation between Asp_{428} and the methylamine cofactor intermediate as the reaction progressed. Proton transfer accompanied by a large change in zero point energy was observed at a C–O separation of 2.64 Å. Such heavy atom compression is common in proton transfer mechanisms and is expected to be a driving force for the reaction. Although the geometries of the QM/MM stationary points were constrained by the link atoms, which were fixed in the enzyme configuration, the initial large separation between H_4 and O_2 has shortened in all the QM/MM profiles as the QM region was optimised to a minimum. This indicates that there are forces acting to compress the Asp_{428} and methylamine groups. A feature of the calculated KIEs is that the only configuration giving a significant KIE is R2 where the separation of $C_5–O_2$ for proton transfer was shortest, 2.9 Å, but this was not very dissimilar to R3–R5 which gave somewhat lower KIEs. The extremely low KIEs for R1 and R5 may be somewhat anomalous due to the flatness of the product side PE surface and the small $\kappa^{CVT/CAG}$ factor as noted in section 2. Despite this, low transmission coefficients would nevertheless be predicted. It should be noted that proton transfer to O_1 usually

Table 3 QM/MM reaction energetics ($\Delta_r V_{MEP}$) and barrier ($\Delta V_{MEP}^\ddagger$) (kcal mol^{-1}) at the PM3 level and KIEs using the CVT/SCT method for enzyme configurations in the 'reactant' ensemble. Energies calculated for a larger 66 atom QM region are shown in parentheses

Enzyme configuration	$\Delta V_{MEP}^\ddagger$	$\Delta_r V_{MEP}$	KIE (CVT/SCT)
R1	15 (14)	8 (4)	0.2
R2	13 (12)	5 (1)	7.2
R3	19 (17)	14 (9)	2.2
R4	19 (17)	14 (5)	2.2
R5	17 (14)	10 (5)	0.2

resulted in higher barriers and similar KIE behaviour to transfer to O_2 for the R-configurations but was more favourable for the P-configurations.

As previously discussed a critical factor to promote tunnelling and thus large KIEs is the width of the barrier to products. Thus reducing the endothermicity of the reaction (or increasing the steepness of the PE curve on the product side) is important to promote tunnelling at lower energies and this can be achieved by either destabilising the reactant, as in R0, or by greater stabilisation of the product structure. As the proton is transferred to Asp_{428}, the resulting negative charge must be delocalised across the iminoquinone. This could be achieved by stabilising the developing oxyanion, O_{10}, of the quinone ring whilst maintaining a quaternary nitrogen on the methylamine. Important hydrogen bonds to perform this role are evident from the Asp_{384} and Ile_{383} protein backbone (see Fig. 6). These interactions are present in the configurations studied. In the configurations R1–R5 good hydrogen bonds of approximately 2 Å are formed as shown in Table 2 for $r(H_7-O_{13})$ and $r(O_{10}-H_{14})$.

Stationary points along the reaction paths for configurations R1–R5 were also obtained for a larger 66 atom QM region and included Asp_{384}, Ile_{383} and part of the Thr_{382} backbone (see Fig. 6(b)). This larger QM region allows polarisation of the additional protein chain resulting in shorter hydrogen bonds to Tr_2. New reaction barriers for R1–R5 and energies of reaction are shown in Table 3. We can see in each case that the reaction barriers are not greatly affected but the products are stabilised resulting in a reduction in endothermicity of approximately 4–5 kcal mol^{-1}. Due to the size of the QM system, direct dynamics calculations were not performed but based upon previous calculations we would expect to see some increased tunnelling and a small increase in the KIE. These results with the larger QM region are important since they show that if we can promote increased stabilisation of product (and TS) species we could obtain reaction profiles which could promote proton tunnelling and which could be better correlated with experimental observations.

Stationary points along the QM/MM reaction paths corresponding to the product enzyme configurations, P1–P4, were thus obtained using the smaller QM region of 31 atoms discussed earlier using the PM3 method. In Table 4 we present a selection of active site geometrical parameters to illustrate the subtle differences in the hydrogen bonds between the Tr_2 and Ile_{383}–Asp_{384} protein backbone. It should be noted in particular that the O_{10}–H_{14} bonds are shorter than in the reactant ensemble structures chosen although there is little difference in the average of this interaction between the reactant and product simulations (Figs. 5(c) and 7(c) respectively). The other hydrogen bonds between Thr_{474} and Asp_{428}, and between Thr_{382} and Tr_2 were relatively constant throughout the simulation.

The QM/MM potential energy barriers and energy changes for P1, P2 and P4 are presented in Table 5. In this case we can see that each of the reaction profiles is exothermic. The shorter

Table 4 Structural parameters for selected active site interactions of enzyme configurations P1, P2 and P4. Distances (Å) are specified for the MD configurations[a] and QM/MM stationary points[b] for the reactant, TS, and product at the PM3 level

Enzyme configuration	Stationary point[b]	$r(O_1-H_4)$	$r(C_5-H_4)$	$r(H_7-O_{13})$	$r(O_{10}-H_{14})$	$r(O_1-C_5)$
P1	MD[a]	0.96	2.70	1.75	1.89	3.35
	Reactant	1.77	1.15	1.97	2.10	2.85
	TS	1.32	1.36	1.95	2.10	2.67
	Product	0.96	2.70	1.78	2.10	3.45
P2	MD[a]	0.96	3.96	2.30	1.99	4.72
	Reactant	2.68	1.16	2.05	1.89	3.71
	TS	1.40	1.57	1.97	1.90	2.89
	Product	0.96	2.89	1.94	1.88	3.38
P4	MD[a]	0.96	2.57	2.28	2.12	3.51
	Reactant	1.76	1.15	2.05	2.02	2.87
	TS	1.33	1.37	2.07	2.00	2.69
	Product	0.96	3.06	1.84	2.02	3.78

[a] The configuration is not a stationary point but is a snapshot taken from the simulation. [b] QM/MM optimised structure within the environment of the fixed enzyme configuration.

Table 5 QM/MM reaction energetics ($\Delta_r V_{MEP}$) and barrier ($\Delta V_{MEP}^{\ddagger}$) (kcal mol^{-1}) for enzyme configurations in the 'product' ensemble with the PM3 method. Potential energies are shown with the zero point energy corrected values in parentheses

Enzyme configuration	$\Delta V_{MEP}^{\ddagger}$	$\Delta_r V_{MEP}$	KIE at 300 K	
			CVT	CVT/SCT
P1	10.6 (7.0)	−4.1 (−3.8)	5.4	13.4
P2	19.1 (16.7)	−17.2 (−17.2)	3.9	18.1
P3	—	—	—	—
P4	9.7 (6.3)	−7.6 (−7.3)	5.3	12.1

hydrogen bonds between the protein backbone and Tr$_2$, particularly to the oxyanion (O$_{10}^-$), are likely to be responsible for stabilising the products (and TS).

A key feature of the energetics using the P1, P2 and P4 configurations is that contrary to using R1–R5, higher activation barriers now give higher KIEs as we would expect. We have summarised the reaction profiles for the P2 and P4 configurations at the PM3 level in Fig. 8. In each case the

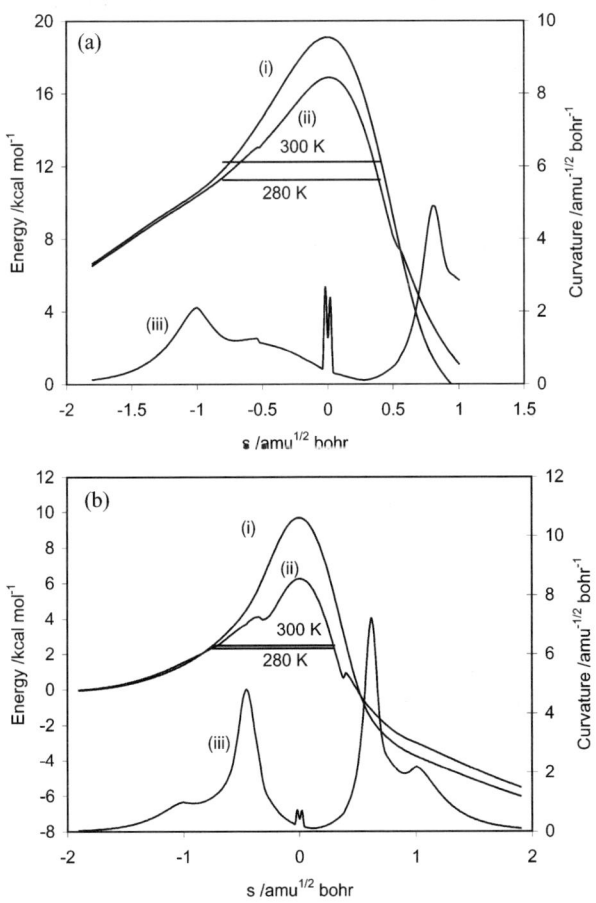

Fig. 8 Energetics and surface curvature along the reaction coordinate for QM/MM PM3 calculations on enzyme configurations (a) P2 and (b) P4. (i) Potential energy relative to reactant. (ii) Vibrationally adiabatic potential energy relative to reactant. (iii) Curvature of the vibrationally adiabatic surface. RTEs at 300 K and 280 K are shown as horizontal lines.

RTEs indicate significant proton tunnelling at least 4 kcal mol^{-1} below the adiabatic PE barrier and large transmission coefficients with $\kappa^{\text{CVT/SCT}}$ = 40 and 29 for P2 and P4 respectively. The activation barriers, including ZPE and tunnelling effects, are now 3.2, 11.6 and 2.8 kcal mol^{-1} for P1, P2 and P4 respectively. At this stage, with few configurations studied, it is difficult to ascertain if P2 or P4 are representative of dominant reaction trajectories and how the availability of, or balance with, other classical reaction pathways with similar activation barriers but little tunnelling, such as R1 to R5, contribute to the overall rate behaviour and observed KIE.

6. Comparison with *ab initio* methods

In order to more accurately model this mechanism it is useful to compare the semi-empirical potential surfaces with the predictions of *ab initio* methods. New reactant, product and transition state stationary points were obtained using the enzyme configurations P1 to P4, at the Hartree–Fock level with a small 3-21G basis set (HF/3-21G).[70] Bond lengths representing the reaction coordinate and important interactions with Tr$_2$ in the active site are shown for P2, P3 and P4 (Table 6) for comparison with previous PM3 results. The bond lengths of the HF/3-21G QM/MM stationary points show roughly the same trends as at the PM3 level with the exception that P4 exhibits a later TS and longer O_1–H_4 and O_1–C_5 reactant separations. As at the PM3 level a higher classical proton transfer barrier (see Table 7) is obtained for P2. KIEs were obtained (Table 7) from direct dynamics calculations using a potential energy profile calculated at the HF/3-21G level.

Preliminary calculations[71] of reaction paths with R0 (R1 is similar) at the HF/3-21G level have similarly resulted in a larger PE barrier (19 kcal mol^{-1}) but a much later transition state with O_1–H_4 and C_5–H_4 distances of 1.13 Å and 1.51 Å respectively. These reactions were also endothermic by 8.6 kcal mol^{-1}, and involved more heavy atom motion, especially to reach the product after the TS. This combined with a relatively flat PE curve (TS imaginary frequency of 1228 cm^{-1}) led to little tunnelling being predicted from direct dynamics calculations and a low transmission coefficient, $\kappa^{\text{CVT/SCT}}$ = 3.2. Other HF calculations performed using 6-31G and 6-31G** basis sets[70] showed similar behaviour but gave higher barriers to reaction. Although giving much lower barriers for the enzyme reaction, density functional calculations with the B3LYP functional gave a similarly endothermic reaction.

Turning now to the results for the product ensemble structures at this level, we note that the PE barriers are larger than at the PM3 level. The higher imaginary frequencies of P2 and P4, 1805i and 1401i cm^{-1}, combined with multidimensional effects give large transmission coefficients, $\kappa^{\text{CVT/SCT}}$, of 165.0 and 5.8 respectively and result in KIEs of 40.3 and 7.2. Although the value for P4 is lower than observed experimentally, we can see that the conformers with higher barriers, such as P2, which in this case has a large acceptor–donor separation, contribute much larger transmission

Table 6 Structural parameters for selected active site interactions of enzyme configurations P2, P3 and P4. Distances (Å) are specified for the MD configurations[a] and QM/MM stationary points[b] for the reactant, TS, and product at the HF/3-21G level

Enzyme configuration	Stationary point[b]	$r(O_1$–$H_4)$	$r(C_5$–$H_4)$	$r(H_7$–$O_{13})$	$r(O_{10}$–$H_{14})$	$r(O_1$–$C_5)$
P2	MD[a]	0.96	3.96	2.30	1.99	4.72
	Reactant	2.95	1.09	2.03	1.87	3.58
	TS	1.29	1.44	2.06	1.89	2.72
	Product	0.98	3.45	1.99	1.82	4.17
P3	MD[a]	0.96	3.54	1.92	1.83	4.39
	Reactant	3.15	1.09	2.27	2.49	3.79
	TS	1.29	1.38	2.16	2.08	2.65
	Product	0.98	3.50	2.04	2.37	4.22
P4	MD[a]	0.96	2.57	2.28	2.12	3.51
	Reactant	2.57	1.08	1.99	1.91	3.33
	TS	1.16	1.50	2.11	1.89	2.66
	Product	0.97	3.08	1.87	1.87	3.70

[a] The configuration is not a stationary point but is a snapshot taken from the simulation. [b] QM/MM optimised structure within the environment of the fixed enzyme configuration

Table 7 QM/MM reaction energetics ($\Delta_r V_{MEP}$) and barrier ($\Delta V_{MEP}^{\ddagger}$) (/kcal mol^{-1}) for enzyme configurations in the 'product' ensemble. Calculated potential energies are shown for the HF/3-21G method and zero point energy corrected values in parentheses

Enzyme configuration	$\Delta V_{MEP}^{\ddagger}$	$\Delta_r V_{MEP}$	KIE at 300 K	
			CVT	CVT/SCT
P1	20.5 (17.5)	5.2 (4.8)	4.0	0.4
P2	36.9 (34.9)	−9.7 (−10.3)	4.8	40.3
P3	30.5 (30.3)	−20.3 (−20.8)	4.6	15.3
P4	20.3 (17.4)	2.6 (2.1)	4.7	7.2

coefficients towards an overall KIE. For P2 the PE barrier is extremely high, 37 kcal mol^{-1}, but the activation barrier taking into consideration zero point effects and tunnelling is considerably lowered to 26 kcal mol^{-1}. The activation energies predicted with ZPEs and tunnelling for P1 and P4 are 15.2 and 15.0 kcal mol^{-1} respectively, in reasonable agreement with experimental predictions for the overall activation enthalpy. These reaction paths are summarised in Fig. 9 where we have also shown the curvature of the potential energy surfaces. It is clear that the curvature of the surfaces at this level is more sensitive to enzyme structure than was observed at the PM3 level, as shown by the differences in KIE between P2 and P4. At the HF/3-21G level this difference is 33.1 whereas at the PM3 level the difference is only 6.0. The predicted KIE for structure P3 at this level is 15.3, a value between that for P2 and P4. Energetically this configuration is not dissimilar to P2 and, even though it is more endothermic, it does not have quite as rapid a drop in potential on the product side. P1 on the other hand, despite its similar energetics to P4, is endothermic and little tunnelling is predicted. We should not forget that HF/3-21G calculations rarely give reaction energetics to experimental accuracy but are in general reliable predictors of stationary point geometries which can be used for higher level energy calculations.

The results presented here clearly reinforce the importance of stabilisation of the oxyanion and product structures to obtain reaction profiles with the correct shape and energetics and pave the way for more detailed high level studies. Although higher level *ab initio* calculations are computationally demanding they can often be used to improve upon the description of the electronic structure given by semi-empirical calculations and have often been used in dual level[37–39] approaches to improve the calculation of reaction rates.

7. Conclusions

Hybrid QM/MM methods, in association with molecular dynamics simulations, have allowed us to study the proton transfer mechanism in MADH and to investigate how specific enzyme interactions and dynamics can affect the energetics of the reaction. This study has illustrated some of the difficulties involved in the computation of accurate potential energy surfaces in enzymes using both semi-empirical and *ab initio* QM methods. Use of the PM3 semi-empirical Hamiltonian has proved useful but consistently gives large transition state imaginary frequencies ($> 2000i$ cm^{-1}) and reaction path curvature even for surfaces with low reaction barriers. *Ab initio* methods tend to give considerably lower imaginary frequencies ($1400i$ cm^{-1}) at the transition state despite their higher barriers.

Different features of the PE surface are important in determining the ease of through barrier as opposed to over barrier motion. Thus, the conventional stabilisation of the TS facilitates over barrier motion. However, for enzymes such as MADH where through barrier motion is very important, as reflected in the large KIEs, it is other aspects of the PE surface, such as the rapid change in PE on the product side, which are critical.

We have shown that C–H bond breakage in methylamine by MADH can involve extensive proton tunnelling which results in high primary deuterium KIEs, although the degree of tunnelling can vary a great deal depending on the enzyme conformation. We have observed a vibrational (compression) mode bringing proton acceptor and donor groups together and have shown that the proximity of this interaction is an integral part of the reaction coordinate to promote proton

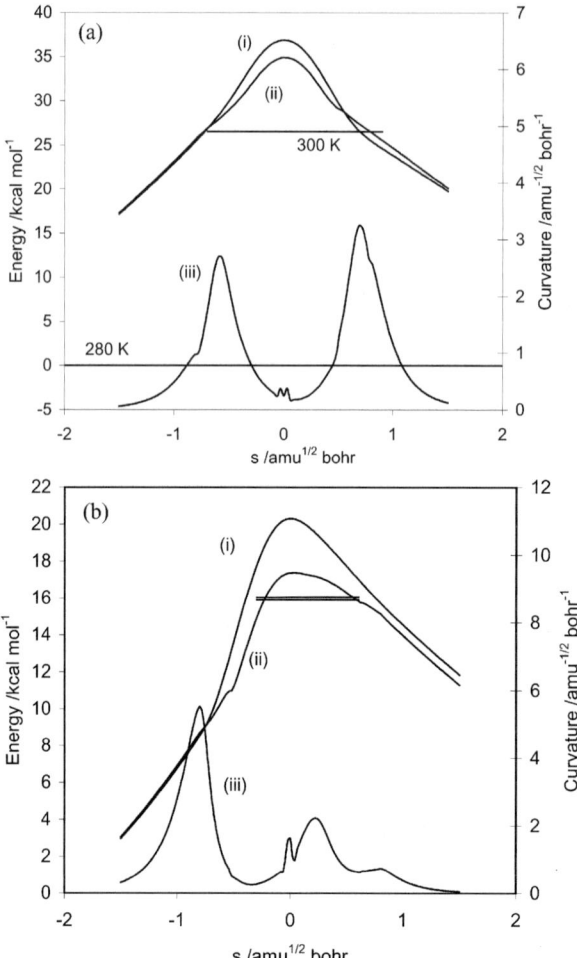

Fig. 9 Energetics and surface curvature along the reaction coordinate for QM/MM HF/3-21G calculations on enzyme configurations (a) P2 and (b) P4. (i) Potential energy relative to reactant. (ii) Vibrationally adiabatic potential energy relative to reactant. (iii) Curvature of the vibrationally adiabatic surface. RTEs at 300 K and 280 K are shown as horizontal lines.

tunnelling and a high KIE. There are however other interactions, such as the hydrogen bonds to residues in the active site, which can indirectly cause changes in the shape and energetics of the reaction profile, particularly on the product side, to promote or inhibit proton transfer. Higher transmission coefficients are clearly favoured when the reaction is exothermic or almost isoenergetic. Although it is difficult to justify at this stage, the temperature independence of the observed KIE for proton transfer in MADH could be as a result of the perturbation of the interactions within the active site, such as with TTQ, via a mechanism involving vibration or thermal motion.

We have demonstrated that for those enzymatic reactions where tunnelling is important, the reaction rate depends critically on the shape of the PE surface, rather than solely on the adiabatic barrier. There are strong indications from our MD simulation that the shape of the surface depends markedly on the enzyme conformation. Both molecular motion and change in the electronic structure of the active site influence the observed kinetics, as reflected in the KIEs. There are therefore grounds for belief that KIE measurements provide an extremely sensitive probe of these effects if computational methods can be developed to accurately disentangle the various effects which we have identified. Clearly there is room for considerable methodological and computational development before this end is achieved.

Acknowledgements

We thank D. G. Truhlar for use of the POLYRATE code and EPSRC for financial support.

References

1. A. Fersht, in *Stucture and Mechanism in Protein Science: A Guide to Enzyme Catalysis and Protein Folding*, Freeman, San Francisco, 1999.
2. J. Villà and A. Warshel, *J. Phys. Chem. B.*, 2001, **105**, 7887.
3. A. Warshel and M. J. Levitt, *Mol. Biol.*, 1976, **103**, 227.
4. U. C. Singh and P. A. Kollman, *J. Comput. Chem.*, 1986, **7**, 718.
5. M. J. Field, P. A. Bash and M. Karplus, *J. Comput. Chem.*, 1990, **11**, 700.
6. J. Gao, in *Reviews in Computational Chemistry*, eds. K. B. Lipkowitz and D. B. Boyd, VCH, New York, 1997, vol. 7, p. 119.
7. N. A. Burton, M. J. Harrison, J. C. Hart, I. H. Hillier and D. W. Sheppard, *Faraday Discuss.*, 1998, **110**, 463.
8. R. M. Nicoll, S. A. Hindle, G. MacKenzie, I. H. Hillier and N. A. Burton, *Theor. Chem. Acc.*, 2001, **106**, 105.
9. J. Basran, M. J. Sutcliffe and N. S. Scrutton, *Biochemistry*, 1999, **38**, 3218.
10. J. Basran, S. Patel, M. J. Sutcliffe and N. S. Scrutton, *J. Biol. Chem.*, 2001, **276**, 6234.
11. A. Kohen and J. P. Klinman, *Acc. Chem. Res.*, 1998, **31**, 397.
12. A. Kohen, R. Cannio, S. Bartolucci and J. P. Klinman, *Nature*, 1999, **399**, 496.
13. J. Rucker and J. P. Klinman, *J. Am. Chem. Soc.*, 1999, **121**, 1997.
14. A. Kohen and J. P. Klinman, *J. Am. Chem. Soc.*, 2000, **122**, 10 738.
15. D. B. Northrop and Y-K. Cho, *Biochemistry*, 2000, **39**, 2406.
16. D. G. Truhlar and B. C. Garrett, *Acc Chem. Res.*, 1980, **13**, 440.
17. D. G. Truhlar, A. D. Isaacson and B. C. Garrett, in *Theory of Chemical Reaction Dynamics.*, ed. M. Baer, CRC Press, Boca Raton, FL, 1985, vol. 4, p. 65.
18. T. C. Allison and D. G. Truhlar, in *Modern Methods for Multidimensional Dynamics Computations in Chemistry*, ed. D. L. Thompson, World Scientific, Singapore, 1998, p. 618.
19. L. Chen, M. Doi, R. C. Durley, A. Y. Christoserdov, M. E. Lidstrom, V. L. Davidson and F. S. Mathews, *J. Mol. Biol.*, 1998, **276**, 131.
20. H. B. Brooks, L. H. Jones and V. L. Davidson, *Biochemistry*, 1993, **32**, 2725.
21. C. J. Cramer and D. G. Truhlar, *Chem. Rev.*, 1999, **99**, 2161.
22. E. A. Carter, G. Ciccotti, J. T. Hynes and R. Kapral, *Chem. Phys. Lett.*, 1989, **156**, 472.
23. M. Sprik and G. Ciccotti, *J. Chem. Phys.*, 1998, **109**, 7737.
24. R. Stanton, M. Peräkylä, D. Bakowies and P. A. Kollman, *J. Am. Chem. Soc.*, 1998, **120**, 3448.
25. J. Chandrasekhar and W. L. Jorgensen, *J. Am. Chem. Soc.*, 1984, **106**, 3049.
26. C. Alhambra, J. Corchado, M. L. Sanchez, M. Garcia-Viloca, J. Gao and D. G. Truhlar, *J. Phys. Chem. B*, 2001, **105**, 11 326.
27. C. Alhambra, M. L. Sanchez, J. Corchado, J. L. Gao and D. G. Truhlar, *Chem. Phys. Lett.*, 2001, **347**, 512.
28. J-K. Hwang, G. King, S. Creighton and A. J. Warshel, *J. Am. Chem. Soc.*, 1988, **110**, 5297.
29. M. E. Tuckerman and D. Marx, *Phys. Rev. Lett.*, 2001, **86**, 4946.
30. E. J. Meijer and M. Sprik, *J. Am. Chem. Soc.*, 1998, **120**, 6345.
31. T. C. Bruice and S. J. Benkovic, *Biochemistry*, 2000, **39**, 6267.
32. M. J. Frisch, G. W. Trucks, H. B. Schlegel, P. M. W. Gill, B. G. Johnson, M. A. Robb, J. R. Cheeseman, T. A. Keith, G. A. Petersson, J. A. Montgomery, K. Raghavachari, M. A. Al-Laham, V. G. Zakrzewski, J. V. Ortiz, J. B. Foresman, J. Cioslowski, B. B. Stefanov, A. Nanayakkara, M. Challacombe, C. Y. Peng, P. Y. Ayala, W. Chen, M. W. Wong, J. L. Andres, E. S. Replogle, R. Gomperts, R. L. Martin, D. J. Fox, J. S. Binkley, D. J. Defrees, J. Baker, J. P. Stewart, M. Head-Gordon, C. Gonzales and J. A. Pople, *GAUSSIAN94*, Gaussian Inc., Pittsburgh, PA, 1995.
33. D. A. Pearlman, D. A. Case, J. W. Caldwell, W. S. Ross, T. E. Cheatham, D. M. Ferguson, G. L. Seibel, U. C. Singh, P. K. Weiner and P. A. Kollman, *AMBER 4.1*, University of California, San Francisco, 1995.
34. W. D. Cornell, P. Cieplak, C. I. Bayly, I. R. Gould, K. M. Merz, D. M. Ferguson, D. C. Spellmeyer, T. Fox, J. W. Caldwell and P. A. Kollman, *J. Am. Chem. Soc.*, 1995, **117**, 5179.
35. R. J. Hall, S. A. Hindle, N. A. Burton and I. H. Hillier, *J. Comput. Chem.*, 2000, **21**, 1433.
36. M. Page and J. W. McIver, *J. Phys. Chem.*, 1988, **88**, 922.
37. W-P. Hu, Y-P. Liu and D. G. Truhlar, *J. Chem. Soc., Faraday Trans.*, 1994, **90**, 1715.

38 Y-Y. Chuang and D. G. Truhlar, *J. Phys. Chem. A.*, 1997, **101**, 3808.
39 Y-Y. Chuang and D. G. Truhlar, *J. Phys. Chem. A.*, 1997, **101**, 8741.
40 J. C. Corchado, Y-Y. Chuang, P. L. Fast, J. Villà, W-P. Hu, Y-P. Liu, G. C. Lynch, J. A. Nguyen, C. F. Jackels, V. S. Melissas, B. J. Lynch, I. Rossi, E. L. Coitiño, A. Fernandez-Ramos, R. Steckler, B. C. Garrett, A. D. Isaacson and D. G. Truhlar., *POLYRATE-version 8.5*, University of Minnesota, Minneapolis, 2000.
41 *GAUSSRATE-version 8.5/P8.5-G94,* by J. C. Corchado, Y-Y. Chuang, E. L. Coitino and D. G. Truhlar, University of Minnesota, Minneapolis, based on *POLYRATE-version 8.5*, 1999.
42 D-H. Lu, T. N. Truong, V. S. Melissas, G. C. Lynch, Y-P. Liu, B. C. Garrett, R. Steckler, A. D. Isaacson, S. N. Rai, G. Hancock, J. G. Lauderdale, T. Joseph and D. G. Truhlar, *Comput. Phys. Commun.*, 1992, **71**, 235.
43 Y-P. Liu, G. C. Lynch, T. N. Truong, D-H. Lu, D. G. Truhlar and B. C. Garrett, *J. Am. Chem. Soc.*, 1993, **115**, 2408.
44 Y-P. Liu, D-H. Lu, A. Gonzalez-Lafont, D. G. Truhlar and B. C. Garrett, *J. Am. Chem. Soc.*, 1993, **115**, 7806.
45 A. Fernandez-Ramos and D. G. Truhlar, *J. Chem. Phys.*, 2001, **114**, 1491.
46 P. F. Faulder, G. Tresadern, K. K. Chohan, N. S. Scrutton, M. J. Sutcliffe, I. H. Hillier and N. A. Burton, *J. Am. Chem. Soc.*, 2001, **123**, 8604.
47 B. C. Garrett, D. G. Truhlar, R. S. Grev, A. W. Magnuson, *J. Phys. Chem.*, 1980, **84**, 1730 B. C. Garrett, D. G. Truhlar, R. S. Grev, A. W. Magnuson, *J. Phys. Chem.*, 1983, **87**, 4554E.
48 B. C. Garrett and D. G. Truhlar, *J. Chem. Phys.*, 1980, **72**, 3460.
49 Y. Kim, D. G. Truhlar and M. M. Kreevoy, *J. Am. Chem. Soc.*, 1991, **113**, 7837.
50 W. J. Bruno and W. Bialek, *Biophys. J.*, 1992, **63**, 689.
51 N. S. Scrutton, J. Basran and M. J. Sutcliffe, *Eur. J. Biochem.*, 1999, **264**, 666.
52 D. Antoniou and S. D. Schwartz, *J. Phys. Chem. B*, 2001, **105**, 5553.
53 A. Kohen and J. P. Klinman, *Acc. Chem. Res.*, 1998, **31**, 397.
54 J. Basran, S. Patel, M. J. Sutcliffe and N. S. Scrutton, *J. Biol. Chem.*, 2001, **276**, 6234.
55 D. B. Northrop and Y-K. Cho, *Biochemistry*, 2000, **39**, 2406.
56 B. J. Bahnson, T. D. Colby, J. K. Chin, B. M. Goldstein and J. P. Klinman, *Proc. Natl. Acad. Sci. USA*, 1997, **94**, 12 797.
57 S-C. Tsai and J. P. Klinman, *Biochemistry*, 2001, **40**, 2303.
58 C. Alhambra, J. C. Corchado, M. L. Sanchez, J. Gao and D. G. Truhlar, *J. Am. Chem. Soc.*, 2000, **122**, 8197.
59 S. P. Webb, P. K. Agarwal and S. Hammes-Schiffer, *J. Phys. Chem.*, 2000, **104**, 8884.
60 S. R. Billeter, S. P. Webb, P. K. Agarwal, T. Iordanov and S. Hammes-Schiffer, *J. Am. Chem. Soc.*, 2001, **123**, 11 262.
61 G. Tresadern, P. F. Faulder, M. P. Gleeson, Z. Tai, G. MacKenzie, N. A. Burton and I. H. Hillier, *Theor. Chem. Acc.*, 2002, , in press.
62 X-ray crystal coordinates from F. S. Mathews, personal communication.
63 P. Moenne-Loccoz, N. Nakamura, S. Itoh, S. Fukuzumi, A. C. F. Gorren, J. A. Duine and J. Sanders-Loehr, *Biochemistry*, 1996, **15**, 4713.
64 R. P. Bell, *The Tunnel Effect in Chemistry*, Chapman & Hall, London, 1980.
65 D. A. Case, D. A. Pearlman, J. W. Caldwell, T. E. Cheatham, W. S. Ross, C. L. Simmerling, T. A. Darden, K. M. Merz, R. V. Stanton, A. L. Cheng, J. J. Vincent, M. Crowley, V. Tsui, R. J. Radmer, Y. Duan, J. Pitera, I. Massova, G. L. Seibel, U. C. Singh, P. K. Weiner and P. A. Kollman, *AMBER 6*, University of California, San Francisco, 1999.
66 D. A. Pearlman, D. A. Case, J. W. Caldwell, W. S. Ross, T. E. Cheatham, S. DeBolt, D. Ferguson, G. Seibel and P. A. Kollman, *Comput. Phys. Commun.*, 1995, **91**, 1.
67 T. Darden, D. York and L. Pedersen, *J. Chem. Phys.*, 1993, **98**, 10 089.
68 J. P. Ryckaert, G. Ciccotti and H. J. C. Berendsen, *J. Comput. Phys.*, 1977, **23**, 327.
69 B. H. Besler, K. M. Merz and P. A. Kollmann, *J. Comput. Chem.*, 1990, **11**, 431.
70 W. J. Hehre, L. Radom, P. vR. Schleyer and J. A. Pople, in *Ab Initio Molecular Orbital Theory*, Wiley, New York, 1986.
71 P. F. Faulder, PhD Thesis, University of Manchester, 2002.

Time-resolved computational protein biochemistry: Solvent effects on interactions, conformational transitions and equilibrium fluctuations

Alexander L. Tournier, Danzhi Huang, Sonja M. Schwarzl, Stefan Fischer and Jeremy C. Smith*

Lehrstuhl für Biocomputing, IWR, Im Neuenheimer Feld 368, Universität Heidelberg, 69120, Heidelberg, Germany

Received 6th February 2002, Accepted 20th March 2002
First published as an Advance Article on the web 30th July 2002

Solvent plays an important role in modulating internal motions of proteins. Here we present a computational method for including solvent effects on charge–charge interactions and on pathways between functional protein conformations, and examine solvent effects on equilibrium internal fluctuations in proteins. A computationally efficient charge reparametrisation method is presented that satisfactorily reproduces the electrostatic interactions present in a full continuum Poisson–Boltzmann representation. The application of charge reparametrisation in the calculation of a large-scale conformational transition pathway in a protein, annexin V, is illustrated. We also examine solvent effects on fast (picosecond timescale) internal protein dynamics. Nosé Hoover dual heatbath molecular dynamics simulations are performed. These simulations allow the solvent region to be fixed at one temperature and the protein at another. The results of the Nosé–Hoover simulations on hydrated myoglobin confirm that the solvent temperature strongly influences the protein fluctuations. We consider to what extent the solvent can be considered to determine the high temperature protein dynamics.

Introduction

A major challenge for computational and experimental biochemistry is to determine the forms and timescales of functional motions in proteins. These motions and their associated free energy changes along a reaction coordinate are essential to our understanding of protein reaction dynamics. Solvent may play an important role in modulating functional dynamics as it affects the protein energy landscape. Here we examine solvent effects on fast equilibrium fluctuations and present a method of modelling solvent screening in the computation of larger-scale conformational transitions.

Understanding large-scale transitions requires characterisation of the end-states and of the pathways between them. The end states are often known from X-ray crystallographic experiments.[1] However, the pathways between the end-states, *i.e.* the sequence of structures accompanying the transition from one stable state to another, are difficult to determine experimentally. Computer simulation techniques can, in principle, provide the required information. Using empirical energy functions, searches of protein conformational space can be used to determine plausible pathways. However, with present-day computer power the sampling obtained with standard MD is

DOI: 10.1039/b201191c

insufficient if the functional conformational change to be studied occurs on a timescale longer than about a nanosecond, as is frequently the case. Therefore, specialised techniques are required. Although the development of these techniques is still in its infancy, a number do exist and have been used to examine important conformational changes in several proteins.[1-5] However, the methods are computationally expensive, and this is particularly so when solvating water molecules are explicitly represented. This extra expense can, in principle, be circumvented by adopting a continuum approach, in which the water molecules are not explicitly included and instead the solvent effect is modelled by modifying the effective intraprotein interaction potential. One common way of doing this has been to adopt a distance-dependent dielectric constant $e.g.$ $\varepsilon = r$. However, this approach is not based on rigorous physics and has been shown to lead to significant errors.[6] Alternatively, physically-based continuum modelling of the solvent can be performed,[7] by use of the Poisson–Boltzmann equation, which enables the electrostatic potential to be calculated at any point in the protein, given that the protein charges are explicitly represented and are embedded in a solvent of uniform dielectric constant. However, methods to solve the Poisson–Boltzmann equation are themselves also computationally demanding. Here, an alternative method is presented, in which the partial atomic charges are reparametrised and fitted to reproduce the electrostatic interactions present in a full continuum Poisson–Boltzmann representation. This is a physically realistic and computationally-efficient way of approximating the solvent effect. The annexin V example given here illustrates the use of a specialised reaction path technique in combination with charge reparametrisation.

A related question concerns the effect of solvent on equilibrium protein fluctuations. Various experimental techniques such as neutron scattering,[8-14] Mössbauer spectroscopy,[15-17] and X-ray scattering[18-20] have shown the presence of a temperature-dependent transition in protein dynamics around 220 K. This dynamical transition has also been seen in MD simulations.[21,22] The transition is thought to be associated with a change in the dynamics from harmonic to anharmonic, and resembles that undergone by glass-forming liquids: proteins and glasses have comparable disordered structures and share the 'freezing-in' feature of the glass transition.[23-28]

Computer simulations can be used to investigate the physical origin of the dynamical transition.[21,29,30] In this context, an innovative method was used to probe features of the dynamical transition due to the protein and those due to the solvent.[31] The approach consisted of using the Nosé–Hoover thermostat[32] to set and maintain the protein and its solvent at two different temperatures. Here we complement the work of ref. 31 with simulations of hydrated myoglobin performed under varying conditions. The results of these simulations confirm the strong influence of the solvent on the protein fluctuations and permit reconsideration of the extent to which solvent determines high-temperature fluctuations.

Methods

Charge reparametrisation

In molecular mechanics-based simulations, the electrostatic interactions between the atoms of the system concerned are modelled by Coulomb interactions between partial atomic charges on each atom. These charges are constant parameters in the potential energy function.

Due to solvent screening the electrostatic interaction energy between two charges in water is about 80 times smaller than in vacuum. Solvent screening is stronger at the solvent-exposed surface of a protein than in the protein core. In order to include the solvent screening effect in simulations without explicit solvent, electrostatic interactions can be represented by specifically scaling the partial atomic charges on the atoms thereby reducing the electrostatic interaction energies to their appropriate values in aqueous solution.

To represent the solvent screening effect, we have developed a charge reparametrisation method for nonuniformly scaling the charges. A similar approach has already been applied successfully to enzymatic[33] and ligand-docking[34] studies. Here, we briefly describe the method, details of which will be published elsewhere. In this method the protein is partitioned into sub-groups I, for which scaling factors λ_I are determined. In the present work the protein is partitioned into residues and each residue into a backbone group and a side-chain group. The scaling factors are determined for each group in such a manner that the Coulombic interaction energy, when computed with the scaled charges, optimally reproduces the calculated solvent-shielded interaction energy of each group with the rest of the protein, as derived using the Poisson–Boltzmann method. The factors, $\lambda_I = \sqrt{\varepsilon_I}$, are determined from group–group interaction energies using the nonscaled partial atomic charges:

$$\varepsilon_I = \frac{\sum_{\substack{J \in \text{cutoff}(I) \\ \varepsilon_{IJ} > 0}} |E_{IJ}^{\text{vac}}|}{\sum_{\substack{J \in \text{cutoff}(I) \\ \varepsilon_{IJ} > 0}} |E_{IJ}^{\text{solv}}|},$$

where E_{IJ}^{vac} is the interaction energy in vacuum between the groups I and J, E_{IJ}^{solv} is the interaction energy in solution calculated with the Poisson–Boltzmann approach, and the sum extends over all groups, J that are within a cut-off distance around the group, I and for which the pair-wise effective dielectric constant $\varepsilon_{IJ} = E_{IJ}^{\text{vac}}/E_{IJ}^{\text{solv}} > 0$, i.e., for which the electrostatic interaction energies in vacuum and solution share the same sign.

The cut-off scheme was implemented in such a way that the scaling factors remain independent of the size of the system under consideration and are consistent with the use of a nonbonded distance cut-off scheme in simulations. The combination rule used for the shielding of the interaction between two groups I and J is $\varepsilon_{IJ} \equiv \sqrt{\varepsilon_I \varepsilon_J}$. Computing the Coulombic interactions with scaled protein charges yields for each group the interaction energy with the rest of the protein, E_I^{shield} whose value can be compared with the corresponding Poisson–Boltzmann energy in solution, E_I^{solv}.

In the example given here, the scaling factors were calculated for the subfragment S1 of the molecular motor myosin including Mg^{2+} and ATP^{4-}. Poisson–Boltzmann calculations were done using the PBEQ module[35] of the program package CHARMM.[36] A finite-difference scheme was used to numerically solve the Poisson–Boltzmann equation with a final grid spacing of 0.5 Å at a temperature of 293 K and an ionic strength of 145 mM. For the vacuum interaction energies, a switch cut-off function ranging from 6.0 Å to 12.0 Å was used.[37]

Conformational pathway

A charge scaling method similar to that described above was used to examine the transition of annexin V. The annexin V system is an example of a protein for which ligand binding is accompanied by a large-scale conformational change. Here we use one of the most extensively tested methods, conjugate peak refinement (CPR) to determine the annexin transition pathway.[2] The CPR algorithm finds the minimum energy path connecting the reactant and product conformations of a process and determines all transition states along this path, allowing every atom to move independently and without applying any constraint to drive the reaction. The resulting path consists of a continuous series of structures. It shows only the motions that are essential to the transition, unlike the trajectories created by other methods used to accelerate slow conformational changes, such as targeted molecular dynamics.[38] Because no artificial strain is created, CPR yields meaningful and easily interpretable energy barriers along the path. The CPR algorithm is implemented in the trajectory refinement algorithm (travel) module of the CHARMM program.

Dynamical transition calculations

Nosé–Hoover dual heat-bath molecular dynamics simulations were used to examine protein atom fluctuations in hydrated myoglobin with the protein and solvent set at different temperatures.

Model system and potential function. The model system and potential function are those given in ref. 31, except where explicitly stated, the protocol in ref. 31 was followed. The CHARMM package[37] version 27b2 was used to perform the simulations. The model system consisted of one myoglobin molecule surrounded by a shell of 492 water molecules simulated in vacuum. The structure was taken from the Protein Data Bank (from the RSCB site: www.rscb.org) structure 1A6G, solved at 1.15 Å resolution using X-ray crystallography.[39] The TIP3P potential function was used to represent the water molecules.[40] The all-atom parameter set 22 was used throughout the simulations.[36] A shift function with a 12 Å cut-off was used to truncate the electrostatic interactions and a switch function was used to truncate the Van der Waals contributions over 10–12 Å. A relative dielectric constant of 1 was used. A coupling constant of 200 kcal mol^{-1} ps^{-2} was used for the Nosé–Hoover algorithm, together with a tolerance of 10^{-10} kcal mol^{-1} and a maximum of 10 cycles for convergence of the predictor–corrector method. Water molecules were taken using a random water box. The protein was placed within the box, only the 492 waters closest to the protein were kept. A time step of 1 fs was used.

Simulation protocols. Again following ref. 31, temperatures of 180 K and 300 K were used in different combinations: Protein Cold/Solvent Cold (PC/SC), Protein Cold/Solvent Hot (PC/SH), Protein Hot/Solvent Cold (PH/SC) and Protein Hot/Solvent Hot (PH/SH). Two simulation protocols were used (Methods 1 and 2). We divide the simulation protocols into three sequential stages: (1) *system relaxation*, (2) *system preparation* and (3) *Nosé–Hoover simulation*. The system relaxation and Nosé–Hoover simulation stages were the same for both methods. The two methods differ in the system preparation stage of the simulation protocol.

(1) System relaxation. The following calculations were sequentially performed: (i) 200 steps of minimisation (SD) with harmonic constraints on the protein of 10 kcal mol^{-1} Å^{-2}. (ii) 200 steps of minimisation (SD) with harmonic constraints on the protein of 1 kcal mol^{-1} Å^{-2}. (iii) 5 ps heating phase up to 180 K by increments of 5 K every 50 steps, fixing the protein atoms. (iv) 5 ps equilibration at 180 K with harmonic constraints on the protein of 1 kcal mol^{-1} Å^{-2}. (v) 5 ps equilibration at 180 K without constraints. (vi) 200 steps of minimisation using steepest descent (SD). (vii) 100 steps of minimisation adopted basis Newton–Raphson (ABNR).[37]

(2) System preparation. Following the system relaxation stage a 'system preparation' stage was performed.

Method 1 resembles as closely as was practically possible the protocol used in ref. 31. Personal communication established that in the work in ref. 31 a 3 ps heating phase to 300 K in 5 K increments was used. This was therefore adopted in Method 1.

Method 2 avoids the instantaneous temperature reduction of the protein from 300 K to 180 K present in the protein cold simulations at the beginning of the third (*i.e.*, Nosé–Hoover simulation) stage of Method 1. The system was heated for 3 ps to the temperature the protein was to have during the Nosé–Hoover run, *i.e.* 180 K for PC/SC PC/SH and 300 K for PH/SC and PH/SH. The system was subsequently equilibrated at that temperature during 50 ps.

(3) Nosé–Hoover simulation stage. The Nosé–Hoover simulation stage was the same for all simulations and follows the protocol used in ref. 31. The Nosé–Hoover thermostat was turned on, setting the protein and the solvent at their respective chosen temperatures. In all methods 50 ps of equilibration were performed followed by 100 ps for the production run.

The simulation model and force field used in the present work (Methods 1 and 2) and in ref. 31 are the same. Consequently, any differences in the results depend on the method of system preparation. The question arises as to which preparation method is most suitable. Methods that equilibrate the system at the temperature at which the protein will be fixed during the Nosé–Hoover run (*e.g.* Method 2, here) may be the least perturbative. These methods avoid the instantaneous reduction of the protein temperature from 300 K to 180 K that was present in ref. 31 and in the closely analogous Method 1 simulation here.

The mean-square-fluctuations of the protein, $\langle u^2 \rangle$, were calculated from the 100 ps production runs and compared with each other. Errors in $\langle u^2 \rangle$ were estimated by calculating the standard error for the $\langle u^2 \rangle$ in 10 bins along the 100 ps of the production runs.

Results

Charge reparametrisation

With the procedure described in Methods, the scaling factors λ_I found for the backbone groups of myosin II subfragment S1 range from 1.0 for Ser181 and Ser260 to 3.6 for Ile132 with an average of 1.6, whereas those for the side chain groups range from 1.0 for Arg654 to 6.9 for Arg402 with an average of 2.2. The distribution of the electrostatic interaction energies between each side chain and the rest of the protein is given in Fig. 1, for the nonuniform charge reparametrisation results, E^{shield}

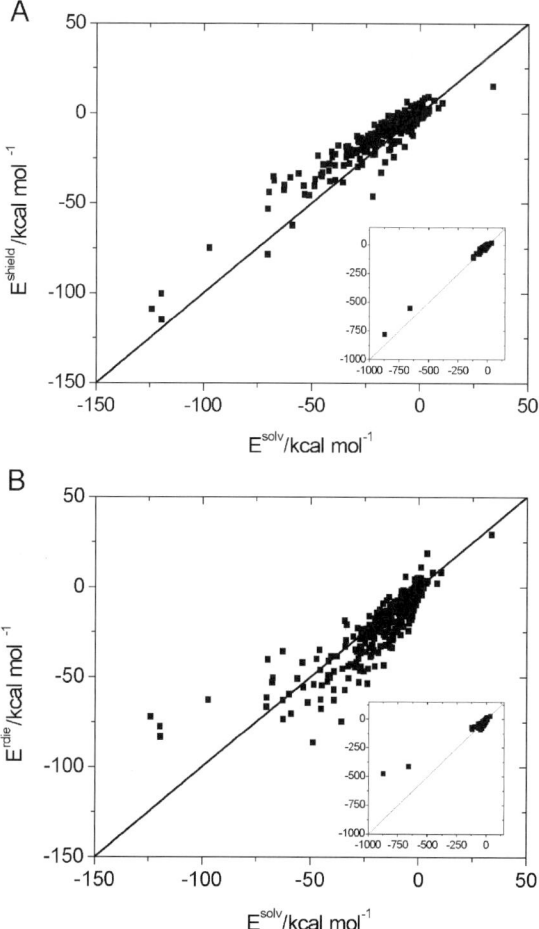

Fig. 1 Electrostatic interaction energies between side-chain groups and the rest of the protein for myosin II subfragment S1 calculated using simplified models and compared with E^{solv} obtained from Poisson–Boltzmann calculations. (A) Energies calculated as Coulomb interactions after nonuniform charge reparametrisation E^{shield}. (B) Energies calculated with the $\varepsilon = r$ distance dependent dielectric constant E^{rdie}.

and those obtained using a distance-dependent dielectric ($\varepsilon = r$) constant E^{rdie}. Both are compared with the reference energies E^{solv} obtained from Poisson–Boltzmann calculations. The root mean square deviation from the reference results is 22.7 kcal mol^{-1} for E^{rdie} but only 9.3 kcal mol^{-1} for E^{shield}. The improvement was found to be particularly large for moieties with large charges, such as for the Mg^{2+} and ATP^{4-} ions. The results indicate that, at least for the myosin S1 system, charge reparametrisation may provide a useful improved approximation to the Poisson–Boltzmann electrostatic representation.

Large-scale conformational transition

Charge scaling was used in the calculation of a large-scale conformational pathway in annexin V. The methods and results of this calculation are described in detail in ref. 41. The modelled pathway involves burial of Trp 187, from the "reactant" (TRP-OUT) to the "product" (TRP-IN) conformations, as shown in Fig. 2. The burial of Trp187 is accompanied by a large increase in conformational strain, compensated by improved protein–protein interaction energies. The pathway obtained is complex, involving > 100 dihedral angle transitions and the complete unwinding of one

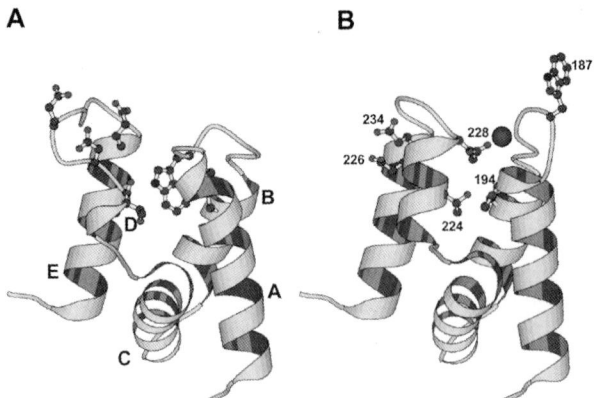

Fig. 2 Crystal structures of the two conformational states of domain II of annexin V (A) with the calcium site (*i.e.*, TRP-OUT) and (B) without the calcium-binding site (*i.e.*, TRP-IN). Important side chains are shown in a ball-and-stick representation. The large sphere in panel B represents the Ca^{2+} ion.

helix. The potential energy profile along the pathway is plotted in Fig. 3. It shows many energy fluctuations locally along the reaction coordinate of ~5–15 kcal mol^{-1} together with slower energy variations of ~20–40 kcal mol^{-1}. The local fluctuations correspond to the energy barriers crossed during the many small discrete conformational rearrangements that are required during the transition, for example, side-chain reorientations. Visual inspection of the pathway using molecular graphics revealed that it can be conveniently divided into the four phases indicated in Fig. 3. Acidic residues are found to play a major role in the conformational change *via* a succession of direct hydrogen bonds with Trp187.

Dynamical transition results

Here we examine the effect of solvent temperature on internal protein fluctuations, using the Nosé–Hoover method. The protein $\langle u^2 \rangle$ results for Methods 1 and 2 are presented in Table 1. Comparison of the $\langle u^2 \rangle$ obtained for PC/SC and PH/SC with those obtained for the hot solvent

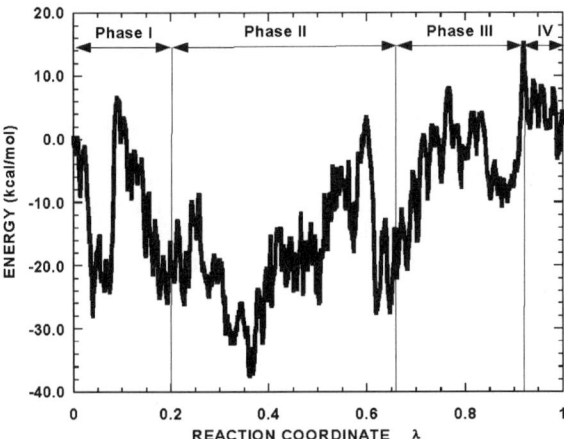

Fig. 3 Potential energy profile along the annexin conformational pathway. The reaction coordinate λ is the sum of all successive coordinate RMS differences λ along the curvilinear path. It is normalised here with respect to the total path length so that $\lambda = 0$ represents the TRP-OUT conformation and $\lambda = 1$ represents the TRP-IN conformation (shown in Fig. 2).

Table 1 Comparison of the $\langle u^2 \rangle$ results obtained using Methods 1 and 2

	PC/SC		PC/SH		PH/SC		PH/SH	
	Meth 1	Meth 2	Meth 1	Meth 2	Meth 1	Meth 2	Meth 1	Meth 2
$\langle u^2 \rangle$ backbone atoms /Å^2	0.07 ± 0.003	0.07 ± 0.007	0.13 ± 0.01	0.13 ± 0.012	0.10 ± 0.005	0.09 ± 0.007	0.18 ± 0.01	0.23 ± 0.03
$\langle u^2 \rangle$ non-H atoms /Å^2	0.10 ± 0.005	0.11 ± 0.009	0.20 ± 0.019	0.21 ± 0.018	0.15 ± 0.009	0.13 ± 0.012	0.30 ± 0.03	0.38 ± 0.05

simulations indicate that the cold solvent has a distinct caging effect on the protein atoms. This effect is significantly stronger using Method 2, as can be deduced from the fact that the ratio of the backbone (and, in brackets, side-chain) atom fluctuations of PH/SC to those of PC/SC is 1.49 (1.5) in Method 1 and 1.28 (1.18) in Method 2, and that the ratio of the backbone atom fluctuations of PH/SH to those of PC/SC is 2.68 (3.0) in Method 1 and 3.28 (3.45) in Method 2.

Comparing PC/SH with PC/SC shows that in both Methods 1 and 2 an effect of hot solvent is to double the protein $\langle u^2 \rangle$. This remarkable result agrees with that found in ref. 31.

Of particular interest is the question as to what fraction of the PH/SH fluctuations can be obtained by heating only the solvent (*i.e.* in PC/SH). The data obtained using both methods (Method 1 and Method 2) show the $\langle u^2 \rangle$ from PC/SH to lie between PC/SC and the PH/SH. One measure of the effect of the solvent on the high temperature protein fluctuations is given by

$$S = (\langle u^2 \rangle_{PC/SH} - \langle u^2 \rangle_{PC/SC})/(\langle u^2 \rangle_{PH/SH} - \langle u^2 \rangle_{PC/SC})$$

If solvent were to drive the high temperature protein fluctuations S should approach 1.0. For the backbone (and, in brackets, side-chain) atoms S is 0.55 (0.50) for Method 1 and 0.37 (0.37) for Method 2. These compare with higher values of 0.64 (0.65) obtained in ref. 31.

Discussion

In the present paper we have examined solvent effects on charge–charge interactions along pathways between functional protein conformations and on equilibrium internal fluctuations in proteins. Electrostatic interactions make a major contribution to interaction energies between protein groups. Thus, it is important to adequately represent these interactions in computer simulations. The surrounding solvent has a strong anisotropic screening effect on these interactions that can, in principle, be described with continuum methods. Here, a computationally-efficient way of doing this is presented in which the partial atomic charges are nonuniformly reparametrised so as to approximate the electrostatic interactions present in a full continuum Poisson–Boltzmann representation. Simulations using nonuniform charge reparametrisation are as computationally efficient as the commonly used distance-dependent dielectric constant approach, yet give an improved representation of the solvent screening effect. This is notably true for residues that exhibit large absolute magnitudes of their charges. It is important to model the interactions of these residues accurately as they lead to the largest interaction energies and strongest forces. The present results suggest that the nonuniform charge reparametrisation method promises to be a valuable simulation tool that includes solvent effects in simulations that, due to computational limitations, must be performed in the absence of explicit solvent. Examples of possible applications are combined quantum mechanical/molecular mechanical (QM/MM) calculations, with which Poisson–Boltzmann-based models have not yet been interfaced in current simulation packages, or simulations that rely on energy minimisation techniques such as ligand docking.

An application of charge reparametrisation is in the determination of large-scale conformational change. A large-scale conformational transition pathway calculated using charge reparametrisation is illustrated here. These pathways are important aspects of time-resolved chemistry and the development of computational tools for their elucidation will be of crucial importance for transforming time-resolved experimental structures into a full atomic-detail description of reaction pathways for conformational change in biological macromolecules. Much, however, remains to be done to explore the ensemble of pathways that may be accessible for any given functional structural change, and to accurately estimate effective reaction coordinates and their associated free energy changes. Charge reparametrisation is proving useful for representing solvent effects in these simulations. However, further improved accuracy will require taking into account the conformation dependence of the charge modification. A simple protocol for correcting the charge scaling by post-processing the energies with full Poisson–Boltzmann has been proposed.[42]

Finally, we have examined here solvent effects on fast (picosecond timescale) internal protein dynamics. Nosé–Hoover dual heatbath molecular dynamics simulations were performed, thus allowing the solvent region to be fixed at one temperature and the protein at another. Two main results are seen: (i) Low temperature solvent cages the protein fluctuations. (ii) Heating the solvent while keeping the protein cold drives the protein fluctuations to values intermediate between those in the fully cold and fully hot systems.

The present Nosé–Hoover results thus confirm, in accord with ref. 14 and 31, that solvent strongly influences the dynamical transition in proteins. However, there is no clear evidence from the present work that, in the hydrated myoglobin system, the high-temperature protein fluctuations are dominated by the solvent, rather, both the protein and the solvent contribute.

Acknowledgements

We thank Professor Dr. Martin Karplus and Dr. Dennis Vitkup for helpful discussions.

References

1. M. A. Ech-Cherif el-Kettani and J. Durup, *Biopolymers*, 1992, **32**, 561.
2. S. Fischer and M. Karplus, *Chem. Phys. Lett.*, 1992, **194**, 252.
3. J. Schlitter, M. Engels and P. Kruger, *J. Mol. Graphics*, 1994, **12**, 84.
4. R. Elber and M. Karplus, *Science*, 1987, **235**, 318.
5. B. Wroblowski, J. F. Diaz, J. Schlitter and Y. Engelborghs, *Protein Eng.*, 1997, **10**, 1163.
6. P. J. Steinbach and B. R. Brooks, *J. Comput. Chem.*, 1994, **15**, 667.
7. B. Honig and A. Nicholls, *Science*, 1995, **268**, 1144.
8. W. Doster, S. Cusack and W. Petry, *Nature*, 1989, **337**, 754.
9. M. Ferrand, A. J. Dianoux, W. Petry and G. Zaccai, *Proc. Natl. Acad. Sci. U. S. A.*, 1993, **90**, 9668.
10. R. V. Dunn, V. Reat, J. Finney, M. Ferrand, J. C. Smith and R. M. Daniel, *Biochem. J.*, 2000, **346**(2), 355.
11. J. Fitter, *Biophys. J.*, 1999, **76**, 1034.
12. J. Fitter, R. E. Lechner and N. A. Dencher, *Biophys. J.*, 1997, **73**, 2126.
13. R. M. Daniel, J. C. Smith, M. Ferrand, S. Hery, R. Dunn and J. L. Finney, *Biophys. J.*, 1998, **75**, 2504.
14. V. Reat, R. Dunn, M. Ferrand, J. L. Finney, R. M. Daniel and J. C. Smith, *Proc. Natl. Acad. Sci. U. S. A.*, 2000, **97**, 9961.
15. E. W. Knapp, S. F. Fischer and F. Parak, *J. Am. Chem. Soc.*, 1982, **86**, 5042.
16. S. G. Cohen, E. R. Bauminger, I. Nowik, S. Ofer and J. Yariv, *Phys. Rev. Lett.*, 1981, **46**, 1244.
17. F. Parak, E. N. Frolov, R. L. Mossbauer and V. I. Goldanskii, *J. Mol. Biol.*, 1981, **145**, 825.
18. H. Frauenfelder, G. A. Petsko and D. Tsernoglou, *Nature*, 1979, **280**, 558.
19. R. F. Tilton, Jr., J. C. Dewan and G. A. Petsko, *Biochemistry*, 1992, **31**, 2469.
20. B. F. Rasmussen, A. M. Stock, D. Ringe and G. A. Petsko, *Nature*, 1992, **357**, 423.
21. J. C. Smith, *Quart. Rev. Biophys.*, 1991, **24**, 227.
22. R. J. Loncharich and B. R. Brooks, *J. Mol. Biol.*, 1990, **215**, 439.
23. J. L. Green, J. Fan and C. A. Angell, *J. Phys. Chem.*, 1994, **98**.
24. F. H. Stillinger, *Science*, 1995, **267**, 1935.
25. H. Frauenfelder, F. Parak and R. D. Young, *Annu. Rev. Biophys. Biophys. Chem.*, 1988, **17**, 451.
26. H. Frauenfelder, S. G. Sligar and P. G. Wolynes, *Science*, 1991, **254**, 1598.
27. I. E. Iben, D. Braunstein, W. Doster, H. Frauenfelder, M. K. Hong, J. B. Johnson, S. Luck, P. Ormos, A. Schulte, P. J. Steinbach, A. H. Xie and R. D. Young, *Phys. Rev. Lett.*, 1989, **62**, 1916.
28. A. P. Sokolov, E. Rossler, A. Kisliuk and D. Quitmann, *Phys. Rev. Lett.*, 1993, **71**, 2062.
29. P. J. Steinbach and B. R. Brooks, *Proc. Natl. Acad. Sci. U. S. A.*, 1993, **90**, 9135.
30. G. R. Kneller and J. C. Smith, *J. Mol. Biol.*, 1994, **242**, 181.
31. D. Vitkup, D. Ringe, G. A. Petsko and M. Karplus, *Nature Struct. Biol.*, 2000, **7**, 34.
32. W. G. Hoover, *Phys. Rev. A*, 1985, **31**, 1695.
33. S. Fischer, S. Michnick and M. Karplus, *Biochemistry*, 1993, **32**, 13830.
34. A. Caflish, S. Fischer and M. Karplus, *J. Comput. Chem.*, 1997, **18**, 723.

35 W. Im, D. Beglov and B. Roux, *Comput. Phys. Commun.*, 1998, **111**, 59.
36 A. D. MacKerell, Jr., D. Bashford, M. Bellott, Jr., R. L. Dunbrack, J. D. Evanseck, M. J. Field, S. Fischer, J. Gao, H. Guo, S. Ha, D. Joseph-McCarthy, L. Kuchnir, K. Kuczera, F. T. K. Lau, C. Mattos, S. Michnick, T. Ngo, D. T. Nguyen, B. Prodhom III, W. E. Reiher, B. Roux, M. Schlenkrich, J. C. Smith, R. Stote, J. Straub, M. Watanabe, J. Wiorkiewicz-Kuczera, D. Yin and M. Karplus, *J. Phys. Chem. B*, 1998, **102**, 3586.
37 B. R. Brooks, R. E. Bruccoleri, B. D. Olafson, D. J. States, S. Swaminathan and M. Karplus, *J. Comput. Chem.*, 1983, **4**, 187.
38 J. Schlitter, M. Engels, P. Kruger, E. Jacoby and A. Wollmer, *Mol. Simul.*, 1993, **10**, 291.
39 J. Vojtechovsky, K. Chu, J. Berendzen, R. M. Sweet and I. Schlichting, *Biophys. J.*, 1999, **77**, 2153.
40 W. L. Jorgensen, J. Chandrasekhar, J. D. Madura, R. W. Impey and M. L. Klein, *J. Chem. Phys.*, 1983, **79**, 926.
41 J. Sopkova-De Oliveira Santos, S. Fischer, C. Guilbert, A. Lewit-Bentley and J. C. Smith, *Biochemistry*, 2000, **39**, 14065.
42 T. Simonson, G. Archontis and M. Karplus, *J. Phys. Chem.*, 1997, **41**, 8347.

Theoretical studies of time-resolved spectroscopy of protein folding

Jonathan D. Hirst,*[a] Samita Bhattacharjee[a] and Alexey V. Onufriev[b]

[a] *School of Chemistry, University of Nottingham, University Park, Nottingham, UK NG7 2RD*
[b] *Department of Molecular Biology, The Scripps Research Institute, 10550 North Torrey Pines Road, La Jolla CA 92037, USA*

Received 24th January 2002, Accepted 7th March 2002
First published as an Advance Article on the web 16th July 2002

Recently, we have made significant improvements in the accuracy of calculations of the circular dichroism of proteins from first principles. The quality of these calculations (especially at 220 nm, a key wavelength, where the intensity of the band correlates well with the helical content of polypeptides) has given us confidence to use such calculations to analyse nanosecond molecular dynamics simulations of the folding of polypeptides. We use this combined approach to explore the influence of dynamics on the circular dichroism spectroscopy of polypeptides. We apply it to equilibrium molecular dynamics simulations of two β-sheet proteins with similar structures, but differing circular dichroism spectra. We analyse a molecular dynamics simulation of the acid-unfolding of myoglobin. For both α-helical and β-sheet conformations, we find that changes in dihedral angles of 30° can change intensities of bands in circular dichroism spectra by up to 5000 degree cm^2 $dmol^{-1}$. Thus, in isolation, moderate differences in circular dichroism spectra cannot be interpreted uniquely in terms of conformational changes. Examination of individual structures allows us to dissect the influence of conformation on the calculated circular dichroism spectra. Our results are aimed at providing a deeper understanding of the optical properties of proteins. An atomic level connection between molecular dynamics simulations and optical spectroscopy is increasingly desirable as theoretical and experimental studies begin to probe protein folding events reliably on the nanosecond timescale.

Introduction

Protein folding is generally rapid and strongly co-operative.[1,2] Knowledge of protein folding pathways and structural characterisation of the states that occur along them are necessary for a thorough understanding of folding. Such an understanding would have an immediate practical impact, as folding and unfolding participate in the control of a variety of cellular processes, such as cross-membrane transport of proteins and cell cycle regulation.[3] The transient nature of intermediates has limited the understanding of the folding process. Intermediate states undergo much larger structural fluctuations than native states, which makes it difficult to resolve their structures fully using techniques such as X-ray crystallography or NMR. In this regard, a quantitative understanding of the relationship between protein conformation and circular dichroism (CD) spectra would be a valuable tool.

CD is the differential absorption of left and right circularly polarised light. It arises from the asymmetry of a chromophore or its environment, and thus provides a tool for measuring both conformation and changes in conformation for proteins and peptides. For decades CD spectroscopy has been an important method used by biochemists to analyse structures in globular proteins[4,5] and it can reveal greater detail than techniques such as routine UV absorption and fluorescence spectroscopies. Most conventional UV absorption and fluorescence studies of proteins provide only qualitative information about tertiary structural changes in the micro-environments of aromatic residues. In contrast, CD spectra provide distinct information about both tertiary and secondary structure and, unlike UV absorption, particular CD spectral features characterise the specific types of secondary structures present in proteins. In particular, CD measurements in the far-UV detect transitions involving primarily the peptide chromophore and are sensitive to secondary structure conformation.[4,5] For example, an α-helical CD spectrum consists of a positive band at 190 nm and two negative bands at 208 nm and 220 nm,[6] whereas the β-sheet proteins have a maximum at 195 nm and a minimum in the region 210–220 nm.

In addition to illuminating equilibrium studies, a detailed connection between the atomic structure of polypeptides and their CD spectra would also have an impact on time-resolved CD studies of protein folding. Several experimental techniques[7] now have the time resolution to follow early events in protein folding on nanosecond time scales.[8] Schemes that rapidly photoinitiate folding through laser temperature jump methods[9] or electron transfer[10] in real-time CD studies are now being pursued by several groups. Meanwhile, the nanosecond time regime is increasingly accessible to molecular dynamics simulations.[11,12] This convergence of experiment and theory makes the development of quantitative protein CD calculations particularly timely. Time-resolved CD is usually limited to a single wavelength, often 220 nm, to monitor helix content. The technique is widely applied, and it is therefore important to understand what factors affect the ellipticity at 220 nm. Thus a detailed understanding of the relationship between conformation, fluctuations and the measured CD spectra will be necessary for the fullest interpretation of these experiments. Clearly the experimental CD intensity of a single band provides only limited information, and we use the combination of CD calculations and molecular dynamics simulations to investigate which mechanisms of protein unfolding would be consistent with the experimentally measured changes in CD.

Although CD is sensitive to protein conformation, its interpretation has been largely empirical,[13] i.e., based on comparison with the CD spectra of proteins of known three-dimensional structure.[14] The validity and success of this approach rests on the structural similarity of different proteins in their native conformations. Whether non-native folding intermediates are sufficiently similar in conformation to fully folded proteins that their CD spectra can be analysed in the same way as those of native proteins is more of an open question. If we could accurately calculate the CD spectra arising from different conformations, we would be much better placed to interpret CD experiments on non-native conformations of peptides and proteins. Recently, we have made encouraging advances in the accuracy of calculations of the CD of proteins from first principles,[15,16] based on modern quantum chemical calculations on the amide group combined with a continuum model of solvent effects. Calculations of similar quality have also been realized by others.[17,18] We begin this paper with some additional benchmarking of our first principles approach against empirical approaches for estimating helicity, using the X-ray crystal structures of 29 proteins. Having established the quality of the first principles calculations on static structures, we investigate the possibility that equilibrium dynamics in solution of some β-sheet-containing proteins may influence their CD spectra.

The CD spectra of β-sheet proteins fall into two classes.[19,20] Class I β-sheet protein (β-I) exhibit a negative band at 216–218 nm and a positive band at 195 nm. The CD spectra of class II β-sheet proteins (β-II) resemble those of random coil models, dominated by an intense negative band near 198 nm. The β-II proteins tend to contain some disulfide bridges (which may contribute to the CD in the far-UV)[21] and have β-sheets that are more irregular than the β-I proteins, reflected by larger content of β-bulge structures. However, the structural origins of the CD spectra of β-II proteins are not fully understood. Calculations of CD based on static structures are unable to distinguish between β-I and β-II proteins, predicting β-I spectra for both classes. To investigate the CD calculations on β-I and β-II proteins further, we analyse the equilibrium dynamics of concanavalin A (a β-I protein) and elastase (a β-II protein). Schematic representations of the structures of these two proteins along with myoglobin are shown in Fig. 1.

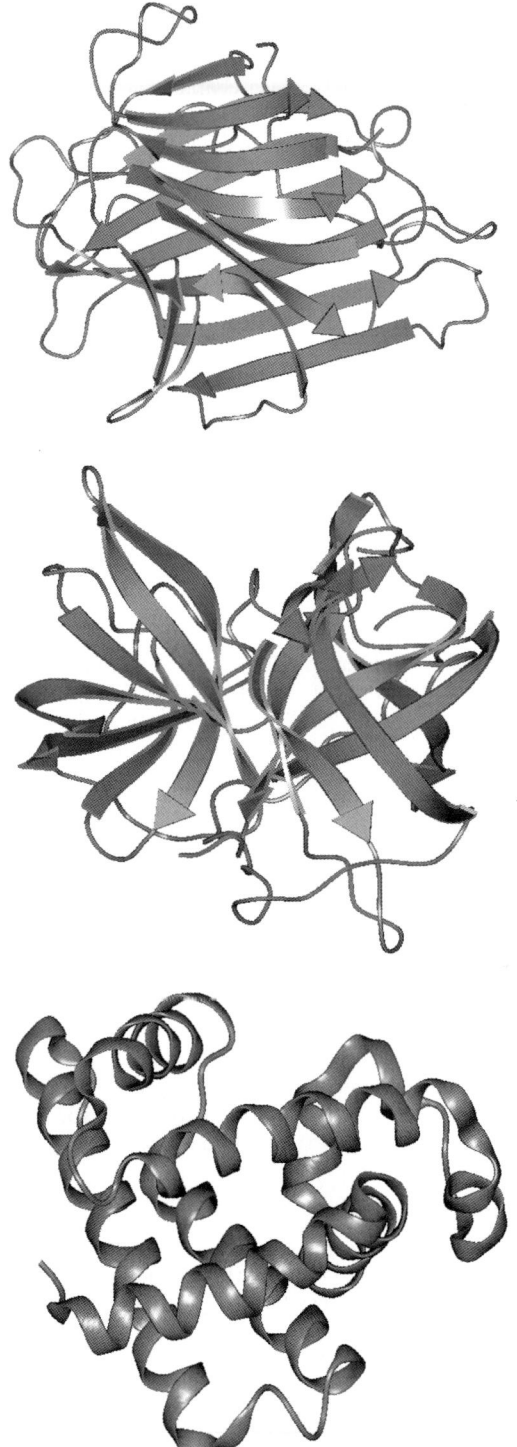

Fig. 1 Ribbon representations, rendered using PREPI (Dr Suhail Islam, Imperial College, London), of the structures of the proteins (PDB accessions codes in parentheses) whose dynamics have been studied: upper – concanavalin A (3cna); centre – elastase (3est); lower – myoglobin (2mb5).

Finally, we explore a non-equilibrium process by calculations of CD based on structures from molecular dynamics simulations of the unfolding of apomyoglobin. Myoglobin has at least two non-native apo states whose structures have been characterised using NMR and CD. These partially unfolded stable states may be good models of folding intermediates, and have attracted much attention from experimentalists and theorists. One difficulty in connecting simulation data to CD experiments is the issue of which conformations contribute to the CD spectrum, especially at 220 nm where the intensity is taken to reflect the helical content of the folding intermediates. Typically, residues are designated 'helical' based on local main-chain dihedral angles and the conformational states of neighbouring residues in any empirical calculations, whereas our calculations of CD from first principles avoid *ad hoc* definitions.

Nanosecond and increasingly microsecond time scales are accessible to molecular dynamics simulations of protein folding and unfolding, providing exquisite detail of these microscopic events.[22] The credibility of such simulations is critical, resting partly upon the quality of force field development, partly on technical issues of sampling and protocol and, perhaps most directly, upon the reproduction of key experimental data. Clear connections to experimental data obviously enhance confidence in molecular dynamics simulations and the atomic level picture that they paint.

Methods

CD calculations

Calculations of the electronic structure of polypeptides are well beyond the scope of fully *ab initio* treatments. The most common method of computing the CD spectra of polypeptides is the matrix method,[23,24] where the excited states of individual chromophores are described quantum mechanically and interactions between these states are computed classically, based on parametrizations of the *ab initio* calculations on the individual chromophores. The intensities of the bands are derived directly from the electronic and magnetic transition dipole moments through the rotational strengths corresponding to each excited state of the polypeptide. The rotational strength can be expressed as the imaginary part of the product of the electronic and magnetic transition dipole moments using the Rosenfeld equation.[25] For an electronic transition $i \leftarrow 0$, the rotational strength R_{0i} is given by

$$R_{0i} = \text{Im}(\langle \psi_0 | \mu_e | \psi_i \rangle) \cdot (\langle \psi_i | \mu_m | \psi_0 \rangle) \quad (1)$$

where Im denotes "the imaginary part of", ψ_0 is the ground state wave function, ψ_i is the excited state wave function and μ_e and μ_m are the electronic and magnetic transition dipole moments, respectively.

In the matrix method, a polypeptide is treated as a collection of M non-interacting chromophoric groups. Electronic excitations may occur only within a group but not between the groups. The excited-state wave function of the whole molecule is expressed as a linear combination of basis functions Φ_{ia} involving the n_i excitations within each chromophoric group:

$$\Psi_T = \sum_i^M \sum_a^{n_i} c_{ia} \Phi_{ia} \quad (2)$$

Each basis function is a product of M monomer wave functions. The basis set is further restricted to allow only one group to be excited. Thus:

$$\Phi_{ia} = \varphi_{10} \cdots \varphi_{ia} \cdots \varphi_{j0} \cdots \varphi_{M0} \quad (3)$$

where φ_{ia} represents the wave function of chromophore i, which has undergone an electronic excitation $a \leftarrow 0$. In general, each transition from the ground state to one of the excited states may have a nonzero rotational strength at its particular transition energy, and the CD spectrum is the sum of all these rotational strengths.

A Hamiltonian matrix is then constructed. The diagonal elements of this matrix are the excitation energies of the single chromophores, and the off-diagonal elements describe the interactions between different chromophoric groups. If the latter are assumed to be purely Coulombic in nature, then the off-diagonal elements are computed from the electrostatic interaction between charge densities and have the form:

$$V_{i0a;j0b} = \int\int \frac{\rho_{i0a}(r_{i1})\rho_{j0b}(r_{j1})}{4\pi\varepsilon_0 r_{i1,j1}} dr_{i1} dr_{j1} \quad (4)$$

where ρ_{i0a} and ρ_{j0b} represent the permanent (when $a = 0$ or $b = 0$) and transition electron densities on chromophores i and j, respectively. Thus, the matrix method requires parameters that describe the above charge distributions associated with the different electronic states of the chromophoric groups of the protein. In the present study, these parameters were taken from calculations on N-methylacetamide (NMA) in solution using the complete-active-space self-consistent field method implemented within a self-consistent reaction field (CASSCF/SCRF).[26–29] The interaction potentials were evaluated by representing the charge densities with a set of point charges (or monopoles). The point charges were fitted to reproduce the *ab initio* electrostatic potential arising from the various states,[30] thereby improving the representation of the monomer.

In the calculations reported here, only the amide electronic transitions $n\pi^*$ (at 220 nm) and $\pi\pi^*$ (at 193 nm) are included. In such a case, for a diamide (considered here solely for illustrative purposes) the Hamiltonian matrix takes the form

$$H = \begin{pmatrix} E^1_{n\pi^*} & V^{11}_{n\pi^*\pi\pi^*} & V^{12}_{n\pi^*n\pi^*} & V^{12}_{n\pi^*\pi\pi^*} \\ V^{11}_{n\pi^*\pi\pi^*} & E^1_{\pi\pi^*} & V^{21}_{n\pi^*\pi\pi^*} & V^{12}_{\pi\pi^*\pi\pi^*} \\ V^{12}_{n\pi^*n\pi^*} & V^{21}_{n\pi^*\pi\pi^*} & E^2_{n\pi^*} & V^{22}_{n\pi^*\pi\pi^*} \\ V^{12}_{n\pi^*\pi\pi^*} & V^{12}_{\pi\pi^*\pi\pi^*} & V^{22}_{n\pi^*\pi\pi^*} & E^2_{\pi\pi^*} \end{pmatrix} \quad (5)$$

Diagonalization of the above matrix by a unitary transformation yields the eigenvalues and eigenvectors of the composite transitions of the protein. The eigenvalues are the energies of the transitions of the polypeptides and the eigenvectors give the mixing coefficients describing contributions of the excited states of the individual groups to the delocalised excited states of the polypeptides. The eigenvectors are then used to calculate the rotational strengths corresponding to each excited state of the peptide, as described in eqn. (1) and subsequently, the CD can be calculated.

Empirical estimates of CD were made using two definitions of helicity, one based on main chain dihedral angles, the other on hydrogen bonds. In the former, a residue was deemed to be helical if its dihedral angles fell within a square region of the Ramanchandran plot[31] centred on the values for an ideal helix, as defined by $\phi = -57° \pm 40°$ and $\psi = -47° \pm 40°$. Occurrences of a single residue or two contiguous residues satisfying the previous constraint were designated non-helical; in other words three (or more) contiguous residues with the necessary dihedral angles were required for these residues to be classified as helical. An alternative empirical definition of helicity was explored based on patterns of hydrogen-bonding and geometrical features calculated by the popular DSSP program.[32] In this program, an ideal hydrogen bond is one where the amide N–H bond and the carbonyl CO bond are collinear and the ideal hydrogen bond length is 2.9 Å. The DSSP definition tolerates deviations in the orientation of up to 63° and a maximum hydrogen bond length of 5.2 Å. Specifically, main-chain $i, i+3$ hydrogen bonds, $i, i+4$ hydrogen bonds and $i, i+5$ hydrogen bonds were counted. Two such hydrogen bonds that were contiguous defined a helical region of the types 3_{10}, α and π, respectively. Helicity was based on the presence of these helical structures; an isolated hydrogen bond did not contribute to the helicity, as it would more likely correspond to a turn-like structure.

CD spectra were calculated for a set of 29 protein structures taken from the Protein Data Bank (PDB)[33] and compared with experimental CD data from the literature.[34–37] This set ranges from highly helical proteins to those that are largely β-sheet. It includes all-α proteins: cytochrome c (PDB accession number: 3cyt), hemoglobin (1hco), myoglobin (1mbn) and bacteriorhodopsin (2brd); some mixed α,β (mainly α) proteins: alcohol dehydrogenase (5adh), glutathione reductase (3grs), lactate dehydrogenase (6ldh), lysozyme (7lyz), papain (9pap), rhodanese (1rhd), subtilisin (1sbt), thermolysin (4tln), triose phosphate isomerase (1tim), flavodoxin (2fx2); some β-I proteins: carbonic anhydrase (1ca2), concanavalin A (3cna), λ-immunoglobulin (1rei), ribonuclease A (3rn3), ribonuclease S (2rns), erabutoxin (3ebx), plastocyanin (1plc), porin (3por), prealbumin (2pab); and some β-II proteins α-chymotrypsinogen A (2cga), α-chymotrypsin II (5cha), elastase (3est), superoxide dismutase (2sod), trypsin inhibitor (4pti) and trypsin (3ptn). The rotational strengths computed *via* the matrix method were used to generate continuous spectra (rather than line spectra) through Gaussian functions centred on each of the transition energies with a bandwidth of 15.5 nm and an area proportional to the rotational strength of the transition.

Effect of conformational dynamics on β-sheet CD

Matrix method calculations of CD using the static X-ray structures are unable to distinguish between β-I and β-II proteins, predicting β-I spectra for both classes. Whilst there may be deficiencies in the CD calculations, we have suggested[15] that relatively minor fluctuations of 30° in backbone dihedral angles would lead to structures whose calculated CD spectra would be much closer to those observed experimentally. We have performed molecular dynamics simulations on concanavalin A (a β-I protein) and elastase (a β-II protein).

Concanavalin A and elastase both comprise approximately 240 residues. Simulations with explicit solvent would require a large number of water molecules. Therefore, to facilitate the sampling of conformational space under equilibrium conditions, a continuum model of solvent was employed. In a continuum model, one eliminates the solvent nuclear degrees of freedom and the interatomic interactions of the biomolecule are reparametrized to give structural, energetic and dynamic properties that are similar to those seen in explicit solvent. The model used here is the generalised Born model.[38] The accuracy of this model has been established in a number of applications to biopolymers. For example, the model has been compared to explicit solvent models in equilibrium simulations of interleukin-8[39] and in folding simulations of a small β-sheet protein.[40]

Simulations under equilibrium conditions were performed at 298 K for 500 ps using the generalised Born model, as implemented[41] within the CHARMM biomolecular simulation code.[42] The PARAM19 parameter set was used. The stability of the simulations was monitored by following the root mean square deviation (rmsd) of backbone atoms from the initial structure. The distributions of main dihedral angles were computed. The dynamics and mobility of the protein backbones were characterised using the generalised order parameter, which measures the angular correlation for the dynamics of the N–H bond. It is calculated from the trajectory as the plateau value of the correlation function $\langle P_2[\mu(t)\cdot\mu(t+\tau)]\rangle$, where μ is a unit vector oriented along the N–H bond and $P_2(x)$ is the second Legendre polynomial.[43] A generalised order parameter with a value close to unity indicates little motion on the picosecond timescale and greater motion for lower values. The CD was calculated using ensembles of 80 structures (one structure sampled every 5 ps from final 400 ps the trajectory) of each of the two proteins.

Molecular dynamic simulations on myoglobin

Holo myoglobin is a globular, *b* heme protein of 153 residues, comprising eight α-helices. Native apomyoglobin is produced by removal of the proto-porphyrin heme prosthetic group from the holomyoglobin, which partially destabilises the tertiary fold of the globin. Apomyoglobin (myoglobin without the heme group) is well suited for both theoretical and experimental studies of folding, as it folds through a set of well-defined intermediate states.[44] Experimental studies[45,46] reveal that the protein is structurally very similar to the native (holo) myoglobin, retaining most of its secondary, and most likely, tertiary structure. With the gradual addition of acid, apomyoglobin undergoes a two-phase unfolding, first to a molten globule intermediate (I-state) at about pH 4, and finally to an unfolded state at pH 2. In re-folding experiments, the I-state is shown to be an obligatory folding intermediate[47,48] suggesting strong similarity between the acid-unfolding and re-folding pathways of apomyoglobin.[44] This observation makes apomyoglobin a particularly interesting system for theoretical studies of folding: one can hope to gain insight into the apomyoglobin folding process by simulating its acid-unfolding, which, unlike direct, fully atomistic simulation of folding, is quite feasible computationally.

To provide a reference point, an equilibrium simulation of native holo-myoglobin was performed. We used version 5.0 of the AMBER suite of programs.[49] An all-atom force field[50] was employed and the SHAKE algorithm[51] was used to restrain hydrogen–heavy atom bond distances. The integration time-step was 2 fs, with a 12 Å cut-off for long-range interactions. The starting structure for the native holo-myoglobin simulation was the structure obtained by neutron scattering[52] (PDB accession number 2mb5). We kept all the hydrogen atoms found in the PDB set. The protonation state of this structure corresponds to neutral pH; its total charge is +5. The protein was solvated by approximately 4000 TIP3P water molecules,[53] forming a spherical droplet of radius 37 Å around the centre of mass of the molecule. This is sufficient for the native structure under neutral pH conditions, as the protein is expected to remain in a compact conformation. A simulation cycle began with a 100 steps of steepest-descent minimization followed by 100 ps equilibration during which the temperature was gradually raised to 305 K, while the protein atom coordinates remain fixed by harmonic restraints (force constant 5 kcal mol^{-1} Å^{-2}) at their crystallographic positions. The Berendsen temperature coupling algorithm[54] was used, with a coupling constant for both solute and solvent of 1.0 ps. After the equilibration was completed the constraints were removed, and the simulation continued for another 200 ps at an average temperature of 305 K. Separate temperature coupling constants of 20 ps and 1 ps, for the solute and solvent respectively, were used. To prevent evaporation of water molecules, a weak (force constant 0.05 kcal mol^{-1} Å^{-2}) spherical cap harmonic restoring potential was applied to atoms further than 37 Å from the centre of mass of the system. Protein coordinates were saved every 0.5 ps. After 200 ps the backbone rmsd from the crystal structure was about 1.3 Å. We used the last 100 ps of the simulation for the analysis.

The starting structure for the unfolding simulation was prepared by removing the heme group from the holo-myoglobin coordinate set used above. To model the conditions of extremely low pH, all aspartate, glutamate, histidine, and the C-terminus side chain groups in the protein were protonated,[55] making the overall charge of the globule +36, in agreement with the experimentally observed value under these conditions. Simulations were carried out using version 5.1 of the AMBER suite of programs;[49] other details were as for the native state simulation, except as noted below. The protein was solvated by 10 000 water molecules, forming a spherical droplet of radius 47 Å around the centre of mass of the molecule. After the equilibration was completed the constraints were removed, and the simulation continued for another 100 ps at 300 K. Protein and solvent coordinates were saved every 10 ps. At the end of this stage, the water molecules were removed, and the protein was re-solvated by 10 000 water molecules forming a spherical droplet of radius 47 Å around the centre of mass of the protein. The above three-step cycle was then repeated 16 times, yielding a total of 1.6 ns of unconstrained trajectory and 160 molecular dynamics trajectory structures. The re-solvation procedure ensured that the protein always stayed well within the droplet during the simulation. The protonation of acidic side-chains to simulate low pH is sufficient to induce unfolding with no added biasing forces or other unusual conditions. By the end of the simulation the protein appears to be completely unfolded; its radius of gyration increased from 15.3 Å of the native holo-myoglobin to 29.6 Å (calculated as an average over the last 200 ps of the trajectory), and was close to that observed experimentally[46] for the acid-unfolded state of apomyoglobin. Other evidence that the simulation yields reasonable structures is provided by the average separations between helices A and G, and A and H. These were calculated as the arithmetic mean of distances between C_α atoms of residues 7 and 103, and 14 and 103; $|AG| = 48$ Å, $|AH| = 57$ Å, consistent with experimental[56] values of $|AG| > 50$ Å, $|AH| > 50$ Å for the acid-unfolded state.

As a further test of the above protocol, a separate simulation of apomyoglobin that models neutral pH conditions was performed. After 20 simulation cycles corresponding to 2.0 ns of unconstrained dynamics, the native fold was preserved, the radius of gyration was only 5% larger, and helical content was 25% lower than that calculated for the native holo-myoglobin. These characteristics were similar to those experimentally observed in apomyoglobin at pH 6.5.[46]

Close quantitative agreement with experiment is not required for the purposes of the current study, and a set of structures reasonably approximating the transition between the native and acid-unfolding states of apomyoglobin is sufficient. The 160 structures taken at 10 ps intervals from the trajectory were used to analyse fluctuations in main chain dihedral angles and hydrogen bonding. The influence of these properties on the predicted helicity has been explored using empirical CD calculations and the matrix method.

Results

Benchmark on static structures

Our benchmark calculations on the set of 29 proteins are summarised in Table 1. The calculation of helicity was based on the mean residue ellipticity at 220 nm, $[\theta]_{220}$. The measured helicity was

Table 1 Comparison of approaches for CD calculations

Method	Spearman rank correlation between calculated and measured helicity	Root mean square error
Matrix method	0.896	0.066
Main chain dihedral angles	0.876	0.089
α-Helical (only) H-bonds	0.874	0.093
All helical H-bonds	0.865	0.107

computed as $[\theta]_{220}/(-37\,000)$, where $[\theta]_{220}$ was taken from experimental spectra reported in the literature. An analogous expression was used to give the helicity calculated using the matrix method, with $[\theta]_{220}$ taken from the calculations. The value of $-37\,000$ degree cm^2 dmol^{-1} is based on experimental[57] and theoretical[15] estimates of the value of $[\theta]_{220}$ for an polypeptide of 100% helicity. Thus, helicity usually ranges from zero to one. Two values of helicity derived from the hydrogen bonding were computed as the fraction of helical residues in the protein, where helical was either restricted to α-helical or included all types of helices. In the former case, the fraction was calculated using the total number of residues less four (as four terminal residues would not be able to form $i, i+4$ hydrogen bonds); in the latter case, the total number of residues less three was used (as three terminal residues would not be able to form $i, i+3$ hydrogen bonds). Table 1 shows two statistical measures of accuracy, the Spearman rank correlation coefficient between the calculated (by various methods) and experimental helicities and the root mean square error in the calculated helicity. Both measures show that the matrix method calculations are marginally better than the empirical approaches, although this difference is probably not statistically significant.

β-Sheet proteins: elastase and concanavalin A

Table 1 presents data on helicity, which are based solely on the intensity at 220 nm. The accuracy of the matrix method at other wavelengths, where there is no comparison with empirical estimates of helicity, has been assessed elsewhere.[15] In contrast to the region at 220 nm, which arises predominantly from the amide $n\pi^*$ transition, the region 190–200 nm is due primarily to the amide $\pi\pi^*$ transition. This part of the spectrum is less well modelled by the matrix method calculations, possibly because the $\pi\pi^*$ transition has a large electric transition dipole moment which can couple with higher energy transitions. Nevertheless, the accuracy of the matrix method appears to be reasonable, based on the static X-ray structures. However, there are some β-sheet proteins (class β-II) for which the matrix method calculations perform poorly. Yet on other β-sheet (class β-I) proteins, with similar structures, the calculations perform well.

To investigate whether conformational dynamics in solution might explain the discrepancy between class β-I and class β-II proteins, simulations on representatives of these two classes were carried out. The chosen proteins were concanavalin A from class β-I and elastase from class β-II. The rmsd of the backbone atoms is shown in Fig. 2 over a 500 ps period. Both proteins undergo some initial rearrangements, but these appear to be complete after 100 ps. In the case of concanavalin A, the ~4.5 Å change in the backbone rmsd corresponds to one of the β-sheets (the upper one in Fig. 1) unfurling and becoming flatter.

The CD spectra, computed using the matrix method, of concanavalin A and elastase, based on the final 400 ps of the simulations are shown in Figs. 3 and 4, respectively. The thick solid line is the mean spectrum computed from 80 snapshots along the trajectory. Spectra from individual structures were qualitatively similar, but varied by up to ± 5000 degree cm^2 dmol^{-1}. The calculated CD for concanavalin A remains close to that calculated for the X-ray crystal structure (Fig. 3), whereas the ensemble of elastase gives a calculated CD spectrum that is markedly different from that of the crystal structure. For the elastase ensemble, the computed intensity at 195 nm is 2400 degree cm^2 dmol^{-1} compared to $10\,000$ degree cm^2 dmol^{-1} calculated for the crystal structure and -7500 degree cm^2 dmol^{-1} observed experimentally (Fig. 4). Whilst a qualitative problem still remains (the sign of the peak is wrong), the results nevertheless represent a significant improvement. Quantitatively, the error in the computed CD spectrum of elastase is much lower. Qualitatively, it appears

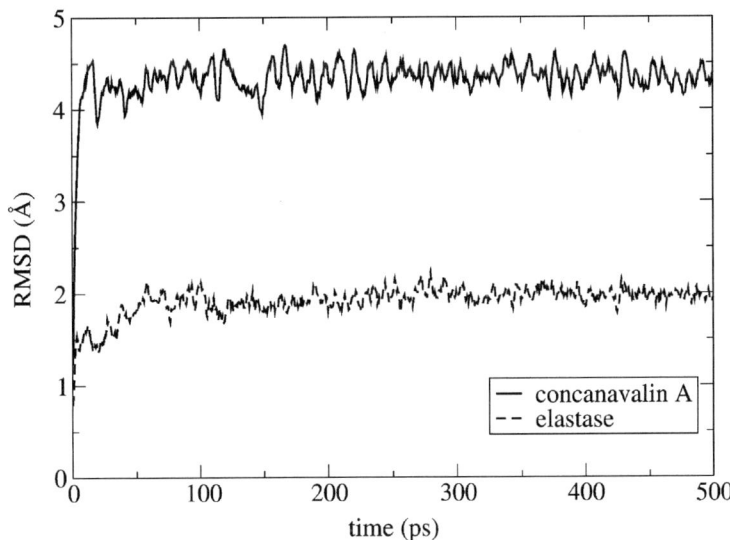

Fig. 2 Root mean square deviation of the backbone atoms during the simulations of elastase (lower curve) and concanavalin A (upper curve).

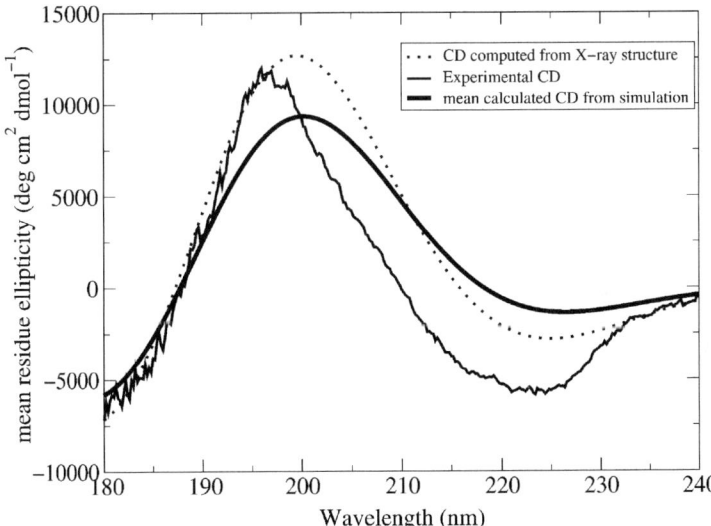

Fig. 3 Circular dichroism spectra of concanavalin A: medium solid line, experimental; dotted line, computed from the X-ray crystal structure; thick solid line, mean computed spectrum from an ensemble of structures from molecular dynamics simulation.

that relaxation of the elastase structure in solution may account for some of the previously unexplained differences between β-I and β-II proteins.

The differences between the ensembles of concanavalin A and elastase have been investigated with respect to both dynamics and structure. To probe whether elastase underwent larger fluctuations than concanavalin A, the generalised order parameters were computed for the last 400 ps of the simulations. From Fig. 5, the two proteins exhibit quite similar backbone flexibility and so this appears unlikely to be the origin of the differing CD spectra. For the last 400 ps of each simulation, the main-chain dihedral angles were computed for structures every 0.5 ps along the

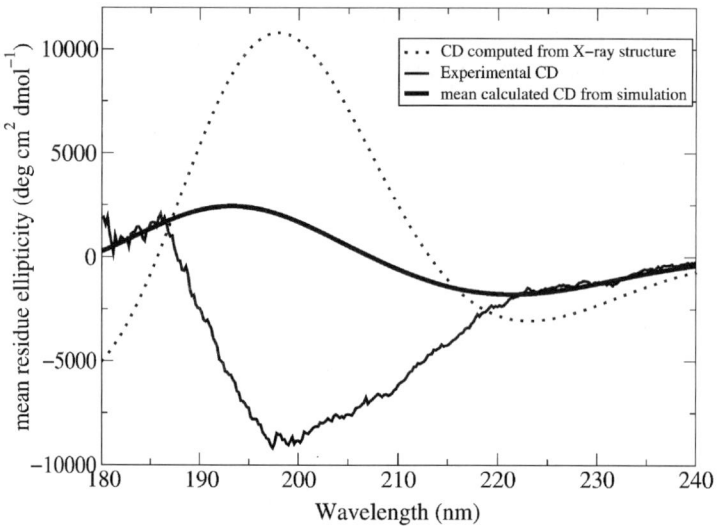

Fig. 4 Circular dichroism spectra of elastase: medium solid line, experimental; dotted line, computed from the X-ray crystal structure; thick solid line, mean computed spectrum from an ensemble of structures from molecular dynamics simulation.

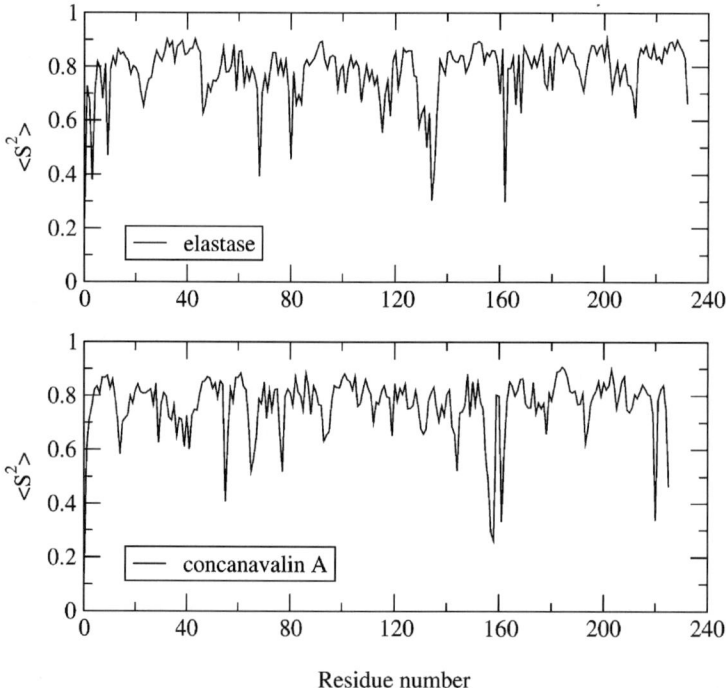

Fig. 5 Generalised order parameters, $\langle S^2 \rangle$, for N–H relaxation.

trajectories. These were used to construct histograms representing the distributions of dihedral angles populated by the ensembles. The difference between the two resulting histograms is plotted in Fig. 6. The darker areas on the figure indicate regions, which are more populated by elastase; the lighter areas indicate a greater population by concanavalin A. A shift in the population in

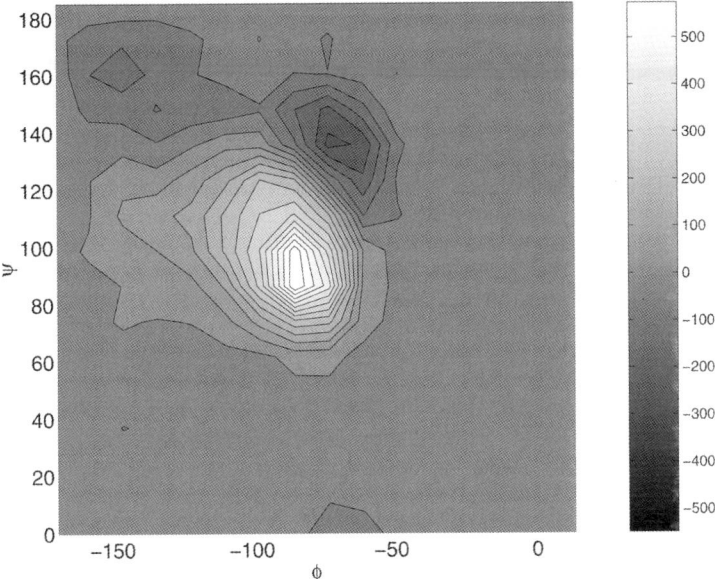

Fig. 6 Difference plot between the distributions of main chain dihedral angles sampled in the simulations (concanavalin A–elastase).

β-conformation portion of the Ramanchandran plot is evident, from (−85°, 95°) for concanavalin A to (−70°, 140°) for elastase. We discuss this further in the next section. The sensitivity of the circular dichroism to changes of this magnitude in the main chain dihedral angles also emerges in the calculations on myoglobin.

Myoglobin

In the benchmark calculations (Table 1) on 29 proteins, the structure of myoglobin 1mbn[58] was considered. In the simulation studies, the structure 2mb5 was used as a starting point.[52] These two structures appear to be very similar, with a backbone rmsd of ∼0.5 Å. The computed CD spectra are compared with experiment in Fig. 7. The calculated CD spectrum is also shown from a third structure, 1bzr, which was solved most recently and to the highest resolution, namely 1.15 Å.[59] Whilst the computed CD spectra agree only qualitatively with the experimental spectrum across the entire wavelength range, the quantitative agreement at 220 nm is evident for the 1mbn structure. The experimental value of $[\theta]_{220}$ is −24 090 degree cm^2 dmol^{-1}; the value computed from structure 1mbn is −23 597 degree cm^2 dmol^{-1} and the value from structure 1bzr is −22 175 degree cm^2 dmol^{-1}. However, the intensity at 220 nm computed from the 2mb5 structure, −19 048 degree cm^2 dmol^{-1}, is less negative than anticipated, which at first glance seemed curious given the similarity of the experimental structures. Closer inspection of the 1mbn and 2mb5 revealed that there were subtle, but significant differences in the main-chain dihedral angles, as shown in Fig. 8. Although in both cases the main chain dihedral angles fall within the helical region and both structures have the same helical assignments the respective centres of the (phi,psi) distribution in the helical region are shifted relative to each other. Analysis of the last 100 ps of the 200 ps simulation of the native state of holo-myoglobin, which used the 2mb5 structure as initial coordinates, showed that over time the dihedral angle distribution moved towards that of the 1mbn structure and so did the value of $[\theta]_{220}$. The value of $[\theta]_{220}$ computed for structures taken every 0.5 ps from the 100 ps portion of the trajectory was −20 110 degree cm^2 dmol^{-1} with a standard deviation of 30 degree cm^2 dmol^{-1}.

The calculated helicity of the structures of apomyoglobin protein as it unfolds in the simulation is depicted in Fig. 9. The different methods give quite similar results, although the inclusion of 3_{10} and π-helical conformations in the hydrogen bond calculation leads to an over-estimate of helicity compared to the consensus. The helicity computed by the empirical approaches (based on dihedral

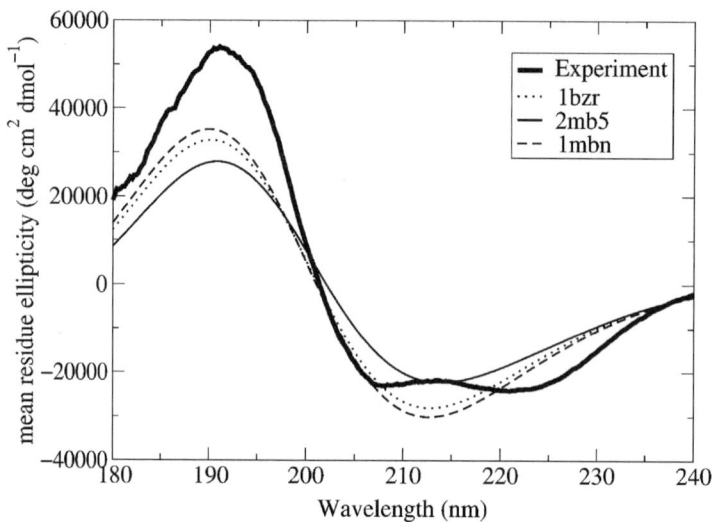

Fig. 7 Experimental and computed CD spectra of myoglobin.

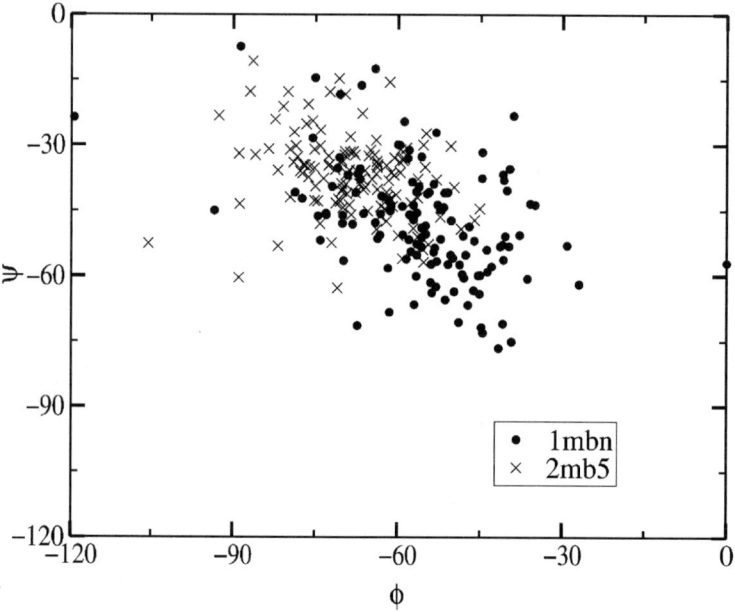

Fig. 8 Ramanchandran plot for the structures 1mbn and 2mb5.

angles or hydrogen bonds) exhibits greater fluctuations compared to the matrix method *ab initio* calculations. After about 300 ps the matrix method helicity remains stable around 0.3, whereas the α-helical hydrogen bond helicity and the helicity computed from the dihedral angles fluctuate between 0.4 and 0.2.

Discussion

We have demonstrated the feasibility of using first principles CD calculations and molecular dynamic simulations to analyse the unfolded and partially unfolded helical states. Earlier work

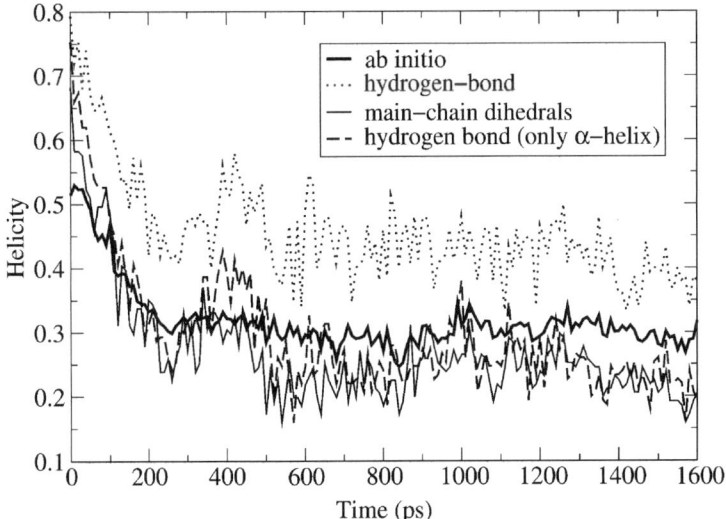

Fig. 9 Time evolution of helicity computed (by several methods) from the unfolding simulation of apo-myoglobin.

adopted this general strategy to study the conformations of cyclic-L-Tyr-L-Tyr.[60] The complexity of the systems that we have investigated using a combined approach of molecular dynamics simulation, to generate statistically meaningful ensembles, and CD calculations is significantly greater. Such calculations allow us to assess precisely when protein conformations are no longer sufficiently helical to be observed by CD spectroscopy. Thus, the theoretical calculation of time resolved spectroscopy of protein folding will provide a direct connection to experimental data.

Many definitions of helicity have been applied in the literature to analyse simulations of conformational transitions in helical peptides and proteins. Examples of the use of hydrogen-bonding patterns include: the DSSP secondary structure assignment[61] and the presence of $i, i+4$ hydrogen bonds.[62] Definitions based on main-chain dihedral angles include: a 15° range centred on $(-58°, -47°)$,[63] a 30° range centred on $(-57°, -47°)$[64] and $(-100° \leqslant \phi \leqslant -30°$ and $-80° \leqslant \psi \leqslant -5°)$.[65,66] In addition to the ambiguity over what constitutes a helical residue, even the definition of a hydrogen bond often involves the stipulation of arbitrary thresholds relating to distances and angles.[67] At one level, most of these definitions appear to be satisfactory. Table 1 and Fig. 9 show that empirical measures reflect the helicity of both native proteins and partially unfolded states in reasonable agreement with either experiment or the first principles calculations. However, counting all helical types seems to over-estimate the helicity of the partially unfolded states, despite strong indications that 3_{10} and π helices do contribute significantly to the intensity at 220 nm.[15,68] Nevertheless, the empirical definitions do involve somewhat arbitrary specifications. The greater fluctuations of the empirical helicities in Fig. 9 are due to the artificially discontinuous nature of the empirical definitions. A change of one degree in a dihedral angle presumably does not lead to an all or nothing change in the CD in reality. Most of the analyses of helicity based on dihedral angles define a square or rectangular window on the Ramanchandran plot. More complex regions have been investigated and the weighting of different helical regions has also been explored.[13] Whilst such an empirical model might be more appropriate, it lacks the appeal of simplicity. Our findings for the β-sheet proteins and myoglobin both suggest, however, that the CD of proteins is more sensitive to the dihedral angles of the backbone than the empirical models allow for.

In the comparison of concanavalin A and elastase, we observed that a shift in the dihedral angle population from $(-85°, 95°)$ to $(-70°, 140°)$ significantly influences the computed CD, bringing the calculated CD spectrum for elastase closer to the experimentally observed spectrum. This result is in accord with earlier work on ideal, regular β-strands where a change of 30° in the ψ dihedral angle from 140° to 170° led to much less intense calculated CD spectrum.[15] There are still obvious deficiencies in the calculated CD spectra, but conformational dynamics in solution at least seems to be one important factor that needs to be accounted for. As discussed earlier, the matrix method performs best around 220 nm, where the amide $n\pi^*$ transitions and helical structures are the prime determinants of the spectrum.

Our results on the α-helical protein myoglobin show that the CD spectra of helical conformations also are sensitive to main chain dihedral angles. The analysis of different structures from the PDB and the simulation of the native state of holo-myoglobin coupled with the CD calculations indicate that accounting for conformational dynamics in solution leads to better agreement with the experimental data. In an earlier study[15] on over 100 helical fragments excised from the 29 proteins used in the benchmark in Table 1, the calculated intensity at 220 nm was shown to depend on the precise conformation of the helix. A weak, but significant, correlation was observed between $[\theta]_{220}$ and the coordinate $0.74\phi - 0.67\psi$, where the dihedral angles were the mean values of all the residues in the helix. A sensitivity to dihedral angles had also been noted elsewhere[68] and has been related to the hydrophobic or hydrophilic nature of the helix, with the latter corresponding to more negative ϕ and less negative ψ.[69] Yet other work[70] has suggested that the CD spectra of helical peptides are also quite sensitive to the length of the main-chain hydrogen bonds.

The first principles calculations of CD have many caveats, as has been discussed elsewhere.[15] Higher energy excitations of the amide chromophore are not included in the calculations. Transitions from side-chain chromophores are not considered. The influence of solvent on the CD itself, as distinct from its influence on the conformation of the protein, has not been accounted for. Whilst these and other factors warrant attention, in this study we have examined the role of conformational dynamics and we have found it to be important. Perhaps the most basic conclusion of the study is to emphasize that moderate differences in CD spectra cannot be interpreted uniquely in terms of conformational changes. In the absence of complementary data, a change in a CD spectrum could be due to several different causes, including the loss of secondary structure, subtle re-distributions of dihedral angles or the re-organization of patterns of secondary structures. To a large extent the detailed structural characterisation of unfolded and partially unfolded states is uncharted terrain and more work is needed in this area. A better understanding of the theoretical basis of protein CD combined with detailed simulations of conformational transitions should help to improve the interpretation of CD experiments on protein folding.

Acknowledgements

We thank BBSRC for financial support through grant 42/B15240. A.V.O. thanks NIH for funding (GM 575513) and Professor David Case for support and encouragement. We thank Professor Robert Woody for his comments on the manuscript.

References

1 T. E. Creighton, *Protein Folding*, Freeman, New York, 1992.
2 C. M. Dobson, A. Sali and M. Karplus, *Angew. Chem. Int. Ed. Engl.*, 1998, **37**, 868.
3 C. M. Dobson and M. Karplus, *Curr. Opin. Struct. Biol.*, 1999, **9**, 92.
4 K. Nakanishi, N. Berova and R. W. Woody, *Circular Dichroism Principles and Applications*, VCH, New York, 1994.
5 G. D. Fasman, *Circular Dichroism and the Conformational Analysis of Biomolecules*, Plenum Press, New York, 1996.
6 G. Holzwarth and P. Doty, *Proc. Natl. Acad. Sci. USA*, 1965, **87**, 218.
7 K. W. Plaxco and C. M. Dobson, *Curr. Opin. Struct. Biol.*, 1996, **6**, 630.
8 C.-F. Zhang, J. W. Lewis, R. Cerpa, I. D. Kuntz and D. S. Kliger, *J. Phys. Chem.*, 1993, **97**, 5499.
9 W. A. Eaton, V. Munoz, P. A. Thompson, E. R. Henry and J. Hofrichter, *Acc. Chem. Res.*, 1998, **31**, 745.
10 J. R. Telford, P. Wittung-Stafshede, H. B. Gray and J. R. Winkler, *Acc. Chem. Res.*, 1998, **31**, 755.
11 Y. Duan and P. A. Kollman, *Science*, 1998, **282**, 740.
12 B. Zagrovic, E. J. Sorin and V. Pande, *J. Mol. Biol.*, 2001, **313**, 151.
13 J. D. Hirst and C. L. Brooks III, *J. Mol. Biol.*, 1994, **243**, 173.
14 W. C. Johnson, *Proteins*, 1990, **7**, 205.
15 N. A. Besley and J. D. Hirst, *J. Am. Chem. Soc.*, 1999, **121**, 9636.
16 J. D. Hirst and N. A. Besley, *J. Chem. Phys.*, 1999, **111**, 2846.
17 R. W. Woody and N. Sreerama, *J. Chem. Phys.*, 1999, **111**, 2844.
18 K. A. Bode and J. Applequist, *J. Am. Chem. Soc.*, 1998, **120**, 10 938.

19 P. Manavalan and W. C. Johnson, Jr., *Nature*, 1983, **305**, 831.
20 J. Wu, J. T. Yang and C.-S. C. Wu, *Anal. Biochem.*, 1992, **200**, 359.
21 R. W. Woody and A. K. Dunker, in *Circular Dichroism and the Conformational Analysis of Biomolecules*, ed. G. D. Fasman, Plenum Press, New York, 1996, p. 109.
22 V. Daggett, *Curr. Opin. Struct. Biol.*, 2000, **10**, 160.
23 P. M. Bayley, E. B. Nielsen and J. A. Schellman, *J. Phys. Chem.*, 1969, **73**, 228.
24 W. J. Goux and T. M. Hooker, Jr., *J. Am. Chem. Soc.*, 1980, **102**, 7080.
25 L. Rosenfeld, *Z. Phys.*, 1928, **52**, 161.
26 G. Karlström, *J. Phys. Chem.*, 1988, **92**, 1315.
27 G. Karlström, *J. Phys. Chem.*, 1989, **93**, 4952.
28 A. Bernhardsson, R. Lindh, G. Karlstrom and B. O. Roos, *Chem. Phys. Lett.*, 1996, **151**, 141.
29 L. Serrano-Andrés, M. P. Fülscher and G. Karlstrom, *Int. J. Quantum Chem.*, 1997, **65**, 167.
30 N. A. Besley and J. D. Hirst, *J. Phys. Chem. A*, 1998, **102**, 10 791.
31 G. N. Ramanchandran, C. Ramakrishnan and V. Sasisekharan, *J. Mol. Biol.*, 1963, **7**, 95.
32 W. Kabsch and C. Sander, *Biopolymers*, 1983, **22**, 2577.
33 F. C. Bernstein, T. F. Koetzle, G. J. B. Williams, E. F. Meer, M. D. Brice, J. R. Rodgers, O. Kennard, T. Shimanouchi and M. Tasumi, *J. Mol. Biol.*, 1977, **112**, 535.
34 P. Pancoska, E. Bitto, V. Janota, M. Urbanova, V. P. Gupta and T. A. Keiderling, *Protein Sci.*, 1995, **4**, 1384.
35 S. Brahms and J. Brahms, *J. Mol. Biol.*, 1980, **138**, 149.
36 T. E. Dahms and A. G. Szabo, *Biophys. J.*, 1995, **69**, 569.
37 J. E. Draheim, G. P. Anderson, J. W. Duane and E. L. Gross, *Biophys. J.*, 1986, **49**, 891.
38 W. C. Still, A. L. Tempczyk, R. C. Hawley and T. Hendrickson, *J. Am. Chem. Soc.*, 1990, **112**, 6127.
39 W. Cornell, R. Abseher, M. Nilges and D. A. Case, *J. Mol. Graphics Mod.*, 2001, **19**, 136.
40 B. D. Bursulaya and C. L. Brooks III, *J. Phys. Chem. B*, 2000, **104**, 12 378.
41 B. N. Dominy and C. L. Brooks III, *J. Phys. Chem. B*, 1999, **103**, 3765.
42 B. R. Brooks, R. E. Bruccoleri, B. D. Olafson, D. J. States, S. Swaminathan and M. Karplus, *J. Comput. Chem.*, 1983, **4**, 187.
43 I. Chandrasekar, G. M. Clore, A. Szabo, A. M. Gronenborn and B. R. Brooks, *J. Mol. Biol.*, 1992, **226**, 239.
44 P. E. Wright and R. L. Baldwin, in *Frontiers in Molecular Biology: Mechanisms of Protein Folding*, ed. R. Pain, Oxford University Press, London, 2000, p. 309.
45 J. T. Lecomte, S. F. Sukits, S. Bhattacharaya and C. J. Falzone, *Protein Sci.*, 1999, **8**, 1484.
46 D. Eliezer, J. Yao, H. J. Dyson and P. E. Wright, *Nature Struct. Biol.*, 1998, **5**, 148.
47 M. Jamin and R. L. Baldwin, *J. Mol. Biol.*, 1998, **276**, 491.
48 V. Tsui, C. Garcia, S. Cavangero, G Sizudak, H. J. Dyson and P. E. Wright, *Protein Sci.*, 1999, **8**, 45.
49 D. A. Pearlman, D. A. Case, J. W. Caldwell, W. S. Ross, T. E. Cheatham, S. DeBolt, D. Ferguson, G. Seibel and P. A. Kollman, *Comput. Phys. Commun.*, 1995, **91**, 1.
50 W. D. Cornell, P. Cieplak, C. I. Bayly, I. R. Gould, K. M. Merz, Jr., D. M. Ferguson, D. C. Spellmeyer, T. Fox, J. W. Caldwell and P. A. Kollman, *J. Am. Chem. Soc.*, 1995, **117**, 5179.
51 J.-P. Ryckaert, G. Ciccotti and H. J. C. Berendsen, *J. Comput. Phys.*, 1977, **23**, 327.
52 X. Cheng and B. Schoenborn, *Acta Crystallogr., Sect. B.*, 1990, **46**, 195.
53 W. L. Jorgensen, J. Chandrasekhar, J. Madura and M. L. Klein, *J. Chem. Phys.*, 1983, **79**, 926.
54 H. J. C. Berendsen, J. P. M. Postma, W. F. van Gunsteren, A. DiNola and J. R. Haak, *J. Chem. Phys.*, 1984, **81**, 3684.
55 L. J. Smith, C. M. Dobson and W. F. van Gunsteren, *Proteins*, 1999, **36**, 77.
56 O. Tcherkasskaya and O. B. Ptitsyn, *FEBS Lett.*, 1999, **455**, 325.
57 J. T. Yang, C. S. C. Wu and H. M. Martinez, *Methods Enzymol.*, 1986, **130**, 208.
58 H. C. Watson, *Prog. Stereochem.*, 1969, **4**, 299.
59 G. S. Kachalova, A. N. Popov and H. D. Bartunik, *Science*, 1999, **284**, 473.
60 J. Fleischhauer, J. Grotzinger, B. Kramer, P. Kruger, A. Wollmer, R. W. Woody and E. Zobel, *Biophys. Chem.*, 1994, **49**, 141.
61 A. R. van Buuren and H. J. C. Berendsen, *Biopolymers*, 1993, **33**, 1159.
62 J. D. Hirst and C. L. Brooks III, *Biochemistry*, 1995, **34**, 7614.
63 M. J. Bodkin and J. M. Goodfellow, *Protein Sci.*, 1995, **4**, 603.
64 S.-S. Sung and X.-W. Wu, *Biopolymers*, 1997, **42**, 633.
65 V. Daggett and M. Levitt, *J. Mol. Biol.*, 1992, **223**, 1121.
66 J. Tirado-Rives and W. L. Jorgensen, *Biochemistry*, 1993, **32**, 4175.
67 G. Ravishanker, S. Vijakumar, and D. L. Beveridge, in *Modeling the Hydrogen Bond*, American Chemical Society, Washington DC, 1994, p. 209.
68 M. C. Manning and R. W. Woody, *Biopolymers*, 1991, **31**, 569.
69 T. Blundell, D. Barlow, N. Borkakorti and J. Thornton, *Nature*, 1983, **306**, 281.
70 Z. Dang and J. D. Hirst, *Angew. Chem. Int. Ed. Engl.*, 2001, **40**, 3619.

General Discussion

Prof. Helliwell opened the discussion of Dr May's paper: Regarding the DNA in cationic vesicle assemblies you put forward what other models might be 'nearly as plausible'? What is the functional significance of these cationic DNA vesicle complexes?

Dr May responded: In general, one must stress that small-angle scattering cannot be used to predict unique models but rather to exclude scattering-incompatible models.

It is known that for the conditions studied in this work DNA–lipid complexes form various condensed multilamellar structures.[1,2] This structure can be altered by varying the shapes of lipid molecules. For example, by increasing the amount of DOPE (cone shaped, natural curvature of the membrane $<0°$) in our cationic liposomes, the complex undergoes a structural transition from the lamellar phase to the inverted hexagonal phase.[3] It is of particular importance to find a structure–function relationship of these DNA–lipid complexes. For example, it was shown that for a range of concentrations the inverted hexagonal DNA–lipid complexes exhibit a higher transfection efficiency than the lamellar complexes.[4]

1 J. Gustafsson, G. Arvidson, G. Karlsson, and M. Almgren, *Biochim. Biophys. Acta*, 1995, **1235**, 305.
2 N. S. Templeton, D. D. Lasic, P. M. Frederik, H. H. Strey, D. D. Roberts and G. N. Pavlakis, *Nature Biotechnol.*, 1997, **15**, 647.
3 B. J. Sternberg, *Liposom. Res.*, 1996, **6**, 515.
4 I. Koltover, T. Salditt, J. O. Rädler and C. R. Safinya, *Science*, 1998, **281**, 78.

Prof. Watts asked: Targeting of drug or DNA loaded liposomes is still a major hurdle, especially if they are required at a particular organ or tissue type. How do you think that this is going to be achieved? Most lipid injected intravenously is cleaned in the liver rather quickly. Are you considering alternative ways of administering liposomes to specific parts of the body?

Dr May answered: Delivering of drug or DNA loaded liposomes to a particular type of tissue may be achieved by docking molecules to the liposomes that can be recognized by certain cell types. There are also recent advances in the technique known as magnetofection[1]—enhanced delivery of therapeutic genes to a specific target site by associating gene vectors with superparamagnetic iron oxide nanoparticles that are drawn to the target tissue with an external magnet. For magnetofection to become practical, research will have to find a way to attract drugs to tissues deeper in the body.

1 F. Scherer, M. Anton, U. Schillinger, J. Henke, C. Bergemann, A. Krüger, B. Gänsbacher and C. Plank, *Gene Ther.*, 2002, in press.

Prof. Watts asked: (i) You have made your liposome $70\% + D_2O$, lipids are ~ 0.98 cm^3 g^{-1} and they will therefore float. Do you see any evidence for free, non-DNA associated liposomes floating in your system? (ii) One definite way to monitor liposome collapse or fusion is through trapped volume measurements. Have you done these with your liposomes on interaction with your DNA to substantiate your model prepared in Fig. 6?

Dr May replied: (i) We have evidence that non-DNA associated liposomes ("free liposomes") exist by visualization techniques; we did not observe that our liposomes were floating in D_2O during the time necessary for our measurements. (ii) The measurement of the intraliposomal aqueous phase would indeed be a good indication of vesicle fusion. We verified the occurrence of vesicle fusion by visualization techniques like for example cryo-TEM.

Prof. Watts said: (i) On mixing in stopped flow methods, it is known that morphological changes can occur in small vesicles. Have you carried out necessary controls to ensure this is not happening and the effects observed are really DNA induced? (ii). Do you think studies in water or D_2O without buffering salts are relevant to physiological conditions of $\sim$150 mM salt, pH$\sim$7.0?

Dr May replied: (i) Our small-angle neutron scattering stopped-flow experiments include control experiments in which the vesicle dispersion was mixed with a solution without DNA. We did not observe any structural changes of the vesicles compared to a steady-state solution measurement. We also performed control experiments by adding DNA to a solution without vesicles.

(ii) The Lund group[1] also addressed the problem of stability of the vesicles, and they studied DNA–lipid vesicles in the presence of higher amounts of salts (*e.g.*, 150 mM salt). Like Rädler *et al.*[2] they observed that the structures of these complexes remain locally lamellar. Rädler *et al.* report that only the *d* spacing of the lipids changes with increasing ionic strength. We controlled the measurement conditions to have the same low-salt conditions using freshly prepared samples (not more than 1–2 days old); the ionic strength is determined by the dilution of the DNA stock solution. pH-controlled experiments are certainly desirable as an extension for future experiments.

1 (a) E. Feitosa, P. C. A. Barreleiro and G. Olofsson, *Chem. Phys. Lipids*, 2000, **105**, 201–213; (b) P. C. A. Barreleiro, M. Cruz, S. Ferreira and G. Olofsson, *J. Phys. Chem. B*, submitted.
2 I. Koltover, T. Salditt and C. R. Safinya, *Biophys. J.*, 1999, **77**, 915.

Prof. Ryan asked: Could orientation in a magnetic or electric field help in the solution of the structure of the final state? This method is widely used in other soft-condensed matter systems.

Dr May answered: Possibly a magnetically well-ordered structure could be observed more easily. This would maybe work for the rods, but presumably not for the final multilamellar (magnetically isotropic) state that we expect. I wonder whether magnetic forces would prevent the rods to turn into the multilamellar structure.

Prof. Watts said: Lipids in bilayers are diamagnetically anisotropic and orient even in moderate magnetic fields. This may, then, be a way to get orientational information of a bilayer associated macromolecule, as used in high resolution solution state NMR with micelles.

Prof. Watts asked: Your DNA is $\sim$20 000 base pairs long. What is the length in nm, and what is the rigid rod correlated length? I ask because vesicle size is presumably $\sim$20–40 nm diameter and the anionic DNA may form the scaffold onto which the cationic vesicles assemble.

Dr May responded: The DNA we used is 2000 (not 20 000) base pairs long, and thus, with a helix rise per base pair of 0.34 nm, its length is 680 nm. The diameter of the vesicles is 100–200 nm. We suggest that the DNA strand is covered by vesicles, and that due to the strong interaction the vesicles rupture and the bilayers roll up around the DNA-cylinder axis.

Prof. Wilson asked: Can measurements over an extended Q-range probe further the slower time constant re-organisation of the complex into the multi-lamellar structure *i.e.* by allowing more extensive modelling?

Dr May replied: Yes, measurements over a wider q range would allow us a more extensive modelling since the pair distribution function would extend over a wider r range. There are technical limitations though, because at very low momentum transfer the neutron flux may become prohibitively low for time-resolved measurements, and at high q, the current count-rate limitation of the detectors do not yet allow us to count neutrons as efficiently as desired. (We are limited by the incoherent background from hydrogen in the samples).

Prof. Wilson asked: Can further deuteration of the various components in the system (as opposed to simply using H_2O/D_2O exchange) help in trying to improve the structural picture?

Dr May answered: Deuteration of the various components in the system (DNA and lipids) would contribute to a clearer structural picture of the DNA–cationic liposome complexes. For example, using (partially) deuterated DNA matched by 100% D_2O for observing the lipids only. The contrast between lipids and natural DNA is not very high, and working at 70% D_2O for matching the DNA contribution infers a still high incoherent background. Fully deuterated DNA would allow one to study its structure with the lipids matched, but the naturally different head group and chain contrasts would have to be matched by partial deuteration.

Prof. Watts said: (i) Are you suggesting then, that the DNA forms the structural scaffold around which the lipid bilayers assemble? (ii) Do you think these rod-shaped DNA–lipid complexes would be stable and flow through the circulatory system intact?

Dr May responded: We suggest that the DNA strand is covered by vesicles and due to the strong interaction the vesicles rupture and the bilayers roll up around the DNA-cylinder axis. Thus, yes we are suggesting that DNA forms the structural scaffold around which the bilayers assemble. The rods then turn into a multilamellar structure. The problem of stability is not so much one of mechanics, but rather one of metabolism, because the DNA–cationic liposome complexes are cleared by the reticuloendothelial system (RES). A way to circumvent this problem is to inject the DNA–cationic liposome complexes directly into the affected area (like for example in a tumor of the skin).

Prof. Helliwell said: I would like to mention Dr May's work with Heumann and the chaperone complex using SANS to follow that process. Please would you give us a summary of that quite recent work?

Dr May responded: The work of Heumann's group (Max-Planck Institut für Biochemie, Martinsried, Germany) on the chaperone from *E. coli* comprised many aspects, including a study of the GroEL–GroES complex,[1] that was really concluded before the X-ray crystallographic work of Xu *et al.*,[2] showed some distinct features of the solution structure.

I wish to concentrate here on the time-resolved studies that have partly been reported by Holzinger in his thesis.[3] Contrary to an X-ray solution investigation by Roessle *et al.*,[4] the rapid-kinetics measurements with neutrons did not allow us to see a sufficiently strong scattering effect for the formation of bullet (1:1) complexes from GroEL and GroES in the presence of ADP using neutrons, although we would have expected to be successful. (A decent neutron signal can be observed with time frames of about 10 s total duration, *i.e.* summing up 8 or 10 experiments with time frames of 1 s.) However, another study that cannot be done without neutrons yielded very nice results.[5] 1:1 complexes of GroEL and of the bacterial chaperonin GroES or its counterpart GP31 from the bacteriophage T4 were preformed in a deuterated buffer solution in the presence of ADP. A deuterated solution containing an excess of partially deuterated GroES, invisible for neutrons in these conditions, was mixed with the former solution, and the time evolution of the scattering from the mixtures was followed by small-angle neutron scattering. The decrease of the scattering intensity due to the replacement of "visible" protein by the "invisible" one allows one to observe the chasing kinetics of the co-chaperone. The decay of both complexes follows two time exponentials, of which one seems to be due to the formation of intermediate football complexes, as can be deduced from experiments with varying GroEL excess concentration.

1 R. Stegmann, S. Nieba-Axmann, E. Manakova, M. Rössle, T. Hermann, R. P. May, A. Wiedenmann, A. Plückthun and H. Heumann, *J. Struct. Biol.*, 1998, **121**, 30–40.
2 Z. Xu, A. L. Horwich and P. B. Sigler, *Nature*, 1997, **388**, 741–750.
3 J. Holzinger, PhD Thesis, Ludwig-Maximilians University, Munich, 2002.
4 M. Roessle, E. Manakova, I. Lauer, T. Nawroth, J. Holzinger, T. Narayanan, S. Bernstorff, H. Amenitsch and H. Heumann, *J. Appl. Crystallogr.*, 2000, **33**, 548–551.
5 J. Holzinger, R. P. May, E. Manakova, S. van der Vies, M. Rössle and H. Heumann, manuscript in preparation.

Prof. Wilson opened the discussion of Dr Sankar's paper: I am interested in the relevance of the time-resolved studies to the materials development in which you are engaged. For example, in your Introduction you described one of your motivations as crystallisation of solid catalysts. In that context, how important is following the mechanism of formation (the time-resolved aspect) to the functionality of the material produced?

Dr Sankar responded: The functionality, whether it is optical, electrical or catalytic, depends largely on the particle size. The property can be altered considerably by controlling the particle size. One of our aims in this time-resolved measurement is to determine the nature of the particle growth which can be used further to optimise and control the formation of a specific particle size

Dr May communicated: (i) The symbols s and q are both used for the scattering vector; I find this misleading. q and s are defined with respect to d, although there is normally no such thing as a crystal plane distance d in small angle scattering.

(ii) Porod's (not quoted) "invariant" Q refers to the volume fraction that is visible for the radiation used, *i.e.* it depends on the resolution of the scattering experiment. The volume fraction changes by the formation of particles from "invisible" molecules, but also the contrast may change by depletion of the solution. This is not explained in the paper.

(iia) How are the scattering curves extrapolated to $s = 0$, and $s = $ infinity for calculating Q? At short times, the scattering curves are rising at q_{max}!

(iib) How are the data normalized to absolute intensity for obtaining the correct invariant(s)?

(iii) The data shown in Fig. 3 of the paper (in which, by the way, the abscissa units are q, not $\ln q$, with missing units) give a clear indication that at short times, there is not the Gaussian behaviour necessary for fitting according to eqn. (2) (radius of gyration). At long times, a structural interference peak seems to develop, which would also not allow you to calculate the radius of gyration. Did you also try to fit the data with the theoretical scattering curves of (a distribution of) spheres?

(iv) The Guinier approximation does not require monodispersed systems, but the region where it can be applied may become very narrow in the case of large polydispersity. The relation $Rq < 2\pi$ is incorrect.

(v) Assuming spheres, Figs. 4 and 5 are not independent. Does the information obtained from the two curves coincide?

Dr Sankar communicated in reponse: (i) We have now altered the text in such a way that we use "q" throughout. (ii) Although not extrapolating the scattering curves to $q = 0$ for calculating the invariant Q can induce errors in the absolute values, the general trend of Q versus time of reaction will remain identical.

(iii) There is a Gaussian behavior that allows us to fit according to eqn. (2). At long times, no structural interference peak seems to develop. The feature observed in Fig. 3 is interpreted as the emergence of a form factor in $I(q)$. The position of the first maxima and minima were fitted using theoretical scattering curves of a distribution of spheres:

$$P(q) = \text{scale} \times \left[\frac{3\sin(qr) - qr\cos(qr)}{(qr)^3} \right]^2$$

The particle size obtained was in good agreement with the one obtained using eqn. (2) and (3).

(iv) I agree that the Guinier approximation does not require monodispersed systems, but in order to apply eqn. (3) and determine the particle size, a monodispersed system is required.

(v) Yes. The information gained from the two curves in Fig. 4 and 5 suggest that, assuming spherical particles, we have particles with an approximate diameter of 110 Å.

Dr Chen asked: What was the particle size of the end product? We observed a very similar phenomenon, lacking the second coordination shell peak in FT-EXAFS spectra in TiO_2 and Fe_2O_3 nanoparticles with a few nm diameter size. We have shown evidence of surface defect sites that are attributed to the disorder of a distant shell, or local lattice disorder. Do you think this is the reason for what you achieved?

Dr Sankar replied: The particle size of the end product (which depends on the temperature and time of synthesis) in this case is *ca* 20 nm. Low temperature EXAFS measurement at *ca*. 20 K is required to extract the second shell information to determine the particle size. This suggests that the

CdS system is dominated by thermal disorder rather than static disorder as seen in other systems.

Dr Dent said: For particle sizes of 7–12.5 nm you get results from SAXS; EXAFS is relatively insensitive. EXAFS is most sensitive to particle sizes below 5 nm.[1] Clearly this problem is even more difficult due to the anharmonic nature of the Cd–Cd interaction.

1 A. Jentys, *Phys. Chem. Chem. Phys.*, 1999, **1**, 4059–4063.

Dr Sankar responded: Yes I agree with this comment. It is well known that beyond a certain particle size the coordination number will be close to the bulk value and the changes will be well within the experimental uncertainty of 10% associated with the estimation of coordination number. Our aim was to follow the particle formation at the early stages of the growth, which will be less than 7 nm. Unfortunately we could not estimate the particle size in the early stages of the formation of CdS using coordination number of the Cd–Cd shell since there is a large thermal disorder associated with Cd–Cd interaction.

Prof. Wilson asked: Is there any long range order apparent in the evolution of these systems *i.e.* any role for WAXS in combination with SAXS?

Dr Sankar answered: There is no direct evidence for long-range order from our combined SAXS/WAXS measurement.

Prof. Ryan said: (i) The maximum yield of solids in your reaction is 0.0028% by mass. In this case eqn. (1) predicts that the invariant would grow linearly with crystallisation and the argument for the fall in the measured invariant is inappropriate. (ii) Does the radius of the particle vary with a power law (such as $t \sim t^{\frac{1}{3}}$) and is this suggestive of the mechanism?

Dr Sankar replied: The main reason for the fall in the measured invariant is because the large particles settle just below the X-ray beam. We took as much care in our design of the *in situ* cell in such a way that the X-ray beam passes through the lowest possible position. Despite this, the X-rays could not see all the particles. We are currently redesigning our *in situ* cell to rotate during the measurement to allow all the particles to come in contact with the X-ray beam.

Prof. Bürgi asked: (i) What is the rate determining step in the formation of the cluster and how can it be controlled? (ii) Does the rate of cluster formation influence the EXAFS spectra?

Dr Sankar answered: (i) The only way to slow down the formation is by lowering the temperature. We also found that, in addition to the temperature, the concentration of the solution has a large effect on the rate and once again the rate can be controlled by appropriate choice of the concentration of cadmium acetate and thioacetamide.

(ii) We do not have direct evidence for whether EXAFS spectra are influenced by the rate of cluster formation, since we are able to obtain reliable information only on the Cd–S first coordination environment. This is not sufficient, since it appears that irrespective of the cluster size, the cluster terminates with sulfur giving rise to a coordination number of four. We need Cd–Cd, second shell information to obtain further information, which could not be extracted, since this shell is dominated by the presence of a large thermal factor which decreases the amplitude.

Prof. Sir John Meurig Thomas commented: In answer to the question as to why one is interested in producing nanoparticles of II–VI compounds, one recalls that the electronic band gap of such materials are tuneable according to their size. Henglein's well known work many years ago showed that good photocatalysts can be fashioned from II–VI nanoparticles; and these are of considerable importance in such fields as the harnessing of solar energy by photocatalytic materials. This is one of the reasons why Schuth and others (at Mülheim) who collaborate with us, are studying various ways of producing CdS and CdSe nanoparticles.

Prof. Hounslow added: From a chemical engineering perspective it is vitally important to be able to identify mechanisms and rates—not just end points. It is only with this knowledge, usually acquired from time-dependant results, that processes for manufacture can be designed.

Precipitation must be driven by chemical potential difference. Is the growth process limited by the rate of precipitation—so particles grow by the acquisition of ions or very small clusters—or by particle–particle coagulation?

Dr Sankar responded: From Fig. 3 (of the paper), we clearly observe a form factor peak. This form factor maximum shifts to lower q values with reaction time, indicating that either the particles increase in size or that the small particles aggregate and therefore form larger structures. After 2 h of reaction, a second order maximum becomes visible. This is typically observed for many systems that represent nucleation and growth processes, which ultimately yield highly monodispersed particles and rules out an aggregation process.

Prof. Hounslow asked: To distinguish between the two extremes of the size-enlargement mechanism it would be very useful to make some *in situ* measure of ion activity in solution, can you do so?

Dr Sankar answered: I do not think we can measure the ion activity in solution by the techniques we have described in this paper.

Prof. Helliwell said: The size of nanoparticle, and evolution time, in your system and that presented in Prof. Greaves's paper are very similar (both ≈ 20 nm); I obviously exclude the trivial explanation that the instrument only allows Q_{min} measurements down to $(20 \text{ nm})^{-1}$! Is there some general size limiting factor occurring (in protein crystal growth there is a limiting size to crystals, under a given set of conditions, which seems a similar phenomenon)? And, in fact, what is the optimum size of nanoparticle that you are after for electrical and optical properties uses?

Dr Sankar replied: It is a coincidence that the size of the nanoparticles presented here and in Prof. Greaves's paper are very similar. It is unlikely that there are some general size-limiting factors operating. The size of the particle produced depends highly on the preparative method, temperature *etc*. For the optical and electrical properties, ideally we would like to prepare *ca*. 3 nm particles.

Prof. Ryan said: This coincidence is simply that 30 nm is the middle of the window of observation on the SAXS beamlines at DC.

Prof. Wilson addressed Prof. Hounslow: I have always understood that one of the most critical aspects of moving from "research" to "production" chemistry was the scale-up from the laboratory to industrial scale. This seems to contradict your earlier contention that detailed information on the time evolution of, for example, particle-size in potential catalytic materials, is very important in moving across the chemistry/chemical engineering divide.

Prof. Hounslow answered: The crucial issue is that of identifying true, intrinsic, kinetics (such as may be obtained from time-resolved laboratory studies). The logic being that the intrinsic kinetics in the lab are the same as in the full-scale plant. Engineers can then take these kinetics, combine them with the available knowledge of transport phenomena (particularly heat and mass transfer) to determine what will happen on the plant. So while the operating conditions on the plant may be very different from in the lab, the underlying kinetics remain the same and it is possible to design efficient, safe, large-scale production equipment.

Prof. Moffat opened the discussion of Prof. Evans's paper: Some of your spectra show features (glitches) that persist from spectrum to spectrum; they would be minimized (or eliminated) in difference measurements. Why do you choose to concentrate on spectra rather than difference spectra?

How do you decide whether intermediate species are present, with distinct XAFS spectra? It would seem that the information is present in the (difference) spectra themselves (*i.e.* consider PCA, SVD, global analysis *etc.*).

Prof. Evans responded: We presented the spectra quite deliberately to inform the reader about the quality of data available by the energy dispersive technique. Our principle aim in the paper was to present the status of its development. In principle a global analysis of the whole dataset should be the best approach, and we have not yet attempted this. Instead we identify regions of the spectrum that show most prominent changes and monitor their time dependence to identify if there is any detectable intermediate. Sometimes difference spectra prove to be disappointing. Beam movement between the acquisition of the background spectrum, I_o, and differing sample spectra, I_t, can still maintain a structured background. As we state in our paper, the highest quality optical and detector systems are required to minimise this problem.

Prof. Wilson said: Presumably the identification of possible intermediate species in your time-resolved EXAFS spectra is somewhat dependent on the resolution you can obtain in those spectra.

Also presumably the availability of simultaneous additional data (*e.g.* XRD) which may identify the presence of such intermediate or transient species will be helpful in the interpretation of the EXAFS spectra.

Prof. Evans replied: Clearly, the ability to identify intermediates is dependent upon time resolution, spectroscopic resolution and high integrity of the absorption intensity. The digital resolution varied between *ca.* 0.4 eV at the Ni K-edge and about 2 eV at the palladium K-edge.

Simultaneous measurement of X-ray diffraction data with a 300–2000 eV bandwidth is unlikely to give optimal data; on the solution described in our paper it would be quite inappropriate. As we indicated, we have utilised stopped-flow uv–visible spectroscopy, and intend to extend this to the IR, which can be structurally more incisive.

Dr Techert said: In Fig. 3 of the paper, the optical density reaches values between 3 and 4. Are there any problems when reaching the non-linear regime of the detector of the spectrometer?

Prof. Evans answered: Obviously this was not ideal. In the spectra presented we used the same concentration in each technique to obtain a good estimate of the reaction rates prior to the SR-based experiments. Even with a 1 mm path length cell, really optimal uv–visible spectra would have been obtained at lower concentrations. In the kinetic plots we restricted our analysis to the early stages of the reaction at a fixed wavelength before the absorption bands became too intense for this to be valid. Recently we have obtained EDE spectra at ~10 mM concentrations, and this will alleviate this incompatibility.

Dr Sagi commented: Sagi and co-workers demonstrated the use of principal component analysis (PCA) to extract intermediates out of an EXAFS spectrum of a mixture. This should be considered as an analytical tool for the analysis of time-resolved XAS. Slowing down the reaction by either cooling or constraining the reaction may aid in trapping the intermediates.

Prof. Evans replied: (i) This is a very helpful suggestion and we should work towards this.

(ii) In the paper we concentrated on the most rapid experiments to demonstrate how far the boundaries of its application have been pushed. In other systems we have lower concentrations of aluminium alkyl (in the Ni experiments) or different pH (in the iron case), and so the quality of data could be improved further. We are interested in a variable temperature stopped flow system for trying to identify very reactive transients.

Dr Cole said: The paper states that it was not possible to structurally differentiate between the alternative intermediates in the iron complex reaction using XAS. Could Mössbauer techniques be a better technique to resolve this issue? (Are time-resolved Mössbauer techniques possible?)

Prof. Evans answered: The reduction of aqueous Fe(III) by hydroquinone has been well studied by uv–visible spectroscopy, and an inner sphere intermediate has been identified by its blue colour. We used this as a test reaction rather than wishing to study this in depth. In the Fe(III) solution itself at the pH used, there are three major species, as we indicate it the paper. From this starting point, trying to carry out a stopped flow experiment on a dilute solution would not be trivial.

Differentiating the Fe(II) and Fe(III) sites would be appropriate to Mössbauer. Freeze–quench techniques have been used on beamline ID18 at the ESRF to study intermediates.[1]

1 Experiment LS728 on ID18 by A. X. Trautwein, H. Winkler and W. Meyer-Klaucke, Reactive intermediates of cytochrome P450 prepared by the freeze–quench method and investigated by nuclear resonant forward scattering, ESRF Annual report 1998.

Prof. Coppens asked: (i) What is the time precision of your stopped-flow technique? (ii) What is exactly your edge shift? Does it correspond to what is recognised as the Fe(III) to Fe(II) shift? Do the different species in your starting mixture have the same edge position?

Prof. Evans replied: (i) The mixing time depends upon the cell used, and varied between 1 ms and 10 ms for different sets of experiments. Commercial cells for other techniques currently offer mixing times down to below 0.5 ms.

(ii) The edge shift (-2 eV) is entirely consistent with Fe(III)/Fe(II). When we varied the pH, thus changing the ratio of the three major Fe(III) species, little change in the XANES spectrum was evident; the three species all have Fe(III) surrounded by six oxygen donor ligands, so this is not very surprising.

Prof. Wilson asked: Is the improvement of time resolution in your EXAFS experiments still dependent on repeated scans to obtain adequate counting statistics, for example, in the projection towards nanosecond timescales in single bunch synchrotron mode.

Prof. Evans answered: Undoubtedly, repeat scans will be necessary in a single bunch mode. An advantage of the dispersive experiment is that about 1000 data points are derived simultaneously, as compared to a step-scan approach. We have shown that single scans can be obtained at the ESRF in 100–200 μs [http://detserv1.dl.ac.uk/xstrip/] at about 200 mA current. With high stability, one might estimate that perhaps 100–1000 might be the minimum required to obtain a single spectrum at the present time, clearly a viable possibility. The total acquisition time will depend upon the repetition rate and also two other important experimental factors: the degree of conversion, say, in a photochemical experiment and also the differences in the XAFS patterns of the species involved.

Prof. Sir John Meurig Thomas asked: In your iridium oxidative scheme, do I take it that the five-coordinate intermediate and the final six-coordinated product are both stoichiometric rather than catalytic processes?

Prof. Evans answered: Indeed, this stopped flow experiment was designed to probe one part of the catalytic cycle for the carbonylation of methanol to form acetic acid. It is the stopped flow experiment with the lowest individual spectrum acquisition time that we have recorded so far (400 μs).

Prof. Evans addressed everyone: Whilst studying the heterogeneous catalyst Rh/alumina with a microreactor cell, we have been able to monitor catalyst function (activity and selectivity for the reaction between NO and H_2) and local structure (by energy dispersive EXAFS) simultaneously. These results show that the metal particles change their structure very rapidly under catalytic conditions, so even after *in situ* studies of material preparation, catalysts may change their structure during their operation in a way which determines their performance.[1]

1 M. A. Newton, A. J. Dent, S. Diaz-Moreno, S. G. Fiddy and J. Evans, *Angew. Chem. Int. Ed. Engl.*, 2002, **41**, 2587–2589.

Prof. Watts opened the discussion of Dr Burton's paper: (i) Is it possible that the substrate vibrations are significantly greater or smaller than those of the protein around the active site? (ii) Are all electrostatic interactions and contributions taken into account?

Dr Burton responded: (i) The 'reactant' in this study is an intermediate in the overall reaction and the motion of the 'substrate' is limited by the immediate protein environment. (ii) Yes, in the QM/MM approach which we have adopted for this study atoms in the QM region have electrostatic interactions with all other atoms.

Prof. J. C. Smith asked: (i) How might one account for changes in protein fluctuations during the reaction (*e.g.* at the transition state) that might influence the barriers? (ii) Can you describe the nature of the "compression mode" that you identify as being correlated with the kinetic isotope effect?

Dr Burton answered: (i) The speculation is that specific vibrational modes of the enzyme may enhance the tunnelling mechanism in MADH (ref. 9 of the paper) although the emphasis of this paper has been to show that the energetics and degree of tunnelling are significantly affected by the protein environment. (ii) We have not analysed the specific nature of the enzyme vibrational modes other than to note that Asp428 does approach the proton before abstraction.

Prof. Coppens asked: How dependent is the kinetic isotope effect on the quality of the treatment in the QM region (such as size of basis set, inclusion of electron correlation, HF or DFT)?

Dr Burton replied: There can be a significant variation in both the classical reaction barrier and the shape of the PE surface depending upon the level of theory (PM3, HF, DFT). The paper highlights the classical barriers at the HF level ($\sim$20 kcal mol^{-1}) which are larger than with the PM3 method ($\sim$10–15 kcal mol^{-1}), although improvement in the basis set makes little difference. We also find that the imaginary frequency at the TS is lower for HF than for PM3. DFT with the BLYP or B3LYP functionals tends to lower the barrier, often considerably.

Dr Grant said: The potential energy surface of a protein can be described as "frustrated" in that there are multiple minima separated by large energy barriers. How does one know that one is working with the correct energy well and how many substates are considered? Does the value of the kinetic isotope effect tend to a certain value so that you know the substate is a good representation of the enzyme configuration during H transfer?

Dr Burton replied: This is a difficult problem for computational methods to treat. Computational studies very much rely on experimental data, such as crystal structures, to reliably determine a reactive enzyme conformation. Our initial structures for this reaction were based upon an experimental structure of the Michaelis complex and the time scales of our simulations are unlikely to sample far from this enzyme structure. In this study we have found certain enzyme configurations which are likely to yield an extreme proton tunnelling event and a large kinetic isotope effect, in agreement with experiment, and others which would not. There is thus potential in this approach to suggest active protein conformations.

Prof. Sir John Meurig Thomas asked: Leaving aside QM/MM as a quantative insight, how am I, acting like an undergraduate, to understand in qualitative terms the fundamental cause of such an enormous kinetic isotope effect?

Dr Burton answered: Primary deuterium kinetic isotope effects, where there is little or no tunnelling through the potential energy barrier, will be small ($<$7) and arising primarily from zero point effects. Larger values reflect considerable tunnelling of the lighter hydrogen compared to deuterium greatly facilitated by a narrow potential energy barrier. Indeed for MADH, the transmission coefficient is $\sim$100 for H and $\sim$40 for D.

Prof. Moffat said: You are focusing on one step, the rate-determining step, in a multi-step, multi-state pathway. You need to know not the ground state structure (nor that of the Michaelis complex), but that of the short-lived intermediate immediately prior to the proton transfer. What is the lifetime of this state, and peak population *i.e.* could time-resolved crystallography reveal it?

Dr Burton replied: The rate constant for the proton transfer step was found experimentally (ref. 9 of the paper) to be 175 s^{-1} but we are not able to comment on the likelihood of resolving this structure.

Dr Hirst asked: Is it straightforward to identify the transition state of the QM region? Was the imaginary frequency reported the only imaginary frequency, indicating a transition state rather than a saddle point?

Dr Burton replied: Certainly some transition states (TSs) can be elusive and they do tend to take longer to find in the condensed phase than in the gas phase, although our use of fixed link atoms has made the process of finding TSs for the many enzyme configurations more tractable. All of the transition states have been fully characterised and have only one imaginary frequency since this is a pre-requisite to generating the reaction path using the IRC algorithm.

Prof. Helliwell asked: What is the diffraction resolution limit? Secondly, can you not harness the B-factor data, *i.e.* from the static structure there would be possibilities to assess the sensitivity of the kinetic isotope effect calculated values to atomic motion in the enzyme active site. [Indeed what are the active site atoms ADPs (atomic displacement parameters)?]

$$\text{Atomic displacement parameters } \left(\sqrt{\langle u^2 \rangle} = \sqrt{\frac{B}{8\pi^2}} \right)$$

Dr Burton answered: Unfortunately we did not have a crystal structure corresponding directly to this reaction step. Certainly diffraction data corresponding to this reaction step could be extremely useful. In general, we do not utilise the B-factor data to full advantage in our computational studies and this may be potentially useful for other reactions.

Prof. Wilson said: I am interested in the reproducibility of the reaction coordinate with respect to "flexing" of the enzyme. You examine multiple reaction coordinates generated by MM (or MD?) simulations. I would like to confirm/emphasise how different or reproducible are these reaction coordinates (and consequent energy barriers) with respect to plausible enzyme configurations.

Dr Burton responded: Multiple reaction paths (coordinates) are generated using the QM/MM method and each one is derived using a different enzyme configuration. The enzyme configurations are taken from an MD simulation, using an MM potential, of the enzyme. In this study we have analysed only a few enzyme configurations but we have subsequently analysed more. At the PM3 level, the reaction coordinates can be broadly split into two categories, with only relatively small deviations for barrier height (see Table 1 presented here).

Dr Hädener asked: (i) Can you comment on the meaning of the symbols H in the Figs. 3 and 6 in you paper? (ii) Can you comment on the way you treat the hydration shell in your calculations and in which way including hydration affects the outcome of the calculations?

Dr Burton replied: (i) The circled H-atoms are the 'link atoms', hydrogen atoms added to the QM calculation to satisfy valency where there should be covalent bonds between QM and MM regions. In this study these are fixed in space along the original C–C bonds to stabilise subsequent geometry optimisations. We and others, have shown that although crude, the approximation works well provided that this region does not significantly influence the reaction.

(ii) The presence of explicit waters in the active site is inconclusive, varying in the different crystal structures. The absence of water may be very important to this reaction step, otherwise the pK_a of Asp428 will be affected and the barrier to the reaction increased. It is interesting to note that the explicit water molecule present within the active site of the initial model (R0) had a strong tendency to leave during the MD simulation and did not influence the reaction in this study. Solvating waters were included in all MD simulations, but remote waters were removed in the QM/MM calculations for computational efficiency.

Table 1 Reaction coordinares at the PM3 level

Category	Reaction energy	Kinetic isotope effect
1	Endothermic	< 5
2	Isoenergetic/exothermic	> 7

Dr Sagi asked: To what degree can we correlate the phenomena we see in very short time scales by computation with actual catalysis occurring in much longer time scales? For example fast fluctuations of specific atoms which contribute to rather slower processes.

Dr Burton answered: The rarity of most reaction events is a major computational challenge. However to some extent this connection may soon be revealed using a range of new rare-event dynamics approaches (*e.g.* refs. 28–30 of the paper) which can focus the reaction event into a shorter time scale whilst including other atomic motions. Direct dynamics methods such as VTST are an effective way to implicitly include these effects for quantitative rate determination.

Prof. Moore opened the discussion of Prof. J. C. Smith's paper: At this meeting we have covered many techniques and looked at dynamic processes on many time scales. Does the energy landscape approach you have used give any guidance on what dynamic processes are functional? I am wondering whether a motion that affects the energy surface in a region away from the path of the reaction coordinate can be considered to be irrelevant for that reaction. The videos of the conformation change mechanisms you have calculated are striking but I am not sure how credible they are. This is partly a reflection of my lack of understanding about the computational procedures you use, but it also reflects my liking for experimental data. So I want to see if there are ways your predictions can be tested experimentally. For example, it should be possible to experimentally determine the effect of increasing pressure on the structure and activity of a protein. Could you, or any of the other theoreticians at this meeting, predict what the effect of pressure would be on a protein? Is it possible that with a change in pressure a different pathway through the landscape is taken so that the activity is dramatically changed?

Prof. J. C. Smith responded: Determining which motions in a protein are functional is an extremely important question which will be a major topic for many years to come. The problem can be reduced to finding a reaction coordinate for a particular process and then determining the free energy as a function of this reaction coordinate. Any motions influencing either of these two properties can be considered to be functionally important.

Concerning the credibility of the videos, I think this is an appropriate point to emphasize the challenges which face us in this type of computational investigation. Firstly, the conformational space in which we are working is extremely large, and the possibility of multiple pathways for any given functional transition exists. Theoretical methods for characterising the complete accessible collection of pathways need to be developed. Secondly, we do not yet have a reliable way of calculating the potential of mean force (free energy) along the pathways. So the calculations we presented should certainly be considered as first estimations. However, they do present energetically reasonable structural pathways, and as such should be considered as considerable improvements over previous descriptions of protein functional mechanics which were based on mere graphical inspection or linear interpolation between end states. Concerning experimental testing, the challenge works both ways, as we ask experimentalists to devise ways of refining their time-resolved methods so as to provide information on more-and-more rarely populated intermediates. Concerning the pressure question, this one is difficult due to the difficultly of including this effect on kinematic pathway calculations, and the long time scales required to derive information on the perturbations using molecular dynamics. I don't think we are yet in a position to provide calculations of direct pressure effects on large-scale conformational pathways. However, one way of testing the calculated pathways is to predict the effect of mutations, as we have recently done successfully for the annexin pathway I presented here.

Prof. Moffat said: In the two "movies" showing the power stroke in muscle contraction, the left hand one shows "flicking" between the two end points; but the right hand one shows a quasi-continuous progression from one end point to the other. Does the right hand one realistically represent the situation (if higher free energy conformers are progressively less-populated and are occupied for shorter and shorter times)?

Prof. J. C. Smith replied: The right hand movie is a representation of the reaction coordinate. It is not a movie of the dynamics of the transition, which would, as you state predominantly populate the lower energy states and would also involve stochastic processes. But the right hand movie does give a clear picture of the rate-limiting events along the pathway.

Prof. Bürgi asked: What is the probability for the occurrence of a large number of transition states with similar energies?

Prof. J. C. Smith answered: This depends on how complicated the conformational pathway is that one wishes to explore, but in the annexin transition that we have already investigated this probability is high. This leads to some interesting questions concerning the kinetics of the overall process.

Prof. Wilson said: It is well known that aspects of structure can be "dominated" by solvent structure *e.g.* humidity-driven conformational changes in DNA. Is it therefore so surprising that your work suggests that dynamics can be solvent-dominated also? In this case, the importance of bound water/solvent dynamics is emphasised, and in real systems is perhaps more vital than the dynamics of the macromolecule itself.

Prof. J. C. Smith replied: Our results do not indicate that the solvent dominates protein dynamics, but that it strongly influences it. The internal energy landscape of an isolated protein in vacuum shows interesting features that certainly play a role in determining the internal motions at physiological temperatures. However, these motions are strongly modulated by solvent. In addition to the results presented here we have more exciting new results on this aspect that we will publish soon.

Prof. Watts asked: Can your simulations accommodate binary solvent mixtures, for example, water and glucose, water and glycerol and other cryoprotectants? Dehydration is, presumably, a major factor here.

Prof. J. C. Smith responded: Yes, certainly. Parametrised potential functions exist for binary solvents and we are now working on simulations of proteins in methanol/water, for example.

Prof. Watts asked: How can parts of proteins be "heated" and the others remain "cold"? This seems an intriguing aspect of the simulation protocol.

Prof. J. C. Smith answered: We use the Nosé–Hoover dual heatbath method to do this. It is described in references given in the present paper. We have implemented a particularly accurate refinement of this method that regulates temperatures using chains of heatbaths together with a precise method for integrating the equations of motion based on the Liouville operator.

Prof. Helliwell said: Stiffness and dynamics would surely be a good place to "fish" to cross-check your calculations (of vibrations of atoms) and observations *e.g.* bacteriorhodopsin and/or extremophiles. (Published by Zaccai, both cases. See www.ill.fr/pages/menu_g/news/mil_pl1/pages/plen_1_5_GZaccai.htm.)

Prof. J. C. Smith replied: Certainly. Indeed we have been doing this for a while and have generally seen good agreement between molecular dynamics and experiment. See, for example, ref. 1 for a review.

1   J. C. Smith, in *Computational Biochemistry and Biophysics*, ed. Becker *et al.*, Dekker, New York, 2001, p. 237–251.

Prof. Finney asked: Where is the experimental evidence that thermophiles are "stiffer" than corresponding mesophiles?

Prof. Helliwell answered: The work of Zaccai on whole cells (personal communication; see www.ill.fr/pages/menu_g/news/mil_pl1/absracts/JOE-ZACCAI.pdf).

Prof. Watts said: From our own solid state NMR studies of ligand binding and protein dynamics, it seems as if ligands are relatively tightly constrained in bonding sites, once bound.

Also, it seems as if bacteriorhosopsin is a relatively 'stiff' protein, but has more flexibility for functional cycles in the membrane than in the crystal, from the work of the others.

Prof. J. C. Smith addressed everyone: Bacteriorhodopsin is an interesting case of a light-driven protein that recently has revealed several intermediates along its photocycle *via* X-ray crystallography. It is now an excellent challenge for time-resolved computational chemistry.

Prof. Watts addressed everyone: For each different photo intermediate of bacteriorhosopsin, a new crystal form seems to be needed and after each intermediate seems to be a mixture of states. This implies that time dependant crystallography on the same crystal, may only be possible in very stable and special circumstances where crystal limits are maintained.

Dr Sagi opened the discussion of Dr Hirst's paper: The possibility of exploring the dynamics of specific residues by simulation of the near-UV CD region is very exciting. For example, one can look at specific residues during protein folding and catalysis. In addition, experimental data (also time-resolved) are available.

Dr Hirst responded: It would indeed be of interest to explore the near-UV CD of proteins in the context of molecular dynamics simulations. Woody and co-workers have reported calculations of the near-UV CD of proteins[1] and the influence of side chains in the far UV was investigated at a previous *Faraday Discussion* meeting.[2] There is still scope to improve the absolute accuracy of calculations of CD in the near-UV.

1 N. Sreerama, M. C. Manning, M. E. Powers, J.-X. Zhang, D. P. Goldenberg and R. W. Woody, *Biochemistry*, 1999, **38**, 10 814.
2 I. B. Grishina and R. W. Woody, *Faraday Discuss.*, 1994, **99**, 245.

Dr Cole said: In an experiment, there is often the assumption of continuity between two data points, by interpolation, when in principle there could be a very fast process occurring in between. With theory, one can obviously have a lot finer time intervals, although not an infinite number, so there is less risk of 'missing' some process/extra intermediate or the like in theory. But how can one select the time interval to be sure that one is not missing something—is there a theoretical test that could be implemented to check for continuity, *e.g.* akin to the area of pure mathematics where limit functions, sequences, *etc.* are used to prove continuity, and could any such theory help check experiments where the danger of 'missing' some change between two data points is much more possible?

Dr Hirst replied: The challenge in molecular dynamics simulations has been attaining longer time scales and much less effort has been focused on very short time scales and issues of continuity. Typical simulations use a time step of one or two femtoseconds. Short time steps are necessary for the stability of the numerical integration that is used to propagate the dynamics.

Prof. J. C. Smith asked: What is the time resolution presently accessible with CD? Is it approaching that accessible to molecular dynamics simulation?

Dr Hirst answered: Kliger and co-workers have reported time-resolved CD measurements at the picosecond, nanosecond and microsecond time scales. The faster time scales are readily accessible to molecular dynamics simulations.[1–3]

1 E. Chen, P. Wittung-Stafshede and D. S. Kliger, *J. Am. Chem. Soc.*, 1999, **121**, 3811.
2 C.-F. Zhang, J. W. Lewis, R. Cerpa, I. D. Kuntz and D. S. Kliger, *J. Phys. Chem.*, 1993, **97**, 5499.
3 J. W. Lewis, R. A. Goldbeck, X. Xie, R. C. Dunn and J. D. Simon, 1992, **96**, 5243.

Prof. J. C. Smith said: There has been some debate in the quantum chemical literature as to whether interacting peptide groups electronically polarize each other. Might such effects influence the accuracy of calculated CD spectra?

Dr Hirst responded: Polarization effects may indeed influence CD spectra. Our calculations account for interactions between the ground state and the $n\pi^*$ and $\pi\pi^*$ excited states. The polarization effects of higher energy transitions may also be taken into account,[1] but we have not investigated this.

1   R. W. Woody and I. Tinoco, *J. Chem. Phys.*, 1967, **46**, 4927.

Prof. Hillier asked: Is it possible to use experimental data on the isolated chromophore to evaluate the important interactions within the protein and to avoid possible inaccuracies in the *ab imtio* calculation of these quantities?

Dr Hirst replied: It is possible to use experimental data to evaluate some of the interactions within the protein. Woody and Sreerama[1] have combined experimental data with semi-empirical INDO/S calculations with some success. However, a complete set of the necessary data is not available. For example, it is difficult to get detailed information on the nπ* electronic transition of the amide. This transition is electrically forbidden, but has a transition quadrupole moment, which is required for the calculation of protein CD. The magnetic transition dipole moments are also difficult to determine experimentally. A fully *ab initio* description of chromophores provides a consistency that is lacking in a mixture of empirical and semi-empirical values.[2]

1   R. W. Woody and N. Sreerama, *J. Chem. Phys.*, 1999, **111**, 2844.
2   J. D. Hirst and N. A. Besley, *J. Chem. Phys.*, 1999, **111**, 2846.

Prof. Watts said: (i) There are several components which have so far not been included in your simulations, even though they already seem rather close to experiment. Are you going to include these, *e.g*; side chains, higher amide excitation levels and solvent effects. (ii) Was the bacteriorhodopsin CD determination made in membranes or detergent? (iii) Do you think the detergent complicates the simulations of CD spectra?

Dr Hirst answered: Inclusion of side chains in calculations of protein CD has been investigated,[1,2] but no improvement in the accuracy of the calculations has been found. Semi-empirical calculations were used to model the electronic structure of side chains. We have realized significant improvements in the accuracy of protein CD calculations, by describing the amide chromophore using modern *ab initio* methods instead of semi-empirical calculations. One might anticipate that a similar approach to side chains is needed and we are currently working on this.

We have characterized some of the higher excited states of the amide.[3] Including these states did not increase the accuracy of the protein CD calculations. There may be charge transfer states that couple with the higher excited states and it may be necessary to include all these states in order to improve the accuracy. We are currently working on including solvent around the protein in the CD calculations. Earlier work by Applequist and Bode[4] did not find a large effect.

The CD spectrum of bacteriorhodopsin that we compared our calculations with was actually determined in water.[5] Fasman notes that it is distorted due to light scattering. The agreement between our calculated spectrum and the measured spectrum is not as good as for the other proteins. We should investigate this further, by comparing our calculated CD with experimental spectra measured under different conditions, such as after sonification in suspension,[6,7] and in detergent.[8]

1   R. W. Woody and N. Sreerama, *J. Chem. Phys.*, 1999, **111**, 2844.
2   N. A. Besley and J. D. Hirst, *J. Am. Chem. Soc.*, 1999, **121**, 9636.
3   N. A. Besley and J. D. Hirst, *J. Phys. Chem. A*, 1998, **102**, 10 791.
4   J. Applequist and K. A. Bode, *J. Phys. Chem. B*, 1999, **103**, 1767.
5   G. D. Fasman, *Circular Dichroism and the Conformational Analysis of Biomolecules*, Plenum Press, New York, 1996.
6   M. M. Long, D. W. Urry and W. Stoeckenius, *Biochem. Biophys. Res. Commun.*, 1977, **75**, 725.
7   D. Mao and B. A. Wallace, *Biochemistry*, 1984, **23**, 2667.
8   J. A. Reynolds and W. Stoecknius, *Proc. Natl. Acad. Sci. USA*, 1977, **74**, 2803.

Chemistry, physics and time: the computer modelling of glassmaking

David Martlew

Pilkington plc, European Technical Centre, Lathom, Ormskirk, Lancashire, UK L40 5UF

Received 8th April 2002, Accepted 29th April 2002
First published as an Advance Article on the web 6th August 2002

A decade or so ago the remains of an early flat glass furnace were discovered in St Helens. Continuous glass production only became feasible after the Siemens Brothers demonstrated their continuous tank furnace at Dresden in 1870. One manufacturer of flat glass enthusiastically adopted the new technology and secretly explored many variations on this theme during the next fifteen years. Study of the surviving furnace remains using today's computer simulation techniques showed how, in 1887, that technology was adapted to the special demands of window glass making. Heterogeneous chemical reactions at high temperatures are required to convert the mixture of granular raw materials into the homogeneous glass needed for windows. Kinetics (and therefore the economics) of glassmaking is dominated by heat transfer and chemical diffusion as refractory grains are converted to highly viscous molten glass. Removal of gas bubbles in a sufficiently short period of time is vital for profitability, but the glassmaker must achieve this in a reaction vessel which is itself being dissolved by the molten glass. Design and operational studies of today's continuous tank furnaces need to take account of these factors, and good use is made of computer simulation techniques to shed light on the way furnaces behave and how improvements may be made. This paper seeks to show how those same techniques can be used to understand how the early Siemens continuous tank furnaces were designed and operated, and how the Victorian entrepreneurs succeeded in managing the thorny problems of what was, in effect, a vulnerable high temperature continuous chemical reactor.

Introduction

From ancient times, glassmaking has involved a complex interaction of chemistry, physics, high temperatures and time. The vast majority of glass products have always been made by dissolving granular silica in some mixture of alkalis, at temperatures sufficiently high to put the containing pots severely at risk. For several thousand years the preferred form of silica has been quartz sand and the alkali has either been naturally occurring (as at the Wadi Natrun in Egypt) or has been laboriously produced by burning vegetation.[1]

By the middle of the nineteenth century the chemical industry had made sufficient progress to give glassmakers reliable alkali supplies, though not as cheaply as they desired. Two further developments were needed to launch glassmaking as a truly industrial process, and both were pioneered in Germany by the Siemens brothers during the 1860s. One was the combined development of the gas producer and the regenerative principle to secure clean, high temperature flames; the other was the continuous glassmaking tank furnace.

The continuous tank furnace for glassmaking was demonstrated at Dresden in the early years of the following decade. The result was sufficiently convincing to cause Mr William Windle Pilkington to build such a furnace in St Helens for the manufacture of sheet glass for windows, but other major flat glass manufacturers were unwilling to take the risk. A leading authority was Sir Henry Chance who, as late as 1883, gave a rather negative review of the continuous tank furnace concept.[2] In his view these furnaces could not yield glass of sufficiently high quality for window glass. In part the defects were due to the dissolution of the fireclay refractory structure by the highly corrosive molten glass, though the same comment could be made about the glassmaking pots conventionally used. Perhaps more serious was the issue of sand grain residues contaminating the end product.

Quartz, the essential precursor for common glassmaking, is itself a refractory material akin to the materials of which the furnace is constructed. The abiding dilemma of the glassmaker is to found the melt just long enough to dissolve the silica grains without breeching the walls which contain the molten glass. When making glass in a pot one can, by skilful adjustment of time and furnace temperature, achieve this on most occasions, but in a continuous tank furnace it was not clear how the glassmaker could prevent undissolved material flooding forward along the melt surface to spoil the end product.

The Dresden furnace

The Siemens brothers had noted that as the alkali and sand reacted together in a pot, the raw material mixture appeared to shrink. Bulk density increases with time as carbon dioxide is evolved and as eutectic melting and reaction between silica and the various alkalis begins to eliminate the inter-granular cavities. As these reactions proceed, the molten material becomes recognisably similar in chemical composition and physical properties to the desired molten glass, but with large numbers of gas bubbles and some undissolved silica grains suspended within its volume. Because of the high viscosity of the melt, removal of these defects takes a considerable time, so the glassmaker's management of furnace temperature and time of founding is geared to achieving good glass quality as quickly as possible. When the glass mixture is contained in a pot, the glassmaker has good control of the time and temperature history of the melt, but as soon as one considers continuous glassmaking on a large scale that element of direct control is no longer possible.

The original Dresden tank furnace was provided with three major chambers, separated by fireclay partitions. Molten glass was transferred from chamber to chamber *via* holes in the partitions at a low level, the theory being that as the glassmaking mixture reacts its bulk density increases, so one imagines that the molten material at the lowest level represents the most completely reacted glass in that partition.[3] Accordingly the tank furnace designer could adjust the size of each partition within the continuous melting furnace and regulate its operating temperature so that each volume element of glass passing through the furnace system would experience the same sort of temperature and time history as was successfully used when the glass was contained in a pot.

Unfortunately the fireclay refractory blocks which were available for building the furnace proved inadequate: the molten glass rapidly corroded the tank structure, with the result that these carefully disposed partitions soon vanished. To combat this problem the Siemens brothers rebuilt their tank furnace with flues running through the furnace sidewall and bottom structures, connected to chimneys to provide updraught which drew ambient air through the passages. Keeping the fireclay structure cool in this way certainly helped prolong its life and helped to avoid disastrous glass leakage through joints between blocks, but at the same time it exacerbated temperature differences within the molten glass, which set up convective flow patterns within the molten mass. Even though the average residence time of glass in each part of the furnace could be made appropriate, the existence of strong convection currents would create paths of very much shorter duration. Undissolved material could therefore find its way into the product, and as Sir Henry Chance observed, this would be singularly prejudicial to the successful production of window glass.

When Mr Windle Pilkington built continuous glassmaking furnaces in St Helens during the twelve or so years from 1873 onwards he experimented with a number of ways of solving this problem. By 1885 there were over fifteen such furnaces making window glass successfully, and in 1887 he made a major design change which set the pattern of such installations for many years to come.[4] Indeed, the furnaces which make float glass today recognisably owe much to his early experiments. So it is tempting to apply some of the theoretical techniques currently used to study the chemistry and physics of today's furnaces to shed light on these pivotal Victorian inventions.

Modelling continuous furnaces

Modern glassmaking furnaces are a capital intensive long-term investment; a float glass furnace may cost up to £30 million and be expected to deliver 5000 tonnes per week of good quality glass for 15 years. Failure to achieve the required glass quality is under these conditions a commercial disaster. Any proposed design changes are therefore subject to careful scrutiny before being adopted, and in recent decades a number of computer-based techniques have been developed for this purpose. Because of the importance of controlling the time–temperature history experienced by each bit of glass in the final product to ensure freedom from defects, the techniques of computational fluid dynamics have been widely applied by the glassmaking community throughout the world to evaluate furnace design and operation. Choudhary[5] has published recently some excellent reviews covering this theme. Other significant recent papers have been published by Nemec and his colleagues,[6] Carvalho[7] and Beerkins.[8]

Although a variety of software codes have been used, the collaborative activities of Technical Committee 21 of the International Commission on Glass have demonstrated that the various groups active in this modelling field around the world come to a surprisingly good consensus when applying their techniques to a common problem. All the codes solve the partial differential equations appropriate to laminar flow in the context of thermally induced buoyancy driven flow with strongly temperature dependent physical properties, mostly using a finite volume approach. Many of the codes acknowledge algorithms derived from the work of Patankhar,[9] in particular the SIMPLER algorithm. In all cases the result of the simulations is an array of orthogonal fluid velocity vectors at nodes distributed throughout the volume of the molten glass, together with temperatures at associated nodes. More or less spectacular graphical post processors are used to express this wealth of numerical information in forms which allow the user to visualise the significant features of the flow patterns within the glass. In the light of practical operating experience of real furnaces, this technique can provide a surprisingly valuable insight into what is happening during glass manufacture and how furnace operation might be realistically improved.

The value of this has led glass manufacturers to sponsor research work in Universities to develop the codes and techniques. At least one independent company offering such flow simulation on a consultancy basis has come into being, and major manufacturers have developed simulation capabilities in house. Pilkington developed its own in-house code (known internally as 3DGLASS) for this purpose;[10] the work described here was carried out using that code.

Glass quality issues

The driving ambition of glass manufacturers is to make high quality glass products as profitably as possible. There is much preoccupation therefore with the occurrence of defects which render units of production unacceptable to the customers, creating reject ware and diminishing profits. Flat glass manufacturers are particularly sensitive to this, because of the high standards demanded on the international market by the major customers. Because the unit of production may be a sheet as large as three metres by six metres weighing half a tonne, the consequences of rejection are costly.

Rejection may be the result of discrete faults, bubbles or undissolved "stones", or of optical defects, some of which originate from quite small variations in chemical composition of the glass. One task of the modeller therefore is to seek the origins of such defects. Occasionally, direct observation of the furnace itself may offer some clues: for example an outbreak of bubbles and stones might be observed to follow some obvious failure of the refractory structure of the furnace. More often, the faults appear without any single causative event which can readily be recognised. Corrective strategy is then very hard to establish.

In common with other glass furnace simulation codes 3DGLASS has a post-processing capability which uses the temperature and velocity information generated by the simulation to track imaginary particles suspended in the molten glass.[10] Since bubbles are of practical importance, the tracking algorithm is able to cope with the buoyancy of a particle with respect to the melt in which it is suspended and which may materially affect the pathway taken by the particle in its transit of the furnace. The post-processor adopts the same mesh as did the solver, following each particle as it moves from cell to cell within the mesh. So, within each cell, the velocity field in the simulated molten glass is assumed to carry the particle with it, and buoyancy effects are catered for by assuming that particles rise or fall at terminal velocity, when an appropriate form of the Stokes' law equation may be pressed into service.

The purpose of this paper is to consider how this kind of capability may be used to account for the time-dependent physico-chemical processes which occur in continuous glassmaking, and how the efficiencies of different furnaces may be compared.

Understanding the behaviour of gas bubbles in molten glass has progressed during the last few decades through the work of Cable,[11] Nemec[12] and Beerkins[13] amongst others. Dissolution of solid grains (such as silica sand grains which form a large part of the mixture fed to the furnace) has been studied by Cable,[14] Cooper,[15] Hlavac[16] and Choudhary,[17] amongst others. The kinetics of the heterogeneous chemical reactions involved are dominated by diffusion of either reagents or reaction products in the viscous medium of the glass melt.

Theory: Diffusion controlled kinetics

In general, kinetic models describing reactions which are diffusion controlled require knowledge of the physical properties of the medium in which diffusion occurs, and the state of motion of that medium.

If a bubble or a silica grain is interacting with a perfectly motionless glass melt, the kinetic models are at first sight analogous with the equations describing heat transfer. The text book by Crank[18] offers the solutions for many detailed geometries, amongst which is that of a sphere in a semi-infinite medium. Initially the rate is limited by the kinetics of species transfer across the particle boundary, but the overall process becomes time dependent as concentration fields develop around the particle. The rate of reaction falls off as the square root of elapsed time.

If the dissolution of a silica grain is being considered, Cooper[15] showed that the motion of the grain interface has a significant effect, serving to accelerate the reaction compared with the truly static case; he introduced a correction term into the descriptive equation to take account of this. Subsequently other authors applied this correction without careful consideration of its applicability to their experimental geometries, with misleading results.

However in the context of transit through a glass tank, the particle would not normally be held within a static melt. Differences in density between the particle and the melt would (especially in the case of bubbles) give rise to buoyancy forces and therefore a vertical movement of the particle relative to the melt. A pseudo-steady state ensues, in which the vertical motion comes to dominate the chemical reactions by compressing the concentration boundary layer over a major portion of the interface. The analogous heat transfer situation is that of the heating or cooling of a sphere in laminar forced convection, and this formed the basis of Nemec's published work[12] on bubble interactions with the glass melt.

As the chemical reactions progress, the molten glass at the interface can change noticeably in chemical composition. The density of the layer of liquid immediately at the interface may therefore be different from that of the original glass melt: this may then induce a buoyancy-driven flow which in turn would influence reaction rate by compressing the concentration boundary layer over part of the surface. This free-convection situation may be treated using some of the correlation equations developed by engineers in the context of heat transfer, but which may, by analogy, be used to describe some kinds of mass transfer situation (see Choudhary[17] and Beerkens[13]).

In addition, the glass flow in which the particle is suspended may involve significant shear, which could influence the reaction rate. This situation virtually never occurs in laboratory experiments, so its treatment in the glass literature is restricted to studies of glass furnaces. In modern glass furnaces, the effects of shear fields in the overall glass flow are usually small from the point of view of a particle less than a millimetre in diameter. The important exception to this is the highly sheared flows next to the electrodes used to provide joule-effect heating in parts of the furnace, or in the vicinity of gas bubblers used as flow inducers under some circumstances. For the purposes of the present comparison, since there is no evidence of the use of either of these technologies in the mid-Victorian glass furnace in St Helens, the role of intense shear fields in the molten glass flow has been neglected.

Interaction of gas bubbles with the glass melt is of considerable importance to glassmakers, but is complicated by the number of gaseous species which are commonly involved. Nitrogen, carbon dioxide, oxygen and water are usually present, together with oxides of sulfur which create their own equilibria within the bubble. Some gases dissolve physically in the melt, whilst others react with components of the molten glass. This complexity multiplies the number of parameters which must be known to create a credible model (not least the diffusivity and gas concentrations in the molten glass). Usually there is not sufficient information of this kind available, so in practical application this often needs to be simplified considerably.

Dissolution of solid grains is somewhat more tractable, because quite often the problem can be treated as single component diffusion. Silica sand grain residues are a known problem of furnaces with deficient design and operation, and silica dissolves to create silicate anions as the diffusing species. It is customary to ignore changes in these anions as they move away from the interface, though it is likely that the size of the anions becomes smaller as they move into regions of higher alkali content. Diffusion models employ an effective binary diffusivity of "SiO_2" which, in a multicomponent melt, is a simplification. But in the light of other difficulties encountered in the study of dissolution perhaps this simplification is justified in order to allow us to make some progress.

Method: Using particle tracking to compare furnaces

For this particular study I chose to explore the use of particle tracking in a simulated furnace as a way of establishing how well the Jubilee furnace of 1887 performed its primary role of glass melter compared with container furnaces of that same period and with the continuous glassmaking furnaces in use today.

3DGLASS will track a specified particle through the calculated flow and temperature fields obtained by the CFD simulation. Simulations have been prepared to represent two furnaces, the mid-Victorian design of Mr Windle Pilkington and a throated container furnace built about a century later and used as a Round Robin subject by ICG TC21. In both cases over a thousand particle tracks were calculated to allow the shortest tracks to be selected. These are the tracks which have the highest risk of failure to dissolve sand grains, so will determine the likely level of glass quality defects from this source.

The Victorian furnace was over 80 ft long by 12 ft wide, built in two roughly equal sized compartments. It made glass at a rate of 150 tonnes per week. By contrast, the more modern furnace was a single chamber 34 ft long by 20 ft wide with a throated offtake, making 1225 tonnes per week of container glass. Flow patterns along the centrelines of these two furnaces are compared in Fig. 1. It should be noted that these diagrams are not to scale, for illustrative purposes the geometrical aspect ratios are deliberately distorted.

Most sand grains in the mixture of raw materials will begin their digestion before entering the molten glass bath. Alkali grains in contact with silica will initiate solid state reactions at the points of physical contact, forming pockets of sodium silicates on the sand grain surfaces. When the alkali melts, the fluid liquid phase formed will tend to spread out over the silica grain surfaces, wetting the silica and initiating dissolution. There is however some experimental evidence that some of the grains will fail to be in contact with the alkalis, so will enter the molten glass substantially unchanged. These are the grains which are most likely to create glass defects.

The key ideas on the basis of which the calculation proceeds are: (1) A silica grain enters the molten glass substantially as an unchanged quartz or crystobalite sphere. (2) The grain diameter is of the order of 1 mm. (3) The density difference between the grain and the molten glass will not introduce significant buoyant deviation from the calculated path. (4) Particle tracks are calculated for a notional zero-sized particle. (5) Dissolution is essentially diffusion controlled. (6) Appropriate engineering correlations may be used to calculate the progress of dissolution along the path.

So it is necessary to select appropriate correlations to express dissolution kinetics and to obtain the various key parameters and physical properties to allow them to be exploited.

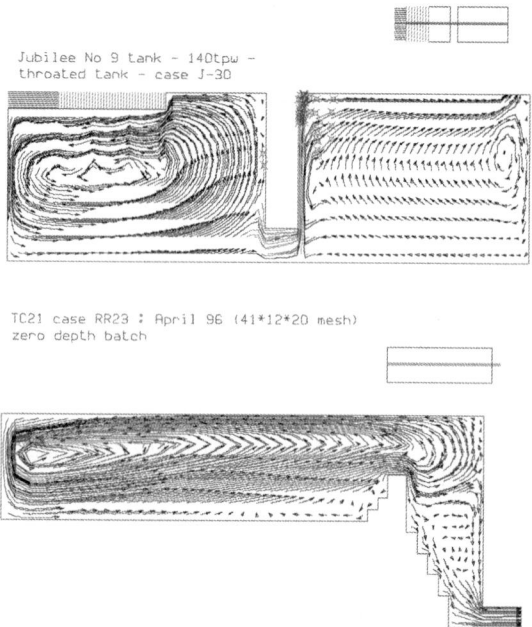

Fig. 1 Centreline flow patterns in the two furnaces.

Theory : Diffusion controlled kinetic models

Kreider and Cooper,[15] Hlavac and Nademlynska[16] and Truhlarova and Veprek[19] all studied the dissolution of silica in sodium silicate melts, in a laboratory context. In each of their papers the applicable equations are clearly stated, and the outcome was some estimate of the effective binary diffusivity of dissolved silica in the melts used. Truhlarova and Veprek extended the work to a soda-lime–silica glass composition which was intended to be representative of common commercial compositions. Cable and Martlew[20] suggested an improvement to their calculation scheme for deriving diffusivities, which has been adopted by other workers (Choudhary[17]). So there are values for this crucial property which may usefully be applied to the dissolution of sand grains in window glass compositions.

Information relating to other physical properties of these melts is not so readily available. In particular the density of the liquid next to the solid sand grain surface is not reported in the open literature. To assess the effects of buoyancy driven free convection it is necessary to have a reasonable estimate of that density so that the difference in density between that interface layer and the bulk liquid may be obtained.

Density data for the interface liquid

For diffusion controlled dissolution it is usual to assume that the liquid immediately in contact with the dissolving solid is in thermodynamic equilibrium with the solid at the temperature of the experiment. The compositions needed to calculate sand grain dissolution may therefore be derived from an appropriate phase diagram. Liquidus data was taken from the soda-lime–silica phase diagram due to Morey and Bowen and later published by the American Ceramic Society.[21] This was the source used by Truhlarova and Veprek[19] in calculating their diffusivity estimates for silica dissolution. They constructed a tieline from their glass composition [16%Na_2O 10%CaO 74%SiO_2] to the silica vertex, then obtained the compositions at each isotherm intersected.

This process was repeated for the present study and the results of the interpolation are given in Table 1.

Table 1 Liquidus temperature *versus* silica content along the tieline

T_{liq}/°C	1710	1600	1500	1400	1300	1200	1100	1000	970
SiO_2(%)	100	91.2	85.4	82.0	79.3	76.7	75.2	74.3	74.0

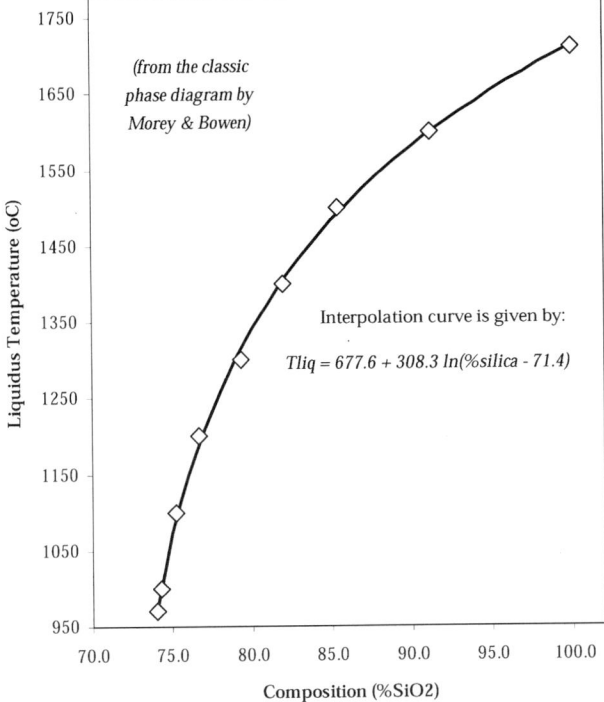

Fig. 2 Liquidus temperatures along the tieline to SiO_2.

A three-parameter equation was constructed to interpolate this data. It fitted remarkably well, though this may have been influenced by the methods used by the original authors for constructing the isotherms on their phase diagram. The equation is:

$$T_{liq} = 677.6 + 308.3 \ln(\%silica - 71.4) \quad (1)$$

Residual standard deviation is about 8 °C which, given the nature of the data, is very satisfactory. Fig. 2 gives the data from the phase diagram along with the suggested interpolation curve. Even though commercial flat glass compositions are more complex than these soda-lime–silica glasses the commercial compositions are strongly clustered and this curve is as good a representation of the equilibrium layer composition as is currently available.

Density measurements by Veprek

In 1968 Veprek carried out some density and viscosity measurements on four melts along this tieline, but the results were published only internally. Professor Hlavac has kindly made this data available,[22] see Table 2.

The viscosity data seem to be very well-behaved, with strong linear adherence to the Arrhenius equation form. Slopes are very similar, and the trend to higher viscosity with increasing silica seems uniform. The dataset at highest silica does betray outlier tendencies at the low temperature end, which the author has judged important enough to cause him to exclude the points from his linear fit.

Table 2 Compositions for which densities were determined

Composition	Na_2O	CaO	SiO_2
1	16.0	10.0	74.0
2	14.3	9.1	76.6
3	12.5	8.2	79.3
4	10.9	6.9	82.2

The density data (not surprisingly) are much less tidy. The two lower silica compositions gave good linear fits on temperature, with virtually the same slope. Composition 3 has a numerically lower slope, but the scatter on the data for composition 4 is such that deriving the slope from the data is not sensible. Within the data set there were nine duplicate determinations: the average difference between duplicates was 0.005 gm cm^{-3}, which is significant compared with the density differences we need to use to estimate free convection effects. This and the observation that the trends of density and of its temperature coefficient with silica content are not as expected cast doubt on the reliability of the measured density values.

Conclusions which may be drawn from this data are: (1) Data at the highest silica content appear to be weakest and most scattered. (2) Melts 2 and 3 give densities less than those for the base composition 1. (3) Surprisingly, densities from melts 2 and 3 are not distinctly different unless the comparison involves extrapolation of the fitted lines. (4) At 1400 °C the densities do not vary linearly with composition, but exhibit an apparent minimum, unlike the viscosities.

In the absence of thoroughly reliable measurement, we would expect both the density of the melt at any particular temperature and its rate of change with temperature to be linear functions of silica content in the melt. This follows from the idea that these macroscopic properties are determined by the molecular structure of the melt, and that as the Na_2O and CaO content of the melt increase (in constant ratio) the number of non-bridging oxygens increases linearly. This suggests an approach based on interpolation.

Estimating the rate of change of density with temperature

Good data exist for the temperature coefficient of density for molten commercial flat glass containing 72% SiO_2: $d\rho/dT$ is -0.000142 g cm^{-3} °C^{-1}.[23] From the CRC Handbook[24] the linear expansion coefficient of vitreous silica is 5.85×10^{-7} which implies $d\rho/dT$ is -3.86×10^{-6} g cm^{-3} °C^{-1}. Above the glass transition region this is likely to be a factor of two higher, so we estimate it to be about 8×10^{-6} g cm^{-3} °C^{-1}. Linear interpolation on silica content yields:

$$d\rho/dT = -0.000488 + (\%SiO_2)4.8 \times 10^{-6} \qquad (2)$$

Fig. 3 shows how this linear trend relates to the $d\rho/dT$ information in the Hlavac data.

Estimating the density of the interface layer

For pure silica, the liquidus temperature is 1710 °C according to Morey and Bowen.[21] At this temperature the sand grain is at equilibrium with molten silica, so the density of the interface liquid may be estimated by taking the density of vitreous silica (2.204 g cm^{-3}) and allowing it to expand from room temperature to 1710 °C. Allowing for the higher expansion coefficient between the glass transition temperature and the liquidus temperature, we estimate the density of the equilibrium liquid silica at the liquidus to be 2.196 g cm^{-3}.

Assuming the bulk melt density at 1200 °C is 2.300 g cm^{-3} for a melt of 72%SiO_2 content we estimate the melt density at 1710 °C would be 2.2274 g cm^{-3}. So if density is linear with silica content at 1710 °C we have:

$$\rho_{1710} = 2.308 - 0.00112(\%SiO_2) \qquad (3)$$

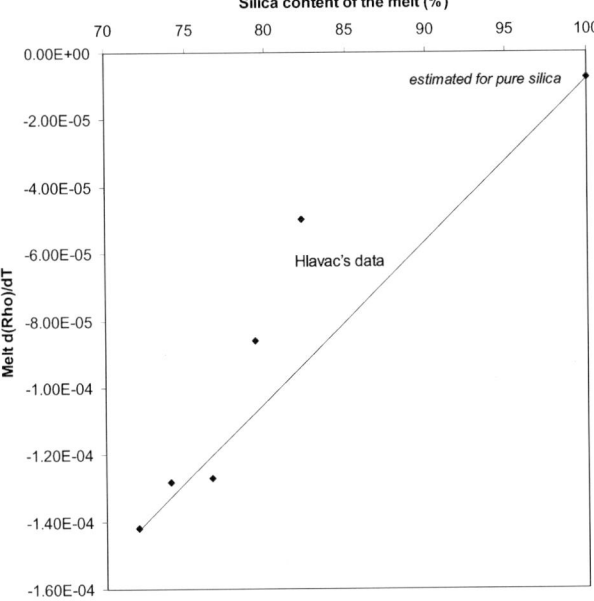

Fig. 3 Temperature coefficient of density along the tieline.

So eqns. (2) and (3) allow us to say that the density at any particular temperature T is given by:

$$\rho_T = \rho_{1710} - (1710 - T)(0.000488 + (\%SiO_2)4.8 \times 10^{-6}) \tag{4}$$

Using these equations in conjunction with Morey & Bowen's phase diagram information (as summarised in eqn. (1)) allows estimation of density values for the equilibrium liquid, and more important for our present purposes, the difference in density between that and the bulk melt over the range of likely temperatures.

Fig. 4 shows that over the temperature range from 960 °C to 1600 °C the estimated density difference is represented sufficiently well by a linear equation:

$$\Delta\rho = 0.046 - 5.05 \times 10^{-5} T \tag{5}$$

Linearising $\Delta\rho$ directly rather than linearising the density of the interface material then obtaining $\Delta\rho$ by difference was judged the better approach. Attempts to model the dissolution of sand grains require robustness and absence of spurious discontinuities more urgently than accuracy. Reliable and accurate density information would be very desirable, but in its absence this scheme of estimation is currently the best tool we have to support comparative studies.

Effect of particle buoyancy

The difference between the density of the silica grain (assumed to be crystobalite rather than quartz) and the bulk melt in which it is suspended is sufficient to generate relative velocity which may be calculated using the familiar Stokes law:

$$V = \frac{2}{9}\frac{D^2}{4}\frac{\Delta\rho g}{\eta} \tag{6}$$

where V is the terminal velocity, D is the diameter of the sphere, $\Delta\rho$ is the difference in density between sphere and melt, g is the acceleration due to gravity and η is the viscosity of the melt.

For a typical path, the velocities involved are of order of 1 µm s^{-1}, so the integrated deviation over the whole transit is of the order of 5 mm in a tank depth of about 0.7 m.

Nevertheless, this causes a significant increase in the rate of dissolution because the concentration boundary layer is compressed over the leading face of the grain.

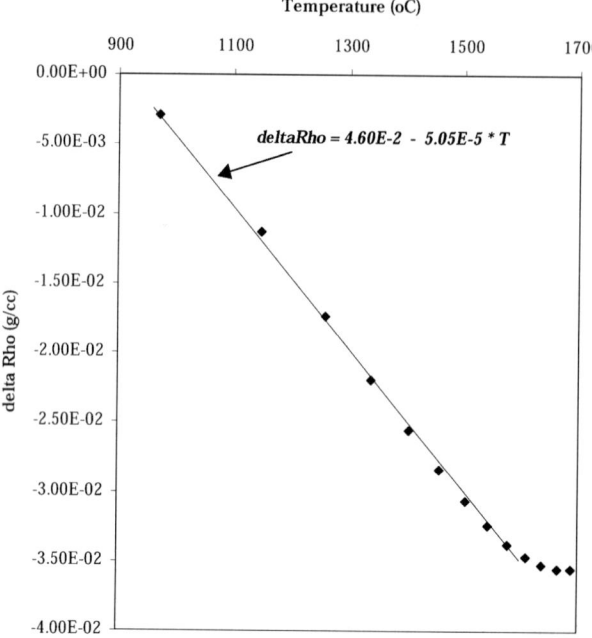

Fig. 4 Estimated density difference between the interface layer and the bulk of the melt.

Table 3 Definitions of the dimensionless groups used in engineering correlations

The mass transfer coefficient, k_c, is defined by: $j_{AB} = k_c(c_i - c_\infty)$
Sherwood number: $Sh = (k_c D)/D_{AB}$
Schmidt number: $Sc = \eta/(\rho D_{AB})$
Reynolds number: $Re = (D V \rho)/\eta$
Grashof number: $Gr = (D^3 g \rho \Delta \rho)/\eta^2$
Peclet number: $Pe = Re\, Sc = (D V)/D_{AB}$
Rayleigh number: $Ra = Gr\, Sc = (D^3 g \Delta \rho)/(\eta D_{AB})$
where j_{AB} is the mass flux of A in B, D_{AB} is the diffusivity of A in B, k_c is the mass transfer coefficient, c_i is the concentration at the interface, c_∞ is the concentration remote from the interface, V is a significant velocity, D is the grain diameter, ρ is the density of the liquid, $\Delta \rho$ is a density difference, η is the viscosity of the liquid and g is the acceleration due to gravity.

The engineering correlations which may be used are based on experimental data generalised in terms of key dimensionless groups. Definitions of these[25] are summarised in Table 3.

From the point of view of mass transfer, the buoyant rise of the particle with respect to the melt creates a forced convection situation. Several correlation equations relating to spheres have been proposed (Table 4).

In the main, the experimental basis for these has been at higher Reynolds numbers than obtained in the present situation. Probably the best to use is that of Beerkens.[13]

Buoyancy of the concentration boundary layer

The expectation is that as silica dissolves in the melt and the interface composition moves towards the silica vertex in the phase diagram, the density of the concentration boundary layer will be reduced. Buoyant instability will therefore cause that layer of liquid to move upwards, in a fashion

Table 4 Correlations for spheres in forced convection

$Sh = 2 + 0.552\, Re^{1/2} Sc^{1/3}$
Ref. 26, p. 584, quoting from Froessling (1938).
$Sh = 2 + 0.6 Re^{1/2} Sc^{1/3}$
Ref. 25, p. 647, quoting from Ranz & Marshall (1952).
$Sh = 2 + (0.4 Re^{1/2} + 0.06 Re^{2/3}) Sc^{0.4} (\eta_\infty/\eta_i)^{1/4}$
Ref. 27, p. 288, quoting from Whitaker on heat transfer for $(3.5 < Re < 80\,000)$
$Sh = 2 + 0.89\, Re^{1/3}\, Sc^{1/3}$
Ref. 13.

Table 5 Correlations for spheres in free convection

$Sh = 2 + 0.6 Gr^{1/4} Sc^{1/3}$
Ref. 25, p. 413, quoting from Ranz & Marshall (1952) on heat transfer when $Gr^{\frac{1}{4}} Sc^{\frac{1}{3}} < 200$.
$Sh = 2 + 0.43 Gr^{1/4} Sc^{1/4}$
Ref. 27, p. 350, quoting from Yuge on heat transfer.
$Sh = 1.7 + 0.3\,(1 + 14.86\, GrSc)^{1/4}$
Ref. 17, quoting from Clift, Grace and Weber (1978) for $(1 < GrSc < 10^{10})$.
$Sh = 2 + 0.89 Gr^{1/3} Sc^{1/4}$
Ref. 13.

analogous to the movement of the layer of liquid adjacent to a hot sphere. This free convection style of flow will compress the concentration boundary layer and enhance dissolution. Correlations which have been derived to express this are summarised in Table 5.

Again, much of the original experimental work (on the basis of which these correlations have been suggested) was carried out using very much less viscous fluids. For present purposes the equation quoted by Holman[27] for heat transfer and used by analogy for mass transfer and that quoted by Choudhary[17] are probably the best. Over the range of values encountered in this work, these two equations yield very similar numerical results: slightly arbitrarily the equation of Holman has been selected for use here.

Method of calculation

A few of the particle tracks which had the shortest transit time from raw material input to furnace exit were selected for each of the furnaces involved in the comparison. For each track a listing was prepared of the points in space visited by the particle in its transit, together with the temperatures and the time spent getting from the previous location. An Excel spreadsheet was then used to carry forward the dissolution calculations: an image of one such spreadsheet is given in Fig. 5 to give an indication of the calculation route.

Each row of the spreadsheet relates sequentially to the particle location nodes along its transit through the furnace. An initial particle diameter for the notional silica grain is set manually, so that after each step of the transit the grain size can be updated. The next nine columns calculate the appropriate physical properties at the node, using eqns. (1) to (5), and the tenth calculates the buoyant rise velocity of the particle using Stokes Law, eqn. (6). Calculation of the important dimensionless groups follows, then the correlations suggested by Beerkins and Holman are used to estimate the Sherwood number for forced convection and free convection mass transfer respectively. The following two columns calculate the corresponding Nernst boundary layer thicknesses, then the concentration difference between the boundary layer and the bulk melt is used to derive mass transfer coefficients for the two scenarios.

The effects of forced and free convection on mass transfer are not simply additive. If both the particle and the boundary layer are less dense than the melt in which the particle is suspended, then one will enhance dissolution on the upper part of the silica grain surface, whilst the other will do so on the lower surface. To analyse the combined effect of these would require detailed work beyond

x (m)	y (m)	z (m)	time (hr)	temp (oC)	grain size (micron)	SiO2 density (g/cc)	glass melt density (g/cc)	glass melt concn. (g/cc)	Estimatd deltaRho (g/cc)	equm. layer density (g/cc)	Equm. layer concn. (%)	Equm. layer concn. (g/cc)	glass viscosity (poise)	diffusivity of silica (sq.micron/s)	Stokes law velocity (mm/s)
2.458	1.683	0.648	0.00	1325	613	2.3346	2.2821	1.6887	-0.0209	2.2612	79.6	1.7990	288	24	3.74E-04
2.373	1.696	0.647	0.05	1311	611	2.3346	2.2839	1.6901	-0.0202	2.2637	79.2	1.7926	326	21	3.16E-04
2.255	1.716	0.647	0.11	1307	608	2.3346	2.2844	1.6905	-0.0200	2.2644	79.1	1.7909	338	20	2.99E-04
2.034	1.756	0.647	0.25	1300	602	2.3347	2.2852	1.6910	-0.0197	2.2655	78.9	1.7883	357	19	2.74E-04
1.695	1.818	0.647	0.48	1292	594	2.3347	2.2862	1.6918	-0.0192	2.2670	78.7	1.7849	386	17	2.42E-04

Reynolds Number	Schmidt Number	DeltaRho over Rho	Grashof Number	Nu for Forced Convection	Nu for Free Convection	Delta for Forced Convection (microns)	Delta for Free Convection (microns)	c(i)-c(inf) (g/cc)	Mass Trsfr coeff (forced) (micron/s)	Mass Trsfr coeff (free) (micron/s)	rate of change of radius (micron/s)	time step (s)	change of diameter during time step (microns)
1.82E-08	5.30E+08	9.16E-03	1.30E-07	3.89	3.24	157	189	0.1103	1.51E-01	1.26E-01	7.14E-03	1.73E+02	2
1.35E-08	6.87E+08	8.84E-03	9.67E-08	3.87	3.23	158	189	0.1025	1.32E-01	1.10E-01	5.79E-03	2.39E+02	3
1.23E-08	7.39E+08	8.75E-03	8.80E-08	3.86	3.22	158	189	0.1004	1.27E-01	1.06E-01	5.47E-03	4.88E+02	5
1.06E-08	8.28E+08	8.61E-03	7.55E-08	3.83	3.21	157	188	0.0973	1.20E-01	1.01E-01	5.01E-03	8.10E+02	8
8.52E-09	9.68E+08	8.42E-03	6.09E-08	3.80	3.19	156	186	0.0931	1.11E-01	9.36E-02	4.44E-03	4.32E+02	4

Fig. 5 Part of a typical dissolution spreadsheet page.

the scope of this study. Holman[17] suggests (p. 347) some correlations for coping with situations of mixed forced and free convection, but those available are for much higher Reynolds numbers than encountered in sand grain dissolution. The approach taken here in the absence of reliable guidance from the literature is to select whichever influence is the dominant one and to ignore the other. This approach may underestimate the dissolution rate somewhat, but this seems less damaging than using inapplicable correlations which risk overestimation.

Results and discussion

The amount of silica dissolution which has occurred in moving from the previous to the current node is calculated using the larger of the two mass transfer coefficients, then the diameter of the particle is updated for the next step of the calculation. The results of this process may conveniently be displayed as a graph of grain diameter *versus* time. An example of this is given in Fig. 6 for a sand grain which is about the largest diameter one would expect to encounter in significant amounts in a modern glassmaking sand.

For the purposes of furnace comparison, it is useful to reduce the starting size of the silica grain until the grain just survives as far as the furnace exit. Comparison of these critical sizes provides a robust indication of relative digestion efficiencies in a form which has some intuitive meaning for the practical glassmaker. Fig. 7 shows this scenario for one of the faster tracks through the Jubilee furnace of 1887.

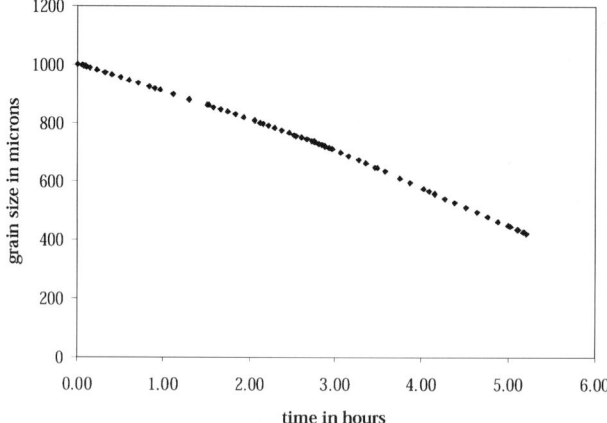

Fig. 6 Calculated diameters for a large silica grain passing through a modern container furnace.

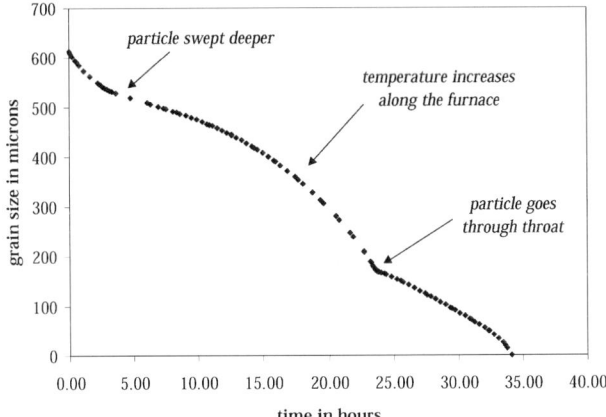

Fig. 7 Digestion curve for a sand grain which just survives transit through the mid-Victorian furnace.

The variation of dissolution rate visible in the figure can be associated with the temperature experienced by the particle at stages along its transit. In spite of the dominant convection flows in a glassmaking furnace, there tends to be a stable stratification of temperature over most of the molten glass volume, with hotter glass in the upper layers. So, initially, the grain dissolves comparatively rapidly but the rate of dissolution falls off as the particle is swept to the deeper layers of glass. After passing through the throat the particle is in warmer glass entering the much cooler conditioning chamber, so the rate of dissolution is significantly diminished.

To establish the repeatability of this pattern, another track within that same furnace was investigated. For this the transit time was four hours longer, so a larger critical sand grain size was anticipated. The result of the calculation is given in Fig. 8, and it may be seen that the dissolution behaviour is qualitatively very similar. Critical grain sizes for these two paths are 613 microns and 639 microns. Thus the result of this calculation is not unreasonably sensitive to the selection of particle track from among those tracks of faster transit time.

Data for a container furnace of the mid-Victorian period have not yet been assembled, but it is known that such furnaces were about half the length of the window glass furnace. To gain a feel for the difference this may have made, the existing track *J30 track01* was used to obtain a critical grain size so that the grain just disappeared at the throat connecting the two chambers. The result is displayed in Fig. 9. The critical grain size has decreased from 613 microns to 540 microns, which

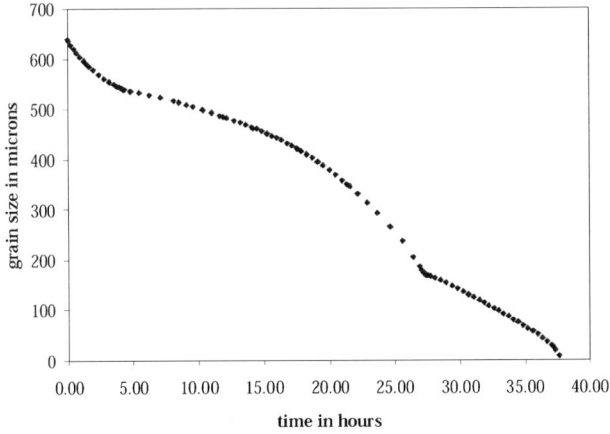

Fig. 8 A second digestion curve for the mid-Victorian furnace.

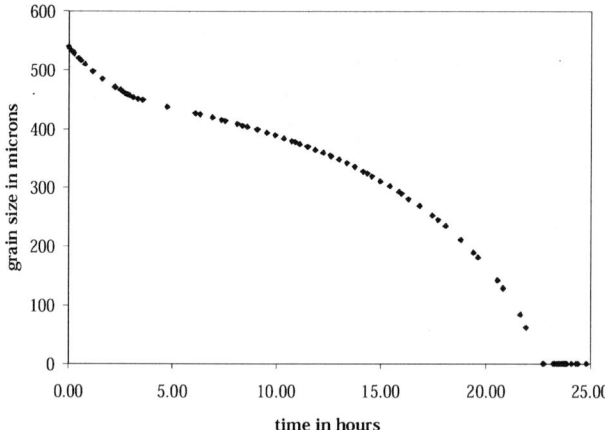

Fig. 9 Digestion curve for a grain which is just dissolved when it reaches the throat.

indicates an inferior digestion performance. It is likely, however, that the temperature regime in a Victorian container furnace would be less advantageous than that in the melting compartment of the flat glass tank, because the bottle-makers would need to have glass at around 1120 °C at the gathering position. The sand grain dissolution rate along the latter part of the path would be adversely affected by this, so the comparison here understates the difference between the two furnace designs. What emerges from this comparison is a clear indication that the flat glass furnace was specifically designed to produce a lower population of discrete faults than the glass tanks in general use at that time.

Modern glass tanks have benefited enormously from the availability of better refractory materials which enable higher throughputs and higher temperatures. The furnace used by ICG TC21 in its Round Robin exercises is an example of the state of furnace technology a century on. Fig. 10 shows a digestion curve for one of the simulations used in that work.

The shape of the curve is not unlike that of the single-chamber curve shown in Fig. 9. The initial dissolution rate is sustained far longer in the more modern furnace, probably as a result of the higher throughput of the furnace and the lower iron content of the glass, both of which would tend

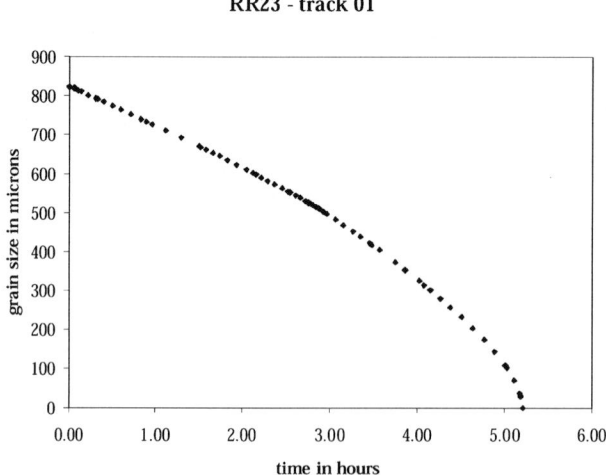

Fig. 10 Digestion curve for a grain passing through a modern container furnace.

to reduce the variation of glass temperature with depth at the upstream end of the melter. Critical grain size is now 823 microns, compared with 540 microns for the single chamber Victorian case.

Making the unwarrantable assumption that critical sand grain size increased linearly with time over this period of glassmaking history, one is tempted to infer that the flat glass furnace of Mr Windle Pilkington was at least twenty five years ahead of its time.

Acknowledgements

Grateful thanks to Michael Cable and David Gelder for most helpful discussions and suggestions. The author is also grateful to Pilkington plc for support and for agreement to the publication of this paper.

References

1. J. W. Smedley, C. M. Jackson and C. A. Booth, in *The History and Prehistory of Glassmaking Technology*, ed. W. P. McCray and W. D. Kingery, American Ceramic Society, Westerville, OH, USA, 1998.
2. H. J. Powell, H. Chance and H. G. Harris, *The Principles of Glassmaking*, George Bell & Sons, London, 1883.
3. R. Gunther, *Glass-Melting Tank Furnaces*, transl. J. Currie, The Society of Glass Technology, Sheffield, 1958, p. 187.
4. T. C. Barker, *The Glassmakers*, Weidenfeld and Nicolson, London, 1977.
5. M. K. Choudhary, in *Proceedings of the ICG Congress "Glass in the New Millenium"*, International Commission on Glass, 2000 (CD ROM).
6. J. Klouzek, L. Nemec, P. Schill and J. Ullrich, *Fundamentals of Glass Science and Technology*, The Glass Research Institute, Växjö, Sweden, 1997.
7. M. G. Carvalho, N. Speranskaia, J. Wang and M. Nogueria, *Proceedings of the 5th International Seminar on the Advances in the Fusion and Processing of Glass*, American Ceramic Society, Westerville, OH, USA, 1998, p. 109.
8. R. G. C. Beerkens, H. P. H. Muysenberg and T. van der Heijen, *Glastechnol. Ber.*, 1994, **67**(7), 179–188.
9. S. V. Patankar, *Numerical Heat Transfer and Fluid Flow*, McGraw-Hill, New York, USA, 1980.
10. A. M. Keeley, *Proceedings of the 1st ESG Conference "Fundamentals of the Glass Manufacturing Process"*, Society of Glass Technology, Sheffield, 1991, p. 178.
11. M. Cable and J. R. Frade, *Glastechnol. Ber.*, 1987, **60**(11), 355–362.
12. L. Nemec and J. Klouzek, *J. Non-Cryst. Solids*, 1998, **231**, 152–160.
13. R. C. G. Beerkens, *Glastechnol. Ber.*, 1990, **63K**, 222–242.
14. M. Cable and D. J. Evans, *J. Appl. Phys.*, 1967, **38**(7), 2899–2906.
15. K. G. Kreider and A. R. Cooper, *Glass Technol.*, 1967, **8**(3), 71–73.
16. J. Hlavac and L. Nademlynska, *Glass Technol.*, 1969, **10**(2), 54–58.
17. M. K. Choudhary, *Glass Technol.*, 1988, **29**(3), 100–102.
18. J. Crank, *The Mathematics of Diffusion*, Oxford University Press, Oxford, 1956.
19. M. Truhlarova and O. Veprek, *Silikaty*, 1970, **14**(1), 1–16.
20. M. Cable and D. Martlew, *Glass Technol.*, 1984, **25**(6), 270–276.
21. G. W. Morey and N. L. Bowen, later published in *Phase Diagrams for Ceramists*, ed. E. M. Levin, C. R. Robbins and H. F. McMurdie, American Ceramic Society, Westerville, OH, USA, 1964.
22. Unpublished notes by O. Veprek (1968), made available by Hlavac in a personal communication.
23. J. Orrel and W. P. Thorley, unpublished report, 1941.
24. *Handbook of Chemistry and Physics*, ed. C. D. Hodgman, Chemical Rubber Publishing Co., Ohio, 40th edn., 1959.
25. R. B. Bird, W. E. Stewart and E. N. Lightfoot, *Transport Phenomena*, Wiley, New York, USA, 1960.
26. J. R. Welty, G. E. Wicks and R. E. Wilson, *Fundamentals of Momentum, Heat and Mass Transfer*, Wiley, New York, USA, 1973.
27. J. P. Holman, *Heat Transfer*, McGraw-Hill, New York, USA, 2002.

A SAXS/WAXS XAFS study of crystallisation in cordierite glass

G. N. Greaves,[a] W. Bras,[b] M. Oversluizen[b] and S. M. Clark[c]

[a] *Department of Physics, University of Wales, Aberystwyth, UK SY23 3BZ*
[b] *DUBBLE CRG/ESRF, Netherlands Organisation for Scientific Research (NWO), PO Box 220, F38043, Grenoble Cedex, France*
[c] *Synchrotron Radiation Source, Daresbury, Warrington, UK WA4 4AD*

Received 5th March 2002, Accepted 8th April 2002
First published as an Advance Article on the web 24th July 2002

New Cr X-ray absorption fine structure (XAFS) data have been combined with the results of small angle X-ray scattering (SAXS) and wide angle X-ray scattering (WAXS) experiments to probe in detail the crystallisation mechanism in cordierite ($Mg_2Al_4Si_5O_{18}$) glass doped with 0.34 mol% Cr_2O_3. By direct comparison with chromo-aluminate spinels ($MgCr_{2x}Al_{2(1-x)}O_4$) Cr XAFS is used to determine the composition of the devitrified Cr species. This is identified as $MgCr_{0.18}Al_{1.82}O_4$, which can be directly related to the Cr content in the starting glass and as a result the total crystalline volume in the fully developed ceramic is predicted to be 4%. *In situ* WAXS not only reveals the presence of the spinel phase but also a silica-rich stuffed quartz phase. This grows independently of the spinel and is probably nucleated from the glass surface. From our knowledge of the compositions of both crystalline phases we are able to deduce that the SAXS contrast between the surrounding glass and the spinel crystallites is 30 times greater than that between the quartz crystallites and the glass matrix, and therefore dominates the measured scattered intensity and the SAXS invariant that is derived from it. As a consequence we are able to show that the spinel crystalline volume fraction inherent in the SAXS is in close agreement with the 4% value obtained from the Cr XAFS. Furthermore *in situ* SAXS reveals the gradual development of the spinel particle size and shape during heat treatment. This is conducted in the super-cooled region just above the glass transition temperature, T_g. By employing a two-step annealing process nucleation can be separated from growth and from time-resolved SAXS measurements the alumino-chromate nanocrystals are found to be closely monodispersed. Over a total time course of 600 min they grow from rough crystallites to smooth spherical particles of radius 21 ± 2 nm, with a final density of $(1.2 \pm 0.4) \times 10^{21}$ m^{-3}. As the process of ceramic formation takes place in the viscous melt, growth is indeed found to be limited by diffusion and is complete when all the Cr is exhausted. We use this comprehensive *in situ* study of crystallisation in cordierite glass to demonstrate the advantages of combining SAXS, WAXS and XAFS for probing the time-resolved chemistry, the microstructure and its development from nucleation sites, that underpins the processing of nanoparticle ceramics.

DOI: 10.1039/b202331h

1. Introduction

Cordierite glass ceramics have the special properties of high resistance to thermal shock, which derives from their low expansion coefficients; low dielectric constants, associated with their optical transparency, and chemical stability, a characteristic which they share with other charge-compensated aluminosilicate network materials. This important family of glass ceramics is not only transparent like glass itself but also incorporates the special properties offered by composite materials.[1–3] These functions in cordierite ceramics currently find application as the chemically inert support for exhaust catalysts. They also offer the promise of thermally tolerant substrates for electronic packaging and, when suitably doped, potential as the matrix for tunable lasers on the one hand and solar concentrators on the other.[3–10] In common with other feldspar glass ceramics cordierite materials can be synthesised in a variety of ways. These include high temperature combustion sintering[11] and controlled devitrification at lower temperatures in the vicinity of T_g which occurs around 805 °C for cordierite.[3,4,12–15] Chemie douce techniques of sol–gel have also been used to prepare cordierite ceramics[16–18] along with colloidal reaction methods.[5] In the present study we have used two-stage devitrification with the objective of preparing fine-grained material.[1] By doping with Cr, annealing close to T_g ensures the creation of numerous nucleation sites and, if this is followed by prolonged heat treatment at slightly higher temperatures, crystalline growth is distributed and can be controlled to limit particles to nanometre dimensions. In this way optical opaqueness can be avoided and enhanced thermal and mechanical properties developed.

In earlier calorimetric work on powdered cordierite, glass crystallisation kinetics were found to depend on particle size,[27] with Avrami analysis pointing to crystallisation growth being promoted by surface nucleation. Two crystallisation exotherms emerged above T_g identified with μ-cordierite, a stuffed quartz, and α-cordierite ($Mg_2Al_4Si_5O_{18}$). Small angle neutron scattering (SANS) and EPR measurements on non-powdered solid samples, doped as here with Cr, revealed the formation of a spinel phase within the cordierite glass matrix with growth dynamics indicative of the formation of spherical crystallites.[15] In our study we have employed combined synchrotron radiation techniques,[20–23] bringing together Cr K-edge XAFS with SAXS/WAXS. This has allowed the structural physics and chemistry of the complex devitrification processes to be clarified. Preliminary results[24–27] established qualitatively the development of crystallization in the Cr environment using XAFS, identified the co-precipitation of a spinel and a stuffed quartz phase with WAXS and, in parallel SAXS measurements, the broad changes in microstructure from the annealed to the devitrified glass. In this paper we present the results of new XAFS experiments on Cr-doped cordierite glass employing the two-tier heat treatment and directly compare those with results from a range of model chromoaluminate spinels ($MgCr_{2x}Al_{2(1-x)}O_4$). Earlier SAXS/WAXS results[26] have now been augmented with additional heat treatments to afford a comprehensive analysis of the development of the microstructure and crystallography. We are now able to report quantitative details of nucleation and growth at each stage of development of these fine-grained cordierite glass ceramics: the geometry of the nucleating site, the size and shape of the crystallites that are precipitated and their density and composition.

2. Experimental methods and results

2.1. Cr XAFS

Glass making techniques are well-catalogued elsewhere.[2] Cr XAFS measurements were made from bulk glass specimens, heated *ex situ* at 875 °C for 4 h to nucleate followed by soaking at 900 °C, 1000 °C and 1100 °C in a muffle furnace for ceramic growth. Quenched material was then powdered for fluorescence measurements on station 8.1[28] at the Synchrotron Radiation Source (SRS) using a multi-element Ge solid state detector.[29] Model chromo-aluminate spinels, $MgCr_{2x}Al_{2(1-x)}O_4$ ($x = 0.09, 0.18, 0.25, 0.35$ and 1) were prepared by sintering $MgAl_2O_4$ with different amounts of Cr_2O_3 at 1200 °C, grinding, resintering and finally powdering for measurement. Because of their higher Cr concentrations, XAFS for the spinels was measured in transmission geometry. With a total data collection time of $\sim$3 h for each spectrum and a 200 mA circulating SRS beam, fine structure was analysable out to a maximum k value of $\sim$12 Å^{-1}. The photoelectron wavevector is defined by $k = \sqrt{2m_e(E - E_0)}/\hbar$, where E is the X-ray energy and E_0 is the origin of the free electron energy. The X-ray energy $E = hc/\lambda$ extended up to 1000 eV above the Cr K-edge at 5.99 keV.

Normalised Cr K-edge XAFS data for the glasses are presented in Fig. 1 and for the chromo-aluminate spinels in Fig. 2. Data reduction was completed using EXBACK and EXCURVE was employed to determine the local structure by least squares refinement.[30] The Cr XAFS spectra and

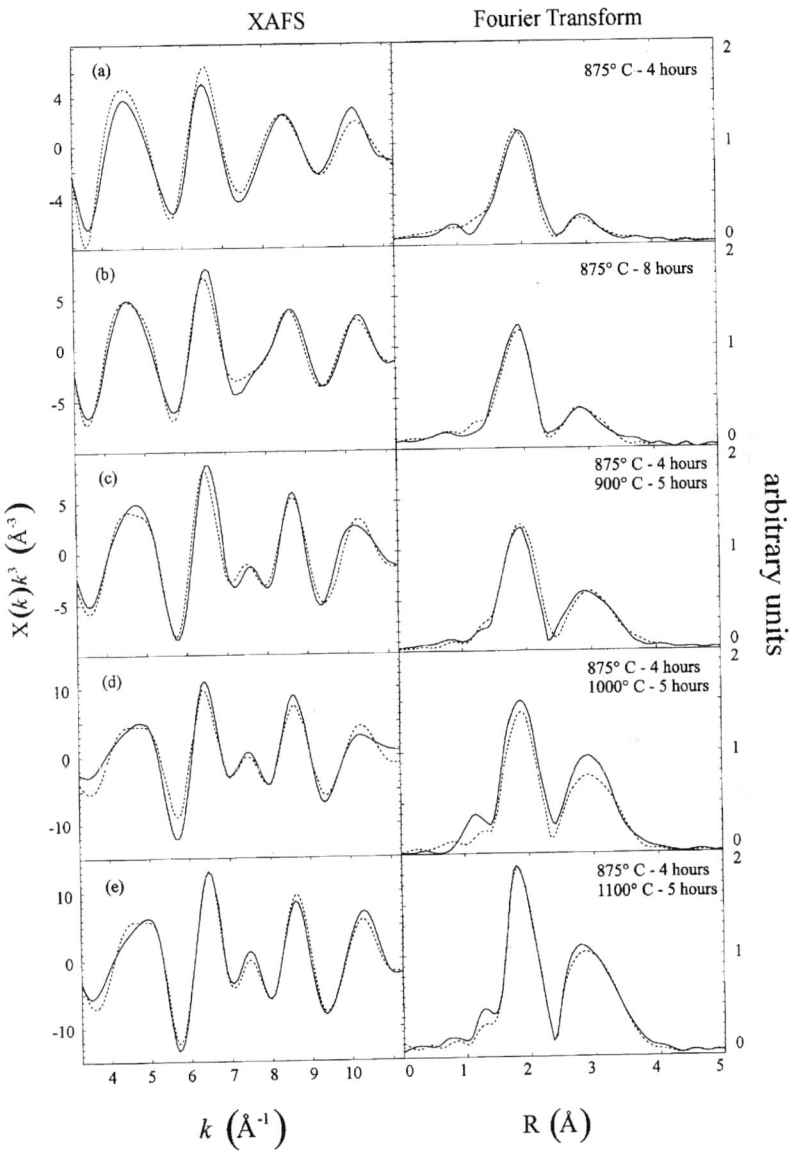

Fig. 1 Chromium K-edge XAFS for Cr-doped $Mg_2Al_4Si_5O_{18}$ powdered glass and glass ceramics obtained using fluorescent detection. Data collection was at room temperature for quenched specimens having the following heat treatment: Annealed at 875 °C for 4 h (a), 875 °C for 8 h (b), 875 °C for 4 h and 900 °C for 5 h (c), 875 °C for 4 h and 1000 °C for 5 h (d), 875 °C for 4 h and 1100 °C for 5 h (e). Experiments are shown by solid curves with theory indicated by dashed curves. The local environments modelled using EXCURVE[30] are listed in Table 1. (Energy range used: 28 eV to 480 eV. Values for Cr 1s photoelectron parameters: AFAC = 0.70, VPI = −4.00 eV, $E_0 = 0$ eV and $E_F = -4.4$ eV).

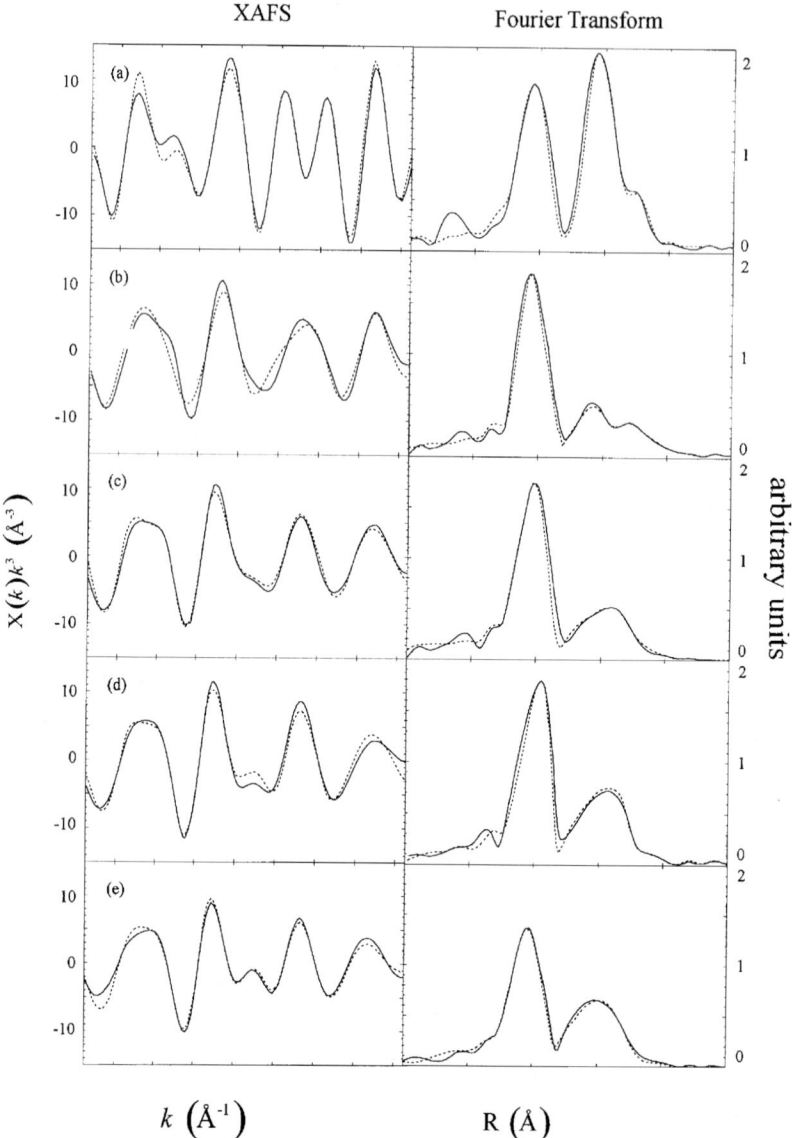

Fig. 2 Chromium K-edge XAFS for $MgCr_{2x}Al_{2(1-x)}O_4$ powdered spinels measured at room temperature in transmission. The compositions are $x = 1$ (a), $x = 0.35$ (b), $x = 0.25$ (c), $x = 0.18$ (d) and $x = 0.09$ (e). Solid curves are experimental data and dashed curves the result of theoretical fitting using EXCURVE[30] to the model environments catalogued in Table 1. (Energy range used: 28 eV to 500 eV. Values for Cr 1s photoelectron parameters: AFAC = 0.70, VPI = -4.00 eV, $E_0 = 0$ eV and $E_F = -4.1$ eV).

the corresponding Fourier transforms in Fig. 1 follow changes in the Cr environment from the annealed $Mg_2Al_4Si_5O_{18}$ glass through nucleation to complete crystallisation of the glass ceramic. The XAFS modulates from the almost single oscillation related to well-defined nearest neighbours typical of a glass (Fig. 1(a)) to the beating of several interatomic distances characteristic of a crystalline environment with several well-defined shells of atoms (Fig. 1(e)).[29] We note in line with earlier EPR data[31] that there is no difference in local structure between the quenched glass and the glass annealed at 875 °C for 4 h. However, when the duration of annealing is increased to 8 h some re-ordering in the Cr environment is discernible. It is also noticeable in Fig. 1 that the average amplitude of the XAFS oscillations steadily increases over the whole temperature range, approximately doubling from that of the homogeneous glass to the heterogeneous devitrified glass ceramic. This reflects significant order developing around Cr sites in the glass ceramic compared to the starting homogeneous glass.[25,26] Radical changes are also evident in the spectra of the $MgCr_{2x}Al_{2(1-x)}O_4$ spinels as the chromate component falls from $MgCr_2O_4$ to $MgCr_{0.18}Al_{1.82}O_4$ (Fig. 2). In this single-phase alloy series, developments in fine structure are almost solely attributable to changes in the Cr next nearest neighbour cations, Al^{3+} and Cr^{3+}. Comparing changes from spectrum to spectrum, it is clear that there are significant spectroscopic differences between compositions, suggesting that this sequence might be used to fingerprint chromo-aluminate spinels of unknown composition. Indeed, if we turn to the Cr XAFS of the fully heat-treated glass ceramic shown in Fig. 1(e), there is quite clearly a striking resemblance between this and the chromium XAFS spectrum for the spinel with composition $MgCr_{0.18}Al_{1.82}O_4$ (Fig. 2(e)).

2.2. SAXS/WAXS

SAXS/WAXS experiments were performed on station 8.2 at the SRS.[22] A collimated X-ray beam of roughly 0.3×2 mm^2 with an X-ray wavelength, λ of 1.5 Å was used. The sample was positioned in the centre of curvature of a curved INEL detector which recorded WAXS patterns dispersively with scattering angles between 5° and 65°. SAXS patterns were collected with a standard Daresbury quadrant detector placed above the direct beam at a distance of 3.5 m behind the sample. The sample holder allowed the collection of a scattering vector range, $q = 4\pi\sin\theta/\lambda = 2\pi/d$, of 0.008–0.2 Å^{-1}, where d is the microstructural length scale.

Monolithic specimens were cut and polished for *in situ* SAXS/WAXS measurements which were conducted in an adapted Linkam THM1500 furnace. Samples were given a pre-heat treatment at 875 °C for 4 h before the temperature was raised to the value for isothermal crystallisation: 920 °C, 940 °C, 970 C and 1040 °C. Representative SAXS/WAXS curves for 970 °C are plotted in Fig. 3. Data reduction of time-resolved SAXS was performed with the XOTOKO package[32] and subsequent analysis by using the software package PDH.[33] Corrected SAXS profiles reveal the microstructural developments that occur with crystalline growth (Fig. 3(a)). As the glass ceramic develops the SAXS intensity saturates and a clear bump in the data can be seen in the wave vector region of 0.03 Å^{-1} moving to lower q-values in time. WAXS patterns for the same frames reveal the diffuse scattering in the starting annealed glass being altered by the growth of diffraction peaks (Fig. 3(b)). We detected no evidence for phase separation taking place within the vitreous phase, either in the pretreatment or in the post treatment. Within the crystallising component the two crystalline phases are readily differentiated, stuffed quartz (sq) and spinel (sp). The development of the features in SAXS and WAXS evident in Fig. 3 is typical for all the temperature treatments we have examined, the main differences between annealing runs relate to the speed with which crystallisation advances. We note that as diffraction lines develop the underlying diffuse scattering diminishes but does not disappear, indicating the retention of glass in the final ceramic.

3. Analysis of Cr XAFS

3.1. Local structure in mixed spinels and the composition of the spinel precipitated in the glass ceramic

The following procedure was employed to ensure consistency in the analysis of the different local structures for Cr in the glass and glass ceramics. $MgCr_2O_4$ was used as the primary model compound to ensure that the electron scattering factors and photoelectron parameters correctly predicted the Cr environment in the spinel structure from crystallography.[34] The first three 6-atom shells: $R_{Cr-O} = 1.99$ Å, $R_{Cr-Cr} = 2.96$ Å and $R_{Cr-Mg} = 3.49$ Å, are all well-reproduced and the theoretical XAFS curve closely follows experiment (Fig. 2(a)). In modelling the chromium XAFS of the mixed spinel series, $MgCr_{2x}Al_{2(1-x)}O_4$ (Fig. 2(b)–(e)), a Cr–Al shell was added to the 2.96 Å Cr–Cr shell and the co-ordination numbers of the two cation shells were weighted in proportion to the composition. Maintaining an overall oxygen co-ordination number, N_O, of 6, R_{Cr-X} and σ^2_{Cr-X} values were then allowed to float for all four shells. The photoelectron wave vector range which is $3 < k < 11$ Å^{-1} gives a bandpass limit on atomic shell separation, ΔR, of ~ 0.3 Å.[35] The chromium

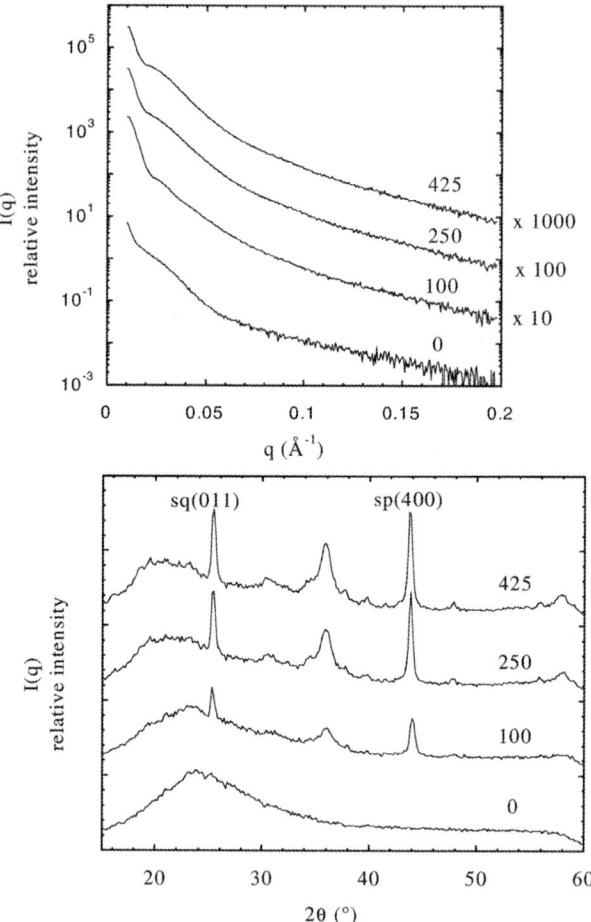

Fig. 3 Representative SAXS profile showing the development of structure during the heat treatment (top). The numbers in the graph denote the elapsed time since the temperature was raised to the final temperature (970 °C). The central intensity, indicating the growth of large-scale structure, increases rapidly and then becomes constant. The broad form factor bump around $q = 0.03$ Å^{-1} increases in intensity and slightly shifts towards lower q-values. The corresponding WAXS curves are shown below. Two peaks belonging to the stuffed quartz and spinel phase respectively are indicated. For clarity all curves are displaced by a constant offset in the vertical direction.

sites analysed from the XAFS spectra are tabulated in Table 1 together with corresponding errors in N_B, R_{A-B} and σ^2_{A-B}.[29] As the chromate component, x, decreases from 1 to 0.09 little or no change is observed in the geometry of the octahedral nearest neighbour oxygen shell (Table 1). The chromium/aluminium shell, however, which is located at 2.96 Å in MgCr$_2$O$_4$, splits into two sub shells as MgAl$_2$O$_4$ replaces MgCr$_2$O$_4$, with $R_{Cr-Al} \sim 2.9$ Å and $R_{Cr-Cr} \sim 3.2$ Å. This is expected for mixed spinel compositions.

We have already noted the close similarity in the Cr XAFS between the mixed spinel MgCr$_{0.18}$Al$_{01.82}$O$_4$ (Fig. 2(e)) and the fully heat-treated glass ceramic structure (Fig. 1(e)). Certainly there is no similarity between Cr XAFS for the heat-treated glasses and Cr XAFS for MgCr$_2$O$_4$, nor with XAFS for any of the mixed spinels, apart from MgCr$_{0.18}$Al$_{01.82}$O$_4$. This points to the latter as the most likely composition of the devitrified chromate species in Cr-doped Mg$_2$Al$_4$Si$_5$O$_{18}$ glass. Accordingly, the O, Al, Cr and Mg shell radii and coordination numbers analysed for MgCr$_{0.18}$Al$_{01.82}$O$_4$ XAFS were used to model the Cr environment in the fully heat-treated glass.

Table 1 Results of fitting with the EXCURVE program room temperature Cr K-edge XAFS spectra for heat-treated Cr-doped cordierite glass $Mg_2Al_4Si_5O_{18}$ and for chromate spinels $MgCr_{2x}Al_{2(1-x)}O_4$ ($x = 0.09$, 0.18, 0.25, 0.35 and 1). Co-ordination numbers, N_X, inter-atomic distances, R_{Cr-X}, and Debye–Waller factors, $2\sigma^2_{Cr-O}$, are given for the nearest neighbour oxygens and the next nearest neighbour cations: aluminium, chromium and magnesium. Photoelectron parameters, $AFAC = 0.7$, $VPI = -4.0$ eV, $E_0 = 0$, were refined against the crystallographic structure of $MgCr_2O_4$. These were then used with an additional aluminium shell to fit the spinels and $Mg_2Al_4Si_5O_{18}$ glass. For the $Mg_2Al_4Si_5O_{18}$ glass ceramics, upper figures refer to the glass component and lower figures to the crystalline component. The percentage of chromium crystallized is given in italics

Sample	$N_O \pm$ 0.5 atom	$R_{Cr-O}/\text{Å} \pm$ 0.01 Å	$2\sigma^2_{Cr-O}/\text{Å}^2 \pm$ 0.002 Å²	$N_{Al} \pm$ 0.5 atom	$R_{Cr-Al}/\text{Å} \pm$ 0.02 Å	$2\sigma^2_{Cr-Al}/\text{Å}^2 \pm$ 0.003 Å²	$N_{Cr} \pm$ 0.5 atom	$R_{Cr-Cr}/\text{Å} \pm$ 0.02 Å	$2\sigma^2_{Cr-Cr}/\text{Å}^2 \pm$ 0.003 Å²	$N_{Mg} \pm$ 0.5 atom	$R_{Cr-Mg}/\text{Å} \pm$ 0.02 Å	$2\sigma^2_{Cr-Mg}/\text{Å}^2 \pm$ 0.003 Å²
$MgCr_2O_4$	6	1.99	0.005	4	2.87	0.018	6	2.96	0.006	6	3.49	0.007
$MgCr_{0.70}Al_{1.30}O_4$	6	1.99	0.004	4.5	2.88	0.021	2	2.96	0.018	6	3.46	0.015
$MgCr_{0.50}Al_{1.50}O_4$	6	1.98	0.004	5	2.88	0.013	1.5	3.10	0.021	6	3.44	0.028
$MgCr_{0.36}Al_{1.64}O_4$	6	1.98	0.005	5.5	2.88	0.013	1	3.12	0.013	6	3.39	0.020
$MgCr_{0.18}Al_{1.82}O_4$	6	1.98	0.008	5.5	2.89	0.013	0.5	3.19	0.013	6	3.36	0.022
g-$Mg_2Al_4Si_5O_{18}$ 875°C 4h 1100°C 5h	6 *100%*	1.98	0.003	5.5	2.88	0.005	0.5	3.20	0.005	6	3.38	0.013
g-$Mg_2Al_4Si_5O_{18}$ 875°C 4h	4.4 *94%* 0.3	1.98	0.003 0.012	4.1 0.3	2.88 2.82	0.005 0.042	0.4	3.20	0.005	4.4	3.38	0.013
g-$Mg_2Al_4Si_5O_{18}$ 875°C 4h 1000°C 5h	3.2 *68%* 1.5	2.00 1.98	0.012 0.003	1.5 2.9	2.82 2.88	0.042 0.005	0.3	3.20	0.005	3.2	3.38	0.013
g-$Mg_2Al_4Si_5O_{18}$ 875°C 4h 900°C 5h	1.3 *24%* 4.2	2.00 1.98	0.012 0.003	1.2 4.2	2.82 2.82	0.005 0.042	0.1	3.20	0.005	1.3	3.38	0.013
g-$Mg_2Al_4Si_5O_{18}$ 875°C 8h	*0%* 6	2.00	0.012	6	2.82	0.042						

From Table 1 it can be seen that there is little or no change in the interatomic distances and coordination numbers returned from analysis of the Cr-doped cordierite glass ceramic, confirming the XAFS for $MgCr_{0.18}Al_{01.82}O_4$ as the spectroscopic fingerprint of the spinel devitrified from $Mg_2Al_4Si_5O_{18}$ glass. On the other hand, the Debye–Waller factors returned from analysing Cr XAFS for the fully heat-treated cordierite glass ceramic (Table 1) are significantly smaller than for the mixed spinel, values lying closer to those found for the ordered spinel $MgCr_2O_4$. This improvement in local order around Cr in nanocrystalline compared to polycrystalline $MgCr_{0.18}Al_{01.82}O_4$ may well result from the fact that crystallites formed in the glass are finely dispersed, in contrast to the model spinel which was prepared by sintering from polycrystalline mixtures. Indeed Wagner and Kampermann[36] conclude that, in general, for a hard particle embedded in a softer matrix, a smooth sphere represents the minimum strain energy shape.

3.2. Progress of crystallisation around Cr in doped cordierite glass

Turning now to the annealed glass, XAFS analysis of Cr (Fig. 1(a)) reveals two 6-fold shells, one containing oxygens for which $R_{Cr-O} = 2.00$ Å and the other aluminiums (or silicons) for which $R_{Cr-Al/Si} = 2.82$ Å (Table 1). In this case the Debye–Waller factors are now much increased compared to the Cr in nanocrystalline spinel within the glass ceramic, with $2\sigma^2_{Cr-O}$ rising from 0.003 Å^2 to 0.012 Å^2 and $2\sigma^2_{Cr-Al/Si}$ rising from 0.005 Å^2 to 0.042 Å^2. In particular, the considerable disorder of the shell of nearest neighbour cations revealed by Cr XAFS is typical of local cation environments in oxide glass structures.[29] Interestingly there is no measurable difference in the Cr XAFS spectra between the glass annealed at 875 °C for 4 h and the as-quenched material. We conclude therefore that Cr remains dissolved in the cordierite glass matrix at 875 °C, for at least 4 h, and that the nucleating sites in subsequent heat treatments are initially non-crystalline. This is consistent with the absence of any SAXS intensity at the start of isothermal growth.

Cr XAFS spectra for intermediate heat-treated states (Fig. 1(b)–(d)) were fitted by constraint using two Cr environments: the annealed cordierite glass (Fig. 1(a)) and the fully heat-treated glass ceramic (Fig. 1(e)). Because the respective differences between R_{Cr-O} and R_{Cr-Cr} analysed for the annealed glass and the fully heat-treated ceramic (see Table 1) are much smaller than 0.3 Å, ΔR set by the bandpass, these and their corresponding Debye–Waller factors were fixed and only the coordination numbers allowed to vary in modelling the different XAFS spectra. The crystalline percentage of $MgCr_{0.18}Al_{01.82}O_4$ in the Cr-doped cordierite glass deduced in this way is shown by italics in Table 1, rising from 0% in the annealed glass to 100% in the fully heat-treated glass ceramic. The XAFS sequence shown in Fig. 1, demonstrates how the 0.21 atom% of chromium dissolved into cordierite glass eventually becomes fully crystalline. Given the level of precision inherent in XAFS modeling,[29] the fraction of nucleating chromium remaining undetected in the vitreous state is estimated to be less than 10%, *i.e.* < 200 ppm.

4. SAXS/WAXS analysis

At low q values the scattered intensity, $I(q)$, is given by

$$I(q) = C\exp\left(-\frac{R_g^2 q^2}{3}\right); q = 2\pi/d \qquad (1)$$

where R_g is the radius of gyration. $I(0)$ can be obtained by extrapolation.[33] In principle eqn. (1) is only correct for small scattering angles and for spherical scatterers but holds surprisingly well for numerous other shapes.[37] In the case of spherical particles R_g is related to the real particle radius, R, via:

$$R_g = \sqrt{\frac{3}{5}}R \qquad (2)$$

In the high q range of the SAXS, the scattered intensity is given by the relation:

$$I(q) = K_1 + \frac{K_2}{q^\alpha} \qquad (3)$$

where K_1 is the so-called thermal background, K_2 is the Porod constant and α is a parameter influenced by the dimensionality and the surface roughness of the scattering particles. For smooth 3-dimensional particles $\alpha = 4$ whereas for rough surfaces or where there are interface density gradients the exponent is smaller.

In a two-phase system the SAXS invariant is given by:

$$Q(t) = \int_{q=0}^{q=\infty} q^2 I(q,t) \mathrm{d}q = C(\Delta\rho)^2 \nu_1 (1-\nu_1) \qquad (4)$$

in which $\Delta\rho$ is the electron density contrast between the two phases and ν_1 the volume fraction of one of the two components. Q is a very sensitive measure of the amount of microstructural development in the sample[37] and is dominated by the intensity in the low q region, being sensitive both to the volume fractions of the phases present as well as to the electron density contrast between them. For smooth particles Q is related to the surface to volume ratio, S/V, for all of the scattering particles whilst $I(0)$ is related to the average volume of each particle.

Crystalline phases can be identified from their powder patterns (Fig. 3) and the proportions of each component from the integrated intensity of characteristic diffraction lines $I_{nlm}(t) = \int_{q_2}^{q_1} I(q,t) \mathrm{d}q$. Similarly the proportions of the amorphous component due to the glass matrix can be obtained approximately from $I_{\mathrm{amorph}}(t) = \int_{q_{\min}}^{q_{\max}} I_{\mathrm{background}}(q,t) \mathrm{d}q$, where $I_{\mathrm{background}}$ is the diffuse scattering $q_{\min}$ and $q_{\max}$ are given by the range of the WAXS measurements, 0.365 and 4.501 Å^{-1} respectively.

4.1. Time dependent SAXS and WAXS parameters and evidence for spherical monodispersed particles

In Fig. 4 the different parameters $I(q=0)$, R_g, S/V, K_2, and Q derived from *in situ* SAXS as a function of time are shown for isothermal heat treatment at 940 °C and 1040 °C. Also included are the proportions of the crystalline phases, spinel and stuffed quartz obtained from the integrated areas, I_{nlm}, determined simultaneously from *in situ* WAXS. A wealth of information is contained in these figures and we will now highlight some of the details.

The time profiles of all the SAXS/WAXS parameters exhibit similar behaviour leading to saturation of crystallisation at the highest temperatures. At these the initial increase in the R_g is followed by an "overshoot" and then a slow decay, which after some time levels out. In general though R_g stabilises around a value of 180 ± 20 Å, which from eqn. (2) leads to a spherical particle radius of 230 ± 25 Å. This is consistent with earlier X-ray experiments on the same system.[24] It is noteworthy in Fig. 4 that at roughly the same moment R_g *stops* increasing the dimension parameter α (eqn. (3)), which identifies surface roughness, stabilises at a value not far from 4 which suggests that particles with a smooth surface have formed. This sequence indicates that, initially, when the crystallites are small but are growing fast a rough surface is formed at the interface with the surrounding glass. Subsequently, as growth slows down, the roughness of the interface reduces in order to minimise the surface energy leading to larger particles being nearly smooth and thus to a q^{-4} dependence in the scattered intensity $I(q,t)$.

For monodispersed spherical particles the coherent scattered intensity at $I(q=0)$ is given by:[38]

$$I(0) = k \frac{N_p V_p^2}{N} (\Delta\rho)^2$$

in which k is a scaling constant, N is the number of atoms in the irradiated sample volume, N_p the number of scattering particles, V_p the volume of each scattering particle and $\Delta\rho$ the electron density difference between the two phases. For spherical particles $V_p = 4\pi R_g^2/3$ so

$$I(0) \propto N_p (\Delta\rho)^2 R_g^6 \qquad (5)$$

If a constant electron density difference, $\Delta\rho$, between the amorphous matrix and the growing particles is assumed, the development of the number of particles N_p can be judged from the ratio of

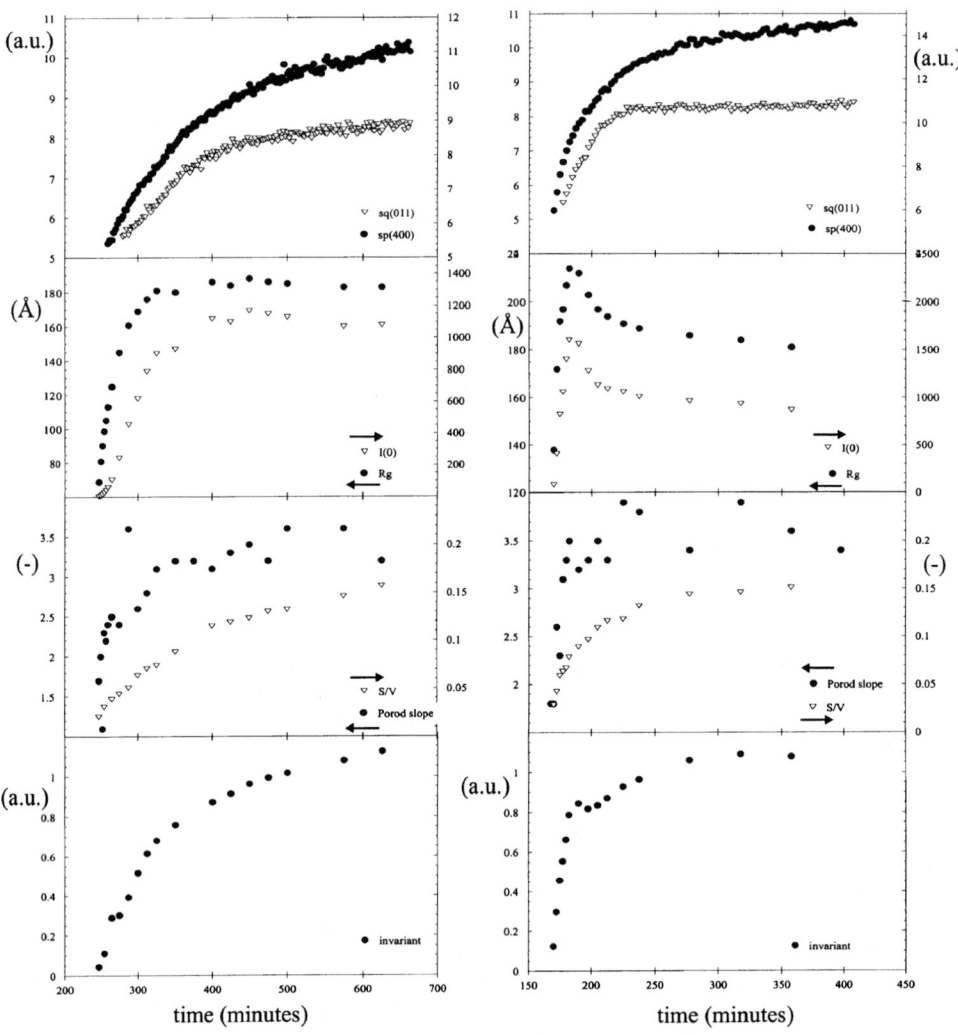

Fig. 4 Parameters derived from SAXS/WAXS for isothermal crystalisation studies on cordierite glasses. The virgin material was given a pre-heat treatment for 4 h at 875 °C before being heated at 920 °C, 940 °C, 970 °C and 1040 °C of which results for 940 °C (left) and 1040 °C (right) are shown here. The top row shows the integrated peak intensity from two representative peaks of spinel and stuffed quartz. The second row shows the size development of R_g (left scale) and the $I(0)$ (right scale). In the third row the evolution of the constants derived from the Porod eqn. (3) are given. In the last row the development of the invariant Q is depicted. For explanations see text.

$I(0)/(R_g)^{6.39}$ In Fig. 5 values of R_g^6 vs. $I(0)$ are plotted for all data sets in the early part of the devitrification whilst the R_g is still growing. Within the error margins we see that R_g^6 vs. $I(0)$ is linear for each isothermal run and hence the particles are spherical in shape. By contrast, if crystalline growth is by Ostwald ripening, where the crystalline volume fraction, V, is fixed, $I(0) \propto R_g^3$. We find no evidence for this type of growth behaviour in any of our experiments. The linearity of R_g^6 vs. $I(0)$ corroborates earlier findings of Durville for a single stage heat treatment SANS measurement.[15] Over the same time course, we also find a linear relation between R_g^2 and t. This is indicative of a diffusive process because if the particle composition is fixed

$$R_g \propto (Dt)^{1/2}$$

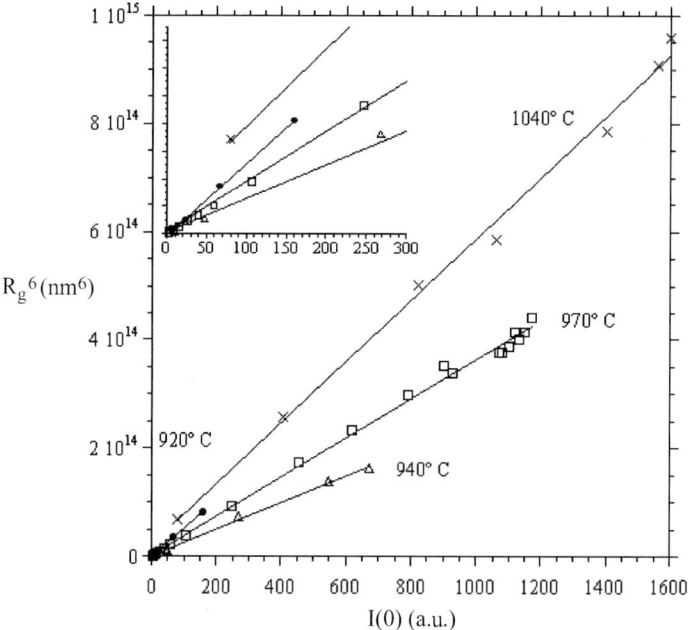

Fig. 5 The relation between R_g^6 and $I(0)$ in the early stages of development when the R_g is still increasing. The insert shows the earliest stage. The determination of $I(0)$ is believed to be accurate to 5% of the value and R_g to approximately 3%. With these error margins the linear correlation between these two parameters is a striking indication of spherical growth for a fixed number of particles in the amorphous matrix.

where D is the diffusion coefficient.[36] At later stages we find that this relation breaks down, which is to be expected if growth is dependent on the supply of Cr from the surrounding glass matrix.

We have already noted in Fig. 3 the development of a form factor feature in the SAXS $I(q,t)$ in the vicinity of 0.03 Å^{-1} as crystallinity advances. An interesting phenomenon, observed in data from the 970 °C experiment, is the appearance of a secondary maximum which is illustrated in Fig. 6, indicating an increased degree of monodispersity. At later stages, beyond the overshoot in R_g and $I(0)$, this secondary maximum disappears. The existence of a time window in which a narrowing of the size distribution curve occurs has been seen in other systems and is considered to be a fingerprint of heterogeneous nucleation.[39] The tendency to become less monodispersed as growth advances is a logical consequence of the statistical distribution of nucleation sites. By the time growth has stabilised and crystallites have attained similar sizes any further development will mean that some crystallites may start to overlap and merge into larger objects.

Since it was difficult to accurately assess the position of the second maximum, the position of the first maxima and minima in Fig. 6 were fitted using

$$I(q) = C \left[3 \frac{\sin qR - qR \cos qR}{(qR)^3} \right]^2 \tag{6}$$

employing the R values obtained earlier from the Guinier region as starting values. The radii obtained in this way closely match the increase in particle size with time determined from eqns. (1) and (2). The final values, however, are approximately 20 Å shorter i.e. $R = 210$ Å compared to 230 Å. It is well known that the Guinier radius from a polydispersed system is biased towards the larger aggregates[38] which again suggests that the system may drift from monodispersion in the final stages of growth.

Using eqn. (3), and the size obtained from determination of the form factor peak positions, we can make an estimate of the volume fraction that the scattering spheres occupy. If we assume that

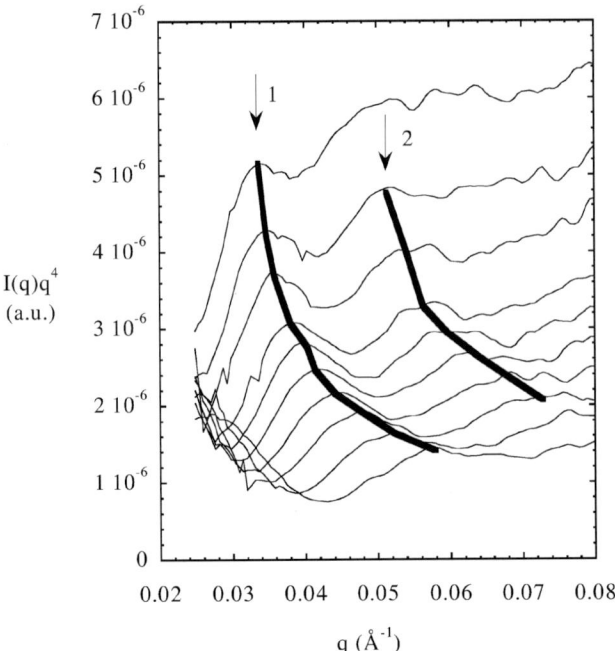

Fig. 6 $I(q)q^4$ vs. q plots of several timeframes of the sample crystallised at 970 °C. The intensity is multiplied by q^4 in order to highlight the weak structural features. No physical significance should be attributed to this. The broad lines connect the maxima of the peaks whose positions were determined by taking the average value between the local minima between the peaks.

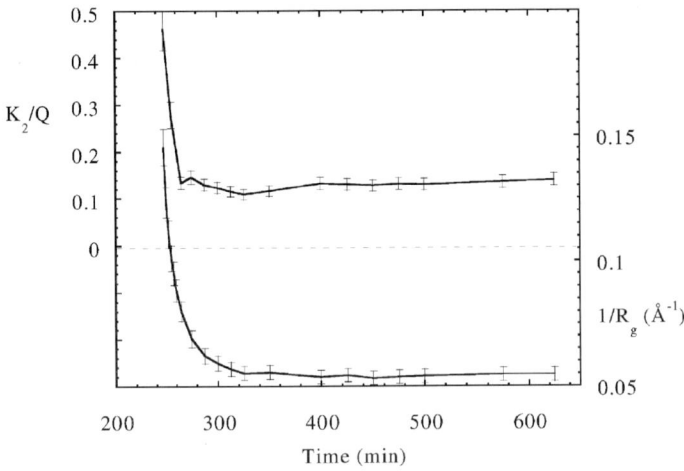

Fig. 7 Time development of the ratio K_2/Q (top) compared with $1/R_g$ (bottom) for treatment at 970 °C. The first ratio has a linear relation with the total internal surface to volume ratio S/V (eqn. (7)). For a system composed of spheres the S/V ratio has a linear relation with $1/R_g$. Within the error margins both curves have the same time development.

there is a fixed number of spherical crystallites, N_p, the total internal surface to volume ratio, S/V, can be determined by taking the ratio of K_2 and Q, which in time will be correlated with $1/R_g$. Both of these curves are plotted in Fig. 7 for the 970 °C measurement and the time correlation between them is accurate within the error margins. By using the exact relation[40]

$$\frac{K_2}{Q} = \frac{1}{\pi}\frac{S}{V} \qquad (7)$$

in combination with assuming a fixed number of particles and applying Babinet's principle we can calculate the total volume fraction occupied by spherical crystallites, ν. This is approximately 0.04 ± 0.02 and is independent of the electron density differences between the scattering phases. It is in reasonable agreement with simulations performed by Durville[15] who reported a value of 2.6% for the crystallised volume.

5. Discussion

Isothermal crystallisation experiments performed at different temperatures in principle enable a glass ceramic system to be studied over a wide range of devitrification, lower temperatures providing insights into the earliest stages of growth with higher temperatures probing the later stages. In this way an artificial time scale can be created allowing detailed analysis of crystallisation from start to finish. The present XAFS (Fig. 1) and SAXS/WAXS (Fig. 4) experiments on Cr-doped cordierite glass demonstrate the usefulness of this approach.

5.1. Cr content and crystalline volume

The degree of crystallinity of chromium sites for the different heat-treatments given in Table 1 taken together with the development of SAXS/WAXS parameters in Fig. 4 reveal how, within experimental error, all of the chromium becomes consumed as the crystallisation advances to the final glass ceramic. Starting with 0.34 mol% dissolved Cr_2O_3 as the nucleating agent and sufficient surrounding cordierite glass to match the chromo-aluminate composition $MgCr_{0.18}Al_{1.82}O_4$, we can write:

$$0.09Cr_2O_3 + 3Mg_2Al_4Si_5O_{18} \Rightarrow MgCr_{0.18}Al_{1.82}O_4 + 3Mg_{1.67}Al_{3.39}Si_5O_{16.7} \qquad (8)$$

If devitrification is restricted by the quantity of chromium present, 0.21 atom%, then the volume crystalline fraction of spinel, ν, is given by

$$\nu = \frac{V_{spinel}}{3V_{glass}} \qquad (9)$$

where V_{spinel} and V_{glass} are the molecular volumes of the spinel and the cordierite glass respectively. From the composition and density of spinel, V_{spinel} equals 60.9 Å^3 whilst for cordierite glass, V_{glass} equals 440 Å^3. Hence from eqn. (9) the crystalline volume fraction of spinel, ν, is 0.046 ± 0.01, the error being given by the 25% uncertainty of the chromo-aluminate composition (Fig. 1(e), Fig. 2(e) and Table 1). This is in excellent agreement with the value of 0.04 ± 0.02 obtained above from the SAXS parameters exploiting eqn. (7).

5.2. Determining crystallite sizes

From our SAXS experiments the particles that devitrify at all isothermal temperatures are clearly closely spherical, certainly initially (Fig. 5), and their final size deduced from R obtained from R_g (eqn. (2)) stabilises around 230 Å. The R_g value of 180 Å obtained here with X-rays is somewhat larger than that of 120 Å reported from SANS measurements.[15] SANS profiles, however, are dominated by oxygen scattering from the alumino-silicate network. For X-rays, on the other hand, scattering from oxygen is least whilst that from Cr is greatest. We conclude, therefore, that most of the SAXS intensity $I(q,t)$ is due to the Cr-rich phase, even though Cr only makes up a small percentage of the total volume. This will be quantified later when the electron densities of the spinel, stuffed quartz and glass phases are compared. By contrast the SANS intensity should carry a prominent contribution from density fluctuations in the glass matrix as well as from the spinel phase nucleated from Cr. On the other hand, since stuffed quartz is the predominant phase precipitated from cordierite glass *in the absence* of Cr and is accentuated by use of powdered specimens,[19] it is reasonable to speculate that spinel is nucleated from Cr centres within the bulk and that stuffed quartz is seeded from intrinsic defects which are likely to reside on the surface. Indeed we find that the time dependence of the two crystalline phases obtained from WAXS shows that the formation of stuffed quartz is always delayed. The growth of stuffed quartz appears to be independent of the growth of spinel, which is also consistent with there being different types of nucleating sites for each crystalline component. There is no sign from Fig. 4 that one crystalline phase grows at the expense of the other.

Morinaga[41] reports devitrification experiments on cordierite glass using a single step heat treatment resulting in crystalline particles with dimensions up to 1000 Å. In the present work particle sizes do not exceed 300 Å, which highlights the role of the two-tier heat treatment employed. The pre-treatment results in the creation of a much larger number of nucleation sites so that the resulting crystallites are smaller and more numerous than single-stage heat treatment at similar temperatures.

In their SANS analysis of Cr-doped cordierite Durville *et al.*[15] utilise the factorisation of the scattered intensity into the form factor $|P(q)|^2$ and the structure factor $S(q)$

$$I(q) = I(0)|P(q)|^2 S(q)$$

in order to calculate $S(q)$ under an assumption for $|P(q)|^2$ based on the size of the particles, $4\pi R_g^3/3$. This technique of dividing out the form factor scattering from the experimental data in order to study the structure factor is not possible with our data, since the expected feature in $S(q)$ is lower in q than we were able to measure. Still it should be remarked that this method, although theoretically sound, becomes dangerous if the population of scattering particles is not completely monodispersed. When we compare our SAXS results with the earlier SANS data we note that the peaks which we see around $q = 0.03$ Å^{-1}, which are due to the form factor, $P(q)$, are absent in the SANS data. We attribute this to the differences between X-ray and neutron scattering lengths, which make SAXS more sensitive to Cr-rich regions than to density fluctuations in the glass matrix and stuffed quartz precipitation, and *vice versa* for SANS.

5.3. Correlations between Cr spinel nanoparticles and why precipitated quartz does not feature in SAXS

The interparticle separation, L, between spinel crystallites can be deduced from:

$$L = \sqrt[1/3]{\frac{4\sqrt{2}\pi\rho_{spinel}}{3\rho_{glass}}} R \qquad (10)$$

Eqn. (10) applies to a close packed system where ρ_{spinel} is the atomic density of Cr atoms in the spinel and ρ_{glass} the atomic density of Cr atoms in the glass. From the spinel composition ρ_{spinel} is 3.0×10^{-3} Å^{-3} and from the doping level used ρ_{glass} is 1.4×10^{-4} Å^{-3}. These are the proportions incorporated into eqn. (8). Taking the spherical particle radius of 210 Å refined from the form factor (Fig. 6), eqn. (10) gives $L = 1050$ Å ± 50 Å. The crystallite number density for such a close-packed distribution of particles is 1.21×10^{15} cm^{-3} in the bulk or 1.14×10^{10} cm^{-2} at the surface. The corresponding interference function, $2\pi/L$, from this distribution of spinel particles would be expected at 0.006 Å^{-1}. This is outside the SAXS q-range but reasonably close to the structure factor peak in $S(q)$ deconvoluted from the SANS profile reported at 0.008 Å^{-1}.[15]

Finally, the electron densities of the various phases in this highly dispersed glass ceramic can be determined. From the composition, MgCr$_{0.18}$Al$_{1.82}$O$_4$, the electron density of the spinel is 1.18 Å^{-3}. By comparison the electron density of Cr-doped cordierite glass is 0.669 Å^{-3}, giving a SAXS contrast between the two, $(\Delta\rho)^2$, of 2.74×10^{-1} Å^{-6}. Taking the density of the stuffed quartz to be 2.5 g cm^{-3} gives an electron density of 0.750 Å^{-3} and so the SAXS contrast between stuffed quartz and cordierite glass is 8.28×10^{-3} Å^{-6}, 33 times smaller than the contrast between spinel and cordierite glass. Hence, since $Q(q)$ (eqn. (4)) and $I(0)$ (eqn. (5)) are both proportional to the respective values of $(\Delta\rho)^2$, it is clear that the contribution of stuffed quartz crystallites to the measured SAXS intensity is minimal, which is confirmed when the development of SAXS parameters are directly compared with the growth of integrated diffraction lines for spinel at different isothermal temperatures (Fig. 4).

6. Conclusions

The XAFS, SAXS and WAXS results presented here follow the devitrification of Cr-doped cordierite glass by a two-tier heat treatment and quantify: the composition of the spinel ceramic as $MgCr_{0.18}Al_{1.82}O_4$; the crystallites as spherical, approximately monodispersed and with a final average radius of 210 Å ± 20 Å; the final crystalline volume fraction as 0.046 ± 0.01; and the intercrystallite separation as 1050 Å ± 50 Å with a crystalline number density of $(1.21 \pm 0.4) \times 10^{15}$ cm^{-3}.

The experiments also reveal how: spinel crystallites initially grow from Cr nucleating sites with rough surfaces which gradually become smooth; the Cr nucleating site in the glass is more disordered than the final Cr site in the spinel nanoparticle; the spinel growth is limited by diffusion and is complete when all the Cr is consumed; and a second stuffed quartz phase follows the bulk nucleation of spinel from Cr but is independent and probably nucleated from surface defects.

The observation that in the intermediate stages of crystallisation a sharper particle size dimension distribution exists, as shown by the occurrence of secondary maxima in the scattering curves, is possibly of technological importance.

Finally we have shown that combined time resolved SAXS and WAXS experiments form a powerful tool for the study of devitrification in glasses. Unfortunately scattering techniques can only provide information by the time large-scale structures are being formed. The crucial stage of the initial creation of crystal nucleation sites cannot be observed with these techniques but we have shown how important XAFS can be in probing nucleation and growth at the atomic level. A combination of real time XAFS spectroscopy combined with *in situ* SAXS and WAXS would enable the structural physics and chemistry of nucleation and growth process in this and other finely dispersed glass ceramics to be elucidated in the fullest detail from beginning to end.

Acknowledgements

O. Glatter, C. M. B. Henderson, G. R. Mant, A. J. Ryan and G. Sankar are thanked for providing useful advice on several aspects of this work and the staff at the SRS are acknowledged for their help during experiments. Access to the SRS was made possible under an agreement of the Netherlands Organisation for Scientific Research (NOW) and the Central Laboratory for the Research Councils (CLRC).

References

1. B. H. W. S. de Jong, J. W. Adams, B. G. Aitken, J. E. Dickinson and G. J. Fine, *Ullman's Encyclopedia of Industrial Chemistry*, 5th edn., 1989, vol. A12, pp. 433–448.
2. J. Zarzycki, *Les Verres et l'état Vitreux*, Masson, Paris, 1982.
3. D. R. Bridge, D. Holland and P. W. McMillan, *Glass Technol.*, 1985, **26**, 286.
4. K. Watanabe and E. A. Giess, *J. Am. Ceram. Soc.*, 1985, **68**, C102–C103.
5. R. W. Dupon, A. C. Tanous and M. S. Thompson, *Chem. Mater.*, 1990, **2**, 728.
6. Y. Hirose, H. Doi and O. Kamigaito, *J. Mater. Sci. Lett.*, 1984, **3**, 153.
7. R. R. Tummala, *J. Am. Ceram. Soc.*, 1991, **66**, 874.
8. B. Andianasolo, B. Chamagnon and C. Esnouf, *J. Non-Cryst. Solids*, 1990, **126**, 103.
9. I. M. Lachman, R. D. Bagley and R. M. Lewis, *Am. Ceram. Soc. Bull.*, 1981, **60**, 202.
10. A. Kisilev, R. Reisfeld, E. Greenberg, A. Buch and M. Ish-Shalom, *Chem. Phys. Lett.*, 1984, **105**.
11. C. S. Hong, P. Ravindranathan, D. K. Agrawal and R. Roy, *J. Mater. Sci. Lett.*, 1994, **13**, 1361.
12. (a) W. Schreyer and J. F. Schairer, *Z. Kristallogr.*, 1961, **60–82**, 116; (b) W. Schreyer and J. P. Schairer, *J. Petrol.*, 1961, **2**, 361.
13. A.G. Gregory and T. J. Veary, *J. Mater. Sci.*, 1971, **6**, 1312.
14. W. Zdaniewski, *J. Am. Ceram. Soc.*, 1975, **58**, 163.
15. F. Durville, B. Champagnon, E. Duval, G. Boulon, F. Gaume, A. F. Wright and A. N. Fitch, *Phys. Chem. Glass.*, 1984, **25**, 126.
16. J. R. Moyer, A. R. Prunier, N. N. Hughes and R. C. Winterton, *Mater. Res. Soc. Symp. Proc.*, 1986, **73**, 117.

17   C. Gensse and U. Chowdry, *Mater. Res. Soc. Symp. Proc.*, 1986, **73**, 693.
18   J. C. Bernier, S. Vilminot, J. L. Rehspringer, El Hadigui and P. Poix, in *High Tech Ceramics*, ed. P. Vincenzini, Elsevier, Amsterdam, 1987, p. 1443.
19   I. W. Donald, *J. Mater. Sci.*, 1995, **30**, 904.
20   J. W. Couves, J. M. Thomas, D. Waller, R. H. Jones, A. J. Dent, G. E. Derbyshire and G. N. Greaves, *Nature*, 1991, **354**, 465.
21   (*a*) G. Sankar, P. A. Wright, N. Srinivasa, J. M. Thomas, G. N. Greaves, A. J. Dent, B. R. Dobson, C. A. Ramsdale and R. H. Jones, *J. Phys. Chem.*, 1993, **97**, 9550; (*b*) L. M. Colyer, G. N. Greaves, S. W. Carr and K. K. Fox, *J. Phys. Chem.*, 1997, **111**, 10 105.
22   W. Bras, G. E. Derbyshire, A. J. Ryan, G. R. Mant, A. Felton, R. A. Lewis, C. J. Hall and G. N. Greaves, *Nucl. Instrum. Methods A*, 1993, **326**, 587.
23   J. M. Thomas and G. N. Greaves, *Science*, 1994, **265**, 1675.
24   M. Oversluizen, S. M. Clark and G. N. Greaves, *Mater. Res. Soc. Symp. Proc.*, 1993, **307**, 39.
25   M. Oversluizen, S. M. Clark, W. Bras and G. N. Greaves, *Supplement to "Rivista della Stazione Sperimentale del Vetro"*, 1993, **XXIII**, 345.
26   M. Oversluizen, W. Bras, G. N. Greaves, S. M. Clark, J. M. Thomas, G. Sankar and B. Tiley, *Nucl. Instrum. Methods Phys. Res. B*, 1995, **97**, 184.
27   S. M. Clark, G. N. Greaves, M. Oversluizen, G. Sankar and J. M. Thomas, *Non-equilibrium Phenomenon in Supercooled Fluids, Glasses and Amorphous Materials*, World Scientific, Singapore, 1996, p. 241.
28   M. J. van der Hoek, W. Werner, P. van Zuylen, B. R. Dobson, S. S. Hasnain, J. S. Worgan and G. Luijcjx, *Nucl. Instrum. Methods Phys. Res. A*, 1989, **276**, 381.
29   G. N. Greaves, in *Glass Science and Technology*, eds. D. R. Uhlmann and N. Kreidl, Academic Press, New York, 1990, p. 1.
30   P. Stephenson, G. N. Greaves and S. J. Gurman, *Synchrotron Radiat. News*, 1991, **4**, 29.
31   A. F. Wright, P. W. McMillan and N. H. Brett, in *Structure of Non-crystalline Materials*, eds. P. H. Gaskell, J. M. Parker and E. A. Davies, Taylor & Francis, London, 1983, p. 569.
32   G. R. Mant, personal communication.
33   O. Glatter, *J. Appl. Cryst.*, 1977, **10**, 415.
34   R. N. G. Wykoff, *Crystal Structures*, Wiley, New York, 1964.
35   G. N. Greaves, N. T. Barrett, G. M. Antonini, F. R. Thornley, B. T. M. Willis and A. Steel, *J. Am. Chem. Soc.*, 1989, **111**, 4313.
36   R. Wagner and R. Kampmann, in *Materials Science and Technology*, eds. R. W. Cahn, P. Haasen and E. J. Kramer, VCH, Mannheim, vol. 5, ch. 4.
37   O. Glatter and O. Kratky, *Small Angle X-ray Scattering*, Academic Press, New York, 1982.
38   A. Guinier and G. Fournet, *Small-Angle X-ray scattering of X-rays*, Wiley, New York, 1955.
39   A. Cummings, P. Wiltzius, F. S. Bates and J. H. Rosedale, *Phys. Rev. A*, 1992, **45**, 885.
40   T. P. Russel, *Handbook on Synchrotron Radiation*, 1991, vol. 3.
41   K. Morinaga and H. Takebe, *Ber. Bunsen-Ges Phys. Chem.*, 1996, **100**(9), 1423.

Excited state molecular structure determination in disordered media using laser pump/X-ray probe time-domain X-ray absorption spectroscopy

Lin X. Chen

Chemistry Division, Argonne National Laboratory, Argonne, Illinois 60439, USA

Received 22nd March 2002, Accepted 9th April 2002
First published as an Advance Article on the web 18th July 2002

Advances in X-ray technologies provide opportunities for solving structures of photoexcited state molecules with short lifetimes. Using X-ray pulses from a modern synchrotron source, the structure of a metal-to-ligand-charge-transfer (MLCT) excited state of $Cu^I(dmp)_2^+$ (dmp = 2,9-dimethyl-1,10-phenanthroline) was investigated by laser pump/X-ray probe X-ray absorption fine structure (LPXP-XAFS) in fluid solution at room temperature on a nanosecond time scale. The experimental requirements for such pump–probe XAFS are described in terms of technical challenges: (1) conversion of optimal excited state population, (2) synchronization of the pump laser pulse and probe X-ray pulse, and (3) timing of the detection. Using a laser pump pulse for the photoexcitation, a photoluminescent MLCT excited state of $Cu^I(dmp)_2(BArF)$, (dmp = 2,9-dimethyl-1,10-phenanthroline, BArF = tetrakis(3,5-bis(trifluoromethylphenyl)borate) with a lifetime of 98 ± 5 ns was created. Probing the structure of this state at its optimal concentration using an X-ray pulse cluster with a total duration of 14.2 ns revealed that (1) a Cu^{II} center was generated *via* a whole charge transfer; (2) the copper in the MLCT state bound an additional ligand to form a penta-coordinate complex with a likely trigonal bipyramidal geometry; and (3) the average Cu–N bond length increases in the MLCT excited state by 0.07 Å. In contrast to previously reported literature, the photoluminescence of this penta-coordinate MLCT state was not quenched upon ligation with the fifth ligand. On the basis of experimental results, we propose that the absorptive and emissive states have distinct geometries. The results represent X-ray characterization of a molecular excited state in fluid solution on a nanosecond time scale.

Introduction

Fundamental processes in photochemistry are interactions between light and molecules, which produce excited states as energetic reactants that undergo various pathways, such as donating electrons, emitting photons, and breaking chemical bonds, to the products.[1,2] Knowledge of the molecular structures of the reactants allows us to predict the energetics and pathways for many chemical reactions, but such knowledge on excited state molecules remains rather incomplete because of the lack of X-ray techniques that are able to characterize the excited state structures during their limited lifetimes ranging from femtoseconds to milliseconds.

X-ray spectroscopy (including XAFS, and X-ray absorption near edge structure, XANES), has been shown to be of tremendous value in the characterization of steady-state molecular structures in

DOI: 10.1039/b202910c

disordered media, but has not been successfully applied to excited states until very recently. The essential requirement for excited state structure determination is a pulsed X-ray source that provides sufficient photons and the proper timing structure for time-domain diffraction, scattering, and absorption measurements. Such a requirement is adequately fulfilled by new generation synchrotron sources that offer X-ray pulses with about 100 ps pulse duration and up to 10^4 times more photons than previous sources.[3,4] In addition, the production of ultrashort X-ray pulses was reported recently using table-top terawatt ultrafast lasers,[5–8] and synchrotron X-ray pulses with an ultrafast laser modulation.[9,10] While these ultrafast X-ray pulses are useful to follow atomic movements from the Franck–Condon excited state to the vibrationally relaxed equilibrated state (Fig. 1), the

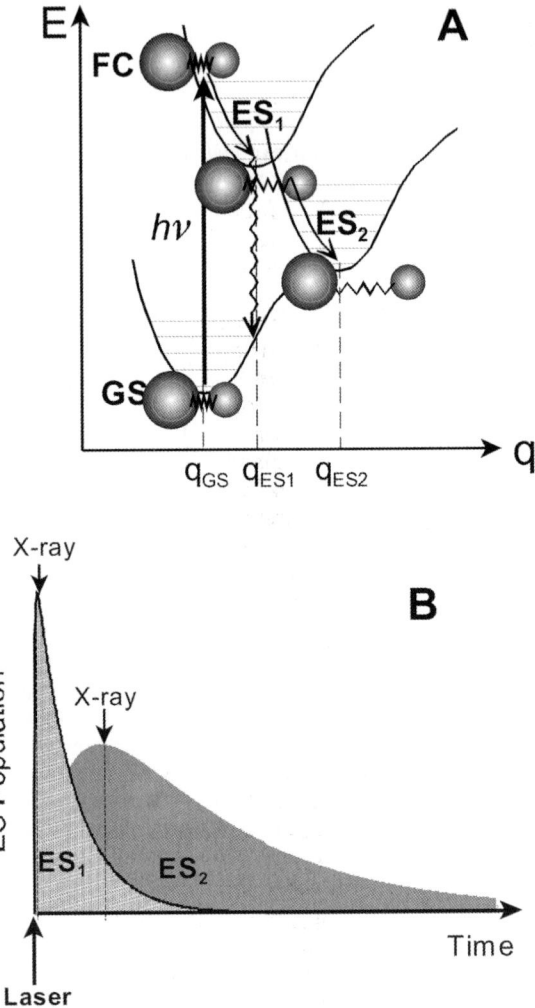

Fig. 1 (A) Illustration of interaction between light and a molecule using the simplest diatomic molecule as an example, where GS, FC, ES_1 and ES_2 stand for the ground state, the Franck–Condon state, the first and the second thermally equilibrated excited states. q stands for the generalized molecular coordinates. While FC has identical coordinates to GS ES_1 and ES_2 may have distinctively different coordination from that of GS. The purpose of the LPXP-XAFS on a nanosecond time scale is to capture the coordinates for ES_1 and ES_2 rather than follow the time evolution of the coordinates from FC to ES_1, which will be accomplished by femtosecond X-ray techniques in the future. (B) The timing delays between the pump laser pulse and the probe X-ray pulse for capturing ES_1 and ES_2 relative to their population decay kinetics. The snapshots of ES_1 and ES_2 were taken when their respective populations were optimal.

X-ray pulses from a synchrotron source with 100 ps duration have much higher X-ray photon flux and are suitable for capturing the structures of thermally equilibrated excited molecules that are reactants in photochemical processes.[11–16]

We report here our recent molecular structure determination for an excited state during a photochemical reaction by laser pump/X-ray probe XAFS (LPXP-XAFS) using a laser and a third generation synchrotron X-ray source. This technique has been successfully applied to capture a nickel porphyrin photodissociation intermediate in solution with 28 ns lifetime.[12] The synchrotron X-ray pulse duration of 100 ps is obviously too long for monitoring atomic movements during vibrational relaxation from the Franck–Condon state to the equilibrated excited state. Therefore, the purpose of the experiments described here is to take one snapshot of the thermally equilibrated excited state at its optimal concentration within 100 ps after the photoexcitation, rather than following the atomic movement during the formation and decay of this state. In circumstances where more than one excited state can be sequentially generated after initial photoexcitation, such as a singlet excited state undergoing inter-system crossing to a triplet excited state, snapshots for each excited state can be taken at proper time delays between the pump and the probe pulses (Fig. 2).

The MLCT excited states of cuprous diimine compounds can be generated *via* absorbing photons of visible light.[17–20] The electron density shift due to the MLCT transition can be manifested by an intramolecular redox reaction where the charge density is transferred from the metal to ligands, resulting in a copper center with a higher oxidation state. These compounds were chosen because of the compelling evidence described in the literature for novel structural reorganization following light absorption.[21–23] These photoinduced structural changes are important in molecular motors and switches and relevant to "gated" electron transfer in proteins[24] and model systems.[25,26] As an example, the MLCT transition of $Cu^I(dmp)_2^+$ is shown below:

$$Cu^I(dmp)_2^+ + h\nu \rightarrow [Cu^{II}(dmp^-)(dmp)^+]^* \qquad (1)$$

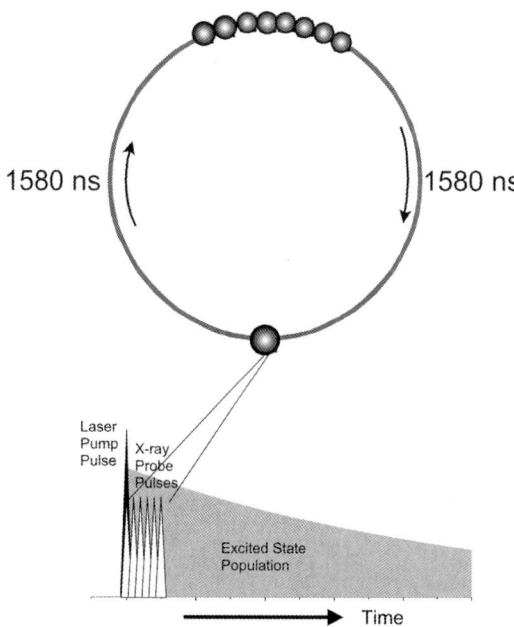

Fig. 2 The special timing mode of the synchrotron during LPXP-XAFS experiments. The large circle represents the storage ring of the synchrotron, and the small circles, electron bunches distributed over the ring. The sextuplet X-ray probe pulse cluster was separated in time from other pulses and consisted of six pulses with interpulse separation of 2.84 ns. The relative timing between the pump and the probe, as well as the excited state population, is illustrated in the lower part of the figure.

The ground state of Cu^I(dmp)$_2{}^+$ has a d^{10} electronic configuration with pseudo-tetrahedral geometry.[27] Photoinduced MLCT transition shifts an electron from Cu(I) to a dmp ligand, creating a Franck–Condon state with a Cu(II) center coordinated to one reduced and one neutral dmp ligand. The excited state Cu(II) center has a d^9 electron configuration and is susceptible to Jahn–Teller distortion,[28] resulting in a thermally equilibrated MLCT state with a structure distinct from that of the ground state. The observations of large "Stokes-like" shifts in the optical spectra and 'exciplex' quenching of the MLCT excited states represent strong evidence for such a significant structural reorganization. For the particular study presented here, we probed structures of the thermally equilibrated MLCT excited state of Cu(I)(dmp)$_2$BArF within 100 ps after photoexcitation. In particular, this work investigates whether the MLCT transition is a whole or partial electron transfer from Cu(I) to the ligand, and how the resulting thermally equilibrated MLCT state structure differs from the corresponding Cu(I) and Cu(II) compounds in the ground state.

Experimental

Pump–probe XAFS

Copper K-edge (8.979 keV) XANES and XAFS measurements were conducted at a wiggler beamline, 11ID-D, Basic Energy Science Synchrotron Research Center of the Advanced Photon Source at Argonne National Laboratory. The energy of the X-rays was selected by a cryogenically cooled fixed offset double crystal Si(220) monochromator that scanned from −100 to 600 eV relative to the copper K-edge energy. The X-rays were focused by a Pd toroidal mirror to a beam size of 0.5 × 1 mm^2 at the sample. The asymmetric fill timing mode of synchrotron X-ray pulses was employed during the experiment (Fig. 2). The following were considered as key aspects for conducting a successful time-domain LPXP-XAFS experiment:

(1) **Creating optimal excited state population.** XAFS measures X-ray absorption or fluorescence signals from both the ground and the excited state molecules. Therefore, creating a significant fraction of the excited state population is crucial for accurate structure determination. Although the quality of XAFS data improves with the concentration of X-ray absorbing atoms, the fraction of the excited state molecules decreases with the concentration because of the finite number of optical photons available in each laser pulse. Therefore, it is important to have an optimal concentration of the sample that satisfies the needs for reasonable XAFS spectra of the excited state. According to the Beer–Lambert law, the fraction of the excited state molecules f_{ex} can be approximated by eqn. (2):

$$f_{ex} = \frac{N_a e^{-kt} Q}{N} = \frac{P e^{-kt} Q}{Nh\nu}[1 - 10^{-\varepsilon(\lambda)lC(1-f_{ex})}] \qquad (2)$$

where N and N_a are the total number of molecules and the number of light absorbing molecules, respectively. k is the excited state decay time constant, and t is the time delay after the pump. Q is the quantum yield of the excitation. P is the pulse energy of the laser, h is the Planck constant, and ν is the frequency of the laser light. C and l are the concentration and the thickness of the sample. $\varepsilon(\lambda)$ are molecular extinction coefficients for the ground and excited states at the wavelength of the photoexcitation, λ. Eqn. (2) assumes that (1) the excited state decay follows a single exponential function; (2) l is small enough so that the absorption gradient through the pathway of the light can be neglected; and (3) the laser photons absorbed by the solvent can be neglected. In the Cu(I)(dmp)$_2$BArF case, applying parameters of the experiment resulted in $f_{ex} \sim 20\%$ for the MLCT state.

(2) **Synchronization of the pump and probe pulses.** The experiment presented here was carried out during an asymmetric fill timing mode of the synchrotron storage ring[29] (Fig. 2) where one sextuplet pulse cluster with a repetition rate of the ring revolution, 271 kHz, was separated by 1.58 μs from other pulses in the storage ring. A replica of the fundamental frequency of the synchrotron (352 MHz) was divided by four and connected to the mode-lock drive of a diode-pumped CW-mode-locked Nd-YLF laser (Lightwave). The output of this laser was used to seed a Q-switched

Nd-YLF regenerative amplifier laser (Quantronix) that produced the second harmonic output of 527 nm light (1 kHz repetition rate, 1 mJ pulse^{-1} and 5 ps fwhm) to illuminate the sample. Thus, the laser pulses and the X-ray pulses were synchronized in time. The relative phase adjustment was accomplished according to the procedure described previously.[12,30,31] The timing overlap between the laser and the sextuplet X-ray pulse clusters was simultaneously monitored by a Si avalanche photodiode. The probe X-ray pulse cluster consisted of six pulses with 2.84 ns time intervals between pulses, so the total time span from this pulse cluster was 14.2 ns. The time delay of the laser pulse was adjusted so it overlapped with the first X-ray pulse within the sextuplet pulse cluster. The accuracy of the timing overlap was limited only by the response times of the photodiode and oscilloscope, at about 200 ps. The laser and X-ray beams were intersected at a continuously flowing sample stream of 2 mM [Cu^I(dmp)$_2$](BArF) toluene solution. The thickness of the sample stream was about 0.5 mm. A transient UV–Vis absorption experiment with the same laser and similar sample conditions was performed prior to X-ray experiments to ensure that the MLCT excited state was generated with the efficiency expected. The sample integrity was monitored periodically by UV–Vis spectroscopy during the pump–probe XAFS experiment. To ensure the quality of the sample, the solution was changed every 3–4 h.

(3) **Timing of the detection.** Many photochemical processes occur in dilute solutions, so excited state quenching and exciton–exciton annihilation can be prevented. Thus, X-ray fluorescence detection was used for the LPXP-XAFS experiments. A nine-element solid state Ge detector array (Canberra) was used to collect the Cu-K$_\alpha$ fluorescence from the sample. In the current experimental set-up, no X-ray shutter was employed. Therefore, extraction of the X-ray fluorescence signals from the pump–probe cycle relied on gating the detector.[31] The output of the Ge detector array was connected to a single channel analyzer (SCAs) module, and the output of the SCA module was then split into two equal parts and connected respectively to two scalar array modules. The gating of a Ge detector array was accomplished by gating the scaler module. A minimum of 1.2 µs time separation was required to prevent interference between signals from adjacent X-ray pulses when the detector was operated with a 0.25 µs shaping time. The first module was gated by a signal derived from the output of the laser with a proper time delay. Therefore, only X-ray signals from the sextuplet X-ray probe pulse cluster that coincided with the laser pump pulse were processed. The sextuplet X-ray pulse cluster had a repetition rate of 271 kHz and 15% of total X-ray photon flux. As a result of gating the scaler module at the laser pulse repetition rate of 1 kHz, only 0.055% of the total X-ray photon flux was used to probe the laser excited sample. Output from the first scaler module was used to obtain the XAFS spectrum of the laser excited sample. The second scaler array module was not gated, so it processed signals from all X-ray pulses to obtain the spectrum of the ground state. This pump–probe cycle was repeated until the XAFS spectrum of the laser excited sample had a satisfactory signal-to-noise ratio to establish the oxidation state, the coordination geometry, and local fine structure around the metal center. The total data acquisition time was approximately 20 h.

Data analysis of XANES and XAFS spectra

The XANES spectrum of the MLCT state was calculated by subtracting the appropriate fraction of ground state spectrum from the measured spectrum. The fraction of the ground state that remained in the laser excited sample was determined using eqn. (2) by the Beer–Lambert law and the measured irradiance, sample concentration, and extinction coefficient with an assumed inter-system crossing yield of unity.

For XAFS data analysis, Cu^I(dmp)$_2$(NO$_3$)[32] and Cu^{II}(dmp)$_2$(NO$_3$)$_2$[33] solids were used as references for the phase and amplitude of the ground state and the MLCT state. The coordination number of four and an average Cu–N distance of 2.07 Å were used for Cu^I(dmp)$_2$(NO$_3$), in accordance with its crystal structure. Similarly, the coordination number of five (four N atoms and one O atom) and the average nearest neighbor distance of 2.09 Å were used for Cu^{II}(dmp)$_2$(NO$_3$)$_2$.[33] WinXAS 97[34] was used for data analysis following standard procedures.[35,36] The experimentally collected data were fit to the equation: $\chi(k) = \sum F_i(k) S_0^2(k) N_i/(k R_i^2) \exp(-2\sigma_i^2 k^2)\sin[2kR_i + \phi_i(k)]$, where $F(k)$ is the magnitude of the backscattering; S_0, the amplitude reduction factor; N, the coordination number; R, the average distance; σ^2, the Debye–Weller factor; and φ_i, the phase shift; the subscript indicates the ith atom; k is the electron wavevector.

Transient optical absorption

Prior to the LPXP-XAFS experiment, a transient optical absorption measurement was made using the same laser and similar sample conditions. The probe was a xenon flash lamp running at 100 Hz and a monochromator was used to select the probe wavelength. The transient absorption signal was collected by a photomultiplier tube (PMT) combined with a digital oscilloscope. The sample was purged with nitrogen. The sample integrity was monitored by its UV–Vis spectra after the experiment and had almost no change during 3–4 h.

Synthesis

The [Cu^I(dmp)$_2$](PF$_6$) and Cu^I(dmp)$_2$(NO$_3$) were synthesized according to previously published procedures.[18,37,38] The [Cu^I(dmp)$_2$](BArF) was synthesized via the metathesis of [Cu^I(dmp)$_2$](PF$_6$) with sodium tetrakis(3,5-bis(trifluoromethylphenyl))borate (Boulder Scientific) in a 1 : 1 ratio in toluene. The [Cu^{II}(dmp)$_2$(NO$_3$)](NO$_3$) compound was synthesized following previously published protocol.[39]

Electrolysis for *in situ* XAFS

Bulk electrolysis of 2 mM Cu(I)(dmp)$_2{}^+$ in acetonitrile with 0.1 M Bu$_4$N$_P$F$_6$ was carried out using a microprocessor controlled potentiostat (Princeton Applied Research, model 273) and a standard three electrode arrangement in a previously described spectroelectrochemical cell designed for XAFS use.[40] The working electrode was a 3 cm^2 platinum mesh, and the auxiliary electrode was a platinum wire located in a portion of the cell separated by a porous glass frit. The applied potential was measured *versus* an aqueous Ag$^+$/AgCl reference electrode. Prior to applying the oxidizing potential, the solution was purged with acetonitrile saturated nitrogen gas. The nitrogen gas continued to bubble through the solution during electrolysis to aid in stirring the solution. After approximately 20 min at +0.80 V, the complex was completely oxidized. During the remainder of the experiments the solution was blanketed with a stream of nitrogen gas.

Photoluminescence

Corrected photoluminescence (PL) spectra were obtained with a Spex Fluorolog that had been calibrated with a standard tungsten–halogen lamp using procedures given by the manufacturer. Quantum yields were measured by the optically dilute technique with Ru(bpy)$_3{}^{2+}$ as a standard.[41] Time-resolved PL measurements were made as previously described in the literature.[42]

Results

Optical absorption and luminescence

The UV–Vis absorption spectrum of [Cu^I(dmp)$_2$](BArF) in toluene displayed characteristic broad MLCT bands centered at 460 nm (Fig. 3A). Light excitation into these bands resulted in room temperature photoluminescence with a corrected maximum at 710 nm, an emission quantum yield, $\varphi_{em} = 1.12 \times 10^{-3}$, and a lifetime of 98 ns. Assuming an inter-system crossing yield of unity, a radiative rate constant, k_r, of 1.14×10^4 s^{-1} and a non-radiative rate constant, k_{nr}, of 1.02×10^7 s^{-1} were obtained. Transient absorption spectroscopy produced difference spectra consistent with positive absorption bands centered at ~350 nm and ~580 nm that were due to the absorption of the reduced dmp ligand and a bleach centered at 460 nm that was due to depletion of the ground state (Fig. 3A). Isosbestic points and first-order kinetics within the experimental time resolution were observed (Fig. 3B) with lifetimes that agree, within experimental error, with those measured independently by time-resolved photoluminescence spectroscopy.

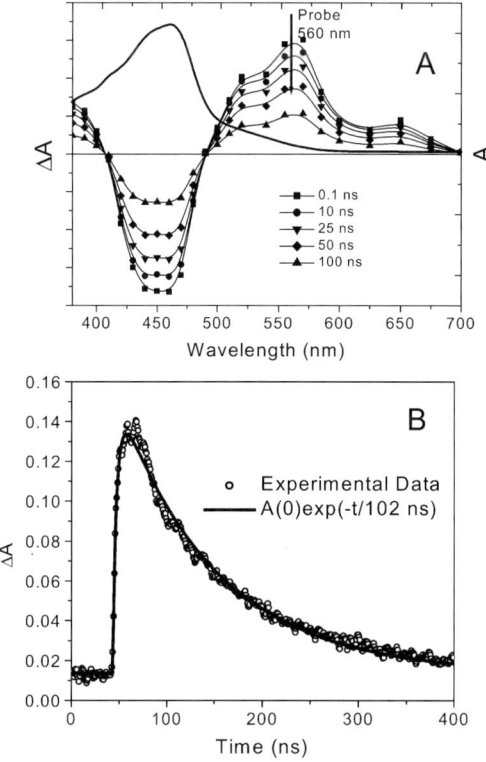

Fig. 3 (A) Left axis: absorption difference spectra after pulsed 532 nm light excitation (5–8 mJ cm^{-2} s fwhm of Cu^I(dmp)$_2$$^+$ in argon-saturated toluene at room temperature (thin lines with symbols). Right axis: the ground state absorption spectrum of Cu^I(dmp)$_2$BArF in toluene at room temperature (thick line). (B) Excited state decay probed at 560 nm.

In situ XAFS measurements of Cu(I) and Cu(I) species during electrolysis

In order to identify the oxidation state of copper in the MLCT excited state, we first measured Cu K-edge XANES spectra of the ground state Cu^I(dmp)$_2$$^+$ and the Cu^{II} product obtained by *in situ* electrolysis (Fig. 4). The starting Cu^I(dmp)$_2$$^+$ solution was bright red and the solution turned bright green after 20 min of electrolysis, indicating formation of the Cu^{II} species. The reaction can be reversed by electrolysis at 0 V relative to the Ag$^+$/AgCl reference electrode, which yielded the same bright red solution as the starting Cu^I(dmp)$_2$$^+$. The following XANES spectral changes were observed as Cu^I(dmp)$_2$$^+$ was converted to Cu(II) species by electrolysis: (1) a transition edge position was shifted 3 eV higher, reflecting the higher positive charges in the copper atoms; (2) a shoulder feature at 8985 eV representing the 1s to 4p$_z$ transition in tetrahedral Cu^I(dmp)$_2$$^+$ was missing, indicating a transformation from tetra- to penta- or hexa-coordinate geometry, because the 4p$_z$ orbital is localized in the former, giving a sharp peak, but delocalized in the latter with a broad, indistinct feature;[43,44] (3) the intensity of the 8997 eV peak was higher, suggesting a higher coordination number in the former, because of the proportionality of the oscillation amplitude with the coordination number; and (4) a pre-edge feature appeared at 8979 eV (Fig. 4 inset) which was attributed to the 1s → 3d transition and was only present for the Cu^{II} (d^9) compound with one vacancy in the 3d orbitals.[45]

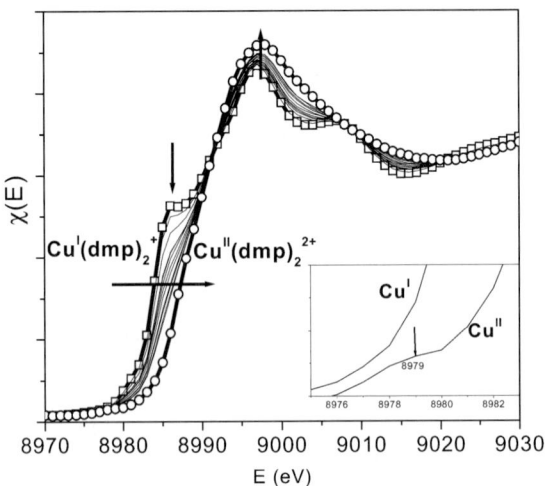

Fig. 4 *In situ* XANES spectra of [Cu^I(dmp)$_2$](BArF) in acetonitrile at room temperature during the electrolysis, where Cu^I was oxidized to Cu^{II} in about 20 min. E is the photon energy of the X-ray and $\mu(E)$ is proportional to the amount of X-rays absorbed by the sample. The initial spectrum of Cu^I(dmp)$_2^+$ before electrolysis is shown as open squares and the final spectrum of Cu^{II}(dmp)$_2^{2+}$ after electrolysis is shown as open circles. Eight intermediate spectra are also shown. The arrows indicate the directions of the changes in the spectra during electrolysis. The inset shows the pre-edge region of the starting and ending spectra only.

LPXP-XAFS measurements of the MLCT excited state of Cu^I(dmp)$_2^+$

XANES spectra of the ground state and laser illuminated Cu^I(dmp)$_2^+$ solution showed clear differences (Fig. 5A). The latter had a reduced shoulder feature at 8985 eV compared to the former, and a weak pre-edge feature at 8979 eV. Changes in the region above the transition edge were also visible, indicated by a slightly higher intensity at 8997 eV and the variations nearby. The spectral changes below and above the transition edge for the laser illuminated sample disappeared when the sample was not illuminated or when the detection was not gated correctly, therefore the spectral changes are due to generation of the MLCT excited state.

The XANES spectrum for the MLCT excited state was extracted from the ground state and the laser illuminated sample. The XANES spectrum of the laser illuminated sample shown in Fig. 5A (circles) represented an algebraic sum of both the MLCT state and the remaining ground state at the time of the X-ray probe. Therefore, finding the right fraction of the ground state molecules was the key to obtaining a correct MLCT excited state spectrum. As mentioned in the Experimental section, the fraction of remaining ground state molecules was calculated based on the Beer–Lambert law, and the set of experimental conditions applied in the experiment. According to our calculation, the laser illuminated spectrum was comprised of 80% ground state and 20% MLCT state spectrum. Therefore, subtraction of this fraction of the known Cu^I(dmp)$_2^+$ spectrum allowed abstraction of the XANES spectrum for the MLCT state in Fig. 5B (circles), which displayed remarkable agreement with the spectrum of the Cu^{II} species generated by the electrolysis of Cu^I(dmp)$_2^+$ solution shown in Fig. 4.

In order to quantify bond lengths from the copper to the ligands for the MLCT excited state of Cu^I(dmp)$_2^+$, the XAFS spectrum of the laser illuminated sample was analyzed. XAFS and Fourier transformed XAFS spectra for the ground state and laser illuminated Cu^I(dmp)$_2^+$ are shown in Fig. 6. Apparent XAFS spectral differences between the ground state and the laser illuminated sample were observed in Fig. 6A, suggesting a phase shift due to the bond alteration in the MLCT state that was 20% of the total molecules. The magnitude of the Cu–N peak in Fig. 6B for the laser illuminated Cu^I(dmp)$_2^+$ was higher and shifted to a longer distance than that of the ground state, suggesting an increase in the coordination number of copper and the lengthening of the average Cu–N bond distance. The results of data analysis for the nearest neighbor distances from the

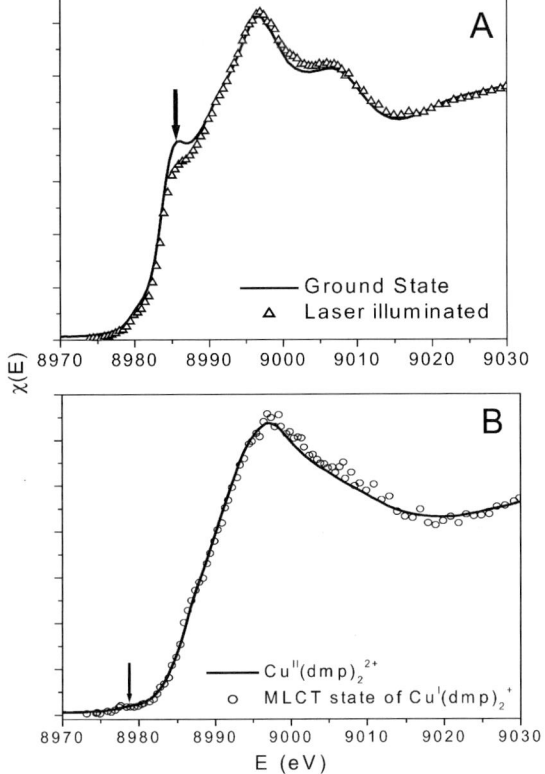

Fig. 5 (A) XANES spectra of the ground state and laser illuminated [Cu^I(dmp)$_2$](BArF) in toluene. (B) XANES spectrum of the MLCT state generated by subtraction of the ground state contributions to the spectrum of the laser illuminated sample. The XANES spectra of Cu^{II}(dmp)$_2^{2+}$ is shown to demonstrate its agreement with that of the MLCT state. $\chi(E)$ is the interference function defined as $[\mu(E) - \mu^0(E)]/\mu^0(E)$, where $\mu(E)$ and $\mu^0(E)$ are absorption coefficients of [Cu^I(dmp)$_2$](BArF) and isolated copper atoms, respectively.

copper ion are listed in Table 1. For the ground state Cu^I(dmp)$_2^+$, an average Cu–N bond distance of $R = 2.06$ Å and a coordination number of four were obtained. However, the Cu–N bond distances for the laser illuminated sample could not be adequately modeled with a single distance, so a two-distance model was used, resulting in a much better fit with two Cu–N bond distances at 2.06 and 2.13 Å and a relative ratio of approximately 80% to 20%. Apparently, the former was from the ground state, and the latter the MLCT excited state. Therefore, the average Cu–N bond distance in the MLCT state increased by 0.07 Å. Unfortunately, the accuracy for coordination number determination from XAFS analysis was normally 10–20%, so it was difficult to establish from the XAFS analysis alone whether the copper coordination number was four or five in the MLCT state. However, the XANES features of the MLCT state described above and the increase in the Cu–N peak height in Fig. 6B supported an increase in copper coordination number in the MLCT state.

Discussion

The above results clearly demonstrated X-ray characterization of a molecular excited state structure under normal conditions for photochemical processes in fluid solution and room temperature. Therefore, such studies can be extended to other inorganic and organic molecular excited states.

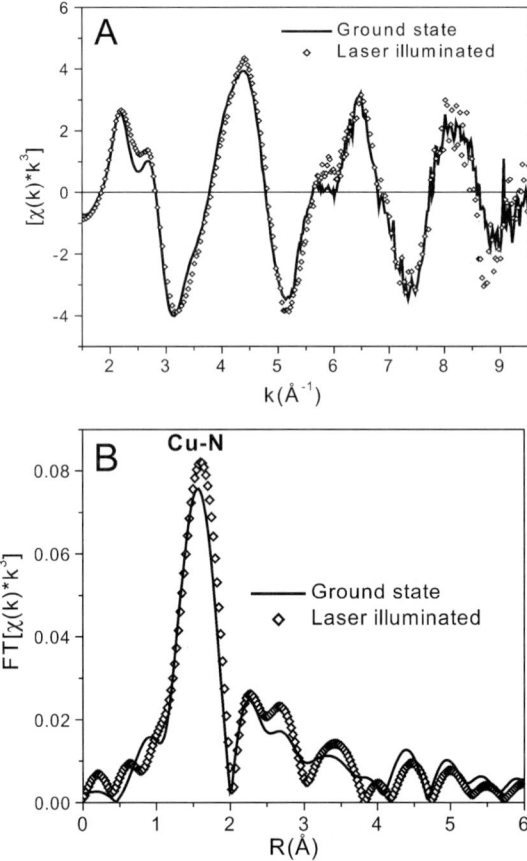

Fig. 6 (A) XAFS spectra of the ground state and laser illuminated [Cu^I(dmp)$_2$](BArF) in toluene where k is the X-ray wave vector, and $\chi(k)$ is the interference function in k space. (B) Fourier transformed XAFS spectra of Fig. 6A where each peak represents one average distance between the copper atom and its neighbors. R is the distance, in Å, from the central copper atom. The shift of the peak and the amplitude change reflects structural changes. The laser illuminated Cu^I(dmp)$_2^+$ solution has a longer average Cu–N distance and a higher coordination number than the ground state. The spectra are not corrected with phase factors.

Table 1 Ground and MLCT state Cu^I(dmp)$_2^+$ structures[a]

	Coordination number	R/Å[c]	σ^2/Å^{2d}
Ground state Cu^I(dmp)$_2^{+b}$	4.0 ± 0.5	2.06 ± 0.02	0.0009
With lght (fit 1 bond length)[b]	4.5 ± 0.5	2.07 ± 0.02	−0.0008
With lght (fit 2 bond lengths)[e]	4.0 ± 0.5 (80%)	2.06 ± 0.02	0.004
	4.0 ± 1.0 (20%)	2.13 ± 0.04	−0.009

[a] Only the nearest neighboring atomic shell is presented. Using Cu^I(dmp)$_2$NO$_3$ solid as reference with an average Cu–N distance of 2.07 Å and a coordination number of 4. [b] Using Cu^I(dmp)$_2$NO$_3$ with an average Cu–N distance of 2.07 Å as reference. [c] Bond distance. [d] Debye–Weller factors. [e] Using Cu^I(dmp)$_2$NO$_3$ and Cu^{II}(dmp)$_2$(NO$_3$)$^+$ (average Cu–N distance of 2.09 Å and a coordination number of 5 as references for the first and second distances respectively.

Below we describe the details of the structure determination for the MLCT excited state of $Cu^I(dmp)_2^+$ and the implications of these results on the photochemistry of Cu(II/I) complexes.

The MLCT excited state structure of $Cu^I(dmp)_2^+$

The transition edge in a K-edge XANES spectrum is related to the energy required for ejecting a 1s electron to the continuum, and is, therefore, sensitive to the oxidation state of the X-ray absorbing atom.[46] Higher oxidation states require higher energy X-ray photons to eject the 1s electron because they bear more positive charges that shield the core electrons. Therefore, the transition edge position generally shifts to a higher energy for the X-ray absorbing atom with a higher oxidation state. However, the transition edge position for the X-ray absorbing atom with the same oxidation state may vary when the central atom chelates with ligands of different electron negativities.[47] The fine XANES features correspond to transitions from the 1s core orbital to valence orbitals, such as 3d, 4s and 4p, that participate in chemical bonding. Consequently, they are sensitive to the coordination geometry of the metal ion and the electron delocalization in the ligand binding.[48-54]

An important issue we intended to explore in the experiment was whether photoexciting $Cu^I(dmp)_2^+$ resulted in whole or partial charge transfer from Cu(I) to a dmp ligand. The copper K-edge XANES spectra for $Cu^I(dmp)_2^+$ and $Cu^{II}(dmp)_2^+$ compounds by *in situ* electrochemical oxidation of $Cu^I(dmp)_2^+$ were measured for comparison with the MLCT excited state spectrum. If the photoexcitation induced a partial charge transfer, the transition edge position was anticipated to be intermediate between those for Cu^I and Cu^{II}. However, the MLCT and Cu^{II} states had virtually identical edge positions, indicative of a complete Cu(I) to dmp charge transfer in the MLCT state. Additional evidence for complete charge transfer in the MLCT state came from the appearance of a pre-edge peak at 8979 eV, due to the 1s to 3d transition induced by the X-ray photon, which is feasible only for Cu^{II} ($3d^9$) with one vacancy in 3d orbitals.

The XANES spectrum of the MLCT excited state in Fig. 5B also revealed the coordination geometry of the copper center. The distinctive shoulder feature at 8985 eV in the ground state of $Cu^I(dmp)_2^+$ was attributed to the $1s \rightarrow 4p_z$ transition when the $4p_z$ was localized on the copper with square-planar or tetrahedral geometry.[43,44,47] When the fifth and sixth ligands bind to the metal along the z direction, the $4p_z$ orbital delocalizes, and the peak due to the $1s \rightarrow 4p_z$ transition is smeared out, resulting in a smooth transition edge. Such changes in the transition edge due to ligation have been well documented for metalloporphyrins without and with one or two axial ligands,[55-60] as well as other transition metal complexes.[61-64] Therefore, the smooth rising edge in the XANES spectrum of the MLCT state in Fig. 4B is consistent with a penta- or hexa-coordination geometry of the copper center. The steric hindrance from the methyl groups on the phenanthroline ligands inhibits octahedral geometries so that a penta-coordinate MLCT structure seems more likely. The other XANES spectral feature that can be used to identify the coordination geometry is the pre-edge feature observed at 8979 eV, which is due to the quadrupole allowed $1s \rightarrow 3d$ transition. However, when certain coordination geometry prompts a mixing between the 3d and 4p orbitals, this transition becomes slightly dipole-allowed, resulting in an enhanced pre-edge intensity. The amount of 4p orbitals mixed with 3d depends on the coordination geometry of the metal center. Therefore, the intensity of the pre-edge peak is sensitive to the coordination geometry. The weak pre-edge peak feature in Fig. 4B for the MLCT excited state indicates that the copper coordination geometry in this state is more likely a centrosymmetric trigonal-bipyramid rather than a square pyramid that is expected to have higher pre-edge intensity.

The average Cu–N bond expansion by 0.07 Å in the MLCT excited state is consistent with the charge transfer to the antibonding orbitals of the ligand, reducing the Cu–N bond order. Although previous excited state Raman studies revealed the localization of the excited state on one dmp ligand, we were unable to resolve discrete Cu–N distances from the current experimental X-ray data with only 20% MLCT state population. The observed Cu–N bond elongation in the MLCT state also agrees with recent theoretical predictions that addition of a water ligand to a copper dmp excited state should substantially increase the Cu–N bond distance.[45] For comparison, the X-ray crystallographically determined bond lengths indicate that the average Cu–N bond length is 0.02 Å longer for $Cu^{II}(dmp)_2NO_3$[33] than for $Cu^I(dmp)_2^+$.[32] Although the XAFS data fitting procedure does not allow us to unambiguously distinguish the coordination number of the excited state, the XANES evidence presented above and the increased amplitude of the Cu–N peak for the laser illuminated sample (Fig. 6B), strongly support a penta-coordinate $Cu^I(dmp)_2^+$, MLCT excited state, despite the uncertainty of the coordination number solely from the XAFS data fitting.

The structural reorganization in Cu^I/Cu^{II} complexes and their photochemistry

The very similar excited state lifetimes from both transient absorption and photoluminescence measurements strongly suggest that the same thermally equilibrated MLCT excited state was examined by both techniques, and this state is photoluminescent at room temperature. The time delay of the 14 ns X-ray probe pulse cluster with the pump laser pulse implied that this is the same state probed by LPXP-XAFS. X-ray data provide strong evidence for penta-coordinated copper in the MLCT state. In addition, the copper center in the MLCT excited state is formally a 17 electron d^9 Cu(II) system prone to the addition of a fifth ligand. There exists a preponderance of indirect literature evidence that indicates a penta-coordinate excited state. Below we discuss the relevant literature results and the implications of an emissive penta-coordinate thermally equilibrated excited state.

A photodriven increase in the copper coordination number has previously been invoked to explain the quenching of copper excited states by Lewis bases. Extensive studies by McMillin and coworkers have provided evidence that Lewis base addition to copper excited states in dichloromethane forms a non-emissive penta-coordinate excited state complex or 'exciplex'.[37,65–67] This differs somewhat from the conclusion drawn from our data that support an emissive penta-coordinate MLCT excited state. However, a review of reported data shows that the past and present results are not mutually exclusive and provide a consistent picture of the MLCT excited state. Copper excited states, and MLCT excited states in general, are known to follow the energy gap law where the nonradiative rate constant increases exponentially with decreasing energy gap between the ground state and the excited state.[68] Therefore, the exciplex quenching is due to the stabilization of the excited state by the coordination of a fifth ligand, decreasing the energy gap and promoting the non-radiative decay. The $Cu(dmp)_2^{+*}$ exciplexes have been identified to have decreased the energy gap to the extent that nonradiative decay is the sole relaxation pathway. However, other copper diimine compounds with more sterically bulky ligands inhibit exciplex formation. Their room temperature photoluminescence is often observed even in Lewis basic solvents. For these sterically congested compounds, the absorption spectra are solvent independent, while the photoluminescence spectra are solvent dependent and red shift in more Lewis basic solvents. These literature data are consistent with an emissive penta-coordinate excited state having weak interactions with the solvent that stabilize the excited state, but not to the extent that radiative decay is kinetically non-competitive.

Our hypothesis is that $Cu(dmp)_2^{+*}$ in toluene behaves in a similar manner to that reported previously for sterically bulky copper compounds. A weak adduct is formed in the excited state, presumably with toluene, or the BArF anion, that stabilizes the excited state but not to the degree where the radiative decay is non-competitive, $k_r = 1.14 \times 10^4 \text{ s}^{-1}$ and $k_{nr} = 1.02 \times 10^7 \text{ s}^{-1}$. There is nothing in the literature that excludes a penta-coordinate excited state for $Cu(dmp)_2^{+*}$. We anticipate stronger ion-pairing in toluene than in dichloromethane. A penta-coordinate emissive excited state would provide an alternative explanation for the relatively slow rate constants reported for Lewis base quenching in dichloromethane where the Lewis base addition is simply slow because there is no open coordination site on copper. Thus, the evidence for exciplex formation in previous work is compelling, but indirect. Exciplexes were only inferred for cases where strong excited state adducts were formed that completely quenched the emission. This draws attention to the utility of X-ray techniques that provide a novel method for determination of the excited state coordination environment.

The conclusion that the MLCT excited state is penta-coordinate has important implications in copper excited states (Fig. 7). Radiative decay is a vertical process and the product must maintain the same nuclear coordinates and geometry as the excited state. Non-radiative decay, on the other hand, can lead directly to ground state products. Therefore, light absorption and light emission involve different states with unique geometries that are not simply vibrational excited states of each

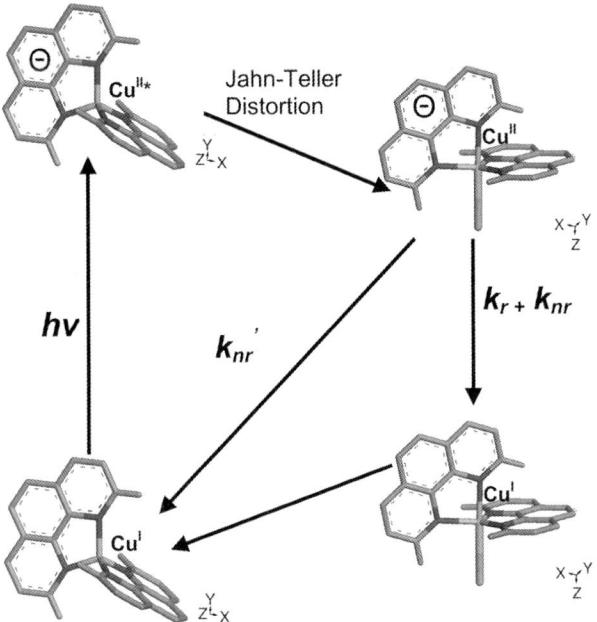

Fig. 7 A four-state model consistent with time-domain X-ray studies of $[Cu^I(dmp)_2^+](BArF)$ in toluene. Light excitation of the ground state $Cu^I(dmp)_2^+$ (T_d symmetry) produces a Franck–Condon state with the same geometry, but with a charge transferred from the copper to the ligand. Within time resolution of the experiment, the Franck–Condon state undergoes vibrational relaxation to the thermally equilibrated MLCT state with a distorted trigonal bi-pyramid geometry with the addition of an exogenous ligand, presumed to be derived from the BArF anion or toluene. Concerted radiative, k_r, and non-radiative decay, k_{nr}, yields a penta-coordinate Cu^I geometry in accord with the Franck–Condon principle.

other as is often the case. This requires a minimum of four states as shown schematically. Furthermore, radiative decay must yield a penta-coordinate Cu(I) compound that subsequently releases the fifth ligand and distorts it to yield the pseudo-tetrahedral ground state.

Conclusions

Structural determination for the MLCT excited states in organometallic complexes by XAFS has been realized for the first time on the nanosecond time scale. The experiments were performed in fluid solution at room temperature, and thus, under conditions meaningful for many photochemical applications. The LPXP-XAFS results not only supported previous studies that have inferred large structural changes in copper diimine excited states, but also revealed previously unrecognized behavior on the dynamics of excited state structural reorganization. Within the experimental time resolution, the X-ray probe pulse cluster captured the Cu^I photo-oxidation induced by the laser pump pulse, and an inner-sphere reorganization that changed the coordination number of the copper center from four to five, and the geometry from tetrahedral to trigonal bipyramidal due to the MLCT transition. An expansion in the average Cu-ligand bond distance was also observed. Because the MLCT excited state is photoluminescent, in accordance with the Franck-Condon principle, the product of radiative recombination must yield a penta-coordinate Cu(I) compound that is not simply a vibrationally excited ground state. Therefore, light absorption and emission involve two distinct geometries, and at least four states are involved, as shown in Fig. 7.

Studies using single X-ray pulses from the synchrotron with 100 ps time resolution are in progress on other metal centered photoactive compounds. In particular, we focus on the investigation on the impact of the excited state structures on the calculations of the internal reorganization energies of the molecules involved in photoinduced electron transfer reactions that are vital in solar energy conversion and storage.

Acknowledgements

This work is supported by the Division of Chemical Sciences, Office of Basic Energy Sciences, U. S. Department of Energy under contract W-31-109-Eng-38. The collaboration with Drs. Wighard Jäger, Guy Jennings, Tao Liu, Anneli Munkholm, David J. Gosztola, Jan P. Hessler of Argonne National Laboratory, and Professor Gerald J. Meyer and Dr. Donald Scaltrito of Johns Hopkins University, has made the work possible. The technical support from the staff of BESSRC-CAT, Advanced Photon Source, Drs. Mark Beno and Jennifer Linton, in particular, is greatly appreciated.

References

1. *Electron Transfer in Chemistry*, ed. V. Balzani, Wiley-VCH, Mannheim, 2001.
2. *Molecular and Supramolecular Photochemistry*, eds. V. Ramamurthy and K. S. Schanze, New York, 1999–2001, vol. 1–7.
3. G. K. Shenoy, P. J. Viccaro and D. M. Mills, Characteristics of the 7-GeV Advanced Photon Source, ANL-88-9, Argonne National Laboratory, 1988.
4. G. S. Knapp, M. A. Beno and H. You, *Annu. Rev. Mater. Sci.*, 1996, **26**, 693.
5. M. M. Murnane, H. C. Kapteyn and R. W. Falcone, *IEEE J. Quantum Electron.*, 1989, **25**, 2417.
6. C. P. J. Barty, F. Raksi, C. Rose-Petruck, K. J. Schafer, K. R. Wilson, V. V. Yakovlev, K. Yamakawa, Z. Jiang, A. Ikhlef, C. Y. Côté and J.-C. Kieffer, *Proc. SPIE-Int. Soc. Opt. Eng.*, 1995, **2521**, 246.
7. C. Rose-Petruck, R. Jimenez, T. Guo, A. Cavalleri, C. W. Siders, F. Raksi, J. A. Squier, B. C. Walker, K. R. Wilson and C. P. J. Barty, *Nature*, 1999, **398**, 310.
8. I. V. Tomov, D. A. Oulianov, P. Chen and P. M. Rentzepis, *J. Phys. Chem. B*, 1999, **103**, 7081.
9. M. F. DeCamp, D. A. Reis, P. H. Bucksbaum, B. Adams, J. M. Caraher, R. Clarke, C. W. S. Conover, E. M. Dufresne, R. Merlin, V. Stoica and J. K. Wahlstrand, *Nature*, 2001, **413**, 825.
10. R. W. Schoenlein, S. Chattopadhyay, H. H. W. Chong, T. E. Glover, P. A. Heimann, C. V. Shank, A. A. Zholents and M. S. Zolotorev, *Science*, 2000, **287**, 2237.
11. A. Geis, M. Bouriau, A. Plech, F. Schotte, S. Techert, H. P. Trommsdroff, M. Wulff and D. Block, *J. Lumin.*, 2001, **94&95**, 493.
12. L. X. Chen, W. J. H. Jager, G. Jennings, D. J. Gosztola, A. Munkholm and J. P. Hessler, *Science*, 2001, **292**, 262.
13. B. Perman, V. Srajer, Z. Ren, T.-Y. Teng, C. Pradervand, M. Wulff, R. Kort, K. Hellingwerf and K. Moffat, *Science*, 1998, **279**, 1946.
14. J. R. Helliwell, Y.-P. Nieh, J. Raftery, A. Cassetta, J. Habash, P. D. Carr, T. Ursby, M. Wulff, A. W. Thompson, A. C. Niemann and A. Hadener, *J. Chem. Soc., Faraday Trans.*, 1998, **94**, 2615.
15. C. Bressler, M. Chergui, P. Pattison, M. Wulff, A. Filipponi and R. Abela, *Proc. SPIE-Int. Soc. Opt. Eng.*, 1998, **3451**, 108.
16. H. Oyanagi, A. Kolobov and K. Tanaka, *J. Synchrotron Radiat.*, 1998, **5**, 1001.
17. B.-T. Ahn and D. R. McMillin, *Inorg. Chem.*, 1978, **17**, 2253.
18. M. W. Blaskie and D. R. McMillin, *Inorg. Chem.*, 1980, **19**, 3519.
19. G. Blasse, P. A. Breddels and D. R. McMillin, *Chem. Phys. Lett.*, 1984, **109**, 24.
20. M. T. Buckner and D. R. McMillin, *J. Chem. Soc., Chem. Commun.*, 1978, 759.
21. K. Kalyanasundaram, *Photochemistry of Polypyridine and Porphyrin Complexes*, Academic Press, New York, 1992.
22. D. V. Scaltrito, D. W. Thompson, J. A. O'Callaghan and G. J. Meyer, *Coord. Chem. Rev.*, 2000, **208**, 243.
23. J.-P. Collin, C. Dietrich-Buchecker, P. Gavina, M. C. Jimenez-Molero and J.-P. Sauvage, *Acc. Chem. Res.*, 2001, **34**, 477.
24. R. H. Holm, P. Kennepohl and E. Solomon, *Chem. Rev.*, 1996, **96**, 2239.
25. N. E. Meagher, K. L. Juntunen, C. A. Salhi, L. A. Ochrymowycz and D. B. Rorabacher, *J. Am. Chem. Soc.*, 1992, **114**, 10411.
26. S. Flanagan, J. Dong, K. Haller, S. Wang, W. R. Scheidt, R. A. Scott, T. R. Webb, D. M. Stanbury and L. J. Wilson, *J. Am. Chem. Soc.*, 1997, **119**, 8857.
27. W. D. Harrison, B. J. Hathaway and D. Kennedy, *Acta Crystallogr., Sect. B*, 1979, **35**, 2301.
28. J. K. Burdett, *Molecular Shapes*, Wiley, New York, 1980.
29. D. M. Mills, *Rev. Sci. Instrum.*, 1989, **60**, 2338.

30 L. X. Chen, *J. Electron Spectrosc. Relat. Phenom.*, 2001, **119**, 161.
31 G. Jennings, W. J. H. Jaeger and L. X. Chen, *Rev. Sci. Instrum.*, 2002, **72**, 362.
32 R. Hamalainen, M. Algren, U. Turpeinen and T. Raikas, *Cryst. Struct. Commun.*, 1979, **8**, 75.
33 M. Van Meerssche, G. Germain and J. P. Declercq, *Cryst. Struct. Commun.*, 1981, **10**, 47.
34 T. Ressler, *J. Synchrotron Radiat.*, 1998, **5**, 118.
35 D. E. Sayers, E. A. Stern and F. Lytle, *Phys. Rev. Lett.*, 1971, **27**, 1204.
36 E. A. Stern, D. E. Sayers and F. W. Lytle, *Phys. Rev. B*, 1975, **11**, 4836.
37 D. R. McMillin, J. R. Kirchhoff and K. V. Goodwin, *Coord. Chem. Rev.*, 1985, **64**, 83.
38 M. T. Miller, P. K. Ganzel and T. B. Karpishin, *J. Am. Chem. Soc.*, 1999, **121**, 4292.
39 E. C. Riesgo, Y.-Z. Hu, F. Bouvier, R. P. Thummel, D. V. Scaltrito and G. J. Meyer, *Inorg. Chem.*, 2001, **40**, 3413.
40 M. R. Antonio, L. Soderholm and I. J. Song, *J. Appl. Electrochem.*, 1997, **27**, 784.
41 J. N. Demas and G. A. Crosby, *J. Phys. Chem.*, 1971, **75**, 991.
42 F. N. Castellano, T. A. Heimer, M. T. Tandhasetti and G. J. Meyer, *Chem. Mater.*, 1994, **6**, 1041.
43 T. A. Smith, J. E. Penner-Hahn, M. A. Berding, S. Doniach and K. O. Hodgson, *J. Am. Chem. Soc.*, 1985, **107**, 5945.
44 L.-S. Kau, D. J. Spira-Solomon, J. E. Penner-Hahn, K. O. Hodgson and E. I. Solomon, *J. Am. Chem. Soc.*, 1987, **109**, 6433.
45 R. G. Shulman, Y. Yafet, P. Eisenberger and W. E. Blumberg, *Proc. Natl. Acad. Sci. U. S. A.*, 1976, **73**, 1384.
46 *X-ray Absorption: Principles, Applications, Techniques of EXAFS, SEXAFS and XANES*, eds. D. C. Koningsberg and R. Prins, Wiley, New York, 1988.
47 T. E. Westre, P. Kennepohl, J. G. DeWitt, B. Hedman, K. O. Hodgson and E. I. Solomon, *J. Am. Chem. Soc.*, 1997, **119**, 6297.
48 F. de Groot, *Chem. Rev.*, 2001, **101**, 1779.
49 J. E. Penner-Hahn, *Coord. Chem. Rev.*, 1999, **190–192**, 1101.
50 E. A. Stern, *Roentgen Centenary*, 1997, p. 323.
51 J. J. Rehr, *Surf. Rev. Lett.*, 1995, **2**, 63.
52 S. M. Heald and J. M. Tranquada, *Phys. Methods Chem.*, 2nd edn., 1990, vol. 5, p. 189.
53 J. Goulon, M. Loos, P. Friant and M. Ruiz-Lopez, *NATO ASI Ser., Ser. C*, 1988, **221**, 247.
54 F. W. Lytle, *Ber. Bunsen-Ges. Phys. Chem.*, 1987, **91**, 1251.
55 I. T. Bae, Y. Tolmachev, Y. Mo, D. Scherson, W. R. Scheidt, M. K. Ellison, M.-C. Cheng, R. S. Armstrong and P. A. Lay, *Inorg. Chem.*, 2001, **40**, 3256.
56 S. Carniato, Y. Luo and H. Agren, *Phys. Rev. B*, 2001, **63**, 085 105/1.
57 L. X. Chen, P. L. Lee, D. Gosztola, W. A. Svec, P. A. Montano and M. R. Wasielewski, *J. Phys. Chem. B*, 1999, **103**, 3270.
58 C. Cartier, M. Momenteau, E. Dartyge, A. Fontaine, G. Tourillon, A. Bianconi and M. Verdaguer, *Biochim. Biophys. Acta*, 1992, **1119**, 169.
59 J. E. Penner-Hahn and K. O. Hodgson, *Phys. Bioinorg. Chem. Ser.*, 1989, **4**, 235.
60 S. P. Cramer, T. K. Eccles, F. Kutzler, K. O. Hodgson and S. Doniach, *J. Am. Chem. Soc.*, 1976, **98**, 8059.
61 V. Briois, P. Sainctavit, G. J. Long and F. Grandjean, *Inorg. Chem.*, 2001, **40**, 912.
62 J.-M. Kern, L. Raehm, J.-P. Sauvage, B. Divisia Blohorn and P.-L. Vidal, *Inorg. Chem.*, 2000, **39**, 1555.
63 J. A. Real, I. Castro, A. Bousseksou, M. Verdaguer, R. Burriel, J. Linares and F. Varret, *Inorg. Chem.*, 1997, **36**, 455.
64 C. R. Randall, L. Shu, Y.-M. Chiou, K. S. Hagen, M. Ito, N. Kitajima, R. J. Lachicotte, Y. Zang and L. Que, Jr., *Inorg. Chem.*, 1995, **34**, 1036.
65 C. T. Cunningham, K. L. H. Cunningham, J. F. Michalec and D. R. McMillin, *Inorg. Chem.*, 1999, **38**, 4388.
66 E. M. Stacy and D. R. McMillin, *Inorg. Chem.*, 1990, **29**, 393.
67 C. E. A. Palmer and D. R. McMillin, *Inorg. Chem.*, 1987, **26**, 3837.
68 M. Bixon, J. Jortner, J. Cortes, H. Heitele and M. E. Michel-Beyerle, *J. Phys. Chem.*, 1994, **98**, 7289.

Recent results from the *in situ* study of hydrothermal crystallisations using time-resolved X-ray and neutron diffraction methods

Richard I. Walton,[a] Alexander Norquist,[b] Ronald I. Smith[c] and Dermot O'Hare*[b]

[a] *School of Chemistry, University of Exeter, Stocker Road, Exeter, UK EX4 4QD*
[b] *Inorganic Chemistry Laboratory, South Parks Road, Oxford, UK OX1 3QR. E-mail: dermot.ohare@chem.ox.ac.uk*
[c] *ISIS Facility, Rutherford Appleton Laboratory, Chilton, Didcot, Oxon, UK OX11 0QX*

Received 25th January 2002, Accepted 29th April 2002
First published as an Advance Article on the web 30th July 2002

We present new time-resolved powder diffraction data measured *in situ* during the hydrothermal crystallisation of two families of crystalline inorganic materials. In the first study, we have used time-resolved energy-dispersive X-ray diffraction (EDXRD) to follow the formation of zeolitic zinc phosphates from amine phosphates and zinc oxide in acidic solutions at 60–150 °C. The advantage of this method is the ability to penetrate a laboratory-sized reaction vessel and to measure data in short (< 1 min) time intervals. Integration of the Bragg peak intensities during the crystallisation of the product allows accurate crystallisation curves to be produced. In addition, in a number of cases, we observe the formation of transient crystalline intermediate phases which can be identified by use of a new three-element detector that allows a large amount of diffraction data to be measured during the experiment. We are thus able to show that three-dimensional zinc phosphate architectures often form *via* low-dimensional chain and layered phases, which is consistent with a recent *aufbau* model proposed for their formation. In the second study, we focus on the hydrothermal formation of ferroelectric barium titanate from TiO_2 and barium salts in alkaline solution using time-resolved neutron diffraction. Although the time resolution of the neutron diffraction experiment is lower than the EDXRD experiment (data are measured in intervals of 5 min), we are able to penetrate reaction mixtures that are highly absorbing towards X-rays, and thus can measure data in a large volume reaction cell. Neutron diffraction data were collected on one of the highest-flux/highest detector-coverage diffractometers currently available; the GEM diffractometer at ISIS, UK. These experiments reveal that $BaTiO_3$ crystallises after a large amount of TiO_2 has been consumed; this implies that a dissolution–crystallisation mechanism predominates. Additional mechanistic information is inferred by the observation of transient crystalline phases under certain reaction conditions.

DOI: 10.1039/b200990k

1. Introduction: *in situ* diffraction studies of the hydrothermal formation of inorganic solids

The hydrothermal preparation of inorganic solids has become of increasing importance in the past few years. The term *hydrothermal* simply refers to the use of water heated above 100 °C in a sealed container as a reaction medium. Under these conditions a mild pressure is developed (typically up to 20 atm when temperatures of less than 250 °C and subcritical conditions are employed) and the solvent properties are rather different from those at ambient conditions.[1] The method has uniquely allowed the synthesis of a diversity of microporous, zeolitic solids, now containing elements from almost all groups of the Periodic Table, and offering a wide range of pore dimensions, with the added attraction of specific chemical activity brought about by the constituent elements.[2] The hydrothermal method has also been used, to a lesser extent, in the preparation of condensed inorganic phases, which are usually synthesised using high temperature ceramic routes.[3] In this case, the advantage of the hydrothermal route lies in the rapid mixing of reagents to form homogeneous products and in the control of particle size and morphology of the material produced.

The use of hydrothermal synthesis as a preparative method in solid-state inorganic chemistry is directed towards materials with practical application: microporous materials already find widespread use in shape-selective catalysis, ion-exchange and gas separation, and condensed inorganic solids have a diversity of important properties from negative thermal expansion and unusual elastic properties, to magnetic properties and superconductivity. One draw-back of the use of hydrothermal synthesis at present is that the method is unable to allow a rational preparation of desired solid materials: the synthesis of new materials is somewhat of a black art with many experimental parameters to vary (such as temperature, time, fill of reaction vessel, choice of reagents *etc.*) by a trial and error approach until a new crystalline material is synthesised in a pure form.

It would be highly advantageous to have knowledge of the reaction mechanisms leading to the formation of crystalline solids under hydrothermal conditions: this would allow the outcome of new reactions to be predicted and control of particle size of the product could be achieved, vital for the optimisation of the properties of a material for commercial application. The complexity of these crystallisations, involving heterogeneous mixtures under elevated temperature and pressure, suggests that, to begin with, the mechanisms will be multi-step reactions, involving equilibria between many competing processes. Thus a large amount of kinetic and mechanistic data will be required to understand the reaction mechanisms. The major limitation on obtaining the required mechanistic data for hydrothermal reactions is that sealed, thick-walled reaction containers are employed, from which it is very difficult to make measurements of even extent of reaction in real time and thus to obtain the kinetic data. Several time-resolved powder diffraction experiments have in the past 7 years or so been developed to allow direct observation of the formation of crystalline solids under hydrothermal conditions.[4] These use either high-intensity synchrotron-generated X-ray beams that can penetrate steel cells, or neutron beams that are little scattered and absorbed by the cell material. Such experiments have become invaluable in developing our understanding of hydrothermal crystallisations, since it is possible to accurately measure crystallisation curves by determining the time dependence of the intensities of characteristic Bragg peaks of particular phases, and the observation of transient crystalline phases has also been possible. In this paper we illustrate the type of data that may currently be obtained using *in situ* powder diffraction by presenting some of our most recent results using state-of-the-art time-resolved X-ray and neutron diffraction methods for following hydrothermal reactions. Before describing the details of the time-resolved diffraction experiments, we will briefly introduce the two systems studied.

The crystallisation of open-framework zinc phosphates

The zinc phosphates are part of a now large family of phosphate-based solids that have open-framework zeolitic structures. It was first shown for the aluminium phosphates in 1982 that zeolite analogue framework structures could be produced,[5] and since then metals from almost every group of the Periodic Table have been incorporated into the open-framework phosphates.[2] The importance of the phosphates is two-fold: (i) the ready inclusion of transition elements infers unusual catalytic properties, and (ii) novel framework architectures are possible based on polyhedral other than the tetrahedral units found in zeolites (for example 5- and 6- coordinate gallium, and 3-coordinate trigonal Sn bipyramids). We have chosen to study the zinc phosphates since it has been postulated by Rao *et al*. that their formation takes place *via* the building up of three-dimensional structures from lower-dimensional structures (chain 1D phases and layered 2D phases).[6] This *aufbau* model for crystallisation requires experimental verification, and we have begun to investigate the syntheses of the zinc phosphates using *in situ* techniques to track changes in crystallinity in real time, with the aim of providing evidence for how crystallisation proceeds. The family of zinc phosphates is particularly attractive to study, because a large number of closely-related phases have been structurally characterised; we thus will be in a favourable position to identify any transient crystalline phases observed during an *in situ* study. In a preliminary *in situ* X-ray diffraction study of the formation of some of the zinc phosphates from amine phosphates, zinc oxide and dilute acid at 150 °C, we have already observed the formation of solids with low dimensional structures before the onset of crystallisation of three-dimensional, zeolitic frameworks.[7] In the current paper we present recent results from a further study of the zinc phosphate system to illustrate the use of time-resolved energy-dispersive X-ray diffraction.

The hydrothermal crystallisation of barium titanate

Tetragonal barium titanate is the most widely used ferroelectric solid. Its high permittivity makes the material an excellent capacitor, and the solid is commonly used in electronic devices such as multilayer capacitors, thermistors, electro-optic devices and dynamic random access memories.[8] Although the synthesis of barium titanate using conventional solid state chemistry is straightforward, and simply involves the direct, stoichiometric solid-state reaction between titania and barium carbonate at ~900 °C, the method has two distinct disadvantages: (i) repeated cycles of sample regrinding and reheating are necessary to achieve sample homogeneity and (ii) control of particle size is extremely difficult to achieve, and often irregularly shaped particles of a wide particle-size distribution are formed. The hydrothermal preparation of barium titanate offers a very attractive alternative to the solid-state reaction, and has been proven to allow the rapid one-step route to homogeneous $BaTiO_3$ from distinct Ba and Ti precursors, and additionally allows the preparation of fine powders of the solid that consist of spherical particles ranging in size from nanometres to microns.[9-11] The control of particle size and morphology that the hydrothermal route offers is of great interest for two reasons: (i) for the preparation of ceramics with few grain boundaries by sintering the fine powders and (ii) in the chemical fabrication of miniaturised devices. For these reasons the hydrothermal crystallisation mechanism of barium titanate has been the focus of some attention in the past few years [see *e.g.* ref. 12 and 13]. All the previous kinetic studies, however, used data obtained by quenching hydrothermal reactions: material was removed from the reaction vessel after it had been cooled to room temperature when a prescribed period of heating time had elapsed. Such studies do provide useful information about the extent of reaction and changes in sample crystallinity with time, but rely on the assumption that the material recovered by quenching is the same as that present under reaction conditions, and has not undergone any irreversible change on cooling and isolation. In this paper we describe recent results from a time-resolved neutron diffraction study of hydrothermal barium titanate formation; this is part of a series of experiments we have performed on the system and is the first study to follow the reaction *in situ*.[14,15]

2. Time-resolved energy-dispersive X-ray diffraction studies of the formation of open-framework zinc phosphates

2.1. The energy-dispersive X-ray diffraction experiment

Station 16.4 of the Daresbury Synchrotron Radiation Source was used to perform time-resolved EDXRD measurements. Station 16.4 is a white-beam diffraction instrument that was constructed 7 years ago with the specific aim of providing an instrument for kinetic studies, and for measuring diffraction data from materials under extreme pressure, a situation that requires confined sample containers.[16] The most significant development in the past few years on Station 16.4 is the installation of a three-element, energy-discriminating, solid-state detector by Barnes *et al.*[17] This device allows three (overlapping) regions of diffraction data to be measured simultaneously. In terms of following chemical reactions *in situ* the synchrotron EDXRD method offers three relevant experimental characteristics: (i) the incident X-ray flux is very high ($\sim 10^{10}$ photons s^{-1}), and this means firstly that data can be collected in extremely short periods of time (sub-second data collection is now possible), and secondly that penetration of thick-walled environmental sample containment is possible; (ii) all data are measured simultaneously by the energy-discriminating detector, which also minimises the data collection time; and (iii) the fixed-angle, energy-discriminating detector means that the path of X-rays through the sample container requires only narrow entrance and exit slits, which in turn allows real heating devices/pressure containers to be modified only slightly to allow the passage of the beam. The Oxford hydrothermal reaction cell has been described in some detail previously.[18] This apparatus is a large-volume hydrothermal reaction cell from which EDXRD data may be collected at up to 250 °C, typical of the temperatures used in hydrothermal synthesis. This reaction cell is virtually identical in design and construction to the 23 mL Parr hydrothermal autoclaves widely used in many research laboratories, but the steel walls of the cell are thinned to 0.3 mm to minimise absorption of X-rays.

In the current study, all chemicals were purchased from chemical companies and used as supplied: ZnO (Aldrich 99%), orthophosphoric acid, H_3PO_4, (BDH, 85% in water), 1,4-diazabicyclo[2.2.2]octane (DABCO), $N_2C_6H_{12}$, (Aldrich 98%), piperazine, $N_2C_4H_{10}$, (Aldrich 99%), N,N,N',N'-tetramethylethylenediamine, $(CH_3)_2NCH_2CH_2N(CH_3)_2$, (Aldrich 99.5%), $ZnSO_4 \cdot 7H_2O$, (Aldrich 99%), HCl (Fisher, 32% in water), methanol (Fisher). $[C_6N_2H_{14}][HPO_4]\cdot H_2O$ (DABCO-P)[19] was synthesised by mixing 6.2 g (0.055 mol) of DABCO with 6.4 g H_3PO_4. 40 mL of methanol was added under stirring. A white precipitate was recovered by filtration. $[C_4N_2H_{12}][HPO_4]\cdot H_2O$ (PIP-P)[20] was synthesised by dissolving 4 g (0.046 mol) piperazine in 40 mL of deionised water. A thick white precipitate formed immediately after the addition of 6.44 g H_3PO_4, and was recovered by filtration. $[C_6N_2H_{18}][HPO_4]\cdot 2H_2O$ (TMED-P)[21] was synthesised by mixing 4.64 g (0.04 mol) of N,N,N',N'-tetramethylethylenediamine with 6.44 g H_3PO_4. The addition of 40 mL of methanol under stirring resulted in the immediate precipitation of a white powder.

2.2. Time-resolved EDXRD studies of the hydrothermal crystallisation of some zinc phosphates

This system was investigated using two synthetic approaches in an attempt to gain understanding of the crystallisation mechanisms and reaction kinetics. The first approach utilised the amine phosphate route,[7,22] while the second involved the transformation of a zinc phosphate monomer ($[C_6N_2H_{18}][Zn(HPO_4)(H_2PO_4)_2]$, ZPM-I)[21] to higher dimensionality structures. The first amine phosphate studied was piperazine phosphate (PIP-P).[7] It was observed that the one-dimensional ladder compound $[C_4N_2H_{12}][Zn(HPO_4)_2(H_2O)]$[23] is formed initially and then transforms to a series of three-dimensional phases; $[C_4N_2H_{12}][Zn_{3.5}(PO_4)_3(H_2O)]$, $[C_4N_2H_{12}][Zn_2(HPO_4)_2(H_2PO_4)_2]$ and $[C_4N_2H_{12}][Zn(H_2O)Zn(HPO_4)(PO_4)]$. In each reaction the PIP-P starting material is not observed owing to dissolution of this soluble species.[7]

Reactions involving another amine phosphate have also been conducted. Fig. 1 shows a stack plot of the time-resolved EDXRD data from the reaction of DABCO-P, zinc oxide, water and concentrated hydrochloric acid at 150 °C. No Bragg reflections were observed from the DABCO-P, suggesting that this starting material immediately dissolves under reaction conditions. After 12 min Bragg reflections from the three-dimensional open-framework material $[C_6N_2H_{14}][Zn_2(HPO_4)_3]$ (ZnPO-DABCO-A)[24] are observed. These reflections increase in intensity for approximately an additional 55 min, at which point these peaks change in neither intensity nor position, Fig. 2. In this case we have not observed any low-dimensional precursor phases.

The second approach involves synthesising zinc phosphates from the zinc phosphate monomer, ZPM-I. The transformation of both ZPM-I and $[C_6N_4H_{21}][Zn(HPO_4)_2(H_2PO_4)]$ (ZPM-II) to one, two and three-dimensional structures was recently reported by Rao *et al.* on the basis of *ex situ* studies whereby solid material was examined before and after reaction using laboratory powder diffraction.[25] Our initial *in situ* investigations have focussed on the formation of ZPM-I and its transformations in the presence of piperazine.

ZPM-I was synthesised by stirring a gel of composition $ZnSO_4 \cdot 7H_2O$:TMED-P:25 H_2O at room temperature. Fig. 3 shows a stack plot of the time-resolved EDXRD data measured during

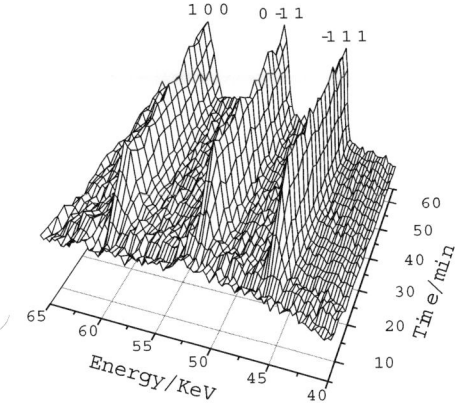

Fig. 1 A stack plot of EDXRD data measured during the crystallisation of ZnPO-DABCO-A from the reaction mixture ZnO:1.5 HCl:2 DABCO-P:50 H_2O.

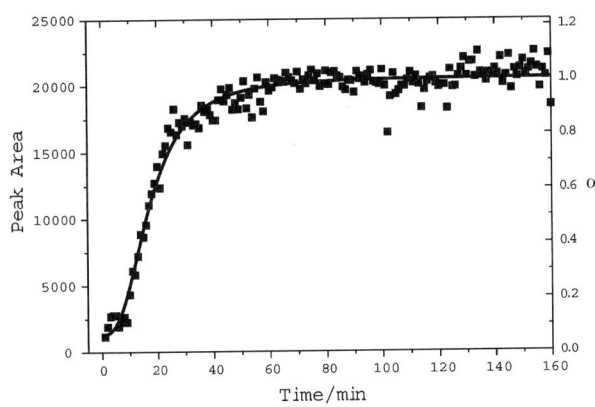

Fig. 2 Integrated peak areas of ZnPO-DABCO-A during crystallisation at 150 °C.

this process. No Bragg reflections were observed during the first 70 min at which point four characteristic reflections of ZPM-I increased in intensity during the next 30 min, until their intensity remained constant for the remainder of the experiment. The ZPM-I zinc phosphate monomer thus forms directly from solution with no transient crystalline phases detected.

The transformation of ZPM-I to higher dimensionality structures was investigated by reacting ZPM-I with piperazine in water at 60 °C. Fig. 4 shows a stack plot of the transformation of ZPM-I to ZnPO-PIP-I from a gel of composition ZPM-I:piperazine:275 H_2O. ZPM-I is only observed during the first 5–6 min while ZnPO-PIP-I Bragg reflections are first detected in the seventh minute. After 20 min the reaction is complete and the ZnPO-PIP-I peak intensities remain constant. The precursor phase is almost completely consumed before the product is observed, which suggests that a solution mediated process is involved rather than a solid-state transformation. The decay of precursor phases and growth of products are expected to mirror one another if a solid-state mechanism is employed. These observations, only made possible by continual monitoring of the reaction under real conditions, provide the first pieces of information towards understanding the hydrothermal formation of these framework solids: we have observed in some cases the presence of a precursor low-dimensional phase prior to the crystallisation of 3D zeolitic phases, and have evidence that the transformation from 1D to 3D zinc phosphates is solution-mediated rather than a direct solid-state process.

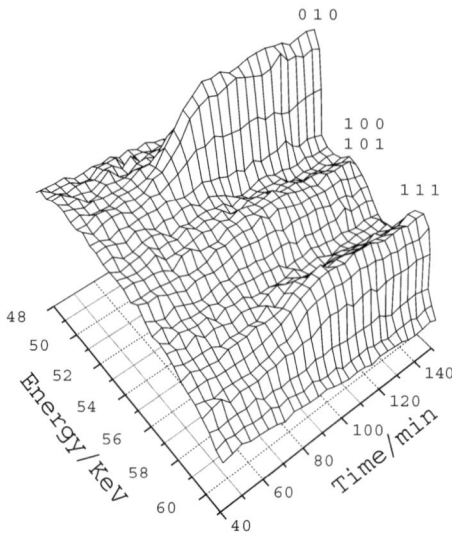

Fig. 3 A stack plot of EDXRD data measured during the crystallisation of ZPM-I.

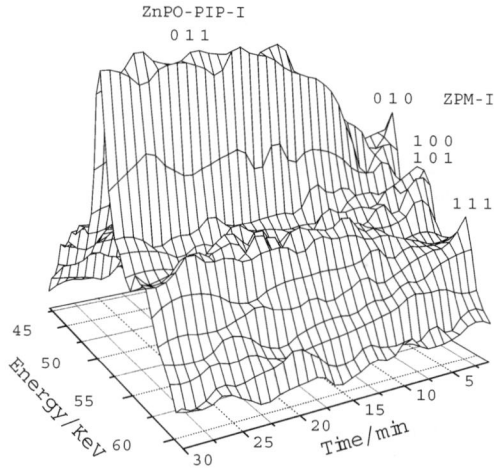

Fig. 4 A stack plot of EDXRD data measured during the transformation of ZPM-I to ZnPO-PIP-I at 60 °C.

3. Time-resolved neutron diffraction studies of the hydrothermal formation of barium titanate

3.1. A hydrothermal reaction cell for time-resolved neutron diffraction studies

We have described previously in some detail, the design, construction and use of a hydrothermal autoclave from which neutron diffraction data can be measured during the crystallisation of inorganic solids.[26] The apparatus was purposely designed to be of the same volume as the 23 mL Parr autoclaves widely used in many chemical laboratories; we are therefore simulating real reaction conditions in our *in situ* studies. Rather than being constructed from steel, as in the laboratory, the Oxford/ISIS reaction vessel is constructed from 0.3 mm thick "null scattering"

Ti–Zr alloy. This material contains Ti and Zr in such a proportion (67.7 atom% Ti and 32.3 atom% Zr) that the negative and positive neutron scattering lengths of Ti and Zr (−3.438 fm and 7.16 fm respectively) cancel completely, so that the average coherent scattering length is zero. The material is thus effectively invisible to neutrons. The alloy has similar mechanical properties to steel so is able to contain the pressure developed in a hydrothermal reaction. We experimented with different means of protecting the Ti–Zr alloy from the corrosive chemicals usually employed in a hydrothermal reaction, and found that Teflon™, usually used in the laboratory as an inert liner for hydrothermal autoclaves, gives rise to substantial scatter (both coherent and incoherent); instead the Oxford/ISIS cell is coated internally with a thin (∼10 μm) layer of gold metal. The cell is heated top and bottom by cartridge heaters inserted into copper blocks, thus exposing a 4 cm high "window" to the neutron beam to which all sample in the reaction container is exposed. In essence our cell gives rise to minimal scattering in the neutron diffraction experiment, and so we are able to collect data from reacting mixtures of solids and liquids at elevated temperature and autogeneous without any contribution to the background from the cell.

Here we report recent data obtained using the Oxford/ISIS hydrothermal cell on one of the most recently constructed neutron diffractometers, the GEM (General Materials Diffractometer) at ISIS, the UK spallation neutron source.[27] GEM is a time-of-flight neutron diffractometer, with an extremely high detector coverage and count rate. Data are measured by a three-dimensional array of seven banks of high count-rate detectors. Combined with the relatively high neutron flux available on GEM, the high count rate means that GEM is ideally suited for time-resolved diffraction studies where data must be collected in short time intervals to maximise kinetic information.

3.2. The hydrothermal crystallisation of barium titanate followed by neutron diffraction

We have previously presented some results on our study of hydrothermal barium titanate crystallisation.[14,15] Since our first studies, performed using the POLARIS diffractometer, the availability of new neutron diffractometers has greatly improved the quality of time-resolved data that we can obtain from the *in situ* experiment, and we have thus gained new insights into the steps involved in the hydrothermal formation of crystalline barium titanate. Using GEM we have now been able to reduce the time taken to record a useful diffraction pattern. With the POLARIS diffractometer we measured data in 15 min intervals; with GEM we can now acquire data in 5 min intervals. This has meant we can follow reactions that take place in shorter times than previously possible, and therefore we have been able to study the barium titanate crystallisation at higher temperatures. Fig. 5 shows a contour plot of data measured during the reaction between barium

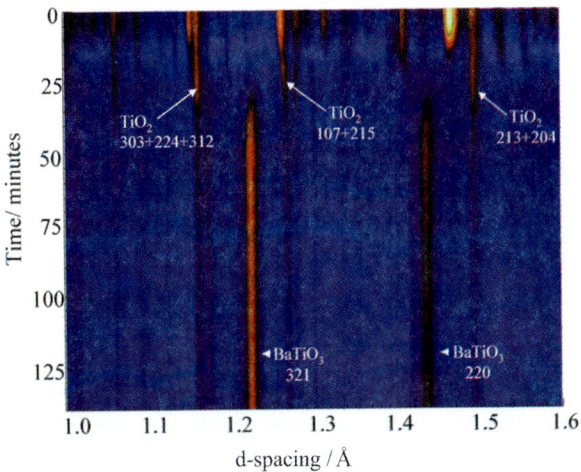

Fig. 5 A contour plot of neutron diffraction data measured during the crystallisation of $BaTiO_3$ from a mixture of composition $1.1BaCl_2:TiO_2:3.33$ NaOD:16.7 D_2O at 200 °C. Pertinent Bragg peaks are marked.

chloride, $BaCl_2$ (10 g), titanium dioxide (anatase), TiO_2 (3.2 g), in a D_2O solution of NaOD at 200 °C in the sealed hydrothermal cell. All chemicals were purchased from chemical companies and transferred to the hydrothermal cell under a flow of nitrogen to prevent aerial contamination and formation of $BaCO_3$. Note that the use of deuterated reagents is required in the neutron diffraction experiment to minimise large backgrounds in the diffraction data due to incoherent scattering from protons. Even qualitative inspection of data such as these allows important observations to be made. For example, the time-scale of the reaction can be easily determined, something which would require probably several days worth of quenching and X-ray diffraction studies in order to estimate fractional crystallinity, and thus to obtain a crude crystallisation curve. In the case of this reaction, we can see that barium titanate begins to crystallise at ~20 min, and at ~40 min the crystallisation is complete, with no further increase in $BaTiO_3$ Bragg peak intensity apparent. A second important feature of these data is that they show that not only does the $BaCl_2$ starting material dissolve rapidly, but also that a significant amount of TiO_2 dissolves (or perhaps is transformed to an amorphous phase) before the onset of crystallisation of barium titanate.

Aside from qualitative observations, we can obtain quantitative information about the kinetics of crystallisation by determining the changing areas of Bragg reflections with time. Since the intensity of Bragg peaks is directly proportional to the amount of substance giving rise to the diffraction, their changing areas with time, allow a crystallisation curve to be calculated. Fig. 6 shows a crystallisation curve of $BaTiO_3$ produced by analysis of the 310 peak of $BaTiO_3$ and also shown are decay curves for both $BaCl_2$, and TiO_2 similarly derived. The intensity data have been normalised to the maximum intensity of the Bragg peak in question. These data convincingly show how a TiO_2 Bragg peak intensity begins to decrease immediately on heating, and how a large amount of the crystalline TiO_2 is consumed before $BaTiO_3$ crystallises; a vital piece of information for establishing the crystallisation mechanism (see below). We also note that some of the TiO_2 does not either dissolve or react in the time the reaction was studied; this is consistent with previous observations that an excess of Ba is always required for the reaction to reach completion.[12]

Additional mechanistic information has been obtained by studying the barium titanate crystallisation at a variety of temperatures. For example, at 125 °C, transient Bragg peaks are observed at higher d-spacings. Fig. 7 shows data from detector bank 6 during this process and two distinct diffraction features can be observed to increase in intensity after the dissolution of $BaCl_2$ and then to decay more slowly as $BaTiO_3$ forms. Fig. 8 shows a narrower d-spacing range of three representative diffraction patterns measured during this time. The two transient diffraction peaks at ~2.53 Å and 2.71 Å, are, alone, extremely difficult to assign unambiguously. A likely candidate responsible for this phase is Ba_2TiO_4; this does exhibit strong Bragg peaks in the same region. Unfortunately, the expected most intense Bragg peak of Ba_2TiO_4, the 103 at 3.05 Å overlaps with strong diffraction features of both the $BaCl_2$ starting material and TiO_2, ruling out confirmation of

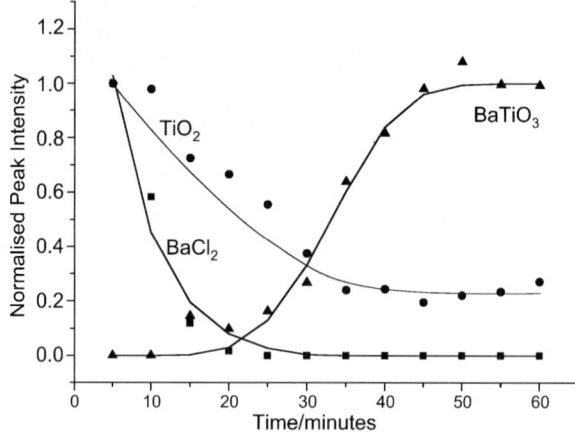

Fig. 6 Normalised integrated Bragg peak intensities obtained during the hydrothermal crystallisation of $BaTiO_3$ at 200 °C. Lines are guides to the eye and have no physical significance.

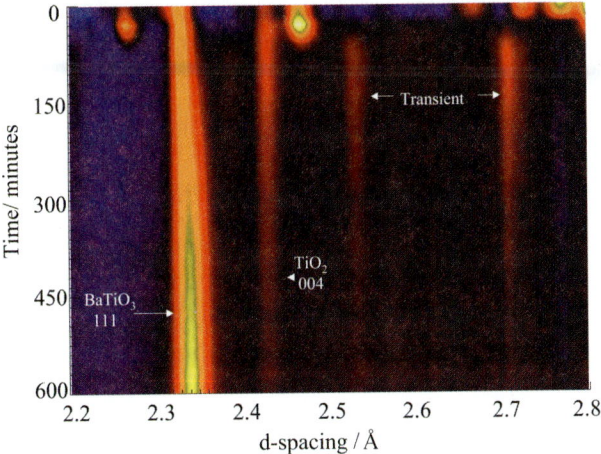

Fig. 7 A contour plot of neutron diffraction data measured during the crystallisation of BaTiO$_3$ from a mixture of composition 1.1 BaCl$_2$:TiO$_2$:3.33 NaOD:16.7 D$_2$O at 125 °C.

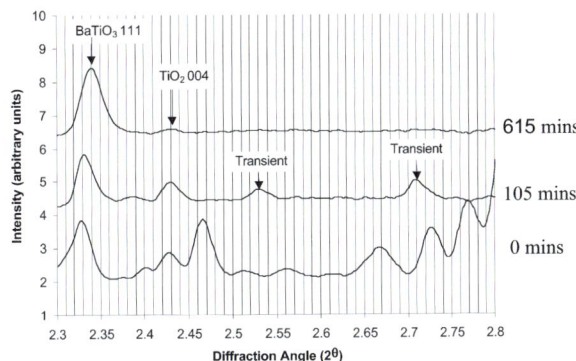

Fig. 8 Selected diffraction patterns recorded during the crystallisation of BaTiO$_3$ from a mixture of composition 1.1 BaCl$_2$:TiO$_2$:3.33 NaOD:16.7 D$_2$O at 125 °C.

our phase assignment. Interestingly Bondioli *et al.* previously reported the presence of Ba$_2$TiO$_4$ during the formation of BaTiO$_3$ in a conventional solid-state reaction.[28] Further experimental evidence is necessary to aid identification of the intermediate material we have observed, but at present we note that the kinetic crystallisation of a barium-rich barium titanate is consistent with a solution rich in Ba^{2+} at the early stages of reaction.

We are able now to postulate that the hydrothermal formation of barium titanate occurs predominantly *via* a dissolution–crystallisation mechanism; the dissolution of both the barium-containing and titanium-containing reagents permits crystallisation directly from solution. This is consistent with our observation of the disappearance of a large amount of TiO$_2$ before the crystallisation of BaTiO$_3$. The new results we have presented here, collected using the GEM diffractometer, compare very favourably with parallel studies we have performed using the constant wavelength diffraction D20 at the ILL.[15] In those studies we were also able to measure diffraction data in intervals of 5 min by virtue of a combination of high incident neutron flux and a 160° position-sensitive detector with rapid data acquisition. The quality of neutron diffraction data obtained using the two diffractometers is comparable, and we have already described the use of the D20 data to obtain rate constants for crystallisation at a number of temperatures, and thus an activation energy for what we believe to be nucleation-controlled crystal growth.[15] Our new corroborative results provide independent evidence for our earlier deductions. Our description of the reaction mechanism as predominantly occurring *via* dissolution of all starting materials is important, since some authors have assumed an alternative heterogeneous-transformation mechanism in which solution Ba^{2+} ions react with solid TiO_2 particles.[12]

4. Conclusions

The two *in situ* studies that we have described in this paper demonstrate the quality of time-resolved diffraction data that currently may be obtained during the crystallisation of inorganic solids under hydrothermal conditions. There now exists a number of specially designed reaction cells for tracking hydrothermal crystallisations using time-resolved diffraction,[4] but our two methods are unique in that laboratory-sized reaction vessels are employed. We therefore study crystallisation under real conditions, and avoid the problems of accurately selecting the correct amounts of starting materials and of achieving reproducibility that might arise if reactions are scaled down to very small volumes. The time-resolved EDXRD method has the advantage of rapid data collection, but a disadvantage in the intrinsically low resolution of the diffraction data. In contrast, the time-resolved neutron diffraction technique offers high resolution diffraction data but lower time resolution (largely due to the fact that the incident neutron flux is considerably lower than that available from X-ray sources). The additional benefit of the time-resolved neutron method is the ability to study reacting mixtures that are highly absorbing towards X-rays (*i.e.* samples that contain high atomic number elements, such as barium).

The results of our time-resolved diffraction studies allow us, for the first time, to build up a picture of the events involved in the nucleation and crystallisation of inorganic materials under hydrothermal conditions. Before a complete reaction mechanism can be put forward, however, experimental results from other techniques need also to be considered. For example, because our time-resolved diffraction studies only detect changes in crystalline material in the hydrothermal reaction vessel and none of the amorphous phases present is probed, the data from spectroscopic methods, which do reveal changes on a local atomic scale, must also be considered. To this end, both NMR[29] and EXAFS[30] spectroscopies have been utilised by other workers to follow hydrothermal crystallisations. Such methods do allow the local atomic environment of specific atom types to be tracked selectively from starting material through any amorphous phases, and small particles of solid (that are too small to be detected by Bragg diffraction). It should be noted that time-resolved diffraction experiments of hydrothermal crystallisation will always be necessary to correlate changes in local atomic structure with the presence of crystalline materials, and thus, we believe, will be at the centre of the ongoing research into understanding how inorganic solids crystallise under hydrothermal conditions.

Acknowledgements

We thank the EPSRC for funding this work, Dr D. J. Taylor for his assistance with running the synchrotron experiments, and Dr P. Radaelli for help with configuring GEM for the neutron studies.

References

1 A. Rabeneau, *Angew. Chem. Int. Ed. Engl.*, 1985, **24**, 1026.
2 A. K. Cheetham, G. Férey and T. Loiseau, *Angew. Chem. Int. Ed. Engl.*, 1999, **38**, 3268.
3 G. Demazeau, *J. Mater. Chem.*, 1999, **9**, 15.
4 R. I. Walton and D. O'Hare, *Chem. Commun.*, 2000, 2283.
5 S. T. Wilson, B. M. Lok, C. A. Messina, T. R. Cannan and E. M. Flannigen, *J. Am. Chem. Soc.*, 1984, **106**, 6092.
6 C. N. R. Rao, S. Natarajan, A. Choudhury, S. Neeraj and A. A. Ayi, *Acc. Chem. Res.*, 2001, **34**, 80.
7 R. I. Walton, A. J. Norquist, S. Neeraj, S. Natarajan, D. O'Hare and C. N. R. Rao, *Chem. Commun.*, 2001, 1990.
8 G. H. Haertling, *J. Am. Ceram. Soc.*, 1999, **82**, 797.
9 P. K. Dutta and J. R. Gregg, *Chem. Mater.*, 1992, **4**, 843.
10 I. J. Clark, T. Takeuchi, N. Ohtori and D. C. Sinclair, *J. Mater. Chem.*, 1999, **8**, 83.
11 S. W. Lu, B. I. Lee, Z. L. Wang and W. D. Samuels, *J. Cryst. Growth*, 2000, **219**, 269.

12. J. O. Eckert, C. C. Hung-Houston, B. L. Gerstan, M. M. Lenka and R. E. Riman, *J. Am. Ceram. Soc.*, 1996, **79**, 2929.
13. I. MacLaren and C. B. Ponton, *J. Eur. Ceram. Soc.*, 2000, **20**, 1267.
14. R. I. Walton, R. I. Smith, F. Millange, I. J. Clark, D. C. Sinclair and D. O'Hare, *Chem. Commun.*, 2000, 1267.
15. R. I. Walton, F. Millange, R. I. Smith, T. C. Hansen and D. O'Hare, *J. Am. Chem. Soc.*, 2001, **123**, 12 547.
16. R. L. Bilsborrow, N. Bliss, J. Bordas, R. J. Cernik, G. F. Clark, S. M. Clark, S. P. Collins, B. R. Dobson, B. D. Fell, A. F. Grant, N. W. Harris, W. Smith and E. Towns-Andrews, *Rev. Sci. Instrum.*, 1995, **66**, 1633.
17. P. Barnes, A. C. Jupe, S. L. Colston, S. D. Jacques, A. Grant, T. Rathbone, M. Miller, S. M. Clark and R. J. Cernik, *Nucl. Instrum. Methods Phys. Res. Sect. B*, 1998, **134**, 310.
18. J. S. O. Evans, R. J. Francis, D. O'Hare, S. J. Price, S. M. Clark, J. Flaherty, J. Gordon, A. Nield and C. C. Tang, *Rev. Sci. Instrum.*, 1995, **66**, 2442.
19. S. Neeraj, S. Natarajan and C. N. R. Rao, *Angew. Chem. Int. Ed. Engl.*, 1999, **38**, 3480.
20. D. Riou, T. Loiseau and G. Férey, *Acta Crystallogr., Sect. C*, 1993, **49**, 1237.
21. S. Neeraj, S. Natarajan and C. N. R. Rao, *J. Solid State Chem.*, 2000, **150**, 417.
22. S. Natarajan, S. Neeraj and C. N. R. Rao, *Solid State Sci.*, 2000, **2**, 87.
23. C. N. R. Rao, S. Natarajan and S. Neeraj, *J. Am. Chem. Soc.*, 2000, **122**, 2810.
24. W. T. A. Harrison, T. E. Martin, T. E. Gier and G. D. Stucky, *J. Mater. Chem.*, 1992, **2**, 75.
25. A. A. Ayi, A. Chourdhury, S. Natarajan, S. Neeraj and C. N. R. Rao, *J. Mater. Chem.*, 2001, **11**, 1181.
26. R. I. Walton, R. J. Francis, P. S. Halasyamani, D. O'Hare, R. I. Smith, R. Done and R. Humphreys, *Rev. Sci. Instrum.*, 1999, **70**, 3391.
27. W. G. Williams, R. M. Ibberson, P. Day and J. E. Enderby, *Physica B*, 1998, **214–243**, 234.
28. K. Bondioli, A. Bonamartini-Corradi, A. M. Ferrari, T. Manfredini and G. C. Pellacani, *Mater. Sci. Forum*, 1998, **278–281**, 379.
29. F. Taulelle, M. Haouas, C. Gerardin, C. Estournes, T. Loiseau and G. Férey, *Colloids Surf. A*, 1999, **158**, 299.
30. G. Sankar, J. M. Thomas, F. Rey and G. N. Greaves, *J. Chem. Soc., Chem. Commun.*, 1995, 2549.

Are metastable, precrystallisation, density-fluctuations a universal phenomena?

Ellen L. Heeley,[a] C. Kit Poh,[b] Wu Li,[a] Anna Maidens,[c] Wim Bras,[d] Igor P. Dolbnya,[d] Anthony J. Gleeson,[e] Nicolas J. Terrill,[e] J. Patrick A. Fairclough,[a] Peter D. Olmsted,[c] Rile I. Ristic,[b] Micheal J. Hounslow[b] and Anthony J. Ryan[a]

[a] *Department of Chemistry, University of Sheffield, Sheffield, UK S3 7HF*
[b] *Department of Chemical and Process Engineering, University of Sheffield, Sheffield, UK S3 7HF*
[c] *Department of Physics, The University of Leeds, Leeds, UK LS 9JT*
[d] *DUBBLE CRG, ESRF, F-38043, Grenoble, France*
[e] *CCLRC Daresbury Laboratory, Warrington, UK WA4 4AD*

Received 18th March 2002, Accepted 29th April 2002
First published as an Advance Article on the web 16th August 2002

In-situ observations of crystallisation in minerals and organic polymers have been made by simultaneous, time-resolved small angle X-ray scattering (SAXS) and wide angle X-ray scattering (WAXS) techniques. In isotactic polypropylene slow quiescent crystallisation shows the onset of large scale ordering prior to crystal growth. Rapid crystallisations studied by melt extrusion indicate the development of well resolved oriented SAXS patterns associated with long range order before the development of crystalline peaks in the WAXS region. Block copolymers self-assemble into mesophases in polymer melts above a critical chain length (or above a critical temperature) and this self-assembly process is shown to be susceptible to an incipient crystallisation. Mesophase formation is observed at anomalously high temperatures in ethylene-oxide containing block copolymers below the normal melting point of the polyoxy ethylene chains. Formation of calcium carbonate from aqueous solutions of sodium carbonate and calcium nitrate is observed to be a two-stage process and precipitation proceeds by the production of an amorphous metastable phase. This phase grows until it is volume filling and leads to the formation of the two polymorphs Calcite and Vaterite. These three sets of results suggest pre-nucleation density fluctuations, leading to a metastable phase, play an integral role in all three classes of crystallisation. In due course, this phase undergoes transformation to "normal" crystals.

Introduction

Homopolymer crystallisation

Recent work on polymer crystallisation has given considerable attention to the possibility that the crystal phase in the final semi-crystalline state is preceded by transient liquid phases of different density from that of the initial quenched bulk isotropic melt or annealed glassy state. Time resolved SAXS shows a peak indicating the growth of structure at length scales approximately corresponding to the long period of the final semi-crystalline material at times significantly before the appearance of crystal Bragg peaks in WAXS. Spinodal kinetics have been reported in a number of materials and using a variety of techniques: Imai and coworkers investigated cold crystallised (annealed from the glassy state) poly(ethylene terephthalate) (PET) using time resolved SAXS and WAXS;[1-4] Matsuba, Kaji and coworkers examined cold crystallised isotactic and sydiotactic polystyrene (iPS and sPS) using FTIR spectroscopy and de-polarized light scattering (DPLS)[5,6] and also cold crystallised poly(ethylene naphthalate) (PEN) using SAXS to reveal Cahn–Hilliard type behaviour at early times and Furakawa scaling behaviour at later times;[7] and Ezquerra's group noted spinodal-type behaviour in cold crystallised poly(ether ketone ketone) (PEKK).[8] We have previously observed spinodal behaviour in melt crystallised iPP[9,10] and with Olmsted et al.[11] interpreted the SAXS peak for the transient liquid phase in terms of spinodal-type kinetics by analogy with Cahn–Hilliard theory.[12,13]

Various studies have suggested that the denser transient phase involves chain orientation. SAXS carried out by Blundell et al. on melt crystallisation of PET and PEN undergoing extension indicates that the strain induces orientation that speeds up crystallisation rates, but that crystallisation only takes place after the strain is released, allowing the chains to relax into crystal order[14,15] with the precursor mesophase taking the form of a transient smectic liquid crystal phase. Crystallisation from oriented states shows a low activation energy, suggesting a process driven by local segmental activity rather than whole chain reptation. However, Blundell's group note that the evidence from these studies is insufficient to decide between the existence of a mesophase and extended linear chains of random monomeric sequence without any long range correlation, though they speculate that a mesophase might form an intermediate state between random extended chains and the final crystalline state.

Investigation of the chain conformational structure suggests that the denser, oriented transient phase is associated with conformational changes. These changes may be understood either as transforming randomly coiled molecules into stiffer chains with rod-like sections or as increasing the mean molecular stiffness (or persistence length). Working on iPS and sPS, Matsuba et al. showed orientation fluctuations using DPLS, increasing *trans* conformation bands during the induction period prior to the emergence of crystalline order, using FTIR, suggesting that the emergence of stiffer, rod-like sections leading to an oriented liquid state is driven by conformational change at the molecular level.[6] Tashiro et al.[16,17] studied a similar mechanism in the case of conformationally disordered (CONDIS) states in the hexagonal phase of PE crystallised from the melt, using SAXS, IR and Raman spectroscopy. They observed a hexagonal phase as a transient phase before the formation of orthorhombic crystals. This phase exhibited *gauche* defects along the chain, and Tashiro et al. speculated on its role as a route to crystallisation, with a CONDIS phase being seen both in rapid quenches and on slower cooling. They noted that it is possible that the hexagonal phase is thermodynamically metastable at atmospheric pressure, though there is no evidence for spinodal behaviour in this particular system.[18] Huang et al. used NMR and differential scanning calorimetry (DSC) to observe conformation changes in amorphous PET annealed above its glass transition temperature.[19] They noted an increase in *trans* content near the onset crystallisation temperature which they analysed with a three domain model of crystalline (all *trans*), constrained non-crystalline (*trans*-rich) and amorphous (*gauche*-rich) states. *Gauche* to *trans* conversion was assumed to proceed before subsequent crystallisation, with the *trans*-rich conformers regarded as precursors for PET crystallisation.

Some theoretical proposals have been made in connection with these findings. Ezquerra and coworkers base their treatment on the proposal that chain straightening and hence parallelization driven by intramolecular forces is followed by a density increase and crystallisation driven by intermolecular forces.[8] They use Doi et al.'s model[20] for the critical concentration above which one would expect to see nematic ordering. Imai et al.[1-3] also use a version of Doi's model in which an isotropic liquid becomes unstable at a critical concentration $C^* \propto 1/L^2$ where L is the length of the "rod" (proportional to the persistence length of the chain). Hence there is a critical length L_{p^*} above which the isotropic liquid becomes unstable to phase separation. Thus as the *trans*-bond number along the chain increases, the chain stiffens, and the critical concentration drops (or, equivalently, the critical length is exceeded) and we see phase separation. Matsuba and coworkers also use a Doi model for the critical "rod" concentration. As before, the critical concentration drops as chains extend with conformational change, with a critical length of about 5 alternate *trans* and *gauche* conformers in iPS (*i.e.* 10 monomer units)[5] and 10 TT sequences in sPS.[6] They note that the Doi model applies to stiff polymers and thus should not apply to a flexible chain like sPS, but speculate that conformational changes along the chain may lead to increase in effective segment length.[6]

The radius of gyration of a (very long) chain changes little during crystallisation, suggesting[21,22] that neighbouring segments adopt the correct conformation and crystallize 'in situ'. While it is commonly assumed that conformational and crystalline ordering occur simultaneously, Olmsted et al.[6] suggest that these processes can occur sequentially. Moreover, chains with different conformations have different densities, and therefore also different energy barriers for reorientation between rotational isomeric states (RIS).[23] Such conformation–density coupling can induce a liquid–liquid phase transition. Physically, the Olmsted model says that at low enough temperatures, the system gives up conformational entropy to relieve packing frustration, and separates into a dense, more conformationally homogeneous liquid and a less dense and more conformationally disordered liquid. In practice, this happens only at appreciable rates by spinodal decomposition, giving rise to two coexisting liquids, with a coarsening interconnected domain texture. The dense liquid is closer in density and conformation to the crystal phase than the original melt, with a lower energy barrier Δ to crystallisation and Δ is expected to decrease with increasing quench depth below the spinodal temperature, T_S.

Several groups have criticised the spinodal hypothesis,[23,24] and offered evidence supporting the traditional picture of nucleation and growth taking the appearance of a SAXS peak to indicate the appearance of crystallites (albeit not within the resolution of the WAXS detector) and hence the end of the induction period. The lag between SAXS and WAXS is then taken to be an issue of detector sensitivity. The induction period is often taken to be the same as the induction time, the time (according to the Avrami equation) after which the calculated crystallinity is non-zero. In this work we shall show that the lag is not due to detector sensitivity and that the emergence of Bragg peaks indicates the end of the induction period. The growth of the SAXS peak prior to this indicates the evolution of additional structure. Hsiao et al. reported the simultaneous growth of SAXS and WAXS peaks in melt crystallised poly(ether ether ketone) (PEEK), though they noted that this might be due to experimental limits on time resolution.[23] In later work,[24] however, they compare their experimental results to the alternative predictions of nucleation and growth, and of spinodal decomposition. They investigate iPP in order to compare their results directly with those of Ryan et al.[9,10] They draw attention to two important issues: analysis and the fitting of models to data; and detector limitations. The detector sensitivity issue is addressed here by the use of a new WAXS detector with a factor of 10^3 improvement in count rate over that used in previous experiments.

Theoretically, the debate is whether nucleation and growth alone explain crystallisation, or whether some spinodal-type mechanism also plays a part. In the first case, small amounts of crystalline material nucleate at random from the surrounding melt, with nuclei above a certain critical size (where the bulk energy outweighs the energetic cost of the interface) growing to form larger crystal lamellae. Clearly, the mechanism for the early stages of polymer crystallisation is an area of considerable controversy. The conflicting results and interpretations show that there is more work to be done. In accounting for the discrepancies, two issues are worth noting: first, a single system may exhibit either nucleation and growth or spinodal-like kinetics, depending on the depth of the quench, as shown in work on the order–disorder transition in polystyrene–*block*–polyisoprene blends.[25] Also, the direction of the shift in q^* may not suffice to confirm or rule out spinodal-type kinetics. The shift to smaller q^* in Cahn–Hilliard theory follows from a model in which the order parameter (concentration in the case of polymers in solution) is conserved. However, the emergence of nematic order involves a non-conserved order parameter (degree of orientation) coupled to the conserved density, so other models for the hydrodynamics may be more appropriate,[12] although such an analysis will not be addressed in this paper.

Order–disorder transitions in block copolymer melts

Theoretical and experimental aspects of microphase separation in block copolymer melts have been reviewed most comprehensively,[26,27] and the many relevant references can be found therein. The brief account which follows is cast in terms of the poly(ethylene oxide), E, and poly(butylene oxide), B, system studied here. E and B units mix endothermically and the positive contribution of the enthalpy of mixing to the Gibbs energy is the primary origin of the microphase separation. The Flory–Huggins mean-field treatment of this effect, which is a natural extension of the regular solution theory for simple liquids, requires definition of a reference segment volume, v_o. It is convenient to equate v_o with the volume occupied by an E unit ($v_E = 39.3$ cm^3 mol^{-1} at 25 °C), and write the overall length of the copolymer molecule in segments as

$$r_v = m + n(v_B/v_E) \qquad (1)$$

where v_B is the volume occupied by a B unit. Room temperature values of the specific volumes of liquid poly(oxyethylene) and poly(oxybutylene) lead to a value of $v_B/v_E = 1.89$, essentially independent of temperature.[28] With values of the Flory–Huggins segment interaction parameter χ based on the same reference volume, the equation for the non-combinatorial part of the Gibbs energy of mixing per chain is

$$\Delta_{mix} G_{nc} = kT(\chi r_v)\phi_E \phi_B \qquad (2)$$

where ϕ_E and ϕ_B are volume fractions. Theory predicts that microphase separation will depend only on χr_v and ϕ_E (or ϕ_B), and requires a phase diagram plotted as χr_v versus ϕ_E. The important feature linking the experimental determination of microphase separation temperatures and structures for real systems with theory is the temperature dependence of parameter χ. With sufficient accuracy this is given by an equation of the form

$$\chi = A/T + B \qquad (3)$$

where A and B are constants for a given system at a given concentration. The equation reflects the fact that endothermic mixing in polymer systems results in χ increasing with decreasing temperature, i.e. microphase separation is favoured by lowering the temperature, but there is a significant temperature independent (or entropic) term which is dependent on the local liquid structure.

For a given copolymer system, the first task is to determine acceptable values of the two constants in eqn. (3). This can be done by measuring the variation of microphase separation temperature as a function of chainlength, thus the experiment is to heat the sample to determine the temperature of the transition from an ordererd to a disordered phase, the so-called order–disorder transition, T_{ODT}. Leibler, using self-consistent mean-field theory (SCFT),[29] first demonstrated that microphase separation would occur for a symmetrical diblock copolymer ($\phi = 0.5$) at $(\chi r_v)_c = 10.5$ and the temperature coefficients of the interaction parameter can be extracted from

$$A/T_{ODT} + B = 10.5/r_v \qquad (4)$$

Composition fluctuations in the disordered melt just above the microphase separation temperature are an important consideration and these have also been reviewed in some detail.[30] The ODT is the transition from a melt with time-independent sinusoidal segment density fluctuations to one with similar but time-dependent fluctuations. A much higher temperature is needed before the melt is homogeneous: for example, for copolymer E$_{74}$B$_{37}$ homogeneity (mean field behaviour) is achieved some 80 °C above T_{ODT}.[31]

The phase behaviours of a number of diblock copolymer systems have been explored. The state of the field was reviewed (at a Faraday Discussion) in 1994 by Bates et al.,[32] who provided a number of illustrative phase diagrams, including those for diblock poly(olefin)s and for poly-(styrene)–block–poly(isoprene) (S$_m$I$_n$). A full account of the phase diagram for the S$_m$I$_n$ system was published later.[33] More recently, phase diagrams have been reported for poly(ethylene-alt-propylene) –block–poly(dimethylsiloxane), (EP)$_m$ (DMS)$_n$,[34] and poly(oxyethylene) –block–poly-(ethylethylene), E$_m$(EE)$_n$,[35] and poly(styrene) –block–poly(2-vinyl pyridine), S$_m$(VP)$_m$.[36] There is obvious universality in the phase behaviour of block copolymers based on non-crystallisable chains and that reported for E$_m$B$_n$ copolymers at temperatures well above the melting point of polyoxy ethylene. The similarity between the E$_n$B$_m$, S$_m$I$_n$ and (EP)$_m$ (DMS)$_n$ systems is striking. Molar masses are higher in the S$_m$I$_n$ system: i.e. $M_n = 10\,000$–$80\,000$ g mol^{-1} compared with 4000–15 000 g mol^{-1} for the other two. This lower molar mass is accompanied (as it must be if microphase separation is to occur at similar values of χr_v) by higher values of χ. Reduced to the same reference volume, $v_o = 100$ cm^3 mol^{-1}, and for $T = 100$ °C, 'fluctuation' values of χ are 0.12 for

S_nI_m, but 0.21 for $(EP)_m (DMS)_n$, and 0.29 for E_mB_n. Bates et al. have used the parameter $\bar{N} = r_v b^6 \rho^2$ calculated for identical reference conditions as an indicator of the importance of composition fluctuations in systems of different chemical composition.[37] Adopting their reference conditions ($\phi_E = 0.5$, $T = 150\,°C$), we find a value of $\bar{N} \approx 800$ for E_mB_n, compared with 1100 for S_mI_n and 500 for $(EP)_m(DMS)_n$, i.e. rather similar values, consistent with the similarity of the phase behaviour of the three systems. We highlight this universality of phase behaviour here before presenting new experimental evidence of a separate branch of microphase separation in the block copolymer melt below the melting point of the E-blocks and suggest that this change in phase behaviour is driven by an intrinsic difference in the rotational isomeric states (chain stiffness) and as a consequence new temperature coefficients in χ.

Calcium carbonate

The precipitation of calcium carbonate has been reviewed in detail.[38] Calcium carbonate is used in large quantities as a filler in materials like paper, plastics and rubber, and in paint, sealants, pharmaceuticals and cosmetics products. In nature calcium carbonate occurs in shells of molluscs (and ultimately chalk and limestone) and gallstones.[39] Calcium carbonate can precipitate into three different anhydrous polymorphs, namely calcite, aragonite and vaterite. Among these, calcite is the most thermodynamically stable polymorph. In addition, the less stable hydrated forms of calcium carbonate hexahydrate,[40] calcium carbonate monohydrate[41] and an "amorphous" calcium carbonate[41-44] are also possible. Many studies of the morphology and size of calcium carbonate precipitates are limited to particles that are at least a few micrometres in size.[45-48] A number of investigations into the so-called "amorphous" metastable phase[42,44,45] claim that these precursor particles are spherical in shape, non-crystalline and sub-micron in size, however, there is no, in situ study to confirm these findings.

However, the use of SAXS and WAXS in the studies of crystallisation from aqueous systems has been scarce. Jalava et al.[49] used SAXS to study the precipitation of hydrous titanium dioxide from aqueous solutions, but this work did not involve in situ observation of the precipitation processes. Rieger et al.[45] studied calcium carbonate precipitation by means of X-ray microscopy using samples that were physically confined to a small volume. We report here time resolved SAXS and WAXS to follow the precipitation and crystallisation of a super-saturated solution of calcium carbonate in a large volume crystalliser, noting the formation of an amorphous precursor phase prior to formation of calcite and vaterite.

Experimental

Time resolved SAXS-WAXS experiments

Simultaneous SAXS/WAXS/DSC measurements were made on beamlines 8.2 and 16.1 at the SRS at the CLRC Daresbury Laboratory, Warrington, UK and on the DUBBLE BM26 at the ESRF, Grenoble, France. The design, layout and operation of these beamlines has been described elsewhere,[50,51] the specific details concerning sample preparation and the scattering set-up are reported below. The scattering pattern from an oriented specimen of collagen (rat-tail tendon) was used to calibrate the SAXS detector and HDPE, aluminium and an NBS silicon standard were used to calibrate the WAXS detectors.[50] At DUBBLE a newly developed position sensitive high countrate microstrip gas chamber (MSGC) detector[52] with high count rate operation has been used. The measurements show local count rate capabilities up to $\sim 4 \times 10^5$ counts s^{-1} channel^{-1}. Parallel-plate ionisation detectors, placed before and after the sample, recorded the incident and transmitted intensities. The experimental data were corrected for background scattering, for sample thickness and transmission, and for any positional non-linearity in the detectors.

Samples and measurement conditions

SAXS/WAXS/DSC. Simultaneous SAXS/WAXS/DSC measurements were made on beamline 8.2 at the SRS and on the DUBBLE BM26 at the ESRF. Disk specimens of polymer (thickness ~ 1 mm, diameter ~ 5 mm) were cut from pre-moulded sheets. A disk specimen for SAXS/WAXS/DSC was encapsulated in a TA Instruments DSC fitted with mica windows (thickness ~ 25 μm, diameter ~6 mm), and the pan was inserted into a Linkam DSC apparatus of the single-pan design that has been described in detail elsewhere.[53] The cell comprises a silver furnace around a heat-flux plate containing a 3×0.5 mm^2 slot, for X-ray access, and the sample is held in contact with the plate by a spring of low thermal-mass. The temperature was calibrated using the melting points of high purity indium and tin. Data were reduced to intensity *versus* scattering vector using the CCP13 programme xotoko and peak intensities and areas were calculated using the CCP13 programme XFIT.[54]

A commercial grade of iPP was obtained from PCD Polymere AG, Daplen iPP has weight-average molar mass (GPC) and polydispersity of 622 kg mol^{-1} and 5.5 respectively, and the crystallisation and melting points by differential scanning calorimetry (heating and cooling at rate of 10 °C min^{-1}) were 99 ± 2 and 165 ± 2 °C respectively. For the SAXS data a Gaussian peak (whose position was a variable) was fitted on top of a Porod background. For the WAXS 4 Pearson VII peaks were fitted on top of a 3rd order polynomial background, where the positions of the 4 peaks were set according to the positions of the α-monoclinic form of isotactic polypropylene with reflections at hkl values of (110), (040), (130) and ((111)(−131)).

The block copolymers were specially synthesised by sequential anionic polymerisation and their characterisation by GPC and NMR has been described previously.[55] The polymers were of low polydispersity ($M_n/M_w < 1.05$) and formulae are quoted as E_mB_n, where m and n are number-average block lengths in ethylene oxide and butylene oxide units respectively, known to $\pm 1\%$. Values of T_{ODT} and T_{DOT} are determined from step changes in the peak-maximum intensity, peak width and peak shape[54] from the SAXS data with a Pearson VII peak (whose position was a variable) fitted on top of a Porod background. T_{DOT} can be determined at temperatures below the melting point if microphase separation occurs in the supercooled melt before crystallisation.

SAXS/WAXS/extrusion. Simultaneous SAXS/WAXS/extrusion[10] measurements were made on beamline 16.1 at the SRS. An extruder above the X-ray position was used to provide a steady stream of crystallising polymer past the X-ray position. Tape extrusion is a steady-state process which shows post-die plug flow so the distance down the spin-line where the observation was made correlates with the time since the material left the extruder die. The material in the X-ray beam is continuously replaced by material with the same shear and temperature history. A tape of polymer melt was extruded from a die (of dimensions 0.5×3 mm^2 at $T_m + 40$ °C) and collected *via* a wind-up mechanism below the X-ray beam. The extruder used was an AXON BX18 which operated in starve feed mode to minimise the time the polymer spent in the melt. The distance from the die head to the beam could be varied between 0.3 and 1.8 m. The beamline is equipped with a multiwire area detector (SAXS) located between 3 and 8 m from the sample position with flight path to the SAXS detector being under vacuum. A CCD area detector was used for WAXS which was offset from the centre line of the beam and located approximately 20 cm from the extruded tape. Time resolved SAXS/WAXS measurements were made with the CCD area detector intersecting either the meridian or the equator.

Calcium carbonate. Simultaneous, time-resolved *in situ* SAXS and WAXS measurements were performed at the DUBBLE BM26 at the ESRF. Solutions of sodium carbonate (Na_2CO_3) and calcium nitrate ($Ca(NO_3)_2$) were prepared from distilled water and AnalaR® grade chemicals obtained from Merck Ltd. Fig. 1 shows the experimental set-up. 200 ml of sodium carbonate solution was recirculated through a glass crystalliser and a glass flow cell of a novel design by means of a magnetic pump. Both the crystalliser and the flow cell were jacketed and thermostatically controlled and stirred by an overhead stirrer using a 45 mm diameter 3-blade upward-flow propeller set at 500 rpm. K-type thermocouples were used to measure the temperature of the solution in the crystalliser and the flow cell. When the solution temperature had stabilised at 10 °C, a background SAXS and WAXS measurement was taken. 200 ml of calcium nitrate solution at 10 °C was then manually mixed into the crystalliser and recording of measurements commenced simultaneously, recording at 10 s intervals. Upon mixing, the temperature of the solution dropped fairly rapidly to 9.4 °C due to an increase in surface area for heat transfer, and thereafter remained constant. After 5000 s, the precipitates were filtered (0.2 μm) from the solution and subsequently dried before weighing.

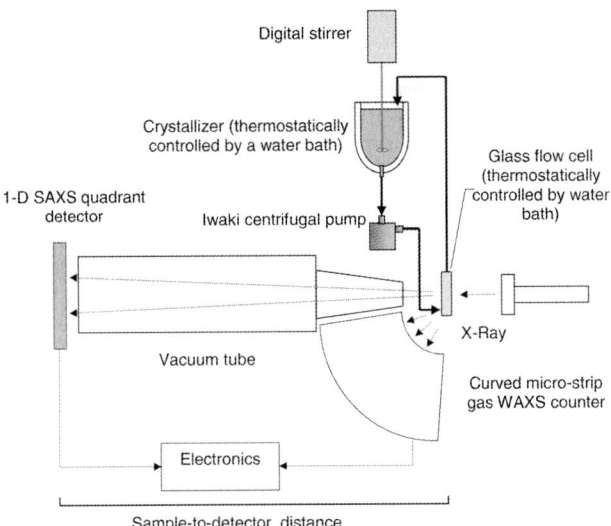

Fig. 1 A schematic diagram of the experimental set-up for CaCO$_3$ crystallisation at DUBBLE BM26.

Results

Homopolymers

It is difficult to separate nucleation from growth in a scattering experiment due to the low concentration of nuclei, which gives rise to poor counting statistics. One potential method is to borrow from elementary chemical kinetics and use a flow apparatus. An extruder operating at steady state provides such a set-up where polymer above the melting point is extruded from a die, the tape or fiber cools in the air (in our case in a column of chilled nitrogen) prior to being wound up as a solid. Extrusion of tape or fiber is a steady-state process where the crystallisation time increases down the spin-line. This allows long data collection times (min) for the very early stages of crystallisation (ms). Prior to the development of crystals, well resolved, oriented small-angle patterns could be observed with length scales (200–500 Å) and intensities that grew down the spin-line. The corresponding WAXS showed no Bragg peaks due to crystals.

Fig. 2 shows the scattering patterns collected during extrusion of iPP. At short times these early patterns have two SAXS peaks at finite q and no WAXS peaks. We interpret this as a signature of density fluctuations. The orientation observed in the scattering is caused by coupling of density fluctuations with the slight elongational flow-field (the take-up speed was approximately twice the extrusion speed). Once crystallisation had been observed in the wide-angle region, the shape of the small-angle pattern changed to that typical of lamellar crystals. Since the elongational flow was weak the crystallisation process dominated and only weakly anisotropic crystals were produced. The SAXS peaks shown at early times in Fig. 2(a) were approximately 100 times weaker than the diffraction ring observed in SAXS once spherulitic crystallisation had occurred (Fig. 2(c)).

There are a number of other possible interpretations of the data. The SAXS peak could be due to the formation of oriented nuclei, the precursor to the "shish" in "shish-kebab" crystals and row nucleation[56] but this should also lead to orientation in the WAXS which is not observed. Furthermore, the elongation is less than a factor of 2, which is very low for formation of such structures.[57] Nucleation could have formed poorly ordered crystals that do not diffract. This would account for the lack of Bragg peaks in the WAXS (peak broadening due to small crystallites), but does not account for the peak in SAXS, the scattering from a low concentration of randomly oriented objects would give a peak at $q = 0$ from the shape factor of the scatterers.[58] Systems with conserved order parameters have nuclei surrounded by a depletion layer and these would give a weak peak in SAXS at low concentration due to the shape factor. However, in this system with a non-conserved order parameter, the nuclei are not surrounded by a depletion layer. Regions of

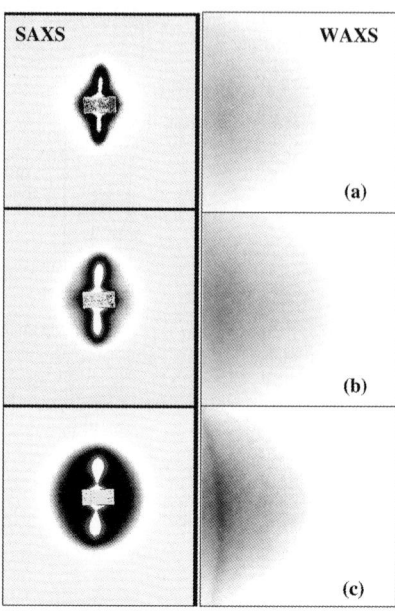

Fig. 2 Evolution of SAXS and WAXS down the spin-line during extrusion of isotactic polypropylene as a function of position down the spin-line. The temperature at the X-ray beam is (a) 117 °C, (b) 84 °C and (c) 65 °C.

high density grow from a background of low density with an overall increase in density and the electron density profile does not have a peak at finite q. The most obvious alternative explanation of the observation is that there is an outer skin of crystalline material, due to the temperature gradient across the tape, which is giving rise to the SAXS. In this situation the crystals formed would be well ordered and one would expect them to diffract at wide angles, which is obviously not the case. Under the current experimental conditions, it is possible to observe diffraction from 1% by volume of a crystalline olefin dispersed in oil.[24] In order to check the temperature of the melt in the scattering volume a number of techniques have been applied, an optical pyrometer indicated that the data taken close to the X-ray position had a surface temperature in excess of 120 °C. Whilst it is undoubtedly true that at long times crystallisation proceeds from the exterior of the tape, it is unlikely that it has occurred in the data presented here.

Previous SAXS/WAXS studies on polymer extrusion have concentrated on the growth and orientation of crystals.[59,60] Interestingly both studies, Cakmak et al.[59] on PVDF tape (using synchrotron radiation) and Katayama et al.[60] on PET fibers (using a sealed tube source and film as a detector) showed SAXS before WAXS down the spin-line, but made no comment on its significance.

More recent reports of flow-induced crystallisation have shown that under shear iPP unambiguously forms metastable precursors to crystallisation. The growth of SAXS peaks shows a difference between isotropic and anisotropic regions in the melt when a sheared melt of iPP is observed above its equilibrium melting point (which prevents crystal formation, enabling the emergence of orientational order to be studied without subsequent crystallisation). Shearing the melt induces orientation and hence alignment, with an Avrami exponent of 0.6 suggesting linear growth of oriented structures consistent with a model of linear aggregation of chains. Even under quiescent conditions the precursor phase is observed, though its exact pathway from mesophase to crystalline structure is uncertain.[61] For quenches of sheared iPP below the melting point the time to the first appearance of precursors decreases with decreasing quench depth (in contrast to the situation for quiescent nucleation, where deeper quenches have shorter times before the emergence of crystals, interpreted as a lowering of the barrier to nucleation for larger quenches). Hsiao and coworkers note that this suggests a non-classical pathway which removes the activation barrier to nucleation, which they speculate is mediated by chain alignment leading to regions of locally parallel segments, increasing the probability that these segments explore a stable, long-lived configuration. However, within their limits of experimental resolution, WAXS and SAXS peaks appear simultaneously, giving no evidence in this case that crystallisation is preceded by emergence of regions of different density.[62]

Slow crystallisations, with long induction times, have been studied by simultaneous SAXS and WAXS by a number of groups who make broadly similar observations but reach radically different conclusions. We shall examine the two crucial issues of detector sensitivity and the appropriate data analysis. The issue of whether the time lag is simply due to low WAXS sensitivity has been resolved using the new MSGC detector which has much higher count-rate than previous delay-line detectors and, consequently, a much improved signal to noise ratio. We apply Cahn–Hilliard theory to calculate the spinodal temperature and compare this with the earlier results on similar samples.[9,10]

These experiments, on quiescent samples, show, at small undercoolings, a clear development of a SAXS peak prior to the presence of crystals identified by WAXS. At large undercoolings the SAXS and WAXS signals grow together and obey a power law throughout the crystallisation process. This is not obvious in the 3-D (intensity *versus* scattering vector *versus* time) SAXS/WAXS patterns in Fig. 3(a) and (b) but the integrated intensity *versus* time data in Fig. 4(a) for iPP at 130 °C show quite clearly the well-established spherulitic growth of polypropylene crystals. The behaviour at small undercoolings is qualitatively different and Fig. 3(c) and (d) shows unequivocally, that the SAXS peak grows before the WAXS peak. In the first 800 s of the experiment there is no scattering above the background intensity. Between 800 and 1500 s there is a measurable SAXS intensity with no WAXS above the background. After 1500 s Bragg peaks are observed and the growth in SAXS and WAXS map onto each other. The crystallinity at 6000 s is ≈ 0.3.

The logarithm of the peak intensity *versus* time, for the period where there is SAXS without WAXS, gives a good straight line as previously reported. Similar behavior has been reported previously for semi-rigid polymers crystallised by devitrifying a glass[1–3,8] and the kinetics of crystallisation after devitrification were analyzed in terms of the Cahn–Hilliard model[15] for spinodal decomposition.

The general form of the variation in scattered intensity, $I(q,t)$, following quench is given by:

$$I(q,t) = I(q,0)\exp[2R(q)t] \tag{5}$$

The variation in $I(q)$ at a given time interval is determined by the scattering law for the objects and $R(q)$ is termed the growth rate constant and is given by:

$$R(q) = -Mq^2\left(\frac{\partial^2 G}{\partial \rho^2} + 2\kappa q^2\right) \tag{6}$$

Here M is the mobility term, G is the Gibbs energy, and κ is a gradient free-energy term. In employing eqn. (5) to analyze the data, the extrema are not strictly correct. The q dependence of the Onsager coefficient relating the diffusive flux of polymer molecules to the local chemical potential has been neglected. This may be valid for the early stages of phase separation and a shallow quench. $R(q)/q^2$ can be taken as a measure of the dynamic driving force for the growth of the concentration fluctuation with wave vector $q/2\pi$. There is a region of q in which $R(q)$, and thus $R(q)/q^2$, is positive and the concentration fluctuations do not decay but grow and give rise to phase separation. These growing concentration fluctuations have upper and lower critical boundaries to their wave numbers. Outside these limits, the concentration fluctuations decay and do not contribute to the phase separation dynamics. The driving force for the growth of the concentration fluctuation with wave vector $q/2\pi$, $R(q)/q^2$, becomes a maximum at $q = q_m = \sqrt{(G''/\kappa)}$. Thus, the wavelength, $q/2\pi$, of the dominant Fourier component of the growing fluctuations in the early stages of phase separation is determined by the maximum dynamic driving force. q_m is time independent in the early stages of phase separation and is controlled by thermodynamics.[63,64] $R(q)$ is further controlled by the transport properties and is related to the flux of molecules where the effective diffusion coefficient, D_{eff}, can be determined from an extrapolation to $q = 0$ of the straight-line portion of $R(q)/q^2$ during phase separation using

$$D_{eff} = \frac{2R(q)}{q^2} \tag{7}$$

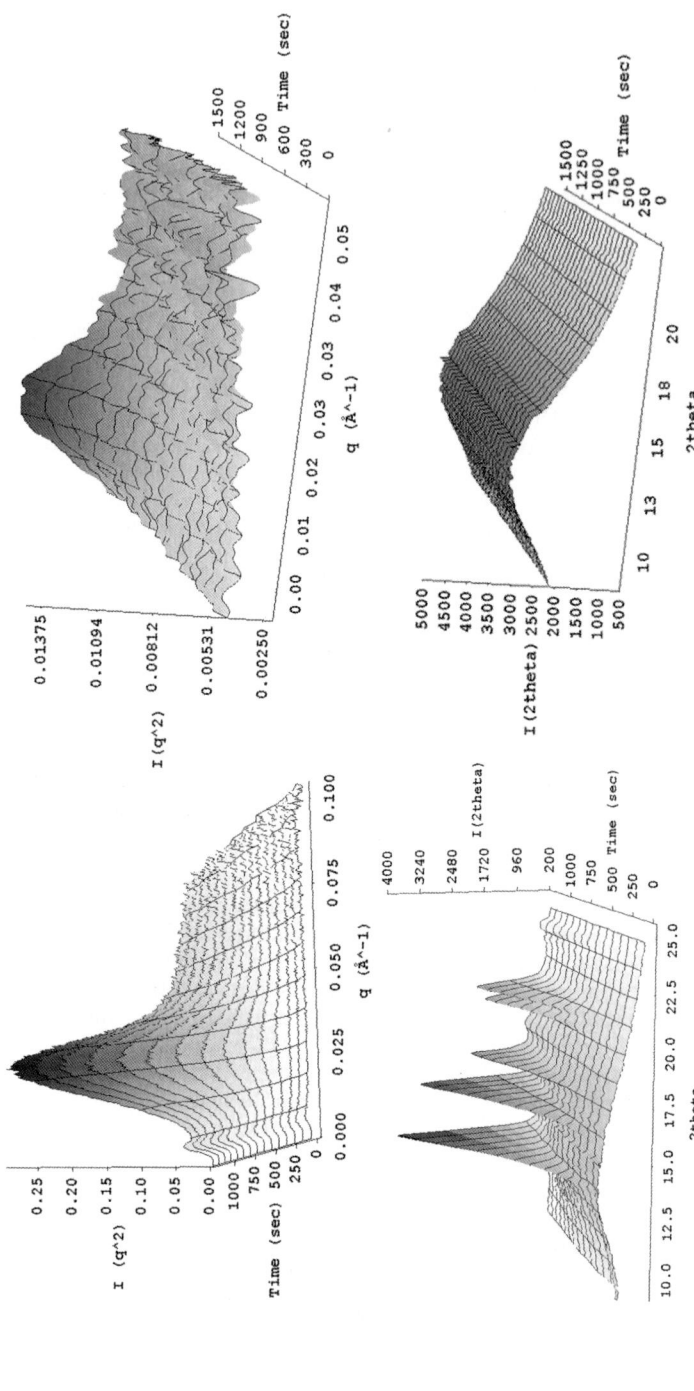

Fig. 3 SAXS/WAXS development during isothermal crystallisation of Daplen iPP at 130 °C where SAXS (a) and WAXS (b) grow contemporaneously and at 142 °C where there is appreciable SAXS (c) before WAXS (d) peaks are observed.

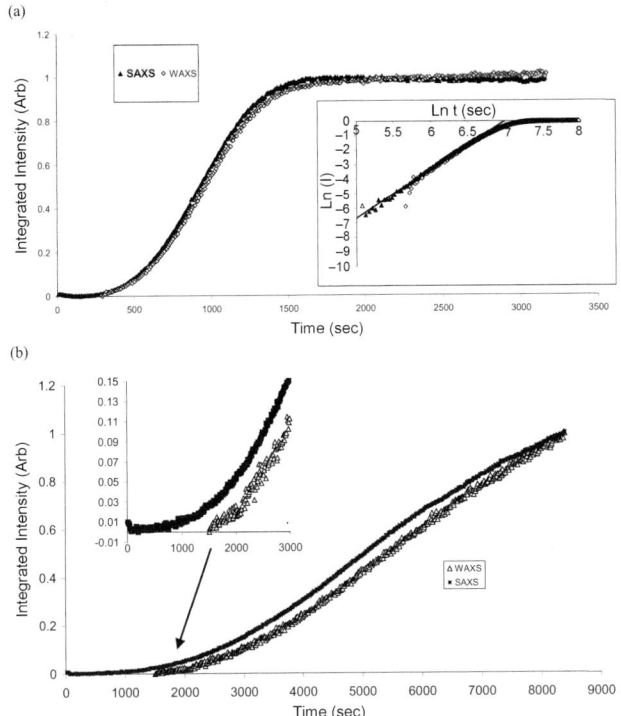

Fig. 4 The SAXS/WAXS data of isothermal crystallisation of Daplen iPP comparing (a) 130 °C, where SAXS and WAXS develop contemporaneously and the data fit to an Avrami model as shown in the inset, with (b) 142 °C, which clearly shows SAXS before WAXS.

and the linearity holds for $q_m < q < \sqrt{2}\, q_m$. Values of the amplification factor $R(q)$, for the early stage of crystallisation where we observe SAXS but no WAXS, were determined by plotting $\ln I$ versus t for discrete wave vectors and finding the slope.[13] $R(q)/q^2$ versus q^2 plots were constructed at a range of temperatures and are shown in Fig. 5. As the crystallisation temperature is increased it

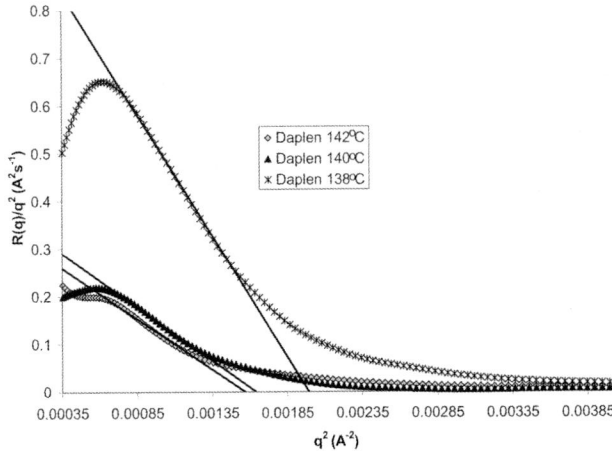

Fig. 5 The Cahn–Hilliard plot of Daplen iPP showing the solid line fit to the data allowing the estimation of D_{eff} from the intercept $q = 0$.

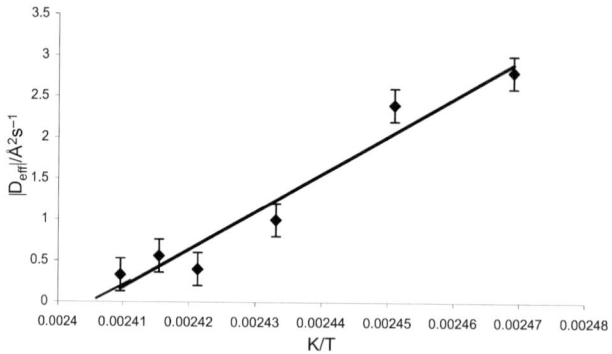

Fig. 6 A plot of D_{eff} versus $1/T$ for Daplen iPP to allow calculation of the spinodal temperature from extrapolation to $D_{eff} = 0$.

should be noted that the data get less noisy (as the kinetics slow down and counting statistics improve) and the linear part of the graph is reduced, this is because q_m moves to lower values.

Fig. 6 shows a plot of D_{eff} versus $1/T$, the spinodal temperature is determined by the $D_{eff} = 0$ intercept. For example, in Daplen iPP at 415 K, we could estimate both the dominant length scale $L \approx 290$ Å and the effective co-operative diffusion coefficient $D_{eff} = -0.4$ Å^2 s^{-1}. By conducting these experiments at a series of temperatures the stability limit of samples of iPP from four different sources could be found at 416 ± 5 K[18] by extrapolation of D_{eff} to zero. The stability limit is the temperature below which the polymer spontaneously separates into two phases. One of the phases is rich in polymer segments of the appropriate chain conformation to crystallize (trans–gauche arrangement of the carbon backbone in isotactic polypropylene) and the other is concentrated in sequences near entanglements and other defects which cannot crystallize. The stability limit is 20 K below the measured melting point for polypropylene with a long spacing of 185 Å and 43 K below the thermodynamic melting point of isotactic polypropylene.[10] Once WAXS from crystals (atomic order on the 1 Å scale) was observed, the kinetics reverted to those of nucleation and growth, that is Avrami kinetics with an exponent $n \approx 3$ (see Fig. 2). Similar behavior has also been observed in devitrified glasses of PET, by Imai and co-workers,[1–3] and PEEK, by Ezquerra and co-workers,[4] however, as the measurements are made close to the glass transition and the dynamics are dominated by the viscosity, estimation of the stability limit is not possible as D_{eff} increases with temperature.

The quiescent time-resolved SAXS/WAXS and extrusion suggest that a process that strongly resembles spinodal decomposition of chain segments with different average conformations is the nucleation step in polymer crystallisation and this is supported by the Olmsted model. That polymer crystallisation occurs with phase separation is in no doubt, since at the end of the process regions of well ordered crystalline polymer coexist with regions of disordered polymer in a layered morphology (lamellae) with a spherulitic super-structure. Sequences that can be oriented with the right conformation and incorporated into the crystal separate from sequences near entanglements and other defects that cannot crystallize and can only be part of the amorphous regions. The transformation from the disordered phase to the better ordered partially crystalline phase proceeds continuously, passing through a sequence of slightly more ordered states rather than building up a crystalline state instantaneously. This is consistent with the evolution of SAXS before WAXS. At some stage secondary nucleation must form crystals directly from the melt and a mechanism of continuous transformation could be consistent with a fast homogeneous nucleation process. It is difficult, however, to make a clear distinction between spinodal decomposition and nucleation and growth with nucleation barriers smaller than $k_B T$.[11] Polymer crystallisation, like any other phase separation, is kinetically controlled. The structure formed is the one with the highest growth rate. Once a crystallite is formed, its lateral growth rate is much higher than that of the fluctuations and so dominates. In this case the growth mechanism of semi-crystalline polymer lamellae, in the form of spherulites, takes over because the lateral growth rate of crystals (typically μm s^{-2}) is much faster than the growth rate of the fluctuations (typically Å^2 s^{-1}). Thus the combination of the

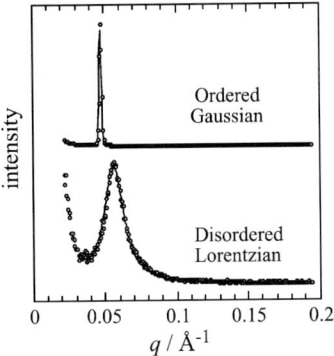

Fig. 7 SAXS patterns for ordered and disordered melts of diblock copolymer $E_{96}B_{47}$ at temperatures 30 °C below and above $T_{ODT} = 163$ °C. The circles are data points and the curves are fits of Gaussian and Lorentzian functions. The maximum intensities are in the approximate ratio, order : disorder = 3500 : 1. The upturn at low q is similar for both copolymers, and originates in parasitic scattering from the camera.

steady-state extrusion and the high intensity, synchrotron X-ray source allows nucleation to be observed.

Block copolymers

SAXS patterns for ordered and fluctuating melts of diblock copolymer $E_{96}B_{47}$ are illustrated in Fig. 7.[31] The data are for the melt at temperatures 30 °C apart on either side of the ODT. The broad peak obtained for the disordered melt is best fitted by a Lorentzian function with width parameter $\sigma/q^* \approx 1/3$ ($q^* = q$ at the first-order maximum), while the narrow peak obtained for the ordered melt is best fitted by a Gaussian function with $\sigma/q^* \approx 1/50$. In fact the narrow peak is resolution limited, a point-spread function of beam profile and detector.

Time resolved SAXS allows detailed investigation of copolymer melts as they are heated through the ODT.[61–66] An example of the data obtained is shown in Fig. 8, i.e. a three-dimensional relief diagram of time-resolved SAXS data obtained during heating and cooling copolymer $B_{46}E_{99}B_{46}$.[67] The SAXS pattern at low temperature is that of the semicrystalline lamellar phase. At 54 °C ⩽ T ⩾ 124 °C, the sharp narrow peak indicates an ordered melt, and the broad scattering peak at T > 124 °C indicates a disordered melt with composition fluctuations. The phase sequence is reversed on cooling. It has been demonstrated that values of T_{ODT} and T_{DOT} can be defined for

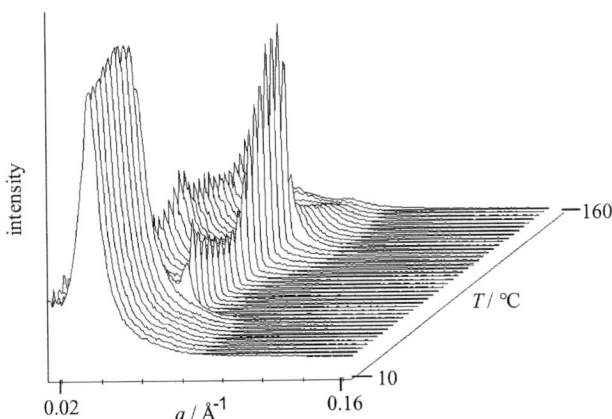

Fig. 8 Three-dimensional relief diagram of time-resolved SAXS obtained while heating triblock copolymer $B_{46}E_{99}B_{46}$. The temperature ramp rate was 10 °C min^{-1}.

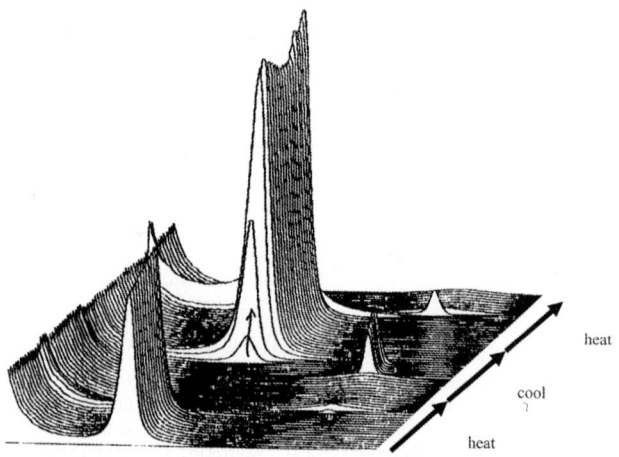

Fig. 9 Three-dimensional relief diagram of time-resolved SAXS obtained while heating and cooling triblock copolymer $E_{68}B_{34}$. The temperature ramp rate was 10 °C min^{-1}.

all E/B copolymers from step changes in the peak-maximum intensity, peak width and peak shape.[32] T_{DOT} can be determined at temperatures below the melting point if microphase separation occurs in the supercooled melt before crystallisation.[54,68–70] A heat–cool–heat cycle is shown for E68B34 in Fig. 9 showing the appearance of such a supercooled, ordered melt with a clearly identifiable DOT. The initial semi-crystalline structure (strong peak at q_c) is heated to form a disordered melt (broad low-intensity peak q_m) which on cooling forms an ordered melt (sharp peak at q_m) prior to crystallisation (strong peak at q_c). The crystals formed during programmed cooling have a lower melting point than those that perfected on storage and a fleeting ordered phase is observed on remelting.

Fig. 10 shows χ determined for E/B copolymers with compositions in the range $\varphi_E = 0.42$ to 0.56 plotted against reciprocal T_{ODT}.[68–70] The values of χ obtained for a wide range of diblocks and triblocks (EBE and BEB) fall on a single straight line above the melting point of the E-blocks. The high T straight line in Fig. 7 is based on the data points (open symbols) for both diblock and triblock copolymers. The equation for the temperature dependence of χ is

$$\chi = 51.6/T - 0.0617 \tag{8}$$

and is based on mean field prediction of $(\chi r_v)_{ODT}$. The data from the DOTs of 4 polymers with $\varphi_E = 0.5$ and $r_V < 100$ are represented by the filled symbols and do not fit the straight line

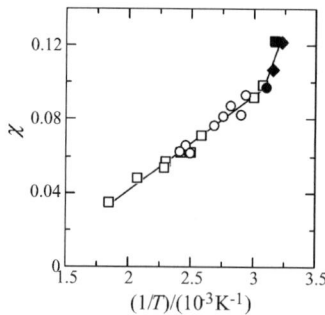

Fig. 10 (a) Flory–Huggins parameter χ versus reciprocal microphase-separation temperature for E/B copolymers with $\phi_E \approx 0.5$. The squares represent linear diblock copolymers, the circles linear triblock copolymers and the diamonds cyclic diblock copolymers. The straight lines are the least-squares fits to the $T > T_m$ (open symbols) and $T < T_m$ (closed symbols) branches of the data.

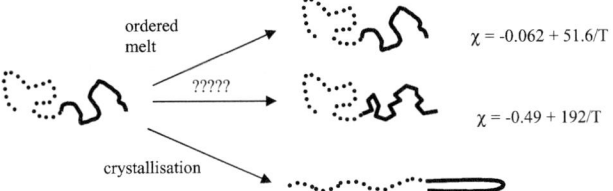

Fig. 11 A schematic representation of the change in the conformation of the E-block around T_m and the subsequent change in the temperature coefficients of χ.

established for the longer copolymers with $T_{ODT} > T_{mE}$. These copolymers fall onto a line with a much stronger slope

$$\chi = 192/T - 0.485 \qquad (9)$$

and one possible reason could be end-group effects. Given the nature of the samples involved (one linear diblock, one linear triblock and two cyclic diblock copolymers) this is unlikely. The simplifying assumption that local (segment scale) and long-range (radius-of-gyration scale) phenomena are decoupled is implicit in the Flory–Huggins theory[71] which introduces χ but this has been shown to be inaccurate in predicting the detailed phase behaviour of polymer blends and block copolymers.[72,73] Higher order corrections to the Flory–Huggins theory were introduced to deal with this problem and they relate the local environment and the liquid chain stiffness (through R_g) to the entropic excess energy of mixing, that is the parameter B in eqn. (4). Kaji and coworkers[1–3,5–7] have shown, by scattering and spectroscopic methods, that there are significant populations of helix conformation in the melt prior to crystallisation and this change in the conformation will result in coil expansion due to increased chain stiffness. Our hypothesis, shown schematically in Fig. 11, is that cooling the block copolymer below a critical temperature causes the conformation of the PEO chains to change due to helix formation, this obviously affects the excess enthalpy of mixing causing an increase in the temperature coefficient of χ, but the increase in chain stiffness, which effects the local liquid structure, has a profound effect on the excess entropy of mixing and this contribution to increases by an order of magnitude, driving the anomalous phase separation.

Calcium carbonate

The precipitation of calcium carbonate proceeded by homogeneous nucleation of a "gelatinous" metastable phase. The gel formed immediately on mixing the sodium carbonate and calcium nitrate solutions. This was evidenced by the immediate increase in turbidity of the solid–solution mixture from visual inspection. Fig. 12(a) shows the time-resolved WAXS results. The absence of any Bragg peak for the initial 350 s strongly suggests that the metastable phase is amorphous. As far as we are aware this is the first *in situ* WAXS study of the metastable phase and its transformation to a crystalline phase, mainly calcite. A little vaterite was also detected. Fig. 12(b) shows the time-resolved SAXS results, demonstrating a change in diffracted intensity corresponding to the metastable phase, the transformation phase, and the crystalline phase. The change in intensity in SAXS during the transformation phase matches the emergence of Bragg reflections in the WAXS pattern.

The (104) reflection was chosen for analysis of the broadening of the Bragg line, primarily due to its much greater intensity, an advantage over the other reflections especially when the signal-to-noise ratio is particularly low. The Gaussian symmetrical profile function has been fitted to the (104) calcite Bragg peak and the width of the diffraction peak at an intensity half the maximum intensity (FWHM) used in the Scherrer formula (crystallite thickness = 0.9λ / FWHM $\cos \theta_B$, where λ = wavelength and θ_B = peak position) to follow the change in crystallite size with time. This is shown in Fig. 13(a). Considering the system as a two-phase system consisting of solution and calcite crystals, the integrated intensity (the area under the curve) of the (104) peak can be used to follow the change in the precipitated mass of calcite in solution with time. We assume here that

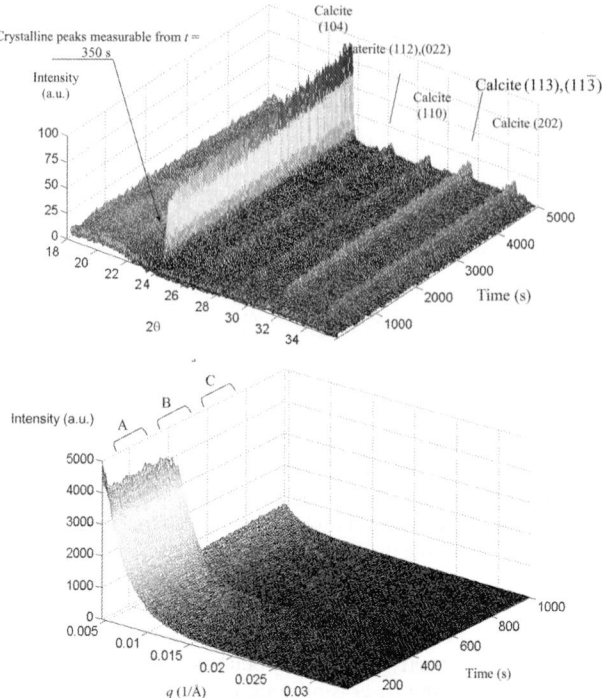

Fig. 12 (a) Time resolved WAXS during precipitation of $CaCO_3$. (b) Time-resolved SAXS during precipitation of $CaCO_3$. Zone A corresponds to the amorphous metastable phase, and Zone B the transformation of the metastable phase to the crystalline phase, indicated by Zone C.

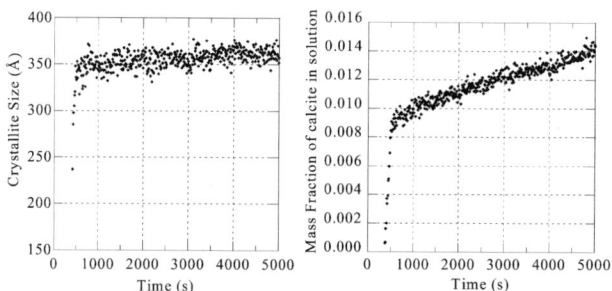

Fig. 13 (a) Evolution of crystallite size with time. (b) Change in mass fraction of calcite in solution, as a function of time.

the amount of vaterite is negligible, especially since the entire vaterite peak shown in Fig. 12 results from sets of planes with two different Miller indices.

For a mixture of two phases the scattered intensity has the following form:

$$I = \frac{K_1 \omega_{calcite}}{\rho_{calcite}[\omega_{calcite}(\mu_{calcite} - \mu_{solution}) + \mu_{solution}]} \quad (10)$$

where K_1 = constant, ω = mass fraction and μ = mass absorption coefficient.

The integrated intensity of the (104) peak at the end of the experiment can be calculated and the corresponding mass of calcite is known from measurement of the mass of the solid precipitate extracted thereafter. Therefore, it is possible to work out the mass at other times for which the integrated intensity can be calculated from the WAXS data. Fig. 13(b) illustrates the change in mass fraction of calcite in solution as a function of time. Both quantitative results demonstrate that once the transformation from the amorphous phase to crystalline phase has started, the process is relatively rapid, lasting for less than 150 s.

An *in situ*, time-resolved simultaneous SAXS and WAXS study on the reactive crystallisation of calcium carbonate in a set-up that mimics industrial crystallizers has been successfully performed. It has to be stressed that in this work, the system was not confined to a small physical volume but allowed to mix, and thus the conditions under which the precipitation occurred closely resembled those that would exist in real, industrial processes. The WAXS results give compelling evidence directly, for the first time, that the "gelatinous" metastable phase is amorphous. Although the mechanism for the transformation from the amorphous phase to the crystalline phase is not yet fully understood, the quantitative analysis shows that this transformation is relatively rapid.

Summary

We describe *in situ* observations of crystallisation minerals and organic polymers by simultaneous, time-resolved SAXS and WAXS techniques. Two types of experiments on homopolymers crystallising from the melt show precrystallisation structures and analysis of the scattering data using the spinodal model allows us to estimate a stability limit for the metastable phase. The justification of this data analysis is in the Olmsted model for polymer crystallisation where fluctuations in a non-conserved order parameter (the chain conformation and stiffness) couple with the density to drive phase separation and subsequent crystallisation. The susceptibility of block copolymer self-assembly to incipient crystallisation has also been demonstrated and mesophase formation is observed at anomalously high temperatures in ethylene oxide-containing block copolymers below the normal melting point of the polyethylene oxide chains. The change in the chain conformation and stiffness below the normal melting point is invoked again to account for the anomalous block copolymer phase separation. Formation of calcium carbonate from aqueous solutions of sodium carbonate and calcium nitrate is observed to be a two-stage process and precipitation proceeds by the production of an amorphous metastable phase. This phase grows until it is volume filling and leads to the subsequent formation of the two polymorphs calcite and vaterite. The reasons behind the metastable behaviour of the calcium carbonate cannot (of course) be analysed in terms of the polymer theory but the coincidence in the phenomenology highlights a common cause deeper than Ostwald's rule of stages. These three sets of results suggest pre-nucleation density fluctuations, leading to a metastable phase, play an integral role in all three classes of crystallisation. In due course, the metastable phase undergoes transformation to "normal" crystals.

Acknowledgements

The authors wish to thank the staff of DUBBLE BM26 beamline at the ESRF, and beamlines 8.2 and 16.1 at the Daresbury SRS for the generous assistance offered to us. The research is supported by the Engineering and Physical Sciences Research Council (EPSRC) *via* grants GR/M73637, GR/M60415 and GR/M22116.

References

1 M. Imai, K. Mori, T. Mizukami, K. Kaji and T. Kanaya, *Polymer*, 1992, **33**, 4451.
2 M. Imai, K. Mori, T. Mizukami, K. Kaji and T. Kanaya, *Polymer*, 1992, **33**, 4457.
3 M. Imai, K. Kaji and T. Kanaya, *Macromolecules*, 1994, **27**, 7103.
4 A. Nogales, T. A. Ezquerra, Z. Denchev, I. Sics, F. J. Balta Calleja and B. S. Hsiao, *Chem. Phys.*, 2001, **115**, 3804.
5 G. Matsuba, K. Kaji, K. Nishida, T. Kanaya and M. Imai, *Polym. J.*, 1999, **31**, 722.
6 G. Matsuba, K. Kaji, K. Nishida, T. Kanaya and M. Imai, *Macromolecules*, 1999, **32**, 8932.
7 G. Matsuba, T. Kanaya, M. Saito, K. Kaji and K. Nishida, *Phys. Rev. E*, 2000, **62**, 1497.
8 T. A. Ezquerra, E. Lopez-Cabarcos, B. S. Hsiao and F. H. Balta-Calleja, *Phys. Rev. E*, 1996, **54**, 989.
9 N. J. Terrill, J. P. A. Fairclough, E. Towns-Andrews, B. U. Komanschek, R. J. Young and A. J. Ryan, *Polymer*, 1998, **39**, 2381.

10 A. J. Ryan, J. P. A. Fairclough, N. J. Terrill, P. D. Olmsted and W. C. K. Poon, *Faraday Discuss.*, 1999, **112**, 13.
11 P. D. Olmsted, W. C. K. Poon, T. C. B McLeish, N. J. Terrill and A. J. Ryan, *Phys. Rev. Lett.*, 1998, **81**, 373–376.
12 P. M. Chaikin and T. C. Lubensky, *Principles of Condensed Matter Physics*, Cambridge University Press, Cambridge, 1995.
13 F. S. Bates and P. Wiltzius, *J. Chem. Phys.*, 1989, **91**, 3258.
14 D. J. Blundell, D. H. MacKerron, W. Fuller, A. Mahendrasingam, C. Martin, R. J. Oldman, R. J. Rule and C. Riekel, *Polymer*, 1996, **37**, 3303.
15 G. E. Welsh, D. J. Blundell and A. H. Windle, *Macromolecules*, 1998, **31**, 7562.
16 K. Tashiro, S. Sasaki and M. Kobayashi, *Macromolecules*, 1996, **29**, 7460.
17 K. Tashiro, S. Sasaki, N. Gose and M. Kobayashi, *Polym. J.*, 1998, **30**, 85.
18 S. Sasaki, K. Tashiro, M. Kobayashi, Y. Izumi and K. Kobajashi, *Polymer*, 1999, **40**, 7125.
19 J.-M. Huang, P. P. Chu and F.-C. Chang, *Polymer*, 2000, **41**, 1741.
20 M. Doi, T. Shimada and K. Okano, *J. Chem Phys.*, 1988, **88**, 4070.
21 M. Dettenmaier, E. W. Fischer and M. Stamm, *Colloid Polymer Sci.*, 1980, **258**, 343.
22 L. R. Pratt, C. S. Hsu and D. Chandler, *J. Chem. Phys.*, 1978, **68**, 4202.
23 B. S. Hsiao, B. B. Sauer, R. K. Verma, G. H. Zachman, S. Seifert, B. Chu and P. Harney, *Macromolecules*, 1995, **28**, 6931.
24 W. Wang, J. M. Schultz and B. S. Hsiao, *Macromolecules*, 1997, **30**, 4544.
25 N. P. Balsara, B. A. Garetz, M. C. Newstein, B. J. Bauer and T. J. Prosa, *Macromolecules*, 1998, **31**, 7668.
26 I. W. Hamley, *The Physics of Block Copolymers*, Oxford University Press, Oxford, 1998.
27 A. J. Ryan, S.-M. Mai, J. P. A. Fairclough, I. W. Hamley and C. Booth, *Phys. Chem. Chem. Phys.*, 2001, **3**, 2961–2971.
28 S.-M. Mai, C. Booth and V. M. Nace, *Eur. Polym. J.*, 1997, **33**, 991.
29 L. Leibler, *Macromolecules*, 1980, **13**, 1602.
30 F. S. Bates, J. H. Rosedale and G. H. Fredrickson, *J. Chem. Phys.*, 1990, **92**, 6255.
31 J. P. A. Fairclough, A. J. Ryan, S. Turner, I. W. Hamley, S.-M. Mai, C. Booth and R. C. Denny, *Phys. Chem. Chem. Phys.*, 1999, **1**, 2093.
32 F. S. Bates, M. F. Schulz, A. K. Khandpur, S. Förster, S. Rosedale, K. Almdal and K. Mortensen, *Faraday Discuss.*, 1994, **98**, 7.
33 A. K. Khandpur, S. Förster, F. S. Bates, I. W. Hamley, A. J. Ryan, W. Bras, K. Almdal and K. Mortensen, *Macromolecules*, 1995, **28**, 8796.
34 M. E. Vigild, K. Almdal, K. Mortensen, I. W. Hamley, J. P. A. Fairclough and A. J. Ryan, *Macromolecules*, 1998, **31**, 5702.
35 D. A. Hadjuk, M. B. Kossuth, M. A. Hillmeyer and F. S. Bates, *J. Phys. Chem. B*, 1998, **102**, 4269.
36 M. F. Schulz, A. K. Khandpur, F. S. Bates, K. Almdal, K. Mortensen, D. A. Hadjuk and S. M. Guner, *Macromolecules*, 1996, **29**, 2857.
37 Y. Matsushita, M. Nomura, J. Watanabe, Y. Mogi, I. Noda and M. Imai, *Macromolecules*, 1995, **25**, 6007.
38 I. Olavi, *Papermaking Sci. Technol.*, 2000, **11**, 140.
39 D. Kralj and L. Brečević, *J. Cryst. Growth*, 1990, **104**, 793.
40 R. Brooks, L. M. Clark and E. F. Thurston, *Philos. Trans. R. Soc. London, Ser. A*, 1950, **243**, 145–167.
41 L. Brečević and A. E. Nielsen, *J. Cryst. Growth*, 1980, **98**, 504.
42 J. R. Clarkson, T. J. Price and C. J. Adams, *J. Chem. Soc., Faraday Trans.*, 1992, **88**, 243.
43 N. Koga, Y. Nakagoe and H. Tanaka, *Thermochim. Acta*, 1998, **318**, 239.
44 J. Rieger, J. Thieme and C. Schmidt, *Langmuir*, 2000, **16**, 8300.
45 J. Hostomský and A. G. Jones, *J. Phys. D*, 1991, **24**, 165.
46 O. Söhnel and J. W. Mullin, *J. Cryst. Growth*, 1982, **60**, 239.
47 S. L. Tracey, C. J. P. François and H. M. Jennings, *J Cryst. Growth*, 1998, **193**, 374.
48 L. Dupont, F. Portemer and M. Figlarz, *J. Mater. Chem.*, 1997, **7**, 797.
49 J. Jalava, E. Hiltunen, H. Kähkönen, H. Erkkilä, H. Härmä and V. Taavitsainen, *Ind. Eng. Chem. Res.*, 2000, **39**, 349.
50 W. Bras, G. E. Derbyshire, A. J. Ryan, G. R. Mant, A. Felton, R. A. Lewis, C. J. Hall and G. N. Greaves, *Nucl. Instrum. Methods Phys. Res., Sect. A*, 1993, **326**, 587.
51 W. Bras, *J. Macromol. Sci.-Phys.*, 1998, **B37**, 557.
52 (*a*) V. Zhukov, F. Udo, O. Marchena, F. G. Hartjes, F. D. van den Berg, W. Bras and E. Vlieg, *Nucl. Instrum. Methods Phys. Res., Sect. A*, 1997, **392**, 83; (*b*) I. P. Dolbnya, H. Alberda, F. G. Hartjes, F. Udo, R. E. Bakker, M. Konijnenburg, E. Homan, I. Cerjak, P. Goedtkindt and W. Bras, *Rev. Sci. Instrum.*, 2002, in press.
53 W. Bras, G. E. Derbyshire, J. Cooke, B. E. Komanschek, A. Devine, S. M. Clark and A. J. Ryan, *J. Appl. Crystallogr.*, 1994, **28**, 26.
54 S. M. Mai, I. W. Hamley, R. C. Denny, M. Matsen, B. Liao, C. Booth and A. J. Ryan, *Macromolecules*, 1997, **38**, 509.
55 Y.-W. Yang, S. Tanodekaew, S.-M. Mai, C. Booth, A. J. Ryan, W. Bras and K. Viras, *Macromolecules*, 1995, **28**, 6029.

56   G. Strobl, *The Physics of Polymers*, Springer-Verlag, Berlin, Germany, 1996.
57   A. N. Wilkinson, A. J. Ryan, *Polymer Processing and Structure Development*, Kluwer, Dordrecht, 1998.
58   F. J. Baltá-Calleja and C. G. Vonk, *X-ray Scattering of Polymers*, Elsevier, Amsterdam, 1989.
59   M. Cakmak, A. Teitge, H. G. Zachmann and J. L. White, *J. Polym. Sci. Polym. Phys. Ed.*, 1993, **31**, 371.
60   K. Katayama, T. Amano and K. Nakamura, *Kolloid Z. Z. Polym.*, 1968, **226**, 125.
61   R. J. Somani, L. Yang and B. S. Hsiao, *Physica A*, 2002, **304**, 145.
62   G. Kumaraswamy, J. A. Kornfield, F. Yeh and B. S. Hsiao, *Macromolecules*, 2002, **35**, 1762.
63   H. E. Cook, *Acta Metall.*, 1970, **18**, 297.
64   P. Pincus, *J. Chem. Phys.*, 1981, **75**, 1996.
65   (*a*) H. Hashimoto and T. Hashimoto, in *Comprehensive Polymer Science, 2nd Supplement*, ed. S. L. Aggarwal and S. Russo, Pergamon, Oxford, 1996, ch. 6; (*b*) N. Sakamoto and T. Hashimoto, *Macromolecules*, 1995, **28**, 6825.
66   (*a*) S. Förster, A. K. Khandpur, J. Zhao, F. S. Bates, I. W. Hamley, A. J. Ryan and W. Bras, *Macromolecules*, 1994, **27**, 6922; (*b*) K. Almdal, K. Mortensen, A. J. Ryan and F. S. Bates, *Macromolecules*, 1996, **29**, 5940.
67   S.-M. Mai, W. Mingvanish, S. C. Turner, C. Chaibundit, J. P. A. Fairclough, F. Heatley, M. W. Matsen, A. J. Ryan and C. Booth, *Macromolecules*, 2000, **33**, 5124.
68   S.-M. Mai, J. P. A. Fairclough, N. J. Terrill, S. C. Turner, I. W. Hamley, M. W. Matsen, A. J. Ryan and C. Booth, *Macromolecules*, 1998, **31**, 8110.
69   S.-M. Mai, W. Mingvanish, S. C. Turner, C. Chaibundit, J. P. A. Fairclough, F. Heatley, M. W. Matsen, A. J. Ryan and C. Booth, *Macromolecules*, 2000, **33**, 5124.
70   C. Chaibundit, W. Mingvanish, S. C. Turner, S.-M. Mai, J. P. A. Fairclough, A. J. Ryan, M. W. Matsen and C. Booth, *Macromol. Rapid Commun.*, 2000, **21**, 964.
71   (*a*) P. J. Flory, *J. Chem. Phys.*, 1942, **10**, 51; (*b*) M. Huggins, *J. Chem. Phys.*, 1942, **46**, 151.
72   G. H. Fredrickson, A. J. Liu and F. S. Bates, *Macromolecules*, 1994, **27**, 2503.
73   W. W. Maurer, F. S. Bates, T. P. Lodge, K. Almdal, K. Mortensen and G. H. Fredrickson, *J. Chem. Phys.*, 1998, **108**, 2989.

In situ neutron diffraction studies of single crystals and powders during microwave irradiation†

Andrew Harrison,*[a] Richard Ibberson,[b] Graeme Robb,[a] Gavin Whittaker,[a] Chick Wilson[b] and Douglas Youngson[a]

[a] *Department of Chemistry, The University of Edinburgh, The King's Buildings, West Mains Rd., Edinburgh, UK EH9 3JJ*
[b] *The ISIS Facility, Rutherford Appleton Laboratory, Chilton, Didcot, Oxon, UK OX11 0QX*

Received 8th April 2002, Accepted 29th April 2002
First published as an Advance Article on the web 9th August 2002

Microwave dielectric heating has become an important method in chemical synthesis and materials processing over the past 15 years, and in the case of the reactions in solutions, there is a well-developed understanding of heating mechanisms and their influence on reaction rate. In the solid-state however, there is much less clarity, despite the advantages to be gained from better insight into the way in which such electromagnetic radiation may couple directly to charge carriers, accelerating reactions in good conductors. The related issue of the influence of microwave irradiation on biological systems, in particular, proteins, and the way in which this may pose hazards to health is similarly poorly understood despite the obvious relevance this may have to the current debate on the influence of electromagnetic radiation, in particular, microwave transmission, on human health. One reason for the paucity of fundamental insight in both fields is because most work has been performed with microwave equipment whose design is derived from that of a domestic oven, and which is not ideal for *in situ* studies of microwave driven processes. We have been developing new methods of irradiating a variety of solid samples while measuring structural parameters through a range of diffraction techniques, and describe apparatus that will enable X-ray or neutron scattering measurements to be performed on powders or single crystals under microwave irradiation with controlled power level. We also describe preliminary studies of a single crystal of the molecular solid aspirin, and a powder of the microwave-susceptible ionic material $BaTiO_3$, during microwave irradiation.

1. Introduction: microwave heating of solids

Microwave heating is now a well-established technique in chemistry and materials processing[1-6] and finds a number of industrial applications due to the direct and energy-efficient nature of the energy transfer to the sample. A microwave field may couple with dipolar species or charge carriers in a wide range of molecular, ionic or metallic materials to produce a heating effect, and in many cases this provides a distinct advantage over conventional heat sources. In particular, it may

---

† Electronic supplementary information (ESI) available: Crystallographic data (powder and single crystal data) in cif format (CCDC reference numbers 185472–185475). See http://www.rsc.org/suppdata/fd/b2/b203379h/

DOI: 10.1039/b203379h

accelerate reactions or processes, in some cases yielding products that differ from those anticipated from conventional heating.[7–9] Much of the work in this field is remarkably uncritical, treating the microwave oven very much as a 'black box', with little attempt to probe what might be happening during microwave irradiation, and what might be the cause of any anomalous effects. Although the cause of many anomalous effects in liquid phases has now been attributed to effects such as superheating,[1] studies of materials in solid phases[9–12] indicate that ion migration may occur due to a non-thermal mechanism. One suggestion is that this is some form of 'ponderomotive' driving force,[13–15] that arises when high frequency electric fields modulate ionic currents near interfaces with abrupt differences in ion mobility.

A number of contentious issues still surround many of the early studies in this field, in particular the reliability of measured temperatures within a microwave-heated solid. One of the original aims of the work reported here was to be able to determine temperatures within the body of a solid, by remote (*i.e.* non-contact) methods that provided more information than mere surface temperatures. The ability to measure sample temperatures in this way would be particularly useful in areas such as catalysis, where specific heating of supported metal particles (to temperatures above that of the support material) has been implicated in the enhanced activity of microwave-heated catalysts.

There are, however, a number of difficulties associated with investigating microwave-driven processes *in situ*. First, the need to enclose the sample and link it to the microwave source using vessels with conducting walls, generally metals whose thickness must be greater than 50 microns, makes it harder to use certain types of probe: light may be brought in and out of the sample chamber using fibre-optic technology, and neutrons will penetrate many metals with relatively weak attenuation,[9] but conventional X-ray diffraction measurements do pose problems.[11] Second, there is a significant problem in measuring the temperature, indeed the whole concept of temperature as an equilibrium phenomenon, is called into question. Fundamental *in situ* studies are also required in non-synthetic applications, and in particular to investigate the manner in which microwave radiation may interact with biological material,[16,17] a subject that is of intense current interest because of the suspicion that exposure to microwave telecommunications equipment may be harmful to health.[18]

Temperature measurement in a microwave cavity is not a trivial process. Whilst conventional heating may be assumed to give rise to uniform temperatures throughout a small sample, microwave heating imparts energy directly to the sample. Within the sample, inhomogeneous heating may occur at the millimetre or even sub-millimetre scale[19] as the rate of conversion from microwave energy to heat is heavily dependent upon the dielectric properties of the sample. As the dielectric properties themselves are often heavily dependent upon the temperature, minor local temperature variations may become amplified through a positive feedback mechanism. It is therefore unreasonable to make the assumption that accurate temperatures in a microwave-heated system may be measured in a conventional manner. The two basic methods for temperature measurement, contact probes (*e.g.* thermocouples) and thermography (*e.g.* pyrometers) are unreliable, as the former may cause perturbation of the microwave field precisely at the point of interest, and the latter only register surface temperatures in an environment where surface cooling is highly significant.

In the absence of clear, critically assessed information on sample temperatures, many authors have alleged that microwave heating enhancement is due to non-thermal effects resulting from the microwave electric or magnetic field.[20] Improved temperature measurement in microwave-heated solids is essential for a full understanding of the processes involved in microwave heating. In this paper we describe novel apparatus that we have designed and built to perform neutron diffraction measurements on single crystals and powders, whilst being heated either conventionally or with microwaves. Such apparatus could be used to study a wide range of structural or chemical problems *in situ*, but we describe here applications of the equipment to the study of the nature of heating effects in carefully selected materials. In particular, we have probed the structure of a single crystal sample of acetylsalicylic acid, an important proprietary painkiller, marketed as aspirin. The molecular structure has been determined by X-rays[21] and more recently by single crystal neutron diffraction.[22,23] In the latter work, the structure was determined at seven temperatures in the range 20–300 K, revealing several significant and interesting temperature-dependent features. Among these are enhanced thermal parameters (which contribute to the anisotropic displacement parameters, or ADPs) on the hydrogen atoms on the terminal methyl group, a common feature in such groups, and also on the hydrogen atom involved in the carboxylic acid dimeric hydrogen bond. This latter effect is particularly interesting, in that the thermal parameters (and associated scattering density) of this atom show clear evidence that increasing temperature allows the anharmonicity of the potential to be sampled and visualised directly.[22] For this reason, i.e. evidence of significant and physically interesting behaviour of the atomic thermal parameters, and, in particular, the possibility of exploring preferentially the "anomalous" thermal parameters, we chose to examine this material in our first single crystal diffraction experiment under microwave irradiation. In this way we hoped that any "preferential" redistribution of energy within the molecule on microwave irradiation compared with conventional heating could be identified.

We also studied a powder sample of $BaTiO_3$, chosen because it is susceptible to microwave heating, and because it has a well-characterised crystal structure that is known to pass through a succession of phases on heating.[24–26] This material would be suitable as a means of probing temperature through structural parameters such as lattice constants and ADPs.

To the best of our knowledge, these measurements constitute the first attempt to study the distribution of thermal energy at microscopic length-scales in a crystalline solid that is heated with microwave radiation in comparison with that for conventional heating. This in turn may have important implications for the use of microwave energy in chemical synthesis and materials processing.

2. Instrument design and diffraction experiments

2.1 Neutron diffraction from a single crystal of aspirin during microwave irradiation

Apparatus for *in situ* irradiation of single crystals was designed to be used in conjunction with the time-of-flight Laue diffractometer SXD at the ISIS Facility at the Rutherford–Appleton laboratories (RAL).[27] SXD is situated on beam line S3, with the sample positioned 8 m from the moderator. The maximum beam diameter at is 15 mm, although this may be modified using B_4C apertures. The scattered radiation is measured by three position-sensitive detectors. Two of the detectors may be rotated to change 2θ for the detector centre between 90° and 130° (detector one) and between 50° and 90° (detector two). The sample to detector distance, L, has a manually adjustable range of $70 < L < 500$ mm, depending upon the sample environment and the detector. A third detector is located opposite detectors one and two, and can be fixed at one of three angles (2θ for the detector centre at $-55°$, $-90°$ or $-125°$). During this experiment a CCR cryostat was employed; this is capable of producing a temperature range of 1.5–300 K in the sample tank. The tails of the cryostat have been adapted to provide reliable ω-rotation and to minimise unwanted scattering. Additional scattering caused by the presence of air in the sample tank was removed by evacuating the sample tank by means of a vacuum pump prior to data collection. Because standard metal pins would interfere with the microwave field, they could not be used for this experiment, and the aspirin crystal was mounted on a custom-made aluminium nitride sample pin instead, using Kapton tape. Aluminium nitride was selected as this machinable ceramic is microwave transparent and has high thermal conductivity, ensuring the maximum possible control of temperature by conventional methods.

The requirements of the sample environment, detectors and temperature measurement apparatus severely limited the space that was available to transmit microwaves to the sample using tubular waveguide techniques, such as we have employed in previous experiments.[9] The minimum dimensions of tubular waveguides are determined by the wavelength of the transmitted wave, which for a rectangular guide is $\lambda/2$ across one face, whilst the minimum cross-sectional radius for a cylindrical guide is $\lambda/3.4$. The size restriction is removed in waveguides where transverse electric and magnetic (TEM) modes are possible, and, for the practical purposes of this work, led to the use of coaxial cables and parallel plate waveguides. Such guides have no theoretical limitation on their size, and vacuum feedthroughs are readily available for coaxial waveguides. The design that was finally used (Fig. 1) for the experiment consisted of a commercial 0–1 kW variable power microwave source (ASTeX 5-1000), which was used to deliver microwaves (2.45 GHz), into the sample tank *via* a flexible 200 W co-axial cable and vacuum feedthrough. The microwaves were then launched in a parallel plate waveguide, constructed from neutron-transparent vanadium foil with 10 mm PTFE dielectric. The vanadium plate waveguide straddled the aspirin crystal, bathing the

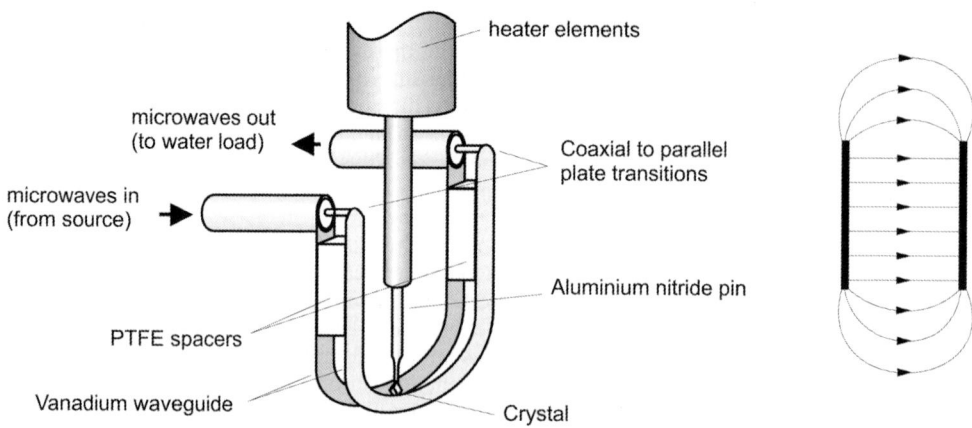

Fig. 1 Schematic representation of the sample arrangement and microwave applicator (left), and of the electric field between the vanadium plates at the sample (right).

crystal with microwaves. To prevent interference with the neutron beam, the section of waveguide that straddled the aspirin crystal had a constant gap of 10 mm, separated by a vacuum. The waveguide downstream of the crystal was designed to prevent the formation of significant standing waves by dumping the forward wave into a water load, located outside the cryostat chamber.

The aspirin crystal was prepared prior to the experiment by dissolving aspirin in acetone. This solution was left in a lightly stoppered sample vial and allowed to evaporate over five days, resulting in the formation of a $8 \times 4 \times 1.5$ mm^3 single crystal of aspirin.

Data were collected on the single crystal diffractometer SXD at the ISIS spallation neutron source under several sets of conditions (see Table 1). We note that due to the constraints of the sample mounting imposed by the needs of the microwave set-up, it was necessary to re-mount the single crystal sample during the experiment in order to obtain a reasonably representative data set with sufficient three-dimensional character to allow the necessary refinement of anisotropic thermal parameters. It is worth pointing out that two recent developments of the neutron diffractometer (SXD is now equipped with a more extensive detector array covering around the solid angle) and of data collection methods (a multiple-crystal method is now fully established[28]) will allow full 3-D data sets to be obtained from vertically-mounted single crystal samples in future experiments.

Data were collected for the crystal at 100, 200 and 300 K, in the presence and absence of a microwave field. The cryostat was used to set the temperature by cooling the sample pin, which in turn controlled the temperature at the crystal. The transmitted microwave power was held at 40 W. The data collection parameters are summarised in Table 1. A total of 8 frames, each containing information from two detectors, were collected at each temperature with the microwave field on. The crystal was remounted in two different orientations: 4 frames were collected under each set of conditions for each orientation. Exposure times for each frame varied from around 60 to 180 min. The intensities were extracted and reduced to structure factors using standard SXD procedures,[29] as detailed in Table 1. The structure factor sets were used for structural refinement in GSAS[30] and SHELXL-97.[31]

2.2 High resolution powder neutron diffraction from BaTiO$_3$ during microwave irradiation

Powder neutron diffraction experiments at elevated temperatures generally use conventional heating methods, and furnaces are optimised for use with particular diffractometers. We aimed to design a microwave applicator that fitted within the space that would otherwise be occupied by a conventional furnace, and thus minimise disruption to experimental procedure. Previous work on the small angle scattering diffractometer LOQ at the ISIS Facility, provided the basis for this apparatus[9,20] and was then modified specifically for use on the high-resolution powder diffractometer HRPD,[32] also at the ISIS Facility at RAL (Fig. 2).

Table 1 Data collection and refinement parameters for the single crystal neutron diffraction study of aspirin under microwave irradiation

Instrumental			
Diffractometer	SXD neutron time-of-flight Laue diffractometer		
Detectors	Three, 64×64 element, 3×3 mm pixel, scintillator PSDs		
Detector position	Detector 1: $2\theta_c = 125°$, $L_2 = 150$ mm.		
	Detector 2: $2\theta_c = 55°$, $L_2 = 190$ mm.		
	Detector 3: $2\theta_c = 95°$, $L_2 = 110$ mm		
Wavelength range	0.5–5.0 Å		
Sample			
Compound	Aspirin		
Formula	$C_9H_8O_4$		
Molecular weight	180.16		
Crystallising solvent	Acetone		
Crystal size	$8 \times 4 \times 1.5$ mm^3		
Data collection and refinement			
Crystal symmetry	Monoclinic		
Space group	$P2_1/c$		
Z	4		
Unit cell (100 K)	$a = 11.233$, $b = 6.544$, $c = 11.231$, $\beta = 95.89°$		
Data collection	8 data frames at each temperature		
T/K	100	200	300
Observed refs	3971	3611	2794
Unique refs $I > 2\sigma(I)$	1151	877	625
R_{int}	0.068	0.078	0.085
Absorption coefficient	μ (cm^{-1}) $= 0.80 + 0.75\lambda$		
Refinement	In program SHELXL-97, refined on F^2		
Refined parameters	190 for full anisotropic refinement		
T/K	100	200	300
$R(F)$	0.096	0.095	0.113
$wR(F^2)$	0.237	0.243	0.268
G of F (S)	1.468	1.424	1.452

2.45 GHz microwaves, generated in a commercial magnetron unit (ASTeX 5-1000), are directed into a cylindrical waveguide operating in the fundamental (TE$_{11}$) mode, with the sample sitting a quarter-wavelength back from the end of the waveguide. When used in this mode, the electric field intensity is greatest at the centre of the circular cross-section of the waveguide. The waveguide is terminated with a sliding plate whose position may be varied so that the standing wave generated by the interaction of the forward travelling wave and the reflected wave has a maximum field strength at the sample. This allows efficient and direct *in situ* heating of the sample, which is simultaneously monitored using conventional pyrometry at elevated temperatures and by fluoro-optic thermometry (Nortech Fibronic Inc, noEMI-TS series) up to 550 K, with a precision of approximately 0.1 K. This temperature is held constant through control of the microwave power *via* a PC. Neutrons passed through the sample *via* vanadium windows incorporated into the stainless steel waveguide; these windows were edged with neutron-absorbing gadolinium sheet to minimise scattering from other components of the microwave heating system.

The sample is supported on a microwave-transparent ceramic holder (Shapal™) within a thin-walled silica crucible; the latter also doubles as a transparent insulating layer. In order to minimise any temperature gradient in the sample, most pronounced at the surface of the sample, a loose powder of the same material surrounded the pellet. The pellet was therefore at the centre of the heated compact and consequently remained at a more uniform temperature than would have been the case with a pellet alone.

The materials we first chose for diffraction studies were selected to have optimal physical properties for these measurements. In particular, they were selected to be chemically and

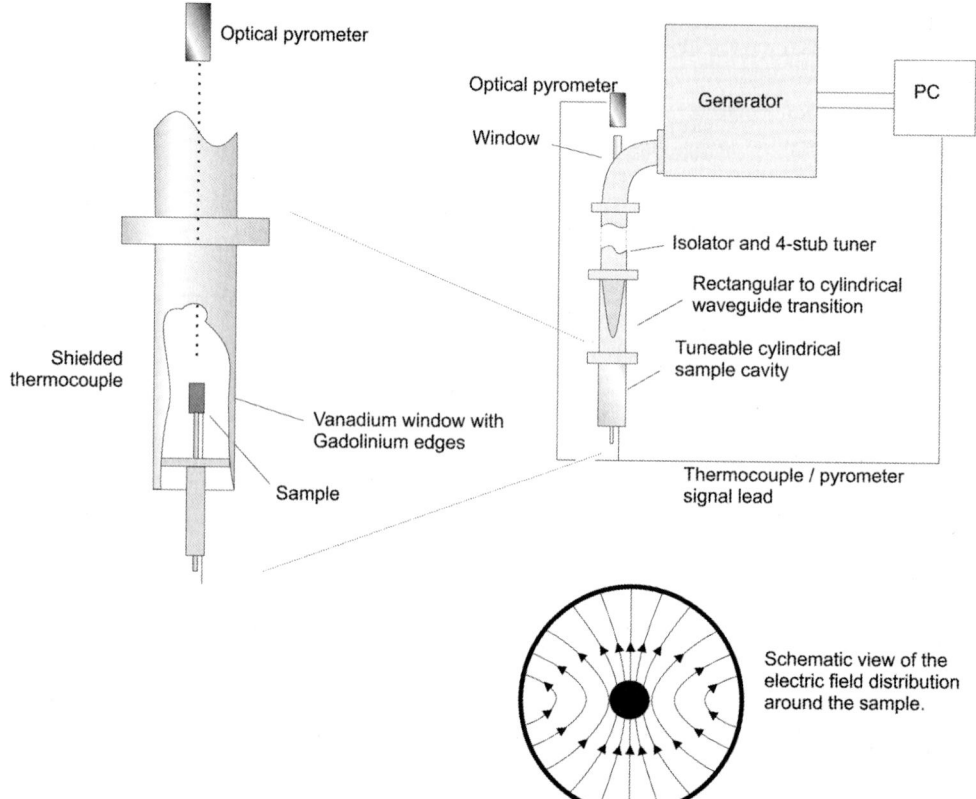

Fig. 2 Schematic view of the apparatus designed and built to irradiate a powder sample during neutron diffraction. The detail of the apparatus indicates how the sample and thermocouple are mounted in a resonant microwave cavity, connected to a microwave source whose output was controlled to maintain a set temperature.

thermally stable, to have a high dielectric loss tangent, an appreciable coefficient of linear expansion, and a high crystal symmetry. The focus of the experiments we report here was $BaTiO_3$, which satisfies the criteria above, and also has a well characterised structure in several crystal phases.[25,26]

$BaTiO_3$ powder (99.99% (metals basis), supplied by Alfa Aesar) was pressed into pellets (diameter 13 mm and approximate height 5 mm) with a force of approximately 10 tonnes. Powder neutron diffraction patterns were taken on HRPD on the bank of backscatter detectors, allowing the greatest resolution to be attained. To provide a basis for comparison between conventional and microwave heating, the sample was first heated in a standard RAL vacuum furnace with vanadium element and heat shields. The furnace temperatures are controlled and monitored using type K, (Chromel/Alumel) thermocouples. Time of flight (TOF) patterns were recorded *in situ*, between 30 and 130 ms, for a time corresponding 18.0 µAh at a series of temperatures, starting at room temperature (295 K) and rising to 1173 K. Having collected these data and allowed the furnace to return to ambient temperature, the sample was transferred to the sample holder of the microwave heating chamber. Generally, longer scan times (30–55 µAh) were used, as there was concern that the background signal from scattering from the microwave equipment would be relatively high. The powder neutron diffraction patterns were recorded *in situ*, first at 295 K without microwaves (for comparison) then at several temperatures *with* microwave heating. Power levels were varied throughout to maintain the temperature to within ±1 K. Unfortunately due to equipment failures and time constraints, data could only be taken with microwave heating at relatively few temperatures: 383 and 473 K.

3. Results

3.1 Aspirin

Largely because of the constraints of the set-up and the available data collection time, the data sets obtained are somewhat limited, and while allowing anisotropic refinements to be undertaken, these refinements result in a rather low data/parameter ratio. Nonetheless, the two 100 K data sets (microwaves off and on) allowed reliable ADPS to be obtained, while the 200 K and 300 K data sets could be refined with isotropic thermal parameters. In addition, we have available good refinements at 300 K from the previous neutron diffraction experiment[22] which we can use again as benchmark "microwave-off" results for comparison.

The refined values for ADPs are summarised in Table 2 and Fig. 3. It can be seen that the thermal parameters for the 100 K "microwave-off" and "microwave-on" refinements are dramatically different. Indeed, comparing the latter with the 300 K refinement of the aspirin structure[22] shows the two to be very similar. It would appear that the application of microwave radiation to the crystal has certainly had a dramatic effect, at the very least in heating the sample. That this is the case is confirmed by the isotropic refinements of the 200 K "microwave-on" data (parameters are not reproduced here). Once again the thermal parameters are akin to the standard 300 K determination.

3.2 BaTiO$_3$

Powder diffraction data for all experiments on BaTiO$_3$ were analysed by Rietveld refinement using the GSAS suite of programs.[30] Above the para- to ferroelectric transition temperature T_c, BaTiO$_3$

Table 2 Refined values of U^{eq} for atoms in aspirin with conventional heating to 100, 200 and 300 K, and with microwave heating at 300 K. Labelling of the atoms is the same as in previous structural studies on aspirin

	No microwaves				Microwaves
T/K	100	200	300	300	100
$a/Å$	11.233	11.233	11.416	11.233	11.233
$b/Å$	6.544	6.544	6.598	6.544	6.544
$c/Å$	11.231	11.231	11.483	11.231	11.231
$\beta/°$	95.89	95.89	95.6	95.89	95.89
$V/Å^3$	762.58	762.58	670.81	762.58	762.58
$U^{eq}/Å^2$					
C1	0.011717	0.020437	0.022550	0.031117	0.029963
C2	0.011957	0.021117	0.038453	0.036613	0.033197
C3	0.017763	0.028620	0.048660	0.045883	0.040730
C4	0.020130	0.029817	0.051037	0.046590	0.043270
C5	0.017727	0.029043	0.046740	0.043770	0.035577
C6	0.015973	0.025770	0.041377	0.042737	0.036917
C7	0.011543	0.021263	0.037220	0.036587	0.030143
C8	0.013920	0.022433	0.044713	0.038890	0.035090
C9	0.021590	0.032927	0.062563	0.049417	0.048163
O1	0.020387	0.029960	0.050937	0.043953	0.044363
O2	0.021220	0.033840	0.051753	0.049593	0.044963
O3	0.013650	0.022733	0.042373	0.043710	0.032583
O4	0.025073	0.039167	0.060673	0.051953	0.049127
H1	0.034827	0.046817	0.082880	0.064540	0.062020
H2	0.033687	0.050300	0.073500	0.066530	0.066477
H3	0.040343	0.046950	0.072340	0.069910	0.057767
H4	0.031363	0.043323	0.068200	0.061000	0.053293
H5	0.059453	0.073377	0.113440	0.099840	0.101673
H6	0.085200	0.161223	0.167093	0.203990	0.146717
H7	0.075087	0.123933	0.174443	0.163580	0.140967
H8	0.030670	0.049227	0.076183	0.077867	0.070010
R	0.0957	0.0954	0.0873	0.1127	0.1302

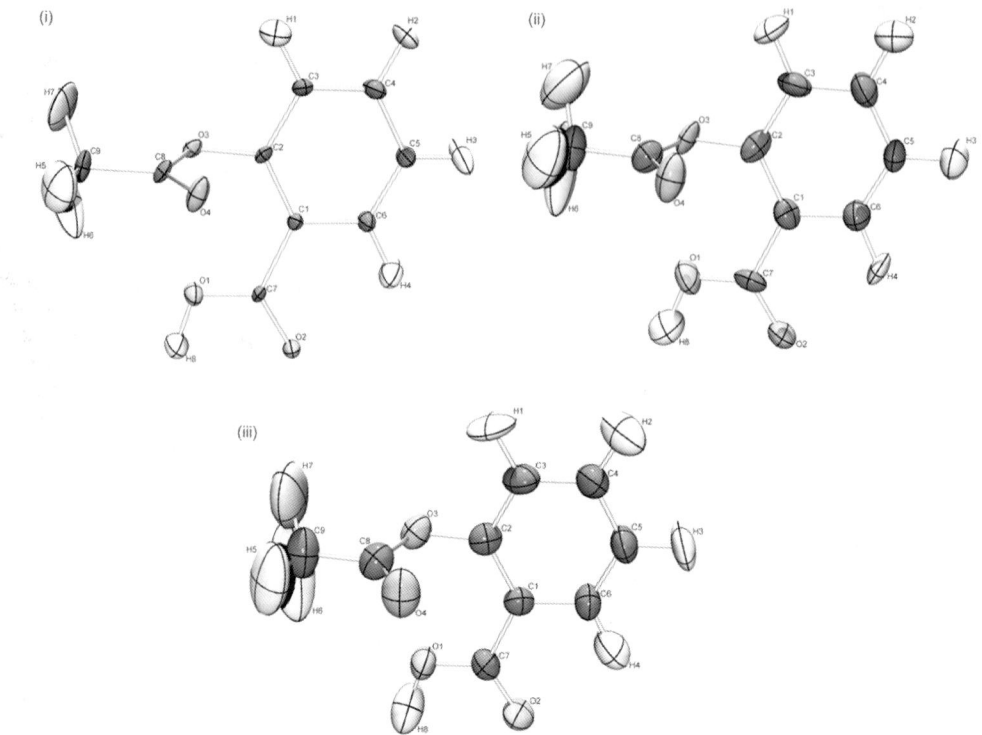

Fig. 3 The structure of aspirin at various temperatures and with different sources of heat: (i) 100 K with conventional heating; (ii) 100 K with microwave heating; (iii) 300 K with conventional heating.

has the simple cubic perovskite structure (space group $Pm3m$); on cooling below T_c the structure first distorts along the [100] axis to give a tetragonal structure (space group $P4mm$), and at yet lower temperatures, beyond the range considered in our experiments, goes through two further structural phase transitions. The value of T_c is known to depend on the state of $BaTiO_3$: although it is generally taken to be in the region of 393 K, reduced particle size, or strain induced by rapid cooling, is known to raise T_c, indeed in the case of thin, strained films of $BaTiO_3$ grown on $SrTiO_3$, T_c may be as high as 500–800 °C.[33]

Data were refined in the appropriate phase, yielding optimised values of cell parameters, atom displacement parameters (ADPs), and where appropriate, atom positions, all of which are summarised in Table 3. In addition, in the tetragonal phase, we report the pseudo-cubic cell parameter $a_c = V^{1/3}$, as well as an isotropic value for the ADP, U^{iso}, calculated as one third of the trace of the diagonalised ADP tensor. In the tetragonal phase it was apparent there was a second, cubic phase present whose structure appeared to be very similar to that of cubic $BaTiO_3$, though the refined percentage of this phase was found to be of the order of 20%, and the cell parameter was consistently larger by about 0.017 Å at the same temperature (Fig. 4). This phase was included in all refinements. Similar effects have been seen before in $BaTiO_3$[34–36] and related materials[37,38] and attributed to small particles stabilized in the cubic phase through local strain. All the structural parameters of this additional phase were refined independently of the majority phase, and optimised parameters are displayed in Table 3; the cell parameter of this phase is given with that of the majority phase in Fig. 4, while the percentage of this phase is given in Fig. 5.

A comparison of the cell parameters for the majority phase (Fig. 4, Table 3) reveals that values under microwave heating are systematically larger. At a set temperature of 473 K for instance, the cell parameters differ by 4–5 standard deviations, indicating that the microwaved sample is effectively hotter as measured through this parameter. The difference is particularly apparent near T_c;

Table 3 Crystallographic data for BaTiO$_3$ in tetragonal (*P4mm*) and cubic (*Pm3m*) phases. All ADPs are scaled up by a factor of 100. The figures in brackets represent one standard deviation in the last decimal place(s) of the quoted figure

	Electric furnace								Microwave			
Temperature/K	295	423	473	573	673	773	873		295	383	473	
Space group	*P4mm*	*Pm3m*	*Pm3m*	*Pm3m*	*Pm3m*	*Pm3m*	*Pm3m*		*P4mm*	*Pm3m*	*Pm3m*	
Phase fraction (%)	75.66	78.79	79.26	79.34	80.03	80.75	82.11		81.23	80.07	81.17	
σ^1	572(24)	448(14)	483(15)	462(14)	403(13)	397(13)	393(13)		598(19)	662(24)	692(17)	
a/Å	3.99218(9)	4.01129(5)	4.01363(5)	4.01786(5)	4.02294(5)	4.02837(5)	4.03200(5)		3.99478(7)	4.01081(7)	4.01389(5)	
c/Å	4.03448(12)								4.03420(9)			
V/Å^3	64.2996(29)	64.5433(14)	64.6565(14)	64.8612(13)	65.1072(14)	65.3713(13)	65.5485(14)		64.3786(22)	64.5204(20)	64.6689(14)	
$V_{1/3}$/Å	4.00623(18)								4.00787(14)			
Ba (0,0,0)												
$U^{11} = U^{22}$/Å^2	0.30(19)	1.11(7)	1.20(7)	1.40(7)	1.44(7)	1.77(7)	1.76(7)		0.55(18)	0.89(11)	0.62(7)	
U^{33}/Å^2	1.4(13)	1.11(7)	1.20(7)	1.40(7)	1.44(7)	1.77(7)	1.76(7)		1.1(21)	0.89(11)	0.62(7)	
U^{eq}/Å^2	0.7(6)	1.11(7)	1.20(7)	1.40(7)	1.44(7)	1.77(7)	1.76(7)		0.7(8)	0.89(11)	0.62(7)	
Ti $(\frac{1}{2},\frac{1}{2},\frac{1}{2} + \Delta z\text{Ti})$												
ΔzTi	−0.035 (5)								−0.009(33)			
$U^{11} = U^{22}$/Å^2	0.73(21)	1.26(9)	1.31(9)	1.51(9)	1.61(9)	1.79(9)	1.75(9)		0.66(19)	0.83(12)	0.80(8)	
U^{33}/Å^2	1(4)	1.26(9)	1.31(9)	1.51(9)	1.61(9)	1.79(9)	1.75(9)		2.2(2.7)	0.83(12)	0.80(8)	
U^{eq}/Å^2	0.8(15)	1.26(9)	1.31(9)	1.51(9)	1.61(9)	1.79(9)	1.75(9)		1.2(11)	0.83(12)	0.80(8)	
O1 $(\frac{1}{2},\frac{1}{2},0 + \Delta z\text{O1})$												
ΔzO1	0.021(4)								0.036(10)			
$U^{11} = U^{22}$/Å^2	0.17(29)	1.14(7)	1.05(7)	1.24(7)	1.46(7)	1.72(7)	1.89(7)		0.30(27)	0.89(10)	0.74(7)	
U^{33}/Å^2	1.0(23)	1.12(12)	1.32(12)	1.49(12)	1.66(12)	1.86(12)	1.93(13)		1.5(13)	0.84(10)	0.74(7)	
U^{eq}/Å^2	0.5(10)	1.13(9)	1.14(9)	1.32(9)	1.53(9)	1.76(9)	1.90(9)		0.7(6)	0.87(10)	0.74(7)	
O2 $(\frac{1}{2},0,\frac{1}{2} + \Delta z\text{O2})$												
ΔzO2	0.006(5)								0.026(12)			
U^{11}/Å^2	0.34(34)								0.28(28)			
U^{22}/Å^2	1.30(26)								0.64(22)			
U^{33}/Å^2	2.0(6)								1.6(4)			
U^{eq}/Å^2	1.2(4)								0.82(30)			
Minority phase												
Space group	*Pm3m*	*Pm3m*	*Pm3m*	*Pm3m*	*Pm3m*	*Pm3m*	*Pm3m*		*Pm3m*	*Pm3m*	*Pm3m*	
a/Å	4.0142(3)	4.0287(7)	4.0338(5)	4.0384(5)	4.0425(5)	4.0480(5)	4.0530(5)		4.01908(25)	4.0238(6)	4.0325(6)	
V/Å^3	64.682(8)	65.389(18)	65.634(15)	65.861(14)	66.064(15)	66.330(15)	66.577(15)		64.920(7)	65.148(16)	65.572(18)	
χ_{red}	1.855	1.422	1.410	1.321	1.402	1.275	1.249		2.958	2.478	1.650	
R_{wp}	0.0551	0.0703	0.0684	0.0666	0.0708	0.0682	0.0679		0.0538	0.0657	0.0492	
R_p	0.0449	0.0600	0.0562	0.0542	0.0590	0.0558	0.0566		0.0439	0.0554	0.0417	

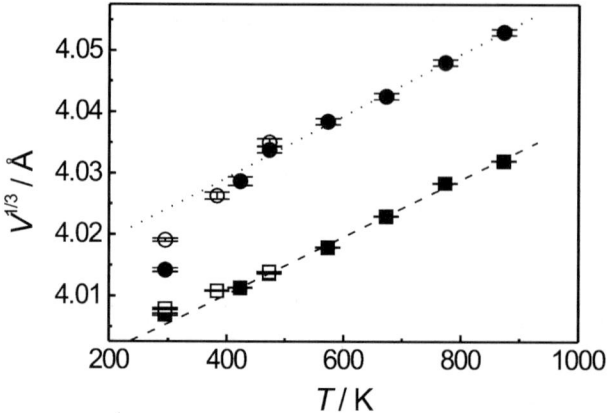

Fig. 4 Comparison of unit cell parameter a of BaTiO$_3$ for microwave (□,○) and conventional heating (■,●). Squares indicate the majority phase while circles correspond to the minority cubic phase. For the tetragonal phase the pseudo-cubic cell parameter is calculated as $V^{1/3}$. The lines through the points are merely guides to the eye.

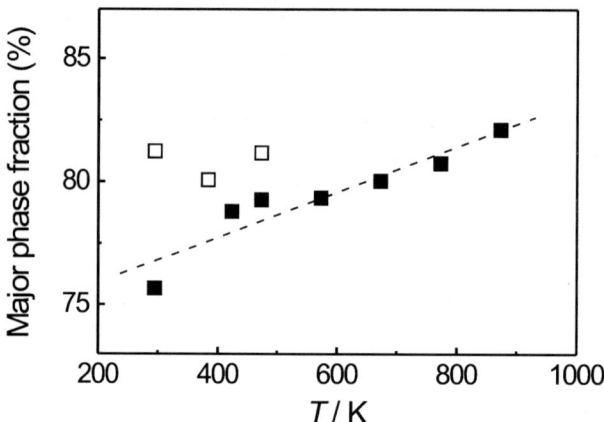

Fig. 5 Variation with temperature of the percentage of the majority phase in BaTiO$_3$. Samples are either heated conventionally (■) or with microwaves (□). The line through some of the points is merely a guide to the eye. The data point for the conventionally heated sample at 295 K is obscured by that for the microwaved sample, and has the smaller error bars.

the data taken from the microwaved sample at 383 K should correspond to the lower temperature phase but the structure at this measured temperature is actually cubic, suggesting a temperature above T_c. However, comparison of the ADPs for the two microwave experiments at elevated temperatures suggested that this measure of temperature gave a *lower* value than for conventional heating (Fig. 6(a)–(c)). It should be noted that strong correlations between several of the fitted parameters at 295 K, where the minority cubic phase and majority tetragonal phase co-exist, gave rise to very large standard deviations in ADPs. Finally, we note that the peak width parameter σ^1 (the second term in the expansion in d^2 (where 'd' is the d-spacing of a reflection) of the Gaussian component of the lineshape in TOF profile function 3 within GSAS, with contributions from both instrumental resolution and isotropic strain broadening of the sample) is significantly higher in the microwaved samples compared to the samples with conventional heating, as displayed in Fig. 7. These data are also afflicted with strong correlation with other parameters in the fit: while the

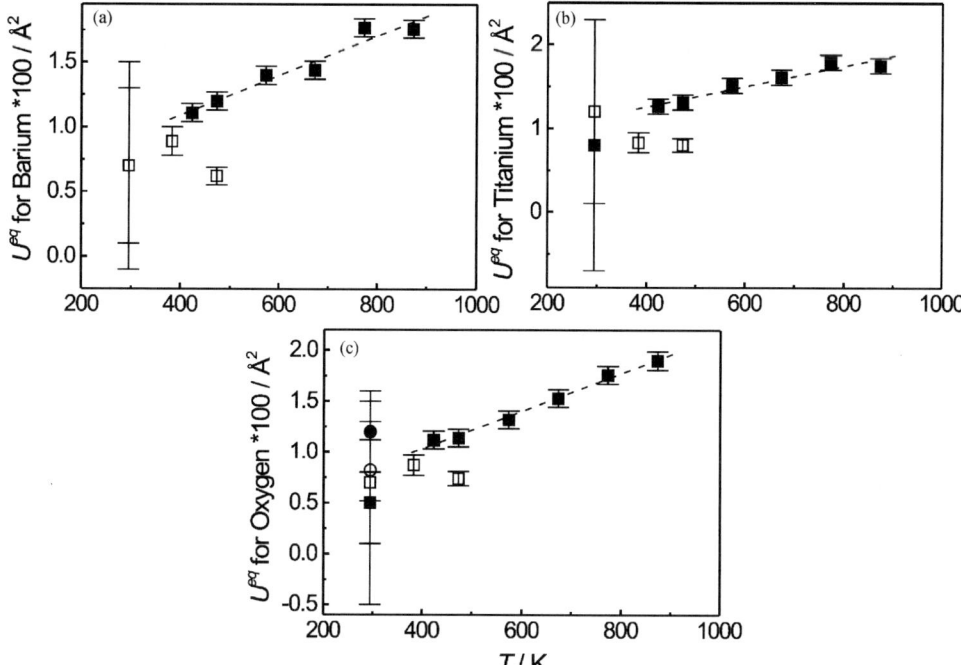

Fig. 6 (a)Comparison of isotropic ADPs for barium atoms in BaTiO$_3$, for microwave (□) and conventional heating (■). The line through some of the points is merely a guide to the eye.(b) Comparison of isotropic ADPs for titanium atoms in BaTiO$_3$, for microwave (□) and conventional heating (■). The line through some of the points is merely a guide to the eye.(c)Comparison of isotropic ADPs for oxygen atoms in BaTiO$_3$, for microwave (□,○) and conventional heating (■,●). In the lower temperature tetragonal phase, the data are in pairs for each mode of heating with symbols distinguishing site O1 (square) and site O2 (circle). The line through some of the points is merely a guide to the eye.

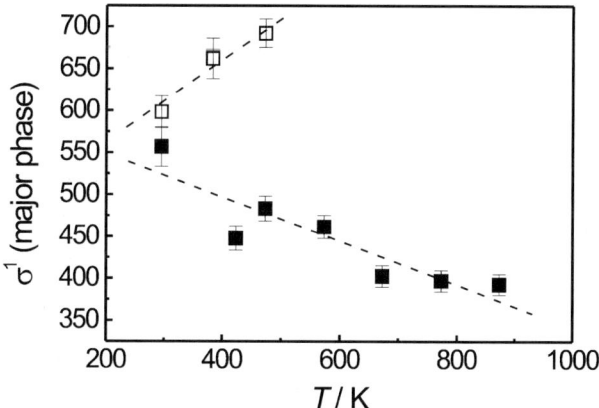

Fig. 7 Refined values of peak width parameter σ^1 (defined in the text) for BaTiO$_3$ with microwave (□) and conventional heating (■). The line through some of the points is merely a guide to the eye.

microwave data taken at the two elevated temperatures unambiguously reveal significantly larger values of σ^1 in relation to the conventionally heated data, values at 295 K depend strongly on the value of cell parameter a of the minority phase. If the value for a of the minority phase was allowed to vary freely, χ^2 was optimised (2.83) at $a = 4.01416$ Å , with a corresponding value for σ^1 of

556.9; alternatively, if a was set to a value of 4.02400 Å, obtained by extrapolating from higher temperature values, χ^2 was optimised (3.381) when σ^1 was 738.9. On the basis of a better value for χ^2, together with closer agreement with the data taken for the conventionally heated data, we decided that the smaller values of σ^1 were more likely to be correct.

4. Discussion

4.1 Heat, phonons and their influence on neutron diffraction patterns

When a crystalline insulator with a wide band gap is heated, the thermal energy is taken up by exciting phonons. The interatomic potential $V(r)$ of the atoms in such a solid may be expressed as a Taylor series written in terms of the displacement of atoms from their equilibrium positions a, to some position r:

$$V(r) = V(a) + \frac{(r-a)^2}{2}\left(\frac{d^2V}{dr^2}\right)_{r=a} + \frac{(r-a)^3}{6}\left(\frac{d^3V}{dr^3}\right)_{r=a} + \ldots \quad (1)$$

The simplest treatments of phonons, truncates this expansion at the second term.[39] One consequence of this 'harmonic' approximation is that there is no coupling between the phonons, and these 'normal modes' may be treated as a collection of independent harmonic oscillators. Such excitations influence the diffraction of X-rays and neutrons,[40,41] weighting the structure factor by the Debye–Waller factor, $\exp(-2W_d)$. For neutron scattering, the nuclear unit-cell structure factor, $F_N(\kappa)$, may be written as:

$$F_N(\kappa) = \sum_d \bar{b}_d \exp(i\kappa.d)\exp(-W_d) \quad (2)$$

where κ is the neutron scattering vector, $\bar{b}_d$ is the mean value of the scattering length of the dth atom in the unit cell at position d, and W_d is defined as:

$$W_d = \frac{\hbar}{4M_d N}\sum_s \frac{(\kappa.e_{ds})^2}{\omega_s}\langle 2n_s + 1\rangle \quad (3)$$

where M_d is the mass of the dth atom in the cell, N is the number of such cells in the crystal, s is an index for the phonon that specifies its wavevector and polarization (typically x, y or z); e_s is the polarisation vector, ω_s the frequency, and n_s is the quantum number of the phonon s. In the case of a Bravais lattice, W_d becomes W, and we can express this quantity simply in terms of the mean square displacement of the atom projected along κ, $\langle u_\kappa^2\rangle$:

$$2W = \langle(\kappa.u)^2\rangle = \kappa^2\langle u_\kappa^2\rangle \quad (4)$$

$\langle u_\kappa^2\rangle$ is commonly written as $\langle u^2\rangle$ and expressed as the anisotropic displacement tensor with components U^{ij}.[42]

$$\langle u^2\rangle = U^{11}l_1^2 + U^{22}l_2^2 + U^{33}l_3^2 + 2U^{12}l_1l_2 + 2U^{23}l_2l_3 + 2U^{31}l_3l_1 \quad (5)$$

where l_i denotes the cosine of the angle between the polarisation of the vibration and the reciprocal axis i. For a non-Bravais lattice, $\langle(\kappa.u)^2\rangle$ must be taken over all non-equivalent atoms, as well as over all cells, and $\langle u^2\rangle$ may then vary from atom to atom in the unit cell. The introduction of anharmonicity[43,44] has a number of important consequences for diffraction from such a solid,[41,45] directly affecting terms in W that are influenced by vibrational amplitudes, and forcing us to modify expression (4):

$$2W = \langle(\kappa.u)^2\rangle - \frac{i}{3}\langle(\kappa.u)^3\rangle - \frac{1}{12}\left\{\langle(\kappa.u)^4\rangle - 3\langle(\kappa.u)^2\rangle^2\right\} + \ldots \quad (6)$$

Anharmonicity may also lead to a change in cell parameters through thermal expansion of the lattice. In the harmonic approximation, the energy of the phonons does not change with volume, V, so they do not contribute to the pressure: a purely harmonic crystal would not expand on heating.

4.2 Microwave excitation of phonons

When a material is heated with microwaves, the input of energy and the manner in which it is distributed among the various degrees of freedom may be quite different compared to the conventional case.[5] There are various ways in which a microwave field may couple with a solid. It may excite charge carriers in the case of a metal, or narrow band-gap material; it may also couple with defects in the solid.[46] In the absence of these two effects, the key mechanism by which energy is absorbed from an electromagnetic field of microwave frequency or below is through a multiphonon process rather than a resonant single-phonon process.[47,48] The reason for this is that the frequency of the microwave radiation is, in general, much lower than that of the phonons with which it can couple (the transverse optic (TO) phonons) and so for energy and momentum to be conserved during microwave absorption, at least two phonons must be involved. Most treatments of this process take a two-phonon process to be the leading term, such that their energy difference is equal to the microwave photon energy. The efficiency of this process depends on the anharmonicity of the phonons, and this is generally treated just to the third-order term in the Taylor expansion of the elastic potential (eqn. (1)). The anharmonicity governs the efficiency of phonon–phonon coupling, and we can express the rate of change of the population of the transverse optic phonons, n_f, as follows:

$$\frac{dn_f}{dt} = \sum_{n_i k_i} \sum_{n_j k_j} (TP_+ - TP_-) \qquad (7)$$

where the sums are over the populations and wavevectors of the two phonons, i and j (which are the phonons that are respectively annihilated and created when the microwave is adsorbed), and $TP_\pm$ indicates the transition probability for creation and destruction of the phonons:

$$TP_\pm = \left(\frac{2\pi}{\hbar}\right) |\langle n_f \pm 1 | H_A | n_f \rangle|^2 \, \delta(E) \qquad (8)$$

The delta function in this expression denotes the energy conservation condition: $E = \hbar\omega - \hbar\omega_{ji}$; $\omega_{ji} \equiv \omega_j - \omega_i$, and H_A is the anharmonic lattice potential. Eqn. (7) may be rewritten as:

$$\frac{dn_f}{dt} = \Gamma(n_f - \bar{n}_f) \qquad (9)$$

where $\bar{n}_f$ is the thermal equilibrium value of n_f, and the relaxation frequency Γ may be written as:

$$\Gamma \approx \int_0^{k_{BZ}} dk \, . k^2 V_{fij}^2 \delta(E)(\bar{n}_i - \bar{n}_j) \qquad (10)$$

where the integral is over the Brillouin zone (BZ) and V_{fij}^2 is proportional to the third-order derivative of the lattice potential, *i.e.* is proportional to the third term in the Taylor expansion (1).[47] This approach has been used successfully to calculate the dielectric response of materials (for example the frequency dependent dielectric constant $\varepsilon(\omega)$ and the value of Q, see for instance ref. 49) in the microwave spectrum, a problem of particular technological importance in microwave communications.

Once the microwave energy has been pumped into particular TO modes in the crystal it will be redistributed, again by anharmonic effects. It is quite conceivable therefore that the energy distribution will differ from that in a conventionally heated sample, where energy is introduced from the bottom up, *via* acoustic modes. However, in order to quantify the populations of various modes and thus predict or rationalise structural parameters such as Debye–Waller factors and thermal expansivity, we need to be able to model the dynamics of the lattice, incorporating anharmonicity and also the polarisability, particularly of the lattice. This is a difficult calculation to do well, because the timescale is relatively long for molecular dynamics simulations,[50] and is beyond the scope of this work. However, the fraction of the energy stored in non-equilibrium excitations in a simple Debye solid has been estimated to be very small, of the order of 10^{-6} for conditions typical for microwave materials processing (10^5 V m^{-1}, 10^3 K).[5]

4.3 Structure of aspirin in a microwave field

Comparing the anisotropic thermal parameters for conventionally heated and microwaved samples, we see no significant evidence for non-uniform equipartition of the microwave energy within the molecular structure. The increase in thermal parameters is approximately the same for all atoms, and the shape and orientation of the thermal ellipsoids show no evidence of potentially significant charges. Our conclusion is thus that the effect of microwave radiation on our single crystal of aspirin is just to heat the structure and the microwave energy deposited in a molecule is distributed rapidly (on the timescale of our neutron diffraction measurements) to all parts of the molecule. Experimentally, this can be explained as the sample was held in the cooling device by an aluminium nitride pin connected to the cold head of the CCR, which was held at the set temperature. Although the thermal conduction path from cold head to sample is made *via* thin Kapton strips, it is not unreasonable to propose that when the microwave radiation is switched on (locally to the sample), the small amount of heat introduced in the small sample mass would not have a significant effect on the temperature measured in the CCR cold head. The possibility of microwave heating having more localised energy effects in different parts of the molecule under study will most probably have to be investigated by more rapid methods than single crystal neutron diffraction, though our preliminary results should not be regarded as conclusive in this respect. Further work on this system using varying microwave set-ups and employing X-ray diffraction along with various spectroscopies including IR, Raman[51] and INS (neutron vibrational spectroscopy) are planned in order to extend this work.

4.4 Structure of $BaTiO_3$ in a microwave field

The simplest interpretation of the data for the cell parameters of $BaTiO_3$ with and without microwave heating is that the microwaved sample is 10–20 K hotter than the temperature measured with the fluoroptic probe over the range considered here. Cell expansion reflects anharmonic effects, and it could be argued that an electric field that is fluctuating at a GHz rate is effectively static compared to phonon frequencies (of the order of THz), and that this might conceivably influence the harmonicity and thence the cell expansion. However, the effective field gradient, of the order of 10^5 V m^{-1}, does not give a particularly high potential difference at atomic length-scales, and therefore one would not anticipate it to have a significant influence on the interatomic potential.

By contrast, the ADPs appear *smaller* under microwave irradiation. It could be argued that the difference between the microwaved and conventionally heated samples is relatively small, of the order of two standard deviations. Care should also be taken to ensure that there are not other effects that are strongly correlated with ADPs, and which might compensate in the refinement. One such effect could be differences in grain size and therefore extinction[37] between the microwaved and conventionally heated cases. In general, an increase in grain size should lead to an increase in extinction, and this in turn leads to a reduced weighting of reflections at larger d-spacings.[52] One would therefore expect an approximately *inverse* correlation between (increased) grain size and (increased) ADPs, and therefore anomalously *small* ADPs for the microwaved sample would correspond to an increase in grain size in that case. This is at odds with the increase in Bragg peak widths during microwave irradiation. Let us imagine how this could arise physically. The microwaved sample is the same as that heated conventionally, with a modest heat treatment (the excursion in temperature to 873 K so it is unlikely that this leads to appreciable structural change). A simple rationalization of the increased peak widths could be that there is an increase in thermal gradients throughout the sample, or fluctuation in sample temperature during microwave heating, leading to a distribution of cell parameters that is manifested as a peak broadening. The temperature stability of the sample over the timescale of the experiment is believed to be of the order of ±1 K, so thermal gradients in the sample are the more likely explanation for such broadening.

Another factor that is sometimes incorporated in ADPs is a degree of static disorder,[45] a phenomenon that is observed in $BaTiO_3$[25] and related materials.[37,38] One inference one might draw from our observation is that microwave irradiation *reduces* the degree of static disorder at a given temperature. Given the complexity of this system, and continued uncertainty of the relative importance of ion disorder and displacive motion in the region of T_c,[53] this proposition requires much more detailed experimental and theoretical analysis. A plausible contribution to such behaviour is the action of the electric component of the microwave field on the ferroelectric domain structure of $BaTiO_3$.[54] Electron microscopy on the tetragonal phase reveals herringbone domain arrangements with 90° boundaries; wall thicknesses range from 0.03 μm to 0.15 μm while the domain width is in the range 0.15 μm to 1 μm, depending on grain size.[55] Even for the paraelectric, cubic phase of perovskite materials it has been shown that the minimisation of energy results in small displacements from the ions' mean positions, giving rise to static disorder in the crystal structure.[56] In the presence of microwave radiation, the external field will move domain walls, resulting in changing ion positions during dipole moment reorientation. With low field amplitude, domain wall positions will resonate within their potential well. However, beyond a certain threshold amplitude, domain walls can be irreversibly displaced.[57] This could lead to a variety of processes, including the growth and change in structure of the domains, both of which are likely to change the static disorder observed for the crystal structure.

The strong dielectric response of $BaTiO_3$, to the microwave field might also influence the thermodynamics of the para- to ferroelectric transition. The driving electric field continuously switches the polarization in the ferroelectric phase, acting to suppress the time-averaged spontaneous polarization.[58] One would anticipate therefore that T_c would be reduced as the field amplitude is increased; there are indeed other observations of other structural transitions whose temperature appears to change in a microwave field.[11,59] It is conceivable that a related effect also has an influence on the ADPs. The fluctuating internal electric field induced by the microwave field has a quite different frequency to most of the phonons in the lattice, and in many cases will act as a damping influence, effectively altering the phonon velocity. It might therefore be possible to reconcile smaller ADPs with higher temperatures if the effective stiffness of the vibrations is increased by the dielectric response induced in the material by microwave heating.

5. Conclusions

We have designed, tested and applied apparatus that allows microwave radiation to be applied to a powder or single crystal sample during a neutron diffraction experiment. Some degree of temperature control may be exerted through moderation of microwave power in conjunction with conventional methods, helium cryogen opposed to electrical heating.

Measurement of the crystal structure of aspirin indicates that microwaves are effective at heating this molecular solid: ADPs for a sample whose temperature was set by the cryostat to be 100 K, corresponded quite closely to those for the same material maintained by conventional heating at 300 K, and were quite different from those taken under the same heating regime at 100 K. There was no evidence for any significant redistribution of thermal energy throughout the molecule as reflected in changes to the ADPs. This is not entirely surprising: one would anticipate thermal equilibration throughout the molecule on the timescale of a vibrational period (10^{-12} s).

High-resolution powder neutron diffraction data taken on the ferroelectric material $BaTiO_3$ with microwave and conventional heating reveal systematic differences between the two. For a given set temperature, the lattice parameter of the microwaved sample is significantly larger, while the ADPs are somewhat smaller. It is difficult to rationalise this difference. The increase in cell parameter under microwave heating suggests a higher temperature, while the change in ADPs suggests the opposite. Of course the microwave field may also excite a strongly fluctuating electric field in the material, and it is conceivable that this gives rise to additional effects: it may damp certain forms of ion motion, perhaps giving rise to anomalous ADPs; it may also alter the energy of the ferroelectric phase relative to the paraelectric phase, in turn influencing T_c for the transition between the two; it may also accelerate structural annealing, for it is now beginning to be appreciated that microwave fields are remarkably efficient at driving ionic motion.[12–15] However, a detailed exploration of these possible effects is beyond the scope of this work, and will required proper modelling of the elastic properties of $BaTiO_3$ in an oscillating GHz electric field. Finally, it should be noted that a significant increase in fitted peak width parameters during microwave heating could provide evidence for hot-spots in the sample, or at least thermal gradients that are significantly greater than in the conventionally heated sample, and again this is entirely consistent with current understanding and observations of the effect of microwave radiation on ceramic dielectrics.[60]

Acknowledgements

The authors would like to thank EPSRC for funding, and the technical support services at both The University of Edinburgh (particularly Stuart Mains and David Paden) and at the ISIS Facility for their invaluable efforts in developing the equipment. They are also grateful for valuable contributions through discussion with Garry Bond, Alastair Bruce, Philip Camp, Kevin Knight and Terry Willis.

References

1. D. M. P. Mingos and D. R. Baghurst, *Chem. Soc. Rev.*, 1991, **20**, 1.
2. A. G. Whittaker and D. M. P. Mingos, *J. Microwave Power Electromag. Energ.*, 1994, **29**, 195.
3. C. R. Strauss and R. W. Trainor, *Aust. J. Chem.*, 1995, **48**, 1665.
4. S. A. Galema, *Chem. Soc. Rev.*, 1997, **26**, 233.
5. Y. V. Bykov, K. I. Rybakov and V. E. Semenov, *J. Phys. D.: Appl. Phys.*, 2001, **34**, R55.
6. P. Lidstrom, J. Tierney, B. Wathey and J. Westman, *Tetrahedron*, 2001, **57**, 9225.
7. D. R. Baghurst, R. C. B. Copley, H. Fleischer, D. M. P. Mingos, G. O. Kyd, L. J. Yellowlees, A. J. Welch, T. R. Spalding and D. O'Connell, *J. Organomet. Chem.*, 1993, **447**, C14.
8. A. G. Whittaker, A. Harrison, G. S. Oakley, I. D. Youngson, S. King and R. Heenan, in *Proceedings of the First International Conference on Microwave Chemistry*, ed. M. Hajek, 1999, Institut National Polytechnique de Toulouse, on behalf of AMPERE, Cambridge, UK, p. 21.
9. A. G. Whittaker, A. Harrison, G. S. Oakley, I. D. Youngson, S. King and R. Heenan, *Rev. Sci. Instrum.*, 2001, **72**, 172.
10. M. Willert-Porada, *Ceram. Trans.*, 1997, **80**, 153.
11. G. Robb, A. G. Whittaker and A. Harrison, in *Proceedings of the Second International Conference on Microwave Chemistry*, ed. A. Gourdenne, 2000, Institut National Polytechnique de Toulouse, on behalf of AMPERE, Cambridge, UK, p. 295.
12. A. G. Whittaker and L. Cronin, in *Proceedings of the Second International Conference on Microwave Chemistry*, ed. A. Gourdenne, 2000, Institut National Polytechnique de Toulouse, on behalf of AMPERE, Cambridge, UK, p. 291.
13. J. H. Booske, R. F. Cooper and I. Dobson, *J. Mater. Res.*, 1992, **7**, 495.
14. J. H. Booske, R. F. Cooper, S. A. Freeman, K. I. Rybakov and V. E. Semenov, *Phys. Plasmas*, 1998, **5**, 1664.
15. S. A. Freeman, J. H. Booske and R. F. Cooper, *J. Appl. Phys.*, 1998, **83**, 5761.
16. H. Bohr and J. Bohr, *Bioelectromagnetism*, 2000, **21**, 68.
17. J. A. Laurence, P. W. French, R. A. Lindner and D. R. McKenzie, *J. Theor. Biol.*, 2000, **206**, 291.
18. W. Stewart, *Mobile Phones and Health: A Report from the Independent Expert Group on Mobile Phones*, IEGMP/National Radiological Protection Board, Chilton, Didcot, UK, 2000.
19. C. Gerk and M. Willert-Porada, in *Proceedings of the Second International Conference on Microwave Chemistry*, ed. A. Gourdenne, 2000, Institut National Polytechnique de Toulouse, on behalf of AMPERE, Cambridge, UK, p. 327.
20. R. Wroe and A. T. Rowley, *J. Mater. Sci.*, 1996, **31**, 2019.
21. Y. Kim, K. Machida, T. Taga and K. Osaki, *Chem. Pharm. Bull.*, 1985, **33**, 2641.
22. C. C. Wilson, *Chem. Phys. Lett.*, 2001, **335**, 57.
23. C. C. Wilson, *New J. Chem.*, submitted.
24. R. Comes, M. Lambert and A. Guinier, *Acta Crystallogr. Sect. A*, 1970, **26**, 244.
25. G. H. Kwei, A. C. Lawson, S. J. L. Billinge and S.-W. Cheong, *J. Phys. Chem.*, 1993, **97**, 2368.
26. C. N. W. Darlington, W. I. F. David and K. S. Knight, *Phase Transitions*, 1994, **48**, 217.
27. http://www.isis.rl.ac.uk/crystallography/sxd/.
28. C. C. Wilson, *J. Appl. Crystallogr.*, 1997, **30**, 184.
29. C. C. Wilson, *J. Mol. Struct.*, 1997, **405**, 207.
30. A. C. Larsen and R. B. Von Dreele, *GSAS, General Structure Analysis System*, 1994, LAUR-86-748, New Mexico, USA.
31. G. M. Sheldrick, *SHELXL97*, University of Göttingen, Germany, 1997.
32. http://www.isis.rl.ac.uk/crystallography/hrpd/.
33. C. Li, Z. Chen, D. Cui, Y. Zhou, H. Lu, C. Dong, F. Wu and H. Chen, *J. Appl. Phys.*, 1999, **86**, 4555.
34. T. Takeuchi, K. Ado, Y. Saito, M. Tabuchi, C. Masquelier and O. Nakamura, *Solid State Ionics*, 1995, **79**, 325.
35. C. Valot, N. Floquet, M. Mesnier and J. C. Niepce, *J. Phys. (Paris) IV*, 1996, **3**, 71.
36. N. Floquet, C. Valot, M. Mesnier, J. C. Niepce, L. Normand, A. Thorel and R. Kilaas, *J. Phys. (Paris) III*, 1997, **7**, 1105.
37. P. U. M. Sastry, A. Sequeira, H. Rajagopal, B. A. Dasanacharya, S. Balakumar, R. Ilangovan and P. Ramasamy, *J. Phys.: Condens. Matter*, 1996, **8**, 2905.

38   C. Bedoya, C. Muller, J.-L. Baudour, F. Bouree, J.-L. Soubeyroux and M. Roubin, *J. Phys.: Condens. Matter*, 2001, **13**, 6453.
39   W. Cochran, *The Dynamics of Atoms in Crystals*, Edward Arnold, London, 1973.
40   G. L. Squires, *Introduction to the Theory of Thermal Neutron Scattering*, Cambridge University Press, Cambridge, 1978.
41   S. W. Lovesey, *Theory of Neutron Scattering from Condensed Matter*, Oxford Science, Oxford, 1986.
42   K. N. Trueblood, H.-B. Bürgi, H. Burzlaff, J. D. Dunitz, C. M. Gramaccioli, H. H. Schulz, U. Shmueli and S. C. Abrahams, *Acta Crystallogr., Sect. A*, 1996, **52**, 770.
43   R. A. Cowley, *Adv. Phys.*, 1963, **12**, 421.
44   A. A. Maradudin and A. E. Fein, *Phys. Rev.*, 1962, **128**, 2589.
45   B. T. M. Willis and A. W. Pryor, *Thermal Vibrations in Crystallography*, Cambridge University Press, Cambridge, 1975.
46   E. Schlömann, *Phys. Rev. A*, 1964, **135**, 413.
47   M. Sparks, D. F. King and D. L. Mills, *Phys. Rev. B*, 1982, **26**, 6987.
48   K. R. Subbaswamy and D. L. Mills, *Phys. Rev. B*, 1986, **33**, 4213.
49   E. J. Wu and G. Ceder, *J. Appl. Phys.*, 2001, **89**, 5630.
50   J. Deppe, M. Balkanski, R. F. Wallis and A. R. McGurn, *Phys. Rev. B*, 1992, **45**, 5687.
51   F. Genet, S. Loridant, C. Ritter and G. Lucazeau, *J. Phys. Chem. Solids*, 1999, **60**, 2009.
52   T. M. Sabine, R. B. Von Dreele and J.-E. Jorgensen, *Acta Crystallogr. Sect. A*, 1988, **44**, 374.
53   J.-M. Kiat, G. Baldinozzi, M. Dunlop, C. Malibert, B. Dkhil, C. Menoret, O. Masson and M.-T. Fernandez-Diaz, *J. Phys.: Condens. Matter*, 2000, **12**, 8411.
54   G. Arlt, U. Böttger and S. Witte, *Appl. Phys. Lett*, 1993, **63**, 602.
55   L. M. Živkovic, B. D. Stojanovic, V. B. Pavlovic, Z. S. Nikolic, B. A. Marinkovic and T. V. Sreckovic, *J. Eur. Ceram. Soc.*, 1999, **19**, 1085.
56   C. Muller, J. L. Baudour, C. Bedoya, F. Bouree, J.-L. Soubeyroux and M. Roubin, *Acta. Crystallogr., Sect. B*, 2000, **56**, 27.
57   D. Damjanovic and M. Demartin, *J. Phys.: Condens. Matter*, 1997, **9**, 4943–4953.
58   H. Frohlich, *Theory of Dielectrics*, Oxford University Press, Oxford, 1986.
59   G. Bond, personal communication, 2002.
60   X. L. Zhang, D. O. Hayward and D. M. P. Mingos, *Chem. Commun.*, 1999, 975.

General Discussion

Prof. Moffat opened the discussion of Dr Martlew's paper: The Roman and Syrians made superb glass two millennia ago—but not window glass. Who is the "Faraday" of window glass making? When was the modern process invented? Where? What were the key novel features?

Dr Martlew replied: It may have been the expansion of the Roman Empire to these chilly islands which provoked the Roman glassmakers to develop methods of creating glass sheets to block up apertures in buildings. Casting molten glass onto a flat rock slab then rolling it out into a sheet was a technique used by the Romans, to create a translucent rather than transparent pane, appropriate to the glare of the Mediterranean lands!

Glass blowing was invented at some time about the beginning of the Christian Era, and naturally provided an easy way to make objects of spherical or cylindrical symmetry or derivatives therefrom. Blowing a glass sphere then flattening it to make a window was quite challenging, and three methods developed. One involved manipulating the sphere to make it into a cylinder, which could then be split axially and flattened to make a flat sheet. A second method (which never became really popular) involved blowing the glass into a suitable mould to create a bottle with four flat sides and a flat base; one could then cut these up to create small flat sheets of glass. The third method, known in England as the Crown Glass process, used the centrifugal forces generated by spinning a sphere on its supporting rod to open the hot glass shape into a flat disc from which small window panes could be cut. The individual inventors of these techniques are not known.

By the middle of the twentieth century continuous glassmaking on an industrial scale had replaced these ancient hand methods of production. Two main kinds of process were used. If cheap window glass was needed it could be drawn vertically upwards from a tank of molten glass in a continuous ribbon, being cooled and annealed in a tower before being cut into handlable sheets at the top. Glass thickness was limited to about 4 mm, but the product answered domestic needs very well, aside from the optical distortion generated in the forming process.

Thicker glass with better optical characteristics was in demand for shop windows and the large windows and mirrors desired by the affluent classes. Polished plate glass to satisfy this demand was made by continuously rolling the stream of molten glass to create a ribbon as thick as needed. To remove the surface scarring introduced by the rolling process it was then necessary to grind and polish both sides of the glass to create optically perfect plates, a tremendously expensive process, and very wasteful of glass.

When the float process was announced in 1959 it was revolutionary in that it amalgamated the strengths of each of the earlier processes. The perfect flatness of polished plate glass was achieved by floating the molten glass on a layer of molten tin. Because the new ribbon didn't touch anything solid whilst it was still deformable, the as-formed surfaces were as brilliant as those of sheet glass drawn up from the melt.

We may not know the individual inventors of antiquity, but we do know that the "Michael Faraday" of industrial window glass production was undoubtedly Sir Alastair Pilkington.

Prof. Hounslow asked: You show particle tracks, yet your velocity maps indicate a great deal of mixing. Would there not be a distribution of residence times?

Dr Martlew answered: There is indeed a very wide spread of residence times over all possible particle tracks. Mixing does occur, but with the generally very high viscosities of the molten glass and the very low Reynolds numbers involved, mixing tends to be slow and relies heavily on chemical diffusion. Homogenising the glass and avoiding the visible effects of non-uniformity of refractive index in the product has exercised glassmakers for several thousand years.

For the present work it has been necessary to prepare several thousand particle tracks for each case, to establish which tracks within the furnace result in the smallest residence times. Dissolution of sand grain residues is favoured by long times and higher temperatures. Generally the particle tracks which have the smallest times yield the worst dissolution efficiency; temperatures are not sufficiently high along these tracks to compensate. For the exploratory research presented here the method of calculation is sufficiently cumbersome to make it necessary to limit the number of tracks studied to a very few. Having established the method and demonstrated some usefulness, the next step is to code the calculation within the 3DGLASS post processor module, so that more complete explorations can be carried out economically.

Dr Cole said: When you add impurities to the glass in order to generate a particular colour of glass, how will this affect the reference data that you have regarding the stability/quality of the glass relating to composition? Do you thus obtain glasses of certain colours being more stable/fragile, *etc.* than clear glass?

Dr Martlew replied: We have talked already about the corrosive nature of molten glass. Though prejudicial to the longevity of the capital equipment needed to make glass products industrially, this attribute enables us to explore many different compositional variants in the quest for desirable properties and performances.

Colouring oxides (notably those of the transition elements) dissolve fairly readily in the molten glass, unconstrained by any rigid stoichiometry. Ligand field effects then do the rest, creating the colour. More often than not, commercial colours require only very small percentages of colouring oxides, so the key macroscopic physical properties are not affected.

Prof. Helliwell asked: I would like to make a connection with Greaves *et al.*'s paper at this *Faraday Discussion* and ask how the new characterisation details are informing new or better products. Also are the SR central facilities currently available, adequate, or needing further development to meet your needs as an industrialist?

Prof. Wilson asked: You mentioned the importance of the surface layer. Could you comment on the use of surface scattering methods to examine the nature of glass surfaces and interfaces *e.g.* neutron or X-ray reflection methods, both specular and off-specular.

To follow up—is this important enough to justify obtaining access to these centralised, often expensive, facilities?

Dr Martlew answered: I may not comment in any detail about novel products which may be emerging from better understanding of glass structures, particularly the structure of glasses within the vicinity of the glass surface. However it is well known that the vagaries of the strength of glass products may be rationalised in terms of Griffith flaws (these are envisaged as sub-microscopic flaws in the glass surface which concentrate any tensile stress being experienced, starting a crack and causing failure). Any techniques which can be used to investigate glass structure at the molecular level are very desirable. With any such technique, however, it seems that the larger the scale of examination the more expensive is the experimental facility. My personal view is that we need to be looking at mesoscale structures in order to gain the working understanding that is needed to be the fundamental foundation of new commercial products. In the current economic climate, manufacturing industry cannot justify spending large amounts of private money on equipping for such techniques. If the United Kingdom is to take the lead in these matters, I believe that some way of financing such expensive facilities needs to be undertaken at Government level to support British industry in the increasingly competitive global marketplace. Having created such capital resources, the Government must ensure that the accountancy conventions used to finance their application to industrial exploitation must be friendly to the industrial budgetary processes. Sadly, the pressures now faced by industry in the current climate mean they can no longer be thought of as any kind of "cash cow"!

Dr May commented: At the ILL (Institut Laue-Langevin), there are no "tickets" to get neutron beam time. You just need to propose an experiment, and you can perform it for free if it is accepted by the relevant subcommittee. The condition is that the results get published. However, one has to pay for secret research.

Dr Martlew replied: Thank you for this helpful comment. The crunch is often the tension between the publication requirement to obtain access to centrally funded capabilities, and the secrecy necessary to protect intellectual property. Defensible IP rights often crucially depend on being able to demonstrate a stance of confidentiality during the early period of the inventive step. Publication of results is directly opposed to this stance.

Prof. Finney opened the discussion of Prof. Greaves' paper: (1) The INEL detector resolution is quite poor, and you are getting a very restricted range in q from it at $\lambda = 1.5$ Å. Is this adequate to be sure of phase identification from one peak for each of two phases (stuffed quartz and spinel)?

(2) Similarly, the detector limits you to only a small part of the Debye–Scherrer rings and hence quantifying amounts of each of the two phases on the basis of integrating under one peak leaves you open to problems of preferred orientation. How can you be sure your quantative phase estimates are not significantly affected by preferred orientation?

(3) In Section 4 you say that the proportions of amorphous content are estimated from integrating the amorphous background. (a) How good do you think this estimate is? (b) Do you have the data available? It is not plotted with the other quantities in Fig. 4 of the paper. (c) Can the variation of the "amorphous content" give a useful constraint on the accuracy of the other quantities (*e.g.* by some kind of sum rule of total material quantity)?

Prof. Greaves answered: (1) The identification of phases were first made through *ex situ* measurements using standard high resolution powder diffraction with a full q range. The INEL system on the station 8.2 at the Synchrotron Radiation Source was then used to provide *in situ* fingerprints. It is worth reporting that in the last few weeks the RAPID II curved multi-wire proportion counter has been commissioned at the SRS on station 6.2. This has a much-improved resolution compared to the INEL, a count rate three decades higher and an overlap geometry with respect to the SAXS detector offering a full q range to the smallest angles. In future it will be possible to identify phases *in situ* as well as to track their development as a function of time and temperature.

(2) Of course we cannot be sure. However, in recent measurements at the ESRF on BM26B we found that the intensity of the quartz pattern was extremely erratic compared to that of spinel, strongly supporting the view that nucleation of stuffed quartz occurs at the surface and for monolithic specimens is prone to preferred orientation. Regarding the quantification of phases at each stage, we have not used the intensity of diffraction lines but have relied on the good agreement between Cr EXAFS and SAXS data (Porod regime plus Invariant) to determine the crystalline fraction, v.

(3) We have chosen here not to use $I_{amorph}(t)$ to square with $I_{nlm}(t)$ from the two phases present because the composition of the glass is changing. In the past, though, we have explored the sum rule approach in crystallisation from gels, for example, where the crystalline phase totally replaces the amorphous one or in amorphisation where the reverse occurs (*e.g.* refs. 1 and 2).

1 J. C. Fernandes, D. A. Hall and G. N. Greaves, *Mater. Sci. Forum*, 1996, **228–231**, 411–416.
2 G. N. Greaves, in *Frontiers of High Pressure Research II: Application of High Pressure to Low Dimensional Novel Electronic Materials, NATO Advanced Research Workshop*, Kluwer, Dordrecht, 2001, p. 53.

Dr Sankar commented: The main limitation in the angular range is primarily due to the *in situ* high temperature facility which has a small window region that permits only up to *ca.* 60° 2θ. In addition only a few strong reflections appear in this 2θ range.

It appears from Fig. 4 (top) of your paper that the stuffed quartz phase is stable. It has been observed in other cordierite-forming systems, for example Mg^{2+}-exchanged zeolite B, that the stuffed quartz phase appears above 900 °C and disappears as soon as the cordierite phase starts to appear. It appears from these studies that the stuffed quartz phase is unstable, whereas this phase appears to be stable in this investigation. Is that due to the presence of chromium?

Prof. Greaves responded: Our view is that the stuffed quartz phase here is not nucleated from Cr at these temperatures but from defects at the glass surface, which will therefore offer some physical stability. However, with accurate unit cell parameters, the composition of stuffed quartz can be determined from the tabulations of Schreyer and Schairer (ref. 12 of the paper) and may not always coincide with stoichiometric cordierite $Mg_2Al_4Si_5O_{18}$. From additional unpublished data the stuffed quartz composition in Cr-doped cordierite glass heat treated at higher temperatures than reported falls on the quartz-rich side of cordierite. This may well be because of the twist in the residual glass composition resulting from the earlier formation of spinel (see eqn. (8) of the paper). Also, energy dispersive XRD results on powders of Cr-doped cordierite glass have shown that for isothermal crystallisation at 1250 °C, 200 °C above the temperatures employed here, the stuffed quartz phase is eventually replaced by cordierite, but that this conversion is slow, suggesting that the stability of stuffed quartz relates to the fact that it does not have the composition of cordierite. In the example of Mg-exchanged zeolite B, as far as I understand, the composition of the stuffed quartz phase is closer to $Mg_2Al_4Si_5O_{18}$ which may explain why the final conversion to cordierite is more rapid and your observation that the stuffed quartz in this case is unstable.

Prof. Wilson said: I am interested in the fact that the time profiles for evolution of the various types of scattering are similar, indicating that equilibration occurs on all length scales simultaneously. That is, are the formation of 210 Å particles and the formation of crystalline phases governed by the kinetics of a single process?

Prof. Greaves replied: Yes, insofar as the spinel phase is concerned, as this almost completely dominates the SAXS. If the composition determined from the final Cr EXAFS spectrum, $MgCr_{0.18}Al_{1.82}O_4$, is the same at nucleation, then the single process is the one described by eqn. (8) in the paper. This of course raises the question as to whether the changing glass composition remains uniform on all length scales as growth advances.

Prof. Ryan asked: The data presented in the paper are truly beautiful and show scattering patterns that look like the form factor of a sphere. The paper indicates that the phase that is growing has a different composition to the glass and that the scattering is dominated by the local Cr concentration. Detailed analysis of the scattering is required, however, as the nucleation and growth process has a dense particle surrounded by a depletion layer, the shape of the depletion layer depending on the thermodynamic driving force for crystallisation and the diffusion coefficients of the components. This effect is not so important at the beginning of the crystallisation and when the reservoir of Cr is exhausted the equilibrium structure could well be dense spherical structures in a uniform background. It is in the intermediate stages (Fig. 1) that a more complex electron density profile needs to be considered.

Prof. Greaves answered: I agree, we have just looked at the start and finish. With improved data coming from the ESRF BM26B and in due course from the SRS 6.2, we can look forward to the possibility of exploring the complete progression from nucleation to full devitrification of Cr.

Prof. Hounslow said: (1) You indicate in the paper that the scaling of radius of gyration with time indicates a diffusion limited process, but that at long times depletion of free Cr slows the process. Does the overall balance on Cr indicate that the amount of free Cr decreases to zero?
(2) For a process with monodisperse particles whose growth is limited by diffusion, is it not surprising that no Ostwald ripening is seen?

Prof. Greaves replied: (1) The R_g^2 vs. t plot is very sensitive to errors in R_g. Nevertheless the initial linear rise is clear, as is the levelling off around the stage at which the intensity of I_{spinel} lines are beginning to saturate. The evidence for the eventual removal of Cr from the glass matrix comes from the composition of the spinel and from the agreement of the crystalline fraction, v, from eqn. (8) in the paper with that obtained from SAXS *via* eqn. (7) in the paper.
(2) Absolutely, but it needs stressing that the greatest degree of monodispersion occurs part way through the heterogeneous growth process, *i.e.* before all the Cr is crystallised and probably at the point at which R_g^2 vs. t ceases to be linear.

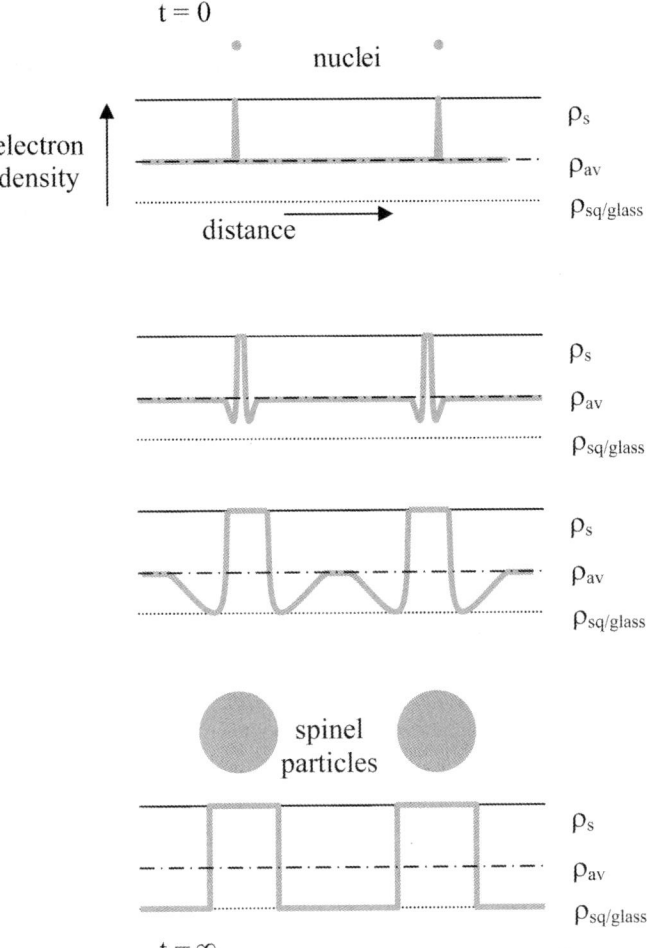

Fig. 1 Plot of electron density throughout the growth process.

Prof. Ryan commented: The formation of monodisperse particles during thermally induced phase separation of a mixture of two polymers has been observed.[1] Mixtures of polyisoprene and ethylene–propylene copolymer were studied using time-resolved elastic light scattering. For off-critical quenches highly monodisperse spheres were observed whose radii grow with a power law. The monodispersity and growth law are rationalised as a heterogeneous nucleation process in a similar manner to the paper under discussion.

1 Cumming, Andrew, Wiltzius, Pierre, Bates and S. Frank, *Phys. Rev. Lett.*, 1990, **65**(7), 863–866.

Prof. Helliwell asked: How has this detailed structural characterisation improved the knowledge of the function of glass?

Prof. Greaves answered: The traditional functions of glasses and ceramics, many with ancient pedigree, have generally developed from the craft sciences. What combined *in situ* structural methods, like those presented here, can now provide is direct observation of the development of high temperature structural chemistry as the optimum conditions that result in a particular function are reached. With serendipity new functions may emerge. For example, fine glass ceramics have been developed for their optical transparency, mechanical and thermal properties, for which monodispersion is not critical. The discovery of monodispersed nanocrystals in Cr-doped cordierite glass, however, promises a bulk quantum dot system with the function of non-linear optical response mouldable into any shape.

Dr Dent opened the discussion of Dr Chen's paper: What are the differences between the electrochemically generated species and the laser induced species?

If the edge data are the same, then how can the EXAFS be different, especially given the signal to noise limitation?

Dr Chen replied: (1) Electrochemically generated Cu(II) species from the starting $Cu(I)(dmp)_2^+$ species had one electron removed from the Cu(II), so the total number of electrons in this species is one less compared to the starting material. The laser excited $Cu(I)(dmp)_2^+$, however, underwent an intramolecular charge separation process where one electron was transferred from Cu(I) to one of the ligands, forming the Cu(II) species. Therefore, the total number of electrons was unchanged. In fact, the metal–ligand charge transfer (MLCT) transition is a reversible process. As the excited state decayed, the intramolecular charge separation recombined.

(2) The edge data for the MLCT state and the electrochemically generated Cu(II) species are almost identical, indicating the generation of Cu(II) species by the laser. However, the edge data for the ground state and the laser excited state are not the same, as indicated by Fig. 5 in the paper. The EXAFS data in Fig. 6 of the paper which we were comparing were the ground state $Cu(I)(dmp)_2^+$ and laser excited mixture with 80% ground state and 20% MLCT state. They are different and from these differences, we extracted the MLCT structure.

Prof. Coppens asked: (1) With acetonitrile you get a shortening on the Cu–N bonds on excitation, while in toluene you get a lengthening. Is it possible that you are looking at the complex before exciplex formation, as we calculate the 4-coordinate Cu(II) excited state to have a C–N bond length shortening of 0.04 Å?

(2) Do you identify the very short-time species visible in the fast laser experiment with the excited state before exciplex formation?

Dr Chen answered: (1) The process of thermal equilibration of the MLCT state takes place on a subpicosecond to a few picosecond timescale. Therefore, it would be too fast for current 100 ps X-ray pulses to probe.

(2) In a recent fs pump–probe laser transient spectroscopic study, we observed two very short components in the kinetic decay trace in addition to the ns longer lifetimes commonly referred to in the literature. We measured transient spectra of $Cu(dmp)_2^+$ in acetonitrile and in ethylene glycol, where both measurements gave a subpicosecond rise time that was longer than our instrumental response time, and a few picoseconds fast decay time. We are in the process of further investigating the origins of these components in the kinetics of the MLCT state. It is likely that they may be related to generation of the thermally equilibrated MLCT state and exciplex formation.

Prof. Evans said: (1) This is a very impressive experiment, but the intrinsic problem is the 2 shell fit for the 2 Cu–N sites. Have you examined the correlation between these 2 shells to make a good error estimate?

(2) It seems surprising that an expansion is observed in the Cu–N distance. The MLCT process would remove an electron from a t_2 M–L σ^* orbital in Cu(I) and transfer it into a phen π^* ligand. So the Cu(II) transient centre would be expected to have a smaller covalent radius.

(3) The BArF anion is an extremely weak binder, with the aryl fluorines the only plausible donors. Acetonitrile, or a linear triatomic ligand, will provide a distinct multiple scattering fingerprint to make it identifiable if it is the fifth ligand.

Dr Chen replied: (1) Yes. In our data analysis, we assumed two Cu–N distances that were associated with the ground state and the MLCT state respectively. From the transient optical absorption experiment and the model calculation with experimental parameters, such as laser pulse energy, sample concentration, sample dimension, *etc.*, we obtained the fraction of the excited state at around 20%. Therefore, in data fitting, we fixed the ratio of the ground state and excited state to 80% *vs.* 20%. The E_0 edge shifts in the fittings for the two Cu–N bond distances were kept the same. The difference in Cu–N bond lengths resulted from such fittings with the above precautions.

(2) That's a very good point. However, the coordination of Cu also changed from tetrahedral to penta-coordinated. I would expect the steric hindrance could force the Cu–N bond to be longer despite the effects that you mentioned.

(3) We are not sure what the fifth ligand was at this point. In the acetonitrile case, you raised a good point.

Dr Techert asked: Despite the fact that triplet annihilation processes quench the population of the triplet state (and therefore the EXAFS difference signal), how would this annihilation process change the structure of the energy-transferring moieties and therefore the EXAFS signal?

Dr Chen answered: The triplet–triplet annihilation due to the adjacent molecules being simultaneously excited will certainly quench the excited state population and shorten the lifetime. Thus, the laser excitation will become less efficient and laser photons will be wasted. More importantly, the excited state annihilation will change fundamental aspects of the photoexcitation of the molecules as the interactions between the same kind of molecules can no longer be neglected. The triplet–triplet annihilation could also result in singlet states at a much later time than the initial photoexcitation. Therefore, it is the fundamental aspects of photochemistry that have been changed due to the strongly interacting molecules. Of course, the XAFS signals expected will no longer be limited to those from isolated molecules due to their photochemical reactions, but come from a mixture of isolated and strongly interacting molecules. Therefore, we can no longer claim the signals are from excited molecules of a certain kind, but from a collection of molecules with a certain configuration.

Dr Sagi commented: Doing a single energy experiment may reveal some correlation between the structural kinetics and the overall kinetics of the system, thus proving that one can identify distinct features in the single energy experiments on EXAFS or edge regions that are directly associated with the structure, for example the transition from one coordination number to another during the excitation process.

Dr Chen replied: In small molecules rather than proteins, the actual atomic movements after the photoexcitation take place in fs or a few ps. After that, the excited state is thermally equilibrated. Therefore, strictly speaking, our experiment is not time resolved, but provides snapshots of the excited state. However, there are circumstances where different excited states could be generated sequentially, such as a singlet state initially generated by photoexcitation, and a triplet generated by intersystem crossing from the initially generated singlet. In this case, we will have to adjust the time delays corresponding to the optimal population of the singlet and the triplet states respectively in order to capture their structures. If this is successful, we will be able to associate certain distinctive spectral features that appear at a certain time after the photoexcitation to particular excited states.

Prof. Helliwell asked: How often does the Advanced Photon Source (APS) offer the "special timing mode"? Is it a limiting factor?

Also the APS operates a "top up mode". How do you allow for that in your experimental design?

Dr Chen responded: APS provides the hybrid fill timing mode about 4 weeks per year. It was split into about one week at a time. So we have the special timing mode every three months. The "top-up" mode from the APS did not affect our experiments, because we average over a long time, and fluctuation caused by the top-up was not obvious to us. We like this mode because it provides 30% more X-ray photon flux.

Prof. Coppens opened the discussion of Prof. O'Hare's paper: We have some experience with hydrothermal synthesis in crystal engineering, where one works with multicomponent (>2) systems. Since we cannot predict which phases will be formed, the stoichiometry, and therefore the products change with time. Have you looked at cases where completely different phases are formed as the cooling process proceeds?

Prof. O'Hare replied: We have not observed any changes in crystalline phase composition of these reactions on cooling.

Prof. Wilson asked: What is the limitation in time resolution for the neutron and X-ray experiments? How well is this matched to "typical" reaction rates in your processes, *i.e.* do you need second-scale time resolution?

Prof. O'Hare answered: The current setup using the GEM diffractometer at the ISIS facility gives us a time resolution of minutes while the synchrotron at the SRS gives us a time resolution of seconds. For most hydrothermal reactions and conventional solid–solid processes this is adequate. For other reactions we would ideally need better time resolution.

Prof Evans said: Have you been able to investigate the solution phase pre-nucleation processes by other techniques, say by high temperature NMR?

Prof. O'Hare replied: We have not. Prof. Taudelle and co-workers at the University of Strasbourg have recently used *in situ* NMR to complement our studies on gallium and aluminium phosphate crystallisation.

Prof. Ryan asked: What evidence is there for precursor structures in hydrothermal synthesis?

Prof. O'Hare responded: We cannot detect precursor structures in our experiment. We need crystalline domains which can diffract X-rays. *In situ* NMR experiments by Taudelle *et al.* suggest the existence of four-membered Al_2P_2 rings in solution prior to crystallisation of aluminium phosphates.

Mr Robb said: You seem to follow the structure by Bragg peak evolution. Is the data you collect sufficiently good for complete structure refinement and, for example, can you obtain atomic displacement parameters for your material and what does this tell you?

Prof. O'Hare replied: The energy dispersive X-day diffraction data we measure is not suitable for complete structure refinement. Different X-ray photon energies are absorbed from the incident and diffracted white X-ray beam by the cell materials and the sample. This means that we cannot define the incident beam profile.

Prof. Finney asked: How much do we know about the variation of conditions within the cell? If there is significant non-uniformity (*e.g.* in temperature or concentration), is there scope for probing spatially as well as temporally?

Prof. O'Hare replied: We try to stir the contents of the hydrothermal cell using a magnetic stirrer which attempts to average out any non-uniformity in temperature or local reagent concentrations.

Prof. Cernik said: Have you used the information from the three-element SSD to show crystallisation differences within the hydrochemical cell? The intensity overlaps should sample different regions of the crystallite distribution and therefore pinpoint non-homogeneous growth.

Following on, do you translate the sample during the experiment to probe preferred regions of synthesis?

Prof. O'Hare answered: The three element detector does allow us to look at different *d*-spacing ranges simultaneously. In the systems we have studied using the three element detector where these regions overlap the variation in the intensity of the common Bragg reflections is identical which suggests isotropic crystal growth.

Prof. Moffat asked: Might the geophysicist's style of large-volume press that affords simultaneous control of pressure and temperature be of use to your style of experiments?

Prof. O'Hare replied: The reagents used in hydrothermal synthesis are quite corrosive viscous gels (acid or alkali) and I wonder whether this would be compatible with their equipment.

Prof. Hounslow asked: (1) Fig. 2 of the paper contains a curve fit—of what form?
(2) Can you quantify the rates in terms of rate constants and orders of reactions?
(3) Are Avrami kinetics appropriate in this case?

Prof. O'Hare responded: (1) The fit is to the Avrami–Erofe'ev equation: $\alpha = 1 - \exp\{-(k(t-t_0))^n\}$.
(2) Yes, the Avrami–Erofe'ev fit gives us an exponent, n, and a rate constant, k.
The value of n, the Avrami exponent, is believed to contain information about the mechanism of reaction. The model was originally developed to describe the growth of crystallites in solid–solid reactions, and assumes the formation of nucleation sites in a uniform mixture of reagents from which crystal growth occurs.
(3) I am not sure; it is a standard analysis but I am not confident that it actually tells us much about the chemistry.

Prof. Ryan asked: What is the path length through the cell?

Prof. O'Hare replied: 20 mm.

Prof. Sir John Meurig Thomas opened the discussion of Prof. Ryan's paper: One wonders whether by changing the conditions (in a well-defined fashion) of precipitation so as to produce aragonite (instead of calcite) you would get the same kind of precursor "phases" being formed.

Prof. Ryan replied: We suspect that a poorly ordered precursor phase could well be found prior to the precipitation or aragonite. We have been able to produce mixed aragonite calcite mixtures under conditions where a precursor phase is observable but cannot distinguish whether there are two precursor phases.

Prof. Finney commented: I would like to add a comment concerning metastable forms occurring in the early stages of crystallisation which then transform to the stable form.
The system is the formation of normal hexagonal ice Ih from ice II (a phase stable at higher pressures) recovered to ambient pressure at 77 K.[1] Neutron powder diffraction on the resulting structure looks like the so-called cubic form Ic, though the resolution of the measurements showed (a) the presence of the 100 hexagonal peak and considerable broadening of the higher angle shoulder of the 111 (cubic) peak. Moreover, various peaks showed hkl-dependent broadening suggesting not only a small particle size of about 160 Å, but also significant stacking faulting. On heating to around 160 K, the structure transforms to normal hexagonal ice, without evidence of any significant disorder.
The simple interpretation of these results would be that the ambient pressure ice phase nucleates first as very small crystallites of the cubic phase, which then transforms as the crystallites grow on heating to the normal stable hexagonal structure ice Ih. However, considering that the difference between the cubic and hexagonal structures is that of different stackings of the hexagonal layers (ABCABC stacking for cubic, ABABAB for hexagonal), an explanation that takes account of the various hkl-dependent broadenings observed suggests that the initial small crystallites may not be identifiable as cubic ice Ih but a structure of random stacking of hexagonal layers. In fact, work on colloidal systems shows similar diffraction features to those observed in the ice case, in particular the simultaneous presence of 111 cubic and 100 hexagonal features, and a high angle shoulder on the 111 peak. Only when the temperature is increased do the molecules have sufficient mobility to begin to anneal out the irregular stackings to approach the stable hexagonal structure.
Thus there is evidence in even this apparently simple system for a metastable phase forming in the early stages of crystallisation. In this case, the metastable phase is clearly not amorphous

(though such might have occurred earlier but not been detected), but it is, in comparison to the stable phase, clearly disordered. Noting electron microscope observations three decades ago of icosahedral structures formed in the early stages of growth of an even simple crystal (fcc gold), we can perhaps suspect that an initial metastable (with respect to the equilibrium phase) structure may be a common occurrence. In fact, there is perhaps little good reason to expect very small microcrystallites to have the structure of the stable phase, considering the large surface/volume ratio compared to the equilibrium (extended) crystal.

1 P. N. Pusey, W. van Megen, P. Bartlett, B. J. Ackerson, J. G. Rarity and S. M. Underwood, *Phys. Rev. Lett.*, 1989, **63**(25), 2753–2756.

Prof. Ryan answered: Thank you for pointing out the relationship to the field of supercooled water and colloidal crystals. The formation of dense, random hexagonally-close-packed structures prior to cubic crystallisation is indeed observed in a wide variety of systems and has been predicted theoretically (see for example refs. 1 and 2).

1 I. Kusaka, D. W. Oxtoby and Z.-G. Wang, *J. Chem. Phys.*, 2001, **115**(15), 6898–6906.
2 V. Talanquer and D. W. Oxtoby, *J. Chem. Phys.*, 1998, **109**(1), 223–227.

Prof. Finney asked: Distinguishing a genuinely amorphous structure from a very small crystal by the presence of clear Bragg peaks can often be controversial: once the "crystallite" is < 3–4 unit cells across, the peak broadening may make it difficult to distinguish the scattering from that of an amorphous structure. How can you be sure that your amorphous precursor phase really is genuinely amorphous and not a very small crystalline nucleus?

Prof. Ryan replied: This is indeed a difficult problem and was the matter of considerable debate at *Faraday Discussion* 112.[1] My colleague Nick Terrill did some modelling, using the scattering geometry of beamline 8.2, and estimated that Bragg peaks could be resolved from a collection of $3 \times 3 \times 3$ unit cells at 1% by volume. Obviously there is considerable line broadening with such small crystals and the wide angle scattering from a metastable, lower-order precursor phase would be even more difficult to resolve. There are some semantic problems in the polymer crystallisation field and the distinction between a collection of chains and a nucleus is often blurred by beliefs.

1 A. J. Ryan, J. P. A. Fairclough, N. J. Terrill, P. D. Olmsted and W. C. K. Poon, *Faraday Discuss.*, 1999, **112**, 13–29.

Prof. Evans commented: The local site symmetry of the carbonate anion differs considerably between calcite and aragonite such that these forms can be differentiated by IR spectroscopy. Perhaps this technique could be used to probe the structure of the pre-crystallisation phase.

Prof. Ryan answered: We are currently working on the use of FTIR and FTIR microscopy to differentiate between aragonite and calcite in our crystalliser geometry. We would anticipate probing the structure of the precursor phase by IR or Raman spectroscopy in the not-too-distant future.

Prof. O'Hare asked: Have you performed an Avrami-type analysis of the crystallization data described in Fig. 13b of the paper?

Prof. Ryan replied: We have indeed performed an Avrami-type analysis on our inorganic crystallisation data but, as was pointed out by Prof. Hounslow, this is not an appropriate model to use for these crystallisation conditions. I bow to his superior knowledge in this regard and leave it to him to explain the reason why the Avrami model is inappropriate and describe the correct model to use.

Dr Chen said: I am impressed by your results of simultaneous collection of SAXS/WAXS data. As a general question, I would like to ask your perspective on using such techniques on other systems, such as protein folding, crystallisation and molecular self-assembly to form nanostructure materials?

Prof. Ryan replied: Thank you, we have worked hard at developing the SAXS/WAXS instrumentation to such a level that it is widely applicable to a wide range of systems. A good account of the work on protein in solution can be obtained from the Daresbury Annual Reports and in refs. 1–6.

1. M. Hirai, H. Iwase, T. Hayakawa, K. Miura and K. Inoue, *J. Synchrotron Radiat.*, 2002, **9**(4), 202–205.
2. W.-Y. Choy, F. A. A. Mulder, K. A. Crowhurst, D. R. Muhandiram, I. S. Millett, S. Doniach, J. D. Forman-Kay and L. E. Kay, *J. Mol. Biol.*, 2002, **316**(1), 101–112.
3. W. Zheng and S. Doniach, *J. Mol. Biol.*, 2002, **316**(1), 173–187.
4. R. Russell, I. S. Millett, S. Doniach and D. Herschlag, *Nat. Struct. Biol.*, 2000, **7**(5), 367–370.
5. D. I. Svergun, G. Zaccai, M. Malfois, R. H. Wade, M. H. J. Koch and F. Kozielski, *J. Biol. Chem.* 2001, **276**(27), 24 826–24 832.
6. D. I. Svergun, M. V. Petoukhov and M. H. J. Koch, *Biophys. J.*, 2001, **80**(6), 2946–2953.

Prof. Helliwell commented: Regarding the literature on protein assembly, protein crystal nucleation *etc.* I refer you to the following authors:
(a) M. H. J. Koch: assembly of multi-macromolecular structures
(b) A. Tardieu: protein crystal nucleation
(c) D. I. Svergun: combined SAXS/WAXS and SANS for protein fold discovery

Prof. Coppens opened the discussion of Prof. Harrison's paper: The discrepancy between the thermal parameters and the cell dimension temperature seems paradoxical, as expansion is driven by anharmonicity, which increases when the thermal parameters increase. So the discrepancy must be in the experiment. My question is: were the crystals in the microwave experiment and the independent measurement the same, or could there be a difference in crystal quality and thus extraction? Or could such a difference be a result of the microwave treatment?

Prof. Harrison† replied: The neutron diffraction experiments were performed on the same sample of $BaTiO_3$, first with conventional heating to 1173 K and then, after slow cooling back to 295 K, with microwave heating. We would not expect that this treatment would lead to any significant change in crystallinity between the conventional and microwave heating measurements, and therefore one would expect little change in factors such as extinction and strain broadening as a consequence of the heat treatment. Indeed, when the sample was remeasured at 295 K just before the microwave heating measurement, the peak widths were essentially unchanged. It should be stressed that the limited time available for neutron data acquisition led to relatively fast scans, and the precision of many of the refined parameters is less than ideal. The parameter that appears to show the most distinct change when the microwave and conventional heating are compared is the peak width parameter, σ^1, as described in our paper.

Prof. O'Hare asked: (1) Have you looked at the effects of using variable microwave frequencies?
(2) Do different solids absorb the microwave energy in different ways?
(3) Do the thermal parameters give you any indication of the types of motion that may be excited by the microwave field?

Prof. Harrison replied: (1) No we haven't: so far our work has been restricted to frequencies of 2.45 GHz, which is one of the small number of frequencies allocated for non-telecommunications work. Microwave sources for those other prescribed frequencies are far more expensive, and the range of devices available at those frequencies is much more limited.
(2) Absolutely: there are several distinct mechanisms of microwave heating, treated in detail in standard references (for example refs. 1 and 2). The most important modes of heating involve coupling of the microwave radiation with phonons (for example the present case of $BaTiO_3$) or mobile species (electrons, for example in metals, or ions, for example in fast-ion conductors), but defects may also play an important role,[3] as may the coupling between the magnetic component of the microwave field and materials with high magnetic susceptibility (such as some ferrites).

---

† Also Dr Whittaker, University of Edinburgh.

(3) In the first instance one would expect rapid equilibration of microwave energy among the various modes, which one would expect to be manifested through increased thermal parameters as an increase in anisotropic displacement parameters, just as one expects with conventional heating. However, one could imagine cases where the thermal parameters respond to the microwave field in a manner that is different from what one would expect from a simple increase in temperature. Where the rate at which particular modes are excited by microwaves is significantly higher than the rate of repartition, and where these modes are either polarised (as might happen when a single crystal is exposed to a linearly polarised microwave field) or in the case of a molecular solid localised to a particular region of the constituent molecules, it is conceivable that there is an anomalous response of either certain components of the thermal parameters, or of thermal parameters for a particular group of atoms.

1   D. M. P Mingos and A. G. Whittaker, in *Chemistry Under Extreme or Non-Classical Conditions*, ed. R. van Eldik and C. D. Hubbard, Wiley, Chichester, 1997, ch. 11, pp. 479–514.
2   Y. V. Bykov, K. I. Rybakov and V. E. Semenov, *J. Phys. D.: Appl. Phys.*, 2001, **34**, R55–57.
3   J. H. Booske, K. I. Rybakov, V. E. Semenov, S. A. Freeman, J. H. Booske and R. F. Cooper, *Phys. Rev. B*, 1997, **55**, 3559–3567.

Prof. Wilson said: (1) Is it possible to decouple microwave heating effects from the electric-field induced issues?

(2) Can you envisage a use for some sort of "spatial scanning" resonance radiography as a means of *in situ* temperature measurement, helping to pin down the temperature fluctuations locally within the samples?

Prof. Harrison responded: (1) Yes. This has been in a particularly elegant piece of work to probe this effect,[1] the essence of which was to study ion migration between similar compounds of different elemental composition in a linearly polarised microwave field. The result was an enhanced diffusion coefficient at a given temperature in the direction of polarisation.

(2) I could imagine that such a technique could provide a spatially resolved probe of temperature, but the length scales involved could well be too large for some of the large and highly localised thermal gradients that can arise in microwave-heated systems, so it is likely to provide only a partial solution to some of the problems we presented.

1   A. G. Whittaker and L. Cronin, in *Proceedings of the Second International Conference on Microwave Chemistry*, ed. A. Gourdenne, 2000, Institut National Polytechnique de Toulouse, on behalf of AMPERE, Cambridge, UK.

Prof. Wilson said: I am interested in the coupling of the microwave frequencies with directional modes within the sample: are these compatible, and is such coupling possible?

Presumably the energy redistribution within the sample/system results from partitioning of "thermal" motion into the various modes.

Prof. Harrison† replied: The microwave radiation couples with the solid through a multiphonon process, such that radiation whose frequency is of the order of GHz is able to excite modes whose frequency is the order of THz (see for example ref. 1). If the microwave field is linearly polarised, one would expect the phonons that are excited to be anisotropic. However, the energy put into these modes is rapidly repartitioned through anharmonic processes with a time-scale typical of the phonon frequencies, that is of the order of THz (ps). For a recent consideration of this sort of process, see ref. 2.

1   M. Sparks, D. F. King and D. L. Mills, *Phys. Rev. B*, 1982, **26**, 6987–7003.
2   Y. V. Bykov, K. I. Rybakov and V. E. Semenov, *J. Phys. D.: Appl. Phys.*, 2001, **34**, R55–57.

Dr Techert asked: What is the expected order of magnitude of the phonon–phonon coupling in *e.g.* $BaTiO_3$?

Prof. Harrison answered: I don't know, and I imagine that it would be very difficult to determine this quantity accurately. When a material such as $BaTiO_3$ is heated with microwaves, phonons are excited through a multiphonon process, and this energy is then repartitioned over the phonon spectrum through anharmonic effects. One therefore needs to know which phonons are involved, and then calculate the appropriate anharmonicity, which is not trivial for a material containing heavy atoms. However, it has been estimated that for electric field strength and temperatures typical of those used in microwave processing, deviations of the population of high-energy phonons from Boltzmann values are very small indeed, implying that this process is fairly efficient in redistributing energy.[1]

1 Y. V. Bykov, K. I. Rybakov and V. E. Semenov, *J. Phys. D.: Appl. Phys.*, 2001, **34**, R55–57.

Dr Techert asked: Since the water in crystalline protein samples cannot rotate freely, as in solution, the energies of the corresponding libration modes should be shifted to higher frequencies. Do any calculations exist concerning these values?

Prof. Harrison† replied: The motion of water molecules bound to protein molecules in a variety of ways has been the subject of extensive studies by NMR with complementary modelling, and reveal a range of amplitudes and correlation times for libration (see for example refs. 1 and 2) extending from relatively fast, small-amplitude motion with a correlation time of the order of 0.07 ps, to slower, larger-amplitude motion correlated with the motion of portions of the molecule, with correlation times in range 1–10 ps. Note that pure water has modes in the region 0.05 ps that have been attributed to libration of H-bonded molecules.

1 V. P. Denisov, K. Venu, J. Peters, H. D. Hörlein and B. Halle, *J. Phys. Chem. B*, 1997, **101**, 9380–9389.
2 V. P. Denisov and B. Halle, *J. Am. Chem. Soc.*, 1995, **117**, 8456–8465.

Dr Grant commented: Michael Levitt published a paper in 1985[1] covering calculations (NMA) he made on bovine pancreatic tripsin inhibitor (BPTI) and he found that the collective motions of groups of up to ten residues have frequencies of 2 cm^{-1} to 10 cm^{-1}. 2 cm$^{-1} \simeq$ 60 GHz, only about one order of magnitude larger than microwave frequency (2.45 GHz for a domestic microwave oven). Therefore the discrepancy between the THz frequency of many of the modes in a protein, and microwave oven and mobile phone frequency (1.8 GHz) is not such a large gap to bridge. The other point is that water in a protein is known to play an integral role in the unfolding and folding of a protein and water obviously couples with 2.45 GHz microwave radiation, so maybe we should be looking at the role of H_2O in conformational changes induced by microwaves as providing a bridge to causing structural changes in the host biomolecule.

1 M. Levitt, C. Sander and C. Stern, *J. Mol. Biol.*, 1985, **181**, 423.

Prof. Helliwell said: (1) You stimulate me to wonder whether the scattering pattern of sectioned brain, with and without microwaves, has been measured.
(2) Assessing the risk of mobile phones, another possible "sample" would be the impact of microwaves on the inner ear. The physiology of the inner ear is studied using guinea pig inner ear, as it is easy to section.[1]

1 F. Mammano, IUPAB '02 Abstract S19-2 (see also www.sissa.it/multidisc/cochlea/homepage/pub-list.htm).

Prof. Harrison answered: (1) I don't believe that experiment has been tried yet, and I imagine it would be difficult to get conclusive information about microwave-induced changes in brain tissue from such measurements because of the complexity of the sample. At the moment the relatively small amount of work that is being done on the effect of microwaves on materials or biological systems, and which involves spectroscopic or structural measurements, has involved relatively simple model systems.
(2) This would indeed be an interesting system for study in that it has been shown to be sensitive to irradiation; however, it is also a relatively complex system and I think it will be some time before conclusive measurements could be performed on it.

Concluding Remarks

Time-resolved chemistry: from structure to function. A summary

John Meurig Thomas

Davy Faraday Research Laboratory, The Royal Institution of Great Britain, 21 Albemarle Street, London W1S 4BS and Department of Materials Science, University of Cambridge, New Museums Site, Cambridge CB2 3QZ

Received 19th July 2002, Accepted 22nd July 2002
First published as an Advance Article on the web 8th October 2002

   Never have I hitherto participated in a Faraday Discussion (over a period of nearly forty years) in which such an enormous range of techniques and such a wide variety of distinct phenomena were displayed. I therefore embark on this summary with some trepidation, as I do not feel adequate to the task required. Forgive me for giving a rather subjective account which inevitably reflects my own tastes, predilections and preferences—even though I have tried conscientiously to reflect a balanced view.
   So far as techniques in general are concerned, it is obvious that faster and ever-more powerful lasers are key features of the time-resolved landscape, and will remain so for as long as one is interested in processes exhibiting shorter and shorter lifetimes. Synchrotron radiation is likewise well-nigh indispensable nowadays as a means of probing the course of both ultra-fast and also very slow processes. (I should like to insert parenthetically that about five or six years ago I heard a group of some of the UK's leading organic chemists declaring that chemistry, and its growth, could flourish perfectly well without synchrotrons. Only an intellectual Luddite would now hold that opinion, in view of the dramatic advances that have been reported at this meeting alone.)
   Synchrotrons serve us best when we use them to record more than one kind of measurement—as I myself have found to my advantage ever since, with collaborators at Daresbury, we carried out parallel studies of our solid catalysts (*in situ*) using X-ray absorption spectroscopy and X-ray diffraction.[1] We heard from Evans *et al.* how much progress there has been recently (and of yet further expected advances) in employing dispersive EXAFS for investigating rapid reactions of transition-metal complexes in solution. Insofar as radically new departures are concerned, the dramatic, unconventional experiment proposed by Moffat involving so-called chirped X-ray pulses merits serious consideration. If one is to attain sub-picosecond (say 100 fs) resolution using synchrotron sources—and such time-scales are necessary to match or compete with what can be done by ultra-fast laser sources in tracking processes such as the rupture and formation of chemical bonds or some electron transfer processes—it follows inexorably that the Laue technique must be implemented. A supreme advantage in doing a time-resolved Laue diffraction experiment in this way (if it can be achieved) is that an energy-chirped pulse maps time into space. One hopes that the proposals made by Moffat can indeed be realised, as they will be of great value to the community of macromolecular crystallographers well represented at this Discussion.
   When it comes to the study of excited states in solids, or probing the course of chemical changes in enzymes, Laue diffraction seems to offer major advantages which were also adumbrated by Moffat, and highlighted in the reflective Introductory Lecture by Coppens. (A recent comprehensive review[2] contains many key items of information concerning this approach). You will recall that, after the interesting presentation by Cole *et al.*, there was a lively debate as to whether future

DOI: 10.1039/b207125h

investigations of the structure of excited-state crystalline materials containing small molecules are better pursued using the re-nascent[3] Laue method or by more conventional goniometric methods. There is a major difference between crystals of small molecules (organic and inorganic materials) on the one hand and of macromolecules on the other, that, as has been said previously[2] "hinders the application of time-resolved crystallography and direct, mechanistic studies to the former and conversely underlies its effective application to the latter".[4] Crystals of small organic and inorganic molecules (such as those studies by Cole *et al.*) generally contain little or no bulk solvent and are stabilised by strong intermolecular or interatomic interactions: they may be regarded as "hard" condensed matter. Seldom do any molecular (as distinct from electronic) transitions occur in such solids without there being a distinct phase change that alters the cell dimensions, the space group or both. By contrast, crystals of macromolecules contain extensive amounts of solvent, the physiochemical properties of which are indistinguishable from those of the bulk. The intermolecular contacts in such (so-called) "soft" condensed matter, are only weakly stabilised. And the large solvent channels permit the ready diffusion of small molecular reactants through the crystal structure. This is why enzyme molecules embedded in a crystal may readily catalyse the conversion of reactant (substrate) to products.

On the subject of monitoring structural changes in an ultra-fast time-frame, it has surprised me a little that we have not heard much at this Discussion about the merits of femtosecond electron diffraction. It is true that Coppens drew attention to the classic Williamson and Zewail experiment[5,6] on $C_2F_4I_2$ in his introduction, but that experiment is already eleven years old, and I myself am a little bemused that, in contrast to femtosecond spectroscopic studies, femtosecond electron diffraction investigations have not been more zealously pursued. I understand that experiments are already underway in the California Institute of Technology to probe uptake and rupture of O_2 to and from myoglobin,[7] under physiological conditions using femtosecond electron diffraction.

Both Helliwell and Coppens rightly emphasised in their introductory remarks that one of the principal aims of this Discussion is to sort out priorities among experimental and theoretical methods and techniques; and I am sure that we can all feel gratified that we have learnt much that is new in this regard. Impressive results were reported by Nibbering, using femtosecond infra red spectroscopy to probe the structural dynamics of condensed-phase hydrogen-bonded systems, and the laser pump/X-ray probe time-domain experiments of Chen (in which she employed X-ray absorption fine structure as her primary tool), and the many elegant experiments with which Wulff was associated (notably Wulff *et al.*) have all greatly enlarged our knowledge of important systems. I, myself, felt particularly pleased to hear the results of Techert *et al.*, by whom topochemical processes in organic molecular crystals were cleverly charted.

Helliwell and Coppens also emphasised that one of the key purposes in conducting time-resolved measurements is ultimately to be better placed to design and synthesize new structures so as to be better able to achieve a desired function, whether it be biological or physiochemical. In this regard, I particularly liked the ingenious way in which Kumita *et al.* set about achieving photo-control of protein conformation and activity by dextrous use of the photo-isomerisable azobenzene chromophore flanked by two iodoacetamide functional groups.

I confess to having been a little disappointed that, in talking about atomic resolution (and time resolution), no-one mentioned any of the various kinds of powerful, real-space imaging techniques that are now at our disposal. I refer, in particular, both to various forms of high-resolution electron microscopy (HREM) (embracing conventional transmission as well as scanning transmission modes)[8] and to the several variants of scanning probe techniques. True, there are problems that sometimes occur with intense beam damage in high-resolution electron microscopy—but this is increasingly a problem as we heard at this Discussion with high intensity, ultra-short X-ray pulses—but many of these can be circumvented and a good deal of structure-function relationships have emerged from the application of HREM to the study of catalysts.[8] Of particular interest is the work of Gai[9] using a special environmental stage, which has enabled her to observe, *in situ*, and at atomic resolution, structural rearrangements in oxide catalysts during the course of chemical conversion.

Insofar as scanning probe methods including both scanning tunnelling, STM, and atomic force microscopy, AFM) are concerned the merit here is that it is not necessary to keep the samples *in vacuo*: these techniques are well-suited to coping with *in situ* studies, especially when metallic solids are in contact with reacting gases or various solutions. The principal drawback of existing scanning microscope techniques is the rate at which images can be collected. In AFM, for example, this is fundamentally limited by the inertia of the force probe (typically a low spring constant-cantilever with a nanometre tip at the end). Although faster imaging rates, down to *ca* 1 frame per second, have been obtained by the construction of smaller, lighter cantilevers this has limited applicability, and has nearly reached its ultimate limit.

At the Department of Physics, University of Bristol, Humphris and colleagues have produced[10–12] an entirely different approach to increasing the imaging rate, in which advantage is taken of a massless optical (near-field) interaction between the specimen and probe. In this new approach the time response is not limited by inertia. A mechanical resonance of the probe is used to scan over the sample and image data are collected continuously during each sweep of the probe. This new scanning microscope is capable of visualising processes that occur on the millisecond time scale and at the nanometre length scale, and is operable in both air and in liquid environments. There is every indication[12] that atomically resolved images of individual DNA molecules (and such important features as molecular motors) will be recorded in real time and under authentic physiological conditions in this way.

Real-time (or time-lapse) photography of nanoscopic or microscopic phenomena is often of great value in elucidating the link between structure and function. Indeed, the merits of the humble optical microscope (provided it is equipped with an appropriate, heatable environmental stage) must not be ignored, as I myself found many years ago when I was able directly to follow the motion of individual particles of catalyst during the oxidation of graphite in oxygen or air, thereby clarifying the influence of structural anisotropy upon kinetic anisotropy, as well as revealing much that was new about the mechanism of catalytic oxidation.[13,14]

Optical microscopy nowadays contributes[15] greatly to time-resolved studies of such phenomena as infection pathways of certain viruses, a subject which merges smoothly with some of the chemical topics raised in this Discussion, where migration of foreign species within and through living cells is of importance. Single-molecule fluorescent imaging, made possible using CCD detectors, enables real-time studies of the trajectories of (fluorescent) labelled single viruses (such as an adeno-associated virus) into and through single cells to be directly recorded under physiological conditions. By overcoming the problem of ensemble averaging, such a technique enables some key questions in molecular biology to be solved (as described by Bräuchle *et al.*[15]). It is conceivable that some of the intricacies of the structural dynamics of the receptor-binding domain of colicin E9 which Moore described to us could be clarified by real-time trajectory studies supplemented by his multi-nuclear NMR methods. And it is not inconceivable that mechanisms of formation of DNA–cationic vesicle complexes, which have benefited much from small-angle neutron scattering (SANS) as May described to us could also be further elaborated by employing time-resolved studies of single-molecule fluorescent probes by direct optical microscopy.

By drawing attention to techniques that have not been highlighted at the Discussion, I do not imply criticism of the organisers for their errors of omission: there are almost as many ways of pursuing time-resolved chemistry as there are techniques within chemistry itself, and it is demonstrably impossible to cover all of them. It is simply my duty to point out areas where significant chemical progress is being achieved in adjacent or parallel areas of chemistry that we should all take note of, areas like electrochemistry (where the dynamic STM studies of Behm[16] and his colleagues at Ulm are noteworthy) or studies of time-dependent surface energies of liquids that lie at the heart of the so-called Marangoni effect, where various (reflection) spectroscopic techniques have been used by Bain[17] at Oxford in his elegant probing of this phenomenon.

The plea by Coppens that strenuous efforts should be made to marry experiment with theory (or computation) has already become a reality in many of the investigations reported here. Thus, the Heidelberg group's effort on time-resolved computational biochemistry has already told us much about the important role that the solvent plays in modulating internal motions of proteins. The joint Nottingham–Scripps Institute work by Hirst *et al.* on time-resolved protein folding depends critically on improvements in the accuracy of calculations of circular dichroism of proteins from first principles. And the Burton *et al.* direct dynamics calculations of reaction rates using hybrid QM-MM (quantum mechanics–molecular mechanics) has been used effectively to rationalise the (relatively) enormous magnitude of the kinetic isotope effect observed[18] for some alcohol dehydrogenases.

In Bürgi's stimulating work, however, it is not so much theory (or computation) but observation allied to insight, deduction and analogy that has led to far-reaching deductions about fast chemical processes from slow diffraction experiments. It will be recalled that I also drew attention in the discussion of that paper to the feasibility of drawing mechanistic conclusions about chemical turnovers at catalytically active centres using steady-state spectroscopic measurements.[19] Helliwell and his colleagues showed us what could be achieved by combining static-ensemble structural chemistry with time-resolved Laue protein crystallography in their study of the carefully chosen enzyme hydroxymethylbilane synthase. This study, which *en route*, took us to the realm of genome sequencing, leads us to believe that it will soon be possible (by crystallography) to pin down the nature and location of the (hitherto "missing") polypeptide loop, composed of residues 47 to 59, at the active site of this enzyme.

Neutron diffraction, as well as neutron scattering in general, has received much less attention here than corresponding studies using X-rays, the papers by Walton *et al.*, by Harrison *et al.*, and Finney *et al.*, being the exceptions. The authors of the first of these papers have also taken advantage of further refinements in the use of energy-dispersive X-ray diffraction (EDXRD) technique (that has been used for some time[20] now to elucidate solid-state and solid-gas reactions) to follow the formation of open-structure metal phosphates; but it is their use of the GEM (neutron) diffractometer at ISIS, UK, which has advanced their time-resolved studies (of the crystallisation of $BaTiO_3$ in particular) the most.

Harrison *et al.*'s work is a promising start to a long awaited thorough (and *in situ*) study of the fundamental physico-chemical processes that occur during microwave irradiation. Apart from neutron diffraction, this group has used several other diffraction techniques on single crystal and powdered samples under microwave irradiation with controlled power levels. The issue of the influence of such irradiation on biological systems, in paticular proteins, and the ways in which is may pose hazards to human health, should be brought sharply into focus by work of this kind.

Neutron scattering measurements were central to Finney *et al.*'s re-assessment of the correlation—spurious or real?—between a perceived dynamic transition in proteins and its activity as an enzyme. Some protein functions have been reported to cease with the loss of equilibrium anharmonic dynamics as the protein is cooled through the dynamic transition. What the authors of this paper convincingly show is that the simple association of a dynamic transition with enzyme activity cannot be made independent of a consideration of the timescale of the measured transition.

The fascinating *in situ*, time-resolved wide angle X-ray scattering (WAXS) studies reported by Ryan *et al.* has brought to light the onset of large-scale ordering prior to regular crystal growth in a variety of distinct circumstances of so-called precrystallisations. The various figures in this paper leave no doubt about the reality of density-fluctuations, the formation of crystalline calcite (or its polymorph vaterite) from aqueous solution, for example, being preceded by the production of an amorphous metastable phase, the precise structural nature of which is, at present, enigmatic. The WAXS technique, together with small-angle X-ray scattering (SAXS) carried out over rather long time scales and supplemented by XAFS studies, enabled Greaves *et al.* to determine the microstructure (and its development during growth of nuclei) of the devitrified form of cordierite glass. Sankar's presentation also dealt with the combined use of SAXS and XAFS as time-resolved techniques. Such studies provide insight into the properties of nanoparticles of II–VI semiconductors such as CdS and ZnS, which, by varying their particle size in the nanometre range, enables one to fine-tune the electronic band gap, thereby facilitating their use as photocatalysts in, for example, the harnessing of solar energy.[21]

Envoi

There are very many other powerful techniques that lend themselves to deployment in time-resolved chemistry—ellipsometry and surface plasmon spectroscopy[22] are but two that now loom large in the study of function in interfacial science—but more important by far than the tools that we use, modify or perfect are the problems that we seek to address and the questions that we endeavour to answer. The most important part of any research is the question(s) that we pose at the outset. We must never forget that whilst almost anything that we may choose as scientists to pursue is interesting, only a few things are both interesting and important.

I feel, Mr Chairman, and I hope that you and everyone attending this Discussion feels, that we are now better equipped to return to our laboratories and to ask and pursue the right questions.

References

1. J. W. Couves, J. M. Thomas, D. Waller, R. H. Jones, A. J. Dent, G. E. Derbyshire and G. N. Greaves, *Nature*, 1991, **354**, 465.
2. K. Moffatt, *Chem. Rev.*, 2001, **101**, 1569.
3. I say re-nascent, because for the first ten years or so after the discovery of X-ray diffraction, it was the Laue method of solving crystal structures that held sway.
4. *Time-Resolved Macromolecular Crystallography*, ed. D. W. J. Cruickshank, J. R. Helliwell and L. R. Johnson, Oxford Science Publications, Oxford 1992.
5. J. C. Williamson and A. H. Zewail, *Proc. Natl. Acad. Sci., USA*, 1991, **88**, 5021.
6. J. M. Thomas, *Nature*, 1991, **351**.
7. B. Steiger, J. S. Baskin, F. C. Anson, A. H. Zewail, *Angew. Chem., Int. Ed. Engl.*, 2000, **39**, 257 and private communication from A. H. Zewail to J. M. Thomas, June 2002.
8. J. M. Thomas, O. Terasaki, P. L. Gai, W. Zhou and J. M. Gonzalez-Calbet, *Acc. Chem. Res.*, 2001, **34**, 583, and references therein.
9. P. L. Gai, *Top. Catal.*, 1999, **8**, 97.
10. A. D. L. Humphris, M. Antognozzi, T. J. McMaster and M. J. Miles, *Langmuir*, 2002, **18**, 1729.
11. J. Jamayo, A. D. L. Humphris, R. J. Owen and M. J. Miles, *Biophys. J.*, 2001, **81**, 526.
12. A. D. L. Humphris, J. Hobbs, P. Mandelin and M. J. Miles, 2002, private communication.
13. J. M. Thomas and P. L. Walker, Jr., *J. Chem. Phys.*, 1964, **41**, 587.
14. (*a*) J. M. Thomas in *Chemistry and Physics of Carbon*, vol. 1, 1966, p. 122; (*b*) see also J. M. Thomas, E. L. Evans and J. O. Williams, *Proc. R. Soc. London, Ser. A*, 1972, **331**, 417, and references therein.
15. G. Seisenberger, M. U. Ried, T. Endress, H. Büning, M. Hallek and C. Bräuchle, *Science*, 2001, **294**, 1929, and references therein.
16. F. Maroun, F. Ozanam, O. M. Magnussen and R. J. Behm, *Science*, 2001, **293**, 1811.
17. C. D. Bain, S. Manning-Benson, S. R. W. Parker, R. C. Darton and J. Penfold, *Langmuir*, 1998, **14**, 990.
18. J. Basran, S. Patel, M. J. Sutcliffe and N. S. Scrutton, *J. Biol. Chem.*, 2001, **276**, 6234.
19. G. Sankar, J. M. Thomas, C. R. A. Catlow, C. M. Barker, D. Gleeson and N. Kaltsoyannis, *J. Phys. Chem. B*, 2001, **105**, 9028, and this Discussion.
20. A. T. Ashcroft, A. K. Cheetham, J. M. Thomas, R. H. Jones, S. Natarajan, D. Waller and S. M. Clark, *J. Phys. Chem.*, 1993, **97**, 3355.
21. J. M. Thomas and W. J. Thomas, *Heterogeneous Catalysis: Principles and Practice*, 1997, ch. 8.
22. S. Flätgen, K. Krischer, B. Pettinger, K. Doblhofer, H. Junkes and G. Ertl, *Science*, 1995, **269**, 668.

List of Posters

Cation ordering, domain growth and zinc loss in the microwave dielectric oxide $Ba_3ZnTa_2O_{9-\delta}$ during processing using real-time synchrotron X-ray powder diffraction **S. M. Moussa, M. Bieringer, R. M. Ibberson** and **M. J. Rosseinsky**, *ISIS, Rutherford Appleton Laboratory, UK*

Photo-control of peptide and protein conformation: The use of computational techniques in the design and implementation of structural switches **J. R. Kumita, D. G. Flint, G. A. Woolley** and **O. S. Smart**, *University of Birmingham, UK*

Using SAXS/WAXS to follow shear-induced crystallization **E. L. Heeley, A. C. Morgovan, W. Bras, I. P. Dolbnya, A. J. Gleeson** and **A. J. Ryan**, *University of Sheffield, UK*

SRS station MPW6.2 — A world class facility for the study of materials processing **N. J. Terrill, G. P. Diakun, C. C. Tang, G. Bushnell-Wye, A. J. Dent, R. J. Cernik, P. Barnes, G. N. Greaves, T. Rayment** and **A. J. Ryan**, *CLRC Daresbury Laboratory, UK*

Scientific highlights of the EPSRC laser loan pool **S. M. Tavender, A. W. Parker** and **M. Towrie**, *ISIS, Rutherford Appleton Laboratory, UK*

Variable temperature studies on a thermotropic liquid crystal at station 9.8 **M. Helliwell, S. Teat** and **S. Coles**, *University of Manchester, UK*

Determination of the low temperature crystal transition temperature of (1,4,8,11,15,18,22,25-octahexylphthalocyaninato)nickel using a time slicing CCD detector and image plate system on station 7.2 of the SRS **M. Helliwell, A. Deacon, K. J. Moon, A. K. Powell** and **M. J. Cook**, *University of Manchester, UK*

A combined *in-situ* X-ray spectroscopy/X-ray diffraction study of the formation of the malaria pigment, β-hematin **I. Harvey** and **T. J. Egan**, *CLRC Daresbury Laboratory, UK*

Application of singular value decomposition to time-resolved X-ray data **M. Schmidt, V. Srajer, R. Pahl, K. Brister, S. Anderson, S. Rajagopal, Z. Ren** and **K. Moffat**, *TU-München, Germany*

Determination of protein structure during microwave irradiation by *in-situ* X-ray diffraction **K. J. Grant, L. Sawyer, A. Harrison** and **G. Whittaker**, *University of Edinburgh, UK*

Through a glass darkly: Techniques for *in-situ* powder x-ray diffraction in microwave chemistry **A. Harrison, G. Robb, G. Whittaker** and **D. Youngson**, *University of Edinburgh, UK*

'Hydration resolved' protein structure details; a methods test at 3.2 Å resolution comparing concanavalin A data (truncated from 1.6 Å) with beta-crustacyanin **A. Minichino, G. Habash, J. Raftery, M. Cianci, P. Rizkallah, N. E. Chayen, P. Zagalsky** and **J. R. Helliwell**, *University of Manchester, UK*

Development of apparatus for *in-situ* X-ray diffraction from single crystals and capilliaries during microwave irradiation **M. Piña-Sandoval, A. Harrison, G. Whittaker, S. Parsons** and **A. Parkin**, *University of Edinburgh, UK*

Structure of concanavalin A exhaustively exchanged in D_2O studied by neutron Laue diffraction at 2.4 Å resolution; The hydrogen/deuterium exchange structural kinetics details **J. Habash, J. Raftery, R. Nuttall, H. J. Price, J. R. Helliwell, C. Wilkinson, M. S. Lehmann** and **A. J. Kalb (Gilboa)**, *University of Manchester, UK*

Crystallographic and theoretical studies of monosaccharide binding to concanavalin A: Explanations for binding affinity differences and enthalpy–entropy compensation **G. M. Bradbrook, J. R. Helliwell** and **I. H. Hillier**, *University of Manchester, UK*

The molecular basis of the coloration mechanism in beta-crustacyanin from lobster shell at 3.2 Å resolution and future prospects for 'hydration resolved' structural studies of beta-crustacyanin **M. Cianci, P. J. Rizkallah, A. Olczak, J. Raftery, N. E. Chayen, P. F. Zagalsky** and **J. R. Helliwell**, *University of Manchester, UK*

Neutron quasi-Laue diffraction study of saccharide-free 1222 concanavalin A at 12 K **M. P. Blakeley, D. A. A. Myles, J. R. Helliwell, J. Habash** and **A. J. Kalb (Gilboa)**, *Institut Laue-Langevin, France*

Pulsed neutron diffraction: New opportunities in time-resolved crystallography **C. C. Wilson**, *ISIS, Rutherford Appleton Laboratory, UK*

4GLS – A fourth generation light source facility for the UK **W. R. Flavell, E. A. Seddon, M. W. Poole** and **P. Weightman**, *CLRC Daresbury Laboratory, UK*

Time-resolved *in situ* EDXRD study of the crystallisation of heterogenous catalysts **A. M. Beale, A. T. Davies, G. Muncaster, G. Sankar, C. R. A. Catlow** and **J. M. Thomas**, *The Royal Institution of GB, UK*

Structural study of the amorphization of zeolite Y by X-ray techniques **F. Meneau, G. Sankar** and **G. N. Greaves**, *The Royal Institution of Great Britain, UK*

Intra- and intermolecular relaxation processes in highly excited near-infrared laser dyes **P. Salen, M. Liu** and **P. van der Meulen**, *Stockholm University, Sweden*

Solvent caging and the dynamical transition in proteins **A. L. Tournier** and **J. C. Smith**, *University of Heidelberg, Germany*

Time-resolved X-ray absorption studies of zinc-dependent enzymes reveal information beyond kinetics **O. Kleifeld, G. Rosenblum, A. Frenkel, J. M. L. Martin** and **I. Sagi**, *The Weizmann Institute of Science, Rehovot, Israel*

Are hPBD combs qualitatively different to linear chains? **A. C. Morgovan, E. L. Heeley, C. M. Ferryhough, W. Bras, N. J. Terrill** and **A. J. Ryan**, *University of Sheffield, UK*

Structural study of the amorphization of zeolite Y by X-ray techniques **F. Meneau, G. Sankar** and **G. N. Greaves**, *University of Aberystwyth, UK*

Timescale dependent dynamical transition in a protein solution **T. Becker, J. L. Finney, R. M. Daniel** and **J. C. Smith**, *University of Heidelberg, Germany*

SANS studies on chaperonins of *E. coli* and *Thermoplasma acidophilum* **J. Holzinger, E. Manakova, I. Gutsche, H. Heumann, K. Vanatalu, S. van der Vies** and **R. P. May**, *Max-Planck Institute for Biochemistry, Martinsried, Germany*

Current progress and future challenges in neutron protein crystallography **M. P. Blakeley, D. A. A. Myles, J. R. Helliwell** and **A. J. Kalb (Gilboa)**, *ILL, Grenoble, France*

List of Participants

Mr C. R. Batchelor, *Royal Society of Chemistry, UK*
Mr T. Becker, *University of Heidelberg, Germany*
Prof. G. S. Beddard, *University of Leeds, UK*
Dr G. Berllier, *The Royal Institution of Great Britain, UK*
Mr J. K. Bjernemose, *University of Southern Denmark, Denmark*
Mr M. P. Blakeley, *Institut Laue–Langevin, France*
Prof. H.-B. Bürgi, *University of Berne, Switzerland*
Dr N. A. Burton, *University of Manchester, UK*
Prof. B. J. Cernik, *CLRC Daresbury Laboratory, UK*
Dr L. X. Chen, *Argonne National Lab, USA*
Mr M. Cianci, *University of Manchester, UK*
Dr J. M. Cole, *University of Cambridge, UK*
Prof. P. Coppens, *University at Buffalo, SUNY, USA*
Prof. D. W. J. Cruickshank
Miss A. D'Alessandro, *Royal Society of Chemistry, UK*
Dr A. Dent, *CLRC Daresbury Laboratory, UK*
Prof. J. Evans, *University of Southampton, UK*
Prof. J. L. Finney, *University College London, UK*
Prof. W. R. Flavell, *UMIST, Manchester, UK*
Mr D. G. Flint, *University of Birmingham, UK*
Dr K. J. Grant, *University of Edinburgh, UK*
Prof. N. Greaves, *University of Wales Aberystwyth, UK*
Dr J. Habash, *University of Manchester, UK*
Dr A. Hädener, *University of Basel, Switzerland*
Miss C. L. Hall, *Royal Society of Chemistry, UK*
Prof. A. Harrison, *University of Edinburgh, UK*
Dr I. Harvey, *Central Laboratory of the Research Councils, UK*
Dr E. L. Heeley, *University of Sheffield, UK*
Prof. J. R. Helliwell, *CLRC Daresbury Laboratory, UK*
Dr M. Helliwell, *University of Manchester, UK*
Mr R. G. Hibbert, *University of Oxford, UK*
Prof. I. H. Hillier, *University of Manchester, UK*
Dr J. D. Hirst, *University of Nottingham, UK*
Prof. M. J. Hounslow, *University of Sheffield, UK*
Prof. J. A. K. Howard, *University of Durham, UK*
Dr P. Johnson, *Ohio University, USA*
Dr N. Kaltsoyannis, *University College London, UK*
Ms J. R. Kumita, *University of Toronto, Canada*
Mr M. Liu, *University of Stockholm, Sweden*
Dr M. MacDonald, *CLRC Daresbury Laboratory, UK*
Dr D. Martlew, *Pilkington Technical Centre, UK*
Dr R. P. May, *Institut LaueLangevin, France*
Mr F. Meneau, *The Royal Institution of Great Britain, UK*
Miss A. Minichino, *University of Manchester, UK*
Prof. K. Moffat, *University of Chicago, USA*
Prof. G. R. Moore, *University of East Anglia, UK*
Mrs N. Morgan, *Royal Society of Chemistry, UK*
Miss A. C. Morgovan, *University of Sheffield, UK*
Dr E. T. J. Nibbering, *Max Born Institut für NOK, Germany*
Prof. D. O'Hare, *University of Oxford, UK*
Miss L. C. Palmer, *Royal Society of Chemistry, UK*
Dr M. Papiz, *CLRC Daresbury Laboratory, UK*
Miss M. Pina-Sandoval, *University of Edinburgh, UK*

Mr C. K. Poh, *University of Sheffield, UK*
Miss N. E. Price, *University of Oxford, UK*
Dr J. Raftery, *University of Manchester, UK*
Prof. P. R. Raithby, *University of Bath, UK*
Miss A. Ramos, *Max-Planck-Institut für Biophysik. Chem., Germany*
Mr G. R. Robb, *University of Edinburgh, UK*
Mr G. Robertson, *University of Oxford, UK*
Prof. A. J. Ryan, *University of Sheffield, UK*
Dr I. Sagi, *Weizmann Institute of Science, Israel*
Mr P. M. Salen, *University of Stockholm, Sweden*
Dr G. Sankar, *The Royal Institution of Great Britain, UK*
Dr M. Schmidt, *Technische Universität München, Germany*
Dr G. H. E. Scott, *Royal Society of Chemistry, UK*
Dr O. S. Smart, *University of Birmingham, UK*
Prof. I. W. M. Smith, *University of Birmingham, UK*
Prof. J. C. Smith, *University of Heidelberg, Germany*
Prof. M. Strauss, *University of Vermont, USA*
Ms S. M. Tavender, *Rutherford Appleton Laboratory, UK*
Dr S. Techert, *Max-Planck-Institut für Biophysik. Chem., Germany*
Mr P. Teriete, *University of Oxford, UK*
Dr N. J. Terrill, *CLRC Daresbury Laboratory, UK*
Dr F. Thibault-Starzyk, *LCMT-ISMRA, France*
Professor Sir John Meurig Thomas, *The Royal Institution of Great Britain, UK*
Mr A. Tournier, *University of Heidelberg, Germany*
Prof. A. Watts, *University of Oxford, UK*
Prof. C. C. Wilson, *Rutherford Appleton Laboratory, UK*
Prof. M. Wulff, *ESRF, France*

Index of Contributors*

Anfinrud, P., **13**
Barrelerio, P. C. A., **191**
Basyaruddin, M., **211**
Bhattacharjee, S., **253**
Boetzel, R., **145**
Bolton, P. R., **211**
Bras, W., **299**, **343**
Bürgi, H.-B., **41**, 79, 83, 84, 86, 176, 273, 280
Bushnell-Wye, G., **119**
Busse, G., **105**
Burton, N. A., **223**, 276, 277, 278, 279
Catlow, C. R. A., **203**
Cernik, B. J., **179**, 388
Chen, L. X., 79, 82, 86, 177, 272, **315**, 386, 387, 390
Cianci, M., **131**
Clark, S. M., **299**
Clayden, N. J., **145**
Cole, J. M., 83, **119**, 177, 178, 179, 186, 275, 281, 382
Collins, E. S., **145**
Coppens, P., **1**, 79, 80, 81, 82, 175, 177, 178, 179, 276, 277, 386, 387, 391
Daniel, R. M., **163**
Dent, A. J., **211**, 273, 386
Diaz-Moreno, S., **211**
Dolbnya, I. P., **343**
Dreyer, J., **27**
Elsaesser, T., **27**
Evans, J., **211**, 275, 276, 386, 388, 390
Eybert, L., **13**
Fairclough, J. P. A., **343**
Faulder, P. F., **131**, **223**
Finney, J. L., 87, **163**, 171, 183, 186, 187, 188, 189, 280, 383, 388, 389, 390
Fischer, S., **243**
Flint, D. G., **89**
Frederichs, B., **105**
Gleeson, A. J., **343**
Grant, K. J., 173, 277, 393
Greaves G. N., 81, 85, 86, 87, **203**, **299**, 383, 384, 385
Habash, J., **131**
Hädener, A., **131**, 172, 181, 182, 278
Harrison, A., **363**, 391, 392, 393
Harvey, I., **211**
Heeley, E. L., **343**
Helliwell, J. R., 79, 80, 83, 85, **131**, 174, 176, 178, 179, 180, 181, 187, 189, 269, 271, 274, 278, 280, 382, 385, 387, 391, 393
Hillier, I. H., **223**, 282
Hirst, J. D., 84, 173, **253**, 277, 281, 282
Hounslow, M. J., 274, **343**, 381, 384, 389
Huang, D., **243**
Ibberson, R., **363**
James, R., **145**
Kleanthous, C., **145**
Kumita, J. R., **89**
Kummrow, A., **27**
Li, W., **343**
Lindman, B., **191**
Maidens, A., **343**

Martlew, D., **283**, 381, 382, 383
May, R. P., 81, 85, **191**, 269, 270, 271, 272, 383
Meneau, F., **203**
Moffat, K., **65**, 81, 85, 86, 87, 88, 173, 174, 178, 179, 188, 274, 277, 279, 381, 389
Moore, G. R., **145**, 181, 183, 184, 185, 187, 188, 189, 279
Morgante, N., **203**
Nibbering, E. T. J., **27**, 80, 81, 82, 83, 87, 176
Nieh, Y. P., **131**
Norquist, A., **331**
Novozhilova, I. V., **1**
Nunez, S., **223**
O'Hare, D., **331**, 388, 389, 390, 391
Olmsted, P. D., **343**
Onufriev, A. V., **253**
Oversluizen, M., **299**
Plech, A., **13**, **105**, **119**
Poh, C. K., **343**
Raftery, J., **131**
Rahman, B. A., **211**
Raithby, P. R., **119**
Randler, R., **13**
Rini, M., **27**
Ristic, R. I., **343**
Robb, G., **363**, 388
Ryan, A. J., 270, 273, 274, **343**, 384, 385, 388, 389, 390, 391
Sagi, I., 83, 171, 184, 275, 279, 281, 387
Sankar, G., **203**, 272, 273, 274, 383
Schmidt, M., 79, 186
Schotte, F., **13**, **119**
Schwarzl, S. M., **243**
Smart, O. S., **89**, 171, 172, 173, 174
Smith, J. C., **163**, 171, 173, 180, 181, 183, 186, 187, **243**, 277, 279, 280, 281
Smith, R. I., **331**
Teat, S. J., **119**
Techert, S., 80, 81, 82, 84, **105**, 171, 175, 176, 177, 178, 179, 182, 275, 387, 392, 393
Teriete, P., 172, 181, 185
Terrill, N. J., **343**
Thomas, J. M., 84, 86, 174, 186, **203**, 273, 276, 277, 389, **395**
Tournier, A. L., **243**
Tresadern, G., **223**
Tschentscher, T., **105**
Walton, R. I., **331**
Wang, H., **223**
Watts, A., 182, 185, 187, 188, 269, 270, 271, 276, 280, 281, 282
Whittaker, G., **363**
Wilson, C. C., 82, 85, 87, 172, 173, 177, 180, 185, 270, 271, 273, 274, 275, 276, 278, 280, **363**, 382, 384, 388, 392
Winter, R., **203**
Woolley, G. A., **89**
Wulff, M., **13**, 80, 81, **105**, **119**, **131**
Youngson, D., **363**

* The page numbers in **bold** type indicate papers submitted for discussions.

General Discussions of the Faraday Society/Faraday Discussions of the Chemical Society

Date of meeting	Subject	Volume
1907	Osmotic Pressure	Trans. 3
1907	Hydrates in Solution	3
1910	The Constitution of Water	6
1911	High Temperature Work	7
1912	Magnetic Properties of Alloys	8
1913	Colloids and their Viscosity	9
1913	The Corrosion of Iron and Steel	9
1913	The Passivity of Metals	9
1914	Optical Rotary Power	10
1914	The Hardening of Metals	10
1915	The Transformation of Pure Iron	11
1916	Methods and Appliances for the Attainment of High Temperatures in a Laboratory	12
1916	Refractory Materials	12
1917	Training and Work of the Chemical Engineer	13
1917	Osmotic Pressure	13
1917	Pyrometers and Pyrometry	13
1918	The Setting of Cements and Plasters	14
1918	Electric Furnaces	14
1918	Co-ordination of Scientific Publication	14
1918	The Occlusion of Gases by Metals	14
1919	The Present Position of the Theory of Ionization	15
1919	The Examination of Materials by X-Rays	15
1920	The Microscope: Its Design, Construction and Applications	16
1920	Basic Slags: Their Production and Utilization in Agriculture	16
1920	Physics and Chemistry of Colloids	16
1920	Electrodeposition and Electroplating	16
1921	Capillarity	17
1921	The Failure of Metals under Internal and Prolonged Stress	17
1921	Physico-Chemical Problems Relating to the Soil	17
1921	Catalysis with special reference to Newer Theories of Chemical Action	17
1922	Some Properties of Powders with special reference to Grading by Elutriation	18
1922	The Generation and Utilization of Cold	18
1923	Alloys Resistant to Corrosion	19
1923	The Physical Chemistry of the Photographic Process	19
1923	The Electronic Theory of Valency	19
1923	Electrode Reactions and Equilibria	19
1923	Atmospheric Corrosion. First Report	19
1924	Investigation on Oppau Ammonium Sulphate-Nitrate	20
1924	Fluxes and Slags in Metal Melting and Working	20
1924	Physical and Physico-Chemical Problems relating to Textile Fibres	20
1924	The Physical Chemistry of Igneous Rock Formation	20
1924	Base Exchange in Soils	20
1925	The Physical Chemistry of Steel-Making Processes	21
1925	Photochemical Reactions of Liquids and Gases	21
1926	Explosive Reactions in Gaseous Media	22
1926	Physical Phenomena at Interfaces, with special reference to Molecular Orientation	22
1927	Atmospheric Corrosion, Second Report	23
1927	The Theory of Strong Electrolytes	23
1927	Cohesion and Related Problems	24
1928	Homogeneous Catalysis	24
1929	Crystal Structure and Chemical Constitution	25
1929	Atmospheric Corrosion of Metals, Third Report	25
1929	Molecular Spectra and Molecular Structure	26
1930	Colloid Science Applied to Biology	26
1931	Photochemical Processes	27
1932	The Adsorption of Gases by Solids	28

Date of meeting	Subject	Volume
1932	The Colloid Aspect of Textile Materials	29
1933	Liquid Crystals and Anisotropic Melts	29
1933	Free Radicals	30
1934	Dipole Moments	30
1934	Colloidal Electrolytes	31
1935	The Structure of Metallic Coatings, Films and Surfaces	31
1935	The Phenomena of Polymerization and Condensation	32
1936	Disperse Systems in Gases: Dust, Smoke and Fog	32
1936	Structure and Molecular Forces in (a) Pure Liquids, and (b) Solutions	33
1937	The Properties and Function of Membranes, Natural and Artificial	33
1937	Reaction Kinetics	34
1938	Chemical Reactions Involving Solids	34
1938	Luminescence	35
1939	Hydrocarbon Chemistry	35
1939	The Electrical Double Layer (owing to the outbreak of the war the meeting was abandoned, but the papers were printed in the *Transactions*)	35
1940	The Hydrogen Bond	36
1941	The Oil-Water Interface	37
1941	The Mechanism and Chemical Kinetics of Organic Reactions in Liquid Systems	37
1942	The Structure and Reactions of Rubber	38
1943	Modes of Drug Action	39
1944	Molecular Weight and Molecular Weight Distribution in High Polymers (Joint Meeting with the Plastics Group, Society of Chemical Industry)	40
1945	The Application of Infra-red Spectra to Chemical Problems	41
1945	Oxidation	42
1946	Dielectrics	42 A
1946	Swelling and Shrinking	42 B
1947	Electrode Processes	Disc. 1
1947	The Labile Molecule	2
1947	Surface Chemistry (Jointly with the Société de Chimie Physique at Bordeaux Published by Butterworths Scientific Publications Ltd	
1947	Colloidal Electrolytes and Solutions	Trans. 43
1948	The Interaction of Water and Porous Materials	Disc. 3
1948	The Physical Chemistry of Process Metallurgy	4
1949	Crystal Growth	5*
1949	Lipo-proteins	6
1949	Chromatographic Analysis	7
1950	Heterogeneous Catalysis	8
1950	Physico-chemical Properties and Behaviour of Nuclear Acids	Trans. 46
1950	Spectroscopy and Molecular Structure and Optical Methods of Investigating Cell Structure	Disc. 9
1950	Electrical Double Layer	Trans. 47
1951	Hydrocarbons	Disc. 10
1951	The Size and Shape Factor in Colloidal Systems	11
1952	Radiation Chemistry	12
1952	The Physical Chemistry of Proteins	13
1952	The Reactivity of Free Radicals	14
1953	The Equilibrium Properties of Solutions on Non-electrolytes	15
1953	The Physical Chemistry of Dyeing and Tanning	16
1954	The Study of Fast Reactions	17
1954	Coagulation and Flocculation	18
1955	Microwave and Radio-frequency Spectroscopy	19
1955	Physical Chemistry of Enzymes	20
1956	Membrane Phenomena	21
1956	Physical Chemistry of Processes at High Pressures	22
1957	Molecular Mechanism of Rate Processes in Solids	23
1957	Interactions in Ionic Solutions	24
1958	Configurations and Interactions of Macromolecules and Liquid Crystals	25
1958	Ions of the Transition Elements	26
1959	Energy Transfer with special reference to Biological Systems	27
1959	Crystal Imperfections and the Chemical Reactivity of Solids	28
1960	Oxidation-Reduction Reactions in Ionizing Solvents	29
1960	The Physical Chemistry of Aerosols	30
1961	Radiation Effects in Inorganic Solids	31
1961	The Structure and Properties of Ionic Melts	32
1962	Inelastic Collisions of Atoms and Simple Molecules	33
1962	High Resolution Nuclear Magnetic Resonance	34
1963	The Structure of Electronically Excited Species in the Gas Phase	35
1963	Fundamental Processes in Radiation Chemistry	36
1964	Chemical Reactions in the Atmosphere	37

Date of meeting	Subject	Volume
1964	Dislocations in Solids	38
1965	The Kinetics of Proton Transfer Processes	39
1965	Intermolecular Forces	40
1966	The Role of the Absorbed State in Heterogeneous Catalysis	41
1966	Colloid Stability in Aqueous and Non-aqueous Media	42
1967	The Structure and Properties of Liquids	43
1967	Molecular Dynamics of the Chemical Reactions of Gases	44
1968	Electrode Reactions of Organic Compounds	45
1968	Homogeneous Catalysis with Special Reference to Hydrogenation and Oxidation	46
1969	Bonding in Metallo-organic Compounds	47
1969	Motions in Molecular Crystals	48
1970	Polymer Solutions	49
1970	The Vitreous State	50
1971	Electrical Conduction in Organic Solids	51
1971	Surface Chemistry of Oxides	52
1972	Reactions of Small Molecules in Excited States	53
1972	The Photoelectron Spectroscopy of Molecules	54
1973	Molecular Beam Scattering	55
1973	Intermediates in Electrochemical Reactions	56
1974	Gels and Gelling Processes	57
1974	Photo-effects in Adsorbed Species	58
1975	Physical Adsorption in Condensed Phases	59
1975	Electron Spectroscopy of Solids and Surfaces	60
1976	Precipitation	61
1977	Potential Energy Surfaces	62
1977	Radiation Effects in Liquids and Solids	63
1977	Ion–Ion and Ion–Solvent Interactions	64
1978	Colloid Stability	65
1978	Structures and Motion in Molecular Liquids	66
1979	Kinetics of State Selected Species	67
1979	Organization of Macromolecules in the Condensed Phase	68
1980	Phase Transitions in Molecular Solids	69
1980	Photoelectrochemistry	70
1981	High Resolution Spectroscopy	71
1981	Selectivity in Heterogeneous Catalysis	72
1982	Van der Waals Molecules	73
1982	Electron and Proton Transfer	74
1983	Intramolecular Kinetics	75
1983	Concentrated Colloidal Dispersions	76
1984	Interfacial Kinetics in Solution	77
1984	Radicals in Condensed Phases	78
1985	Polymer Liquid Crystals	79
1985	Physical Interactions and Energy Exchange at the Gas–Solid Interface	80
1986	Lipid Vesicles and Membranes	81
1986	Dynamics of Molecular Photofragmentation	82
1987	Brownian Motion	83
1987	Dynamics of Elementary Gas-phase Reactions	84
1988	Solvation	85
1988	Spectroscopy at Low Temperatures	86
1989	Catalysis by Well Characterised Materials	87
1989	Charge Transfer in Polymeric Systems	88
1990	Structure of Surfaces and Interfaces as studied using Synchrotron Radiation	89
1990	Colloidal Dispersions	90
1991	Structure and Dynamics of Reactive Transition States	91
1991	The Chemistry and Physics of Small Metallic Particles	92
1992	Structure and Activity of Enzymes	93
1992	The Liquid/Solid Interface at High Resolution	94
1993	Crystal Growth	95
1993	Dynamics at the Gas/Solid Interface	96
1994	Structure and Dynamics of Van der Waals Complexes	97
1994	Polymers at Surfaces and Interfaces	98
1994	Vibrational Optical Activity: From Fundamentals to Biological Applications	99
1995	Atmospheric Chemistry: Measurements, Mechanisms and Models	100
1995	Gels	101
1995	Unimolecular Reaction Dynamics	102
1996	Hydration Processes in Biological and Macromolecular Systems	103
1996	Complex Fluids at Interfaces	104
1996	Catalysis and Surface Science at High Resolution	105
1997	Solid State Chemistry: New Opportunities from Computer Simulations	106
1997	Interactions of Acoustic Waves with Thin Films and Interfaces	107

Date of meeting	Subject	Volume
1997	Dynamics of Electronically Excited States in Gaseous, Clusters and Condensed Media	108
1998	Chemistry and Physics of Molecules and Grains in Space	109
1998	Chemical Reaction Theory	110
1998	Molecular Interactions of Biomembranes	111
1999	Physical Chemistry in the Mesoscopic Regime	112
1999	Stereochemistry and Control in Molecular Reaction Dynamics	113*
1999	The Surface Science of Metal Oxides	114*
2000	Molecular Photoionisation	115*
2000	Bioelectrochemistry	116*
2000	Excited States at Surfaces	117*
2001	Cluster Dynamics	118*
2001	Combustion Chemistry: Elementary Reactions to Macroscopic Processes	119*
2001	Nonlinear Chemical Kinetics: Complex Dynamics and Spatiotemporal Patterns	120*
2002	The Dynamic Electrode Surface	121*

* *Available for purchase, for current information on prices* etc. *please contact the Sales and Promotion Department, The Royal Society of Chemistry, Thomas Graham House, Science Park, Milton Road, Cambridge, U. CB4 0WF.*